THE WORDSWORTH COLLECTION OF
Science Fiction

The Wordsworth Collection of
Science Fiction

Selected and introduced by
David Stuart Davies

Wordsworth Editions

I

Readers interested in other titles from
Wordsworth Editions are invited to visit our
website at www.wordsworth-editions.com

For our latest list and a full mail-order service, contact
Bibliophile Books, Unit 5 Datapoint,
South Crescent, London E16 4TL
TEL: +44 (0)20 7474 2474
FAX: +44 (0)20 7474 8589
ORDERS: orders@bibliophilebooks.com
WEBSITE: www.bibliophilebooks.com

This edition published 2011 by
Wordsworth Editions Limited
8B East Street, Ware,
Hertfordshire SG12 9HJ

ISBN   978 1 84022 656 0

Typeset in Great Britain by Roperford Editorial
Printed and bound by Clays Ltd, St Ives plc

CONTENTS

From the Earth to the Moon, Jules Verne   1

Into the Sun, Robert Duncan Milne   155

A Tale of Negative Gravity, Frank R. Stockton   171

To Whom This May Come, Edward Bellamy   189

The Scarlet Plague, Jack London   203

A Thousand Deaths, Jack London   245

The Great Keinplatz Experiment, Arthur Conan Doyle   255

The Thames Valley Catastrophe, Grant Allen   269

A Martian Odyssey, Stanley G. Weinbaum   285

Valley of Dreams, Stanley G. Weinbaum   307

The Adaptive Ultimate, Stanley G. Weinbaum   329

Parasite Planet, Stanley G. Weinbaum   351

Pygmalion's Spectacles, Stanley G. Weinbaum   377

Shifting Seas, Stanley G. Weinbaum   395

The Worlds of If, Stanley G. Weinbaum   417

The Mad Moon, Stanley G. Weinbaum   431

Redemption Cairn, Stanley G. Weinbaum   451

The Ideal, Stanley G. Weinbaum   479

The Lotus Eaters, Stanley G. Weinbaum   497

Proteus Island, Stanley G. Weinbaum   523

The Purple Death, W. L. Alden   553

Flatland, Edwin A. Abbott   565

The Last Stand of the Decapods, Frank T. Bullen   645

Three Go Back, J. Leslie Mitchell   661

The Crystal Man, Edward Page Mitchell   829

The Balloon Tree, Edward Page Mitchell   841

The Ablest Man in the World, Edward Page Mitchell   849

The Tachypomp, Edward Page Mitchell   865

The Man Without a Body, Edward Page Mitchell   879

The Clock That Went Backward, Edward Page Mitchell   887

The Senator's Daughter, Edward Page Mitchell   899

Old Squids and Little Speller, Edward Page Mitchell   915

The Facts in the Ratcliff Case, Edward Page Mitchell   927

The Story of the Deluge, Edward Page Mitchell   935

The Professor's Experiment, Edward Page Mitchell   943

The Soul Spectroscope, Edward Page Mitchell   955

The Inside of the Earth, Edward Page Mitchell   961

Stories of Other Worlds, George Griffith   969

    A Visit to the Moon   971

    The World of the War God   989

    A Glimpse of the Sinless Star   1009

    The World of the Crystal Cities   1027

    In Saturn's Realm   1045

    Homeward Bound   1063

The Dust of Death, Fred M. White   1073

The Four Days' Night, Fred M. White   1089

The Invisible Force, Fred M. White   1107

The Purple Terror, Fred M. White   1125

Around the Moon, Jules Verne   1139

INTRODUCTION

It always amuses me that numerous beginners' guides to writing fiction advise would-be scribes to 'write about what you know'. While there is an element of truth in this suggestion, it does seem to deny the power of the imagination so essential in creating an absorbing, challenging and entertaining narrative. If all authors just wrote exactly about what they knew, what a limited and rather dull selection of reads would be available to us from the bookshelf. Writers are artistic dreamers, and while some dream of characters, plots and environments they are intimately familiar with, others reach beyond these confines into the uncharted terrain of the unknown. They become pioneers into realms of their own creation, and if successful, they convince us to join them on this ground-breaking journey. With the magic of carefully spun words and revolutionary ideas we are exposed to characters, situations and environments we ourselves could never have imagined. Authors of fantasy and science fiction are our guides to these unique and very special worlds.

It was in the nineteenth century that writers very gradually began to construct what we would regard today as 'science fiction'. This was partly due, of course, to the great leaps that science made in all fields from medicine to industry during this remarkable century. The nineteenth century began with horse-drawn carriages, gas-lamps and musical boxes, and ended with motor cars, electric lighting, phonographs and numerous other inventions which would have been deemed incredible in an earlier age. The further and faster science and technology advances, the more it makes it possible for the writer to stretch his and our imaginations. Possible and necessary, for the fantastic becomes less fantastic as science supersedes fiction.

Isaac Asimov, the great exponent of the genre in the twentieth century, stated that: 'True science fiction, by its modern definition (or at least, my modern definition) could not have been written prior to the nineteenth century, then, because it was only with the coming of the Industrial Revolution in the last decades of the eighteenth century that the rate of technological change became great enough to notice in a single lifetime – in those areas of the globe affected by that revolution.'

However the growth of science fiction was not due to technological advances alone; it was also due to man's increasing curiosity about his world, its limits and its possibilities. There was a fascination with what constitutes life and what happens after death – it could be claimed that Mary Shelley's *Frankenstein* (1818), which encapsulates these concerns, is the first science fiction novel – and this in turn gave rise to the popularity of the ghost story. But other writers looked not to the spirit world for their subject matter, but to other fantastic realms either in the future, or hidden from our view, or indeed, beyond the confines of this mortal coil.

This collection features a set of stories and novellas from the pioneers of this most fascinating and challenging of genres. It is a rich seam and these writers were the first to mine it.

The greatest of all science fiction writers in the nineteenth century was Jules Verne (1828–1905). In fact he was regarded as the 'Father of Science Fiction', although the actual phrase was not coined until the early twentieth century. Verne referred to his works as 'scientific romances'. In fact he was the first professional writer who made a good living out of creating fantastic tales. He is well known for his novels *A Journey to the Centre of the Earth* (1864), *From the Earth to the Moon* (1865), *Twenty Thousand Leagues Under the Sea* (1869–1870), *Around the World in Eighty Days* (1873) and *The Mysterious Island* (1875). Verne wrote about space, air, and underwater travel before navigable aircraft and practical submarines were invented, and before any means of space travel had been devised. The third in his series of novels that came to be regarded as 'Les Voyages Extraordinaires' was *From the Earth to the Moon* in which two Americans and a Frenchman are launched into orbit from the muzzle of an enormous gun embedded in the ground on the coast of Florida. The story has certain remarkable aspects to it. Verne attempted to do some rough calculations as to the requirements for the cannon and, considering the total lack of any data on the subject at the time, a great number of his calculations are surprisingly close to reality. The author shows amazing prescience in some of the details in the novel. Verne's cannon is called Columbiad and the Apollo II space mission command module was named Columbia. This was manned by three astronauts as in the novel. Verne's rocket base is in 'Tampa Town' in Florida, not many miles away from where Cape Canaveral is now located. The story is more of an adventurous romp than a gripping drama but it is a significant work in the annals of science fiction.

Surprisingly it took Verne three years to write the sequel, *Around the Moon* (1868) Actually this work is less of a sequel, rather a completion of the original tale. It recounts what the travellers experience on reaching the moon and how they returned to earth. To simulate the gap between the publication of the first part and the second, we have placed the final segment of Verne's space story at the end of this collection.

Apart from Verne, most of the authors featured in these pages will be unfamiliar to the many. True there is a neat little offering from Arthur Conan Doyle (1859–1930) who tried his hand at many genres, his Professor Challenger stories being the most notable in the field of fantasy fiction; and there is a stunning novella from Jack London (1876–1916) of *The Call of the Wild* and *White Fang* fame. London's *The Scarlet Plague* is a post-apocalyptic tale (written in 1912 when post-apocalyptic tales were rare) presenting a future where only a few individuals have survived the virulent eponymous Scarlet Plague. The central character is an old man who still holds the memories and images of the past civilised age and the horrors brought about by the plague. This dystopian vision of the future remains a terrifying and prescient prophecy of man's hell-bent destruction of his own world.

The remaining authors chosen for this volume have languished in the shadows of this genre for a long time and it is with great delight that I have been able to bring some of their work back into print. The major contributors to this collection deserve a special mention.

There are eleven stories here by Stanley G. Weinbaum who, writing in the late twenties and early thirties, was light years ahead of his time. He would have been a major star in the science fiction galaxy had it not been for his tragically early death, in 1935, at the age of thirty-three – only eighteen months after the publication of his first work of fiction. At the time of his death, he had published just twelve stories; eleven more appeared posthumously. The story that heads the section devoted to Weinbaum, 'A Martian Odyssey' (1934), is not only his best but one of the most effective space travel tales ever. In 1970 the Science Fiction Writers of America voted on the best science-fiction short stories of all time and 'A Martian Odyssey' proved to be one of their choices. It was one of the first, if not *the* first, stories to present a realistic vision of space travel unlike the somewhat whimsical approach taken by Verne and Fred M. White (another of our chosen authors). The dialogue remains modern and realistic today, as are the attitude and behaviour of his characters.

Not all Weinbaum's stories are set in outer space, but like all great writers in this genre he deals with complex ideas as well as emotions and revolutionary concepts. This approach is beautifully illustrated in the story 'The Adaptive Ultimate' (1935), where he takes the notion of experimenting with adaptive characteristics in humans – artificially enhancing the ability to adjust and modify their behaviour to all environments and circumstances – with remarkable and tragic results.

Weinbaum was a true loss to the world of storytelling and I am so pleased to include so much of his work in this volume.

If we are moving into mind-stretching territory, it is appropriate that we next mention Edwin A. Abbott (1838–1926) and his bizarre and challenging novella *Flatland* (1884) which has been called a 'classic of the Fourth Dimension' and 'a capricious and delicious mathematical fantasy of life in a sunless, shadowless, two-dimensional country'. It is also a brilliant satire on human nature and in particular on Victorian mores and morals. The reader needs to throw away all maps and compasses used for traditional fiction in order to navigate the delightful and bizarre route of this plot. The narrator is A. Square, whose flat middle-class life is given an exciting new shape by his encounter with a sphere. The sphere introduces A. Square to the joys and sorrows of the third dimension, and the reader is drawn into the subtleties and irrepressible logic of multidimensional thinking. With the advent of modern science fiction from the 1950s to the present day, *Flatland* has seen a revival in popularity. There has even been a movie based on the novel in 2007, but, in reality, no cinema can rival the one in your head, stimulated by Abbott's prose.

I am delighted to be able to include John Leslie Mitchell's complete novel, *Three Go Back* (1932) in this collection. This is another work of fascinating imagination which takes us into the territory of Conan Doyle's *The Lost World* (1912) and Michael Crichton's *Jurassic Park* (1990). The three characters of the title are Clair Stranlay, a novelist, Sir John Mullaghan, head of an armament combine; and Keith Sinclair, an American president of the League of Militant Pacifists. When the luxury airship on which they are travelling across the Atlantic crashes, they find themselves on a beach edged by strange jungle terrain. As they explore, they discover that they have been transported back twenty-five thousand years and are in fact on the lost continent of Atlantis. Here they encounter great pre-historic beasts, such as mammoths and sabre-toothed tigers, and the Cro-Magnards, the ancient race of men who turn out not to be savages as envisaged by historians, but a kind, noble people leading an idyllic existence. Despite the element of boy's own adventure inherent in this tale, Mitchell uses his story to argue Rousseau's theory that men are naturally good – noble savages – and that it is civilisation that corrupts and taints the human spirit.

John Leslie Mitchell (1901–1935) is another writer who died very young – he succumbed to peritonitis at the age of thirty-five. Mitchell wrote a number of novels under the pseudonym Lewis Grassic Gibbon which dealt with Scottish rural life, but his other fantasy works *The Lost Trumpet* (1932) and *Gay Hunter* (1934), published under his own name, will be of particular interest to readers of this volume and are worth seeking out.

Of all the authors presented in this book, Edward Page Mitchell (1852–1927) is perhaps the most enigmatic in that despite the brilliant ideas he presents in his stories – quite a few of them foreshadowing those of H. G. Wells – his name was hardly known during his lifetime, let alone today. The reason for this is that Mitchell was a journalist and most of his stories were originally published anonymously in newspapers. We have to thank Sam Moskowitz, one of science fiction's leading historians and anthologists, for bringing Mitchell's work to the attention of modern readers. Because Mitchell's stories were not by-lined on original publication, Moskowitz had to do some serious detective work to track down and collect these works by an author whom Moskowitz cited as 'the lost giant of American science fiction'. It is amazing to discover how original and advanced Mitchell was in his sci-fi scenarios. For example, in 'The Crystal Man' (1881), he wrote a story about a man rendered invisible by scientific means, long before H. G. Wells (1866–1946) published *The Invisible Man* (1897); he wrote about a time-travel machine ('The Clock that Went Backward', 1881) before Wells's *The Time Machine* (1895); he wrote about faster-than-light travel in 'The Tachypomp' (1874); he wrote the earliest known stories about matter transmission or teleportation in 'The Man without a Body' (1877); and about mind transference in 'Exchanging Their Souls' (1877).

The range of Mitchell's imagination is thrilling and, like all great science fiction writers who presented a view of the future, so many of his predictions came true in one form or another. For example, the story 'The Senator's Daughter', written in 1879 but set fifty-eight years ahead in 1937, contains several technological predictions which were daring for the time: travel by pneumatic tube, electric heating, newspapers printed in the home by electrical transmission, food-pellet concentrates, international broadcasts, and cryogenics, the suspended animation of humans through freezing.

Many of Mitchell's stories reflect the strong influence of Edgar Allan Poe. Moskowitz pointed out that, among other traits, Mitchell shares Poe's habit of giving a basically serious and dignified fictional character a jokey name, such as 'Professor Dummkopf' in Mitchell's 'The Man Without a Body' (1877). Since Mitchell's fictions were originally published in newspapers, typeset in the same format as news articles and therefore not identified as fiction, he may possibly have used this device to signal to his readers that this text should not be taken seriously.

On a par with Jules Verne for fantasy fancifulness is the work of George Griffith (George Chetwyn Griffith-Jones, 1857–1906), who provides a very entertaining section in this volume. He was a prolific British science fiction writer and noted explorer who wrote during the late Victorian and Edwardian age. Many of his visionary tales appeared in periodicals such as *Pearson's Magazine* and *Pearson's Weekly* before being published as novels. I have chosen his series of short connected tales *Stories of Other Worlds*, which first appeared in *Pearson's Magazine* circa 1900. These stories chart the adventures of the Earl of Redgrave and his bride Lilla Zaidie as they spend their honeymoon in space visiting various planets in the solar system. Whimsical though they may be, the stories are also exciting and thoroughly entertaining.

Fred M. White (born 1859), who provides us with four stories, is another forgotten titan of the early age of sci-fi. Like George Griffith, he was a regular contributor to *Pearson's Magazine*, and it was in this publication that he presented a series of tales in which various catastrophes beset London in the early part of the twentieth century. We feature three of those stories here, all published in 1903: 'The Dust of Death' describes what happens when a great plague ravages the city; 'The Four Day's Night' sees the metropolis smothered by a strange, impenetrable fog; and 'The Invisible Force' plunges London into crisis because of violent explosions in the Underground. White creates realistic and spectacular drama out of these not too fantastic scenarios. However, his final offering in this volume, 'The Purple Terror' (1898), lives up to its name by being a wonderful pulp-type horror story featuring a dreadful jungle 'creature'.

Other authors who provide just one offering add an extra sparkle to this shining collection. W. L. Alden (1837–1908), American diplomat and fairly prolific scribbler of adventure-type yarns, gives us a stirring 'threat to civilisation' thriller in 'The Purple Death' (1895).

Robert Duncan Milne (1844–1899) is another author, like Edward Page Mitchell, whose work appeared mainly in newspapers and therefore was neglected for many years. Although born in Scotland, he spent most of his adult life in America, mainly as a resident in San Francisco. He was a friend of Ambrose Bierce and Robert Louis Stevenson. 'Into the Sun' (1882) is a splendid cosmic disaster story, remarkably modern in its style and content.

'A Tale of Negative Gravity' (1884) by Frank R. Stockton (1834–1902) is typical of the satirical, witty and anecdotal style of this American author. Entertainment was the primary purpose of Stockton's writing, which is refreshingly free of messages or social comment.

Edward Bellamy (1850–1898) became a tremendously successful science fiction writer because of his novel *Looking Backward 2000–1887*, which was published in 1888. The book sold several million copies, was translated into over twenty languages and led to the founding of more than one hundred and sixty-five Bellamy Clubs in the United States. The novel presents a visionary view of history from the then futuristic year of 2000, and charts the development of a system of state capitalism that was intensely democratic. Bellamy's belief that an ideal society would evolve naturally from capitalism without a class struggle influenced the work of other writers including William Morris (*News from Nowhere*, 1891) and H. G. Wells (*When the Sleeper Wakes* (1899). Bellamy's contribution here, 'To Whom This May Come' (1888), is a fascinating exploration of the implications of a telepathic society.

Frank T. Bullen (1857–1915), spent some time at sea in his youth and later specialised in stories with a nautical flavour. With 'The Last Stand of the Decapods' (1901) he introduces a strong, rather gruesome, fantasy ingredient to his usual seafaring elements.

Grant Allen (1848–1899) is best remembered today for his crime stories featuring the heroic rogue Colonel Clay. However, Allen was a versatile wordsmith and contributed many a ripping yarn in various genres to the periodicals of the day such as the *Strand Magazine* which first published 'The Thames Valley Catastrophe' (1897), a story that falls into the category of 'unnatural disasters'. It is also a gripping account of love and survival in the face of imminent peril.

In aiming at variety and range in this collection of classic science fiction tales, I believe that the target has been well and truly hit with this fantastic mélange of stories. From the wonders of outer space, to the predictions of the future and the startling possibilities of scientific development for the potentials of human development, the writers of these early science fiction scenarios tick all the boxes and provide a thrilling and mind-expanding experience for all those who love to take a step beyond the familiar. Your journey into various unknowns is about to begin: I know you will enjoy the trip!

DAVID STUART DAVIES

From the Earth to the Moon
Jules Verne

CONTENTS

1   *The Gun Club*

2   *President Barbicane's communication*

3   *Effect of Barbicane's communication*

4   *Reply from the Cambridge Observatory*

5   *The romance of the moon*

6   *Things that all must know, and things that none are allowed to believe, in the United States*

7   *The song of the shot*

8   *The history of the cannon*

9   *The powder question*

10 *One enemy amongst twenty-five million friends*

11 *Florida and Texas*

12 *'Urbi et orbi'*

13 *Stone's Hill*

14 *Spade and trowel*

15 *The festival of the casting*

16 *The columbiad*

17 *A telegram*

18 *The passenger by the* Atlanta

19 *A meeting*

20 *Thrust and parry*

21 *How a Frenchman settles an affair of honour*

22 *The new citizen of the United States*

23 *The projectile-carriage*

24 *The telescope of the Rocky Mountains*

25 *Last details*

26 *Fire!*

27 *Murky weather*

28 *A new star*

CHAPTER ONE

The Gun Club

During the American War of Secession a new and very influential club was formed in the city of Baltimore, Maryland. We all know with what rapidity the military instinct developed itself in this people of ship-owners, merchants, and mechanics. Simple shopkeepers stepped over their counters transformed into captains, colonels, and generals, without having passed through the School of Application at West Point; never-theless, they were soon equal in the art of war to their colleagues of the Old World, and, like them, obtained their victories at the cost of an immense expenditure of bullets, money, and men.

The main point in which the Americans were so much superior to the Europeans was the science of gunnery; not that their arms had attained a greater degree of perfection, but they were of unusual dimensions, and consequently reached distances until then unknown. As regards grazing, plunging, point-blank, or enfilading and side-firing, the English, French, and Prussians have nothing to learn; but their cannons, howitzers, and mortars are but pocket-pistols compared with the formidable engines of the American artillery.

Nor is this matter for surprise. The Yankees, the first mechanics in the world, are born engineers, as Italians are born musicians, and Germans metaphysicians. What is therefore more natural than to see them bring their audacious ingenuity to bear upon the science of gunnery? Hence these gigantic cannons, less useful than sewing-machines, but just as astonishing and yet more admired. We have seen in this respect the marvels of Parrot, of Dahlgren, and Rodman; Armstrong, Palliser, and Treuille de Beaulieu must bow before their transatlantic rivals.

Thus, in the terrible struggle between the North and South, the artillery played the great part. Each new invention was celebrated with enthusiasm by the newspapers of the Union, and, down to the smallest storekeeper, every American citizen devoted his time to the calculation of extraordinary trajectories.

When an American has an idea he looks out for a second American to share it. If there are three of them they elect a chairman and two secret-aries. If four, they appoint a recorder, and the committee is in working order. If five, they convene a general meeting, and a club is formed. This is what happened in Baltimore. The first who invented a new cannon allied himself with the second, who cast it, and the third, who bored it. This was the nucleus of the Gun Club. One month after its formation it counted 1,833 effective members, and 30,575 corresponding members.

One condition, *sine quâ non*, was required of each person desirous of joining the association; this condition was to have invented, or at least perfected, a cannon; if not a cannon, at any rate some sort of firearm. However, inventors of fifteen-shooters, revolving rifles, or sword-pistols, were not much thought of. Artillerists took precedence of such on every occasion.

'The amount of esteem which each obtains,' said, one day, one of the most learned orators of the Gun Club, 'is proportionate to the weight of his gun, and in direct ratio of the square of the ranges attained by his projectiles.' A social application, so to speak, of Newton's law of universal gravitation.

So soon as the Gun Club was established, it is easy to imagine what the inventive genius of the Americans would produce. Engines of war attained colossal proportions, and projectiles flew beyond their proper limits, much to the detriment of inoffensive spectators. All these inventions far surpassed the timid instruments of European artillery. Witness the following figures –

Formerly (in the good old time) the shot from a 36-pounder, at a distance of 300 feet, cut through 36 horses standing flank to flank and 68 men. This was but the infancy of science. Since that time projectiles have improved. Rodman's cannon, which sent a shot weighing half a ton to a distance of seven miles, would easily have cut through 150 horses and 300 men. At one time there was a question of making a solemn trial at the Gun Club. But even had the horses consented to the experiment, the men unfortunately could not be found.

Joking apart, the effect of these cannons was tremendous, and at each discharge the combatants fell like blades of grass before the scythe. Of what account beside such projectiles was the famous cannon-ball which, in 1587, at Coutras, put 25 men *hors de combat*, and that other which, in 1758, at Zorndorff, is reported to have killed 40 foot soldiers? Or, again, the Austrian cannon of Kesselsdorf, in 1742, each shot of which took the lives of 70 enemies? What was the extraordinary cannonading of Jena or Austerlitz which decided the fate of the battle? Something very different was seen during the War of Secession. At the battle of Gettysburg a conic projectile, fired from a rifled cannon, brought to the ground 173 Confederates; and at the passage of the Potomac a shot from Rodman's gun sent

215 southerners into a better world. Nor must we forget a formidable mortar invented by J. T. Maston, a distinguished member and perpetual secretary of the Gun Club, which attained yet more murderous results, for at its trial shot it killed 337 persons – by bursting.

What can be added to these figures, so eloquent in themselves? Nothing. So we must admit without contestation the following calculation by the statistician Pitcairn: dividing the sum total of the victims by the number of the members of the Gun Club, it was found that each of the latter had killed for his own account an average of 2,375 men and a fraction.

In presence of such results it is evident that the sole preoccupation of this learned society was the destruction of humanity from motives of philanthropy, and the perfecting of firearms considered as instruments of civilisation: an assembly of exterminating angels, otherwise the best fellows in the world.

It is but just to add that these Yankees, brave beyond a doubt, did not confine themselves to mere formulae, but risked their persons without hesitation. They counted amongst them officers of every grade, from lieutenants to generals, military men of all ages – those who were making their *débuts* in the career of arms, and those who had grown old in the service. Many remained upon the field of battle whose names figure in the book of honour of the Gun Club, and, of those who returned, many bore marks of their undaunted intrepidity. Crutches, wooden legs, cork arms, hooks instead of hands, india-rubber jaws, silver skulls, platinum noses – nothing was wanting to the collection; and the above-mentioned Pitcairn calculated that in the Gun Club there was not quite one arm to four persons, and only two legs to six.

But those valiant artillerists were not very particular on such points, and they were justly proud when despatches from the field of battle showed a number of victims ten times in excess of the number of projectiles used.

One day, however – sad and lamentable day! – peace was signed by the survivors of the war. The firing gradually ceased, mortars were silent, muzzled howitzers and cannons returned to their arsenals, shot and shell were piled up in the parks, bloody remembrances were wiped out, cotton trees flourished luxuriantly in the well-manured fields, and the garments of woe were laid aside with the griefs of their wearers, and the Gun Club relapsed into a state of profound inactivity.

Certain of the members, hard-working fellows, still applied themselves to abstruse calculations in the science of gunnery. They still dreamt of gigantic shells and incomparable shot. But without practical application theory soon loses its charm. So the club was deserted, the servants slept in the ante-rooms, the newspapers mildewed on the table, snores were heard to issue from the darker corners of the rooms, and the members of the Gun Club, formerly so noisy, but now reduced to silence by disastrous peace, resigned themselves to visions of Platonic artillery.

'This is dreadful,' said, one evening, bold Tom Hunter, carbonising his wooden legs in the smoking-room grate. 'Nothing to do! Nothing to hope for! What a dreadful existence! Where is the time when the cannon awoke us each morning with its welcome boom?'

'That time is no more,' said the sprightly Bilsby, stretching what remained of his arms. 'There was some fun to be had then! One could invent a howitzer, and, as soon as it was cast, run off and try it on the enemy, and return to the camp with a word of encouragement from Sherman, or a clasp of the hand from MacClellan. But now the generals have gone back to their stores, and, instead of cannon-balls, send off inoffensive bales of cotton. Alas! artillery is of no further account in America.'

'Yes, Bilsby,' said Colonel Blomsberry, 'these are cruel disappointments! We leave our accustomed habits, we learn the use of arms, we leave Baltimore for the fields of battle, we fight like heroes, and two or three years later we lose the fruit of so many fatigues, relapse into hateful inactivity, and may keep our hands in our pockets.'

Notwithstanding which statement, the valiant colonel would have found great difficulty in giving this latter proof of his inactivity; not from want of pockets, however.

'And no prospect of war,' said the famous J. T. Maston, scratching his gutta-percha skull with his iron hook, 'not a cloud in the horizon, and so much still to be done in the science of artillery! For instance, this very morning I completed the drawings, with plan, section, and elevation, of a mortar which will alter the whole theory of war.'

'You don't mean to say so!' said Tom Hunter, involuntarily thinking of the Hon. J. T. Maston's last attempt.

'It is quite true,' said the latter. 'But to what purpose all these studies, these difficulties overcome? I am working in pure waste, for the people of the New World seem to have made up their minds to live in peace, and our warlike *Tribune* is already prophesying a catastrophe from the scandalous increase of population.'

'Nevertheless, Maston,' replied Colonel Blomsberry, 'there is still fighting in Europe to maintain the principle of nationalities.'

'What then?'

'Why, we might be able to do something there, and if they would accept our services – '

'What are you thinking of?' cried Bilsby. 'Give foreigners the benefit of our science!'

'That would be better than doing nothing,' replied the colonel.

'No doubt,' said J. T. Maston, 'but unfortunately that expedient is not to be thought of.'

'Why not?' asked the colonel.

'Because in the Old World they have ideas about promotion quite contrary to our American notions. People do not believe it possible for a man to become a general until he has served as a sub-lieutenant, which is almost tantamount to asserting that one cannot be a good marksman without serving one's time in a cannon foundry, which is simply – '

'Bosh,' said Tom Hunter, whittling the arm of his chair with a large bowie-knife. 'And since matters have gone so far, it only remains for us to plant tobacco or refine spermaceti.'

'What!' cried J. T. Maston, in a stentorian voice, 'are we not to employ the last years of our existence in improving firearms? Are we to have no new opportunity of testing the range of our projectiles? Are we never again to light up the air with the flash of our cannon? Will no international difficulty arise, that we may declare war against some transatlantic power? Won't the French run down a single one of our steamers? Won't the English hang a few of our compatriots, in defiance of international law?'

'No, Maston,' replied Colonel Blomsberry. 'No such luck! None of those opportunities will arise, and if one did, we should not take advantage of it. American susceptibility is daily decreasing; we are degenerating into old women.'

'We are eating humble-pie,' said Bilsby.

'We are daily subjected to humiliations,' said Tom Hunter.

'It is but too true,' replied J. T. Maston, with renewed vehemence. 'We have a thousand reasons for fighting, yet we don't fight! We economise arms and legs for people who don't know what to do with them. Why, look here! Without seeking farther for a *casus belli*, did not North America formerly belong to the English?'

'Doubtless,' replied Tom Hunter, poking the fire savagely with the end of his crutch.

'Then,' continued J. T. Maston, 'why should not England, in its turn, belong to the Americans?'

'It would only be fair,' replied Colonel Blomsberry.

'Go and propose it to the President of the United States,' cried J. T. Maston, 'and see how he'll receive you.'

'He'd receive us badly enough,' grumbled Bilsby, through the four molars which the wars had left him.

'Bedad!' cried J. T. Maston, 'he need not count on my vote at the next election.'

'Nor on ours,' cried the warlike invalids with one voice.

'Meanwhile,' continued J. T. Maston, 'and to conclude, if I am not given an opportunity of trying my new mortar on a real battle-field, I shall send in my resignation to the Gun Club, and withdraw to the plains of the Arkansas.'

'We'll all follow you,' replied the interlocutors of the audacious J. T. Maston.

Such was the state of affairs. The feeling of discontent was becoming more and more general, and the club was threatened with early dissolution, but this catastrophe was averted by an unexpected event.

The very day following the above conversation, each member of the club received a circular to this effect.

Baltimore, 3rd October
The President of the Gun Club has the honour to inform his colleagues that he proposes to make a communication of great interest at the meeting of the 5th instant; he therefore begs that members will make a point of attending the said meeting, in answer to the present invitation.

And remains, very cordially,

IMPEY BARBICANE, P.G.C.

CHAPTER TWO

President Barbicane's communication

On the 5th of October, at eight o'clock in the evening, a compact crowd filled the rooms of the Gun Club, at 21, Union Square. All the members of the club living in Baltimore were present in compliance with their president's invitation. As for the corresponding members, special trains brought them by hundreds to the town, and notwithstanding the size of the great hall, was insufficient to contain this crowd of *savants* which filled up the adjoining rooms and passages, and even half the exterior courtyards. They were met by masses of the public pressing in through the gates, each trying to force his way to a front rank; all anxious to hear President Barbicane's important communication, pushing, shoving, and crushing each other with that liberty of action peculiar to crowds educated in ideas of self-government.

On that evening no stranger in Baltimore would have been able for any sum of money to penetrate into the great hall, which was specially reserved for resident and corresponding members. None others were admitted, and the notabilities, the magistrates and magnates of the city, had to mix with the crowd of citizens, eager to catch, if possible, some item of news from the great hall.

The immense hall presented a curious spectacle; the vast space was marvellously well suited to its purpose. High columns formed by cannons, superposed with mortars for their base, supported the elegant framework of the dome, itself a real lacework of wrought iron. Trophies of blunderbusses, matchlocks, arquebuses, rifles, and all kinds of ancient and modern firearms spread over the wall in picturesque arrangement. Flames of gas issued from a thousand revolvers grouped as lustres, while girandoles of pistols, and chandeliers of stands of guns, completed the splendid illumination. Models of cannons, specimens of bronze, targets riddled with bullets, plates of metal broken by the shot of the Gun Club, rammers and sponges, chaplets of shell, collars and projectiles, garlands of grapeshot – in a word all the weapons of the artillerists, surprised the eye by the tastefulness of their arrangement, and led one to believe that their destination was rather decorative than murderous.

In the place of honour, under a splendid glass case, might be seen a piece of the breach of a cannon, broken and twisted by the force of an explosion. This was the precious relic of J. T. Maston's gun.

At the extremity of the hall, the president and his four secretaries occupied a large daïs. A seat raised upon a sculptured base, represented a thirty-two-inch mortar, pointed at an angle of 90°, and suspended by the trunnions, so that the president could give it a backward and forward motion like a rocking-chair, which was most agreeable in the great heats. On the bureau, formed by an immense sheet of iron, supported by six carronades, lay an inkbottle of most exquisite taste, made from a delicately-chiselled cannon-ball, and a detonating handbell, which went off when required with a report like a revolver. During vehement discussions, this new kind of bell could hardly make itself heard above the roars of this legion of excited artillerists.

In front of the bureau, benches placed in zigzag, like the circumvallations of an intrenchment, formed a succession of bastions and curtains where the members of the Gun Club were seated; and on this evening it might truly be said that the ramparts were fully manned. They knew the president too well to think that he would have assembled his colleagues without motives of the highest gravity.

Impey Barbicane was a man of about forty; calm, cold, austere; of a character eminently serious and concentrated; as exact as a chronometer, of a temperament above proof, of immovable force of mind; not romantic, although adventuresome, but bringing practical ideas to bear upon the wildest undertakings; a true son of New England, a colonising northerner, a descendant of those Roundheads who proved so fatal to the Stuarts, an implacable enemy to the southern gentlemen, those ancient cavaliers of the mother-country. In a word, a Yankee all over.

Barbicane had made a great fortune in the timber trade. Appointed Director of Artillery during the war, he had shown himself fertile in inventions. By the audacity of his conceptions, he contributed powerfully to the progress of that arm, and gave incomparable impulse to experimental researches.

He was a personage of middle height, possessing, by a rare exception in the Gun Club, all his members intact; his marked features seemed traced by the rule and square; and if it be true that a man's instincts are shown by his profile, Barbicane, in this respect, afforded the most perfect indications of energy, audacity, and self-possession.

At that moment he was seated immovable on his chair, mute, absorbed, with a preoccupied look beneath his tall hat – one of those black silk cylinders which seem screwed on to American heads.

His colleagues were talking noisily around him without attracting his attention; they asked each other questions; they made suppositions; they examined their president; and sought, but in vain, to work out the unknown quantity from his imperturbable countenance.

When eight o'clock had struck from the fulminating clock of the great hall, Barbicane rose suddenly, as though moved by a spring, and there was a general silence, while the speaker, in somewhat emphatic tones, began as follows: 'Worthy colleagues, for some time past a disastrous peace has plunged the members of the Gun Club in a state of deplorable inaction. After a few eventful happy years, we have been obliged to renounce our labours, and to come to a sudden halt in the path of progress. I do not fear to proclaim loudly that any war which would put arms into our hands would be welcome.'

'War for ever!' cried the impetuous J. T. Maston.

'Hear, hear!' echoed from all sides.

'But,' said Barbicane, 'war is impossible under present circumstances, and, notwithstanding the hopes of my honourable interrupter, long years will pass ere the thunder of our cannons will be again heard on the field of battle. We must make up our minds to this, and seek elsewhere food for our all-devouring energies.'

The meeting felt that the president was nearing the delicate point, and attention was redoubled.

'For some months, my worthy colleagues,' continued Barbicane, 'I have put the question to myself whether, whilst remaining within the limits of our speciality, we could not undertake some great experiment worthy of the nineteenth century, and whether the progress we have made in the art of gunnery would not enable us to carry such an experiment to a successful issue. I have studied deeply, worked and calculated, and from my studies the conviction has arisen that we ought to succeed in an undertaking which would appear impracticable in any other country. This project, carefully worked out, will form the subject of my communication. It is worthy of you, worthy of the reputation of the Gun Club, and cannot fail to make a stir in the world.'

'A great stir?' asked an enthusiastic artillerist.

'A great stir, in the true acceptation of the word,' replied Barbicane.

'Don't interrupt,' cried several voices.

'I therefore beg, worthy colleagues,' continued the president, 'that you will give me all your attention.'

A thrill of impatience ran through the assembly, and Barbicane, having rapidly pressed down his hat over his forehead, continued his speech in a calm voice.

'There is no one amongst you, worthy colleagues, who has not seen the moon, or, at least, heard about her; so you will not be astonished if I speak to you about the orb of night. It is, perhaps, reserved for us to be the discoverers of a new world. Follow me, assist me with all your power, and I will lead you to her conquest, and her name shall be added to the other thirty-six states which form this great country of the Union.'

'Hurrah for the moon!' shouted the Gun Club, with one voice.

'The moon has been the subject of much study,' continued Barbicane. 'Her mass, her density, her weight, her volume, her constitution, her movements, her distance, the part she plays in the solar system, are all perfectly well defined; selenographic maps have been prepared with equal, if not greater, minuteness than the terrestrial maps; photography has given us proofs of our satellite, of an incomparable beauty – in a word we know all about the moon that the mathematical sciences, astronomy, geology, and optics can teach us; but, up to the present time, no direct communication has ever been established with the luminary.'

This statement occasioned a general movement of interest and surprise amongst the audience.

'Allow me,' continued the speaker, 'to recall, in a few words, how certain enterprising minds – thanks to their vivid imagination! – claimed at various times to have penetrated the secrets of our satellite. In the seventeenth century a certain David Fabricius boasted that he had seen inhabitants in the moon. In 1649 a Frenchman, named Jean Baudouin, published a *Journey from the World to the Moon*, by Domingo Gonzalez, a Spanish adventurer. About the same time, Cyrano de Bergerac instituted that celebrated expedition which had so much success in France. Later on, another Frenchman (those people seem to take a great interest in the moon!), a certain Fontenelle, wrote the *Plurality of Worlds*, a masterpiece for his time; but the advance of science crushes even masterpieces! Towards 1835, a small work, translated from *The New York American*, related how Sir John Herschel – sent to the Cape of Good Hope to make certain astronomical observations – had, by means of a telescope perfected with an interior light, brought the moon to a distance of eighty yards. He then is stated to have seen distinctly caverns, in which dwelt hippopotami, green mountains fringed with golden lace, sheep with ivory horns, white deer, and men and women with membraned wings like bats. This book, written by an American named Locke, met with great success at first, but was soon discovered to be a scientific hoax, and the French were the first to laugh at it.'

'Laugh at an American?' cried J. T. Maston; 'that is a *casus belli*!'

'Do not alarm yourself, worthy friend! The French, before laughing, had been thoroughly duped by our countryman. To close this rapid sketch, I may add that a certain Hans Pfaal, of Rotterdam, travelling in a balloon, filled with an oxygen gas thirty-seven times lighter than hydrogen, reached the moon after a nineteen-days' journey. This journey, like the other attempts, was merely imaginary, being the work of a popular writer in America, a strange, contemplative genius. I refer to Poe.'

'Hurrah for Edgar Poe!' cried the electrified assembly.

'I have done,' continued Barbicane, 'with these attempts, which I may call purely literary, and quite insufficient to establish any real communication with the Queen of the Night. However, I must add that some practical minds have endeavoured to establish such communication. A few years ago, a German mathematician proposed to send a commission of scientists into the steppes of Siberia. There, on the vast plains, immense geometrical figures were to be described by means of luminous reflectors; amongst others, the problem of the square of the hypothenuse, called by Frenchmen, the *pons asinorum*. "Every intelligent person must understand the scientific value of this figure. If there are any inhabitants in the moon they will reply by a similar figure; and, communication once established, it will be easy to create an alphabet, which will allow of intercourse with the inhabitants of the moon." Thus reasoned the German mathematician; but his project was not put into execution, and, up to the present time, no direct means of communication exists between the earth and its satellite. It is reserved for the practical genius of Americans to place themselves in communication with the sidereal world. The way to arrive at this is simple, easy, and certain, and will form the subject of my communication.'

A very tempest of exclamation here burst from the assembly; not one of the audience but was dominated and carried away by the words of the orator.

'Hear, hear! Silence!' was cried from every side.

When the agitation had subsided, Barbicane, in a grave tone of voice, continued his interrupted speech.

'You know,' said he, 'what progress the science of gunnery has made in the last few years, and to what degree of perfection firearms would have reached if the war had but continued. You are aware, also, that in a general way, the resisting power of cannon and the expansive power of gunpowder are unlimited. Acting upon this principle, I have asked myself whether, by means of a sufficient apparatus, manufactured under given conditions of resistance, it would not be possible to send a shot to the moon.'

At these words a cry of stupefaction burst from a thousand excited breasts, followed by a moment of silence like the calm before a storm. Then came a roll of thunder; but it was the thunder of applause, shouts, and clamours, which shook the hall to its foundations. The president tried to speak, but could not. For ten minutes, at least, he was unable to make himself heard.

'Let me finish,' said he calmly. 'I have examined the question in all its phases, and the result of my calculations is, that any projectile having an initial velocity of 12,000 yards per second, and fired in the direction of the moon, must necessarily reach her. I have, therefore, the honour to propose to you, worthy colleagues, to try this little experiment.'

CHAPTER THREE

Effect of Barbicane's communication

It is impossible to describe the effect produced by the hon. president's last words. The cries, the vociferations, the succession of cheers, Hip, hip, hurrahs! and other onomatopoeia in which the American language is so rich. The scene of disorder was utterly indescribable. Shouts were raised, hands clapped, and the very foundations were shaken by the stamping of many feet. Had all the firearms in the Museum of Artillery exploded at once, they would not have produced a greater volume of sound. Nor is this to be wondered at, for some cannoniers are almost as noisy as their cannons.

Barbicane remained calm in the midst of this enthusiastic clamour. Perhaps he wished to address some further words to his colleagues, for his gesticulations seemed to ask for silence, and his detonating hand-bell fired a perfect volley of shots, but was not even heard; and soon the president was snatched from his seat, carried in triumph, and passed from the shoulders of his faithful comrades into the arms of the not less excited crowd outside.

Nothing surprises an American. It has often been repeated that the word 'impossible' was not French, but this last word is evidently a *lapsus linguae*. In America all is easy, all is simple; and as regards mechanical difficulties, they are conquered before they arise. Between Barbicane's project and its realisation, no true Yankee would have allowed himself to admit the appearance of a difficulty. A thing was carried out as soon as decided upon.

The president's triumphal progress lasted till evening, when it became a real torch-light procession. Irishmen, Germans, Frenchmen, and Scotchmen – in fact all that heterogeneous assemblage which composes the population of Maryland – cheered in their mother-tongues, and their shouts and bravoes combined in an inexpressible burst of acclamation.

At that moment, as if fully understanding that the question was of her, the moon shone forth with serene magnificence, and eclipsed with her intense brilliancy all the surrounding illumination. All eyes were turned towards her lambent disc; some waved their hands to her, others called her by the most endearing names, some tried to measure her with the

eye, whilst others shook their fists at her. From eight o'clock to midnight, an optician in Jones' Falls Street made his fortune by the sale of tele-scopes. The Queen of the Night was the object of as much attention as any fine lady. The Americans treated her as if she were their property. It seemed as though fair-haired Phoebe belonged to these audacious conquerors, and already formed part of the territory of the Union; and yet they were only proposing to take a shot at her, which was certainly a rather brutal way of entering into communication, even with a satellite, though greatly in vogue amongst civilised nations.

Midnight had struck, but the enthusiasm had not calmed down. It was equally shared by all classes of the population: the magistrate, the man of science, the merchant, the shopkeeper, the porter, intelligent men as well as fools, were subject to the same excitement. It was a question of a national undertaking: so the upper and lower parts of the town, the quays bathed by the waters of the Patapsco, and the ships floating in the docks, were crowded with men and women intoxicated with pleasure, gin, and whisky. Everyone was talking, speechifying, discussing, disputing, approving, applauding, from the gentleman reclining easily on the sofa of the bar-room before his glass of sherry-cobbler, to the waterman getting drunk upon knock-me-down in the dark taverns of the Fells.

However, about two o'clock in the morning the agitation subsided. President Barbicane succeeded in reaching his home, literally dead with fatigue. Hercules could not have borne so much enthusiasm. The crowd gradually withdrew from the squares and the streets. The four lines of railway to Ohio, Susquehanna, Philadelphia, and Washington, which meet in Baltimore, carried back the visitors to the four corners of the United States, and the town relapsed into comparative tranquillity.

It would, however, be erroneous to think that during this memorable evening Baltimore alone was a prey to this agitation. The great towns of the Union – New York, Boston, Albany, Washington, Richmond, New Orleans, Charlestown, and Mobile – from Texas to Massachusetts, from Michigan to Florida – all had their share in the delirium. In fact, the 30,000 correspondents of the Gun Club were acquainted with the letter of the president, and were awaiting, with equal impatience, the famous communication of the 5th of October. So that, that very evening, in proportion as the words left the lips of the speaker, they were transmitted by the telegraph through all the States of the Union with a rapidity of 248,447 miles per second. We may therefore say, with absolute certainty, that at the same instant the United States of America, ten times as large as France, sent up one great shout, and that twenty-five millions of hearts inflated with pride, beat with the same pulsation.

The next day 1,500 papers – daily, weekly, fortnightly, and monthly – took up the question and examined it in its different bearings – physical, meteorological, economical, and moral – as well as in its relation to political preponderance and to civilisation. They discussed the question whether the moon was a completed world, and whether it would not undergo some further transformation. Was it like the earth at the time when the atmosphere did not exist? Of what nature and formation was the face invisible to the terrestrial spheroid?

Although it was as yet only a question of firing a shot at the Queen of the Night, all saw therein the commencement of a series of experiments, all hoped that one day America would penetrate the last secrets of this mysterious disc, and some were even afraid that its conquest might seriously disturb European equilibrium. Whilst discussing the project, not a single paper doubted its realisation.

The reviews, the pamphlets, the magazines, published by learned societies, literary or religious, pointed out its advantages; and the Society of Natural History of Boston, the American Society of Arts and Sciences of Albany, the Geographical and Statistical Society of New York, the American Philosophical Society of Philadelphia, the Smithsonian Institution of Washington – all sent a thousand letters of congratulation to the Gun Club, with immediate offers of service and of money.

We may therefore say that no proposal ever met with so large a number of admirers. There was no question whatever of hesitation, doubts, or uncertainties. As regards jokes, caricatures, or songs, which in Europe – especially in France – would have ridiculed the idea of sending a projectile to the moon, they would have done bad service to their authors: all the life-preservers in the world would have been powerless to protect them from general indignation. There are some things at which one dare not laugh in the New World.

So Impey Barbicane became, from that day, one of the greatest citizens of the United States, something like a Washington of science. And one very characteristic fact, amongst many others, shows to what pitch the respect of a nation for one man can be carried.

Some days after the famous meeting of the Gun Club, the manager of an English troupe advertised the play of *Much Ado about Nothing*, at the theatre of Baltimore; but the population of the town, who saw in this title an allusion to the projects of President Barbicane, broke into the theatre, tore up the seats, and obliged the unfortunate manager to alter his programme. He, like a sensible fellow, complied with the public wish, and replaced the above popular comedy by *As You Like It*; and during several weeks his receipts were phenomenal.

CHAPTER FOUR

Reply from the Cambridge Observatory

Meanwhile Barbicane did not lose a minute in the midst of these ovations. His first care was to assemble his colleagues in the committeeroom of the Gun Club, where, after long discussion, it was resolved to consult the most learned astronomers upon the astronomical part of the undertaking, and when their reply was known, to discuss the mechanical means, so that nothing should be neglected to ensure the success of this great experiment.

A very precise note, containing special questions, was drawn up and addressed to the Observatory of Cambridge, Massachusetts. This town, which contains the first university of the United States, is justly celebrated for its astronomical college. There are collected *savants* of the highest merit. There is to be found the powerful telescope which enabled Bond to resolve the nebulae of Andromeda, and Clark to discover the satellite of Syrius. This celebrated establishment fully justified in all respects the confidence of the Gun Club, and two days later the reply, so impatiently expected, reached the hands of President Barbicane.

It was couched in the following terms –

From the Director of the Cambridge University to
the President of the Gun Club at Baltimore

Cambridge, 7th October

Upon receipt of your favour of the 6th instant, addressed to the Cambridge Observatory in the name of the members of the Gun Club of Baltimore, our committee immediately met and resolved to reply as follows.

The questions asked are these:

(1st) Is it possible to send a projectile to the moon?

(2nd) What is the exact distance which separates the earth from its satellite?

(3rd) What would be the duration of the passage of a projectile to which a sufficient velocity had been imparted, and consequently at what moment ought the same to be despatched to reach the moon at a fixed spot?

(4th) At what precise moment will the moon be in the most favourable position to be reached by the projectile?

(5th) At what point of the sky must the cannon be aimed which is to despatch the projectile?

(6th) What position will the moon occupy in the sky at the moment the projectile is despatched?

As regards the first question – Is it possible to send a projectile to the moon?

Yes. It is possible to send a projectile to the moon, if you are able to endow the projectile with an initial velocity of 12,000 yards per second.

Calculations prove that this velocity is sufficient. As it leaves the earth the action of gravitation diminishes in inverse ratio of the square of the distances – that is to say, for a distance three times greater the action is nine times less. Consequently the weight of the projectile will decrease rapidly, until it becomes completely null at the moment when the attraction of the moon equals that of the earth, that is to say, at 47-52nds of the distance. The projectile will then have no further weight, and if it passes this point it will reach the moon by the mere effect of lunar attraction. The theoretical possibility of the experiment is thus absolutely proved. As regards its success, that will depend solely upon the power of the gun employed.

'As regards the second question – What is the exact distance which separates the earth from its satellite?

The moon does not describe around the earth a circle, but an ellipse, of which our globe occupies one of the foci; hence the moon is sometimes nearer and sometimes farther from the earth, or, in astronomical terms, sometimes in her apogee and sometimes in her perigee. The difference between her greatest and smallest distances is sufficiently important not to be neglected in the present instance. When in her apogee the moon is 247,552 miles, and in her perigee only 218,657 miles distant, which makes a difference of 28,895 miles, or more than a ninth part of the whole distance. Consequently it is the distance of the moon when in her perigee which must serve as a basis of our calculations.

As regards the third question – What will be the duration of the passage of a projectile to which a sufficient initial velocity has been imparted, and, consequently, at what moment must it be despatched to reach the moon at a given point?

If the projectile retained indefinitely the initial velocity of 12,000 yards per second, with which it was endowed at its departure, it would only take about nine hours to reach its destination; but as this initial velocity will continually decrease, it results from calculations made that the projectile will take 300,000 seconds, or 83 hours and 20 minutes, to reach the point where the terrestrial and lunary attractions are equal, and from this point it will reach the moon in 50,000 seconds, or 13 hours, 53 minutes, and 20 seconds. It will therefore be necessary to despatch the projectile 97 hours, 13 minutes, and 20 seconds before the arrival of the moon at the point aimed at.

As to the fourth question – At what precise moment will the moon be in the most favourable position to be reached by the projectile?

It results from what has been above stated that you must choose not only the moment when the moon is in her perigee, but also the moment when she crosses the zenith, which will again diminish the distance by a length equal to the radius of the earth, or 3,919 miles, so that the whole distance will be 214,976 miles. But although the moon reaches her perigee each month, she does not always at the same moment cross the zenith; she only unites these two conditions at long intervals. You must therefore wait for the coincidence of the passage to the perigee with that of the zenith. By a fortunate circumstance, on the 4th of December of next year the moon will unite these two conditions. At midnight she will be in perigee, that is at the shortest distance from the earth, and she will cross the zenith at the same time.

As regards the fifth question – At what point of the sky must we aim the cannon which is to discharge the projectile?

The preceding observations being admitted, the cannon must be aimed at the zenith of the spot so that its line of fire will be perpendicular to the plane of the horizon, and the projectile will escape more rapidly from the effects of gravitation. But in order that the moon should reach the zenith of a certain spot, it is necessary that that spot should not be situated in a higher latitude than the declination of the satellite – that is to say, it must be situate between 0° and 28° north or south. In any other spot the line of fire must necessarily be oblique, which would impair the success of the experiment.

To the sixth question – What place in the sky will the moon occupy at the moment the projectile is despatched?

At the moment the projectile is despatched into space, the moon, which advances each day 13° 10' 35'', must be distant from the point of the zenith four times that number, or say, 52° 42' 20'', which distance corresponds with the distance she will travel during the flight of the projectile. But as we must also take into account the deviation caused to the projectile by the rotatory movement of the earth, and as the projectile will only reach the moon after having deviated a distance equal to 16 radii of the earth – which, computed upon the orbit of the moon, make about 11° – we must add these 11° to those which represent the delay of the moon already mentioned, making, in round numbers, 64°. Thus, at the moment of firing, the line of sight drawn direct to the moon will form, with a perpendicular erected on the spot, an angle of 64°.

Such are the replies to the questions proposed to the Cambridge Observatory by the members of the Gun Club.

To recapitulate: –

(1st) The cannon must be established in a country within 0° and 28° of latitude north or south.

(2nd) It must be pointed at the zenith of the spot.

(3rd) The projectile must be endowed with an initial velocity of 12,000 yards per second.

(4th) It must be discharged on the 1st of December of next year, at 13 minutes and 20 seconds to 11 p.m.

(5th) It will reach the moon four days after its departure, on the 4th of December at midnight, at the moment when the moon crosses the zenith.

The members of the Gun Club should therefore lose no time in commencing the works necessary for such an undertaking, and should be ready to operate at the moment fixed; for if they allow the date of the 4th of December to pass, they will not again find the moon in the same conditions as to perigee and zenith for 18 years and 11 days.

The committee of the Cambridge Observatory place themselves entirely at the disposal of the Gun Club upon all questions of theoretical astronomy, and they beg to add herewith their congratulations to those of the whole of America.

For the Committee,

J. M. Belfast
Director of the Cambridge Observatory

CHAPTER FIVE

The romance of the moon

An observer gifted with an infinitely penetrating sight, and placed at that unknown centre around which the world revolves, would have seen, at the chaotic period of the universe, myriads of atoms floating in space. But gradually, with the centuries, a change was produced: a law of attraction manifested itself which the floating atoms obeyed. These atoms chemically combined according to their affinities, became molecules, and formed the nebulous masses which are scattered over the depths of the sky.

Then these masses were animated by a movement of rotation around their central point. This centre, formed by inchoate molecules, revolved upon itself and became progressively condensed. According to the immutable law of mechanics, in proportion as its volume diminished by condensation its rotatory movement increased, and both these effects continuing there resulted one principal star, the centre of the nebulous agglomeration.

By careful attention, an observer would have perceived other molecules from the masses follow the example of the central star, condense in the same way – by a rotatory movement progressively increased – and gravitate round the same in the form of innumerable stars.

Thus were the nebulae formed, of which astronomy counts nearly 5,000.

Among these 5,000 nebulae there is one called the Milky Way, containing millions of stars, of which each has become the centre of a solar system.

Had the observer then specially examined, amongst these 18 millions of stars, one of the most modest and the least brilliant, a star of the fourth order, which is proudly called the Sun, all the phenomena to which the formation of the universe is due would have been successively accomplished before his eyes.

That sun, still in a gaseous state, and composed of floating molecules, might have been seen revolving on its axis to complete its work of concentration. This movement, true to the laws of mechanics, would have increased with the diminution of volume; and at a certain moment the centrifugal force would have conquered the centripetal force, which latter attracts molecules towards the centre.

Then another phenomenon would have happened before the observer's eyes, and the molecules situated on the plane of the equator, escaping like a stone from a broken sling, would have formed round the sun several concentric rings, like that of Saturn. In their turn these rings of cosmical matter, gaining a rotatory movement around the central mass, would have been broken up and decomposed into secondary nebulosities – that is to say, into planets.

If the observer had then concentrated his attention upon these planets, he would have seen them act in the same manner as the sun, and each give birth to one or more cosmical rings, which are the origin of those stars of inferior order which are called satellites.

Thus, in tracing back from the atom to the molecule, from the molecule to the nebulous agglomeration, from the nebulous agglomeration to the nebulae, from the nebulae to the principal star, from the principal star to the sun, from the sun to the planet, from the planet to the satellite, we have the whole series of transformations undergone by the celestial bodies since the first days of the world.

The sun seems lost in the immensity of the starry world, and yet it is connected by the present theories of science with the nebulae of the Milky Way. It is the centre of the world, and however diminutive it may appear in the midst of the ethereal regions, it is nevertheless enormous, for its size is 1,400,000 times that of the earth. Around it gravitate eight planets, which were drawn from its very entrails during the first epoch of creation. These are – to commence with the nearest – Mercury, Venus, the Earth, Mars, Jupiter, Saturn, Uranus, and Neptune. Farther, between Mars and Jupiter, there are other bodies of less size, the floating remnants, perhaps, of some star shattered into a thousand pieces, and of which the telescope has hitherto revealed ninety-seven. Some of these attendant bodies, which the sun maintains in their elliptical orbit by the universal law of gravitation, have satellites in their turn. Uranus has eight; Jupiter four; Neptune three, perhaps; and the Earth one.

The latter is one of the most important in the solar system, and is called the Moon, which the audacious genius of the Americans aimed to conquer.

The Queen of the Night, by her comparative proximity and the frequently-renewed spectacle of her several phases, was the first to divide with the sun the attention of the inhabitants of the earth. But the sun is fatiguing to the glance, and the splendour of its light dazzles the eyes of its observers.

Fair-haired Phoebe, on the contrary, complacently shows herself, robed in her modest graces; she is soft to the eye and not ambitious, although she sometimes takes upon herself to eclipse her radiant brother Apollo, and is never eclipsed by him. The Mahomedans understood the gratitude which they owed to this faithful friend of the earth, and have regulated their months by her revolutions.

This chaste goddess was the object of particular adoration by the first inhabitants of the earth. The Egyptians called her Isis; the Phoenicians, Astarte; the Greeks adored her under the name of Phoebe, daughter of Latona and Jupiter, and they explained her eclipses by the mysterious visits of Diana to the beautiful Endymion. If we are to believe the legends of mythology, the Nemean lion ranged over the countries of the moon before his appearance upon earth; and the poet Agesianax, cited by Plutarch, celebrated in his verses the soft eyes, the charming nose and adorable mouth formed by the luminous parts of the beauteous Selene.

However the ancients may have understood the character and temperament, in a word the moral qualities of the moon from a mythological point of view, the most learned amongst them were very ignorant of selenography.

Many astronomers in earlier times discovered, it is true, certain particulars which science confirms today, although the Arcadians pretended that they had inhabited the earth at a time when the moon did not yet exist. Simplicius thought her immovable, and fixed to a dome of crystal; Tacitus thought her a fragment detached from the solar disc; and Clearchus, a disciple of Aristotle, called her a polished mirror in which the images of the ocean were reflected. Whilst others only saw in her a mass of vapour exhaled by the earth, or a globe half fire and half ice, revolving upon its own axis, some learned men, by sagacious observation, though unassisted by optical instruments, suspected most of the laws which govern the Queen of the Night.

Thus Thales of Miletus, 460 B.C., gave as his opinion that the moon borrowed her light from the sun. Aristarchus, of Samos, gave the true explanation of her phases. Cleomedes thought that she shone with a reflected light. The Chaldean, Berose, discovered that the duration of her movement of rotation was equal to that of her movement of revolution; and he explained in this way the fact that the moon always presents the same face. Lastly, Hipparchus, 200 B.C., discovered some inequality in the apparent movements of the earth's satellite.

These several observations were confirmed later, and were useful to new astronomers. Ptolemaeus, in the second century, and the Arab, Aboul Wefa, in the tenth, completed the observations of Hipparchus as to the inequalities which the moon undergoes when following the undulated line of her orbit under the action of the sun; then Copernicus, in the fifteenth century, and Tycho Brahe, in the sixteenth century, completely unfolded the system of the world and the part which the moon plays amongst the celestial bodies.

At this epoch the movements of the moon were pretty well determined, but little was known about her physical constitution. It was then that Galileo explained the phenomena of light produced in certain phases by the existence of mountains, to which he assigned an average height of 4,400 fathoms. Subsequently Hevelius, an astronomer from Dantzic, reduced the greatest altitudes to 2,600 fathoms; but his colleague, Riccioli, set them down at 7,000. Herschel, at the end of the eighteenth century, with the aid of a powerful telescope, reduced the above measures considerably. He fixed the highest mountains at 1,900 fathoms, and reduced the average of different altitudes to only 400 fathoms. But Herschel was still wrong, and it required the observations of Schroeter, Louville, Halley, Nasmyth, Bianchini, Pastorf, Lohrman, Gruithuisen, and especially the patient studies of Messrs Beer and Moedler, to solve the question definitively. Thanks to these learned men, the altitude of the mountains of the moon is thoroughly well known today. Messrs Beer and Moedler have measured 1,905 summits, six of which are above 2,600 fathoms, and twenty-two above 2,400. Their highest summit rises to a height of 3,801 fathoms above the surface of the lunar disc.

At the same time the examination of the moon was completed; this luminary appeared covered with craters, and its essentially volcanic nature was confirmed by each successive observation.

From the absence of refraction in the rays of the planet occulted by the moon, it was concluded that the latter could have no atmosphere. This absence of air necessitated absence of water. It was thus manifest that the Selenites, to be able to live under these conditions, must be endowed with a special organisation and be very different from the inhabitants of the earth. At last, thanks to new inventions, more perfect instruments examined the moon without ceasing, and left not a single spot of her surface unexplored. Her diameter measures 2,500 miles; her surface is 1/13th part of the surface of the globe; her volume 1/49th part of the volume of the terrestrial spheroid; yet none of her secrets could escape the eyes of astronomers, and these clever *savants* carried their prodigious observations farther still.

Thus they observed that during the full moon the disc appeared in certain parts marked with white lines, and during the phases with black lines. By examining with yet greater precision they succeeded in discovering the exact nature of these lines. They are long and narrow furrows dug between parallel lines, generally terminating at the edge of the craters; they are from about 10 to 100 miles long, and 800 fathoms wide. Astronomers call them rifts, but are only able to give them a name. As to knowing whether these rifts are dry, the beds of ancient rivers or not, they could come to no satisfactory conclusion. The Americans hope one day or other to decide this question. They also hoped to reconnoitre that series of parallel ramparts discovered on the surface of the moon by Gruithuisen, the learned professor of Munich, who thought them a system of fortifications thrown up by Selenite engineers. These two points, still obscure, and many others no doubt, could only be definitively settled when direct communication had been established with the moon.

As to the intensity of her light, there was nothing further to learn on that head; it was known to be 3,000 times weaker than that of the sun, and that its heat has no appreciable action on the thermometer. As to the phenomenon known as the ash light, it is naturally explained by the effect of the rays of the sun reflected from the earth to the moon, which seem to complete the lunar disc when the latter presents itself under the form of a crescent in its first and last phases.

Such was the state of knowledge acquired with reference to the earth's satellite which the Gun Club proposed to complete in all respects, whether cosmographical, geological, political, or moral.

CHAPTER SIX

Things that all must know, and things that none are
allowed to believe in the United States

The immediate result of Barbicane's proposal was to draw attention to all astronomical facts relating to the Queen of the Night. Everyone gave himself up to the study of the matter. It was as though Luna had just made her first appearance above the horizon and no one had yet perceived her in the heavens. She became quite the fashion; she was the lion of the day without appearing the less modest on that account, and she took her place amongst the 'stars' without any signs of pride. The papers revived all the old anecdotes about the 'Sun of the Wolves'; they remembered the various influences which were attributed to her by the ignorance of former ages; she was the universal topic of conversation; they nearly went to the extent of retailing her latest witticisms; the whole of America was struck with selenomania.

The various scientific reviews published treatises upon questions relating to the undertaking of the Gun Club, and the letter from the Cambridge Observatory was published, commented on, and unreservedly approved.

In short, it was impossible for the most illiterate Yankee to ignore a single fact relating to his satellite, nor was it possible for the most bigoted old woman to entertain any superstitious terror on the subject. Science reached them in every shape; it penetrated by the eyes and by the ears; it was quite impossible to be an ass – in astronomy.

Until this time many people had been unaware by what means it was possible to calculate the distance between the moon and the earth. They were now informed that this distance was obtained by measuring the parallax of the moon. If the word parallax was unfamiliar to them, it was explained to be the angle formed by two straight lines drawn from each extremity of the eye's radius to the moon. If they had any doubt as to the exactness of this method, it was immediately proved to them that not only the average distance was in reality 234,347 miles, but that astronomers could not possibly be more than seventy miles out in their calculations.

To such as were not familiar with the movements of the moon, the daily papers showed that she possesses two distinct movements, the first known as rotation upon her axis, the second, revolution around the earth, both being executed in the same time, say 27 days and one-third.

The movement of rotation is that which causes day and night on the surface of the moon, only there is but one day and one night in each lunar month, and each of these lasts 354 hours and one-third. Fortunately for the moon, the face turned towards the terrestrial globe is illuminated by the latter with an intensity equal to the light of fourteen moons. As regards the other face, which is always invisible, it has, naturally, 354 hours of absolute night, only tempered by that pale glimmer which falls from the stars. This phenomenon is solely due to the particular circumstance that the movements of rotation and revolution are each completed in exactly the same time. Cassini and Herschel declare that this phenomenon is observable in the satellites of Jupiter, and very probably in all other satellites.

Some well-intentioned people were inclined to cavil, and did not at first understand how, if the moon invariably shows the same face to the earth during her revolution, she could possibly in the same lapse of time rotate upon her axis. To such as these the following explanation was given: 'Go into your dining-room and walk round your table, always keeping your eye on the centre. When your circular walk is completed you will find that you have made one turn upon your axis, for your eye will have successively glanced over all the parts of the room. There you have it – the room is the sky, the table is the earth, and you are the moon.' And they went away delighted with the comparison.

Thus the moon turns continually the same face towards the earth; however, to be exact, we must add that on account of a certain oscillation from north to south, and to the west, which is called libration, she shows rather more than half of her disc, in all about 57-100ths.

So soon as the most ignorant were as well informed as the Director of the Cambridge Observatory with regard to the rotation of the moon, they at once took a great interest in her movement of revolution around the earth, and twenty scientific reviews immediately undertook to instruct them. They learned that the firmament, with its infinity of stars, may be compared to an immense dial, round which the moon travels, marking the exact time to all the inhabitants of the earth. During this movement the Queen of the Night presents her various phases. The moon is full when she is in opposition with the sun, that is, when the three orbs are in the same line, the earth being the centre; the moon is new when she is in conjunction with the sun, that is, when she stands between the earth and it; lastly, she is in her first or last quarter when she forms with the sun and earth a right angle, of which she is the apex.

Certain perspicacious Yankees arrived at the conclusion that eclipses could only occur at times of conjunction or opposition, and their reasoning was correct. When in conjunction the moon can eclipse the sun, whereas, in opposition the earth eclipses it in its turn, and if these eclipses do not happen twice in each revolution it is because the plane on which the moon moves is elliptically inclined, like the plane on which the earth moves.

The letter from the Cambridge Observatory had said all that was requisite with reference to the height which the orb of night can attain above the horizon. Everyone knew that this height varies according to the latitude of the spot from which the moon is observed. But the only zones of the globe in which the moon attains the zenith – that is to say, places herself directly above the heads of the observers – are necessarily comprised between the equator and the twenty-eighth parallel. Hence the important recommendation to make the experiment upon some spot in this portion of the globe, so that the projectile might be discharged perpendicularly, and thus escape sooner from the action of gravitation. This was a condition essential to the success of the undertaking and greatly preoccupied public opinion.

The Cambridge Observatory had sufficiently taught even the most ignorant in the country that the line followed by the moon in her revolution around the earth is not a circle but an ellipse, of which the earth forms one of the foci. These elliptic orbits are common to all the planets as well as to all the satellites, and the laws of mechanics prove that things could not be otherwise. It is well understood that the moon in her apogee is farthest removed from the earth, and nearest to it in her perigee.

Every American learnt the above, whether he would or not, and indeed no one could decently be ignorant upon such matters. But if true principles spread rapidly, many errors and illusory fears were not the less difficult to uproot.

Thus, for instance, some well-meaning people maintained that the moon was nothing but an old comet which, travelling on its long orbit around the sun, had come so near to the earth as to be retained within its circle of attraction. These drawing-room astronomers tried to explain in this way the burnt appearance of the moon, which irreparable misfortune they attributed to the solar rays. But when it was pointed out to them that comets have an atmosphere, and the moon has little or none, they were somewhat at a loss for a reply.

Others, of more timid nature, entertained certain fears concerning the moon. They had heard that, since the observations taken in the time of the Khalifs, its movement of rotation had increased in a certain proportion, whence they deduced, and with a certain amount of reason, that as an increase of velocity must entail a diminution in the distance separating the two orbs, the moon would one day come into collision with the earth. However, they were reassured, and their fears on behalf of future generations were dissipated, when they learned that, according to the calculation of Laplace, a well-known French mathematician, this increase of movement was restrained within very narrow limits, and will soon be succeeded by a proportionate diminution. Thus the equilibrium of the solar system will not be disturbed in future ages.

Lastly, there remained the superstitious class of ignoramuses. These people are not only ignorant, but they know what does not exist, and in this manner their knowledge of the moon was inexhaustible. Some considered its disc merely as a polished mirror in which they could see themselves from various points of the earth, and communicate their thoughts to each other. Others declared that out of a thousand new moons which had been observed, nine hundred and fifty had brought about most notable changes, such as cataclysms, revolutions, earthquakes, deluges, &c.; they therefore believed in some mystical influence of the orb of night upon human destinies. They looked upon it as the real counterbalance of existence: they thought that each Selenite was attached by some sympathetic bond to each inhabitant of the earth; they joined with Dr Mead in maintaining that the vital system is completely under lunar influence, that boys especially are born during the new moon, and girls during the last quarter, &c. However, these vulgar errors had to be given up and the real facts recognised; and if the moon, thus shorn of her influence, lost ground in the opinion of some, the immense majority pronounced in her favour. As to the Yankees, they had but one other ambition, which was to take possession of this new continent, and plant on its highest summit the stars and stripes of the United States of America.

CHAPTER SEVEN

The song of the shot

In their memorable letter of the 7th of October, the Cambridge Observatory had treated the question in its astronomical aspect; it now became necessary to resolve it by mechanics. The practical difficulties which this offered would have appeared insurmountable in any other country, but in America they were only matter for amusement.

President Barbicane had lost no time in appointing an acting committee in the Gun Club. This committee was to elucidate, in three sittings, the three great questions of the cannon, the projectile, and the powder. It was composed of four members learned in these matters: Barbicane (with a casting vote in case of equality), General Morgan, Major Elphiston, and lastly the irrepressible J. T. Maston, who acted as secretary to the committee.

On the 8th of October the committee held their first meeting at President Barbicane's, 3, Republican Street. As it was desirable that the wants of the stomach should not interrupt so important a discussion, the four members of the Gun Club took their seats at a table spread with sandwiches and teapots. J. T. Maston screwed his pen on his iron hook, and the meeting was declared opened. Barbicane spoke first.

'My dear colleagues,' he said, 'we have to resolve one of the most important problems in the science of gunnery, that noble science which treats of the movement of projectiles, *i.e.*, bodies thrown into space by some force of impulsion and then left to themselves.'

'Gunnery for ever!' cried J. T. Maston, already somewhat excited.

'Perhaps it would have been somewhat more consistent,' continued Barbicane, 'to discuss at this first meeting the apparatus.'

'It would indeed,' said General Morgan.

'However,' continued Barbicane, 'after much reflection, it does appear to me that the question of the projectile should have precedence of the cannon, and that the dimensions of the latter should depend upon the dimensions of the former.'

'Let me speak,' said J. T. Maston.

Permission was granted to him with a readiness justified by his splendid antecedents.

'My good friends,' said he in inspired tones, 'our president is right in giving the question of the projectile precedence over all others. This shot, which we are going to fire at the moon, is our messenger – our ambassador – and I ask permission to consider it in its purely moral aspect.'

This new mode of considering a projectile raised the curiosity of all the members of the committee, and they listened with deep attention to J. T. Maston's words.

'My dear colleagues,' continued the latter, 'I will be brief. I will leave on one side the physical shot – the shot that kills – and only consider the mathematical or moral shot. A shot, to my mind, is the most startling manifestation of human power, which it sums up in its entirety.'

'Bravo!' said Major Elphiston.

'God,' said the orator, 'has made the stars and planets; man has pro-duced the cannon-ball, which is the great criterion of terrestrial velocity – a reproduction of wandering stars, which after all are only projectiles. Leave to the Deity the swiftness of electricity, the swiftness of light, the swiftness of stars, the swiftness of comets, the swiftness of satellites, the swiftness of planets, the swiftness of sound, the swiftness of wind; we have the swiftness of the cannon-ball – one hundred times greater than the swiftness of the most rapid trains and horses.'

J. T. Marston was carried away by his enthusiasm; his voice assumed lyrical accents, as he sang this sacred song of the shot.

'Would you have figures,' continued he, 'these are truly eloquent. Take, for instance, the ball of a 24-pounder. If it travels 800,000 times slower than electricity, 640,000 times slower than light, 76 times slower than the earth in its movement around the sun, at least, when it issues from the cannon's mouth, it exceeds the rapidity of sound; it travels 200 fathoms in a second, 2,000 fathoms in ten seconds, 14 miles in a minute, 840 miles in an hour, 20,100 miles per day; which is equal to the rapidity of the points of the equator in the rotatory movement of the globe, or 7,336,500 miles per annum. It would therefore take eleven days to reach the moon, twelve years to reach the sun, and 360 years to reach Neptune on the limits of the solar system. See what a small cannon-ball is capable of! What would it be when its velocity is increased twenty-fold, and the shot is discharged with a rapidity of seven miles to the second? Superb shot! Splendid projectile! Doubtless it would be received above with the honours due to a terrestrial ambassador.'

This high-flown speech was received with cheers; and J. T. Maston, overcome by his feelings, seated himself amidst the congratulations of his colleagues.

'Now,' said Barbicane, 'having devoted so much time to poetry, let us commence the practical discussion of the question.'

'We are ready,' said the members of the committee as each bolted half-a-dozen sandwiches.

'You know the problem we have to resolve,' continued the president; 'it is necessary to endow a projectile with a velocity of 12,000 yards per second. I believe we shall succeed. But, let us commence by examining the velocities obtained up to the present time; General Morgan can give us information on this point.'

'The more easily,' replied the general, 'that during the war I was a member of the committee of experiments. I may tell you that the Dahlgren 100-pounders, carrying to a distance of 2,500 fathoms, despatched their projectiles with an initial velocity of 500 yards per second.'

'What about Rodman's columbiad?' asked the president.

'Rodman's columbiad, tested at Fort Hamilton, near New York, threw a shot weighing half a ton to a distance of six miles with a velocity of 800 yards per second, which result has never been attained by either Armstrong or Palliser in England.'

'Pooh! Englishmen!' said J. T. Maston, jerking his formidable hook towards the eastern horizon.

'It appears, then,' said Barbicane, 'that 800 yards represent the maximum velocity hitherto obtained.'

'Yes,' replied Morgan.

'I wish to say,' interrupted J. T. Maston, 'that if my mortar had not burst –'

'Yes, but it did burst,' said Barbicane with a good-natured smile. 'We can therefore only take into consideration this velocity of 800 yards. It must be increased twenty-fold. But setting aside for the moment the means for obtaining this velocity, I wish to call your attention, dear colleagues, to the dimensions which it would be necessary to give to the projectile. Of course you quite understand that there can be no question here of projectiles weighing half a ton.'

'Why not?' asked the major.

'Because the shot,' said J. T. Maston, 'must be large enough to attract the attention of the inhabitants of the moon if there are any.'

'Yes,' said Barbicane, 'and for another reason still more important.'

'What is that, Barbicane?' asked the major.

'I mean that it is not sufficient to send off a projectile, and then take no more interest in it; we must follow it during its passage, until the very moment when it reaches its goal.'

'What!' said the general and the major, somewhat surprised at the proposal.

'Doubtless,' continued Barbicane, with a confident mien; 'doubtless, or our experiment will produce no result.'

'But in that case,' said the major, 'the dimensions of the projectile must be enormous.'

'No, be good enough to listen. You know that optical instruments have attained a great pitch of perfection. With certain telescopes we are able to enlarge an object 6,000 times, and to bring the moon to within about forty miles. At this distance, objects sixty feet long are easily visible. The penetrating power of telescopes would have been carried farther still but for the fact that this power can only be exercised to the detriment of clearness, and the moon, which is after all but a reflecting mirror, does not emit sufficient light to allow of enlargements beyond this limit.'

'What will you do, then?' asked the general. 'Will your projectile have a diameter of sixty feet?'

'Certainly not.'

'Would you render the moon more luminous?'

'I would.'

'That's a little too strong,' cried J. T. Maston.

'Yet it is very simple,' said Barbicane. 'I have only to diminish the density of the atmosphere traversed by the rays of the moon; that will make the light more intense.'

'Quite so.'

'Well, to obtain this result, it is only necessary to erect a telescope on some very high mountains. We can surely do that.'

'I give in,' said the major; 'you have such a way of simplifying things. And what enlargement do you hope to obtain in this way?'

'Forty-eight thousand times, which would bring the moon to within five miles, when objects having nine feet in diameter will be easily visible.'

'Bravo!' cried J. T. Maston; 'our projectile will therefore be nine feet in diameter.'

'Precisely so.'

'Allow me to remark, however,' said Major Elphiston, 'that the weight will still be so great – '

'Oh, major,' said Barbicane, 'before discussing the weight let me tell you that our ancestors did wonders in that way. I should be the last to assert that the science of gunnery has made no progress, but we must not forget that the middle ages obtained astonishing results, I might say more astonishing than we.'

'How so?' said Morgan.

'Prove your words,' said J. T. Maston.

'Nothing is more easy,' replied Barbicane. 'I can bring examples to prove my assertions. During the siege of Constantinople by Mahomet II in 1543, stone shots were fired weighing 1,900 pounds. They must have been large enough!'

'One thousand nine hundred pounds!' said the major, 'that's a very big figure.'

'At Malta, when the knights had possession of the island, one of the cannons from Fort St Elme fired projectiles weighing 2,500 pounds.'

'You don't mean to say so!'

'According to a French historian, in Louis XI's time a mortar threw a shell weighing only 500 pounds; but this shell, fired from the Bastille, where fools imprisoned wise men, fell into Charenton, a place where wise men lock up fools.'

'Hear! hear!' said J. T. Maston.

'Since then what have we seen? Armstrong guns throwing shot weighing 500 pounds, and Rodman's columbiad projectiles weighing half a ton. It would seem, then, that projectiles have gained in range and lost in weight. But if we give our attention to this side of the question we ought to be able, with our advanced science, to manage ten times the weight of the shot used by Mahomet II and the Knights of Malta.'

'That is clear,' said the major, 'but what metal will you use for your projectile?'

'Merely cast-iron,' said General Morgan.

'Cast-iron!' said J. T. Maston with great disdain, 'that's a very common sort of metal for a shot intended for the moon.'

'Don't let us be extravagant, my good friend,' replied Morgan, 'cast-iron is quite sufficient.'

'Well, then,' said Major Elphiston, 'as the weight of the shot is proportionate to its volume, a cast-iron shot of nine feet in diameter will still be a tremendous weight.'

'Yes, if it is massive, but not if it is hollow,' said Barbicane.

'Hollow? That will be a shell.'

'We might put despatches into it,' said J. T. Maston, 'and samples of our terrestrial products.'

'It must be a shell. A massive shot of 108 inches would weigh more than 200,000 pounds – that would clearly be too heavy; however, as this projectile must have a certain strength of resistance, I propose that it shall weigh 20,000 pounds.'

'What would be the thickness of the sides?' asked the major.

'If we follow out the regular proportions,' said Morgan, 'a diameter of 108 inches would require a thickness of at least two feet.'

'That would be too much,' said Barbicane. 'You see we are not making a shot for piercing iron plates; it will only require sufficient thickness to withstand the pressure of the powder gas. This is the problem: What would be the thickness of a cast-iron shell only weighing 20,000 pounds? Mr Maston will tell us at once.'

'Nothing can be easier,' replied the hon. secretary; whereupon he traced some rapid algebraic formulae on the paper. x, y, and z followed each other in quick succession. He appeared to extract a certain cubic root, and said: 'The sides will only be two inches thick.'

'Will that be sufficient?' asked the major, doubtfully.

'No,' replied President Barbicane, 'evidently not.'

'Well, what's to be done?' said Elphiston, looking somewhat embarrassed.

'We must use another metal.'

'Copper?' said Morgan.

'No; that's too heavy. I have something better to propose.'

'What is it?' said the major.

'Aluminum,' answered Barbicane.

'Aluminum?' cried the president's three colleagues.

'Certainly, my friends. You are aware that an illustrious French chemist, Henri St Clair-Deville, succeeded in 1854 in producing aluminum in large masses. This precious metal is as white as silver, as inalterable as gold, as tenacious as iron, as fusible as copper, and as light as glass; it is easily worked, easily found, as alumina forms the basis of most rocks; it is three times as light as iron, and would seem to have been specially created to supply the material for our projectile.'

'Three cheers for aluminum!' cried the secretary of the committee, always very noisy in his moments of enthusiasm.

'But, my dear president,' said the major, 'is not aluminum very expensive?'

'It was,' replied Barbicane; 'a short time after its discovery a pound of aluminum cost from 260 to 280 dollars; later on it fell to 27 dollars, and today it costs only 9 dollars a pound.'

'But nine dollars a pound,' replied the major, who was not easily beaten off, 'will make a tremendous sum.'

'No doubt, my dear major, but not an impossible one.'

'What will the projectile weigh?' asked Morgan.

'Here are my calculations,' replied Barbicane: 'a shot 108 inches in diameter and 12 inches thick, would weigh, in cast-iron, 67,440 pounds;

in aluminum its weight would be reduced to 19,250 pounds.'

'Hear, hear!' said Maston; 'that comes within our programme.'

'Hear, hear!' replied the major; 'but don't you know that at nine dollars a pound this projectile will cost – '

'One hundred and seventy-three thousand two hundred and fifty dollars. I am well aware of it; but fear nothing, my friends, money will not be wanting for our undertaking. I'll answer for that.'

'We shall get more than we want,' replied J. T. Maston.

'Well, what do you think of aluminum?' asked the president.

'Accepted!' replied the three members of the committee.

'As to the shape of the projectile,' continued Barbicane, 'that is of little importance, for once the atmosphere is passed the projectile will be in vacuum. I should propose, therefore, a round shot which can turn upon its own axis, or otherwise behave as it thinks proper.'

So terminated the first meeting of the committee. The question of the projectile was definitively resolved, and J. T. Maston was delighted at the idea of sending an aluminum cannon-ball to the Selenites, 'which would give them a great idea of the inhabitants of the earth.'

CHAPTER EIGHT

The history of the cannon

The resolutions taken at this meeting produced a great effect on the outside world. Some timid persons were rather afraid at the idea of a shot weighing 20,000 pounds travelling through space. It was a question whether a cannon could ever endow such a mass with a sufficient initial velocity. The minutes of the second meeting of the committee fully answered all these questions.

On the evening of the next day the four members of the Gun Club seated themselves before new mountains of sandwiches, on the brink of a very ocean of tea. The discussion was continued, but this time without any preamble.

'Worthy colleagues,' said Barbicane, 'we are going to discuss the apparatus and its construction, its length, its weight, its form and composition. It is probable we may have to make it of gigantic dimensions; but, however great the difficulties, our mechanical genius will overcome them. Listen, then, and don't spare your objections; I do not fear them.'

This declaration was met by a murmur of approval.

'Do not let us forget,' continued Barbicane, 'the point at which our discussion finished yesterday. This is the present form of the problem: how to impart an initial velocity of 12,000 yards per second to a shell 108 inches in diameter, weighing 20,000 pounds?'

'That is the question,' said Major Elphiston.

'Let me continue,' said Barbicane. 'When a projectile is discharged into space, what happens? It is subjected to three separate independent forces: the resistance of the atmosphere, the attraction of the earth, and the force of impulsion given to it. Let us examine these three forces. The resistance of the atmosphere is not very important, as the terrestrial atmosphere only extends for forty miles. Possessing a velocity of 12,000 yards per second, the projectile will have passed through it in five seconds, which is so short a space of time that the resistance of the atmosphere may be considered as insignificant. Let us pass to the attraction of the earth *i.e.*, the weight of the shell. We know that this weight will diminish in the inverse ratio of the square of the distance. The laws of physics teach us that when any substance is left to itself, and falls to the surface of the earth, it travels fifteen feet in the first second; and if this same substance be carried to a height of 257,542 miles, which is the distance from the moon to the earth, its fall would be reduced to about half the width of a line in the first second, or almost immobility. It is necessary to conquer progressively this action of gravitation. How is it to be done? By the force of impulsion.'

'Therein lies the difficulty,' said the major.

'You are quite right,' said the president; 'but we will conquer it, for this force of impulsion which we require is the result of the length of the gun and the quantity of powder used; the latter being only limited by the resistance of the former. Let us take into consideration today the dimensions to be given to the cannon. It is well understood that we can construct it to resist almost any possible pressure, for it will not have to be moved about.'

'Very good,' said the general.

'Until now,' said Barbicane, 'our longest cannons – our enormous columbiads – have not exceeded twenty-five feet in length. Many people will be astonished at the dimensions which we shall now be forced to adopt.'

'For my part,' said J. T. Maston, 'I vote for a cannon half a mile long at least.'

'Half a mile!' cried the major and general.

'Yes, half a mile; and that will be too short by half.'

'Maston,' said Morgan, 'you are exaggerating.'

'No, I am not,' said the irrepressible secretary; 'I do not know why you should accuse me of exaggeration.'

'Because you are going too far.'

'Learn, sir,' said J. T. Maston with his grand air, 'learn that an artillerist is like a cannon-ball – he can never go too far.'

As the discussion was taking a personal turn the president interfered.

'Don't excite yourselves, my friends, but let us examine the question. The cannon must evidently be a long one, for the length of the gun will increase the detention of gas behind the projectile; but it is useless to exceed certain limits.'

'Quite so,' said the major.

'What are the usual rules in such cases? Generally the length of a cannon is from 20 to 25 times the diameter of the shot, and weighs from 235 to 240 times the weight of the latter.'

'That is not sufficient,' cried J. T. Maston.

'I agree with you, my worthy friend. According to these proportions the gun for a projectile nine feet broad, weighing 30,000 pounds, would only be 225 feet long, and would only weigh 7,200,000 pounds.'

'That is ridiculous,' said J. T. Maston. 'Why not take a pocket-pistol.'

'I am of the same opinion,' replied Barbicane; 'so I propose to quadruple that length and construct a cannon 900 feet long.'

The general and the major offered some objections, but nevertheless the proposal, seconded by the secretary of the Gun Club, was definitively adopted.

'Now,' said Elphiston, 'what is to be the thickness of the tube?'

'Six feet,' said Barbicane.

'You'll never be able to put such a mass on to a carriage,' said the major.

'It would look magnificent,' said J. T. Maston.

'But impracticable,' replied Barbicane. 'No, I am going to cast the gun in the earth, fit it with rings of forged iron, and surround it with a mass of stone masonry, so that it shall have the advantage of the resistance of the surrounding ground. So soon as the gun is cast, it shall be carefully bored and polished so as to avoid any possible windage; thus there will be no loss of gas, and all the expansive force of the powder will be applied to the impulsion.'

'Hear, hear,' said J. T. Maston, 'there we have our cannon.'

'Not yet,' replied Barbicane, motioning his impatient friend to be still.

'Why not?'

'Because we have not yet discussed its form. Is it to be a cannon, a howitzer, or a mortar?'

'A cannon,' replied Morgan.

'A howitzer,' said the major.

'A mortar,' cried J. T. Maston.

A new discussion was on the point of commencing, each one supporting his favourite arm; but the president stopped it short.

'My friends,' said he, 'you shall all be satisfied. Our columbiad shall have something of all three. It shall be a cannon, for its powder chamber shall have the same diameter as the bore; it shall be a howitzer, for it will fire a shell; lastly, it shall be a mortar, for it will be fixed at an angle of 90° without any possibility of recoil so as to transmit all its accumulated power of impulsion to the projectile.'

'Hear, hear,' said the members of the committee.

'I wish to ask one question,' said Elphiston; 'will the gun be rifled?'

'No,' answered Barbicane, 'it will not. We require an enormous initial velocity, and you are aware that the shot leaves a rifled cannon much less rapidly than a smooth-bore.'

'That is true.'

'We have got it this time,' repeated J. T. Maston.

'Not quite,' replied the president.

'Why not?'

'Because we have not yet decided what metal shall be used.'

'Let us decide at once.'

'I was going to make a proposal.'

The four members of the committee swallowed a dozen sandwiches, washed down by a dish of tea, and the discussion recommenced.

'My worthy colleagues,' said Barbicane, 'our cannon must be of great tenacity, of great hardness, unfusible by heat, and proof against the corrosive action of acids.'

'There can be no doubt about that,' said the major, 'and as we shall want an immense quantity of metal we have not much choice in the matter.'

'I propose,' said Maston, 'to employ the best alloy known. That is, one hundred parts of copper, twelve parts of tin, and six parts of brass.'

'My friends,' replied the president, 'I admit that this composition has given excellent results, but in the present instance it would cost too much, and would be difficult to employ. So I think we must adopt something good but cheap, such as cast-iron. What do you think, major?'

'I think the same,' said Elphiston.

'Cast-iron,' said Barbicane, 'costs ten times less than bronze, is easily melted, can be run into a sand mould, and is easily manipulated. It therefore offers an economy of money and of time. Besides, it is an excellent substance, and I remember that during the war, at the siege of Atlanta, some cast-iron guns fired 1,000 shots each, at intervals of twenty minutes, without being any the worse.'

'Cast-iron is very brittle,' said Morgan.

'Yes, but very resisting too; besides, I answer for it we shall not burst.'

'One may burst, and yet remain honest,' said J. T. Maston, sententiously.

'No doubt,' replied Barbicane. 'I am going to beg our worthy secretary to calculate the weight of a cast-iron gun 900 feet long, having an interior diameter of nine feet, and a tube six feet thick.'

'In a minute,' replied Maston.

And, as on the previous evening, he arranged his formulae with marvellous facility, and said, at the end of a minute: 'The cannon will weigh 68,040 tons; which will cost, at two cents the pound, 2,510,701 dollars.'

J. T. Maston, the major, and the general looked at Barbicane with some alarm.

'Gentlemen,' said the president, 'I beg to repeat what I said yesterday: Be without fear – the millions will be forthcoming.'

With this assurance the committee adjourned until the following evening.

CHAPTER NINE

The powder question

The powder question remained to be discussed, and the public awaited the decision with great anxiety. Given the thickness of the projectile and the length of the gun, what would be the quantity of powder necessary to produce the impulsion? The terrible agent, which man has been able to subdue, was to be called upon to play its part in unusual proportions.

It is very generally considered that gunpowder was invented in the fourteenth century, by a monk named Schwartz, who paid for his invention with his life; but it is proved now that this story is only a legend of the middle ages. No one invented gunpowder; it is directly derived from Greek fire, which, like it, was composed of sulphur and saltpetre, with this difference, that the one is only a slow-burning mixture, and the other a detonating mixture.

Although many learned men are well acquainted with the false history of gunpowder, very few know anything about its mechanical power. Yet it is necessary to understand this point, in order to comprehend the importance of the question submitted to the committee.

A litre of gunpowder weighs about two pounds, and produces by combustion 400 litres of gas; this liberated gas, under the action of a temperature raised to 2,400°, fills a space of 4,000 litres. Thus the volume of powder is, to the volume of gas produced by its combustion, as 1 is to 4,000. Judge from this the frightful propelling power of this gas when compressed in a space 4,000 times too small.

This was well known to the members of the committee when, next day, they opened their meeting. Barbicane called upon Major Elphiston to speak, he having been Director of Powder Magazines during the war.

'My dear comrade,' said this distinguished chemist, 'I will commence by referring to the irrefutable figures which will form the basis of our discussion. The shot of the 24-pounder, mentioned the day before yesterday by the Hon. J. T. Maston in such poetic language, is discharged from the gun by sixteen pounds of powder only.'

'Are you certain of the figures?' asked Barbicane.

'Absolutely certain,' replied the major. 'Armstrong's gun employs seventy-five pounds of powder for a projectile weighing 800 pounds, and Rodman's columbiad takes 160 pounds of powder to throw a shot weighing half a ton a distance of six miles. These facts are beyond all doubt, for I extracted them myself from the minutes of the Committee of Artillery.'

'Very well,' said the general.

'The conclusion I draw from these figures,' continued the major, 'is that the quantity of powder does not increase with the weight of the shot. If it requires sixteen pounds of powder for the shot of a 24-pounder – in other terms, if, in ordinary cannons, the amount of powder used is two-thirds the weight of the projectile, the proportions are not maintained elsewhere. Make your calculations, and you will see that for a shot weighing half a ton the amount of powder has been reduced from 333 pounds to 160 pounds.'

'What do you conclude?' said the president.

'That if you carry your theory to its extreme limit, my dear major,' said J. T. Maston, 'you will arrive at the conclusion that when the shot attains a sufficient weight no more powder will be required at all.'

'Our friend Maston must have his joke,' said the major; 'but he need be under no apprehension. I intend to propose a quantity of powder which will satisfy even his *amour propre*. Only I wish to remark that during the war the weight of the powder for the largest cannons was reduced, after experiment, to one-tenth the weight of the shot.'

'Nothing could be more exact,' said Morgan; 'but, before we decide on the quantity of powder necessary, I think we had better decide as to its quality.'

'We will employ large-grained powder; its combustion is more rapid than that of smaller grains.'

'Doubtless,' replied Morgan; 'but it is very damaging and ends by destroying the bore of the gun.'

'That may be an objection if the cannon is to undergo a long service, but it cannot apply to our columbiad. We don't run any risk of bursting, and the combustion of our powder must be instantaneous, so that its mechanical effect may be complete.'

'We may,' said J. T. Maston, 'make several touch-holes, so as to ignite the powder in different parts at the same time.'

'No doubt,' replied Elphiston, 'but that would be creating difficulties. I prefer to adopt the coarse-grained powder at once.'

'Very well,' said the general.

'Rodman,' continued the major, 'used for his columbiad powder with grains as large as chestnuts, made from willow charcoal, carbonised in cast-iron vessels. This powder was hard and glossy, left no mark on the hand, contained a large proportion of hydrogen and oxygen, ignited instantaneously, and, though very powerful, did not damage the bore to any great extent.'

'It appears to me,' said J. T. Maston, 'that we ought not to hesitate one moment.'

'Unless you prefer tooth-powder,' replied the major, laughing at his susceptible friend, who shook his hook at him threateningly.

Up to this time Barbicane had abstained from the discussion; he let them speak and merely listened; he evidently had formed his opinion, and asked: 'Now, my friends, what quantity of powder do you propose?'

The three members of the Gun Club looked at each other.

'Two hundred thousand pounds,' said Morgan.

'Five hundred thousand pounds,' said the major.

'Eight hundred thousand pounds,' cried J. T. Maston.

This time Elphiston could not accuse his colleague of exaggeration. It was a question of sending to the moon a projectile weighing 20,000 pounds, and of giving it an initial velocity of 12,000 yards per second. A moment of silence followed the triple proposal made by the three colleagues.

Silence was broken by President Barbicane.

'My worthy comrades,' said he, quietly, 'I start from the principle that the resistance of our cannon, properly constructed, is unlimited; I shall therefore astonish the Hon. J. T. Maston by telling him that he has been too timid in his calculation, and I shall propose to double his 800,000 pounds of powder.'

'One million six hundred thousand pounds?' said J. T. Maston, excitedly.

'At least.'

'Then we shall require my cannon half a mile long?'

'That is evident,' said the major.

'One million six hundred thousand pounds of powder,' continued the secretary of the committee, 'will fill a space of 22,000 cubic feet, or thereabouts. Now, as your cannon has only a total capacity of 54,000 cubic feet, it will be half filled, and the bore will not be long enough to allow the expansion of gas to give a sufficient impulsion to the projectile.'

There was nothing to reply to this; J. T. Maston was right; all looked towards Barbicane.

'Nevertheless,' continued the president, 'I shall require that quantity of powder. One million six hundred thousand pounds of powder will create six milliards of litres of gas. Six milliards! You understand?'

'What is to be done, then?' asked the general.

'It is very simple: we must reduce this enormous quantity of powder whilst retaining its mechanical power.'

'How is that to be done?'

'I will tell you,' said Barbicane. His interlocutors were all attention. 'Nothing is easier,' he continued, 'than to reduce this mass of powder to a volume four times less. You are all acquainted with that curious substance which forms the elementary tissues of vegetable matter, and is called cellulose.'

'Ah!' said the major. 'I can see what you mean, my dear Barbicane.'

'This substance is found in a state of perfect purity in cotton, which latter is nothing but the fibre from the seeds of the cotton tree. Cotton, combined in a cold state with azotic acid, forms a substance eminently insoluble, eminently combustible, and eminently explosive. Some years ago (in 1832) a French chemist, named Bracconot, discovered this substance, and called it xyloidine. In 1838 another Frenchman, Pelouze, made a study of its several properties; and lastly, in 1846, Schönbein, a professor of chemistry at Basle, proposed its adoption for purposes of war. This powder is azotic cotton.'

'Or pyroxyle,' replied Elphiston.

'Or gun-cotton,' said Morgan.

'Is there no American name connected with this discovery?' cried J. T. Maston, whose sentiments of national *amour propre* were very highly developed.

'Not one, unfortunately,' cried the major.

'However, to satisfy Maston,' continued the president, 'I may tell him that the labours of one of our fellow-countrymen are connected with the study of cellulose, for colodium, which is one of the principal agents in photography, is merely pyroxyle dissolved in alcoholic ether, and was discovered by Maynard, when medical student in Boston.'

'Three cheers, then, for Maynard and gun-cotton!' cried the noisy secretary of the Gun Club.

'To return to pyroxyle,' continued Barbicane. 'You know its properties, which will make it so precious to us. It is prepared with the greatest facility. Some cotton is plunged into smoking azotic acid, left there for fifteen minutes, then washed in water and dried.'

'Nothing can be more simple,' said Morgan.

'Further, gun-cotton does not suffer from damp, which is an important quality in our eyes, as we shall require several days to load the cannon; it ignites at 170° instead of 240°, and its deflagration is so sudden that you can light it upon ordinary gunpowder without the latter having time to take fire.'

'Nothing could be better,' said the major, 'only it is more expensive.'

'What does that matter?' said J. T. Maston.

'Further, it transmits to projectiles a velocity four times superior to that of gunpowder. I may add that if it is mixed with eight-tenths of its own weight of nitrate of potash its expansive power is greatly increased.'

'Is that necessary?' asked the major.

'I do not think so,' replied Barbicane. 'Thus, instead of 1,600,000 pounds of gunpowder, we shall only require 400,000 pounds of gun-cotton; and as 500 pounds of cotton can, without danger, be compressed into twenty-seven cubic feet, this substance will only occupy a height of thirty fathoms in the columbiad. In this way the shot will have more than 700 feet of bore to travel under pressure of six milliards of litres of gas before taking its flight towards the Queen of the Night.'

At this period J. T. Maston could not contain his emotion. He flung himself into the arms of his friend with the force of a projectile, and would certainly have gone through him had not Barbicane, fortunately, been bomb-proof.

This incident closed the third meeting of the committee. Barbicane and his audacious colleagues, to whom nothing seemed impossible, had resolved the complex question of the projectile, the cannon, and the powder. Their plan was complete, and only required to be put into execution.

'Which is a mere detail, a bagatelle,' said J. T. Maston.

CHAPTER TEN

One enemy amongst twenty-five millions of friends

The American public took an immense interest in the minutest details connected with the undertaking of the Gun Club. They followed, day by day, the discussions of the committee, and got quite excited over the most simple preparation for this great experiment, and the question of figures which it raised, and the mechanical difficulties to be overcome.

More than one year would elapse between the commencement of the works and their completion; but this lapse of time would not be absolutely void of emotions; the place had to be chosen for the boring, for the construction of the mould, for the casting of the columbiad, and its dangerous loading.

This was more than was necessary to excite public curiosity. Once the projectile was despatched it would escape from their sight in some tenths of a second, and only a small number of privileged persons would be able to see what became of it, how it acted in space, and how it reached the moon. Thus the real interest in the matter was concentrated upon the preparations for the experiment and the precise details of its execution.

However, the purely scientific attraction was suddenly increased by an incident.

We know what legions of admirers and friends Barbicane's project had gained for its author; nevertheless, however honourable, however extraordinary it might be, this majority did not make unanimity. One man, one only, in all the states of the Union, protested against the attempt of the Gun Club. He attacked it with violence on every occasion; and human nature is so constituted that Barbicane was more sensitive to the opposition of this one man than to the applause of all the others.

However, he knew the motive of this antipathy, and whence this solitary enmity arose; he knew that it was personal and of ancient date, and he knew what had given rise to this rivalry of *amour propre*. The president of the Gun Club had never seen his persevering enemy, and this was fortunate; for a meeting of these two men would certainly have led to disastrous consequences. His rival was a scientist, like Barbicane – a proud, audacious, self-sufficient, violent man – in a word a pure Yankee. His name was Captain Nicholl, and he dwelt in Philadelphia.

Everyone is acquainted with the interesting struggle which was carried on during the American war between projectiles and the armour-plating of ironclads – the former intended to pierce, the latter firmly determined not to be pierced. Hence a radical transformation of the navies of the two continents. Shot and iron plate fought with unexampled persistence, the one increasing in size, the other thickening in the same proportion. Vessels armed with formidable guns went boldly into fire under shelter of their invulnerable armour-plates. The *Merrimac*, the *Monitor*, the ram *Tennessee*, and the *Weckhausen* discharged enormous projectiles, and were themselves plated to withstand the projectiles of others. They did unto others as they would should not be done unto them, upon which immoral principle the whole art of war reposes.

If Barbicane was a great shot-founder, Nicholl was a great manufacturer of iron-plates. The one worked day and night at Baltimore, the other worked day and night at Philadelphia. Each one followed a train of ideas essentially opposed to the other.

So, when Barbicane invented a new shot, Nicholl invented a new armour-plate. The president of the Gun Club passed his life in piercing holes, and the captain in endeavouring to stop him. Hence a continual rivalry which became personal. Nicholl appeared to Barbicane in his dreams in the form of an impenetrable armour-plate, against which he was shattered into pieces, and Barbicane in the visions of Nicholl became a projectile which pierced him through and through.

Although these two scientists followed diverging lines they would have finished by meeting, despite all the axioms of geometry; but then they would have met in duel. Happily for these citizens, so useful to their country, a distance of fifty or sixty miles divided them from each other, and their friends threw so many obstacles in the way that they never met.

It was very uncertain which of the two inventors had the best of it, for the results obtained made it difficult to form an exact opinion. All things considered, it would appear that the armour-plate must ultimately give way to the cannon-ball, yet competent men were undecided. At the latest experiments Barbicane's cylindro-conic projectiles stuck like pins in Nicholl's armour-plates. On that day the Philadelphian iron-founder considered himself victorious, and entertained the utmost contempt for his rival. But when the latter, a short time afterwards, substituted shells weighing 600 pounds for the conic projectiles, the captain had to lower his flag; for these projectiles, though discharged with moderate velocity, broke through, and smashed into a thousand pieces, the armour-plates of the best metal.

When things were at this point, and victory seemed to remain with the shot, the war ceased on the very same day that Nicholl had completed a new armour-plate of wrought-steel. It was a masterpiece of its kind, and defied all the projectiles of the world. The captain had it carried to the Polygon at Washington, and defied the president of the Gun Club to break it. As the peace had been signed, Barbicane declined to try the experiment.

In a great state of fury Nicholl offered to expose his armour-plate to any imaginable kind of shot – massive, hollow, round, or conical; but the president refused, not caring to endanger his last success.

Nicholl, angered beyond all bounds by Barbicane's obstinacy, endeavoured to tempt him by leaving him all the chances of success. He proposed to set up his plates 200 yards from the cannon. Barbicane still refused. 'At 100 yards?' 'Not even at 75.' 'At 50, then!' cried the captain through the organ of the press. 'I'll put it at 25 yards, and get behind it myself.'

Barbicane replied that even if Captain Nicholl were to get in front of it he would not fire.

At this reply Nicholl could contain himself no longer. He became personal; insinuated that cowardice was indivisible; that the man who refused to fire a cannon was very near being afraid of it; that in reality artillerists who now fight at a distance of six miles have prudently replaced individual courage by mathematical formulae; and, further, that there is as much bravery in quietly awaiting a shot behind an armour-plate as in firing off the projectile according to all the rules of science.

To these insinuations Barbicane did not reply. Perhaps, even, he did not know of them, for at that time he was completely absorbed by his calculations for the great undertaking.

When he made his famous communication to the Gun Club, Captain Nicholl's anger reached its paroxysm. It was mixed with an intense jealousy and a feeling of absolute powerlessness. How could he invent anything better than this 900-feet columbiad? What armour-plate could ever withstand a projectile weighing 30,000 pounds? At first Nicholl was overwhelmed and annihilated by this monstrous cannon, but he soon recovered himself, and resolved to crush the proposition by the weight of his arguments.

He violently attacked the works of the Gun Club; he published a number of letters which the papers were delighted to insert; he tried to pick Barbicane's work to pieces – scientifically. Once the war was commenced, any kind of argument served its purpose; and, in truth, they were often specious and illogical.

In the first place Barbicane's figures were attacked. Nicholl tried to prove by $a + b$ that his formulae were incorrect, and that he was ignorant of the very rudiments of gunnery. Amongst other errors, according to Nicholl's calculations, it was utterly impossible to transmit to any object whatever a velocity of 12,000 yards per second. He maintained – algebra in hand – that even with this velocity no projectile, however heavy, could possibly pass the limits of the terrestrial atmosphere; it would not even go a distance of eight leagues. Better still: admitting the velocity, and admitting that it was sufficient, the shell would never resist the pressure of the gas developed by the combustion of 1,600,000 pounds of gunpowder, and, if it did resist this pressure, at least it could not support the temperature, but would melt as it issued from the columbiad, and fall back in boiling rain on the heads of the imprudent spectators.

Barbicane met these attacks without wincing, and continued his work.

Nicholl then considered the question in its other aspects. Without speaking of its general uselessness, he considered the experiment exceedingly dangerous, both for the citizens who countenanced such a spectacle by their presence and for the towns in the neighbourhood of the deplorable cannon. He also remarked that if the projectile did not reach its goal, which it could not possibly do, it would naturally fall back upon the earth, and the fall of such a mass, multiplied by the square of its velocity, would create great damage in some part of the globe. Under such circumstances, without wishing to infringe the rights of free citizens, this was certainly a case in which the intervention of the Government became necessary, for the safety of all could not be endangered for the pleasure of one man.

It was plain that Captain Nicholl was addicted to exaggeration. He was alone of his opinion, and no one paid the slightest attention to his prophecies. He was allowed to say what he pleased and write what he pleased; he was defending a cause which was lost beforehand. He was heard, but not listened to; and he did not gain over one of the president's admirers. The latter did not even take the trouble of refuting his rival's arguments.

Nicholl, driven into his last intrenchments, determined to risk his money, as he could not risk his person, and he proposed, through the columns of the *Richmond Inquirer*, the following series of wagers. He offered to bet: –

(1st) That the funds necessary for the undertaking of the Gun Club would not be forthcoming – 1,000 dollars.

(2nd) That the operation of casting a cannon 900 feet long was impracticable, and would not succeed – 2,000 dollars.

(3rd) That it would be impossible to load the columbiad, and that the gun-cotton would ignite under the pressure of the projectile – 3,000 dollars.

(4th) That the columbiad would burst at the first shot – 4,000 dollars.

(5th) That the projectile would not travel even six miles, but would fall back to earth a few seconds after the discharge – 5,000 dollars.

Thus the captain's stubbornness induced him to risk a considerable sum, for the total of the bets amounted to no less than 15,000 dollars. Notwithstanding which, on the 19th of October he received this note of Spartan brevity –

Baltimore, 18th October

Done

BARBICANE

CHAPTER ELEVEN

Florida and Texas

One question yet remained to be decided; it was necessary to choose the most favourable spot for the experiment. According to the recommendation of the Cambridge Observatory, a shot was to be fired perpendicularly to the plane of the horizon, *i.e.*, towards the zenith; but the moon only crosses the zenith in places situated between 0° and 28° of latitude; in other words, its declination is only 28°. It was therefore necessary to determine exactly the point of the globe where the enormous columbiad was to be cast.

On the 28th of October, at a general meeting of the Gun Club, Barbicane produced an immense map of the United States, by L. Belltropp. But before he had time to open it, J. T. Maston, with his usual vehemence, had claimed permission to speak, and commenced in the following terms.

'Honorable colleagues, the question to be discussed today has a truly national importance, and will give us an opportunity of showing a great deal of patriotism.'

The members of the Gun Club looked at each other without understanding what the speaker was coming to.

'No one amongst you,' continued he, 'would harbour the thought of diminishing this country's glory; and if the Union can claim one right above all others, it is to receive in its bosom the formidable cannon of the Gun Club. Under present circumstances – '

'Worthy Maston – ' said the president.

'Don't interrupt,' said the speaker. 'Under present circumstances we are obliged to choose a spot sufficiently near the equator, that the experiment may be made under favourable conditions – '

'If you will allow me – ' said Barbicane.

'I claim the freedom of discussion,' replied the choleric J. T. Maston; 'and I maintain that the ground from which our glorious projectile will be discharged should belong to the Union.'

'Quite right,' said several members.

'Well! As our frontiers are not sufficiently wide; as the ocean forms an impassable barrier to the south, as the 28th parallel must be sought in a neighbouring country beyond the United States – that, I say, constitutes a legitimate *casus belli*, and I demand that war be declared against Mexico.'

'No, no, no,' was echoed from every side.

'No?' replied J. T. Maston. 'I am astonished to hear such sentiments in this place.'

'But listen.'

'Never,' cried the impetuous orator. 'Sooner or later this war must occur, and I demand that it should commence at once.'

'Maston,' said Barbicane, firing a volley from his handbell, 'I must ask you to be silent.'

Maston wished to reply, but several of his colleagues succeeded in restraining him.

'I admit,' said Barbicane, 'that the experiment cannot and ought not to be tried elsewhere than on American soil; but, if our impatient friend had allowed me to speak, if he had only cast a glance at a map, he would have seen that it is quite unnecessary to declare war against our neighbours, inasmuch as certain frontiers of the United States extend beyond the 28th parallel. Look here! We have at our disposal all the southern portions of Texas and Florida.'

The incident then dropped, though J. T. Maston was not convinced without difficulty. It was decided that the columbiad should be cast either in Texas or Florida. But this decision created much rivalry between the towns of these two states.

The 28th parallel, on meeting the American coast, traverses the peninsula of Florida, which it cuts into two almost equal parts. Then passing through the Gulf of Mexico, to the south of Georgia, Alabama, and Louisiana, it reaches Texas, of which it cuts off a corner, stretches through Mexico, passes the Sonora, cuts through Old California, and is lost in the Pacific Ocean. Thus only those portions of Florida and Texas which lie below this parallel presented the conditions as to latitude recommended by the Cambridge Observatory.

Florida, in its southern parts, has no important towns, but only a few forts constructed to keep the wandering Indians in check. Tampa Town was the only city which could have any claim in regard to its situation.

In Texas, on the other hand, the towns are more numerous and more important. Corpus Christi in Nuace's County, and all the towns situated on the Rio Bravo; Laredo; Comalites; San Ignacio on the Webb; Roma and Rio Grande city on the Starr; Edinburg on the Hidalgo; and Santa Rita, Elpanda, and Brownsville, on the Cameron, formed an imposing league against the pretensions of Florida.

The decision was hardly known when Texan and Floridan deputies reached Baltimore by express train. From that moment President Barbicane, and the more influential members of the Gun Club, were besieged day and night by these formidable claimants. Seven towns of Greece disputed the honour of Homer's birthplace, but two states of America were ready to annihilate each other merely on account of a cannon.

These 'ferocious brothers' carried arms in the streets of the town. At each meeting some conflict was feared entailing disastrous consequences, but happily the danger was averted by President Barbicane's prudence and address. Personal animosities found an outlet in the papers of the different states. Thus the *New York Herald* and the *Tribune* supported Texas, whereas the *Times* and the *American Review* advocated the cause of the Floridan deputies. The Gun Club was unable to decide between the two.

Texas bravely brought its twenty-six counties into line of battle; but Florida replied that twelve counties were worth more than twenty-six in a country six times smaller.

Texas laid great stress on its 330,000 natives, but Florida, though not so large, maintained that it was more densely populated with 56,000. Further, it accused Texas of having a speciality of paludal fevers which carried off, on an average, several thousand inhabitants each year; and Florida was right.

In its turn Texas replied that as regards fevers Florida had enough of her own, and that it was at least imprudent to call other countries unhealthy when she suffered chronically from *vomito negro*; and herein Texas was not wrong.

Further, the Texans maintained, in the columns of the *New York Herald*, that every consideration is due to a state which grows the finest cotton in America and the best oak for ship-building; a state which contains excellent coal and iron-ore yielding fifty per cent. of pure metal.

To this the *American Review* replied that the soil of Florida, without being so rich, offered greater advantages for casting the columbiad, as it was composed of sand and clay.

'But,' said the Texans, 'before casting anything in a country, you have to get there, and communication with Florida is difficult; whereas the Texan coast contains the bay of Galveston, which is fourteen leagues round, and might contain the united fleets of the whole world.'

'Very well,' replied the papers in the Floridan interest, 'but what is the good of your bay of Galveston situated above the 29th parallel? Have we not the bay of Espiritu Santo situated precisely on the 28th degree of latitude, and by which ships may reach Tampa Town?'

'A nice bay, indeed,' replied Texas, 'it's half full of sand.'

'Full of sand yourselves,' cried Florida; 'why don't you say at once that we're a country of savages?'

'I really don't know; there are still some Seminoles to be found in your prairies.'

'Well, and how about your Apaches and your Comanches – are they civilised?'

Thus the war had been waged for several days when Florida tried a change of tactics, and one morning the *Times* insinuated that the undertaking, being essentially American, could only be tried upon essentially American territory.

'American!' cried Texas; 'are we not as American as you? Were not Texas and Florida both incorporated in the Union in 1844?'

'No doubt,' replied the *Times*, 'but we belonged to the Americans since 1820.'

'I should think so,' sneered the *Tribune*, 'after having been Spanish or English during 200 years, you were sold to the United States for 5,000,000 dollars.'

'What does that matter?' replied the Floridans. 'Are we to be ashamed of it? Was not Louisiana purchased from Napoleon for 16,000,000 dollars in 1803?'

'It is a shame,' cried the Texan deputies, 'for a miserable slip of land like Florida to dare to compare itself with Texas, which, instead of being sold, achieved its own independence, drove out the Mexicans on the 2nd of March, 1836, and declared itself a federative republic after the victory gained by Samuel Houston, on the banks of the San Jacinto, over the troops of Santa Anna. A country, in fact, which voluntarily joined the United States of America.'

'Because it was afraid of the Mexicans,' replied Florida.

'Afraid!' From the day this unparliamentary word was pronounced the situation became intolerable. A massacre of the two parties was daily expected in the streets of Baltimore. The authorities had to keep the deputies under constant supervision.

President Barbicane was at his wits' end. Notes, documents, and threatening letters literally poured into his house. What was he to do? As regards soils, facility of communication, and rapidity of transports, the rights of the two states were equal. As to political personalities, they had nothing to do with the question.

This hesitation and embarrassment had lasted for some time when Barbicane resolved to put an end to it, so he called his colleagues together, and proposed the following wise resolutions.

'When we consider,' said he, 'what has just taken place between Florida and Texas, it is evident that the same difficulties will arise between the towns of the favoured state. The rivalry will descend from the genus to the species, from the state to the city, and that is all we shall gain. Now Texas possesses eleven towns in the required conditions, which will each claim the honour of the undertaking and cause us an infinity of bother; whereas Florida has only one. I vote, therefore, for Florida and Tampa Town.'

When this decision was made public, the Texan deputies were astounded. Their fury knew no bounds, and they sent personal challenges to the several members of the Gun Club. The Baltimore magistrates had but one course open, which they took; a special train was prepared, and the Texan deputies were hurried from the town, *nolens volens*, at a rate of thirty miles an hour.

Notwithstanding the speed of their departure they found time to discharge a last threatening sarcasm at their adversaries. Alluding to the narrowness of Florida – which is merely a peninsula sandwiched between two seas – they maintained that she would not resist the shock of the discharge, but would blow up at the first fire.

'Well, let her blow up,' replied the Floridans, with a brevity worthy of ancient times.

CHAPTER TWELVE

'Urbi et Orbi'

The astronomical, mechanical, and topographical difficulties having been settled, there arose the question of money. It was necessary to procure an enormous sum for the execution of the project; and no individual, nor any single state even, would have been able to supply the required millions.

President Barbicane therefore decided that, although the undertaking was American, it should be made a matter of universal interest, to which the financial co-operation of every nation might be invited. It was at once the right and the duty of all the earth to take a share in the affairs of its satellite. The subscription opened for this purpose extended from Baltimore to the entire world, *urbi et orbi*.

The subscription succeeded beyond all expectation, although the money was to be given and not lent. The operation was purely disinterested, in the literal sense of the word, and held out no hopes of profit.

The effect of Barbicane's communication had not been confined within the frontiers of the United States; it had crossed the Atlantic and the Pacific, and invaded at once Europe, Asia, Africa, and Oceania. The observatories of the Union placed themselves in communication with the observatories of foreign countries. Those of Paris, St Petersburg, the Cape, Berlin, Altona, Stockholm, Warsaw, Hamburg, Breda, Bologna, Malta, Lisbon, Benares, Madras, and Pekin sent their compliments to the Gun Club; others maintained a prudent reserve.

As to the Greenwich Observatory, backed up by the twenty-two other astronomical establishments of Great Britain, it was very concise: it denied all possibility of success, and adopted the theories of Captain Nicholl.

When the different learned societies promised to send delegates to Tampa Town, the Greenwich committee declined to entertain Barbicane's proposal; but this was merely English jealousy, and nothing else.

As a general rule the effect upon the scientific world was excellent, and from thence it was disseminated amongst the masses who took a great interest in the question. This was a matter of great importance, as these masses were about to be called upon to subscribe an immense sum.

On the 8th of October, President Barbicane had issued a manifesto, couched in enthusiastic language, appealing to 'All Men of Good Will upon Earth.' This document was translated into all languages, and met with great success.

Subscriptions were opened in the Union to the credit of the Bank of Baltimore, 9, Baltimore Street, and in the different countries of the two continents:

In Vienna, at S. M. de Rothschild's.
In St Petersburg, at Stieglitz & Co.'s.
In Paris, at the Crédit Mobilier.
In Stockholm, at Tottie and Arfuredson's.
In London, at N. M. de Rothschild & Son's.
In Turin, at Ardouin & Co.'s.
In Berlin, at Mendelssohn's.
In Geneva, at Lombard, Odie, & Co.'s.
In Constantinople, at the Ottoman Bank.
In Brussels, at S. Lambert's.
In Madrid, at Daniel Weisweller's.
In Amsterdam, at the Credit Neerlandais.
In Rome, at Torlonia & Co.'s.
In Lisbon, at Lecesne's.
In Copenhagen, at the Private Bank.
In Buenos Ayres, at Maua's Bank.
In Rio de Janeiro, at Maua's Bank.
In Montevideo, at Maua's Bank.
In Valparaiso, at Thomas La Chambre & Co.'s.
In Mexico, at Martin Daran & Co.'s.
In Lima, at Thomas La Chambre & Co.'s.

Three days after President Barbicane's manifesto, four millions of dollars had been paid in at the different towns of the Union. With such an amount in hand the Gun Club could commence operations.

Some days later, telegrams to America brought news that the foreign subscriptions were yielding largely. Some countries distinguished themselves by their generosity, others were more penurious. It was a mere question of temperament. However, figures are more eloquent than words, and the following is an official statement of the sums credited to the Gun Club at the close of the subscription.

Russia subscribed for its share the enormous sum of 368,733 roubles. Those who are astonished at this evidently misunderstand the Russian taste for science and the impulse which they have given to astronomical studies by means of their numerous observatories, the chief of which cost two million roubles.

France began by laughing at the American pretensions. The moon served as a pretext for a thousand stale jokes, and twenty or thirty vaudevilles equally remarkable for ignorance and bad taste; but as the French formerly paid for singing they now paid for laughing, and subscribed a sum of 1,253,930 francs, at which price they certainly had the right to be jovial if they liked.

Austria was generous in the midst of her financial embarrassments. Her share in the public subscription reached 216,000 florins, which were well received.

Fifty-two thousand rix-dollars were subscribed by Sweden and Norway. This figure is comparatively high for the country, but it would certainly have been higher had the subscription been opened at Christiania as well as at Stockholm. For some reason or other, Norwegians do not like sending their money to Sweden.

Prussia showed its approval of the enterprise by sending 250,000 thalers. The different observatories readily contributed a large amount, and were amongst the warmest of President Barbicane's encouragers.

Turkey acted generously. It is true she had a personal interest in the matter, as the moon regulates the course of her years and her fast of the Ramadân. She could not give less than 1,372,640 piastres, but she gave them in a manner which indicated a certain pressure on the part of the Government of the Porte.

Belgium distinguished herself amongst secondary states by giving 513,000 francs, or about twelve centimes per head of her inhabitants.

Holland and her colonies took an interest in the operation to the extent of 110,000 florins, but they claimed five per cent. discount for paying cash.

Denmark, notwithstanding the diminutive size of its territory, subscribed 9,000 ducats, which proves the love of the Danes for scientific expeditions.

The Germanic Confederation undertook to subscribe 34,285 florins. More could not have been expected. At any rate no more would have been given.

Although very hard up, Italy found 200,000 lire in the pockets of her children, after much searching. If she had had Venice she would have done more; but then she had not got Venice.

The States of the Church did not think it necessary to send more than 7,040 Roman crowns, and Portugal went so far in its devotion to science as to subscribe 30,000 crusados.

As regards Mexico, it was the widow's mite – eighty-six piastres. But then, empires in course of formation are always in monetary difficulties.

Two hundred and fifty-seven francs was the modest subscription of the Swiss to the American undertaking. The fact is, Switzerland could not see the practical side of the operation. She could not understand how the mere fact of sending a cannon-ball to the moon would establish business relations with that satellite, and it seemed to her very imprudent to risk money in such an uncertain undertaking. And, after all, perhaps Switzerland was right.

As for Spain, she could not collect more than 110 reals. The pretext given was that her railways were not completed, but the truth is that science is not much thought of in that country, which is still rather backward. Then some of the better-taught Spaniards did not exactly understand the mass of the projectile as compared with that of the moon. They feared it might damage its orbit, interfere with its action as a satellite, and, perhaps, cause its fall upon the surface of the terrestrial globe, in which case it was better to abstain; which they did, except to the extent of some few reals.

England yet remained. We have seen the contemptuous antipathy with which she received Barbicane's proposal. Englishmen have but one and the same mind for the 25 millions of inhabitants contained in Great Britain. They intimated that the Gun Club's undertaking was contrary to the 'principle of non-intervention', and declined to subscribe a farthing.

At this news the Gun Club shrugged their shoulders, and went on with their business. When South America – that is to say Peru, Chili, Brazil, and the provinces of La Plata and Columbia – had paid up their share of 300,000 dollars, the club found itself at the head of a very considerable capital, composed as follows: –

Subscriptions in the United States	$4,000,000
Ditto abroad	$1,446,675
Total	$5,446,675

which the public had paid in to the credit of the Gun Club.

Let no one be surprised at the importance of the sum. The works of casting, boring; of masonry, and transport of workmen; the establishment of the latter in an almost uninhabited country; the construction of furnaces and buildings, the machinery for the works; the powder, the projectile, and the general expenses would, according to the estimates, fully absorb the whole amount.

During the American War some cannons are said to have cost 1,000 dollars a shot. President Barbicane's gun, unique in the history of artillery, would probably cost 5,000 times as much.

On the 28th of October an agreement was signed with the Goldspring Works near New York, which, during the war, had supplied Parrott with his best cast-iron cannons.

It was stipulated between the contracting parties that the Goldspring Works undertook to transport to Tampa Town, South Florida, the plant and machinery necessary for casting the columbiad.

This operation was to be completed, at latest, by the 15th of October next, and the gun delivered in good condition, under penalty of a fine of 100 dollars per day up to the moment when the moon should again present herself in the same conditions – that is to say, eighteen years and eleven days.

The hiring of the workmen, their payment, and all necessary arrangements, were to be at the charge of the Goldspring Works.

This agreement, executed in duplicate and in good faith, was signed by J. Barbicane, President of the Gun Club, and J. Murphison, Director of the Goldspring Works, and delivered under their respective hands and seals.

CHAPTER THIRTEEN

Stone's Hill

As soon as the choice made by the members of the Gun Club to the detriment of Texas was known to the public, everyone in America, where the ability to read is universal, applied himself to study the geography of Florida. Publishers had never sold so many copies of Bertram's *Travels in Florida*, Roman's *Natural History of East and West Florida*, Williams's *Territory of Florida*, and Clelland on the *Culture of Sugar-Cane in East Florida*. Such was the rush for these works that new editions had to be printed.

But Barbicane had no time for reading. He had to inspect and mark out the site for the columbiad. So, without loss of time, he placed the necessary funds at the disposal of the Cambridge Observatory for the construction of a monster telescope, and gave Messrs Breadwill and Co., of Albany, an order for the manufacture of the projectile in aluminum, and then left Baltimore, accompanied by J. T. Maston, Major Elphiston, and the director of the Goldspring Works.

Next day the four travellers reached New Orleans, where the Government had placed the despatch-boat *Tampico* at their disposal, and, getting up steam, the coasts of Louisiana were soon hidden from their view.

The passage was not a long one. Two days after starting the *Tampico* had steamed 490 miles, and was in sight of the coast of Florida. As they approached, Barbicane perceived a long stretch of barren, low-lying land, and after passing a series of creeks, abounding in oysters and lobsters, the *Tampico* steamed into the bay of Espiritu Santo.

This bay terminates in two narrow inlets, one leading to Tampa and the other to Hillisborough, up the former of which the steamer held its way. In a short time the batteries of Fort Brooke were seen towering above the water-line, and soon the town of Tampa appeared at the extremity of a small harbour formed by the mouth of the River Hillisborough.

Here the *Tampico* cast anchor on the 22nd of October, at 7 p.m., and the four passengers immediately went on shore.

Barbicane's heart beat with violence as he stepped on to Floridan soil, and he stamped with his foot as an architect would try the solidity of a building. J. T. Maston scratched the ground with his hook.

'Gentlemen,' said Barbicane, 'we have no time to lose; tomorrow we must be off on horseback to explore the country.'

When it was known that Barbicane had landed, the 3,000 inhabitants of Tampa Town flocked out to greet the president of the Gun Club, who had honoured them with his choice; but Barbicane escaped from the oration, and shut himself in a room of Franklin's Hotel, where he refused to receive anybody. The honours of celebrity were evidently not to his taste.

The next morning, which was the 23rd of October, they were awakened by the snorting and pawing of some small Spanish-bred horses beneath their windows; but instead of four, they found fifty, already mounted.

When Barbicane came down with his three companions, he was at first astonished to find himself in the midst of such a cavalcade, the more so that each horseman had a rifle slung over his shoulder and pistols in his holsters. A young Floridan explained the reason for this display of forces as follows.

'It is on account of the Seminoles, sir.'

'What Seminoles?'

'Wandering Indians of the prairies. We thought it more prudent to escort you.'

'Pooh!' said J. T. Maston, climbing into his saddle.

'At any rate,' said the young Floridan, 'it will be safer.'

'Gentlemen,' said Barbicane, 'I thank you for your kind attention. Let us be off.'

The little troop put itself in motion, and soon disappeared in a cloud of dust. Although only 5 a.m., the sun was shining brightly, and the thermometer registered 84°; but fresh breezes from the sea tempered the excessive heat.

After leaving Tampa Town, Barbicane travelled southwards, and followed the coast till he came to Alifia Creek. This little river flows into Hillisborough Bay about twelve miles below Tampa Town. Barbicane and his escort skirted its right bank in an easterly direction, and soon the waters of the bay disappeared behind the rising land, and the plains of Florida were alone visible.

Florida is divided into two parts. The northern part is more populous – or, rather, less deserted – and has for its capitals Tallahassee and Pensacola, one of the principal naval arsenals of the United States. The other part, which lies between the Atlantic and the Gulf of Mexico, forms a narrow peninsula worn by the action of the Gulf Stream – a slip of earth in the midst of a small archipelago, incessantly doubled by the numerous vessels of the Bahama Canal. It is the advanced guard of the Gulf of Tempests. The superficial area of the state is 38,033,267 acres, from which a site was to be chosen within the 28th parallel, for the purposes of the undertaking. So Barbicane, during his ride, examined attentively the configuration of the ground and its general distribution.

Florida was discovered in 1512, by Juan Ponce de Leon, on Palm Sunday, and was first named Pasca Florida, though its burnt and arid coast but little deserved this charming appellation; however, a few miles from the sea, the nature of the ground gradually changes, and becomes more worthy of its name. The country is cut up by a network of creeks, rios, watercourses, ponds, and small lakes, which remind one of Holland or Guiana; but the highlands spread out into cultivated plains, teeming with the vegetable productions of the north and south, immense fields rendered productive by the action of a tropical sun upon the water, retained by a clay soil, where pineapples, yams, tobacco, rice, cotton, and the sugarcane display their boundless riches with heedless prodigality.

Barbicane appeared well satisfied with the gradually increasing elevation of the ground, and when J. T. Maston spoke to him on the subject: 'My worthy friend,' he replied, 'it is very important that our columbiad should be cast in the higher ground.'

'To be nearer the moon?' asked the secretary of the Gun Club.

'No,' replied Barbicane, smiling; 'what difference can a few fathoms make? In the midst of the higher grounds our works will be carried out more easily, for we shall not have to contend against the water, and can therefore dispense with a costly system of drainage, which is an important matter when sinking a shaft 900 feet deep.'

'You are right,' said Murchison, the engineer, 'it is very important to avoid water when sinking the pit. But our pumping-engines will soon get the better of any springs we may meet with. There is no question here of an artesian well, dark and narrow, where the boring apparatus works out of sight. Our operations will be carried on in the light of day; with the aid of pickaxe, shovel, and blasting powder, we will carry the matter through in no time.'

'Nevertheless,' said Barbicane, 'if by the choice of our site we can avoid all trouble from subterranean waters our work will be done better and more rapidly, so let us look out for a spot some hundreds of fathoms above the level of the sea.'

'Very true, Mr Barbicane, and I am much mistaken or we shall find such a spot before long.'

'I should like to see the first stroke given at once,' said the president.

'And I should like to see the last,' said J. T. Maston.

'We are arrived, gentlemen,' said the engineer, 'and believe me the Goldspring Works will not have to pay you any penalty for delay.'

'So much the better for you,' said J. T. Maston. 'Are you aware that 100 dollars a day, until the moon presents herself in the same condition – that is for eighteen years and eleven days – would amount to 658,100 dollars?'

'No, I am not, sir,' replied the engineer; 'and I do not want to be.'

At about ten o'clock the little troop had got over twelve miles, and the fertile plains were succeeded by forest lands. Here they found the most varied kinds of trees in tropical profusion. These almost impenetrable forests were composed of pomegranate trees, orange trees, lemon trees, fig trees, olive trees, apricot trees, banana trees, and vines, whose fruits and flowers rivalled each other in colour and perfume. The odoriferous shade of these magnificent trees was peopled by a world of brilliantly-plumaged birds, amongst which the crab-eaters (*cancroma*) were particularly notice- able. Surely these, feathered jewels must have caskets for their nests!

J. T. Maston and the major were lost in admiration of these beautiful works of nature.

But President Barbicane, who cared little for such marvels, was anxious to get on. The very fertility of the country was displeasing to him, for without being a hydroscope, he could feel the water beneath his feet, and what he was searching for was a site of incontestable dryness.

So they pushed on, fording several rivers, and not without danger, for they were infested with alligators from fifteen to eighteen feet long. J. T. Maston bravely shook his redoubtable hook at them, but he only frightened the pelicans, the seals, and the phaetons, which peopled the banks of the rivers, whilst large red flamingos stared at him in stupid wonder.

At last they left behind them this too-well irrigated country, and the size of the trees diminished. As they advanced the underwood became less dense, until nothing was left but isolated clumps scattered over im- mense plains, where troops of wild deer ranged in primitive freedom.

'At last,' cried Barbicane, raising himself in his stirrups, 'we are in the region of pines.'

'And of savages,' replied the major.

Just then some Seminoles appeared on the horizon, galloping their swift horses and brandishing long lances, and occasionally firing off their guns; but they confined themselves to these hostile demonstrations, and did not otherwise interfere with Barbicane and his party.

The latter had reached the centre of a vast rocky plain, inundated by the burning rays of the sun, and formed by a large extumescence of the ground, which appeared to the members of the Gun Club to combine all the conditions requisite for the manufacture of their columbiad.

'Halt!' said Barbicane, pulling up; 'has this spot a name in the country?'

'It is called Stone's Hill,' answered one of the Floridans.

Barbicane dismounted without a word, and drawing out his instruments, set himself to take the most precise observations of the spot, whilst the little troop stood around, watching him in profound silence.

At this moment the sun passed the meridian. Barbicane having completed his calculations, gave the result of his observations as follows.

'This spot is situated 300 fathoms above the level of the sea, in 27° 7' latitude and 5° 7' W. longitude. It seems to me, from its rocky and arid character, to offer the most favourable conditions for our experiment. On this plain we will erect our stores, our workshops, our furnaces, and the huts for our workmen; and from this spot,' he continued, stamping his foot on the summit of Stone's Hill, 'our projectile will take its flight to the vast regions of the solar world.'

CHAPTER FOURTEEN
Spade and trowel

Barbicane and his companions returned the same evening to Tampa Town, and the engineer, Murchison, re-embarked on the *Tampico*, for New Orleans, to engage an army of workmen and bring back the greater portion of the plant. The members of the Gun Club remained at Tampa Town to organise the commencement of the works, with the aid of the people of the country.

Eight days later the *Tampico* re-entered the bay of Espiritu Santo, surrounded by a flotilla of steamers transporting 1,500 workmen.

In the bad days of slavery this number could not have been collected, but since America, the land of freedom, had none but free men for her inhabitants, workpeople crowded to every spot where their labour was likely to be required and liberally remunerated. The Gun Club did not want for money, and offered liberal pay and proportionate bonuses. Each workman engaged for Florida, could count, after completion of the work, upon a certain sum of money deposited in his name at the Bank of Baltimore; consequently Murchison could pick and choose amongst the most intelligent and most skilful of the working-classes. You may imagine that he only enrolled in his staff the *élite* of mechanicians, stokers, founders, boiler-makers, miners, brick-makers, and labourers of every kind, white or black, without distinction of colour. Many of them brought their families with them, as if for a permanent emigration.

At 10 a.m. on the 31st of October the troop landed on the quays of Tampa Town. The movement and activity in this little town, whose population was thus doubled in one day, may be better imagined than described. Tampa Town was a great gainer by this initiative of the Gun Club, not so much from the workpeople, who were immediately sent on to Stone's Hill, but from the number of visitors who arrived in the Floridan peninsula from all points of the globe.

The first days were occupied with unloading the machinery, tools, and provisions brought by the flotilla, as well as some iron huts which had been packed in separate pieces, each properly numbered. At the same time Barbicane commenced marking out a line of railway, fifteen miles long, uniting Stone's Hill with Tampa Town.

We all know how American railways are constructed – with what capricious curves and steep inclines, with what disregard for railings and masonry, scaling hills and dipping into valleys without any regard for the straight line. They are not costly or troublesome, but are allowed every liberty for blowing up or running off the rails. The line from Tampa Town to Stone's Hill was a mere bagatelle, requiring neither much time nor much money.

Barbicane was the moving spirit in all this world of workmen. He imparted to them his enthusiasm and his conviction; he was everywhere at once, as though gifted with ubiquity, and J. T. Maston was constantly at his side. There was no limit to the inventions of his practical mind. For him there were no obstacles, no difficulties, no embarrassments. He was as much a miner, a mason or a mechanician, as an artillerist. He had answers to every question, and solutions for every problem. He corresponded actively with the Gun Club and Goldspring Works, and the *Tampico*, with lighted furnaces and steam up, awaited his orders, day and night, in the harbour of Hillisborough.

On the 1st of November, Barbicane left Tampa Town with a detachment of workmen, and the next day a city of iron houses had arisen on the summit of Stone's Hill. These were surrounded by palisades, and, from the movement and activity therein displayed, the whole might have been taken for one of the great cities of the Union. Perfect discipline was maintained, and the works commenced in perfect order.

The nature of the ground had been ascertained by careful borings; and, on the 4th of November, everything was ready for commencing the sinking of the principal shaft. On that day Barbicane called a meeting of his chief foremen, and said: 'You all know, my friends, why I have brought you together in this wild part of Florida. We are to cast a cannon measuring 9 feet in diameter, 6 feet in thickness, and surrounded by 19½ feet of masonry, which will give the shaft a total width of 60 feet and a depth of 900 feet. This great work must be completed in eight months. You have 2,543,400 cubic feet of earth to extract in 255 days, which makes, in round figures, about 10,000 cubic feet per day. This would be no great task for 1,000 workmen in an open space, but in our case it will be more difficult. However, as the work must be done it will be done, and I count upon your zeal as much as upon your skill.'

At 8 a.m. the first stroke of the pickaxe was given to Floridan soil, and from that moment the tool was allowed no rest in the hands of the miners, who worked in relays of three hours each.

However colossal the undertaking might appear, it did not exceed the limits of human strength. Far from it. Many works of more real difficulty have been successfully carried out, even where it has been necessary to contend against the elements. Amongst other extraordinary works, the 'Father Joseph's Well' may be cited, which descends below the very level of the Nile, near Cairo, to a depth of 300 feet, and was constructed by Sultan Saladin at a time when machinery had not increased one hundred-fold the power of man; and another well at Coblentz, sunk by Margrave John of Baden, to a depth of 600 feet. What was required now? Merely to triple the depth and double the width – which latter rendered the work much easier; consequently not one of the foremen or workpeople had any doubt as to the success of the operation.

An important decision taken by the engineer Murchison, with the consent of President Barbicane, considerably accelerated the progress of the work. One clause in the agreement stipulated that the columbiad should be circled with rings of wrought-iron, applied when hot. This precaution was manifestly unnecessary, for the gun could evidently dispense with these rings. The clause was consequently cancelled, which proved a great economy of time, as it enabled them to adopt the new system of boring, by which the masonry is constructed at the same time as the pit is sunk. Thanks to this very simple arrangement, it is no longer necessary to shore up the earth by means of stays; the masonry keeps up the sides of the shaft, and sinks by its own weight. This work was not commenced until the pickaxe had reached the harder part of the ground.

On the 4th of November, fifty workmen sank a circular pit 60 feet wide, in the very centre of the palisaded enclosure, that is to say the upper portion of Stone's Hill. The pickaxe first met about 6 inches of black soil, which was easily removed. Below this soil were 2 feet of fine sand, which was carefully put on one side for the construction of the interior mould. Below this sand was compact white clay, like English marl, in a layer 4 feet thick. Then the iron of the pickaxe struck sparks out of a hard sort of rock, formed by petrified shells, at which time the pit was 6½ feet deep, and the works of masonry commenced.

At the bottom of this excavation, a sort of wheel or strong disc of oak was laid down and securely bolted. A hole was bored in its centre, of a diameter equal to the exterior diameter of the columbiad. Upon this wheel the masonry was erected and rendered of indubitable solidity by means of hydraulic cement. When the workmen had built from the circumference towards the centre, they were enclosed in a sort of well, 21 feet wide.

When this was completed, the miners set to work with pick and spade to dig out the rock beneath the wheel, taking care, however, to leave a sufficient number of supports. When the pit had gained 2 feet in depth, these supports were removed, and the wheel with the masonry gradually settled down, while the masons continued their work at the top of the stonework, leaving a certain number of vent-holes to allow of the escape of gas during the operation of casting.

This sort of work called for extreme skill and continuous attention on the part of the workmen. More than one, whilst excavating beneath the wheel, was dangerously and even mortally wounded by the stone splinters; but their ardour did not diminish on that account, and the work continued night and day. In the daytime the rays of the sun shed, some months later, 99° of heat over these calcined plains; at night, under the white glare of the electric light, the blows of picks upon the rock, the explosions of the mines, the grinding of the machinery, and the clouds of smoke which filled the air, traced round Stone's Hill a magic circle, into which neither bisons nor Seminoles had dared to penetrate.

The works advanced regularly. Steam-cranes assisted to remove the excavated soil. No unexpected obstacles arose, but only foreseen difficulties, which were skilfully overcome.

At the end of the first month the shaft had attained the given depth of 112 feet. In December this depth was doubled, and tripled in January. During the month of February the workmen had to contend against a sheet of water which rushed in from every side. It was necessary to employ the most powerful pumps and air machines to enable the workmen to cement the orifices of the springs, as a gap is stopped on board ship. At last they conquered this difficulty, but by reason of the increased softness of the soil the wheel gave way slightly, and there was a partial collapse. You may fancy the terrible effect produced by the fall of this mass of masonry, 75 fathoms high, and will not be astonished that the accident cost the lives of several workmen.

Three weeks were spent in shoring up the stonework, repairing it below, and restoring the wheel to its original solidity. Thanks to the skill of the engineer and the power of the machinery employed, the endangered edifice was set straight, and the boring continued.

No further incident delayed the progress of the work, and on the 10th of June, twenty days before the term fixed by Barbicane, the shaft was completely lined with its facing of stone, and had attained a depth of 900 feet. At the bottom the masonry rested on a massive cube measuring 30 feet in thickness, whilst its upper portion was on a level with the ground.

President Barbicane and the members of the Gun Club warmly congratulated the engineer, Murchison, who had completed this cyclopean task with such unusual rapidity.

During these eight months Barbicane had not quitted Stone's Hill for one instant. Whilst inspecting each of the operations connected with the boring, he had given his special attention to the well-being and health of his workmen, and was so fortunate as to escape those epidemics which are common to great agglomerations of men, and specially disastrous in those regions of the globe which are exposed to tropical influences.

Of course the carelessness which is inseparable from dangerous works cost the lives of several workmen; but such misfortunes cannot be avoided, and are details to which Americans pay but little attention. They think more of humanity in general than in particular instances. Barbicane, however, professed contrary principles, and took every opportunity of putting them into practice. Thanks to his care, his intelligence, his useful intervention in difficult cases, and his prodigious and humane sagacity, the average of accidents did not exceed that of many countries which are quoted for the numerous precautionary measures they enforce, amongst others France, where there is one accident for every 200,000 francs' worth of work done.

CHAPTER FIFTEEN

The festival of the casting

During the eight months occupied in sinking the shaft, the preparatory works for the casting had been carried on simultaneously and with equal rapidity. A stranger arriving at Stone's Hill would have been much surprised at the spectacle offered to his view.

Twelve hundred smelting furnaces, each 6 feet wide and standing 3 feet apart from each other, rose in a circle round the shaft at a distance of 600 yards from the central point. The circle described by these 1,200 furnaces measured 2 miles in circumference. All were constructed on the same model, and their square, high chimneys presented a most singular spectacle. J. T. Maston considered the architectural disposition superb, and said that it recalled to his mind the monuments of Washington. To his mind there could be nothing more beautiful, not even in Greece, although, as he said himself, he had never been there.

It will be remembered that at their third meeting the committee decided to use cast-iron for their columbiad, and particularly the white description. This metal is, in fact, more tenacious, more ductile, softer, more easily bored, more applicable to all moulding operations, and when smelted with coal attains a superior quality for all articles requiring a great resisting power, such as cannons, cylinders of steam-engines, hydraulic-presses, &c.

But cast-iron which has been only once smelted is rarely sufficiently homogeneous, and requires to be smelted a second time, to be purified and refined, so as to be separated from all earthy matter.

The iron-ore, before being sent to Tampa Town, was smelted in the Goldspring furnaces, and being brought in contact with coal and silicum heated to a high temperature, became impregnated with carbon and transformed into cast-iron. After this first operation the metal was despatched to Stone's Hill. As the mass of cast-iron to be transported amounted to 36 millions of pounds, the carriage by railway would have been too expensive and would have doubled the cost of the material, so it was considered preferable to load the pigs of iron on vessels at New York. No less than sixty-eight vessels, each of 1,000 tons registered burden, were chartered for this purpose, and this fleet sailed from New York on the 3rd of May into the Atlantic Ocean, along the American coast, south-wards to the Bahama Canal; doubled the Cape of Florida, and entering the Bay of Espiritu Santo on the 10th of the same month, cast anchor in the port of Tampa Town. There the cargoes were discharged into the trucks of the Stone's Hill railway, and towards the middle of January the enormous mass of metal had reached its destination.

It will readily be understood that 1,200 furnaces were not too many to liquefy at the same time the 60,000 tons of castings. Each furnace could contain about 114,000 pounds of metal. They had been constructed on the same model as those used for casting Rodman's gun; they were trapezoidal in form and extremely low-slung. The heating apparatus and the flue were at the two extremities of the furnace, so that the latter could be equally heated over its whole extent. These furnaces were constructed of fire-brick, and were composed merely of a grating for the coal, and a sole on which the pigs of iron were laid. This sole inclined at an angle of 25°, and allowed the metal to flow into the receiving drafts, from whence 1,200 converging trenches carried it to the central shaft.

The day after the works of masonry and boring were completed, Barbi-cane commenced the manufacture of the interior mould. It was necessary to build in the centre of the shaft, and on the same axis, a cylinder 900 feet long and 9 feet wide, which would exactly fill the space reserved for the bore of the columbiad. This cylinder was composed of a mixture of clay and sand, with some hay and straw. The interval between the mould and the masonry was to be filled with the molten metal, which would thus form the tube 6 feet thick.

To maintain this cylinder in equilibrium it was necessary to surround it with iron sheeting, and support it at certain distances by stays fixed into the stone wall; after the casting these stays would be lost in the block of metal, but this was of no importance.

This operation was completed on the 8th of July, and the casting was fixed for the next day.

'The festival of the casting will be a magnificent ceremony,' said J. T. Maston to his friend Barbicane.

'No doubt,' replied Barbicane, 'but it will not be a public festival.'

'Why, won't you allow everyone to be present?'

'Most certainly not, Maston. The casting of the columbiad is a delicate operation, not to say perilous, and I prefer to have it carried out in private. When the projectile is fired off you may have a festival if you like, but not until then.'

The president was right, the operation might give rise to unforeseen dangers which could not be averted if a large influx of spectators were allowed. It was necessary to retain complete liberty of action. No one, therefore, was admitted into the enclosure except a delegation of members of the Gun Club who had arrived from Tampa Town. There were to be seen the sprightly Bilsby, Tom Hunter, Colonel Blomsberry, Major Elphiston, General Morgan and the rest, who considered the casting of the columbiad a personal matter. J. T. Maston acted as cicerone, and did not omit a single detail; he took them everywhere – to the stores, to the workshops, through all the machinery – and forced them to visit the 1,200 furnaces in succession. At the 1,200th visit they were rather sick of furnaces.

The casting was to take place at noon precisely. On the previous day each furnace had been charged with 114,000 pounds of metal in pigs, laid in crossed piles, so that the hot air might freely circulate between them. From early morning the 1,200 chimneys vomited torrents of flame into the air, and the earth was shaken as with subterranean tremblings. For each pound of metal to be smelted, a pound of coal had to be burnt, so that 68,000 tons of coal hid the face of the sun behind a dense cloud of smoke.

The heat soon became unbearable within this circle of furnaces, whose roarings resembled the growling of distant thunder. Powerful ventilators added their continuous blast, and saturated with oxygen these incandescent fires.

The operation, to be successful, had to be executed rapidly. At a signal given by firing a cannon, each furnace was to give vent to the molten metal and empty itself completely.

When these arrangements had been made, the foremen and workpeople awaited the appointed time with an impatience not unmixed with anxiety. There was no longer anyone in the enclosure, and each foreman took his post at the aperture of the run.

Barbicane and his colleagues took their stands on a neighbouring hill to view the operation. Before them stood the cannon ready to be fired at a sign from the engineer.

A few minutes before noon the first drops of metal commenced to flow, and the receiving-troughs filled gradually. When the metal was completely liquid, it was kept in suspense for a few minutes, so as to facilitate the removal of all foreign substances.

Twelve o'clock struck. The cannon thundered and flashed its yellow flame into the air. One thousand two hundred runs were opened simultaneously, and 1,200 fiery serpents crawled towards the central shaft, unrolling their incandescent coils, and plunged with fearful noise to a depth of 900 feet. It was an exciting and magnificent spectacle. The earth

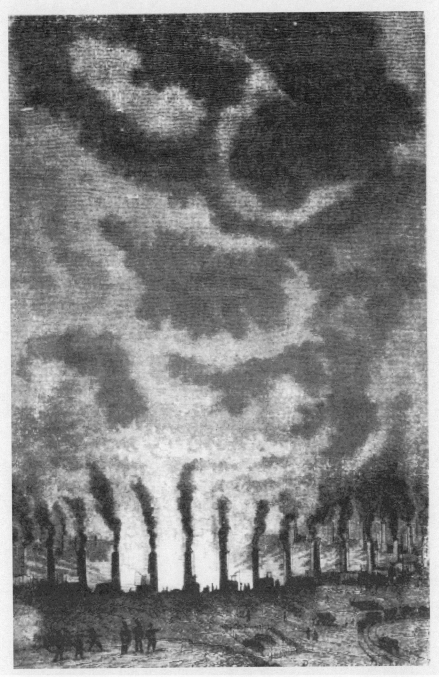

quaked while these waves of molten metal, launching clouds of smoke towards the sky, evaporated at the same time the moisture in the mould, and hurled it through the wind holes of the stone lining in the shape of dense masses of vapour. These artificial clouds rolled upwards in thick spirals to a height of 500 fathoms. A savage roaming beyond the limits of the horizon, might have imagined that a new crater had been formed in Floridan soil. Yet there was neither an eruption nor a waterspout, nor a storm nor a struggle of the elements, nor any of those terrible phenomena which nature is capable of producing. Man alone had caused these ruddy vapours, these gigantic flames, worthy of a volcano; these terrific tremblings, as from the shocks of an earthquake; these roarings, which rivalled the noise of hurricanes and tempests; and it was his deed which plunged into the abyss, dug by himself, a whole Niagara of molten metal.

CHAPTER SIXTEEN

The columbiad

Had the casting been successful? This could only be matter for conjecture, although the probabilities were in favour of success, since the mould had absorbed the whole of the metal melted in the furnaces. In any case it would be some time before the result could be ascertained.

When Major Rodman cast his 160-pounder, the cooling of the metal took fifteen days. How long, then, would the monstrous columbiad, crowned with wreaths of vapour, and defended by its intense heat, remain hidden from the eyes of its admirers? This was difficult to calculate.

The patience of the members of the Gun Club was sorely tried during this time. But nothing could be done, and J. T. Maston was near being roasted for his impetuosity. Fifteen days after the casting an immense cloud of vapour still filled the sky, and the ground was burning for 200 paces round the summit of Stone's Hill.

Days and weeks passed, and yet the immense cylinder showed no signs of cooling. It was impossible to get near it. There was nothing for it but to wait, and the members of the Gun Club had to make the best of it they could.

'This is the 10th of August,' said J. T. Maston, one morning, 'and there are now hardly four months to the 1st of December. We have still to remove the centre mould, bore the tube of the columbiad, and load it. We shall not be ready in time! We cannot get near the cannon! What a cruel thing it would be if it should never cool!'

They tried to calm the impatient secretary, but without success. Barbicane said nothing, but his silence hid a growing irritation. It was hard for such doughty warriors to find themselves stopped by an obstacle which time alone could conquer, and to be at the discretion of so redoubtable an enemy.

However, daily observations showed a certain change in the state of the ground. Towards the 15th of August the vapour had notably diminished in thickness and intensity. A few days later only a few small puffs appeared occasionally above the surface of the ground, like the last breathings of the monster hidden below in its stony vault. Little by little the quaking of the earth diminished, and the circle of heat became narrower. The more impatient spectators advanced as far as possible; one day they gained two fathoms, the next day four, and on the 22nd of August Barbicane and his colleagues were able to stand upon the sheet of cast-iron which appeared upon the surface of Stone's Hill. This was certainly a most salubrious standpoint, preventing all possibility of cold feet.

'At last!' said the president of the Gun Club, heaving an immense sigh of satisfaction.

The works were recommenced next day. They began by breaking up the interior mould to clear out the bore of the gun. Pickaxes, shovels, and drilling machines worked without ceasing, and although the clay and sand had become greatly hardened by the action of the heat, they were able, with the help of their powerful machinery, to remove the burning mixture from the sides of the cannon. The excavated matter was rapidly loaded upon trucks worked by steam, and such was the ardour with which the work was carried on, so pressing was Barbicane's intervention, and such the force of his arguments, which generally took the form of dollars, that on the 3rd of September all trace of the mould had disappeared.

The boring operations commenced at once; machinery was fixed, and powerful drills were brought to bear upon the uneven parts of the cast-iron, with such effect that a few weeks later the whole inner surface of the immense tube was accurately bored and had acquired a perfect polish.

On the 22nd of September, less than one year after Barbicane's communication, the enormous gun was accurately bored and declared ready for use, after having been proved by the most delicate instruments to be pointed in an exactly vertical line. They had now only the moon to wait for, and they were quite sure she would keep her appointment.

J. T. Maston's joy knew no bounds, and he nearly had a terrific fall when looking into the tube 900 feet deep. Without Blomsberry's right arm, which the worthy colonel had fortunately retained, the secretary of the Gun Club, like a second Erostratus, would have met his death in the depths of the columbiad.

So the gun was completed and there could be no further doubt possible as to its perfect execution. On the 6th of October, therefore, Captain Nicholl was obliged to settle with President Barbicane, who credited himself in his books with a sum of 2,000 dollars. It will readily be believed that the captain's wrath was so great that he was ill for a whole week. However, there were still three bets of 3,000, 4,000, and 5,000 dollars respectively, and if he should win two the business would not be a bad one, although nothing extraordinary. But money had no share in his calculations, and his rival's success in casting a cannon which 10-fathom plates could not have resisted, was a very severe blow.

Since the 23rd of September the enclosure of Stone's Hill had been thrown open to the public, and the influx of visitors will be easily imagined. In fact they came in streams from all points of the United States. The city of Tampa had increased prodigiously during the year of the works, and now contained a population of 150,000 souls. After having swallowed up Fort Brooke in a network of streets, it now covered the narrow slip of land which divided the Bay of Espiritu Santo. New streets, new squares, and a perfect forest of houses had suddenly sprung up upon these deserted shores under the heat of the American sun. Companies had been formed for the erection of churches, schools, and private houses, and in less than a year the extent of the town had increased tenfold.

It is well known that Yankees are born traders. Wherever fate has thrown them, whether in the torrid or the frozen zone, this business instinct prevails. Thus mere idlers who had come to Florida for the sole purpose of following the operations of the Gun Club, were tempted into commercial speculations as soon as they were established in Tampa Town. The ships chartered for conveying the plant and workmen had imparted unexampled activity to the port; soon vessels of all sizes and tonnage, laden with provisions and merchandise, ploughed the waters of the bay or lay at anchor before the town. Vast offices of shipowners and brokers were built in the town, and the *Shipping Gazette* daily registered the new arrivals in the port of Tampa.

While roads were multiplying round the town, the latter, in consideration of its increased importance, was placed in railway communication with the southern states of the Union. A railway united Mobile with Pensacola, the great naval arsenal of the south, and ran from this important point to Tallahassee. Here there was already a short line of railway 21 miles long, placing Tallahassee in communication with St Marks, on the coast. This railway was extended to Tampa Town, spreading along its passage new life amongst the dead or sleeping parts of Florida. Thus Tampa, thanks to the marvels of industry, caused by an idea hatched one day in the brain of one man, was entitled to consider itself an important town. It had been surnamed Moon City, and the capital of Florida suffered a total eclipse, visible from all parts of the world.

It will now be easily understood why such rivalry existed between Florida and Texas, and why the irritation of the Texans was so great when their claims were disallowed by the decision of the Gun Club. In their sagacious foresight they had understood how much a country would gain through Barbicane's experiment, and by how much good such a cannon-shot would be accompanied. Texas lost by this choice a vast trade centre, railways, and a considerable increase of population, all which advantages had been reaped by that miserable Floridan peninsula, which had been thrown like a breakwater between the waters of the Gulf and the waves of the Atlantic Ocean. So Barbicane shared with Santa Anna the most violent Texan antipathies.

The inhabitants of Tampa Town took care not to forget the operations of the Gun Club in the midst of their commercial and industrial occupations. On the contrary, the most minute details of the undertaking, even the smallest stroke of a pickaxe, had its interest for them. There was a continual procession, or rather pilgrimage, between Stone's Hill and the town.

It was easy to foresee that, on the day of the experiment, the influx of visitors would be counted by millions, for they were already collecting, on the narrow peninsula, from all parts of the world. Europe was emigrating to America.

It is true that up to this time but little satisfaction had been given to the visitors' curiosity, and many who were counting upon the spectacle of the casting, only saw the smoke. This was not much for their hungry eyes, but Barbicane would admit no one to the operation. Hence grumblings, discontent, and murmurs. The president was blamed; he was considered autocratic; his proceeding was styled un-American. There was almost a revolt round the palisade of Stone's Hill, but, as we have seen, Barbicane remained immovable in his decision.

But when the columbiad was completely finished, this privacy could not be maintained. It would have been ungracious to keep the gates closed any longer, and might even have been dangerous in the then state of public feeling. So Barbicane threw open the enclosure to everyone; but, like a practical man, he determined to make money out of the public's curiosity.

To see the immense columbiad was worth a great deal, but to descend into its depths appeared to these Americans the *ne plus ultra* of happiness in this world, and every visitor was desirous of tasting the joys of a descent into the interior of this abyss of metal. Cages, suspended from steam pulleys, gave the spectators the means of satisfying their curiosity. There was a perfect rage. Women, children and old men, all considered it their duty to penetrate the mysteries of the colossal gun to the very bottom of the bore. The cost of each descent was fixed at 5 dollars per head, but notwithstanding this high figure the influx of visitors during the two months which preceded the experiment realised to the Gun Club nearly 500,000 dollars.

It is unnecessary to add that the first visitors to the columbiad were the members of the Gun Club, the privilege being very justly reserved to that august assembly. This solemnity took place on the 25th of September. A special cage lowered President Barbicane, J. T. Maston, Major Elphiston, General Morgan, Colonel Blomsberry, the engineer Murchison, and other distinguished members of the celebrated club to the number of ten. It was still rather warm at the bottom of the long metal tube, and the atmosphere was somewhat stifling; but what joy! what ecstasy! There was a table laid for ten on the massive block of stone supporting the columbiad, which was lighted *à giorno* by the rays of an electric light. Numerous exquisite dishes descended as from the sky, and were placed in succession before the guests; and the best wines of France flowed in profusion during this splendid repast served 900 feet below the ground.

The feast was animated and even noisy. Numerous toasts were proposed. They drank to the terrestrial globe, to its satellite, to the Union, to the Gun Club, to the moon, to Phoebe, to Selene, to the Queen of the Night, to the 'peaceful messenger of the firmament'. The noisy cheers, borne upon the sonorous waves of the immense acoustic tube, burst from its extremity with a sound like thunder, and the crowd surrounding Stone's Hill joined their acclamations with the shouts of the ten revellers at the bottom of the gigantic columbiad.

J. T. Maston's ecstasy knew no bounds. It is difficult to decide whether he shouted more than he gesticulated, or drank more than he ate. At any rate, he would not have given his place for an empire, 'Not even if the cannon, loaded, primed, and fired on the spot, were to distribute his fragments amongst the planetary regions.'

CHAPTER SEVENTEEN

A telegram

The great work undertaken by the Gun Club was, so to speak, completed, and yet two months had to elapse ere the projectile could be despatched to the moon; two months which, to the general impatience, would appear like two years. Until now the smallest details of the operation had been each day published in the papers and greedily devoured by a million eyes; but now it was to be feared that the instalment of interest given to the public would diminish daily, and each was afraid to lose his share of diurnal emotion.

This, however, was not the case. A most unexpected, most extraordinary, most incredible, most improbable incident, again attracted public attention, and plunged the world into a new state of excitement.

One day – it was the 30th of September, at 3.47 p.m. – a telegram, sent by the submarine cable between Valentia, Newfoundland, and the American coast, arrived for President Barbicane.

President Barbicane tore open the envelope, read the despatch, and, notwithstanding his power of self-control, his lips grew pale and his eyes dim on reading the twenty words contained in this telegram.

The following is the text of the telegram, which is still in the archives of the Gun Club –

Paris, France
30th September, 4 a.m.
To BARBICANE, Tampa, Florida, United States

REPLACE SPHERICAL SHELL BY CYLINDRO-CONIC PROJECTILE. WILL START INSIDE. ARRIVE PER STEAMER *ATLANTA*.

MICHEL ARDAN

CHAPTER EIGHTEEN

The passenger by the Atlanta

If this astounding news had been sent by post in a sealed cover instead of by electric wire, and if the French, Irish, Newfoundland, and American clerks had not necessarily shared the confidence of the telegraph, Barbicane would not have hesitated a single instant. He would have prudently held his tongue so as not to bring his work into disrepute. The telegram might be a hoax, especially as it emanated from a Frenchman. What probability was there that anyone could be so foolhardy as to conceive the idea of such a journey? And if such a man really existed, must he not be some madman to be confined in a madhouse rather than in a cannon-ball?

But the telegram was known, for telegraphic apparatuses are not very discreet, and Michel Ardan's proposal had already spread through the different states of the Union. So Barbicane had no reason to be silent. He assembled such of his colleagues as were present at Tampa Town, and without discussing the question as to what credence was to be given to the telegram, he calmly read out the laconic message.

'It can't be possible!' 'It's improbable!' 'It's a joke!' 'He is laughing at us!' 'It's ridiculous!' 'It's absurd!' And the whole series of expressions of doubt, incredulity, stupidity and folly, circulated through the assembly with the usual accompaniment of gesticulations.

The members smiled, laughed, shrugged their shoulders or burst into loud cachinnations, each according to his humour. J. T. Maston alone was equal to the occasion.

'It is a magnificent idea,' said he.

'Yes,' replied the major, 'but it is only permissible to have ideas like that on the condition of never even thinking of putting them into practice.'

'Why not?' replied the secretary of the Gun Club, always ready for a discussion. But the matter was not followed up.

Meanwhile the name of Michel Ardan had already reached Tampa Town. Natives and foreigners were very facetious, not about this European – who was a myth, a chimerical personage – but about J. T. Maston, who had believed in his existence. When Barbicane had proposed to send a projectile to the moon, everyone thought the undertaking natural, practical, and a mere matter of gunnery. But that any reasonable being should offer to make the journey in the projectile, and hazard this improbable voyage, was looked upon as a fantastic proposal, a joke, a hoax, and, to use a very familiar word, a piece of humbug.

These mockings lasted till the evening without ceasing, and it may be said that the whole Union held its sides with laughter, which is very unusual in a country where the most impossible undertakings find promoters and partisans.

However, Michel Ardan's proposal, like all new ideas, did not fail to disquiet some minds. It altered the course of accustomed emotions: 'We never thought of that.' The very strangeness of the proposal gave it a certain interest, and people turned it over in their minds. How many things considered impossible yesterday have become realities today! Why should this journey not be made some day or other? In any case, a man who would run the risk must be mad, and as his proposal could not be taken into serious consideration, he would have done much better to have held his tongue and not trouble a whole nation with his nonsensical hallucinations.

The first question was, did this person really exist? The name of Michel Ardan was not unknown in America. It belonged to a European often quoted for his audacious undertakings. Then there was the telegram flashed through the depths of the Atlantic, the name of the ship in which the Frenchman was said to have taken his passage, the date fixed for its arrival: all these circumstances gave a certain probability to the proposal. Something more must be known about it. Isolated individuals formed themselves into groups, the groups thickened under the action of curiosity like atoms in virtue of molecular attraction, and finally a dense crowd was formed which directed its steps towards President Barbicane's dwelling.

The latter, since the arrival of the telegram, had not made known his opinion. He had allowed J. T. Maston's expressions to go unchallenged without manifesting either approval or blame. He was remaining quiet in the background, determined to watch the course of events, but he had not taken public impatience into account, and was but little gratified at the sight of the population of Tampa crowding beneath his window. However, the murmurs and vociferations of the crowd obliged him to make his appearance, for celebrity has its duties, and consequently its trials.

When he appeared there was a dead silence, and one of the citizens, acting as spokesman, asked him point-blank the following questions.

'Is the person mentioned in the telegram under the name of Michel Ardan on his way to America; yes or no?'

'Gentlemen,' replied Barbicane, 'I know no more than you.'

'You ought to know,' exclaimed some impatient voices.

'Time will show,' replied the president calmly.

'Time has no right to keep a whole country in suspense,' continued the speaker. 'Have you altered the plans of the projectile as the telegram requires?'

'Not yet, gentlemen; but you are quite right, we must know all about it. The telegraph which has caused all this excitement must be good enough to complete the information.'

'To the telegraph!' roared the crowd.

Barbicane came down and walked at the head of the immense assemblage to the offices of the telegraph company.

Some minutes later a telegram had been despatched to Lloyd's agent at Liverpool requesting a reply to the following questions.

'What sort of a vessel is the *Atlanta*? When did she leave Europe? Had she a Frenchman named Michel Ardan on board?'

Two hours later, Barbicane was in possession of such precise information that there was no longer any room for doubt.

'The *Atlanta*, steamer, from Liverpool, sailed on the 2nd of October, for Tampa Town, having on board a Frenchman, entered in the list of passengers under the name of Michel Ardan.'

At this confirmation of the first telegram, the president's eyes shone with a sudden fire, his hands closed violently, and he was heard to murmur: 'It *is* true, then! It *is* possible! This Frenchman exists, and will be here in a fortnight. But he must be mad! I will never consent – '

And yet that same evening he wrote to Messrs Breadwill and Co., begging them to suspend, for the present, the manufacture of the projectile.

It would be impossible to describe the excitement which spread over the whole of America; how the effect of Barbicane's communication was thrown in the shade; what the papers of the Union said on the subject, how they received the news, and how they gloried in the arrival of this hero from the Old World. It would be impossible to paint the agitation in which all lived, counting the hours, the minutes, and the seconds; to give even a small idea how minds were dominated by this one thought; to show how all occupations gave way to one single preoccupation; how works were stopped, commerce suspended; how ships on the point of sailing remained in port, so as not to miss the arrival of the *Atlanta*; how trains arrived full and returned empty; how the Bay of Espiritu Santo was incessantly ploughed by steamers, packet-boats, pleasure-yachts, and fly-boats of all dimensions. And to count the thousands of visitors who quadrupled in a fortnight the population of Tampa Town, and camped out in tents like an invading army, would be a task beyond human strength, which could not be attempted without temerity.

On the 20th of October, at 9 a.m., the semaphores of the Bahama Canal signalled a thick smoke on the horizon. Two hours later the signals were answered by a large steamer, and the name of the *Atlanta* was telegraphed to Tampa Town. At 4 o'clock the English vessel entered the Bay of Espiritu Santo, and at 6 o'clock it cast anchor in the port of Tampa.

The anchor had hardly touched the sandy bottom, when 500 embarkations surrounded the *Atlanta*, and the steamer was taken by assault. Barbicane was the first over the gunwale, and shouted with a voice, of which he vainly tried to conceal the emotion: 'Michel Ardan!'

'Here,' replied an individual, standing on the bridge.

Barbicane, with crossed arms, inquiring eye, and compressed lips, looked fixedly at the passenger of the *Atlanta*.

He was a man of about forty-two years of age, tall and slightly round-shouldered, like those caryatides which support terraces on their shoulders. His massive, lion-like head was covered with thick yellow hair, as with a mane. A short face, broad at the temples, ornamented with a stiff moustache bristling like that of a cat, small tufts of yellow hair planted in the middle of his cheeks, and round eyes with a wildish though short-sighted look, completed this eminently feline physiognomy. But the nose was well shaped, the mouth wore a kindly expression, and the forehead was high and intellectual, and furrowed like a field which is never left fallow. Lastly, a body strongly developed and firmly established on two long legs, and two muscular arms, powerful and well knit, gave this European the general appearance of a well-built fellow, 'rather wrought than cast', to borrow one of the expressions of metallurgical science.

Disciples of Lavater or Gratiolet would have easily traced on the skull and physiognomy of this personage indubitable signs of combativeness – that is to say, courage in danger and a tendency to break through obstacles; also signs of benevolence and love of the marvellous, an instinct which leads certain temperaments to a passionate interest in superhuman things. On the other hand the bumps of acquisitiveness, that desire to possess and to acquire, were absolutely wanting.

To complete the description of the outward appearance of the passenger by the *Atlanta* it is necessary to mention his wide-cut dress fitting

loosely to his person – his trousers and coat containing so much cloth that Michel Ardan called himself a 'cloth eater' – his loose cravat, his shirt-collar thrown widely open, fully displaying his robust neck, and his cuffs – which were invariably unbuttoned – discovering a pair of febrile hands. One felt that, even in the greatest dangers or the coldest winters, that man's blood would never run cold.

On the deck of the steamer, in the midst of the crowd, he walked up and down, and was never two minutes in the same place – 'dragging his anchor', as sailors say – gesticulating, chatting familiarly with everybody, and biting his nails with nervous eagerness. He was one of those originals which Nature invents in a moment of fancy, and of which she breaks the mould directly afterwards.

The character of Michel Ardan offered a large field to the observations of an analyst. The man lived in a state of perpetual inclination to hyperbole, and had not yet passed the age of superlatives. Objects were reflected on the retina of his eye in unusual dimensions; hence an association of gigantic ideas. Everything appeared great to him except difficulties and men.

Otherwise he was of a luxuriant nature. He was an artist by instinct and wit; not one who kept up a rolling fire of jokes, but affecting rather the dropping fire of a sharpshooter. In discussion he was heedless of logic, and a declared enemy of syllogisms; but he had his own way of coming to the point. He was fond of the *argumentum ad hominem* and of defending hopeless causes.

Amongst other manias, he called himself 'a sublime ignoramus', as did Shakespeare, and professed a great contempt for men of science: 'People,' said he, 'who mark the points while we play the game.' In one word, he was a Bohemian from the world of the marvellous – adventuresome, but not an adventurer; a breakneck; a Phaethon, driving at full gallop the chariot of the sun; an Icarus with a change of wings. He never spared his person, but threw himself with open eyes into the most dangerous undertakings. He burnt his ships with greater readiness than Agathocles; and being always ready for the worst, invariably fell upon his feet, like those little pith acrobats which children play with.

In two words his motto was 'What matter?' and the love of the impossible was his 'ruling passion' – to borrow Pope's beautiful expression.

Yet this adventuresome fellow possessed all the defects inherent to his qualities. 'Who risks nothing gains nothing,' said he. Ardan risked often and yet gained nothing. He was a thorough spendthrift; he was perfectly unselfish, and listened to his heart much more than to his head; open-handed and chivalrous, he would not have signed the death-warrant of his greatest enemy, and would have sold himself to purchase the freedom of a slave.

All over France and Europe this brilliant and noisy personage was well known to everybody. The hundred voices of renown had grown hoarse in his service. He lived in a glass house, taking the whole world into the confidence of his most intimate secrets. At the same time he possessed an imposing collection of enemies amongst those whom he had brushed against, wounded, or upset, whilst elbowing his way through the crowd.

However, he was generally liked and treated as a spoilt child. People took him as they found him, and all were interested in his audacious undertakings, which were followed with uneasy attention, for he was known to be so imprudently foolhardy. When a friend tried to stay him by prophesying a catastrophe, he replied with a jovial smile, 'The forest is burnt through its own trees,' and was not aware that he quoted the prettiest of all Arabian proverbs.

Such was the passenger of the *Atlanta*. Always agitated, always boiling under the action of an internal fire, and always in a state of excitement, not by reason of what he had come to do in America – he never gave that a thought – but by reason of his feverish organisation. If ever two persons offered a striking contrast, they were certainly the Frenchman Michel Ardan and the Yankee Barbicane, though each was enterprising, hardy, and audacious in his way.

The reflections into which Barbicane was plunged at the sight of this rival, who had come to throw him in the background, were soon interrupted by the cheers and shouts of the crowd. The shouting became so frantic, and the enthusiasm took such a personal turn, that Michel Ardan, after shaking a thousand hands till he nearly lost the use of his fingers, was obliged to escape into his cabin.

Barbicane followed him without having yet spoken.

'Are you Barbicane?' asked Michel Ardan, as soon as they were alone, and with the tone of a friend of twenty years' standing.

'Yes,' replied the president of the Gun Club.

'Well, good-day, Barbicane; how are you? Very well? So much the better; that is all right!'

'So,' said Barbicane, without further preamble, 'you have made up your mind to start?'

'Quite so.'

'Nothing would stop you?'

'Nothing. Have you altered your projectile as stated in my telegram?'

'I was awaiting your arrival. But,' continued Barbicane, 'have you well considered – '

'Considered! Have I any time to lose? I come across an opportunity of making a tour in the moon, and I take advantage of it; that is all. I don't think that requires so much reflection.'

Barbicane examined this man who spoke of his proposed journey with such light-heartedness, such complete carelessness and with such a perfect absence of all disquietude.

'But at least,' said he, 'you have arranged some plan, and some means of execution?'

'I have, my dear Barbicane; but allow me to make one remark: I prefer to tell my story to everybody at once, and to make an end of it. That avoids repetitions. So, if agreeable to you, call together your friends, your colleagues – the whole town, all Florida, all America if you like – and tomorrow I will be ready to state my means of action, and to reply to any objections. Believe me I am ready to meet them. Does that suit you?'

'It does,' replied Barbicane.

Whereupon the president left the cabin, and informed the crowd of Michel Ardan's proposal. His words were met by hand-clappings and shouts of joy, for that put an end to all difficulty. The next day everyone could see the European hero at his ease. However, certain of the more obstinate spectators refused to quit the deck of the *Atlanta*; amongst others J. T. Maston had screwed his hook into the paddle-box, and it would have been necessary to use the capstan to drag him away.

'He is a hero – a real hero!' was cried on every side, 'and we are but silly women compared with this European.'

As to the president, after having begged the visitors to withdraw, he returned to the passengers' cabin, and only left it when the ship's bells struck a quarter to twelve; at which time the two rivals in popularity shook each other warmly by the hand, and Michel Ardan was on terms of the most perfect familiarity with President Barbicane.

CHAPTER NINETEEN

A meeting

The next day the sun rose much too late for the impatient wishes of the public; much too late for the luminary which was to shine on such a festival. Barbicane, fearing that indiscreet questions would be put to Michel Ardan, would have wished to reduce the audience to a small number of adepts – his colleagues for instance. But he might as well have tried to dam Niagara; and he was obliged to give up the project and let his new friend run the chances of a public conference. The new hall of the Tampa Exchange was considered insufficient for the ceremony, notwithstanding its colossal dimensions, for the proposed assembly took the proportions of a mass meeting.

The place chosen was a vast plain just outside the town, and in a few hours a sufficient space was sheltered from the rays of the sun, for the ships in the port lent their sails, spare masts, and spars, and all the accessories necessary for the construction of a colossal tent. An immense canvas roofing spread over the scorched prairies, which it protected from the rays of the sun, and beneath this covering 300,000 persons supported for hours the stifling temperature whilst waiting for the Frenchman's arrival. Of this crowd of spectators about one-third could see and hear; another third saw and heard but little; while the remainder saw nothing and heard less, but were not on that account the less enthusiastic in their applause.

At three o'clock Michel Ardan made his appearance, accompanied by the principal members of the Gun Club, giving his right arm to President Barbicane and his left to J. T. Maston, who was as radiant as the sun and almost as glowing.

Ardan mounted a hustings from which his glances spread over an ocean of black hats. He was not embarrassed, he did not try to show off, but was easy, jovial, familiar, and amiable. He replied by a graceful bow to the shouts which greeted his appearance, and then, claiming silence by a movement of his hand, he spoke as follows in very correct English.

'Gentlemen,' said he, 'notwithstanding the heat, I am going to occupy a few moments of your time to offer you some explanations with reference to projects in which you appear to take an interest. I am neither an orator nor a man of learning, and I had no intention of speaking in public; but my friend Barbicane tells me that you wish to hear me, and I bow to your wishes, so listen with your six hundred thousand ears and kindly excuse the mistakes of the speaker.'

This familiar address was much to the taste of the audience, who expressed their satisfaction in the usual way.

'Gentlemen,' said he, 'no sign of approval or disapproval is forbidden, with which stipulation I will begin. In the first place, do not forget that you have to do with an ignoramus, but one whose ignorance is so great that he ignores even difficulties. It has appeared to him a very simple matter, an easy thing, to take a seat in a projectile, and so start for the moon. It is a journey which, sooner or later, would have to be made; and as to the mode of locomotion, that merely follows the laws of progress. Man commenced by travelling on all-fours, then one day on two feet, then on a cart, then in a coach, then in post-chaise, then in a diligence, and at last in a railway. The projectile is the carriage of the future, and in point of fact the planets are but projectiles – mere cannon-balls thrown from the hand of the Creator. But to return to our vehicle. Some of you, gentlemen, may have thought that its rapidity is excessive. That is not the case; all the stars exceed it in velocity, and the earth itself carries us three times more rapidly in its movement round the sun. I will give you some instances; but I must ask your permission to state them in leagues, as American measures are not very familiar to me, and I am afraid of becoming confused in my calculations.'

This request appeared very reasonable, and, as no objections were raised, the speaker continued in the following terms.

'Gentlemen, these are the velocities of the different planets. I am constrained to admit that, notwithstanding my ignorance, I am well acquainted with these astronomical details; but in two minutes you will be as learned as myself. Know, then, that Neptune travels at the rate of 5,000 leagues an hour, Uranus at the rate of 7,000, Saturn at the rate of 8,858, Jupiter at the rate of 8,675, Mars at the rate of 22,011, the earth at the rate of 22,500, Venus at the rate of 32,590, Mercury at the rate of 52,520, and certain comets travel at the rate of 1,400,000 leagues in their perihelion. As to ourselves, we are mere idlers and loungers, for our velocity will not exceed 9,900 leagues, and will decrease as we continue. I put it to you whether there is anything to boast of in this, and whether it is not evident that it will be some day exceeded by greater velocities of which light or electricity will probably be the mechanical agents.'

As no one seemed to doubt this assertion, Michel Ardan continued.

'My dear hearers, if we were to believe what certain narrow-minded people maintain, humanity would be enclosed within a magic circle, and condemned to vegetate on this globe, without ever being able to reach the planetary spheres. This must not be. We shall travel to the moon, we shall travel to the planets and to the stars, as we journey today from Liverpool to New York – easily, rapidly, and with safety; and the atmospheric ocean will soon be crossed as well as the oceans of the moon. Distance is a relative term which will soon be reduced to zero.'

The meeting, though well disposed in favour of the French hero, was somewhat astounded by this audacious theory, and Michel Ardan perceived it at once.

'You do not seem convinced, my worthy hosts,' said he, with an amiable smile; 'well, let us discuss the matter. Do you know how long an express train would take to reach the moon? 300 days – not an hour more. What is, after all, a journey of 86,410 leagues? Not even nine times the circumference of the earth; and certainly the majority of sailors and travellers have been over a greater distance in their lifetime. Remember that I shall only be 97 hours on the road. Oh, you think that the moon is at an immense distance from the earth, and that one should hesitate before risking the journey! but what would you say if it were a question of going to Neptune, which gravitates 1,147 millions of leagues from the sun! There you have a journey which few people could undertake, if it cost only five cents per kilometer. Baron Rothschild himself, with his milliard of money, would not be able to pay for his ticket, and would be left on the road for want of 147 millions.'

This system of argument seemed to please the meeting immensely; besides which Michel Ardan was full of his subject, and plunged into it with great animation. Feeling that he was eagerly listened to, he continued with admirable assurance.

'Well, my friends, this distance of Neptune from the sun is nothing if compared with that of the stars. To calculate the distance of the latter, we are carried into those dazzling sums where the smallest number has nine figures and a milliard is taken as unity. I beg your pardon for being so learned on this point, but it is really a question of immense interest. Listen and judge for yourself! Alpha, of Centaurus, is distant 8,000 milliards of leagues; Wega, 50,000 milliards; Sirius, 50,000 milliards; Arcturus, 52,000 milliards; the Polar Star, 117,000 milliards; Capella, 170,000; and the other stars thousands, millions, and milliards of milliards of leagues. And after that you would talk of the distance which separates the planets from the sun! You would maintain that distance exists! Error! Falsehood! Ridiculous nonsense! Do you know what I think of the world, which commences at the orb of day and finishes with Neptune? Would you know my theory? It is very simple! To me the solar world is one solid homogeneous

body; the planets which compose it are pressed together, touch each other, and adhere; and the spaces which exist between them are no more than the spaces which separate the molecules of the most compact metal, silver, iron, or platinum. I have therefore the right to assert, and I repeat it with a conviction which you all must share: "Distance is a vain word, distance does not exist."'

'Well spoken! Bravo! Hurrah!' cried the assembly with one voice, electrified by the manner and the words of the orator, and by the boldness of his conceptions.

'No,' cried J. T. Maston, more energetically than the rest; 'distance does not exist.' And carried away by the violence of his feelings, he nearly fell from the top of the hustings to the ground. Fortunately he succeeded in regaining his equilibrium, and saved himself from a fall which would have proved, somewhat brutally, that distance after all is not such a vain word.

The orator then resumed his speech.

'My friends,' said Michel Ardan, 'I think the question is now settled. If I have not convinced you, all my demonstrations and my arguments must have been too weak, and the fault must lie in my theoretic studies. However that may be, I repeat that the distance from the earth to its satellite is really very unimportant, and quite unworthy of preoccupying a serious mind. I shall not go too far, I think, in asserting that trains of projectiles will soon be established, in which the journey from the earth to the moon may be comfortably made; there will be neither shock, nor shaking, nor accident to be feared, and the goal will be reached rapidly, without fatigue, in a straight line, "as the bee flies", to use the language of your trappers. Before twenty years have passed, half the earth will have visited the moon.'

'Three cheers for Michel Ardan!' cried the audience, even such as were least convinced.

'Cheers for Barbicane,' modestly replied the speaker.

This act of graceful courtesy towards the promoter of the undertaking was received with unanimous applause.

'Now, my friends,' continued Michel Ardan, 'if you have any questions to ask, you will certainly embarrass such a poor scholar as I am, but I will try to answer them.'

Up to this time the president of the Gun Club had every reason to be satisfied with the turn the discussion was taking. It was dealing with speculative theory, in which Michel Ardan, carried away by his vivid imagination, showed to great advantage. It was necessary to keep from entering into practical questions, with which no doubt he would be less able to deal. Barbicane therefore hastened to take up the discussion, and asked his new friend if he thought that the moon or the planets were inhabited.

'That is a difficult problem, my worthy president,' replied the orator
with a smile; 'but unless I am mistaken men of great intelligence, Plutarch,
Swedenborg, Bernardin de St Pierre, and many others, have given their
opinion in the affirmative. Taking natural philosophy as the standpoint, I
should feel inclined to think with them. I should say that nothing useless
exists in creation; and replying to your question by another question, my
friend Barbicane, I should assert that if these worlds are inhabitable, they
either are, or have been, or will be inhabited.'

'Hear, hear!' cried the front ranks of the spectators, whose opinion
naturally decided that of the rear.

'No one could reply more logically or more justly,' said the president
of the Gun Club. 'The question, therefore, resolves itself into this: are
these worlds inhabitable? For my part I think they are.'

'And I am certain of it,' replied Michel Ardan.

'However,' said one of the spectators, 'there are arguments against the
inhabitableness of these worlds. It would be evidently necessary in most
cases that the principles of life should be modified. Take, for instance,
the planets: we should be burnt up in some and frozen in others, according as they are more or less distant from the sun.'

'I regret,' replied Michel Ardan, 'that I am not personally acquainted
with my hon. contradictor, for I would try to answer him. His objection
has its value, but I think it may be successfully combated as well as all
such as deal with the inhabitableness of these worlds. If I were a natural
philosopher, I should say that if there is less caloric put in motion in the
planets nearer the sun, and more, on the contrary, in the distant planets,
this simple phenomenon is sufficient to equalise the heat and render the
temperature of these worlds supportable to beings organised as we are.
If I were a naturalist, I would say, with many illustrious *savants*, that
nature supplies us on this earth with examples of animals living under
very opposite conditions; that fishes breathe in an element which is
mortal to other animals; that the *amphibii* have a double existence which
is very difficult to explain; that certain inhabitants of the sea live at a great
depth, and support, without being crushed, pressures of 50 or 60 atmospheres; that certain aquatic insects are utterly insensible to temperature,
and are found at once in springs of boiling waters and in the icy plains of
the Polar Ocean; consequently, that we must acknowledge in Nature a
diversity in her means of action which is often incomprehensible, but not
the less real, and which almost reaches omnipotence. If I were a chemist I
would tell him that the aerolites, which are bodies evidently formed
outside the terrestrial world, have revealed, under analysis, indubitable
traces of carbon, which substance owes its existence solely to organised

beings, Reichenbach's experiments having proved that it must necessarily have been "animalised". Lastly, if I were a theologian, I would say, with St Paul, that the Divine redemption seems to be applicable, not only to the earth but to all the celestial worlds. But I am neither a theologian, nor a chemist, nor a naturalist, nor a natural philosopher; so, in my complete ignorance of the grand laws which rule the universe, I confine myself to answering: I do not know if these worlds are inhabited, and as I don't know I shall go and see.'

Did the opposers of Michel Ardan's theory hazard any further arguments? It is impossible to say, for the frantic shouts of the crowd would have drowned any further expression of opinion, but when silence was restored the triumphant orator added the following observations.

'As you may well think, worthy Yankees, I have only touched superficially on so great a question. I have not come here to give a public lecture and maintain a thesis on this vast subject. There is quite a series of other arguments in favour of the habitableness of these worlds, but I will not enter into them. Allow me only to insist on one point. To people who maintain that the planets are not inhabited, we may reply: you may be right if it is proved that the earth is the best possible world; but such is not the case, Voltaire notwithstanding. It has but one satellite, while Jupiter, Uranus, Saturn, and Neptune have several at their service, which advantage is not to be disdained. But what renders our globe especially uncomfortable is the inclination of its axis towards its orbit, whence arises the inequality of days and nights; hence, also, the unpleasant diversity of seasons. On our unfortunate spheroid it is always too hot or too cold. We are frozen in winter and scorched in summer. Colds, influenzas, and bronchitis prevail on our planet, whereas on the surface of Jupiter, for instance, where the axis is but slightly inclined, the inhabitants may enjoy uniform temperatures. There is a zone of spring, a zone of summer, a zone of autumn, and a zone of perpetual winter. Each Jovite can choose the climate which he pleases, and remain protected for his lifetime from all variations of temperature. You will easily understand this superiority of Jupiter over our planet, without speaking of its cycles, which last twelve years each. Further, it is evident to me, that under such auspices, and under such marvellous conditions of existence, the inhabitants of that fortunate world must be superior beings, that their scientific men are more learned, their artists more skilful, the wicked less depraved, and the good people better in all respects. Alas! what is wanting to our spheroid? Little indeed! An axis of rotation less inclined to the plane of its orbit.'

'In that case,' cried an impetuous voice, 'let us unite our efforts; let us invent machinery and straighten the axis of the earth!'

A thunder of applause was elicited by this observation, which could only have emanated from J. T. Maston. It is probable that the impetuous secretary had been carried away by his engineering instincts to risk this bold proposal; but it must be added, in the interest of truth, that many supported it with their shouts, and doubtless, could they have found the standpoint required by Archimedes, the Americans would have constructed a lever capable of raising the world and straightening its axis. Unfortunately the standpoint was wanting to these hardy mechanicians. Nevertheless this eminently practical idea met with extraordinary success; the discussion was suspended for a good quarter of an hour, and long afterwards the proposal so energetically formulated by the perpetual secretary of the Gun Club furnished a topic of conversation to all the states of the Union.

CHAPTER TWENTY

Thrust and parry

This incident would seem to have closed the discussion. It was the last word, and better could not have been found. However, when the agitation had subsided, a clear, firm voice was heard to pronounce the following words – 'Now that the speaker has treated us to so much fiction, will he have the goodness to resume his subject, give us less theory, and discuss the practical side of his expedition?'

Everyone looked towards the man who spoke these words. He was a thin, dry man, with an energetic cast of countenance, wearing his beard, in American fashion, in a tuft beneath his chin. Profiting by the successive movements in the crowd, he had gradually made his way to the front rank of spectators. There, with crossed arms and a bright, bold glance, he stared imperturbably at the hero of the meeting. After having made his request he remained silent, and appeared in no way concerned by the thousands of glances which converged towards him, nor by the murmur of disapprobation which his words excited. As the reply did not come immediately, he repeated his question in a sharp, precise tone, and added: 'We are here to discuss the moon, and not the earth.'

'You are right, sir,' replied Michel Ardan; 'the discussion has been irregular. Let us return to the moon.'

'Sir,' continued the unknown, 'you maintain that our satellite is inhabited. Very well. But if there are any Selenites, those people most certainly live without breathing; for I must remind you, in your own interest, there is not the smallest particle of air on the surface of the moon.'

At this assertion Ardan shook his yellow mane, for he understood that a struggle was about to commence with this man upon the main question. He stared fixedly at him, and said: 'So there is no air in the moon. And who says so, if you please?'

'Men of science.'

'Really?'

'Really.'

'Sir,' continued Michel, 'joking apart, I have a great esteem for men of science who know what they are talking about, and a great contempt for those who do not.'

'Do you know any who belong to that last category?'

'Very many. In France there is one who maintains that, mathematically, a bird cannot fly; and another whose theories prove that fishes were not made to live in the water.'

'It is no question of those, sir; and I could back up my statement by names to which even you would have to defer.'

'In that case, sir, you would cruelly embarrass a poor ignoramus – who, however, would be only too happy to learn.'

'Why, then, do you enter into scientific questions, if you have not studied them?' asked the unknown, somewhat coarsely.

'Why!' replied Ardan, 'for the reason that the man is always brave who suspects no danger. I know nothing, it is true; but it is precisely my weakness which constitutes my force.'

'Your weakness will lead you into follies,' cried the unknown in a tone of great ill-humour.

'So much the better,' replied the Frenchman, 'if my folly leads me to the moon.'

Barbicane and his colleagues examined this intruder, who thus placed himself in opposition to the undertaking. None of them knew him, and the president, somewhat uneasy as to the results of a discussion on such a basis, looked at his new friend with some apprehension. The audience were attentive, but seriously uneasy, for the result of the discussion had been to draw their attention to the dangers and even to the real impossibilities of the expedition.

'Sir,' continued Michel Ardan's adversary, 'the reasons which prove the absence of all atmosphere around the moon are numerous and indisputable. I will even say that, *a priori*, if such atmosphere has ever existed it must have been drawn from the earth. But I prefer to bring forward incontrovertible facts.'

'Bring forward as many as you please, sir,' replied Michel Ardan, with great courtesy.

'You are aware,' said the unknown, 'that when luminous rays pass through a medium such as air, they deviate from the straight line, or, in other words, undergo refraction. Well, when the stars are occulted by the moon, their rays, whilst grazing the edges of the disc, do not undergo the slightest deviation, nor give the smallest indication of refraction; the evident consequence is that the moon is not surrounded by an atmosphere.'

All looked towards the Frenchman, for if this proposition was admitted the consequences were inevitable.

'That,' replied Michel Ardan, 'is your best argument, not to say your only one, and a man of science might have some difficulty in answering;

but I merely say that this argument has no absolute value, for it is based on the supposition that the angular diameter of the moon is accurately defined, which is not the case. But let that pass; and tell me, my dear sir, if you admit the existence of volcanoes on the surface of the moon?'

'Extinct volcanoes, yes; not volcanoes in activity.'

'You will admit, however, that these volcanoes have been in activity during a certain period?'

'That is positive; but as they could themselves supply the oxygen necessary for combustion, the fact of their eruption in no way proves the presence of a lunar atmosphere.'

'Let that pass, then,' replied Michel Ardan; 'and let us give up this class of arguments and come to direct observations. But I warn you that I am going to put forward names.'

'As many as you like.'

'Very well then. In 1715 the astronomers Louville and Halley, when observing the eclipse of the 3rd of May, remarked certain fulminations of an unusual nature. These flashes of light were rapid and frequently renewed, and were attributed by them to storms occurring in the atmosphere of the moon.'

'In 1715,' replied the unknown, 'the astronomers Louville and Halley mistook, for lunar phenomena, phenomena of a purely terrestrial character, such as meteoric or other bodies which are produced in our atmosphere. That is what men of science reply to the facts stated by you, and my reply is the same.'

'Let us seek further, then,' said Ardan, quite unruffled by the *riposte*. 'Herschel, in 1787, observed a large number of luminous spots on the surface of the moon. Is that not so?'

'Doubtless, but without giving any explanation as to their origin, Herschel himself did not conclude from their appearance that there must necessarily be a lunar atmosphere.'

'Well answered,' said Ardan, complimenting his adversary; 'I see you are well up in selenography.'

'I have made it my study, sir; and, I may add, that the most skilful observers, those who have best studied the orb of night, Messrs Beer and Moedler, in fact, are agreed as to the complete absence of air from its surface.'

There was a movement amongst the audience, who appeared to be growing excited by the arguments of this singular personage.

'Let us go farther still,' replied Michel Ardan with the utmost calmness, 'and let me mention an important fact. A learned French astronomer,

Monsieur Laussedat, when observing the eclipse of the 18th of July, 1860, remarked that the points of the solar crescent were rounded and truncated. This phenomenon could only have been produced by a deviation of the rays of the sun through the atmosphere of the moon, and there is no other explanation possible.'

'But is this fact certain?' asked the unknown.

'Absolutely certain.'

A movement in a contrary sense brought back the audience to their favourite hero, whose adversary remained silent. Ardan continued, without appearing vain of his last advantage, and said simply: 'You see, then, my dear sir, that one must not decide absolutely against the existence of an atmosphere on the surface of the moon; probably the atmosphere is not very dense – but science today generally admits its existence.'

'Not on the mountains, with your permission,' replied the unknown, who would not give in completely.

'No, but at the bottom of the valleys, and at a height not exceeding a few hundred feet.'

'In any case you will do well to take your precautions, for the air will be terribly rarefied.'

'Oh, my good sir, there will be always enough for one man. Besides, once I am up there I will try and economise, and only breathe upon great occasions.'

A formidable shout of laughter here arose at the expense of the mysterious interlocutor, who glared defiance at the assembly.

'Therefore,' continued Michel Ardan in his easy way, 'since we are agreed as to the presence of a certain atmosphere, we are obliged to admit the presence of a certain quantity of water, which is a matter of personal satisfaction to myself. Besides, my amiable contradictor will perhaps allow me to offer one other remark; we only know one side of the moon's disc, and if there is but little air on the side which looks towards us, there may possibly be a great deal on the other side.'

'And for what reason?'

'Because the moon, under the action of terrestrial attraction, has assumed the form of an egg, of which we see the smaller end; hence the conclusion arrived at by Hansen's calculations, that its central gravity is situated in the other hemisphere. Hence also the conclusion that all the masses of air and water must have been attracted to the other face of our satellite in the first days of its creation.'

'Mere speculations,' cried the unknown.

'Not so: they are theories based upon the laws of mechanics, and they appear to me very difficult to refute. I appeal to this meeting, and I put to the vote the question, whether life, such as it exists on our earth, is possible on the surface of the moon?'

Three hundred thousand auditors applauded the proposal simultaneously. Michel Ardan's adversary still wished to speak, but could not make himself heard. Cries and threats fell upon him like hail.

'Enough, enough,' cried some.

'Turn him out,' said others.

'Turn him out,' roared the infuriated crowd.

But he clung firmly to the hustings and refused to move, notwithstanding the storm, which would have gained formidable proportions if Michel Ardan had not appeased it by a gest. He was too chivalrous to abandon his contradictor in such an extremity.

'You wished to add a few words?' he said in a most gracious tone of voice.

'Yes, a hundred,' replied the unknown angrily. 'Or, rather, no, only one! To persevere in your undertaking you must be – '

'Rash! How can you call me so? I who have asked my friend Barbicane for a cylindro-conic projectile so as not to turn like a squirrel on my journey.'

'But, unhappy man, the terrible shock will kill you at the start.'

'My dear contradictor, you have just put your finger upon the only real difficulty. However, I have too good an opinion of the industrial genius of Americans not to believe that they will be able to obviate it.'

'But the heat developed by the velocity of the projectile through the air?'

'Oh, the sides are thick, and I shall soon have got through the atmosphere.'

'But how about provisions and water?'

'I have calculated that I can take sufficient for one year, and my journey will only last four days!'

'What air will you breathe on the journey?'

'I will make it by chemical process.'

'How about your fall upon the moon, if you ever reach it?'

'It will be six times less rapid than a fall upon the earth, because the gravitation is six times less upon the surface of the moon.'

'But it will still be sufficient to smash you like glass!'

'I shall lessen the fall by means of rockets, properly placed and let off when necessary.'

'But even supposing all the difficulties are overcome, and all the obstacles removed – supposing that all the chances are in your favour, and admitting that you reach the moon – how will you return?'

'I will not return.'

At this reply, which was almost sublime in its simplicity, the audience were dumfounded. But their silence was more eloquent than the loudest shouts of enthusiasm. The unknown took advantage of the pause to protest once more.

'You will infallibly be killed,' cried he, 'and your death will be but the death of an insensate, of no service whatever to science.'

'Go on, generous unknown, for truly your prophecies are most agreeable!'

'This is too much,' cried Michel Ardan's adversary. 'I don't know why I continue such a useless discussion! Carry out your mad undertaking. It is not you who are to blame!'

'Oh, don't mind me!'

'No, there is another who will bear the responsibility of your actions.'

'And who is that, if you please?' asked Michel Ardan, imperiously.

'The ignoramus who organised this impossible and ridiculous attempt.'

The attack was direct. Barbicane, since the intervention of the unknown, was making violent efforts to contain himself and 'consume his own smoke', like certain boiler furnaces; but seeing himself so outrageously insulted, he started up, and was on the point of throwing himself upon the adversary who thus defied him, when he suddenly found himself separated from him.

The platform was suddenly lifted up by a hundred vigorous arms, and the president of the Gun Club had to share with Michel Ardan the honour of being carried in triumph. The burden was heavy, but the bearers relieved each other incessantly, and each one pushed, struggled, and fought to lend the aid of his shoulders to this manifestation.

However, the unknown had not taken advantage of the tumult to escape from the spot, nor could he have done so in the midst of the compact crowd. He remained in the first rank, his arms crossed, glaring at President Barbicane.

The latter did not lose sight of him, and the glances of the two men crossed each other like the blades of two duellists.

The shouts of the immense crowd were maintained at their maximum of intensity during the triumphal march. That Michel Ardan evidently enjoyed his position was shown by his beaming face; and though the platform occasionally pitched and rolled like a ship in a storm, the two heroes of the meeting proved themselves good sailors, and held firm till their bark arrived, without damage, at the port of Tampa Town.

Michel Ardan was fortunately able to escape from the last embraces of his vigorous admirers. He rushed into Franklin's hotel, gained his bedchamber, and slipped into bed, whilst an army of 100,000 men kept watch under his window.

During this time a short but decisive scene took place between the mysterious personage and the president of the Gun Club.

Barbicane, the moment he was free, had gone straight to his adversary.

'Come with me,' said he, abruptly.

The other followed him on to the quay, and soon they were both standing alone at the entrance of a wharf opening into Jones's Fall.

There these enemies, still strangers to each other, stopped simultaneously.

'Who are you?' asked Barbicane.

'Captain Nicholl.'

'I expected as much. Until now we have never chanced to meet – '

'I came here for that purpose.'

'You have insulted me.'

'Publicly.'

'And you will give me satisfaction for this insult?'

'At once.'

'No; I wish all to pass secretly between us. There is a wood situated three miles from Tampa – Skersnaw. You know it?'

'I do.'

'Would you be good enough to enter this wood on one side, tomorrow, at 5 a.m.?'

'Yes, if you will enter by the other side at the same hour.'

'You will not forget your rifle?' said Barbicane.

'Nor will you forget yours,' replied Nicholl.

After which words, spoken with great calmness, the president of the Gun Club and the captain separated. Barbicane returned to his dwelling, but instead of taking a few hours' rest he passed the night in searching for the means to obviate the shock of the projectile, and to solve the difficult problem suggested by Michel Ardan during the discussion at the meeting.

CHAPTER TWENTY-ONE

How a Frenchman settles an affair of honour

While the president and the captain were discussing the preliminaries for the duel – (terrible and savage duel, in which each adversary becomes a man-hunter!) – Michel Ardan was resting after the fatigues of his triumph. Resting is hardly the correct expression, for American beds rival for hardness their marble or granite tables. Ardan therefore slept very badly, twisting and turning between the napkins which served for sheets, and was dreaming of establishing a more comfortable couch in his projectile, when a violent noise awoke him suddenly from his slumbers. A shower of blows was beating on his door, apparently produced by some iron instrument, whilst loud shouts mingled with this too matutinal hubbub.

'Open!' someone was crying; 'for Heaven's sake, open at once!'

Ardan had no reason for complying with this noisy request; however, he rose and opened the door, at the moment when it was on the point of giving way before the efforts of the obstinate visitor.

The secretary of the Gun Club rushed into the room. A bombshell would not have entered with less ceremony.

'Yesterday evening,' cried J. T. Maston, *ex abrupto*, 'our president was publicly insulted during the meeting. He has challenged his adversary, who is no other than Captain Nicholl, and they fight this morning in Skersnaw Wood. I learned it from Barbicane's own mouth. If he is killed our project will be annihilated. This duel must be stopped. There is but one man in the world with sufficient influence over Barbicane to stop it, and that man is Michel Ardan.'

While J. T. Maston was speaking, Michel Ardan, renouncing all idea of interrupting him, had slipped on his wide trousers, and in less than two minutes afterwards the two friends were making their way towards the suburbs of Tampa Town. During their rapid walk, Maston told Ardan the facts of the case. He informed him of the true causes of enmity between Barbicane and Nicholl; how this enmity was of ancient date; how, until then, thanks to mutual friends, the president and the captain had never met. He added that it was nothing but a rivalry between armour-plate and cannon ball, and that the scene at the meeting had

been nothing but an opportunity long sought for by Nicholl to gratify a resentment of old standing.

Nothing can be more terrible than these duels, which are special to America, and during which the two adversaries seek each other through the underwood, await each other on the edge of the clearings, and draw each other from the thickets, like wild beasts. Each of them must envy those marvellous qualities which distinguish the Indians of the prairies – their quick intelligence, their ingenious cunning, their knowledge of tracks, and their scent of an enemy; for an error, a hesitation, or a false step, may prove fatal. In these duels the Yankees are often accompanied by their dogs, and, at once hunters and hunted, they follow each other's tracks for hours together.

'What a devil of a set you are,' cried Michel Ardan, when his companion had described this scene to him with much energy.

'We are as we are made,' replied J. T. Maston, modestly; 'but let us make haste.'

It was, however, in vain that Michel Ardan and he raced across the plain, still wet with dew, taking the shortest cuts through rivulets and creeks – they could not reach Skersnaw Wood before half-past five; Barbicane had headed them by at least half an hour. An old wood-cutter was there, splitting into faggots the trees which had fallen beneath his axe. Maston ran to him, crying: 'Did you see a man go into the wood with a rifle? Barbicane, the president – my best friend?'

The worthy secretary of the Gun Club naïvely thought that his president must be known to everybody, but the wood-cutter did not appear to understand.

'A sportsman,' said Ardan.

'A sportsman! Yes,' replied the wood-cutter.

'How long since?'

'About one hour.'

'We are too late,' cried Maston.

'Have you heard any shots?' asked Michel Ardan.

'No.'

'Not one?'

'Not one. That sportsman does not appear to have much luck.'

'What's to be done?' said Maston.

'We must enter the wood, even at the risk of getting a ball which is not intended for us.'

'Oh!' cried Maston, in a tone which could not be misunderstood, 'I would rather get ten balls in my head, than one in Barbicane's.'

'Forward then,' said Ardan, wringing his companion's hand.

A few seconds later the two friends disappeared in the thicket formed of giant cypress trees, sycamores, tulip trees, olive trees, tamarinds, oaks, and magnolias. These different trees interlaced their branches in an inextricable pell-mell which made it impossible to see any distance ahead. Michel Ardan and Maston walked side by side, passing silently through the tall grass, cutting a path through the thick creepers, examining the bushes and the thick depths of foliage, and expecting to hear at each step the redoubtable crack of the rifles. As regards any traces which Barbicane might have left of his passage through the wood, they were unable to discover them, but walked blindly through the half-formed tracks, on which an Indian would have followed the march of his adversary step by step.

After one hour of vain searching, the two companions made a halt, for their uneasiness had redoubled.

'All must be over,' said Maston, in a tone of discouragement. 'A man like Barbicane would not *finesse* with his enemy, nor lay traps, nor practise any manoeuvre! He is too straightforward, too courageous. He has gone straight to the danger, and doubtless so far from the wood-cutter that the wind has carried away the sound of the rifles.'

'But we!' replied Michel Ardan, 'since our entry into the wood – we would have heard.'

'And if we had arrived too late!' cried Maston despairingly.

Michel Ardan found nothing to answer to this, and he and Maston resumed their interrupted walk. From time to time they shouted and hallooed, calling now for Barbicane, now for Nicholl, but neither of the two adversaries answered their shouts. Frightened at the noise, joyous flights of birds disappeared among the branches, and some scared deer fled precipitately into the thicket. For a whole hour the search was prolonged, and the greater portion of the wood had been explored without discovering any trace of the combatants. They began to doubt the wood-cutter's statement, and Ardan was on the point of giving up a search which he considered as hopeless, when Maston stopped suddenly.

'Hush,' said he, 'there is someone there.'

'Where?' said Michel Ardan.

'There! A man! He seems motionless. He has no rifle – what can he be doing?'

'Do you recognise him?' asked Michel Ardan, whose shortsightedness was rather against him under such circumstances.

'Yes, yes; he is turning round,' replied Maston.

'And who is it?'

'Captain Nicholl.'

'Nicholl!' cried Michel Ardan; and his heart beat rapidly.

Nicholl – unarmed! Then he could have nothing further to fear from his adversary.

'Let us go to him,' said Michel Ardan, 'we will soon know how the matter stands.'

But his companion and he had not advanced more than fifty paces when they again stopped to examine the captain more attentively. They had expected to find a bloodthirsty man gloating over his revenge. What they did see filled them with stupefaction.

A closely-spun net stretched between two gigantic tulip trees, and in the very centre of this snare a little bird with entangled wings was struggling and uttering its plaintive cries. The birdcatcher who had laid this trap was not a human being, but a venomous spider, indigenous to the country, of the size of a pigeon's egg, with eight enormous legs. At the moment when this hideous insect had been on the point of seizing its prey it had been obliged to retreat and seek safety on the high branches of the tulip tree, for it was threatened in its turn by a redoubtable enemy.

In fact Captain Nicholl, with his gun lying by his side, and quite forgetful of the danger of his situation, was engaged in delivering, as delicately as possible, the victim caught in the web of the monstrous spider. When he had finished he let the little creature go, and the bird flew joyfully away and disappeared.

Nicholl was watching its flight between the branches, when he heard the following words, pronounced in a tone full of emotion: 'You are a real good fellow, you are.'

He turned round, and Michel Ardan was before him, repeating: 'And an amiable man!'

'Michel Ardan,' cried the captain, 'what are you here for, sir?'

'To shake your hand, Nicholl, and to prevent your killing Barbicane, or being killed by him.'

'Barbicane,' cried the captain, 'I have been looking for him for the last two hours, and cannot find him. Where is he hiding?'

'Nicholl,' said Michel Ardan, 'that is not polite; a man should always respect his adversary. Do not be afraid; if Barbicane is alive we will find him, and the more easily that if he is not amusing himself like you in getting little birds out of trouble he must be on the lookout for you. But when we do find him, take Michel Ardan's word for it, there shall be no duel between you.'

'Between President Barbicane and myself,' replied Nicholl gravely, 'there is such rivalry that only the death of one of us – '

'Nonsense, nonsense,' replied Michel Ardan, 'such good fellows as you may hate each other, but you must esteem each other as well; you shall not fight.'

'I will fight, sir.'

'You will not.'

'Captain,' said J. T. Maston, with much feeling, 'I am the president's friend, his *alter ego*, his second self. If you absolutely wish to kill someone, fire at me; it will be just the same thing.'

'Sir,' said Nicholl, grasping his rifle convulsively, 'these pleasantries – '

'My friend Maston is not joking,' replied Michel Ardan, 'and I quite understand his readiness to be killed for the man he loves! But neither he nor Barbicane shall fall before Captain Nicholl's fire, for I have such a seductive proposal to make to the two rivals that they will be sure to accept it.'

'What is that?' asked Nicholl with visible incredulity.

'Be patient,' replied Ardan; 'I can only communicate it in the presence of Barbicane.'

'Let us look for him, then,' cried the captain; and the three men set off together. The captain, having uncocked his rifle, threw it over his shoulder, and stepped out in silence.

For half an hour their researches were useless. A sinister presentiment arose in Maston's mind; he watched Nicholl closely, wondering whether the captain had not already satisfied his vengeance, and whether the unfortunate Barbicane was not lying, shot through the heart, in some blood-bespattered thicket. Michel Ardan appeared to have the same suspicion, and both were observing Captain Nicholl with inquiring eyes when Maston suddenly stopped. The motionless head and shoulders of a man appeared about twenty paces off, leaning against the trunk of a gigantic catalpa, and half hidden by the grass.

'It is he,' said Maston.

Barbicane did not move. Ardan looked suspiciously at the captain, but the latter appeared unmoved. Ardan stepped forward, crying out: 'Barbicane! Barbicane!'

There was no reply. Ardan rushed towards his friend, but at the moment when he was going to seize him by the arm he stopped short and uttered a cry of surprise. Barbicane, pencil in hand, was tracing formulae and geometrical figures in his note-book, whilst his rifle lay uncocked by his side.

Absorbed in his work, Barbicane had forgotten his duel and his vengeance, and had seen and heard nothing.

But when Michel Ardan laid his hand upon him he rose, started, and looked up at him with astonishment.

'Hallo!' said he, 'you here? *Eureka*, my friend, *eureka*!'

'What is it?'

'The means!'

'What means?'

'The means to nullify the shock at the despatch of the projectile!'

'Really!' said Michel, glancing at the captain from the corner of his eye.

'Yes, with water; the water will act as a spring – Hallo, Maston, you here too?' cried Barbicane.

'*In propriâ personâ*,' replied Michel Ardan; 'and let me introduce, at the same time, worthy Captain Nicholl.'

'Nicholl!' cried Barbicane, jumping up. 'I beg your pardon, captain,' he said; 'I had forgotten – I am ready – '

But Michel Ardan interfered, without leaving the two enemies time to provoke each other.

'By Jove!' said he, 'it is fortunate that two good fellows like you did not meet sooner; we should now be mourning one or the other; but, thank Heaven, there is nothing further to fear! Hatred that can be forgotten to work out mechanical problems, or to play tricks upon spiders, cannot be very dangerous for anyone.'

Michel Ardan related to the president how he had found the captain.

'I leave you to judge,' said he in conclusion, 'if two good fellows such as you were intended to blow each other's brains out with a rifle-bullet?'

There was something so unexpected in this rather ridiculous situation that Barbicane and Nicholl hardly knew how to face each other. Michel Ardan felt this, and resolved to hasten the reconciliation.

'My good friends,' said he, with his most fascinating smile, 'there has never been more between you than a misunderstanding – nothing else. Well, to prove that all animosity is at an end, and as you are not afraid of a little danger, accept frankly the proposal which I am going to make to you.'

'Say on,' said Nicholl.

'Our friend Barbicane believes that his projectile will fly straight to the moon?'

'Most decidedly,' replied the president.

'And our friend Nicholl is convinced that it will fall back to the earth?'

'I am certain it will,' cried the captain.

'Very good!' continued Michel Ardan. 'I have not the pretension to make you agree, but what I say is this: start with me, and see if we are stopped on our journey!'

'What?' said J. T. Maston, stupefied.

The two rivals at this sudden proposal had raised their eyes and observed each other attentively. Barbicane awaited the captain's reply, and Nicholl waited for Barbicane to speak.

'Well,' said Michel, in his most insinuating tone, 'since there is no shock to be feared!'

'Agreed,' cried Barbicane.

Notwithstanding the quickness with which he uttered the word, Nicholl had completed it at the same time as he.

'Three cheers! Bravo! Hip, hip, hurrah!' cried Michel Ardan, offering a hand to each of the two adversaries. 'And now the matter is settled, my friends, allow me to treat you à la Française. Let us go to breakfast.'

CHAPTER TWENTY-TWO

The new citizen of the United States

That same day all America learnt at once the meeting of Captain Nicholl and President Barbicane, and its singular termination. The part played therein by the chivalrous European, his unexpected proposal, which had settled the difficulty; the simultaneous acceptance by the two rivals; this conquest of the lunar continent, to which France and America were to march side by side – all combined to increase Michel Ardan's popularity. It is well known with what frenzy Yankees become enamoured of an individual. In a country where sedate magistrates harness themselves to a ballet-girl's carriage, and drag her in triumph through the streets, it is easy to imagine the enthusiasm provoked by the audacious Frenchman. If the horses were not taken out of his carriage it was probably because he had none; but he was overwhelmed with all the other proofs of enthusiastic regard. Every citizen had a personal affection for him: '*e pluribus unum*', according to the motto of the United States. From that day Michel Ardan had not a moment's repose. Deputations from all points of the Union harassed him without ceasing. He was obliged to receive them, whether he would or not. The hands he shook and the people he spoke with were beyond all count, and he was soon completely knocked up. His voice had become hoarse through innumerable speechifyings, only unintelligible sounds escaped from his lips, and he nearly caught a gastro-enteritis from the toasts he was obliged to drink to all the counties of the Union. So much success would have probably intoxicated any other man from the first day, but he was able to maintain himself in a charming and witty state of semi-sobriety.

Among the deputations of every kind which assailed him on all sides, that of the lunatics was careful not to forget what they owed to the future conqueror of the moon. One day some of these poor people, who are sufficiently numerous in America, begged to be allowed to return with him to their native country. Some amongst them pretended to speak 'Selenite', and wanted to teach it to Michel Ardan. The latter willingly humoured their harmless mania, and took all sorts of messages for their friends in the moon.

'What a singular hallucination,' said he to Barbicane, after having got rid of them; 'yet it is an hallucination to which the finest intelligences are subject. One of our most illustrious *savants*, M. Arago, tells me that many of the wisest people, even such as are most cautious in their conceptions, give way to great exaltation and extraordinary singularities whenever the moon is in question. Do you believe in the influence of the moon in sicknesses?'

'Not much,' replied the president of the Gun Club.

'Nor do I; yet history furnishes some astonishing facts. For instance, in 1693, during an epidemic, the greatest number of persons died on the 21st of January, during an eclipse. The celebrated Bacon fainted during eclipses of the moon, and only recovered after the complete emersion of that satellite. King Charles VI relapsed six times into idiocy during the year 1399, either at the new or at the full moon. Doctors have classed epilepsy amongst the disorders which follow the phases of the moon. All nervous disorders appear to be subject to her influence. Mead speaks of a child who fell into convulsions whenever the moon entered into opposition. Gall observed that the exaltation of weak-minded people increased twice in each month, at the time of the new and full moon. There are a thousand other observations of this sort upon vertigoes, malignant fevers, and somnambulisms, which go far to prove that the Queen of the Night has a mysterious influence on terrestrial illnesses.'

'But how? Why?' asked Barbicane.

'Why?' replied Ardan. 'By George, I'll give you the same answer which Arago repeated nineteen centuries after Plutarch: "Perhaps because it is not true."'

In the midst of his triumph Ardan could escape from none of the annoyances to which celebrities are exposed. Caterers for the public wished to exhibit him. Barnum offered him a million if he would allow himself to be carried from town to town through the United States, to be shown off like some curious animal. Michel Ardan called him 'impertinent showman', and told him to go and exhibit himself.

However, though he refused to satisfy public curiosity in this manner, his portraits were soon spread over the world, and filled the place of honour in all the albums. Copies were made in all sizes, from a full-size picture down to microscopic reductions of the size of a postage-stamp. Everyone could possess his hero in all imaginable postures – his head, his bust, his full-length figure, full face, in profile, in three-fourths, or with his back turned. More than 1,500,000 proofs were taken, and he had, further, an excellent opportunity to dispose of himself for relics, but he did not take advantage of it. He had still hairs enough left on his head to make his fortune by selling them at a dollar apiece.

In truth this popularity was not displeasing to him; on the contrary, he placed himself at the disposal of the public, and corresponded with the entire universe. His jokes were repeated and widely propagated, especially such as were not his own. Like Sheridan, more witty sayings were attributed to him than a lifetime would have sufficed to utter.

Not only he had the men on his side, but the women also. What an infinity of 'advantageous matches' he might have made, had he been desirous of 'settling'. Old maids especially, who had been withering for forty years, remained day and night in contemplation before his photograph. Most certainly he could have found wives by the hundred, even if he had stipulated that they should follow him into the air, for women are intrepid unless afraid of everything. But it was not his intention to settle on the lunar continent, and to bring up a progeny of little Franco-Americans. So he refused.

'Go up there,' said he, 'to play the part of Adam with a daughter of Eve? No, thank you; I should be afraid of serpents.'

As soon as he could escape from the too-oft-repeated joys of his triumph, he accompanied his friends on a visit to the columbiad, which he certainly owed to the monster cannon. Besides, he had become very learned in gunnery since he had lived with Barbicane, J. T. Maston, and that lot. His greatest pleasure consisted in repeating to these worthy artillerists, that they were nothing but amiable and learned murderers. He was always making jokes on this subject. On the day that he visited the columbiad he greatly admired it, and was lowered to the bottom of the bore of this gigantic mortar, which was soon to launch him to the lunar sphere.

'At least,' said he, 'that cannon will do no harm to anybody, which is rather unusual as cannons go; but as regards your machines – which destroy, and burn, and break, and kill – don't talk to me about them, and don't tell me that they are to be admired, for I do not believe it.'

We must mention here a proposal connected with J. T. Maston. When the secretary of the Gun Club heard Barbicane and Nicholl accept Michel Ardan's proposal, he resolved to join them, and make up a party of four. One day he asked to be allowed to accompany them, but Barbicane, although sorry to refuse him anything, pointed out to him that the projectile could not contain such a large number of passengers. J. T. Maston, in despair, addressed himself to Michel Ardan, who begged him to be resigned, and made use of his usual *argumenta ad hominem*.

'You see, old fellow,' said he, 'you must not be offended, but really between ourselves you are too incomplete to appear in the moon.'

'Incomplete!' cried the valiant invalid.

'Yes, my worthy friend. Think for one moment, if we were to meet inhabitants up there, would you like to give them such a sad idea of what goes on down here as to teach them what war is, and show them that we employ the best part of our time in devouring each other, and breaking legs and arms, on a globe which could maintain one hundred milliards of inhabitants, and where there are only about twelve hundred millions? Why, my worthy friend, you would have us turned out!'

'But if you arrive there in pieces,' replied J. T. Maston, 'you will be as incomplete as I am.'

'No doubt,' replied Michel Ardan; 'but we shall not arrive there in pieces.'

In fact, a preparatory experiment which was tried on the 18th of October had yielded the best results, and encouraged legitimate hopes of success. Barbicane, who was desirous of forming an opinion as to the effect of the shock at the moment of the departure of the projectile, had sent for a 32-inch mortar from the arsenal of Pensacola. It was fixed on the shore of Hillisborough Bay, so that the shell might fall into the sea, and its fall be thus broken. They wanted to ascertain the shock at the departure, and not the shock on arrival.

A hollow projectile was prepared with the greatest care for this experiment. A thick quilting, covering a network of springs made of the best steel, lined it internally. It formed a perfect nest, carefully wadded.

'What a pity not to be able to get inside,' said J. T. Maston, regretting that his size did not allow him to try the adventure.

In this charming shell, which closed by means of a screw-lid, a large cat was first placed, and then a squirrel belonging to the perpetual secretary of the Gun Club, and to which J. T. Maston was particularly attached. They wanted to find out how this little animal, which is not much subject to vertigo, would stand this experimental journey.

The mortar was loaded with 160 pounds of powder, and the shell was then inserted and the gun fired.

The projectile flew upwards with great velocity, described a majestic parabola, reached a height of nearly a thousand feet, and then with a graceful curve plunged into the midst of the waves.

Without losing an instant a boat was despatched to the spot; skilful divers plunged beneath the water and fixed cables to the handles of the shell, which was immediately hauled on board. Five minutes had not elapsed between the moment when the animals were shut in and the moment when the lid of their prison was unscrewed.

Ardan, Barbicane, Maston, and Nicholl were in the boat, and assisted at the operation with a feeling of interest easily understood. Hardly was the shell opened when the cat jumped out, a little frightened, but full of life, and without any appearance of having returned from an aerial expedition. But where was the squirrel? They searched for it, but in vain, and were driven at last to the conclusion that the cat had eaten its travelling companion.

J. T. Maston was much grieved at the loss of his poor squirrel, and resolved to inscribe its name amongst the list of martyrs to science.

After this experiment all hesitation and fear disappeared; besides, Barbicane's plans would render the projectile yet more perfect, and almost completely nullify the effects of the shock.

Nothing remained now but to start.

Two days later Michel Ardan received a message from the President of the Union, an honour of which he showed himself particularly sensible. As in the case of his chivalrous fellow-countryman, the Marquis de Lafayette, the Government conferred on him the title of Citizen of the United States of America.

CHAPTER TWENTY-THREE

The projectile-carriage

After the completion of the celebrated columbiad, public interest was immediately drawn to the projectile, the new vehicle which was to carry through space our three bold adventurers. Nobody had forgotten that Michel Ardan in his telegram of the 30th of September had asked for an alteration of the plans which had been settled by the members of the committee.

At that time President Barbicane considered with reason that the form of the projectile was of small importance, for after traversing the atmosphere in a few seconds its passage would be made in absolute vacuum. The committee had chosen the round shape, so that the shot might turn upon its axis and act as it thought fit. But from the moment that it was to become a vehicle the matter was different. Michel Ardan had no desire to travel like a squirrel, he wished to ascend with his head uppermost and his feet below, as much at his ease as in the car of a balloon – more rapidly, no doubt, but without turning a series of very undignified somersaults.

New plans were therefore sent to Messrs Breadwill and Co., of Albany, with the request to have them executed without delay. The projectile thus modified was cast on the 2nd of November, and despatched immediately to Stone's Hill by the Eastern Railway.

On the 10th, it reached its destination without accident. Michel Ardan, Barbicane, and Nicholl awaited with the greatest impatience this 'projectile-carriage' in which they were to journey to the discovery of a new world.

They were fain to admit that it was a magnificent piece of metal, and a metallurgical product which did the greatest honour to the industrial genius of the Americans. It was the first time that aluminum had been obtained in so considerable a mass, and it might justly be considered a prodigious result. The precious projectile gleamed in the rays of the sun. To see it, with its imposing size, covered with its conical roof, it might easily have been taken for one of those turretlike pepper-boxes which the architects of the middle ages erected at the angles of their castles. It only wanted loopholes and a weathercock.

'I fully expect,' cried Michel Ardan, 'to see a man-at-arms come out of it with a partisan and steel corsolet. We shall be like feudal lords in there, and with a cannon or two we might stand a siege from a whole army of Selenites, if there be any in the moon.'

'So you like the carriage?' asked Barbicane.

'Yes, pretty well,' replied Michel Ardan, who examined it from an artist's standpoint, 'only I am sorry that the shape is not more slender and the cone more graceful. It ought to have been finished off with some ornaments in metal-work, with a griffin, for instance, or a gargoyle, or a salamander rising from the fire with spread wings and an open mouth.'

'What would be the good of that?' said Barbicane, whose matter-of-fact mind was but little sensible of the beauties of art.

'What good, friend Barbicane? Alas! since you put such a question I am afraid you would never understand.'

'Never mind that; tell me, worthy comrade.'

'Well, to my mind, one ought always to introduce art into everything that one does. Do you know an Indian piece called the "Chariot and the Child?"'

'Never heard the name,' replied Barbicane.

'I am not surprised,' continued Michel Ardan. 'Learn, then, that in this piece there is a robber who stays to consider, when on the point of breaking into a house, whether he will make his hole in the form of a lyre, of a flower, of a bird, or of a vase! Now tell me, friend Barbicane, if you had been a member of the jury, would you have brought that thief in guilty?'

'Without hesitation,' replied the president of the Gun Club, 'and with a recommendation that the full penalty might be inflicted.'

'And I would have acquitted him, friend Barbicane. That is why you will never understand me.'

'I shall not even try, most radiant artist.'

'At any rate,' continued Michel Ardan, 'since the exterior of our "projectile-carriage" is not to my taste, I must be allowed to furnish it as I like, and with all the luxury which is proper for ambassadors from the earth.'

'In that respect, my worthy Michel,' replied Barbicane, 'you shall act as you think proper. We give you full permission.'

But before going into the question of what might be agreeable, the president of the Gun Club had given his attention to what was more useful, and the means invented by him to lessen the effects of the shock were most intelligently applied.

Barbicane had said to himself, not without reason, that no spring would be sufficiently powerful to deaden the shock, and during his famous promenade in Skersnaw Wood he had arrived at an ingenious solution of this great difficulty. He intended to use water as the medium in this matter.

The projectile was to be filled to a height of three feet with a bed of water supporting a perfectly water-tight wooden disc, which worked easily against the interior walls of the projectile. Upon this raft the passengers would take their stand. As to the mass of liquid, it was divided by horizontal separations which the shock of departure would break in succession. Then each bed of water, from the lowest to the highest, escaping through service-pipes to the upper portion of the projectile, acted as a spring; and the disc, which was itself provided with extremely powerful buffers, could only reach the bottom of the projectile when the different separations had been broken through. Doubtless the travellers would still feel a violent shock after the complete escape of the liquid mass, but the first shock would be almost completely destroyed by this powerful spring.

It is true that 3 feet of water on a surface of 54 square feet would weigh nearly 11,500 pounds, but the pressure of gas accumulated in the columbiad would be sufficient, in Barbicane's opinion, to deal with this increase of weight; besides which, the shock would force out all the water in less than a second, and the projectile would promptly recover its normal weight.

This is what the president of the Gun Club had imagined, and the manner in which he considered the great question of the shock to have been solved.

In all other respects the work which had been undertaken by Messrs Breadwill's engineers had been marvellously well executed; and once the effect was produced, and the water driven out, the travellers could easily get rid of the broken partitions, and take to pieces the movable disc which supported them at the moment of their departure.

As regards the upper walls of the projectile, they had been thickly padded with leather placed over spirals of the best steel, as elastic as watch-springs; the service-pipes were hidden by this lining. Thus all imaginable precautions had been taken to deaden the first shock, and, as Michel Ardan said, 'One must have been very ill-conditioned indeed to allow oneself to be hurt.'

The projectile measured, exteriorly, 9 feet in width by 12 feet in height. In order not to exceed the given weight, the thickness of the walls had been slightly reduced and the lower portion strengthened, as the latter had to support the whole force of the gas developed by the combustion of the gun-cotton. This is the reason why, in all cylindro-conic shells, the lower portion is always the thickest. The entrance to this metal tower was by a narrow opening made in the side of the cone, and resembling the manhole of a steam boiler. It shut hermetically, by means of an aluminum plate fixed to the interior by powerful screws, so that the travellers could leave their movable prison, at will, upon arrival at the moon.

It was not sufficient, however, to make the journey, it was necessary to be able to see during the passage. Nothing could be easier! Under the padding were four lenticular glass scuttles of great thickness – two in the circular wall of the projectile, a third in its lower portion, and a fourth in the conic roof. Thus the travellers would be able to observe during their passage the earth which they were leaving, the moon which they neared, and the constellated regions of the heavens. As a precautionary measure these scuttles were protected from the shock of the departure by plates let into grooves, but which could easily be got rid of by unscrewing the bolts from within. By this means the air contained in the projectile could not escape, and observations were rendered possible.

All these mechanisms were admirably constructed and worked with the greatest ease, and the engineers had not shown themselves less intelligent in the interior arrangements of the 'projectile-carriage'.

Reservoirs, firmly fixed down, contained water and the necessary provisions for three travellers; the latter could even obtain fire and light by means of gas contained in a special reservoir, under a pressure of several atmospheres. It was only necessary to turn a tap, and during six days the gas would light and heat this comfortable vehicle. As you see, nothing was wanting of things essential to life or even to comfort. Further, thanks to the artistic instincts of Michel Ardan, taste was combined with utility, and the projectile would have become quite an artist's studio had there been sufficient space. It would be wrong to suppose that three persons would be much crowded in this metal tower. It possessed an area of 54 square feet and a height of 10 feet, which allowed the passengers a certain freedom of movement. They would not have been so much at their ease in the most comfortable railway carriage in the United States.

The question of provisions and light being thus settled, there only remained the question of air. It was evident that the air contained in the projectile would not suffice for the travellers' breathing during four days, inasmuch as each man consumes, in about one hour, all the oxygen contained in 100 litres of air. Barbicane and his two companions, with two dogs which they intended to take with them, would consume, in twenty-four hours, 2,400 litres of oxygen, or about seven pounds in weight. It was, therefore, necessary to renew the air in the projectile. But how? By a very simple process – that of Messrs Reiset and Regnault, mentioned by Michel Ardan during the discussion at the meeting.

It is known that air is composed principally of 21 parts of oxygen and 79 parts of azote (nitrogen). Now what takes place when we breathe? A very simple phenomenon. Man absorbs the oxygen of the air which is necessary to maintain life, and exhales the nitrogen intact. The air thus exhaled has lost nearly five per cent. of its oxygen, and contains then an almost equal volume of carbonic acid, produced by the combustion of the elements of blood by the inhaled oxygen. Thus, in a confined space, after a certain lapse of time, all the oxygen of the air is replaced by carbonic acid, which is a very deleterious gas.

The question was therefore reduced to this – the nitrogen remaining intact – first, how to replace the oxygen absorbed? Secondly, how to destroy the carbonic acid exhaled? Nothing could be more easy by means of chlorate of potash and caustic potash.

Chlorate of potash is a salt which presents itself in the form of white crystals; at a temperature of more than 400° it is transformed into chloride of potassium, and the oxygen which it contains is entirely liberated. Eighteen pounds of chlorate of potash produce seven pounds of oxygen, which is just the quantity required by the travellers during twenty-four hours. There you have the supply of oxygen.

Caustic potash has a great affinity for carbonic acid, and it is only necessary to wave it through the air and it will absorb all that is therein contained, and form a bi-carbonate of potash. There you have the means of getting rid of the carbonic acid.

By combining these two means, it was easy to restore all its vivifying qualities to the vitiated air – an experiment which Messrs Reiset and Regnault had successfully carried out.

It is true that the experiments, hitherto, had been made *in anima vili*, and notwithstanding the scientific precision thereby attained it was quite unknown how men would be able to bear it.

This latter remark was made at the meeting when this important question was under discussion. Michel Ardan would not admit the possibility of a doubt as to their being able to live in this artificial air, and he offered to make a trial before their departure. But the honour of making this experiment was energetically claimed by J. T. Maston.

'As I am not going with you,' said the worthy artillerist, 'at least you may allow me to pass a week in the projectile.'

It would have been ungracious to refuse him this, so his wish was granted. A sufficient quantity of chlorate of potash and caustic potash was placed at his disposal, together with provisions for eight days. Then,

having shaken his friends by the hand, he let himself down into the projectile, on the 12th of November, at 6 a.m., with the express command
that his prison was not to be opened before the 20th, at 6 p.m. The plate
covering the aperture was hermetically closed.

What took place during these eight days? It was impossible to tell, for the thickness of the sides of the projectile prevented any sound from being heard outside.

On the 20th of November, at 6 p.m. precisely, the plate was removed. J. T. Maston's friends had not been free from some anxiety, but they were promptly reassured on hearing a loud hurrah shouted by a jovial voice. Soon the secretary of the Gun Club appeared at the summit of the cone in a triumphant attitude.

He had grown fat!

CHAPTER TWENTY-FOUR

The telescope of the Rocky Mountains

On the 20th of October of the preceding year, after the close of the subscription, the president of the Gun Club had credited the Cambridge Observatory with the amount necessary for the construction of an enormous optical instrument.

This instrument was to be either a lunette or a telescope, and sufficiently powerful to render any object, more than 9 feet in length, visible on the surface of the moon.

There is an important difference between a lunette and a telescope, which it is well to mention here. The lunette is composed of a tube, having at its upper extremity a convex lens called the object-glass, and at its lower extremity another lens called the eyeglass, to which the observer's eye is applied. The rays emanating from a luminous body pass through the first lens, and form by refraction a reversed figure in its focus. This figure is seen through the eyeglass, which magnifies it just like a magnifying-glass. So the tube of the lunette is closed at either extremity by an object-glass and an eye-glass.

The tube of the telescope, on the contrary, is open at its upper extremity. The rays of the object under observation enter freely and strike on a concave metallic mirror – that is to say, they converge. From thence the reflected rays are met by a small mirror which reflects them on to the eye-glass, by which latter the figure is magnified.

Thus in lunettes refraction plays the principal part, and reflection in telescopes. Hence the name of refractors given to the former, and that of reflectors attributed to the latter. The great difficulty of execution in these optical instruments lies in the manufacture of the object-glasses, whether lenses or metallic mirrors.

However, at the time when the Gun Club undertook its great experiment, these instruments had attained a high degree of perfection, and produced magnificent results. The time was far distant, when Galileo had observed the stars through his poor lunette which only magnified seven times. Since the sixteenth century, optical instruments had considerably increased in breadth and in length, and enabled astronomers to examine the starry firmament, to an extent hitherto unknown. Amongst the refracting instruments in existence at that time, the most notable were the lunette in the observatory of Polkowa, in Russia, of which the object-glass measured 15 inches in diameter; the lunette of the French optician Lerebours, which had an object-glass of similar dimensions; and, lastly, the lunette in the Cambridge Observatory, which was provided with an object-glass 19 inches in diameter.

Amongst the telescopes there were two of remarkable power and gigantic dimensions. The first, constructed by Herschel, was 36 feet long, and possessed a mirror 4½ feet wide; by it objects were magnified 6,000 times. The second was in Ireland, in Birr Castle, Parsonstown Park, and belonged to Lord Rosse; the length of its tube was 48 feet, the width of its mirror 6 feet, it magnified 6,400 times, and it had been found necessary to erect an immense construction in brickwork to contain the apparatus requisite for working the instrument, which weighed 28,000 pounds.

It will be seen, however, that notwithstanding these colossal dimensions, the magnifying power obtained did not exceed 6,000 times in round numbers; but an enlargement of 6,000 times would only bring the moon to a distance of 39 miles, and only render visible objects having 60 feet in diameter, unless these objects were of considerable length.

In the present instance, the projectile was only 9 feet wide by 15 feet in length; therefore the moon must be brought to 5 miles at the utmost, and, consequently, the magnifying power must be 48,000 times.

This was what the Cambridge Observatory had to execute. There were no financial difficulties in the way, so they had only to contend with the material difficulties.

In the first place they had to choose between telescopes and lunettes. The latter offered some advantages over telescopes. With equal object-glasses they possessed greater magnifying power, because the rays of light, passing through lenses, lose less by absorption than by reflection from the metallic mirror of a telescope. On the other hand, the thickness that can be given to a lens is limited, for if made too thick, it no longer allows the rays of light to pass. Further, the construction of large lenses is excessively difficult, and requires a considerable time – sometimes even years.

For this reason – although figures were to be seen with greater clearness through lunettes, which advantage would be inappreciable as regards the moon, whose light is merely reflected – it was decided to employ the telescope, which is more easily constructed and can be endowed with a greater magnifying power. However, as rays of light lose a great portion of their intensity by passing through the atmosphere, the Gun Club resolved to set up their instrument on one of the highest mountains of the Union, by which means the thickness of the stratum of air would be considerably lessened.

We have seen that in telescopes the eye-glass – that is, the magnifying-glass to which the observer places his eye – produces the enlargements; and that the object-glass, or mirror, which bears the greatest number of enlargements, is the one with the largest diameter and the greatest focal distance. To magnify 48,000 times it was necessary to greatly exceed the object-glasses constructed by Herschel and Lord Rosse. Therein lay the difficulty, for the construction of these mirrors is a very delicate operation.

Happily, some years ago, a member of the French Institute named Léon Foucault, had invented a process which greatly facilitated the polishing of object-glasses, by substituting silver-plated glasses for metallic mirrors. It was merely necessary to manufacture a sheet of glass, of the requisite size, and to give a metal back to it by means of a salt of silver. This process had given excellent results, and was adopted for the manufacture of the object-glass.

The latter was fixed in the way invented by Herschel for his telescope. In the immense instrument, constructed by the Slough astronomer, the image of the object reflected by the inclined mirror at the lower extremity of the tube, was concentrated at the other extremity where the eye-glass was situated. Thus the observer, instead of placing himself at the lower end of the tube, stationed himself at the upper end, and there looked through his magnifying-glass down into the enormous cylinder. The advantage of this arrangement was that it allowed of the suppression of the small mirror which reflected the figure on to the eye-glass. By this means the latter only received one reflection instead of two; so the stoppage of luminous rays was much less, the image was less weakened, and finally greater clearness was obtained, which was a great advantage in the observations they were about to make.

So soon as these resolutions had been taken, the work commenced. According to calculations made by the committee of the Cambridge Observatory, the tube of the new reflector was to be 280 feet long and its mirror 16 feet in diameter.

However colossal such an instrument might appear, it was not to be compared to the telescope, 10,000 feet long, which the astronomer Hook proposed to construct a few years ago. Nevertheless, such an instrument was not to be made without difficulty.

The question as to the site was quickly settled. A high mountain had to be chosen, and high mountains are not numerous in the United States.

In fact the mountain system of this great country is reduced to two chains of medium height, between which flows the magnificent Mississippi, which Americans would call 'the King of Rivers', if they admitted any sort of royalty whatever.

To the east lie the Appalachians, of which the highest point is in New Hampshire, and does not exceed the moderate height of 5,600 feet.

To the west are the Rocky Mountains, an immense chain which commences at the Straits of Magellan, follows the west coast of South America under the name of the Andes, or Cordilleras, crosses the Isthmus of Panama, and runs through North America up to the borders of the Polar Sea.

These mountains are not of any great height, and the Alps or Himalayas look down upon them with supreme contempt, for the highest point only rises to 10,701 feet, whereas Mont Blanc measures 14,439, and Kintschindjinga towers 26,776 feet above the level of the sea.

But as the Gun Club desired that the telescope, as well as the columbiad, should be established within the states of the Union, they were obliged to content themselves with the Rocky Mountains, and all the necessary apparatus was despatched to the summit of Long's Peak in the Missouri territory.

Words would be powerless to describe the difficulties of all kinds which the American engineers had to conquer, and the prodigies of audacity and skill which they accomplished. They had to raise enormous stones, heavy blocks of wrought-iron, weighty corner-clamps, huge portions of the cylinder, and the object-glass (alone weighing nearly 30,000 pounds), beyond the line of perpetual snow, to a height of more than 10,000 feet, after crossing desert plains, impenetrable forests, and frightful rapids, far from the centres of population, in the midst of wild regions where every detail of existence became an almost insoluble problem. Nevertheless, American genius triumphed over these thousand obstacles, and in less than one year from the commencement of the works, in the last days of September, the gigantic reflector raised its tube, 290 feet long, towards the sky. It was suspended from an enormous framework of iron, and, by an ingenious mechanism, it could easily be turned towards all points of the firmament, and follow the movements of the stars from one horizon to the other.

It had cost more than 400,000 dollars. The first time it was directed towards the moon the observers sustained a thrill of curiosity mingled with uneasiness. What were they going to discover by means of this telescope which magnified objects 48,000 times? Populations, troops of lunar animals, cities, lakes, or oceans? No, nothing that science was not already acquainted with; but at all points of its disc the volcanic nature of the moon could be determined with absolute precision.

But before being used for the purposes of the Gun Club, the telescope of the Rocky Mountains rendered considerable service to astronomy. Thanks to its power of penetration, the depths of the heavens were scanned to their utmost limits. The apparent diameter of a large number of stars could be accurately measured, and Mr Clarke, of the Cambridge Observatory, decomposed the Crab nebulae of Taurus, which Lord Rosse's telescope had never been able to resolve.

CHAPTER TWENTY-FIVE

Last details

The 22nd of November had arrived, and the departure was to take place ten days later. Only one operation now remained, but it was delicate and perilous in the extreme, requiring infinite precautions; and Captain Nicholl had laid his third wager against its success. It was, in fact, the loading of the columbiad with 400,000 pounds of gun-cotton. Nicholl had thought, not without reason perhaps, that the manipulation of such an enormous quantity of pyroxyle would infallibly lead to some great catastrophe, and that, in any case, so explosive a substance would ignite under the pressure of the projectile.

These serious dangers were greatly increased by the carelessness of the Americans, who did not hesitate during the Federal war to smoke their cigars whilst loading bomb-shells. But Barbicane was anxious to succeed, and not fall through at the last moment, so he chose the best workmen, and made them act under his personal inspection. He did not leave them for one minute, and by his prudence and precautions managed to bring the chances of success on his side.

In the first place, he took care not to have the whole charge brought to the enclosure of Stone's Hill at once, but had it conveyed there gradually in carefully-sealed cases. The 400,000 pounds of pyroxyle had been divided into charges of 500 pounds each, so that there were 800 gigantic cartridges carefully manufactured by the most skilful artificers of Pensacola. Each case contained ten of these, and they arrived one after the other by the Tampa Town railway. In this way there were never more than 5,000 pounds of pyroxyle at one time in the enclosure. As soon as it arrived each case was unloaded by barefooted workmen, and each cartridge was carried to the orifice of the columbiad, into which it was let down by means of hand-worked cranes. Every steam-engine had been removed, and the smallest fires extinguished for two miles round. It was difficult enough to preserve this mass of gun-cotton from the heat of the sun even in November, therefore they preferred working during the night by a light produced in vacuum by means of Ruhmkorff's apparatus, which shed an artificial daylight down to the bottom of the columbiad. There the cartridges were arranged in perfect regularity, and united by

means of a metallic wire which would carry the electric spark simultaneously to the centre of each. It was, in fact, by means of electricity that
this mass of gun-cotton was to be ignited. All these wires, covered with an
isolating substance, united at a narrow aperture, pierced at the height
where the projectile would lie; there they passed through the thick wall of
cast-iron, and ascended to the ground through one of the vent-holes
constructed for this purpose in the stone facing. Once at the summit of
Stone's Hill the wire passed on telegraph posts for a distance of two
miles, and was then connected with a powerful Bunsen battery, fitted
with an interruptor. Thus it was only necessary to place one's finger on
the knob of the interruptor to re-establish the electric current and set fire
to the 400,000 pounds of gun-cotton. It is unnecessary to add that this
was only to be done at the last moment.

On the 28th of November the 800 cartridges were deposited at the
bottom of the columbiad. This portion of the operation had succeeded;
but what trouble, what anxieties, what struggles had not President Barbicane undergone! In vain he had forbidden admission into Stone's Hill;
every day an inquisitive crowd climbed over the palisades, and some
carried their imprudence to the extent of smoking amongst the bales of
gun-cotton. Barbicane was in a continual state of fury. J. T. Maston
assisted him as best he could, chasing the intruders and collecting the still
burning cigar-ends which the Yankees scattered on all sides. This was a
difficult task indeed, for more than 300,000 persons pressed round the
palisades. Michel Ardan, it is true, had offered to escort the cases to
the very mouth of the columbiad, but having been discovered with an
immense cigar in his mouth at the very moment when hunting out the
intruders to whom he was setting so bad an example, the president of the
Gun Club perceived that he could not depend upon this intrepid smoker,
and was obliged to place him under special guard.

However, as there is a Providence even for artillerists, no explosion
occurred, and the loading was happily completed. Captain Nicholl's third
wager was therefore lost, and there only remained to insert the projectile
into the columbiad and place it upon the thick layer of gun-cotton.

Before commencing this operation, the articles required for the journey were placed in order in the 'projectile carriage'. They were sufficiently numerous, and if Michel Ardan had been allowed his way there
would have been no space left for the travellers. You can have no idea of
the extraordinary things which this amiable Frenchman wished to take
with him to the moon – a veritable stock-in-trade of useless trifles. But
Barbicane interfered, and he was obliged to confine himself to what was
strictly necessary.

Several thermometers, barometers, and lunettes were placed in the instrument-case.

The travellers were to examine the moon during the passage, and, to facilitate their observations of this new world, they took with them an excellent map, by Beer and Moedler, entitled, *Mappa Selenographica*, which is published in four sheets, and is rightly considered a masterpiece of patient observation. It reproduced with scrupulous accuracy the minutest details of that portion of the orb which is turned towards the earth. Mountains, valleys, craters, holes, and grooves are drawn according to their exact dimensions and situations, each with its proper denomination, from mounts Doerfel and Leibnitz, which raise their high summits on the eastern portion of the disc, to the *Mare frigoris*, which lies in the region surrounding the North Pole.

This was a precious document for our travellers, since it enabled them to study the country before they reached it. They carried with them also three rifles and three fowling-pieces, with explosive balls, also a large quantity of powder and lead.

'We don't know what we may meet,' said Michel Ardan. 'Men or beasts may take umbrage at our visit. We must be prepared for everything.'

Besides these defensive arms, they had pickaxes, spades, hand-saws, and other indispensable tools, not to mention garments adapted to all temperatures, from the cold of the polar regions to the heat of the torrid zone.

Michel Ardan would have wished to take with him on the expedition a certain number of animals, though not a pair of each species – for he did not see the necessity of colonising the moon with serpents, tigers, alligators, and other harmful beasts.

'No,' said he to Barbicane; 'but a few beasts of burden – oxen or cows, horses or asses – would look well and be of great use to us.'

'I agree with you, my dear Ardan,' said the president of the Gun Club; 'but our "projectile-carriage" is not a Noah's ark. It is neither big enough nor in any way adapted to such a purpose, so we must remain within the limits of what is possible.'

At last, after many discussions, it was agreed that the travellers should only take with them a well-trained setter bitch belonging to Nicholl, and a vigorous Newfoundland of prodigious strength. Several boxes of the most useful seeds were added to the number of indispensable articles. If Michel Ardan had had his way he would have taken also a few sacks of earth to sow them in. However, he took a dozen shrubs, which were carefully wrapped in straw cases and placed in a corner of the projectile.

There yet remained the important question of provisions, for they had to take into account the probability of arriving at a perfectly barren part of the moon. Barbicane managed to collect enough for one year, but, it must be added, lest people should be surprised, that these provisions consisted of preserved meats and vegetables, reduced to their smallest volume under the action of the hydraulic press, and containing a large amount of nutriment. They were not very varied, but, for such an expedition, one could not be very particular. There was also a reserve of brandy, which might amount to about fifty gallons, but water for two months only; for after the last observations of astronomers, no one doubted the existence of a certain quantity of water on the surface of the moon. As to the provisions, it would have been ridiculous to imagine that inhabitants of the earth could not find food up there. Michel Ardan had no doubt on this head, otherwise he could not have made up his mind to start.

'Besides,' said he, one day to his friends, 'we shall not be completely abandoned by our comrades on the earth, and they will take care not to forget us.'

'Certainly not,' replied J. T. Maston.

'How do you mean?' asked Nicholl.

'Nothing can be easier,' replied Ardan. 'Will not the columbiad be always there? Well, each time that the moon presents herself in favourable conditions as to zenith if not of perigee – that is to say about once a year – you can send us a shell laden with provisions, which we will expect on the day fixed.'

'Hear, hear!' cried Maston, with the tone of a man who had made up his mind to say something. 'Bravo! certainly, my good friends, we shall not forget you.'

'I depend upon it. So you see we shall have news from the globe very regularly, and for our part we shall be very unskilful indeed if we do not find some means of communicating with our good friends on the earth.'

These words were impregnated with such confidence that Michel Ardan, with his determined air and perfect self-possession, would have carried away the whole Gun Club in his wake. What he said appeared simple, elementary, easy, and of assured success. One must have been sordidly attached to this miserable globe not to follow the three travellers on their lunar expedition.

When the different articles had been arranged in the projectile, the water, which was to act as a spring, was introduced between the partitions, and the gas for lighting was forced into its reservoirs; as to the chlorate of potash and the caustic potash, Barbicane, fearing unforeseen delays on the road, took a sufficient quantity to renew the oxygen and absorb the carbonic acid during two months. An extremely ingenious apparatus, which acted automatically, restored to the air its vivifying qualities and purified it completely. The projectile was thus ready, and there only remained to lower it in the columbiad, an operation, however, which was full of difficulties and perils.

The enormous shell was carried to the summit of Stone's Hill, where powerful cranes seized upon it and held it suspended over the metal shaft.

The excitement of the moment was intense. If a chain had broken under this enormous weight the fall of such a mass would have certainly fired the gun-cotton.

Happily this did not occur, and, a few hours later, the 'projectile-carriage' had been slowly lowered into the bore of the cannon, and was reposing on its bed of pyroxyle. Its pressure had no other effect than to ram down more compactly the charge of the columbiad.

'I have lost,' said the captain, handing to Barbicane a sum of 3,000 dollars.

Barbicane did not wish to receive this money from his travelling companion; but he was forced to give way to Nicholl's obstinacy, for the latter made a point of paying all his debts before leaving the earth.

'In that case,' said Michel Ardan, 'I have only one thing to wish for you, my worthy captain.'

'And that is?' asked Nicholl.

'That you should lose your two other bets; in which case we shall be certain not to be stopped on our journey.'

CHAPTER TWENTY-SIX

Fire!

The momentous date of the 1st of December had arrived, and if the departure of the projectile did not take place that same evening at 46 minutes and 40 seconds past 10 p.m., more than 18 years must elapse before the moon would again be found in the same conditions of zenith and perigee.

The weather was magnificent. Notwithstanding the approach of winter, the sun shone forth in all its splendour, and bathed in its radiant light that earth which was about to be abandoned by three of its inhabitants in search of a new world. How many people found themselves unable to sleep during the night which preceded this ardently-expected day! How many bosoms were oppressed by the heavy burden of expectation! The hearts of all beat faster, except the heart of Michel Ardan. This unimpressionable personage ran backwards and forwards in his accustomed busy manner, but there were no signs apparent of any unusual preoccupation. His slumbers had been as peaceful as the sleep of Turenne, on a gun-carriage, before the battle.

From early morning an innumerable crowd covered the plains which spread around Stone's Hill. Every quarter of an hour the Tampa railway brought new visitors. The immigration soon attained fabulous proportions, and according to the statistics of the *Tampa Town Observer*, on that memorable day five millions of spectators stood upon Floridan soil.

For a month past, the greater portion of this crowd bivouacked around the enclosure, and laid the foundations of a city which has since been called Ardanstown. Sheds, cabins, huts, and tents were scattered over the plain, and these ephemeral habitations contained a population so numerous as to be envied by the greatest cities of Europe.

All the nations of the earth were represented there: all the dialects of the world were to be heard at the same time. It was like the confusion of tongues as in the biblical times of the Tower of Babel. There the several classes of American society mingled in absolute equality. Bankers, farmers, sailors, commission agents, brokers, cotton planters, merchants, watermen, and magistrates, elbowed each other with the most primitive unceremoniousness. Creoles from Louisiana fraternised with farmers from Indiana, gentlemen from Kentucky and Tennessee; elegant and haughty Virginians chatted with half-savage trappers from the lakes, and with cattle-dealers from Cincinnati. There was a varied display of broad-brimmed white beaver hats, and the inevitable panamas; trousers of blue cottonade from the manufactories of Opelousas; elegant blouses of brown holland, boots of startling colours, extravagant cambric frills; and on fingers, in ears, in shirts, in cuffs, and in cravats, an assortment of rings, pins, diamonds, chains, drops, and pendants, as costly as they were in bad taste. Women, children, and servants, in not less opulent dresses, accompanied, followed, preceded, and surrounded their husbands, fathers, and masters, who looked like chiefs of tribes in the midst of their innumerable families.

·It was a sight at dinner-time to see this crowd throw themselves on the viands peculiar to the southern states, and devour, with an appetite that threatened exhaustion of all Floridan supplies, dishes most repugnant to European stomachs – such as fricasséed frogs, stewed monkeys, fish chowder, underdone opossum, or grilled raccoon.

Then what a varied series of liquors and drinks to wash down this indigestible food! What excited shouts! What engaging vociferations re-echoed in the bar-rooms and taverns, ornamented with glasses, vials, caraffes, and bottles of improbable shapes, mortars for pounding sugar, and bundles of straw!

'Here is the mint-julep,' cried one of the barmen, in a loud voice.

'Claret-sangaree,' cries another.

'Gin-sling,' on one side.

'Cocktail and brandy-smash! Real mint-julep from the latest receipt!' cried the men, skilfully passing from one glass to another, as a conjuror would, the nutmeg, sugar, lemon, green mint, powdered ice, water, brandy, and fresh pineapple, of which this refreshing drink is composed.

Such, on general occasions, were the invitations addressed from every side to throats parched by the burning action of spices, producing a bewildering and deafening hubbub. But on that day, the 1st of December, such cries were unheard, as though the barmen had lost their voices by vaunting their wares. No one thought of eating or drinking, and many people in the crowd at 4 p.m. had not even taken their accustomed luncheon. A yet more significant symptom still was the fact that the national passion for games seemed quelled by a stronger excitement. The sight of the ninepins scattered through the bowling-alleys, the dice lying hid in their boxes, the packs of cards for whist, vingt-et-un, rouge-et-noir, monte, and faro, still wrapped up in their covers, proved that the event of the day absorbed every other desire, and left no room for amusement.

Until evening, a low, noiseless agitation, such as precedes great catastrophes, pervaded the anxious crowd. An indescribable uneasiness filled the minds of all; a distressing torpor, an indefinable sensation which oppressed the heart. Everyone wished that it was over.

However, about seven o'clock this heavy silence was suddenly broken. The moon appeared above the horizon, and several millions of cheers greeted her appearance. She was punctual at the rendezvous. Shouts ascended to the sky, applause burst forth from every side, whilst fair-haired Phoebe shone peacefully, in a clear sky, and caressed the excited crowd with her most affectionate rays.

At this moment, the three intrepid travellers made their appearance. At their sight, the shouts were redoubled; and unanimously, instantaneously, the national song of the United States burst from every throat, and the strains of 'Yankee Doodle', sung by five million voices, arose in a tempest of sound to the uttermost limits of the atmosphere.

Then, after this irresistible outburst, the song was hushed; the last sounds faded little by little, the noises ceased, and profound silence reigned throughout the crowd. Meanwhile the Frenchman and the two Americans had entered the reserved enclosure, round which the immense crowd was assembled. They were accompanied by the members of the Gun Club and the deputations sent by European observatories. Barbicane, calm as ever, was quietly giving his last instructions; Nicholl, with compressed lips and hands crossed behind his back, walked with a firm and measured step; Michel Ardan – always easy, dressed like a thorough traveller, with leather gaiters and a game-bag at his side, in his loosest suit of brown velvet, and a cigar between his teeth – distributed nods and smiles amongst the crowd with princely prodigality. His spirits and gaiety were inexhaustible, and he laughed, joked, and played schoolboy tricks upon the worthy J. T. Maston, remaining a true Frenchman, or, what is worse, a true Parisian, to the last second.

Ten o'clock struck. The moment was come to take seats in the projectile. The work of lowering, of securing the aperture, and removing the cranes and scaffolding which overhung the mouth of the columbiad required a certain time. Barbicane had regulated his chronometer to a tenth of a second by that of Murchison, the engineer who was entrusted with the firing of the gun-cotton by means of the electric spark. In this way the travellers, shut up in the projectile, could keep a watchful eye upon the hand which would mark the precise moment of their departure.

The moment had now arrived to say farewell. The scene was touching, and even Michel Ardan was moved, in despite of his feverish gaiety. J. T. Maston had found, beneath his withered eyelids, an ancient tear, which he doubtless reserved for this occasion, and he dropped it on the fore-head of his dear and worthy president.

'Let me go too,' said he; 'there is still time.'

'It is not possible, old fellow,' replied Barbicane.

A few minutes later the three fellow-travellers were installed within the projectile, and had securely screwed down the plate which covered the entrance-hole. The mouth of the columbiad, completely freed from incumbrances, lay open towards the sky.

Nicholl, Barbicane, and Michel Ardan were definitively walled up in their metal carriage. Who could describe the general excitement which now reached its paroxysm?

The moon rose in a firmament of limpid purity, dimming along her passage the sparkling fires of the stars; she was then passing through the constellation of Gemini, and was almost half-way between the zenith and the horizon. Everyone could easily understand that they were aiming beyond the mark, as a sportsman aims ahead of the hare which he is desirous of shooting.

A fearful silence weighed upon the whole scene. Not a breath of air upon the earth – not a breath escaping from the assembled crowd! Hearts feared to beat; all eyes were fixed upon the yawning mouth of the columbiad.

Murchison watched the hands of his chronometer. There remained hardly forty seconds before the moment of departure and each second seemed a century.

At the twentieth there was a general shudder, and a sudden thought struck the crowd that the audacious travellers enclosed within the projectile were also counting the terrible seconds. Isolated cries were heard: 'Thirty-five – thirty-six – thirty-seven – thirty-eight – thirty-nine – forty – FIRE!!!'

And Murchison, pressing his finger upon the interruptor, restored the electric current, and flashed a spark to the bottom of the columbiad.

The detonation which instantly followed was frightful, unheard of, superhuman; resembling nothing ever heard before – neither the bursting of a thunderbolt nor the eruption of a volcano. An immense column of flame leapt from the entrails of the earth as from a crater. The ground heaved, and but few of the spectators caught a momentary glimpse of the projectile victoriously cleaving the air in the midst of the flames and smoke.

CHAPTER TWENTY-SEVEN

Murky weather

The column of flame which rose to a prodigious height towards the sky illumined the whole of Florida, and, for the space of one moment, night was turned into day over a vast expanse of country. The immense pyramid of fire was seen to a distance of 100 miles out at sea – in the Gulf as well as in the Atlantic – and more than one ship's captain entered in his log the appearance of this gigantic meteor.

The discharge of the columbiad was accompanied by an earthquake. Florida was shaken to her very entrails. The gas from the gun-cotton, dilated by the heat, forced back the atmospheric strata with incomparable violence; and this artificial hurricane, one hundred times more rapid than the hurricane of tempests, rushed like a whirlwind through the air.

Not a single spectator remained on his feet. Men, women, and children, all lay prostrate, like ears of corn before a storm. There was an indescribable tumult; a great number of persons seriously hurt; and J. T. Maston, who had stood most imprudently to the fore, was thrown 20 fathoms back, and passed like a cannon-ball over the heads of his fellow-citizens. Three hundred thousand persons remained momentarily deaf and stupefied.

The atmospheric wave, after destroying the sheds and cabins, uprooting the trees within a radius of 20 miles, and driving the trains upon the railway back to Tampa, swept over that town and destroyed 100 buildings, amongst which were St Mary's church and the new Exchange. Some of the ships in the port were dashed against each other and sank immediately, whilst several others, anchored at a greater distance from the shore, broke their chains like threads and were driven on to the coast.

But the circle of these devastations extended farther still, beyond the limits of the United States. The effect of the shock, aided by a westerly wind, was felt upon the Atlantic to a distance of more than 300 miles from the American coast. An artificial storm, utterly unexpected, which even Admiral Fitzroy would have been unable to foresee, seized upon the ships with untold violence. Several vessels, caught by the terrific whirlwinds without time for preparation, sank with all hands on board; amongst these was the *Childe Harold*, from Liverpool, the loss of which formed the subject of bitter recriminations on the part of England. To this may be added, although the fact has no other guarantee than the statement of certain natives, that, half an hour after the departure of the projectile, the inhabitants of Gorea and Sierra Leone heard a muffled sound, produced by the last vibrations of the atmospheric wave which had crossed the Atlantic Ocean to expire on the African coast.

But to return to Florida. When the first moment of tumult had passed, the wounded, the deaf, in fact the whole crowd awoke, and frantic cries of 'Hurrah for Ardan! Hurrah for Barbicane! Hurrah for Nicholl!' rose towards the sky. Several millions of men, armed with telescopes, lunettes, and field-glasses, scanned the air, forgetful of all contusions and emotions, and thinking only of the projectile. But they sought it in vain; it could not be discovered, and they were obliged to wait for telegrams from Long's Peak. The director of the Cambridge Observatory was at his post in the Rocky Mountains, and to this learned and persevering astronomer the observations had been entrusted.

An unforeseen phenomenon, but which might have been expected, and against which it was impossible to guard, subjected public impatience to a severe trial.

The weather – so fine until then – suddenly changed, and the sky became covered with clouds. Could it be otherwise, after the terrible displacement of atmospheric strata, and the dispersion of the enormous mass of vapour arising from the combustion of 400,000 pounds of pyroxyle? The whole order of nature had been troubled. This could not be matter for astonishment, inasmuch as, in naval battles, the state of the atmosphere has been often suddenly changed by the discharges of artillery.

The next day, the sun rose upon a horizon covered with thick clouds, forming a heavy and impenetrable curtain between the earth and the sky, which unfortunately extended to the regions of the Rocky Mountains. It was a stroke of bad luck, and a concert of expostulations arose from every part of the globe. But nature took little heed thereat; and, certainly, since men had disturbed the atmosphere by their own act, they ought not to have grumbled at the consequences.

During the first day, each one sought to pierce this opaque veil of clouds, but without success; besides which, they were all wrong in looking towards the sky, for, in consequence of the diurnal movement of the globe, the projectile was necessarily flying at that time in a straight line from the antipodes.

However that may be, when night again enveloped the earth in impenetrable darkness, when the moon had again risen above the horizon, she was completely hidden from sight, as though purposely withdrawing from the view of those rash men who had dared to fire at her. No observation was possible, and telegrams from Long's Peak confirmed this disagreeable mischance.

However, if the experiment had succeeded, the travellers, who left on the 1st of December at 46 minutes and 40 seconds past 10 p.m., would reach their destination on the 4th at midnight. Up to that time, inasmuch as it would after all have been difficult to observe a body so small as the projectile, people waited with more or less patience and without too much grumbling.

On the 4th of December, it would have been possible to follow the track of the projectile, which would then have appeared like a black spot upon the shining disc of the moon; but the weather remained cloudy, which provoked public exasperation to a fearful pitch. Insults were uttered against the moon for not showing herself, which proves the sad instability of human regard.

J. T. Maston, in despair, started for Long's Peak to make an observation for himself. He did not doubt for one instant that his friends had reached the goal of their journey. Besides, he had not heard that the projectile had fallen back upon any point of the terrestrial islands or continents, and J. T. Maston did not admit, for one instant, the possibility of its fall into the oceans which cover three-fourths of the globe.

On the 5th, the weather was the same. The large telescopes of the old world – those of Herschel, Rosse, and Foucault, were constantly directed towards the moon, for the weather in Europe was magnificent, but the comparative weakness of these instruments prevented any reliable observation.

On the 6th the weather was the same. Three-fourths of the globe were wild with impatience. The most insensate means were proposed for dispersing the clouds accumulated in the air.

On the 7th the sky changed slightly. People began to hope, but their hope did not last long, for, in the evening, thick clouds again hid the starry firmament from their eyes.

Matters were becoming serious, for on the 11th, at 9.11 a.m., the moon would enter her last quarter, after which she would daily become less, and even if the sky were to clear, the chances of an observation would be considerably diminished. In fact the moon would no longer show more than an ever-decreasing portion of her disc, and would end by becoming new – that is to say, she would set and rise with the sun, whose rays would render her almost invisible. It would consequently be necessary to wait until the 3rd of January, at 44 minutes past noon, to commence observations.

The newspapers published these objections with a thousand comments, and did not hide from the public that they would have to call all their patience to their aid.

On the 8th, nothing. On the 9th the sun appeared for a minute, as though to taunt the Americans. It was received with groans and hisses, and being no doubt offended at such conduct, withdrew almost immediately.

On the 10th, no change. J. T. Maston was nearly wild, and fears were entertained for the worthy man's brain, which had been hitherto so well preserved beneath his gutta-percha cranium.

But on the 11th one of those terrible tempests which occur in inter-tropical regions broke upon the atmosphere. Strong easterly winds swept away the clouds amassed for so long, and in the evening the lambent crescent of the Queen of Night floated majestically amid the limpid constellations of the heavens.

CHAPTER TWENTY-EIGHT

A new star

That same night the exciting news so impatiently awaited burst like a thunderclap upon the States of the Union, and thence through the ocean it flashed along all the telegraph wires of the globe. The projectile had been perceived by the gigantic reflector at Long's Peak.

This is the note despatched by the Director of the Cambridge Observatory; it contains the scientific conclusion as to the great experiment of the Gun Club.

Long's Peak, December 12th

To the Members of the Committee of the Cambridge Observatory

The projectile discharged by the columbiad from Stone's Hill was perceived by Messrs Belfast and J. T. Maston on the 12th of December, at 8.47 p.m., the moon being then in her last quarter.

The projectile has not reached its goal; it has passed beside it, but near enough, however, to be retained by lunar attraction.

There, its rectilinear movement has been changed to a circular movement of extreme velocity, and it is describing an elliptic orbit round the moon, whose satellite it has become.

The elements of this new star have not yet been determined. We neither know its velocity of translation nor its velocity of rotation. The distance which separates it from the surface of the moon may be estimated at about 2,833 miles.

Two hypotheses are possible, one of which may modify this state of things.

Either the attraction of the moon will end by dragging the travellers to their destination, or the projectile, following an immutable law, will gravitate round the lunar disc till the end of time.

Future observations will decide the question, but up to the present the only result of the experiment of the Gun Club has been to endow our solar system with a new star.

J. BELFAST

What questions were raised by this unexpected result! What mysteries were reserved to the future investigations of science! Thanks to the courage and devotion of three men, the apparently futile undertaking of sending a cannon-ball to the moon had attained a result of incalculable importance. The travellers, imprisoned in a new satellite, even if they had not attained their purpose, at least formed part of the lunar world; they were gravitating round the orb of night, and for the first time a human eye would be able to penetrate all its mysteries. The names of Nicholl, Barbicane, and Michel Ardan will therefore be for ever celebrated in the records of astronomy, for these intrepid explorers, anxious to increase the sphere of human knowledge, had boldly rushed through space and risked their lives in the strangest experiment of modern times.

However, the note from Long's Peak elicited in the whole universe a feeling of surprise and terror. Was it possible to come to the assistance of these bold inhabitants of the earth? No, for they had placed themselves beyond the pale of humanity by crossing the limits imposed by Providence on terrestrial creatures.

They could obtain air during two months. They had provisions for a year. But after that? . . . The most unfeeling hearts beat rapidly at this terrible question.

One man alone would not admit that the situation was hopeless. One alone had confidence, and that was their devoted friend, audacious and resolute as themselves, worthy J. T. Maston.

Besides which, he did not lose sight of them. He took up his abode at Long's Peak, and his horizon was the mirror of the immense reflector. So soon as the moon rose above the horizon, he brought her within the focus of the telescope, and without losing sight of her, followed her assiduously in her journey through the starry regions. He observed with untiring patience the passage of the projectile over the disc of silver, and in reality, the worthy man remained in perpetual communication with his three friends, whom he did not despair of seeing again some day.

'We will correspond with them,' said he to whoever would listen to him, 'as soon as circumstances will permit. We shall hear from them, and they from us. Besides, I know them well! they are men of ingenuity. Amongst the three of them, they have carried into space all the resources of art, science, and industry. With that they can do almost anything, and you will see that they will get out of their difficulties.'

Into the Sun

Robert Duncan Milne

Scene – San Francisco: Time – 1883

'And so you think, doctor, that the comet which has just been reported from South Africa is the same as last year's comet – the one discovered first by Cruls at Rio Janeiro, I mean, and which was afterward so plainly visible to us here all through the month of October?'

'Judging from the statement in the papers regarding its general appearance, and the course in which it is traveling, I do not see to what other conclusion we can come. It is approaching the sun from the same quarter as last year's comet; it resembles it in appearance; its rate of motion is as great, if not greater; all these things are very strong arguments of identity.'

'But, then, how do you account for so speedy a return? This is only the end of August, and last year's comet was computed to have passed its perihelion about the eighteenth of September – scarcely a year ago. Even Encke's and Biela's comets, which are denizens of our solar system, so to speak, have longer periods than that.'

'I account for it simply on the hypothesis that this comet passes so close to the sun that its motion is retarded, and its course consequently changed after every such approach. I believe, with Mr Proctor and Professor Boss, that this is the comet of 1843 and 1880; that it is moving in a succession of eccentric spirals, the curvatures of which have reduced its periods of revolution from perhaps many hundreds of years to – at its last recorded return – thirty-seven years, then to two and a fraction, and now to less than one; and that its ultimate destination is to be precipitated into the sun.'

'This is certainly startling, supposing your hypothesis to be correct; and should such a casualty happen, what result would you anticipate?'

'That demands some consideration. Take another cigar, and we shall look into the matter.'

The foregoing conversation took place in the rooms of my friend Doctor Arkwright, upon Market Street; the time was about eleven o'clock at night; the date, the twenty-seventh of August; the interrogations had been mine and the answers the doctor's. I may add that the doctor was a chemist of no mean attainments, and took great interest in all scientific discussions and experiments.

'The effect of the collision of a comet with the sun,' observed the doctor, as he lit his cigar, 'would depend upon a good many conditions. It would depend primarily upon the mass, momentum, and velocity of the comet – something, too, upon its constitution. Let me see that paragraph again. Ah, here it is,' and the doctor proceeded to read from the paper.

'"RIO JANEIRO, August 18th. The comet was again visible last evening, before and after sunset, about thirty degrees from the sun. Mr Cruls pronounces it identical with the comet of last year. It is approaching the sun at the rate of two and a half degrees a day. R.A., at noon, yesterday, 178 degrees, 24 minutes; Dec. 83 degrees, 40 minutes, S."

'Now this,' he went on, 'corresponds exactly with the position and motion of last year's comet. It came from a point nearly due south of the sun, consequently was invisible to the northern hemisphere before perihelion.'

'Pardon me,' I interrupted, 'but you remember the newspaper predictions regarding last year's comet were to the effect that it would speedily become invisible to us here, whereas it continued to adorn the morning skies for weeks, till it faded away in the remote distance.'

'That was because the nature of its orbit was not distinctly understood. The plane of the comet's orbit cut the plane of the earth's orbit nearly at right angles, but the major axis or general direction of this orbit in space, was also inclined some fifty degrees to our plane; and so it came about that while the approach of the comet was from a point somewhat east of south, its return journey into space was along a line some twenty degrees south of west, which threw its course nearly along the line of the celestial equator; consequently, last year's comet was visible in the early morning, not only to us, but to every inhabitant of the earth between the sixtieth parallel north and the south pole, until the vast distance caused it to disappear. But, as I was going to say when you interrupted me, if the distance of the comet from the sun was only thirty degrees when observed at Rio Janeiro, nine days ago, and its speed was then two and a half degrees a day, it can not be far from perihelion now, especially as its speed increases as it approaches the sun.'

'Suppose it should strike the sun this time,' said I. 'What results would you predict?'

'A solid globe,' replied the doctor, 'of the size of our earth, if falling upon the sun with the momentum resulting from direct attraction from its present position in space, would engender sufficient heat to maintain the solar fires at their existing standard, without further supply, for about ninety years. This calculation does not involve great scientific or mathematical knowledge, but, on the contrary, is as simple as it is reliable, because we have positive data to go upon in the mass and momentum of our planet. But with a comet the case is different. We do not know what elements its nucleus is composed of. It is true we know the value of its momentum; but what does that tell us if we do not know its density or its mass? A momentum of four hundred miles a second – the estimated rate of speed of the present comet at perihelion – would undoubtedly engender fierce combustion were the comet a ponderable body. On the other hand, large bodies composed of fluid matter highly volatilized might collide with the sun without an appreciable effect.'

'Have we any data to go upon in this matter?' I inquired.

'With regard to our own sun,' replied the doctor, 'we have not; but several suggestive circumstances have occurred in the case of other suns which lead us to infer that something similar might happen to our own. Some years ago, a star in the constellation Cygnus was observed to suddenly blaze out with extraordinary brilliancy, its luster increasing from that of a star of the sixth magnitude – but faintly distinguishable to the unaided eye – to that of a star of the first. This brilliancy was maintained for several days, when it resumed its original condition. Now, it is fair to infer that this great increase of light may have been caused by the precipitation of some large solid body – a planet, a comet, or perhaps another sun – upon the sun in question; and, as light and heat are now understood to be merely different modes or expressions of the same quality of motion, it is fair to infer further that the increment of heat corresponded to that of light.'

'What, then, do you suppose would be the natural effect upon ourselves here, on this planet, by some such catastrophe as you have just imagined happening to our own sun!' I asked.

'The light and heat of our luminary might be increased a hundredfold, or a thousandfold, according to the nature of the collision. One can conceive of combustion so fierce as to evaporate all of our oceans in one short minute, or even to volatilize the solid matter of our planet in less than that time, like a globule of mercury in a hot-air chamber. "Large" and "small" are not absolute, but relative, terms in Nature's vocabulary; both are equally amenable to her laws,' sententiously observed the doctor.

'A comforting reflection, certainly,' I remarked. 'Let us hope we shall not be favored with any such experience.'

'Who can tell?' rejoined the doctor, as he rose from his seat. 'Excuse me for a minute. You know there is a balloon ascension from Woodward's

Gardens tomorrow, and there is a new ingredient I am going to introduce at the inflation. The stuff wants a little more mixing. Take another
cigar. I won't be a minute.'

I sat back and meditated as I listened to the retreating footsteps of the
doctor, as he passed into an adjoining room. I looked at the clock. It was
half past eleven. It was a warm night for San Francisco in August –
remarkably so, in fact. I got up to open the window, and as I did so the
doctor entered the room again.

'What is that?' I exclaimed involuntarily, as I threw up the sash. And
the spectacle which met my gaze as I did so, certainly warranted the
exclamation.

Doctor Arkwright's rooms were on the north side of Market Street,
and the inferior height of the buildings opposite afforded an uninterrupted view of the horizon to the south and east. Over the tops of the
houses to the east could be seen a thin, livid line, marking the waters
of the bay, and beyond it the serrated outline of the Alameda hills. All
this was normal and just as I had seen it a hundred times before,
but in the northeast the sky was lit up with a lurid, dull-red glow,
which extended northward along the horizon in a broadening arc,
till the view was shut out by the street line to our left. This light resembled in all respects the *aurora borealis*, except that of color. Instead of
the cold, clear radiance of the northern light, we were confronted by an
angry, blood-red glare which ever and anon shot forks, and tongues,
and streamers of fire upward toward the zenith. It was as if some
vast conflagration were in progress to our north. But what, I asked
myself, could produce so extensive, so powerful an illumination? Vast
forest fires, or the burning of large cities, make themselves manifest by
a sky-reflected glare for great distances, but they do not display the
regularity – or the harmony, so to speak – which was apparent in the
present instance. The conclusion was inevitable that the phenomenon
was not local in its source.

As we looked out at the window we could see that the scene had
arrested the attention of others besides ourselves. Little knots of people
had collected on the sidewalk; larger knots at the street corners; and the
passers-by kept turning their heads to gaze at the strange spectacle. At
the same time the air was growing heavier and more sultry every minute.
There was not a breath stirring, but an ominous and preternatural calm
seemed to brood over the city, like that which in some climates is the
precursor of a storm, and which here is frequently known as 'earthquake
weather'.

The doctor broke the silence.

'This is something quite out of the common run of events,' he exclaimed. 'That light in the north must have a cause. All the Sonoma and Mendocino redwoods, with the pineries of Oregon and Washington Territory thrown in, would not make such a blaze as that. Besides, that is not the sort of sky-reflection a forest fire would cause.'

'Just my own idea,' I asserted.

'Let us see if we can not connect it with a wider origin. It is now nearly midnight. That light is in the north. The sun's rays are now illuminating the other side of the globe. It is, therefore, sunrise on the Atlantic, noon in eastern Europe, and sunset in Western Asia. When you came here, scarcely an hour ago, the heavens were clear, and the temperature normal. Whatever has given rise to this extraordinary phenomenon has done so within the last hour. Even since we began to look I see that the extremity of the illuminated arc has shifted further to the east. That light has its origin in the sun, but it altogether passes the bounds of experience.'

'Might we not connect it with the comet we have just been speaking about?' I suggested. 'It should now be near its perihelion point.'

'That must be it,' acquiesced the doctor. 'Who knows but that the fiery wanderer has actually come in contact with the sun? Let us go out.'

We put on our hats, and left the building. All along the sidewalks we came upon excited groups staring at the strange light, and speculating upon its cause. The general expression of opinion referred it to some vast forest fire, though there were not wanting religions enthusiasts who saw in it a manifestation of all things; for in the uninformed human mind there is no middle ground between the grossly practical and the purely fanatical. We hurried along Market Street and turned down Kearny, where the crowds were even denser and more anxious-looking. Arrived at the *Chronicle* office, I noticed that a succession of messengers from the various telegraph offices were encountering each other on the stairs of the building.

'If you will wait a minute,' I said to the doctor, 'I will run upstairs and find out what is the matter.'

'Strange news from the East,' said the telegraphic editor, hurriedly, in answer to my question, at the same time pointing to a little pile of dispatches. 'These have been coming in for the last half hour from all points of the Union.'

I took up one, and read the contents:

NEW YORK, 3:15 A.M. EXTRAORDINARY LIGHT JUST BROKE OUT OVER THE EASTERN HORIZON. VERY RED AND THREATENING. SEEMS TO PROCEED FROM A GREAT DISTANCE OUT AT SEA. PEOPLE UNABLE TO ASSIGN CAUSE.

Another ran as follows:

NEW ORLEANS, 4:10 A.M. VIVID CONFLAGRATION REFLECTED IN THE
SKY. A LITTLE NORTH OF EAST. GENERAL SENTIMENT THAT VAST
FIRES HAVE SPRUNG UP IN THE CANE-BRAKES. POPULATION ABROAD
AND ANXIOUS.

'There are a score more,' remarked the editor, 'from Chicago, Memphis, Canada – everywhere, in fact – all to the same purpose. What do you make of it?'

'The phenomenon is evidently universal,' I said. 'It must have its origin in the sun. Do you notice how hot and stifling the air is getting? Have you any dispatches from Europe?'

'None yet. Ah, here is a cablegram repeated from New York,' said the editor, taking a dispatch from the hand of a messenger who just then entered. 'This may tell us something. Listen.

' "LONDON, 7:45 a.m. Five minutes ago sun's heat became overpowering. Business stopped. People falling dead in streets. Thermometer risen from 52 degrees to 113. Still rising. Message from Greenwich Observatory says – "

'The dispatch stops abruptly there,' interpolated the editor, 'and the New York operator goes on thus: "Message cut short. Nothing more through cable. Intense alarm everywhere. Light and heat increasing." '

'Well,' said I, 'it must be as Doctor Arkwright suggested. The comet observed again at Rio Janeiro, ten days ago, has fallen into the sun. Heaven only knows what we had better do.'

'I shall edit these dispatches and get the paper out, at any rate,' said the editor with determination. 'Ah, here comes the ice for the printers,' as half a dozen men filed past the door, each with a sack upon his shoulder. 'The paper must come out if the earth burns for it. I fancy we can hold out until sunrise, and before then the worst may be over.'

I left the office, rejoined the doctor in the street, and told him the news.

'There is no doubt about it,' he remarked at once. 'The comet of last year has fallen into the sun. All the telegraphic messages were nearly identical in time, as it is now just midnight here, and consequently about four o'clock in New York, and eight o'clock in England.'

'What had we better do?' queried I.

'I do not think there is any cause for immediate alarm,' replied the doctor. 'We shall see whether the heat increases materially between now and sunrise, and take measures accordingly. Meanwhile, let us look about us.'

The scenes of alarm were intensified in the streets as we passed along. It seemed as if half the population of the city had left their houses, and gathered in the most public places. Thousands of people were pushing and jostling each other in the neighborhood of the various newspaper offices in frantic endeavors to get a glimpse of the bulletin boards, where the substance of the various telegrams was posted up as fast as they came in. Multitudes of hacks and express wagons were driving hither and thither, crowded with family parties seemingly intent upon leaving the city, and probably without any definite aim or accurate comprehension of what they were doing or whither they were going.

As the hours wore on toward morning the angry red arch moved farther along the horizon, its outlines grew bolder and brighter, and its flaming crest towered higher in the heavens. Nothing could be conceived more ominous or ghastly, more calculated to produce feelings of brutish terror, and to convince the spectator of his utter powerlessness to cope with an inevitable and inexorable event, than this blood-red arch of flame which spread over one fourth of the apparent horizon. The air, too, was momentarily growing heavier and more stifling. A glance at a thermometer in one of the hotels gave a temperature of 114 degrees.

Between two and three o'clock four successive alarms of fire were sounded from the lower quarters of the city. Two large wholesale houses and a liquor store, in three contiguous blocks, caught fire, evidently the work of incendiaries. Multitudes of the worst rabble collected, as if by concert, in the business quarters. Shops and warehouses were broken into and looted – the police force, though working vigorously, not being strong enough to arrest the work of pillage, backed as it was by the moral terrors of the night, and the general paralysis which unnerved the better class of citizens. Strange scenes were being enacted at every corner and on every street. Groups of women kneeling upon sidewalks, and rending the air with prayers and lamentations, were jostled aside by ruffians wild and furious with liquor. A procession of religious fanatics, chanting shrill and discordant hymns, and bearing lanterns in their hands, passed unheeded through the crowded streets, and we could afterward watch them threading their way up the steep side of Telegraph Hill. In short, the terrible and bizarre effects of that fearful night would overtax the pen of a Dante to describe, or the pencil of a Doré to portray.

'Let us go home,' said the doctor, looking at his watch. 'It is now half past three. The temperature of the atmosphere is evidently rising. The chances are that it will become unbearable after sunrise. We must consider what is best to do.'

We pushed our way back through the crowded streets, past despairing and terror-stricken men and wailing women; but as we passed the bulletin boards at the corner of Bush and Kearny streets, it was encouraging to mark that at least one earthly industry would continue to go on till the mechanism could run no longer, and that the world would, at any rate, get full particulars of its approaching doom, so long as wires could transmit them, compositors set them in type, and pressmen print them. I felt that the power and grandeur of the press had never been more fully exemplified than in the regular and ceaseless pulsations of its machinery as the daily issue was being thrown off, with the news that the other hemisphere was in conflagration, and that a few short hours would in all probability witness the same catastrophe in our own.

The last two wagons which had driven up with ice for the employees had been boarded and sacked by the thirsty mob, and, looking down into the pressroom as I entered the building, I could see the pressmen stripped to the waist in that terrible hot-air bath, while upstairs the telegraphic editor was in similar *déshabille*, with the additional feature of a wet towel bound round his temples. He motioned to the last dispatch from New York as I entered. I took it up and read as follows:

NEW YORK, 6 A.M. SUN JUST RISEN. HEAT TERRIBLE. AIR SUFFOC-
ATING. PEOPLE SEEKING SHADE. THOUSANDS BATHING OFF THE
DOCKS. THOUSANDS KILLED BY SUNSTROKE.

'Almost a recapitulation of the London message of three hours ago.' I said, as I hurried out. 'Three hours hence we may expect the same here.'

I rejoined the doctor in the street, and together we proceeded to his apartments.

'Now,' said he, as I told him the purport of the last message, 'there is only one thing to be done if we wish to save our lives. It is a chance if even this plan will succeed, but at all events there *is* a chance.'

'What is it?' I asked eagerly.

'I take it,' answered he, 'that the increase of heat and light which will accrue as soon as the sun rises above the horizon must prove fatal to all animal life beneath the influence of his beams. The population of Europe, and by this time, I doubt not, of all this country east of the Mississippi, is next to annihilated. With us it is but a question of time unless – '

'Unless what?' I exlaimed excitedly, as he paused meditatively.

'Unless we are willing to run a great risk,' he added. 'You are a philosopher enough to know that heat and light are simply modes of motion – expressions, so to speak, of the same molecular action of the elements they pass through or agitate. They have no intrinsic being in themselves, no entity, no existence, as it were, independent of outside matter. In their case the two forms of outside matter affected by them are the ether pervading space and the atmosphere of our planet. Do you follow?'

'Certainly,' I replied impatiently, for I dreaded one of the doctor's disquisitions at such a critical moment as this. 'But my dear sir, what is the practical application of your theorem? How can we apply it to the case in point?'

'In this wise, he went on: 'heat – that is, the heat we have to do with now – is caused by the action of the sun's rays upon our atmosphere. If we get beyond the limits of that atmosphere, what then? Simply, we have no heat. Ascend to a sufficient altitude, even under the cloudless rays of the vertical sun, and you will freeze to death. The limit of perpetual snow is not an extreme one.'

'I catch your idea perfectly,' I assented. 'I concede the accuracy of your premises. But what does it avail us? The Sierra Nevada mountains are practically as far off as the peaks of the Himalayas.'

'There are other means,' rejoined the doctor, 'of attaining the necessary altitude. A balloon ascension, as you are aware, was to have taken place today from Woodward's Gardens. I was going to assist at the inflation, to test a new method of generating gas. I now propose that we endeavor to gain possession of the balloon and make the ascension. I do not think we shall be anticipated or thwarted in doing so.

'We must remember that the risk of the balloon bursting, through the expansion of the gas, is great; for we shall be exposed, not only to its normal expansion, should we penetrate the upper atmospheric strata, but to its abnormal expansion through heat, should we fail to do so in time.'

'It is shaking the dice with Death in any case,' I answered, and proceeded to assist the doctor in packing the apparatus and chemicals he had prepared overnight; and, having done so, we left the building and hastened southward along Market Street. The cars were not running, and the carriages we saw paid no heed to our importunities; so the precious time seemed to fly past, while we swiftly covered the mile which separated us from the gardens. The gates were luckily open, and none of the employees visible, so we made for the spot where the balloon, half-inflated, lay like some slimy antediluvian monster in its lair. We adjusted the apparatus and arranged the ropes as speedily as possible, and waited anxiously while the great bag slowly swelled and shook, rearing itself and falling back by turns, but gradually assuming more and more spherical proportions.

Meanwhile, we had again opportunity to observe the condition of the atmosphere and the heavens. It was already half past four, and in less than an hour the sun would spring up in the east. The pale, bluish tints of daybreak were beginning to assert themselves beside the lurid semi-circle which flamed above them. This latter changed to a hard, coppery hue as daylight became stronger, but preserved its contour unchanged. The heat became more oppressive, the thermometer we had brought with us now registering 133 degrees. Strange sounds were wafted in from the city – meaningless indeed, but rendered fearfully suggestive by the circumstances of the morning. The animals howled unceasingly from their cages, and we could hear their frantic struggles for liberty. One catlike form that had made good its escape shot past us in the gloom. Had the whole managerie been set free at that moment, we should have had nothing to fear from them, so great is the influence elemental crises exert over the brute creation.

We had at last the satisfaction of seeing the great globe swing clear of the gound, though not yet fully inflated, and tug at the ropes which moored it. We had already placed the ballast-bags and other necessary articles in the car, when, perspiring at every pore, we simultaneously cut the last ropes, and rose heavily into the air. There was not a breath of wind stirring, but our course was guided slightly east in the direction of the bay.

It was now broad daylight, and the upper limb of the sun appeared above the horizon as we estimated our altitude from surrounding objects at about a thousand feet. As the full orb appeared the heat became more intense, and by the doctor's direction we swathed our heads in flannel, sprinkled sparingly with a preparation of ether and alcohol, the swift evap-oration of which imparted coolness for a short time. The sky had now assumed the appearance of a vast brazen dome, and the waters of the ocean to the west and the bay beneath us reflected the dull, dead, pitiless glare with horrible fidelity. We had taken the precaution to hang heavy blankets upon the ropes sustaining the car, and these we kept sparingly moistened with water. Our own thirst was as intense as our perspiration was profuse, and we had divested ourselves of everything but our woolen underclothing – wool being a nonconductor, and therefore as effective in excluding heat as retaining it.

We were provided with a powerful ship telescope, and also a large binocular glass of long range, and so far as the discomforts of the situ-ation would permit us we took observations of the prospect beneath. To the unaided eye the city simply presented a patch of little rectangles at the end of a brown peninsula, but through our glasses the streets and houses became surprisingly plain. Little squat black forms were to be seen moving, falling down, and lying in the streets. Down by the city front the wharves were seen to be lined with nude, or semi-nude bodies, which dived into the water and remained submerged, with the exception of their heads, though these disappeared at short intervals below the surface. Thousands upon thousands of people were thus engaged. The spectacle would have been utterly absurd and ludicrous had it not been tremendous in its awful suggestiveness.

'The mortality will be terrible, I fear,' said the doctor, 'if things do not change for the better soon, and I see no prospect of that. Our thermometer already marks 147 degrees even at this altitude. We are in the *tepidarium* of a thrice-heated Turkish bath. And if this is the case at a barometric altitude of eleven thousand feet – nearly two perpendicular miles – what must it be down there? It is too terrible to contemplate!'

'It is only seven o'clock yet,' I remarked, looking at my watch. 'The sun is scarcely an hour high.'

'We must throw out more ballast,' said the doctor, 'and reach the higher strata at all hazards.' He threw out a forty-pound bag of sand.

We shot upward with tremendous velocity for several minutes, when our ascent again became regular. We now remarked, with intense relief, that the thermometer did not rise – that, in fact, it had fallen about two degrees; though this relief was counterbalanced by the extreme difficulty of breathing the rarefied air at this immense altitude, which we estimated by the barometer at twenty-five thousand feet, or nearly five perpendicular miles. We therefore opened the valve and discharged a quantity of gas, and presently descended into a stratum of dense fog. This fog reminded me of the steam which rises from tropical vegetation during the rainy season, and I mentioned the fact to the doctor.

'If these fogs,' replied he, 'would only rest upon the city, they might shield it from destruction, but in a case of this kind we have no meteorological data to go on. No one can estimate either the amount of heat or the meteorological results it is now producing on the surface of the earth five miles below us.'

The stratum of fog in which we now were was dense and impenetrable. We lay in it as in a steam bath, the balloon not seeming to drift, but swaying sluggishly from side to side, like a sail flapping idly against a mast in a calm.

Hour after hour passed like this, the temperature still ranging from 130 to 140 degrees Fahrenheit. The doctor preserved his wonted equanimity.

'I have grave apprehensions,' he remarked impressively, as if in answer to my thoughts, 'that the final fiery cataclysm, a foreboding of which has run through all systems of philosophies and religions through all ages, and which seems to be, as it were, ingrained in the inner consciousness of man, is now upon us. I am determined, however, not to fall a victim to the fiery energy that has been evoked, and shall anticipate such a fate by an easier and less disagreeable one,' and as he spoke he motioned significantly toward his right hip.

'Do you think, then,' said I, 'that an act under such circumstances' – designedly employing a vague periphrasis on such an unpleasant topic – 'is morally defensible?'

'What can it matter?' returned the doctor, with a shrug. 'Of two alternatives, both leading to the same end, common sense accepts the easier. A refusal to touch the hemlock would not have saved Socrates.'

In spite of the terrible forebodings which filled me, the exigencies of the situation seemed to render my brain preternaturally concentrated and abnormally active. The surrounding stillness, the lack of sound of any description, the dreamy warmth of the dense mist in which we lay, exercised a sedative influence, and rendered the mind peculiarly impressionable to action from within.

'We have no means, then, of calculating the probable intensity of the heat at the earth's surface?' I asked.

'None whatever,' replied the doctor. 'We are now at an indicated elevation, by barometrical pressure, of twenty-two thousand feet. We are probably actually much higher, as the steam in which we lie is acting on the barometer. Atmospheric conditions like the present, at such an altitude, are totally beyond the experience of science. They might be, and probably are, caused by the action of intense heat upon hotter surfaces below us. To the fact of their presence, however, we owe our existence. This atmosphere, though peculiarly favorable to the passage of heat rays through it, is incapable of retaining them.'

'Supposing,' I went on, in a wildly speculative mood, engendered by the excitement of the occasion, 'supposing that the heat of the surface of the earth were sufficiently intense to melt metals – iron, for instance – the most refractory substances, in fact. Take a further flight: supposing that such heat were ten times intensified, what would be its effect upon our planet?'

'The solid portions – the crust with everything upon it – would be the first to experience the effects of such a catastrophe. Then the oceans would boil, and their surface waters, at any rate, be converted into steam.'

'What then?' I continued.

'This steam would ascend to the upper regions of the atmosphere till it reached an equilibrium of rarefaction, when its expansion would cool it, upon which rapid condensation would follow, and it would descend to earth in the form of rain. The more sudden and energetic the heat, the sooner would this result be accomplished, and the more copious the precipitation of the succeeding rain. After the first terrible crisis, the grand compensation of natural law would come into play, and the face of the planet would be protected from further harm by the shield of humid vapor – the *vis medicatrix naturae*, so to speak. Equilibrium would be restored, but most organisms would meanwhile have perished.'

'Most organisms, you say?' I repeated, inquiringly.

'It is possible,' said the doctor, 'that ocean infusoria, and even some of the comparatively higher forms of ocean life, might survive. It is also possible that terrestrial animals occupying high altitudes – mountaineers for example, whose homes are deep snows and glaciers, denizens of the frozen zone, and beings similarly situated – might escape. This would altogether depend upon the intensity and duration of the heat. We must remember that *size*, looked at from a universal point of view, is merely relative. If we consider our planet as a six-inch ball, our oceans, with their insignificant average depth of a few miles, would be aptly represented by a film of the finest writing paper. How long, think you, would a watery film, such as that, last a few feet from a suddenly stirred fire?'

I bowed acquiescence to the conclusion drawn from the simile, and the doctor proceeded.

'There can be no longer any doubt that the present elemental convulsion is due to the collision of the comet with the sun. Knowing what we do of its orbit from last year's computation, its precipitation upon the solar surface has taken place on the side farthest from our own position in space. We do not, therefore, experience so sudden and so fierce atmospherical excitement as would otherwise have followed. It now remains to be seen what the duration of the effect will be.'

During the latter portion of our conversation a low moaning sound, which had been heard for the past few minutes, was growing more pronounced and seemingly coming nearer. At the same time the barometer was observed to be falling rapidly.

'That is the sound of wind,' I exclaimed. 'I have heard it on tropical deserts and on tropical seas. I can not be mistaken. It comes from the east.'

'The hot air from the parched continent is approaching,' said the doctor. 'Scientifically speaking, atmospheric convection is taking place, and we shall bear the brunt of it.'

As he spoke the balloon was seized with a violent tremor. It vibrated from apex to car, and the next moment was struck by the most terrific tornado it is possible to imagine. The blast was like the torrid breath of a furnace, and we involuntarily covered our heads with our blankets, and clutched convulsively to the frail bulwarks of the car, which was being dragged on at a tremendous velocity, and at a horribly acute angle, by the distended gas-bag which towered ahead of us. Luckily we had both clutched mechanically at the railing on the side whence the wind came, to let go which hold would have meant instant precipitation over the opposite side of the car into the yawning gulf beneath. For less than a minute, so far as my stricken and scattered senses could compute, we were borne on by this terrific simoom, when, suddenly, we found ourselves as before, in the midst of a preternatural calm. We had evidently drifted into an eddy of the cyclone; for I could hear its sullen and awful roar at some distance to our right. Hardly had we composed ourselves when the blast struck us again; this time on the opposite side of the car. Again we were hurled forward by the resistless elemental fury; but this time in a sensibly downward direction. The blast had struck us from above, and was hurling us before it – down, down, to inevitable destruction. Fortunately the comparative bulk of the balloon offered more resistance than the car to this downward progress. Down, down we sped, till, of a sudden, we emerged from the cloud-strata and obtained a brief and abrupt glimpse of the scene below. The counter-blasts of the past few minutes had apparently compensated each other's action, for we found ourselves just over the city.

The city? There was no city. I recognized, indeed, the contour of the peninsula, and the well-known outlines of the bay and islands, through casual rifts in the dense clouds of steam which rose in volumes from below. Well-nigh stupefied and maddened as I was by the intense heat, a horrible curiosity seized me to peer into the dread mystery beneath, and while with one scorched and writhing hand I held the blankets, which had not yet parted with the moisture gathered from the clouds above, to my aching head and temples, with the other I raised the powerful binocular to my eyes, I caught glimpses which filled me with unutterable and nameless horror. Neither streets nor buildings were decipherable where the city once had been. The eye rested upon nothing but irregular and misshapen piles of vitrified slag and calcined ashes. Everything was as scarred in a ruinous silence as the ruined surface of the moon. There was neither flame nor fire to be seen. Things seemed to have long passed the stage of active combustion, as though all the elements necessary to sustain flame had already been abstracted from them. Here and there an ominous dark-red glow showed, however, that the lava into which the fair city had been transformed was still incandescent. The sand dunes to the west shone like glaciers or dull mirrors through the steam fissures, and long shapeless masses of what resembled charred wood were strewn here and there over the surface of the bay. Less than five seconds served to reveal all that I have taken so long to describe. The binocular, too hot to hold, dropped from my hand. At the same moment the balloon was again struck by the cyclone, and dashed eastward with the same fury as before. The doctor caught convulsively at the railing of the car, missed his hold, and with a wild, despairing shriek, outstretched arms, and starting eyes fixed upon mine, disappeared headlong in the abyss.

I am alone in the balloon – perhaps alone in the world. My companion has been hurled to a fiery death below. His awful shriek still rings in my ears. It sounds over the sullen roar of the cyclone. I am whirled resistlessly onward.

The blast shifts. Again the balloon pauses in one of the strange eddies formed by this strange simoom. The wind dies away to a moan. It rises again. It writhes around the car like the convulsive struggles of some gigantic reptile in the throes of death. It seizes me again in its resistless clutch. The balloon is being whirled toward the earth.

I am falling. But no – it seemed to me that the earth – the plutonic, igneous earth – is rising toward me. With lightning-like rapidity it seems to hurl itself up through the air to meet me. I hear the roar of flames mingling with the roar of the blast. I see the seething, bubbling waste of waters through rifts in the clouds of steam.

I am nearing the molten surface. My feeling has changed. I am conscious that it has ceased to seem to rise. I feel that I am falling now – falling into the fiery depths below. Nearer – nearer yet; scorched and blackened by the awful heat as I approach – I fall – down – down – down –

A Tale of Negative Gravity

Frank R. Stockton

My wife and I were staying at a small town in northern Italy; and on a certain pleasant afternoon in spring we had taken a walk of six or seven miles to see the sun set behind some low mountains to the west of the town. Most of our walk had been along a hard, smooth highway, and then we turned into a series of narrower roads, sometimes bordered by walls, and sometimes by light fences of reed or cane. Nearing the mountain, to a low spur of which we intended to ascend, we easily scaled a wall about four feet high, and found ourselves upon pasture-land, which led, some-times by gradual ascents, and sometimes by bits of rough climbing, to the spot we wished to reach. We were afraid we were a little late, and therefore hurried on, running up the grassy hills, and bounding briskly over the rough and rocky places. I carried a knapsack strapped firmly to my shoulders, and under my wife's arm was a large, soft basket of a kind much used by tourists. Her arm was passed through the handles and around the bottom of the basket, which she pressed closely to her side. This was the way she always carried it. The basket contained two bottles of wine, one sweet for my wife, and another a little acid for myself. Sweet wines give me a headache.

When we reached the grassy bluff, well known thereabouts to lovers of sunset views, I stepped immediately to the edge to gaze upon the scene, but my wife sat down to take a sip of wine, for she was very thirsty; and then, leaving her basket, she came to my side. The scene was indeed one of great beauty. Beneath us stretched a wide valley of many shades of green, with a little river running through it, and red-tiled houses here and there. Beyond rose a range of mountains, pink, pale green, and purple where their tips caught the reflection of the setting sun, and of a rich gray-green in shadows. Beyond all was the blue Italian sky, illumined by an especially fine sunset.

My wife and I are Americans, and at the time of this story were middle-aged people and very fond of seeing in each other's company whatever there was of interest or beauty around us. We had a son about twenty-two years old, of whom we were also very fond; but he was not with us, being at that time a student in Germany. Although we had good health, we were not very robust people, and, under ordinary circumstances, not much given to long country tramps. I was of medium size, without much muscular development, while my wife was quite stout, and growing stouter.

The reader may, perhaps, be somewhat surprised that a middle-aged couple, not very strong, or very good walkers, the lady loaded with a basket containing two bottles of wine and a metal drinking-cup, and the gentleman carrying a heavy knapsack, filled with all sorts of odds and ends, strapped to his shoulders, should set off on a seven-mile walk, jump over a wall, run up a hillside, and yet feel in very good trim to enjoy a sunset view. This peculiar state of things I will proceed to explain.

I had been a professional man, but some years before had retired upon a very comfortable income. I had always been very fond of scientific pursuits, and now made these the occupation and pleasure of much of my leisure time. Our home was in a small town; and in a corner of my grounds I built a laboratory, where I carried on my work and my experiments. I had long been anxious to discover the means not only of producing, but of retaining and controlling, a natural force, really the same as centrifugal force, but which I called negative gravity. This name I adopted because it indicated better than any other the action of the force in question, as I produced it. Positive gravity attracts everything toward the centre of the earth. Negative gravity, therefore, would be that power which repels everything from the centre of the earth, just as the negative pole of a magnet repels the needle, while the positive pole attracts it. My object was, in fact, to store centrifugal force and to render it constant, controllable, and available for use. The advantages of such a discovery could scarcely be described. In a word, it would lighten the burdens of the world.

I will not touch upon the labors and disappointments of several years. It is enough to say that at last I discovered a method of producing, storing, and controlling negative gravity.

The mechanism of my invention was rather complicated, but the method of operating it was very simple. A strong metallic case, about eight inches long, and half as wide, contained the machinery for producing the force; and this was put into action by means of the pressure of a screw worked from the outside. As soon as this pressure was produced, negative gravity began to be evolved and stored, and the greater the pressure the greater the force. As the screw was moved outward, and the pressure diminished, the force decreased, and when the screw was withdrawn to its fullest extent, the action of negative gravity entirely ceased. Thus this force could be produced or dissipated at will to such degrees as might be desired, and its action, so long as the requisite pressure was maintained, was constant.

When this little apparatus worked to my satisfaction I called my wife into my laboratory and explained to her my invention and its value. She had known that I had been at work with an important object, but I had never told her what it was. I had said that if I succeeded I would tell her all, but if I failed she need not be troubled with the matter at all. Being a very sensible woman, this satisfied her perfectly. Now I explained every-thing to her – the construction of the machine, and the wonderful uses to which this invention could be applied. I told her that it could diminish, or entirely dissipate, the weight of objects of any kind. A heavily loaded wagon, with two of these instruments fastened to its sides, and each screwed to a proper force, would be so lifted and supported that it would press upon the ground as lightly as an empty cart, and a small horse could draw it with ease. A bale of cotton, with one of these machines attached, could be handled and carried by a boy. A car, with a number of these machines, could be made to rise in the air like a balloon. Everything, in fact, that was heavy could be made light; and as a great part of labor, all over the world, is caused by the attraction of gravitation, so this repellent force, wherever applied, would make weight less and work easier. I told her of many, many ways in which the invention might be used, and would have told her of many more if she had not suddenly burst into tears.

'The world has gained something wonderful,' she exclaimed, between her sobs, 'but I have lost a husband!'

'What do you mean by that?' I asked, in surprise.

'I haven't minded it so far,' she said, 'because it gave you something to do, and it pleased you, and it never interfered with our home pleasures and our home life. But now that is all over. You will never be your own master again. It will succeed, I am sure, and you may make a great deal of money, but we don't need money. What we need is the happiness which we have always had until now. Now there will be companies, and patents, and lawsuits, and experiments, and people calling you a humbug, and other people saying they discovered it long ago, and all sorts of persons coming to see you, and you'll be obliged to go to all sorts of places, and you will be an altered man, and we shall never be happy again. Millions of money will not repay us for the happiness we have lost.'

These words of my wife struck me with much force. Before I had called her my mind had begun to be filled and perplexed with ideas of what I ought to do now that the great invention was perfected. Until now the matter had not troubled me at all. Sometimes I had gone backward and sometimes forward, but, on the whole, I had always felt encouraged.

I had taken great pleasure in the work, but I had never allowed myself to be too much absorbed by it. But now everything was different. I began to feel that it was due to myself and to my fellow-beings that I should properly put this invention before the world. And how should I set about it? What steps should I take? I must make no mistakes. When the matter should become known hundreds of scientific people might set themselves to work; how could I tell but that they might discover other methods of producing the same effect? I must guard myself against a great many things. I must get patents in all parts of the world. Already, as I have said, my mind began to be troubled and perplexed with these things. A turmoil of this sort did not suit my age or disposition. I could not but agree with my wife that the joys of a quiet and contented life were now about to be broken into.

'My dear,' said I, 'I believe, with you, that the thing will do us more harm than good. If it were not for depriving the world of the invention I would throw the whole thing to the winds. And yet,' I added, regretfully, 'I had expected a great deal of personal gratification from the use of this invention.'

'Now listen,' said my wife, eagerly; 'don't you think it would be best to do this: use the thing as much as you please for your own amusement and satisfaction, but let the world wait? It has waited a long time, and let it wait a little longer. When we are dead let Herbert have the invention. He will then be old enough to judge for himself whether it will be better to take advantage of it for his own profit, or simply to give it to the public for nothing. It would be cheating him if we were to do the latter, but it would also be doing him a great wrong if we were, at his age, to load him with such a heavy responsibility. Besides, if he took it up, you could not help going into it, too.'

I took my wife's advice. I wrote a careful and complete account of the invention, and, sealing it up, I gave it to my lawyers to be handed to my son after my death. If he died first, I would make other arrangements. Then I determined to get all the good and fun out of the thing that was possible without telling anyone anything about it. Even Herbert, who was away from home, was not to be told of the invention.

The first thing I did was to buy a strong leathern knapsack, and inside of this I fastened my little machine, with a screw so arranged that it could be worked from the outside. Strapping this firmly to my shoulders, my wife gently turned the screw at the back until the upward tendency of the knapsack began to lift and sustain me. When I felt myself so gently supported and upheld that I seemed to weigh about thirty or forty pounds, I would set out for a walk. The knapsack did not raise me from the ground, but it gave me a very buoyant step. It was no labor at all to walk; it was a delight, an ecstasy. With the strength of a man and the weight of a child, I gayly strode along. The first day I walked half a dozen miles at a very brisk pace, and came back without feeling in the least degree tired. These walks now became one of the greatest joys of my life. When nobody was looking, I would bound over a fence, sometimes just touching it with one hand, and sometimes not touching it at all. I delighted in rough places. I sprang over streams. I jumped and I ran. I felt like Mercury himself.

I now set about making another machine, so that my wife could accompany me in my walks; but when it was finished she positively refused to use it. 'I can't wear a knapsack,' she said, 'and there is no other good way of fastening it to me. Besides, everybody about here knows I am no walker, and it would only set them talking.'

I occasionally made use of this second machine, but I will give only one instance of its application. Some repairs were needed to the foundation-walls of my barn, and a two-horse wagon, loaded with building-stone, had been brought into my yard and left there. In the evening, when the men had gone away, I took my two machines and fastened them, with strong chains, one on each side of the loaded wagon. Then, gradually turning the screws, the wagon was so lifted that its weight became very greatly diminished. We had an old donkey which used to belong to Herbert, and which was now occasionally used with a small cart to bring packages from the station. I went into the barn and put the harness on the little fellow, and, bringing him out to the wagon, I attached him to it. In this position he looked very funny with a long pole sticking out in front of him and the great wagon behind him. When all was ready I touched him up; and, to my great delight, he moved off with the two-horse load of stone as easily as if he were drawing his own cart. I led him out into the public road, along which he proceeded without difficulty. He was an opinionated little beast, and sometimes stopped, not liking the peculiar manner in which he was harnessed; but a touch of the switch made him move on, and I soon turned him and brought the wagon back into the yard. This determined the success of my invention in one of its most important uses, and with a satisfied heart I put the donkey into the stable and went into the house.

Our trip to Europe was made a few months after this, and was mainly on our son Herbert's account. He, poor fellow, was in great trouble, and so, therefore, were we. He had become engaged, with our full consent, to a young lady in our town, the daughter of a gentleman whom we esteemed very highly. Herbert was young to be engaged to be married, but as we felt that he would never find a girl to make him so good a wife, we were entirely satisfied, especially as it was agreed on all hands that the marriage was not to take place for some time. It seemed to us that, in marrying Janet Gilbert, Herbert would secure for himself, in the very beginning of his career, the most important element of a happy life. But suddenly, without any reason that seemed to us justifiable, Mr Gilbert, the only surviving parent of Janet, broke off the match; and he and his daughter soon after left the town for a trip to the West.

This blow nearly broke poor Herbert's heart. He gave up his professional studies and came home to us, and for a time we thought he would be seriously ill. Then we took him to Europe, and after a Continental tour of a month or two we left him, at his own request, in Göttingen, where he thought it would do him good to go to work again. Then we went down to the little town in Italy where my story first finds us. My wife had suffered much in mind and body on her son's account, and for this reason I was anxious that she should take outdoor exercise, and enjoy as much as possible the bracing air of the country. I had brought with me both my little machines. One was still in my knapsack, and the other I had fastened to the inside of an enormous family trunk. As one is obliged to pay for nearly every pound of his baggage on the Continent, this saved me a great deal of money. Everything heavy was packed into this great trunk – books, papers, the bronze, iron, and marble relics we had picked up, and all the articles that usually weigh down a tourist's baggage. I screwed up the negative-gravity apparatus until the trunk could be handled with great ease by an ordinary porter. I could have made it weigh nothing at all, but this, of course, I did not wish to do. The lightness of my baggage, however, had occasioned some comment, and I had overheard remarks which were not altogether complimentary about people travelling around with empty trunks; but this only amused me.

Desirous that my wife should have the advantage of negative gravity while taking our walks, I had removed the machine from the trunk and fastened it inside of the basket, which she could carry under her arm. This assisted her wonderfully. When one arm was tired she put the basket under the other, and thus, with one hand on my arm, she could easily keep up with the free and buoyant steps my knapsack enabled me to take. She did not object to long tramps here, because nobody knew that she was not a walker, and she always carried some wine or other refreshment in the basket, not only because it was pleasant to have it with us, but because it seemed ridiculous to go about carrying an empty basket.

There were English-speaking people stopping at the hotel where we were, but they seemed more fond of driving than walking, and none of them offered to accompany us on our rambles, for which we were very glad. There was one man there, however, who was a great walker. He was an Englishman, a member of an Alpine Club, and generally went about dressed in a knickerbocker suit, with gray woollen stockings covering an enormous pair of calves. One evening this gentleman was talking to me and some others about the ascent of the Matterhorn, and I took occasion to deliver in pretty strong language my opinion upon such exploits. I declared them to be useless, foolhardy, and, if the climber had anyone who loved him, wicked.

'Even if the weather should permit a view,' I said, 'what is that compared to the terrible risk to life? Under certain circumstances,' I added (thinking of a kind of waistcoat I had some idea of making, which, set about with little negative-gravity machines, all connected with a conveniently handled screw, would enable the wearer at times to dispense with his weight altogether), 'such ascents might be divested of danger, and be quite admissible; but ordinarily they should be frowned upon by the intelligent public.'

The Alpine Club man looked at me, especially regarding my somewhat slight figure and thinnish legs.

'It's all very well for you to talk that way,' he said, 'because it is easy to see that you are not up to that sort of thing.'

'In conversations of this kind,' I replied, 'I never make personal allusions; but since you have chosen to do so, I feel inclined to invite you to walk with me tomorrow to the top of the mountain to the north of this town.'

'I'll do it,' he said, 'at any time you choose to name.' And as I left the room soon afterward I heard him laugh.

The next afternoon, about two o'clock, the Alpine Club man and myself set out for the mountain.

'What have you got in your knapsack?' he said.

'A hammer to use if I come across geological specimens, a field-glass, a flask of wine, and some other things.'

'I wouldn't carry any weight, if I were you,' he said.

'Oh, I don't mind it,' I answered, and off we started.

The mountain to which we were bound was about two miles from the town. Its nearest side was steep, and in places almost precipitous, but it sloped away more gradually toward the north, and up that side a road led by devious windings to a village near the summit. It was not a very high mountain, but it would do for an afternoon's climb.

'I suppose you want to go up by the road,' said my companion.

'Oh no,' I answered, 'we won't go so far around as that. There is a path up this side, along which I have seen men driving their goats. I prefer to take that.'

'All right, if you say so,' he answered, with a smile; 'but you'll find it pretty tough.'

After a time he remarked: 'I wouldn't walk so fast, if I were you.'

'Oh, I like to step along briskly,' I said. And briskly on we went.

My wife had screwed up the machine in the knapsack more than usual, and walking seemed scarcely any effort at all. I carried a long alpenstock, and when we reached the mountain and began the ascent, I found that with the help of this and my knapsack I could go uphill at a wonderful rate. My companion had taken the lead, so as to show me how to climb. Making a *détour* over some rocks, I quickly passed him and went ahead. After that it was impossible for him to keep up with me. I ran up steep places, I cut off the windings of the path by lightly clambering over rocks, and even when I followed the beaten track my step was as rapid as if I had been walking on level ground.

'Look here!' shouted the Alpine Club man from below, 'you'll kill yourself if you go at that rate! That's no way to climb mountains.'

'It's my way!' I cried. And on I skipped.

Twenty minutes after I arrived at the summit my companion joined me, puffing, and wiping his red face with his handkerchief.

'Confound it!' he cried, 'I never came up a mountain so fast in my life.'

'You need not have hurried,' I said, coolly.

'I was afraid something would happen to you,' he growled, 'and I wanted to stop you. I never saw a person climb in such an utterly absurd way.'

'I don't see why you should call it absurd,' I said, smiling with an air of superiority. 'I arrived here in a perfectly comfortable condition, neither heated nor wearied.'

He made no answer, but walked off to a little distance, fanning himself with his hat and growling words which I did not catch. After a time I proposed to descend.

'You must be careful as you go down,' he said. 'It is much more dangerous to go down steep places than to climb up.'

'I am always prudent,' I answered, and started in advance. I found the descent of the mountain much more pleasant than the ascent. It was positively exhilarating. I jumped from rocks and bluffs eight and ten feet in height, and touched the ground as gently as if I had stepped down but two feet. I ran down steep paths, and, with the aid of my alpenstock, stopped myself in an instant. I was careful to avoid dangerous places, but the runs and jumps I made were such as no man had ever made before upon that mountain-side. Once only I heard my companion's voice.

'You'll break your — neck!' he yelled.

'Never fear!' I called back, and soon left him far above.

When I reached the bottom I would have waited for him, but my activity had warmed me up, and as a cool evening breeze was beginning to blow I thought it better not to stop and take cold. Half an hour after my arrival at the hotel I came down to the court, cool, fresh, and dressed for dinner, and just in time to meet the Alpine man as he entered, hot, dusty, and growling.

'Excuse me for not waiting for you,' I said; but without stopping to hear my reason, he muttered something about waiting in a place where no one would care to stay, and passed into the house.

There was no doubt that what I had done gratified my pique and tickled my vanity.

'I think now,' I said, when I related the matter to my wife, 'that he will scarcely say that I am not up to that sort of thing.'

'I am not sure,' she answered, 'that it was exactly fair. He did not know how you were assisted.'

'It was fair enough,' I said. 'He is enabled to climb well by the in-herited vigor of his constitution and by his training. He did not tell me what methods of exercise he used to get those great muscles upon his legs. I am enabled to climb by the exercise of my intellect. My method is my business and his method is his business. It is all perfectly fair.'

Still she persisted.

'He *thought* that you climbed with your legs, and not with your head.'

And now, after this long digression, necessary to explain how a middle-aged couple of slight pedestrian ability, and loaded with a heavy knapsack and basket, should have started out on a rough walk and climb, fourteen miles in all, we will return to ourselves, standing on the little bluff and gazing out upon the sunset view. When the sky began to fade a little we turned from it and prepared to go back to the town.

'Where is the basket?' I said.

'I left it right here,' answered my wife. 'I unscrewed the machine and it lay perfectly flat.'

'Did you afterward take out the bottles?' I asked, seeing them lying on the grass.

'Yes, I believe I did. I had to take out yours in order to get at mine.'

'Then,' said I, after looking all about the grassy patch on which we stood, 'I am afraid you did not entirely unscrew the instrument, and that when the weight of the bottles was removed the basket gently rose into the air.'

'It may be so,' she said, lugubriously. 'The basket was behind me as I drank my wine.'

'I believe that is just what has happened,' I said. 'Look up there! I vow that is our basket!'

I pulled out my field-glass and directed it at a little speck high above our heads. It was the basket floating high in the air. I gave the glass to my wife to look, but she did not want to use it.

'What shall I do?' she cried. 'I can't walk home without that basket. It's perfectly dreadful!' And she looked as if she was going to cry.

'Do not distress yourself,' I said, although I was a good deal disturbed myself. 'We shall get home very well. You shall put your hand on my shoulder, while I put my arm around you. Then you can screw up my machine a good deal higher, and it will support us both. In this way I am sure that we shall get on very well.'

We carried out this plan, and managed to walk on with moderate comfort. To be sure, with the knapsack pulling me upward, and the weight of my wife pulling me down, the straps hurt me somewhat, which they had not done before. We did not spring lightly over the wall into the road, but, still clinging to each other, we clambered awkwardly over it. The road for the most part declined gently toward the town, and with moderate ease we made our way along it. But we walked much more slowly than we had done before, and it was quite dark when we reached our hotel. If it had not been for the light inside the court it would have been difficult for us to find it. A travelling-carriage was standing before the entrance, and against the light. It was necessary to pass around it, and my wife went first. I attempted to follow her, but, strange to say, there was nothing under my feet. I stepped vigorously, but only wagged my legs in the air. To my horror I found that I was rising in the air! I soon saw, by the light below me, that I was some fifteen feet from the ground. The carriage drove away, and in the darkness I was not noticed. Of course I knew what had happened. The instrument in my knapsack had been screwed up to such an intensity, in order to support both myself and my wife, that when her weight was removed the force of the negative gravity was sufficient to raise me from the ground. But I was glad to find that when I had risen to the height I have mentioned I did not go up any higher, but hung in the air, about on a level with the second tier of windows of the hotel.

I now began to try to reach the screw in my knapsack in order to reduce the force of the negative gravity; but, do what I would, I could not get my hand to it. The machine in the knapsack had been placed so as to support me in a well-balanced and comfortable way; and in doing this it had been impossible to set the screw so that I could reach it. But in a temporary arrangement of the kind this had not been considered necessary, as my wife always turned the screw for me until sufficient lifting power had been attained. I had intended, as I have said before, to construct a negative-gravity waistcoat, in which the screw should be in front, and entirely under the wearer's control; but this was a thing of the future.

When I found that I could not turn the screw I began to be much alarmed. Here I was, dangling in the air, without any means of reaching the ground. I could not expect my wife to return to look for me, as she would naturally suppose I had stopped to speak to someone. I thought of loosening myself from the knapsack, but this would not do, for I should fall heavily, and either kill myself or break some of my bones. I did not dare to call for assistance, for if any of the simple-minded inhabitants of the town had discovered me floating in the air they would have taken me for a demon, and would probably have shot at me. A moderate breeze was blowing, and it wafted me gently down the street. If it had blown me against a tree I would have seized it, and have endeavored, so to speak, to climb down it; but there were no trees. There was a dim street-lamp here and there, but reflectors above them threw their light upon the pavement, and none up to me. On many accounts I was glad that the night was so dark, for, much as I desired to get down, I wanted no one to see me in my strange position, which, to anyone but myself and wife, would be utterly unaccountable. If I could rise as high as the roofs I might get on one of them, and, tearing off an armful of tiles, so load myself that I would be heavy enough to descend. But I did not rise to the eaves of any of the houses. If there had been a telegraph-pole, or anything of the kind that I could have clung to, I would have taken off the knapsack, and would have endeavored to scramble down as well as I could. But there was nothing I could cling to. Even the water-spouts, if I could have reached the face of the houses, were embedded in the walls. At an open window, near which I was slowly blown, I saw two little boys going to bed by the light of a dim candle. I was dreadfully afraid that they would see me and raise an alarm. I actually came so near to the window that I threw out one foot and pushed against the wall with such force that I went nearly across the street. I thought I caught sight of a frightened look on the face of one of the boys; but of this I am not sure, and I heard no cries. I still floated, dangling, down the street. What was to be done? Should I call out? In that case, if I were not shot or stoned, my strange predicament, and the secret of my invention, would be exposed to the world. If I did not do this, I must either let myself drop and be killed or mangled, or hang there and die. When, during the course of the night, the air became more rarefied, I might rise higher and higher, perhaps to an altitude of one or two hundred feet. It would then be impossible for the people to reach me and get me down, even if they were convinced that I was not a demon. I should then expire, and when the birds of the air had eaten all of me that they could devour, I should forever hang above the unlucky town, a dangling skeleton with a knapsack on its back.

Such thoughts were not reassuring, and I determined that if I could find no means of getting down without assistance, I would call out and run all risks; but so long as I could endure the tension of the straps I would hold out, and hope for a tree or a pole. Perhaps it might rain, and my wet clothes would then become so heavy that I would descend as low as the top of a lamp-post.

As this thought was passing through my mind I saw a spark of light upon the street approaching me. I rightly imagined that it came from a tobacco-pipe, and presently I heard a voice. It was that of the Alpine Club man. Of all people in the world I did not want him to discover me, and I hung as motionless as possible. The man was speaking to another person who was walking with him.

'He is crazy beyond a doubt,' said the Alpine man. 'Nobody but a maniac could have gone up and down that mountain as he did! He hasn't any muscles, and one need only look at him to know that he couldn't do any climbing in a natural way. It is only the excitement of insanity that gives him strength.'

The two now stopped almost under me, and the speaker continued: 'Such things are very common with maniacs. At times they acquire an unnatural strength which is perfectly wonderful. I have seen a little fellow struggle and fight so that four strong men could not hold him.'

Then the other person spoke.

'I am afraid what you say is too true,' he remarked. 'Indeed, I have known it for some time.'

At these words my breath almost stopped. It was the voice of Mr Gilbert, my townsman, and the father of Janet. It must have been he who had arrived in the travelling-carriage. He was acquainted with the Alpine Club man, and they were talking of me. Proper or improper, I listened with all my ears.

'It is a very sad case,' Mr Gilbert continued. 'My daughter was engaged to marry his son, but I broke off the match. I could not have her marry the son of a lunatic, and there could be no doubt of his condition. He has been seen – a man of his age, and the head of a family – to load himself up with a heavy knapsack, which there was no earthly necessity for him to carry, and go skipping along the road for miles, vaulting over fences and jumping over rocks and ditches like a young calf or a colt. I myself saw a most heartrending instance of how a kindly man's nature can be changed by the derangement of his intellect. I was at some distance from his house, but I plainly saw him harness a little donkey which he owns to a large two-horse wagon loaded with stone, and beat and lash the poor little beast until it drew the heavy load some distance along the public road. I would have remonstrated with him on this horrible cruelty, but he had the wagon back in his yard before I could reach him.'

'Oh, there can be no doubt of his insanity,' said the Alpine Club man, 'and he oughtn't to be allowed to travel about in this way. Some day he will pitch his wife over a precipice just for the fun of seeing her shoot through the air.'

'I am sorry he is here,' said Mr Gilbert, 'for it would be very painful to meet him. My daughter and I will retire very soon, and go away as early tomorrow morning as possible, so as to avoid seeing him.'

And then they walked back to the hotel.

For a few moments I hung, utterly forgetful of my condition, and absorbed in the consideration of these revelations. One idea now filled my mind. Everything must be explained to Mr Gilbert, even if it should be necessary to have him called to me, and for me to speak to him from the upper air.

Just then I saw something white approaching me along the road. My eyes had become accustomed to the darkness, and I perceived that it was an upturned face. I recognized the hurried gait, the form; it was my wife. As she came near me, I called her name, and in the same breath entreated her not to scream. It must have been an effort for her to restrain herself, but she did it.

'You must help me to get down,' I said, 'without anybody seeing us.'

'What shall I do?' she whispered.

'Try to catch hold of this string.'

Taking a piece of twine from my pocket, I lowered one end to her. But it was too short; she could not reach it. I then tied my handkerchief to it, but still it was not long enough.

'I can get more string, or handkerchiefs,' she whispered, hurriedly.

'No,' I said; 'you could not get them up to me. But, leaning against the hotel wall, on this side, in the corner, just inside of the garden gate, are some fishing-poles. I have seen them there every day. You can easily find them in the dark. Go, please, and bring me one of those.'

The hotel was not far away, and in a few minutes my wife returned with a fishing-pole. She stood on tiptoe, and reached it high in air; but all she could do was to strike my feet and legs with it. My most frantic exertions did not enable me to get my hands low enough to touch it.

'Wait a minute,' she said; and the rod was withdrawn.

I knew what she was doing. There was a hook and line attached to the pole, and with womanly dexterity she was fastening the hook to the extreme end of the rod. Soon she reached up, and gently struck at my legs. After a few attempts the hook caught in my trousers, a little below my right knee. Then there was a slight pull, a long scratch down my leg, and the hook was stopped by the top of my boot. Then came a steady downward pull, and I felt myself descending. Gently and firmly the rod was drawn down; carefully the lower end was kept free from the ground; and in a few moments my ankle was seized with a vigorous grasp. Then someone seemed to climb up me, my feet touched the ground, an arm was thrown around my neck, the hand of another arm was busy at the back of my knapsack, and I soon stood firmly in the road, entirely divested of negative gravity.

'Oh that I should have forgotten,' sobbed my wife, 'and that I should have dropped your arms and let you go up into the air! At first I thought that you had stopped below, and it was only a little while ago that the truth flashed upon me. Then I rushed out and began looking up for you. I knew that you had wax matches in your pocket, and hoped that you would keep on striking them, so that you would be seen.'

'But I did not wish to be seen,' I said, as we hurried to the hotel; 'and I can never be sufficiently thankful that it was you who found me and brought me down. Do you know that it is Mr Gilbert and his daughter who have just arrived? I must see him instantly. I will explain it all to you when I come upstairs.'

I took off my knapsack and gave it to my wife, who carried it to our room, while I went to look for Mr Gilbert. Fortunately I found him just as he was about to go up to his chamber. He took my offered hand, but looked at me sadly and gravely.

'Mr Gilbert,' I said, 'I must speak to you in private. Let us step into this room. There is no one here.'

'My friend,' said Mr Gilbert, 'it will be much better to avoid discussing this subject. It is very painful to both of us, and no good can come from talking of it.'

'You cannot now comprehend what it is I want to say to you,' I replied. 'Come in here, and in a few minutes you will be very glad that you listened to me.'

My manner was so earnest and impressive that Mr Gilbert was constrained to follow me, and we went into a small room called the smoking-room, but in which people seldom smoked, and closed the door. I immediately began my statement. I told my old friend that I had discovered, by means that I need not explain at present, that he had considered me crazy, and that now the most important object of my life was to set myself right in his eyes. I thereupon gave him the whole history of my invention, and explained the reason of the actions that had appeared to him those of a lunatic. I said nothing about the little incident of that evening. That was a mere accident, and I did not care now to speak of it.

Mr Gilbert listened to me very attentively.

'Your wife is here?' he asked, when I had finished.

'Yes,' I said; 'and she will corroborate my story in every item, and no one could ever suspect her of being crazy. I will go and bring her to you.'

In a few minutes my wife was in the room, had shaken hands with Mr Gilbert, and had been told of my suspected madness. She turned pale, but smiled.

'He did act like a crazy man,' she said, 'but I never supposed that anybody would think him one.' And tears came into her eyes.

'And now, my dear,' said I, 'perhaps you will tell Mr Gilbert how I did all this.'

And then she told him the story that I had told.

Mr Gilbert looked from the one to the other of us with a troubled air.

'Of course I do not doubt either of you, or rather I do not doubt that you believe what you say. All would be right if I could bring myself to credit that such a force as that you speak of can possibly exist.'

'That is a matter,' said I, 'which I can easily prove to you by actual demonstration. If you can wait a short time, until my wife and I have had something to eat – for I am nearly famished, and I am sure she must be – I will set your mind at rest upon that point.'

'I will wait here,' said Mr Gilbert, 'and smoke a cigar. Don't hurry yourselves. I shall be glad to have some time to think about what you have told me.'

When we had finished the dinner, which had been set aside for us, I went upstairs and got my knapsack, and we both joined Mr Gilbert in the smoking-room. I showed him the little machine, and explained, very briefly, the principle of its construction. I did not give any practical demonstration of its action, because there were people walking about the corridor who might at any moment come into the room; but, looking out of the window, I saw that the night was much clearer. The wind had dissipated the clouds, and the stars were shining brightly.

'If you will come up the street with me,' said I to Mr Gilbert, 'I will show you how this thing works.'

'That is just what I want to see,' he answered.

'I will go with you,' said my wife, throwing a shawl over her head. And we started up the street.

When we were outside the little town I found the starlight was quite sufficient for my purpose. The white roadway, the low walls, and objects about us, could easily be distinguished.

'Now,' said I to Mr Gilbert, 'I want to put this knapsack on you, and let you see how it feels, and how it will help you to walk.' To this he assented with some eagerness, and I strapped it firmly on him. 'I will now turn this screw,' said I, 'until you shall become lighter and lighter.'

'Be very careful not to turn it too much,' said my wife, earnestly.

'Oh, you may depend on me for that,' said I, turning the screw very gradually.

Mr Gilbert was a stout man, and I was obliged to give the screw a good many turns.

'There seems to be considerable hoist in it,' he said, directly. And then I put my arms around him, and found that I could raise him from the ground.

'Are you lifting me?' he exclaimed, in surprise.

'Yes; I did it with ease,' I answered.

'Upon – my – word!' ejaculated Mr Gilbert.

I then gave the screw a half-turn more, and told him to walk and run. He started off, at first slowly, then he made long strides, then he began to run, and then to skip and jump. It had been many years since Mr Gilbert had skipped and jumped. No one was in sight, and he was free to gambol as much as he pleased. 'Could you give it another turn?' said he, bounding up to me. 'I want to try that wall.' I put on a little more negative gravity, and he vaulted over a five-foot wall with great ease. In an instant he had leaped back into the road, and in two bounds was at my side. 'I came down as light as a cat,' he said. 'There was never anything like it.' And away he went up the road, taking steps at least eight feet long, leaving my wife and me laughing heartily at the preternatural agility of our stout friend. In a few minutes he was with us again. 'Take it off,' he said. 'If I wear it any longer I shall want one myself, and then I shall be taken for a crazy man, and perhaps clapped into an asylum.'

'Now,' said I, as I turned back the screw before unstrapping the knapsack, 'do you understand how I took long walks, and leaped and jumped; how I ran uphill and downhill, and how the little donkey drew the loaded wagon?'

'I understand it all,' cried he. 'I take back all I ever said or thought about you, my friend.'

'And Herbert may marry Janet?' cried my wife.

'*May* marry her!' cried Mr Gilbert. 'Indeed, he *shall* marry her, if I have anything to say about it! My poor girl has been drooping ever since I told her it could not be.'

My wife rushed at him, but whether she embraced him or only shook his hands I cannot say; for I had the knapsack in one hand and was rubbing my eyes with the other.

'But, my dear fellow,' said Mr Gilbert, directly, 'if you still consider it to your interest to keep your invention a secret, I wish you had never made it. No one having a machine like that can help using it, and it is often quite as bad to be considered a maniac as to be one.'

'My friend,' I cried, with some excitement, 'I have made up my mind on this subject. The little machine in this knapsack, which is the only one I now possess, has been a great pleasure to me. But I now know it has also been of the greatest injury indirectly to me and mine, not to mention some direct inconvenience and danger, which I will speak of another time. The secret lies with us three, and we will keep it. But the invention itself is too full of temptation and danger for any of us.'

As I said this I held the knapsack with one hand while I quickly turned the screw with the other. In a few moments it was high above my head, while I with difficulty held it down by the straps. 'Look!' I cried. And then I released my hold, and the knapsack shot into the air and disappeared into the upper gloom.

I was about to make a remark, but had no chance, for my wife threw herself upon my bosom, sobbing with joy.

'Oh, I am so glad – so glad!' she said. 'And you will never make another?'

'Never another!' I answered.

'And now let us hurry in and see Janet,' said my wife.

'You don't know how heavy and clumsy I feel,' said Mr Gilbert, striving to keep up with us as we walked back. 'If I had worn that thing much longer, I should never have been willing to take it off!'

Janet had retired, but my wife went up to her room.

'I think she has felt it as much as our boy,' she said, when she rejoined me. 'But I tell you, my dear, I left a very happy girl in that little bedchamber over the garden.'

And there were three very happy elderly people talking together until quite late that evening. 'I shall write to Herbert tonight,' I said, when we separated, 'and tell him to meet us all in Geneva. It will do the young man no harm if we interrupt his studies just now.'

'You must let me add a postscript to the letter,' said Mr Gilbert, 'and I am sure it will require no knapsack with a screw in the back to bring him quickly to us.'

And it did not.

There is a wonderful pleasure in tripping over the earth like a winged Mercury, and in feeling one's self relieved of much of that attraction of gravitation which drags us down to earth and gradually makes the movement of our bodies but weariness and labor. But this pleasure is not to be compared, I think, to that given by the buoyancy and lightness of two young and loving hearts, reunited after a separation which they had supposed would last forever.

What became of the basket and the knapsack, or whether they ever met in upper air, I do not know. If they but float away and stay away from ken of mortal man, I shall be satisfied.

And whether or not the world will ever know more of the power of negative gravity depends entirely upon the disposition of my son Herbert, when – after a good many years, I hope – he shall open the packet my lawyers have in keeping.

[Note. – It would be quite useless for anyone to interview my wife on this subject, for she has entirely forgotten how my machine was made. And as for Mr Gilbert, he never knew.]

To Whom This May Come

Edward Bellamy

It is now about a year since I took passage at Calcutta in the ship *Adelaide* for New York. We had baffling weather till New Amsterdam Island was sighted, where we took a new point of departure. Three days later, a terrible gale struck us. Four days we flew before it, whither, no one knew, for neither sun, moon, nor stars were at any time visible, and we could take no observation. Toward midnight of the fourth day, the glare of lightning revealed the *Adelaide* in a hopeless position, close in upon a low-lying shore, and driving straight toward it. All around and astern far out to sea was such a maze of rocks and shoals that it was a miracle we had come so far. Presently the ship struck, and almost instantly went to pieces, so great was the violence of the sea. I gave myself up for lost, and was indeed already past the worst of drowning, when I was recalled to consciousness by being thrown with a tremendous shock upon the beach. I had just strength enough to drag myself above the reach of the waves, and then I fell down and knew no more.

When I awoke, the storm was over. The sun, already halfway up the sky, had dried my clothing, and renewed the vigor of my bruised and aching limbs. On sea or shore I saw no vestige of my ship or my companions, of whom I appeared the sole survivor. I was not, however, alone. A group of persons, apparently the inhabitants of the country, stood near, observing me with looks of friendliness which at once freed me from apprehension as to my treatment at their hands. They were a white and handsome people, evidently of a high order of civilization, though I recognized in them the traits of no race with which I was familiar.

Seeing that it was evidently their idea of etiquette to leave it to strangers to open conversation, I addressed them in English, but failed to elicit any response beyond deprecating smiles. I then accosted them successively in the French, German, Italian, Spanish, Dutch, and Portuguese tongues, but with no better results. I began to be very much puzzled as to what could possibly be the nationality of a white and evidently civilized race to which no one of the tongues of the great seafaring nations was intelligible. The oddest thing of all was the unbroken silence with which they contemplated my efforts to open communication with them. It was as if they were agreed not to give me a clue to their language by even a whisper; for while they regarded one another with looks of smiling intelligence, they did not once open their lips. But if this behavior suggested that they were amusing themselves at my expense, that presumption was negatived by the unmistakable friendliness and sympathy which their whole bearing expressed.

A most extraordinary conjecture occurred to me. Could it be that these strange people were dumb? Such a freak of nature as an entire race thus afflicted had never indeed been heard of, but who could say what wonders the unexplored vasts of the great Southern Ocean might thus far have hid from human ken? Now, among the scraps of useless information which lumbered my mind was an acquaintance with the deaf-and-dumb alphabet, and forthwith I began to spell out with my fingers some of the phrases I had already uttered to so little effect. My resort to the sign language overcame the last remnant of gravity in the already profusely smiling group. The small boys now rolled on the ground in convulsions of mirth, while the grave and reverend seniors, who had hitherto kept them in check, were fain momentarily to avert their faces, and I could see their bodies shaking with laughter. The greatest clown in the world never received a more flattering tribute to his powers to amuse than had been called forth by mine to make myself understood. Naturally, however, I was not flattered, but on the contrary entirely discomfited. Angry I could not well be, for the deprecating manner in which all, excepting of course the boys, yielded to their perception of the ridiculous, and the distress they showed at their failure in self-control, made me seem the aggressor. It was as if they were very sorry for me, and ready to put themselves wholly at my service, if I would only refrain from reducing them to a state of disability by being so exquisitely absurd. Certainly this evidently amiable race had a very embarrassing way of receiving strangers.

Just at this moment, when my bewilderment was fast verging on exasperation, relief came. The circle opened, and a little elderly man, who had evidently come in haste, confronted me, and, bowing very politely, addressed me in English. His voice was the most pitiable abortion of a voice I had ever heard. While having all the defects in articulation of a child's who is just beginning to talk, it was not even a child's in strength of tone, being in fact a mere alternation of squeaks and whispers inaudible a rod away. With some difficulty I was, however, able to follow him pretty nearly.

'As the official interpreter,' he said, 'I extend you a cordial welcome to these islands. I was sent for as soon as you were discovered, but being at some distance, I was unable to arrive until this moment. I regret this, as my presence would have saved you embarrassment. My countrymen desire me to intercede with you to pardon the wholly involuntary and uncontrollable mirth provoked by your attempts to communicate with them. You see, they understood you perfectly well, but could not answer you.'

'Merciful heavens!' I exclaimed, horrified to find my surmise correct; 'can it be that they are all thus afflicted? Is it possible that you are the only man among them who has the power of speech?'

Again it appeared that, quite unintentionally, I had said something excruciatingly funny; for at my speech there arose a sound of gentle laughter from the group, now augmented to quite an assemblage, which drowned the plashing of the waves on the beach at our feet. Even the interpreter smiled.

'Do they think it so amusing to be dumb?' I asked.

'They find it very amusing,' replied the interpreter, 'that their inability to speak should be regarded by anyone as an affliction; for it is by the voluntary disuse of the organs of articulation that they have lost the power of speech, and, as a consequence, the ability even to understand speech.'

'But,' said I, somewhat puzzled by this statement, 'didn't you just tell me that they understood me, though they could not reply, and are they not laughing now at what I just said?'

'It is you they understood, not your words,' answered the interpreter. 'Our speech now is gibberish to them, as unintelligible in itself as the growling of animals; but they know what we are saying, because they know our thoughts. You must know that these are the islands of the mind-readers.'

Such were the circumstances of my introduction to this extraordinary people. The official interpreter being charged by virtue of his office with the first entertainment of shipwrecked members of the talking nations, I became his guest, and passed a number of days under his roof before going out to any considerable extent among the people. My first impression had been the somewhat oppressive one that the power to read the thoughts of others could be possessed only by beings of a superior order to man. It was the first effort of the interpreter to disabuse me of this notion. It appeared from his account that the experience of the mind-readers was a case simply of a slight acceleration, from special causes, of the course of universal human evolution, which in time was destined to lead to the disuse of speech and the substitution of direct mental vision on the part of all races. This rapid evolution of these islanders was accounted for by their peculiar origin and circumstances.

Some three centuries before Christ, one of the Parthian kings of Persia, of the dynasty of the Arsacids, undertook a persecution of the soothsayers and magicians in his realms. These people were credited with super-natural powers by popular prejudice, but in fact were merely persons of special gifts in the way of hypnotizing, mind-reading, thought trans-ference, and such arts, which they exercised for their own gain.

Too much in awe of the soothsayers to do them outright violence, the king resolved to banish them, and to this end put them, with their families, on ships and sent them to Ceylon. When, however, the fleet was in the neighborhood of that island, a great storm scattered it, and one of the ships, after being driven for many days before the tempest, was wrecked upon one of an archipelago of uninhabited islands far to the south, where the survivors settled. Naturally, the posterity of the parents possessed of such peculiar gifts had developed extraordinary psychical powers.

Having set before them the end of evolving a new and advanced order of humanity, they had aided the development of these powers by a rigid system of stirpiculture. The result was that, after a few centuries, mind-reading became so general that language fell into disuse as a means of communicating ideas. For many generations the power of speech still remained voluntary, but gradually the vocal organs had become atrophied, and for several hundred years the power of articulation had been wholly lost. Infants for a few months after birth did, indeed, still emit inartic-ulate cries, but at an age when in less advanced races these cries began to be articulate, the children of the mind-readers developed the power of direct vision, and ceased to attempt to use the voice.

The fact that the existence of the mind-readers had never been found out by the rest of the world was explained by two considerations. In the first place, the group of islands was small, and occupied a corner of the Indian Ocean quite out of the ordinary track of ships. In the second place, the approach to the islands was rendered so desperately perilous by terrible currents, and the maze of outlying rocks and shoals, that it was next to impossible for any ship to touch their shores save as a wreck. No ship at least had ever done so in the two thousand years since the mind-readers' own arrival, and the *Adelaide* had made the one hundred and twenty-third such wreck.

Apart from motives of humanity, the mind-readers made strenuous efforts to rescue shipwrecked persons, for from them alone, through the interpreters, could they obtain information of the outside world. Little enough this proved when, as often happened, the sole survivor of the shipwreck was some ignorant sailor, who had no news to communicate beyond the latest varieties of forecastle blasphemy. My hosts gratefully assured me that, as a person of some little education, they considered me a veritable godsend. No less a task was mine than to relate to them the history of the world for the past two centuries, and often did I wish, for their sakes, that I had made a more exact study of it.

It is solely for the purpose of communicating with shipwrecked strangers of the talking nations that the office of the interpreters exists. When, as from time to time happens, a child is born with some powers of articulation, he is set apart, and trained to talk in the interpreters' college. Of course the partial atrophy of the vocal organs, from which even the best interpreters suffer, renders many of the sounds of language impossible for them. None, for instance, can pronounce *v, f*, or *s*; and as to the sound represented by *th*, it is five generations since the last interpreter lived who could utter it. But for the occasional intermarriage of shipwrecked strangers with the islanders, it is probable that the supply of interpreters would have long ere this quite failed.

I imagine that the very unpleasant sensations which followed the realization that I was among people who, while inscrutable to me, knew my every thought, were very much what anyone would have experienced in the same case. They were very comparable to the panic which accidental nudity causes a person among races whose custom it is to conceal the figure with drapery. I wanted to run away and hide myself. If I analyzed my feeling, it did not seem to arise so much from the consciousness of any particularly heinous secrets, as from the knowledge of a swarm of fatuous, ill-natured, and unseemly thoughts and half thoughts concerning those around me, and concerning myself, which it was insufferable that any person should peruse in however benevolent a spirit. But while my chagrin and distress on this account were at first intense, they were also very shortlived, for almost immediately I discovered that the very knowledge that my mind was overlooked by others operated to check thoughts that might be painful to them, and that, too, without more effort of the will than a kindly person exerts to check the utterance of disagreeable remarks. As a very few lessons in the elements of courtesy cures a decent person of inconsiderate speaking, so a brief experience among the mind-readers went far in my case to check inconsiderate thinking. It must not be supposed, however, that courtesy among the mind-readers prevents them from thinking pointedly and freely concerning one another upon serious occasions, any more than the finest courtesy among the talking races restrains them from speaking to one another with entire plainness when it it desirable to do so. Indeed, among the mind-readers, politeness never can extend to the point of insincerity, as among talking nations, seeing that it is always one another's real and inmost thought that they read. I may fitly mention here, though it was not till later that I fully understood why it must necessarily be so, that one need feel far less chagrin at the complete revelation of his weaknesses to a mind-reader than at the slightest betrayal of them to one of another race. For the very reason that the mind-reader reads all your thoughts, particular thoughts are judged with reference to the general tenor of thought. Your characteristic and habitual frame of mind is what he takes account of. No one need fear being misjudged by a mind-reader on account of sentiments or emotions which are not representative of the real character or general attitude. Justice may, indeed, be said to be a necessary consequence of mind-reading.

As regards the interpreter himself, the instinct of courtesy was not long needed to check wanton or offensive thoughts. In all my life before, I had been very slow to form friendships, but before I had been three days in the company of this stranger of a strange race, I had become enthusiastically devoted to him. It was impossible not to be. The peculiar joy of friendship is the sense of being understood by our friend as we are not by others, and yet of being loved in spite of the understanding. Now here was one whose every word testified to a knowledge of my secret thoughts and motives which the oldest and nearest of my former friends had never, and could never, have approximated. Had such a knowledge bred in him contempt of me, I should neither have blamed him nor been at all surprised. Judge, then, whether the cordial friendliness which he showed was likely to leave me indifferent.

Imagine my incredulity when he informed me that our friendship was not based upon more than ordinary mutual suitability of temperaments. The faculty of mind-reading, he explained, brought minds so close together, and so heightened sympathy, that the lowest order of friendship between mind-readers implied a mutual delight such as only rare friends enjoyed among other races. He assured me that later on, when I came to know others of his race, I should find, by the far greater intensity of sympathy and affection I should conceive for some of them, how true this saying was.

It may be inquired how, on beginning to mingle with the mind-readers in general, I managed to communicate with them, seeing that, while they could read my thoughts, they could not, like the interpreter, respond to them by speech. I must here explain that, while these people have no use for a spoken language, a written language is needful for purposes of record. They consequently all know how to write. Do they, then, write Persian? Luckily for me, no. It appears that, for a long period after mind-reading was fully developed, not only was spoken language disused, but also written, no records whatever having been kept during this period. The delight of the people in the newly found power of direct mind-to-mind vision, whereby pictures of the total mental state were communicated, instead of the imperfect descriptions of single thoughts which words at best could give, induced an invincible distaste for the laborious impotence of language.

When, however, the first intellectual intoxication had, after several generations, somewhat sobered down, it was recognized that records of the past were desirable, and that the despised medium of words was needful to preserve it. Persian had meanwhile been wholly forgotten. In order to avoid the prodigious task of inventing a complete new language, the institution of the interpreters was now set up, with the idea of acquiring through them a knowledge of some of the languages of the outside world from the mariners wrecked on the islands.

Owing to the fact that most of the castaway ships were English, a better knowledge of that tongue was acquired than of any other, and it was adopted as the written language of the people. As a rule, my acquaintances wrote slowly and laboriously, and yet the fact that they knew exactly what was in my mind rendered their responses so apt that, in my conversations with the slowest speller of them all, the interchange of thought was as rapid and incomparably more accurate and satisfactory than the fastest talkers attain to.

It was but a very short time after I had begun to extend my acquaintance among the mind-readers before I discovered how truly the interpreter had told me that I should find others to whom, on account of greater natural congeniality, I should become more strongly attached than I had been to him. This was in no wise, however, because I loved him less, but them more. I would fain write particularly of some of these beloved friends, comrades of my heart, from whom I first learned the undreamed-of possibilities of human friendship, and how ravishing the satisfactions of sympathy may be. Who, among those who may read this, has not known that sense of a gulf fixed between soul and soul which mocks love? Who has not felt that loneliness which oppresses the heart that loves it best? Think no longer that this gulf is eternally fixed, or is any necessity of human nature. It has no existence for the race of our fellow-men which I describe, and by that fact we may be assured that eventually it will be bridged also for us. Like the touch of shoulder to shoulder, like the clasping of hands, is the contact of their minds and their sensation of sympathy.

I say that I would fain speak more particularly of some of my friends, but waning strength forbids, and moreover, now that I think of it, another consideration would render any comparison of their characters rather confusing than instructive to a reader. This is the fact that, in common with the rest of the mind-readers, they had no names. Every one had, indeed, an arbitrary sign for his designation in records, but it has no sound value. A register of these names is kept, so they can at any time be ascertained, but it is very common to meet persons who have forgotten titles which are used solely for biographical and official purposes. For social intercourse names are of course superfluous, for these people accost one another merely by a mental act of attention, and refer to third persons by transferring their mental pictures – something as dumb persons might by means of photographs. Something so, I say, for in the pictures of one another's personalities which the mind-readers conceive, the physical aspect, as might be expected with people who directly con-template each other's minds and hearts, is a subordinate element.

I have already told how my first qualms of morbid self-consciousness at knowing that my mind was an open book to all around me disappeared as I learned that the very completeness of the disclosure of my thoughts and motives was a guarantee that I would be judged with a fairness and a sympathy such as even self-judgment cannot pretend to, affected as that is by so many subtle reactions. The assurance of being so judged by everyone might well seem an inestimable privilege to one accustomed to a world in which not even the tenderest love is any pledge of com-prehension, and yet I soon discovered that open-mindedness had a still greater profit than this. How shall I describe the delightful exhilaration of moral health and cleanness, the breezy oxygenated mental condition, which resulted from the consciousness that I had absolutely nothing concealed! Truly I may say that I enjoyed myself. I think surely that no one needs to have had my marvelous experience to sympathize with this portion of it. Are we not all ready to agree that this having a curtained chamber where we may go to grovel, out of the sight of our fellows, troubled only by a vague apprehension that God may look over the top, is the most demoralizing incident in the human condition? It is the exist-ence within the soul of this secure refuge of lies which has always been the despair of the saint and the exultation of the knave. It is the foul cellar which taints the whole house above, be it never so fine.

What stronger testimony could there be to the instinctive conscious-ness that concealment is debauching, and openness our only cure, than the world-old conviction of the virtue of confession for the soul, and that the uttermost exposing of one's worst and foulest is the first step toward moral health? The wickedest man, if he could but somehow attain to writhe himself inside out as to his soul, so that its full sickness could be seen, would feel ready for a new life. Nevertheless, owing to the utter impotence of the words to convey mental conditions in their totality, or to give other than mere distortions of them, confession is, we must needs admit, but a mockery of that longing for self-revelation to which it testifies. But think what health and soundness there must be for souls among a people who see in every face a conscience which, unlike their own, they cannot sophisticate, who confess one another with a glance, and shrive with a smile! Ah, friends, let me now predict, though ages may elapse before the slow event shall justify me, that in no way will the mutual vision of minds, when at last it shall be perfected, so enhance the blessedness of mankind as by rending the veil of self, and leaving no spot of darkness in the mind for lies to hide in. Then shall the soul no longer be a coal smoking among ashes, but a star in a crystal sphere.

From what I have said of the delights which friendship among the mind-readers derives from the perfection of the mental rapport, it may be imagined how intoxicating must be the experience when one of the friends is a woman, and the subtle attractions and correspondences of sex touch with passion the intellectual sympathy. With my first venturing into society I had begun, to their extreme amusement, to fall in love with the women right and left. In the perfect frankness which is the condition of all intercourse among this people, these adorable women told me that what I felt was only friendship, which was a very good thing, but wholly different from love, as I should well know if I were beloved. It was difficult to believe that the melting emotions which I had experienced in their company were the result merely of the friendly and kindly attitude of their minds toward mine; but when I found that I was affected in the same way by every gracious woman I met, I had to make up my mind that they must be right about it, and that I should have to adapt myself to a world in which, friendship being a passion, love must needs be nothing less than rapture.

The homely proverb, 'Every Jack has his Gill', may, I suppose, be taken to mean that for all men there are certain women expressly suited by mental and moral as well as by physical constitution. It is a thought painful, rather than cheering, that this may be the truth, so altogether do the chances preponderate against the ability of these elect ones to recognize each other even if they meet, seeing that speech is so inadequate and so misleading a medium of self-revelation. But among the mind-readers, the search for one's ideal mate is a quest reasonably sure of being crowned with success, and no one dreams of wedding unless it be; for so to do, they consider, would be to throw away the choicest blessing of life, and not alone to wrong themselves and their unfound mates, but likewise those whom they themselves and those un-discovered mates might wed. Therefore, passionate pilgrims, they go from isle to isle till they find each other, and, as the population of the islands is but small, the pilgrimage is not often long.

When I met her first we were in company, and I was struck by the sudden stir and the looks and smiling interest with which all around turned and regarded us, the women with moistened eyes. They had read her thought when she saw me, but this I did not know, neither what was the custom in these matters, till afterward. But I knew, from the moment she first fixed her eyes on me, and I felt her mind brooding upon mine, how truly I had been told by those other women that the feeling with which they had inspired me was not love.

With people who become acquainted at a glance, and old friends in an hour, wooing is naturally not a long process. Indeed, it may be said that between lovers among mind-readers there is no wooing, but merely recognition. The day after we met, she became mine.

Perhaps I cannot better illustrate how subordinate the merely physical element is in the impression which mind-readers form of their friends than by mentioning an incident that occurred some months after our union. This was my discovery, wholly by accident, that my love, in whose society I had almost constantly been, had not the least idea what was the color of my eyes, or whether my hair and complexion were light or dark. Of course, as soon as I asked her the question, she read the answer in my mind, but she admitted that she had previously had no distinct impression on those points. On the other hand, if in the blackest midnight I should come to her, she would not need to ask who the comer was. It is by the mind, not the eye, that these people know one another. It is really only in their relations to soulless and inanimate things that they need eyes at all.

It must not be supposed that their disregard of one another's bodily aspect grows out of any ascetic sentiment. It is merely a necessary consequence of their power of directly apprehending mind, that whenever mind is closely associated with matter the latter is comparatively neglected on account of the greater interest of the former, suffering as lesser things always do when placed in immediate contrast with greater. Art is with them confined to the inanimate, the human form having, for the reason mentioned, ceased to inspire the artist. It will be naturally and quite correctly inferred that among such a race physical beauty is not the important factor in human fortune and felicity that it elsewhere is. The absolute openness of their minds and hearts to one another makes their happiness far more dependent on the moral and mental qualities of their companions than upon their physical. A genial temperament, a wide-grasping, godlike intellect, a poet soul, are incomparably more fascinating to them than the most dazzling combination conceivable of mere bodily graces.

A woman of mind and heart has no more need of beauty to win love in these islands than a beauty elsewhere of mind or heart. I should mention here, perhaps, that this race, which makes so little account of physical beauty, is itself a singularly handsome one. This is owing doubtless in part to the absolute compatibility of temperaments in all the marriages, and partly also to the reaction upon the body of a state of ideal mental and moral health and placidity.

Not being myself a mind-reader, the fact that my love was rarely beautiful in form and face had doubtless no little part in attracting my devotion. This, of course, she knew, as she knew all my thoughts, and, knowing my limitations, tolerated and forgave the element of sensuousness in my passion. But if it must have seemed to her so little worthy in comparison with the high spiritual communion which her race know as love, to me it became, by virtue of her almost superhuman relation to me, an ecstasy more ravishing surely than any lover of my race tasted before. The ache at the heart of the intensest love is the impotence of words to make it perfectly understood to its object. But my passion was without this pang, for my heart was absolutely open to her I loved. Lovers may imagine, but I cannot describe, the ecstatic thrill of communion into which this consciousness transformed every tender emotion. As I considered what mutual love must be where both parties are mind-readers, I realized the high communion which my sweet companion had sacrificed for me.

She might indeed comprehend her lover and his love for her, but the higher satisfaction of knowing that she was comprehended by him and her love understood, she had foregone. For that I should ever attain the power of mind-reading was out of the question, the faculty never having been developed in a single lifetime.

Why my inability should move my dear companion to such depths of pity I was not able fully to understand until I learned that mind-reading is chiefly held desirable, not for the knowledge of others which it gives its possessors, but for the self-knowledge which is its reflex effect. Of all they see in the minds of others, that which concerns them most is the reflection of themselves, the photographs of their own characters. The most obvious consequence of the self-knowledge thus forced upon them is to render them alike incapable of self-conceit or self-depreciation. Everyone must needs always think of himself as he is, being no more able to do otherwise than is a man in a hall of mirrors to cherish delusions as to his personal appearance.

But self-knowledge means to the mind-readers much more than this – nothing less, indeed, than a shifting of the sense of identity. When a man sees himself in a mirror, he is compelled to distinguish between the bodily self he sees and his real self, which is within and unseen. When in turn the mind-reader comes to see the mental and moral self reflected in other minds as in mirrors, the same thing happens. He is compelled to distinguish between this mental and moral self which has been made objective to him, and can be contemplated by him as impartially as if it were another's, and the inner ego which still remains subjective, unseen, and indefinable. In this inner ego the mind-readers recognize the essential identity and being, the noumenal self, the core of the soul, and the true hiding of its eternal life, to which the mind as well as the body is but the garment of a day.

The effect of such a philosophy as this – which, indeed, with the mind-readers is rather an instinctive consciousness than a philosophy – must obviously be to impart a sense of wonderful superiority to the vicissitudes of this earthly state, and a singular serenity in the midst of the haps and mishaps which threaten or befall the personality. They did indeed appear to me, as I never dreamed men could attain to be, lords of themselves.

It was because I might not hope to attain this enfranchisement from the false ego of the apparent self, without which life seemed to her race scarcely worth living, that my love so pitied me.

But I must hasten on, leaving a thousand things unsaid, to relate the lamentable catastrophe to which it is owing that, instead of being still a resident of those blessed islands, in the full enjoyment of that intimate and ravishing companionship which by contrast would forever dim the pleasures of all other human society, I recall the bright picture as a memory under other skies.

Among a people who are compelled by the very constitution of their minds to put themselves in the places of others, the sympathy which is the inevitable consequence of perfect comprehension renders envy, hatred, and uncharitableness impossible. But of course there are people less genially constituted than others, and these are necessarily the objects of a certain distaste on the part of associates. Now, owing to the unhindered impact of minds upon one another, the anguish of persons so regarded, despite the tenderest consideration of those about them, is so great that they beg the grace of exile, that, being out of the way, people may think less frequently upon them. There are numerous small islets, scarcely more than rocks, lying to the north of the archipelago, and on these the unfortunates are permitted to live. Only one lives on each islet, as they cannot endure each other even as well as the more happily constituted can endure them. From time to time supplies of food are taken to them, and of course, any time they wish to take the risk, they are permitted to return to society.

Now, as I have said, the fact which, even more than their out-of-the-way location, makes the islands of the mind-readers unapproachable, is the violence with which the great antarctic current, owing probably to some configuration of the ocean bed, together with the innumerable rocks and shoals, flows through and about the archipelago.

Ships making the islands from the southward are caught by this current and drawn among the rocks, to their almost certain destruction; while, owing to the violence with which the current sets to the north, it is not possible to approach at all from that direction, or at least it has never been accomplished. Indeed, so powerful are the currents that even the boats which cross the narrow straits between the main islands and the islets of the unfortunate, to carry the latter their supplies, are ferried over by cables, not trusting to oar or sail.

The brother of my love had charge of one of the boats engaged in this transportation, and, being desirous of visiting the islets, I accepted an invitation to accompany him on one of his trips. I know nothing of how the accident happened, but in the fiercest part of the current of one of the straits we parted from the cable and were swept out to sea. There was no question of stemming the boiling current, our utmost endeavors barely sufficing to avoid being dashed to pieces on the rocks. From the first, there was no hope of our winning back to the land, and so swiftly did we drift that by noon – the accident having befallen in the morning – the islands, which are low-lying, had sunk beneath the southwestern horizon.

Among these mind-readers, distance is not an insuperable obstacle to the transfer of thought. My companion was in communication with our friends, and from time to time conveyed to me messages of anguish from my dear love; for, being well aware of the nature of the currents and the unapproachableness of the islands, those we had left behind, as well as we ourselves, knew well we should see each other's faces no more. For five days we continued to drift to the northwest, in no danger of starvation, owing to our lading of provisions, but constrained to unintermitting watch and ward by the roughness of the weather. On the fifth day my companion died from exposure and exhaustion. He died very quietly – indeed, with great appearance of relief. The life of the mind-readers while yet they are in the body is so largely spiritual that the idea of an existence wholly so, which seems vague and chill to us, suggests to them a state only slightly more refined than they already know on earth.

After that I suppose I must have fallen into an unconscious state, from which I roused to find myself on an American ship bound for New York, surrounded by people whose only means of communicating with one another is to keep up while together a constant clatter of hissing, guttural, and explosive noises, eked out by all manner of facial contortions and bodily gestures. I frequently find myself staring open-mouthed at those who address me, too much struck by their grotesque appearance to bethink myself of replying.

I find that I shall not live out the voyage, and I do not care to. From my experience of the people on the ship, I can judge how I should fare on land amid the stunning Babel of a nation of talkers. And my friends – God bless them! how lonely I should feel in their very presence! Nay, what satisfaction or consolation, what but bitter mockery, could I ever more find in such human sympathy and companionship as suffice others and once sufficed me – I who have seen and known what I have seen and known! Ah, yes, doubtless it is far better I should die; but the knowledge of the things that I have seen I feel should not perish with me. For hope's sake, men should not miss the glimpse of the higher, sun-bathed reaches of the upward path they plod. So thinking, I have written out some account of my wonderful experience, though briefer far, by reason of my weakness, than fits the greatness of the matter. The captain seems an honest, well-meaning man, and to him I shall confide the narrative, charging him, on touching shore, to see it safely in the hands of someone who will bring it to the world's ear.

Note. – The extent of my own connection with the foregoing document is sufficiently indicated by the author himself in the final paragraph.

                                                                    E. B.

The Scarlet Plague

Jack London

I

The way led along upon what had once been the embankment of a
railroad. But no train had run upon it for many years. The forest on
either side swelled up the slopes of the embankment and crested across it
in a green wave of trees and bushes. The trail was as narrow as a man's
body, and was no more than a wild-animal runway. Occasionally, a piece
of rusty iron, showing through the forest-mold, advertised that the rail
and the ties still remained. In one place, a ten-inch tree, bursting through
at a connection, had lifted the end of a rail clearly into view. The tie had
evidently followed the rail, held to it by the spike long enough for its bed
to be filled with gravel and rotten leaves, so that now the crumbling,
rotten timber thrust itself up at a curious slant. Old as the road was, it was
manifest that it had been of the monorail type.

An old man and a boy travelled along this runway. They moved slowly,
for the old man was very old, a touch of palsy made his movements
tremulous, and he leaned heavily upon his staff. A rude skull-cap of
goatskin protected his head from the sun. From beneath this fell a scant
fringe of stained and dirty-white hair. A visor, ingeniously made from a
large leaf, shielded his eyes, and from under this he peered at the way of
his feet on the trail. His beard, which should have been snow-white but
which showed the same weather-wear and camp-stain as his hair, fell
nearly to his waist in a great tangled mass. About his chest and shoulders
hung a single, mangy garment of goatskin. His arms and legs, withered
and skinny, betokened extreme age, as well as did their sunburn and scars
and scratches betoken long years of exposure to the elements.

The boy, who led the way, checking the eagerness of his muscles to the
slow progress of the elder, likewise wore a single garment – a ragged-
edged piece of bearskin, with a hole in the middle through which he had
thrust his head. He could not have been more than twelve years old.
Tucked coquettishly over one ear was the freshly severed tail of a pig. In
one hand he carried a medium-sized bow and an arrow. On his back was a
quiverful of arrows. From a sheath hanging about his neck on a thong,
projected the battered handle of a hunting knife. He was as brown as a

berry, and walked softly, with almost a catlike tread. In marked contrast
with his sunburned skin were his eyes – blue, deep blue, but keen and
sharp as a pair of gimlets. They seemed to bore into all about him in a
way that was habitual. As he went along he smelled things, as well, his
distended, quivering nostrils carrying to his brain an endless series of
messages from the outside world. Also, his hearing was acute, and had
been so trained that it operated automatically. Without conscious effort,
he heard all the slight sounds in the apparent quiet – heard, and differentiated, and classified these sounds – whether they were of the wind
rustling the leaves, of the humming of bees and gnats, of the distant
rumble of the sea that drifted to him only in lulls, or of the gopher, just
under his foot, shoving a pouchful of earth into the entrance of his hole.

Suddenly he became alertly tense. Sound, sight, and odor had given
him a simultaneous warning. His hand went back to the old man, touching him, and the pair stood still. Ahead, at one side of the top of the
embankment, arose a crackling sound, and the boy's gaze was fixed on the
tops of the agitated bushes. Then a large bear, a grizzly, crashed into
view, and likewise stopped abruptly, at sight of the humans. He did not
like them, and growled querulously. Slowly the boy fitted the arrow to
the bow, and slowly he pulled the bowstring taut. But he never removed
his eyes from the bear.

The old man peered from under his green leaf at the danger, and
stood as quietly as the boy. For a few seconds this mutual scrutinizing
went on; then, the bear betraying a growing irritability, the boy, with a
movement of his head, indicated that the old man must step aside from
the trail and go down the embankment. The boy followed, going backward, still holding the bow taut and ready. They waited till a crashing
among the bushes from the opposite side of the embankment told them
the bear had gone on. The boy grinned as he led back to the trail. 'A big
un, Granser,' he chuckled.

The old man shook his head.

'They get thicker every day,' he complained in a thin, undependable
falsetto. 'Who'd have thought I'd live to see the time when a man would
be afraid of his life on the way to the Cliff House? When I was a boy,
Edwin, men and women and little babies used to come out here from San
Francisco by tens of thousands on a nice day. And there weren't any bears
then. No, sir. They used to pay money to look at them in cages, they were
that rare.'

'What is money, Granser?'

Before the old man could answer, the boy recollected and triumphantly shoved his hand into a pouch under his bearskin and pulled forth a

battered and tarnished silver dollar. The old man's eyes glistened, as he held the coin close to them. 'I can't see,' he muttered. 'You look and see if you can make out the date, Edwin.'

The boy laughed.

'You're a great Granser,' he cried delightedly, 'always making believe them little marks mean something.'

The old man manifested an accustomed chagrin as he brought the coin back again close to his own eyes.

'2012,' he shrilled, and then fell to cackling grotesquely. 'That was the year Morgan the Fifth was appointed President of the United States by the Board of Magnates. It must have been one of the last coins minted, for the Scarlet Death came in 2013. Lord! Lord! – think of it! Sixty years ago, and I am the only person alive today that lived in those times. Where did you find it, Edwin?' The boy, who had been regarding him with the tolerant curiousness one accords to the prattlings of the feeble-minded, answered promptly.

'I got it off of Hoo-Hoo. He found it when we was herdin' goats down near San José last spring. Hoo-Hoo said it was *money*. Ain't you hungry, Granser?'

The ancient caught his staff in a tighter grip and urged along the trail, his old eyes shining greedily.

'I hope Hare-Lip's found a crab . . . or two,' he mumbled. 'They're good eating, crabs, mighty good eating when you've no more teeth and you've got grandsons that love their old grandsire and make a point of catching crabs for him. When I was a boy – '

But Edwin, suddenly stopped by what he saw, was drawing the bow-string on a fitted arrow. He had paused on the brink of a crevasse in the embankment. An ancient culvert had here washed out, and the stream, no longer confined, had cut a passage through the fill. On the opposite side, the end of a rail projected and overhung. It showed rustily through the creeping vines which overran it. Beyond, crouching by a bush, a rabbit looked across at him in trembling hesitancy. Fully fifty feet was the distance, but the arrow flashed true; and the transfixed rabbit, crying out in sudden fright and hurt, struggled painfully away into the brush. The boy himself was a flash of brown skin and flying fur as he bounded down the steep wall of the gap and up the other side. His lean muscles were springs of steel that released into graceful and efficient action. A hundred feet beyond, in a tangle of bushes, he overtook the wounded creature, knocked its head on a convenient tree-trunk, and turned it over to Granser to carry.

'Rabbit is good, very good,' the ancient quavered, 'but when it comes to a toothsome delicacy I prefer crab. When I was a boy – '

'Why do you say so much that ain't got no sense?' Edwin impatiently interrupted the other's threatened garrulousness.

The boy did not exactly utter these words, but something that remotely resembled them and that was more guttural and explosive and economical of qualifying phrases. His speech showed distant kinship with that of the old man, and the latter's speech was approximately an English that had gone through a bath of corrupt usage.

'What I want to know,' Edwin continued, 'is why you call crab "toothsome delicacy"? Crab is crab, ain't it? No one I never heard calls it such funny things.'

The old man sighed but did not answer, and they moved on in silence. The surf grew suddenly louder, as they emerged from the forest upon a stretch of sand dunes bordering the sea. A few goats were browsing among the sandy hillocks, and a skin-clad boy, aided by a wolfish-looking dog that was only faintly reminiscent of a collie, was watching them. Mingled with the roar of the surf was a continuous, deep-throated barking or bellowing, which came from a cluster of jagged rocks a hundred yards out from shore. Here huge sea-lions hauled themselves up to lie in the sun or battle with one another. In the immediate foreground arose the smoke of a fire, tended by a third savage-looking boy. Crouched near him were several wolfish dogs similar to the one that guarded the goats.

The old man accelerated his pace, sniffing eagerly as he neared the fire.

'Mussels!' he muttered ecstatically. 'Mussels! And ain't that a crab, Hoo-Hoo? Ain't that a crab? My, my, you boys are good to your old grandsire.'

Hoo-Hoo, who was apparently of the same age as Edwin, grinned. 'All you want, Granser. I got four.'

The old man's palsied eagerness was pitiful. Sitting down in the sand as quickly as his stiff limbs would let him, he poked a large rock-mussel from out of the coals. The heat had forced its shells apart, and the meat, salmon-colored, was thoroughly cooked. Between thumb and forefinger, in trembling haste, he caught the morsel and carried it to his mouth. But it was too hot, and the next moment was violently ejected. The old man spluttered with the pain, and tears ran out of his eyes and down his cheeks.

The boys were true savages, possessing only the cruel humor of the savage. To them the incident was excruciatingly funny, and they burst into loud laughter. Hoo-Hoo danced up and down, while Edwin rolled gleefully on the ground. The boy with the goats came running to join in the fun.

'Set 'em to cool, Edwin, set 'em to cool,' the old man besought, in the midst of his grief, making no attempt to wipe away the tears that flowed from his eyes. 'And cool a crab, Edwin, too. You know your grandsire likes crabs.'

From the coals arose a great sizzling, which proceeded from the many mussels bursting open their shells and exuding their moisture. They were large shellfish, running from three to six inches in length. The boys raked them out with sticks and placed them on a large piece of driftwood to cool.

'When I was a boy, we did not laugh at our elders; we respected them.'

The boys took no notice, and Granser continued to babble an incoherent flow of complaint and censure. But this time he was more careful, and did not burn his mouth. All began to eat, using nothing but their hands and making loud mouth-noises and lip-smackings. The third boy, who was called Hare-Lip, slyly deposited a pinch of sand on a mussel the the ancient was carrying to his mouth; and when the grit of it bit into the old fellow's mucous membrane and gums, the laughter was again uproarious. He was unaware that a joke had been played on him, and spluttered and spat until Edwin, relenting, gave him a gourd of fresh water with which to wash out his mouth.

'Where's them crabs, Hoo-Hoo?' Edwin demanded. 'Granser's set upon having a snack.'

Again Granser's eyes burned with greediness as a large crab was handed to him. It was a shell with legs and all complete, but the meat had long since departed. With shaky fingers and babblings of anticipation, the old man broke off a leg and found it filled with emptiness.

'The crabs, Hoo-Hoo?' he wailed. 'The crabs?'

'I was foolin', Granser. They ain't no crabs. I never found one.'

The boys were overwhelmed with delight at sight of the tears of senile disappointment that dribbled down the old man's cheeks. Then, unnoticed, Hoo-Hoo replaced the empty shell with a fresh-cooked crab. Already dismembered, from the cracked legs the white meat sent forth a small cloud of savory steam. This attracted amazement.

The change of his mood to one of joy was immediate. He snuffled and muttered and mumbled, making almost a croon of delight, as he began to eat. Of this the boys took little notice, for it was an accustomed spectacle. Nor did they notice his occasional exclamations and utterances of phrases which meant nothing to them, as, for instance, when he smacked his lips and champed his gums while muttering: 'Mayonnaise! Just think – mayonnaise! And it's sixty years since the last was ever made! Two generations and never a smell of it! Why, in those days it was served in every restaurant with crab.' When he could eat no more, the old man sighed, wiped his hands on his naked legs, and gazed out over the sea. With the content of a full stomach, he waxed reminiscent.

'To think of it! I've seen this beach alive with men, women, and children on a pleasant Sunday. And there weren't any bears to eat them up, either. And right up there on the cliff was a big restaurant where you could get anything you wanted to eat. Four million people lived in San Francisco then. And now, in the whole city and county there aren't forty all told. And out there on the sea were ships and ships always to be seen, going in for the Golden Gate or coming out. And airships in the air – dirigibles and flying machines. They could travel two hundred miles an hour. The mail contracts with the New York and San Francisco Limited demanded that for the minimum. There was a chap, a Frenchman, I forget his name, who succeeded in making three hundred; but the thing was risky, too risky for conservative persons. But he was on the right clue, and he would have managed it if it hadn't been for the Great Plague. When I was a boy, there were men alive who remembered the coming of the first aeroplanes, and now I have lived to see the last of them, and that sixty years ago.'

The old man babbled on, unheeded by the boys, who were long accustomed to his garrulousness, and whose vocabularies, besides, lacked the greater portion of the words he used. It was noticeable that in these rambling soliloquies his English seemed to recrudesce into better construction and phraseology. But when he talked directly with the boys it lapsed, largely, into their own uncouth and simpler forms.

'But there weren't many crabs in those days,' the old man wandered on. 'They were fished out, and they were great delicacies. The open season was only a month long, too. And now crabs are accessible the whole year around. Think of it – catching all the crabs you want, any time you want, in the surf of the Cliff House beach!'

A sudden commotion among the goats brought the boys to their feet. The dogs about the fire rushed to join their snarling fellow who guarded the goats, while the goats themselves stampeded in the direction of their human protectors. A half dozen forms, lean and gray, glided about on the sand hillocks or faced the bristling dogs. Edwin arched an arrow that fell short. But Hare-Lip, with a sling such as David carried into battle against Goliath, hurled a stone through the air that whistled from the speed of its flight. It fell squarely among the wolves and caused them to slink away toward the dark depths of the eucalyptus forest.

The boys laughed and lay down again in the sand, while Granser sighed ponderously. He had eaten too much, and, with hands clasped on his paunch, the fingers interlaced, he resumed his maunderings.

' "The fleeting systems lapse like foam",' he mumbled what was evidently a quotation. 'That's it – foam, and fleeting. All man's toil upon the planet was just so much foam. He domesticated the serviceable animals, destroyed the hostile ones, and cleared the land of its wild vegetation. And then be passed, and the flood of primordial life rolled back again, sweeping his handiwork away – the weeds and the forest inundated his fields, the beasts of prey swept over his flocks, and now there are wolves on the Cliff House beach.' He was appalled by the thought. 'Where four million people disported themselves, the wild wolves roam today, and the savage progeny of our loins, with prehistoric weapons, defend themselves against the fanged despoilers. Think of it! And all because of the Scarlet Death – '

The adjective had caught Hare-Lip's ear.

'He's always saying that,' he said to Edwin. 'What is scarlet?'

' "The scarlet of the maples can shake me like the cry of bugles going by",' the old man quoted.

'It's red,' Edwin answered the question. 'And you don't know it because you come from the Chauffeur Tribe. They never did know nothing, none of them. Scarlet is red – I know that.'

'Red is red, ain't it?' Hare-Lip grumbled. 'Then what's the good of gettin' cocky and calling it scarlet?'

'Granser, what for do you always say so much what nobody knows?' he asked. 'Scarlet ain't anything, but red is red. Why don't you say red, then?'

'Red is not the right word,' was the reply. 'The plague was scarlet. The whole face and body turned scarlet in a hour's time. Don't I know? Didn't I see enough of it? And I am telling you it was scarlet because – well, because it was scarlet. There is no other word for it.'

'Red is good enough for me,' Hare-Lip muttered obstinately. 'My dad calls red red, and he ought to know. He says everybody died of the Red Death.'

'Your dad is a common fellow, descended from a common fellow,' Granser retorted heatedly. 'Don't I know the beginnings of the Chauffeurs? Your grandsire was a chauffeur, a servant, and without education. He worked for other persons. But your grandmother was of good stock, only the children did not take after her. Don't I remember when I first met them catching fish at Lake Temescal?'

'What is education?' Edwin asked.

'Calling red scarlet,' Hare-Lip sneered, then returned to the attack on Granser. 'My dad told me, an' he got it from his dad afore he croaked, that your wife was a Santa Rosan, an' that she was sure no account. He said she was a hash-slinger before the Red Death, though I don't know what a hash-slinger is. You can tell me, Edwin.'

But Edwin shook his head in token of ignorance.

'It is true, she was a waitress,' Granser acknowledged. 'But she was a good woman, and your mother was her daughter. Women were very scarce in the days after the Plague. She was the only wife I could find, even if she was a hash-slinger, as your father calls it. But it is not nice to talk about our progenitors that way.'

'Dad says that the wife of the first Chauffeur was a *lady* – '

'What's a *lady*?' Hoo-Hoo demanded.

'A *Lady's* a Chauffeur squaw,' was the quick reply of Hare-Lip.

'The first Chauffeur was Bill, a common fellow, as I said before,' the old man expounded; 'but his wife was a lady, a great lady. Before the Scarlet Death she was the wife of Van Warden. He was President of the Board of Industrial Magnates, and was one of the dozen men who ruled America. He was worth one billion, eight hundred millions of dollars – coins like you have there in your pouch, Edwin. And then came the Scarlet Death, and his wife became the wife of Bill, the first Chauffeur. He used to beat her, too. I have seen it myself.'

Hoo-Hoo, lying on his stomach and idly digging his toes in the sand, cried out and investigated, first, his toe-nail, and next, the small hole he had dug. The other two boys joined him, excavating the sand rapidly with their hands till there lay three skeletons exposed. Two were of adults, the third being that of a part-grown child. The old man nudged along on the ground and peered at the find.

'Plague victims,' he announced. 'That's the way they died everywhere in the last days. This must have been a family, running away from the contagion and perishing here on the Cliff House beach. They – what are you doing, Edwin?'

This question was asked in sudden dismay, as Edwin, using the back of his hunting knife, began to knock out the teeth from the jaws of one of the skulls.

'Going to string 'em,' was the response.

The three boys were now hard at it; and quite a knocking and hammering arose, in which Granser babbled on unnoticed.

'You are true savages. Already has begun the custom of wearing human teeth. In another generation you will be perforating your noses and ears and wearing ornaments of bone and shell. I know. The human race is doomed to sink back farther and farther into the primitive night ere again it begins its bloody climb upward to civilization. When we increase and feel the lack of room, we will proceed to kill one another. And then I suppose you will wear human scalp-locks at your waist, as well – as you, Edwin, who are the gentlest of my grandsons, have already begun with that vile pigtail. Throw it away, Edwin, boy; throw it away.'

'What a gabble the old geezer makes,' Hare-Lip remarked, when, the teeth all extracted, they began an attempt at equal division.

They were very quick and abrupt in their actions, and their speech, in moments of hot discussion over the allotment of the choicer teeth, was truly a gabble. They spoke in monosyllables and short jerky sentences that was more a gibberish than a language. And yet, through it ran hints of grammatical construction, and appeared vestiges of the conjugation of some superior culture. Even the speech of Granser was so corrupt that were it put down literally it would be almost so much nonsense to the reader. This, however, was when he talked with the boys. When he got into the full swing of babbling to himself, it slowly purged itself into pure English. The sentences grew longer and were enunciated with a rhythm and ease that was reminiscent of the lecture platform.

'Tell us about the Red Death, Granser,' Hare-Lip demanded, when the teeth affair had been satisfactorily concluded.

'The Scarlet Death,' Edwin corrected.

'An' don't work all that funny lingo on us,' Hare-Lip went on. 'Talk sensible, Granser, like a Santa Rosan ought to talk. Other Santa Rosans don't talk like you.'

2

The old man showed pleasure in being thus called upon. He cleared his throat and began.

'Twenty or thirty years ago my story was in great demand. But in these days nobody seems interested – '

'There you go!' Hare-Lip cried hotly. 'Cut out the funny stuff and talk sensible. What's interested? You talk like a baby that don't know how.'

'Let him alone,' Edwin urged, 'or he'll get mad and won't talk at all. Skip the funny places. We'll catch on to some of what he tells us.'

'Let her go, Granser,' Hoo-Hoo encouraged; for the old man was already maundering about the disrespect for elders and the reversion to cruelty of all humans that fell from high culture to primitive conditions.

The tale began.

'There were very many people in the world in those days. San Francisco alone held four millions – '

'What is millions?' Edwin interrupted.

Granser looked at him kindly.

'I know you cannot count beyond ten, so I will tell you. Hold up your two hands. On both of them you have altogether ten fingers and thumbs. Very well. I now take this grain of sand – you hold it, Hoo-Hoo.' He dropped the grain of sand into the lad's palm and went on. 'Now that grain of sand stands for the ten fingers of Edwin. I add another grain. That's ten more fingers. And I add another, and another, and another, until I have added as many grains as Edwin has fingers and thumbs. That makes what I call one hundred. Remember that word – one hundred. Now I put this pebble in Hare-Lip's hand. It stands for ten grains of sand, or ten tens of fingers, or one hundred fingers. I put in ten pebbles. They stand for a thousand fingers. I take a mussel-shell, and it stands for ten pebbles, or one hundred grains of sand, or one thousand fingers . . . .'

And so on, laboriously, and with much reiteration, he strove to build up in their minds a crude conception of numbers. As the quantities increased, he had the boys holding different magnitudes in each of their hands. For still higher sums, he laid the symbols on the log of driftwood; and for symbols he was hard put, being compelled to use the teeth from the skulls for millions, and the crab-shells for billions. It was here that he stopped, for the boys were showing signs of becoming tired.

'There were four million people in San Francisco – four teeth.'

The boys' eyes ranged along from the teeth and from hand to hand, down through the pebbles and sand-grains to Edwin's fingers. And back again they ranged along the ascending series in the effort to grasp such inconceivable numbers.

'That was a lot of folks, Granser,' Edwin at last hazarded.

'Like sand on the beach here, like sand on the beach, each grain of sand a man, or woman, or child. Yes, my boy, all those people lived right here in San Francisco. And at one time or another all those people came out on this very beach – more people than there are grains of sand. More – more – more. And San Francisco was a noble city. And across the bay – where we camped last year, even more people lived, clear from Point Richmond, on the level ground and on the hills, all the way around to San Leandro – one great city of seven million people. – Seven teeth . . . there, that's it, seven millions.' Again the boys' eyes ranged up and down from Edwin's fingers to the teeth on the log.

'The world was full of people. The census of 2010 gave eight billions for the whole world – eight crab-shells, yes, eight billions. It was not like today. Mankind knew a great deal more about getting food. And the more food there was, the more people there were. In the year 1800, there were one hundred and seventy millions in Europe alone. One hundred years later – a grain of sand, Hoo-Hoo – one hundred years later, at 1900, there were five hundred millions in Europe – five grains of sand, Hoo-Hoo, and this one tooth. This shows how easy was the getting of food, and how men increased. And in the year 2000, there were fifteen hundred millions in Europe. And it was the same all over the rest of the world. Eight crab-shells there, yes, eight billion people were alive on the earth when the Scarlet Death began.

'I was a young man when the Plague came – twenty-seven years old; and I lived on the other side of San Francisco Bay, in Berkeley. You remember those great stone houses, Edwin, when we came down the hills from Contra Costa? That was where I lived, in those stone houses. I was a professor of English literature.'

Much of this was over the heads of the boys, but they strove to comprehend dimly this tale of the past.

'What was them stone houses for?' Hare-Lip queried.

'You remember when your dad taught you to swim?' The boy nodded. 'Well, in the University of California – that is the name we had for the houses – we taught young men and women how to think, just as I have taught you now, by sand and pebbles and shells, to know how many people lived in those days. There was very much to teach. The young men and women we taught were called students. We had large rooms in which we taught. I talked to them, forty or fifty at a time, just as I am talking to you now. I told them about the books other men had written before their time, and even, sometimes, in their time – '

'Was that all you did? – just talk, talk, talk?' Hoo-Hoo demanded. 'Who hunted your meat for you? and milked the goats? and caught the fish?'

'A sensible question, Hoo-Hoo, a sensible question. As I have told you, in those days food-getting was easy. We were very wise. A few men got the food for many men. The other men did other things. As you say, I talked. I talked all the time, and for this food was given me – much food, fine food, beautiful food, food that I have not tasted in sixty years and shall never taste again. I sometimes think the most wonderful achievement of our tremendous civilization was food – its inconceivable abundance, its infinite variety, its marvellous delicacy. O my grandsons, life was life in those days, when we had such wonderful things to eat.'

This was beyond the boys, and they let it slip by, words and thoughts, as a mere senile wandering in the narrative.

'Our food-getters were called freemen. This was a joke. We of the ruling classes owned all the land, all the machines, everything. These food-getters were our slaves. We took almost all the food they got, and left them a little so that they might eat, and work, and get us more food – '

'I'd have gone into the forest and got food for myself,' Hare-Lip announced; 'and if any man tried to take it away from me, I'd have killed him.'

The old man laughed.

'Did I not tell you that we of the ruling class owned all the land, all the forest, everything? Any food-getter who would not get food for us, him we punished or compelled to starve to death. And very few did that. They preferred to get food for us, and make clothes for us, and prepare and administer to us a thousand – a mussel-shell, Hoo-Hoo – a thousand satisfactions and delights. And I was Professor Smith in those days – Professor James Howard Smith. And my lecture courses were very popular – that is, very many of the young men and women liked to hear me talk about the books other men had written.

'And I was very happy, and I had beautiful things to eat. And my hands were soft, because I did no work with them, and my body was clean all over and dressed in the softest garments – ' He surveyed his mangy goatskin with disgust. 'We did not wear such things in those days. Even the slaves had better garments. And we were most clean. We washed our faces and hands often every day. You boys never wash unless you fall into the water or go in swimming.'

'Neither do you, Granser,' Hoo-Hoo retorted.

'I know, I know. I am a filthy old man. But times have changed. Nobody washes these days, and there are no conveniences. It is sixty years since I have seen a piece of soap. You do not know what soap is, and I shall not tell you, for I am telling the story of the Scarlet Death. You know what sickness is. We called it a disease. Very many of the diseases came from what we called germs. Remember that word – germs. A germ is a very small thing. It is like a woodtick, such as you find on the dogs in the spring of the year when they run in the forest. Only the germ is very small. It is so small that you cannot see it – '

Hoo-Hoo began to laugh.

'You're a queer un, Granser, talking about things you can't see. If you can't see 'em, how do you know they are? That's what I want to know. How do you know anything you can't see?'

'A good question, a very good question, Hoo-Hoo. But we did see – some of them. We had what we called microscopes and ultramicroscopes, and we put them to our eyes and looked through them, so that we saw things larger than they really were, and many things we could not see without the microscopes at all. Our best ultramicroscopes could make a germ look forty thousand times larger. A mussel-shell is a thousand fingers like Edwin's. Take forty mussel-shells, and by as many times larger was the germ when we looked at it through a microscope. And after that, we had other ways, by using what we called moving pictures, of making the forty-thousand-times germ many, many thousand times larger still. And thus we saw all these things which our eyes of themselves could not see. Take a grain of sand. Break it into ten pieces. Take one piece and break it into ten. Break one of those pieces into ten, and one of those into ten, and one of those into ten, and one of those into ten, and do it all day, and maybe, by sunset, you will have a piece as small as one of the germs.'

The boys were openly incredulous. Hare-Lip sniffed and sneered and Hoo-Hoo snickered, until Edwin nudged them to be silent.

'The woodtick sucks the blood of the dog, but the germ, being so very small, goes right into the blood of the body, and there it has many children. In those days there would be as many as a billion – a crab-shell, please – as many as that crab-shell in one man's body. We called germs micro-organisms. When a few million, or a billion, of them were in a man, in all the blood of a man, he was sick. These germs were a disease. There were many different kinds of them – more different kinds than there are grains of sand on this beach. We knew only a few of the kinds. The micro-organic world was an invisible world, a world we could not see, and we knew very little about it. Yet we did know something. There was the *bacillus anthracis*; there was the *micrococcus*; there was the *bacterium termo*, and the *bacterium lactis* – that's what turns the goat milk sour even to this day, Hare-Lip; and there were *schizomycetes* without end. And there were many others . . . '

Here the old man launched into a disquisition on germs and their natures, using words and phrases of such extraordinary length and meaninglessness, that the boys grinned at one another and looked out over the deserted ocean till they forgot the old man was babbling on.

'But the Scarlet Death, Granser,' Edwin at last suggested. Granser recollected himself, and with a start tore himself away from the rostrum of the lecture-hall, where, to another-world audience, he had been expounding the latest theory, sixty years gone, of germs and germ-diseases.

'Yes, yes, Edwin; I had forgotten. Sometimes the memory of the past is very strong upon me, and I forget that I am a dirty old man, clad in goatskin, wandering with my savage grandsons who are goatherds in the primeval wilderness. "The fleeting systems lapse like foam", and so lapsed our glorious, colossal civilization. I am Granser, a tired old man. I belong to the tribe of Santa Rosans. I married into that tribe. My sons and daughters married into the Chauffeurs, the Sacramentos, and the Palo-Altos. You, Hare-Lip, are of the Chauffeurs. You, Edwin, are of the Sacramentos. And you, Hoo-Hoo, are of the Palo-Altos. Your tribe takes its name from a town that was near the seat of another great institution of learning. It was called Stanford University. Yes, I remember now. It is perfectly clear. I was telling you of the Scarlet Death. Where was I in my story?'

'You was telling about germs, the things you can't see but which make men sick,' Edwin prompted.

'Yes, that's where I was. A man did not notice at first when only a few of these germs got into his body. But each germ broke in half and became two germs, and they kept doing this very rapidly so that in a short time there were many millions of them in the body. Then the man was sick. He had a disease, and the disease was named after the kind of germ that was in him. It might be measles, it might be influenza, it might be yellow fever; it might be any of thousands and thousands of kinds of diseases.

'Now this is the strange thing about these germs. There were always new ones coming to live in men's bodies. Long and long and long ago, when there were only a few men in the world, there were few diseases. But as men increased and lived closely together in great cities and civilizations, new diseases arose, new kinds of germs entered their bodies. Thus were countless millions and billions of human beings killed. And the more thickly men packed together, the more terrible were the new diseases that came to be. Long before my time, in the middle ages, there was the Black Plague that swept across Europe. It swept across Europe many times. There was tuberculosis, that entered into men wherever they were thickly packed. A hundred years before my time there was the bubonic plague. And in Africa was the sleeping sickness. The bacteriologists fought all these sicknesses and destroyed them, just as you boys fight the wolves away from your goats, or squash the mosquitoes that light on you. The bacteriologists – '

'But, Granser, what is a what-you-call-it?' Edwin interrupted.

'You, Edwin, are a goatherd. Your task is to watch the goats. You know a great deal about goats. A bacteriologist watches germs. That's his task, and he knows a great deal about them. So, as I was saying, the bacteriologists fought with the germs and destroyed them – sometimes. There was leprosy, a horrible disease. A hundred years before I was born, the bacteriologists discovered the germ of leprosy. They knew all about it. They made pictures of it. I have seen those pictures. But they never found a way to kill it. But in 1984, there was the Pantoblast Plague, a disease that broke out in a country called Brazil and that killed millions of people. But the bacteriologists found it out, and found the way to kill it, so that the Pantoblast Plague went no farther. They made what they called a serum, which they put into a man's body and which killed the pantoblast germs without killing the man. And in 1910, there was pellagra, and also the hookworm. These were easily killed by the bacteriologists. But in 1947 there arose a new disease that had never been seen before. It got into the bodies of babies of only ten months old or less, and it made them unable to move their hands and feet, or to eat, or anything; and the bacteriologists were eleven years in discovering how to kill that particular germ and save the babies.

'In spite of all these diseases, and of all the new ones that continued to arise, there were more and more men in the world. This was because it was easy to get food. The easier it was to get food, the more men there were; the more men there were, the more thickly were they packed together on the earth; and the more thickly they were packed, the more new kinds of germs became diseases. There were warnings. Soldervetzsky, as early as 1929, told the bacteriologists that they had no guaranty against some new disease, a thousand times more deadly than any they knew, arising and killing by the hundreds of millions and even by the billion. You see, the micro-organic world remained a mystery to the end. They knew there was such a world, and that from time to time armies of new germs emerged from it to kill men. And that was all they knew about it. For all they knew, in that invisible micro-organic world there might be as many different kinds of germs as there are grains of sand on this beach. And also, in that same invisible world it might well be that new kinds of germs came to be. It might be there that life originated – the "abysmal fecundity", Soldervetzsky called it, applying the words of other men who had written before him...'

It was at this point that Hare-Lip rose to his feet, an expression of huge contempt on his face.

'Granser,' he announced, 'you make me sick with your gabble. Why don't you tell about the Red Death? If you ain't going to, say so, an' we'll start back for camp.'

The old man looked at him and silently began to cry. The weak tears of age rolled down his cheeks, and all the feebleness of his eighty-seven years showed in his grief-stricken countenance.

'Sit down,' Edwin counselled soothingly. 'Granser's all right. He's just gettin' to the Scarlet Death, ain't you, Granser? He's just goin' to tell us about it right now. Sit down, Hare-Lip. Go ahead, Granser.'

3

The old man wiped the tears away on his grimy knuckles and took up the tale in a tremulous, piping voice that soon strengthened as he got the swing of the narrative.

'It was in the summer of 2013 that the Plague came. I was twenty-seven years old, and well do I remember it. Wireless dispatches – '

Hare-Lip spat loudly his disgust, and Granser hastened to make amends.

'We talked through the air in those days, thousands and thousands of miles. And the word came of a strange disease that had broken out in New York. There were seventeen millions of people living then in that noblest city of America. Nobody thought anything about the news. It was only a small thing. There had been only a few deaths. It seemed, though, that they had died very quickly, and that one of the first signs of the disease was the turning red of the face and all the body. Within twenty-four hours came the report of the first case in Chicago. And on the same day, it was made public that London, the greatest city in the world, next to Chicago, had been secretly fighting the plague for two weeks and censoring the news dispatches – that is, not permitting the word to go forth to the rest of the world that London had the plague.

'It looked serious, but we in California, like everywhere else, were not alarmed. We were sure that the bacteriologists would find a way to overcome this new germ, just as they had overcome other germs in the past. But the trouble was the astonishing quickness with which this germ destroyed human beings, and the fact that it inevitably killed any human body it entered. No one ever recovered. There was the old Asiatic cholera, when you might eat dinner with a well man in the evening, and the next morning, if you got up early enough, you would see him being hauled by your window in the death-cart. But this new plague was quicker than that – much quicker. From the moment of the first signs of it, a man would be dead in an hour. Some lasted for several hours. Many died within ten or fifteen minutes of the appearance of the first signs.

'The heart began to beat faster and the heat of the body to increase. Then came the scarlet rash, spreading like wildfire over the face and body. Most persons never noticed the increase in heat and heart-beat, and the first they knew was when the scarlet rash came out. Usually, they had convulsions at the time of the appearance of the rash. But these convulsions did not last long and were not very severe. If one lived through them, he became perfectly quiet, and only did he feel a numbness swiftly creeping up his body from the feet. The heels became numb first, then the legs, and hips, and when the numbness reached as high as his heart he died. They did not rave or sleep. Their minds always remained cool and calm up to the moment their heart numbed and stopped. And another strange thing was the rapidity of decomposition. No sooner was a person dead than the body seemed to fall to pieces, to fly apart, to melt away even as you looked at it. That was one of the reasons the plague spread so rapidly. All the billions of germs in a corpse were so immediately released.

'And it was because of all this that the bacteriologists had so little chance in fighting the germs. They were killed in their laboratories even as they studied the germ of the Scarlet Death. They were heroes. As fast as they perished, others stepped forth and took their places. It was in London that they first isolated it. The news was telegraphed everywhere. Trask was the name of the man who succeeded in this, but within thirty hours he was dead. Then came the struggle in all the laboratories to find something that would kill the plague germs. All drugs failed. You see, the problem was to get a drug, or serum, that would kill the germs in the body and not kill the body. They tried to fight it with other germs, to put into the body of a sick man germs that were the enemies of the plague germs – '

'And you can't see these germ-things, Granser,' Hare-Lip objected, 'and here you gabble, gabble, gabble about them as if they was anything, when they're nothing at all. Anything you can't see, ain't, that's what. Fighting things that ain't with things that ain't! They must have been all fools in them days. That's why they croaked. I ain't goin' to believe in such rot, I tell you that.'

Granser promptly began to weep, while Edwin hotly took up his defense.

'Look here, Hare-Lip, you believe in lots of things you can't see.' Hare-Lip shook his head.

'You believe in dead men walking about. You never seen one dead man walk about.'

'I tell you I seen 'em, last winter, when I was wolf-hunting with dad.'

'Well, you always spit when you cross running water,' Edwin challenged.

'That's to keep off bad luck,' was Hare-Lip's defence.

'You believe in bad luck?'

'Sure.'

'An' you ain't never seen bad luck,' Edwin concluded triumphantly. 'You're just as bad as Granser and his germs. You believe in what you don't see. Go on, Granser.'

Hare-Lip, crushed by this metaphysical defeat, remained silent, and the old man went on. Often and often, though this narrative must not be clogged by the details, was Granser's tale interrupted while the boys squabbled among themselves. Also, among themselves they kept up a constant, low-voiced exchange of explanation and conjecture, as they strove to follow the old man into his unknown and vanished world.

'The Scarlet Death broke out in San Francisco. The first death came on a Monday morning. By Thursday they were dying like flies in Oakland and

San Francisco. They died everywhere – in their beds, at their work, walking along the street. It was on Tuesday that I saw my first death – Miss Colibran, one of my students, sitting right there before my eyes, in my lecture-room. I noticed her face while I was talking. It had suddenly turned scarlet. I ceased speaking and could only look at her, for the first fear of the plague was already on all of us and we knew that it had come. The young women screamed and ran out of the room. So did the young men run out, all but two. Miss Colibran's convulsions were very mild and lasted less than a minute. One of the young men fetched her a glass of water. She drank only a little of it, and cried out: "My feet! All sensation has left them."

'After a minute she said, "I have no feet. I am unaware that I have any feet. And my knees are cold. I can scarcely feel that I – have knees."

'She lay on the floor, a bundle of notebooks under her head. And we could do nothing. The coldness and the numbness crept up past her hips to her heart, and when it reached her heart she was dead. In fifteen minutes, by the clock – I timed it – she was dead, there, in my own classroom, dead. And she was a very beautiful, strong, healthy young woman. And from the first sign of the plague to her death only fifteen minutes elapsed. That will show you how swift was the Scarlet Death.

'Yet in those few minutes I remained with the dying woman in my classroom, the alarm had spread over the university; and the students, by thousands, all of them, had deserted the lecture-room and laboratories. When I emerged, on my way to make report to the President of the Faculty, I found the university deserted. Across the campus were several stragglers hurrying for their homes. Two of them were running.

'President Hoag I found in his office, all alone, looking very old and very gray, with a multitude of wrinkles in his face that I had never seen before. At the sight of me, he pulled himself to his feet and tottered away to the inner office, banging the door after him and locking it. You see, he knew I had been exposed, and he was afraid. He shouted to me through the door to go away. I shall never forget my feelings. as I walked down the silent corridors and out across that deserted campus. I was not afraid. I had been exposed, and I looked upon myself as already dead. It was not that, but a feeling of awful depression that impressed me. Everything had stopped. It was like the end of the world to me – my world. I had been born within sight and sound of the university. It had been my predestined career. My father had been a professor there before me, and his father before him. For a century and a half had this university, like a splendid machine, been running steadily on. And now, in an instant, it had stopped. It was like seeing the sacred flame die down on some thrice-sacred altar. I was shocked, unutterably shocked.

'When I arrived home, my housekeeper screamed as I entered, and fled away. And when I rang, I found the housemaid had likewise fled. I investigated. In the kitchen I found the cook on the point of departure. But she screamed, too, and in her haste dropped a suitcase of her personal belongings and ran out of the house and across the grounds, still screaming. I can hear her scream to this day. You see, we did not act in this way when ordinary diseases smote us. We were always calm over such things, and sent for the doctors and nurses who knew just what to do. But this was different. It struck so suddenly, and killed so swiftly, and never missed a stroke. When the scarlet rash appeared on a person's face, that person was marked by death. There was never a known case of a recovery.

'I was alone in my big house. As I have told you often before, in those days we could talk with one another over wires or through the air. The telephone bell rang, and I found my brother talking to me. He told me that he was not coming home for fear of catching the plague from me, and that he had taken our two sisters to stop at Professor Bacon's home. He advised me to remain where I was, and wait to find out whether or not I had caught the plague.

'To all of this I agreed, staying in my house and for the first time in my life attempting to cook. And the plague did not come out on me. By means of the telephone I could talk with whomsoever I pleased and get the news. Also, there were the newspapers, and I ordered all of them to be thrown up to my door so that I could know what was happening with the rest of the world.

'New York City and Chicago were in chaos. And what happened with them was happening in all the large cities. A third of the New York police were dead. Their chief was also dead, likewise the mayor. All law and order had ceased. The bodies were lying in the streets unburied. All railroads and vessels carrying food and such things into the great city had ceased running, and mobs of the hungry poor were pillaging the stores and warehouses. Murder and robbery and drunkenness were everywhere. Already the people had fled from the city by millions – at first the rich, in their private motor-cars and dirigibles, and then the great mass of the population, on foot, carrying the plague with them, themselves starving and pillaging the farmers and all the towns and villages on the way.

'The man who sent this news, the wireless operator, was alone with his instrument on the top of a lofty building. The people remaining in the city – he estimated them at several hundred thousand – had gone mad from fear and drink, and on all sides of him great fires were raging. He was a hero, that man who stayed by his post – an obscure newspaperman, most likely.

'For twenty-four hours, he said, no transatlantic airships had arrived, and no more messages were coming from England. He did state, though, that a message from Berlin – that's in Germany – announced that Hoffmeyer, a bacteriologist of the Metchnikoff School, had discovered the serum for the plague. That was the last word, to this day, that we of America ever received from Europe. If Hoffmeyer discovered the serum, it was too late, or otherwise, long ere this, explorers from Europe would have come looking for us. We can only conclude that what happened in America happened in Europe, and that, at the best, some several score may have survived the Scarlet Death on that whole continent.

'For one day longer the dispatches continued to come from New York. Then they, too, ceased. The man who had sent them, perched in his lofty building, had either died of the plague or been consumed in the great conflagrations he had described as raging around him. And what had occurred in New York had been duplicated in all the other cities. It was the same in San Francisco, and Oakland, and Berkeley. By Thursday the people were dying so rapidly that their corpses could not be handled, and dead bodies lay everywhere. Thursday night the panic outrush for the country began. Imagine, my grandsons, people, thicker than the salmon-run you have seen on the Sacramento River, pouring out of the cities by millions, madly over the country, in vain attempt to escape the ubiquitous death. You see, they carried the germs with them. Even the airships of the rich, fleeing for mountain and desert fastnesses, carried the germs.

'Hundreds of these airships escaped to Hawaii, and not only did they bring the plague with them, but they found the plague already there before them. This we learned by the dispatches, until all order in San Francisco vanished, and there were no operators left at their posts to receive or send. It was amazing, astounding, this loss of communication with the world. It was exactly as if the world had ceased, been blotted out. For sixty years that world has no longer existed for me. I know there must be such places as New York, Europe, Asia, and Africa; but not one word has been heard of them – not in sixty years. With the coming of the Scarlet Death the world fell apart, absolutely, irretrievably. Ten thousand years of culture and civilization passed in the twinkling of an eye, "lapsed like foam".

'I was telling about the airships of the rich. They carried the plague with them and no matter where they fled, they died. I never encountered but one survivor of any of them – Mungerson. He was afterwards a Santa Rosan, and he married my eldest daughter. He came into the tribe eight years after the plague. He was then nineteen years old, and he was compelled to wait twelve years more before he could marry. You see, there were no unmarried women, and some of the older daughters of the Santa Rosans were already bespoken. So he was forced to wait until my Mary had grown to sixteen years. It was his son, Gimp-Leg, who was killed last year by the mountain lion.

'Mungerson was eleven years old at the time of the plague. His father was one of the Industrial Magnates, a very wealthy, powerful man. It was on his airship, the *Condor*, that they were fleeing, with all the family, for the wilds of British Columbia, which is far to the north of here. But there was some accident, and they were wrecked near Mount Shasta. You have heard of that mountain. It is far to the north. The plague broke out amongst them, and this boy of eleven was the only survivor. For eight years he was alone, wandering over a deserted land and looking vainly for his own kind. And at last, travelling south, he picked up with us, the Santa Rosans.

'But I am ahead of my story. When the great exodus from the cities around San Francisco Bay began, and while the telephones were still working, I talked with my brother. I told him this flight from the cities was insanity, that there were no symptoms of the plague in me, and that the thing for us to do was to isolate ourselves and our relatives in some safe place. We decided on the Chemistry Building, at the university, and we planned to lay in a supply of provisions, and by force of arms to prevent any other persons from forcing their presence upon us after we had retired to our refuge.

'All this being arranged, my brother begged me to stay in my own house for at least twenty-four hours more, on the chance of the plague developing in me. To this I agreed, and he promised to come for me next day. We talked on over the details of the provisioning and the defending of the Chemistry Building until the telephone died. It died in the midst of our conversation. That evening there were no electric lights, and I was alone in my house in the darkness. No more newspapers were being printed, so I had no knowledge of what was taking place outside. I heard sounds of rioting and of pistol shots, and from my windows I could see the glare in the sky of some conflagration in the direction of Oakland. It was a night of terror. I did not sleep a wink. A man – why and how I do not know – was killed on the sidewalk in front of the house. I heard the rapid reports of an automatic pistol, and a few minutes later the wounded wretch crawled up to my door, moaning and crying out for help. Arming myself with two automatics, I went to him. By the light of a match I ascertained that while he was dying of the bullet wounds, at the same time the plague was on him. I fled indoors, whence I heard him moan and cry out for half an hour longer.

'In the morning, my brother came to me. I had gathered into a hand-bag what things of value I purposed taking, but when I saw his face I knew that he would never accompany me to the Chemistry Building. The plague was on him. He intended shaking my hand, but I went back hurriedly before him.

'Look at yourself in the mirror,' I commanded.

'He did so, and at sight of his scarlet face, the color deepening as he looked at it, he sank down nervelessly in a chair.

' "My God!" he said. "I've got it. Don't come near me. I am a dead man." Then the convulsions seized him. He was two hours in dying, and he was conscious to the last, complaining about the coldness and loss of sensation in his feet, his calves, his thighs, until at last it was his heart and he was dead.

'That was the way the Scarlet Death slew. I caught up my handbag and fled. The sights in the streets were terrible. One stumbled on bodies everywhere. Some were not yet dead. And even as you looked, you saw men sink down with the death fastened upon them. There were numerous fires burning in Berkeley, while Oakland and San Francisco were apparently being swept by vast conflagrations. The smoke of the burning filled the heavens, so that the mid-day was as a gloomy twilight, and, in the shifts of wind, sometimes the sun shone through dimly, a dull red orb. Truly, my grandsons, it was like the last days of the end of the world.

'There were numerous stalled motor-cars, showing that the gasoline and the engine supplies of the garages had given out. I remember one such car. A man and a woman lay back dead in the seats, and on the pavement near it were two more women and a child. Strange and terrible sights there were on every hand. People slipped by silently, furtively, like ghosts – white-faced women carrying infants in their arms; fathers leading children by the hand; singly, and in couples, and in families – all fleeing out of the city of death. Some carried supplies of food, others blankets and valuables, and there were many who carried nothing.

'There was a grocery store – a place where food was sold. The man to whom it belonged – I knew him well – a quiet, sober, but stupid and obstinate fellow, was defending it. The windows and doors had been broken in, but he, inside, hiding behind a counter, was discharging his pistol at a number of men on the sidewalk who were breaking in. In the entrance were several bodies – of men, I decided, whom he had killed earlier in the day. Even as I looked on from a distance, I saw one of the robbers break the windows of the adjoining store, a place where shoes were sold, and deliberately set fire to it. I did not go to the groceryman's assistance. The time for such acts had already passed. Civilization was crumbling, and it was each for himself.'

4

'I went away hastily, down a cross-street, and at the first corner I saw another tragedy. Two men of the working class had caught a man and a woman with two children, and were robbing them. I knew the man by sight though I had never been introduced to him. He was a poet whose verses I had long admired. Yet I did not go to his help, for at the moment I came upon the scene there was a pistol shot, and I saw him sinking to the ground. The woman screamed, and she was felled with a fist-blow by one of the brutes. I cried out threateningly, whereupon they discharged their pistols at me and I ran away around the corner. Here I was blocked by an advancing conflagration. The buildings on both sides were burning, and the street was filled with smoke and flame. From somewhere in that murk came a woman's voice calling shrilly for help. But I did not go to her. A man's heart turned to iron amid such scenes, and one heard all too many appeals for help.

'Returning to the corner, I found the two robbers were gone. The poet and his wife lay dead on the pavement. It was a shocking sight. The two children had vanished – whither I could not tell. And I knew, now, why it was that the fleeing persons I encountered slipped along so furtively and with such white faces. In the midst of our civilization, down in our slums and labor-ghettos, we had bred a race of barbarians, of savages; and now, in the time of our calamity, they turned upon us like the wild beasts they were and destroyed us. And they destroyed themselves as well. They inflamed themselves with strong drink and committed a thousand atrocities, quarreling and killing one another in the general madness. One group of working-men I saw, of the better sort, who had banded together, and, with their women and children in their midst, the sick and aged in litters and being carried, and with a number of horses pulling a truck-load of provisions, they were fighting their way out of the city. They made a fine spectacle as they came down the street through the drifting smoke, though they nearly shot me when I first appeared in their path. As they went by, one of their leaders shouted out to me in apologetic explanation. He said they were killing the robbers and looters on sight, and that they had thus banded together as the only means by which to escape the prowlers.

'It was here that I saw for the first time what I was soon to see so often. One of the marching men had suddenly shown the unmistakable mark of the plague. Immediately those about him drew away, and he, without a remonstrance, stepped out of his place to let them pass on. A woman, most probably his wife, attempted to follow him. She was leading a little boy by the hand. But the husband commanded her sternly to go on, while others laid hands on her and restrained her from following him. This I saw, and I saw the man also, with his scarlet blaze of face, step into a doorway on the opposite side of the street. I heard the report of his pistol, and saw him sink lifeless to the ground.

'After being turned aside twice again by advancing fires, I succeeded in getting through to the university. On the edge of the campus I came upon a party of university folk who were going in the direction of the Chemistry Building. They were all family men, and their families were with them, including the nurses and the servants. Professor Badminton greeted me, and I had difficulty in recognizing him. Somewhere he had gone through flames, and his beard was singed off. About his head was a bloody bandage, and his clothes were filthy. He told me he had been cruelly beaten by prowlers, and that his brother had been killed the previous night, in the defence of their dwelling.

'Midway across the campus, he pointed suddenly to Mrs Swinton's face. The unmistakable scarlet was there. Immediately all the other women set up a screaming and began to run away from her. Her two children were with a nurse, and these also ran with the women. But her husband, Doctor Swinton, remained with her.

'"Go on, Smith," he told me. "Keep an eye on the children. As for me, I shall stay with my wife. I know she is as already dead, but I can't leave her. Afterwards, if I escape, I shall come to the Chemistry Building, and do you watch for me and let me in."

'I left him bending over his wife and soothing her last moments, while I ran to overtake the party. We were the last to be admitted to the Chemistry Building. After that, with our automatic rifles we maintained our isolation. By our plans, we had arranged for a company of sixty to be in this refuge. Instead, every one of the number originally planned had added relatives and friends and whole families until there were over four hundred souls. But the Chemistry Building was large, and, standing by itself, was in no danger of being burned by the great fires that raged everywhere in the city.

'A large quantity of provisions had been gathered, and a food committee took charge of it, issuing rations daily to the various families and groups that arranged themselves into messes. A number of committees were appointed, and we developed a very efficient organization. I was on the committee of defence, though for the first day no prowlers came near. We could see them in the distance, however, and by the smoke of their fires knew that several camps of them were occupying the far edge of the campus. Drunkenness was rife, and often we heard them singing ribald songs or insanely shouting. While the world crashed to ruin about them and all the air was filled with the smoke of its burning, these low creatures gave rein to their bestiality and fought and drank and died. And after all, what did it matter? Everybody died anyway, the good and the bad, the efficients and the weaklings, those that loved to live and those that scorned to live. They passed. Everything passed.

'When twenty-four hours had gone by and no signs of the plague were apparent, we congratulated ourselves and set about digging a well. You have seen the great iron pipes which in those days carried water to all the city-dwellers. We feared that the fires in the city would burst the pipes and empty the reservoirs. So we tore up the cement floor of the central court of the Chemistry Building and dug a well. There were many young men, undergraduates, with us, and we worked night and day on the well. And our fears were confirmed. Three hours before we reached water, the pipes went dry.

'A second twenty-four hours passed, and still the plague did not appear among us. We thought we were saved. But we did not know what I afterwards decided to be true, namely, that the period of the incubation of the plague germs in a human's body was a matter of a number of days. It slew so swiftly when once it manifested itself, that we were led to believe that the period of incubation was equally swift. So, when two days had left us unscathed, we were elated with the idea that we were free of the contagion.

'But the third day disillusioned us. I can never forget the night preceding it. I had charge of the night guards from eight to twelve, and from the roof of the building I watched the passing of all man's glorious works. So terrible were the local conflagrations that all the sky was lighted up. One could read the finest print in the red glare. All the world seemed wrapped in flames. San Francisco spouted smoke and fire from a score of vast conflagrations that were like so many active volcanoes. Oakland, San Leandro, Haywards – all were burning; and to the northward, clear to Point Richmond, other fires were at work. It was an awe-inspiring spectacle. Civilization, my grandsons, civilization was passing in a sheet of flame and a breath of death. At ten o'clock that night, the great powder magazines at Point Pinole exploded in rapid succession. So terrific were the concussions that the strong building rocked as in an earthquake, while every pane of glass was broken. It was then that I left the roof and went down the long corridors, from room to room, quieting the alarmed women and telling them what had happened.

'An hour later, at a window on the ground floor, I heard pandemonium break out in the camps of the prowlers. There were cries and screams, and shots from many pistols. As we afterward conjectured, this fight had been precipitated by an attempt on the part of those that were well to drive out those that were sick. At any rate, a number of the plague-stricken prowlers escaped across the campus and drifted against our doors. We warned them back, but they cursed us and discharged a fusillade from their pistols. Professor Merryweather, at one of the windows, was instantly killed, the bullet striking him squarely between the eyes. We opened fire in turn, and all the prowlers fled away with the exception of three. One was a woman. The plague was on them and they were reckless. Like foul fiends, there in the red glare from the skies, with faces blazing, they continued to curse us and fire at us. One of the men I shot with my own hand. After that the other man and the woman, still cursing us, lay down under our windows, where we were compelled to watch them die of the plague.

'The situation was critical. The explosions of the powder magazines had broken all the windows of the Chemistry Building, so that we were exposed to the germs from the corpses. The sanitary committee was called upon to act, and it responded nobly. Two men were required to go out and remove the corpses, and this meant the probable sacrifice of their own lives, for, having performed the task, they were not to be permitted to re-enter the building. One of the professors, who was a bachelor, and one of the undergraduates volunteered. They bade goodbye to us and went forth. They were heroes. They gave up their lives that four hundred others might live. After they had performed their work, they stood for a moment, at a distance, looking at us wistfully. Then they waved their hands in farewell and went away slowly across the campus toward the burning city.

'And yet it was all useless. The next morning the first one of us was smitten with the plague – a little nurse-girl in the family of Professor Stout. It was no time for weak-kneed, sentimental policies. On the chance that she might be the only one, we thrust her forth from the building and commanded her to be gone. She went away slowly across the campus, wringing her hands and crying pitifully. We felt like brutes, but what were we to do? There were four hundred of us, and individuals had to be sacrificed.

'In one of the laboratories three families had domiciled themselves, and that afternoon we found among them no less than four corpses and seven cases of the plague in all its different stages.

'Then it was that the horror began. Leaving the dead lie, we forced the living ones to segregate themselves in another room. The plague began to break out among the rest of us, and as fast as the symptoms appeared, we sent the stricken ones to these segregated rooms. We compelled them to walk there by themselves, so as to avoid laying hands on them. It was heartrending. But still the plague raged among us, and room after room was filled with the dead and dying. And so we who were yet clean retreated to the next floor and to the next, before this sea of the dead, that, room by room and floor by floor, inundated the building.

'The place became a charnel house, and in the middle of the night the survivors fled forth, taking nothing with them except arms and ammunition and a heavy store of tinned foods. We camped on the opposite side of the campus from the prowlers, and, while some stood guard, others of us volunteered to scout into the city in quest of horses, motor-cars, carts, and wagons, or anything that would carry our provisions and enable us to emulate the banded working-men I had seen fighting their way out to the open country.

'I was one of these scouts; and Doctor Hoyle, remembering that his motor-car had been left behind in his home garage, told me to look for it. We scouted in pairs, and Dombey, a young undergraduate, accompanied me. We had to cross half a mile of the residence portion of the city to get to Doctor Hoyle's home. Here the buildings stood apart, in the midst of trees and grassy lawns, and here the fires had played freaks, burning whole blocks, skipping blocks and often skipping a single house in a block. And here, too, the prowlers were still at their work . . . We carried our automatic pistols openly in our hands, and looked desperate enough, forsooth, to keep them from attacking us. But at Doctor Hoyle's house the thing happened. Untouched by fire, even as we came to it the smoke of flames burst forth.

'The miscreant who had set fire to it staggered down the steps and out along the driveway. Sticking out of his coat pockets were bottles of whiskey, and he was very drunk. My first impulse was to shoot him, and I have never ceased regretting that I did not. Staggering and maundering to himself, with bloodshot eyes, and a raw and bleeding slash down one side of his bewhiskered face, he was altogether the most nauseating specimen of degradation and filth I had ever encountered. I did not shoot him, and he leaned against a tree on the lawn to let us go by. It was the most absolute, wanton act. Just as we were opposite him, he suddenly drew a pistol and shot Dombey through the head. The next instant I shot him. But it was too late. Dombey expired without a groan, immediately. I doubt if he even knew what had happened to him.

'Leaving the two corpses, I hurried on past the burning house to the garage, and there found Doctor Hoyle's motor-car. The tanks were filled with gasoline, and it was ready for use. And it was in this car that I threaded the streets of the ruined city and came back to the survivors on the campus. The other scouts returned, but none had been so fortunate. Professor Fairmead had found a Shetland pony, but the poor creature, tied in a stable and abandoned for days, was so weak from want of food and water that it could carry no burden at all. Some of the men were for turning it loose, but I insisted that we should lead it along with us, so that, if we got out of food, we would have it to eat.

'There were forty-seven of us when we started, many being women and children. The President of the Faculty, an old man to begin with, and now hopelessly broken by the awful happenings of the past week, rode in the motor-car with several young children and the aged mother of Professor Fairmead. Wathope, a young professor of English, who had a grievous bullet-wound in his leg, drove the car. The rest of us walked, Professor Fairmead leading the pony.

'It was what should have been a bright summer day, but the smoke from the burning world filled the sky, through which the sun shone murkily, a dull and lifeless orb, blood-red and ominous. But we had grown accustomed to that blood-red sun. With the smoke it was different. It bit into our nostrils and eyes, and there was not one of us whose eyes were not bloodshot. We directed our course to the south-east through the endless miles of suburban residences, travelling along where the first swells of low hills rose from the flat of the central city. It was by this way, only, that we could expect to gain the country.

'Our progress was painfully slow. The women and children could not walk fast. They did not dream of walking, my grandsons, in the way all people walk today. In truth, none of us knew how to walk. It was not until after the plague that I learned really to walk. So it was that the pace of the slowest was the pace of all, for we dared not separate on account of the prowlers. There were not so many now of these human beasts of prey. The plague had already well diminished their numbers, but enough still lived to be a constant menace to us. Many of the beautiful residences were untouched by fire, yet smoking ruins were everywhere. The prowlers, too, seemed to have got over their insensate desire to burn, and it was more rarely that we saw houses freshly on fire.

'Several of us scouted among the private garages in search of motor-cars and gasoline. But in this we were unsuccessful. The first great flights from the cities had swept all such utilities away. Calgan, a fine young man, was lost in this work. He was shot by prowlers while crossing a lawn. Yet this was our only casualty, though, once, a drunken brute deliberately opened fire on all of us. Luckily, he fired wildly, and we shot him before he had done any hurt.

'At Fruitvale, still in the heart of the magnificent residence section of the city, the plague again smote us. Professor Fairmead was the victim. Making signs to us that his mother was not to know, he turned aside into the grounds of a beautiful mansion. He sat down forlornly on the steps of the front veranda, and I, having lingered, waved him a last farewell. That night, several miles beyond Fruitvale and still in the city, we made camp. And that night we shifted camp twice to get away from our dead. In the morning there were thirty of us. I shall never forget the President of the Faculty. During the morning's march his wife, who was walking, betrayed the fatal symptoms, and when she drew aside to let us go on, he insisted on leaving the motor-car and remaining with her. There was quite a discussion about this, but in the end we gave in. It was just as well, for we knew not which ones of us, if any, might ultimately escape.

'That night, the second of our march, we camped beyond Haywards in the first stretches of country. And in the morning there were eleven of us that lived. Also, during the night, Wathope, the professor with the wounded leg, deserted us in the motor-car. He took with him his sister and his mother and most of our tinned provisions. It was that day, in the afternoon, while resting by the wayside, that I saw the last airship I shall ever see. The smoke was much thinner here in the country, and I first sighted the ship drifting and veering helplessly at an elevation of two thousand feet. What had happened I could not conjecture, but even as we looked we saw her bow dip down lower and lower. Then the bulkheads of the various gas-chambers must have burst, for, quite perpendicular, she fell like a plummet to the earth. And from that day to this I have not seen another airship. Often and often, during the next few years, I scanned the sky for them, hoping against hope that somewhere in the world civiliz-ation had survived. But it was not to be. What happened with us in California must have happened with everybody everywhere.

'Another day, and at Niles there were three of us. Beyond Niles, in the middle of the highway, we found Wathope. The motor-car had broken down, and there, on the rugs which they had spread on the ground, lay the bodies of his sister, his mother, and himself. 'Wearied by the unusual exercise of continual walking, that night I slept heavily. In the morning

I was alone in the world. Canfield and Parsons, my last companions, were dead of the plague. Of the four hundred that sought shelter in the Chemistry Building, and of the forty-seven that began the march, I alone remained – I and the Shetland pony. Why this should be so there is no explaining. I did not catch the plague, that is all. I was immune. I was merely the one lucky man in a million – just as every survivor was one in a million, or, rather, in several millions, for the proportion was at least that.'

5

'For two days I sheltered in a pleasant grove where there had been no deaths. In those two days, while badly depressed and believing that my turn would come at any moment, nevertheless I rested and recuperated. So did the pony. And on the third day, putting what small store of tinned provisions I possessed on the pony's back, I started on across a very lonely land. Not a live man, woman, child, did I encounter, though the dead were everywhere. Food, however, was abundant. The land then was not as it is now. It was all cleared of trees and brush, and it was cultivated. The food for millions of mouths was growing, ripening, and going to waste. From the fields and orchards I gathered vegetables, fruits, and berries. Around the deserted farmhouses I got eggs and caught chickens. And frequently I found supplies of tinned provisions in the store-rooms.

'A strange thing was what was taking place with all the domestic animals. Everywhere they were going wild and preying on one another. The chickens and ducks were the first to be destroyed, while the pigs were the first to go wild, followed by the cats. Nor were the dogs long in adapting themselves to the changed conditions. There was a veritable plague of dogs. They devoured the corpses, barked and howled during the nights, and in the daytime slunk about in the distance. As the time went by, I noticed a change in their behavior. At first they were apart from one another, very suspicious and very prone to fight. But after a not very long while they began to come together and run in packs. The dog, you see, always was a social animal, and this was true before ever he came to be domesticated by man. In the last days of the world before the plagues there were many many very different kinds of dogs – dogs without hair and dogs with warm fur, dogs so small that they would make scarcely a mouthful for other dogs that were as large as mountain lions. Well, all the small dogs, and the weak types were killed by their fellows. Also, the very large ones not adapted for the wild life bred out. As a result, the many different kinds of dogs disappeared, and there remained, running in packs, the medium-sized wolfish dogs that you know today.'

'But the cats don't run in packs, Granser,' Hoo-Hoo objected.

'The cat was never a social animal. As one writer in the nineteenth century said, the cat walks by himself. He always walked by himself, from before the time he was tamed by man, down through the long ages of domestication, to today when once more he is wild.

'The horses also went wild, and all the fine breeds we had degenerated into the small mustang horse you know today. The cows likewise went wild, as did the pigeons and the sheep. And that a few of the chickens survived you know yourself. But the wild chicken of today is quite a different thing from the chickens we had in those days.

'But I must go on with my story. I travelled through a deserted land. As the time went by I began to yearn more and more for human beings. But I never found one, and I grew lonelier and lonelier. I crossed Livermore Valley and the mountains between it and the great valley of the San Joaquin. You have never seen that valley, but it is very large and it is the home of the wild horse. There are great droves there, thousands and tens of thousands. I revisited it thirty years after, so I know. You think there are lots of wild horses down here in the coast valleys, but they are as nothing compared with those of the San Joaquin. Strange to say, the cows, when they went wild, went back into the lower mountains. Evidently they were better able to protect themselves there.

'In the country districts the ghouls and prowlers had been less in evidence, for I found many villages and towns untouched by fire. But they were filled by the pestilential dead, and I passed by without exploring them. It was near Lathrop that, out of my loneliness, I picked up a pair of collie dogs that were so newly free that they were urgently willing to return to their allegiance to man. These collies accompanied me for many years, and the strains of them are in those very dogs there that you boys have today. But in sixty years the collie strain has worked out. These brutes are more like domesticated wolves than anything else.'

Hare-Lip rose to his feet, glanced to see that the goats were safe, and looked at the sun's position in the afternoon sky, advertising impatience at the prolixity of the old man's tale. Urged to hurry by Edwin, Granser went on.

'There is little more to tell. With my two dogs and my pony, and riding a horse I had managed to capture, I crossed the San Joaquin and went on to a wonderful valley in the Sierras called Yosemite. In the great hotel there I found a prodigious supply of tinned provisions. The pasture was abundant, as was the game, and the river that ran through the valley was full of trout. I remained there three years in an utter loneliness that none but a man who has once been highly civilized can understand. Then I could stand it no more. I felt that I was going crazy. Like the dog, I

was a social animal and I needed my kind. I reasoned that since I had
survived the plague, there was a possibility that others had survived. Also,
I reasoned that after three years the plague germs must all be gone and
the land be clean again.

'With my horse and dogs and pony, I set out. Again I crossed the San
Joaquin Valley, the mountains beyond, and came down into Livermore
Valley. The change in those three years was amazing. All the land had
been splendidly tilled, and now I could scarcely recognize it, such was the
sea of rank vegetation that had overrun the agricultural handiwork of
man. You see, the wheat, the vegetables, and orchard trees had always
been cared for and nursed by man, so that they were soft and tender. The
weeds and wild bushes and such things, on the contrary, had always
been fought by man, so that they were tough and resistant. As a result,
when the hand of man was removed, the wild vegetation smothered and
destroyed practically all the domesticated vegetation. The coyotes were
greatly increased, and it was at this time that I first encountered wolves,
straying in twos and threes and small packs down from the regions where
they had always persisted.

'It was at Lake Temescal, not far from the one-time city of Oakland, that I came upon the first live human beings. Oh, my grandsons,
how can I describe to you my emotion, when, astride my horse and
dropping down the hillside to the lake, I saw the smoke of a campfire
rising through the trees. Almost did my heart stop beating. I felt that I
was going crazy. Then I heard the cry of a babe – a human babe. And
dogs barked, and my dogs answered. I did not know but what I was the
one human alive in the whole world. It could not be true that here were
others – smoke and the cry of a babe.

'Emerging on the lake, there, before my eyes, not a hundred yards
away, I saw a man, a large man. He was standing on an outjutting rock
and fishing. I was overcome. I stopped my horse. I tried to call out but
could not. I waved my hand. It seemed to me that the man looked at me,
but he did not appear to wave. Then I laid my head on my arms there in
the saddle. I was afraid to look again, for I knew it was an hallucination,
and I knew that if I looked the man would be gone. And so precious was
the hallucination, that I wanted it to persist yet a little while. I knew, too,
that as long as I did not look it would persist.

'Thus I remained, until I heard my dogs snarling, and a man's voice.
What do you think the voice said? I will tell you. It said: "Where in hell
did you come from?"

'Those were the words, the exact words. That was what your other
grandfather said to me, Hare-Lip, when he greeted me there on the

shore of Lake Temescal fifty-seven years ago. And they were the most ineffable words I have ever heard. I opened my eyes, and there he stood before me, a large, dark, hairy man, heavy jawed, slant-browed, fierce-eyed. How I got off my horse I do not know. But it seemed that the next I knew I was clasping his hand with both of mine and crying. I would have embraced him, but he was ever a narrow-minded, suspicious man, and he drew away from me. Yet did I cling to his hand and cry.'

Granser's voice faltered and broke at the recollection, and the weak tears streamed down his cheeks while the boys looked on and giggled. 'Yet did I cry,' he continued, 'and desire to embrace him, though the Chauffeur was a brute, a perfect brute – the most abhorrent man I have ever known. His name was . . . strange, how I have forgotten his name. Everybody called him Chauffeur – it was the name of his occupation, and it stuck. That is how, to this day, the tribe he founded is called the Chauffeur Tribe.

'He was a violent, unjust man. Why the plague germs spared him I can never understand. It would seem, in spite of our old metaphysical notions about absolute justice, that there is no justice in the universe. Why did he live? – an iniquitous, moral monster, a blot on the face of nature, a cruel, relentless, bestial cheat as well. All he could talk about was motor-cars, machinery, gasoline, and garages – and especially, and with huge delight, of his mean pilferings and sordid swindlings of the persons who had employed him in the days before the coming of the plague. And yet he was spared, while hundreds of millions, yea, billions, of better men were destroyed.

'I went on with him to his camp, and there I saw her, Vesta, the one woman. It was glorious and . . . pitiful. There she was, Vesta Van Warden, the young wife of John Van Warden, clad in rags, with marred and scarred and toil-calloused hands, bending over the campfire and doing scullion work – she, Vesta, who had been born to the purple of the greatest baronage of wealth the world has ever known. John Van Warden, her husband, worth one billion, eight hundred millions and President of the Board of Industrial Magnates, had been the ruler of America. Also, sitting on the International Board of Control, he had been one of the seven men who ruled the world. And she herself had come of equally noble stock. Her father, Philip Saxon, had been President of the Board of Industrial Magnates up to the time of his death. This office was in process of becoming hereditary, and had Philip Saxon had a son that son would have succeeded him. But his only child was Vesta, the perfect flower of generations of the highest culture this planet has ever pro-duced. It was not until the engagement between Vesta and Van Warden took place, that Saxon indicated the latter as his successor. It was, I am sure, a political marriage. I have reason to believe that Vesta never really loved her husband in the mad passionate way of which the poets used to sing. It was more like the marriages that obtained among crowned heads in the days before they were displaced by the Magnates.

'And there she was, boiling fish-chowder in a soot-covered pot, her glorious eyes inflamed by the acrid smoke of the open fire. Hers was a sad story. She was the one survivor in a million, as I had been, as the Chauffeur had been. On a crowning eminence of the Alameda Hills, overlooking San Francisco Bay, Van Warden had built a vast summer palace. It was surrounded by a park of a thousand acres. When the plague broke out, Van Warden sent her there. Armed guards patrolled the boundaries of the park, and nothing entered in the way of provisions or even mail matter that was not first fumigated. And yet did the plague enter, killing the guards at their posts, the servants at their tasks, sweeping away the whole army of retainers – or, at least, all of them who did not flee to die elsewhere. So it was that Vesta found herself the sole living person in the palace that had become a charnel house.

'Now the Chauffeur had been one of the servants that ran away. Returning, two months afterward, he discovered Vesta in a little summer pavilion where there had been no deaths and where she had established herself. He was a brute. She was afraid, and she ran away and hid among the trees. That night, on foot, she fled into the mountains – she, whose tender feet and delicate body had never known the bruise of stones nor the scratch of briars. He followed, and that night he caught her. He struck her. Do you understand? He beat her with those terrible fists of his and made her his slave. It was she who had to gather the firewood, build the fires, cook, and do all the degrading camp-labor – she, who had never performed a menial act in her life. These things he compelled her to do, while he, a proper savage, elected to lie around camp and look on. He did nothing, absolutely nothing, except on occasion to hunt meat or catch fish.'

'Good for Chauffeur,' Hare-Lip commented in an undertone to the other boys. 'I remember him before he died. He was a corker. But he did things, and he made things go. You know, Dad married his daughter, an' you ought to see the way he knocked the spots outa Dad. The Chauffeur was a son-of-a-gun. He made us kids stand around. Even when he was croakin', he reached out for me, once, an' laid my head open with that long stick he kept always beside him.' Hare-Lip rubbed his bullet head reminiscently, and the boys returned to the old man, who was maundering ecstatically about Vesta, the squaw of the founder of the Chauffeur Tribe.

'And so I say to you that you cannot understand the awfulness of the situation. The Chauffeur was a servant, understand, a servant. And he cringed, with bowed head, to such as she. She was a lord of life, both by birth and by marriage. The destinies of millions, such as he, she carried in the hollow of her pink-white hand. And, in the days before the plague, the slightest contact with such as he would have been pollution. Oh, I have seen it. Once, I remember, there was Mrs Goldwin, wife of one of the great magnates. It was on a landing stage, just as she was embarking in her private dirigible, that she dropped her parasol. A servant picked it up and made the mistake of handing it to her – to her, one of the greatest royal ladies of the land! She shrank back, as though he were a leper, and indicated her secretary to receive it. Also, she ordered her secretary to ascertain the creature's name and to see that he was immediately discharged from service. And such a woman was Vesta Van Warden. And her the Chauffeur beat and made his slave.

' . . . Bill – that was it; Bill, the Chauffeur. That was his name. He was a wretched, primitive man, wholly devoid of the finer instincts and chivalrous promptings of a cultured soul. No, there is no absolute justice, for to him fell that wonder of womanhood, Vesta Van Warden. The grievousness of this you will never understand, my grandsons; for you are yourselves primitive little savages, unaware of aught else but savagery. Why should Vesta not have been mine? I was a man of culture and refinement, a professor in a great university. Even so, in the time before the plague, such was her exalted position, she would not have deigned to know that I existed. Mark, then, the abysmal degradation to which she fell at the hands of the Chauffeur. Nothing less than the destruction of all mankind had made it possible that I should know her, look in her eyes, converse with her, touch her hand – ay, and love her and know that her feelings toward me were very kindly. I have reason to believe that she, even she, would have loved me, there being no other man in the world except the Chauffeur. Why, when it destroyed eight billions of souls, did not the plague destroy just one more man, and that man the Chauffeur?

'Once, when the Chauffeur was away fishing, she begged me to kill him. With tears in her eyes she begged me to kill him. But he was a strong and violent man, and I was afraid. Afterwards, I talked with him. I offered him my horse, my pony, my dogs, all that I possessed, if he would give Vesta to me. And he grinned in my face and shook his head. He was very insulting. He said that in the old days he had been a servant, had been dirt under the feet of men like me and of women like Vesta, and that now he had the greatest lady in the land to be servant to him and cook his food and nurse his brats. "You had your day before the plague," he said;

"but this is my day, and a damned good day it is. I wouldn't trade back to the old times for anything." Such words he spoke, but they are not his words. He was a vulgar, low-minded man, and vile oaths fell continually from his lips.

'Also, he told me that if he caught me making eyes at his woman he'd wring my neck and give her a beating as well. What was I to do? I was afraid. He was a brute. That first night, when I discovered the camp, Vesta and I had great talk about the things of our vanished world. We talked of art, and books, and poetry; and the Chauffeur listened and grinned and sneered. He was bored and angered by our way of speech which he did not comprehend, and finally he spoke up and said: "And this is Vesta Van Warden, one-time wife of Van Warden the Magnate – a high and stuck-up beauty, who is now my squaw. Eh, Professor Smith, times is changed, times is changed. Here, you, woman, take off my moccasins, and lively about it. I want Professor Smith to see how well I have you trained."

'I saw her clench her teeth, and the flame of revolt rise in her face. He drew back his gnarled fist to strike, and I was afraid, and sick at heart. I could do nothing to prevail against him. So I got up to go, and not be witness to such indignity. But the Chauffeur laughed and threatened me with a beating if I did not stay and behold. And I sat there, perforce, by the campfire on the shore of lake Temescal, and saw Vesta, Vesta Van Warden, kneel and remove the moccasins of that grinning, hairy, ape-like human brute.

'Oh, you do not understand, my grandsons. You have never known anything else, and you do not understand.

'"Halter-broke and bridle-wise," the Chauffeur gloated, while she performed that dreadful, menial task. "A trifle balky at times, Professor, a trifle balky; but a clout alongside the jaw makes her as meek and gentle as a lamb."

'And another time he said: "We've got to start all over and replenish the earth and multiply. You're handicapped, Professor. You ain't got no wife, and we're up against a regular Garden-of-Eden proposition. But I ain't proud. I'll tell you what, Professor." He pointed at their little infant, barely a year old. "There's your wife, though you'll have to wait till she grows up. It's rich, ain't it? We're all equals here, and I'm the biggest toad in the splash. But I ain't stuck up – not I. I do you the honor, Professor Smith, the very great honor of betrothing to you my and Vesta Van Warden's daughter. Ain't it cussed bad that Van Warden ain't here to see?"

6

'I lived three weeks of infinite torment there in the Chauffeur's camp. And then, one day, tiring of me, or of what to him was my bad effect on Vesta, he told me that the year before, wandering through the Contra Costa Hills to the Straits of Carquinez, across the Straits he had seen a smoke. This meant that there were still other human beings, and that for three weeks he had kept this inestimably precious information from me. I departed at once, with my dogs and horses, and journeyed across the Contra Costa Hills to the Straits. I saw no smoke on the other side, but at Port Costa discovered a small steel barge on which I was able to embark my animals. Old canvas which I found served me for a sail, and a southerly breeze fanned me across the Straits and up to the ruins of Vallejo. Here, on the outskirts of the city, I found evidences of a recently occupied camp. Many clam-shells showed me why these humans had come to the shores of the Bay. This was the Santa Rosa Tribe, and I followed its track along the old railroad right of way across the salt marshes to Sonoma Valley. Here, at the old brickyard at Glen Ellen, I came upon the camp. There were eighteen souls all told. Two were old men, one of whom was Jones, a banker. The other was Harrison, a retired pawnbroker, who had taken for wife the matron of the State Hospital for the Insane at Napa. Of all the persons of the city of Napa, and of all the other towns and villages in that rich and populous valley, she had been the only survivor. Next, there were the three young men – Cardiff and Hale, who had been farmers, and Wainwright, a common day-laborer. All three had found wives. To Hale, a crude, illiterate farmer, had fallen Isadore, the greatest prize, next to Vesta, of the women who came through the plague. She was one of the world's most noted singers, and the plague had caught her at San Francisco. She has talked with me for hours at a time, telling me of her adventures, until, at last, rescued by Hale in the Mendocino Forest Reserve, there had remained nothing for her to do but become his wife. But Hale was a good fellow, in spite of his illiteracy. He had a keen sense of justice and right-dealing, and she was far happier with him than was Vesta with the Chauffeur.

'The wives of Cardiff and Wainwright were ordinary women, accustomed to toil, with strong constitutions just the type for the wild new life which they were compelled to live. In addition were two adult idiots from the feeble-minded home at Eldredge, and five or six young children and infants born after the formation of the Santa Rosa Tribe. Also, there was Bertha. She was a good woman, Hare-Lip, in spite of the sneers of your father. Her I took for wife. She was the mother of your father, Edwin, and of yours, Hoo-Hoo. And it was our daughter, Vera, who married your father, Hare-Lip – your father, Sandow, who was the oldest son of Vesta Van Warden and the Chauffeur.

'And so it was that I became the nineteenth member of the Santa Rosa Tribe. There were only two outsiders added after me. One was Mungerson, descended from the Magnates, who wandered alone in the wilds of Northern California for eight years before he came south and joined us. He it was who waited twelve years more before he married my daughter, Mary. The other was Johnson, the man who founded the Utah Tribe. That was where he came from, Utah, a country that lies very far away from here, across the great deserts, to the east. It was not until twenty-seven years after the plague that Johnson reached California. In all that Utah region he reported but three survivors, himself one, and all men. For many years these three men lived and hunted together, until at last, desperate, fearing that with them the human race would perish utterly from the planet, they headed westward on the possibility of finding women survivors in California. Johnson alone came through the great desert, where his two companions died. He was forty-six years old when he joined us, and he married the fourth daughter of Isadore and Hale, and his eldest son married your aunt, Hare-Lip, who was the third daughter of Vesta and the Chauffeur. Johnson was a strong man, with a will of his own. And it was because of this that he seceded from the Santa Rosans and formed the Utah Tribe at San José. It is a small tribe – there are only nine in it; but, though he is dead, such was his influence and the strength of his breed, that it will grow into a strong tribe and play a leading part in the recivilization of the planet.

'There are only two other tribes that we know of – the Los Angelitos and the Carmelitos. The latter started from one man and woman. He was called Lopez, and he was descended from the ancient Mexicans and was very black. He was a cowherd in the ranges beyond Carmel, and his wife was a maidservant in the great Del Monte Hotel. It was seven years before we first got in touch with the Los Angelitos. They have a good country down there, but it is too warm. I estimate the present population of the world at between three hundred and fifty and four hundred – provided, of course, that there are no scattered little tribes elsewhere in the world. If there be such, we have not heard from them. Since Johnson crossed the desert from Utah, no word nor sign has come from the East or anywhere else. The great world which I knew in my boyhood and early manhood is gone. It has ceased to be. I am the last man who was alive in the days of the plague and who knows the wonders of that far-off time. We, who mastered the planet – its earth, and sea, and sky – and who were as very gods, now live in primitive savagery along the water-courses of this California country.

'But we are increasing rapidly – your sister, Hare-Lip, already has four children. We are increasing rapidly and making ready for a new climb toward civilization. In time, pressure of population will compel us to spread out, and a hundred generations from now we may expect our descendants to start across the Sierras, oozing slowly along, generation by generation, over the great continent to the colonization of the East – a new Aryan drift around the world.

'But it will be slow, very slow; we have so far to climb. We fell so hopelessly far. If only one physicist or one chemist had survived! But it was not to be, and we have forgotten everything. The Chauffeur started working in iron. He made the forge which we use to this day. But he was a lazy man, and when he died he took with him all he knew of metals and machinery. What was I to know of such things? I was a classical scholar, not a chemist. The other men who survived were not educated. Only two things did the Chauffeur accomplish – the brewing of strong drink and the growing of tobacco. It was while he was drunk, once, that he killed Vesta. I firmly believe that he killed Vesta in a fit of drunken cruelty though he always maintained that she fell into the lake and was drowned.

'And, my grandsons, let me warn you against the medicine-men. They call themselves doctors, travestying what was once a noble profession, but in reality they are medicine-men, devil-devil men, and they make for superstition and darkness. They are cheats and liars. But so debased and degraded are we, that we believe their lies. They, too, will increase in numbers as we increase, and they will strive to rule us. Yet are they liars and charlatans. Look at young Cross-Eyes, posing as a doctor, selling charms against sickness, giving good hunting, exchanging promises of fair weather for good meat and skins, sending the death stick, performing a thousand abominations. Yet I say to you, that when he says he can do these things, he lies. I, Professor Smith, Professor James Howard Smith, say that he lies. I have told him so to his teeth. Why has he not sent me the death-stick? Because he knows that with me it is without avail. But you, Hare-Lip, so deeply are you sunk in black superstition that did you awake this night and find the death-stick beside you, you would surely die. And you would die, not because of any virtues in the stick, but because you are a savage with the dark and clouded mind of a savage.

'The doctors must be destroyed, and all that was lost must be discovered over again. Wherefore, earnestly, I repeat unto you certain things which you must remember and tell to your children after you. You must tell them that when water is made hot by fire, there resides in it a wonderful thing called steam, which is stronger than ten thousand men and which can do all man's work for him. There are other very useful things. In the lightning flash resides a similarly strong servant of man, which was of old his slave and which some day will be his slave again.

'Quite a different thing is the alphabet. It is what enables me to know the meaning of fine markings, whereas you boys know only rude picture-writing. In that dry cave on Telegraph Hill, where you see me often go when the tribe is down by the sea, I have stored many books. In them is great wisdom Also, with them, I have placed a key to the alphabet, so that one who knows picture-writing may also know print. Some day men will read again; and then, if no accident has befallen my cave, they will know that Professor James Howard Smith once lived and saved for them the knowledge of the ancients.

'There is another little device that men inevitably will rediscover. It is called gunpowder. It was what enabled us to kill surely and at long distances. Certain things which are found in the ground, when combined in the right proportions, will make this gunpowder. What these things are, I have forgotten, or else I never knew. But I wish I did know. Then would I make powder, and then would I certainly kill Cross-Eyes and rid the land of superstition – '

'After I am man-grown I am going to give Cross-Eyes all the goats, and meat, and skins I can get, so that he'll teach me to be a doctor,' Hoo-Hoo asserted. 'And when I know, I'll make everybody else sit up and take notice. They'll get down in the dirt to me, you bet.'

The old man nodded his head solemnly, and murmured: 'Strange it is to hear the vestiges and remnants of the complicated Aryan speech falling from the lips of a filthy little skin-clad savage. All the world is topsy-turvy. And it has been topsy-turvy ever since the plague.'

'You won't make me sit up,' Hare-Lip boasted to the would-be medicine-man. 'If I paid you for a sending of the death-stick and it didn't work, I'd bust in your head – understand, you Hoo-Hoo, you?'

'I'm going to get Granser to remember this here gunpowder stuff,' Edwin said softly, 'and then I'll have you all on the run. You, Hare-Lip, will do my fighting for me and get my meat for me, and you, Hoo-Hoo, will send the death-stick for me and make everybody afraid. And if I catch Hare-Lip trying to bust your head, Hoo-Hoo, I'll fix him with that same gunpowder. Granser ain't such a fool as you think, and I'm going to listen to him and some day I'll be boss over the whole bunch of you.'

The old man shook his head sadly, and said: 'The gunpowder will come. Nothing can stop it – the same old story over and over. Man will increase, and men will fight. The gunpowder will enable men to kill millions of men, and in this way only, by fire and blood, will a new civilization, in some remote day, be evolved. And of what profit will it be? Just as the old civilization passed, so will the new. It may take fifty thousand years to build, but it will pass. All things pass.

'Only remain cosmic force and matter, ever in flux, ever acting and reacting and realizing the eternal types – the priest, the soldier, and the king. Out of the mouths of babes comes the wisdom of all the ages. Some will fight, some will rule, some will pray; and all the rest will toil and suffer sore while on their bleeding carcasses is reared again, and yet again, without end, the amazing beauty and surpassing wonder of the civilized state. It were just as well that I destroyed those cave-stored books – whether they remain or perish, all their old truths will be discovered, their old lies lived and handed down. What is the profit – '

Hare-Lip leaped to his feet, giving a quick glance at the pasturing goats and the afternoon sun.

'Gee!' he muttered to Edwin. 'The old geezer gets more long-winded every day. Let's pull for camp.'

While the other two, aided by the dogs, assembled the goats and started them for the trail through the forest, Edwin stayed by the old man and guided him in the same direction. When they reached the old right of way, Edwin stopped suddenly and looked back. Hare-Lip and Hoo-Hoo and the dogs and the goats passed on. Edwin was looking at a small herd of wild horses which had come down on the hard sand. There were at least twenty of them, young colts and yearlings and mares, led by a beautiful stallion which stood in the foam at the edge of the surf, with arched neck and bright wild eyes, sniffing the salt air from off the sea.

'What is it?' Granser queried.

'Horses,' was the answer. 'First time I ever seen 'em on the beach. It's the mountain lions getting thicker and thicker and driving 'em down.'

The low sun shot red shafts of light, fanshaped, up from a cloud-tumbled horizon. And close at hand, in the white waste of shore-lashed waters, the sea-lions, bellowing their old primeval chant, hauled up out of the sea on the black rocks and fought and loved.

'Come on, Granser,' Edwin prompted.

And old man and boy, skin-clad and barbaric, turned and went along the right of way into the forest in the wake of the goats.

A Thousand Deaths

Jack London

I had been in the water about an hour, and cold, exhausted, with a terrible cramp in my right calf, it seemed as though my hour had come. Fruitlessly struggling against the strong ebb tide, I had beheld the maddening procession of the water-front lights slip by, but now I gave up attempting to breast the stream and contented myself with the bitter thoughts of a wasted career, now drawing to a close.

It had been my luck to come of good, English stock, but of parents whose account with the bankers far exceeded their knowledge of child-nature and the rearing of children. While born with a silver spoon in my mouth, the blessed atmosphere of the home circle was to me unknown. My father, a very learned man and a celebrated antiquarian, gave no thought to his family, being constantly lost in the abstractions of his study; while my mother, noted far more for her good looks than her good sense, sated herself with the adulation of the society in which she was perpetually plunged. I went through the regular school and college routine of a boy of the English bourgeoisie, and as the years brought me increasing strength and passions, my parents suddenly became aware that I was possessed of an immortal soul, and endeavoured to draw the curb. But it was too late; I perpetrated the wildest and most audacious folly, and was disowned by my people, ostracised by the society I had so long outraged, and with the thousand pounds my father gave me, with the declaration that he would neither see me again nor give me more, I took a first-class passage to Australia.

Since then my life had been one long peregrination – from the Orient to the Occident, from the Arctic to the Antarctic – to find myself at last, an able seaman at thirty, in the full vigour of my manhood, drowning in San Francisco bay because of a disastrously successful attempt to desert my ship.

My right leg was drawn up by the cramp, and I was suffering the keenest agony. A slight breeze stirred up a choppy sea, which washed into my mouth and down my throat, nor could I prevent it. Though I still contrived to keep afloat, it was merely mechanical, for I was rapidly becoming unconscious. I have a dim recollection of drifting past the sea-wall, and of catching a glimpse of an upriver steamer's starboard light; then everything became a blank.

I heard the low hum of insect life, and felt the balmy air of a spring morning fanning my cheek. Gradually it assumed a rhythmic flow, to whose soft pulsations my body seemed to respond. I floated on the gentle bosom of a summer's sea, rising and falling with dreamy pleasure on each crooning wave. But the pulsations grew stronger; the humming, louder; the waves, larger, fiercer – I was dashed about on a stormy sea. A great agony fastened upon me. Brilliant, intermittent sparks of light flashed athwart my inner consciousness; in my ears there was the sound of many waters; then a sudden snapping of an intangible some-thing, and I awoke.

The scene, of which I was protagonist, was a curious one. A glance sufficed to inform me that I lay on the cabin floor of some gentleman's yacht, in a most uncomfortable posture. On either side, grasping my arms and working them up and down like pump handles, were two peculiarly clad, dark-skinned creatures. Though conversant with most aboriginal types, I could not conjecture their nationality. Some attach-ment had been fastened about my head, which connected my respiratory organs with the machine I shall next describe. My nostrils, however, had been closed, forcing me to breathe through my mouth. Foreshortened by the obliquity of my line of vision, I beheld two tubes, similar to small hosing but of different composition, which emerged from my mouth and went off at an acute angle from each other. The first came to an abrupt termination and lay on the floor beside me; the second traversed the floor in numerous coils, connecting with the apparatus I have promised to describe.

In the days before my life had become tangential, I had dabbled not a little in science, and, conversant with the appurtenances and general paraphernalia of the laboratory, I appreciated the machine I now beheld. It was composed chiefly of glass, the construction being of that crude sort which is employed for experimental purposes. A vessel of water was surrounded by an air chamber, to which was fixed a vertical tube, sur-mounted by a globe. In the centre of this was a vacuum gauge. The water in the tube moved upwards and downwards, creating alternate inhal-ations and exhalations, which were in turn communicated to me through the hose. With this, and the aid of the men who pumped my arms, so vigorously, had the process of breathing been artificially carried on, my chest rising and falling and my lungs expanding and contracting, till nature could be persuaded to again take up her wonted labour.

As I opened my eyes the appliance about my head, nostrils and mouth was removed. Draining a stiff three fingers of brandy, I staggered to my feet to thank my preserver, and confronted – my father. But long years of fellowship with danger had taught me self-control, and I waited to see if he would recognise me. Not so; he saw in me no more than a runaway sailor and treated me accordingly.

Leaving me to the care of the blackies, he fell to revising the notes he had made on my resuscitation. As I ate of the handsome fare served up to me, confusion began on deck, and from the chanteys of the sailors and the rattling of blocks and tackles I surmised that we were getting under way. What a lark! Off on a cruise with my recluse father into the wide Pacific! Little did I realise, as I laughed to myself, which side the joke was to be on. Aye, had I known, I would have plunged overboard and welcomed the dirty fo'c'sle from which I had just escaped.

I was not allowed on deck till we had sunk the Farallones and the last pilot boat. I appreciated this forethought on the part of my father and made it a point to thank him heartily, in my bluff seaman's manner. I could not suspect that he had his own ends in view, in thus keeping my presence secret to all save the crew. He told me briefly of my rescue by his sailors, assuring me that the obligation was on his side, as my appearance had been most opportune. He had constructed the apparatus for the vindication of a theory concerning certain biological phenomena, and had been waiting for an opportunity to use it.

"You have proved it beyond all doubt," he said; then added with a sigh, "But only in the small matter of drowning." But, to take a reef in my yarn – he offered me an advance of two pounds on my previous wages to sail with him, and this I considered handsome, for he really did not need me. Contrary to my expectations, I did not join the sailor' mess, for'ard, being assigned to a comfortable stateroom and eating at the captain's table. He had perceived that I was no common sailor, and I resolved to take this chance for reinstating myself in his good graces. I wove a fictitious past to account for my education and present position, and did my best to come in touch with him. I was not long in disclosing a predilection for scientific pursuits, nor he in appreciating my aptitude. I became his assistant, with a corresponding increase in wages, and before long, as he grew confidential and expounded his theories, I was as enthusiastic as himself.

The days flew quickly by, for I was deeply interested in my new studies, passing my waking hours in his well-stocked library, or listening to his plans and aiding him in his laboratory work. But we were forced to forego many enticing experiments, a rolling ship not being exactly the proper place for delicate or intricate work. He promised me, however, many delightful hours in the magnificent laboratory for which we were bound. He had taken possession of an uncharted South Sea island, as he said, and turned it into a scientific paradise.

We had not been on the island long, before I discovered the horrible mare's nest I had fallen into. But before I describe the strange things which came to pass, I must briefly outline the causes which culminated in as startling an experience as ever fell to the lot of man.

Late in life, my father had abandoned the musty charms of antiquity and succumbed to the more fascinating ones embraced under the general head of biology. Having been thoroughly grounded during his youth in the fundamentals, he rapidly explored all the higher branches as far as the scientific world had gone, and found himself in the no man's land of the unknowable. It was his intention to pre-empt some of this unclaimed territory, and it was at this stage of his investigations that we had been thrown together. Having a good brain, though I say it myself, I had mastered his speculations and methods of reasoning, becoming almost as mad as himself. But I should not say this. The marvellous results we afterwards obtained can only go to prove his sanity. I can but say that he was the most abnormal specimen of cold-blooded cruelty I have ever seen.

After having penetrated the dual mysteries of physiology and psychology, his thought had led him to the verge of a great field, for which, the better to explore, he began studies in higher organic chemistry, pathology, toxicology and other sciences and sub-sciences rendered kindred as accessories to his speculative hypotheses. Starting from the proposition that the direct cause of the temporary and permanent arrest of vitality was due to the coagulation of certain elements and compounds in the protoplasm, he had isolated and subjected these various substances to innumerable experiments. Since the temporary arrest of vitality in an organism brought coma, and a permanent arrest death, he held that by artificial means this coagulation of the protoplasm could be retarded, prevented, and even overcome in the extreme states of solidification. Or, to do away with the technical nomenclature, he argued that death, when not violent and in which none of the organs had suffered injury, was merely suspended vitality; and that, in such instances, life could be induced to resume its functions by the use of proper methods. This, then, was his idea: to discover the method – and by practical experimentation prove the possibility – of renewing vitality in a structure from which life had seemingly fled. Of course, he recognised the futility of such endeavour after decomposition had set in; he must have organisms which but the moment, the hour, or the day before, had been quick with life. With me, in a crude way, he had proved this theory. I was really drowned, really dead, when picked from the water of San Francisco bay – but the vital spark had been renewed by means of his aerotherapeutical apparatus, as he called it.

Now to his dark purpose concerning me. He first showed me how completely I was in his power. He had sent the yacht away for a year, retaining only his two blackies, who were utterly devoted to him. He then made an exhaustive review of his theory and outlined the method of proof he had adopted, concluding with the startling announcement that I was to be his subject.

I had faced death and weighed my chances in many a desperate venture, but never in one of this nature. I can swear I am no coward, yet this proposition of journeying back and forth across the borderland of death put the yellow fear upon me. I asked for time, which he granted, at the same time assuring me that but the one course was open – I must submit. Escape from the Island was out of the question; escape by suicide was not to be entertained, though really preferable to what it seemed I must undergo; my only hope was to destroy my captors. But this latter was frustrated through the precautions taken by my father. I was subjected to a constant surveillance, even in my sleep being guarded by one or the other of the blacks.

Having pleaded in vain, I announced and proved that I was his son. It was my last card, and I had played all my hopes upon it. But he was inexorable; he was not a father but a scientific machine. I wonder yet how it ever came to pass that he married my mother or begat me, for there was not the slightest grain of emotion in his make-up. Reason was all in all to him, nor could he understand such things as love or sympathy in others, except as petty weaknesses which should be overcome. So he informed me that in the beginning he had given me life, and who had better right to take it away than he? Such, he said, was not his desire, however; he merely wished to borrow it occasionally, promising to return it punctually at the appointed time. Of course, there was a liability of mishaps, but I could do no more than take the chances, since the affairs of men were full of such.

The better to ensure success, he wished me to be in the best possible condition, so I was dieted and trained like a great athlete before a decisive contest. What could I do? If I had to undergo the peril, it were best to be in good shape. In my intervals of relaxation he allowed me to assist in the arranging of the apparatus and in the various subsidiary experiments. The interest I took in all such operations can be imagined. I mastered the work as thoroughly as he, and often had the pleasure of seeing some of my suggestions or alterations put into effect. After such events I would smile grimly, conscious of officiating at my own funeral.

He began by inaugurating a series of experiments in toxicology. When all was ready, I was killed by a stiff dose of strychnine and allowed to lie dead for some twenty hours. During that period my body was dead, absolutely dead. All respiration and circulation ceased; but the frightful part of it was, that while the protoplasmic coagulation proceeded, I retained consciousness and was enabled to study it in all its ghastly details.

The apparatus to bring me back to life was an air-tight chamber, fitted to receive my body. The mechanism was simple – a few valves, a rotary shaft and crank, and an electric motor. When in operation, the interior atmosphere was alternately condenses and rarefied, thus communicating to my lungs an artificial respiration without the agency of the hosing previously used. Though my body was inert, and, for all I knew, in the first stages of decomposition, I was cognizant of everything that transpired. I knew when they placed me in the chamber, and though all my senses were quiescent, I was aware of hypodermic injections of a compound to react upon the coagulatory process. Then the chamber was closed and the machinery started. My anxiety was terrible; but the circulation became gradually restored, the different organs began to carry on their respective functions, and in an hour's time I was eating a hearty dinner.

It cannot be said that I participated in this series, nor in the subsequent ones, with much verve; but after two ineffectual attempts of escape, I began to take quite an interest. Besides, I was becoming accustomed. My father was beside himself at his success, and as the months rolled by his speculations took wilder and yet wilder flights. We ranged through the three great classes of poisons, the neurotics, the gaseous and the irritants, but carefully avoided some of the mineral irritants and passed the whole group of corrosives. During the poison regime I became quite accustomed to dying, and had but one mishap to shake my growing confidence. Scarifying a number of lesser blood vessels in my arm, he introduced a minute quantity of that most frightful of poisons, the arrow poison, or curare. I lost consciousness at the start, quickly followed by the cessation of respiration and circulation, and so far had the solidification of the protoplasm advanced, that he gave up all hope. But at the last moment he applied a discovery he had been working upon, receiving such encouragement as to redouble his efforts.

In a glass vacuum, similar but not exactly like a Crookes' tube, was placed a magnetic field. When penetrated by polarised light, it gave no phenomena of phosphorescence nor the rectilinear projection of atoms, but emitted non-luminous rays, similar to the x-ray. While the x-ray could reveal opaque objects hidden in dense mediums, this was possessed of far subtler penetration. By this he photographed my body, and found on the negative an infinite number of blurred shadows, due to the chemical and electric motions still going on. This was an infallible proof that the rigor mortis in which I lay was not genuine; that is, those mysterious forces, those delicate bonds which held my soul to my body, were still in action. The resultants of all other poisons were unapparent, save those of mercurial compounds, which usually left me languid for several days.

Another series of delightful experiments was with electricity. We verified Tesla's assertion that high currents were utterly harmless by passing 100,000 volts through my body. As this did not affect me, the current was reduced to 2,500, and I was quickly electrocuted. This time he ventured so far as to allow me to remain dead, or in a state of suspended vitality, for three days. It took four hours to bring me back.

Once, he superinduced lockjaw; but the agony of dying was so great that I positively refused to undergo similar experiments. The easiest deaths were by asphyxiation, such as drowning, strangling, and suffocation by gas; while those by morphine, opium, cocaine and chloroform, were not at all hard.

Another time, after being suffocated, he kept me in cold storage for three months, not permitting me to freeze or decay. This was without my knowledge, and I was in a great fright on discovering the lapse of time. I became afraid of what he might do with me when I lay dead, my alarm being increased by the predilection he was beginning to betray towards vivisection. The last time I was resurrected, I discovered that he had been tampering with my breast. Though he had carefully dressed and sewed the incisions up, they were so severe that I had to take to my bed for some time. It was during this convalescence that I evolved the plan by which I ultimately escaped.

While feigning unbounded enthusiasm in the work, I asked and received a vacation from my moribund occupation. During this period I devoted myself to laboratory work, while he was too deep in the vivisection of the many animals captured by the blacks to take notice of my work.

It was on these two propositions that I constructed my theory: First, electrolysis, or the decomposition of water into its constituent gases by means of electricity; and, second, by the hypothetical existence of a force, the converse of gravitation, which Astor has named 'apergy'. Terrestrial attraction, for instance, merely draws objects together but does not combine them; hence, apergy is merely repulsion. Now, atomic or molecular attraction not only draws objects together but integrates them; and it was the converse of this, or a disintegrative force, which I wished to not only discover and produce, but to direct at will. Thus, the molecules of hydrogen and oxygen reacting on each other, separate and create new molecules, containing both elements and forming water. Electrolysis causes these molecules to split up and resume their original condition, producing the two gases separately. The force I wished to find must not only do this with two, but with all elements, no matter in what compounds they exist. If I could then entice my father within its radius, he would be instantly disintegrated and sent flying to the four quarters, a mass of isolated elements.

It must not be understood that this force, which I finally came to control, annihilated matter; it merely annihilated form. Nor, as I soon discovered, had it any effect on inorganic structure; but to all organic form it was absolutely fatal. This partiality puzzled me at first, though had I stopped to think deeper I would have seen through it. Since the number of atoms in organic molecules is far greater than in the most complex mineral molecules, organic compounds are characterised by their instability and the ease with which they are split up by physical forces and chemical reagents.

By two powerful batteries, connected with magnets constructed specially for this purpose, two tremendous forces were projected. Considered apart from each other, they were perfectly harmless; but they accomplished their purpose by focusing at an invisible point in mid-air. After practically demonstrating its success, besides narrowly escaping being blown into nothingness, I laid my trap. Concealing the magnets, so that their force made the whole space of my chamber doorway a field of death, and placing by my couch a button by which I could throw on the current from the storage batteries, I climbed into bed.

The blackies still guarded my sleeping quarters, one relieving the other at midnight. I turned on the current as soon as the first man arrived. Hardly had I begun to doze, when I was aroused by a sharp, metallic tinkle. There, on the mid-threshold, lay the collar of Dan, my father's St Bernard. My keeper ran to pick it up. He disappeared like a gust of wind, his clothes falling to the floor in a heap. There was a slight wiff of ozone in the air, but since the principal gaseous components of his body were hydrogen, oxygen and nitrogen, which are equally colourless and odourless, there was no other manifestation of his departure. Yet when I shut off the current and removed the garments, I found a deposit of carbon in the form of animal charcoal; also other powders, the isolated, solid elements of his organism, such as sulphur, potassium and iron. Resetting the trap, I crawled back to bed. At midnight I got up and removed the remains of the second black, and then slept peacefully till morning.

I was awakened by the strident voice of my father, who was calling to me from across the laboratory. I laughed to myself. There had been no one to call him and he had overslept. I could hear him as he approached my room with the intention of rousing me, and so I sat up in bed, the better to observe his translation – perhaps apotheosis were a better term. He paused a moment at the threshold, then took the fatal step. Puff! It was like the wind sighing among the pines. He was gone. His clothes fell in a fantastic heap on the floor. Besides ozone, I noticed the faint, garlic-like odour of phosphorus. A little pile of elementary solids lay among his garments. That was all. The wide world lay before me. My captors were no more.

The Great Keinplatz Experiment

Arthur Conan Doyle

Of all the sciences which have puzzled the sons of men, none had such an attraction for the learned Professor von Baumgarten as those which relate to psychology and the ill-defined relations between mind and matter. A celebrated anatomist, a profound chemist, and one of the first physiologists in Europe, it was a relief for him to turn from these subjects and to bring his varied knowledge to bear upon the study of the soul and the mysterious relationship of spirits. At first, when as a young man he began to dip into the secrets of mesmerism, his mind seemed to be wandering in a strange land where all was chaos and darkness, save that here and there some great unexplainable and disconnected fact loomed out in front of him. As the years passed, however, and as the worthy Professor's stock of knowledge increased, for knowledge begets knowledge as money bears interest, much which had seemed strange and unaccountable began to take another shape in his eyes. New trains of reasoning became familiar to him, and he perceived connecting links where all had been incomprehensible and startling. By experiments which extended over twenty years, he obtained a basis of facts upon which it was his ambition to build up a new exact science which should embrace mesmerism, spiritualism, and all cognate subjects. In this he was much helped by his intimate knowledge of the more intricate parts of animal physiology which treat of nerve currents and the working of the brain; for Alexis von Baumgarten was Regius Professor of Physiology at the University of Keinplatz, and had all the resources of the laboratory to aid him in his profound researches.

Professor von Baumgarten was tall and thin, with a hatchet face and steel-grey eyes, which were singularly bright and penetrating. Much thought had furrowed his forehead and contracted his heavy eyebrows, so that he appeared to wear a perpetual frown, which often misled people as to his character, for though austere he was tender-hearted. He was popular among the students, who would gather round him after his lectures and listen eagerly to his strange theories. Often he would call for volunteers from amongst them in order to conduct some experiment, so that eventually there was hardly a lad in the class who had not, at one time or another, been thrown into a mesmeric trance by his Professor.

Of all these young devotees of science there was none who equalled in enthusiasm Fritz von Hartmann. It had often seemed strange to his fellow-students that wild, reckless Fritz, as dashing a young fellow as ever hailed from the Rhinelands, should devote the time and trouble which he did in reading up abstruse works and in assisting the Professor in his strange experiments. The fact was, however, that Fritz was a knowing and long-headed fellow. Months before he had lost his heart to young Elise, the blue-eyed, yellow-haired daughter of the lecturer. Although he had succeeded in learning from her lips that she was not indifferent to his suit, he had never dared to announce himself to her family as a formal suitor. Hence he would have found it a difficult matter to see his young lady had he not adopted the expedient of making himself useful to the Professor. By this means he frequently was asked to the old man's house, where he willingly submitted to be experimented upon in any way as long as there was a chance of his receiving one bright glance from the eyes of Elise or one touch of her little hand.

Young Fritz von Hartmann was a handsome lad enough. There were broad acres, too, which would descend to him when his father died. To many he would have seemed an eligible suitor; but Madame frowned upon his presence in the house, and lectured the Professor at times on his allowing such a wolf to prowl around their lamb. To tell the truth, Fritz had an evil name in Keinplatz. Never was there a riot or a duel, or any other mischief afoot, but the young Rhinelander figured as a ringleader in it. No one used more free and violent language, no one drank more, no one played cards more habitually, no one was more idle, save in the one solitary subject. No wonder, then, that the good Frau Professorin gathered her Fräulein under her wing, and resented the attentions of such a *mauvais sujet*. As to the worthy lecturer, he was too much engrossed by his strange studies to form an opinion upon the subject one way or the other.

For many years there was one question which had continually obtruded itself upon his thoughts. All his experiments and his theories turned upon a single point. A hundred times a day the Professor asked himself whether it was possible for the human spirit to exist apart from the body for a time and then to return to it once again. When the possibility first suggested itself to him his scientific mind had revolted from it. It clashed too violently with preconceived ideas and the prejudices of his early training. Gradually, however, as he proceeded farther and farther along the pathway of original research, his mind shook off its old fetters and became ready to face any conclusion which could reconcile the facts. There were many things which made him believe that it was possible for mind to exist apart from matter. At last it occurred to him that by a daring and original experiment the question might be definitely decided.

'It is evident,' he remarked in his celebrated article upon invisible entities, which appeared in the *Keinplatz wochenliche Medicalschrift* about this time, and which surprised the whole scientific world – 'it is evident that under certain conditions the soul or mind does separate itself from the body. In the case of a mesmerised person, the body lies in a cataleptic condition, but the spirit has left it. Perhaps you reply that the soul is there, but in a dormant condition. I answer that this is not so, otherwise how can one account for the condition of clairvoyance, which has fallen into disrepute through the knavery of certain scoundrels, but which can easily be shown to be an undoubted fact? I have been able myself, with a sensitive subject, to obtain an accurate description of what was going on in another room or another house. How can such knowledge be accounted for on any hypothesis save that the soul of the subject has left the body and is wandering through space? For a moment it is recalled by the voice of the operator and says what it has seen, and then wings its way once more through the air. Since the spirit is by its very nature invisible, we cannot see these comings and goings, but we see their effect in the body of the subject, now rigid and inert, now struggling to narrate impressions which could never have come to it by natural means. There is only one way which I can see by which the fact can be demonstrated. Although we in the flesh are unable to see these spirits, yet our own spirits, could we separate them from the body, would be conscious of the presence of others. It is my intention, therefore, shortly to mesmerise one of my pupils. I shall then mesmerise myself in a manner which has become easy to me. After that, if my theory holds good, my spirit will have no difficulty in meeting and communing with the spirit of my pupil, both being separated from the body. I hope to be able to communicate the result of this interesting experiment in an early number of the *Keinplatz wochenliche Medicalschrift*.'

When the good Professor finally fulfilled his promise, and published an account of what occurred, the narrative was so extraordinary that it was received with general incredulity. The tone of some of the papers was so offensive in their comments upon the matter that the angry savant declared that he would never open his mouth again or refer to the subject in any way – a promise which he has faithfully kept. This narrative has been compiled, however, from the most authentic sources, and the events cited in it may be relied upon as substantially correct.

It happened, then, that shortly after the time when Professor von Baumgarten conceived the idea of the above-mentioned experiment, he was walking thoughtfully homewards after a long day in the laboratory, when he met a crowd of roystering students who had just streamed out from a beer-house. At the head of them, half-intoxicated and very noisy, was young Fritz von Hartmann. The Professor would have passed them, but his pupil ran across and intercepted him.

'Heh! my worthy master,' he said, taking the old man by the sleeve, and leading him down the road with him. 'There is something that I have to say to you, and it is easier for me to say it now, when the good beer is humming in my head, than at another time.'

'What is it, then, Fritz?' the physiologist asked, looking at him in mild surprise.

'I hear, *mein Herr*, that you are about to do some wondrous experiment in which you hope to take a man's soul out of his body, and then to put it back again. Is it not so?'

'It is true, Fritz.'

'And have you considered, my dear sir, that you may have some difficulty in finding someone on whom to try this? *Potztausend*! Suppose that the soul went out and would not come back. That would be a bad business. Who is to take the risk?'

'But, Fritz,' the Professor cried, very much startled by this view of the matter, 'I had relied upon your assistance in the attempt. Surely you will not desert me. Consider the honour and glory.'

'Consider the fiddlesticks!' the student cried angrily. 'Am I to be paid always thus? Did I not stand two hours upon a glass insulator while you poured electricity into my body? Have you not stimulated my phrenic nerves, besides ruining my digestion with a galvanic current round my stomach? Four-and-thirty times you have mesmerised me, and what have I got from all this? Nothing. And now you wish to take my soul out, as you would take the works from a watch. It is more than flesh and blood can stand.'

'Dear, dear!' the Professor cried in great distress. 'That is very true, Fritz. I never thought of it before. If you can but suggest how I can compensate you, you will find me ready and willing.'

'Then listen,' said Fritz solemnly. 'If you will pledge your word that after this experiment I may have the hand of your daughter, then I am willing to assist you; but if not, I shall have nothing to do with it. These are my only terms.'

'And what would my daughter say to this?' the Professor exclaimed, after a pause of astonishment.

'Elise would welcome it,' the young man replied. 'We have loved each other long.'

'Then she shall be yours,' the physiologist said with decision, 'for you are a good-hearted young man, and one of the best neurotic subjects that I have ever known – that is when you are not under the influence of alcohol. My experiment is to be performed upon the fourth of next month. You will attend at the physiological laboratory at twelve o'clock. It will be a great occasion, Fritz. Von Gruben is coming from Jena, and Hinterstein from Basle. The chief men of science of all South Germany will be there.'

'I shall be punctual,' the student said briefly; and so the two parted. The Professor plodded homeward, thinking of the great coming event, while the young man staggered along after his noisy companions, with his mind full of the blue-eyed Elise, and of the bargain which he had concluded with her father.

The Professor did not exaggerate when he spoke of the widespread interest excited by his novel psychophysiological experiment. Long before the hour had arrived the room was filled by a galaxy of talent. Besides the celebrities whom he had mentioned, there had come from London the great Professor Lurcher, who had just established his reputation by a remarkable treatise upon cerebral centres. Several great lights of the Spiritualistic body had also come a long distance to be present, as had a Swedenborgian minister, who considered that the proceedings might throw some light upon the doctrines of the Rosy Cross.

There was considerable applause from this eminent assembly upon the appearance of Professor von Baumgarten and his subject upon the platform. The lecturer, in a few well-chosen words, explained what his views were, and how he proposed to test them. 'I hold,' he said, 'that when a person is under the influence of mesmerism, his spirit is for the time released from his body, and I challenge anyone to put forward any other hypothesis which will account for the fact of clairvoyance. I therefore hope that upon mesmerising my young friend here, and then putting myself into a trance, our spirits may be able to commune together, though our bodies lie still and inert. After a time nature will resume her sway, our spirits will return into our respective bodies, and all will be as before. With your kind permission, we shall now proceed to attempt the experiment.'

The applause was renewed at this speech, and the audience settled down in expectant silence. With a few rapid passes the Professor mesmerised the young man, who sank back in his chair, pale and rigid. He then took a bright globe of glass from his pocket, and by concentrating his gaze upon it and making a strong mental effort, he succeeded in throwing himself into the same condition. It was a strange and impressive

sight to see the old man and the young sitting together in the same
cataleptic condition. Whither, then, had their souls fled? That was the
question which presented itself to each and every one of the spectators.

Five minutes passed, and then ten, and then fifteen, and then fifteen
more, while the Professor and his pupil sat stiff and stark upon the platform. During that time not a sound was heard from the assembled
savants, but every eye was bent upon the two pale faces, in search of the
first signs of returning consciousness. Nearly an hour had elapsed before
the patient watchers were rewarded. A faint flush came back to the cheeks
of Professor von Baumgarten. The soul was coming back once more to
its earthly tenement. Suddenly he stretched out his long thin arms, as one
awaking from sleep, and rubbing his eyes, stood up from his chair and
gazed about him as though he hardly realised where he was. '*Tausend
Teufel*!' he exclaimed, rapping out a tremendous South German oath,
to the great astonishment of his audience and to the disgust of the
Swedenborgian. 'Where the *Henker* am I then, and what in thunder has
occurred? Oh yes, I remember now. One of these nonsensical mesmeric
experiments. There is no result this time, for I remember nothing at all
since I became unconscious; so you have had all your long journeys for
nothing, my learned friends, and a very good joke too;' at which the
Regius Professor of Physiology burst into a roar of laughter and slapped
his thigh in a highly indecorous fashion. The audience were so enraged
at this unseemly behaviour on the part of their host, that there might
have been a considerable disturbance, had it not been for the judicious
interference of young Fritz von Hartmann, who had now recovered
from his lethargy. Stepping to the front of the platform, the young man
apologised for the conduct of his companion. 'I am sorry to say,' he said,
'that he is a harum-scarum sort of fellow, although he appeared so grave
at the commencement of this experiment. He is still suffering from
mesmeric reaction, and is hardly accountable for his words. As to the
experiment itself, I do not consider it to be a failure. It is very possible
that our spirits may have been communing in space during this hour;
but, unfortunately, our gross bodily memory is distinct from our spirit,
and we cannot recall what has occurred. My energies shall now be
devoted to devising some means by which spirits may be able to recollect
what occurs to them in their free state, and I trust that when I have
worked this out, I may have the pleasure of meeting you all once again in
this hall, and demonstrating to you the result.' This address, coming
from so young a student, caused considerable astonishment among
the audience, and some were inclined to be offended, thinking that he
assumed rather too much importance. The majority, however, looked

upon him as a young man of great promise, and many comparisons were made as they left the hall between his dignified conduct and the levity of his professor, who during the above remarks was laughing heartily in a corner, by no means abashed at the failure of the experiment.

Now although all these learned men were filing out of the lecture-room under the impression that they had seen nothing of note, as a matter of fact one of the most wonderful things in the whole history of the world had just occurred before their very eyes. Professor von Baumgarten had been so far correct in his theory that both his spirit and that of his pupil had been for a time absent from his body. But here a strange and unforeseen complication had occurred. In their return the spirit of Fritz von Hartmann had entered into the body of Alexis von Baumgarten, and that of Alexis von Baumgarten had taken up its abode in the frame of Fritz von Hartmann. Hence the slang and scurril-ity which issued from the lips of the serious Professor, and hence also the weighty words and grave statements which fell from the careless student. It was an unprecedented event, yet no one knew of it, least of all those whom it concerned.

The body of the Professor, feeling conscious suddenly of a great dryness about the back of the throat, sallied out into the street, still chuckling to himself over the result of the experiment, for the soul of Fritz within was reckless at the thought of the bride whom he had won so easily. His first impulse was to go up to the house and see her, but on second thoughts he came to the conclusion that it would be best to stay away until Madame Baumgarten should be informed by her husband of the agreement which had been made. He therefore made his way down to the *Grüner Mann*, which was one of the favourite trysting-places of the wilder students, and ran, boisterously waving his cane in the air, into the little parlour, where sat Spiegler and Muller and half a dozen other boon companions.

'Ha, ha! my boys,' he shouted. 'I knew I should find you here. Drink up, every one of you, and call for what you like, for I'm going to stand treat today.'

Had the green man who is depicted upon the signpost of that well-known inn suddenly marched into the room and called for a bottle of wine, the students could not have been more amazed than they were by this unexpected entry of their revered professor. They were so astonished that for a minute or two they glared at him in utter bewilderment without being able to make any reply to his hearty invitation.

'*Donner und Blitzen!*' shouted the Professor angrily. 'What the deuce is the matter with you, then? You sit there like a set of stuck pigs staring at me. What is it, then?'

'It is the unexpected honour,' stammered Spiegel, who was in the chair.

'Honour – rubbish!' said the Professor testily. 'Do you think that just because I happen to have been exhibiting mesmerism to a parcel of old fossils, I am therefore too proud to associate with dear old friends like you? Come out of that chair, Spiegel my boy, for I shall preside now. Beer, or wine, or schnapps, my lads – call for what you like, and put it all down to me.'

Never was there such an afternoon in the *Grüner Mann*. The foaming flagons of lager and the green-necked bottles of Rhenish circulated merrily. By degrees the students lost their shyness in the presence of their Professor. As for him, he shouted, he sang, he roared, he balanced a long tobacco-pipe upon his nose, and offered to run a hundred yards against any member of the company. The Kellner and the barmaid whispered to each other outside the door their astonishment at such proceedings on the part of a Regius Professor of the ancient university of Keinplatz. They had still more to whisper about afterwards, for the learned man cracked the Kellner's crown, and kissed the barmaid behind the kitchen door.

'Gentlemen,' said the Professor, standing up, albeit somewhat totteringly, at the end of the table, and balancing his high old-fashioned wineglass in his bony hand, 'I must now explain to you what is the cause of this festivity.'

'Hear! hear!' roared the students, hammering their beer glasses against the table; 'a speech, a speech! – silence for a speech!'

'The fact is, my friends,' said the Professor, beaming through his spectacles, 'I hope very soon to be married.'

'Married!' cried a student, bolder than the others. 'Is Madame dead, then?'

'Madame who?'

'Why, Madame von Baumgarten, of course.'

'Ha, ha!' laughed the Professor; 'I can see, then, that you know all about my former difficulties. No, she is not dead, but I have reason to believe that she will not oppose my marriage.'

'That is very accommodating of her,' remarked one of the company.

'In fact,' said the Professor, 'I hope that she will now be induced to aid me in getting a wife. She and I never took to each other very much; but now I hope all that may be ended, and when I marry she will come and stay with me.'

'What a happy family!' exclaimed some wag.

'Yes, indeed; and I hope you will come to my wedding, all of you. I won't mention names, but here is to my little bride!' and the Professor waved his glass in the air.

'Here's to his little bride!' roared the roysterers, with shouts of laughter. 'Here's her health. *Sie soll leben – Hoch!*' And so the fun waxed still more fast and furious, while each young fellow followed the Professor's example, and drank a toast to the girl of his heart.

While all this festivity had been going on at the *Grüner Mann*, a very different scene had been enacted elsewhere. Young Fritz von Hartmann, with a solemn face and a reserved manner, had, after the experiment, consulted and adjusted some mathematical instruments; after which, with a few peremptory words to the janitors, he had walked out into the street and wended his way slowly in the direction of the house of the Professor. As he walked he saw von Althaus, the professor of anatomy, in front of him, and quickening his pace he overtook him.

'I say, von Althaus,' he exclaimed, tapping him on the sleeve, 'you were asking me for some information the other day concerning the middle coat of the cerebral arteries. Now I find –'

'*Donnerwetter!*' shouted von Althaus, who was a peppery old fellow. 'What the deuce do you mean by your impertinence! I'll have you up before the Academical Senate for this, sir;' with which threat he turned on his heel and hurried away. Von Hartmann was much surprised at this reception. 'It's on account of this failure of my experiment,' he said to himself, and continued moodily on his way.

Fresh surprises were in store for him, however. He was hurrying along when he was overtaken by two students. These youths, instead of raising their caps or showing any other sign of respect, gave a wild whoop of delight the instant that they saw him, and rushing at him, seized him by each arm and commenced dragging him along with them.

'*Gott in Himmel!*' roared von Hartmann. 'What is the meaning of this unparalleled insult? Where are you taking me?'

'To crack a bottle of wine with us,' said the two students. 'Come along! That is an invitation which you have never refused.'

'I never heard of such insolence in my life!' cried von Hartmann. 'Let go my arms! I shall certainly have you rusticated for this. Let me go, I say!' and he kicked furiously at his captors.

'Oh, if you choose to turn ill-tempered, you may go where you like,' the students said, releasing him. 'We can do very well without you.'

'I know you. I'll pay you out,' said von Hartmann furiously, and continued in the direction which he imagined to be his own home, much incensed at the two episodes which had occurred to him on the way.

Now, Madame von Baumgarten, who was looking out of the window and wondering why her husband was late for dinner, was considerably astonished to see the young student come stalking down the road. As already remarked, she had a great antipathy to him, and if ever he ventured into the house it was on suffrance, and under the protection of the Professor. Still more astonished was she, therefore, when she beheld him undo the wicket-gate and stride up the garden path with the air of one who is master of the situation. She could hardly believe her eyes, and hastened to the door with all her maternal instincts up in arms. From the upper windows the fair Elise had also observed this daring move upon the part of her lover, and her heart beat quick with mingled pride and consternation.

'Good day, sir,' Madame Baumgarten remarked to the intruder, as she stood in gloomy majesty in the open doorway.

'A very fine day indeed, Martha,' returned the other. 'Now, don't stand there like a statue of Juno, but bustle about and get the dinner ready, for I am well-nigh starved.'

'Martha! Dinner!' ejaculated the lady, falling back in astonishment.

'Yes, dinner, Martha, dinner!' howled von Hartmann, who was becoming irritable. 'Is there anything wonderful in that request when a man has been out all day? I'll wait in the dining-room. Anything will do. Schinken, and sausage, and prunes – any little thing that happens to be about. There you are, standing staring again. Woman, will you or will you not stir your legs?'

This last address, delivered with a perfect shriek of rage, had the effect of sending good Madame Baumgarten flying along the passage and through the kitchen, where she locked herself up in the scullery and went into violent hysterics. In the meantime von Hartmann strode into the room and threw himself down upon the sofa in the worst of tempers.

'Elise!' he shouted. 'Confound the girl! Elise!'

Thus roughly summoned, the young lady came timidly downstairs and into the presence of her lover. 'Dearest!' she cried, throwing her arms round him, 'I know this is all done for my sake! It is a *ruse* in order to see me.'

Von Hartmann's indignation at this fresh attack upon him was so great that he became speechless for a minute from rage, and could only glare and shake his fists, while he struggled in her embrace. When he at last regained his utterance, he indulged in such a bellow of passion that the young lady dropped back, petrified with fear, into an armchair.

'Never have I passed such a day in my life,' von Hartmann cried, stamping upon the floor. 'My experiment has failed. Von Althaus has insulted me. Two students have dragged me along the public road. My wife nearly faints when I ask her for dinner, and my daughter flies at me and hugs me like a grizzly bear.'

'You are ill, dear,' the young lady cried. 'Your mind is wandering. You have not even kissed me once.'

'No, and I don't intend to either,' von Hartmann said with decision. 'You ought to be ashamed of yourself. Why don't you go and fetch my slippers, and help your mother to dish the dinner?'

'And is it for this,' Elise cried, burying her face in her handkerchief – 'is it for this that I have loved you passionately for upwards of ten months? Is it for this that I have braved my mother's wrath? Oh, you have broken my heart; I am sure you have!' and she sobbed hysterically.

'I can't stand much more of this,' roared von Hartmann furiously. 'What the deuce does the girl mean? What did I do ten months ago which inspired you with such a particular affection for me? If you are really so very fond, you would do better to run away down and find the schinken and some bread, instead of talking all this nonsense'

'Oh, my darling!' cried the unhappy maiden, throwing herself into the arms of what she imagined to be her lover, 'you do but joke in order to frighten your little Elise.'

Now it chanced that at the moment of this unexpected embrace von Hartmann was still leaning back against the end of the sofa, which, like much German furniture, was in a somewhat rickety condition. It also chanced that beneath this end of the sofa there stood a tank full of water in which the physiologist was conducting certain experiments upon the ova of fish, and which he kept in his drawing-room in order to ensure an equable temperature. The additional weight of the maiden, combined with the impetus with which she hurled herself upon him, caused the precarious piece of furniture to give way, and the body of the unfortunate student was hurled backwards into the tank, in which his head and shoulders were firmly wedged, while his lower extremities flapped helplessly about in the air. This was the last straw. Extricating himself with some difficulty from his unpleasant position, von Hartmann gave an inarticulate yell of fury, and dashing out of the room, in spite of the entreaties of Elise, he seized his hat and rushed off into the town, all dripping and dishevelled, with the intention of seeking in some inn the food and comfort which he could not find at home.

As the spirit of von Baumgarten encased in the body of von Hartmann strode down the winding pathway which led down to the little town, brooding angrily over his many wrongs, he became aware that an elderly man was approaching him who appeared to be in an advanced state of intoxication. von Hartmann waited by the side of the road and watched this individual, who came stumbling along, reeling from one side of the road to the other, and singing a student song in a very husky and drunken voice. At first his interest was merely excited by the fact of seeing a man of so venerable an appearance in such a disgraceful condition, but as he approached nearer, he became convinced that he knew the other well, though he could not recall when or where he had met him. This impression became so strong with him, that when the stranger came abreast of him he stepped in front of him and took a good look at his features.

'Well, sonny,' said the drunken man, surveying von Hartmann and swaying about in front of him, 'where the *Henker* have I seen you before? I know you as well as I know myself. Who the deuce are you?'

'I am Professor von Baumgarten,' said the student. 'May I ask who you are? I am strangely familiar with your features.'

'You should never tell lies, young man,' said the other. 'You're certainly not the Professor, for he is an ugly snuffy old chap, and you are a big broad-shouldered young fellow. As to myself, I am Fritz von Hartmann at your service.'

'That you certainly are not,' exclaimed the body of von Hartmann. 'You might very well be his father. But hullo, sir, are you aware that you are wearing my studs and my watch-chain?'

'*Donnerwetter*!' hiccoughed the other. ' If those are not the trousers for which my tailor is about to sue me, may I never taste beer again.'

Now as von Hartmann, overwhelmed by the many strange things which had occurred to him that day, passed his hand over his forehead and cast his eyes downwards, he chanced to catch the reflection of his own face in a pool which the rain had left upon the road. To his utter astonishment he perceived that his face was that of a youth, that his dress was that of a fashionable young student, and that in every way he was the antithesis of the grave and scholarly figure in which his mind was wont to dwell. In an instant his active brain ran over the series of events which had occurred and sprang to the conclusion. He fairly reeled under the blow.

'*Himmel*!' he cried, 'I see it all. Our souls are in the wrong bodies. I am you and you are I. My theory is proved – but at what an expense! Is the most scholarly mind in Europe to go about with this frivolous exterior? Oh the labours of a lifetime are ruined!' and he smote his breast in his despair.

'I say,' remarked the real von Hartmann from the body of the Professor, 'I quite see the force of your remarks, but don't go knocking my body about like that. You received it in excellent condition, but I perceive that you have wet it and bruised it, and spilled snuff over my ruffled shirt-front.'

'It matters little,' the other said moodily. 'Such as we are so must we stay. My theory is triumphantly proved, but the cost is terrible.'

'If I thought so,' said the spirit of the student, 'it would be hard indeed. What could I do with these stiff old limbs, and how could I woo Elise and persuade her that I was not her father? No, thank Heaven, in spite of the beer which has upset me more than ever it could upset my real self, I can see a way out of it.'

'How?' gasped the Professor.

'Why, by repeating the experiment. Liberate our souls once more, and the chances are that they will find their way back into their respective bodies.'

No drowning man could clutch more eagerly at a straw than did von Baumgarten's spirit at this suggestion. In feverish haste he dragged his own frame to the side of the road and threw it into a mesmeric trance; he then extracted the crystal ball from the pocket, and managed to bring himself into the same condition.

Some students and peasants who chanced to pass during the next hour were much astonished to see the worthy Professor of Physiology and his favourite student both sitting upon a very muddy bank and both completely insensible. Before the hour was up quite a crowd had assembled, and they were discussing the advisability of sending for an ambulance to convey the pair to hospital, when the learned savant opened his eyes and gazed vacantly around him. For an instant he seemed to forget how he had come there, but next moment he astonished his audience by waving his skinny arms above his head and crying out in a voice of rapture, '*Gott sei gedankt*! I am myself again. I feel I am!' Nor was the amazement lessened when the student, springing to his feet, burst into the same cry, and the two performed a sort of *pas de joie* in the middle of the road.

For some time after that people had some suspicion of the sanity of both the actors in this strange episode. When the Professor published his experiences in the *Medicalschrift* as he had promised, he was met by an intimation, even from his colleagues, that he would do well to have his mind cared for, and that another such publication would certainly consign him to a madhouse. The student also found by experience that it was wisest to be silent about the matter.

When the worthy lecturer returned home that night he did not receive the cordial welcome which he might have looked for after his strange adventures. On the contrary, he was roundly upbraided by both his female relatives for smelling of drink and tobacco, and also for being absent while a young scapegrace invaded the house and insulted its occupants. It was long before the domestic atmosphere of the lecturer's house resumed its normal quiet, and longer still before the genial face of von Hartmann was seen beneath its roof. Perseverance, however, conquers every obstacle, and the student eventually succeeded in pacifying the enraged ladies and in establishing himself upon the old footing. He has now no longer any cause to fear the enmity of Madame, for he is Hauptmann von Hartmann of the Emperor's own Uhlans, and his loving wife Elise has already presented him with two little Uhlans as a visible sign and token of her affection.

The Thames Valley Catastrophe

Grant Allen

It can scarcely be necessary for me to mention, I suppose, at this time of day, that I was one of the earliest and fullest observers of the sad series of events which finally brought about the transference of the seat of Government of these islands from London to Manchester. Nor need I allude here to the conspicuous position which my narrative naturally occupies in the Blue-book on the Thames Valley Catastrophe (vol. ii., part vii), ordered by Parliament in its preliminary session under the new regime at Birmingham. But I think it also incumbent upon me, for the benefit of posterity, to supplement that necessarily dry and formal statement by a more circumstantial account of my personal adventures during the terrible period.

I am aware, of course, that my poor little story can possess little interest for our contemporaries, wearied out as they are with details of the disaster, and surfeited with tedious scientific discussions as to its origin and nature. But in after years, I venture to believe, when the crowning calamity of the nineteenth century has grown picturesque and, so to speak, ivy-clad, by reason of its remoteness (like the Great Plague or the Great Fire of London with ourselves), the world may possibly desire to hear how this unparalleled convulsion affected the feelings and fortunes of a single family in the middle rank of life, and in a part of London neither squalid nor fashionable.

It is such personal touches of human nature that give reality to history, which without them must become, as a great writer has finely said, nothing more than an old almanac. I shall not apologize, therefore, for being frankly egoistic and domestic in my reminiscences of that appalling day: for I know that those who desire to seek scientific information on the subject will look for it, not in vain, in the eight bulky volumes of the recent Blue-book. I shall concern myself here with the great event merely as it appeared to myself, a Government servant of the second grade, and in its relations to my own wife, my home, and my children.

On the morning of the 21st of August, in the memorable year of the calamity, I happened to be at Cookham, a pleasant and pretty village which then occupied the western bank of the Thames just below the spot where the Look-out Tower of the Earthquake and Eruption Department now dominates the whole wide plain of the Glassy Rock Desert. In place of the black lake of basalt which young people see nowadays winding its solid bays in and out among the grassy downs, most men still living can well remember a gracious and smiling valley, threaded in the midst by a beautiful river.

I had cycled down from London the evening before (thus forestalling my holiday), and had spent the night at a tolerable inn in the village. By a curious coincidence, the only other visitor at the little hotel that night was a fellow-cyclist, an American, George W. Ward by name, who had come over with his 'wheel', as he called it, for six weeks in England, in order to investigate the geology of our southern counties for himself, and to compare it with that of the far western cretaceous system. I venture to describe this as a curious coincidence, because, as it happened, the mere accident of my meeting him gave me my first inkling of the very existence of that singular phenomenon of which we were all so soon to receive a startling example. I had never so much as heard before of fissure-eruptions; and if I had not heard of them from Ward that evening, I might not have recognised at sight the actuality when it first appeared, and therefore I might have been involved in the general disaster. In which case, of course, this unpretentious narrative would never have been written.

As we sat in the little parlour of the White Hart, however, over our evening pipe, it chanced that the American, who was a pleasant, conversable fellow, began talking to me of his reasons for visiting England. I was at that time a clerk in the General Post Office (of which I am now secretary), and was then no student of science; but his enthusiastic talk about his own country and its vastness amused and interested me. He had been employed for some years on the Geological Survey in the Western States, and he was deeply impressed by the solemnity and the colossal scale of everything American. 'Mountains!' he said, when I spoke of Scotland; 'why, for mountains, your Alps aren't in it, and as for volcanoes, your Vesuviuses and Etnas just spit fire a bit at infrequent intervals; while ours do things on a scale worthy of a great country, I can tell you. Europe is a circumstance: America is a continent.'

'But surely,' I objected, 'that was a pretty fair eruption that destroyed Pompeii!'

The American rose and surveyed me slowly. I can see him to this day, with his close-shaven face and his contemptuous smile at my European ignorance. 'Well,' he said, after a long and impressive pause, 'the lava-flood that destroyed a few acres about the Bay of Naples was what we call a trickle: it came from a crater; and the crater it came from was nothing more than a small round vent-hole; the lava flowed down from it in a moderate stream over a limited area. But what do you say to the earth opening in a huge crack, forty or fifty miles long – say, as far as from here right away to London, or farther – and lava pouring out from the orifice, not in a little rivulet as at Etna or Vesuvius, but in a sea or inundation, which spread at once over a tract as big as England? That's something like volcanic action, isn't it? And that's the sort of thing we have out in Colorado.'

'You are joking,' I replied, 'or bragging. You are trying to astonish me with the familiar spread eagle.'

He smiled a quiet smile. 'Not a bit of it,' he answered. 'What I tell you is at least as true as Gospel. The earth yawns in Montana. There are fissure-eruptions, as we call them, in the Western States, out of which the lava has welled like wine out of a broken skin – welled up in vast roaring floods, molten torrents of basalt, many miles across, and spread like water over whole plains and valleys.'

'Not within historical times!' I exclaimed.

'I'm not so sure about that,' he answered, musing. 'I grant you, not within times which are historical right there – for Colorado is a very new country: but I incline to think some of the most recent fissure eruptions took place not later than when the Tudors reigned in England. The lava oozed out, red-hot – gushed out – was squeezed out – and spread instantly everywhere; it's so comparatively recent that the surface of the rock is still bare in many parts, unweathered sufficiently to support vegetation. I fancy the stream must have been ejected at a single burst, in a huge white-hot dome, and then flowed down on every side, filling up the valleys to a certain level, in and out among the hills, exactly as water might do. And some of these eruptions, I tell you, by measured survey, would have covered more ground than from Dover to Liverpool, and from York to Cornwall.'

'Let us be thankful,' I said, carelessly, 'that such things don't happen in our own times.'

He eyed me curiously. 'Haven't happened, you mean,' he answered. 'We have no security that they mayn't happen again tomorrow. These fissure-eruptions, though not historically described for us, are common events in geological history – commoner and on a larger scale in America than elsewhere. Still, they have occurred in all lands and at various epochs; there is no reason at all why one shouldn't occur in England at present.'

I laughed, and shook my head. I had the Englishman's firm conviction – so rudely shattered by the subsequent events, but then so universal – that nothing very unusual ever happened in England.

Next morning I rose early, bathed in Odney Weir (a picturesque pool close by), breakfasted with the American, and then wrote a hasty line to my wife, informing her that I should probably sleep that night at Oxford; for I was off on a few days' holiday, and I liked Ethel to know where a letter or telegram would reach me each day, as we were both a little anxious about the baby's teething. Even while I pen these words now, the grim humour of the situation comes back to me vividly. Thousands of fathers and mothers were anxious that morning about similar trifles, whose pettiness was brought home to them with an appalling shock in the all-embracing horror of that day's calamity.

About ten o'clock I inflated my tyres and got under way. I meant to ride towards Oxford by a leisurely and circuitous route, along the windings of the river, past Marlow and Henley; so I began by crossing Cookham Bridge, a wooden or iron structure, I scarcely remember which. It spanned the Thames close by the village: the curious will find its exact position marked in the maps of the period.

In the middle of the bridge, I paused and surveyed that charming prospect, which I was the last of living men perhaps to see as it then existed. Close by stood a weir; beside it, the stream divided into three separate branches, exquisitely backed up by the gentle green slopes of Hedsor and Cliveden. I could never pass that typical English view without a glance of admiration; this morning, I pulled up my bicycle for a moment, and cast my eye downstream with more than my usual enjoyment of the smooth blue water and the tall white poplars whose leaves showed their gleaming silver in the breeze beside it. I might have gazed at it too long – and one minute more would have sufficed for my destruction – had not a cry from the tow-path a little farther up attracted my attention.

It was a wild, despairing cry, like that of a man being overpowered and murdered.

I am confident this was my first intimation of danger. Two minutes before, it is true, I had heard a faint sound like distant rumbling of thunder; but nothing else. I am one of those who strenuously maintain that the catastrophe was not heralded by shocks of earthquake.

I turned my eye upstream. For half a second I was utterly bewildered. Strange to say, I did not perceive at first the great flood of fire that was advancing towards me. I saw only the man who had shouted – a miserable, cowering, terror-stricken wretch, one of the abject creatures who used to earn a dubious livelihood in those days (when the river was a boulevard of pleasure) by towing boats upstream. But now, he was rushing wildly forward, with panic in his face; I could see he looked as if close pursued by some wild beast behind him. 'A mad dog!' I said to myself at the outset; 'or else a bull in the meadow!'

I glanced back to see what his pursuer might be; and then, in one second, the whole horror and terror of the catastrophe burst upon me. Its whole horror and terror, I say, but not yet its magnitude. I was aware at first just of a moving red wall, like dull, red-hot molten metal. Trying to recall at so safe a distance in time and space the feelings of the moment and the way in which they surged and succeeded one another, I think I can recollect that my earliest idea was no more than this: 'He must run, or the moving wall will overtake him!' Next instant, a hot wave seemed to strike my face. It was just like the blast of heat that strikes one in a glasshouse when you stand in front of the boiling and seething glass in the furnace. At about the same point in time, I was aware, I believe, that the dull red wall was really a wall of fire. But it was cooled by contact with the air and the water. Even as I looked, however, a second wave from behind seemed to rush on and break: it overlaid and outran the first one. This second wave was white, not red – at white heat, I realized. Then, with a burst of recognition, I knew what it all meant. What Ward had spoken of last night – a fissure eruption!

I looked back. Ward was coming towards me on the bridge, mounted on his Columbia. Too speechless to utter one word, I pointed upstream with my hand. He nodded and shouted back, in a singularly calm voice: 'Yes; just what I told you. A fissure-eruption!'

They were the last words I heard him speak. Not that he appreciated the danger less than I did, though his manner was cool; but he was wearing no clips to his trousers, and at that critical moment he caught his leg in his pedals. The accident disconcerted him; he dismounted hurriedly, and then, panic-stricken as I judged, abandoned his machine. He tried to run. The error was fatal. He tripped and fell. What became of him afterward I will mention later.

But for the moment I saw only the poor wretch on the tow-path. He was not a hundred yards off, just beyond the little bridge which led over the opening to a private boat-house. But as he rushed forwards and shrieked, the wall of fire overtook him. I do not think it quite caught him. It is hard at such moments to judge what really happens; but I believe I saw him shrivel like a moth in a flame a few seconds before the advancing wall of fire swept over the boat-house. I have seen an insect shrivel just so when flung into the midst of white-hot coals. He seemed to go off in gas, leaving a shower or powdery ash to represent his bones behind him. But of this I do not pretend to be positive; I will allow that my own agitation was far too profound to permit of my observing anything with accuracy.

How high was the wall at that time? This has been much debated. I
should guess, thirty feet (though it rose afterwards to more than two
hundred), and it advanced rather faster than a man could run down the
centre of the valley. (Later on, its pace accelerated greatly with subsequent outbursts.) In frantic haste, I saw or felt that only one chance of
safety lay before me: I must strike uphill by the field path to Hedsor.

I rode for very life, with grim death behind me. Once well across the
bridge, and turning up the hill, I saw Ward on the parapet, with his arms
flung up, trying wildly to save himself by leaping into the river. Next
instant he shrivelled I think, as the beggar had shrivelled; and it is to this
complete combustion before the lava flood reached them that I attribute
the circumstance (so much commented upon in the scientific excavations
among the ruins) that no cast of dead bodies, like those at Pompeii, have
anywhere been found in the Thames Valley Desert. My own belief is that
every human body was reduced to a gaseous condition by the terrific heat
several seconds before the molten basalt reached it.

Even at the distance which I had now attained from the central mass,
indeed, the heat was intolerable. Yet, strange to say, I saw few or no
people flying as yet from the inundation. The fact is, the eruption came
upon us so suddenly, so utterly without warning or premonitory symptoms (for I deny the earthquake shocks), that whole towns must have
been destroyed before the inhabitants were aware that anything out of
the common was happening. It is a sort of alleviation to the general
horror to remember that a large proportion of the victims must have
died without even knowing it; one second, they were laughing, talking,
bargaining; the next, they were asphyxiated or reduced to ashes as you
have seen a small fly disappear in an incandescent gas flame.

This, however, is what I learned afterward. At that moment, I was
only aware of a frantic pace uphill, over a rough, stony road, and with
my pedals working as I had never before worked them; while behind
me, I saw purgatory let loose, striving hard to overtake me. I just knew
that a sea of fire was filling the valley from end to end, and that its heat
scorched my face as I urged on my bicycle in abject terror.

All this time, I will admit, my panic was purely personal. I was too
much engaged in the engrossing sense of my own pressing danger to be
vividly alive to the public catastrophe. I did not even think of Ethel and
the children. But when I reached the hill by Hedsor Church – a neat,
small building, whose shell still stands, though scorched and charred, by
the edge of the desert – I was able to pause for half a minute to recover
breath, and to look back upon the scene of the first disaster.

It was a terrible and yet I felt even then a beautiful sight – beautiful with the awful and unearthly beauty of a great forest fire, or a mighty conflagration in some crowded city. The whole river valley, up which I looked, was one sea of fire. Barriers of red-hot lava formed themselves for a moment now and again where the outer edge or vanguard of the inundation had cooled a little on the surface by exposure: and over these temporary dams, fresh cataracts of white-hot material poured themselves afresh into the valley beyond it. After a while, as the deeper portion of basalt was pushed out all was white alike. So glorious it looked in the morning sunshine that one could hardly realize the appalling reality of that sea of molten gold; one might almost have imagined a splendid triumph of the scene painter's art, did one not know that it was actually a river of fire, overwhelming, consuming, and destroying every object before it in its devastating progress.

I tried vaguely to discover the source of the disaster. Looking straight upstream, past Bourne End and Marlow, I descried with bleared and dazzled eyes a whiter mass than any, glowing fiercely in the daylight like an electric light, and filling up the narrow gorge of the river towards Hurley and Henley. I recollected at once that this portion of the valley was not usually visible from Hedsor Hill, and almost without thinking of it I instinctively guessed the reason why it had become so now: it was the centre of disturbance – the earth's crust just there had bulged upward slightly, till it cracked and gaped to emit the basalt.

Looking harder, I could make out (though it was like looking at the sun) that the glowing white dome-shaped mass, as of an electric light, was the molten lava as it gurgled from the mouth of the vast fissure. I say vast, because so it seemed to me, though, as everybody now knows, the actual gap where the earth opened measures no more than eight miles across, from a point near what was once Shiplake Ferry to the site of the old lime-kilns at Marlow. Yet when one saw the eruption actually taking place, the colossal scale of it was what most appalled one. A sea of fire, eight to twelve miles broad, in the familiar Thames Valley, impressed and terrified one a thousand times more than a sea of fire ten times as vast in the nameless wilds of Western America.

I could see dimly, too, that the flood spread in every direction from its central point, both up and down the river. To right and left, indeed, it was soon checked and hemmed in by the hills about Wargrave and Medmenham; but downward, it had filled the entire valley as far as Cookham and beyond; while upward, it spread in one vast glowing sheet towards Reading and the flats by the confluence of the Kennet. I did not then know, of course, that this gigantic natural dam or barrier was later on to fill up the whole low-lying level, and so block the course of the two rivers as to form those twin expanses of inland water, Lake Newbury and Lake Oxford. Tourists who now look down on still summer evenings where the ruins of Magdalen and of Merton may be dimly descried through the pale green depths, their broken masonry picturesquely overgrown with tangled water-weeds, can form but little idea of the terrible scene which that peaceful bank presented while the incandescent lava was pouring forth in a scorching white flood towards the doomed district. Merchants who crowd the busy quays of those mushroom cities which have sprung up with greater rapidity than Chicago or Johannesburg on the indented shore where the new lakes abut upon the Berkshire Chalk Downs have half forgotten the horror of the intermediate time when the waters of the two rivers rose slowly, slowly, day after day, to choke their valleys and overwhelm some of the most glorious architecture in Britain. But though I did not know and could not then foresee the remoter effects of the great fire-flood in that direction, I saw enough to make my heart stand still within me. It was with difficulty that I grasped my bicycle, my hands trembled so fiercely. I realized that I was a spectator of the greatest calamity which had befallen a civilized land within the ken of history.

I looked southward along the valley in the direction of Maidenhead. As yet it did not occur to me that the catastrophe was anything more than a local flood, though even as such it would have been one of unexampled vastness. My imagination could hardly conceive that London itself was threatened. In those days one could not grasp the idea of the destruction of London. I only thought just at first, 'It will go on towards Maiden-head!' Even as I thought it, I saw a fresh and fiercer gush of fire well out from the central gash, and flow still faster than ever down the centre of the valley, over the hardening layer already cooling on its edge by contact with the air and soil. This new outburst fell in a mad cataract over the end or van of the last, and instantly spread like water across the level expanse between the Cliveden hills and the opposite range at Pink-neys. I realized with a throb that it was advancing towards Windsor. Then a wild fear thrilled through me. If Windsor, why not Staines and Chertsey and Hounslow? If Hounslow, why not London?

In a second I remembered Ethel and the children. Hitherto, the immediate danger of my own position alone had struck me. The fire was so near; the heat of it rose up in my face and daunted me. But now I felt I must make a wild dash to warn – not London – no, frankly, I forgot those millions; but Ethel and my little ones. In that thought, for the first moment, the real vastness of the catastrophe came home to me. The Thames Valley was doomed! I must ride for dear life if I wished to save my wife and children!

I mounted again, but found my shaking feet could hardly work the pedals. My legs were one jelly. With a frantic effort, I struck off inland in the direction of Burnham. I did not think my way out definitely; I hardly knew the topography of the district well enough to form any clear conception of what route I must take in order to keep to the hills and avoid the flood of fire that was deluging the lowlands. But by pure instinct, I believe, I set my face Londonwards along the ridge of the chalk downs. In three minutes I had lost sight of the burning flood, and was deep among green lanes and under shadowy beeches. The very contrast frightened me. I wondered if I was going mad. It was all so quiet. One could not believe that scarce five miles off from that devastating sheet of fire, birds were singing in the sky and men toiling in the fields as if nothing had happened.

Near Lambourne Wood I met a brother cyclist, just about to descend the hill. A curve in the road hid the valley from him I shouted aloud: 'For Heaven's sake, don't go down! There is danger, danger!'

He smiled and looked back at me. 'I can take any hill in England,' he answered.

'It's not the hill,' I burst out. 'There has been an eruption – a fissure-eruption at Marlow – great floods of fire – and all the valley is filled with burning lava!'

He stared at me derisively. Then his expression changed of a sudden. I suppose he saw I was white-faced and horror-stricken. He drew away as if alarmed. 'Go back to Colney Hatch!' he cried, pedalling faster and rode hastily down the hill, as if afraid of me. I have no doubt he must have ridden into the very midst of the flood, and been scorched by its advance, before he could check his machine on so sudden a slope.

Between Lambourne Wood and Burnham I did not see the fire-flood. I rode on at full speed among green fields and meadows. Here and there I passed a labouring man on the road. More than one looked up at me and commented on the oppressive heat, but none of them seemed to be aware of the fate that was overtaking their own homes close by, in the valley. I told one or two, but they laughed and gazed after me as if I were a madman. I grew sick of warning them. They took no heed of my words, but went on upon their way as if nothing out of the common were happening to England.

On the edge of the down, near Burnham, I caught sight of the valley again. Here, people were just awaking to what was taking place near them. Half the population was gathered on the slope, looking down with wonder on the flood of fire, which had now just turned the corner of the hills by Taplow. Silent terror was the prevailing type of expression. But when I told them I had seen the lava bursting forth from the earth in a white dome above Marlow, they laughed me to scorn; and when I assured them I was pushing forward in hot haste to London, they answered, 'London! It won't never get as far as London!' That was the only place on the hills, as is now well known, where the flood was observed long enough beforehand to telegraph and warn the inhabitants of the great city; but nobody thought of doing it; and I must say, even if they had done so, there is not the slightest probability that the warning would have attracted the least attention in our ancient Metropolis. Men on the Stock Exchange would have made jests about the slump, and proceeded to buy and sell as usual.

I measured with my eye the level plain between Burnham and Slough, calculating roughly with myself whether I should have time to descend upon the well-known road from Maidenhead to London by Colnbrook and Hounslow. (I advise those who are unacquainted with the topography of this district before the eruption to follow out my route on a good map of the period.) But I recognised in a moment that this course would be impossible. At the rate that the flood had taken to progress from Cookham Bridge to Taplow, I felt sure it would be upon me before I reached Upton, or Ditton Park at the outside. It is true the speed of the advance might slacken somewhat as the lava cooled; and strange to say, so rapidly do realities come to be accepted in one's mind, that I caught myself thinking this thought in the most natural manner, as if I had all my life long been accustomed to the ways of fissure-eruptions. But on the other hand, the lava might well out faster and hotter than before, as I had already seen it do more than once; and I had no certainty even that it would not rise to the level of the hills on which I was standing. You who read this narrative nowadays take it for granted, of course, that the extent and height of the inundation was bound to be exactly what you know it to have been; we at the time could not guess how high it might rise and how large an area of the country it might overwhelm and devastate. Was it to stop at the Chilterns, or to go north to Birmingham, York, and Scotland?

Still, in my trembling anxiety to warn my wife and children, I debated with myself whether I should venture down into the valley, and hurry along the main road with a wild burst for London. I thought of Ethel, alone in our little home at Bayswater, and almost made up my mind to risk it. At that moment, I became aware that the road to London was already crowded with carriages, carts, and cycles, all dashing at a mad pace unanimously towards London. Suddenly a fresh wave turned the corner by Taplow and Maidenhead Bridge, and began to gain upon them visibly. It was an awful sight. I cannot pretend to describe it. The poor creatures on the road, men and animals alike, rushed wildly, despairingly on; the fire took them from behind, and, one by one, before the actual sea reached them, I saw them shrivel and melt away in the fierce white heat of the advancing inundation. I could not look at it any longer. I certainly could not descend and court instant death. I felt that my one chance was to strike across the downs, by Stoke Poges and Uxbridge, and then try the line of northern heights to London.

Oh, how fiercely I pedalled! At Farnham Royal (where again nobody seemed to be aware what had happened) a rural policeman tried to stop me for frantic riding. I tripped him up, and rode on. Experience had taught me it was no use telling those who had not seen it of the disaster. A little beyond, at the entrance to a fine park, a gatekeeper attempted to shut a gate in my face, exclaiming that the road was private. I saw it was the only practicable way without descending to the valley, and I made up my mind this was no time for trifling. I am a man of peace, but I lifted my fist and planted it between his eyes. Then, before he could recover from his astonishment, I had mounted again and ridden on across the park, while he ran after me in vain, screaming to the men in the pleasure-grounds to stop me. But I would not be stopped; and I emerged on the road once more at Stoke Poges.

Near Galley Hill, after a long and furious ride, I reached the descent to Uxbridge. Was it possible to descend? I glanced across, once more by pure instinct, for I had never visited the spot before, towards where I felt the Thames must run. A great white cloud hung over it. I saw what that cloud must mean: it was the steam of the river, where the lava sucked it up and made it seethe and boil suddenly. I had not noticed this white fleece of steam at Cookham, though I did not guess why till afterwards. In the narrow valley where the Thames ran between hills, the lava flowed over it all at once, bottling the steam beneath; and it is this imprisoned steam that gave rise in time to the subsequent series of appalling earthquakes, to supply forecasts of which is now the chief duty of the Seismologer Royal; whereas, in the open plain, the basalt advanced more gradually and in a thinner stream, and therefore turned the whole mass of water into white cloud as soon as it reached each bend of the river.

At the time, however, I had no leisure to think out all this. I only knew by such indirect signs that the flood was still advancing, and, therefore, that it would be impossible for me to proceed towards London by the direct route via Uxbridge and Hanwell. If I meant to reach town (as we called it familiarly), I must descend to the valley at once, pass through Uxbridge streets as fast as I could, make a dash across the plain, by what I afterwards knew to be Hillingdon (I saw it then as a nameless village), and aim at a house-crowned hill which I only learned later was Harrow, but which I felt sure would enable me to descend upon London by Hampstead or Highgate.

I am no strategist; but in a second, in that extremity, I picked out these points, feeling dimly sure they would lead me home to Ethel and the children.

The town of Uxbridge (whose place you can still find marked on many maps) lay in the valley of a small river, a confluent of the Thames. Up this valley it was certain that the lava-stream must flow; and, indeed, at the present day, the basin around is completely filled by one of the solidest and most forbidding masses of black basalt in the country. Still, I made up my mind to descend and cut across the low-lying ground towards Harrow. If I failed, I felt, after all, I was but one unit more in what I now began to realize as a prodigious national calamity.

I was just coasting down the hill, with Uxbridge lying snug and unconscious in the glen below me, when a slight and unimportant accident occurred which almost rendered impossible my further progress. It was past the middle of August; the hedges were being cut; and this particular lane, bordered by a high thorn fence, was strewn with the mangled branches of the may-bushes. At any other time, I should have remembered the danger and avoided them; that day, hurrying downhill for dear life and for Ethel, I forgot to notice them. The consequence was, I was pulled up suddenly by finding my front wheel deflated;* this untimely misfortune almost unmanned me. I dismounted and examined the tyre; it had received a bad puncture. I tried inflating again, in hopes the hole might be small enough to make that precaution sufficient. But it was quite useless. I found I must submit to stop and doctor up the puncture. Fortunately, I had the necessary apparatus in my wallet.

I think it was the weirdest episode of all that weird ride – this sense of stopping impatiently, while the fiery flood still surged on towards London, in order to go through all the fiddling and troublesome little details of mending a pneumatic tyre. The moment and the operation seemed so sadly out of harmony. A countryman passed by on a cart, obviously suspecting nothing; that was another point which added horror to the occasion – that so near the catastrophe, so very few people were even aware what was taking place beside them. Indeed, as is well known, I was one of the very few who saw the eruption during its course, and yet managed to escape from it. Elsewhere, those who tried to run before it,

---

* The bicycles of this period were fitted with pneumatic tubes of india rubber as tires – a clumsy device, now long superseded.

either to escape themselves or to warn others of the danger, were over-taken by the lava before they could reach a place of safety. I attribute this mainly to the fact that most of them continued along the high roads in the valley, or fled instinctively for shelter towards their homes, instead of making at once for the heights and the uplands.

The countryman stopped and looked at me.

'The more haste the less speed!' he said, with proverbial wisdom.

I glanced up at him, and hesitated. Should I warn him of his doom, or was it useless? 'Keep up on the hills,' I said, at last. 'An unspeakable calamity is happening in the valley. Flames of fire are flowing down it, as from a great burning mountain. You will be cut off by the eruption.'

He stared at me blankly, and burst into a meaningless laugh. 'Why, you're one of them Salvation Army fellows,' he exclaimed, after a short pause. 'You're trying to preach to me. I'm going to Uxbridge.' And he continued down the hill towards certain destruction.

It was hours, I feel sure, before I had patched up that puncture, though I did it by the watch in four and a half minutes. As soon as I had blown out my tyre again I mounted once more, and rode at a breakneck pace to Uxbridge. I passed down the straggling main street of the suburban town, crying aloud as I went, 'Run, run, to the downs! A flood of lava is rushing up the valley! To the hills, for your lives! All the Thames bank is blazing!' Nobody took the slightest heed; they stood still in the street for a minute with open mouths: then they returned to their customary occupations. A quarter of an hour later, there was no such place in the world as Uxbridge.

I followed the main road through the village which I have since identi-fied as Hillingdon; then I diverged to the left, partly by roads and partly by field paths of whose exact course I am still uncertain, towards the hill at Harrow. When I reached the town, I did not strive to rouse the people, partly because my past experience had taught me the futility of the attempt, and partly because I rightly judged that they were safe from the inund-ation; for as it never quite covered the dome of St Paul's, part of which still protrudes from the sea of basalt, it did not reach the level of the northern heights of London. I rode on through Harrow without one word to any-body. I did not desire to be stopped or harassed as an escaped lunatic.

From Harrow I made my way tortuously along the rising ground, by the light of nature, through Wembley Park, to Willesden. At Willesden, for the first time, I found to a certainty that London was threatened. Great crowds of people in the profoundest excitement stood watching a dense cloud of smoke and steam that spread rapidly over the direction of Shepherd's Bush and Hammersmith. They were speculating as to its meaning, but laughed incredulously when I told them what it portended. A few minutes later, the smoke spread ominously towards Kensington and Paddington. That settled my fate. It was clearly impossible to descend into London; and indeed, the heat now began to be unendurable. It drove us all back, almost physically. I thought I must abandon all hope. I should never even know what had become of Ethel and the children.

My first impulse was to lie down and await the fire-flood. Yet the sense of the greatness of the catastrophe seemed somehow to blunt one's own private grief. I was beside myself with fear for my darlings; but I realized that I was but one among hundreds of thousands of fathers in the same position. What was happening at that moment in the great city of five million souls we did not know, we shall never know; but we may conjecture that the end was mercifully too swift to entail much needless suffering. All at once, a gleam of hope struck me. It was my father's birthday. Was it not just possible that Ethel might have taken the children up to Hampstead to wish their grandpa many happy returns of the day? With a wild determination not to give up all for lost, I turned my front wheel in the direction of Hampstead Hill, still skirting the high ground as far as possible. My heart was on fire within me. A restless anxiety urged me to ride my hardest. As all along the route, I was still just a minute or two in front of the catastrophe. People were beginning to be aware that something was taking place; more than once as I passed they asked me eagerly where the fire was. It was impossible for me to believe by this time that they knew nothing of an event in whose midst I seemed to have been living for months; how could I realize that all the things which had happened since I started from Cookham Bridge so long ago were really compressed into the space of a single morning? – nay, more, of an hour and a half only?

As I approached Windmill Hill, a terrible sinking seized me. I seemed to totter on the brink of a precipice. Could Ethel be safe? Should I ever again see little Bertie and the baby? I pedalled on as if automatically; for all life had gone out of me. I felt my hip-joint moving dry in its socket. I held my breath; my heart stood still. It was a ghastly moment.

At my father's door I drew up, and opened the garden gate. I hardly dared to go in. Though each second was precious, I paused and hesitated.

At last I turned the handle. I heard somebody within. My heart came up in my mouth. It was little Bertie's voice: 'Do it again, Granpa; do it again; it amooses Bertie!'

I rushed into the room. 'Bertie, Bertie!' I cried. 'Is Mammy here?'

He flung himself upon me. 'Mammy, Mammy, Daddy has comed home.' I burst into tears. 'And Baby?' I asked, trembling.

'Baby and Ethel are here, George,' my father answered, staring at me. 'Why, my boy, what's the matter?'

I flung myself into a chair and broke down. In that moment of relief, I felt that London was lost, but I had saved my wife and children.

I did not wait for explanations. A crawling four-wheeler was loitering by. I hailed it and hurried them in. My father wished to discuss the matter, but I cut him short. I gave the driver three pounds – all the gold I had with me. 'Drive on!' I shouted, 'drive on! Towards Hatfield – anywhere!'

He drove as he was bid. We spent that night, while Hampstead flared like a beacon, at an isolated farm-house on the high ground in Hertfordshire. For, of course, though the flood did not reach so high, it set fire to everything inflammable in its neighbourhood.

Next day, all the world knew the magnitude of the disaster. It can only be summed up in five emphatic words: there was no more London.

I have one other observation alone to make. I noticed at the time how, in my personal relief, I forgot for the moment that London was perishing. I even forgot that my house and property had perished. Exactly the opposite, it seemed to me, happened with most of those survivors who lost wives and children in the eruption. They moved about as in a dream, without a tear, without a complaint, helping others to provide for the needs of the homeless and houseless. The universality of the catastrophe made each man feel as though it were selfishness to attach too great an importance at such a crisis to his own personal losses. Nay, more; the burst of feverish activity and nervous excitement, I might even say enjoyment, which followed the horror, was traceable, I think, to this self-same cause. Even grave citizens felt they must do their best to dispel the universal gloom; and they plunged accordingly into around of dissipations which other nations thought both unseemly and un-English. It was one way of expressing the common emotion. We had all lost heart – and we flocked to the theatres to pluck up our courage. That, I believe, must be our national answer to M. Zola's strictures on our untimely levity. 'This people,' says the great French author, 'which took its pleasures sadly while it was rich and prosperous, begins to dance and sing above the ashes of its capital – it makes merry by the open graves of its wives and children. What an enigma! What a puzzle! What chance of an Oedipus!'

A Martian Odyssey

Stanley G. Weinbaum

Jarvis stretched himself as luxuriously as he could in the cramped general quarters of the *Ares*.

'Air you can breathe!' he exulted. 'It feels as thick as soup after the thin stuff out there!' He nodded at the Martian landscape stretching flat and desolate in the light of the nearer moon, beyond the glass of the port.

The other three stared at him sympathetically – Putz, the engineer, Leroy, the biologist, and Harrison, the astronomer and captain of the expedition. Dick Jarvis was chemist of the famous crew, the *Ares* expedition, first human beings to set foot on the mysterious neighbor of the earth, the planet Mars. This, of course, was in the old days, less than twenty years after the mad American Doheny perfected the atomic blast at the cost of his life, and only a decade after the equally mad Cardoza rode on it to the moon. They were true pioneers, these four of the *Ares*. Except for a half-dozen moon expeditions and the ill-fated de Lancey flight aimed at the seductive orb of Venus, they were the first men to feel other gravity than earth's, and certainly the first successful crew to leave the earth-moon system. And they deserved that success when one considers the difficulties and discomforts – the months spent in acclimatization chambers back on earth, learning to breathe the air as tenuous as that of Mars, the challenging of the void in the tiny rocket driven by the cranky reaction motors of the twenty-first century, and mostly the facing of an absolutely unknown world.

Jarvis stretched and fingered the raw and peeling tip of his frostbitten nose. He sighed again contentedly.

'Well,' exploded Harrison abruptly, 'are we going to hear what happened? You set out all shipshape in an auxiliary rocket, we don't get a peep for ten days, and finally Putz here picks you out of a lunatic ant-heap with a freak ostrich as your pal! Spill it, man!'

'Speel?' queried Leroy perplexedly. 'Speel what?'

'He means "*spiel*",' explained Putz soberly. 'It iss to tell.'

Jarvis met Harrison's amused glance without the shadow of a smile. 'That's right, Karl,' he said in grave agreement with Putz. '*Ich spiel es!*' He grunted comfortably and began.

'According to orders,' he said, 'I watched Karl here take off toward the North, and then I got into my flying sweat-box and headed south. You'll remember, Cap – we had orders not to land, but just scout about for points of interest. I set the two cameras clicking and buzzed along, riding pretty high – about two thousand feet – for a couple of reasons. First, it gave the cameras a greater field, and second, the under-jets travel so far in this half-vacuum they call air here that they stir up dust if you move low.'

'We know all that from Putz,' grunted Harrison. 'I wish you'd saved the films, though. They'd have paid the cost of this junket; remember how the public mobbed the first moon pictures?'

'The films are safe,' retorted Jarvis. 'Well,' he resumed, 'as I said, I buzzed along at a pretty good clip; just as we figured, the wings haven't much lift in this air at less than a hundred miles per hour, and even then I had to use the under-jets.

'So, with the speed and the altitude and the blurring caused by the under-jets, the seeing wasn't any too good. I could see enough, though, to distinguish that what I sailed over was just more of this gray plain that we'd been examining the whole week since our landing – same blobby growths and the same eternal carpet of crawling little plant-animals, or biopods, as Leroy calls them. So I sailed along, calling back my position every hour as instructed, and not knowing whether you heard me.'

'I did!' snapped Harrison.

'A hundred and fifty miles south,' continued Jarvis imperturbably, 'the surface changed to a sort of low plateau, nothing but desert and orange-tinted sand. I figured that we were right in our guess then, and this gray plain we dropped on was really the Mare Cimmerium, which would make my orange desert the region called Xanthus. If I were right, I ought to hit another gray plain, the Mare Chronium, in another couple of hundred miles, and then another orange desert, Thyle I or II. And so I did.'

'Putz verified our position a week and a half ago!' grumbled the captain. 'Let's get to the point.'

'Coming!' remarked Jarvis. 'Twenty miles into Thyle – believe it or not – I crossed a canal!'

'Putz photographed a hundred! Let's hear something new!'

'And did he also see a city?'

'Twenty of 'em, if you call those heaps of mud cities!'

'Well,' observed Jarvis, 'from here on I'll be telling a few things Putz didn't see!' He rubbed his tingling nose, and continued. 'I knew that I had sixteen hours of daylight at this season, so eight hours – eight hundred miles – from here, I decided to turn back. I was still over Thyle, whether I or II I'm not sure, not more than twenty-five miles into it. And right there, Putz's pet motor quit!'

'Quit? How?' Putz was solicitous.

'The atomic blast got weak. I started losing altitude right away, and suddenly there I was with a thump right in the middle of Thyle! Smashed my nose on the window, too!' He rubbed the injured member ruefully.

'Did you maybe try vashing der combustion chamber mit acid sulphuric?' inquired Putz. 'Sometimes der lead giffs a secondary radiation –'

'Naw!' said Jarvis disgustedly. 'I wouldn't try that, of course – not more than ten times! Besides, the bump flattened the landing gear and busted off the under-jets. Suppose I got the thing working – what then? Ten miles with the blast coming right out of the bottom and I'd have melted the floor from under me!' He rubbed his nose again. 'Lucky for me a pound only weighs seven ounces here, or I'd have been mashed flat!'

'I could have fixed!' ejaculated the engineer. 'I bet it vas not serious.'

'Probably not,' agreed Jarvis sarcastically. 'Only it wouldn't fly. Nothing serious, but I had the choice of waiting to be picked up or trying to walk back – eight hundred miles, and perhaps twenty days before we had to leave! Forty miles a day! Well,' he concluded, 'I chose to walk. Just as much chance of being picked up, and it kept me busy.'

'We'd have found you,' said Harrison.

'No doubt. Anyway, I rigged up a harness from some seat straps, and put the water tank on my back, took a cartridge belt and revolver, and some iron rations, and started out.'

'Water tank!' exclaimed the little biologist, Leroy. 'She weigh one-quarter ton!'

'Wasn't full. Weighed about two hundred and fifty pounds earth-weight, which is eighty-five here. Then, besides, my own personal two hundred and ten pounds is only seventy on Mars, so, tank and all, I grossed a hundred and fifty-five, or fifty-five pounds less than my every-day earth-weight. I figured on that when I undertook the forty-mile daily stroll. Oh – of course I took a thermo-skin sleeping bag for these wintry Martian nights.

'Off I went, bouncing along pretty quickly. Eight hours of daylight meant twenty miles or more. It got tiresome, of course – plugging along over a soft sand desert with nothing to see, not even Leroy's crawling bio-pods. But an hour or so brought me to the canal – just a dry ditch about four hundred feet wide, and straight as a railroad on its own company map.

'There'd been water in it sometime, though. The ditch was covered with what looked like a nice green lawn. Only, as I approached, the lawn moved out of my way!'

'Eh?' said Leroy.

'Yeah, it was a relative of your biopods. I caught one, a little grass-like blade about as long as my finger, with two thin, stemmy legs.'

'He is where?' Leroy was eager.

'He is let go! I had to move, so I plowed along with the walking grass opening in front and closing behind. And then I was out on the orange desert of Thyle again.

'I plugged steadily along, cussing the sand that made going so tiresome, and, incidentally, cussing that cranky motor of yours, Karl. It was just before twilight that I reached the edge of Thyle, and looked down over the gray Mare Chronium. And I knew there was seventy-five miles of *that* to be walked over, and then a couple of hundred miles of that Xanthus desert, and about as much more Mare Cimmerium. Was I pleased? I started cussing you fellows for not picking me up!'

'We were trying, you sap!' said Harrison.

'That didn't help. Well, I figured I might as well use what was left of daylight in getting down the cliff that bounded Thyle. I found an easy place, and down I went. Mare Chronium was just the same sort of place as this – crazy leafless plants and a bunch of crawlers; I gave it a glance and hauled out my sleeping bag. Up to that time, you know, I hadn't seen anything worth worrying about on this half-dead world – nothing dangerous, that is.'

'Did you?' queried Harrison.

'*Did I!* You'll hear about it when I come to it. Well, I was just about to turn in when suddenly I heard the wildest sort of shenanigans!'

'Vot iss shenanigans?' inquired Putz.

'He says, "*Je ne sais quoi*",' explained Leroy. 'It is to say, "I don't know what".'

'That's right,' agreed Jarvis. 'I didn't know what, so I sneaked over to find out. There was a racket like a flock of crows eating a bunch of canaries – whistles, cackles, caws, trills, and what have you. I rounded a clump of stumps, and there was Tweel!'

'Tweel?' said Harrison, and 'Tveel?' said Leroy and Putz.

'That freak ostrich,' explained the narrator. 'At least, Tweel is as near as I can pronounce it without sputtering. He called it something like "Trrrweerrll!".'

'What was he doing?' asked the Captain.

'He was being eaten! And squealing, of course, as any one would.'

'Eaten! By what?'

'I found out later. All I could see then was a bunch of black ropy arms tangled around what looked like, as Putz described it to you, an ostrich. I wasn't going to interfere, naturally; if both creatures were dangerous, I'd have one less to worry about.

'But the bird-like thing was putting up a good battle, dealing vicious blows with an eighteen-inch beak, between screeches. And besides, I caught a glimpse or two of what was on the end of those arms!' Jarvis shuddered. 'But the clincher was when I noticed a little black bag or case hung about the neck of the bird-thing! It was intelligent. That or tame, I assumed. Anyway, it clinched my decision. I pulled out my automatic and fired into what I could see of its antagonist.

'There was a flurry of tentacles and a spurt of black corruption, and then the thing, with a disgusting sucking noise, pulled itself and its arms into a hole in the ground. The other let out a series of clacks, staggered around on legs about as thick as golf sticks, and turned suddenly to face me. I held my weapon ready, and the two of us stared at each other.

'The Martian wasn't a bird, really. It wasn't even bird-like, except just at first glance. It had a beak all right, and a few feathery appendages, but the beak wasn't really a beak. It was somewhat flexible; I could see the tip bend slowly from side to side; it was almost like a cross between a beak and a trunk. It had four-toed feet, and four-fingered things – hands, you'd have to call them, and a little roundish body, and a long neck ending in a tiny head – and that beak. It stood an inch or so taller than I, and – well, Putz saw it!'

The engineer nodded. '*Ja*! I saw!'

Jarvis continued. 'So – we stared at each other. Finally the creature went into a series of clackings and twitterings and held out its hands toward me, empty. I took that as a gesture of friendship.'

'Perhaps,' suggested Harrison, 'it looked at that nose of yours and thought you were its brother!'

'Huh! You can be funny without talking! Anyway, I put up my gun and said "Aw, don't mention it", or something of the sort, and the thing came over and we were pals.

'By that time, the sun was pretty low and I knew that I'd better build a fire or get into my thermo-skin. I decided on the fire. I picked a spot at the base of the Thyle cliff where the rock could reflect a little heat on my back. I started breaking off chunks of this desiccated Martian vegetation, and my companion caught the idea and brought in an armful. I reached for a match, but the Martian fished into his pouch and brought out something that looked like a glowing coal; one touch of it, and the fire was blazing – and you all know what a job we have starting a fire in this atmosphere!

'And that bag of his!' continued the narrator. 'That was a manufactured article, my friends; press an end and she popped open – press the middle and she sealed so perfectly you couldn't see the line. Better than zippers.

'Well, we stared at the fire for a while and I decided to attempt some sort of communication with the Martian. I pointed at myself and said "Dick"; he caught the drift immediately, stretched a bony claw at me and repeated "Tick". Then I pointed at him, and he gave that whistle I called Tweel; I can't imitate his accent. Things were going smoothly; to emphasize the names, I repeated "Dick", and then, pointing at him, "Tweel".

'There we stuck! He gave some clacks that sounded negative, and said something like "P-p-p-root". And that was just the beginning; I was always "Tick", but as for him – part of the time he was "Tweel", and part of the time he was "P-p-p-proot", and part of the time he was sixteen other noises!

'We just couldn't connect. I tried "rock", and I tried "star", and "tree", and "fire". and Lord knows what else, and try as I would, I couldn't get a single word! Nothing was the same for two successive minutes, and if that's a language, I'm an alchemist. Finally I gave it up and called him Tweel, and that seemed to do.

'But Tweel hung on to some of my words. He remembered a couple of them, which I suppose is a great achievement if you're used to a language you have to make up as you go along. But I couldn't get the hang of his talk; either I missed some subtle point or we just didn't *think* alike – and I rather believe the latter view.

'I've other reasons for believing that. After a while I gave up the language business, and tried mathematics. I scratched two plus two equals four on the ground, and demonstrated it with pebbles. Again Tweel caught the idea, and informed me that three plus three equals six. Once more we seemed to be getting somewhere.

'So, knowing that Tweel had at least a grammar school education, I drew a circle for the sun, pointing first at it, and then at the last glow of the sun. Then I sketched in Mercury, and Venus, and Mother Earth, and Mars, and finally, pointing to Mars, I swept my hand around in a sort of inclusive gesture to indicate that Mars was our current environment. I was working up to putting over the idea that my home was on the earth.

'Tweel understood my diagram all right. He poked his beak at it, and with a great deal of trilling and clucking, he added Deimos and Phobos to Mars, and then sketched in the earth's moon!

'Do you see what that proves? It proves that Tweel's race uses telescopes – that they're civilized!'

'Does not!' snapped Harrison. 'The moon is visible from here as a fifth magnitude star. They could see its revolution with the naked eye.'

'The moon, yes!' said Jarvis. 'You've missed my point. Mercury isn't visible! And Tweel knew of Mercury because he placed the Moon at the *third* planet, not the second. If he didn't know Mercury, he'd put the earth second, and Mars third, instead of fourth! See?'

'Humph!' said Harrison.

'Anyway,' proceeded Jarvis, 'I went on with my lesson. Things were going smoothly, and it looked as if I could put the idea over. I pointed at the earth on my diagram, and then at myself, and then, to clinch it, I pointed to myself and then to the earth itself shining bright green almost at the zenith.

'Tweel set up such an excited clacking that I was certain he understood. He jumped up and down, and suddenly he pointed at himself and then at the sky, and then at himself and at the sky again. He pointed at his middle and then at Arcturus, at his head and then at Spica, at his feet and then at half a dozen stars, while I just gaped at him. Then, all of a sudden, he gave a tremendous leap. Man, what a hop! He shot straight up into the starlight, seventy-five feet if an inch! I saw him silhouetted against the sky, saw him turn and come down at me head first, and land smack on his beak like a javelin! There he stuck square in the center of my sun-circle in the sand – a bull's eye!'

'Nuts!' observed the captain. 'Plain nuts!'

'That's what I thought, too! I just stared at him openmouthed while he pulled his head out of the sand and stood up. Then I figured he'd missed my point, and I went through the whole blamed rigmarole again, and it ended the same way, with Tweel on his nose in the middle of my picture!'

'Maybe it's a religious rite,' suggested Harrison.

'Maybe,' said Jarvis dubiously. 'Well, there we were. We could exchange ideas up to a certain point, and then – blooey! Something in us was different, unrelated; I don't doubt that Tweel thought me just as screwy as I thought him. Our minds simply looked at the world from different viewpoints, and perhaps his viewpoint is as true as ours. But – we couldn't get together, that's all. Yet, in spite of all difficulties, I *liked* Tweel, and I have a queer certainty that he liked me.'

'Nuts!' repeated the captain. 'Just daffy!'

'Yeah? Wait and see. A couple of times I've thought that perhaps we – ' He paused, and then resumed his narrative. 'Anyway, I finally gave it up, and got into my thermo-skin to sleep. The fire hadn't kept me any too warm, but that damned sleeping bag did. Got stuffy five minutes after I closed myself in. I opened it a little and bingo! Some eighty-below-zero air hit my nose, and that's when I got this pleasant little frostbite to add to the bump I acquired during the crash of my rocket.

'I don't know what Tweel made of my sleeping. He sat around, but when I woke up, he was gone. I'd just crawled out of my bag, though, when I heard some twittering, and there he came, sailing down from that three-story Thyle cliff to alight on his beak beside me. I pointed to myself and toward the north, and he pointed at himself and toward the south, and when I loaded up and started away, he came along.

'Man, how he traveled! A hundred and fifty feet at a jump, sailing through the air stretched out like a spear, and landing on his beak. He seemed surprised at my plodding, but after a few moments he fell in beside me, only every few minutes he'd go into one of his leaps, and stick his nose into the sand a block ahead of me. Then he'd come shooting back at me; it made me nervous at first to see that beak of his coming at me like a spear, but he always ended in the sand at my side.

'So the two of us plugged along across the Mare Chronium. Same sort of place as this – same crazy plants and same little green biopods growing in the sand, or crawling out of your way. We talked – not that we understood each other, you know, but just for company. I sang songs, and I suspected Tweel did too; at least, some of his trillings and twitterings had a subtle sort of rhythm.

'Then, for variety, Tweel would display his smattering of English words. He'd point to an outcropping and say "rock", and point to a pebble and say it again; or he'd touch my arm and say "Tick", and then repeat it. He seemed terrifically amused that the same word meant the same thing twice in succession, or that the same word could apply to two different objects. It set me wondering if perhaps his language wasn't like the primitive speech of some earth people – you know, Captain, like the Negritoes, for instance, who haven't any generic words. No word for food or water or man – words for good food and bad food, or rainwater and seawater, or strong man and weak man – but no names for general classes. They're too primitive to understand that rain water and sea water are just different aspects of the same thing. But that wasn't the case with Tweel; it was just that we were somehow mysteriously different – our minds were alien to each other. And yet – we *liked* each other!'

'Looney, that's all,' remarked Harrison. 'That's why you two were so fond of each other.'

'Well, I like *you*!' countered Jarvis wickedly. 'Anyway,' he resumed, 'don't get the idea that there was anything screwy about Tweel. In fact, I'm not so sure but that he couldn't teach our highly praised human intelligence a trick or two. Oh, he wasn't an intellectual superman, I guess; but don't overlook the point that he managed to understand a little of my mental workings, and I never even got a glimmering of his.'

'Because he didn't have any!' suggested the captain, while Putz and Leroy blinked attentively.

'You can judge of that when I'm through,' said Jarvis. 'Well, we plugged along across the Mare Chronium all that day, and all the next. Mare Chronium – Sea of Time! Say, I was willing to agree with Schiaparelli's name by the end of that march! Just that gray, endless plain of weird plants, and never a sign of any other life. It was so monotonous that I was even glad to see the desert of Xanthus toward the evening of the second day.

'I was fair worn out, but Tweel seemed as fresh as ever, for all I never saw him drink or eat. I think he could have crossed the Mare Chronium in a couple of hours with those block-long nose dives of his, but he stuck along with me. I offered him some water once or twice; he took the cup from me and sucked the liquid into his beak, and then carefully squirted it all back into the cup and gravely returned it.

'Just as we sighted Xanthus, or the cliffs that bounded it, one of those nasty sand clouds blew along, not as bad as the one we had here, but mean to travel against. I pulled the transparent flap of my thermo-skin bag across my face and managed pretty well, and I noticed that Tweel used some feathery appendages growing like a mustache at the base of his beak to cover his nostrils, and some similar fuzz to shield his eyes.'

'He is a desert creature!' ejaculated the little biologist, Leroy.

'Huh? Why?'

'He drink no water – he is adapt' for sand storm – '

'Proves nothing! There's not enough water to waste anywhere on this desiccated pill called Mars. We'd call all of it desert on earth, you know.' He paused. 'Anyway, after the sand storm blew over, a little wind kept blowing in our faces, not strong enough to stir the sand. But suddenly things came drifting along from the Xanthus cliffs – small, transparent spheres, for all the world like glass tennis balls! But light – they were almost light enough to float even in this thin air – empty, too; at least, I cracked open a couple and nothing came out but a bad smell. I asked Tweel about them, but all he said was "No, no, no", which I took to mean that he knew nothing about them. So they went bouncing by like tumbleweeds, or like soap bubbles, and we plugged on toward Xanthus. Tweel pointed at one of the crystal balls once and said "rock", but I was too tired to argue with him. Later I discovered what he meant.

'We came to the bottom of the Xanthus cliffs finally, when there wasn't much daylight left. I decided to sleep on the plateau if possible;

anything dangerous, I reasoned, would be more likely to prowl through the vegetation of the Mare Chronium than the sand of Xanthus. Not that I'd seen a single sign of menace, except the rope-armed black thing that had trapped Tweel, and apparently that didn't prowl at all, but lured its victims within reach. It couldn't lure me while I slept, especially as Tweel didn't seem to sleep at all, but simply sat patiently around all night. I wondered how the creature had managed to trap Tweel, but there wasn't any way of asking him. I found that out too, later; it's devilish!

'However, we were ambling around the base of the Xanthus barrier looking for an easy spot to climb. At least, I was. Tweel could have leaped it easily, for the cliffs were lower than Thyle – perhaps sixty feet. I found a place and started up, swearing at the water tank strapped to my back – it didn't bother me except when climbing – and suddenly I heard a sound that I thought I recognized!

'You know how deceptive sounds are in this thin air. A shot sounds like the pop of a cork. But this sound was the drone of a rocket, and sure enough, there went our second auxiliary about ten miles to westward, between me and the sunset!'

'Vas me!' said Putz. 'I hunt for you.'

'Yeah; I knew that, but what good did it do me? I hung on to the cliff and yelled and waved with one hand. Tweel saw it too, and set up a trilling and twittering, leaping to the top of the barrier and then high into the air. And while I watched, the machine droned on into the shadows to the south.

'I scrambled to the top of the cliff. Tweel was still pointing and trilling excitedly, shooting up toward the sky and coming down head-on to stick upside down on his back in the sand. I pointed toward the south, and at myself, and he said, "Yes – Yes – Yes"; but somehow I gathered that he thought the flying thing was a relative of mine, probably a parent. Perhaps I did his intellect an injustice; I think now that I did.

'I was bitterly disappointed by the failure to attract attention. I pulled out my thermo-skin and crawled into it, as the night chill was already apparent. Tweel stuck his beak into the sand and drew up his legs and arms and looked for all the world like one of those leafless shrubs out there. I think he stayed that way all night.'

'Protective mimicry!' ejaculated Leroy. 'See? He is desert creature!'

'In the morning,' resumed Jarvis, 'we started off again. We hadn't gone a hundred yards into Xanthus when I saw something queer! This is one thing Putz didn't photograph, I'll wager!

'There was a line of little pyramids – tiny ones, not more than six inches high, stretching across Xanthus as far as I could see! Little buildings made of pygmy bricks, they were, hollow inside and truncated, or at least broken at the top and empty. I pointed at them and said "What?" to Tweel, but he gave some negative twitters to indicate, I suppose, that he didn't know. So off we went, following the row of pyramids because they ran north, and I was going north.

'Man, we trailed that line for hours! After a while, I noticed another queer thing: they were getting larger. Same number of bricks in each one, but the bricks were larger.

'By noon they were shoulder high. I looked into a couple – all just the same, broken at the top and empty. I examined a brick or two as well; they were silica, and old as creation itself!'

'How do you know?' asked Leroy.

'They were weathered – edges rounded. Silica doesn't weather easily even on earth, and in this climate – !'

'How old you think?'

'Fifty thousand – a hundred thousand years. How can I tell? The little ones we saw in the morning were older – perhaps ten times as old. Crumbling. How old would that make *them*? Half a million years? Who knows?' Jarvis paused a moment. 'Well,' he resumed, 'we followed the line. Tweel pointed at them and said "rock" once or twice, but he'd done that many times before. Besides, he was more or less right about these.

'I tried questioning him. I pointed at a pyramid and asked "People?" and indicated the two of us. He set up a negative sort of clucking and said, "No, no, no. No one – one – two. No two – two – four," meanwhile rubbing his stomach. I just stared at him and he went through the business again. "No one – one – two. No two – two – four." I just gaped at him.'

'That proves it!' exclaimed Harrison. 'Nuts!'

'You think so?' queried Jarvis sardonically. 'Well, I figured it out different! "No one – one – two!" You don't get it, of course, do you?'

'Nope – nor do you!'

'I think I do! Tweel was using the few English words he knew to put over a very complex idea. What, let me ask, does mathematics make you think of?'

'Why – of astronomy. Or – or logic!'

'That's it! "No one – one – two!" Tweel was telling me that the builders of the pyramids weren't people – or that they weren't intelligent, that they weren't reasoning creatures! Get it?'

'Huh! I'll be damned!'

'You probably will.'

'Why,' put in Leroy, 'he rub his belly?'

'Why? Because, my dear biologist, that's where his brains are! Not in his tiny head – in his middle!'

'*C'est impossible!*'

'Not on Mars, it isn't! This flora and fauna aren't earthly; your biopods prove that!' Jarvis grinned and took up his narrative. 'Anyway, we plugged along across Xanthus and in about the middle of the afternoon, something else queer happened. The pyramids ended.'

'Ended!'

'Yeah; the queer part was that the last one – and now they were ten-footers – was capped! See? Whatever built it was still inside; we'd trailed 'em from their half-million-year-old origin to the present.

'Tweel and I noticed it about the same time. I yanked out my automatic (I had a clip of Boland explosive bullets in it) and Tweel, quick as a sleight-of-hand trick, snapped a queer little glass revolver out of his bag. It was much like our weapons, except that the grip was larger to accommodate his four-taloned hand. And we held our weapons ready while we sneaked up along the lines of empty pyramids.

'Tweel saw the movement first. The top tiers of bricks were heaving, shaking, and suddenly slid down the sides with a thin crash. And then – something – something was coming out!

'A long, silvery-gray arm appeared, dragging after it an armored body. Armored, I mean, with scales, silver-gray and dull-shining. The arm heaved the body out of the hole; the beast crashed to the sand.

'It was a nondescript creature – body like a big gray cask, arm and a sort of mouth-hole at one end; stiff, pointed tail at the other – and that's all. No other limbs, no eyes, ears, nose – nothing! The thing dragged itself a few yards, inserted its pointed tail in the sand, pushed itself upright, and just sat.

'Tweel and I watched it for ten minutes before it moved. Then, with a creaking and rustling like – oh, like crumpling stiff paper – its arm moved to the mouth-hole and out came a brick! The arm placed the brick carefully on the ground, and the thing was still again.

'Another ten minutes – another brick. Just one of Nature's bricklayers. I was about to slip away and move on when Tweel pointed at the thing and said "rock"! I went "huh?" and he said it again. Then, to the accompaniment of some of his trilling, he said, "No – no – " and gave two or three whistling breaths.

'Well, I got his meaning, for a wonder! I said, "No breathe!" and demonstrated the word. Tweel was ecstatic; he said, "Yes, yes, yes! No, no, no breet!" Then he gave a leap and sailed out to land on his nose about one pace from the monster!

'I was startled, you can imagine! The arm was going up for a brick, and I expected to see Tweel caught and mangled, but – nothing happened! Tweel pounded on the creature, and the arm took the brick and placed it neatly beside the first. Tweel rapped on its body again, and said "rock", and I got up nerve enough to take a look myself.

'Tweel was right again. The creature *was* rock, and it didn't breathe!'

'How you know?' snapped Leroy, his black eyes blazing interest.

'Because I'm a chemist. The beast was made of silica! There must have been pure silicon in the sand, and it lived on that. Get it? We, and Tweel, and those plants out there, and even the biopods are *carbon* life; this thing lived by a different set of chemical reactions. It was silicon life!'

'*La vie silicieuse!*' shouted Leroy. 'I have suspect, and now it is proof! I must go see! *Il faut que je* – '

'All right! All right!' said Jarvis. 'You can go see. Anyhow, there the thing was, alive and yet not alive, moving every ten minutes, and then only to remove a brick. Those bricks were its waste matter. See, Frenchy? We're carbon, and our waste is carbon dioxide, and this thing is silicon and *its* waste is silicon dioxide – silica. But silica is a solid, hence the bricks. And it builds itself in, and when it is covered, it moves over to a fresh place to start over. No wonder it creaked! A living creature a half a million years old!'

'How you know how old?' Leroy was frantic.

'We trailed its pyramids from the beginning, didn't we? If this weren't the original pyramid builder, the series would have ended somewhere before we found him, wouldn't it? – ended and started over with the small ones. That's simple enough, isn't it?

'But he reproduces, or tries to. Before the third brick came out, there was a little rustle and out popped a whole stream of those little crystal balls. They're his spores, or seeds – call 'em what you want. They went bouncing by across Xanthus just as they'd bounced by us back in the Mare Chronium. I've a hunch how they work, too – this is for your information, Leroy. I think the crystal shell of silica is no more than protective covering, like an eggshell, and that the active principle is the smell inside. It's some sort of gas that attacks silicon, and if the shell is broken near a supply of that element, some reaction starts that ultimately develops into a beast like that one.'

'You should try!' exclaimed the little Frenchman. 'We must break one to see!'

'Yeah? Well, I did. I smashed a couple against the sand. Would you like to come back in about ten thousand years to see if I planted some pyramid monsters? You'd most likely be able to tell by that time!' Jarvis paused and drew a deep breath. 'Lord! That queer creature Do you picture it? Blind, deaf, nerveless, brainless – just a mechanism, and yet – immortal! Bound to go on making bricks, building pyramids, as long as silicon and oxygen exist, and even afterwards it'll just stop. It won't be dead. If the accidents of a million years bring it its food again, there it'll be, ready to run again, while brains and civilizations are part of the past. A queer beast – yet I met a stranger one!'

'If you did, it must have been in your dreams!' growled Harrison.

'You're right!' said Jarvis soberly. 'In a way, you're right. The dream-beast! That's the best name for it – and it's the most fiendish, terrifying creation one could imagine! More dangerous than a lion, more insidious than a snake!'

'Tell me!' begged Leroy. 'I must go see!'

'Not *this* devil!' He paused again. 'Well,' he resumed, 'Tweel and I left the pyramid creature and plowed along through Xanthus. I was tired and a little disheartened by Putz's failure to pick me up, and Tweel's trilling got on my nerves, as did his flying nosedives. So I just strode along without a word, hour after hour across that monotonous desert.

'Toward mid-afternoon we came in sight of a low dark line on the horizon. I knew what it was. It was a canal; I'd crossed it in the rocket and it meant that we were just one-third of the way across Xanthus. Pleasant thought, wasn't it? And still, I was keeping up to schedule.

'We approached the canal slowly; I remembered that this one was bordered by a wide fringe of vegetation and that Mudheap City was on it.

'I was tired, as I said. I kept thinking of a good hot meal, and then from that I jumped to reflections of how nice and home-like even Borneo would seem after this crazy planet, and from that, to thoughts of little old New York, and then to thinking about a girl I know there, Fancy Long. Know her?'

'Vision entertainer,' said Harrison. 'I've tuned her in. Nice blonde – dances and sings on the *Yerba Mate* hour.'

'That's her,' said Jarvis ungrammatically. 'I know her pretty well – just friends, get me? – though she came down to see us off in the *Ares*. Well, I was thinking about her, feeling pretty lonesome, and all the time we were approaching that line of rubbery plants.

'And then – I said, "What 'n Hell!" and stared. And there she was – Fancy Long, standing plain as day under one of those crack-brained trees, and smiling and waving just the way I remembered her when we left!'

'Now you're nuts, too!' observed the captain.

'Boy, I almost agreed with you! I stared and pinched myself and closed my eyes and then stared again – and every time, there was Fancy Long

smiling and waving! Tweel saw something, too; he was trilling and clucking away, but I scarcely heard him. I was bounding toward her over the
sand, too amazed even to ask myself questions.

'I wasn't twenty feet from her when Tweel caught me with one of his
flying leaps. He grabbed my arm, yelling, "No – no – no!" in his squeaky
voice. I tried to shake him off – he was as light as if he were built of
bamboo – but he dug his claws in and yelled. And finally some sort of
sanity returned to me and I stopped less than ten feet from her. There she
stood, looking as solid as Putz's head!'

'Vot?' said the engineer.

'She smiled and waved, and waved and smiled, and I stood there dumb
as Leroy, while Tweel squeaked and chattered. I *knew* it couldn't be real,
yet – there she was!

'Finally I said, "Fancy! Fancy Long!" She just kept on smiling and
waving, but looking as real as if I hadn't left her thirty-seven million
miles away.

'Tweel had his glass pistol out, pointing it at her. I grabbed his arm,
but he tried to push me away. He pointed at her and said, "No breet! No
breet!" and I understood that he meant that the Fancy Long thing
wasn't alive.

'Man, my head was whirling!

'Still, it gave me the jitters to see him pointing his weapon at her. I
don't know why I stood there watching him take careful aim, but I did.
Then he squeezed the handle of his weapon; there was a little puff of
steam, and Fancy Long was gone! And in her place was one of those
writhing, black rope-armed horrors like the one I'd saved Tweel from!

'The dream-beast! I stood there dizzy, watching it die while Tweel
trilled and whistled. Finally he touched my arm, pointed at the twisting
thing, and said, "You one – one – two, he one – one – two." After he'd
repeated it eight or ten times, I got it. Do any of you?'

'*Oui*,' shrilled Leroy. '*Moi – je le comprends*! He mean you think of
something, the beast he know, and you see it! *Un chien* – a hungry dog, he
would see the big bone with meat! Or smell it – not?'

'Right!' said Jarvis. 'The dream-beast uses its victim's longings and
desires to trap its prey. The bird at nesting season would see its mate, the
fox, prowling for its own prey, would see a helpless rabbit!'

'How he do?' queried Leroy.

'How do I know? How does a snake back on earth charm a bird into its
very jaws? And aren't there deep-sea fish that lure their victims into their
mouths? Lord!' Jarvis shuddered. 'Do you see how insidious the monster
is? We're warned now – but henceforth we can't trust even our eyes. You

might see me – I might see one of you – and back of it may be nothing but another of those black horrors!'

'How'd your friend know?' asked the captain abruptly.

'Tweel? I wonder! Perhaps he was thinking of something that couldn't possibly have interested me, and when I started to run, he realized that I saw something different and was warned. Or perhaps the dream-beast can only project a single vision, and Tweel saw what I saw – or nothing. I couldn't ask him. But it's just another proof that his intelligence is equal to ours or greater.'

'He's daffy, I tell you!' said Harrison. 'What makes you think his intellect ranks with the human?'

'Plenty of things! First the pyramid-beast. He hadn't seen one before; he said as much. Yet he recognized it as a dead-alive automaton of silicon.'

'He could have heard of it,' objected Harrison. 'He lives around here, you know.'

'Well how about the language? I couldn't pick up a single idea of his and he learned six or seven words of mine. And do you realize what complex ideas he put over with no more than those six or seven words? The pyramid monster – the dream-beast! In a single phrase he told me that one was a harmless automaton and the other a deadly hypnotist. What about that?'

'Huh!' said the captain.

'*Huh* if you wish! Could you have done it knowing only six words of English? Could you go even further, as Tweel did, and tell me that another creature was of a sort of intelligence so different from ours that understanding was impossible – even more impossible than that between Tweel and me?'

'Eh? What was that?'

'Later. The point I'm making is that Tweel and his race are worthy of our friendship. Somewhere on Mars – and you'll find I'm right – is a civilization and culture equal to ours, and maybe more than equal. And communication is possible between them and us; Tweel proves that. It may take years of patient trial, for their minds are alien, but less alien than the next minds we encountered – if they *are* minds.'

'The next ones? What next ones?'

'The people of the mud cities along the canals.' Jarvis frowned, then resumed his narrative. 'I thought the dream-beast and the silicon-monster were the strangest beings conceivable, but I was wrong. These creatures are still more alien, less understandable than either and far less comprehensible than Tweel, with whom friendship is possible, and even, by patience and concentration, the exchange of ideas.

'Well,' he continued, 'we left the dream-beast dying, dragging itself back into its hole, and we moved toward the canal. There was a carpet of that queer walking-grass scampering out of our way, and when we reached the bank, there was a yellow trickle of water flowing. The mound city I'd noticed from the rocket was a mile or so to the right and I was curious enough to want to take a look at it.

'It had seemed deserted from my previous glimpse of it, and if any creatures were lurking in it – well, Tweel and I were both armed. And by the way, that crystal weapon of Tweel's was an interesting device; I took a look at it after the dream-beast episode. It fired a little glass splinter, poisoned, I suppose, and I guess it held at least a hundred of 'em to a load. The propellant was steam – just plain steam!'

'Shteam!' echoed Putz. 'From vot come, shteam?'

'From water, of course! You could see the water through the transparent handle and about a gill of another liquid, thick and yellowish. When Tweel squeezed the handle – there was no trigger – a drop of water and a drop of the yellow stuff squirted into the firing chamber, and the water vaporized – pop! – like that. It's not so difficult; I think we could develop the same principle. Concentrated sulfuric acid will heat water almost to boiling, and so will quicklime, and there's potassium and sodium –

'Of course, his weapon hadn't the range of mine, but it wasn't so bad in this thin air, and it *did* hold as many shots as a cowboy's gun in a Western movie. It was effective, too, at least against Martian life; I tried it out, aiming at one of the crazy plants, and darned if the plant didn't wither up and fall apart! That's why I think the glass splinters were poisoned.

'Anyway, we trudged along toward the mud-heap city and I began to wonder whether the city builders dug the canals. I pointed to the city and then at the canal, and Tweel said "No – no – no!" and gestured toward the south. I took it to mean that some other race had created the canal system, perhaps Tweel's people. I don't know; maybe there's still another intelligent race on the planet, or a dozen others. Mars is a queer little world.

'A hundred yards from the city we crossed a sort of road – just a hard-packed mud trail, and then, all of a sudden, along came one of the mound builders!

'Man, talk about fantastic beings! It looked rather like a barrel trotting along on four legs with four other arms or tentacles. It had no head, just body and members and a row of eyes completely around it. The top end of the barrel-body was a diaphragm stretched as tight as a drumhead, and that was all. It was pushing a little coppery cart and tore right past us like the proverbial bat out of Hell. It didn't even notice us, although I thought the eyes on my side shifted a little as it passed.

'A moment later another came along, pushing another empty cart. Same thing – it just scooted past us. Well, I wasn't going to be ignored by a bunch of barrels playing train, so when the third one approached, I planted myself in the way – ready to jump, of course, if the thing didn't stop.

'But it did. It stopped and set up a sort of drumming from the diaphragm on top. And I held out both hands and said, "We are friends!" And what do you suppose the thing did?'

'Said, "Pleased to meet you," I'll bet!' suggested Harrison.

'I couldn't have been more surprised if it had! It drummed on its diaphragm, and then suddenly boomed out, "We are v-r-r-riends" and gave its pushcart a vicious poke at me! I jumped aside, and away it went while I stared dumbly after it.

'A minute later another one came hurrying along. This one didn't pause, but simply drummed out, "We are v-r-r-riends!" and scurried by. How did it learn the phrase? Were all of the creatures in some sort of communication with each other? Were they all parts of some central organism? I don't know, though I think Tweel does.

'Anyway, the creatures went sailing past us, every one greeting us with the same statement. It got to be funny; I never thought to find so many friends on this God-forsaken ball! Finally I made a puzzled gesture to Tweel; I guess he understood, for he said, "One-one-two – yes! – Two-two-four – no!" Get it?'

'Sure,' said Harrison. 'It's a Martian nursery rhyme.'

'Yeah! Well, I was getting used to Tweel's symbolism, and I figured it out this way. "One-one-two – yes!" The creatures were intelligent. "Two-two-four – no!" Their intelligence was not of our order, but something different and beyond the logic of two and two is four. Maybe I missed his meaning. Perhaps he meant that their minds were of low degree, able to figure out the simple things. "One-one-two – yes! – but not more difficult things – Two-two-four – no!" But I think from what we saw later that he meant the other.

'After a few moments, the creatures came rushing back – first one, then another. Their pushcarts were full of stones, sand, chunks of rubbery plants, and such rubbish as that. They droned out their friendly greeting, which didn't really sound so friendly, and dashed on. The third one I assumed to be my first acquaintance and I decided to have another chat with him. I stepped into his path again and waited.

'Up he came, booming out his "We are v-r-r-riends" and stopped. I looked at him; four or five of his eyes looked at me. He tried his password again and gave a shove on his cart, but I stood firm. And then the – the dashed creature reached out one of his arms, and two finger-like nippers tweaked my nose!'

'Haw!' roared Harrison. 'Maybe the things have a sense of beauty!'

'Laugh!' grumbled Jarvis. 'I'd already had a nasty bump and a mean frostbite on that nose. Anyway, I yelled "Ouch!" and jumped aside and the creature dashed away; but from then on, their greeting was "We are v-r-r-riends! Ouch!" Queer beasts!

'Tweel and I followed the road squarely up to the nearest mound. The creatures were coming and going, paying us not the slightest attention, fetching their loads of rubbish. The road simply dived into an opening, and slanted down like an old mine, and in and out darted the barrel-people, greeting us with their eternal phrase.

'I looked in; there was a light somewhere below, and I was curious to see it. It didn't look like a flame or torch, you understand, but more like a civilized light, and I thought that I might get some clue as to the creatures' development. So in I went and Tweel tagged along, not without a few trills and twitters, however.

'The light was curious; it sputtered and flared like an old arc light, but came from a single black rod set in the wall of the corridor. It was electric, beyond doubt. The creatures were fairly civilized, apparently.

'Then I saw another light shining on something that glittered and I went on to look at that, but it was only a heap of shiny sand. I turned toward the entrance to leave, and the Devil take me if it wasn't gone!

'I supposed the corridor had curved, or I'd stepped into a side passage. Anyway, I walked back in that direction I thought we'd come, and all I saw was more dimlit corridor. The place was a labyrinth! There was nothing but twisting passages running every way, lit by occasional lights, and now and then a creature running by, sometimes with a pushcart, sometimes without.

'Well, I wasn't much worried at first. Tweel and I had only come a few steps from the entrance. But every move we made after that seemed to get us in deeper. Finally I tried following one of the creatures with an empty cart, thinking that he'd be going out for his rubbish, but he ran around aimlessly, into one passage and out another. When he started dashing around a pillar like one of these Japanese waltzing mice, I gave up, dumped my water tank on the floor, and sat down.

'Tweel was as lost as I. I pointed up and he said "No – no – no!" in a sort of helpless trill. And we couldn't get any help from the natives. They paid no attention at all, except to assure us they were friends – ouch!

'Lord! I don't know how many hours or days we wandered around there! I slept twice from sheer exhaustion; Tweel never seemed to need sleep. We tried following only the upward corridors, but they'd run up-hill a ways and then curve downwards. The temperature in that damned ant hill was constant; you couldn't tell night from day and after my first sleep I didn't know whether I'd slept one hour or thirteen, so I couldn't tell from my watch whether it was midnight or noon.

'We saw plenty of strange things. There were machines running in some of the corridors, but they didn't seem to be doing anything – just wheels turning. And several times I saw two barrel-beasts with a little one growing between them, joined to both.'

'Parthenogenesis!' exulted Leroy. 'Parthenogenesis by budding like *les tulipes!*'

'If you say so, Frenchy,' agreed Jarvis. 'The things never noticed us at all, except, as I say, to greet us with "We are v-r-r-riends! Ouch!" They seemed to have no home-life of any sort, but just scurried around with their pushcarts, bringing in rubbish. And finally I discovered what they did with it.

'We'd had a little luck with a corridor, one that slanted upwards for a great distance. I was feeling that we ought to be close to the surface when suddenly the passage debouched into a domed chamber, the only one we'd seen. And man! – I felt like dancing when I saw what looked like daylight through a crevice in the roof.

'There was a – a sort of machine in the chamber, just an enormous wheel that turned slowly, and one of the creatures was in the act of dump-ing his rubbish below it. The wheel ground it with a crunch – sand, stones, plants, all into powder that sifted away somewhere. While we watched, others filed in, repeating the process, and that seemed to be all. No rhyme nor reason to the whole thing – but that's characteristic of this crazy planet. And there was another fact that's almost too bizarre to believe.

'One of the creatures, having dumped his load, pushed his cart aside with a crash and calmly shoved himself under the wheel! I watched him being crushed, too stupefied to make a sound, and a moment later, another followed him! They were perfectly methodical about it, too; one of the cartless creatures took the abandoned pushcart.

'Tweel didn't seem surprised; I pointed out the next suicide to him, and he just gave the most human-like shrug imaginable, as much as to say, "What can I do about it?" He must have known more or less about these creatures.

'Then I saw something else. There was something beyond the wheel, something shining on a sort of low pedestal. I walked over; there was a little crystal, about the size of an egg, fluorescing to beat Tophet. The light from it stung my hands and face, almost like a static discharge, and then I noticed another funny thing. Remember that wart I had on my left thumb? Look!' Jarvis extended his hand. 'It dried up and fell off – just like that! And my abused nose – say, the pain went out of it like magic! The thing had the property of hard x-rays or gamma radiations, only more so; it destroyed diseased tissue and left healthy tissue unharmed!

'I was thinking what a present *that*'d be to take back to Mother Earth when a lot of racket interrupted. We dashed back to the other side of the wheel in time to see one of the pushcarts ground up. Some suicide had been careless, it seems.

'Then suddenly the creatures were booming and drumming all around us and their noise was decidedly menacing. A crowd of them advanced toward us; we backed out of what I thought was the passage we'd entered by, and they came rumbling after us, some pushing carts and some not. Crazy brutes! There was a whole chorus of "We are v-r-r-riends! Ouch!" I didn't like the "ouch"; it was rather suggestive.

'Tweel had his glass gun out and I dumped my water tank for greater freedom and got mine. We backed up the corridor with the barrel-beasts following – about twenty of them. Queer thing – the ones coming in with loaded carts moved past us inches away without a sign.

'Tweel must have noticed that. Suddenly, he snatched out that glowing coal cigar-lighter of his and touched a cartload of plant limbs. Puff! The whole load was burning – and the crazy beast pushing it went right along without a change of pace. It created some disturbance among our "v-v-r-riends", however – and then I noticed the smoke eddying and swirling past us, and sure enough, there was the entrance!

'I grabbed Tweel and out we dashed and after us our twenty pursuers. The daylight felt like Heaven, though I saw at first glance that the sun was all but set, and that was bad, since I couldn't live outside my thermo-skin bag in a Martian night – at least, without a fire.

'And things got worse in a hurry. They cornered us in an angle between two mounds, and there we stood. I hadn't fired nor had Tweel; there wasn't any use in irritating the brutes. They stopped a little dist-ance away and began their booming about friendship and ouches.

'Then things got still worse! A barrel-brute came out with a pushcart and they all grabbed into it and came out with handfuls of foot-long copper darts – sharp-looking ones – and all of a sudden one sailed past my ear – zing! And it was shoot or die then.

'We were doing pretty well for a while. We picked off the ones next to the pushcart and managed to keep the darts at a minimum, but suddenly there was a thunderous booming of "v-v-r-riends" and "ouches", and a whole army of 'em came out of their hole.

'Man! We were through and I knew it! Then I realized that Tweel wasn't. He could have leaped the mound behind us as easily as not. He was staying for me!

'Say, I could have cried if there'd been time! I'd liked Tweel from the first, but whether I'd have had gratitude to do what he was doing – suppose I *had* saved him from the first dream-beast – he'd done as much for me, hadn't he? I grabbed his arm, and said "Tweel", and pointed up, and he understood. He said, "No – no – no, Tick!" and popped away with his glass pistol.

'What could I do? I'd be a goner anyway when the sun set, but I couldn't explain that to him. I said, "Thanks, Tweel. You're a man!" and felt that I wasn't paying him any compliment at all. A man! There are mighty few men who'd do that.

'So I went "bang" with my gun and Tweel went "puff" with his, and the barrels were throwing darts and getting ready to rush us, and booming about being friends. I had given up hope. Then suddenly an angel dropped right down from Heaven in the shape of Putz, with his underjets blasting the barrels into very small pieces!

'Wow! I let out a yell and dashed for the rocket; Putz opened the door and in I went, laughing and crying and shouting! It was a moment or so before I remembered Tweel; I looked around in time to see him rising in one of his nosedives over the mound and away.

'I had a devil of a job arguing Putz into following! By the time we got the rocket aloft, darkness was down; you know how it comes here – like turning off a light. We sailed out over the desert and put down once or twice. I yelled "Tweel!" and yelled it a hundred times, I guess. We couldn't find him; he could travel like the wind and all I got – or else I imagined it – was a faint trilling and twittering drifting out of the south. He'd gone, and damn it! I wish – I wish he hadn't!'

The four men of the *Ares* were silent – even the sardonic Harrison. At last little Leroy broke the stillness.

'I should like to see,' he murmured.

'Yeah,' said Harrison. 'And the wart-cure. Too bad you missed that; it might be the cancer cure they've been hunting for a century and a half.'

'Oh, that!' muttered Jarvis gloomily. 'That's what started the fight!' He drew a glistening object from his pocket.

'Here it is.'

Valley of Dreams
Stanley G. Weinbaum

Captain Harrison of the *Ares* expedition turned away from the little telescope in the bow of the rocket. 'Two weeks more, at the most,' he remarked. 'Mars only retrogrades for seventy days in all, relative to the earth, and we've got to be homeward bound during that period, or wait a year and a half for old Mother Earth to go around the sun and catch up with us again. How'd you like to spend a winter here?'

Dick Jarvis, chemist of the party, shivered as he looked up from his notebook. 'I'd just as soon spend it in a liquid air tank!' he averred. 'These eighty-below-zero summer nights are plenty for me.'

'Well,' mused the captain, 'the first successful Martian expedition ought to be home long before then.'

'Successful if we get home,' corrected Jarvis. 'I don't trust these cranky rockets – not since the auxiliary dumped me in the middle of Thyle last week. Walking back from a rocket ride is a new sensation to me.'

'Which reminds me,' returned Harrison, 'that we've got to recover your films. They're important if we're to pull this trip out of the red. Remember how the public mobbed the first moon pictures? Our shots ought to pack 'em to the doors. And the broadcast rights, too; we might show a profit for the Academy.'

'What interests me,' countered Jarvis, 'is a personal profit. A book, for instance; exploration books are always popular. *Martian Deserts* – how's that for a title?'

'Lousy!' grunted the captain. 'Sounds like a cookbook for desserts. You'd have to call it *Love Life of a Martian*, or something like that.'

Jarvis chuckled. 'Anyway,' he said, 'if we once get back home, I'm going to grab what profit there is, and never, never, get any farther from the earth than a good stratosphere plane'll take me. I've learned to appreciate the planet after plowing over this dried-up pill we're on now.'

'I'll lay you odds you'll be back here year after next,' grinned the captain. 'You'll want to visit your pal – that trick ostrich.'

'Tweel?' The other's tone sobered. 'I wish I hadn't lost him, at that. He was a good scout. I'd never have survived the dream-beast but for him. And that battle with the pushcart things – I never even had a chance to thank him.'

'A pair of lunatics, you two,' observed Harrison. He squinted through the port at the gray gloom of the Mare Cimmerium. 'There comes the sun.' He paused. 'Listen, Dick – you and Leroy take the other auxiliary rocket and go out and salvage those films.'

Jarvis stared. 'Me and Leroy?' he echoed ungrammatically. 'Why not me and Putz? An engineer would have some chance of getting us there and back if the rocket goes bad on us.'

The captain nodded toward the stem, whence issued at that moment a medley of blows and guttural expletives. 'Putz is going over the insides of the *Ares*,' he announced. 'He'll have his hands full until we leave, because I want every bolt inspected. It's too late for repairs once we cast off.'

'And if Leroy and I crack up? That's our last auxiliary.'

'Pick up another ostrich and walk back,' suggested Harrison gruffly. Then he smiled. 'If you have trouble, we'll hunt you out in the *Ares*,' he finished. 'Those films are important.' He turned. 'Leroy!'

The dapper little biologist appeared, his face questioning.

'You and Jarvis are off to salvage the auxiliary,' the captain said. 'Everything's ready and you'd better start now. Call back at half-hour intervals; I'll be listening.'

Leroy's eyes glistened. 'Perhaps we land for specimens – no?' he queried.

'Land if you want to. This golf ball seems safe enough.'

'Except for the dream-beast,' muttered Jarvis with a faint shudder. He frowned suddenly. 'Say, as long as we're going that way, suppose I have a look for Tweel's home! He must live off there somewhere, and he's the most important thing we've seen on Mars.'

Harrison hesitated. 'If I thought you could keep out of trouble,' he muttered. 'All right,' he decided. 'Have a look. There's food and water aboard the auxiliary; you can take a couple of days. But keep in touch with me, you saps!'

Jarvis and Leroy went through the airlock out to the gray plain. The thin air, still scarcely warmed by the rising sun, bit flesh and lung like needles, and they gasped with a sense of suffocation. They dropped to a sitting posture, waiting for their bodies, trained by months in acclimatization chambers back on earth, to accommodate themselves to the tenuous air. Leroy's face, as always, turned a smothered blue, and Jarvis heard his own breath rasping and rattling in his throat. But in five minutes, the discomfort passed; they rose and entered the little auxiliary rocket that rested beside the black hull of the *Ares*.

The under-jets roared out their fiery atomic blast; dirt and bits of shattered biopods spun away in a cloud as the rocket rose. Harrison watched the projectile trail its flaming way into the south, then turned back to his work.

It was four days before he saw the rocket again. Just at evening, as the sun dropped behind the horizon with the suddenness of a candle falling into the sea, the auxiliary flashed out of the southern heavens, easing gently down on the flaming wings of the under-jets. Jarvis and Leroy emerged, passed through the swiftly gathering dusk, and faced him in the light of the *Ares*. He surveyed the two; Jarvis was tattered and scratched, but apparently in better condition than Leroy, whose dapperness was completely lost. The little biologist was pale as the nearer moon that glowed outside; one arm was bandaged in thermo-skin and his clothes hung in veritable rags. But it was his eyes that struck Harrison most strangely; to one who lived these many weary days with the diminutive Frenchman, there was something queer about them. They were frightened, plainly enough, and that was odd, since Leroy was no coward or he'd never have been one of the four chosen by the Academy for the first Martian expedition. But the fear in his eyes was more understandable than that other expression, that queer fixity of gaze like one in a trance, or like a person in an ecstasy. 'Like a chap who's seen Heaven and Hell together,' Harrison expressed it to himself. He was yet to discover how right he was.

He assumed a gruffness as the weary pair sat down. 'You're a fine looking couple!' he growled. 'I should've known better than to let you wander off alone.' He paused. 'Is your arm all right, Leroy? Need any treatment?'

Jarvis answered. 'It's all right – just gashed. No danger of infection here, I guess; Leroy says there aren't any microbes on Mars.'

'Well,' exploded the captain, 'let's hear it, then! Your radio reports sounded screwy. "Escaped from Paradise!" Huh!'

'I didn't want to give details on the radio,' said Jarvis soberly. 'You'd have thought we'd gone loony.'

'I think so, anyway.'

'*Moi aussi*!' muttered Leroy. 'I too!'

'Shall I begin at the beginning?' queried the chemist. 'Our early reports were pretty nearly complete.' He stared at Putz, who had come in silently, his face and hands blackened with carbon, and seated himself beside Harrison.

'At the beginning,' the captain decided.

'Well,' began Jarvis, 'we got started all right, and flew due south along the meridian of the *Ares*, same course I'd followed last week. I was getting used to this narrow horizon, so I didn't feel so much like being cooped under a big bowl, but one does keep overestimating distances. Something four miles away looks eight when you're used to terrestrial curvature, and that makes you guess its size just four times too large. A little hill looks like a mountain until you're almost over it.'

'I know that,' grunted Harrison.

'Yes, but Leroy didn't, and I spent our first couple of hours trying to explain it to him. By the time he understood (if he does yet) we were past Cimmerium and over that Xanthus desert, and then we crossed the canal with the mud city and the barrel-shaped citizens and the place where Tweel had shot the dream-beast. And nothing would do for Pierre here but that we put down so he could practice his biology on the remains. So we did.

'The thing was still there. No sign of decay; couldn't be, of course, without bacterial forms of life, and Leroy says that Mars is as sterile as an operating table.'

'*Comme le coeur d'une fileuse*,' corrected the little biologist, who was beginning to regain a trace of his usual energy. 'Like an old maid's heart!'

'However,' resumed Jarvis, 'about a hundred of the little gray-green biopods had fastened onto the thing and were growing and branching. Leroy found a stick and knocked 'em off, and each branch broke away and became a biopod crawling around with the others. So he poked around at the creature, while I looked away from it; even dead, that rope-armed devil gave me the creeps. And then came the surprise; the thing was part plant!'

'*C'est vrai!*' confirmed the biologist. 'It's true!'

'It was a big cousin of the biopods,' continued Jarvis. 'Leroy was quite excited; he figures that all Martian life is of that sort – neither plant nor animal. Life here never differentiated, he says; everything has both natures in it, even the barrel-creatures – even Tweel! I think he's right, especially when I recall how Tweel rested, sticking his beak in the ground and staying that way all night. I never saw him eat or drink, either; perhaps his beak was more in the nature of a root, and he got his nourishment that way.'

'Sounds nutty to me,' observed Harrison.

'Well,' continued Jarvis, 'we broke up a few of the other growths and they acted the same way – the pieces crawled around, only much slower than the biopods, and then stuck themselves in the ground. Then Leroy had to catch a sample of the walking grass, and we were ready to leave when a parade of the barrel creatures rushed by with their pushcarts. They hadn't forgotten me, either; they all drummed out, "We are v-r-r-iends –

ouch!" just as they had before. Leroy wanted to shoot one and cut it up, but I remembered the battle Tweel and I had had with them, and vetoed the idea. But he did hit on a possible explanation as to what they did with all the rubbish they gathered.'

'Made mud-pies, I guess,' grunted the captain.

'More or less,' agreed Jarvis. 'They use it for food, Leroy thinks. If they're part vegetable, you see, that's what they'd want – soil with organic remains in it to make it fertile. That's why they ground up sand and biopods and other growths all together. See?'

'Dimly,' countered Harrison. 'How about the suicides?'

'Leroy had a hunch there, too. The suicides jump into the grinder when the mixture has too much sand and gravel; they throw themselves in to adjust the proportions.'

'Rats!' said Harrison disgustedly. 'Why couldn't they bring in some extra branches from outside?'

'Because suicide is easier. You've got to remember that these creatures can't be judged by earthly standards; they probably don't feel pain, and they haven't got what we'd call individuality. Any intelligence they have is the property of the whole community – like an ant-heap. That's it! Ants are willing to die for their ant-hill; so are these creatures.'

'So are men,' observed the captain, 'if it comes to that.'

'Yes, but men aren't exactly eager. It takes some emotion like patriotism to work 'em to the point of dying for their country; these things do it all in the day's work.' He paused.

'Well, we took some pictures of the dream-beast and the barrel-creatures, and then we started along. We sailed over Xanthus, keeping as close to the meridian of the *Ares* as we could, and pretty soon we crossed the trail of the pyramidbuilder. So we circled back to let Leroy take a look at it, and when we found it, we landed. The thing had completed just two rows of bricks since Tweel and I left it, and there it was, breathing in silicon and breathing out bricks as if it had eternity to do it in – which it has. Leroy wanted to dissect it with a Boland explosive bullet, but I thought that anything that had lived for ten million years was entitled to the respect due to old age, so I talked him out of it. He peeped into the hole on top of it and nearly got beaned by the arm coming up with a brick, and then he chipped off a few pieces of it, which didn't disturb the creature a bit. He found the place I'd chipped, tried to see if there was any sign of healing, and decided he could tell better in two or three thousand years. So we took a few shots of it and sailed on.

'Mid-afternoon we located the wreck of my rocket. Not a thing disturbed; we picked up my films and tried to decide what next. I wanted to find Tweel if possible; I figured from the fact of his pointing south that he lived somewhere near Thyle. We plotted our route and judged that the desert we were in now was Thyle II; Thyle I should be east of us. So, on a hunch, we decided to have a look at Thyle I, and away we buzzed.'

'*Der* motors?' queried Putz, breaking his long silence.

'For a wonder, we had no trouble, Karl. Your blast worked perfectly. So we bummed along, pretty high to get a wider view, I'd say about fifty thousand feet. Thyle II spread out like an orange carpet, and after a while we came to the gray branch of the Mare Chronium that bounded it. That was narrow; we crossed it in half an hour, and there was Thyle I – same orange-hued desert as its mate. We veered south, toward the Mare Australe, and followed the edge of the desert. And toward sunset we spotted it.'

'Shpotted?' echoed Putz. 'Vot vas shpotted?'

'The desert was spotted – with buildings! Not one of the mud cities of the canals, although a canal went through it. From the map we figured the canal was a continuation of the one Schiaparelli called Ascanius.

'We were probably too high to be visible to any inhabitants of the city, but also too high for a good look at it, even with the glasses. However, it was nearly sunset, anyway, so we didn't plan on dropping in. We circled the place; the canal went out into the Mare Australe, and there, glittering in the south, was the melting polar ice-cap! The canal drained it; we could distinguish the sparkle of water in it. Off to the southeast, just at the edge of the Mare Australe, was a valley – the first irregularity I'd seen on Mars except the cliffs that bounded Xanthus and Thyle II. We flew over the valley – ' Jarvis paused suddenly and shuddered; Leroy, whose color had begun to return, seemed to pale. The chemist resumed, 'Well, the valley looked all right – then! Just a gray waste, probably full of crawlers like the others.

'We circled back over the city; say, I want to tell you that place was – well, gigantic! It was colossal; at first I thought the size was due to that illusion I spoke of – you know, the nearness of the horizon – but it wasn't that. We sailed right over it, and you've never seen anything like it!

'But the sun dropped out of sight right then. I knew we were pretty far south – latitude 60 – but I didn't know just how much night we'd have.'

Harrison glanced at a Schiaparelli chart. 'About 60 – eh?' he said. 'Close to what corresponds to the Antarctic Circle. You'd have about four hours of night at this season. Three months from now you'd have none at all.'

'Three months!' echoed Jarvis, surprised. Then he grinned. 'Right! I forget the seasons here are twice as long as ours. Well, we sailed out into the desert about twenty miles, which put the city below the horizon in case we overslept, and there we spent the night.

'You're right about the length of it. We had about four hours of darkness which left us fairly rested. We ate breakfast, called our location to you, and started over to have a look at the city.

'We sailed toward it from the east and it loomed up ahead of us like a range of mountains. Lord, what a city! Not that New York mightn't have higher buildings, or Chicago cover more ground, but for sheer mass, those structures were in a class by themselves. Gargantuan!

'There was a queer look about the place, though. You know how a terrestrial city sprawls out, a nimbus of suburbs, a ring of residential sections, factory districts, parks, highways, There was none of that here; the city rose out of the desert as abruptly as a cliff. Only a few little sand mounds marked the division, and then the walls of those gigantic structures.

'The architecture was strange, too. There were lots of devices that are impossible back home, such as set-backs in reverse, so that a building with a small base could spread out as it rose. That would be a valuable trick in New York, where land is almost priceless, but to do it, you'd have to transfer Martian gravitation there!

'Well, since you can't very well land a rocket in a city street, we put down right next to the canal side of the city, took our small cameras and revolvers, and started for a gap in the wall of masonry. We weren't ten feet from the rocket when we both saw the explanation for a lot of the queerness.

'The city was in ruin! Abandoned, deserted, dead as Babylon! Or at least, so it looked to us then, with its empty streets which, if they *had* been paved, were now deep under sand.'

'A ruin, eh?' commented Harrison. 'How old?'

'How could we tell?' countered Jarvis. 'The next expedition to this golf ball ought to carry an archeologist – and a philologist, too, as we found out later. But it's a devil of a job to estimate the age of anything here; things weather so slowly that most of the buildings might have been put up yesterday. No rainfall, no earthquakes, no vegetation is here to spread cracks with its roots – nothing. The only aging factors here are the erosion of the wind – and that's negligible in this atmosphere – and the cracks caused by changing temperature. And one other agent – meteorites. They must crash down occasionally on the city, judging from the thinness of the air, and the fact that we've seen four strike ground right here near the *Ares*.'

'Seven,' corrected the captain. 'Three dropped while you were gone.'

'Well, damage by meteorites must be slow, anyway. Big ones would be as rare here as on earth, because big ones get through in spite of the atmosphere, and those buildings could sustain a lot of little ones. My guess at the city's age – and it may be wrong by a big percentage – would be fifteen thousand years. Even that's thousands of years older than any human civilization; fifteen thousand years ago was the Late Stone Age in the history of mankind.

'So Leroy and I crept up to those tremendous buildings feeling like pygmies, sort of awe-struck, and talking in whispers. I tell you, it was ghostly walking down that dead and deserted street, and every time we passed through a shadow, we shivered, and not just because shadows are cold on Mars. We felt like intruders, as if the great race that had built the place might resent our presence even across a hundred and fifty centuries. The place was as quiet as a grave, but we kept imagining things and peeping down the dark lanes between buildings and looking over our shoulders. Most of the structures were windowless, but when we did see an opening in those vast walls, we couldn't look away, expecting to see some horror peering out of it.

'Then we passed an edifice with an open arch; the doors were there, but blocked open by sand. I got up nerve enough to take a look inside, and then, of course, we discovered we'd forgotten to take our flashes. But we eased a few feet into the darkness and the passage debouched into a colossal hall. Far above us a little crack let in a pallid ray of daylight, not nearly enough to light the place; I couldn't even see if the hall rose clear to the distant roof. But I know the place was enormous; I said something to Leroy and a million thin echoes came clipping back to us out of the darkness. And after that, we began to hear other sounds – slithering rustling noises, and whispers, and sounds like suppressed breathing – and something black and silent passed between us and that far-away crevice of light.

'Then we saw three little greenish spots of luminosity in the dusk to our left. We stood staring at them, and suddenly they all shifted at once. Leroy yelled "*Ce sont des yeux!*" and they were! They were eyes! Well, we stood frozen for a moment, while Leroy's yell reverberated back and forth between the distant walls, and the echoes repeated the words in queer, thin voices. There were mumblings and mutterings and whisperings and sounds like strange soft laughter, and then the three-eyed thing moved again. Then we broke for the door!

'We felt better out in the sunlight; we looked at each other sheepishly, but neither of us suggested another look at the buildings inside – though we *did* see the place later, and that was queer, too – but you'll hear about it when I come to it. We just loosened our revolvers and crept on along that ghostly street.

'The street curved and twisted and subdivided. I kept careful note of our directions, since we couldn't risk getting lost in that gigantic maze. Without our thermo-skin bags, night would finish us, even if what lurked in the ruins didn't. By and by, I noticed that we were veering back toward the canal, the buildings ended and there were only a few dozen ragged stone huts which looked as though they might have been built of débris from the city. I was just beginning to feel a bit disappointed at finding no trace of Tweel's people here when we rounded a corner and there he was!

'I yelled "Tweel!" but he just stared, and then I realized that he wasn't Tweel, but another Martian of his sort. Tweel's feathery appendages were more orange-hued and he stood several inches taller than this one. Leroy was sputtering in excitement, and the Martian kept his vicious beak directed at us, so I stepped forward as peace-maker.

'I said "Tweel?" very questioningly, but there was no result. I tried it a dozen times, and we finally had to give it up; we couldn't connect.

'Leroy and I walked toward the huts, and the Martian followed us. Twice he was joined by others, and each time I tried yelling "Tweel" at them but they just stared at us. So we ambled on with the three trailing us, and then it suddenly occurred to me that my Martian accent might be at fault. I faced the group and tried trilling it out the way Tweel himself did: "T-r-r-rweee-r-rl!" Like that.

'And that worked! One of them spun his head around a full ninety degrees, and screeched "T-r-r-rweee-r-rl!" and a moment later, like an arrow from a bow, Tweel came sailing over the nearer huts to land on his beak in front of me!

'Man, we were glad to see each other! Tweel set up a twittering and chirping like a farm in summer and went sailing up and coming down on his beak, and I would have grabbed his hands, only he wouldn't keep still long enough.

'The other Martians and Leroy just stared, and after a while, Tweel stopped bouncing, and there we were. We couldn't talk to each other any more than we could before, so after I'd said "Tweel" a couple of times and he'd said "Tick", we were more or less helpless. However, it was only mid-morning, and it seemed important to learn all we could about Tweel and the city, so I suggested that he guide us around the place if he weren't busy. I put over the idea by pointing back at the buildings and then at him and us.

'Well, apparently he wasn't too busy, for he set off with us, leading the way with one of his hundred and fifty-foot nosedives that set Leroy

gasping. When we caught up, he said something like "one, one, two –
two, two, four – no, no – yes, yes – rock – no breet!" That didn't seem to
mean anything; perhaps he was just letting Leroy know that he could
speak English, or perhaps he was merely running over his vocabulary to
refresh his memory.

'Anyway, he showed us around. He had a light of sorts in his black
pouch, good enough for small rooms, but simply lost in some of the
colossal caverns we went through. Nine out of ten buildings meant
absolutely nothing to us – just vast empty chambers, full of shadows and
rustlings and echoes. I couldn't imagine their use; they didn't seem
suitable for living quarters, or even for commercial purposes – trade and
so forth; they might have been all right as power-houses, but what could
have been the purpose of a whole city full? And where were the remains
of the machinery?

'The place was a mystery. Sometimes Tweel would show us through
a hall that would have housed an ocean-liner, and he'd seem to swell
with pride – and we couldn't make a damn thing of it! As a display of
architectural power, the city was colossal; as anything else it was just
nutty!

'But we did see one thing that registered. We came to that same
building Leroy and I had entered earlier – the one with the three eyes
in it. Well, we were a little shaky about going in there, but Tweel
twittered and trilled and kept saying, "Yes, yes, yes!" so we followed
him, staring nervously about for the thing that had watched us. However, that hall was just like the others, full of murmurs and slithering
noises and shadowy things slipping away into corners. If the three-eyed
creature were still there, it must have slunk away with the others.

'Tweel led us along the wall; his light showed a series of little alcoves,
and in the first of these we ran into a puzzling thing – a very weird thing.
As the light flashed into the alcove, I saw first just an empty space, and
then, squatting on the floor, I saw – it! A little creature about as big
as a large rat, it was, gray and huddled and evidently startled by our
appearance. It had the queerest, most devilish little face! – pointed ears
or horns and satanic eyes that seemed to sparkle with a sort of fiendish
intelligence.

'Tweel saw it, too, and let out a screech of anger, and the creature rose
on two pencil-thin legs and scuttled off with a half-terrified, half-defiant
squeak. It darted past us into the darkness too quickly even for Tweel,
and as it ran, something waved on its body like the fluttering of a cape.
Tweel screeched angrily at it and set up a shrill hullabaloo that sounded
like genuine rage.

'But the thing was gone, and then I noticed the weirdest of imaginable details. Where it had squatted on the floor was – a book! It had been hunched over a book!

'I took a step forward; sure enough, there was some sort of inscription on the pages – wavy white lines like a seismograph record on black sheets like the material of Tweel's pouch. Tweel fumed and whistled in wrath, picked up the volume and slammed it into place on a shelf full of others. Leroy and I stared dumbfounded at each other.

'Had the little thing with the fiendish face been reading? Or was it simply eating the pages, getting physical nourishment rather than mental? Or had the whole thing been accidental?

'If the creature were some rat-like pest that destroyed books, Tweel's rage was understandable, but why should he try to prevent an intelligent being, even though of an alien race, from *reading* – if it *was* reading. I don't know; I did notice that the book was entirely undamaged, nor did I see a damaged book among any that we handled. But I have an odd hunch that if we knew the secret of the little cape-clothed imp, we'd know the mystery of the vast abandoned city and of the decay of Martian culture.

'Well, Tweel quieted down after a while and led us completely around that tremendous hall. It had been a library, I think; at least, there were thousands upon thousands of those queer black-paged volumes printed in wavy lines of white. There were pictures, too, in some; and some of these showed Tweel's people. That's a point, of course; it indicated that his race built the city and printed the books. I don't think the greatest philologist on earth will ever translate one line of those records; they were made by minds too different from ours.

'Tweel could read them, naturally. He twittered off a few lines, and then I took a few of the books, with his permission; he said "no, no!" to some and "yes, yes!" to others. Perhaps he kept back the ones his people needed, or perhaps he let me take the ones he thought we'd understand most easily. I don't know; the books are outside there in the rocket.

'Then he held that dim torch of his toward the walls, and they were pictured. Lord, what pictures! They stretched up and up into the blackness of the roof, mysterious and gigantic. I couldn't make much of the first wall; it seemed to be a portrayal of a great assembly of Tweel's people. Perhaps it was meant to symbolize Society or Government. But the next wall was more obvious; it showed creatures at work on a colossal machine of some sort, and that would be Industry or Science. The back wall had corroded away in part; from what we could see, I suspected the scene was meant to portray Art, but it was on the fourth wall that we got a shock that nearly dazed us.

'I think the symbol was Exploration or Discovery. This wall was a little plainer, because the moving beam of daylight from that crack lit up the higher surface and Tweel's torch illuminated the lower. We made out a giant seated figure, one of the beaked Martians like Tweel, but with every limb suggesting heaviness, weariness. The arms dropped inertly on the chair, the thin neck bent and the beak rested on the body, as if the creature could scarcely bear its own weight. And before it was a queer kneeling figure, and at sight of it, Leroy and I almost reeled against each other. It was, apparently, a man!'

'A man!' bellowed Harrison. 'A man you say?'

'I said apparently,' retorted Jarvis. 'The artist had exaggerated the nose almost to the length of Tweel's beak, but the figure had black shoulder-length hair, and instead of the Martian four, there were *five* fingers on its outstretched hand! It was kneeling as if in worship of the Martian, and on the ground was what looked like a pottery bowl full of some food as an offering. Well! Leroy and I thought we'd gone screwy!'

'And Putz and I think so, too!' roared the captain.

'Maybe we all have,' replied Jarvis, with a faint grin at the pale face of the little Frenchman, who returned it in silence. 'Anyway,' he continued, 'Tweel was squeaking and pointing at the figure, and saying "Tick! Tick!" so he recognized the resemblance – and never mind any cracks about my nose!' he warned the captain. 'It was Leroy who made the important comment; he looked at the Martian and said "Thoth! The god Thoth!"'

'*Oui*!' confirmed the biologist. '*Comme l'Egypte*!'

'Yeah,' said Jarvis. 'Like the Egyptian ibis-headed god – the one with the beak. Well, no sooner did Tweel hear the name Thoth than he set up a clamor of twittering and squeaking. He pointed at himself and said "Thoth! Thoth!" and then waved his arm all around and repeated it. Of course he often did queer things, but we both thought we understood what he meant. He was trying to tell us that his race called themselves Thoth. Do you see what I'm getting at?'

'I see, all right,' said Harrison. 'You think the Martians paid a visit to the earth, and the Egyptians remembered it in their mythology. Well, you're off, then; there wasn't any Egyptian civilization fifteen thousand years ago.'

'Wrong!' grinned Jarvis. 'It's too bad we haven't an archeologist with us, but Leroy tells me that there was a stone-age culture in Egypt then, the pre-dynastic civilization.'

'Well, even so, what of it?'

'Plenty! Everything in that picture proves my point. The attitude of the Martian, heavy and weary – that's the unnatural strain of terrestrial gravitation. The name Thoth; Leroy tells me Thoth was the Egyptian god of philosophy and the inventor of writing! Get that? They must have picked up the idea from watching the Martian take notes. It's too much for coincidence that Thoth should be beaked and ibis-headed, and that the beaked Martians call themselves Thoth.'

'Well, I'll be hanged! But what about the nose on the Egyptian? Do you mean to tell me that stone-age Egyptians had longer noses than ordinary men?'

'Of course not! It's just that the Martians very naturally cast their paintings in Martianized form. Don't human beings tend to relate everything to themselves? That's why dugongs and manatees started the mermaid myths – sailors thought they saw human features on the beasts. So the Martian artist, drawing either from descriptions or imperfect photographs, naturally exaggerated the size of the human nose to a degree that looked normal to him. Or anyway, that's my theory.'

'Well, it'll do as a theory,' grunted Harrison. 'What I want to hear is why you two got back here looking like a couple of year-before-last bird's nests.'

Jarvis shuddered again, and cast another glance at Leroy. The little biologist was recovering some of his accustomed poise, but he returned the glance with an echo of the chemist's shudder.

'We'll get to that,' resumed the latter. 'Meanwhile I'll stick to Tweel and his people. We spent the better part of three days with them, as you know. I can't give every detail, but I'll summarize the important facts and give our conclusions, which may not be worth an inflated franc. It's hard to judge this dried-up world by earthly standards.

'We took pictures of everything possible; I even tried to photograph that gigantic mural in the library, but unless Tweel's lamp was unusually rich in actinic rays, I don't suppose it'll show. And that's a pity, since it's undoubtedly the most interesting object we've found on Mars, at least from a human viewpoint.

'Tweel was a very courteous host. He took us to all the points of interest – even the new water-works.'

Putz's eyes brightened at the word. 'Vater-vorks?' he echoed. 'For vot?'

'For the canal, naturally. They have to build up a head of water to drive it through; that's obvious.' He looked at the captain. 'You told me yourself that to drive water from the polar caps of Mars to the equator was equivalent to forcing it up a twenty-mile hill, because Mars is flattened at the poles and bulges at the equator just like the earth.'

'That's true,' agreed Harrison.

'Well,' resumed Jarvis, 'this city was one of the relay stations to boost the flow. Their power plant was the only one of the giant buildings that seemed to serve any useful purpose, and that was worth seeing. I wish you'd seen it, Karl; you'll have to make what you can from our pictures. It's a sun-power plant!'

Harrison and Putz stared. 'Sun-power!' grunted the captain. 'That's primitive!' And the engineer added an emphatic '*Ja!*' of agreement.

'Not as primitive as all that,' corrected Jarvis. 'The sunlight focused on a queer cylinder in the center of a big concave mirror, and they drew an electric current from it. The juice worked the pumps.'

'A t'ermocouple' ejaculated Putz.

'That sounds reasonable; you can judge by the pictures. But the power plant had some queer things about it. The queerest was that the machinery was tended, not by Tweel's people, but by some of the barrel-shaped creatures like the ones in Xanthus!' He gazed around at the faces of his auditors; there was no comment.

'Get it?' he resumed. At their silence, he proceeded, 'I see you don't. Leroy figured it out, but whether rightly or wrongly, I don't know. He thinks that the barrels and Tweel's race have a reciprocal arrangement like – well, like bees and flowers on earth. The flowers give honey for the bees; the bees carry the pollen for the flowers. See? The barrels tend the works and Tweel's people build the canal system. The Xanthus city must have been a boosting station; that explains the mysterious machines I saw. And Leroy believes further that it isn't an intelligent arrangement – not on the part of the barrels, at least – but that it's been done for so many thousands of generations that it's become instinctive, a tropism – just like the actions of ants and bees. The creatures have been bred to it!'

'Nuts!' observed Harrison. 'Let's hear you explain the reason for that big empty city, then.'

'Sure. Tweel's civilization is decadent, that's the reason. It's a dying race, and out of all the millions that must once have lived there, Tweel's couple of hundred companions are the remnant. They're an outpost, left to tend the source of the water at the polar cap; probably there are still a few respectable cities left somewhere on the canal system, most likely near the tropics. It's the last gasp of a race – and a race that reached a higher peak of culture than Man!'

'Huh?' said Harrison. 'Then why are they dying? Lack of water?'

'I don't think so,' responded the chemist. 'If my guess at the city's age is right, fifteen thousand years wouldn't make enough difference in the water supply – nor a hundred thousand for that matter. It's something else, though the water's doubtless a factor.'

'*Das wasser*,' cut in Putz. 'Vere goes dot?'

'Even a chemist knows that!' scoffed Jarvis. 'At least on earth. Here I'm not so sure, but on earth, every time there's a lightning flash, it electrolyzes some water vapor into hydrogen and oxygen, and then the hydrogen escapes into space, because terrestrial gravitation won't hold it permanently. And every time there's an earthquake, some water is lost to the interior. Slow – but damned certain.' He turned to Harrison. 'Right, Cap?'

'Right,' conceded the captain. 'But here, of course – no earthquakes, no thunderstorms – the loss must be very slow. Then why is the race dying?'

'The sunpower plant answers that,' countered Jarvis. 'Lack of fuel! Lack of power! No oil left, no coal left – if Mars ever had a Carboniferous Age – and no water-power – just the driblets of energy they can get from the sun. That's why they're dying.'

'With the limitless energy of the atom?' exploded Harrison.

'They don't know about atomic energy. Probably never did. Must have used some other principle in their space-ship.'

'Then,' snapped the captain, 'what makes you rate their intelligence above the human? *We've* finally cracked open the atom!'

'Sure we have. We had a clue, didn't we? Radium and uranium. Do you think we'd ever have learned how without those elements? We'd never even have suspected that atomic energy existed!'

'Well? Haven't they – '

'No, they haven't. You've told me yourself that Mars has only 73 per cent of the earth's density. Even a chemist can see that that means a lack of heavy metals – no osmium, no uranium, no radium. They didn't have the clue.'

'Even so, that doesn't prove they're more advanced than we are. If they were *more* advanced, they'd have discovered it anyway.'

'Maybe,' conceded Jarvis. 'I'm not claiming that we don't surpass them in some ways. But in others, they're far ahead of us.'

'In what, for instance?'

'Well – socially, for one thing.'

'Huh? How do you mean?'

Jarvis glanced in turn at each of the three that faced him. He hesitated. 'I wonder how you chaps will take this,' he muttered. 'Naturally, everybody likes his own system best.' He frowned. 'Look here – on the earth we have three types of society, haven't we? And there's a member of each type right here. Putz lives under a dictatorship – an autocracy. Leroy's a citizen of the Sixth Commune in France. Harrison and I are Americans, members of a democracy. There you are – autocracy, democracy, communism – the three types of terrestrial societies. Tweel's people have a different system from any of us.'

'Different? What is it?'

'The one no earthly nation has tried. Anarchy!'

'Anarchy!' the captain and Putz burst out together.

'That's right.'

'But – ' Harrison was sputtering. 'What do you mean, they're ahead of us? Anarchy! Bah!'

'All right – bah!' retorted Jarvis. 'I'm not saying it would work for us, or for any race of men. But it works for them.'

'But – anarchy!' The captain was indignant.

'Well, when you come right down to it,' argued Jarvis defensively, 'anarchy is the ideal form of government, if it works. Emerson said that the best government was that which governs least, and so did Wendell Phillips, and I think George Washington. And you can't have any form of government which governs less than anarchy, which is no government at all!'

The captain was sputtering. 'But – it's unnatural! Even savage tribes have their chiefs! Even a pack of wolves has its leader!'

'Well,' retorted Jarvis defiantly, 'that only proves that government is a primitive device, doesn't it? With a perfect race you wouldn't need it at all; government is a confession of weakness, isn't it? It's a confession that part of the people won't cooperate with the rest and that you need laws to restrain those individuals which a psychologist calls anti-social. If there were no anti-social persons – criminals and such – you wouldn't need laws or police, would you?'

'But government! You'd need government! How about public works – wars – taxes?'

'No wars on Mars, in spite of being named after the War God. No point in wars here; the population is too thin and too scattered, and besides, it takes the help of every single community to keep the canal system functioning. No taxes because apparently all individuals cooperate in building public works. No competition to cause trouble, because anybody can help himself to anything. As I said, with a perfect race government is entirely unnecessary.'

'And do you consider the Martians a perfect race?' asked the captain grimly.

'Not at all! But they've existed so much longer than man that they're evolved, socially at least, to the point where they don't need government. They work together, that's all.' Jarvis paused. 'Queer, isn't it – as if Mother Nature were carrying on two experiments, one at home and one on Mars. On earth it's the trial of an emotional, highly competitive race in a world of plenty; here it's the trial of a quiet, friendly race on a desert, unproductive, and inhospitable world. Everything here makes for cooperation. Why, there isn't even the factor that causes so much trouble at home – sex!'

'Huh?'

'Yeah: Tweel's people reproduce just like the barrels in the mud cities; two individuals grow a third one between them. Another proof of Leroy's theory that Martian life is neither animal nor vegetable. Besides, Tweel was a good enough host to let him poke down his beak and twiddle his feathers, and the examination convinced Leroy.'

'*Oui*,' confirmed the biologist. 'It is true.'

'But anarchy!' grumbled Harrison disgustedly. 'It *would* show up on a dizzy, half-dead pill like Mars!'

'It'll be a good many centuries before you'll have to worry about it on earth,' grinned Jarvis. He resumed his narrative.

'Well, we wandered through that sepulchral city, taking pictures of everything. And then – ' Jarvis paused and shuddered – 'then I took a notion to have a look at that valley we'd spotted from the rocket. I don't know why. But when we tried to steer Tweel in that direction, he set up such a squawking and screeching that I thought he'd gone batty.'

'If possible!' jeered Harrison.

'So we started over there without him; he kept wailing and screaming, "No – no – no! Tick!" but that made us the more curious. He sailed over our heads and stuck on his beak, and went through a dozen other antics, but we ploughed on, and finally he gave up and trudged disconsolately along with us.

'The valley wasn't more than a mile southeast of the city. Tweel could have covered the distance in twenty jumps, but he lagged and loitered and kept pointing back at the city and wailing "No – no – no!" Then he'd sail up into the air and zip down on his beak directly in front of us, and we'd have to walk around him. I'd seen him do lots of crazy things before, of course; I was used to them, but it was as plain as print that he didn't want us to see that valley.'

'Why?' queried Harrison.

'You asked why we came back like tramps,' said Jarvis with a faint shudder. 'You'll learn. We plugged along up a low rocky hill that bounded it, and as we neared the top, Tweel said, "No breet, Tick! No breet!" Well, those were the words he used to describe the silicon monster; they were also the words he had used to tell me that the image of Fancy Long, the one that had almost lured me to the dream-beast, wasn't real. I remembered that, but it meant nothing to me then!

'Right after that, Tweel said, "You one – one – two, he one – one – two," and then I began to see. That was the phrase he had used to explain the dream-beast to tell me that what I thought, the creature thought – to tell me how the thing lured its victims by their own desires. So I warned Leroy; it seemed to me that even the dream-beast couldn't be dangerous if we were warned and expecting it. Well, I was wrong!

'As we reached the crest, Tweel spun his head completely around, so his feet were forward but his eyes looked backward, as if he feared to gaze into the valley. Leroy and I stared out over it, just a gray waste like this around us, with the gleam of the south polar cap far beyond its southern rim. That's what it was one second; the next it was – Paradise!'

'What?' exclaimed the captain.

Jarvis turned to Leroy. 'Can you describe it?' he asked.

The biologist waved helpless hands, 'C'est impossible!' he whispered. 'Il me rend muet!'

'It strikes me dumb, too,' muttered Jarvis. 'I don't know how to tell it; I'm a chemist, not a poet. Paradise is as good a word as I can think of, and that's not at all right. It was Paradise and Hell in one!'

'Will you talk sense?' growled Harrison.

'As much of it as makes sense. I tell you, one moment we were looking at a gray valley covered with blobby plants, and the next – Lord! You can't imagine that next moment! How I would you like to see all your dreams made real? Every desire you'd ever had gratified? Everything you'd ever wanted there for the taking?'

'I'd like it fine!' said the captain.

'You're welcome, then! – not only your noble desires, remember! Every good impulse, yes – but also every nasty little wish, every vicious thought, everything you'd ever desired, good or bad! The dream-beasts are marvelous salesmen, but they lack the moral sense!'

'The dream-beasts?'

'Yes. It was a valley of them. Hundreds, I suppose, maybe thousands. Enough, at any rate, to spread out a complete picture of your desires, even all the forgotten ones that must have been out of the subconscious. A Paradise – of sorts. I saw a dozen Fancy Longs, in every costume I'd ever admired on her, and some I must have imagined. I saw every beautiful woman I've ever known, and all of them pleading for my attention. I saw every lovely place I'd ever wanted to be, all packed queerly into that little valley. And I saw other things.' He shook his head soberly. 'It wasn't all exactly pretty. Lord! How much of the beast is left in us! I suppose if every man alive could have one look at that weird valley, and could see just once what nastiness is hidden in him – well, the world might gain by it. I thanked heaven afterwards that Leroy – and even Tweel – saw their own pictures and not mine!'

Jarvis paused again, then resumed, 'I turned dizzy with a sort of ecstasy. I closed my eyes – and with eyes closed, I still saw the whole thing! That beautiful, evil, devilish panorama was in my mind, not my eyes. That's how those fiends work – through the mind. I knew it was the dream-beasts; I didn't need Tweel's wail of "No breet! No breet!" But – *I couldn't keep away*! I knew it was death beckoning, but it was worth it for one moment with the vision.'

'Which particular vision?' asked Harrison dryly.

Jarvis flushed. 'No matter,' he said. 'But beside me I heard Leroy's cry of "Yvonne! Yvonne!" and I knew he was trapped like myself. I fought for sanity; I kept telling myself to stop, and all the time I was rushing head-long into the snare!

'Then something tripped me. Tweel! He had come leaping from behind; as I crashed down I saw him flash over me straight toward – toward what I'd been running to, with his vicious beak pointed right at her heart!'

'Oh!' nodded the captain. '*Her heart!*'

'Never mind that. When I scrambled up, that particular image was gone, and Tweel was in a twist of black ropey arms, just as when I first saw him. He'd missed a vital point in the beast's anatomy, but was jab-bing away desperately with his beak.

'Somehow, the spell had lifted, or partially lifted. I wasn't five feet from Tweel, and it took a terrific struggle, but I managed to raise my revolver and put a Boland shell into the beast. Out came a spurt of horrible black corruption, drenching Tweel and me – and I guess the sickening smell of it helped to destroy the illusion of that valley of beauty. Anyway, we managed to get Leroy away from the devil that had him, and the three of us staggered to the ridge and over. I had presence of mind enough to raise my camera over the crest and take a shot of the valley, but I'll bet it shows nothing but gray waste and writhing horrors. What we saw was with our minds, not our eyes.'

Jarvis paused and shuddered. 'The brute half poisoned Leroy,' he con-tinued. 'We dragged ourselves back to the auxiliary, called you, and did what we could to treat ourselves. Leroy took a long dose of the cognac that we had with us; we didn't dare try anything of Tweel's because his metabolism is so different from ours that what cured him might kill us. But the cognac seemed to work, and so, after I'd done one other thing I wanted to do, we came back here – and that's all.'

'All, is it?' queried Harrison. 'So you've solved all the mysteries of Mars, eh?'

'Not by a damned sight!' retorted Jarvis. 'Plenty of unanswered questions are left.'

'*Ja!*' snapped Putz. 'Der evaporation – dot iss shtopped how?'

'In the canals? I wondered about that, too; in those thousands of miles, and against this low air pressure, you'd think they'd lose a lot. But the answer's simple; they float a skin of oil on the water.'

Putz nodded, but Harrison cut in. 'Here's a puzzler. With only coal and oil – just combustion or electric power – where'd they get the energy to build a planet-wide canal system, thousands and thousands of miles of 'em? Think of the job we had cutting the Panama Canal to sea level, and then answer that!'

'Easy!' grinned Jarvis. 'Martian gravity and Martian air – that's the answer. Figure it out: First, the dirt they dug only weighed a third its earth-weight. Second, a steam engine here expands against ten pounds per square inch less air pressure than on earth. Third, they could build the engine three times as large here with no greater internal weight. And fourth, the whole planet's nearly level. Right, Putz?'

The engineer nodded. '*Ja!* Der shteam-engine – it iss *sieben-und-zwanzig* – twenty-seven times – so effective here.'

'Well, there does go the last mystery then,' mused Harrison.

'Yeah?' queried Jarvis sardonically. 'You answer these, then. What was the nature of that vast empty city? Why do the Martians *need* canals, since we never saw them eat or drink? Did they really visit the earth before the dawn of history, and, if not atomic energy, what powered their ship? Since Tweel's race seems to need little or no water, are they merely operating the canals for some higher creature that does? Are there other intelligences on Mars? If not, what was the demon-faced imp we saw with the book? There are a few mysteries for you!'

'I know one or two more!' growled Harrison, glaring suddenly at little Leroy. 'You and your visions! "Yvonne!" eh? Your wife's name is Marie, isn't it?'

The little biologist turned crimson. '*Oui,*' he admitted unhappily. He turned pleading eyes on the captain. 'Please,' he said. 'In Paris *tout le monde* – everybody he think differently of those things – no?' He twisted uncomfortably. 'Please you will not tell Marie, *n'est-ce pas?*'

Harrison chuckled. 'None of my business,' he said. 'One more question, Jarvis. What was the one other thing you did before returning here?'

Jarvis looked diffident. 'Oh – that.' He hesitated. 'Well I sort of felt we owed Tweel a lot, so after some trouble, we coaxed him into the rocket and sailed him out to the wreck of the first one, over on Thyle II. Then,' he finished apologetically, 'I showed him the atomic blast, got it working – and gave it to him!'

'You *what*?' roared the captain. 'You turned something as powerful as that over to an alien race – maybe some day an enemy race?'

'Yes, I did,' said Jarvis. 'Look here,' he argued defensively. 'This lousy, dried-up pill of a desert called Mars'll never support much human population. The Sahara desert is just as good a field for imperialism, and a lot closer to home. So we'll never find Tweel's race enemies. The only value we'll find here is commercial trade with the Martians. Then why shouldn't I give Tweel a chance for survival? With atomic energy, they can run their canal system a hundred per cent instead of only one out of five, as Putz's observations showed. They can repopulate those ghostly cities; they can resume their arts and industries; they can trade with the nations of the earth – and I'll bet they can teach us a few things,' he paused, 'if they can figure out the atomic blast, and I'll lay odds they can. They're no fools, Tweel and his ostrich-faced Martians!'

The Adaptive Ultimate

Stanley G. Weinbaum

Dr Daniel Scott, his dark and brilliant eyes alight with the fire of enthusiasm, paused at last and stared out over the city, or that portion of it visible from the office windows of Herman Bach – the Dr Herman Bach of Grand Mercy Hospital. There was a moment of silence; the old man smiled a little indulgently, a little wistfully, at the face of the youthful biochemist.

'Go on, Dan,' he said. 'So it occurred to you that getting well of a disease or injury is merely a form of adaptation – then what?'

'Then,' flashed the other, 'I began to look for the most adaptive of living organisms. And what are they? Insects! Insects, of course. Cut off a wing, and it grows back. Cut off a head, stick it to the headless body of another of the same species, and that grows back on. And what's the secret of their great adaptability?'

Dr Bach shrugged. 'What is?'

Scott was suddenly gloomy. 'I'm not sure,' he muttered. 'It's glandular, of course – a matter of hormones.' He brightened again. 'But I'm off the track. So then I looked around for the most adaptive insect. And which is that?'

'Ants?' suggested Dr Bach. 'Bees? Termites?'

'Bah! They're the most highly evolved, not the most adaptable. No; there's one insect that is known to produce a higher percentage of mutants than any other, more freaks, more biological sports. The one Morgan used in his experiments on the effect of hard x-rays on heredity – the fruit fly, the ordinary fruit fly. Remember? They have reddish eyes, but under x-rays they produced white-eyed offspring – and that was a true mutation, because the white eyes bred true! Acquired characteristics can't be inherited, but these were. Therefore – '

'I know,' interrupted Dr Bach.

Scott caught his breath. 'So I used fruit flies,' he resumed. 'I putrefied their bodies, injected a cow, and got a serum at last, after weeks of clarifying with albumen, evaporating *in vacuo*, rectifying with – But you're not interested in the technique. I got a serum. I tried it on tubercular guinea pigs, and' – he paused dramatically – 'it cured! They adapted themselves to the tubercle bacillus. I tried it on a rabid dog. He adapted. I tried it on a cat with a broken spine. That knit. And now, I'm asking you for the chance to try it on a human being!'

Dr Bach frowned. 'You're not ready,' he grunted. 'You're not ready by two years. Try it on an anthropoid. Then try it on yourself. I can't risk a human life in an experiment that's as raw as this.'

'Yes, but I haven't got anything that needs curing, and as for an anthropoid, you get the board to allow funds to buy an ape – if you can. I've tried.'

'Take it up with the Stoneman Foundation, then.'

'And have Grand Mercy lose the credit? Listen, Dr Bach, I'm asking for just one chance – a charity case – anything.'

'Charity cases are human beings.' The old man scowled down at his hands. 'See here, Dan. I shouldn't even offer this much, because it's against all medical ethics, but if I find a hopeless case – utterly hopeless, you understand – where the patient himself consents, I'll do it. And that's the final word.'

Scott groaned. 'And try to find a case like that. If the patient's conscious, you think there's hope, and if he isn't how can he consent? That settles it!'

But it didn't. Less than a week later Scott looked suddenly up at the annunciator in the corner of his tiny laboratory. 'Dr Scott,' it rasped. 'Dr Scott. Dr Scott. To Dr Bach's office.'

He finished his titration, noted the figures, and hurried out. The old man was pacing the floor nervously as Scott entered.

'I've got your case, Dan,' he muttered. 'It's against all ethics – yet I'll be damned if I can see how you can do this one any harm. But you'd better hurry. Come on – isolation ward.'

They hurried. In the tiny cubical room Scott stared appalled. 'A girl!' he muttered.

She could never have been other than drab and plain, but lying there with the pallor of death already on her cheeks, she had an appearance of somber sweetness. Yet that was all the charm she could ever have possessed; her dark, cropped, oily hair was unkempt and stringy, her features flat and unattractive. She breathed with an almost inaudible rasp, and her eyes were closed.

'Do you,' asked Scott, 'consider this a test? She's all but dead now.'

Dr Bach nodded. 'Tuberculosis,' he said, 'final stage. Her lungs are hemorrhaging – a matter of hours.'

The girl coughed; flecks of blood appeared on her pallid lips. She opened dull, watery blue eyes.

'So!' said Bach, 'conscious, eh? This is Dr Scott. Dan, this is – uh' – he peered at the card at the foot of the bed – 'Miss – uh – Kyra Zelas. Dr Scott has an injection, Miss Zelas. As I warned you, it probably won't help, but I can't see how it can hurt. Are you willing?'

She spoke in faint, gurgling tones. 'Sure, I'm through anyway. What's the odds?'

'All right. Got the hypo, Dan?' Bach took the tube of water-clear serum. 'Any particular point of injection? No? Give me the cubital, then.'

He thrust the needle into the girl's arm. Dan noted that she did not even wince at the bite of the steel point, but lay stoical and passive as thirty cc. of liquid flowed into her veins. She coughed again, then closed her eyes.

'Come out of here,' ordered Bach gruffly, as they moved into the hall, 'I'm damned if I like this. I feel like a dirty dog.'

He seemed to feel less canine, however, the following day. 'That Zelas case is still alive,' he reported to Scott. 'If I dared trust my eyes, I'd say she's improved a little. A very little. I'd still call it hopeless.'

But the following day Scott found him seated in his office with a puzzled expression in his old gray eyes. 'Zelas is better,' he muttered. 'No question of it. But you keep your head, Dan. Such miracles have happened before, and without serums. You wait until we've had her under long observation.'

By the end of the week it became evident that the observation was not to be long. Kyra Zelas flourished under their gaze like some swift-blooming tropical weed. Queerly, she lost none of her pallor, but flesh softened the angular features, and a trace of light grew in her eyes.

'The spots on her lungs are going,' muttered Bach. 'She's stopped coughing, and there's no sign of bugs in her culture. But the queerest thing, Dan – and I can't figure it out, either – is the way she reacts to abrasions and skin punctures. Yesterday I took a blood specimen for a Wasserman, and – this sounds utterly mad – the puncture closed almost before I had a c.c.! Closed and healed!'

And in another week, 'Dan, I can't see any reason for keeping Kyra here. She's well. Yet I want her where we can keep her under observation. There's a queer mystery about this serum of yours. And besides, I hate to turn her out to the sort of life that brought her here.'

'What did she do?'

'Sewed. Piece work in some sweatshop, when she could work at all. Drab, ugly, uneducated girl, but there's something appealing about her. She adapts quickly.'

Scott gave him a strange look. 'Yes,' he said, 'she adapts quickly.'

'So,' resumed Bach, 'it occurred to me that she could stay at my place. We could keep her under observation, you see, and she could help the housekeeper. I'm interested – damn' interested. I think I'll offer her the chance.'

Scott was present when Dr Bach made his suggestion. The girl Kyra smiled. 'Sure,' she said. Her pallid, plain face lighted up. 'Thanks.'

Bach gave her the address. 'Mrs Getz will let you in. Don't do anything this afternoon. In fact, it might not hurt you to simply walk in the park for a few hours.'

Scott watched the girl as she walked down the hall toward the elevator. She had filled out, but she was still spare to the point of emaciation, and her worn black suit hung on her as if it were on a frame of sticks. As she disappeared, he moved thoughtfully about his duties, and a quarter hour later descended to his laboratory.

On the first floor, turmoil met him. Two officers were carrying in the body of a nondescript old man, whose head was a bloody ruin. There was a babble of excited voices, and he saw a crowd on the steps outside.

'What's up?' he called. 'Accident?'

'Accident!' snapped an officer. 'Murder, you mean. Woman steps up to this old guy, picks a hefty stone from the park border, slugs him, and takes his wallet. Just like that!'

Scott peered out of the window. The Black Maria was backing toward a crowd on the park side of the street.

A pair of hulking policemen flanked a thin figure in black, thrusting it toward the doors of the vehicle. Scott gasped. It was Kyra Zelas!

A week later Dr Bach stared into the dark fireplace of his living room. 'It's not our business,' he repeated. 'My God!' blazed Scott. 'Not our busi-ness! How do we know we're not responsible? How do we know that our injection didn't unsettle her mind? Glands can do that; look at Mongoloid idiots and cretins. Our stuff was glandular. Maybe we drove her crazy!'

'All right,' said Bach. 'Listen. We'll attend the trial tomorrow, and if it looks bad for her, we'll get hold of her lawyer and let him put us on the stand. We'll testify that she's just been released after a long and dangerous illness, and may not be fully responsible. That's entirely true.'

Mid-morning of the next day found them hunched tensely on benches in the crowded courtroom. The prosecution was opening; three witnesses testified to the event.

'This old guy buys peanuts for the pigeons. Yeah, I sell 'em to him every day – or did. So this time he hasn't any change, and he pulls out his wallet, and I see it's stuffed with bills. And one minute later I see the dame pick up the rock and conk him. Then she grabs the dough – '

'Describe her, please.'

'She's skinny, and dressed in black. She ain't no beauty, neither. Brownish hair, dark eyes, I don't know whether dark-blue or brown.'

'Your witness!' snapped the prosecutor.

A young and nervous individual – appointed by the court, the paper said – rose. 'You say,' he squeaked, 'that the assailant had brown hair and dark eyes?'

'Yeah.'

'Will the defendant please rise?'

Her back was toward Scott and Bach as Kyra Zelas arose, but Scott stiffened. Something strangely different about her appearance; surely her worn black suit no longer hung so loosely about her. What he could see of her figure seemed – well, magnificent.

'Take off your hat, Miss Zelas,' squeaked the attorney.

Scott gasped. Radiant as aluminum glowed the mass of hair she revealed!

'I submit, your honor, that this defendant does not possess dark hair, nor, if you will observe, dark eyes. It is, I suppose, conceivable that she could somehow have bleached her hair while in custody, and I therefore' – he brandished a pair of scissors – 'submit a lock to be tested by any chemist the court appoints. The pigmentation is entirely natural. And as for her eyes – does my esteemed opponent suggest that they, too, are bleached?'

He swung on the gaping witness. 'Is this lady the one you claim to have seen committing the crime?'

The man goggled. 'Uh – I can't – say.'

'Is she?'

'N-no!'

The speaker smiled. 'That's all. Will you take the stand, Miss Zelas?'

The girl moved lithe as a panther. Slowly she turned, facing the court. Scott's brain whirled, and his fingers dug into Bach's arm. Silver-eyed, aluminum-haired, alabaster pale, the girl on the stand was beyond doubt the most beautiful woman he had ever seen!

The attorney was speaking again. 'Tell the court in your own words what happened, Miss Zelas.'

Quite casually the girl crossed her trim ankles and began to speak. Her voice was low, resonant, and thrilling; Scott had to fight to keep his attention on the sense of her words rather than the sound.

'I had just left Grand Mercy Hospital,' she said, 'where I had been ill for some months. I had crossed the park when suddenly a woman in black rushed at me, thrust an empty wallet into my hands, and vanished.

A moment later I was surrounded by a screaming crowd, and – well, that's all.'

'An empty wallet, you say?' asked the defense lawyer. 'What of the money found in your own bag, which my eminent colleague believes stolen?'

'It was mine,' said the girl, 'about seven hundred dollars.'

Bach hissed, 'That's a lie! She had two dollars and thirty-three cents on her when we took her in.'

'Do you mean you think she's the same Kyra Zelas we had at the hospital?' gasped Scott.

'I don't know. I don't know anything, but if I ever touch that damned serum of yours – Look! Look, Dan!' This last was a tense whisper.

'What?'

'Her hair! When the sun strikes it!'

Scott peered more closely. A vagrant ray of noon sunlight filtered through a high window, and now and again the swaying of a shade permitted it to touch the metallic radiance of the girl's hair. Scott stared and saw; slightly but unmistakable, whenever the light touched that glowing aureole, her hair darkened from bright aluminum to golden blond!

Something clicked in his brain. There was a clue somewhere – if he could but find it. The pieces of the puzzle were there, but they were woefully hard to fit together. The girl in the hospital and her reaction to incisions; this girl and her reaction to light.

'I've got to see her,' he whispered. 'There's something I have to find – Listen!'

The speaker was orating. 'And we ask the dismissal of the whole case, your honor, on the grounds that the prosecution has utterly failed even to identify the defendant.'

The judge's gavel crashed. For a moment his aging eyes rested on the girl with the silver eyes and, incredible hair, then: 'Case dismissed!' he snapped. 'Jury discharged!'

There was a tumult of voices. Flashlights shot instantaneous sheets of lightning. The girl on the witness stand rose with perfect poise, smiled with lovely, innocent lips, and moved away. Scott waited until she passed close at hand then:

'Miss Zelas!' he called.

She paused. Her strange silver eyes lighted with unmistakable recognition. 'Dr Scott!' said the voice of tinkling metal. 'And Dr Bach!'

She was, then. She was the same girl. This was the drab sloven of the isolation ward, this weirdly beautiful creature of exotic coloring. Staring, Scott could trace now the very identity of her features, but changed as by a miracle.

He pushed through the mob of photographers, press men, and curiosity seekers. 'Have you a place to stay?' he asked. 'Dr Bach's offer still stands.'

She smiled. 'I am very grateful,' she murmured, and then, to the crowd of reporters. 'The doctor is an old friend of mine.' She was completely at ease, unruffled, poised.

Something caught Scott's eye, and he purchased a paper, glancing quickly at the photograph, the one taken at the moment the girl had removed her hat. He started; her hair showed raven black! There was a comment below the picture, too, to the effect that 'her striking hair photographs much darker than it appears to the eye.'

He frowned. 'This way,' he said to the girl, then goggled in surprise again. For in the broad light of noon her complexion was no longer the white of alabaster; it was creamy tan, the skin of one exposed to long hours of sunlight; her eyes were deep violet, and her hair – that tiny wisp unconcealed by her hat – was as black as the basalt columns of hell!

Kyra had insisted on stopping to purchase a substitute for the worn black suit, and had ended by acquiring an entire outfit. She sat now curled in the deep davenport before the fireplace in Dr Bach's library, sheathed in silken black from her white throat to the tiny black pumps on her feet. She was almost unearthly in her weird beauty, with her aluminum hair, silver eyes, and marble-pale skin against the jet silk covering.

She gazed innocently at Scott. 'But why shouldn't I?' she asked. 'The court returned my money; I can buy what I please with it.'

'Your money?' he muttered. 'You had less than three dollars when you left the hospital.'

'But this is mine now.'

'Kyra,' he said abruptly, 'where did you get that money?'

Her face was saintlike in its purity. 'From the old man.'

'You – you did murder him!'

'Why, of course I did.'

He choked. 'My Lord!' he gasped. 'Don't you realize we'll have to tell?'

She shook her head, smiling, gently from one to the other of them. 'No, Dan. You won't tell, for it wouldn't do any good. I can't be tried twice for the same crime. Not in America.'

'But why, Kyra? Why did you –'

'Would you have me resume the life that sent me into your hands? I needed money; money was there; I took it.'

'But murder!'

'It was the most direct way.'

'Not if you happened to be punished for it,' he returned grimly.

'But I wasn't,' she reminded him gently.

He groaned. 'Kyra,' he said, shifting the subject suddenly, 'why do your eyes and skin and hair darken in sunlight or when exposed to flashlight?'

She smiled. 'Do they?' she asked. 'I hadn't noticed.' She yawned, stretched her arms above her head and her slim legs before her. 'I think I shall sleep now,' she announced. She swept her magnificent eyes over them, rose, and disappeared into the room Dr Bach had given her – his own.

Scott faced the older man, his features working in emotion. 'Do you see?' he hissed. 'Good Lord, do you see?'

'Do you, Dan?'

'Part of it. Part of it, anyway.'

'And I see part as well.'

'Well,' said Scott, 'here it is as I see it. That serum – that accursed serum of mine – has somehow accentuated this girl's adaptability to an impossible degree. What is it that differentiates life from non-living matter? Two things, irritation and adaptation. Life adapts itself to its environment, and the greater the adaptability, the more successful the organism.

'Now,' he proceeded, 'all human beings show a very considerable adaptivity. When we expose ourselves to sunlight, our skin shows pigmentation – we tan. That's adaptation to an environment containing sunlight. When a man loses his right hand, he learns to use his left. That's another adaptation. When a person's skin is punctured, it heals and rebuilds, and that's another angle of the same thing. Sunny regions produce dark-skinned, dark-haired people; northern lands produce blonds – and that's adaptation again.

'So what's happened to Kyra Zelas, by some mad twist I don't understand, is that her adaptive powers have been increased to an extreme. She adapts instantly to her environment; when sun strikes her, she tans at once, and in shade she fades immediately. In sunlight her hair and eyes are those of a tropical race; in shadow, those of a Northerner. And – good Lord, I see it now – when she was faced with danger there in the courtroom, faced by a jury and judge who were men, she adapted to that! She met that danger, not only by changed appearance, but by a beauty so great, that she couldn't have been convicted!' He paused. 'But how? How?'

'Perhaps medicine can tell how,' said Bach. 'Undoubtedly man is the creature of his glands. The differences between races – white, red, black, yellow – is doubtless glandular. And perhaps the most effective agent of adaptation is the human brain and neural system, which in itself is controlled partly by a little greasy mass on the floor of the brain's third ventricle, before the cerebellum, and supposed by the ancients to be the seat of the soul.

'I mean, of course, the pineal gland. I suspect that what your serum contains is the long-sought hormone *pinealin*, and that it has caused hypertrophy of Kyra's pineal gland. And Dan, do you realize that if her adaptability is perfect, she's not only invincible, but invulnerable?'

'That's true!' gulped Scott. 'Why, she couldn't be electrocuted, because she'd adapt instantly to an environment containing an electric current, and she couldn't be killed by a shot, because she'd adapt to that as quickly as to your needle pricks. And poison – but there must be a limit somewhere!'

'There doubtless is,' observed Bach. 'I hardly believe she could adapt herself to an environment containing a fifty-ton locomotive passing over her body. And yet there's an important point we haven't considered. Adaptation itself is of two kinds.'

'Two kinds?'

'Yes. One kind is biological; the other, human. Naturally a biochemist like you would deal only with the first, and equally naturally a brain surgeon like me has to consider the second as well. Biological adaptation is what all life – plant, animal, and human – possesses, and it is merely conforming to one's environment. A chameleon, for instance, shows much the same ability as Kyra herself, and so, in lesser degree, does the arctic fox, white in winter, brown in summer; or the snow-shoe rabbit, for that matter, or the weasel. All life conforms to its environment to a great extent, because if it doesn't, it dies. But human life does more.'

'More?'

'Much more. Human adaptation is not only conformity to environment, but also the actual changing of environment to fit human needs! The first cave man who left his cave to build a grass hut changed his environment, and so, in exactly the same sense, did Steinmetz, Edison, and as far as that goes, Julius Caesar and Napoleon. In fact, Dan, all human invention, genius, and military leadership boils down to that one fact – changing the environment instead of conforming to it.'

He paused, then continued, 'Now we know that Kyra possesses the biological adaptivity. Her hair and eyes prove that. But what if she possesses the other to the same degree? If she does, God knows what the result will be. We can only watch to see what direction she takes – watch and hope.'

'But I don't see,' muttered Scott, 'how that could be glandular.'

'Anything can be glandular. In a mutant – and Kyra's as much a mutant as your white-eyed fruit flies – anything is possible.' He frowned reflectively. 'If I dared phrase a philosophical interpretation, I'd say that Kyra – perhaps – represents a stage in human evolution. A mutation. If one ventured to believe that, then de Vries and Weissman are justified.'

'The mutation theory of evolution, you mean?'

'Exactly. You see, Dan, while it is very obvious from fossil remains that evolution occurred, yet it is very easy to prove it couldn't possibly have occurred!'

'How?'

'Well, it couldn't have occurred slowly, as Darwin believed, for many reasons. Take the eye, for instance. He thought that very gradually, over thousands of generations, some sea creature developed a spot on its skin that was sensitive to light, and that this gave it an advantage over its blind fellows. Therefore its kind survived and others perished. But see here. If this eye developed slowly, why did the very first ones, the ones that couldn't yet see, have any better chance than the others? And take a wing. What good is a wing until you can fly with it? Just because a jumping lizard had a tiny fold of skin between foreleg and breast wouldn't mean that that lizard could survive where others died. What kept the wing developing to a point where it could actually have value?'

'What did?'

'De Vries and Weissman say nothing did. They answer that evolution must have progressed in jumps, so that when the eye appeared, it was already efficient enough to have survival value, and likewise the wing. Those jumps they named mutations. And in that sense, Dan, Kyra's a mutation, a jump from the human to – something else. Perhaps the superhuman.'

Scott shook his head in perplexity. He was thoroughly puzzled, completely baffled, and more than a little unnerved. In a few moments more he bade Bach good night, wandered home, and lay for hours in sleepless thought.

The next day Bach managed a leave of absence for both of them from Grand Mercy, and Scott moved in. This was in part simply out of his fascinated interest in the case of Kyra Zelas, but in part it was altruistic. She had confessedly murdered one man; it occurred to Scott that she might with no more compunction murder Dr Bach, and he meant to be at hand to prevent it.

He had been in her company no more than a few hours before Bach's words on evolution and mutations took on new meaning. It was not only Kyra's chameleon-like coloring, nor her strangely pure and saintlike features, nor even her incredible beauty. There was something more; he could not at once identify it, but decidedly the girl Kyra was not quite human.

The event that impressed this on him occurred in the late afternoon. Bach was away somewhere on personal business, and Scott had been questioning the girl about her own impressions of her experience.

'But don't you know you've changed?' he asked. 'Can't you see the difference in yourself?'

'Not I. It is the world that has changed.'

'But your hair was black. Now it's light as ashes.'

'Was it?' she asked. 'Is it?'

He groaned in exasperation. 'Kyra,' he said, 'you must know something about yourself.'

Her exquisite eyes turned their silver on him. 'I do,' she said. 'I know that what I want is mine, and' – her pure lips smiled – 'I think I want you, Dan.'

It seemed to him, that she changed at that moment. Her beauty was not quite as it had been, but somehow more wildly intoxicating than before. He realized what it meant; her environment now contained a man she loved, or thought she loved, and she was adapting to that, too. She was becoming – he shivered slightly – irresistible!

Bach must have realized the situation, but he said nothing. As for Scott, it was sheer torture, for he realized only too well that the girl he loved was a freak, a biological sport, and worse than that, a cold murderess and a creature not exactly human. Yet for the next several days things went smoothly. Kyra slipped easily into the routine; she was ever a willing subject for their inquiries and investigations.

Then Scott had an idea. He produced one of the guinea pigs that he had injected, and they found that the creature evinced the same reaction as Kyra to cuts. They killed the thing by literally cutting it in half with an ax, and Bach examined its brain.

'Right!' he said at last. 'It's hypertrophy of the pineal.' He stared intently at Scott. 'Suppose,' he said, 'that we could reach Kyra's pineal and correct the hypertrophy. Do you suppose that might return her to normal?'

Scott suppressed a pang of fear. 'But why? She can't do any harm as long as we guard her here. Why do we have to gamble with her life like that?'

Bach laughed shortly. 'For the first time in my life I'm glad I'm an old man,' he said. 'Don't you see we have to do something? She's a menace. She's dangerous. Heaven only knows how dangerous. We'll have to try.'

Scott groaned and assented. An hour later, under the pretext of experiment, he watched the old man inject five grains of morphia into the girl's arm, watched her frown and blink – and adjust. The drug was powerless.

It was at night that Bach got his next idea. 'Ethyl chloride!' he whispered. 'The instantaneous anaesthetic. Perhaps she can't adjust to lack of oxygen. We'll try.'

Kyra was asleep. Silently, carefully, the two crept in, and Scott stared down in utter fascination at the weird beauty of her features, paler than ever in the faint light of midnight. Carefully, so carefully, Bach held the cone above her sleeping face, drop by drop he poured the volatile, sweet-scented liquid into it. Minutes passed.

'That should anaesthetize an elephant,' he whispered at last, and jammed the cone full upon her face.

She awoke. Fingers like slim steel rods closed on his wrist, forcing his hand away. Scott seized the cone, and her hand clutched his wrist as well, and he felt the strength of her grasp.

'Stupid,' she said quietly, sitting erect. 'This is quite useless – look!'

She snatched a paper knife from the table beside the bed. She bared her pale throat to the moonlight, and then, suddenly, drove the knife to its hilt into her bosom!

Scott gulped in horror as she withdrew it. A single spot of blood showed on her flesh, she wiped it away, and displayed her skin, pale, unscarred, beautiful.

'Go away,' she said softly, and they departed.

The next day she made no reference to the incident. Scott and Bach spent a worried morning in the laboratory, doing no work, but simply talking. It was a mistake, for when they returned to the library, she was gone, having, according to Mrs Getz, simply strolled out of the door and away. A hectic and hasty search of the adjacent blocks brought no sign of her.

At dusk she was back, pausing hatless in the doorway to permit Scott, who was there alone, to watch the miraculous change as she passed from sunset to chamber, and her hair faded from mahogany to aluminum.

'Hello,' she said smiling. 'I killed a child.'

'What? My Lord, Kyra!'

'It was an accident. Surely you don't feel that I should be punished for an accident, Dan, do you?'

He was staring in utter horror. 'How – '

'Oh, I decided to walk a bit. After a block or two, it occurred to me that I should like to ride. There was a car parked there with the keys in it, and the driver was talking on the sidewalk, so I slipped in, started it, and drove away. Naturally I drove rather fast, since he was shouting, and at the second corner I hit a little boy.'

'And – you didn't stop?'

'Of course not. I drove around the corner, turned another corner or two, and then parked the car and walked back. The boy was gone, but the crowd was still there. Not one of them noticed me.' She smiled her saintlike smile. 'We're quite safe. They can't possibly trace me.'

Scott dropped his head on his hands and groaned. 'I don't know what to do!' he muttered. 'Kyra, you're going to have to report this to the police.'

'But it was an accident,' she said gently, her luminous silver eyes pityingly on Scott.

'No matter. You'll have to.'

She placed her white hand on his head. 'Perhaps tomorrow,' she said. 'Dan, I have learned something. What one needs in this world is power. As long as there are people in the world with more power than I, I run afoul of them. They keep trying to punish me with their laws – and why? Their laws are not for me. They cannot punish me.'

He did not answer.

'Therefore,' she said softly, 'tomorrow I go out of here to seek power. I will be more powerful than any laws.'

That shocked him to action. 'Kyra!' he cried. 'You're not to try to leave here again.' He gripped her shoulders. 'Promise me! Swear that you'll not step beyond that door without me!'

'Why, if you wish,' she said quietly.

'But swear it! Swear it by everything sacred!'

Her silver eyes looked steadily into his from a face like that of a marble angel. 'I swear it,' she murmured. 'By anything you name, I swear it, Dan.'

And in the morning she was gone, taking what cash and bills had been in Scott's wallet, and in Bach's as well. And, they discovered later, in Mrs Getz's also.

'But if you could have seen her!' muttered Scott. 'She looked straight into my eyes and promised, and her face was pure as a madonna's. I can't believe she was lying.'

'The lie as an adaptive mechanism,' said Bach, 'deserves more attention than it has received. Probably the original liars are those plants and animals that use protective mimicry – harmless snakes imitating poisonous ones, stingless flies that look like bees. Those are living lies.'

'But she couldn't – '

'She has, however. What you've told me about her desire for power is proof enough. She's entered the second adaptive phase – that of adapting her environment to herself instead of herself to her environment.

How far will her madness – or her genius – carry her? There is very little difference between the two, Dan. And what is left now for us to do but watch?'

'Watch? How? Where is she?'

'Unless I'm badly mistaken, watching her will be easy once she begins to achieve. Wherever she is, I think we – and the rest of the world – will know of it soon enough.'

But weeks dropped away without sign of Kyra Zelas. Scott and Bach returned to their duties at Grand Mercy, and down in his laboratory the biochemist disposed grimly of the remains of three guinea pigs, a cat, and a dog, whose killing had been an exhausting and sickening task. In the crematory as well went a tube of water-clear serum.

Then one day the annunciator summoned him to Bach's office, where he found the old man hunched over a copy of the *Post Record*.

'Look here!' he said, indicating a political gossip column called 'Whirls of Washington'.

Scott read, 'And the surprise of the evening was the *soi disant* confirmed bachelor of the cabinet, upright John Callan, who fluttered none other than the gorgeous Kyra Zelas, the lady who affects a dark wig by day and a white by night. Some of us remember her as the acquittee of a murder trial.'

Scott looked up. 'Callan, eh? Secretary of the treasury, no less! When she said power she meant power, apparently.'

'But will she stop there?' mused Bach gloomily. 'I have a premonition that she's just beginning.'

'Well, actually, how far can a woman go?'

The old man looked at him. 'A woman? This is Kyra Zelas, Dan. Don't set your limits yet. There will be more of her.'

Bach was right. Her name began to appear with increasing frequency, first in social connections, then with veiled references to secret intrigues and influences.

Thus: 'Whom do the press boys mean by the tenth cabineteer?' Or later: 'Why not a secretary of personal relations? She has the powers; give her the name.' And still later: 'One has to go back to Egypt for another instance of a country whose exchequer was run by a woman. And Cleopatra busted that one.'

Scott grinned a little ruefully to himself as he realized that the thrusts were becoming more indirect, as if the press itself were beginning to grow cautious. It was a sign of increasing power, for nowhere are people as sensitive to such trends as among the Washington correspondents.

Kyra's appearance in the public prints began to be more largely restrained to purely social affairs, and usually in connection with John Callan, the forty-five-year-old bachelor secretary of the treasury.

Waking or sleeping, Scott never for a moment quite forgot her, for there was something mystical about her, whether she were mad or a woman of genius, whether freak or superwoman. The only thing he did forget was a thin girl with drab features and greasy black hair who had lain on a pallet in the isolation ward and coughed up flecks of blood.

It was no surprise to either Scott or Dr Bach to return one evening to Bach's residence for a few hours' conversation, and find there, seated as comfortably as if she had never left it, Kyra Zelas. Outwardly she had changed but little; Scott gazed once more in fascination on her incredible hair and wide, innocent silver eyes. She was smoking a cigarette, and she exhaled a long, blue plume of smoke and smiled up at him.

He hardened himself. 'Nice of you to honor us,' he said coldly. 'What's the reason for this visit? Did you run out of money?'

'Money? Of course not. How could I run out of money?'

'You couldn't, not as long as you replenished your funds the way you did when you left.'

'Oh, that!' she said contemptuously. She opened her handbag, indicating a green mass of bills. 'I'll give that back, Dan. How much was it?'

'To hell with the money!' he blazed. 'What hurts me is the way you lied. Staring into my eyes as innocent as a baby, and lying all the time!'

'Was I?' she asked. 'I won't lie to you again, Dan. I promise.'

'I don't believe you,' he said bitterly. 'Tell us what you're doing here, then.'

'I wanted to see you. I haven't forgotten what I said to you, Dan.' With the words she seemed to grow more beautiful than ever, and this time poignantly wistful as well.

'And have you,' asked Bach suddenly, 'abandoned your idea of power?'

'Why should I want power?' she rejoined innocently, flashing her magnificent eyes to him.

'But you said,' began Scott impatiently, 'that you – '

'Did I?' There was a ghost of a smile on her perfect lips. 'I won't lie to you, Dan,' she went on, laughing a little. 'If I want power, it is mine for the taking – more power than you dream.'

'Through John Callan?' he rasped.

'He offers a simple way,' she said impassively. 'Suppose, for instance, that in a day or so he were to issue a statement – a supremely insulting statement – about the war debts. The administration couldn't afford to reprimand him openly, because most of the voters feel that a supremely insulting statement is called for. And if it were insulting enough – and I assure you it would be – you would see the animosity of Europe directed westward.

'Now, if the statement were one that no national government could ignore and yet keep its dignity in the eyes of its people, it would provoke counter-insults. And there are three nations – you know their names as well as I – who await only such a diversion of interest. Don't you see?' She frowned.

'How stupid you both are!' she murmured, and then, stretching her glorious figure and yawning, 'I wonder what sort of empress I would make. A good one, doubtless.'

But Scott was aghast. 'Kyra, do you mean you'd urge Callan into such a colossal blunder as that?'

'Urge him!' she echoed contemptuously. 'I'd force him.'

'Do you mean you'd do it?'

'I haven't said so,' she smiled. She yawned again, and snapped her cigarette into the dark fireplace. 'I'll stay here a day or two,' she added pleasantly, rising. 'Good night.'

Scott faced Dr Bach as she vanished into the old man's chamber. 'Damn her!' he grated, his lips white. 'If I believed she meant all of that – '

'You'd better believe it,' said Bach.

'Empress, eh! Empress of what?'

'Of the world, perhaps. You can't set limits to madness or genius.'

'We've got to stop her!'

'How? We can't keep her locked up here. In the first place, she'd doubtless develop strength enough in her wrists to break the locks on the doors, and if she didn't, all she'd need to do is shout for help from a window.'

'We can have her adjudged insane!' flared Scott. 'We can have her locked up where she can't break out or call for help.'

'Yes, we could. We could if we could get her committed by the Sanity Commission. And if we got her before them, what chance do you think we'd have?'

'All right, then,' said Scott grimly, 'we're going to have to find her weakness. Her adaptability can't be infinite. She's immune to drugs and immune to wounds, but she can't be above the fundamental laws of biology. What we have to do is to find the law we need.'

'You find it then,' said Bach gloomily.

'But we've got to do something. At least we can warn people – ' He broke off, realizing the utter absurdity of the idea.

'Warn people!' scoffed Bach. 'Against what? We'd be the ones to go before the Sanity Commission then. Callan would ignore us with dignity, and Kyra would laugh her pretty little laugh of contempt, and that would be that.'

Scott shrugged helplessly. 'I'm staying here tonight,' he said. 'At least we can talk to her again tomorrow.'

'If she's still here,' remarked Bach ironically.

But she was. She came out as Scott was reading the morning papers alone in the library, and sat silently opposite him, garbed in black silk lounging pajamas against which her alabaster skin and incredible hair glowed in startling contrast. He watched skin and hair turn faintly golden as the morning sun lightened the chamber. Somehow it angered him that she should be so beautiful and at the same time deadly with an inhuman deadliness.

He spoke first. 'You haven't committed any murders since our last meeting, I hope.' He said it spitefully, viciously.

She was quite indifferent. 'Why should I? It has not been necessary.'

'You know, Kyra,' he said evenly, 'that you ought to be killed.'

'But not by you, Dan. You love me.'

He said nothing. The fact was too obvious to deny.

'Dan,' she said softly, 'if you only had my courage, there is no height we might not reach together. No height – if you had the courage to try. That is why I came back here, but – ' She shrugged. 'I go back to Washington tomorrow.'

Later in the day Scott got Bach alone. 'She's going tomorrow!' he said tensely. 'Whatever we can do has to be done tonight.'

The old man gestured helplessly. 'What can we do? Can you think of any law that limits adaptability?'

'No, but – ' He paused suddenly. 'By Heaven!' he cried. 'I can! I've got it!'

'What?'

'The law! A fundamental biological law that must be Kyra's weakness!'

'But what?'

'This! No organism can live in its own waste products! Its own waste is poison to any living thing!'

'But – '

'Listen. Carbon dioxide is a human waste product. Kyra can't adapt to an atmosphere of carbon dioxide!'

Bach stared. 'By Heaven!' he cried. 'But even if you're right, how – '

'Wait a minute. You can get a couple of cylinders of carbonic acid gas from Grand Mercy. Can you think of any way of getting the gas into her room?'

'Why – this is an old house. There's a hole from her room to the one I'm using, where the radiator connection goes through. It's not tight; we could get a rubber tube past the pipe.'

'Good!'

'But the windows! She'll have the windows open.'

'Never mind that,' said Scott. 'See that they're soaped so they'll close easily, that's all.'

'But even if it works, what good – Dan! You don't mean to kill her?'

He shook his head. 'I – couldn't,' he whispered. 'But once she's helpless, once she's overcome – if she is – you'll operate. That operation on the pineal you suggested before. And may Heaven forgive me!'

Scott suffered the tortures of the damned that evening. Kyra was, if possible, lovelier than ever, and for the first time she seemed to exert herself to be charming. Her conversation was literally brilliant; she sparkled, and over and over Scott found himself so fascinated that the thought of the treachery he planned was an excruciating pain. It seemed almost a blasphemy to attempt violence against one whose outward appearance was so pure, so innocent, so saintlike.

'But she isn't quite – human!' he told himself. 'She's not an angel but a female demon, a – what were they called? – an incubus!'

Despite himself, when at last Kyra yawned luxuriously and dropped her dainty feet to the floor to depart, he pleaded for a few moments more.

'But it's early,' he said, 'and tomorrow you leave.'

'I will return, Dan. This is not the end for us.'

'I hope not,' he muttered miserably, watching the door of her room as it clicked shut.

He gazed at Bach. The older man, after a moment's silence, whispered, 'It is likely that she sleeps almost at once. That's also a matter of adaptability.'

In tense silence they watched the thin line of light below the closed door. Scott started violently when, after a brief interval, her shadow crossed it and it disappeared with a faint click.

'Now, then,' he said grimly. 'Let's get it over.'

He followed Bach into the adjacent room. There, cold and metallic, stood the gray cylinders of compressed gas. He watched as the old man attached a length of tubing, ran it to the opening around the steam pipe, and began to pack the remaining space with wet cotton.

Scott turned to his own task. He moved quietly into the library. With utmost stealth he tried the door of Kyra's room; it was unlocked as he had known it would be, for the girl was supremely confident of her own invulnerability.

For a long moment he gazed across at the mass of radiant silver hair on her pillow, then, very cautiously, he placed a tiny candle on the chair by the window, so that it should be at about the level of the bed, lighted it with a snap of his cigarette lighter, withdrew the door key, and departed.

He locked the door on the outside, and set about stuffing the crack below it with cotton. It was far from airtight, but that mattered little, he mused, since one had to allow for the escape of the replaced atmosphere.

He returned to Bach's room. 'Give me a minute,' he whispered. 'Then turn it on.'

He stepped to a window. Outside was a two-foot ledge of stone, and he crept to this precarious perch. He was visible from the street below, but not markedly noticeable, for he was directly above an areaway between Bach's house and its neighbor. He prayed fervently that he might escape attention.

He crept along the ledge. The two windows of Kyra's chamber were wide, but Bach had done his work. They slid downward, without a creak, and he pressed close against the glass to peer in.

Across the room glowed the faint and steady flame of his little taper. Close beside him, within a short arm's length had no pane intervened, lay Kyra, quite visible in the dusk. She lay on her back, with one arm thrown above her unbelievable hair, and she had drawn only a single sheet over her. He could watch her breathing, quiet, calm, peaceful.

It seemed as if a long time passed. He fancied at last that he could hear the gentle hiss of gas from Bach's window, but he knew that that must be fancy. In the chamber he watched there was no sign of anything unusual; the glorious Kyra slept as she did everything else – easily, quietly, and confidently.

Then there was a sign. The little candle flame, burning steadily in the draughtless air, flickered suddenly. He watched it, certain now that its color was changing. Again it flickered, flared for a moment, then died. A red spark glowed on the wick for a bare instant, then that was gone.

The candle flame was smothered. That meant a concentration of eight or ten per cent of carbon dioxide in the room's temperature – far too high to support ordinary life. Yet Kyra was living. Except that her quiet breathing seemed to have deepened, she gave not even a sign of inconvenience. She had adapted to the decreased oxygen supply.

But there must be limits to her powers. He blinked into the darkness. Surely – surely her breathing was quickening. He was positive now; her breast rose and fell in convulsive gasps, and somewhere in his turbulent mind the scientist in him recorded the fact.

'Cheyne-Stokes breathing,' he muttered. In a moment the violence of it would waken her.

It did. Suddenly the silver eyes started open. She brushed her hand across her mouth, then clutched at her throat. Aware instantly of danger, she thrust herself erect, and her bare legs flashed as she pushed herself from the bed. But she must have been dazed, for she turned first to the door.

He saw the unsteadiness in her movements. She twisted the doorknob, tugged frantically, then whirled toward the window. He could see her swaying as she staggered through the vitiated air, but she reached it. Her face was close to his, but he doubted if she saw him, for her eyes were wide and frightened, and her mouth and throat were straining violently for breath. She raised her hand to smash the pane; the blow landed, but weakly, and the window shook but did not shatter.

Again her arm rose, but that blow was never delivered. For a moment she stood poised, swaying slowly, then her magnificent eyes misted and closed, she dropped to her knees, and at last collapsed limply on the floor.

Scott waited a long, torturing moment, then thrust up the window. The rush of lifeless air sent him whirling dizzily on his dangerous perch, and he clutched the casement. Then a slow breeze moved between the buildings, and his head cleared.

He stepped gingerly into the chamber. It was stifling, but near the open window he could breathe. He kicked thrice against Bach's wall.

The hiss of gas ceased. He gathered Kyra's form in his arms, waited until he heard the key turn, then dashed across the room and into the library.

Bach stared as if fascinated at the pure features of the girl. 'A goddess overcome,' he said. 'There is something sinful about our part in this.'

'Be quick!' snapped Scott. 'She's unconscious, not anaesthetized. God knows how quickly she'll readjust.'

But she had not yet recovered when Scott laid her on the operating table in Bach's office, and drew the straps about her arms and body and slim bare legs. He looked down on her still, white face and bright hair, and he felt his heart contract with pain to see them darken ever so faintly and beautifully under the brilliant operating light, rich in actinic rays.

'You were right,' he whispered to the unhearing girl. 'Had I your courage there is nothing we might not have attained together.'

Bach spoke brusquely. 'Nasal?' he asked. 'Or shall I trephine her?'

'Nasal.'

'But I should like a chance to observe the pineal gland. This case is unique, and – '

'Nasal!' blazed Scott. 'I won't have her scarred!'

Bach sighed and began. Scott, despite his long hospital experience, found himself quite unable to watch this operation; he passed the old man his instruments as needed, but kept his eyes averted from the girl's passive and lovely face.

'So!' said Bach at last. 'It is done.' For the first time he himself had a moment's leisure to survey Kyra's features.

Bach started violently. Gone was the exquisite aluminum hair, replaced by the stringy, dark, and oily locks of the girl in the hospital! He pried open her eye, silver no longer, but pallid blue. Of all her loveliness, there remained – what? A trace, perhaps; a trace in the saintlike purity of her pale face, and in the molding of her features. But a flame had died; she was a goddess no longer, but a mortal – a human being. The superwoman had become no more than a suffering girl.

An ejaculation had almost burst from his lips when Scott's voice stopped him.

'How beautiful she is!' he whispered. Bach stared. He realized suddenly that Scott was not seeing her as she was, but as she once had been. To his eyes, colored by love, she was still Kyra the magnificent.

Parasite Planet

Stanley G. Weinbaum

Luckily for 'Ham' Hammond it was mid-winter when the mudspout came. Mid-winter, that is, in the Venusian sense, which is nothing at all like the conception of the season generally entertained on Earth, except possibly by dwellers in the hotter regions of the Amazon basin or the Congo.

They, perhaps, might form a vague mental picture of winter on Venus by visualizing their hottest summer days, multiplying the heat, discomfort and unpleasant denizens of the jungle by ten or twelve.

On Venus, as is now well known, the seasons occur alternately in opposite hemispheres, as on the Earth, but with a very important difference. Here, when North America and Europe swelter in summer, it is winter in Australia and Cape Colony and Argentina. It is the northern and southern hemispheres which alternate their seasons.

But on Venus, very strangely, it is the eastern and western hemispheres, because the seasons of Venus depend, not on inclination to the plane of the echliptic, but on libration. Venus does not rotate, but keeps the same face always toward the Sun, just as the Moon does toward the earth. One face is forever daylight, and the other forever night, and only along the twilight zone, a strip five hundred miles wide, is human habitation possible, a thin ring of territory circling the planet.

Toward the sunlit side it verges into the blasting heat of a desert where only a few Venusian creatures live, and on the night edge the strip ends abruptly in the colossal ice barrier produced by the condensation of the upper winds that sweep endlessly from the rising air of the hot hemisphere to cool and sink and rush back again from the cold one.

The chilling of warm air always produces rain, and at the edge of the darkness the rain freezes to form these great ramparts. What lies beyond, what fantastic forms of life may live in the starless darkness of the frozen face, or whether that region is as dead as the airless Moon – those are mysteries.

But the slow libration, a ponderous wobbling of the planet from side to side, does produce the effect of seasons. On the lands of the twilight zone, first in one hemisphere and then the other, the cloud-hidden Sun seems to rise gradually for fifteen days, then sink for the same period. It never ascends far, and only near the ice barrier does it seem to touch the horizon; for the libration is only seven degrees, but it is sufficient to produce noticeable fifteen-day seasons.

But such seasons! In the winter the temperature drops sometimes to a humid but bearable ninety, but, two weeks later, a hundred and forty is a cool day near the torrid edge of the zone. And always, winter and summer, the intermittent rains drip sullenly down to be absorbed by the spongy soil and given back again as sticky, unpleasant, unhealthy steam.

And that, the vast amount of moisture on Venus, was the greatest surprise of the first human visitors; the clouds had been seen, of course, but the spectroscope denied the presence of water, naturally, since it was analyzing light reflected from the upper cloud surfaces, fifty miles above the planet's face.

That abundance of water has strange consequences. There are no seas or oceans on Venus, if we except the probability of vast, silent, and eternally frozen oceans on the sunless side. On the hot hemisphere evaporation is too rapid, and the rivers that flow out of the ice mountains simply diminish and finally vanish, dried up.

A further consequence is the curiously unstable nature of the land of the twilight zone. Enormous subterranean rivers course invisibly through it, some boiling, some cold as the ice from which they flow. These are the cause of the mud eruptions that make human habitation in the Hotlands such a gamble; a perfectly solid and apparently safe area of soil may be changed suddenly into a boiling sea of mud in which buildings sink and vanish, together, frequently, with their occupants.

There is no way of predicting these catastrophes; only on the rare outcroppings of bed rock is a structure safe, and so all permanent human settlements cluster about the mountains.

Sam Hammond was a trader. He was one of those adventurous individuals who always appear on the frontiers and fringes of habitable regions. Most of these fall into two classes; they are either reckless daredevils pursuing danger, or outcasts, criminal or otherwise, pursuing either solitude or forgetfulness.

Ham Hammond was neither. He was pursuing no such abstractions, but the good, solid lure of wealth. He was, in fact, trading with the natives for the spore-pods of the Venusian plant xixtchil, from which terrestrial chemists would extract trihydroxyl-tertiary-tolunitrile-beta-anthraquinone, the xixtline or triple-T-B-A that was so effective in rejuvenation treatments.

Ham was young and sometimes wondered why rich old men – and women – would pay such tremendous prices for a few more years of virility, especially as the treatments didn't actually increase the span of life, but just produced a sort of temporary and synthetic youth.

Gray hair darkened, wrinkles filled out, bald heads grew fuzzy, and then, in a few years, the rejuvenated person was just as dead as he would have been, anyway. But as long as triple-T-B-A commanded a price about equal to its weight in radium, why, Ham was willing to take the gamble to obtain it.

He had never really expected the mudspout. Of course it was an ever-present danger, but when, staring idly through the window of his shack over the writhing and steaming Venusian plain, he had seen the sudden boiling pools erupting all around, it had come as a shocking surprise.

For a moment he was paralyzed; then he sprang into immediate and frantic action. He pulled on his enveloping suit of rubberlike transkin; he strapped the great bowls of mudshoes to his feet; he tied the precious bag of spore-pods to his shoulders, packed some food, and then burst into the open.

The ground was still semisolid, but even as he watched, the black soil boiled out around the metal walls of the shack, the cube tilted a trifle, and then sank deliberately from sight, and the mud sucked and gurgled as it closed gently above the spot.

Ham caught himself. One couldn't stand still in the midst of a mud-spout, even with the bowl-like mudshoes as support. Once let the viscous stuff flow over the rim and the luckless victim was trapped; he couldn't raise his foot against the suction, and first slowly, then more quickly, he'd follow the shack.

So Ham started off over the boiling swamp, walking with the peculiar sliding motion he had learned by much practice, never raising the mud-shoes above the surface, but sliding them along, careful that no mud topped the curving rim.

It was a tiresome motion, but absolutely necessary. He slid along as if on snowshoes, bearing west because that was the direction of the dark side, and if he had to walk to safety, he might as well do it in coolness. The area of swamp was unusually large; he covered at least a mile before he attained a slight rise in the ground, and the mudshoes clumped on solid, or nearly solid, soil.

He was bathed in perspiration; and his transkin suit was hot as a boiler room, but one grows accustomed to that on Venus. He'd have given half his supply of xixtchil pods for the opportunity to open the mask of the suit, to draw a breath of even the steamy and humid Venusian air, but that was impossible; impossible, at least, if he had any inclination to continue living.

One breath of unfiltered air anywhere near the warm edge of the twilight zone was quick and very painful death; Ham would have drawn in uncounted millions of the spores of those fierce Venusian molds, and they'd have sprouted in furry and nauseating masses in his nostrils, his mouth, his lungs, and eventually in his ears and eyes.

Breathing them wasn't even a necessary requirement; once he'd come upon a trader's body with the molds springing from his flesh. The poor fellow had somehow torn a rip in his transkin suit, and that was enough.

The situation made eating and drinking in the open a problem on Venus; one had to wait until a rain had precipitated the spores, when it was safe for half an hour or so. Even then the water must have been recently boiled and the food just removed from its can; otherwise, as had happened to Ham more than once, the food was apt to turn abruptly into a fuzzy mass of molds that grew about as fast as the minute hand moved on a clock. A disgusting sight! A disgusting planet!

That last reflection was induced by Ham's view of the quagmire that had engulfed his shack. The heavier vegetation had gone with it, but already avid and greedy life was emerging, wriggling mud grass and the bulbous fungi called 'walking balls'. And all around a million little slimy creatures slithered across the mud, eating each other rapaciously, being torn to bits, and each fragment re-forming to a complete creature.

A thousand different species, but all the same in one respect; each of them was all appetite. In common with most Venusian beings, they had a multiplicity of both legs and mouths; in fact some of them were little more than blobs of skin split into dozens of hungry mouths, and crawling on a hundred spidery legs.

All life on Venus is more or less parasitic. Even the plants that draw their nourishment directly from soil and air have also the ability to absorb and digest – and, often enough, to trap – animal food. So fierce is the competition on that humid strip of land between the fire and the ice that one who has never seen it must fail even to imagine it.

The animal kingdom wars incessantly on itself and the plant world; the vegetable kingdom retaliates, and frequently outdoes the other in the production of monstrous predatory horrors that one would even hesitate to call plant life. A terrible world!

In the few moments that Ham had paused to look back, ropy creepers had already entangled his legs; transkin was impervious, of course, but he had to cut the things away with his knife, and the black, nauseating juices that flowed out of them smeared on his suit and began instantly to grow furry as the molds sprouted. He shuddered.

'Hell of a place!' Ham growled, stooping to remove his mudshoes, which he slung carefully over his back.

He slogged away through the writhing vegetation, automatically dodging the awkward thrusts of the Jack Ketch trees as they cast their nooses hopefully toward his arms and head.

Now and again he passed one that dangled some trapped creature, usually unrecognizable because the molds had enveloped it in a fuzzy shroud, while the tree itself was placidly absorbing victim and molds alike.

'Horrible place!' Ham muttered, kicked a writhing mass of nameless little vermin from his path.

He mused; his shack had been situated rather nearer the hot edge of the twilight zone; it was a trifle over two hundred and fifty miles to the shadow line, though of course that varied with the libration. But one couldn't approach the line too closely, anyway, because of the fierce, almost inconceivable, storms that raged where the hot upper winds encountered the icy blasts of the night side, giving rise to the birth throes of the ice barrier.

So a hundred and fifty miles due west would be sufficient to bring coolness, to enter a region too temperate for the molds, where he could walk in comparative comfort. And then, not more than fifty miles north, lay the American settlement Erotia, named, obviously, after that troublesome mythical son of Venus, Cupid.

Intervening, of course, were the ranges of the Mountains of Eternity, not those mighty twenty-mile-high peaks whose summits are occasionally glimpsed by Earthly telescopes, and that forever sunder British Venus from the American possessions, but, even at the point he planned to cross, very respectable mountains indeed. He was on the British side now; not that any one cared. Traders came and went as they pleased.

Well, that meant about two hundred miles. No reason why he couldn't make it; he was armed with both automatic and flame-pistol, and water was no problem, if carefully boiled. Under pressure of necessity, one could even eat Venusian life – but it required hunger and thorough cooking and a sturdy stomach.

It wasn't the taste so much as the appearance, or so he'd been told. He grimaced; beyond doubt he'd be driven to find out for himself, since his canned food couldn't possibly last out the trip. Nothing to worry about, Ham kept telling himself. In fact, plenty to be glad about; the xixtchil pods in his pack represented as much wealth as he could have accumulated by ten years of toil back on Earth.

No danger – and yet, men had vanished on Venus, dozens of them. The molds had claimed them, or some fierce unearthly monster, or perhaps one of the many unknown living horrors, both plant and animal.

Ham trudged along, keeping always to the clearings about the Jack Ketch trees, since these vegetable omnivores kept other life beyond the reach of their greedy nooses. Elsewhere progress was impossible, for the Venusian jungle presented such a terrific tangle of writhing and struggling forms that one could move only by cutting the way, step by step, with infinite labor.

Even then there was the danger of Heaven only knew what fanged and venomous creatures whose teeth might pierce the protective membrane of transkin, and a crack in that meant death. Even the unpleasant Jack Ketch trees were preferable company, he reflected, as he slapped their questing lariats aside.

Six hours after Ham had started his involuntary journey, it rained. He seized the opportunity, found a place where a recent mudspout had cleared the heavier vegetation away, and prepared to eat. First, however, he scooped up some scummy water, filtered it through the screen attached for that purpose to his canteen, and set about sterilizing it.

Fire was difficult to manage, since dry fuel is rare indeed in the Hotlands of Venus, but Ham tossed a thermide tablet into the liquid, and the chemicals boiled the water instantly, escaping themselves as gases. If the water retained a slight ammoniacal taste – well, that was the least of his discomforts, he mused, as he covered it and set it by to cool.

He uncapped a can of beans, watched a moment to see that no stray molds had remained in the air to infect the food, then opened the visor of his suit and swallowed hastily. Thereafter he drank the blood-warm water and poured carefully what remained into the water pouch within his transkin, where he could suck it through a tube to his mouth without the deadly exposure to the molds.

Ten minutes after he had completed the meal, while he rested and longed for the impossible luxury of a cigarette, the fuzzy coat sprang suddenly to life on the remnants of food in the can.

An hour later, weary and thoroughly soaked in perspiration, Ham found a Friendly tree, so named by the explorer Burlingame because it is one of the few organisms on Venus sluggish enough to permit one to rest in its branches. So Ham climbed it, found the most comfortable position available, and slept as best he could.

It was five hours by his wrist watch before he awoke, and the tendrils and little sucking cups of the Friendly tree were fastened all over his transkin. He tore them away very carefully, climbed down, and trudged westward.

It was after the second rain that he met the doughpot, as the creature is called in British and American Venus. In the French strip, it's the *pot à colle*, the 'paste pot'; in the Dutch – well, the Dutch are not prudish, and they call the horror just what they think it warrants.

Actually, the doughpot is a nauseous creature. It's a mass of white, dough-like protoplasm, ranging in size from a single cell to perhaps twenty tons of mushy filth. It has no fixed form; in fact, it's merely a mass of de Proust cells – in effect, a disembodied, crawling, hungry cancer.

It has no organization and no intelligence, nor even any instinct save hunger. It moves in whatever direction food touches its surfaces; when it touches two edible substances, it quietly divides, with the larger portion invariably attacking the greater supply.

It's invulnerable to bullets; nothing less than the terrific blast of a flame-pistol will kill it, and then only if the blast destroys every individual cell. It travels over the ground absorbing everything, leaving bare black soil where the ubiquitous molds spring up at once – a noisome, nightmarish creature.

Ham sprang aside as the doughpot erupted suddenly from the jungle to his right. It couldn't absorb the transkin, of course, but to be caught in that mess meant quick suffocation. He glared at it disgustedly and was sorely tempted to blast it with his flame-pistol as it slithered past at running speed. He would have, too, but the experienced Venusian frontiersman is very careful with the flame-pistol.

It has to be charged with a diamond, a cheap black one, of course, but still an item to consider. The crystal, when fired, gives up all its energy in one terrific blast that roars out like a lightning stroke for a hundred yards, incinerating everything in its path.

The thing rolled by with a sucking and gulping sound. Behind it opened the passage it had cleared; creepers, snake vines, Jack Ketch trees – everything had been swept away down to the humid earth itself, where already the molds were springing up on the slime of the doughpot's trail.

The alley led nearly in the direction Ham wanted to travel; he seized the opportunity and strode briskly along, with a wary eye, nevertheless, on the ominous walls of jungle. In ten hours or so the opening would be filled once more with unpleasant life, but for the present it offered a much quicker progress than dodging from one clearing to the next.

It was five miles up the trail, which was already beginning to sprout inconveniently, that he met the native galloping along on his four short legs, his pincerlike hands shearing a path for him. Ham stopped for a palaver.

'*Murra*,' he said.

The language of the natives of the equatorial regions of the Hotlands is a queer one. It has, perhaps, two hundred words, but when a trader has learned those two hundred, his knowledge of the tongue is but little greater than the man who knows none at all.

The words are generalized, and each sound has anywhere from a dozen to a hundred meanings. *Murra*, for instance, is a word of greeting; it may mean something much like 'hello', or 'good morning'. It also may convey a challenge – 'on guard!' It means besides, 'Let's be friends', and also, strangely, 'Let's fight this out.'

It has, moreover, certain noun senses; it means peace, it means war, it means courage, and, again, fear. A subtle language; it is only recently that studies of inflection have begun to reveal its nature to human philologists. Yet, after all, perhaps English, with its 'to', 'too' and 'two', its 'one', 'won', 'wan', 'wen', 'win', 'when', and a dozen other similarities, might seem just as strange to Venusian ears, untrained in vowel distinctions.

Moreover, humans can't read the expressions of the broad, flat, three-eyed Venusian faces, which in the nature of things must convey a world of information among the natives themselves.

But this one accepted the intended sense. '*Murra*,' he responded, pausing. '*Usk*?' That was, among other things, 'Who are you?' or 'Where did you come from?' or 'Where are you bound?'

Ham chose the latter sense. He pointed off into the dim west, then raised his hand in an arc to indicate the mountains. 'Erotia,' he said. That had but one meaning, at least.

The native considered this in silence. At last he grunted and volunteered some information. He swept his cutting claw in a gesture west along the trail. '*Curky*,' he said, and then, '*Murra*.' The last was farewell; Ham pressed against the wriggling jungle wall to permit him to pass.

'*Curky*' meant, together with twenty other senses, trader. It was the word usually applied to humans, and Ham felt a pleasant anticipation in the prospect of human company. It had been six months since he had heard a human voice other than that on the tiny radio now sunk with his shack.

True enough, five miles along the doughpot's trail Ham emerged suddenly in an area where there had been a recent mudspout. The vegetation was only waist-high, and across the quarter-mile clearing he saw a structure, a trading hut. But far more pretentious than his own iron-walled cubicle; this one boasted three rooms, an unheard-of luxury in the Hotlands, where every ounce had to be laboriously transported by rocket from one of the settlements. That was expensive, almost prohibitive. Traders took a real gamble, and Ham knew he was lucky to have come out so profitably.

He strode over the still spongy ground. The windows were shaded against the eternal daylight, and the door – the door was locked. This was a violation of the frontier code. One always left doors unlocked; it might mean the salvation of some strayed trader, and not even the most dishonorable would steal from a hut left open for his safety.

Nor would the natives; no creature is as honest as a Venusian native, who never lies and never steals, though he might, after due warning, kill a trader for his trade goods. But only after a fair warning.

Ham stood puzzled. At last he kicked and tramped a clear space before the door, sat down against it, and fell to snapping away the numerous and loathsome little creatures that swarmed over his transkin. He waited.

It wasn't half an hour before he saw the trader plowing through the clearing – a short, slim fellow; the transkin shaded his face, but Ham could make out large, shadowed eyes. He stood up.

'Hello!' he said jovially. 'Thought I'd drop in for a visit. My name's Hamilton Hammond – you guess the nickname!'

The newcomer stopped short, then spoke in a curiously soft and husky voice, with a decidedly English accent. 'My guess would be "Boiled Pork", I fancy.' The tones were cold, unfriendly. 'Suppose you step aside and let me in. Good day!'

Ham felt anger and amazement. 'The devil!' he snapped. 'You're a hospitable sort, aren't you?'

'No. Not at all.' The other paused at the door. 'You're an American. What are you doing on British soil? Have you a passport?'

'Since when do you need a passport in the Hotlands?'

'Trading, aren't you?' the slim man said sharply. 'In other words, poaching. You've no rights here. Get on.'

Ham's jaw set stubbornly behind his mask. 'Rights or none,' he said, 'I'm entitled to the consideration of the frontier code. I want a breath of air and a chance to wipe my face, and also a chance to eat. If you open that door I'm coming in after you.'

An automatic flashed into view. 'Do, and you'll feed the molds.'

Ham, like all Venusian traders, was of necessity bold, resourceful, and what is called in the States 'hard-boiled'. He didn't flinch, but said in apparent yielding: 'All right; but listen, all I want is a chance to eat.'

'Wait for a rain,' said the other coolly and half turned to unlock the door.

As his eyes shifted, Ham kicked at the revolver; it went spinning against the wall and dropped into the weeds. His opponent snatched for the flame-pistol that still dangled on his hip; Ham caught his wrist in a mighty clutch.

Instantly the other ceased to struggle, while Ham felt a momentary surprise at the skinny feel of the wrist through its transkin covering.

'Look here!' he growled. 'I want a chance to eat, and I'm going to get it. Unlock that door!'

He had both wrists now; the fellow seemed curiously delicate. After a moment he nodded, and Ham released one hand. The door opened, and he followed the other in.

Again, unheard-of magnificence. Solid chairs, a sturdy table, even books, carefully preserved, no doubt, by lycopodium against the ravenous molds that sometimes entered Hotland shacks in spite of screen filters and automatic spray. An automatic spray was going now to destroy any spores that might have entered with the opening door.

Ham sat down, keeping an eye on the other, whose flame-pistol he had permitted to remain in its holster. He was confident of his ability to outdraw the slim individual, and, besides, who'd risk firing a flame-pistol indoors? It would simply blow out one wall of the building.

So he set about opening his mask, removing food from his pack, wiping his steaming face, while his companion – or opponent – looked on silently. Ham watched the canned meat for a moment; no molds appeared, and he ate.

'Why the devil,' he rasped, 'don't you open your visor?' At the other's silence, he continued: 'Afraid I'll see your face, eh? Well, I'm not interested; I'm no cop.'

No reply.

He tried again. 'What's your name?'

The cool voice sounded: 'Burlingame. Pat Burlingame.'

Ham laughed. 'Patrick Burlingame is dead, my friend. I knew him.' No answer. 'And if you don't want to tell your name, at least you needn't insult the memory of a brave man and a great explorer.'

'Thank you.' The voice was sardonic. 'He was my father.'

'Another lie. He had no son. He had only a – ' Ham paused abruptly; a feeling of consternation swept over him. 'Open your visor!' he yelled.

He saw the lips of the other, dim through the transkin, twitch into a sarcastic smile.

'Why not?' said the soft voice, and the mask dropped.

Ham gulped; behind the covering were the delicately modeled features of a girl, with cool gray eyes in a face lovely despite the glistening perspiration on cheeks and forehead.

The man gulped again. After all, he was a gentleman despite his profession as one of the fierce, adventurous traders of Venus. He was university-educated – an engineer – and only the lure of quick wealth had brought him to the Hotlands.

'I – I'm sorry,' he stammered.

'You brave American poachers!' she sneered. 'Are all of you so valiant as to force yourselves on women?'

'But – how could I know? What are you doing in a place like this?'

'There's no reason for me to answer your questions, but' – she gestured toward the room beyond – 'I'm classifying Hotland flora and fauna. I'm Patricia Burlingame, biologist.'

He perceived now the jar-enclosed specimens of a laboratory in the next chamber. 'But a girl alone in the Hotlands! It's – it's reckless!'

'I didn't expect to meet any American poachers,' she retorted.

He flushed. 'You needn't worry about me. I'm going.' He raised his hands to his visor.

Instantly Patricia snatched an automatic from the table drawer. 'You're going, indeed, Mr Hamilton Hammond,' she said coolly. 'But you're leaving your xixtchil with me. It's crown property; you've stolen it from British territory, and I'm confiscating it.'

He stared. 'Look here!' he blazed suddenly. 'I've risked all I have for that xixtchil. If I lose it I'm ruined – busted. I'm not giving it up!'

'But you are.'

He dropped his mask and sat down. 'Miss Burlingame,' he said, 'I don't think you've nerve enough to shoot me, but that's what you'll have to do to get it. Otherwise I'll sit here until you drop of exhaustion.'

Her gray eyes bored silently into his blue ones. The gun held steadily on his heart, but spat no bullet. It was a deadlock.

At last the girl said, 'You win, poacher.' She slapped the gun into her empty holster. 'Get out, then.'

'Gladly!' he snapped.

He rose, fingered his visor, then dropped it again at a sudden startled scream from the girl. He whirled, suspecting a trick, but she was staring out of the window with wide, apprehensive eyes.

Ham saw the writhing of vegetation and then a vast whitish mass. A doughpot – a monstrous one, bearing steadily toward their shelter. He heard the gentle clunk of impact, and then the window was blotted out by the pasty mess, as the creature, not quite large enough to engulf the building, split into two masses that flowed around and merged on the other side. Another cry from Patricia. 'Your mask, fool!' she rasped. 'Close it!'

'Mask? Why?' Nevertheless, he obeyed automatically.

'Why? That's why! The digestive acids – look!' She pointed at the walls; indeed, thousands of tiny pinholes of light were appearing. The digestive acids of the monstrosity, powerful enough to attack whatever food chance brought, had corroded the metal; it was porous; the shack was ruined. He gasped as fuzzy molds shot instantly from the remains of his meal, and a red-and-green fur sprouted from the wood of chairs and table.

The two faced each other.

Ham chuckled. 'Well,' he said, 'you're homeless, too. Mine went down in a mudspout.'

'Yours would!' Patricia retorted acidly. 'You Yankees couldn't think of finding shallow soil, I suppose. Bed rock is just six feet below here, and my place is on pylons.'

'Well, you're a cool devil! Anyway, your place might as well be sunk. What are you going to do?'

'Do? Don't concern yourself. I'm quite able to manage.'

'How?'

'It's no affair of yours, but I have a rocket call each month.'

'You must be a millionaire, then,' he commented.

'The Royal Society,' she said coldly, 'is financing this expedition. The rocket is due – '

She paused; Ham thought she paled a little behind her mask.

'Due when?'

'Why – it just came two days ago. I'd forgotten.'

'I see. And you think you'll just stick around for a month waiting for it. Is that it?'

Patricia stared at him defiantly.

'Do you know,' he resumed, 'what you'd be in a month? It's ten days to summer and look at your shack.' He gestured at the walls, where brown and rusty patches were forming; at his motion a piece the size of a saucer tumbled in with a crackle. 'In two days this thing will be a caved-in ruin. What'll you do during fifteen days of summer? What'll you do without shelter when the temperature reaches a hundred and fifty – a hundred and sixty? I'll tell you – you'll die.' She said nothing.

'You'll be a fuzzy mass of molds before the rocket returns,' Ham said. 'And then a pile of clean bones that will go down with the first mudspout.'

'Be still!' she blazed.

'Silence won't help. Now I'll tell you what you can do. You can take your pack and your mudshoes and walk along with me. We may make the Cool Country before summer – if you can walk as well as you talk.'

'Go with a Yankee poacher? I fancy not!'

'And then,' he continued imperturbably, 'we can cross comfortably to Erotia, a good American town.'

Patricia reached for her emergency pack, slung it over her shoulders. She retrieved a thick bundle of notes, written in aniline ink on transkin, brushed off a few vagrant molds, and slipped it into the pack. She picked up a pair of diminutive mudshoes and turned deliberately to the door.

'So you're coming?' he chuckled.

'I'm going,' she retorted coldly, 'to the good British town of Venoble. Alone!'

'Venoble!' he gasped. 'That's two hundred miles south! And across the Greater Eternities, too!'

Patricia walked silently out of the door and turned west toward the Cool Country. Ham hesitated a moment, then followed. He couldn't permit the girl to attempt that journey alone; since she ignored his presence, he simply trailed a few steps behind her, plodding grimly and angrily along.

For three hours or more they trudged through the endless daylight, dodging the thrusts of the Jack Ketch trees, but mostly following the still fairly open trail of the first doughpot.

Ham was amazed at the agile and lithe grace of the girl, who slipped along the way with the sure skill of a native. Then a memory came to him; she was a native, in a sense. He recalled now that Patrick Burlingame's daughter was the first human child born on Venus, in the colony of Venoble, founded by her father.

Ham remembered the newspaper articles when she had been sent to Earth to be educated, a child of eight; he had been thirteen then. He was twenty-seven now, which made Patricia Burlingame twenty-two.

Not a word passed between them until at last the girl swung about in exasperation.

'Go away,' she blazed.

Ham halted. 'I'm not bothering you.'

'But I don't want a bodyguard. I'm a better Hotlander than you!'

He didn't argue the point. He kept silent, and after a moment she flashed: 'I hate you, Yankee! Lord, how I hate you!' She turned and trudged on.

An hour later the mudspout caught them. Without warning, watery muck boiled up around their feet, and the vegetation swayed wildly.

Hastily, they strapped on their mudshoes, while the heavier plants sank with sullen gurgles around them. Again Ham marveled at the girl's skill; Patricia slipped away across the unstable surface with a speed he could not match, and he shuffled far behind.

Suddenly he saw her stop. That was dangerous in a mudspout; only an emergency could explain it. He hurried; a hundred feet away he perceived the reason. A strap had broken on her right shoe, and she stood helpless, balancing on her left foot, while the remaining bowl was sinking slowly. Even now black mud slopped over the edge.

She eyed him as he approached. He shuffled to her side; as she saw his intention, she spoke.

'You can't,' she said.

Ham bent cautiously, slipping his arms about her knees and shoulders. Her mudshoes were already embedded, but he heaved mightily, driving the rims of his own dangerously close to the surface. With a great sucking gulp, she came free and lay very still in his arms, so as not to unbalance him as he slid again into careful motion over the treacherous surface. She was not heavy, but it was a hairbreadth chance, and the mud slipped and gurgled at the very edge of his shoe-bowls. Even though Venus has slightly less surface gravitation than Earth, a week or so gets one accustomed to it, and the twenty per cent advantage in weight seems to disappear.

A hundred yards brought firm footing. He sat her down and unstrapped her mudshoes.

'Thank you,' she said coolly. 'That was brave.'

'You're welcome,' he returned dryly. 'I suppose this will end any idea of your traveling alone. Without both mudshoes, the next spout will be the last for you. Do we walk together now?'

Her voice chilled. 'I can make a substitute shoe from tree skin.'

'Not even a native could walk on tree skin.'

'Then,' she said, 'I'll simply wait a day or two for the mud to dry and dig up my lost one.'

He laughed and gestured at the acres of mud. 'Dig where?' he countered. 'You'll be here till summer if you try that.'

She yielded. 'You win again, Yankee. But only to the Cool Country; then you'll go north and I south.'

They trudged on. Patricia was as tireless as Ham himself and was vastly more adept in Hotland lore. Though they spoke but little, he never ceased to wonder at the skill she had in picking the quickest route, and she seemed to sense the thrusts of the Jack Ketch trees without looking. But it was when they halted at last, after a rain had given opportunity for a hasty meal, that he had real cause to thank her.

'Sleep?' he suggested, and as she nodded: 'There's a Friendly tree.'

He moved toward it, the girl behind.

Suddenly she seized his arm. 'It's a Pharisee!' she cried, jerking him back.

None too soon! The false Friendly tree had lashed down with a terrible stroke that missed his face by inches. It was no Friendly tree at all, but an imitator, luring prey within reach by its apparent harmlessness, then striking with knife-sharp spikes.

Ham gasped. 'What is it? I never saw one of those before.'

'A Pharisee! It just looks like a Friendly tree.'

She took out her automatic and sent a bullet into the black, pulsing trunk. A dark stream gushed, and the ubiquitous molds sprang into life about the hole. The tree was doomed.

'Thanks,' said Ham awkwardly. 'I guess you saved my life.'

'We're quits now.' She gazed levelly at him. 'Understand? We're even.'

Later they found a true Friendly tree and slept. Awakening, they trudged on again, and slept again, and so on for three nightless days. No more mudspouts burst about them, but all the other horrors of the Hotlands were well in evidence. Doughpots crossed their path, snake vines hissed and struck, the Jack Ketch trees flung sinister nooses, and a million little crawling things writhed underfoot or dropped upon their suits.

Once they encountered a uniped, that queer, kangaroolike creature that leaps, crashing through the jungle on a single mighty leg, and trusts to its ten-foot beak to spear its prey.

When Ham missed his first shot, the girl brought it down in mid-leap to thresh into the avid clutches of the Jack Ketch trees and the merciless molds.

On another occasion, Patricia had both feet caught in a Jack Ketch noose that lay for some unknown cause on the ground. As she stepped within it, the tree jerked her suddenly, to dangle head down a dozen feet in the air, and she hung helplessly until Ham managed to cut her free. Beyond doubt, either would have died alone on any of several occasions; together they pulled through.

Yet neither relaxed the cool, unfriendly attitude that had become habitual. Ham never addressed the girl unless necessary, and she in the rare instances when they spoke, called him always by no other name than Yankee poacher. In spite of this, the man found himself sometimes remembering the piquant loveliness of her features, her brown hair and level gray eyes, as he had glimpsed them in the brief moments when rain made it safe to open their visors.

At last one day a wind stirred out of the west, bringing with it a breath of coolness that was like the air of heaven to them. It was the under-wind, the wind that blew from the frozen half of the planet, that breathed cold from beyond the ice barrier. When Ham experimentally shaved the skin from a writhing weed, the molds sprang out more slowly and with encouraging sparseness; they were approaching the Cool Country.

They found a Friendly tree with lightened hearts; another day's trek might bring them to the uplands where one could walk unhooded, in safety from the molds, since these could not sprout in a temperature much below eighty.

Ham woke first. For a while he gazed silently across at the girl, smiling at the way the branches of the tree had encircled her like affectionate arms. They were merely hungry, of course, but it looked like tenderness. His smile turned a little sad as he realized that the Cool Country meant parting, unless he could discourage that insane determination of hers to cross the Greater Eternities.

He sighed, and reached for his pack slung on a branch between them, and suddenly a bellow of rage and astonishment broke from him.

His xixtchil pods! The transkin pouch was slit; they were gone.

Patricia woke startled at his cry. Then, behind her mask, he sensed an ironic, mocking smile.

'My xixtchil!' he roared. 'Where is it?'

She pointed down. There among the lesser growths was a little mound of molds.

'There,' she said coolly. 'Down there, poacher.'

'You – ' He choked with rage.

'Yes. I slit the pouch while you slept. You'll smuggle no stolen wealth from British territory.'

Ham was white, speechless. 'You damned devil!' he bellowed at last. 'That's every cent I had!'

'But stolen,' she reminded him pleasantly, swinging her dainty feet.

Rage actually made him tremble. He glared at her; the light struck through the translucent transkin, outlining her body and slim rounded legs in shadow. 'I ought to kill you!' he muttered tensely.

His hand twitched, and the girl laughed softly. With a groan of desperation, he slung his pack over his shoulders and dropped to the ground.

'I hope – I hope you die in the mountains,' he said grimly, and stalked away toward the west.

A hundred yards distant he heard her voice.

'Yankee! Wait a moment!'

He neither paused nor glanced back, but strode on.

Half an hour later, glancing back from the crest of a rise, Ham perceived that she was following him. He turned and hurried on. The way was upward now, and his strength began to outweigh her speed and skill.

When next he glimpsed her, she was a plodding speck far behind, moving, he imagined, with a weary doggedness. He frowned back at her; it had occurred to him that a mudspout would find her completely helpless, lacking the vitally important mudshoes.

Then he realized that they were beyond the region of mudspouts, here in the foothills of the Mountains of Eternity, and anyway, he decided grimly, he didn't care.

For a while Ham paralleled a river, doubtless an unnamed tributary of the Phlegethon. So far there had been no necessity to cross watercourses, since naturally all streams on Venus flow from the ice barrier across the twilight zone to the hot side, and therefore, had coincided with their own direction.

But now, once he attained the tablelands and turned north, he would encounter rivers. They had to be crossed either on logs or, if opportunity offered and the stream was narrow, through the branches of Friendly trees. To set foot in the water was death; fierce fanged creatures haunted the streams.

He had one near catastrophe at the rim of the tableland. It was while he edged through a Jack Ketch clearing; suddenly there was a heave of white corruption, and tree and jungle wall disappeared in the mass of a gigantic doughpot.

He was cornered between the monster and an impenetrable tangle of vegetation, so he did the only thing left to do. He snatched his flame-pistol and sent a terrific, roaring blast into the horror, a blast that incinerated tons of pasty filth and left a few small fragments crawling and feeding on the débris.

The blast also, as it usually does, shattered the barrel of the weapon. He sighed as he set about the forty-minute job of replacing it – no true Hotlander ever delays that – for the blast had cost fifteen good American dollars, ten for the cheap diamond that had exploded, and five for the barrel. Nothing at all when he had had his xixtchil, but a real item now. He sighed again as he discovered that the remaining barrel was his last; he been forced to economize on everything when he set out.

Ham came at last to the table-land. The fierce and predatory vegetation of the Hotlands grew scarce; he began to encounter true plants, with no power of movement, and the underwind blew cool in his face.

He was in a sort of high valley; to his right were the gray peaks of the Lesser Eternities, beyond which lay Erotia, and to his left, like a mighty, glittering rampart, lay the vast slopes of the Greater Range, whose peaks were lost in the clouds fifteen miles above.

He looked at the opening of the rugged Madman's Pass where it separated two colossal peaks; the pass itself was twenty-five thousand feet in height, but the mountains out-topped it by fifty thousand more. One man had crossed that jagged crack on foot – Patrick Burlingame – and that was the way his daughter meant to follow.

Ahead, visible as a curtain of shadow, lay the night edge of the twilight zone, and Ham could see the incessant lightnings that flashed forever in this region of endless storms. It was here that the ice barrier crossed the ranges of the Mountains of Eternity, and the cold underwind, thrust up by the mighty range, met the warm upper winds in a struggle that was one continuous storm, such a storm as only Venus could provide. The river Phlegethon had its source somewhere back in there.

Ham surveyed the wildly magnificent panorama. Tomorrow, or rather, after resting, he would turn north. Patricia would turn south, and, beyond doubt, would die somewhere on Madman's Pass. For a moment he had a queerly painful sensation, then he frowned bitterly.

Let her die, if she was fool enough to attempt the pass alone just because she was too proud to take a rocket from an American settlement. She deserved it. He didn't care; he was still assuring himself of that as he prepared to sleep, not in a Friendly tree, but in one of the far more friendly specimens of true vegetation and in the luxury of an open visor.

The sound of his name awakened him. He gazed across the table-land to see Patricia just topping the divide, and he felt a moment's wonder at how she managed to trail him, a difficult feat indeed in a country where the living vegetation writhes instantly back across one's path. Then he recalled the blast of his flame-pistol; the flash and sound would carry for miles, and she must have heard or seen it.

Ham saw her glancing anxiously around.

'Ham!' she shouted again – not Yankee or poacher, but 'Ham!'

He kept a sullen silence; again she called. He could see her bronzed and piquant features now; she had dropped her transkin hood. She called again; with a despondent little shrug, she turned south along the divide, and he watched her go in grim silence. When the forest hid her from view, he descended and turned slowly north.

Very slowly; his steps lagged; it was as if he tugged against some invisible elastic bond. He kept seeing her anxious face and hearing in memory the despondent call. She was going to her death, he believed, and, after all, despite what she had done to him, he didn't want that.

She was too full of life, too confident, too young, and above all, too lovely to die.

True, she was an arrogant, vicious, self-centered devil, cool as crystal, and as unfriendly, but – she had gray eyes and brown hair, and she was courageous. And at last, with a groan of exasperation, he halted his lagging steps, turned, and rushed with almost eager speed into the south.

Trailing the girl was easy here for one trained in the Hotlands. The vegetation was slow to mend itself, here in the Cool Country, and now again he found imprints of her feet, or broken twigs to mark her path. He found the place where she had crossed the river through tree branches, and he found a place where she had paused to eat.

But he saw that she was gaining on him; her skill and speed outmatched his, and the trail grew steadily older. At last he stopped to rest; the table-land was beginning to curve upward toward the vast Mountains of Eternity, and on rising ground he knew he could overtake her. So he slept for a while in the luxurious comfort of no transkin at all, just the shorts and shirt that one wore beneath. That was safe here; the eternal underwind, blowing always toward the Hotlands, kept drifting mold spores away, and any brought in on the fur of animals died quickly at the first cool breeze. Nor would the true plants of the Cool Country attack his flesh.

He slept five hours. The next 'day' of traveling brought another change in the country. The life of the foothills was sparse compared to the table-lands; the vegetation was no longer a jungle, but a forest, an unearthly forest, true, of treelike growths whose boles rose five hundred feet and then spread, not into foliage, but flowery appendages. Only an occasional Jack Ketch tree reminded him of the Hotlands.

Farther on, the forest diminished. Great rock outcroppings appeared, and vast red cliffs with no growths of any kind. Now and then he encountered swarms of the planet's only aerial creatures, the gray, moth-like dusters, large as hawks, but so fragile that a blow shattered them. They darted about, alighting at times to seize small squirming things, and tinkling in their curiously bell-like voices. And apparently almost above him, though really thirty miles distant, loomed the Mountains of Eternity, their peaks lost in the clouds that swirled fifteen miles overhead.

Here again it grew difficult to trail, since Patricia scrambled often over bare rock. But little by little the signs grew fresher; once again his greater strength began to tell. And then he glimpsed her, at the base of a colossal escarpment split by a narrow, tree-filled canyon.

She was peering first at the mighty precipice, then at the cleft, obviously wondering whether it offered a means of scaling the barrier, or whether it was necessary to circle the obstacle. Like himself, she had discarded her transkin and wore the usual shirt and shorts of the Cool Country, which, after all, is not very cool by terrestrial standards. She looked, he thought, like some lovely forest nymph of the ancient slopes of Pelion.

He hurried as she moved into the canyon. 'Pat!' he shouted; it was the first time he had spoken her given name. A hundred feet within the passage he overtook her.

'You!' she gasped. She looked tired; she had been hurrying for hours, but a light of eagerness flashed in her eyes. 'I thought you had – I tried to find you.'

Ham's face held no responsive light. 'Listen here, Pat Burlingame,' he said coldly. 'You don't deserve any consideration, but I can't see you walking into death. You're a stubborn devil but you're a woman. I'm taking you to Erotia.'

The eagerness vanished. 'Indeed, poacher? My father crossed here. I can, too.'

'Your father crossed in midsummer, didn't he? And midsummer's to-day. You can't make Madman's Pass in less than five days, a hundred and twenty hours, and by then it will nearly winter, and this longitude will be close to the storm line. You're a fool.'

She flushed. 'The pass is high enough to be in the upper winds. It will be warm.'

'Warm! Yes – warm with lightning.' He paused; the faint rumble of thunder rolled through the canyon. 'Listen to that. In five days that will be right over us.' He gestured up at the utterly barren slopes. 'Not even Venusian life can get a foothold up there – or do you think you've got brass enough to be a lightning rod? Maybe you're right.'

Anger flamed. 'Rather the lightning than you!' Patricia snapped, and then as suddenly softened. 'I tried to call you back,' she said irrelevantly.

'To laugh at me,' he retorted bitterly.

'No. To tell you I was sorry, and that – '

'I don't want your apology.'

'But I wanted to tell you that – '

'Never mind,' he said curtly. 'I'm not interested in your repentance. The harm's done.' He frowned coldly down on her.

Patricia said meekly: 'But I – '

A crashing and gurgling interrupted her, and she screamed as a gigantic doughpot burst into view, a colossus that filled the canyon from wall to wall to a six-foot height as it surged toward them. The horrors were rarer in the Cool Country, but larger, since the abundance of food in the Hotlands kept subdividing them. But this one was a giant, a behemoth, tons and tons of nauseous, ill-smelling corruption heaving up the narrow way. They were cut off.

Ham snatched his flame-pistol, but the girl seized his arm.

'No, no!' she cried. 'Too close! It will spatter!'

Patricia was right. Unprotected by transkin, the touch of a fragment of that monstrosity was deadly, and, beyond that, the blast of a flame-pistol would shower bits of it upon them. He grasped her wrist and they fled up the canyon, striving for vantage way enough to risk a shot. And a dozen feet behind surged the doughpot, traveling blindly in the only direction it could – the way of food.

They gained. Then, abruptly, the canyon, which had been angling southwest, turned sharply south. The light of the eternally eastward Sun was hidden; they were in a pit of perpetual shadow, and the ground was bare and lifeless rock. And as it reached that point, the doughpot halted; lacking any organization, any will, it could not move when no food gave it direction. It was such a monster as only the life-swarming climate of Venus could harbor; it lived only by endless eating.

The two paused in the shadow.

'Now what?' muttered Ham.

A fair shot at the mass was impossible because of the angle; a blast would destroy only the portion it could reach.

Patricia leaped upward, catching a snaky shrub on the wall, so placed that it received a faint ray of light. She tossed it against the pulsing mass; the whole doughpot lunged forward a foot or two.

'Lure it in,' she suggested.

They tried. It was impossible; vegetation was too sparse.

'What will happen to the thing?' asked Ham.

'I saw one stranded on the desert edge of the Hotlands,' replied the girl. 'It quivered around for a long time, and then the cells attacked each other. It ate itself.' She shuddered. 'It was – horrible!'

'How long?'

'Oh, forty to fifty hours.'

'I won't wait that long,' growled Ham. He fumbled in his pack, pulling out his transkin.

'What will you do?'

'Put this on and try to blast that mass out of here at close range.' He fingered his flame-pistol. 'This is my last barrel,' he said gloomily, then more hopefully: 'But we have yours.'

'The chamber of mine cracked last time I used it, ten or twelve hours ago. But I have plenty of barrels.'

'Good enough!' said Ham.

He crept cautiously toward the horrible, pulsating wall of white. He thrust his arm so as to cover the greatest angle, pulled the trigger, and the roar and blazing fire of the blast bellowed echoing through the canyon. Bits of the monster spattered around him, and the thickness of the remainder, lessened by the incineration of tons of filth, was now only three feet.

'The barrel held!' he called triumphantly. It saved much time in recharging.

Five minutes later the weapon crashed again. When the mass of the monstrosity stopped heaving, only a foot and a half of depth remained, but the barrel had been blown to atoms.

'We'll have to use yours,' he said.

Patricia produced one, he took it, and then stared at it in dismay. The barrels of her Enfield-made weapon were far too small for his American pistol stock!

He groaned. 'Of all the idiots!' he burst out.

'Idiots!' she flared. 'Because you Yankees use trench mortars for your barrels?'

'I meant myself. I should have guessed this.' He shrugged. 'Well, we have our choice now of waiting here for the doughpot to eat himself, or trying to find some other way out of this trap. And my hunch is that this canyon's blind.'

It was probable, Patricia admitted. The narrow cleft was the product of some vast, ancient upheaval that had split the mountain in halves. Since it was not the result of water erosion, it was likely enough that the cleft ended abruptly in an unscalable precipice, but it was possible, too, that somewhere those sheer walls might be surmountable.

'We've time to waste, anyway,' she concluded. 'We might as well try it. Besides – ' She wrinkled her dainty nose distastefully at the doughpot's odor.

Still in his transkin, Ham followed her through the shadowy half dusk. The passage narrowed, then veered west again, but now so high and sheer were the walls that the Sun, slightly south of east, cast no light into it. It was a place of shades like the region of the storm line that divides the twilight zone from the dark hemisphere, not true night, nor yet honest day, but a dim middle state.

Ahead of him Patricia's bronzed limbs showed pale instead of tan, and when she spoke her voice went echoing queerly between the opposing cliffs. A weird place, this chasm, a dusky, unpleasant place.

'I don't like this,' said Ham. 'The pass is cutting closer and closer to the dark. Do you realize no one knows what's in the dark parts of the Mountains of Eternity?'

Patricia laughed; the sound was ghostly. 'What danger could there be? Anyway, we still have our automatics.'

'There's no way up here,' Ham grumbled. 'Let's turn back.'

Patricia faced him. 'Frightened, Yankee?' Her voice dropped. 'The natives say these mountains are haunted,' she went on mockingly. 'My father told me he saw queer things in Madman's Pass. Do you know that if there is life on the night side, here is the one place it would impinge on the twilight zone? Here in the Mountains of Eternity?'

She was taunting him; she laughed again. And suddenly her laughter was repeated in a hideous cacophony that hooted out from the sides of the cliffs above them in a horrid medley.

She paled; it was Patricia who was frightened now. They stared apprehensively up at the rock walls where strange shadows flickered and shifted.

'What – what was it?' she whispered. And then: 'Ham! Did you see that?'

Ham had seen it. A wild shape had flung itself across the strip of sky, leaping from cliff to cliff far above them. And again came a peal of hooting that sounded like laughter, while shadowy forms moved, flylike, on the sheer walls.

'Let's go back!' she gasped. 'Quickly!'

As she turned, a small black object fell and broke with a sullen pop before them. Ham stared at it. A pod, a spore-sac, of some unknown variety. A lazy, dusky cloud drifted over it, and suddenly both of them were choking violently. Ham felt his head spinning in dizziness, and Patricia reeled against him.

'It's narcotic!' she gasped. 'Back!'

But a dozen more plopped around them. The dusty spores whirled in dark eddies, and breathing was a torment. They were being drugged and suffocated at the same time.

Ham had a sudden inspiration. 'Mask!' he choked, and pulled his tran-skin over his face.

The filter that kept out the molds of the Hotlands cleaned the air of these spores as well; his head cleared. But the girl's covering was somewhere in her pack; she was fumbling for it. Abruptly she sat down, swaying.

'My pack,' she murmured. 'Take it out with you. Your – your – ' She broke into a fit of coughing.

He dragged her under a shallow overhang and ripped her transkin from the pack. 'Put it on!' he snapped.

A score of pods were popping.

A figure flitted silently far up on the wall of rock. Ham watched its progress, then aimed his automatic and fired. There was a shrill, rasping scream, answered by a chorus of dissonant ululations, and something as large as a man whirled down to crash not ten feet from him.

The thing was hideous. Ham stared appalled at a creature not unlike a native, three-eyed, two-handed, four-legged, but the hands, though two-fingered like the Hotlanders', were not pincer-like, but white and clawed.

And the face! Not the broad, expressionless face of the others, but a slanting, malevolent, dusky visage with each eye double the size of the natives'. It wasn't dead; it glared hatred and seized a stone, flinging it at him with weak viciousness. Then it died.

Ham didn't know what it was, of course. Actually it was a *triops nocti- vivans* – the 'three-eyed dweller in the dark', the strange, semi-intelligent being that is as yet the only known creature of the night side, and a member of that fierce remnant still occasionally found in the sunless parts of the Mountains of Eternity. It is perhaps the most vicious creature in the known planets, absolutely unapproachable, and delighting in slaughter.

At the crash of the shot, the shower of pods had ceased, and a chorus of laughing hoots ensued. Ham seized the respite to pull the girl's transkin over her face; she had collapsed with it only half on.

Then a sharp crack sounded, and a stone rebounded to strike his arm. Others pattered around him, whining past, swift as bullets. Black figures flickered in great leaps against the sky, and their fierce laughter sounded mockingly. He fired at one in mid-air; the cry of pain rasped again, but the creature did not fall.

Stones pelted him. They were all small ones, pebble-sized, but they were flung so fiercely that they hummed in passage, and they tore his flesh through his transkin. He turned Patricia on her face, but she moaned faintly as a missile struck her back. He shielded her with his own body.

The position was intolerable. He must risk a dash back, even though the doughpot blocked the opening. Perhaps, he thought, armored in transkin he could wade through the creature. He knew that was an insane idea; the gluey mass would roll him into itself to suffocate – but it had to be faced. He gathered the girl in his arms and rushed suddenly down the canyon.

Hoots and shrieks and a chorus of mocking laughter echoed around him. Stones struck him everywhere. One glanced from his head, sending him stumbling and staggering against the cliff. But he ran doggedly on;

he knew now what drove him. It was the girl he carried; he had to save Patricia Burlingame.

Ham reached the bend. Far up on the west wall glowed cloudy sunlight, and his weird pursuers flung themselves to the dark side. They couldn't stand daylight, and that gave him some assistance; by creeping very close to the eastern wall he was partially shielded.

Ahead was the other bend, blocked by the doughpot. As he neared it, he turned suddenly sick. Three of the creatures were grouped against the mass of white, eating – actually eating! – the corruption. They whirled, hooting, as he came, he shot two of them, and as the third leaped for the wall, he dropped that one as well, and it fell with a dull gulping sound into the doughpot.

Again he sickened; the doughpot drew away from it, leaving the thing lying in a hollow like the hole of a giant doughnut. Not even that monstrosity would eat these creatures.*

But the thing's leap had drawn Ham's attention to a twelve-inch ledge. It might be – yes, it was possible that he could traverse that rugged trail and so circle the doughpot. Nearly hopeless, no doubt, to attempt it under the volley of stones, but he must. There was no alternative.

He shifted the girl to free his right arm. He slipped a second clip in his automatic and then fired at random into the flitting shadows above. For a moment the hail of pebbles ceased, and with a convulsive, painful struggle, Ham dragged himself and Patricia to the ledge.

Stones cracked about him once more. Step by step he edged along the way, poised just over the doomed doughpot. Death below and death above! And little by little he rounded the bend; above him both walls glowed in sunlight, and they were safe.

At least, he was safe. The girl might be already dead, he thought frantically, as he slipped and slid through the slime of the doughpot's passage. Out on the daylit slope he tore the mask from her face and gazed on white, marble-cold features.

It was not death, however, but only drugged torpor. An hour later she was conscious, though weak and very badly frightened. Yet almost her first question was for her pack.

'It's here,' Ham said. 'What's so precious about that pack? Your notes?'

'My notes? Oh, no!' A faint flush covered her features. 'It's – I kept trying to tell you – it's your xixtchil.'

'What?'

---

* It was not known then that while the night-side life of Venus can eat and digest that of the day side, the reverse is not true. No day-side creature can absorb the dark life because of the presence of various metabolic alcohols, all poisonous.

'Yes. I – of course I didn't throw it to the molds. It's yours by rights, Ham. Lots of British traders go into the American Hotlands. I just slit the pouch and hid it here in my pack. The molds on the ground were only some twigs I threw there to – to make it look real.'

'But – but – why?'

The flush deepened. 'I wanted to punish you,' Patricia whispered, 'for being so – so cold and distant.'

'I?' Ham was amazed. 'It was you!'

'Perhaps it was, at first. You forced your way into my house, you know. But – after you carried me across the mudspout, Ham – it was different.'

Ham gulped. Suddenly he pulled her into his arms. 'I'm not going to quarrel about whose fault it was,' he said. 'But we'll settle one thing immediately. We're going to Erotia, and that's where we'll be married, in a good American church if they've put one up yet, or by a good American justice if they haven't. There's no more talk of Madman's Pass and crossing the Mountains of Eternity. Is that clear?'

She glanced at the vast, looming peaks and shuddered. 'Quite clear!' she replied meekly.

Pygmalion's Spectacles

Stanley G. Weinbaum

'But what is reality?' asked the gnomelike man. He gestured at the tall banks of buildings that loomed around Central Park, with their countless windows glowing like the cave fires of a city of Cro-Magnon people. 'All is dream, all is illusion; I am your vision as you are mine.'

Dan Burke, struggling for clarity of thought through the fumes of liquor, stared without comprehension at the tiny figure of his companion. He began to regret the impulse that had driven him to leave the party to seek fresh air in the park, and to fall by chance into the company of this diminutive old madman. But he had needed escape; this was one party too many, and not even the presence of Claire with her trim ankles could hold him there. He felt an angry desire to go home – not to his hotel, but home to Chicago and to the comparative peace of the Board of Trade. But he was leaving tomorrow anyway.

'You drink,' said the elfin, bearded face, 'to make real a dream. Is it not so? Either to dream that what you seek is yours, or else to dream that what you hate is conquered. You drink to escape reality, and the irony is that even reality is a dream.'

'Cracked!' thought Dan again.

'Or so,' concluded the other, 'says the philosopher Berkeley.'

'Berkeley?' echoed Dan.

His head was clearing; memories of a sophomore course in Elementary Philosophy drifted back. 'Bishop Berkeley, eh?'

'You know him, then? The philosopher of Idealism – no? – the one who argues that we do not see, feel, hear, taste the object, but that we have only the sensation of seeing, feeling, hearing, tasting.'

'I – sort of recall it.'

'Hah! But sensations are *mental* phenomena. They exist in our minds. How, then, do we know that the objects themselves do not exist only in our minds?' He waved again at the light-flecked buildings. 'You do not see that wall of masonry; you perceive only a *sensation*, a feeling of sight. The rest you interpret.'

'You see the same thing,' retorted Dan.

'How do you know I do? Even if you knew that what I call red would not be green could you see through my eyes – even if you knew that, how do you know that I too am not a dream of yours?'

Dan laughed. 'Of course nobody *knows* anything. You just get what information you can through the windows of your five senses, and then make your guesses. When they're wrong, you pay the penalty.' His mind was clear now save for a mild headache. 'Listen,' he said suddenly. 'You can argue a reality away to an illusion; that's easy. But if your friend Berkeley is right, why can't you take a dream and make it real? If it works one way, it must work the other.'

The beard waggled; elf-bright eyes glittered queerly at him. 'All artists do that,' said the old man softly. Dan felt that something more quivered on the verge of utterance.

'That's an evasion,' he grunted. 'Anybody can tell the difference between a picture and the real thing, or between a movie and life.'

'But,' whispered the other, 'the realer the better, no? And if one could make a – a movie – *very* real indeed, what would you say then?'

'Nobody can, though.'

The eyes glittered strangely again. 'I can!' he whispered. 'I *did*!'

'Did what?'

'Made real a dream.' The voice turned angry. 'Fools! I bring it here to sell to Westman, the camera people, and what do they say? "It isn't clear. Only one person can use it at a time. It's too expensive." Fools! Fools!'

'Huh?'

'Listen! I'm Albert Ludwig – *Professor* Ludwig.' As Dan was silent, he continued, 'It means nothing to you, eh? But listen – a movie that gives one sight and sound. Suppose now I add taste, smell, even touch, if your interest is taken by the story. Suppose I make it so that you are in the story, you speak to the shadows, and the shadows reply, and instead of being on a screen, the story is all about you, and you are in it. Would that be to make real a dream?'

'How the devil could you do that?'

'How? How? But simply! First my liquid positive, then my magic spectacles. I photograph the story in a liquid with light-sensitive chromates. I build up a complex solution – do you see? I add taste chemically and sound electrically. And when the story is recorded, then I put the solution in my spectacles – my movie projector. I electrolyze the solution, the story, sight, sound, smell, taste all!'

'Touch?'

'If your interest is taken, your mind supplies that.' Eagerness crept into his voice. 'You will look at it, Mr – '

'Burke,' said Dan. 'A swindle!' he thought. Then a spark of recklessness glowed out of the vanishing fumes of alcohol. 'Why not?' he grunted.

He rose; Ludwig, standing, came scarcely to his shoulder. A queer gnomelike old man, Dan thought as he followed him across the park and into one of the scores of apartment hotels in the vicinity.

In his room Ludwig fumbled in a bag, producing a device vaguely reminiscent of a gas mask. There were goggles and a rubber mouthpiece; Dan examined it curiously, while the little bearded professor brandished a bottle of watery liquid.

'Here it is!' he gloated. 'My liquid positive, the story. Hard photography – infernally hard, therefore the simplest story. A Utopia – just two characters and you, the audience. Now, put the spectacles on. Put them on and tell me what fools the Westman people are!' He decanted some of the liquid into the mask, and trailed a twisted wire to a device on the table. 'A rectifier,' he explained. 'For the electrolysis.'

'Must you use all the liquid?' asked Dan. 'If you use part, do you see only part of the story? And which part?'

'Every drop has all of it, but you must fill the eye-pieces.' Then as Dan slipped the device gingerly on, 'So! Now what do you see?'

'Not a damn thing. Just the windows and the lights across the street.'

'Of course. But now I start the electrolysis. Now!'

There was a moment of chaos. The liquid before Dan's eyes clouded suddenly white, and formless sounds buzzed. He moved to tear the device from his head, but emerging forms in the mistiness caught his interest. Giant things were writhing there.

The scene steadied; the whiteness was dissipating like mist in summer. Unbelieving, still gripping the arms of that unseen chair, he was staring at a forest. But what a forest! Incredible, unearthly, beautiful! Smooth boles ascended inconceivably toward a brightening sky, trees bizarre as the forests of the Carboniferous age. Infinitely overhead swayed misty fronds, and the verdure showed brown and green in the heights. And there were birds – at least, curiously loving pipings and twitterings were all about him though he saw no creatures – thin elfin whistlings like fairy bugles sounded softly.

He sat frozen, entranced. A louder fragment of melody drifted down to him, mounting in exquisite, ecstatic bursts, now clear as sounding metal, now soft as remembered music. For a moment he forgot the chair whose arms he gripped, the miserable hotel room invisibly about him, old Ludwig, his aching head. He imagined himself alone in the midst of that lovely glade. 'Eden!' he muttered, and the swelling music of unseen voices answered.

Some measure of reason returned. 'Illusion!' he told himself. Clever optical devices, not reality. He groped for the chair's arm, found it, and clung to it; he scraped his feet and found again an inconsistency. To his eyes the ground was mossy verdure; to his touch it was merely a thin hotel carpet.

The elfin buglings sounded gently. A faint, deliciously sweet perfume breathed against him; he glanced up to watch the opening of a great crimson blossom on the nearest tree, and a tiny reddish sun edged into the circle of sky above him. The fairy orchestra swelled louder in its light, and the notes sent a thrill of wistfulness through him. Illusion? If it were, it made reality almost unbearable; he wanted to believe that somewhere – somewhere this side of dreams, there actually existed this region of loveliness. An outpost of Paradise? Perhaps.

And then – far through the softening mists, he caught a movement that was not the swaying of verdure, a shimmer of silver more solid than mist. Something approached. He watched the figure as it moved, now visible, now hidden by trees; very soon he perceived that it was human, but it was almost upon him before he realized that it was a girl.

She wore a robe of silvery, half-translucent stuff, luminous as starbeams; a thin band of silver bound glowing black hair about her forehead, and other garment or ornament she had none. Her tiny white feet were bare to the mossy forest floor as she stood no more than a pace from him, staring dark-eyed. The thin music sounded again; she smiled.

Dan summoned stumbling thoughts. Was this being also – illusion? Had she no more reality than the loveliness of the forest? He opened his lips to speak, but a strained excited voice sounded in his ears. 'Who are you?' Had he spoken? The voice had come as if from another, like the sound of one's words in fever.

The girl smiled again. 'English!' she said in queer soft tones. 'I can speak a little English.' She spoke slowly, carefully. 'I learned it from' – she hesitated – 'my mother's father, whom they call the Grey Weaver.'

Again came the voice in Dan's ears. 'Who are you?'

'I am called Galatea,' she said. 'I came to find you.'

'To find me?' echoed the voice that was Dan's.

'Leucon, who is called the Grey Weaver, told me,' she explained smiling. 'He said you will stay with us until the second noon from this.' She cast a quick slanting glance at the pale sun now full above the clearing, then stepped closer. 'What are you called?'

'Dan,' he muttered. His voice sounded oddly different.

'What a strange name!' said the girl. She stretched out her bare arm. 'Come,' she smiled.

Dan touched her extended hand, feeling without any surprise the living warmth of her fingers. He had forgotten the paradoxes of illusion; this was no longer illusion to him, but reality itself. It seemed to him that he followed her, walking over the shadowed turf that gave with springy crunch beneath his tread, though Galatea left hardly an imprint. He glanced down, noting that he himself wore a silver garment, and that his feet were bare; with the glance he felt a feathery breeze on his body and a sense of mossy earth on his feet.

'Galatea,' said his voice. 'Galatea, what place is this? What language do you speak?'

She glanced back laughing. 'Why, this is Paracosma, of course, and this is our language.'

'Paracosma,' muttered Dan. 'Paracosma!' A fragment of Greek that had survived somehow from a Sophomore course a decade in the past came strangely back to him. Paracosma! Land-beyond-the-world!

Galatea cast a smiling glance at him. 'Does the real world seem strange,' she queried, 'after that shadow land of yours?'

'Shadow land?' echoed Dan, bewildered. '*This* is shadow, not my world.'

The girl's smile turned quizzical. 'Poof!' she retorted with an impudently lovely pout. 'And I suppose, then, that I am the phantom instead of you!' She laughed. 'Do I seem ghost-like?'

Dan made no reply; he was puzzling over unanswerable questions as he trod behind the lithe figure of his guide. The aisle between the unearthly trees widened, and the giants were fewer. It seemed a mile, perhaps, before a sound of tinkling water obscured that other strange music; they emerged on the bank of a little river, swift and crystalline, that rippled and gurgled its way from glowing pool to flashing rapids, sparkling under the pale sun. Galatea bent over the brink and cupped her hands, raising a few mouthfuls of water to her lips; Dan followed her example, finding the liquid stinging cold.

'How do we cross?' he asked.

'You can wade up there' – the dryad who led him gestured to a sun-lit shallows above a tiny falls – 'but I always cross here.' She poised herself for a moment on the green bank, then dove like a silver arrow into the pool. Dan followed; the water stung his body like champagne, but a stroke or two carried him across to where Galatea had already emerged with a glistening of creamy bare limbs. Her garment clung tight as a metal sheath to her wet body; he felt a breathtaking thrill at the sight of her. And then, miraculously, the silver cloth was dry, the droplets rolled off as if from oiled silk, and they moved briskly on.

The incredible forest had ended with the river; they walked over a meadow studded with little, many-hued, star-shaped flowers, whose fronds underfoot were soft as a lawn. Yet still the sweet pipings followed them, now loud, now whisper-soft, in a tenuous web of melody.

'Galatea!' said Dan suddenly. 'Where is the music coming from?'

She looked back amazed. 'You silly one!' she laughed. 'From the flowers, of course. See!' she plucked a purple star and held it to his ear; true enough, a faint and plaintive melody hummed out of the blossom. She tossed it in his startled face and skipped on.

A little copse appeared ahead, not of the gigantic forest trees, but of lesser growths, bearing flowers and fruits of iridescent colors, and a tiny brook bubbled through. And there stood the objective of their journey – a building of white, marble-like stone, single-storied and vine-covered, with broad glassless windows. They trod upon a path of bright pebbles to the arched entrance, and here, on an intricate stone bench, sat a grey-bearded patriarchal individual. Galatea addressed him in a liquid language that reminded Dan of the flower-pipings; then she turned. 'This is Leucon,' she said, as the ancient rose from his seat and spoke in English.

'We are happy, Galatea and I, to welcome you, since visitors are a rare pleasure here, and those from your shadowy country most rare.'

Dan uttered puzzled words of thanks, and the old man nodded, re-seating himself on the carven bench; Galatea skipped through the arched entrance, and Dan, after an irresolute moment, dropped to the remaining bench. Once more his thoughts were whirling in perplexed turbulence. Was all this indeed but illusion? Was he sitting, in actuality, in a prosaic hotel room, peering through magic spectacles that pictured this world about him, or was he, transported by some miracle, really sitting here in this land of loveliness? He touched the bench; stone, hard and unyielding, met his fingers.

'Leucon,' said his voice, 'how did you know I was coming?'

'I was told,' said the other.

'By whom?'

'By no one.'

'Why – *someone* must have told you!'

The Grey Weaver shook his solemn head. 'I was just told.'

Dan ceased his questioning, content for the moment to drink in the beauty about him, and then Galatea returned bearing a crystal bowl of the strange fruits. They were piled in colorful disorder, red, purple, orange and yellow, pear-shaped, egg-shaped, and clustered spheroids –

fantastic, unearthly. He selected a pale, transparent ovoid, bit into it, and was deluged by a flood of sweet liquid, to the amusement of the girl. She laughed and chose a similar morsel; biting a tiny puncture in the end, she squeezed the contents into her mouth. Dan took a different sort, purple and tart as Rhenish wine, and then another, filled with edible, almond-like seeds. Galatea laughed delightedly at his surprises, and even Leucon smiled a grey smile. Finally Dan tossed the last husk into the brook beside them, where it danced briskly toward the river.

'Galatea,' he said, 'do you ever go to a city? What cities are in Paracosma?'

'Cities? What are cities?'

'Places where many people live close together.'

'Oh,' said the girl frowning. 'No. There are no cities here.'

'Then where are the people of Paracosma? You must have neighbors.'

The girl looked puzzled. 'A man and a woman live off there,' she said, gesturing toward a distant blue range of hills dim on the horizon. 'Far away over there. I went there once, but Leucon and I prefer the valley.'

'But Galatea!' protested Dan. 'Are you and Leucon alone in this valley? Where – what happened to your parents – your father and mother?'

'They went away. That way – toward the sunrise. They'll return some day.'

'And if they don't?'

'Why, foolish one! What could hinder them?'

'Wild beasts,' said Dan. 'Poisonous insects, disease, flood, storm, lawless people, death!'

'I never heard those words,' said Galatea. 'There are no such things here.' She sniffed contemptuously. 'Lawless people!'

'Not – death?'

'What is death?'

'It's – ' Dan paused helplessly. 'It's like falling asleep and never waking. It's what happens to everyone at the end of life.'

'I never heard of such a thing as the end of life!' said the girl decidedly. 'There isn't such a thing.'

'What happens, then,' queried Dan desperately, 'when one grows old?'

'Nothing, silly! No one grows old unless he wants to, like Leucon. A person grows to the age he likes best and then stops. It's a law!'

Dan gathered his chaotic thoughts. He stared into Galatea's dark, lovely eyes. 'Have you stopped yet?'

The dark eyes dropped; he was amazed to see a deep, embarrassed flush spread over her cheeks. She looked at Leucon nodding reflectively on his bench, then back to Dan, meeting his gaze.

'Not yet,' she said.

'And when will you, Galatea?'

'When I have had the one child permitted me. You see – ' she stared down at her dainty toes – 'one cannot – bear children – afterwards.'

'Permitted? Permitted by whom?'

'By a law.'

'Laws! Is everything here governed by laws? What of chance and accidents'

'What are those – chance and accidents?'

'Things unexpected – things unforeseen.'

'Nothing is unforeseen,' said Galatea, still soberly. She repeated slowly, 'Nothing is unforeseen.' He fancied her voice was wistful.

Leucon looked up. 'Enough of this,' he said abruptly. He turned to Dan, 'I know these words of yours – chance, disease, death. They are not for Paracosma. Keep them in your unreal country.'

'Where did you hear them, then?'

'From Galatea's mother,' said the Grey Weaver, 'who had them from your predecessor – a phantom who visited here before Galatea was born.'

Dan had a vision of Ludwig's face. 'What was he like?'

'Much like you.'

'But his name?'

The old man's mouth was suddenly grim. 'We do not speak of him,' he said and rose, entering the dwelling in cold silence.

'He goes to weave,' said Galatea after a moment. Her lovely piquant face was still troubled.

'What does he weave?'

'This.' She fingered the silver cloth of her gown. 'He weaves it out of metal bars on a very clever machine. I do not know the method.'

'Who made the machine?'

'It was here.'

'But – Galatea! Who built the house? Who planted these fruit trees?'

'They were here. The house and trees were always here,' She lifted her eyes. 'I told you everything had been foreseen, from the beginning until eternity – everything. The house and trees and machine were ready for Leucon and my parents and me. There is a place for my child, who will be a girl, and a place for her child – and so on forever.'

Dan thought a moment. 'Were you born here?'

'I don't know.' He noted in sudden concern that her eyes were glistening with tears.

'Galatea, dear! Why are you unhappy? What's wrong?'

'Why, nothing!' She shook her black curls, sniffed suddenly at him.

'What could be wrong? How can one be unhappy in Paracosma?' She sprang erect and seized his hand. 'Come! Let's gather fruit for tomorrow.'

She darted off in a whirl of flashing silver, and Dan followed her around the wing of the edifice. Graceful as a dancer she leaped for a branch above her head, caught it laughingly, and tossed a great golden globe to him. She loaded his arms with the bright prizes and sent him back to the bench, and when he returned, she piled it so full of fruit that a deluge of colorful spheres dropped around him. She laughed again, and sent them spinning into the brook with thrusts of her rosy toes, while Dan watched her with an aching wistfulness. Then suddenly she was facing him; for a long, tense instant they stood motionless, eyes upon eyes, and then she turned away and walked slowly around to the arched portal. He followed her with his burden of fruit; his mind was once more in a turmoil of doubt and perplexity.

The little sun was losing itself behind the trees of that colossal forest to the west, and a coolness stirred among long shadows. The brook was purple-hued in the dusk, but its cheery notes mingled still with the flower music. Then the sun was hidden; the shadow fingers darkened the meadow; of a sudden the flowers were still, and the brook gurgled alone in a world of silence. In silence too, Dan entered the doorway.

The chamber within was a spacious one, floored with large black and white squares; exquisite benches of carved marble were here and there. Old Leucon, in a far corner, bent over an intricate, glistening mechanism, and as Dan entered he drew a shining length of silver cloth from it, folded it, and placed it carefully aside. There was a curious, unearthly fact that Dan noted; despite windows open to the evening, no night insects circled the globes that glowed at intervals from niches in the walls.

Galatea stood in a doorway to his left, leaning half-wearily against the frame; he placed the bowl of fruit on a bench at the entrance and moved to her side.

'This is yours,' she said, indicating the room beyond. He looked in upon a pleasant, smaller chamber; a window framed a starry square, and a thin, swift, nearly silent stream of water gushed from the mouth of a carved human head on the left wall, curving into a six-foot basin sunk in the floor. Another of the graceful benches covered with the silver cloth completed the furnishings; a single glowing sphere, pendant by a chain from the ceiling, illuminated the room. Dan turned to the girl, whose eyes were still unwontedly serious.

'This is ideal,' he said, 'but, Galatea, how am I to turn out the light?'

'Turn it out?' she said. 'You must cap it – so!' A faint smile showed again on her lips as she dropped a metal covering over the shining sphere.

They stood tense in the darkness; Dan sensed her nearness achingly, and then the light was on once more. She moved toward the door, and there paused, taking his hand.

'Dear shadow,' she said softly, 'I hope your dreams are music.' She was gone.

Dan stood irresolute in his chamber; he glanced into the large room where Leucon still bent over his work, and the Grey Weaver raised a hand in a solemn salutation, but said nothing. He felt no urge for the old man's silent company and turned back into his room to prepare for slumber.

Almost instantly, it seemed, the dawn was upon him and bright elfin pipings were all about him, while the odd ruddy sun sent a broad slanting plane of light across the room. He rose as fully aware of his surroundings as if he had not slept at all; the pool tempted him and he bathed in stinging water. Thereafter he emerged into the central chamber, noting curiously that the globes still glowed in dim rivalry to the daylight. He touched one casually; it was cool as metal to his fingers, and lifted freely from its standard. For a moment he held the cold flaming thing in his hands, then replaced it and wandered into the dawn.

Galatea was dancing up the path, eating a strange fruit as rosy as her lips. She was merry again, once more the happy nymph who had greeted him, and she gave him a bright smile as he chose a sweet green ovoid for his breakfast.

'Come on!' she called. 'To the river!'

She skipped away toward the unbelievable forest; Dan followed, marveling that her lithe speed was so easy a match for his stronger muscles. Then they were laughing in the pool, splashing about until Galatea drew herself to the bank, glowing and panting. He followed her as she lay relaxed; strangely, he was neither tired nor breathless, with no sense of exertion. A question recurred to him, as yet unasked.

'Galatea,' said his voice, 'whom will you take as mate?'

Her eyes went serious. 'I don't know,' she said. 'At the proper time he will come. That is a law.'

'And will you be happy?'

'Of course.' She seemed troubled. 'Isn't everyone happy?'

'Not where I live, Galatea.'

'Then that must be a strange place – that ghostly world of yours. A rather terrible place.'

'It is, often enough,' Dan agreed. 'I wish – ' He paused. What did he wish? Was he not talking to an illusion, a dream, an apparition? He looked at the girl, at her glistening black hair, her eyes, her soft white skin, and then, for a tragic moment, he tried to feel the arms of that drab hotel chair beneath his hands – and failed. He smiled; he reached out his fingers to touch her bare arm, and for an instant she looked back at him with startled, sober eyes, and sprang to her feet.

'Come on! I want to show you my country.' She set off down the stream, and Dan rose reluctantly to follow.

What a day that was! They traced the little river from still pool to singing rapids, and ever about them were the strange twitterings and pipings that were the voices of the flowers. Every turn brought a new vista of beauty; every moment brought a new sense of delight. They talked or were silent; when they were thirsty, the cool river was at hand; when they were hungry, fruit offered itself. When they were tired, there was always a deep pool and a mossy bank; and when they were rested, a new beauty beckoned. The incredible trees towered in numberless forms of fantasy, but on their own side of the river was still the flower-starred meadow. Galatea twisted him a bright-blossomed garland for his head, and thereafter he moved always with a sweet singing about him. But little by little the red sun slanted toward the forest, and the hours dripped away. It was Dan who pointed it out, and reluctantly they turned homeward.

As they returned, Galatea sang a strange song, plaintive and sweet as the medley of river and flower music. And again her eyes were sad.

'What song is that?' he asked.

'It is a song sung by another Galatea,' she answered, 'who is my mother.' She laid her hand on his arm. 'I will make it into English for you.' She sang:

> 'The River lies in flower and fern,
>   In flower and fern it breathes a song.
> It breathes a song of your return,
>   Of your return in years too long.
> In years too long its murmurs bring,
>   Its murmurs bring their vain replies,
> Their vain replies the flowers sing,
>   The flowers sing, 'The River lies!'

Her voice quavered on the final notes; there was silence save for the tinkle of water and the flower bugles. Dan said, 'Galatea – ' and paused. The girl was again somber-eyed, tearful. He said huskily, 'That's a sad song, Galatea. Why was your mother sad? You said everyone was happy in Paracosma.'

'She broke a law,' replied the girl tonelessly. 'It is the inevitable way to sorrow.' She faced him. 'She fell in love with a phantom!' Galatea said.

'One of your shadowy race, who came and stayed and then had to go back. So when her appointed lover came, it was too late; do you understand? But she yielded finally to the law, and is forever unhappy, and goes wandering from place to place about the world.' She paused. 'I shall never break a law,' she said defiantly.

Dan took her hand. 'I would not have you unhappy, Galatea. I want you always happy.'

She shook her head. 'I am happy,' she said, and smiled a tender, wistful smile.

They were silent a long time as they trudged the way homeward. The shadows of the forest giants reached out across the river as the sun slipped behind them. For a distance they walked hand in hand, but as they reached the path of pebbly brightness near the house, Galatea drew away and sped swiftly before him. Dan followed as quickly as he might; when he arrived, Leucon sat on his bench by the portal, and Galatea had paused on the threshold. She watched his approach with eyes in which he again fancied the glint of tears.

'I am very tired,' she said, and slipped within.

Dan moved to follow, but the old man raised a staying hand.

'Friend from the shadows,' he said, 'will you hear me a moment?'

Dan paused, acquiesced, and dropped to the opposite bench. He felt a sense of foreboding; nothing pleasant awaited him.

'There is something to be said,' Leucon continued, 'and I say it without desire to pain you, if phantoms feel pain. It is this: Galatea loves you, though I think she has not yet realized it.'

'I love her too,' said Dan.

The Grey Weaver stared at him. 'I do not understand. Substance, indeed, may love shadow, but how can shadow love substance?'

'I love her,' insisted Dan.

'Then woe to both of you! For this is impossible in Paracosma; it is a confliction with the laws. Galatea's mate is appointed, perhaps even now approaching.'

'Laws! Laws!' muttered Dan. 'Whose laws are they? Not Galatea's nor mine!'

'But they are,' said the Grey Weaver. 'It is not for you nor for me to criticize them – though I yet wonder what power could annul them to permit your presence here!'

'I had no voice in your laws.'

The old man peered at him in the dusk. 'Has anyone, anywhere, a voice in the laws?' he queried.

'In my country we have,' retorted Dan.

'Madness!' growled Leucon. 'Man-made laws! Of what use are man-made laws with only man-made penalties, or none at all? If you shadows make a law that the wind shall blow only from the east, does the west wind obey it?'

'We do pass such laws,' acknowledged Dan bitterly. 'They may be stupid, but they're no more unjust than yours.'

'Ours,' said the Grey Weaver, 'are the unalterable laws of the world, the laws of Nature. Violation is always unhappiness. I have seen it; I have known it in another, in Galatea's mother, though Galatea is stronger than she.' He paused. 'Now,' he continued, 'I ask only for mercy; your stay is short, and I ask that you do no more harm than is already done. Be merciful; give her no more to regret.'

He rose and moved through the archway; when Dan followed a moment later, he was already removing a square of silver from his device in the corner. Dan turned silent and unhappy to his own chamber, where the jet of water tinkled faintly as a distant bell.

Again he rose at the glow of dawn, and again Galatea was before him, meeting him at the door with her bowl of fruit. She deposited her burden, giving him a wan little smile of greeting, and stood facing him as if waiting.

'Come with me, Galatea,' he said.

'Where?'

'To the river bank. To talk.'

They trudged in silence to the brink of Galatea's pool. Dan noted a subtle difference in the world about him; outlines were vague, the thin flower pipings less audible and the very landscape was queerly unstable, shifting like smoke when he wasn't looking at it directly. And strangely, though he had brought the girl here to talk to her, he had now nothing to say, but sat in aching silence with his eyes on the loveliness of her face.

Galatea pointed at the red ascending sun. 'So short a time,' she said, 'before you go back to your phantom world. I shall be sorry, very sorry.' She touched his cheek with her fingers. 'Dear shadow!'

'Suppose,' said Dan huskily, 'that I won't go. What if I won't leave here?' His voice grew fiercer. 'I'll not go! I'm going to stay!'

The calm mournfulness of the girl's face checked him; he felt the irony of struggling against the inevitable progress of a dream. She spoke. 'Had I the making of the laws, you should stay. But you can't, dear one. You can't!'

Forgotten now were the words of the Grey Weaver. 'I love you, Galatea,' he said.

'And I you,' she whispered. 'See, dearest shadow, how I break the same law my mother broke, and am glad to face the sorrow it will bring.' She placed her hand tenderly over his. 'Leucon is very wise and I am bound to obey him, but this is beyond his wisdom because he let himself grow old.' She paused. 'He let himself grow old,' she repeated slowly. A strange light gleamed in her dark eyes as she turned suddenly to Dan.

'Dear one!' she said tensely. 'That thing that happens to the old – that death of yours! What follows it?'

'What follows death?' he echoed. 'Who knows?'

'But – ' her voice was quivering. 'But one can't simply – vanish! There must be an awakening.'

'Who knows?' said Dan again. 'There are those who believe we wake to a happier world, but – ' He shook his head hopelessly.

'It must be true! Oh, it must be!' Galatea cried. 'There must be more for you than the mad world you speak of!' She leaned very close. 'Suppose, dear,' she said, 'that when my appointed lover arrives, I send him away. Suppose I bear no child, but let myself grow old, older than Leucon, old until death. Would I join you in your happier world?'

'Galatea!' he cried distractedly. 'Oh, my dearest – what a terrible thought!'

'More terrible than you know,' she whispered, still very close to him. 'It is more than violation of a law; it is rebellion. Everything is planned, everything was foreseen, except this; and if I bear no child, her place will be left unfilled, and the places of her children, and of *their* children, and so on until some day the whole great plan of Paracosma fails of whatever its destiny was to be.' Her whisper grew very faint and fearful. 'It is destruction, but I love you more than I fear death!'

Dan's arms were about her. 'No, Galatea! No! Promise me!'

She murmured, 'I can promise and then break my promise.' She drew his head down; their lips touched, and he felt a fragrance and a taste like honey in her kiss. 'At least,' she breathed. 'I can give you a name by which to love you. Philometros! Measure of my love!'

'A name?' muttered Dan. A fantastic idea shot through his mind – a way of proving to himself that all this was reality, and not just a page that any one could read who wore old Ludwig's magic spectacles. If Galatea would speak his name! Perhaps, he thought daringly, perhaps then he could stay! He thrust her away.

'Galatea!' he cried. 'Do you remember my name?'

She nodded silently, her unhappy eyes on his.

'Then say it! Say it, dear!'

She stared at him dumbly, miserably, but made no sound.

'Say it, Galatea!' he pleaded desperately. 'My name, dear – just my name!' Her mouth moved; she grew pale with effort and Dan could

have sworn that his name trembled on her quivering lips, though no
sound came.

At last she spoke. 'I can't, dearest one! Oh, I can't. A law forbids it!'
She stood suddenly erect, pallid as an ivory carving. 'Leucon calls!' she
said, and darted away. Dan followed along the pebbled path, but her
speed was beyond his powers; at the portal he found only the Grey
Weaver standing cold and stern. He raised his hand as Dan appeared.

'Your time is short,' he said. 'Go, thinking of the havoc you have
done.'

'Where's Galatea?' gasped Dan.

'I have sent her away.' The old man blocked the entrance; for a moment Dan would have struck him aside, but something withheld him. He
stared wildly about the meadow – there! A flash of silver beyond the river,
at the edge of the forest. He turned and raced toward it, while motionless
and cold the Grey Weaver watched him go.

'Galatea!' he called. 'Galatea!'

He was over the river now, on the forest bank, running through col-
umned vistas that whirled about him like mist. The world had gone cloudy;
fine flakes danced like snow before his eyes; Paracosma was dissolving
around him. Through the chaos he fancied a glimpse of the girl, but closer
approach left him still voicing his hopeless cry of 'Galatea!'

After an endless time, he paused; something familiar about the spot
struck him, and just as the red sun edged above him, he recognized the
place – the very point at which he had entered Paracosma! A sense of
futility overwhelmed him as for a moment he gazed at an unbelievable
apparition – a dark window hung in mid-air before him through which
glowed rows of electric lights. Ludwig's window!

It vanished. But the trees writhed and the sky darkened, and he swayed
dizzily in turmoil. He realized suddenly that he was no longer standing,
but sitting in the midst of the crazy glade, and his hands clutched something smooth and hard – the arms of that miserable hotel chair. Then at
last he saw her, close before him – Galatea, with sorrow-stricken features,
her tear-filled eyes on his. He made a terrific effort to rise, stood erect,
and fell sprawling in a blaze of coruscating lights.

He struggled to his knees; walls – Ludwig's room – encompassed him;
he must have slipped from the chair. The magic spectacles lay before
him, one lens splintered and spilling a fluid no longer water-clear, but
white as milk.

'God!' he muttered. He felt shaken, sick, exhausted, with a bitter
sense of bereavement, and his head ached fiercely. The room was drab,
disgusting; he wanted to get out of it. He glanced automatically at his

watch: four o'clock – he must have sat here nearly five hours. For the first time he noticed Ludwig's absence; he was glad of it and walked dully out of the door to an automatic elevator. There was no response to his ring; someone was using the thing. He walked three flights to the street and back to his own room.

In love with a vision! Worse – in love with a girl who had never lived, in a fantastic Utopia that was literally nowhere! He threw himself on his bed with a groan that was half a sob.

He saw finally the implication of the name Galatea. Galatea – Pygmalion's statue, given life by Venus in the ancient Grecian myth. But *his* Galatea, warm and lovely and vital, must remain forever without the gift of life, since he was neither Pygmalion nor God.

He woke late in the morning, staring uncomprehendingly about for the fountain and pool of Paracosma. Slow comprehension dawned; how much – *how much* – of last night's experience had been real? How much was the product of alcohol? Or had old Ludwig been right, and was there no difference between reality and dream?

He changed his rumpled attire and wandered despondently to the street. He found Ludwig's hotel at last; inquiry revealed that the diminutive professor had checked out, leaving no forwarding address.

What of it? Even Ludwig couldn't give what he sought, a living Galatea. Dan was glad that he had disappeared; he hated the little professor. Professor? Hypnotists called themselves 'professors'. He dragged through a weary day and then a sleepless night back to Chicago.

It was mid-winter when he saw a suggestively tiny figure ahead of him in the Loop. Ludwig! Yet what use to hail him? His cry was automatic. 'Professor Ludwig!'

The elfin figure turned, recognized him, smiled. They stepped into the shelter of a building.

'I'm sorry about your machine, Professor. I'd be glad to pay for the damage.'

'Ach, that was nothing – a cracked glass. But you – have you been ill? You look much the worse.'

'It's nothing,' said Dan. 'Your show was marvelous, Professor – marvelous! I'd have told you so, but you were gone when it ended.'

Ludwig shrugged. 'I went to the lobby for a cigar. Five hours with a wax dummy, you know!'

'It was marvelous,' repeated Dan.

'So real?' smiled the other. 'Only because you co-operated, then. It takes self-hypnosis.'

'It was real, all right,' agreed Dan glumly. 'I don't understand it – that strange beautiful country.'

'The trees were club-mosses enlarged by a lens,' said Ludwig. 'All was trick photography, but stereoscopic, as I told you – three-dimensional. The fruits were rubber; the house is a summer building on our campus – Northern University. And the voice was mine; you didn't speak at all, except your name at the first, and I left a blank for that. I played your part, you see; I went around with the photographic apparatus strapped on my head, to keep the viewpoint always that of the observer. See?' He grinned wryly. 'Luckily I'm rather short, or you'd have seemed a giant.'

'Wait a minute!' said Dan, his mind whirling. 'You say you played my part. Then Galatea – is *she* real too?'

'She's real enough,' said the Professor. 'My niece, a senior at Northern, and likes dramatics. She helped me out with the thing. Why? Want to meet her?'

Dan answered vaguely, happily. An ache had vanished; a pain was eased. Paracosma was attainable at last!

Shifting Seas

Stanley G. Weinbaum

It developed later that Ted Welling was one of the very few eye-witnesses of the catastrophe, or rather, that among the million and a half eye-witnesses, he was among the half dozen that survived. At the time, he was completely unaware of the extent of the disaster, although it looked bad enough to him in all truth!

He was in a Colquist gyro, just north of the spot where Lake Nicaragua drains its brown overflow into the San Juan, and was bound for Managua, seventy-five miles north and west across the great inland sea. Below him, quite audible above the muffled whir of his motor, sounded the intermittent clicking of his tripanoramic camera, adjusted delicately to his speed so that its pictures could be assembled into a beautiful relief map of the terrain over which he passed. That, in fact, was the sole purpose of his flight; he had left San Juan del Norte early that morning to traverse the route of the proposed Nicaragua Canal, flying for the Topographical branch of the U. S. Geological Survey. The United States, of course, had owned the rights to the route since early in the century – a safeguard against any other nation's aspirations to construct a competitor for the Panama Canal.

Now, however, the Nicaragua Canal was actually under consideration. The over-burdened ditch that crossed the Isthmus was groaning under vastly increased traffic, and it became a question of either cutting the vast trench another eighty-five feet to sea-level or opening an alternate passage. The Nicaragua route was feasible enough; there was the San Juan emptying from the great lake into the Atlantic, and there was Lake Managua a dozen miles or so from the Pacific. It was simply a matter of choice, and Ted Welling, of the Topographical Service of the Geological Survey, was doing his part to aid the choice.

At precisely 10:40 it happened. Ted was gazing idly through a faintly misty morning toward Ometepec, its cone of a peak plumed by dusky smoke. A hundred miles away, across both Lake Nicaragua and Lake Managua, the fiery mountain was easily visible from his altitude. All week, he knew, it had been rumbling and smoking, but now, as he watched it, it burst like a mighty Roman candle.

There was a flash of white fire not less brilliant than the sun. There was a column of smoke with a red core that spouted upward like a fountain and then mushroomed out. There was a moment of utter silence in which the camera clicked methodically, and then there was a roar as if the very roof of Hell had blown away to let out the bellows of the damned!

Ted had one amazed thought – the sound had followed too quickly on the eruption! It should have taken minutes to reach him at that distance – and then his thoughts were forcibly diverted as the Colquist tossed and skittered like a leaf in a hurricane. He caught an astonished glimpse of the terrain below, of Lake Nicaragua heaving and boiling as if it were the seas that lash through the Straits of Magellan instead of a body of land-locked fresh water. On the shore to the east a colossal wave was breaking, and there in a banana grove frightened figures were scampering away. And then, exactly as if by magic, a white mist condensed about him, shutting out all view of the world below.

He fought grimly for altitude. He had had three thousand feet, but now, tossed in this wild ocean of fog, of up-drafts and down-drafts, of pockets and humps, he had no idea at all of his position. His altimeter needle quivered and jumped in the changing pressure, his compass spun, and he had not the vaguest conception of the direction of the ground. So he struggled as best he could, listening anxiously to the changing whine of his blades as strain grew and lessened. And below, deep as thunder, came intermittent rumblings that were, unless he imagined it, accompanied by the flash of jagged fires.

Suddenly he was out of it. He burst abruptly into clear air, and for a horrible instant it seemed to him that he was actually flying inverted. Apparently below him was the white sea of mist, and above was what looked at first glance like dark ground, but a moment's scrutiny revealed it as a world-blanketing canopy of smoke or dust, through which the sun shone with a fantastic blue light. He had heard of blue suns, he recalled; they were one of the rarer phenomena of volcanic eruptions.

His altimeter showed ten thousand. The vast plain of mist heaved in gigantic ridges like rolling waves, and he fought upward away from it. At twenty thousand the air was steadier, but still infinitely above was the sullen ceiling of smoke. Ted leveled out, turning at random north-east, and relaxed.

'Whew!' he breathed. 'What – what happened?'

He couldn't land, of course, in that impenetrable fog. He flew doggedly north and east, because there was an airport at Bluefields, if this heaving sea of white didn't blanket it.

But it did. He had still half a tank of fuel, and, he bored grimly north. Far away was a pillar of fire, and beyond it to the right, another and a third. The first, of course, was Ometepec, but what were the others? Fuego and Tajumulco? It seemed impossible.

Three hours later the fog was still below him, and the grim roof of smoke was dropping as if to crush him between. He was going to have to land soon; even now he must have spanned Nicaragua and be somewhere over Honduras. With a sort of desperate calm he slanted down toward the fog and plunged in. He expected to crash; curiously, the only thing he really regretted was dying without a chance to say goodbye to Kay Lovell, who was far off in Washington with her father, old Sir Joshua Lovell, Ambassador from Great Britain.

When the needle read two hundred, he leveled off – and then, like a train bursting out of a tunnel, he came clear again! But under him was wild and raging ocean, whose waves seemed almost to graze the ship. He spun along at a low level, wondering savagely how he could possibly have wandered out to sea. It must, he supposed, be the gulf of Honduras.

He turned west. Within five minutes he had raised a storm-lashed coast, and then – miracle of all miracles! – a town! And a landing field, He pancaked over it, let his vanes idle, and dropped as vertically as he could in that volley of gusty winds.

It was Belize in British Honduras. He recognized the port even before the attendants had reached him.

'A Yankee!' yelled the first. 'Ain't that Yankee luck for you!'

Ted grinned. 'I needed it. What happened?'

'The roof over this part of Hell blew off. That's all.'

'Yeah. I saw that much. I was over it.'

'Then you know more'n any of us. Radio's dead and there ain't no bloomin' telegraph at all.'

It began to rain suddenly, a fierce, pattering rain with drops as big as marbles. The men broke for the shelter of a hangar, where Ted's information, meager as it was, was avidly seized upon, for sensational news is rare below the Tropic of Cancer. But none of them yet realized just how sensational it was.

It was three days before Ted, and the rest of the world as well, began to understand in part what had happened. This was after hours of effort at Belize had finally raised Havana on the beam, and Ted had reported through to old Asa Gaunt, his chief at Washington. He had been agreeably surprised by the promptness of the reply ordering him instantly to the Capital; that meant a taste of the pleasant life that Washington reserved for young departmentals, and most of all, it meant a glimpse of Kay Lovell after two months of letter-writing. So he had flown the Colquist gayly across Yucatan Channel, left it at Havana, and was now comfortably settled in a huge Caribbean plane bound for Washington, boring steadily north through a queerly misty mid-October morning.

At the moment, however, his thoughts were not of Kay. He was reading a grim newspaper account of the catastrophe, and wondering what thousand-to-one shot had brought him unscathed through the very midst of it. For the disaster overshadowed into insignificance such little disturbances as the Yellow River flood in China, the eruption of Krakatoa, the holocaust of Mount Pelée, or even the great Japanese earthquake of 1923, or any other terrible visitation ever inflicted on a civilized race.

For the Ring of Fire, that vast volcanic circle that surrounds the Pacific Ocean, perhaps the last unhealed scars of the birththroes of the Moon, had burst into flame. Aniakchak in Alaska had blown its top away, Fujiyama had vomited lava, on the Atlantic side La Soufrière and the terrible Pelée had awakened again.

But these were minor. It was at the two volcanic foci, in Java and Central America, that the fire-mountains had really shown their powers. What had happened in Java was still a mystery, but on the Isthmus – that was already too plain. From Mosquito Bay to the Rio Coco, there was – ocean! Half of Panama, seven-eighths of Nicaragua – and as for Costa Rica, that country was as if it had never been. The Canal was a wreck, but Ted grinned a wry grin at the thought that it was now as unnecessary as a pyramid. North and South America had been cut adrift, and the Isthmus, the land that had once known Atlantis, had gone to join it.

In Washington Ted reported at once to Asa Gaunt. That dry Texan questioned him closely concerning his experience, grunted disgustedly at the paucity of information, and then ordered him tersely to attend a meeting at his office in the evening. There remained a full afternoon to devote to Kay, and Ted lost little time in so devoting it.

He didn't see her alone. Washington, like the rest of the world, was full of excitement because of the earthquake, but in Washington more than elsewhere the talk was less of the million and a half deaths and more largely of the other consequences. After all, the bulk of the deaths had been among the natives, and it was a sort of remote tragedy, like the perishing of so many Chinese. It affected only those who had friends or relatives in the stricken region, and these were few in number.

But at Kay's home Ted encountered an excited group arguing physical results. Obviously, the removal of the bottleneck of the Canal strengthened the naval power of the United States enormously. No need now to guard the vulnerable Canal so intensively. The whole fleet could stream abreast through the four hundred mile gap left by the subsidence. Of course the country would lose the revenues of the toll-charges, but that was balanced by the cessation of the expense of fortifying and guarding.

Ted fumed until he managed a few moments of greeting with Kay alone. Once that was concluded to his satisfaction, he joined the discussion as eagerly as the rest. But no one even considered the one factor in the whole catastrophe that could change the entire history of the world.

At the evening meeting Ted stared around him in surprise. He recognized all those present, but the reasons for their presence were obscure. Of course there was Asa Gaunt, head of the Geological Survey, and of course there was Golsborough, Secretary of the Interior, because the Survey was one of his departments. But what was Maxwell, joint Secretary of War and the Navy, doing there? And why was silent John Parish, Secretary of State, frowning down at his shoes in the corner?

Asa Gaunt cleared his throat and began. 'Do any of you like eels?' he asked soberly.

There was a murmur. 'Why, I do,' said Golsborough, who had once been Consul at Venice. 'What about it?'

'This – that you'd better buy some and eat 'em tomorrow. There won't be any more eels.'

'No more eels?'

'No more eels. You see, eels breed in the Sargasso Sea, and there won't be any Sargasso Sea.'

'What *is* this?' growled Maxwell. 'I'm a busy man. No more Sargasso Sea, huh!'

'You're likely to be busier soon,' said Asa Gaunt dryly. He frowned. 'Let me ask one other question. Does anyone here know what spot on the American continent is opposite London, England?'

Golsborough shifted impatiently, 'I don't see the trend of this, Asa,' he grunted, 'but my guess is that New York City and London are nearly in the same latitude. Or maybe New York's a little to the north, since I know its climate is somewhat colder.'

'Hah!' said Asa Gaunt. 'Any disagreement?'

There was none. 'Well,' said the head of the Survey, 'you're all wrong, then. London is about one thousand miles north of New York. It's in the latitude of southern Labrador!'

'Labrador! That's practically the Arctic!'

Asa Gaunt pulled down a large map on the wall behind him, a Mercator projection of the world.

'Look at it,' he said. 'New York's in the latitude of Rome, Italy. Washington's opposite Naples. Norfolk's level with Tunis in Africa, and Jacksonville with the Sahara Desert. And gentlemen, these facts lead to the conclusion that next summer is going to see the wildest war in the history of the world!'

Even Ted, who knew his superior well enough to swear to his sanity, could not resist a glance at the faces of the others, and met their eyes with full understanding of the suspicion in them.

Maxwell cleared his throat. 'Of course, of course,' he said gruffly. 'So there'll be a war and no more eels. That's very easy to follow, but I believe I'll ask you gentlemen to excuse me. You see, I don't care for eels.'

'Just a moment more,' said Asa Gaunt. He began to speak, and little by little a grim understanding dawned on the four he faced.

Ted remained after the appalled and sobered group had departed. His mind was too chaotic as yet for other occupations, and it was already too late in the evening to find Kay, even had he dared with these oppressive revelations weighing on him.

'Are you sure?' he asked nervously. 'Are you quite certain?'

'Well, let's go over it again,' grunted Asa Gaunt, turning to the map. He swept his hand over the white lines drawn in the Pacific Ocean. 'Look here. This is the Equatorial Counter Current, sweeping east to wash the shores of Guatemala, Salvador, Honduras, Nicaragua, Costa Rica, and Panama.'

'I know. I've flown over every square mile of that coast.'

'Uh.' The older man turned to the blue-mapped expanse of the Atlantic. 'And here,' he resumed, 'is the North Equatorial Drift, coming west out of the Atlantic to sweep around Cuba into the Gulf, and to emerge as – the Gulf Stream. It flows at an average speed of three knots per hour, is sixty miles broad, a hundred fathoms deep, and possesses, to start with, an average temperature of 50°. And here – it meets the Labrador Current and turns east to carry warmth to all of Western Europe. *That's* why England is habitable; that's why southern France is semi-tropical; that's why men can live even in Norway and Sweden. Look at Scandinavia, Ted; it's in the latitude of central Greenland, level with Baffin Bay. Even Eskimos have difficulty scraping a living on Baffin Island.'

'I know,' said Ted in a voice like a groan. 'But are you certain about – the rest of this?'

'See for yourself,' growled Asa Gaunt. 'The barrier's down now. The Equatorial Counter Current, moving two knots per hour, will sweep right over what used to be Central America and strike the North Equatorial Drift just south of Cuba. Do you see what will happen – is happening –

to the Gulf Stream? Instead of moving north-east along the Atlantic coast, it will flow almost due east, across what used to be the Sargasso Sea. Instead of bathing the shores of Northern Europe, it will strike the Spanish peninsula, just as the current called the West Wind Drift does now, and instead of veering north it will turn *south*, along the coast of Africa. At three knots an hour it will take less than three months for the Gulf Stream to deliver its last gallon of warm water to Europe. That brings us to January – and after January, what?'

Ted said nothing.

'Now,' resumed Asa Gaunt grimly, 'the part of Europe occupied by countries dependent on the Gulf Stream consists of Norway, Sweden, Denmark, Germany, the British Isles, the Netherlands, Belgium, France, and to a lesser extent, several others. Before six months have passed, Ted, you're going to see a realignment of Europe. The Gulf Stream countries are going to be driven together; Germany and France are suddenly going to become bosom friends, and France and Russia, friendly as they are today, are going to be bitter enemies. Do you see why?'

'N-no.'

'Because the countries I've named now support over two hundred million inhabitants. *Two hundred million*, Ted! And without the Gulf Stream, when England and Germany have the climate of Labrador, and France of Newfoundland, and Scandinavia of Baffin Land – how many people can those regions support then? Three or four million, perhaps, and that with difficulty. *Where will the others go?*'

'Where?'

'I can tell you where they'll *try* to go. England will try to unload its surplus population on its colonies. India's hopelessly overcrowded, but South Africa, Canada, Australia, and New Zealand can absorb some. About twenty-five of its fifty millions, I should estimate, because Canada's a northern country and Australia desert in a vast part of it. France has Northern Africa, already nearly as populous as it can be. The others – well, *you* guess, Ted.'

'I will. Siberia, South America, and – the United States!'

'A good guess. That's why Russia and France will no longer be the best of friends. South America is a skeleton continent, a shell. The interior is unfit for white men, and so – it leaves Siberia and North America. What a war's in the making!'

'It's almost unbelievable!' muttered Ted. 'Just when the world seemed to be settling down, too.'

'Oh, it's happened before,' observed Asa Gaunt. 'This isn't the only climatic change that brought on war. It was decreasing rainfall in central

Asia that sent the Huns scouring Europe, and probably the Goths and Vandals as well. But it's never happened to two hundred million civilized people before!' He paused. 'The newspapers are all shrieking about the million and a half deaths in Central America. By this time next year they'll have forgotten that a million and a half deaths ever rated a headline!'

'But good Lord!' Ted burst out. 'Isn't there anything to be done about it?'

'Sure, sure,' said Asa Gaunt. 'Go find a nice tame earthquake that will raise back the forty thousand square miles the last one sunk. That's all you have to do, and if you can't do that, Maxwell's suggestion is the next best: build submarines *and* submarines. They can't invade a country if they can't get to it.'

Asa Gaunt was beyond doubt the first man in the world to realize the full implications of the Central American disaster, but he was not very much ahead of the brilliant Sir Phineas Grey of the Royal Society. Fortunately (or unfortunately, depending on which shore of the Atlantic you call home), Sir Phineas was known to the world of journalism as somewhat of a sensationalist, and his warning was treated by the English and Continental newspapers as on a par with those recurrent predictions of the end of the world. Parliament noticed the warning just once, when Lord Rathmere rose in the Upper House to complain of the unseasonably warm weather and to suggest dryly that the Gulf Stream be turned off a month early this year. But now and again some oceanographer made the inside pages by agreeing with Sir Phineas.

So Christmas approached very quietly, and Ted, happy enough to be stationed in Washington, spent his days in routine topographical work in the office and his evenings, as many as she permitted, with Kay Lovell. And she did permit an increasing number, so that the round of gaiety during the holidays found them on the verge of engagement. They *were* engaged so far as the two of them were concerned, and only awaited a propitious moment to inform Sir Joshua, whose approval Kay felt, with true English conservatism, was a necessity.

Ted worried often enough about the dark picture Asa Gaunt had drawn, but an oath of secrecy kept him from ever mentioning it to Kay. Once, when she had casually brought up the subject of Sir Phineas Grey and his warning, Ted had stammered some inanity and hastily switched the subject. But with the turn of the year and January, things began to change.

It was on the fourteenth that the first taste of cold struck Europe. London shivered for twenty-four hours in the unheard-of temperature of twenty below zero, and Paris argued and gesticulated about its *grands froids*. Then the high pressure area moved eastward and normal temperatures returned.

But not for long. On the twenty-first another zone of frigid temperature came drifting in on the Westerlies, and the English and Continental papers, carefully filed at the Congressional Library, began to betray a note of panic. Ted read the editorial comments avidly: of course Sir Phineas Grey was crazy; of course he was – but just suppose he were right. Just suppose he were. Wasn't it unthinkable that the safety and majesty of Germany (or France or England or Belgium, depending on the particular capital whence the paper came) was subject to the disturbances of a little strip of land seven thousand miles away? Germany (or France, *et al*) must control its own destiny.

With the third wave of Arctic cold, the tone became openly fearful. Perhaps Sir Phineas was right. What then? What was to be done? There were rumblings and mutterings in Paris and Berlin, and even staid Oslo witnessed a riot, and conservative London as well. Ted began to realize that Asa Gaunt's predictions were founded on keen judgment; the German government made an openly friendly gesture toward France in a delicate border matter, and France reciprocated with an equally indulgent note. Russia protested and was politely ignored; Europe was definitely realigning itself, and in desperate haste.

But America, save for a harassed group in Washington, had only casual interest in the matter. When reports of suffering among the poor began to come during the first week in February, a drive was launched to provide relief funds, but it met with only nominal success. People just weren't interested; a cold winter lacked the dramatic power of a flood, a fire, or an earthquake. But the papers reported in increasing anxiety that the immigration quotas, unapproached for a half a dozen years, were full again; there was the beginning of an exodus from the Gulf Stream countries.

By the second week in February stark panic had gripped Europe, and echoes of it began to penetrate even self-sufficient America. The realignment of the Powers was definite and open now, and Spain, Italy, the Balkans, and Russia found themselves herded together, facing an ominous thunderhead on the north and west. Russia instantly forgot her longstanding quarrel with Japan, and Japan, oddly, was willing enough to forget her own grievances. There was a strange shifting of sympathies; the nations which possessed large and thinly populated areas – Russia, the United States, Mexico, and all of South America – were glaring back at a frantic Europe that awaited only the release of summer to launch a greater invasion than any history had recorded.

Attila and his horde of Huns – the Mongol waves that beat down on China – even the vast movements of the white race into North and South America – all these were but minor migrations to that which threatened now. Two hundred million people, backed by colossal fighting power, glaring panic-stricken at the empty places of the world. No one knew where the thunderbolt would strike first, but that it would strike was beyond doubt.

While Europe shivered in the grip of an incredible winter, Ted shivered at the thought of certain personal problems of his own. The frantic world found an echo in his own situation, for here was he, America in miniature, and there was Kay Lovell, a small edition of Britannia. Their sympathies clashed like those of their respective nations.

The time for secrecy was over. Ted faced Kay before the fireplace in her home and stared from her face to the cheery fire, whose brightness merely accentuated his gloom.

'Yeah,' he admitted. 'I knew about it. I've known it since a couple of days after the Isthmus earthquake.'

'Then why didn't you tell me? You should have.'

'Couldn't. I swore not to tell.'

'It isn't fair!' blazed Kay. 'Why should it fall on England? I tell you it sickens me even to think of Merecroft standing there in snow, like some old Norse tower. I was *born* in Warwickshire, Ted, and so was my father, and his father, and *his*, and all of us back to the time of William the Conqueror. Do you think it's a pleasant thing to think of my mother's rose garden as barren as – as a tundra?'

'I'm sorry,' said Ted gently, 'but what can I – or anyone – do about it? I'm just glad you're here on this side of the Atlantic, where you're safe.'

'Safe!' she flashed. 'Yes, I'm safe, but what about my people? I'm safe because I'm in America, the lucky country, the chosen land! Why did this have to happen to England? The Gulf Stream washes your shores too. Why aren't Americans shivering and freezing and frightened and hopeless, instead of being warm and comfortable and indifferent? Is that fair?'

'The Gulf Stream,' he explained miserably, 'doesn't affect our climate so definitely because in the first place we're much farther south than Europe and in the second place our prevailing winds are from the west, just as England's. But our winds blow from the land to the Gulf Stream, and England's from the Gulf Stream to the land.'

'But it's not fair! It's not fair!'

'Can I help it, Kay?'

'Oh, I suppose not,' she agreed in suddenly weary tones, and then, with a resurgence of anger, 'But you people can do something about it! Look here! Listen to this!'

She spied a week-old copy of the London *Times*, fingered rapidly through it, and turned on Ted. 'Listen – just listen! "And in the name of humanity it is not asking too much to insist that our sister nation open her gates to us. Let us settle the vast areas where now only Indian tribes hunt and buffalo range. We would not be the only ones to gain by such a settlement, for we would bring to the new country a sane, industrious, law-abiding citizenry, no harborers of highwaymen and gangsters – a point well worth considering. We would bring a great new purchasing public for American manufacturers, carrying with us all our portable wealth. And finally, we would provide a host of eager defenders in the war for territory, a war that now seems inevitable. Our language is one with theirs; surely this is the logical solution, especially when one remembers that the state of Texas alone contains land enough to supply two acres to every man, woman, and child on earth!" ' She paused and stared defiantly at Ted. 'Well?'

He snorted. 'Indians and buffalo!' he snapped. 'Have you seen either one in the United States?'

'No, but – '

'And as for Texas, *sure* there's enough land there for two acres to everybody in the world, but why didn't your editor mention that two acres won't even support a cow over much of it? The Llano Estacado's nothing but an alkali desert, and there's a scarcity of water in lots of the rest of it. On that argument, you ought to move to Greenland; I'll bet there's land enough there for six acres per person!'

'That may be true, but – '

'And as for a great new purchasing public, your portable wealth is gold and paper money, isn't it? The gold's all right, but what good is a pound if there's no British credit to back it? Your great new public would simply swell the ranks of the unemployed until American industry could absorb them, which might take years! And meanwhile wages would go down to nothing because of an enormous surplus of labor, and food and rent would go skyhigh because of millions of extra stomachs to feed and bodies to shelter.'

'All right!' said Kay bleakly. 'Argue all you wish. I'll even concede that your arguments are right, but there's one thing I know is wrong, and that's leaving fifty million English people to starve and freeze and suffer in a country that's been moved, as far as climate goes, to the North Pole.

Why, you even get excited over a newspaper story about one poor family in an unheated hovel! Thenwhat about a whole nation whose furnace has gone out?'

'What,' countered Ted grimly, 'about the seven or eight other nations whose furnaces have also gone out?'

'But England deserves priority!' she blazed. 'You took your language from us, your literature, your laws, your whole civilization. Why, even now you ought to be nothing but an English colony! That's all you *are*, if you want the truth!'

'We think differently. Anyway, you know as well as I that the United States can't open the door to one nation and exclude the others. It must be all or none, and that means – none!'

'And that means war,' she said bitterly. 'Oh, Ted! I can't help the way I feel. I have people over there – aunts, cousins, friends. Do you think I can stand indifferently aside while they're ruined? Although they're ruined already, as far as that goes. Land's already dropped to nothing there. You can't sell it at any price now.'

'I know. I'm sorry, Kay, but it's no one's fault. No one's to blame.'

'And so no one needs to do anything about it, I suppose. Is that your nice American theory?'

'You know that isn't fair! What *can* we do?'

'You could let us in! As it is we'll have to fight our way in, and you can't blame us!'

'Kay, no nation and no group of nations can invade this country. Even if our navy were utterly destroyed, how far from the sea do you think a hostile army could march? It would be Napoleon in Russia all over again; your army marches in and is swallowed up. And where is Europe going to find the food to support an invading army? Do you think it could live on the land as it moved? I tell you no sane nation would try that!'

'No *sane* nation, perhaps!' she retorted fiercely. 'Do you think you're dealing with sane nations?'

He shrugged gloomily.

'They're desperate!' she went on. 'I don't blame them. Whatever they do, you've brought it on yourselves. Now you'll be fighting all of Europe, when you could have the British navy on your side. It's stupid. It's worse than stupid; it's selfish!'

'Kay,' he said miserably, 'I can't argue with you. I know how you feel, and I know it's a hell of a situation. But even if I agreed with everything you've said – which I don't – what could I do about it? I'm not the President and I'm not Congress. Let's drop the argument for this evening, honey; it's just making you unhappy.'

'Unhappy! As if I could ever be anything else when everything I value, everything I love, is doomed to be buried under Arctic snow.'

'Everything, Kay?' he asked gently. 'Haven't you forgotten that there's something for you on this side of the Atlantic as well?'

'I haven't forgotten anything,' she said coldly. 'I said everything, and I mean it. America! I hate America. Yes, and I hate Americans too!'

'Kay!'

'And what's more,' she blazed, 'I wouldn't marry an American if he – if he could rebuild the Isthmus! If England's to freeze, I'll freeze with her, and if England's to fight, her enemies are mine!'

She rose suddenly to her feet, deliberately averted her eyes from his troubled face, and stalked out of the room.

Sometimes, during those hectic weeks in February, Ted wormed his way into the Visitor's Gallery in one or the other Congressional house. The outgoing Congress, due to stand for re-election in the fall, was the focal point of the dawning hysteria in the nation, and was battling sensationally through its closing session. Routine matters were ignored, and day after day found both houses considering the unprecedented emergency with a sort of appalled inability to act in any effective unison. Freak bills of all description were read, considered, tabled, reconsidered, put to a second reading, and tabled again. The hard-money boom of a year earlier had swept in a Conservative majority in the off-year elections, but they had no real policy to offer, and the proposals of the minority group of Laborites and Leftists were voted down without substitutes being suggested.

Some of the weirdest bills in all the weird annals of Congress appeared at this time. Ted listened in fascination to the Leftist proposal that each American family adopt two Europeans, splitting its income into thirds; to a suggestion that Continentals be advised to undergo voluntary sterilization, thus restraining the emergency to the time of one generation; to a fantastic paper money scheme of the Senator from the new state of Alaska, that was to provide a magic formula to permit Europe to purchase its livelihood without impoverishing the rest of the world. There were suggestions of outright relief, but the problem of charity to two hundred million people was so obviously staggering that this proposal at least received little attention. But there were certain bills that passed both houses without debate, gaining the votes of Leftists, Laborites, and Conservatives alike; these were the grim appropriations for submarines, super-bombers and interceptors, and aircraft-carriers.

Those were strange, hectic days in Washington. Outwardly there was still the same gay society that gathers like froth around all great capitals, and Ted, of course, being young and decidedly not unattractive, received his full share of invitations. But not even the least sensitive could have overlooked the dark undercurrents of hysteria that flowed just beneath the surface. There was dancing, there was gay dinner conversation, there was laughter, but beneath all of it was fear. Ted was not the only one to notice that the diplomatic representatives of the Gulf Stream countries were conspicuous by their absence from all affairs save those of such importance that their presence was a matter of policy. And even then, incidents occurred; he was present when the Minister from France stalked angrily from the room because some hostess had betrayed the poor taste of permitting her dance orchestra to play a certain popular number called 'The Gulf Stream Blues'. Newspapers carefully refrained from mentioning the occurrence, but Washington buzzed with it for days.

Ted looked in vain for Kay. Her father appeared when appearance was necessary, but Ted had not seen the girl since her abrupt dismissal of him, and in reply to his inquiries, Sir Joshua granted only the gruff and double-edged explanation that she was 'indisposed'. So Ted worried and fumed about her in vain, until he scarcely knew whether his own situation or that of the world was more important. In the last analysis, of course, the two were one and the same.

The world was like a crystal of nitrogen iodide, waiting only the drying-out of summer to explode. Under its frozen surface Europe was seething like Mounts Erebus and Terror that blaze in the ice of Antarctica. Little Hungary had massed its army on the west, beyond doubt to oppose a similar massing on the part of the Anschluss. Of this particular report, Ted heard Maxwell say with an air of relief that it indicated that Germany had turned her face inland; it meant one less potential enemy for America.

But the maritime nations were another story, and especially mighty Britain, whose world-girdling fleet was gathering day by day in the Atlantic. That was a crowded ocean indeed, for on its westward shore was massed the American battle fleet, built at last to treaty strength, and building far beyond it, while north and south piled every vessel that could raise a pound of steam, bearing those fortunates who could leave their European homes to whatever lands hope called them. Africa and Australia, wherever Europe had colonies, were receiving an unheard of stream of immigrants. But this stream was actually only the merest trickle, composed of those who possessed sufficient liquid wealth to encompass the journey. Untold millions remained chained to their homes, bound by the possession of unsaleable lands, or by investments in business, or by sentiment, or by the simple lack of sufficient funds to buy passage for families. And throughout all of the afflicted countries were those who clung stubbornly to hope, who believed even in the grip of that unbelievable winter that the danger would pass, and that things would come right in the end.

Blunt, straightforward little Holland was the first nation to propose openly a wholesale transfer of population. Ted read the note, or at least the version of it given the press on February 21st. In substance it simply repeated the arguments Kay had read from the London paper – the plea to humanity, the affirmation of an honest and industrious citizenry, and the appeal to the friendship that had always existed between the two nations; and the communication closed with a request for an immediate reply because of 'the urgency of the situation'. And an immediate reply was forthcoming.

This was also given to the press. In suave and very polished diplomatic language it pointed out that the United States could hardly admit nationals of one country while excluding those of others. Under the terms of the National Origins Act, Dutch immigrants would be welcomed to the full extent of their quota. It was even possible that the quota might be increased, but it was not conceivable that it could be removed entirely. The note was in effect a suave, dignified, diplomatic No.

March drifted in on a southwest wind. In the Southern states it brought spring, and in Washington a faint forerunner of balmy weather to come, but to the Gulf Stream countries it brought no release from the Arctic winter that had fallen on them with its icy mantle. Only in the Basque country of Southern France, where vagrant winds slipped at intervals across the Pyrenees with the warm breath of the deflected Stream, was there any sign of the relaxing of that frigid clutch. But that was a promise; April would come, and May – and the world flexed its steel muscles for war.

Everyone knew now that war threatened. After the first few notes and replies, no more were released to the press, but everyone knew that notes, representatives, and communiqués were flying between the powers like a flurry of white doves, and everyone knew, at least in Washington, that the tenor of those notes was no longer dove-like. Now they carried brusque demands and blunt refusals.

Ted knew as much of the situation as any alert observer, but no more. He and Asa Gaunt discussed it endlessly, but the dry Texan, having made his predictions and seen them verified, was no longer in the middle of the turmoil, for his bureau had, of course, nothing to do with the affair now. So the Geological Survey staggered on under a woefully reduced appropriation, a handicap shared by every other governmental function that had no direct bearing on defense.

All the American countries, and for that matter, every nation save those in Western Europe, were enjoying a feverish, abnormal, hectic boom. The flight of capital from Europe, and the incessant, avid, frantic cry for food, had created a rush of business, and exports mounted unbelievably. In this emergency, France and the nations under her hegemony, those who had clung so stubbornly to gold ever since the second revaluation of the franc, were now at a marked advantage, since their money would buy more wheat, more cattle, and more coal. But the paper countries, especially Britain, shivered and froze in stone cottage and draughty manor alike.

On the eleventh of March, that memorable Tuesday when the thermometer touched twenty-eight below in London, Ted reached a decision toward which he had been struggling for six weeks. He was going to swallow his pride and see Kay again. Washington was buzzing with rumors that Sir Joshua was to be recalled, that diplomatic relations with England were to be broken as they had already been broken with France. The entire nation moved about its daily business in an air of tense expectancy, for the break with France meant little in view of that country's negligible sea power, but now, if the colossus of the British navy were to align itself with the French army –

But what troubled Ted was a much more personal problem. If Sir Joshua Lovell were recalled to London, that meant that Kay would accompany him, and once she were caught in the frozen Hell of Europe, he had a panicky feeling that she was lost to him forever. When war broke, as it surely must, there would go his last hope of ever seeing her again. Europe, apparently, was doomed, for it seemed impossible that any successful invasion could be carried on over thousands of miles of ocean, but if he could save the one fragment of Europe that meant everything to him, if he could somehow save Kay Lovell, it was worth the sacrifice of pride or of anything else. So he called one final time on the telephone, received the same response from an unfriendly maid, and then left the almost idle office and drove directly to her home.

The same maid answered his ring. 'Miss Lovell is not in,' she said coldly. 'I told you that when you telephoned.'

'I'll wait,' returned Ted grimly, and thrust himself through the door. He seated himself stolidly in the hall, glared back at the maid, and waited. It was no more than five minutes before Kay herself appeared, coming wearily down the steps.

'I wish you'd leave,' she said. She was pallid and troubled, and he felt a great surge of sympathy.

'I won't leave.'

'What do I have to do to make you go away? I don't want to see you, Ted.'

'If you'll talk to me just half an hour, I'll go.'

She yielded listlessly, leading the way into the living room where a fire still crackled in cheerful irony. 'Well?' she asked.

'Kay, do you love me?'

'I – No, I don't!'

'Kay,' he persisted gently, 'do you love me enough to marry me and stay here where you're safe?'

Tears glistened suddenly in her brown eyes. 'I hate you,' she said. 'I hate all of you. You're a nation of murderers. You're like the East Indian Thugs, only they call murder religion and you call it patriotism.'

'I won't even argue with you, Kay. I can't blame you for your viewpoint, and I can't blame you for not understanding mine. But – do you love me?'

'All right,' she said in sudden weariness. 'I do.'

'And will you marry me?'

'No. No, I won't marry you, Ted. I'm going back to England.'

'Then will you marry me first? I'll let you go back, Kay, but afterwards – if there's any world left after what's coming – I could bring you back here. I'll have to fight for what I believe in, and I won't ask you to stay with me during the time our nations are enemies, but afterwards, Kay – if you're my wife I could bring you here. Don't you see?'

'I see, but – no.'

'Why, Kay? You said you loved me.'

'I do,' she said almost bitterly. 'I wish I didn't, because I can't marry you hating your people the way I do. If you were on my side, Ted, I swear I'd marry you tomorrow, or today, or five minutes from now – but as it is, I can't. It just wouldn't be fair.'

'You'd not want me to turn traitor,' he responded gloomily. 'One thing I'm sure of, Kay, is that you couldn't love a traitor.' He paused. 'Is it goodbye, then?'

'Yes.' There were tears in her eyes again. 'It isn't public yet, but father has been recalled. Tomorrow he presents his recall to the Secretary of State, and the day after we leave for England. This is goodbye.'

'That *does* mean war!' he muttered. 'I've been hoping that in spite of everything – God knows I'm sorry, Kay. I don't blame you for the way you feel. You couldn't feel differently and still be Kay Lovell, but – it's damned hard. It's damned hard!'

She agreed silently. After a moment she said, 'Think of my part of it, Ted – going back to a home that's like – well, the Rockefeller Mountains in Antarctica. I tell you, I'd rather it had been England that sunk into the sea! That would have been easier, much easier than this. If it had sunk until the waves rolled over the very peak of Ben Macduhl – ' She broke off.

'The waves are rolling over higher peaks than Ben Macduhl,' he responded drearily. 'They're – ' Suddenly he paused, staring at Kay with his jaw dropping and a wild light in his eyes!

'The Sierra Madre!' he bellowed, in such a roaring voice that the girl shrank away. 'The Mother range! The Sierra Madre! The Sierra Madre!'

'Wh-what?' she gasped.

'The Sierra – ! Listen to me, Kay! Listen to me! Do you trust me! Will you do something – something for both of us? *Us?* I mean for the world! Will you?

'I know you will! Kay, keep your father from presenting his recall! Keep him here another ten days – even another week. Can you?'

'How? How can I?'

'I don't know. Any way at all. Get sick. Get too sick to travel, and beg him not to present his papers until you can leave. Or – or tell him that the United States will make his country an alternate proposal in a few days. That's the truth. I swear that's true, Kay.'

'But – but he won't believe me!'

'He's got to! I don't care how you do it, but keep him here! And have him report to the Foreign Office that new developments – vastly import-ant developments – have come up. That's true, Kay.'

'True? Then what are they?'

'There isn't time to explain. Will you do what I ask?'

'I'll try!'

'You're – well you're marvelous!' he said huskily. He stared into her tragic brown eyes, kissed her lightly, and rushed away.

Asa Gaunt was scowling down at a map of the dead Salton Sea when Ted dashed unannounced into the office. The rangy Texan looked up with a dry smile at the unceremonious entry.

'I've got it!' yelled Ted.

'A bad case of it,' agreed Asa Gaunt. 'What's the diagnosis?'

'No, I mean – Say, has the Survey taken soundings over the Isthmus?'

'The *Dolphin*'s been there for weeks,' said the older man. 'You know you can't map forty thousand square miles of ocean bed during the lunch hour.'

'Where,' shouted Ted, 'are they sounding?'

'Over Pearl Cay Point, Bluefields, Monkey Point, and San Juan del Norte, of course. Naturally they'll sound the places where there were cities first of all.'

'Oh, naturally!' said Ted, suppressing his voice to a tense quiver. 'And where is the *Marlin*?'

'Idle at Newport News. We can't operate both of them under this year's budget.'

'To hell with the budget!' flared Ted. 'Get the *Marlin* there too, and any other vessel that can carry an electric plumb!'

'Yes, sir – right away, sir,' said Asa Gaunt dryly. 'When did you relieve Golsborough as Secretary of the Interior, Mr Welling?'

'I'm sorry,' replied Ted. 'I'm not giving orders, but I've thought of something. Something that may get all of us out of this mess we're in.'

'Indeed? Sounds mildly interesting. Is it another of these international fiat-money schemes?'

'No!' blazed Ted. 'It's the Sierra Madre! Don't you see?'

'In words of one syllable, no.'

'Then listen! I've flown over every square mile of the sunken territory. I've mapped and photographed it, and I've laid out the geodetics. I know that buried strip of land as well as I know the humps and hollows in my own bed.'

'Congratulations, but what of it?'

'This!' snapped Ted. He turned to the wall, pulled down the topographical map of Central America, and began to speak. After a while Asa Gaunt leaned forward in his chair and a queer light gathered in his pale blue eyes.

What follows has been recorded and interpreted in a hundred ways by numberless historians. The story of the *Dolphin* and the *Marlin*, sounding in frantic haste the course of the submerged Cordilleras, is in itself romance of the first order. The secret story of diplomacy, the holding of Britain's neutrality so that the lesser sea powers dared not declare war across three thousand miles of ocean, is another romance that will never be told openly. But the most fascinating story of all, the building of the Cordilleran Intercontinental Wall, has been told so often that it needs little comment.

The soundings traced the irregular course of the sunken Sierra Madre mountains. Ted's guess was justified; the peaks of the range were not inaccessibly far below the surface. A route was found where the Equatorial Counter Current swept over them with a depth at no point greater than forty fathoms, and the building of the Wall began on March the 31st, began in frantic haste, for the task utterly dwarfed the digging of the abandoned Canal itself. By the end of September some two hundred miles had been raised to sea-level, a mighty rampart seventy-five feet broad at its narrowest point, and with an extreme height of two hundred and forty feet and an average of ninety.

There was still almost half to be completed when winter swept out of the north over a frightened Europe, but the half that had been built was the critical sector. On one side washed the Counter Current, on the other the Equatorial Drift, bound to join the Gulf Stream in its slow march toward Europe. And the mighty Stream, traced by a hundred oceanographic vessels, veered slowly northward again, and bathed first the shores of France, then of England, and finally of the high northern Scandinavian Peninsula. Winter came drifting in as mildly as of old, and a sigh of relief went up from every nation in the world.

Ostensibly the Cordilleran Inter-continental Wall was constructed by the United States. A good many of the more chauvinistic newspapers bewailed the appearance of Uncle Sam as a sucker again, paying for the five hundred million dollar project for the benefit of Europe. No one noticed that there was no Congressional appropriation for the purpose, nor has anyone since wondered why the British naval bases on Trinidad, Jamaica, and at Belize have harbored so large a portion of His Majesty's Atlantic Fleet. Nor, for that matter, has anyone inquired why the dead war debts were so suddenly exhumedand settledso cheerfully by the European powers.

A few historians and economists may suspect. The truth is that the Cordilleran Inter-continental Wall has given the United States a world hegemony, in fact almost a world empire. From the south tip of Texas, from Florida, from Puerto Rico, and from the otherwise useless Canal Zone, a thousand American planes could bomb the Wall into ruin. No European nation dares risk that.

Moreover, no nation in the world, not even in the orient where the Gulf Stream has no climatic influence, dares threaten war on America. If Japan, for instance, should so much as speak a hostile word, the whole military might of Europe would turn against her. Europe simply cannot risk an attack on the Wall, and certainly the first effort of a nation at war with the United States would be to force a passage through the Wall.

In effect the United States can command the armies of Europe with a few bombing planes, though not even the most ardent pacifists have yet suggested that experiment. But such are the results of the barrier officially known as the Cordilleran Intercontinental Wall, but called by every newspaper after its originator, the Welling Wall.

It was mid-summer before Ted had time enough to consider marriage and a honeymoon. He and Kay spent the latter on the Caribbean, cruising that treacherous sea in a sturdy fifty-foot sloop lent for the occasion

by Asa Gaunt and the Geological Survey. They spent a good share of
the time watching the great dredges and construction vessels working
desperately at the task of adding millions of cubic yards to the peaks of
the submarine range that was once the Sierra Madre. And one day as they
lay on the deck in swimming suits, bent on acquiring a tropical tan, Ted
asked her a question.

'By the way,' he began, 'you've never told me how you managed to
keep Sir Joshua in the States. That stalled off war just long enough for
this thing to be worked out and presented. How'd you do it?'

Kay dimpled. 'Oh, first I tried to tell him I was sick. I got desperately
sick.'

'I knew he'd fall for that.'

'But he didn't. He said a sea voyage would help me.'

'Then – what *did* you do?'

'Well, you see he has a sort of idiosyncrasy toward quinine. Ever since
his service in India, where he had to take it day after day, he develops
what doctors call a quinine rash, and he hasn't taken any for years.'

'Well?'

'Don't you see? His before-dinner cocktail had a little quinine in it,
and so did his wine, and so did his tea, and the sugar and the salt. He kept
complaining that everything he ate tasted bitter to him, and I convinced
him that it was due to his indigestion.'

'And then?'

'Why, then I brought him one of his indigestion capsules, only it
didn't have his medicine in it. It had a nice dose of quinine, and in two
hours he was pink as a salmon, and so itchy he couldn't sit still!'

Ted began to laugh. 'Don't tell me that kept him there!'

'Not that alone,' said Kay demurely. 'I made him call in a doctor, a
friend of mine who – well, who kept asking me to marry him – and I sort
of bribed him to tell father he had – I think it was erysipelas he called it.
Something violently contagious, anyway.'

'And so – ?'

'And so we were quarantined for two weeks! And I kept feeding father
quinine to keep up the bluff, and – well, we were very strictly quarantined.
He just couldn't present his recall!'

The Worlds of If

Stanley G. Weinbaum

I stopped on the way to the Staten Island Airport to call up, and that was a mistake, doubtless, since I had a chance of making it otherwise. But the office was affable. 'We'll hold the ship five minutes for you,' the clerk said. 'That's the best we can do.'

So I rushed back to my taxi and we spun off to the third level and sped across the Staten Bridge like a comet treading a steel rainbow. I had to be in Moscow by evening, by eight o'clock in fact, for the opening of bids on the Ural Tunnel. The Government required the personal presence of an agent of each bidder, but the firm should have known better than to send me, Dixon Wells, even though the N. J. Wells Corporation is, so to speak, my father. I have a – well, an undeserved reputation for being late to everything; something always comes up to prevent me from getting anywhere on time. It's never my fault; this time it was a chance encounter with my old physics professor, old Haskel van Manderpootz. I couldn't very well just say hello and goodbye to him; I'd been a favorite of his back in the college days of 2014.

I missed the airliner, of course. I was still on the Staten Bridge when I heard the roar of the catapult and the Soviet rocket *Baikal* hummed over us like a tracer bullet with a long tail of flame.

We got the contract anyway; the firm wired our man in Beirut and he flew up to Moscow, but it didn't help my reputation. However, I felt a great deal better when I saw the evening papers; the *Baikal*, flying at the north edge of the eastbound lane to avoid a storm, had locked wings with a British fruitship and all but a hundred of her five hundred passengers were lost. I had almost become 'the late Mr Wells' in a grimmer sense.

I'd made an engagement for the following week with old van Manderpootz. It seems he'd transferred to N.Y.U. as head of the department of Newer Physics – that is, of Relativity. He deserved it; the old chap was a genius if ever there was one, and even now, eight years out of college, I remember more from his course than from half a dozen in calculus, steam and gas, mechanics, and other hazards on the path to an engineer's education, So on Tuesday night I dropped in an hour or so late, to tell the truth, since I'd forgotten about the engagement until mid-evening.

He was reading in a room as disorderly as ever. 'Humph!' he granted. 'Time changes everything but habit, I see. You were a good student, Dick, but I seem to recall that you always arrived in class toward the middle of the lectures.'

'I had a course in East Hall just before,' I explained. 'I couldn't seem to make it in time.'

'Well, it's time you learned to be on time,' he growled. Then his eyes twinkled. 'Time!' he ejaculated. 'The most fascinating word in the language. Here we've used it five times (there goes the sixth time – and the seventh!) in the first minute of conversation; each of us understands the other, yet science is just beginning to learn its meaning, Science? I mean that *I* am beginning to learn.'

I sat down. 'You and science are synonymous,' I grinned. 'Aren't you one of the world's outstanding physicists?'

'One of them!' he snorted. '*One* of them! And who are the others?'

'Oh, Corveille and Hastings and Shrimski –'

'Bah! Would you mention them in the same breath with the name of van Manderpootz? A pack of jackals, eating the crumbs of ideas that drop from my feast of thoughts! Had you gone back into the last century, now – had you mentioned Einstein and de Sitter – there, perhaps, are names worthy to rank with (or just below) van Manderpootz!'

I grinned again in amusement. 'Einstein was considered pretty good, wasn't he?' I remarked. 'After all, he was the first to tie time and space to the laboratory. Before him they were just philosophical concepts.'

'He didn't!' rasped the professor. 'Perhaps, in a dim, primitive fashion, he showed the way, but I – I, van Manderpootz – am the first to seize time, drag it into my laboratory, and perform an experiment on it.'

'Indeed? And what sort of experiment?'

'What experiment, other than simple measurement, is it possible to perform?' he snapped.

'Why – I don't know. To travel in it?'

'Exactly.'

'Like these time-machines that are so popular in the current magazines? To go into the future or the past?'

'Bah! Many bahs! The future or the past – pfui! It needs no van Manderpootz to see the fallacy in that. Einstein showed us that much.'

'How? It's conceivable, isn't it?'

'Conceivable? And you, Dixon Wells, studied under van Manderpootz!' He grew red with emotion, then grimly calm. 'Listen to me. You know how time varies with the speed of a system – Einstein's relativity.'

'Yes.'

'Very well. Now suppose then that the great engineer Dixon Wells invents a machine capable of traveling very fast, enormously fast, nine-tenths as fast as light. Do you follow? Good. You then fuel this miracle ship for a little jaunt of a half-million miles, which, since mass (and with it inertia) increases according to the Einstein formula with increasing speed, takes all the fuel in the world. But you solve that. You use atomic energy. Then, since at nine-tenths light-speed, your ship weighs about as much as the sun, you disintegrate North America to give you sufficient motive power. You start off at that speed, a hundred and sixty-eight thousand miles per second, and you travel for two hundred and four thousand miles. The acceleration has now crushed you to death, but you have penetrated the future.' He paused, grinning sardonically. 'Haven't you?'

'Yes.'

'And how far?'

I hesitated.

'Use your Einstein formula!' he screeched. 'How far? I'll tell you. *One second*!' He grinned triumphantly. 'That's how possible it is to travel into the future. And as for the past – in the first place, you'd have to exceed light-speed, which immediately entails the use of more than an infinite number of horsepowers. We'll assume that the great engineer Dixon Wells solves that little problem too, even though the energy output of the whole universe is not an infinite number of horsepowers. Then he applies this more than infinite power to travel at two hundred and four thousand miles per second for ten seconds. He has then penetrated the past. How far?'

Again I hesitated.

'I'll tell you. *One second*!' He glared at me. 'Now all you have to do is to design such a machine, and then van Manderpootz will admit the possibility of traveling into the future – for a limited number of seconds. As for the past, I have just explained that all the energy in the universe is insufficient for that.'

'But,' I stammered, 'you just said that you – '

'I did not say anything about traveling into either future or past, which I have just demonstrated to you to be impossible – a practical impossibility in the one case and an absolute one in the other.'

'Then how do you travel in time?'

'Not even van Manderpootz can perform the impossible,' said the professor, now faintly jovial. He tapped a thick pad of typewriter paper on the table beside him. 'See, Dick, this is the world, the universe.' He swept a finger down it. 'It is long in time, and' – sweeping his hand across it – 'it is broad in space, but' – now jabbing his finger against its center – 'it is very thin in the fourth dimension. Van Manderpootz takes always the shortest, the most logical course. I do not travel along time, into past or future. No. Me, I travel across time, sideways!'

I gulped. 'Sideways into time! What's there?'

'What would naturally be there?' he snorted. 'Ahead is the future; behind is the past. Those are real, the worlds of past and future. What worlds are neither past nor future, but contemporary and yet – extemporal – existing, as it were, in time parallel to our time?'

I shook my head.

'Idiot!' he snapped. 'The conditional worlds, of course! The worlds of "if". Ahead are the worlds to be; behind are the worlds that were; to either side are the worlds that might have been – the worlds of "if"!'

'Eh?' I was puzzled. 'Do you mean that you can see what will happen if I do such and such?'

'No!' he snorted. 'My machine does not reveal the past nor predict the future. It will show, as I told you, the conditional worlds. You might express it, by "if I had done such and such, so and so would have happened." The worlds of the subjunctive mode.'

'Now how the devil does it do that?'

'Simple, for van Manderpootz! I use polarized light, polarized not in the horizontal or vertical planes, but in the direction of the fourth dimension – an easy matter. One uses Iceland spar under colossal pressure, that is all. And since the worlds are very thin in the direction of the fourth dimension, the thickness of a single light wave, though it be but millionths of an inch, is sufficient. A considerable improvement over time-traveling in past or future, with its impossible velocities and ridiculous distances!'

'But – are those – worlds of "if" – real?'

'Real? What is real? They are real, perhaps, in the sense that two is a real number as opposed to the square root of –2, which is imaginary. They are the worlds that would have been *if* – do you see?'

I nodded. 'Dimly. You could see, for instance, what New York would have been like if England had won the Revolution instead of the Colonies.'

'That's the principle, true enough, but you couldn't see that on the machine. Part of it, you see, is a Horsten psychomat (stolen from one of *my* ideas, by the way) and you, the user, become part of the device. Your own mind is necessary to furnish the background. For instance, if George Washington could have used the mechanism after the signing of peace, he could have seen what you suggest. We can't. You can't even see what would have happened if I hadn't invented the thing, but *I* can. Do you understand?'

'Of course. You mean the background has to rest in the past experiences of the user.'

'You're growing brilliant,' he scoffed. 'Yes. The device will show ten hours of what would have happened *if* – condensed, of course, as in a movie, to half an hour's actual time.'

'Say, that sounds interesting!'

'You'd like to see it? Is there anything you'd like to find out? Any choice you'd alter?'

'I'll say – a thousand of 'em. I'd like to know what would have happened if I'd sold out my stocks in 2009 instead of '10. I was a millionaire in my own right then, but I was a little – well, a little late in liquidating.'

'As usual,' remarked van Manderpootz. 'Let's go over to the laboratory then.'

The professor's quarters were but a block from the campus. He ushered me into the Physics Building, and thence into his own research laboratory, much like the one I had visited during my courses under him. The device – he called it his 'subjunctivisor', since it operated in hypothetical worlds – occupied the entire center table. Most of it was merely a Horsten psychomat, but glittering crystalline and glassy was the prism of Iceland spar, the polarizing agent that was the heart of the instrument.

Van Manderpootz pointed to the headpiece. 'Put it on,' he said, and I sat staring at the screen of the psychomat. I suppose everyone is familiar with the Horsten psychomat; it was as much a fad a few years ago as the ouija board a century back. Yet it isn't just a toy; sometimes, much as the ouija board, it's a real aid to memory. A maze of vague and colored shadows is caused to drift slowly across the screen, and one watches them, meanwhile visualizing whatever scene or circumstances he is trying to remember. He turns a knob that alters the arrangement of lights and shadows, and when, by chance, the design corresponds to his mental picture – presto! There is his scene re-created under his eyes. Of course his own mind adds the details. All the screen actually shows are these tinted blobs of light and shadow, but the thing can be amazingly real. I've seen occasions when I could have sworn the psychomat showed pictures almost as sharp and detailed as reality itself; the illusion is sometimes as startling as that.

Van Manderpootz switched on the light, and the play of shadows began. 'Now recall the circumstances of, say, a half-year after the market crash. Turn the knob until the picture clears, then stop. At that point I direct the light of the subjunctivisor upon the screen, and you have nothing to do but watch.'

I did as directed. Momentary pictures formed and vanished. The inchoate sounds of the device hummed like distant voices, but without the added suggestion of the picture, they meant nothing. My own face flashed and dissolved and then, finally, I had it. There was a picture of myself sitting in an ill-defined room; that was all. I released the knob and gestured.

A click followed. The light dimmed, then brightened. The picture cleared, and amazingly, another figure emerged, a woman, I recognized her; it was Whimsy White, erstwhile star of television and première actress of the 'Vision Varieties of '09'. She was changed on that picture, but I recognized her.

I'll say I did! I'd been trailing her all through the boom years of '07 to '10, trying to marry her, while old N. J. raved and ranted and threatened to leave everything to the Society for Rehabilitation of the Gobi Desert. I think those threats were what kept her from accepting me, but after I took my own money and ran it up to a couple of million in that crazy market of '08 and '09, she softened.

Temporarily, that is. When the crash of the spring of '10 came and bounced me back on my father and into the firm of N. J. Wells, her favor dropped a dozen points to the market's one. In February we were engaged, in April we were hardly speaking. In May they sold me out. I'd been late again.

And now, there she was on the psychomat screen, obviously plumping out, and not nearly so pretty as memory had pictured her. She was staring at me with an expression of enmity, and I was glaring back. The buzzes became voices.

'You nit-wit!' she snapped. 'You can't bury me out here. I want to go back to New York, where there's a little life. I'm bored with you and your golf.'

'And I'm bored with you and your whole dizzy crowd.'

'At least they're *alive*. You're a walking corpse! Just because you were lucky enough to gamble yourself into the money, you think you're a tin god.'

'Well, I don't think *you're* Cleopatra! Those friends of yours – they trail after you because you give parties and spend money – *my* money.'

'Better than spending it to knock a white walnut along a mountain-side!'

'Indeed? You ought to try it, Marie.' (That was her real name.) 'It might help your figure – though I doubt if anything could!'

She glared in rage and – well, that was a painful half-hour. I won't give all the details, but I was glad when the screen dissolved into meaningless colored clouds.

'Whew!' I said, staring at van Manderpootz, who had been reading. 'You liked it?'

'Liked it! Say, I guess I was lucky to be cleaned out. I won't regret it from now on.'

'That,' said the professor grandly, 'is van Manderpootz's great contribution to human happiness. "Of all sad words of tongue or pen, the saddest are these: it might have been!" True no longer, my friend Dick. Van Manderpootz has shown that the proper reading is, "it might have been – worse!" '

It was very late when I returned home, and as a result, very late when I rose, and equally late when I got to the office. My father was unnecessarily worked up about it, but he exaggerated when he said I'd never been on time. He forgets the occasions when he's awakened me and dragged me down with him. Nor was it necessary to refer so sarcastically to my missing the *Baikal*; I reminded him of the wrecking of the liner, and he responded very heartlessly that if I'd been aboard, the rocket would have been late, and so would have missed colliding with the British fruitship. It was likewise superfluous for him to mention that when he and I had tried to snatch a few weeks of golfing in the mountains, even the spring had been late. I had nothing to do with that.

'Dixon,' he concluded, 'you have no conception whatever of time. None whatever.'

The conversation with van Manderpootz recurred to me. I was impelled to ask, 'And have you, sir?'

'I have,' he said grimly. 'I most assuredly have. Time,' he said oracularly 'is money.'

You can't argue with a viewpoint like that.

But those aspersions of his rankled, especially that about the *Baikal*. Tardy I might be, but it was hardly conceivable that my presence aboard the rocket could have averted the catastrophe. It irritated me; in a way, it made me responsible for the deaths of those unrescued hundreds among the passengers and crew, and I didn't like the thought.

Of course, if they'd waited an extra five minutes for me, or if I'd been on time and they'd left on schedule instead of five minutes late, or if – *if*!

If! The word called up van Manderpootz and his subjunctivisor – the worlds of 'if', the weird, unreal worlds that existed beside reality, neither past nor future, but contemporary, yet extemporal. Somewhere among their ghostly infinities existed one that represented the world that would have been had I made the liner. I had only to call up Haskel van Manderpootz, make an appointment, and then – find out.

Yet it wasn't an easy decision. Suppose – just suppose that I found myself responsible – not legally responsible, certainly; there'd be no question of criminal negligence, or anything of that sort – not even morally responsible, because I couldn't possibly have anticipated that my presence or absence could weigh so heavily in the scales of life and death, nor could I have known in which direction the scales would tip. Just – responsible; that was all. Yet I hated to find out.

I hated equally not finding out. Uncertainty has its pangs too, quite as painful as those of remorse. It might be less nerve-racking to know myself responsible than to wonder, to waste thoughts in vain doubts and futile reproaches. So I seized the visiphone, dialed the number of the University and at length gazed on the broad, humorous, intelligent features of van Manderpootz, dragged from a morning lecture by my call.

I was all but prompt for the appointment the following evening, and might actually have been on time but for an unreasonable traffic officer who insisted on booking me for speeding. At any rate, van Manderpootz was impressed.

'Well!' he rumbled. 'I almost missed you, Dixon. I was just going over to the club, since I didn't expect you for an hour. You're only ten minutes late.'

I ignored this. 'Professor, I want to use your – uh – your subjunctivisor.'

'Eh? Oh, yes. You're lucky, then. I was just about to dismantle it.'

'Dismantle it! Why?'

'It has served its purpose. It has given birth to an idea far more important than itself. I shall need the space it occupies.'

'But what is the idea, if it's not too presumptuous of me to ask?'

'It is not too presumptuous. You and the world which awaits it so eagerly may both know, but you bear it from the lips of the author. It is nothing less than the autobiography of van Manderpootz!' He paused impressively.

I gaped. 'Your autobiography?'

'Yes. The world, though perhaps unaware, is crying for it. I shall detail my life, my work. I shall reveal myself as the man responsible for the three years' duration of the Pacific War of 2004.'

'You?'

'None other. Had I not been a loyal Netherlands subject at that time, and therefore neutral, the forces of Asia would have been crushed in three months instead of three years. The subjunctivisor tells me so; I would have invented a calculator to forecast the chances of every engagement; van

Manderpootz would have removed the hit or miss element in the conduct of war.' He frowned solemnly. 'There is my idea. The autobiography of van Manderpootz. What do you think of it?'

I recovered my thoughts. 'It's – uh – it's colossal!' I said vehemently. 'I'll buy a copy myself. Several copies. I'll send 'em to my friends.'

'I,' said van Manderpootz expansively, 'shall autograph your copy for you. It will be priceless. I shall write in some fitting phrase, perhaps something like *Magnificus sed non superbus*. "Great but not proud!" That well described van Manderpootz, who despite his greatness is simple, modest, and unassuming. Don't you agree?'

'Perfectly! A very apt description of you. But – couldn't I see your subjunctivisor before it's dismantled to make way for the greater work?'

'Ah! You wish to find out something?'

'Yes, professor. Do you remember the *Baikal* disaster of a week or two ago? I was to have taken that liner to Moscow. I just missed it.' I related the circumstances.

'Humph!' he grunted. 'You wish to discover what would have happened had you caught it, eh? Well, I see several possibilities. Among the worlds of "if" is the one that would have been real if you had been on time, the one that depended on the vessel waiting for your actual arrival, and the one that hung on your arriving within the five minutes they actually waited. In which are you interested?'

'Oh – the last one.' That seemed the likeliest. After all, it was too much to expect that Dixon Wells could ever be on time, and as to the second possibility – well, they *hadn't* waited for me, and that in a way removed the weight of responsibility.

'Come on,' rumbled van Manderpootz. I followed him across to the Physics Building and into his littered laboratory. The device still stood on the table and I took my place before it, staring at the screen of the Horsten psychomat. The clouds wavered and shifted as I sought to impress my memories on their suggestive shapes, to read into them some picture of that vanished morning.

Then I had it. I made out the vista from the Staten Bridge, and was speeding across the giant span toward the airport. I waved a signal to van Manderpootz, the thing clicked, and the subjunctivisor was on.

The grassless clay of the field appeared. It is a curious thing about the psychomat that you see only through the eyes of your image on the screen. It lends a strange reality to the working of the toy; I suppose a sort of self-hypnosis is partly responsible.

I was rushing over the ground toward the glittering, silver-winged projectile that was the *Baikal*. A glowering officer waved me on, and I dashed up the slant of the gangplank and into the ship; the port dropped and I heard a long 'Whew!' of relief.

'Sit down!' barked the officer, gesturing toward an unoccupied seat. I fell into it; the ship quivered under the thrust of the catapult, grated harshly into motion, and then was flung bodily into the air. The blasts roared instantly, then settled to a more muffled throbbing, and I watched Staten Island drop down and slide back beneath me. The giant rocket was under way.

'Whew!' I breathed again. 'Made it!' I caught an amused glance from my right. I was in an aisle seat; there was no one to my left, so I turned to the eyes that had flashed, glanced, and froze staring.

It was a girl. Perhaps she wasn't actually as lovely as she looked to me; after all, I was seeing her through the half-visionary screen of a psycho-mat. I've told myself since that she *couldn't* have been as pretty as she seemed, that it was due to my own imagination filling in the details. I don't know; I remember only that I stared at curiously lovely silver-blue eyes and velvety brown hair, and a small amused mouth, and an impudent nose. I kept staring until she flushed.

'I'm sorry,' I said quickly. 'I – was startled.'

There's a friendly atmosphere aboard a trans-oceanic rocket. The passengers are forced into a crowded infirmary for anywhere from seven to twelve hours, and there isn't much room for moving about. Generally, one strikes up an acquaintance with his neighbors; introductions aren't at all necessary, and the custom is simply to speak to anybody you choose – something like an all-day trip on the railroad trains of the last century, I suppose. You make friends for the duration of the journey, and then, nine times out of ten, you never hear of your traveling companions again.

The girl smiled. 'Are you the individual responsible for the delay in starting?'

I admitted it. 'I seem to be chronically late. Even watches lose time as soon as I wear them.'

She laughed. 'Your responsibilities can't be very heavy.'

Well, they weren't of course, though it's surprising how many clubs, caddies, and chorus girls have depended on me at various times for appreciable portions of their incomes. But somehow I didn't feel like mentioning those things to the silvery-eyed girl.

We talked. Her name, it developed, was Joanna Caldwell, and she was going as far as Paris. She was an artist, or hoped to be one day, and of course there is no place in the world that can supply both training and inspiration like Paris. So it was there she was bound for a year of study, and despite her demurely humorous lips and laughing eyes, I could see that the business was of vast importance to her. I gathered that she had worked hard for the year in Paris, had scraped and saved for three years as fashion illustrator for some woman's magazine, though she couldn't have been many months over twenty-one. Her painting meant a great deal to her, and I could understand it. I'd felt that way about polo once.

So you see, we were sympathetic spirits from the beginning. I knew that she liked me, and it was obvious that she didn't connect Dixon Wells with the N. J. Wells Corporation. And as for me – well, after that first glance into her cool silver eyes, I simply didn't care to look anywhere else. The hours seemed to drip away like minutes while I watched her.

You know how those things go. Suddenly I was calling her Joanna and she was calling me Dick, and it seemed as if we'd been doing just that all our lives. I'd decided to stop over in Paris on my way back from Moscow, and I'd secured her promise to let me see her. She was different, I tell you; she was nothing like the calculating Whimsy White, and still less like the dancing, simpering, giddy youngsters one meets around at social affairs. She was just Joanna, cool and humorous, yet sympathetic and serious, and as pretty as a Majolica figurine.

We could scarcely realize it when the steward passed along to take orders for luncheon. Four hours out? It seemed like forty minutes. And we had a pleasant feeling of intimacy in the discovery that both of us liked lobster salad and detested oysters. It was another bond; I told her whimsically that it was an omen, nor did she object to considering it so.

Afterwards we walked along the narrow aisle to the glassed-in observation room up forward. It was almost too crowded for entry, but we didn't mind that at all, as it forced us to sit very close together. We stayed long after both of us had begun to notice the stuffiness of the air.

It was just after we had returned to our seats that the catastrophe occurred. There was no warning save a sudden lurch, the result, I suppose, of the pilot's futile last-minute attempt to swerve – just that and then a grinding crash and a terrible sensation of spinning, and after that a chorus of shrieks that were like the sounds of a battle.

It *was* battle. Five hundred people were picking themselves up from the floor, were trampling each other, milling around, being cast helplessly down as the great rocket-plane, its left wing but a broken stub, circled downward toward the Atlantic.

The shouts of officers sounded and a loudspeaker blared. 'Be calm,' it kept repeating, and then, 'There has been a collision. We have contacted a surface ship. There is no danger – There is no danger – '

I struggled up from the débris of shattered seats. Joanna was gone; just as I found her crumpled between the rows, the ship struck the water with a jar that set everything crashing again. The speaker blared, 'Put on the cork belts under the seats. The life-belts are under the seats.'

I dragged a belt loose and snapped it around Joanna, then donned one myself. The crowd was surging forward now, and the tail end of the ship began to drop. There was water behind us, sloshing in the darkness as the lights went out. An officer came sliding by, stooped, and fastened a belt about an unconscious woman ahead of us. 'You all right?' he yelled, and passed on without waiting for an answer.

The speaker must have been cut on to a battery circuit. 'And get as far away as possible,' it ordered suddenly. 'Jump from the forward port and get as far away as possible. A ship is standing by. You will be picked up. Jump from the – '. It went dead again.

I got Joanna untangled from the wreckage. She was pale; her silvery eyes were closed. I started dragging her slowly and painfully toward the forward port, and the slant of the floor increased until it was like the slide of a ski-jump. The officer passed again. 'Can you handle her?' he asked, and again dashed away.

I was getting there. The crowd around the port looked smaller, or was it simply huddling closer? Then suddenly, a wail of fear and despair went up, and there was a roar of water. The observation room walls had given. I saw the green surge of waves, and a billowing deluge rushed down upon us. I had been late again.

That was all. I raised shocked and frightened eyes from the subjunct-ivisor to face van Manderpootz, who was scribbling on the edge of the table.

'Well?' he asked.

I shuddered. 'Horrible!' I murmured. 'We – I guess we wouldn't have been among the survivors.'

'We, eh? We?' His eyes twinkled.

I did not enlighten him.

I thanked him, bade him good-night and went dolorously home.

Even my father noticed something queer about me. The day I got to the office only five minutes late, he called me in for some anxious questioning as to my health. I couldn't tell him anything, of course. How could I explain that I'd been late once too often, and had fallen in love with a girl two weeks after she was dead?

The thought drove me nearly crazy. Joanna! Joanna with her silvery eyes now lay somewhere at the bottom of the Atlantic. I went around half dazed, scarcely speaking. One night I actually lacked the energy to go home and sat smoking in my father's big overstuffed chair in his private office until I finally dozed off. The next morning, when old N. J. entered and found me there before him, he turned pale as paper, staggered, and gasped, 'My heart!' It took a lot of explaining to convince him that I wasn't early at the office but just very late going home.

At last I felt that I couldn't stand it. I had to do something – anything at all. I thought finally of the subjunctivisor. I could see – yes, I could see what would have transpired if the ship hadn't been wrecked! I could trace out that weird, unreal romance hidden somewhere in the worlds of 'if'. I could, perhaps, wring a somber, vicarious joy from the things that might have been. I could see Joanna once more!

It was late afternoon when I rushed over to van Manderpootz's quarters. He wasn't there; I encountered him finally in the hall of the Physics Building.

'Dick!' he exclaimed. 'Are you sick?'

'Sick? No, not physically. Professor, I've got to use your subjunctivisor again. I've *got* to!'

'Eh? Oh – that toy. You're too late, Dick. I've dismantled it. I have a better use for the space.'

I gave a miserable groan and was tempted to damn the autobiography of the great van Manderpootz. A gleam of sympathy showed in his eyes, and he took my arm, dragging me into the little office adjoining his laboratory. 'Tell me,' he commanded.

I did. I guess I made the tragedy plain enough, for his heavy brows knit in a frown of pity. 'Not even van Manderpootz can bring back the dead,' he murmured. 'I'm sorry, Dick. Take your mind from the affair. Even were my subjunctivisor available, I wouldn't permit you to use it. That would be but to turn the knife in the wound.' He paused. 'Find something else to occupy your mind. Do as van Manderpootz does. Find forgetfulness in work.'

'Yes,' I responded dully. 'But who'd want to read my autobiography? That's all right for you.'

'Autobiography? Oh! I remember. No, I have abandoned that. History itself will record the life and works of van Manderpootz. Now I am engaged in a far grander project.'

'Indeed?' I was utterly, gloomily disinterested.

'Yes. Gogli has been here, Gogli the sculptor. He is to make a bust of me. What better legacy can I leave to the world than a bust of van Manderpootz, sculptured from life? Perhaps I shall present it to the city, perhaps to the university. I would have given it to the Royal Society if they had been a little more receptive, if they – if – *if*!' The last in a shout.

'Huh?'

'*If!*' cried van Manderpootz. 'What you saw in the subjunctivisor was what would have happened if you had caught the ship!'

'I know that.'

'But something quite different might really have happened! Don't you see? She – she – Where are those old newspapers?'

He was pawing through a pile of them. He flourished one finally. 'Here! Here are the survivors!'

Like letters of flame, Joanna Caldwell's name leaped out at me. There was even a little paragraph about it, as I saw once my reeling brain permitted me to read.

> At least a score of survivors owe their lives to the bravery of twenty-eight-year-old Navigator Orris Hope, who patrolled both aisles during the panic, lacing lifebelts on the injured and helpless, and carrying many to the port. He remained on the sinking liner until the last, finally fighting his way to the surface through the broken walls of the observation room. Among those who owe their lives to the young officer are: Patrick Owensby. New York City; Mrs Campbell Warren, Boston; Miss Joanna Caldwell, New York City –

I suppose my shout of joy was heard over in the Administration Building, blocks away. I didn't care; if van Manderpootz hadn't been armored in stubby whiskers, I'd have kissed him. Perhaps I did anyway; I can't be sure of my actions during those chaotic minutes in the professor's tiny office.

At last I calmed. 'I can look her up!' I gloated. 'She must have landed with the other survivors, and they were all on that British tramp freighter the *Osgood*, that docked here last week. She must be in New York – and if she's gone over to Paris, I'll find out and follow her!'

Well, it's a queer ending. She was in New York, but – you see, Dixon Wells had, so to speak, known Joanna Caldwell by means of the professor's subjunctivisor, but Joanna had never known Dixon Wells. What the ending might have been if – *if* – but it wasn't; she had married Orris Hope, the young officer who had rescued her. I was late again.

The Mad Moon

Stanley G. Weinbaum

'Idiots!' howled Grant Calthorpe. 'Fools – nitwits – imbeciles!' He sought wildly for some more expressive terms, failed and vented his exasperation in a vicious kick at the pile of rubbish on the ground.

Too vicious a kick, in fact; he had again forgotten the one-third normal gravitation of Io, and his whole body followed his kick in a long, twelve-foot arc.

As he struck the ground the four loonies giggled. Their great, idiotic heads, looking like nothing so much as the comic faces painted on Sunday balloons for children, swayed in unison on their five-foot necks, as thin as Grant's wrist.

'Get out!' he blazed, scrambling erect. 'Beat it, skiddoo, scram! No chocolate. No candy. Not until you learn that I want ferva leaves, and not any junk you happen to grab. Clear out!'

The loonies – *Lunae Jovis Magnicapites*, or literally, Bigheads of Jupiter's Moon – backed away, giggling plaintively. Beyond doubt, they considered Grant fully as idiotic as he considered them, and were quite unable to understand the reasons for his anger. But they certainly realized that no candy was to be forthcoming, and their giggles took on a note of keen disappointment.

So keen, indeed, that the leader, after twisting his ridiculous blue face in an imbecilic grin at Grant, voiced a last wild giggle and dashed his head against a glittering stone-bark tree. His companions casually picked up his body and moved off, with his head dragging behind them on its neck like a prisoner's ball on a chain.

Grant brushed his hand across his forehead and turned wearily toward his stone-bark log shack. A pair of tiny, glittering red eyes caught his attention, and a slinker – *Mus Sapiens* – skipped his six-inch form across the threshold, bearing under his tiny, skinny arm what looked very much like Grant's clinical thermometer.

Grant yelled angrily at the creature, seized a stone, and flung it vainly. At the edge of the brush, the slinker turned its ratlike, semi-human face toward him, squeaked its thin gibberish, shook a microscopic fist in manlike wrath, and vanished, its batlike cowl of skin fluttering like a cloak. It looked, indeed, very much like a black rat wearing a cape.

It had been a mistake, Grant knew, to throw the stone at it. Now the tiny fiends would never permit him any peace, and their diminutive size and pseudo-human intelligence made them infernally troublesome as enemies. Yet, neither that reflection nor the loony's suicide troubled him particularly; he had witnessed instances like the latter too often, and besides, his head felt as if he were in for another siege of white fever.

He entered the shack, closed the door, and stared down at his pet parcat. 'Oliver,' he growled, 'you're a fine one. Why the devil don't you watch out for slinkers? What are you here for?'

The parcat rose on its single, powerful hind leg, clawing at his knees with its two forelegs. 'The red jack on the black queen,' it observed placidly. 'Ten loonies make one half-wit.'

Grant placed both statements easily. The first was, of course, an echo of his preceding evening's solitaire game, and the second of yesterday's session with the loonies. He grunted abstractedly and rubbed his aching head. White fever again, beyond doubt.

He swallowed two ferverin tablets, and sank listlessly to the edge of his bunk, wondering whether this attack of *blancha* would culminate in delirium.

He cursed himself for a fool for ever taking this job on Jupiter's third habitable moon, Io. The tiny world was a planet of madness, good for nothing except the production of ferva leaves, out of which Earthly chemists made as many potent alkaloids as they once made from opium.

Invaluable to medical science, of course, but what difference did that make to him? What difference, even, did the munificent salary make, if he got back to Earth a raving maniac after a year in the equatorial regions of Io? He swore bitterly that when the plane from Junopolis landed next month for his ferva, he'd go back to the polar city with it, even though his contract with Neilan Drug called for a full year, and he'd get no pay if he broke it. What good was money to a lunatic?

The whole little planet was mad – loonies, parcats, slinkers and Grant Calthorpe – all crazy. At least, anybody who ever ventured outside either of the two polar cities, Junopolis on the north and Herapolis on the south, was crazy. One could live there in safety from white fever, but anywhere below the twentieth parallel it was worse than the Cambodian jungles on Earth.

He amused himself by dreaming of Earth. Just two years ago he had been happy there, known as a wealthy, popular sportsman. He had been just that too; before he was twenty-one he had hunted knife-kite and threadworm on Titan, and *triops* and uniped on Venus.

That had been before the gold crisis of 2110 had wiped out his fortune. And – well, if he had to work, it had seemed logical to use his interplanetary experience as a means of livelihood. He had really been enthusiastic at the chance to associate himself with Neilan Drug.

He had never been on Io before. This wild little world was no sportsman's paradise, with its idiotic loonies and wicked, intelligent, tiny slinkers. There wasn't anything worth hunting on the feverish little moon, bathed in warmth by the giant Jupiter only a quarter million miles away.

If he *had* happened to visit it, he told himself ruefully, he'd never have taken the job; he had visualized Io as something like Titan, cold but clean.

Instead it was as hot as the Venus Hotlands because of its glowing primary, and subject to half a dozen different forms of steamy daylight – sun day, Jovian day, Jovian and sun day, Europa light, and occasionally actual and dismal night. And most of these came in the course of Io's forty-two-hour revolution, too – a mad succession of changing lights. He hated the dizzy days, the jungle, and Idiots' Hills stretching behind his shack.

It was Jovian and solar day at the present moment, and that was the worst of all, because the distant sun added its modicum of heat to that of Jupiter. And to complete Grant's discomfort now was the prospect of a white fever attack. He swore as his head gave an additional twinge, and then swallowed another ferverin tablet. His supply of these was diminishing, he noticed; he'd have to remember to ask for some when the plane called – no, he was going back with it.

Oliver rubbed against his leg. 'Idiots, fools, nitwits, imbeciles,' remarked the parcat affectionately. 'Why did I have to go to that damn dance?'

'Huh?' said Grant. He couldn't remember having said anything about a dance. It must, he decided, have been said during his last fever madness.

Oliver creaked like the door, then giggled like a loony. 'It'll be all right,' he assured Grant. 'Father is bound to come soon.'

'Father!' echoed the man. His father had died fifteen years before. 'Where'd you get that from, Oliver?'

'It must be the fever,' observed Oliver placidly. 'You're a nice kitty, but I wish you had sense enough to know what you're saying. And I wish father would come.' He finished with a suppressed gurgle that might have been a sob.

Grant stared dizzily at him. He hadn't said any of those things; he was positive. The parcat must have heard them from somebody else – Somebody else? Where within five hundred miles was there anybody else?

'Oliver!' he bellowed. 'Where'd you hear that? Where'd you hear it?'

The parcat backed away, startled. 'Father is idiots, fools, nitwits, imbeciles,' he said anxiously. 'The red jack on the nice kitty.'

'Come here!' roared Grant. 'Whose father? Where have you – Come here, you imp!'

He lunged at the creature. Oliver flexed his single hind leg and flung himself frantically to the cowl of the wood stove. 'It must be the fever!' he squalled. 'No chocolate!'

He leaped like a three-legged flash for the flue opening. There came a sound of claws grating on metal, and then he had scrambled through.

Grant followed him. His head ached from the effort, and with the still sane part of his mind he knew that the whole episode was doubtless white fever delirium, but he plowed on.

His progress was a nightmare. Loonies kept bobbing their long necks above the tall bleeding-grass, their idiotic giggles and imbecilic faces adding to the general atmosphere of madness.

Wisps of fetid, fever-bearing vapors spouted up at every step on the spongy soil. Somewhere to his right a slinker squeaked and gibbered; he knew that a tiny slinker village was over in that direction, for once he had glimpsed the neat little buildings, constructed of small, perfectly fitted stones like a miniature medieval town, complete to towers and battlements. It was said that there were even slinker wars.

His head buzzed and whirled from the combined effects of ferverin and fever. It was an attack of *blancha*, right enough, and he realized that he was an imbecile, a loony, to wander thus away from his shack. He should be lying on his bunk; the fever was not serious, but more than one man had died on Io, in the delirium, with its attendant hallucinations.

He was delirious now. He knew it as soon as he saw Oliver, for Oliver was placidly regarding an attractive young lady in perfect evening dress of the style of the second decade of the twenty-second century. Very obviously that was a hallucination, since girls had no business in the Ionian tropics, and if by some wild chance one should appear there, she would certainly not choose formal garb.

The hallucination had fever, apparently, for her face was pale with the whiteness that gave *blancha* its name. Her gray eyes regarded him without surprise as he wound his way through the bleeding-grass to her.

'Good afternoon, evening, or morning,' he remarked, giving a puzzled glance at Jupiter, which was rising, and the sun, which was setting. 'Or perhaps merely good day, Miss Lee Neilan.'

She gazed seriously at him. 'Do you know,' she said, 'you're the first one of the illusions that I haven't recognized? All my friends have been around, but you're the first stranger. Or are you a stranger? You know my name – but you ought to, of course, being my own hallucination.'

'We won't argue about which of us is the hallucination,' he suggested. 'Let's do it this way. The one of us that disappears first is the illusion. Bet you five dollars you do.'

'How could I collect?' she said. 'I can't very well collect from my own dream.'

'That is a problem.' He frowned. 'My problem, of course, not yours. I know I'm real.'

'How do you know my name?' she demanded.

'Ah!' he said. 'From intensive reading of the society sections of the newspapers brought by my supply plane. As a matter of fact, I have one of your pictures cut out and pasted next to my bunk. That probably accounts for my seeing you now. I'd like to really meet you some time.'

'What a gallant remark for an apparition!' she exclaimed. 'And who are you supposed to be?'

'Why, I'm Grant Calthorpe. In fact, I work for your father, trading with the loonies for ferva.'

'Grant Calthorpe,' she echoed. She narrowed her fever-dulled eyes as if to bring him into better focus. 'Why, you are!'

Her voice wavered for a moment, and she brushed her hand across her pale brow. 'Why should you pop out of my memories? It's strange. Three or four years ago, when I was a romantic schoolgirl and you the famous sportsman, I was madly in love with you. I had a whole book filled with your pictures – Grant Calthorpe dressed in parka for hunting thread-worms on Titan – Grant Calthorpe beside the giant uniped he killed near the Mountains of Eternity. You're – you're really the pleasantest hallucination I've had so far. Delirium would be – fun' – she pressed her hand to her brow again – 'if one's head – didn't ache so!'

'Gee!' thought Grant, 'I wish that were true, that about the book. This is what psychology calls a wish-fulfillment dream.' A drop of warm rain plopped on his neck. 'Got to get to bed,' he said aloud. 'Rain's bad for *blancha*. Hope to see you next time I'm feverish.'

'Thank you,' said Lee Neilan with dignity. 'It's quite mutual.'

He nodded, sending a twinge through his head. 'Here, Oliver,' he said to the drowsing parcat. 'Come on.'

'That isn't Oliver,' said Lee. 'It's Polly. It's kept me company for two days, and I've named it Polly.'

'Wrong gender,' muttered Grant. 'Anyway, it's my parcat, Oliver. Aren't you Oliver?'

'Hope to see you,' said Oliver sleepily.

'It's Polly. Aren't you, Polly?'

'Bet you five dollars,' said the parcat. He rose, stretched and loped off into the underbrush. 'It must be the fever,' he observed as he vanished.

'It must be,' agreed Grant. He turned away. 'Goodbye, Miss – or I might as well call you Lee, since you're not real. Goodbye, Lee.'

'Goodbye, Grant. But don't go that way. There's a slinker village over in the grass.'

'No. It's over there.'

'It's *there*,' she insisted. 'I've been watching them build it. But they can't hurt you anyway, can they? Not even a slinker could hurt an apparition. Goodbye, Grant.' She closed her eyes wearily.

It was raining harder now. Grant pushed his way through the bleeding-grass, whose red sap collected in bloody drops on his boots. He had to get back to his shack quickly, before the white fever and its attendant delirium set him wandering utterly astray. He needed ferverin.

Suddenly he stopped short. Directly before him the grass had been cleared away, and in the little clearing were the shoulder-high towers and battlements of a slinker village – a new one, for half-finished houses stood among the others, and hooded six-inch forms toiled over the stones.

There was an outcry of squeaks and gibberish. He backed away, but a dozen tiny darts whizzed about him. One stuck like a toothpick in his boot, but none, luckily, scratched his skin, for they were undoubtedly poisoned. He moved more quickly, but all around in the thick, fleshy grasses were rustlings, squeakings, and incomprehensible imprecations.

He circled away. Loonies kept popping their balloon heads over the vegetation, and now and again one giggled in pain as a slinker bit or stabbed it. Grant cut toward a group of the creatures, hoping to distract the tiny fiends in the grass, and a tall, purple-faced loony curved its long neck above him, giggling and gesturing with its skinny fingers at a bundle under its arm.

He ignored the thing, and veered toward his shack. He seemed to have eluded the slinkers, so he trudged doggedly on, for he needed a ferverin tablet badly. Yet, suddenly he came to a frowning halt, turned, and began to retrace his steps.

'It can't be so,' he muttered. 'But she told me the truth about the slinker village. I didn't know it was there. Yet how could a hallucination tell me something I didn't know?'

Lee Neilan was sitting on the stone-bark log exactly as he had left her with Oliver again at her side. Her eyes were closed, and two slinkers were cutting at the long skirt of her gown with tiny, glittering knives.

Grant knew that they were always attracted by Terrestrial textiles; apparently they were unable to duplicate the fascinating sheen of satin, though the fiends were infernally clever with their tiny hands. As he approached, they tore a strip from thigh to ankle, but the girl made no move. Grant shouted, and the vicious little creatures mouthed unutterable curses at him, as they skittered away with their silken plunder.

Lee Neilan opened her eyes. 'You again,' she murmured vaguely. 'A moment ago it was father. Now it's you.' Her pallor had increased; the white fever was running its course in her body.

'Your father! Then that's where Oliver heard – Listen, Lee. I found the slinker village. I didn't know it was there, but I found it just as you said. Do you see what that means? We're both real!'

'Real?' she said dully. 'There's a purple loony grinning over your shoulder. Make him go away. He makes me feel – sick.'

He glanced around; true enough, the purple-faced loony was behind him. 'Look here,' he said, seizing her arm. The feel of her smooth skin was added proof. 'You're coming to the shack for ferverin.' He pulled her to her feet. 'Don't you understand? I'm real!'

'No, you're not,' she said dazedly.

'Listen, Lee. I don't know how in the devil you got here or why, but I know Io hasn't driven me that crazy yet. You're real and I'm real.' He shook her violently. 'I'm *real*!' he shouted.

Faint comprehension showed in her dazed eyes. 'Real?' she whispered. 'Real! Oh, Lord! Then take – me out of this mad place!' She swayed, made a stubborn effort to control herself, then pitched forward against him.

Of course on Io her weight was negligible, less than a third Earth normal. He swung her into his arms and set off toward the shack, keeping well away from both slinker settlements. Around him bobbed excited loonies, and now and again the purple-faced one, or another exactly like him, giggled and pointed and gestured.

The rain had increased, and warm rivulets flowed down his neck, and to add to the madness, he blundered near a copse of stinging palms, and their barbed lashes stung painfully through his shirt. Those stings were virulent too, if one failed to disinfect them; indeed, it was largely the stinging palms that kept traders from gathering their own ferva instead of depending on the loonies.

Behind the low rain clouds, the sun had set and it was ruddy Jupiter daylight, which lent a false flush to the cheeks of the unconscious Lee Neilan, making her still features very lovely.

Perhaps he kept his eyes too steadily on her face, for suddenly Grant was among slinkers again; they were squeaking and sputtering, and the purple loony leaped in pain as teeth and darts pricked his legs. But, of course, loonies were immune to the poison.

The tiny devils were around his feet now. He swore in a low voice and kicked vigorously, sending a ratlike form spinning fifty feet in the air. He had both automatic and flame pistol at his hip, but he could not use them for several reasons.

First, using an automatic against the tiny hordes was much like firing into a swarm of mosquitoes; if the bullet killed one or two or a dozen, it made no appreciable impression on the remaining thousands. And as for the flame pistol, that was like using a Big Bertha to swat a fly. Its vast belch of fire would certainly incinerate all the slinkers in its immediate path, along with grass, trees, and loonies, but that again would make but little impress on the surviving hordes, and it meant laboriously recharging the pistol with another black diamond and another barrel.

He had gas bulbs in the shack, but they were not available at the moment, and besides, he had no spare mask, and no chemist has yet succeeded in devising a gas that would kill slinkers without being also deadly to humans. And, finally, he couldn't use any weapon whatsoever right now, because he dared not drop Lee Neilan to free his hands.

Ahead was the clearing around the shack. The space was full of slinkers, but the shack itself was supposed to be slinkerproof, at least for reasonable lengths of time, since stone-bark logs were very resistant to their tiny tools.

But Grant perceived that a group of the diminutive devils were around the door, and suddenly he realized their intent. They had looped a cord of some sort over the knob, and were engaged now in twisting it!

Grant yelled and broke into a run. While he was yet half a hundred feet distant, the door swung inward and the rabble of slinkers flowed into the shack.

He dashed through the entrance. Within was turmoil. Little hooded shapes were cutting at the blankets on his bunk, his extra clothing, the sacks he hoped to fill with ferva leaves, and were pulling at the cooking utensils, or at any and all loose objects.

He bellowed and kicked at the swarm. A wild chorus of squeaks and gibberish arose as the creatures skipped and dodged about him. The fiends were intelligent enough to realize that he could do nothing with his arms occupied by Lee Neilan. They skittered out of the way of his kicks, and while he threatened a group at the stove, another rabble tore at his blankets.

In desperation he charged the bunk. He swept the girl's body across it to clear it, dropped her on it, and seized a grass broom he had made to facilitate his housekeeping. With wide strokes of its handle he attacked the slinkers, and the squeals were checkered by cries and whimpers of pain.

A few broke for the door, dragging whatever loot they had. He spun around in time to see half a dozen swarming around Lee Neilan, tearing at her clothing, at the wrist watch on her arm, at the satin evening pumps on her small feet. He roared a curse at them and battered them away, hoping that none had pricked her skin with virulent dagger or poisonous tooth.

He began to win the skirmish. More of the creatures drew their black capes close about them and scurried over the threshold with their plunder. At last, with a burst of squeaks, the remainder, laden and empty-handed alike, broke and ran for safety, leaving a dozen furry, impish bodies slain or wounded.

Grant swept these after the others with his erstwhile weapon, closed the door in the face of a loony that bobbed in the opening, latched it against any repetition of the slinker's trick, and stared in dismay about the plundered dwelling.

Cans had been rolled or dragged away. Every loose object had been pawed by the slinkers' foul little hands, and Grant's clothes hung in ruins on their hooks against the wall. But the tiny robbers had not succeeded in opening the cabinet nor the table drawer, and there was food left.

Six months of Ionian life had left him philosophical; he swore heartily, shrugged resignedly, and pulled his bottle of ferverin from the cabinet.

His own spell of fever had vanished as suddenly and completely as *blancha* always does when treated, but the girl, lacking ferverin, was paper-white and still. Grant glanced at the bottle; eight tablets remained.

'Well, I can always chew ferva leaves,' he muttered. That was less effective than the alkaloid itself, but it would serve, and Lee Neilan needed the tablets. He dissolved two of them in a glass of water, and lifted her head.

She was not too inert to swallow, and he poured the solution between her pale lips, then arranged her as comfortably as he could. Her dress was a tattered silken ruin, and he covered her with a blanket that was no less a ruin. Then he disinfected his palm stings, pulled two chairs together, and sprawled across them to sleep.

He started up at the sound of claws on the roof, but it was only Oliver, gingerly testing the flue to see if it were hot. In a moment the parcat scrambled through, stretched himself, and remarked, 'I'm real and you're real.'

'Imagine that!' grunted Grant sleepily.

When he awoke it was Jupiter and Europa light, which meant he had slept about seven hours, since the brilliant little third moon was just rising. He rose and gazed at Lee Neilan, who was sleeping soundly with a tinge of color in her face that was not entirely due to the ruddy daylight. The *blancha* was passing.

He dissolved two more tablets in water, then shook the girl's shoulder. Instantly her gray eyes opened, quite clear now, and she looked up at him without surprise. 'Hello, Grant,' she murmured. 'So it's you again. Fever isn't so bad, after all.'

'Maybe I ought to let you stay feverish,' he grinned. 'You say such nice things. Wake up and drink this, Lee.'

She became suddenly aware of the shack's interior. 'Why – Where is this? It looks – real!'

'It is. Drink this ferverin.'

She obeyed, then lay back and stared at him perplexedly. 'Real?' she said. 'And you're real?'

'I think I am.'

A rush of tears clouded her eyes. 'Then – I'm out of that place? That horrible place?'

'You certainly are.' He saw signs of her relief becoming hysteria, and hastened to distract her. 'Would you mind telling me how you happened to be there – and dressed for a party too?'

She controlled herself. 'I was dressed for a party. A party. A party in Herapolis. But I was in Junopolis, you see.'

'I don't see. In the first place, what are you doing on Io, anyway? Every time I ever heard of you, it was in connection with New York or Paris society.'

She smiled. 'Then it wasn't all delirium, was it? You did say that you had one of my pictures – Oh, that one!' She frowned at the print on the wall. 'Next time a news photographer wants to snap my picture, I'll remember not to grin like – like a loony. But as to how I happen to be on Io, I came with father, who's looking over the possibilities of raising ferva on plantations instead of having to depend on traders and loonies. We've been here three months, and I've been terribly bored. I thought Io would be exciting, but it wasn't – until recently.'

'But what about that dance? How'd you manage to get here, a thousand miles from Junopolis?'

'Well,' she said slowly, 'it was terribly tiresome in Junopolis. No shows, no sport, nothing but an occasional dance. I got restless. When there were dances in Herapolis, I formed the habit of flying over there. It's only four or five hours in a fast plane, you know. And last week – or whatever it was – I'd planned on flying down, and Harvey – that's father's secretary – was to take me. But at the last minute father needed him and forbade my flying alone.'

Grant felt a strong dislike for Harvey. 'Well?' he asked.

'So I flew alone,' she finished demurely.

'And cracked up, eh?'

'I can fly as well as anybody,' she retorted. 'It was just that I followed a different route, and suddenly there were mountains ahead.'

He nodded. 'The Idiots' Hills,' he said. 'My supply plane detours five hundred miles to avoid them. They're not high, but they stick right out above the atmosphere of this crazy planet. The air here is dense but shallow.'

'I know that. I knew I couldn't fly above them, but I thought I could hurdle them. Work up full speed, you know, and then throw the plane upward. I had a closed plane, and gravitation is so weak here. And besides, I've seen it done several times, especially with a rocket-driven craft. The jets help to support the plane even after the wings are useless for lack of air.'

'What a damn fool stunt!' exclaimed Grant. 'Sure it can be done, but you have to be an expert to pull out of it when you hit the air on the other side. You hit fast, and there isn't much falling room.'

'So I found out,' said Lee ruefully. 'I almost pulled out, but not quite, and I hit in the middle of some stinging palms. I guess the crash dazed them, because I managed to get out before they started lashing around. But I couldn't reach my plane again, and it was – I only remember two days of it – but it was horrible!'

'It must have been,' he said gently.

'I knew that if I didn't eat or drink, I had a chance of avoiding white fever. The not eating wasn't so bad, but the not drinking – well, I finally gave up and drank out of a brook. I didn't care what happened if I could have a few moments that weren't thirst-tortured. And after that it's all confused and vague.'

'You should have chewed ferva leaves.'

'I didn't know that. I wouldn't have even known what they looked like, and besides, I kept expecting father to appear. He must be having a search made by now.'

'He probably is,' rejoined Grant ironically. 'Has it occurred to you that there are thirteen million square miles of surface on little Io? And that for all he knows, you might have crashed on any square mile of it? When you're flying from north pole to south pole, there *isn't* any shortest route. You can cross any point on the planet.'

Her gray eyes started wide. 'But I – '

'Furthermore,' said Grant, 'this is probably the *last* place a searching party would look. They wouldn't think anyone but a loony would try to hurdle Idiots' Hills, in which thesis I quite agree. So it looks very much, Lee Neilan, as if you're marooned here until my supply plane gets here next month!'

'But father will be crazy! He'll think I'm dead!'

'He thinks that now, no doubt.'

'But we can't – ' She broke off, staring around the tiny shack's single room. After a moment she sighed resignedly, smiled, and said softly, 'Well, it might have been worse, Grant. I'll try to earn my keep.'

'Good. How do you feel, Lee?'

'Quite normal. I'll start right to work.' She flung off the tattered blanket, sat up, and dropped her feet to the floor. 'I'll fix dinn– Good night! My dress!' She snatched the blanket about her again.

He grinned. 'We had a little run-in with the slinkers after you had passed out. They did for my spare wardrobe too.'

'It's ruined!' she wailed.

'Would needle and thread help? They left that, at least, because it was in the table drawer.'

'Why, I couldn't make a good swimming suit out of this!' she retorted. 'Let me try one of yours.'

By dint of cutting, patching, and mending, she at last managed to piece one of Grant's suits to respectable proportions. She looked very lovely in shirt and trousers, but he was troubled to note that a sudden pallor had overtaken her.

It was the *riblancha*, the second spell of fever that usually followed a severe or prolonged attack. His face was serious as he cupped two of his last four ferverin tablets in his hand.

'Take these,' he ordered. 'And we've got to get some ferva leaves somewhere. The plane took my supply away last week, and I've had bad luck with my loonies ever since. They haven't brought me anything but weeds and rubbish.'

Lee puckered her lips at the bitterness of the drug, then closed her eyes against its momentary dizziness and nausea. 'Where can you find ferva?' she asked.

He shook his head perplexedly, glancing out at the setting mass of Jupiter, with its bands glowing creamy and brown, and the Red Spot boiling near the western edge. Close above it was the brilliant little disk of Europa. He frowned suddenly, glanced at his watch and then at the almanac on the inside of the cabinet door.

'It'll be Europa light in fifteen minutes,' he muttered, 'and true night in twenty-five – the first true night in half a month. I wonder – '

He gazed thoughtfully at Lee's face. He knew where ferva grew. One dared not penetrate the jungle itself, where stinging palms and arrow vines and the deadly worms called toothers made such a venture sheer suicide for any creatures but loonies and slinkers. But he knew where ferva grew –

In Io's rare true night even the clearing might be dangerous. Not merely from slinkers, either; he knew well enough that in the darkness creatures crept out of the jungle who otherwise remained in the eternal shadows of its depths – toothers, bullet-head frogs, and doubtless many unknown slimy, venomous, mysterious beings never seen by man. One heard stories in Herapolis and –

But he had to get ferva, and he knew where it grew. Not even a loony would try to gather it there, but in the little gardens or farms around the tiny slinker towns, there was ferva growing.

He switched on a light in the gathering dusk. 'I'm going outside a moment,' he told Lee Neilan. 'If the *blancha* starts coming back, take the other two tablets. Wouldn't hurt you to take 'em anyway. The slinkers got away with my thermometer, but if you get dizzy again, you take 'em.'

'Grant! Where – '

'I'll be back,' he called, closing the door behind him.

A loony, purple in the bluish Europa light, bobbed up with a long giggle. He waved the creature aside and set off on a cautious approach to the neighborhood of the slinker village – the old one, for the other could hardly have had time to cultivate its surrounding ground. He crept warily through the bleeding-grass, but he knew his stealth was pure optimism. He was in exactly the position of a hundred-foot giant trying to approach a human city in secrecy – a difficult matter even in the utter darkness of night.

He reached the edge of the slinker clearing. Behind him, Europa, moving as fast as the second hand on his watch, plummeted toward the horizon. He paused in momentary surprise at the sight of the exquisite little town, a hundred feet away across the tiny square fields, with lights flickering in its hand-wide windows. He had not known that slinker culture included the use of lights, but there they were, tiny candles or perhaps diminutive oil lamps.

He blinked in the darkness. The second of the ten-foot fields looked like – it was – ferva. He stooped low, crept out, and reached his hand for the fleshy, white leaves. And at that moment came a shrill giggle and the crackle of grass behind him. The loony! The idiotic purple loony!

Squeaking shrieks sounded. He snatched a double handful of ferva, rose, and dashed toward the lighted window of his shack. He had no wish to face poisoned barbs or disease-bearing teeth, and the slinkers were certainly aroused. Their gibbering sounded in chorus; the ground looked black with them.

He reached the shack, burst in, slammed and latched the door. 'Got it!' he grinned. 'Let 'em rave outside now.'

They were raving. Their gibberish sounded like the creaking of worn machinery. Even Oliver opened his drowsy eyes to listen. 'It must be the fever,' observed the parcat placidly.

Lee was certainly no paler; the *riblancha* was passing safely. 'Ugh!' she said, listening to the tumult without. 'I've always hated rats, but slinkers are worse. All the shrewdness and viciousness of rats plus the intelligence of devils.'

'Well,' said Grant thoughtfully, 'I don't see what they can do. They've had it in for me anyway.'

'It sounds as if they're going off,' said the girl, listening. 'The noise is fading.'

Grant peered out of the window. 'They're still around. They've just passed from swearing to planning, and I wish I knew what. Some day, if this crazy little planet ever becomes worth human occupation, there's going to be a showdown between humans and slinkers.'

'Well? They're not civilized enough to be really a serious obstacle, and they're so small, besides.'

'But they learn,' he said. 'They learn so quickly, and they breed like flies. Suppose they pick up the use of gas, or suppose they develop little rifles for their poisonous darts. That's possible, because they work in metals right now, and they know fire. That would put them practically on a par with man as far as offense goes, for what good are our giant cannons and rocket planes against six-inch slinkers? And to be just on even terms would be fatal; one slinker for one man would be a hell of a trade.'

Lee yawned. 'Well, it's not our problem. I'm hungry, Grant.'

'Good. That's a sign the *blancha*'s through with you. We'll eat and then sleep a while, for there's five hours of darkness.'

'But the slinkers?'

'I don't see what they can do. They couldn't cut through stone-bark walls in five hours, and anyway, Oliver would warn us if one managed to slip in somewhere.'

It was light when Grant awoke, and he stretched his cramped limbs painfully across his two chairs. Something had wakened him, but he didn't know just what. Oliver was pacing nervously beside him, and now looked anxiously up at him.

'I've had bad luck with my loonies,' announced the parcat plaintively. 'You're a nice kitty.'

'So are you,' said Grant. Something had wakened him, but what?

Then he knew, for it came again – the merest trembling of the stone-bark floor. He frowned in puzzlement. Earthquakes? Not on Io, for the tiny sphere had lost its internal heat untold ages ago. Then what?

Comprehension dawned suddenly. He sprang to his feet with so wild a yell that Oliver scrambled sideways with an infernal babble. The startled parcat leaped to the stove and vanished up the flue. His squall drifted faintly back.

'It must be the fever!'

Lee had started to a sitting position on the bunk, her gray eyes blinking sleepily.

'Outside!' he roared, pulling her to her feet. 'Get out! Quickly!'

'Wh-what – why –'

'Get out!' He thrust her through the door, then spun to seize his belt and weapons, the bag of ferva leaves, a package of chocolate. The floor trembled again, and he burst out of the door with a frantic leap to the side of the dazed girl.

'They've undermined it!' he choked. 'The devils undermined the –'

He had no time to say more. A corner of the shack suddenly subsided; the stone-bark logs grated, and the whole structure collapsed like a child's house of blocks. The crash died into silence, and there was no motion save a lazy wisp of vapor, a few black, ratlike forms scurrying toward the grass, and a purple loony bobbing beyond the ruins.

'The dirty devils!' he swore bitterly. 'The damn little black rats! The –'

A dart whistled so close that it grazed his ear and then twitched a lock of Lee's tousled brown hair. A chorus of squeaking sounded in the bleeding-grass.

'Come on!' he cried. 'They're out to exterminate us this time. No – this way. Toward the hills. There's less jungle this way.'

They could outrun the tiny slinkers easily enough. In a few moments they had lost the sound of squeaking voices, and they stopped to gaze ruefully back on the fallen dwelling.

'Now,' he said miserably, 'we're both where you were to start with.'

'Oh, no.' Lee looked up at him. 'We're together now, Grant. I'm not afraid.'

'We'll manage,' he said with a show of assurance. 'We'll put up a temporary shack somehow. We'll – '

A dart struck his boot with a sharp *blup*. The slinkers had caught up to them.

Again they ran toward Idiots' Hills. When at last they stopped, they could look down a long slope and far over the Ionian jungles. There was the ruined shack, and there, neatly checkered, the fields and towers of the nearer slinker town. But they had scarcely caught their breath when gibbering and squeaking came out of the brush.

They were being driven into Idiots' Hills, a region as unknown to man as the icy wastes of Pluto. It was as if the tiny fiends behind them had determined that this time their enemy, the giant trampler and despoiler of their fields, should be pursued to extinction.

Weapons were useless. Grant could not even glimpse their pursuers, slipping like hooded rats through the vegetation. A bullet, even if chance sped it through a slinker's body, was futile, and his flame pistol, though its lightning stroke should incinerate tons of brush and bleeding-grass, could no more than cut a narrow path through the horde of tormentors. The only weapons that might have availed, the gas bulbs, were lost in the ruins of the shack.

Grant and Lee were forced upward. They had risen a thousand feet above the plain, and the air was thinning. There was no jungle here, but only great stretches of bleeding-grass, across which a few loonies were visible, bobbing their heads on their long necks.

'Toward – the peaks!' gasped Grant, now painfully short of breath. 'Perhaps we can stand rarer air than they.'

Lee was beyond answer. She panted doggedly along beside him as they plodded now over patches of bare rock. Before them were two low peaks, like the pillars of a gate. Glancing back, Grant caught a glimpse of tiny black forms on a clear area, and in sheer anger he fired a shot. A single slinker leaped convulsively, its cape flapping, but the rest flowed on. There must have been thousands of them.

The peaks were closer, no more than a few hundred yards away. They were sheer, smooth, unscalable.

'Between them,' muttered Grant.

The passage that separated them was bare and narrow. The twin peaks had been one in ages past; some forgotten volcanic convulsion had split them, leaving this slender canyon between.

He slipped an arm about Lee, whose breath, from effort and altitude, was a series of rasping gasps. A bright dart tinkled on the rocks as they reached the opening, but looking back, Grant could see only a purple loony plodding upward, and a few more to his right. They raced down a straight fifty-foot passage that debouched suddenly into a sizable valley – and there, thunderstruck for a moment, they paused.

A city lay there. For a brief instant Grant thought they had burst upon a vast slinker metropolis, but the merest glance showed otherwise. This was no city of medieval blocks, but a poem in marble, classical in beauty, and of human or near-human proportions. White columns, glorious arches, pure curving domes, an architectural loveliness that might have been born on the Acropolis. It took a second look to discern that the city was dead, deserted, in ruins.

Even in her exhaustion, Lee felt its beauty. 'How – how exquisite!' she panted. 'One could almost forgive them – for being – slinkers!'

'They won't forgive us for being human,' he muttered. 'We'll have to make a stand somewhere. We'd better pick a building.'

But before they could move more than a few feet from the canyon mouth, a wild disturbance halted them. Grant whirled, and for a moment found himself actually paralyzed by amazement. The narrow canyon was filled with a gibbering horde of slinkers, like a nauseous, heaving black carpet. But they came no further than the valley end, for grinning, giggling, and bobbing, blocking the opening with tramping three-toed feet, were four loonies!

It was a battle. The slinkers were biting and stabbing at the miserable defenders, whose shrill keenings of pain were less giggles than shrieks. But with a determination and purpose utterly foreign to loonies, their clawed feet tramped methodically up and down, up and down.

Grant exploded, 'I'll be damned!' Then an idea struck him. 'Lee! They're packed in the canyon, the whole devil's brood of 'em!'

He rushed toward the opening. He thrust his flame pistol between the skinny legs of a loony, aimed it straight along the canyon, and fired.

Inferno burst. The tiny diamond, giving up all its energy in one terrific blast, shot a jagged stream of fire that filled the canyon from wall to wall and vomited out beyond to cut a fan of fire through the bleeding-grass of the slope.

Idiots' Hills reverberated to the roar, and when the rain of débris settled, there was nothing in the canyon save a few bits of flesh and the head of an unfortunate loony, still bouncing and rolling.

Three of the loonies survived. A purple-faced one was pulling his arm, grinning and giggling in imbecile glee. He waved the thing aside and returned to the girl.

'Thank goodness!' he said. 'We're out of that, anyway.'

'I wasn't afraid, Grant. Not with you.'

He smiled. 'Perhaps we can find a place here,' he suggested. 'The fever ought to be less troublesome at this altitude. But – say, this must have been the capital city of the whole slinker race in ancient times. I can scarcely imagine those fiends creating an architecture as beautiful as this – or as large. Why, these buildings are as colossal in proportion to slinker size as the skyscrapers of New York to us!'

'But so beautiful,' said Lee softly, sweeping her eyes over the glory of the ruins. 'One might almost forgive – Grant! Look at those!'

He followed the gesture. On the inner side of the canyon's portals were gigantic carvings. But the thing that set him staring in amazement was the subject of the portrayal. There, towering far up the cliff sides, were the figures, not of slinkers, but of – loonies! Exquisitely carved, smiling rather than grinning, and smiling somehow sadly, regretfully, pityingly – yet beyond doubt, loonies!

'Good night!' he whispered. 'Do you see, Lee? This must once have been a loony city. The steps, the doors, the buildings, all are on their scale of size. Somehow, some time, they must have achieved civilization, and the loonies we know are the degenerate residue of a great race.'

'And,' put in Lee, 'the reason those four blocked the way when the slinkers tried to come through is that they still remember. Or probably they don't actually remember, but they have a tradition of past glories, or more likely still, just a superstitious feeling that this place is in some way sacred. They let us pass because, after all, we look more like loonies than like slinkers. But the amazing thing is that they still possess even that dim memory, because this city must have been in ruins for centuries. Or perhaps even for thousands of years.'

'But to think that loonies could ever have had the intelligence to create a culture of their own,' said Grant, waving away the purple one bobbing and giggling at his side. Suddenly he paused, turning a gaze of new respect on the creature. 'This one's been following me for days. All right, old chap, what is it?'

The purple one extended a sorely bedraggled bundle of bleeding-grass and twigs, giggling idiotically. His ridiculous mouth twisted; his eyes popped in an agony of effort at mental concentration.

'Canny!' he giggled triumphantly.

'The imbecile!' flared Grant. 'Nitwit! Idiot!' He broke off, then laughed. 'Never mind. I guess you deserve it.' He tossed his package of chocolate to the three delighted loonies. 'Here's your candy.'

A scream from Lee startled him. She was waving her arms wildly, and over the crest of Idiots' Hills a rocket plane roared, circled, and nosed its way into the valley.

The door opened. Oliver stalked gravely out, remarking casually. 'I'm real and you're real.' A man followed the parcat – two men.

'Father!' screamed Lee.

It was some time later that Gustavus Neilan turned to Grant. 'I can't thank you,' he said. 'If there's ever any way I can show my appreciation for – '

'There is. You can cancel my contract.'

'Oh, you work for me?'

'I'm Grant Calthorpe, one of your traders, and I'm about sick of this crazy planet.'

'Of course, if you wish,' said Neilan. 'If it's a question of pay – '

'You can pay me for the six months I've worked.'

'If you'd care to stay,' said the older man, 'there won't be trading much longer. We've been able to grow ferva near the polar cities, and I prefer plantations to the uncertainties of relying on loonies. If you'd work out your year, we might be able to put you in charge of a plantation by the end of that time.'

Grant met Lee Neilan's gray eyes, and hesitated. 'Thanks,' he said slowly, 'but I'm sick of it.' He smiled at the girl, then turned back to her father. 'Would you mind telling me how you happened to find us? This is the most unlikely place on the planet.'

'That's just the reason,' said Neilan. 'When Lee didn't get back, I thought things over pretty carefully. At last I decided, knowing her as I did, to search the least likely places first. We tried the shores of the Fever Sea, and then the White Desert, and finally Idiots' Hills. We spotted the ruins of a shack, and on the débris was this chap' – he indicated Oliver – 'remarking that Ten loonies make one half-wit.' Well, the half-wit part sounded very much like a reference to my daughter, and we cruised about until the roar of your flame pistol attracted our attention.'

Lee pouted, then turned her serious gray eyes on Grant. 'Do you remember,' she said softly, 'what I told you there in the jungle?'

'I wouldn't even have mentioned that,' he replied. 'I knew you were delirious.'

'But – perhaps I wasn't. Would companionship make it any easier to work out your year? I mean if – for instance – you were to fly back with us to Junopolis and return with a wife?'

'Lee,' he said huskily, 'you know what a difference that would make, though I can't understand why you'd ever dream of it.'

'It must,' suggested Oliver, 'be the fever.'

Redemption Cairn

Stanley G. Weinbaum

Have you ever been flat broke, hungry as the very devil, and yet so down and out that you didn't even care? Looking back now, after a couple of months, it's hard to put it into words, but I think the low point was the evening old Captain Harris Henshaw dropped into my room – my room, that is, until the twenty-four-hour notice to move or pay up expired.

There I sat, Jack Sands, ex-rocket pilot. Yeah, the same Jack Sands you're thinking of, the one who cracked up the Gunderson Europa expedition trying to land at Young's Field, Long Island, in March, 2110. Just a year and a half ago! It seemed like ten and a half. Five hundred idle days. Eighteen months of having your friends look the other way when you happened to pass on the street, partly because they're ashamed to nod to a pilot that's been tagged yellow, and partly because they feel maybe it's kinder to just let you drop out of sight peacefully.

I didn't even look up when a knock sounded on my door, because I knew it could only be the landlady. 'Haven't got it,' I growled. 'I've got a right to stay out my notice.'

'You got a right to make a damn fool of yourself,' said Henshaw's voice. 'Why don't you tell your friends your address?'

'Harris!' I yelled. It was 'Captain' only aboard ship. Then I caught myself. 'What's the matter?' I asked, grinning bitterly. 'Did you crack up, too? Coming to join me on the dust heap, eh?'

'Coming to offer you a job,' he growled.

'Yeah? It must be a swell one, then. Carting sand to fill up the blast pits on a field, huh? And I'm damn near hungry enough to take it – but not quite.'

'It's a piloting job,' said Henshaw quietly.

'Who wants a pilot who's been smeared with yellow paint? What outfit will trust its ships to a coward? Don't you know that Jack Sands is tagged forever?'

'Shut up, Jack,' he said briefly. 'I'm offering you the job as pilot under me on Interplanetary's new Europa expedition.'

I started to burn up then. You see, it was returning from Jupiter's third moon, Europa, that I'd smashed up the Gunderson outfit, and now I got a wild idea that Henshaw was taunting me about that. 'By Heaven!' I screeched, 'if you're trying to be funny – '

But he wasn't. I quieted down when I saw he was serious, and he went on slowly, 'I want a pilot I can trust, Jack. I don't know anything about your cracking up the *Hera*; I was on the Venus run when it happened. All I know is that I can depend on you.'

After a while I began to believe him. When I got over the shock a little, I figured Henshaw was friend enough to be entitled to the facts.

'Listen, Harris,' I said. 'You're taking me on, reputation and all, and it looks to me as if you deserve an explanation. I haven't been whining about the bump I got, and I'm not now. I cracked up Gunderson and his outfit all right, only – ' I hesitated; it's kind of tough to feel that maybe you're squirming in the pinch – 'only my co-pilot, that fellow Kratska, forgot to mention a few things, and mentioned a few others that weren't true. Oh, it was my shift, right enough, but he neglected to tell the investigating committee that I'd stood his shift and my own before it. I'd been on for two long shifts, and this was my short one.'

'Two long ones!' echoed Henshaw. 'You mean you were on sixteen hours before the landing shift?'

'That's what I mean. I'll tell you just what I told the committee, and maybe you'll believe me. They didn't. But when Kratska showed up to relieve me he was hopped. He had a regular hexylamine jag, and he couldn't have piloted a tricycle. So I did the only possible thing to do; I sent him back to sleep it off, and I reported it to Gunderson, but that still left me the job of getting us down.

'It wouldn't have been so bad if it had happened in space, because there isn't much for a pilot to do out there except follow the course laid out by the captain, and maybe dodge a meteor if the alarm buzzes. But I had sixteen solid hours of teetering down through a gravitational field, and by the time my four-hour spell came around I was bleary.'

'I don't wonder,' said the captain. 'Two long shifts!'

Maybe I'd better explain a rocket's pilot system. On short runs like Venus or Mars, a vessel could carry three pilots, and then it's a simple matter of three eight-hour shifts. But on any longer run, because air and weight and fuel and food are all precious, no rocket ever carries more than two pilots.

So a day's run is divided into four shifts, and each pilot has one long spell of eight hours, then four hours off, then four hours on again for his short shift, and then eight hours to sleep. He eats two of his meals right at the control desk, and the third during his short free period. It's a queer life, and sometimes men have been co-pilots for years without really seeing each other except at the beginning and the end of their run.

I went on with my story, still wondering whether Henshaw would feel as if I were whining. 'I was bleary,' I repeated, 'but Kratska showed up still foggy, and I didn't dare trust a hexylamine dope with the job of landing. Anyway, I'd reported to Gunderson, and that seemed to shift some of the responsibility to him. So I let Kratska sit in the control cabin, and I began to put down.'

Telling the story made me mad all over. 'Those lousy reporters!' I blazed. 'All of them seemed to think landing a rocket is like settling down in bed; you just cushion down on your underblast. Yeah; they don't realize that you have to land blind, because three hundred feet down from the ground the blast begins to splash against it.

'You watch the leveling poles at the edge of the field and try to judge your altitude from them, but you don't see the ground; what you see under you are the flames of Hell. And another thing they don't realize: lowering a ship is like bringing down a dinner plate balanced on a fishing rod. If she starts to roll sideways – blooey! The underjets only hold you up when they're pointing down, you know.'

Henshaw let me vent my temper without interruption, and I returned to my story. 'Well, I was getting down as well as could be expected. The *Hera* always did have a tendency to roll a little, but she wasn't the worst ship I've put to ground.

'But every time she slid over a little, Kratska let out a yell; he was nervous from his dope jag, and he knew he was due to lose his license, and on top of that he was just plain scared by the side roll. We got to seventy feet on the leveling poles when she gave a pretty sharp roll, and Kratska went plain daffy.'

I hesitated. 'I don't know exactly how to tell what happened. It went quick, and I didn't see all of it, of course. But suddenly Kratska, who had been fumbling with the air lock for ten minutes, shrieked something like "She's going over!" and grabbed the throttle. He shut off the blast before I could lift an eyelash, shut it off and flung himself out. Yeah; he'd opened the air lock.

'Well, we were only seventy feet – less than that – above the field. We dropped like an overripe apple off a tree. I didn't have time even to move before we hit, and when we hit, all the fuel in all the jets must have let go. And for what happened after that you'd better read the newspapers.'

'Not me,' said Henshaw. 'You spill it.'

'I can't, not all of it, because I was laid out. But I can guess, all right. It seems that when the jets blew off, Kratska was just picked up in a couple of cubic yards of the soft sand he had landed in, and tossed clear. He had nothing but a broken wrist. And as for me, apparently I was shot out of the control room, and banged up considerably. And as for Gunderson, his professors, and everyone else on the Hera – well, they were just stains on the pool of molten ferralumin that was left.'

'Then how,' asked Henshaw, 'did they hang it on you?'

I tried to control my voice. 'Kratska,' I said grimly. 'The field was clear for landing; nobody can stand in close with the blast splashing in a six-hundred-foot circle. Of course, they saw someone jump from the nose of the ship after the jets cut off, but how could they tell which of us? And the explosion shuffled the whole field around, and nobody knew which was what.'

'Then it should have been his word against yours.'

'Yeah; it should have been. But the field knew it was my shift because I'd been talking over the landing beam, and besides, Kratska got to the reporters first. I never even knew of the mess until I woke up at Grand Mercy Hospital thirteen days later. By that time Kratska had talked and I was the goat.'

'But the investigating committee?'

I grunted. 'Sure, the investigating committee. I'd reported to Gunderson, but he made a swell witness, being just an impurity in a mass of ferralumin alloy. And Kratska had disappeared anyway.'

'Couldn't they find him?'

'Not on what I knew about him. We picked him up at Junopolis on Io, because Briggs was down with white fever. I didn't see him at all except when we were relieving each other, and you know what that's like, seeing somebody in a control cabin with the sun shields up. And on Europa we kept to space routine, so I couldn't even give you a good description of him. He had a beard, but so have ninety per cent of us after a long hop, and he said when we took him on that he'd just come over from the Earth.' I paused. 'I'll find him some day.'

'Hope you do,' said Henshaw briskly. 'About this present run, now. There'll be you and me, and then there'll be Stefan Coretti, a physical chemist, and an Ivor Gogrol, a biologist. That's the scientific personnel of the expedition.'

'Yeah, but who's my co-pilot? That's what interests me.'

'Oh, sure,' said Henshaw, and coughed. 'Your co-pilot. Well, I've been meaning to tell you. It's Claire Avery.'

'*Claire Avery!*'

'That's right,' agreed the captain gloomily. 'The Golden Flash herself.

The only woman pilot to have her name on the Curry Cup, winner of this year's Apogee race.'

'She's no pilot!' I snapped. 'She's a rich publicity hound with brass nerves. I was just curious enough to blow ten bucks rental on a 'scope to watch that race. She was ninth rounding the Moon. Ninth! Do you know how she won? She gunned her rocket under full acceleration practically all the way back, and then fell into a braking orbit.

'Any sophomore in Astronautics II knows that you can't calculate a braking orbit without knowing the density of the stratosphere and ionosphere, and even then it's a gamble. That's what she did – simply gambled, and happened to be lucky. Why do you pick a rich moron with a taste for thrills on a job like this?'

'I didn't pick her, Jack. Interplanetary picked her for publicity purposes. To tell the truth, I think this whole expedition is an attempt to get a little favorable advertising to offset that shady stock investigation this spring. Interplanetary wants to show itself as the noble patron of exploration. So Claire Avery will take off for the television and papers, and you'll be politely ignored.'

'And that suits me! I wouldn't even take the job if things were a little different, and – ' I broke off suddenly, frozen 'Say,' I said weakly, 'did you know they'd revoked my license?'

'You don't say,' said Henshaw. 'And after all the trouble I had talking Interplanetary into permission to take you on, too.' Then he grinned. 'Here,' he said, tossing me an envelope. 'See how long it'll take you to lose this one.'

But the very sight of the familiar blue paper was enough to make me forget a lot of things – Kratska, Claire Avery, even hunger.

The take-off was worse than I had expected. I had sense enough to wear my pilot's goggles to the field, but of course I was recognized as soon as I joined the group at the rocket. They'd given us the *Minos*, an old ship, but she looked as if she'd handle well.

The newsmen must have had orders to ignore me, but I could hear plenty of comments from the crowd. And to finish things up, there was Claire Avery, a lot prettier than she looked on the television screens, but with the same unmistakable cobalt-blue eyes, and hair closer to the actual shade of metallic gold than any I'd ever seen. The 'Golden Flash', the newsmen called her. Blah!

She accepted her introduction to me with the coolest possible nod, as if to say to the scanners and cameras that it wasn't her choice she was teamed with yellow Jack Sands. But for that matter, Coretti's black Latin eyes were not especially cordial either, nor were Gogrol's broad features. I'd met Gogrol somewhere before, but couldn't place him at the moment.

Well, at last the speeches were over, and the photographers and broadcast men let the Golden Flash stop posing, and she and I got into the control cabin for the take-off. I still wore my goggles, and huddled down low besides, because there were a dozen telescopic cameras and scanners recording us from the field's edge. Claire Avery simply ate it up, though, smiling and waving before she cut in the underblast. But finally we were rising over the flame.

She was worse than I'd dreamed. The *Minos* was a sweetly balanced ship, but she rolled it like a baby's cradle. She had the radio on the field broadcast, and I could hear the description of the take-off: ' – heavily laden. There – she rolls again. But she's making altitude. The blast has stopped splashing now, and is coming down in a beautiful fan of fire. A difficult take-off, even for the Golden Flash.' A difficult take-off! Bunk!

I was watching the red bubble in the level, but I stole a glance to Claire Avery's face, and it wasn't so cool and stand-offish now. And just then the bubble in the level bobbed way over, and I heard the girl at my side give a frightened little gasp. This wasn't cradle rocking any more – we were in a real roll!

I slapped her hands hard and grabbed the U-bar. I cut the underjets completely off, letting the ship fall free, then shot the full blast through the right laterals. It was damn close, I'm ready to swear, but we leveled, and I snapped on the under-blast before we lost a hundred feet of altitude. And there was that inane radio still talking: 'They're over! No – they've leveled again, but what a roll! She's a real pilot, this Golden Flash – '

I looked at her; she was pale and shaken, but her eyes were angry. 'Golden Flash, eh?' I jeered. 'The gold must refer to your money, but what's the flash? It can't have much to do with your ability as a pilot.' But at that time I had no idea how pitifully little she really knew about rocketry.

She flared. 'Anyway,' she hissed, her lips actually quivering with rage, 'the gold doesn't refer to color, Mr Malaria Sands!' She knew that would hurt; the 'Malaria' was some bright columnist's idea of a pun on my name. You see, malaria's popularly called Yellow Jack. 'Besides,' she went on defiantly, 'I could have pulled out of that roll myself, and you know it.'

'Sure,' I said, with the meanest possible sarcasm. We had considerable upward velocity now, and plenty of altitude, both of which tend toward safety because they give one more time to pull out of a roll. 'You can take over again now. The hard part's over.'

She gave me a look from those electric blue eyes, and I began to realize just what sort of trip I was in for. Coretti and Gogrol had indicated their unfriendliness plainly enough, and heaven knows I couldn't mistake the hatred in Claire Avery's eyes, so that left just Captain Henshaw. But the captain of the ship dare not show favoritism; so all in all I saw myself doomed to a lonely trip.

Lonely isn't the word for it. Henshaw was decent enough, but since Claire Avery had started with a long shift and so had the captain, they were having their free spells and meals on the same schedule, along with Gogrol, and that left me with Coretti. He was pretty cool, and I had pride enough left not to make any unwanted advances.

Gogrol was worse; I saw him seldom enough, but he never addressed a word to me except on routine. Yet there was something familiar about him – As for Claire Avery, I simply wasn't in her scheme of things at all; she even relieved me in silence.

Offhand, I'd have said it was the wildest sort of stupidity to send a girl with four men on a trip like this. Well, I had to hand it to Claire Avery; in *that* way she was a splendid rocketrix. She took the inconveniences of space routine without a murmur, and she was so companionable – that is, with the others – that it was like having a young and unusually entertaining man aboard.

And, after all, Gogrol was twice her age and Henshaw almost three times; Coretti was younger, but I was the only one who was really of her generation. But as I say, she hated me; Coretti seemed to stand best with her.

So the weary weeks of the journey dragged along. The Sun shrunk up to a disk only a fifth the diameter of the terrestrial Sun, but Jupiter grew to an enormous moon-like orb with its bands and spots gloriously tinted. It was an exquisite sight, and sometimes, since eight hours' sleep is more than I can use, I used to slip into the control room while Claire Avery was on duty, just to watch the giant planet and its moons. The girl and I never said a word to each other.

We weren't to stop at Io, but were landing directly on Europa, our destination, the third moon outward from the vast molten globe of Jupiter. In some ways Europa is the queerest little sphere in the Solar System, and for many years it was believed to be quite uninhabitable. It is, too, as far as seventy per cent of its surface goes, but the remaining area is a wild and weird region.

This is the mountainous hollow in the face toward Jupiter, for Europa, like the Moon, keeps one face always toward its primary. Here in this vast depression, all of the tiny world's scanty atmosphere is collected, gathered like little lakes and puddles into the valleys between mountain ranges that often pierce through the low-lying air into the emptiness of space.

Often enough a single valley forms a microcosm sundered by nothingness from the rest of the planet, generating its own little rainstorms under pygmy cloud banks, inhabited by its indigenous life, untouched by, and unaware of, all else.

In the ephemeris, Europa is dismissed prosaically with a string of figures: diameter, 2099 m. – period, 3 days, 13 hours, 14 seconds – distance from primary, 425,160 m. For an astronomical ephemeris isn't concerned with the thin film of life that occasionally blurs a planet's surface; it has nothing to say of the slow libration of Europa that sends intermittent tides of air washing against the mountain slopes under the tidal drag of Jupiter, nor of the waves that sometimes spill air from valley to valley, and sometimes spill alien life as well.

Least of all is the ephemeris concerned with the queer forms that crawl now and then right up out of the air pools, to lie on the vacuum-bathed peaks exactly as strange fishes flopped their way out of the Earthly seas to bask on the sands at the close of the Devonian age.

Of the five of us, I was the only one who had ever visited Europa – or so I thought at the time. Indeed, there were few men in the world who had actually set foot on the inhospitable little planet; Gunderson and his men were dead, save me and perhaps Kratska, and we had been the first organized expedition.

Only a few stray adventurers from Io had preceded us. So it was to me that Captain Henshaw directed his orders when he said, 'Take us as close as possible to Gunderson's landing.'

It began to be evident that we'd make ground toward the end of Claire's long shift, so I crawled out of the coffinlike niche I called my cabin an hour early, and went up to the control room to guide her down. We were seventy or eighty miles up, but there were no clouds or air distortion here, and the valleys crisscrossed under us like a relief map.

It was infernally hard to pick Gunderson's valley; the burned spot from the blast was long since grown over, and I had only memory to rely on, for, of course, all charts were lost with the *Hera*. But I knew the general region, and it really made less difference than it might have, for practically all the valleys in that vicinity were connected by passes; one could walk between them in breathable air.

After a while I picked one of a series of narrow parallel valleys, one with what I knew was a salt pool in the center – though most of them had that; they'd be desert without it – and pointed it out to Claire. 'That one,' I said, adding maliciously, 'and I'd better warn you that it's narrow and deep – a ticklish landing place.'

She flashed me an unfriendly glance from sapphire eyes, but said nothing. But a voice behind me sounded unexpectedly: 'To the left! The one to the left. It – it looks easier.'

Gogrol! I was startled for a moment, then turned coldly on him. 'Keep out of the control room during landings,' I snapped.

He glared, muttered something, and retired. But he left me a trifle worried; not that his valley to the left was any easier to land in – that was pure bunk – but it looked a little familiar! Actually, I wasn't sure but that Gogrol had pointed out Gunderson's valley.

But I stuck to my first guess. The irritation I felt I took out on Claire. 'Take it slow!' I said gruffly. 'This isn't a landing field. Nobody's put up leveling poles in these valleys. You're going to have to land completely blind from about four hundred feet, because the blast begins to splash sooner in this thin air. You go down by level and guess, and Heaven help us if you roll her! There's no room for rolling between those cliffs.'

She bit her lip nervously. The *Minos* was already rolling under the girl's inexpert hand, though that wasn't dangerous while we still had ten or twelve miles of altitude. But the ground was coming up steadily.

I was in a cruel mood. I watched the strain grow in her lovely features, and if I felt any pity, I lost it when I thought of the way she had treated me. So I taunted her.

'This shouldn't be a hard landing for the Golden Flash. Or maybe you'd rather be landing at full speed, so you could fall into a braking ellipse – only that wouldn't work here, because the air doesn't stick up high enough to act as a brake.'

And a few minutes later, when her lips were quivering with tension, I said, 'It takes more than publicity and gambler's luck to make a pilot, doesn't it?'

She broke. She screamed suddenly, 'Oh, take it! Take it, then!' and slammed the U-bar into my hands. Then she huddled back in her corner sobbing, with her golden hair streaming over her face.

I took over; I had no choice. I pulled the *Minos* out of the roll Claire's gesture had put her in, and then started teetering down on the underjets. It was pitifully easy because of Europa's low gravitation and the resulting low falling acceleration; it gave the pilot so much time to compensate for side sway.

I began to realize how miserably little the Golden Flash really knew about rocketry, and, despite myself, I felt a surge of pity for her. But why pity her? Everyone knew that Claire Avery was simply a wealthy, thrill-intoxicated daredevil, with more than her share of money, of beauty, of adulation. The despised Jack Sands pitying her? That's a laugh!

The underblast hit and splashed, turning the brown-clad valley into black ashes and flame. I inched down very slowly now, for there was nothing to see below save the fiery sheet of the blast, and I watched the bubble on the level as if my life depended on it – which it did.

I knew the splash began at about four hundred feet in this density of air, but from then on it was guesswork, and a question of settling down so slowly that when we hit we wouldn't damage the underjets. And if I do say it, we grounded so gently that I don't think Claire Avery knew it until I cut off the blast.

She rubbed the tears away with her sleeve and glared blue-eyed defiance at me, but before she could speak, Henshaw opened the door. 'Nice landing, Miss Avery,' he said.

'Wasn't it?' I echoed, with a grin at the girl.

She stood up. She was trembling and I think that under Earthly gravitation she would have fallen back into the pilot's seat, for I saw her knees shaking below her trim, black shorts.

'I didn't land us,' she said grimly. 'Mr Sands put us to ground.'

Somehow my pity got the best of me then. 'Sure,' I said. 'It's into my shift. Look.' It was; the chronometer showed three minutes in. 'Miss Avery had all the hard part – '

But she was gone. And try as I would, I could not bring myself to see her as the hard, brilliant thrill-seeker which the papers and broadcasts portrayed her. Instead, she left me with a strange and by no means logical impression of – wistfulness.

Life on Europa began uneventfully. Little by little we reduced the atmospheric pressure in the *Minos* to conform to that outside. First Coretti and then Claire Avery had a spell of altitude sickness, but by the end of twenty hours we were all acclimated enough to be comfortable outside.

Henshaw and I were first to venture into the open. I scanned the valley carefully for familiar landmarks, but it was hard to be sure; all these canyonlike ditches were much alike. I know that a copse of song-bushes had grown high on the cliff when the *Hera* had landed, but our blast had splashed higher, and if the bushes had been there, they were only a patch of ashes now.

At the far end of the valley there should have been a cleft in the hills, a pass leading to the right into the next valley. That wasn't there; all I could distinguish was a narrow ravine cutting the hills to the left.

'I'm afraid I've missed Gunderson's valley,' I told Henshaw. 'I think it's the next one to our left; it's connected to this one by a pass, if I'm right, and this is one I came in several times to hunt.' It recurred to me suddenly that Gogrol had said the left one.

'You say there's a pass?' mused Henshaw. 'Then we'll stay here rather than chance another take-off and another landing. We can work in Gunderson's valley through the pass. You're sure it's low enough so we won't have to use oxygen helmets?'

'If it's the right pass, I am. But work at what in Gunderson's valley? I thought this was an exploring expedition.'

Henshaw gave me a queer, sharp look, and turned away. Right then I saw Gogrol standing in the port of the *Minos*, and I didn't know whether Henshaw's reticence was due to his presence or mine. I moved a step to follow him, but at that moment the outer door of the air lock opened and Claire Avery came out.

It was the first time I had seen her in a fair light since the take-off at Young's Field, and I had rather forgotten the loveliness of her coloring. Of course, her skin had paled from the weeks in semidarkness, but her cadmium-yellow hair and sapphire-blue eyes were really startling, especially when she moved into the sun shadow of the cliff and stood bathed only in the golden Jupiter light.

Like Henshaw and myself, she had slipped on the all-enveloping ski suit one wore on chilly little Europa. The small world received only a fourth as much heat as steamy Io, and would not have been habitable at all, except for the fact that it kept its face always toward its primary, and therefore received heat intermittently from the Sun, but eternally from Jupiter.

The girl cast an eager look over the valley; I knew this was her first experience on an uninhabited world, and there is always a sense of strangeness and the fascination of the unknown in one's first step on an alien planet.

She looked at Henshaw, who was methodically examining the scorched soil on which the *Minos* rested, and then her glance crossed mine. There was an electric moment of tension, but then the anger in her blue eyes – if it had been anger – died away, and she strode deliberately to my side.

She faced me squarely. 'Jack Sands,' she said with an undertone of defiance, 'I owe you an apology. Don't think I'm apologizing for my opinion of you, but only for the way I've been acting toward you. In a small company like this there isn't room for enmity, and as far as I'm concerned, your past is yours from now on. What's more, I want to thank you for helping me during the take-off, and' – her defiance was cracking a bit – 'd-during the – the landing.'

I stared at her. That apology must have cost her an effort, for the Golden Flash was a proud young lady, and I saw her wink back her tears. I choked back the vicious reply I had been about to make, and said only, 'O.K. You keep your opinion of me to yourself and I'll do the same with my opinion of you.'

She flushed, then smiled. 'I guess I'm a rotten pilot,' she admitted ruefully. 'I hate take-offs and landings. To tell the truth, I'm simply scared of the *Minos*. Up to the time we left Young's Field, I'd never handled anything larger than my little racing rocket, the *Golden Flash*.'

I gasped. That wouldn't have been credible if I hadn't seen with my own eyes how utterly unpracticed she was. 'But why?' I asked in perplexity. 'If you hate piloting so, why do it? Just for publicity? With your money you don't have to, you know.'

'Oh, my money!' she echoed irritably. She stared away over the narrow valley, and started suddenly. 'Look!' she cried. 'There's something moving on the peaks – like a big ball. And way up where there's no air at all!'

I glanced over. 'It's just a bladder bird,' I said indifferently. I'd seen plenty of them; they were the commonest mobile form of life on Europa. But of course Claire hadn't, and she was eagerly curious.

I explained. I threw stones into a tinkling grove of song-bushes until I flushed up another, and it went gliding over our heads with its membrane stretched taut.

I told her that the three-foot creature that had sailed like a flying squirrel was the same sort as the giant ball she had glimpsed among the airless peaks, only the one on the peaks had inflated its bladder. The creatures were able to cross from valley to valley by carrying their air with them in their big, balloonlike bladders. And, of course, bladder birds weren't really birds at all; they didn't fly, but glided like the lemurs and flying squirrels of Earth, and naturally, couldn't even do that when they were up on the airless heights.

Claire was so eager and interested and wide-eyed that I quite forgot my grudge. I started to show her my knowledge of things Europan; I led her close to the copse of song-bushes so that she could listen to the sweet and plaintive melody of their breathing leaves, and I took her down to the salt pool in the center of the valley to find some of the primitive creatures which Gunderson's men had called 'nutsies', because they looked very much like walnuts with the hulls on. But within was a small mouthful of delicious meat, neither animal nor vegetable, which was quite safe to eat raw, since bacterial life did not exist on Europa.

I guess I was pretty exuberant, for after all, this was the first chance at companionship I'd had for many weeks. We wandered down the valley and I talked, talked about anything. I told her of the various forms life assumed on the planets, how on Mars and Titan and Europa sex was unknown, though Venus and Earth and Io all possessed it; and how on Mars and Europa vegetable and animal life had never differentiated, so that even the vastly intelligent beaked Martians had a tinge of vegetable nature, while conversely the song-bushes on the hills of Europa had a vaguely animal content. And meanwhile we wandered aimlessly along until we stood below the narrow pass or ravine that led presumably into Gunderson's valley to our left.

Far up the slope a movement caught my eye. A bladder bird, I thought idly, though it was a low altitude for one to inflate; they usually expanded their bladders just below the point where breathing became impossible. Then I saw that it wasn't a bladder bird; it was a man. In fact, it was Gogrol.

He was emerging from the pass, and his collar was turned up about his throat against the cold of the altitude. He hadn't seen us, apparently, as he angled down what mountaineers call a *col*, a ledge or neck of rock that slanted from the mouth of the ravine along the hillside toward the *Minos*. But Claire, following the direction of my gaze, saw him in the moment before brush hid him from view.

'Gogrol!' she exclaimed. 'He must have been in the next valley. Stefan will want – ' She caught herself sharply.

'Why,' I asked grimly, 'should your friend Coretti be interested in Gogrol's actions? After all, Gogrol's supposed to be a biologist, isn't he? Why shouldn't he take a look in the next valley?'

Her lips tightened. 'Why shouldn't he?' she echoed. 'I didn't say he shouldn't. I didn't say anything like that.'

And thenceforward she maintained a stubborn silence. Indeed, something of the old enmity and coolness seemed to have settled between us as we walked back through the valley toward the *Minos*.

That night Henshaw rearranged our schedule to a more convenient plan than the requirements of space. We divided our time into days and nights, or rather into sleeping and waking periods, for, of course, there is no true night on Europa. The shifts of light are almost as puzzling as those on its neighbor Io, but not quite, because Io has its own rotation to complicate matters.

On Europa, the nearest approach to true night is during the eclipse that occurs every three days or so, when the landscape is illumined only by the golden twilight of Jupiter, or at the most, only by Jupiter and Io light. So we set our own night time by arbitrary Earth reckoning, so that we might all work and sleep during the same periods.

There was no need for any sort of watch to be kept; no one had ever reported life dangerous to man on little Europa. The only danger came from the meteors that swarm about the giant Jupiter's orbit, and sometimes came crashing down through the shallow air of his satellites; we couldn't dodge them here as we could in space. But that was a danger against which a guard was unavailing.

It was the next morning that I cornered Henshaw and forced him to listen to my questions.

'Listen to me, Harris,' I said determinedly. 'What is there about this expedition that everybody knows but me? If this is an exploring party, I'm the Ameer of Yarkand. Now I want to know what it's all about.'

Henshaw looked miserably embarrassed. He kept his eyes away from mine, and muttered unhappily, 'I can't tell you, Jack. I'm damned sorry, but I can't tell you.'

'Why not?'

He hesitated. 'Because I'm under orders not to, Jack.'

'Whose orders?'

Henshaw shook his head. 'Damn it!' he said vehemently. 'I trust you. If it were my choice, you'd be the one I'd pick for honesty. But it isn't my choice.' He paused. 'Do you understand that? All right' – he stiffened into his captain's manner – 'no more questions, then. I'll ask the questions and give the orders.'

Well, put on that basis, I couldn't argue. I'm a pilot, first, last, and always, and I don't disobey my superior's orders even when he happens to be as close a friend as Henshaw. But I began to kick myself for not seeing something queer in the business as soon as Henshaw offered me the job.

If Interplanetary was looking for favorable publicity, they wouldn't get it by signing me on. Moreover, the government wasn't in the habit of reissuing a revoked pilot's license without good and sufficient reason, and I knew I hadn't supplied any such reason by loafing around brooding over my troubles. That alone should have tipped me off that something was screwy.

And there were plenty of hints during the voyage itself. True, Gogrol seemed to talk the language of biology, but I'll be dogged if Coretti talked like a chemist. And there was that haunting sense of familiarity about Gogrol, too. And to cap the climax was the incongruity of calling this jaunt an exploring expedition; for all the exploring we were doing we might as well have landed on Staten Island or Buffalo. Better, as far as I was concerned, because I'd seen Europa but had never been to Buffalo.

Well, there was nothing to be done about it now. I suppressed my disgust and tried as hard as I could to cooperate with the others in whatever project we were supposed to be pursuing. That was rather difficult, too, because suspicious-appearing incidents kept cropping up to make me feel like a stranger or an outcast.

There was, for instance, the time Henshaw decided that a change in diet would be welcome. The native life of Europa was perfectly edible, though not all as tasty as the tiny shell creatures of the salt pools. However, I knew of one variety that had served the men of the *Hera*, a plant-like growth consisting of a single fleshy hand-sized member, that we had called liver-leaf because of its taste.

The captain detailed Coretti and myself to gather a supply of this delicacy, and I found a specimen, showed it to him, and then set off dutifully along the north – that is, the left – wall of the valley.

Coretti appeared to take the opposite side, but I had not gone far before I glimpsed him skirting my edge of the salt pool. That meant nothing; he was free to search anywhere for liver-leaf, but it was soon evident to me that he was not searching. He was following me; he was shadowing my movements.

I was thoroughly irritated, but determined not to show it. I plodded methodically along, gathering the fat leaves in my basket, until I reached the valley's far end and the slopes back and succeeded in running square into Coretti before he could maneuver himself out of a copse of song-bushes.

He grinned at me. 'Any luck?' he asked.

'More than you, it seems,' I retorted, with a contemptuous look at his all but empty basket.

'I had no luck at all. I thought maybe in the next valley, through the pass there, we might find some.'

'I've found my share,' I grunted.

I thought I noticed a flicker of surprise in his black eyes. 'You're not going over?' he asked sharply. 'You're going back?'

'You guessed it,' I said sharply. 'My basket's full and I'm going back.'

I knew that he watched me most of the way back, because halfway to the *Minos* I turned around, and I could see him standing there on the slope below the pass.

Along toward what we called evening the Sun went into our first eclipse. The landscape was bathed in the aureate light of Jupiter alone, and I realized that I'd forgotten how beautiful that golden twilight could be.

I was feeling particularly lonesome, too; so I wandered out to stare at the glowing peaks against the black sky, and the immense, bulging sphere of Jupiter with Ganymede swinging like a luminous pearl close beside it. The scene was so lovely that I forgot my loneliness, until I was suddenly reminded of it.

A glint of more brilliant gold caught my eye, up near the grove of song-bushes. It was Claire's head; she was standing there watching the display, and beside her was Coretti. While I looked, he suddenly turned and drew her into his arms; she put her hands against his chest, but she wasn't struggling; she was perfectly passive and content. It was none of my business, of course, but – well, if I'd disliked Coretti before, I hated him now, because I was lonely again.

I think it was the next day that things came to a head, and trouble really began. Henshaw had been pleased with our meal of indigenous life, and decided to try it again. This time Claire was assigned to accompany me, and we set off in silence. A sort of echo of the coolness that had attended our last parting survived, and besides, what I had seen last night in the eclipse light seemed to make a difference to me. So I simply stalked along at her side, wondering what to choose for the day's menu.

We didn't want liver-leaves again. The little nutsies from the salt pool were all right, but it was a half-day's job to gather enough, and besides, they were almost too salty to be pleasant fare for a whole meal. Bladder birds were hopeless; they consisted of practically nothing except thin skin stretched over a framework of bones. I remembered that once we had tried a brown, fungoid lump that grew in the shade under the song-bushes; some of Gunderson's men had liked it.

Claire finally broke the silence. 'If I'm going to help you look,' she suggested, 'I ought to know what we're looking for.'

I described the lumpy growths. 'I'm not so sure all of us will like them. Near as I can remember, they tasted something like truffles, with a faint flavor of meat added. We tried them both raw and cooked, and cooked was best.'

'I like truffles,' said the girl. 'They're – '

A shot! There was no mistaking the sharp crack of a .38, though it sounded queerly thin in the rare atmosphere. But it sounded again, and a third time, and then a regular fusillade!

'Keep back of me!' I snapped as we turned and raced for the *Minos*. The warning was needless; Claire was unaccustomed to the difficulties of running on a small planet. Her weight on Europa must have been no more than twelve or fifteen pounds, one eighth Earth normal, and though she had learned to walk easily enough – one learned that on any space journey – she had had no opportunity to learn to run. Her first step sent her half a dozen feet in the air; I sped away from her with the long, sliding stride one had to use on such planets as Europa.

I burst out of the brush into the area cleared by the blast, where already growth had begun. For a moment I saw only the *Minos* resting peacefully in the clearing, then I reeled with shock. At the air lock lay a man – Henshaw – with his face a bloody pulp, his head split by two bullets.

There was a burst of sound, voices, another shot. Out of the open air lock reeled Coretti; he staggered backward for ten steps, then dropped on his side, while blood welled up out of the collar of his suit. And standing grimly in the opening, an automatic smoking in his right hand, a charged flame-pistol in his left, was Gogrol!

I had no weapon; why should one carry arms on airless Europa? For an instant I stood frozen, appalled, uncomprehending, and in that moment Gogrol glimpsed me. I saw his hand tighten on his automatic, then he shrugged and strode toward me.

'Well,' he said with a snarl in his voice, 'I had to do it. They went crazy. Anerosis. It struck both of them at once, and they went clean mad. Self-defense, it was.'

I didn't believe him, of course. People don't get anerosis in air no rarer than Europa's; one could live his whole life out there without ever suffering from air starvation. But I couldn't argue those points with a panting murderer armed with the most deadly weapon ever devised, and with a girl coming up behind me. So I said nothing at all.

Claire came up; I heard her shocked intake of breath, and her almost inaudible wail, 'Stefan!' Then she saw Gogrol holding his guns, and she flared out, 'So you did it! I knew they suspected you! But you'll never get away with it, you – '

She broke off under the sudden menace of Gogrol's eyes, and I stepped in front of her as he raised the automatic. For an instant death looked squarely at both of us, then the man shrugged and the evil light in his eyes dimmed.

'A while yet,' he muttered. 'If Coretti dies – ' He backed to the air lock and pulled a helmet from within the *Minos*, an air helmet that we had thought might serve should we ever need to cross the heights about a blind valley.

Then Gogrol advanced toward us, and I felt Claire quiver against my shoulder. But the man only glared at us and spat out a single word. 'Back!' he rasped. 'Back!'

We backed. Under the menace of that deadly flame-pistol he herded us along the narrow valley, eastward to the slope whence angled the ravine that led toward Gunderson's valley. And up the slope, into the dim shadows of the pass itself, so narrow in places that my outstretched hands could have spanned the gap between the walls. A grim, dark, echo-haunted, and forbidding place; I did not wonder that the girl shrank against me. The air was thin to the point of insufficiency, and all three of us were gasping for breath.

There was nothing I could do, for Gogrol's weapons bore too steadily on Claire Avery. So I slipped my arm about her to hearten her and inched warily along that shadowy canyon, until at last it widened, and a thousand feet below stretched a valley – Gunderson's valley, I knew at once. Far away was the slope where the *Hera* had rested, and down in the lower end was the heart-shaped pool of brine.

Gogrol had slipped on the helmet, leaving the visor open, and his flat features peered out at us like a gargoyle's. On he drove us, and down into the valley. But as he passed the mouth of the ravine, which by now was no more than a narrow gorge between colossal escarpments that loomed heavenward like the battlements of Atlantis, he stooped momentarily into the shadows, and when he rose again I fancied that a small sound like the singing of a tea-kettle followed us down the slope. It meant nothing to me then.

He waved the automatic. 'Faster!' he ordered threateningly. We were down in the talus now, and we scrambled doggedly among the rocks and fallen débris. On he drove us, until we stumbled among the boulders around the central pond. Then, suddenly, he halted.

'If you follow,' he said with a cold intensity, 'I shoot!' He strode away not toward the pass, but toward the ridge itself, back along the slopes that lay nearest the *Minos*, hidden from view in the other valley. Of course, Gogrol could cross those airless heights, secure in this helmet, carrying his air supply like the bladder birds.

He seemed to seek the shelter of an ascending ridge. As the jutting rock concealed him, I leaped to a boulder.

'Come on!' I said. 'Perhaps we can beat him through the pass to the ship!'

'No!' screamed Claire, so frantically that I halted. 'My Lord, no! Didn't you see the blaster he left?'

The singing tea-kettle noise! I had barely time to throw myself beside the girl crouching behind a rock when the little atomic bomb let go.

I suppose everybody has seen, either by eye or television, the effect of atomic explosions. All of us, by one means or the other, have watched old buildings demolished, road grades or canals blasted, and those over forty may even remember the havoc-spreading bombs of the Pacific War. But none of you could have seen anything like this, for this explosion had a low air pressure and a gravitation only one-eighth normal as the sole checks to its fury.

It seemed to me that the whole mountain lifted. Vast masses of crumbling rock hurtled toward the black sky. Bits of stone, whistling like bullets and incandescent like meteors, shot past us, and the very ground we clung to heaved like the deck of a rolling rocket.

When the wild turmoil had subsided, when the débris no longer sang about us, when the upheaved masses had either fallen again or had spun beyond Europa's gravitation to crash on indifferent Jupiter, the pass had vanished. Mountain and vacuum hemmed us into a prison.

Both of us were slightly stunned by the concussion, although the thin atmosphere transmitted a strangely high-pitched sound instead of the resounding *b-o-o-m* one would have heard on the Earth. When my head stopped ringing, I looked around for Gogrol, and saw him at last seven or eight hundred feet up the slope of the mountain. Anger surged in me; I seized a stone from the margin of the pool, and flung it viciously at him. One can throw amazing distances on small worlds like Europa; I watched the missile raise dust at his very feet.

He turned; very deliberately he raised the automatic, and stone splinters from the boulder beside me stung my face. I dragged Claire down behind the shelter, knowing beyond doubt that he had meant that bullet to kill. In silence we watched him climb until he was but a tiny black speck, nearing the crest.

He approached a bladder bird crawling its slow way along the airless heights. Up there the creatures were slow as snails, for their flight membranes were useless in the near vacuum. But they had normally no enemies on the peaks.

I saw Gogrol change his course purposely to intercept the thing. Intentionally, maliciously, he kicked a hole in the inflated bladder, collapsing it like a child's balloon. He stood watching while the miserable creature flopped in the agonies of suffocation, then moved methodically on. It was the coldest exhibition of wanton cruelty I had ever witnessed.

Claire shuddered; still in silence we watched the man's leisurely progress along the ridge. There was something in his attitude that suggested searching, seeking, hunting. Suddenly he quickened his pace and then halted abruptly, stooping over what looked to me like a waist-high heap of stones, or perhaps merely a hummock on the ridge.

But he was burrowing in it, digging, flinging stones and dirt aside. And at last he stood up; if he held anything, distance hid it, but he seemed to wave some small object at us in derisive triumph. Then he moved over the crest of the hills and disappeared.

Claire sighed despondently; she seemed very little like the proud and rather arrogant Golden Flash. 'That settles it,' she murmured disconsolately. 'He's got it, and he's got us trapped; so we're quite helpless.'

'Got what?' I asked. 'What was he digging for up there?'

Her blue eyes widened in amazement. 'Don't you know?'

'I certainly don't. I seem to know less about this damn trip than anybody else on it.'

She gazed steadily at me. 'I knew Stefan was wrong,' she said softly. 'I don't care what you were when you wrecked the *Hera*, Jack Sands; on this trip you've been decent and brave and a gentleman.'

'Thanks,' I said dryly, but I was a little touched for all that because, after all, the Golden Flash was a very beautiful girl. 'Then suppose you let me in on a few of the secrets. For instance, what was Coretti wrong about? And what did Gogrol dig for?'

'Gogrol,' she said, watching me, 'was digging in Gunderson's cairn.'

I looked blank. 'Gunderson's what? This is news to me.'

She was silent for a moment. 'Jack Sands,' she said at last, 'I don't care what Stefan or the government or anybody thinks of you. I think you're honest, and I think you've had an injustice done you somehow, and I don't believe you were to blame in the *Hera* crash. And I'm going to tell you all I know about this matter. But first, do you know the object of Gunderson's expedition to Europa?'

'I never knew it. I'm a pilot; I took no interest in their scientific gibberish.'

She nodded. 'Well, you know how a rocket motor works, of course. How they use a minute amount of uranium or radium as catalyst to release the energy in the fuel. Uranium has low activity; it will set off only metals like the alkalis, and ships using uranium motors burn salt. And radium, being more active, will set off the metals from iron to copper; so ships using a radium initiator usually burn one of the commoner iron or copper ores.'

'I know all that,' I grunted. 'And the heavier the metal, the greater the power from its disintegration.'

'Exactly.' She paused a moment. 'Well, Gunderson wanted to use still heavier elements. That required a source of rays more penetrating than those from radium, and he knew of only one available source – Element 91, protactinium. And it happens that the richest deposits of protactinium so far discovered are those in the rocks of Europa; so to Europa he came for his experiments.'

'Well?' I asked. 'Where do I fit in this mess?'

'I don't quite know, Jack. Let me finish what I know, which is all Stefan would tell me. Gunderson succeeded, they think; he's supposed to have worked out the formula by which protactinium could be made to set off lead, which would give much more power than any present type of initiator. But if he did succeed, his formula and notes were destroyed when the *Hera* crashed!'

I began to see. 'But what – what about that cairn?'

'You really don't know?'

'I'll be double damned if I do! If Gunderson built a cairn, it must have been that last day. I had the take-off, so I slept through most of it. But – why, they did have some sort of ceremony!'

'Yes. Gunderson mentioned something about it when your ship touched at Junopolis on Io. What the government hopes is that he buried a copy of his formula in that cairn. They do, you know. Well, nobody could possibly know of the location except you and a man named Kratska, who had disappeared.

'So Interplanetary, which is in bad anyway because of some stock transactions, was ordered to back this expedition with you as pilot – or at least, that's what Stefan told me. I guess I was taken along just to give the corporation a little more publicity, and, of course, Stefan was sent to watch you, in hopes you'd give away the location. The formula's immensely valuable, you see.'

'Yeah, I see. And how about Gogrol?'

She frowned. 'I don't know. Stefan hinted that he had some connections with Harrick of Interplanetary, or perhaps some hold over him. Harrick insisted on his being a member.'

'The devil!' I exploded suddenly. 'He knew about the cairn! He knew where to look!'

Her eyes grew wide. 'Why, he did! He's – could he be the representative of some foreign government? If we could stop him! But he's left us absolutely helpless here. Why didn't he kill us?'

'I can guess that,' I said grimly. 'He can't fly the *Minos* alone. Henshaw's dead, and if Coretti dies – well, one of us is due for the job of pilot.'

A tremor shook her. 'I'd rather be dead, too,' she murmured, 'than travel with him alone.'

'And I'd rather see you so,' I agreed glumly. 'I wish to heaven you had stayed out of this. You could be home enjoying your money.'

'My money!' she flashed. 'I haven't any money. Do you think I take these chances for publicity or thrills or admiration?'

I gaped; of course, I'd thought exactly that.

She was literally blazing. 'Listen to me, Jack Sands. There's just one reason for the fool things I do – money! There isn't any Avery fortune, and hasn't been since my father died. I've needed money desperately these last two years, to keep the Connecticut place for my mother, because she'd die if she had to leave it. It's been our family home for two hundred years, since 1910, and I won't be the one to lose it!'

It took a moment to adjust myself to what she was saying. 'But a racing rocket isn't a poor man's toy,' I said feebly. 'And surely a girl like you could find – '

'A girl like me!' she cut in bitterly. 'Oh, I know I have a good figure and a passable voice, and perhaps I could have found work in a television chorus, but I needed real money. I had my choice of two ways to get it: I could marry it, or I could gamble my neck against it. You see which way I chose. As the Golden Flash, I can get big prices for endorsing breakfast foods and beauty preparations. That's why I gambled in that race; my racing rocket was all I had left to gamble with. And it worked, only' – her voice broke a little – 'I wish I could stop gambling. I – I hate it!'

It wasn't only pity I felt for her then. Her confession of poverty had changed things; she was no longer the wealthy, unattainable being I had always imagined the Golden Flash to be. She was simply a forlorn and un-happy girl, one who needed to be loved and comforted. And then I remem-bered the evening of the eclipse, and Coretti's arms about her. So I gazed for an instant at the sunlight on her hair, and then turned slowly away.

After a while we gathered some liver-leaves and cooked them, and I tried to tell Claire that we were certain to be rescued. Neither of us believed it; we knew very well that Gogrol would carry no living com-panion to Io; whoever helped him run the *Minos* would certainly be dead and cast into space before landing. And we knew that Gogrol's story, whatever it might be, would not be one likely to encourage a rescue party. He'd simply report us all dead somehow or other.

'I don't care,' said Claire. 'I'm glad I'm with you.'

I thought of Coretti and said nothing. We were just sitting in glum silence near the fire when Gogrol came over the hills again.

Claire saw him first and cried out. Despite his helmet, neither of us could mistake his broad, squat figure. But there was nothing we could do except wait, though we did draw closer to the area of wild and tumbled boulders about the central pool.

'What do you suppose – ' asked Claire nervously. 'Coretti may have died, or may be too injured to help.' Pain twisted her features. 'Yes, or – Oh, I know, Jack! It's that Gogrol can't plot a course. He can pilot; he can follow a course already laid out, but he can't plot one – and neither can Stefan!'

Instantly I knew she must be right. Piloting a ship is just a question of following directions, but plotting a course involves the calculus of function, and that, let me tell you, takes a mathematician. I could do it, and Claire handled a simple route well enough – one had to in rocket racing – but astrogators were not common even among pilots.

You see, the difficulty is that you don't just point the ship at your destination, because that destination is moving; you head for where the planet will be when you arrive. And in this case, assuming Gogrol meant to make for Io, a journey from Europa to that world meant speeding in the direction of the colossal mass of Jupiter, and if a rocket once passed the critical velocity in that direction – good night!

A hundred feet away Gogrol halted. 'Listen, you two,' he yelled, 'I'm offering Miss Avery the chance to join the crew of the *Minos*.'

'You're the crew,' I retorted. 'She's not taking your offer.'

Without warning he leveled his revolver and fired, and a shock numbed my left leg. I fell within the shelter of a boulder, thrusting Claire before me, while Gogrol's bellow followed the crash of his shot: 'I'll shut your mouth for you!'

There began the weirdest game of hide and seek I've ever played, with Claire and me crawling among the tumbled boulders, scarcely daring to breathe. Gogrol had all the advantage, and he used it. I couldn't stand upright, and my legs began to hurt so excruciatingly that I was afraid each minute of an involuntary groan forcing its way through my lips. Claire suffered with me; her eyes were agonized blue pools of torment, but she dared not even whisper to me.

Gogrol took to leaping atop the boulders. He glimpsed me, and a second bullet struck that same burning leg. He was deliberately hunting me down, and I saw it was the end.

We had a momentary shelter. Claire whispered to me, 'I'm going to him. He'll kill you otherwise, and take me anyway.'

'No!' I croaked. 'No!'

Gogrol heard, and was coming. Claire said hastily. 'He's – bestial. At least I can plot a course that will – kill us!' Then she called, 'Gogrol! I'll surrender.'

I snatched at her ankle – too late. I went crawling after her as she strode into the open, but her steps were too rapid. I heard her say, 'I give up, if you won't – shoot him again.'

Gogrol mumbled, and then Claire's voice again, 'Yes, I'll plot your course, but how can I cross the peaks?'

'Walk,' he said, and laughed.

'I can't breathe up there.'

'Walk as far as you can. You won't die while I take you the rest of the way.'

There was no reply. When I finally crept into the open, they were a hundred feet up the slope.

Helpless, raging, pain-maddened, I seized a stone and flung it. It struck Gogrol in the back, but it struck with no more force than if I'd tossed it a dozen feet on Earth. He spun in fury, thrust the screaming Claire aside, and sent another bullet at me. Missed me, I thought, though I wasn't sure, for pain had numbed me. I couldn't be sure of anything.

Claire saw that I still retained some semblance of consciousness. 'Goodbye!' she called, and added something that I could not hear because of the red waves of pain, but I knew Gogrol laughed at it. Thereafter, for what seemed like a long time, I knew only that I was crawling doggedly through an inferno of torture.

When the red mist lifted, I was only at the base of the rise. Far above I could see the figures of Claire and Gogrol, and I perceived that though he strode with easy steps, protected by his helmet, the girl was already staggering from breathlessness. While I watched, she stumbled, and then began to struggle frantically and spasmodically to jerk away from him. It wasn't that she meant to break her promise, but merely that the agonies of suffocation drove her to attempt any means of regaining breathable air.

But the struggle was brief. It was less than a minute before she fainted, passed out from air starvation, and Gogrol slung her carelessly under one arm – as I said, she weighed about twelve pounds on Europa – and pressed on. At the very crest he paused and looked back, and in that thin, clear air I could see every detail with telescopic distinctness, even to the shadow he cast across Claire's drooping golden head.

He raised the revolver to his temple, waved it at me with a derisive gesture, and then flung it far down the mountainside toward me. His meaning was unmistakable; he was advising me to commit suicide. When I reached the revolver, there was a single unused cartridge in the clip; I looked up, tempted to try it on Gogrol himself, but he was gone across the ridge.

Now I knew all hope was gone. Perhaps I was dying from that last bullet anyway, but whether I were or not, Claire was lost, and all that remained for me was the madness of solitude, forever imprisoned by empty space in this valley. That or – suicide.

I don't know how many times I thought of that single cartridge, but I know the thought grew very tempting after a few more hours of pain. By that time, for all I knew, the *Minos* might have taken off on its dash to death, for the roar of its blast could not carry over the airless heights, and it would be so high and small by the time I could see it above the hills that I might have missed it.

If only I could cross those hills! I began to realize that more important than my own life was Claire's safety, even if it meant saving her for Coretti. But I couldn't save her; I couldn't even get to her unless I could walk along the hills like a bladder bird.

Like a bladder bird! I was sure that it was only the delirium of fever that suggested that wild thought. Would it work? I answered myself that whether it worked or failed it was better than dying here without ever trying.

I stalked that bladder bird like a cat. Time after time I spent long minutes creeping toward a copse of song-bushes only to have the creature sail blithely over my head and across the valley. But at last I saw the thing crouched for flight above me; I dared not delay longer lest my wounds weaken me too much for the trial of my plan, and I fired. There went my single cartridge.

The bladder bird dropped! But that was only the beginning of my task. Carefully – so very carefully – I removed the creature's bladder, leaving the vent tube intact. Then, through the opening that connects to the bird's single lung, I slipped my head, letting the bloody rim contract about my throat.

I knew that wouldn't be air-tight, so I bound it with strips torn from my clothing, so closely that it all but choked me. Then I took the slimy vent tube in my mouth and began an endless routine. Breathe in through the vent tube, pinch it shut, breathe out into the bladder – over and over and over. But gradually the bladder expanded with filthy, vitiated, stinking, and once-breathed air.

I had it half filled when I saw that I was going to have to start if I were to have a chance of living long enough for a test. Breathing through the vent tube as long as there was air enough, peering dully through the semitransparent walls of the bladder, I started crawling up the hill.

I won't describe that incredible journey. On Earth it would have been utterly impossible; here, since I weighed but eighteen pounds, it was barely within the bounds of possibility. As I ascended, the bladder swelled against the reduced pressure; by the time I had to start breathing the fearful stuff, I could feel it escaping and bubbling through the blood around my neck.

Somehow I made the crest, almost directly above the *Minos*. It was still there, anyway. Gogrol hadn't come this way, and now I saw why. There was a sheer drop here of four hundred feet. Well, that only equaled fifty on Earth, but even fifty – But I had to try it, because I was dying here on the peaks. I jumped.

I landed with a wrench of pain on my wounded leg, but much more lightly than I had feared. Of course! Jumping down into denser air, the great bladder had acted like a parachute, and, after all, my weight here was but eighteen pounds. I crawled onward, in agony for the moment when I could cast off the stinking, choking bladder.

That moment came. I had crossed the peaks, and before me lay the *Minos*. I crawled on, around to the side where the air lock was. It was open, and a voice bellowed out of it. Gogrol!

'You'll trick me, eh!' he screeched. 'You'll lay a course that will crash us! We'll see! We'll see!' There came the unmistakable sound of a blow, and a faint whimper of pain.

Somewhere I found the strength to stand up. Brandishing the empty automatic, I swayed into the air lock, sliding along the walls to the control room.

There was something about the figure that bent in the dusk above a sobbing girl that aroused a flash of recognition. Seeing him thus in a shadowed control room with the sun shields up – I knew what I should have known weeks ago. Gogrol was – Kratska!

'Kratska!' I croaked, and he whirled. Both he and Claire were frozen into utter rigidity by surprise and disbelief. I really think they were both convinced that I was a ghost.

'How – how – ' squeaked Gogrol, or rather Kratska.

'I walked across. I'd walk across hell to find you, Kratska.' I brandished the gun. 'Get out and get away quick, if you expect to escape the blast. We're leaving you here until police from Io can pick you up – on that *Hera* matter among others.' I spoke to the dazed Claire. 'Close the air lock after him. We're taking off.'

'Jack!' she cried, comprehending at last. 'But Stefan's wired to a tree out there. The blast will incinerate him!'

'Then loose him, and for Heaven's sake, quickly!'

But no sooner had she vanished than Kratska took his chance. He saw how weak I was, and he gambled on the one shot he thought remained in the magazine of my weapon. He rushed me.

I think he was mad. He was screaming curses. 'Damn you!' he screeched. 'You can't beat me! I made you the goat on the *Hera*, and I can do it here.'

And I knew he could, too, if he could overcome me before Claire released Coretti. She couldn't handle him, and we'd all be at his mercy. So I fought with all the life I had left, and felt it draining out of me like acid out of burette. And after a while it was all drained, and darkness filled up the emptiness.

I heard curious sounds. Someone was saying, 'No, I'll take off first and lay out the course after we reach escape velocity. Saves time. We've got to get him to Io.' And a little later, 'Oh, Lord, Stefan! If I roll her now – Why am I such a rotten pilot?' And then there was the roar of the blast for hours upon hours.

A long time later I realized that I was lying on the chart room table, and Coretti was looking down at me. He said, 'How you feel, Jack!' It was the first time he had used my name.

'O.K.,' I said, and then memory came back. 'Gogrol! He's Kratska!'

'He was,' said Coretti. 'He's dead.'

'Dead!' There went any chance of squaring that *Hera* mess.

'Yep. You killed him, smashed in his head with that automatic before we could pull you off. But he had it coming.'

'Yeah, maybe, but the *Hera* – '

'Never mind the *Hera*, Jack. Both Claire and I beard Kratska admit his responsibility. We'll clear you of that, all right.' He paused. 'And it might make you feel a little more chipper it I tell you that we got the formula, too, and that there's a reward for it that will leave us sitting in the clover field, even split three ways. That is, Claire keeps insisting on three ways; I know I don't deserve a split.'

'Three ways is right,' I said. 'It'll give you and Claire a good send-off.'

'Me and Claire?'

'Listen, Coretti. I didn't mean to, but I saw you the evening of the eclipse. Claire didn't look as if she was fighting you.'

He smiled. 'So you saw that,' he said slowly. 'Then you listen. A fellow who's asking a girl to marry him is apt to hold the girl a little close. And if she's got any heart, she doesn't push him away. She just says no as gently as possible.'

'She says no?'

'She did that time. I'd bet different with you.'

'She – she – ' Something about the familiar sound of the blast caught my attention. 'We're landing!'

'Yeah, on Io. We've been landing for two hours.'

'Who took off?'

'Claire did. She took off and kept going. She's been sitting there fifty hours. She thinks you need a doctor, and I don't know a damn thing about running a rocket. She's taken it clear from Europa.'

I sat up. 'Take me in there,' I said grimly. 'Don't argue. Take me in there!'

Claire barely raised her eyes when Coretti slid me down beside her. She was all but exhausted, sitting there all those weary hours, and now up against her old terror of landing.

'Jack, Jack!' she whispered as if to herself. 'I'm glad you're better.'

'Honey,' I said – her hair did look like honey – 'I'm taking half the U-bar. Just let me guide you.'

We came down without a roll, and landed like a canary feather. But I hadn't a thing to do with it; I was so weak I couldn't even move the U-bar, but she didn't know that. Confidence was all she needed; she had the makings of a damn good pilot. Yeah; I've proved that. She is a damn good pilot. But all the same, she went to sleep in the middle of our first kiss.

The Ideal

Stanley G. Weinbaum

'This,' said the Franciscan, 'is my Automaton, who at the proper time will speak, answer whatsoever question I may ask, and reveal all secret knowledge to me.' He smiled as he laid his hand affectionately on the iron skull that topped the pedestal.

The youth gazed open-mouthed, first at the head and then at the Friar. 'But it's iron!' he whispered. 'The head is iron, good father.'

'Iron without, skill within, my son,' said Roger Bacon. 'It will speak, at the proper time and in its own manner, for so have I made it. A clever man can twist the devil's arts to God's ends, thereby cheating the fiend – Sst! There sounds vespers! Plena gratia, ave Virgo.'

But it did not speak. Long hours, long weeks, the doctor mirabilis watched his creation, but iron lips were silent and the iron eyes dull, and no voice but the great man's own sounded in his monkish cell, nor was there ever an answer to all the questions that he asked – until one day when he sat surveying his work, composing a letter to Duns Scotus in distant Cologne – one day –

'Time is!' said the image, and smiled benignly.

The Friar looked up. 'Time is, indeed,' he echoed. 'Time it is that you give utterance, and to some assertion less obvious than that time is. For of course time is, else there were nothing at all. Without time – '

'Time was!' rumbled the image, still smiling, but sternly, at the statue of Draco.

'Indeed time was,' said the monk, 'Time was, is, and will be, for time is that medium in which events occur. Matter exists in space, but events – '

The image smiled no longer. 'Time is past!' it roared in tones deep as the cathedral bell outside, and burst into ten thousand pieces.

'There,' said old Haskel van Manderpootz, shutting the book, 'is my classical authority in this experiment. This story, overlaid as it is with medieval myth and legend, proves that Roger Bacon himself attempted the experiment and failed.' He shook a long finger at me. 'Yet do not get the impression, Dixon, that Friar Bacon was not a great man. He was – extremely great, in fact; he lighted the torch that his namesake Francis Bacon took up four centuries later, and that now van Manderpootz rekindles.'

I stared in silence,

'Indeed,' resumed the Professor, 'Roger Bacon might almost be called a thirteenth-century van Manderpootz, or van Manderpootz a twenty-first-century Roger Bacon. His *Opus Majus*, *Opus Minus*, and *Opus Tertium* –'

'What,' I interrupted impatiently, 'has all this to do with – that?' I indicated the clumsy metal robot standing in the corner of the laboratory.

'Don't interrupt!' snapped van Manderpootz.

At this point I fell out of my chair. The mass of metal had ejaculated something like 'A-a-gh-rasp!' and had lunged a single pace toward the window, arms upraised. 'What the devil!' I sputtered as the thing dropped its arms and returned stolidly to its place.

'A car must have passed in the alley,' said van Manderpootz indifferently. 'Now as I was saying, Roger Bacon – '

I ceased to listen. When van Manderpootz is determined to finish a statement, interruptions are worse than futile. As an ex-student of his, I know. So I permitted my thoughts to drift to certain personal problems of my own, particularly Tips Alva, who was the most pressing problem of the moment. Yes, I mean Tips Alva the 'vision dancer, the little blonde imp who entertains on the Yerba Mate hour for that Brazilian company. Chorus girls, dancers, and television stars are a weakness of mine; maybe it indicates that there's a latent artistic soul in me. Maybe.

I'm Dixon Wells, you know, scion of the N. J. Wells Corporation, Engineers Extraordinary. I'm supposed to be an engineer myself; I say supposed, because in the seven years since my graduation, my father hasn't given me much opportunity to prove it. He has a strong sense of the value of time, and I'm cursed with the unenviable quality of being late to anything and for everything. He even asserts that the occasional designs I submit are late Jacobean, but that isn't fair. They're post-Romanesque.

Old N. J. also objects to my penchant for ladies of the stage and 'vision screen, and periodically threatens to cut my allowance, though that's supposed to be a salary. It's inconvenient to be so dependent, and sometimes I regret that unfortunate market crash of 2009 that wiped out my own money, although it did keep me from marrying Whimsy White, and van Manderpootz, through his subjunctivisor, succeeded in proving that that would have been a catastrophe. But it turned out nearly as much of a disaster anyway, as far as my feelings were concerned. It took me months to forget Joanna Caldwell and her silvery eyes. Just another instance when I was a little late.

Van Manderpootz himself is my old Physics Professor, head of the Department of Newer Physics at N.Y.U., and a genius, but a bit eccentric. Judge for yourself.

'And that's the thesis,' he said suddenly, interrupting my thoughts.

'Eh? Oh, of course. But what's that grinning robot got to do with it?'

He purpled. 'I've just told you!' he roared. 'Idiot! Imbecile! to dream while van Manderpootz talks! Get out! Get out!'

I got. It was late anyway, so late that I overslept more than usual in the morning, and suffered more than the usual lecture on promptness from my father at the office.

Van Manderpootz had forgotten his anger by the next time I dropped in for an evening. The robot still stood in the corner near the window, and I lost no time asking its purpose.

'It's just a toy I had some of the students construct,' he explained. 'There's a screen of photoelectric cells behind the right eye, so connected that when a certain pattern is thrown on them, it activates the mechanism. The thing's plugged into the light-circuit, but it really ought to run on gasoline.'

'Why?'

'Well, the pattern it's set for is the shape of an automobile. See here.' He picked up a card from his desk, and cut in the outlines of a streamlined car like those of that year. 'Since only one eye is used,' he continued, 'the thing can't tell the difference between a full-sized vehicle at a distance and this small outline nearby. It has no sense of perspective.'

He held the bit of cardboard before the eye of the mechanism. Instantly came its roar of 'A-a-gh-rasp!' and it leaped forward a single pace, arms upraised. Van Manderpootz withdrew the card, and again the thing relapsed stolidly into its place.

'What the devil!' I exclaimed. 'What's it for?'

'Does van Manderpootz ever do work without reason back of it? I use it as a demonstration in my seminar.'

'To demonstrate what?'

'The power of reason,' said van Manderpootz solemnly.

'How? And why ought it to work on gasoline instead of electric power?'

'One question at a time, Dixon. You have missed the grandeur of van Manderpootz's concept. See here, this creature, imperfect as it is, represents the predatory machine. It is the mechanical parallel of the tiger, lurking in its jungle to leap on living prey. This monster's jungle is the city; its prey is the unwary machine that follows the trails called streets. Understand?'

'No.'

'Well, picture this automaton, not as it is, but as van Manderpootz could make it if he wished. It lurks gigantic in the shadows of buildings;

it creeps stealthily through dark alleys; it skulks on deserted streets, with its gasoline engine purring quietly. Then – an unsuspecting automobile flashes its image on the screen behind its eyes. It leaps. It seizes its prey, swinging it in steel arms to its steel jaws. Through the metal throat of its victim crash steel teeth; the blood of its prey – the gasoline, that is – is drained into its stomach, or its gas-tank. With renewed strength it flings away the husk and prowls on to seek other prey. It is the machine-carnivore, the tiger of mechanics.'

I suppose I stared dumbly. It occurred to me suddenly that the brain of the great van Manderpootz was cracking. 'What the – ?' I gasped.

'That,' he said blandly, 'is but a concept. I have many another use for the toy. I can prove anything with it, anything I wish.'

'You can? Then prove something.'

'Name your proposition, Dixon.'

I hesitated, nonplussed.

'Come!' he said impatiently. 'Look here; I will prove that anarchy is the ideal government, or that Heaven and Hell are the same place, or that – '

'Prove that!' I said. 'About Heaven and Hell.'

'Easily. First we will endow my robot with intelligence. I add a mechanical memory by means of the old Cushman delayed valve; I add a mathematical sense with any of the calculating machines; I give it a voice and a vocabulary with the magnetic-impulse wire phonograph. Now the point I make is this: granted an intelligent machine, does it not follow that every other machine constructed like it must have the identical qualities? Would not each robot given the same insides have exactly the same character?'

'No!' I snapped. 'Human beings can't make two machines exactly alike. There'd be tiny differences; one would react quicker than others, or one would prefer Fox Airsplitters as prey, while another reacted most vigorously to Carnecars. In other words, they'd have – individuality!' I grinned in triumph.

'My point exactly,' observed van Manderpootz. 'You admit, then, that this individuality is the result of imperfect workmanship. If our means of manufacture were perfect, all robots would be identical, and this individuality would not exist. Is that true?'

'I – suppose so.'

'Then I argue that our own individuality is due to our falling short of perfection. All of us – even van Manderpootz – are individuals only because we are not perfect. Were we perfect, each of us would be exactly like everyone else. True?'

'Uh – yes.'

'But Heaven, by definition, is a place where all is perfect. Therefore, in Heaven everybody is exactly like everybody else; and therefore, everybody thoroughly and completely bored. There is no torture like boredom, Dixon, and – well, have I proved my point?'

I was floored. 'But – about anarchy, then?' I stammered.

'Simple. Very simple for van Manderpootz. See here; with a perfect nation – that is, one whose individuals are all exactly alike, which I have just proved to constitute perfection – with a perfect nation, I repeat, laws and government are utterly superfluous. If everybody reacts to stimuli in the same way, laws are quite useless, obviously. If, for instance, a certain event occurred that might lead to a declaration of war, why, everybody in such a nation would vote for war at the same instant. Therefore government is unnecessary, and therefore anarchy is the ideal government, since it is the proper government for a perfect race.' He paused. 'I shall now prove that anarchy is not the ideal government – '

'Never mind!' I begged. 'Who am I to argue with van Manderpootz? But is that the whole purpose of this dizzy robot? Just a basis for logic?' The mechanism replied with its usual rasp as it leaped toward some vagrant car beyond the window.

'Isn't that enough?' growled van Manderpootz. 'However' – his voice dropped – 'I have even a greater destiny in mind. My boy, van Manderpootz has solved the riddle of the universe!' He paused impressively. 'Well, why don't you say something?'

'Uh!' I gasped. 'It's – uh – marvelous!'

'Not for van Manderpootz,' he said modestly.

'But – what is it?'

'Eh – oh!' He frowned. 'Well, I'll tell you, Dixon. You won't understand, but I'll tell you.' He coughed. 'As far back as the early twentieth century,' he resumed, 'Einstein proved that energy is particular. Matter is also particular, and now van Manderpootz adds that space and time are discrete!' He glared at me.

'Energy and matter are particular,' I murmured, 'and space and time are discrete! How very moral of them!'

'Imbecile!' he blazed. 'To pun on the words of van Manderpootz! You know very well that I mean particular and discrete in the physical sense. Matter is composed of particles, therefore it is particular. The particles of matter are called electrons, protons, and neutrons, and those of energy, quanta. I now add two others, the particles of space I call spations, those of time, chronons.'

'And what in the devil,' I asked, 'are particles of space and time?'

'Just what I said!' snapped van Manderpootz. 'Exactly as the particles of matter are the smallest pieces of matter that can exist, just as there is no such thing as a half of an electron, or for that matter, half a quantum, so the chronon is the smallest possible fragment of time, and the spation the smallest possible bit of space. Neither time nor space is continuous; each is composed of these infinitely tiny fragments.'

'Well, how long is a chronon in time? How big is a spation in space?'

'Van Manderpootz has even measured that. A chronon is the length of time it takes one quantum of energy to push one electron from one electronic orbit to the next. There can obviously be no shorter interval of time, since an electron is the smallest unit of matter and the quantum the smallest unit of energy. And a spation is the exact volume of a proton. Since nothing smaller exists, that is obviously the smallest unit of space.'

'Well, look here,' I argued. 'Then what's in between these particles of space and time? If time moves, as you say, in jerks of one chronon each, what's between the jerks?'

'Ah!' said the great van Manderpootz. 'Now we come to the heart of the matter. In between the particles of space and time, must obviously be something that is neither space, time, matter, nor energy. A hundred years ago Shapley anticipated van Manderpootz in a vague way when he announced his cosmo-plasma, the great underlying matrix in which time and space and the universe are embedded. Now van Manderpootz announces the ultimate unit, the universal particle, the focus in which matter, energy, time, and space meet, the unit from which electrons, protons, neutrons, quanta, spations, and chronons are all constructed. The riddle of the universe is solved by what I have chosen to name the cosmon.' His blue eyes bored into me.

'Magnificent!' I said feebly, knowing that some such word was expected. 'But what good is it?'

'What good is it?' he roared. 'It provides – or will provide, once I work out a few details – the means of turning energy into time, or space into matter, or time into space, or – ' He sputtered into silence. 'Fool!' he muttered. 'To think that you studied under the tutelage of van Manderpootz. I blush; I actually blush!'

One couldn't have told it if he were blushing. His face was always rubicund enough. 'Colossal!' I said hastily. 'What a mind!'

That mollified him. 'But that's not all,' he proceeded. 'Van Manderpootz never stops short of perfection. I now announce the unit particle of thought – the psychon!'

This was a little too much. I simply stared.

'Well may you be dumbfounded,' said van Manderpootz. 'I presume you are aware, by hearsay at least, of the existence of thought. The psychon, the unit of thought, is one electron plus one proton, which are bound so as to form one neutron, embedded in one cosmon, occupying a volume of one spation, driven by one quantum for a period of one chronon. Very obvious; very simple.'

'Oh, very!' I echoed. 'Even I can see that that equals one psychon.'

He beamed. 'Excellent! Excellent!'

'And what,' I asked, 'will you do with the psychons?'

'Ah,' he rumbled. 'Now we go even past the heart of the matter, and return to Isaak here.' He jammed a thumb toward the robot. 'Here I will create Roger Bacon's mechanical head. In the skull of this clumsy creature will rest such intelligence as not even van Manderpootz – I should say, as only van Manderpootz – can conceive. It remains merely to construct my idealizator.'

'Your idealizator?'

'Of course. Have I not just proven that thoughts are as real as matter, energy, time, or space? Have I not just demonstrated that one can be transformed, through the cosmon, into any other? My idealizator is the means of transforming psychons to quanta, just as, for instance, a Crookes tube or X-ray tube transforms matter to electrons. I will make your thoughts visible! And not your thoughts as they are in that numb brain of yours, but in ideal form. Do you see? The psychons of your mind are the same as those from any other mind, just as all electrons are identical, whether from gold or iron. Yes! your psychons' – his voice quavered – 'are identical with those from the mind of – van Manderpootz!' He paused, shaken.

'Actually?' I gasped.

'Actually. Fewer in number, of course, but identical. Therefore, my idealizator shows your thought released from the impress of your personality. It shows it – ideal!'

Well, I was late to the office again.

A week later I thought of van Manderpootz. Tips was on tour somewhere, and I didn't dare take anyone else out because I'd tried it once before and she'd heard about it. So, with nothing to do, I finally dropped around to the professor's quarter, found him missing, and eventually located him in his laboratory at the Physics Building. He was puttering around the table that had once held that damned subjunctivisor of his, but now it supported an indescribable mess of tubes and tangled wires, and as its most striking feature, a circular plane mirror etched with a grating of delicately scratched lines.

'Good evening, Dixon,' he rumbled.

I echoed his greeting. 'What's that?' I asked.

'My idealizator. A rough model, much too clumsy to fit into Isaak's iron skull. I'm just finishing it to try it out.' He turned glittering blue eyes on me. 'How fortunate that you're here. It will save the world a terrible risk.'

'A risk?'

'Yes. It is obvious that too long an exposure to the device will extract too many psychons, and leave the subject's mind in a sort of moronic condition. I was about to accept the risk, but I see now that it would be woefully unfair to the world to endanger the mind of van Manderpootz. But you are at hand, and will do very well.'

'Oh, no I won't!'

'Come, come!' he said, frowning. 'The danger is negligible. In fact, I doubt whether the device will be able to extract any psychons from your mind. At any rate, you will be perfectly safe for a period of at least half an hour. I, with a vastly more productive mind, could doubtless stand the strain indefinitely, but my responsibility to the world is too great to chance it until I have tested the machine on someone else. You should be proud of the honor.'

'Well, I'm not!' But my protest was feeble, and after all, despite his overbearing mannerisms, I knew van Manderpootz liked me, and I was positive he would not have exposed me to any real danger. In the end I found myself seated before the table facing the etched mirror.

'Put your face against the barrel,' said van Manderpootz, indicating a stovepipe-like tube. 'That's merely to cut off extraneous sights, so that you can see only the mirror. Go ahead, I tell you! It's no more than the barrel of a telescope or microscope.'

I complied. 'Now what?' I asked.

'What do you see?'

'My own face in the mirror.'

'Of course. Now I start the reflector rotating.' There was a faint whir, and the mirror was spinning smoothly, still with only a slightly blurred image of myself. 'Listen, now,' continued van Manderpootz. 'Here is what you are to do. You will think of a generic noun. "House", for instance. If you think of house, you will see, not an individual house, but your ideal house, the house of all your dreams and desires. If you think of a horse, you will see what your mind conceives as the perfect horse, such a horse as dream and longing create. Do you understand? Have you chosen a topic?'

'Yes.' After all, I was only twenty-eight; the noun I had chosen was – girl.

'Good,' said the professor. 'I turn on the current.'

There was a blue radiance behind the mirror. My own face still stared back at me from the spinning surface, but something was forming behind it, building up, growing. I blinked; when I focused my eyes again, it was – she was – there.

Lord! I can't begin to describe her. I don't even know if I saw her clearly the first time. It was like looking into another world and seeing the embodiment of all longings, dreams, aspirations, and ideals. It was so poignant a sensation that it crossed the borderline into pain. It was – well, exquisite torture or agonized delight. It was at once unbearable and irresistible.

But I gazed. I had to. There was a haunting familiarity about the impossibly beautiful features. I had seen the face – somewhere – sometime. In dreams? No; I realized suddenly what was the source of that familiarity. This was no living woman, but a synthesis. Her nose was the tiny, impudent one of Whimsy White at her loveliest moment; her lips were the perfect bow of Tips Alva; her silvery eyes and dusky velvet hair were those of Joan Caldwell. But the aggregate, the sum total, the face in the mirror – that was none of these; it was a face impossibly, incredibly, outrageously beautiful.

Only her face and throat were visible, and the features were cool, expressionless, and still as a carving. I wondered suddenly if she could smile, and with the thought, she did. If she had been beautiful before, now her beauty flamed to such a pitch that it was – well, insolent; it was an affront to be so lovely; it was insulting. I felt a wild surge of anger that the image before me should flaunt such beauty, and yet be – non-existent! It was deception, cheating, fraud, a promise that could never be fulfilled.

Anger died in the depths of that fascination. I wondered what the rest of her was like, and instantly she moved gracefully back until her full figure was visible. I must be a prude at heart, for she wasn't wearing the usual cuirass-and-shorts of that year, but an iridescent four-paneled costume that all but concealed her dainty knees. But her form was slim and erect as a column of cigarette smoke in still air, and I knew that she could dance like a fragment of mist on water. And with that thought she did move, dropping in a low curtsy, and looking up with the faintest possible flush crimsoning the curve of her throat. Yes, I must be a prude at heart; despite Tips Alva and Whimsey White and the rest, my ideal was modest.

It was unbelievable that the mirror was simply giving back my thoughts. She seemed as real as myself, and – after all – I guess she was. As real as myself, no more, no less, because she was part of my own mind. And at this point I realized that van Manderpootz was shaking me and bellowing, 'Your time's up. Come out of it! Your half-hour's up!'

'O-o-o-o-o-oh!' I groaned.

'How do you feel?' he snapped.

'Feel? All right – physically.' I looked up.

Concern flickered in his blue eyes. 'What's the cube root of 4913?' he crackled sharply.

I've always been quick at figures. 'It's – uh – 17,' I returned dully. 'Why the devil – ?'

'You're all right mentally,' he announced. 'Now – why were you sitting there like a dummy for half an hour? My idealizator must have worked, as is only natural for a van Manderpootz creation, but what were you thinking of?'

'I thought – I thought of "girl",' I groaned.

He snorted. 'Hah! You would, you idiot! "House" or "horse", wasn't good enough; you had to pick something with emotional connotations. Well, you can start right in forgetting her, because she doesn't exist.'

I couldn't give up hope as easily as that. 'But can't you – can't you – ' I didn't even know what I meant to ask.

'Van Manderpootz,' he announced, 'is a mathematician, not a magician. Do you expect me to materialize an ideal for you?' When I had no reply but a groan, he continued. 'Now I think it safe enough to try the device myself. I shall take – let's see – the thought "man". I shall see what the superman looks like, since the ideal of van Manderpootz can be nothing less than superman.' He seated himself. 'Turn that switch,' he said. 'Now!'

I did. The tubes glowed into low blue light. I watched dully, disinterestedly; nothing held any attraction for me after that image of the ideal.

'Huh!' said van Manderpootz suddenly. 'Turn it on, I say! I see nothing but my own reflection.'

I stared, then burst into a hollow laugh. The mirror was spinning; the banks of tubes were glowing; the device was operating.

Van Manderpootz raised his face, a little redder than usual. I laughed half hysterically. 'After all,' he said huffily, 'one might have a lower ideal of man than van Manderpootz. I see nothing nearly so humorous as your situation.'

The laughter died. I went miserably home, spent half the remainder of the night in morose contemplation, smoked nearly two packs of cigarettes, and didn't get to the office at all the next day.

Tips Alva got back to town for a weekend broadcast, but I didn't even bother to see her, just phoned her and told her I was sick. I guess my face lent credibility to the story, for she was duly sympathetic, and her face in the phone screen was quite anxious. Even at that, I couldn't keep my eyes away from her lips because, except for a bit too lustrous make-up, they were the lips of the ideal. But they weren't enough; they just weren't enough.

Old N. J. began to worry again. I couldn't sleep late of mornings any more, and after missing that one day, I kept getting down earlier and earlier until one morning I was only ten minutes late. He called me in at once.

'Look here, Dixon,' he said. 'Have you been to a doctor recently?'

'I'm not sick,' I said listlessly.

'Then for Heaven's sake, marry the girl! I don't care what chorus she kicks in, marry her and act like a human being again.'

'I can't.'

'Oh. She's already married, eh?'

Well, I couldn't tell him she didn't exist. I couldn't say I was in love with a vision, a dream, an ideal. He thought I was a little crazy, anyway, so I just muttered 'Yeah', and didn't argue when he said gruffly: 'Then you'll get over it. Take a vacation. Take two vacations. You might as well for all the good you are around here.'

I didn't leave New York; I lacked the energy. I just mooned around the city for a while, avoiding my friends, and dreaming of the impossible beauty of the face in the mirror. And by and by the longing to see that vision of perfection once more began to become overpowering. I don't suppose anyone except me can understand the lure of that memory; the face, you see, had been my ideal, my concept of perfection. One sees beautiful woman here and there in the world; one falls in love – but always, no matter how great their beauty or how deep one's love, they fall short in some degree of the secret vision of the ideal. But not the mirrored face; she was my ideal, and therefore, whatever imperfections she might have had in the minds of others, in my eyes she had none. None, that is, save the terrible one of being only an ideal, and therefore unattainable – but that is a fault inherent in all perfection.

It was a matter of days before I yielded. Common sense told me it was futile, even foolhardy, to gaze again on the vision of perfect desirability. I fought against the hunger, but I fought hopelessly, and was not at all surprised to find myself one evening rapping on van Manderpootz's door in the University Club. He wasn't there; I'd been hoping he wouldn't be, since it gave me an excuse to seek him in his laboratory in the Physics Building to which I would have dragged him anyway.

There I found him, writing some sort of notations on the table that held the idealizator. 'Hello, Dixon,' he said. 'Did it ever occur to you that the ideal university cannot exist? Naturally not, since it must be composed of perfect students and perfect educators, in which case the former could have nothing to learn and the latter, therefore, nothing to teach.'

What interest had I in the perfect university and its inability to exist? My whole being was desolate over the nonexistence of another ideal. 'Professor,' I said tensely, 'may I use that – that thing of yours again? I want to – uh – see something.'

My voice must have disclosed the situation, for van Manderpootz looked up sharply. 'So!' he snapped. 'So you disregarded my advice! Forget her, I said. Forget her because she doesn't exist.'

'But – I can't! Once more, Professor – only once more!'

He shrugged, but his blue, metallic eyes were a little softer than usual. After all, for some inconceivable reason, he likes me. 'Well, Dixon,' he said, 'you're of age and supposed to be of mature intelligence. I tell you that this is a very stupid request, and van Manderpootz always knows what he's talking about. If you want to stupefy yourself with the opium of impossible dreams, go ahead. This is the last chance you'll have, for tomorrow the idealizator of van Manderpootz goes into the Bacon head of Isaak there. I shall shift the oscillators so that the psychons, instead of becoming light quanta, emerge as an electron flow – a current which will actuate Isaak's vocal apparatus and come out as speech.' He paused musingly. 'Van Manderpootz will hear the voice of the ideal. Of course Isaak can return only what psychons he receives from the brain of the operator, but just as the image in the mirror, the thoughts will have lost their human impress, and the words will be those of an ideal.' He perceived that I wasn't listening, I suppose. 'Go ahead, imbecile!' he grunted.

I did. The glory that I hungered after flamed slowly into being, incredible in loveliness, and somehow, unbelievably, even more beautiful than on that other occasion. I know why now; long afterwards, van Manderpootz explained that the very fact that I had seen an ideal once before had altered my ideal, raised it to a higher level. With that face among my memories, my concept of perfection was different than it had been.

So I gazed and hungered. Readily and instantly the being in the mirror responded to my thoughts with smile and movement. When I thought of love, her eyes blazed with such tenderness that it seemed as if – I – I, Dixon Wells – were part of those pairs who had made the great romances of the world, Heloise and Abelard, Tristram and Isolde, Aucassin and Nicolette. It was like the thrust of a dagger to feel van Manderpootz shaking me, to hear his gruff voice calling, 'Out of it! Out of it! Time's up.'

I groaned and dropped my face on my hands. The professor had been right, of course; this insane repetition had only intensified an unfulfillable longing, and had made a bad mess ten times as bad. Then I heard him muttering behind me. 'Strange!' he murmured. 'In fact, fantastic. Oedipus – Oedipus of the magazine covers and billboards.'

I looked dully around. He was standing behind me, squinting, apparently, into the spinning mirror beyond the end of the black tube. 'Huh?' I grunted wearily.

'That face,' he said. 'Very queer. You must have seen her features on a hundred magazines, on a thousand billboards, on countless 'vision broadcasts. The Oedipus Complex in a curious form.'

'Eh? Could *you* see her?'

'Of course!' he grunted. 'Didn't I say a dozen times that the psychons are transmuted to perfectly ordinary quanta of visible light? If you could see her, why not I?'

'But – what about billboards and all?'

'That face,' said the professor slowly. 'It's somewhat idealized, of course, and certain details are wrong. Her eyes aren't that pallid silver-blue you imagined; they're green, sea-green, emerald-colored.'

'What the devil,' I asked hoarsely, 'are you talking about?'

'About the face in the mirror. It happens to be, Dixon, a close approximation of the features of de Lisle d'Agrion, the Dragon Fly!'

'You mean – she's real? She exists? She lives? She – '

'Wait a moment, Dixon. She's real enough, but in accordance with your habit, you're a little late. About twenty-five years too late, I should say. She must now be somewhere in the fifties – let's see – fifty-three, I think. But during your very early childhood, you must have seen her face pictured everywhere, de Lisle d'Agrion, the Dragon Fly.'

I could only gulp. That blow was devastating.

'You see,' continued van Manderpootz, 'one's ideals are implanted very early. That's why you continually fall in love with girls who possess one or another features that reminds you of her, her hair, her nose, her mouth, her eyes. Very simple, but rather curious.'

'Curious!' I blazed. 'Curious, you say! Every time I look into one of your damned contraptions I find myself in love with a myth! A girl who's dead, or married, or unreal, or turned into an old woman! Curious, eh? Damned funny, isn't it?'

'Just a moment,' said the professor placidly. 'It happens, Dixon, that she has a daughter. What's more, Denise resembles her mother. And what's still more, she's arriving in New York next week to study American letters at the University here. She writes, you see.'

That was too much for immediate comprehension. 'How – how do you know?' I gasped.

It was one of the few times I have seen the colossal blandness of van Manderpootz ruffled. He reddened a trifle, and said slowly, 'It also happens, Dixon, that many years ago in Amsterdam, Haskel van Manderpootz and de Lisle d'Agrion were – very friendly – more than friendly, I might say, but for the fact that two such powerful personalities as the Dragon Fly and van Manderpootz were always at odds.' He frowned. 'I was almost her second husband. She's had seven, I believe; Denise is the daughter of her third.'

'Why – why is she coming here?'

'Because,' he said with dignity, 'van Manderpootz is here. I am still a friend of de Lisle's.' He turned and bent over the complex device on the table. 'Hand me that wrench,' he ordered. 'Tonight I dismantle this, and tomorrow start reconstructing it for Isaak's head.'

But when, the following week, I rushed eagerly back to van Manderpootz's laboratory, the idealizator was still in place. The professor greeted me with a humorous twist to what was visible of his bearded mouth. 'Yes, it's still here,' he said, gesturing at the device. 'I've decided to build an entirely new one for Isaak, and besides, this one has afforded me considerable amusement. Furthermore, in the words of Oscar Wilde, who am I to tamper with a work of genius? After all, the mechanism is the product of the great van Manderpootz.'

He was deliberately tantalizing me. He knew that I hadn't come to hear him discourse on Isaak, or even on the incomparable van Manderpootz. Then he smiled and softened, and turned to the little inner office adjacent, the room where Isaak stood in metal austerity. 'Denise!' he called. 'Come here.'

I don't know exactly what I expected, but I do know that the breath left me as the girl entered. She wasn't exactly my image of the ideal, of course; she was perhaps the merest trifle slimmer, and her eyes – well, they must have been much like those of de Lisle d'Agrion, for they were the clearest emerald I've ever seen. They were impudently direct eyes, and I could imagine why van Manderpootz and the Dragon Fly might have been forever quarreling; that was easy to imagine, looking into the eyes of the Dragon Fly's daughter.

Nor was Denise, apparently, quite as femininely modest as my image of perfection. She wore the extremely unconcealing costume of the day, which covered, I suppose, about as much of her as one of the one-piece swimming suits of the middle years of the twentieth century. She gave an impression, not so much of fleeting grace as of litheness and supple strength, an air of independence, frankness, and – I say it again – impudence.

'Well!' she said coolly as van Manderpootz presented me. 'So *you're* the scion of the N. J. Wells Corporation. Every now and then your escapades enliven the Paris Sunday supplements. Wasn't it you who snared a million dollars in the market so you could ask Whimsy White – ?'

I rushed. 'That was greatly exaggerated,' I said hastily, 'and anyway I lost it before we – uh – before I – '

'Not before you made somewhat of a fool of yourself, I believe,' she finished sweetly.

Well, that's the sort she was. If she hadn't been so infernally lovely, if she hadn't looked so much like the face in the mirror, I'd have flared up, said 'Pleased to have met you', and never have seen her again. But I couldn't get angry, not when she had the dusky hair, the perfect lips, the saucy nose of the being who to me was ideal.

So I did see her again, and several times again. In fact, I suppose I occupied most of her time between the few literary courses she was taking, and little by little I began to see that in other respects besides the physical she was not so far from my ideal. Beneath her impudence was honesty, and frankness, and, despite herself, sweetness, so that even allowing for the head-start I'd had, I fell in love pretty hastily. And what's more, I knew she was beginning to reciprocate.

That was the situation when I called for her one noon and took her over to van Manderpootz's laboratory. We were to lunch with him at the University Club, but we found him occupied in directing some experiment in the big laboratory beyond his personal one, untangling some sort of mess that his staff had blundered into. So Denise and I wandered back into the smaller room, perfectly content to be alone together. I simply could not feel hungry in her presence; just talking to her was enough of a substitute for food.

'I'm going to be a good writer,' she was saying musingly. 'Some day, Dick, I'm going to be famous.'

Well, everyone knows how correct that prediction was. I agreed with her instantly.

She smiled. 'You're nice, Dick,' she said. 'Very nice.'

'Very?'

'*Very!*' she said emphatically. Then her green eyes strayed over to the table that held the idealizator. 'What crack-brained contraption of Uncle Haskel's is that?' she asked.

I explained, rather inaccurately, I'm afraid, but no ordinary engineer can follow the ramifications of a van Manderpootz conception. Nevertheless, Denise caught the gist of it and her eyes glowed emerald fire.

'It's fascinating!' she exclaimed. She rose and moved over to the table. 'I'm going to try it.'

'Not without the professor, you won't! It might be dangerous.'

That was the wrong thing to say. The green eyes glowed brighter as she cast me a whimsical glance. 'But I am,' she said. 'Dick, I'm going to – see my ideal man!' She laughed softly.

I was panicky. Suppose her ideal turned out tall and dark and powerful, instead of short and sandy-haired and a bit – well, chubby, as I am. 'No!' I said vehemently. 'I won't let you!'

She laughed again. I suppose she read my consternation, for she said softly, 'Don't be silly, Dick.' She sat down, placed her face against the opening of the barrel, and commanded, 'Turn it on.'

I couldn't refuse her. I set the mirror whirling, then switched on the bank of tubes. Then immediately I stepped behind her, squinting into what was visible of the flashing mirror, where a face was forming, slowly – vaguely.

I thrilled. Surely the hair of the image was sandy. I even fancied now that I could trace a resemblance to my own features. Perhaps Denise sensed something similar, for she suddenly withdrew her eyes from the tube and looked up with a faintly embarrassed flush, a thing most unusual for her.

'Ideals are dull!' she said. 'I want a real thrill. Do you know what I'm going to see? I'm going to visualize ideal horror. That's what I'll do. I'm going to see absolute horror!'

'Oh, no you're not!' I gasped. 'That's a terribly dangerous idea.' Off in the other room I heard the voice of van Manderpootz, 'Dixon!'

'Dangerous – bosh!' Denise retorted. 'I'm a writer, Dick. All this means to me is material. It's just experience, and I want it.'

Van Manderpootz again. 'Dixon! Dixon! Come here.' I said, 'Listen, Denise. I'll be right back. Don't try anything until I'm here – please!'

I dashed into the big laboratory. Van Manderpootz was facing a cowed group of assistants, quite apparently in extreme awe of the great man.

'Hah, Dixon!' he rasped. 'Tell these fools what an Emmerich valve is, and why it won't operate in a free electronic stream. Let 'em see that even an ordinary engineer knows that much.'

Well, an ordinary engineer doesn't, but it happened that I did. Not that I'm particularly exceptional as an engineer, but I did happen to know that because a year or two before I'd done some work on the big tidal turbines up in Maine, where they have to use Emmerich valves to guard against electrical leakage from the tremendous potentials in their condensers. So I started explaining, and van Manderpootz kept interpolating sarcasms about his staff, and when I finally finished, I suppose I'd been in there about half an hour. And then – I remembered Denise!

I left van Manderpootz staring as I rushed back, and sure enough, there was the girl with her face pressed against the barrel, and her hands gripping the table edge. Her features were hidden, of course, but there was something about her strained position, her white knuckles –

'Denise!' I yelled. 'Are you all right? *Denise!*'

She didn't move. I stuck my face in between the mirror and the end of the barrel and peered up the tube at her visage, and what I saw left me all but stunned. Have you ever seen stark, mad, infinite terror on a human face? That was what I saw in Denise's – inexpressible, unbearable horror, worse than the fear of death could ever be. Her green eyes were widened so that the whites showed around them; her perfect lips were contorted, her whole face strained into a mask of sheer terror.

I rushed for the switch, but in passing I caught a single glimpse of – of what showed in the mirror. Incredible! Obscene, terror-laden, horrifying things – there just aren't words for them. There are no words.

Denise didn't move as the tubes darkened. I raised her face from the barrel and when she glimpsed me she moved. She flung herself out of that chair and away, facing me with such mad terror that I halted.

'Denise!' I cried. 'It's just Dick. Look, Denise!'

But as I moved toward her, she uttered a choking scream, her eyes dulled, her knees gave, and she fainted. Whatever she had seen, it must have been appalling to the uttermost, for Denise was not the sort to faint.

It was a week later that I sat facing van Manderpootz in his little inner office. The grey metal figure of Isaak was missing, and the table that had held the idealizator was empty.

'Yes,' said van Manderpootz. 'I've dismantled it. One of van Manderpootz's few mistakes was to leave it around where a pair of incompetents like you and Denise could get to it. It seems that I continually overestimate the intelligence of others. I suppose I tend to judge them by the brain of van Manderpootz.'

I said nothing. I was thoroughly disheartened and depressed, and whatever the professor said about my lack of intelligence, I felt it justified.

'Hereafter,' resumed van Manderpootz, 'I shall credit nobody except myself with intelligence, and will doubtless be much more nearly correct.' He waved a hand at Isaak's vacant corner. 'Not even the Bacon head,' he continued. 'I've abandoned that project, because, when you come right down to it, what need has the world of a mechanical brain when it already has that of van Manderpootz?'

'Professor,' I burst out suddenly, 'why won't they let me see Denise? I've been at the hospital every day, and they let me into her room just once – just once, and that time she went right into a fit of hysterics. Why? Is she – ?' I gulped.

'She's recovering nicely, Dixon.'

'Then why can't I see her?'

'Well,' said van Manderpootz placidly, 'it's like this. You see, when you rushed into the laboratory there, you made the mistake of pushing your face in front of the barrel. She saw your features right in the midst of all those horrors she had called up. Do you see? From then on your face was associated in her mind with the whole hell's brew in the mirror. She can't even look at you without seeing all of it again.'

'*Good – God!*' I gasped. 'But she'll get over it, won't she? She'll forget that part of it?'

'The young psychiatrist who attends her – a bright chap, by the way, with a number of my own ideas – believes she'll be quite over it in a couple of months. But personally, Dixon, I don't think she'll ever welcome the sight of your face, though I myself have seen uglier visages somewhere or other.'

I ignored that. 'Lord!' I groaned. 'What a mess!' I rose to depart, and then – then I knew what inspiration means!

'Listen!' I said, spinning back. 'Listen, professor Why can't you get her back here and let her visualize the ideally beautiful? And then stick my face into that' Enthusiasm grew. '*It can't fail!*' I cried. 'At the worst, it'll cancel that other memory. It's marvelous!'

'But as usual,' said van Manderpootz, 'a little late.'

'Late? Why? You can put up your idealizator again. You'd do that much, wouldn't you?'

'Van Manderpootz,' he observed, 'is the very soul of generosity. I'd do it gladly, but it's still a little late, Dixon. You see, she married the bright young psychiatrist this noon.'

Well, I've a date with Tips Alva tonight, and I'm going to be late for it, just as late as I please. And then I'm going to do nothing but stare at her lips all evening.

The Lotus Eaters

Stanley G. Weinbaum

'Whew!' whistled 'Ham' Hammond, staring through the right forward observation port. 'What a place for a honeymoon!'

'Then you shouldn't have married a biologist,' remarked Mrs Hammond over his shoulder, but he could see her gray eyes dancing in the glass of the port. 'Nor an explorer's daughter,' she added. For Pat Hammond, until her marriage to Ham a scant four weeks ago, had been Patricia Burlingame, daughter of the great Englishman who had won so much of the twilight zone of Venus for Britain, exactly as Crowly had done for the United States.

'I didn't,' observed Ham, 'marry a biologist. I married a girl who happened to be interested in biology; that's all. It's one of her few drawbacks.'

He cut the blast to the underjets, and the rocket settled down gently on a cushion of flame toward the black landscape below. Slowly, carefully, he dropped the unwieldy mechanism until there was the faintest perceptible jar; then he killed the blast suddenly, the floor beneath them tilted slightly, and a strange silence fell like a blanket after the cessation of the roaring blast.

'We're here,' he announced.

'So we are,' agreed Pat. 'Where's here?'

'It's a point exactly seventy-five miles east of the Barrier opposite Venoble, in the British Cool Country. To the north is, I suppose, the continuation of the Mountains of Eternity, and to the south is Heaven knows what. And this last applies to the east.'

'Which is a good technical description of nowhere.' Pat laughed. 'Let's turn off the lights and look at nowhere.'

She did, and in the darkness the ports showed as faintly luminous circles.

'I suggest,' she proceeded, 'that the Joint Expedition ascend to the dome for a less restricted view. We're here to investigate; let's do a little investigating.'

'This joint of the expedition agrees,' chuckled Ham.

He grinned in the darkness at the flippancy with which Pat approached the serious business of exploration. Here they were, the Joint Expedition of the Royal Society and the Smithsonian Institute for the Investigation of Conditions on the Dark Side of Venus, to use the full official title.

Of course Ham himself, while technically the American half of the project, was in reality a member only because Pat wouldn't consider anything else; but she was the one to whom the bearded society and institute members addressed their questions, their terms, and their instructions.

And this was no more than fair, for Pat, after all, was the leading authority on Hotland flora and fauna, and, moreover, the first human child born on Venus, while Ham was only an engineer lured originally to the Venusian frontier by a dream of quick wealth in *xixtchil* trading in the Hotlands.

It was there he had met Patricia Burlingame, and there, after an adventurous journey to the foothills of the Mountains of Eternity, that he had won her. They had been married in Erotia, the American settlement, less than a month ago, and then had come the offer of the expedition to the dark side.

Ham had argued against it. He had wanted a good terrestrial honeymoon in New York or London, but there were difficulties. Primarily there was the astronomical one; Venus was past perigee, and it would be eight long months before its slow swing around the Sun brought it back to a point where a rocket could overtake the Earth. Eight months in primitive, frontier-built Erotia, or in equally primitive Venoble, if they chose the British settlement, with no amusement save hunting, no radio, no plays, even very few books. And if they must hunt, Pat argued, why not add the thrill and danger of the unknown?

No one knew what life, if any, lurked on the dark side of the planet; very few had even seen it, and those few from rockets speeding over vast mountain ranges or infinite frozen oceans. Here was a chance to explain the mystery, and explore it, expenses paid.

It took a multimillionaire to build and equip a private rocket, but the Royal Society and the Smithsonian Institute, spending government money, were above such considerations. There'd be danger, perhaps, and breathtaking thrills, but – they could be alone.

The last point had won Ham. So they had spent two busy weeks provisioning and equipping the rocket, had ridden high above the ice barrier that bounds the twilight zone, and dashed frantically through the storm line, where the cold Underwind from the sunless side meets the hot Upper Winds that sweep from the desert face of the planet.

For Venus, of course, has no rotation, and hence no alternate days and nights. One face is forever sunlit, and one forever dark, and only the planet's slow libration gives the twilight zone a semblance of seasons. And this twilight zone, the only habitable part of the planet, merges through the Hotlands on one side to the blazing desert, and on the other side ends abruptly in the ice barrier where the Upper Winds yield their moisture to the chilling breaths of the Underwind.

So here they were, crowded into the tiny glass dome above the navigation panel, standing close together on the top rung of the ladder, and with just room in the dome for both their heads. Ham slipped his arm around the girl as they stared at the scene outside.

Away off to the west was the eternal dawn – or sunset, perhaps – where the light glistened on the ice barrier. Like vast columns, the Mountains of Eternity thrust themselves against the light, with their mighty peaks lost in the lower clouds twenty-five miles above. There, a little south, were the ramparts of the Lesser Eternities, bounding American Venus, and between the two ranges were the perpetual lightnings of the storm line.

But around them, illuminated dimly by the refraction of the sunlight, was a scene of dark and wild splendor. Everywhere was ice – hills of it, spires, plains, boulders, and cliffs of it, all glowing a pallid green in the trickle of light from beyond the barrier. A world without motion, frozen and sterile, save for the moaning of the Underwind outside, not hindered here as the barrier shielded it from the Cool Country.

'It's – glorious!' Pat murmured.

'Yes,' he agreed, 'but cold, lifeless, yet menacing. Pat, do you think there is life here?'

'I should judge so. If life can exist on such worlds as Titan and Iapetus, it should exist here. How cold is it?' She glanced at the thermometer outside the dome, its column and figures self-luminous. 'Only thirty below zero, Fahrenheit. Life exists on Earth at that temperature.'

'Exists, yes. But it couldn't have developed at a temperature below freezing. Life has to be lived in liquid water.'

She laughed softly. 'You're talking to a biologist, Ham. No; life couldn't have *evolved* at thirty below zero, but suppose it originated back in the twilight zone and migrated here? Or suppose it was pushed here by the terrific competition of the warmer regions? *You* know what conditions are in the Hotlands, with the molds and doughpots and Jack Ketch trees, and the millions of little parasitic things, all eating each other.'

He considered this. 'What sort of life should you expect?'

She chuckled. 'Do you want a prediction? Very well. I'd guess, first of all, some sort of vegetation as a base, for animal life can't keep eating itself without some added fuel. It's like the story of the man with the cat farm, who raised rats to feed the cats, and then when he skinned the cats, he fed the bodies to the rats, and then fed more rats to the cats. It sounds good, but it won't work.'

'So there ought to be vegetation. Then what?'

'Then? Heaven knows. Presumably the dark side life, if it exists, came originally from the weaker strains of twilight-zone life, but what it might have become – well, I can't guess. Of course, there's the *triops noctivivans* that I discovered in the Mountains of Eternity – '

'*You* discovered!' He grinned. 'You were out as cold as ice when I carried you away from the nest of devils. You never even saw one!'

'I examined the dead one brought into Venoble by the hunters,' she returned imperturbably. 'And don't forget that the society wanted to name it after me – the *triops Patriciae*'. Involuntarily a shudder shook her at the memory of those satanic creatures that had all but destroyed the two of them. 'But I chose the other name – *triops noctivivans*, the three-eyed dweller in the dark.'

'Romantic name for a devilish beast!'

'Yes; but what I was getting at is this – that it's probable that *triops* – or *triopses* – Say, what is the plural of *triops*?'

'*Trioptes*,' he grunted. 'Latin root.'

'Well, it's probable that *trioptes*, then, are among the creatures to be found here on the night side, and that those fierce devils who attacked us in that shadowed canyon in the Mountains of Eternity are an outpost, creeping into the twilight zone through the dark and sunless passes in the mountains. They can't stand light; you saw that yourself.'

'So what?'

Pat laughed at the Americanism. 'So this: from their form and structure – six limbs, three eyes, and all – it's plain that the *trioptes* are related to ordinary native Hotlanders. Therefore I conclude that they're recent arrivals on the dark side; that they didn't evolve here, but were driven here quite lately, geologically speaking. Or geologically isn't quite the word, because *geos* means earth. *Venusologically* speaking, I should say.'

'You shouldn't say. You're substituting a Latin root for a Greek one. What you mean is aphrodisiologically speaking.'

She chuckled again. 'What I mean, and should have said right away to avoid argument, is palaeontologically speaking, which is better English. Anyway, I mean that *trioptes* haven't existed on the dark side for more than twenty to fifty thousand Earth years, or maybe less, because what do we know about the speed of evolution on Venus? Perhaps it's faster than on the Earth; maybe a *triops* could adapt itself to night life in five thousand.'

'I've seen college students adapt themselves to night life in one semester!' He grinned.

She ignored this. 'And therefore,' she proceeded, 'I argue that there must have been life here before *triops* arrived, since it must have found something to eat when it got here or it couldn't have survived. And since my examination showed that it's partly a carnivorous feeder, there must have been not only life here, but animal life. And that's as far as pure reason can carry the argument.'

'So you can't guess what sort of animal life. Intelligent, perhaps?'

'I don't know. It might be. But in spite of the way you Yankees worship intelligence, biologically it's unimportant. It hasn't even much survival value.'

'What? How can you say that, Pat? What except human intelligence has given man the supremacy of the Earth – and of Venus, too, for that matter?'

'But *has* man the supremacy of the Earth? Look here, Ham, here's what I mean about intelligence. A gorilla has a far better brain than a turtle, hasn't it? And yet which is the more successful – the gorilla, which is rare and confined only to a small region in Africa, or the turtle, which is common everywhere from the arctic to the antarctic? And as for man – well, if you had microscopic eyes, and could see every living thing on the Earth, you'd decide that man was just a rare specimen, and that the planet was really a nematode world – that is, a worm world – because the nematodes far outnumber all the other forms of life put together.'

'But that isn't supremacy, Pat.'

'I didn't say it was. I merely said that intelligence hasn't much survival value. If it has, why are the insects that have no intelligence, but just instinct, giving the human race such a battle? Men have better brains than corn borers, boll weevils, fruit flies, Japanese beetles, gypsy moths, and all the other pests, and yet they match our intelligence with just one weapon – their enormous fecundity. Do you realize that every time a child is born, until it's balanced by a death, it can be fed in only one way? And that way is by taking the food away from the child's own weight of insects.'

'All that sounds reasonable enough, but what's it got to do with intelligence on the dark side of Venus?'

'I don't know,' replied Pat, and her voice took on a queer tinge of nervousness. 'I just mean – look at it this way, Ham. A lizard is more intelligent than a fish, but not enough to give it any advantage. Then *why* did the lizard and its descendants keep on developing intelligence? Why – unless all life tends to become intelligent in time? And if that's true, then there may be intelligence even here – strange, alien, incomprehensible intelligence.'

She shivered in the dark against him. 'Never mind,' she said in suddenly altered tones. 'It's probably just fancy. The world out there is so weird, so unearthly – I'm tired, Ham. It's been a long day.'

He followed her down into the body of the rocket. As the lights flicked on the strange landscape beyond the ports was blotted out, and he saw only Pat, very lovely in the scanty costume of the Cool Country.

'Tomorrow, then,' he said. 'We've food for three weeks.'

Tomorrow, of course, meant only time and not daylight. They rose to the same darkness that had always blanketed the sunless half of Venus, with the same eternal sunset green on the horizon at the barrier. But Pat was in better humor, and went eagerly about the preparations for their first venture into the open. She brought out the parkas of inch-thick wool sheathed in rubber, and Ham, in his capacity as engineer, carefully inspected the hoods, each with its crown of powerful lamps.

These were primarily for vision, of course, but they had another purpose. It was known that the incredibly fierce *trioptes* could not face light, and thus, by using all four beams in the helmet, one could move, surrounded by a protective aura. But that did not prevent both of them from including in their equipment two blunt blue automatics and a pair of the terrifically destructive flame pistols. And Pat carried a bag at her belt, into which she proposed to drop specimens of any dark-side flora she encountered, and fauna, too, if it proved small and harmless enough.

They grinned at each other through their masks. 'Makes you look fat,' observed Ham maliciously, and enjoyed her sniff of annoyance.

She turned, threw open the door, and stamped into the open.

It was different from looking out through a port. Then the scene had some of the unreality and all of the immobility and silence of a picture, but now it was actually around them, and the cold breath and mournful voice of the Underwind proved definitely enough that the world was real. For a moment they stood in the circlet of light from the rocket ports, staring awe-struck at the horizon where the unbelievable peaks of the Greater Eternities towered black against the false sunset.

Nearer, for as far as vision reached through that sunless, moonless, starless region, was a desolate tumbled plain where peaks, minarets, spires, and ridges of ice and stone rose in indescribable and fantastic shapes, carved by the wild artistry of the Underwind.

Ham slipped a padded arm around Pat, and was surprised to feel her shiver. 'Cold?' he asked, glancing at the dial thermometer on his wrist. 'It's only thirty-six below.'

'I'm not cold,' replied Pat. 'It's the scenery; that's all.' She moved away. 'I wonder what keeps the place as warm as it is. Without sunlight you'd think – '

'Then you'd be wrong,' cut in Ham. 'Any engineer knows that gases diffuse. The Upper Winds are going by just five or six miles over our heads, and they naturally carry a lot of heat from the desert beyond the twilight zone. There's some diffusion of the warm air into the cold, and then, besides, as the warm winds cool, they tend to sink. And what's more, the contour of the country has a lot to do with it.'

He paused. 'Say,' he went on reflectively, 'I shouldn't be surprised if we found sections near the Eternities where there was a down draft, where the Upper Winds slid right along the slope and gave certain places a fairly bearable climate.'

He followed Pat as she poked around the boulders near the edge of the circle of light from the rocket.

'Ha!' she exclaimed. 'There it is, Ham! There's our specimen of dark-side plant life.'

She bent over a gray bulbous mass. 'Lichenous or fungoid,' she continued. 'No leaves, of course; leaves are only useful in sunlight. No chlorophyl for the same reason. A very primitive, very simple plant, and yet – in some ways – not simple at all. Look, Ham – a highly developed circulatory system!'

He leaned closer, and in the dim yellow light from the ports he saw the fine tracery of veins she indicated.

'That,' she proceeded, 'would indicate a sort of heart and – I wonder!' Abruptly she thrust her dial thermometer against the fleshy mass, held it there a moment, and then peered at it. 'Yes! Look how the needle's moved, Ham. It's warm! A warm-blooded plant. And when you think of it, it's only natural, because that's the one sort of plant that could live in a region forever below freezing. Life *must* be lived in liquid water.'

She tugged at the thing, and with a sullen plump it came free, and dark driblets of liquid welled out of the torn root.

'Ugh!' exclaimed Ham. 'What a disgusting thing! "And tore the bleeding mandragore", eh? Only they were supposed to scream when you uprooted them.'

He paused. A low, pulsing, wailing whimper came out of the quivering mass of pulp, and he turned a startled gaze on Pat. 'Ugh!' he grunted again. 'Disgusting!'

'Disgusting? Why, it's a beautiful organism! It's adapted perfectly to its environment.'

'Well, I'm glad I'm an engineer,' he growled, watching Pat as she opened the rocket's door and laid the thing on a square of rubber within. 'Come on. Let's look around.'

Pat closed the door and followed him away from the rocket. Instantly the night folded in around them like a black mist, and it was only by glancing back at the lighted ports that Pat could convince herself that they stood in a real world.

'Should we light our helmet lamps?' asked Ham. 'We'd better, I suppose, or risk a fall.'

Before either could move farther, a sound struck through the moaning of the Underwind, a wild, fierce, unearthly shrieking like laughter in hell, hoots and howls and mirthless chuckling noises.

'It's *triops*!' gasped Pat, forgetting plurals and grammar alike.

She was frightened; ordinarily she was as courageous as Ham, and rather more reckless and daring, but those uncanny shrieks brought back the moments of torment when they had been trapped in the canyon in the Mountains of Eternity. She was badly frightened and fumbled frantically and ineffectually at light switch and revolver.

Just as half a dozen stones hummed fast as bullets around them, and one crashed painfully on Ham's arm, he flicked on his lights. Four beams shot in a long cross on the glittering peaks, and the wild laughter rose in a crescendo of pain. He had a momentary glimpse of shadowy figures flinging themselves from pinnacle and ridge, flitting specterlike into the darkness, and then silence.

'O-o-oh!' murmured Pat. 'I – was scared, Ham.' She huddled against him, then continued more strongly: 'But there's proof. *Triops noctivivans* actually is a night-side creature, and those in the mountains are outposts or fragments that've wandered into the sunless chasms.'

Far off sounded the hooting laughter. 'I wonder,' mused Ham, 'if that noise of theirs is in the nature of a language.'

'Very probably. After all, the Hotland natives are intelligent, and these creatures are a related species. Besides, they throw stones, and they know the use of those smothering pods they showered on us in the canyon – which, by the way, must be the fruit of some night-side plant. The *trioptes* are doubtless intelligent in a fierce, bloodthirsty, barbaric fashion, but the beasts are so unapproachable that I doubt if human beings ever learn much of their minds or language.'

Ham agreed emphatically, the more so as a viciously cast rock suddenly chipped glittering particles from an icy spire a dozen paces away. He twisted his head, sending the beams of his helmet lamps angling over the plain, and a single shrill cachinnation drifted out of the dark.

'Thank Heaven the lights keep 'em fairly out of range,' he muttered. 'These are pleasant little subjects of His Majesty,* aren't they? God save the king if he had many more like 'em!'

But Pat was again engaged in her search for specimens. She had switched on her lamps now, and scrambled agilely in and out among the fantastic monuments of that bizarre plain. Ham followed her, watching as she wrenched up bleeding and whimpering vegetation. She found a dozen varieties, and one little wriggling cigar-shaped creature that she gazed at in perplexity, quite unable to determine whether it was plant, animal, or neither. And at last her specimen bag was completely filled, and they turned back over the plain toward the rocket, whose ports gleamed afar like a row of staring eyes.

But a shock awaited them as they opened the door to enter. Both of them started back at the gust of warm, stuffy, putrid, and unbreathable air that gushed into their faces with an odor of carrion.

'What – ' gasped Ham, and then laughed. 'Your mandragore!' He chuckled. 'Look at it!'

The plant she had placed within was a mass of decayed corruption. In the warmth of the interior it had decomposed rapidly and completely and was now but a semiliquid heap on the rubber mat. She pulled it through the entrance and flung mat and all away.

They clambered into an interior still reeking, and Ham set a ventilator spinning. The air that came in was cold, of course, but pure with the breath of the Underwind, sterile and dustless from its sweep across five thousand miles of frozen oceans and mountains. He swung the door closed, set a heater going, and dropped his visor to grin at Pat.

'So that's your beautiful organism!' he chuckled.

'It was. It *was* a beautiful organism, Ham. You can't blame it because we exposed it to temperatures it was never supposed to encounter.' She sighed and slung her specimen pouch to the table. 'I'll have to prepare these at once, I suppose, since they don't keep.'

Ham grunted and set about the preparation of a meal, working with the expert touch of a true Hotlander. He glanced at Pat as she bent over her specimens, injecting the bichloride solution.

'Do you suppose,' he asked, 'that the *triops* is the highest form of life on the dark side?'

* They were on British territory, being in the latitude of Venoble. The International Congress at Lisle had in 2020 apportioned the dark-side rights by giving to each nation owning Venusian possessions a wedge extending from the twilight zone to a point on the planet directly opposite the Sun in mid-autumn.

'Beyond doubt,' replied Pat. 'If any higher form existed, it would long ago have exterminated those fierce devils.'

But she was utterly wrong.

Within the span of four days they had exhausted the possibilities of the tumbled plain around the rocket. Pat had accumulated a variegated group of specimens, and Ham had taken an endless series of observations on temperature, on magnetic variations, on the direction and velocity of the Underwind.

So they moved their base, and the rocket flared into flight southward, toward the region where, presumably, the vast and mysterious Mountains of Eternity towered across the ice barrier into the dusky world of the night side. They flew slowly, throttling the reaction motors to a bare fifty miles an hour, for they were flying through night, depending on the beam of the forward light to warn against looming peaks.

Twice they halted, and each time a day or two sufficed to indicate that the region was similar to that of their first base. The same veined and bulbous plants, the same eternal Underwind, the same laughter from blood-thirsty trioptic throats.

But on the third occasion, there was a difference. They came to rest on a wild and bleak plateau among the foothills of the Greater Eternities. Far away to the westward, half the horizon still glowed green with the false sunset, but the whole span south of the due-west point was black, hidden from view by the vast ramparts of the range that soared twenty-five miles above them into the black heavens. The mountains were invisible, of course, in that region of endless night, but the two in the rocket felt the colossal nearness of those incredible peaks.

And there was another way in which the mighty presence of the Mountains of Eternity affected them. The region was warm – not warm by the standards of the twilight zone, but much warmer than the plain below. Their thermometers showed zero on one side of the rocket, five above on the other. The vast peaks, ascending into the level of the Upper Winds, set up eddies and stray currents that brought warm air down to temper the cold breath of the Underwind.

Ham stared gloomily over the plateau visible in the lights. 'I don't like it,' he grunted. 'I never did like these mountains, not since you made a fool of yourself by trying to cross 'em back in the Cool Country.'

'A fool!' echoed Pat. 'Who named these mountains? Who crossed them? Who discovered them? My father, that's who!'

'And so you thought you inherited 'em,' he retorted, 'and that all you had to do was to whistle and they'd lie down and play dead, and Madman's Pass would turn into a park walk. With the result that you'd now be a heap of clean-picked bones in a canyon if I hadn't been around to carry you out of it.'

'Oh, you're just a timid Yankee!' she snapped. 'I'm going outside to have a look.' She pulled on her parka and stepped to the door, and there paused. 'Aren't you – aren't you coming, too?' she asked hesitantly.

He grinned. 'Sure! I just wanted to hear you ask.' He slipped into his own outdoor garb and followed.

There was a difference here. Outwardly the plateau presented the same bleak wilderness of ice and stone that they had found on the plain below. There were wind-eroded pinnacles of the utmost fantasy of form, and the wild landscape that glittered in the beams from their helmet lamps was the same bizarre terrain that they had first encountered.

But the cold was less bitter here; strangely, increasing altitude on this curious planet brought warmth instead of cold, as on the Earth, because it raised one closer to the region of the Upper Winds, and here in the Mountains of Eternity the Underwind howled less persistently, broken into gusts by the mighty peaks.

And the vegetation was less sparse. Everywhere were the veined and bulbous masses, and Ham had to tread carefully lest he repeat the unpleasant experience of stepping on one and hearing its moaning whimper of pain. Pat had no such scruples, insisting that the whimper was but a tropism; that the specimens she pulled up and dissected felt no more pain than an apple that was eaten; and that, anyway, it was a biologist's business to be a biologist.

Somewhere off among the peaks shrilled the mocking laughter of a *triops*, and in the shifting shadows at the extremities of their beams, Ham imagined more than once that he saw the forms of these demons of the dark. If there they were, however, the light kept them at a safe distance, for no stones hummed past.

Yet it was a queer sensation to walk thus in the center of a moving circle of light; he felt continually as if just beyond the boundary of visibility lurked Heaven only knew what weird and incredible creatures, though reason argued that such monsters couldn't have remained undetected.

Ahead of them their beams glistened on an icy rampart, a bank or cliff that stretched right and left across their course.

Pat gestured suddenly toward it. 'Look there!' she exclaimed, holding her light steady. 'Caves in the ice – burrows, rather. See?'

He saw – little black openings as large, perhaps, as a manhole cover, a whole row of them at the base of the ice rampart. Something black skittered laughing up the glassy slope and away – a *triops*. Were these the dens of the beasts? He squinted sharply.

'Something's there!' he muttered to Pat. 'Look! Half the openings have something in front of them – or are those just rocks to block the entrance?'

Cautiously, revolvers in hand, they advanced. There was no more motion, but in the growing intensity of the beams, the objects were less and less rocklike, and at last they could make out the veinings and fleshy bulbousness of life.

At least the creatures were a new variety. Now Ham could distinguish a row of eyelike spots, and now a multiplicity of legs beneath them. The things were like inverted bushel baskets, about the size and contour, veined, flabby, and featureless save for a complete circle of eye spots. And now he could even see the semitransparent lids that closed, apparently, to shield the eyes from the pain of their lights.

They were barely a dozen feet from one of the creatures. Pat, after a moment of hesitation, moved directly before the motionless mystery.

'Well!' she said. 'Here's a new one, Ham. Hello, old fella!'

An instant later both of them were frozen in utter consternation, completely overwhelmed by bewilderment, amazement, and confusion. Issuing, it seemed, from a membrane at the top of the creature, came a clicking, high-pitched voice.

'Hello, fella!' it said.

There was an appalled silence. Ham held his revolver, but had there been need, he couldn't have used it, nor even remembered it. He was paralyzed; stricken dumb.

But Pat found her voice. 'It – isn't real,' she said faintly. 'It's a tropism. The thing just echoed whatever sounds strike it. Doesn't it, Ham? Doesn't it?'

'I – I – of course!' He was staring at the lidded eyes. 'It must be. Listen!' He leaned forward and yelled, 'Hello!' directly at the creature. 'It'll answer.'

It did. 'It isn't a tropism,' it clicked in shrill but perfect English.

'*That's* no echo!' gasped Pat. She backed away. 'I'm scared,' she whimpered, pulling at Ham's arm. 'Come away – quick!'

He thrust her behind him. 'I'm just a timid Yankee,' he grunted, 'but I'm going to cross-question this living phonograph until I find out what – or who makes it tick.'

'No! No, Ham! I'm scared!'

'It doesn't look dangerous,' he observed.

'It isn't dangerous,' remarked the thing on the ice.

Ham gulped, and Pat gave a horrified little moan.

'Who – who are you?' he faltered.

There was no answer. The lidded eyes stared steadily at him.

'What are you?' he tried again.

Again no reply.

'How do you know English?' he ventured.

The clicking voice sounded: 'I isn't know English.'

'Then – uh – then why do you speak English?'

'You speak English,' explained the mystery, logically enough.

'I don't mean why. I mean *how*?'

But Pat had overcome a part of her terrified astonishment, and her quick mind perceived a clue. 'Ham,' she whispered tensely, 'it uses the words we use. It gets the meaning from us!'

'I gets the meaning from you,' confirmed the thing ungrammatically.

Light dawned on Ham. 'Lord!' he gasped. 'Then it's up to us to give it a vocabulary.'

'You speak, I speak,' suggested the creature.

'Sure! See, Pat? We can say just anything.' He paused. 'Let's see – "When in the course of human events it – "

'Shut up!' snapped Pat. 'Yankee! You're on crown territory now. "To be or not to be; that is the question just – "

Ham grinned and was silent. When she had exhausted her memory, he took up the task: 'Once upon a time there were three bears – '

And so it went. Suddenly the situation struck him as fantastically ridiculous – there was Pat carefully relating the story of Little Red Riding Hood to a humorless monstrosity of the night-side of Venus! The girl cast him a perplexed glance as he roared into a gale of laughter.

'Tell him the one about the traveling man and the farmer's daughter!' he said, choking. 'See if you can get a smile from him!'

She joined his laughter. 'But it's really a serious matter,' she concluded. 'Imagine it, Ham! Intelligent life on the dark side! Or *are you* intelligent?' she asked suddenly of the thing on the ice.

'I am intelligent,' it assured her. 'I'm intelligently intelligent.'

'At least you're a marvelous linguist,' said the girl. 'Did you ever hear of learning English in half an hour, Ham? Think of that!' Apparently her fear of the creature had vanished.

'Well; let's make use of it,' suggested Ham. 'What's your name, friend?' There was no reply.

'Of course,' put in Pat. 'He can't tell us his name until we give it to him in English, and we can't do that because – Oh, well, let's call him Oscar, then. That'll serve.'

'Good enough. Oscar, what are you, anyway?'

'Human, I'm a man.'

'Eh? I'll be damned if you are!'

'Those are the words you've given me. To me I am a man to you.'

'Wait a moment. "To me I am – " I see, Pat. He means that the only words we have for what he considers himself are words like man and human. Well, what are your people, then?'

'People.'

'I mean your race. What race do you belong to?'

'Human.'

'Ow!' groaned Ham. 'You try, Pat.'

'Oscar,' said the girl, 'you say you're human. Are you a mammal?'

'To me man is a mammal to you.'

'Oh, good heavens!' She tried again. 'Oscar, how does your race reproduce?'

'I have not the words.'

'Are you born?'

The queer face, or faceless body, of the creature changed slightly. Heavier lids dropped over the semi-transparent ones that shielded its many eyes; it was almost as if the thing frowned in concentration.

'We are not born,' he clicked.

'Then – seeds, spores, parthenogenesis? Or fissure?'

'Spores,' shrilled the mystery, 'and fissure.'

'But –'

She paused, nonplussed. In the momentary silence came the mocking hoot of a *triops* far to their left, and both turned involuntarily, stared, and recoiled aghast. At the very extremity of their beam one of the laughing demons had seized and was bearing away what was beyond doubt one of the creatures of the caves. And to add to the horror, all the rest squatted in utter indifference before their burrows.

'Oscar!' Pat screamed. 'They got one of you!'

She broke off suddenly at the crack of Ham's revolver, but it was a futile shot.

'O-oh!' she gasped. 'The devils! They got one!' There was no comment at all from the creature before them. 'Oscar,' she cried, 'don't you care? They murdered one of you! Don't you understand?'

'Yes.'

'But – doesn't it affect you at all?' The creatures had come, somehow, to hold a sort of human sympathy in Pat's mind. They could talk; they were more than beasts. 'Don't you care at all?'

'No.'

'But what are those devils to you? What do they do that you let them murder you?'

'They eat us,' said Oscar placidly.

'Oh!' gasped Pat in horror. 'But – but why don't – '

She broke off; the creature was backing slowly and methodically into its burrow.

'Wait!' she cried. 'They can't come here! Our lights – '

The clicking voice drifted out: 'It is cold. I go because of the cold.'

There was silence.

It was colder. The gusty Underwind moaned more steadily now, and glancing along the ridge, Pat saw that every one of the cave creatures was slipping like Oscar into his burrow. She turned a helpless gaze on Ham.

'Did I – dream this?' she whispered.

'Then both of us dreamed it, Pat.' He took her arm and drew her back toward the rocket, whose round ports glowed an invitation through the dusk.

But once in the warm interior, with her clumsy outer garments removed, Pat drew her dainty legs under her, lighted a cigarette, and fell to more rational consideration of the mystery.

'There's something we don't understand about this, Ham. Did you sense anything queer about Oscar's mind?'

'It's a devilishly quick one!'

'Yes; he's intelligent enough. Intelligence of the human level, or even' – she hesitated – 'above the human. But it isn't a human mind. It's different, somehow – alien, strange. I can't quite express what I felt, but did you notice Oscar never asked a question? Not one!'

'Why – he didn't, did he? That's queer!'

'It's darn queer. Any human intelligence, meeting another thinking form of life, would ask plenty of questions. We did.' She blew a thoughtful puff of smoke. 'And that isn't all. That – that indifference of his when the *triops* attacked his fellow – was that human, or even earthly? I've seen a hunting spider snatch one fly from a swarm of them without disturbing the rest, but could that happen to intelligent creatures? It couldn't; not even to brains as undeveloped as those in a herd of deer, or a flock of sparrows. Kill one and you frighten all.'

'That's true, Pat. They're damn queer ducks, these fellow citizens of Oscar's. Queer animals.'

'Animals? Don't tell me you didn't notice, Ham!'

'Notice what?'

'Oscar's no animal. He's a plant – a warm-blooded, mobile vegetable! All the time we were talking to him he was rooting around below him with his – well, his root. And those things that looked like legs – they were pods. He didn't walk on them; he dragged himself on his root. And what's more he – '

'What's more?'

'What's more, Ham, those pods were the same sort as the ones that the *triops* threw at us in the canyon of the Mountains of Eternity, the ones that choked and smothered us so – '

'The ones that laid you out so cold, you mean.'

'Anyway, I had wits enough to notice them!' she retorted, flushing. 'But there's part of the mystery, Ham. Oscar's mind is a vegetable mind!' She paused, puffing her cigarette as he packed his pipe.

'Do you suppose,' she asked suddenly, 'that the presence of Oscar and his crew represents a menace to human occupancy of Venus? I know they're dark-side creatures, but what if mines are discovered here? What if there turns out to be a field for commercial exploitation? Humans can't live indefinitely away from sunlight, I know, but there might be a need for temporary colonies here, and what then?'

'Well, what then?' rejoined Ham.

'Yes; what then? Is there room on the same planet for two intelligent races? Won't there be a conflict of interests sooner or later?'

'What of it?' he grunted. 'Those things are primitive, Pat. They live in caves, without culture, without weapons. They're no danger to man.'

'But they're magnificently intelligent. How do you know that these we've seen aren't just a barbaric tribe and that somewhere on the vastness of the dark side there isn't a vegetable civilization? You know civilization isn't the personal prerogative of mankind, because look at the mighty decadent culture on Mars and the dead remnants on Titan. Man has simply happened to have the strangest brand of it, at least so far.'

'That's true enough, Pat,' he agreed. 'But if Oscar's fellows aren't any more pugnacious than they were toward that murderous *triops*, then they aren't much of a menace.'

She shuddered. 'I can't understand that at all. I wonder if – ' She paused, frowning.

'If what?'

'I – don't know. I had an idea – a rather horrible idea.' She looked up suddenly. 'Ham, tomorrow I'm going to find out exactly how intelligent Oscar really is. Exactly how intelligent – if I can.'

There were certain difficulties, however. When Ham and Pat approached the ice ridge, plodding across the fantastic terrain, they found themselves in utter perplexity as to which of the row of caves was the one before which they had stood in conversation with Oscar. In the glittering reflections from their lamps each opening appeared exactly like every other, and the creatures at their mouths stared at them with lidded eyes in which there was no readable expression.

'Well,' said Pat in puzzlement, 'we'll just have to try. You there, are you Oscar?'

The clicking voice sounded: 'Yes.'

'I don't believe it,' objected Ham. 'He was over more to the right. Hey! Are you Oscar?'

Another voice clicked: 'Yes.'

'You can't *both* be Oscar!'

Pat's choice responded: 'We are all Oscar.'

'Oh, never mind,' cut in Pat, forestalling Ham's protests. 'Apparently what one knows they all know, so it doesn't make any difference which we choose. Oscar, you said yesterday you were intelligent. Are you more intelligent than I am?'

'Yes. Much more intelligent.'

'Hah!' snickered Ham. 'Take that, Pat!'

She sniffed. 'Well, that puts him miles above you, Yankee! Oscar, do you ever lie?'

Opaque lids dropped over translucent ones. 'Lie,' repeated the shrill voice. 'Lie. No. There is no need.'

'Well, do you – ' She broke off suddenly at the sound of a dull pop. 'What's that? Oh! Look, Ham, one of his pods burst!' She drew back.

A sharply pungent odor assailed them, reminiscent of that dangerous hour in the canyon, but not strong enough this time to set Ham choking or send the girl reeling into unconsciousness. Sharp, acrid, and yet not entirely unpleasant.

'What's that for, Oscar?'

'It is so we – ' The voice cut short.

'Reproduce?' suggested Pat.

'Yes. Reproduce. The wind carries our spores to each other. We live where the wind is not steady.'

'But yesterday you said fissure was your method.'

'Yes. The spores lodge against our bodies and there is a – ' Again the voice died.

'A fertilization?' suggested the girl.

'No.'

'Well, a – I know! An irritation!'

'Yes.'

'That causes a tumorous growth?'

'Yes. When the growth is complete, we split.'

'Ugh!' snorted Ham. 'A tumor!'

'Shut up!' snapped the girl. 'That's all a baby is – a normal tumor.'

'A normal – Well, I'm glad I'm not a biologist! Or a woman!'

'So'm I,' said Pat demurely. 'Oscar, how much do you know?'

'Everything.'

'Do you know where my people come from?'

'From beyond the light.'

'Yes; but before that?'

'No.'

'We come from another planet,' said the girl impressively. At Oscar's silence she said: 'Do you know what a planet is?'

'Yes.'

'But did you know before I said the word?'

'Yes. Long before.'

'But how? Do you know what machinery is? Do you know what weapons are? Do you know how to make them?'

'Yes.'

'Then – why don't you?'

'There is no need.'

'No need!' she gasped. 'With light – even with fire – you could keep the *triopses* – *trioptes*, I mean – away. You could keep them from eating you!'

'There is no need.'

She turned helplessly to Ham.

'The thing's lying,' he suggested.

'I – don't think so,' she murmured. 'It's something else – something we don't understand. Oscar, how do you know all those things?'

'Intelligence.'

At the next cave another pod popped sullenly.

'But how? Tell me how you discover facts.'

'From any fact,' clicked the creature on the ice, 'intelligence can build a picture of the – ' There was silence.

'Universe?' she suggested.

'Yes. The universe. I start with one fact and I reason from it. I build a picture of the universe. I start with another fact. I reason from it. I find that the universe I picture is the same as the first. I know that the picture is true.'

Both listeners stared in awe at the creature. 'Say!' gulped Ham. 'If that's true we could find out anything from Oscar! Oscar, can you tell us secrets that we don't know?'

'No.'

'Why not?'

'You must first have the words to give me. I cannot tell you that for which you have no words.'

'It's true!' whispered Pat. 'But, Oscar, I have the words time and space and energy and matter and law and cause. Tell me the ultimate law of the universe?'

'It is the law of – ' Silence.

'Conservation of energy or matter? Gravitation?'

'No.'

'Of – of God?'

'No.'

'Of – life?'

'No. Life is of no importance.'

'Of – what? I can't think of another word.'

'There's a chance,' said Ham tensely, 'that there is no word!'

'Yes,' clicked Oscar. 'It is the law of chance. Those other words are different sides of the law of chance.'

'Good Heaven!' breathed Pat. 'Oscar, do you know what I mean by stars, suns, constellations, planets, nebulae, and atoms, protons, and electrons?'

'Yes.'

'But – how? Have you ever seen the stars that are above these eternal clouds? Or the Sun there beyond the barrier?'

'No. Reason is enough, because there is only one possible way in which the universe could exist. Only what is possible is real; what is not real is also not possible.'

'That – that seems to mean something,' murmured Pat. 'I don't see exactly what. But Oscar, why – why don't you use your knowledge to protect yourselves from your enemies?'

'There is no need. There is no need to do anything. In a hundred years we shall be – ' Silence.

'Safe?'

'Yes – no.'

'What?' A horrible thought struck her. 'Do you mean – extinct?'

'Yes.'

'But – oh, Oscar! Don't you *want* to live? Don't your people want to survive?'

'Want,' shrilled Oscar. 'Want – want – want. That word means nothing.'

'It means – it means desire, need.'

'Desire means nothing. Need – need. No. My people do not need to survive.'

'Oh,' said Pat faintly. 'Then why do you reproduce?'

As if in answer, a bursting pod sent its pungent dust over them. 'Because we must,' clicked Oscar. 'When the spores strike us, we must.'

'I – see,' murmured Pat slowly. 'Ham, I think I've got it. I think I understand. Let's get back to the ship.'

Without farewell she turned away and he followed her thoughtfully. A strange listlessness oppressed him.

They had one slight mishap. A stone flung by some stray *trioptes* sheltered behind the ridge shattered the left lamp in Pat's helmet. It seemed hardly to disturb the girl; she glanced briefly aside and plodded on. But all the way back, in the gloom to their left now illumined only by his own lamp, hoots and shrieks and mocking laughter pursued them.

Within the rocket Pat swung her specimen bag wearily to the table and sat down without removing her heavy outer garment. Nor did Ham; despite the oppressive warmth of it, he, too, dropped listlessly to a seat on the bunk.

'I'm tired,' said the girl, 'but not too tired to realize what that mystery out there means.'

'Then let's hear it.'

'Ham,' she said, 'what's the big difference between plant and animal life?'

'Why – plants derive their sustenance directly from soil and air. Animals need plants or other animals as food.'

'That isn't entirely true, Ham. Some plants are parasitic, and prey on other life. Think of the Hotlands, or think, even, of some terrestrial plants – the fungi, the pitcher plant, the *Dionaea* that trap flies.'

'Well, animals move, then, and plants don't.'

'That's not true, either. Look at microbes; they're plants, but they swim about in search of food.'

'Then what *is* the difference?'

'Sometimes it's hard to say,' she murmured, 'but I think I see it now. It's this: Animals have desire and plants necessity. Do you understand?'

'Not a damn bit.'

'Listen, Then. A plant – even a moving one – acts the way it does because it *must*, because it's made so. An animal acts because it *wants* to, or because it's made so that it wants to.'

'What's the difference?'

'There is a difference. An animal has will, a plant hasn't. Do you see now? Oscar has all the magnificent intelligence of a god, but he hasn't the will of a worm. He has reactions, but no desire. When the wind is warm he comes out and feeds; when it's cold he crawls back into the cave melted by his body heat, but that isn't will, it's just a reaction. He has no desires!'

Ham stared, roused out of his lassitude. 'I'll be damned if it isn't true!' he cried. 'That's why he – or they – never ask questions. It takes desire or will to ask a question! And that's why they have no civilization and never will have!'

'That and other reasons,' said Pat. 'Think of this: Oscar has no sex, and in spite of your Yankee pride, sex has been a big factor in building civilization. It's the basis of the family, and among Oscar's people there is no such thing as parent and child. He splits; each half of him is an adult, probably with all the knowledge and memory of the original.

'There's no need for love, no place for it, in fact, and therefore no call to fight for mate and family, and no reason to make life easier than it already is, and no cause to apply his intelligence to develop art or science or – or anything!' She paused. 'And did you ever hear of the Malthusian law, Ham?'

'Not that I remember.'

'Well, the law of Malthus says that population presses on the food supply. Increase the food and the population increases in proportion. Man evolved under that law; for a century or so it's been suspended, but our race grew to be human under it.'

'Suspended! It sounds sort of like repealing the law of gravitation or amending the law of inverse squares.'

'No, no,' she said. 'It was suspended by the development of machinery in the nineteenth and twentieth centuries, which shot the food supply so far ahead, that population hasn't caught up. But it will and the Malthusian law will rule again.'

'And what's that got to do with Oscar?'

'This, Ham: he never evolved under that law. Other factors kept his numbers below the limit of the food supply, and so his species developed free of the need to struggle for food. He's so perfectly adapted to his environment that he needs nothing more. To him a civilization would be superfluous!'

'But – then what of the *triops*?'

'Yes, the *triops*. You see, Ham, just as I argued days ago, the *triops* is a newcomer, pushed over from the twilight zone. When those devils arrived, Oscar's people were already evolved, and they couldn't change to meet the new conditions, or couldn't change quickly enough. So – they're doomed.

'As Oscar says, they'll be extinct soon – and – and they don't even care.' She shuddered. 'All they do, all they can do, is sit before their caves and think. Probably they think godlike thoughts, but they can't summon even a mouse-like will. That's what a vegetable intelligence is; that's what it has to be!'

'I think – I think you're right,' he muttered. 'In a way it's horrible, isn't it?'

'Yes.' Despite her heavy garments she shivered. 'Yes; it's horrible. Those vast, magnificent minds and no way for them to work. It's like a powerful gasoline motor with its drive shaft broken, and no matter how well it runs it can't turn the wheels. Ham, do you know what I'm going to name them? The *Lotophagi Veneris* – the Lotus Eaters! Content to sit and dream away existence while lesser minds – ours and the *trioptes*' – battle for their planet.'

'It's a good name, Pat.' As she rose he asked in surprise: 'Your specimens? Aren't you going to prepare them?'

'Oh, tomorrow.' She flung herself, parka and all, on her bunk.

'But they'll spoil! And your helmet light – I ought to fix it.'

'Tomorrow,' she repeated wearily, and his own languor kept him from further argument.

When the nauseous odor of decay awakened him some hours later Pat was asleep, still garbed in the heavy suit. He flung bag and specimens from the door, and then slipped the parka from her body. She hardly stirred as he tucked her gently into her bunk.

Pat never missed the specimen bag at all, and, somehow, the next day, if one could call that endless night a day, found them trudging over the bleak plateau with the girl's helmet lamp still unrepaired. Again at their left, the wildly mocking laughter of the night dwellers followed them, drifting eerily down on the Underwind, and twice far-flung stones chipped glittering ice from neighboring spires. They plodded listlessly and silently, as if in a sort of fascination, but their minds seemed strangely clear.

Pat addressed the first Lotus Eater they saw. 'We're back, Oscar,' she said with a faint rebirth of her usual flippancy. 'How'd you spend the night?'

'I thought,' clicked the thing.

'What'd you think about?'

'I thought about – ' The voice ceased.

A pod popped, and the curiously pleasant pungent odor was in their nostrils.

'About – us?'

'No.'

'About – the world?'

'No.'

'About – what's the use?' she ended wearily. 'We could keep that up forever, and perhaps never hit on the right question.'

'If there is a right question,' added Ham. 'How do you know there are words to fit it? How do you even know that it's the kind of thought our minds are capable of conceiving? There must be thoughts that are beyond our grasp.'

Off to their left a pod burst with a dull *pop*. Ham saw the dust move like a shadow across their beams as the Underwind caught it, and he saw Pat draw a deep draft of the pungent air as it whirled around her. Queer how pleasant the smell was, especially since it was the same stuff which in higher concentration had nearly cost their lives. He felt vaguely worried as that thought struck him, but could assign no reason for worry.

He realized suddenly that both of them were standing in complete silence before the Lotus Eater. They had come to ask questions, hadn't they?

'Oscar,' he said, 'what's the meaning of life?'

'No meaning. There is no meaning.'

'Then why fight for it so?'

'We do not fight for it. Life is unimportant.'

'And when you're gone, the world goes on just the same? Is that it?'

'When we are gone it will make no difference to any except the *trioptes* who eat us.'

'Who eat you,' echoed Ham.

There was something about that thought that did penetrate the fog of indifference that blanketed his mind. He peered at Pat, who stood passively and silently beside him, and in the glow of her helmet lamp he could see her clear gray eyes behind her goggles, staring straight ahead in what was apparently abstraction or deep thought. And beyond the ridge sounded suddenly the yells and wild laughter of the dwellers in the dark.

'Pat,' he said.

There was no answer.

'Pat!' he repeated, raising a listless hand to her arm. 'We have to go back.' To his right a pod popped. 'We have to go back,' he repeated.

A sudden shower of stones came glancing over the ridge. One struck his helmet, and his forward lamp burst with a dull explosion. Another struck his arm with a stinging pain, though it seemed surprisingly unimportant.

'We have to go back,' he reiterated doggedly.

Pat spoke at last without moving. 'What's the use?' she asked dully.

He frowned over that. What *was* the use? To go back to the twilight zone? A picture of Erotia rose in his mind, and then a vision of that honeymoon they had planned on the Earth, and then a whole series of terrestrial scenes – New York, a tree-girt campus, the sunny farm of his boyhood. But they all seemed very far away and unreal.

A violent blow that stung his shoulder recalled him, and he saw a stone bound from Pat's helmet. Only two of her lamps glowed now, the rear and the right, and he realized vaguely that on his own helmet shone only the rear and the left. Shadowy figures were skittering and gibbering along the crest of the ridge now left dark by the breaking of their lights, and stones were whizzing and spattering around them.

He made a supreme effort and seized her arm. 'We've got to go back!' he muttered.

'Why? Why should we?'

'Because we'll be killed if we stay.'

'Yes. I know that, but – '

He ceased to listen and jerked savagely at Pat's arm. She spun around and staggered after him as he turned doggedly toward the rocket.

Shrill hoots sounded as their rear lamps swept the ridge, and as he dragged the girl with infinite slowness, the shrieks spread out to the right and left. He knew what that meant; the demons were circling them to get in front of them where their shattered forward lamps cast no protecting light.

Pat followed listlessly, making no effort of her own. It was simply the drag of his arm that impelled her, and it was becoming an intolerable effort to move even himself. And there directly before him, flitting shadows that howled and hooted, were the devils that sought their lives.

Ham twisted his head so that his right lamp swept the area. Shrieks sounded as they found shelter in the shadows of peaks and ridges, but Ham, walking with his head sidewise, tripped and tumbled.

Pat wouldn't rise when he tugged at her. 'There's no need of it,' she murmured, but made no resistance when he lifted her.

An idea stirred vaguely; he bundled her into his arms so that her right lamp shot its beam forward, and so he staggered at last to the circle of light about the rocket, opened the door, and dumped her on the floor within.

He had one final impression. He saw the laughing shadows that were the *trioptes* skipping and skittering across the darkness toward the ridge where Oscar and his people waited in placid acceptance of their destiny.

The rocket was roaring along at two hundred thousand feet, because numberless observations and photographs from space had shown that not even the vast peaks of the Mountains of Eternity project forty miles above the planet's surface. Below them the clouds glistened white before and black behind, for they were just entering the twilight zone. At that height one could even see the mighty curvature of the planet.

'Half cue ball, half eight ball,' said Ham, staring down. 'Hereafter we stick to the cue-ball half.'

'It was the spores,' proceeded Pat, ignoring him. 'We *knew* they were narcotic before, but we couldn't be expected to guess that they'd carry a drug as subtle as that – to steal away your will and undermine your strength. Oscar's people are the Lotus Eaters and the Lotus, all in one. But I'm – somehow – I'm sorry for them. Those colossal, magnificent, useless minds of theirs!' What snapped you out of it?'

'Oh, it was a remark of Oscar's, something about his being only a square meal for a *triops.*'

'Well?'

'Well, did you know we've used up all our food? That remark reminded me that I hadn't eaten for two days!'

Proteus Island

Stanley G. Weinbaum

The brown Maori in the bow of the outrigger stared hard at Austin Island slowly swimming nearer; then he twisted to fix his anxious brown eyes on Carver. 'Taboo!' he exclaimed. 'Taboo! *Aussitan* taboo!'

Carver regarded him without change of expression. He lifted his gaze to the island. With an air of sullen brooding the Maori returned to his stroke. The second Polynesian threw the zoologist a pleading look.

'Taboo,' he said. '*Aussitan* taboo!'

The white man studied him briefly, but said nothing. The soft brown eyes fell and the two bent to their work. But as Carver stared eagerly shoreward there was a mute, significant exchange between the natives.

The proa slid over green combers toward the foam-skirted island, then began to sheer off as if reluctant to approach. Carver's jaw squared. '*Malloa*! Put in, you chocolate pig. Put in, do you hear?'

He looked again at the land. Austin Island was not traditionally sacred, but these natives had a fear of it for some reason. It was not the concern of a zoologist to discover why. The island was uninhabited and had been charted only recently. He noted the fern forests ahead, like those of New Zealand, the Kauri pine and dammar – dark wood hills, a curve of white beach, and between them a moving dot – an *apteryx mantelli*, thought Carver – a kiwi.

The proa worked cautiously shoreward.

'Taboo,' Malloa kept whispering. 'Him plenty *bunyip*!'

'Hope there is,' the white man grunted. 'I'd hate to go back to Jameson and the others at Macquarie without at least one little *bunyip*, or anyway a ghost of a fairy.' He grinned. '*Bunyip Carveris*. Not bad, eh? Look good in natural-history books with pictures.'

On the approaching beach the kiwi scuttled for the forest – if it *was* a kiwi after all. It looked queer, somehow, and Carver squinted after it. Of course, it had to be an *apteryx*; these islands of the New Zealand group were too deficient in fauna for it to be anything else. One variety of dog, one sort of rat, and two species of bat – that covered the mammalian life of New Zealand.

Of course, there were the imported cats, pigs and rabbits that ran wild on the North and Middle Islands, but not here. Not on the Aucklands, not on Macquarie, least of all here on Austin, out in the lonely sea between Macquarie and the desolate Balleny Islands, far down on the edge of Antarctica. No; the scuttling dot *must* have been a kiwi.

The craft grounded. Kolu, in the bow, leaped like a brown flash to the beach and drew the proa above the gentle inwash of the waves. Carver stood up and stepped out, then paused sharply at a moan from Malloa in the stern.

'See!' he gulped. 'The trees, *wahi*! The *bunyip* trees!'

Carver followed his pointing figure. The trees – what about them? There they were beyond the beach as they had fringed the sands of Macquarie and of the Aucklands. Then he frowned. He was no botanist; that was Halburton's field, back with Jameson and the *Fortune* at Macquarie Island. He was a zoologist, aware only generally of the variations of flora. Yet he frowned.

The trees *were* vaguely queer. In the distance they had resembled the giant ferns and towering kauri pine that one would expect. Yet here, close at hand, they had a different aspect – not a markedly different one, it is true, but none the less, a strangeness. The kauri pines were not exactly kauri, nor were the tree ferns quite the same Cryptogamia that flourished on the Aucklands and Macquarie. Of course, those islands were many miles away to the north, and certain local variations might be expected. All the same –

'Mutants,' he muttered, frowning. 'Tends to substantiate Darwin's isolation theories. I'll have to take a couple of specimens back to Halburton.'

'*Wahi*,' said Kolu nervously, 'we go back now?'

'Now!' exploded Carver. 'We just got here! Do you think we came all the way from Macquarie for one look? We stay here a day or two, so I have a chance to take a look at this place's animal life. What's the matter, anyway?'

'The trees, *wahi*!' wailed Malloa. '*Bunyip*! – the walking trees, the talking trees!'

'Bah! Walking and talking, eh?' He seized a stone from the pebbled beach and sent it spinning into the nearest mass of dusky green. 'Let's hear 'em say a few cuss words, then.'

The stone tore through leaves and creepers, and the gentle crash died into motionless silence. Or not entirely motionless; for a moment something dark and tiny fluttered there, and then soared briefly into black silhouette against the sky. It was small as a sparrow, but bat-like, with membranous wings. Yet Carver stared at it amazed, for it trailed a twelve-inch tail, thin as a pencil, but certainly an appendage no normal bat ought to possess.

For a moment or two the creature fluttered awkwardly in the sunlight, its strange tail lashing, and then it swooped again into the dusk of the forest whence his missile had frightened it. There was only an echo of its wild, shrill cry remaining, something that sounded like '*Wheer*! *Whe-e-e-r*!'

'What the devil!' said Carver. 'There are two species of Chiroptera in New Zealand and neighboring islands, and that was neither of them! No bat has a tail like that!'

Kolu and Malloa were wailing in chorus. The creature had been too small to induce outright panic, but it had flashed against the sky with a sinister appearance of abnormality. It was a monstrosity, an aberration, and the minds of Polynesians were not such as to face unknown strangeness without fear. Nor for that matter, reflected Carver, were the minds of whites; he shrugged away a queer feeling of apprehension. It would be sheer stupidity to permit the fears of Kolu and Malloa to influence a perfectly sane zoologist.

'Shut up!' he snapped. 'We'll have to trap that fellow, or one of his cousins. I'll want a specimen of his tribe. Rhimolophidae, I'll bet a trade dollar, but a brand-new species. We'll net one tonight.'

The voices of the two brown islanders rose in terror. Carver cut in sharply on the protests and expostulations and fragmentary descriptions of the horrors of *bunyips*, walking and talking trees, and the bat-winged spirits of evil.

'Come on,' he said gruffly. 'Turn out the stuff in the proa. I'll look along the beach for a stream of fresh water. Mawson reported water on the north side of the island.'

Malloa and Kolu were muttering as he turned away. Before him the beach stretched white in the late afternoon sun; at his left rolled the blue Pacific and at his right slumbered the strange, dark, dusky quarter; he noted curiously the all but infinite variety of the vegetable forms, marveling that there was scarcely a tree or shrub that he could identify with any variety common on Macquarie or the Aucklands, or far-away New Zealand. But of course, he mused, he was no botanist.

Anyway, remote islands often produced their own particular varieties of flora and fauna. That was part of Darwin's original evolution theory, this idea of isolation. Look at Mauritius and its dodo, and the Galapagos turtles, or for that matter, the kiwi of New Zealand, or the gigantic, extinct moa. And yet – he frowned over the thought – one never found an island that was entirely covered by its own unique forms of plant life. Windblown seeds of ocean-borne débris always caused an interchange of vegetation among islands; birds carried seeds clinging to their feathers, and even the occasional human visitors aided in the exchange.

Besides, a careful observer like Mawson in 1911 would certainly have reported the peculiarities of Austin Island. He hadn't; nor, for that matter, had the whalers who touched here at intervals as they headed into the antarctic, brought back any reports. Of course, whalers had become very rare of late years; it might have been a decade or more since one had made anchorage at Austin. Yet what change could have occurred in ten or fifteen years?

Carver came suddenly upon a narrow tidal arm into which dropped a tinkling trickle of water from a granite ledge at the verge of the jungle. He stooped, moistened his finger, and tasted it. It was brackish but drinkable, and therefore quite satisfactory. He could hardly expect to find a larger stream on Austin, since the watershed was too small on an island only seven miles by three. With his eyes he followed the course of the brook up into the tangle of fern forest, and a flash of movement arrested his eyes. For a moment he gazed in complete incredulity, knowing that he couldn't possibly be seeing – what he was seeing!

The creature had apparently been drinking at the brink of the stream, for Carver glimpsed it first in kneeling position. That was part of the surprise – the fact that it was kneeling – for no animal save man ever assumes that attitude, and this being, whatever it might be, was not human.

Wild, yellow eyes glared back at him, and the thing rose to an erect posture. It was a biped, a small travesty of man, standing no more than twenty inches in height. Little clawed fingers clutched at hanging creepers. Carver had a shocked glimpse of a body covered in patches with ragged gray fur, of an agile tail, of needle-sharp teeth in a little red mouth. But mostly he saw only malevolent yellow eyes and a face that was not human, yet had a hideous suggestion of humanity gone wild, a stunning miniature synthesis of manlike and feline characteristics. Carver had spent much time in the wastelands of the planet. His reaction was almost in the nature of a reflex, without thought or volition; his blue-barreled gun leaped and flashed as if it moved of itself. This automatism was a valuable quality in the wilder portions of the earth; more than once he had saved his life by shooting first when startled, and reflecting afterward. But the quickness of the reaction did not lend itself to accuracy.

His bullet tore a leaf at the very cheek of the creature. The thing snarled, and then, with a final flash of yellow flame from its wild eyes, leaped headlong into the tangle of foliage and vanished.

Carver whistled. 'What in Heaven's name,' he muttered aloud, 'was that?' But he had small time for reflection; long shadows and an orange tint to the afternoon light warned that darkness – sudden, twilightless darkness – was near. He turned back along the curving beach toward the outrigger.

A low coral spit hid the craft and the two Maoris, and the ridge jutted like a bar squarely across the face of the descending sun. Carver squinted against the light and trudged thoughtfully onward – to freeze into sudden immobility at the sound of a terrified scream from the direction of the proa!

He broke into a run. It was no more than a hundred yards to the coral ridge, but so swiftly did the sun drop in these latitudes that dusk seemed to race him to the crest. Shadows skittered along the beach as he leaped to the top and stared frantically toward the spot where his craft had been beached.

Something was there. A box – part of the provisions from the proa. But the proa itself – was gone!

Then he saw it, already a half dozen cables' lengths out in the bay. Malloa was crouching in the stern, Kolu was partly hidden by the sail, as the craft moved swiftly and steadily out toward the darkness gathering in the north.

His first impulse was to shout, and shout he did. Then he realized that they were beyond earshot, and very deliberately, he fired his revolver three times. Twice he shot into the air, but since Malloa cast not even a glance backward, the third bullet he sent carefully in the direction of the fleeing pair. Whether or not it took effect he could not tell, but the proa only slid more swiftly into the black distance.

He stared in hot rage after the deserters until even the white sail had vanished; then he ceased to swear, sat glumly on the single box they had unloaded, and fell to wondering what had frightened them. But that was something he never discovered.

Full darkness settled. In the sky appeared the strange constellations of the heaven's under-hemisphere; south-east glowed the glorious Southern Cross, and south the mystic Clouds of Magellan. But Carver had no eyes for these beauties; he was already long familiar with the aspect of the Southern skies.

He mused over his situation. It was irritating rather than desperate, for he was armed, and even had he not been, there was no dangerous animal life on these tiny islands south of the Aucklands, nor, excepting man, on New Zealand itself. But not even man lived in the Aucklands, or on Macquarie, or here on remote Austin. Malloa and Kolu had been terrifically frightened, beyond doubt; but it took very little to rouse the superstitious fears of a Polynesian. A strange species of bat was enough, or even a kiwi passing in the shadows of the brush, or merely their own fancies, stimulated by whatever wild tales had ringed lonely Austin Island with taboos.

And as for rescue, that too was certain. Malloa and Kolu might recover their courage and return for him. If they didn't, they still might make for Macquarie Island and the *Fortune* expedition. Even if they did what he supposed they naturally would do – head for the Aucklands, and then to their home on the Chathams – still Jameson would begin to worry in three or four days, and there'd be a search made.

There was no danger, he told himself – nothing to worry about. Best thing to do was simply to go about his work. Luckily, the box on which he sat was the one that contained his cyanide jar for insect specimens, nets, traps, and snares. He could proceed just as planned, except that he'd have to devote some of his time to hunting and preparing food.

Carver lighted his pipe, set about building a fire of the plentiful driftwood, and prepared for the night. He delivered himself of a few choice epithets descriptive of the two Maoris as he realized that his comfortable sleeping bag was gone with the proa, but the fire would serve against the chill of the high Southern latitude. He puffed his pipe reflectively to its end, lay down near his driftwood blaze, and prepared to sleep.

When, seven hours and fifty minutes later, the edge of the sun dented the eastern horizon, he was ready to admit that the night was something other than a success. He was hardened to the tiny, persistent fleas that skipped out of the sand, and his skin had long been toughened to the bloodthirsty night insects of the islands. Yet he had made a decided failure at the attempt to sleep.

Why? It surely couldn't be nervousness over the fact of strange surroundings and loneliness. Alan Carver had spent too many nights in wild and solitary places for that. Yet the night sounds had kept him in a perpetual state of half-wakeful apprehension, and at least a dozen times he had started to full consciousness in a sweat of nervousness. Why?

He knew why. It was the night sounds themselves. Not their loudness nor their menace, but their – well, their *variety*. He knew what darkness ought to bring forth in the way of noises; he knew every bird call and bat squeak indigenous to these islands. But the noises of night here on Austin Island had refused to conform to his pattern of knowledge. They were strange, unclassified, and far more varied than they should have been; and yet, even through the wildest cry, he fancied a disturbing note of familiarity.

Carver shrugged. In the clear daylight his memories of the night seemed like foolish and perverse notions, quite inexcusable in the mind of one as accustomed to lonely places as himself. He heaved his powerful form erect, stretched, and gazed toward the matted tangle of plant life under the tree ferns.

He was hungry, and somewhere in there was breakfast, either fruit or bird. Those represented the entire range of choice, since he was not at present hungry enough to consider any of the other possible variations – rat, bat, or dog. That covered the fauna of these islands.

Did it, indeed? He frowned as sudden remembrance struck him. What of the wild, yellow-eyed imp that had snarled at him from the brookside? He had forgotten that in the excitement of the desertion of Kolu and Malloa. That was certainly neither bat, rat, nor dog. What was it?

Still frowning, he felt his gun, glancing to assure himself of its readiness. The two Maoris might have been frightened away by an imaginary menace, but the thing by the brook was something he could not ascribe to superstition. He had seen that. He frowned more deeply as he recalled the tailed bat of earlier in the preceding evening. That was no native fancy either.

He strode toward the fern forest. Suppose Austin Island *did* harbor a few mutants, freaks, and individual species. What of it? So much the better; it justified the *Fortune* expedition. It might contribute to the fame of one Alan Carver, zoologist, if he were the first to report this strange, insular animal world. And yet – it was queer that Mawson had said nothing of it, nor had the whalers.

At the edge of the forest he stopped short. Suddenly he perceived what was responsible for its aspect of queerness. He saw what Malloa had meant when he gestured toward the trees. He gazed incredulously, peering from tree to tree. It was true. There were no related species. There were no two trees alike. Not two alike. Each was individual in leaf, bark, stem. There were no two the same. *No two trees were alike!*

But that was impossible. Botanist or not, he knew the impossibility of it. It was all the more impossible on a remote islet where inbreeding must of necessity take place. The living forms might differ from those of other islands, but not from each other – at least, not in such incredible profusion. The number of species must be limited by the very intensity of competition on an island. *Must* be!

Carver stepped back a half dozen paces, surveying the forest wall. It was true. There were ferns innumerable; there were pines; there were deciduous trees – but there were, in the hundred yard stretch he could scan accurately, *no two alike!* No two, even, with enough similarity to be assigned to the same species, perhaps not even to the same genus.

He stood frozen in uncomprehending bewilderment. What was the meaning of it? What was the origin of this unnatural plenitude of species and genera? How could any one of the numberless forms reproduce unless there were somewhere others of its kind to fertilize it? It was true, of course, that blossoms on the same tree could cross-fertilize each other, but where, then, were the offspring? It is a fundamental aspect of nature that from acorns spring oaks, and from kauri cones spring kauri pines.

In utter perplexity, he turned along the beach, edging away from the wash of the waves into which he had almost backed. The solid wall of forest was immobile save where the sea breeze ruffled its leaves, but all that Carver saw was the unbelievable variety of those leaves. Nowhere – nowhere – was there a single tree that resembled any he had seen before.

There were compound leaves, and digitate, palmate, cordate, acuminate, bipinnate, and ensiform ones. There were specimens of every variety he could name, and even a zoologist can name a number if he has worked with a botanist like Halburton. But there were *no* specimens that looked as if they might be related, however distantly, to any one of the others. It was as if, on Austin Island, the walls between the genera had dissolved, and only the grand divisions remained.

Carver had covered nearly a mile along the beach before the pangs of hunger recalled his original mission to his mind. He had to have food of some sort, animal or vegetable. With a feeling of distinct relief, he eyed the beach birds quarreling raucously up and down the sand; at least, they were perfectly normal representatives of the genus Larus. But they made, at best, but tough and oily fare, and his glance returned again to the mysterious woodlands.

He saw now a trail or path, or perhaps just a chance thinning of the vegetation along a subsoil ridge of rock, that led into the green shades, slanting toward the forested hill at the western end of the island. That offered the first convenient means of penetration he had encountered, and in a moment he was slipping through the dusky aisle, watching sharply for either fruit or bird.

He saw fruit in plenty. Many of the trees bore globes and ovoids of various sizes, but the difficulty, so far as Carver was concerned, was that he saw none he could recognize as edible. He dared not chance biting into some poisonous variety, and Heaven alone knew what wild and deadly alkaloids this queer island might produce.

Birds fluttered and called in the branches, but for the moment he saw none large enough to warrant a bullet. And besides, another queer fact had caught his attention; he noticed that the farther he proceeded from the sea, the more bizarre became the infinite forms of the trees of the forest. Along the beach he had been able at least to assign an individual growth to its family, if not its genus, but here even those distinctions began to vanish.

He knew why. 'The coastal growths are crossed with strays from other islands,' he muttered. 'But in here they've run wild. The whole island's run wild.'

The movement of a dark mass against the leaf-sprinkled sky caught his attention. A bird? If it were, it was a much larger one than the inconsiderable passerine songsters that fluttered about him. He raised his revolver carefully, and fired.

The weird forest echoed to the report. A body large as a duck crashed with a long, strange cry, thrashed briefly among the grasses of the forest floor, and was still. Carver hurried forward to stare in perplexity at his victim.

It was not a bird. It was a climbing creature of some sort, armed with viciously sharp claws and wicked, needle-pointed white teeth in a triangular little red mouth. It resembled quite closely a small dog – if one could imagine a tree-climbing dog – and for a moment Carver froze in surprise at the thought that he had inadvertently shot somebody's mongrel terrier, or at least some specimen of Canis.

But the creature was no dog. Even disregarding its plunge from the treetops, Carver could see that. The retractile claws, five on the forefeet, four on the hind, were evidence enough, but stronger still was the evidence of those needle teeth. This was one of the Felidae. He could see further proof in the yellow, slitted eyes that glared at him in moribund hate, to lose their fire now in death. This was no dog, but a cat!

His mind flashed to that other apparition on the bank of the stream. That had borne a wild aspect of feline nature, too. What was the meaning of it? Cats that looked like monkeys; cats that looked like dogs!

He had lost his hunger. After a moment he picked up the furry body and set off toward the beach. The zoologist had superseded the man; this dangling bit of disintegrating protoplasm was no longer food, but a rare specimen. He had to get to the beach to do what he could to preserve it. It would be named after him – *Felis Carveri* – doubtless.

A sound behind him brought him to an abrupt halt. He peered cautiously back through the branch-roofed tunnel. He was being trailed. Something, bestial or human, lurked back there in the forest shadows. He saw it – or them – dimly, as formless as darker shades in the shifting array that marked the wind-stirred leaves.

For the first time, the successive mysteries began to induce a sense of menace. He increased his pace. The shadows slid and skittered behind him, and, lest he ascribe the thing to fancy, a low cry of some sort, a subdued howl, rose in the dusk of the forest at his left, and was answered at his right.

He dared not run, knowing that the appearance of fear too often brought a charge from both beasts and primitive humans. He moved as quickly as he could without the effect of flight from danger, and at last saw the beach. There in the opening he would at least distinguish his pursuers, if they chose to attack.

But they didn't. He backed away from the wall of vegetation, but no forms followed him. Yet they were there. All the way back to the box and the remains of his fire, he knew that just within the cover of the leaves lurked wild forms.

The situation began to prey on his mind. He couldn't simply remain on the beach indefinitely, waiting for an attack. Sooner or later he'd have to sleep, and then – better to provoke the attack at once, see what sort of creatures he faced, and try to drive them off or exterminate them. He had, after all, plenty of ammunition.

He raised his gun, aimed at the skittering shadow, and fired. There was a howl that was indubitably bestial; before it had quivered into silence, others answered. Then Carver started violently backward, as the bushes quivered to the passage of bodies, and he saw what sort of beings had lurked there.

A line of perhaps a dozen forms leaped from the fringe of underbrush to the sand. For the space of a breath they were motionless, and Carver knew that he was in the grip of a zoologist's nightmare, for no other explanation was at all adequate.

The pack was vaguely doglike; but by no means did its members resemble the indigenous hunting dogs of New Zealand, nor the dingoes of Australia. Nor, for that matter, did they resemble any other dogs in his experience, nor, if the truth be told, any dogs at all, except perhaps in their lupine method of attack, their subdued yelps, their slavering mouths, and the arrangement of their teeth – what Carver could see of that arrangement.

But the fact that bore home to him now was another stunning repetition of all his observations of Austin Island – they did not resemble each other! Indeed, it occurred to Carver with the devastating force of a blow that, so far on this mad island, he had seen no two living creatures, animal or vegetable, that appeared to belong to related species!

The nondescript pack inched forward. He saw the wildest extremes among the creatures – beings with long hind legs and short forelimbs; a creature with hairless, thorn-scarred skin and a face like the half-human visage of a werewolf; a tiny, rat-sized thing that yelped with a shrill, yapping voice; and a mighty, barrel-chested creature whose body seemed almost designed for erect posture, and who loped on its hinder limbs with its fore-paws touching the ground at intervals like the knuckles of an orangutan. That particular being was a horrible, yellow-fanged monstrosity, and Carver chose it for his first bullet.

The thing dropped without a sound; the slug had split its skull. As the report echoed back and forth between the hills on the east and west extremities of Austin, the pack answered with a threatening chorus of bays, howls, growls, and shrieks. They shrank back momentarily from their companion's body, then came menacingly forward.

Again Carver fired. A red-eyed hopping creature yelped and crumpled. The line halted nervously, divided now by two dead forms. Their cries were no more than a muffled growling as they eyed him with red and yellowish orbs.

He started suddenly as a different sound rose, a cry whose nature he could not determine, though it seemed to come from a point where the forested bank rose sharply in a little cliff. It was as if some watcher urged on the nondescript pack, for they gathered courage again to advance. And it was at this moment that a viciously flung stone caught the man painfully on the shoulder.

He staggered, then scanned the line of brush. A missile meant humankind. The mad island harbored something more than aberrant beasts.

A second cry sounded, and another stone hummed past his ear. But this time he had caught the flash of movement at the top of the cliff, and he fired instantly.

There was a scream. A human figure reeled from the cover of foliage, swayed, and pitched headlong into the brush at the base, ten feet below. The pack of creatures broke howling, as if their courage had vanished before this evidence of power. They fled like shadows into the forest.

But something about the figure that had fallen from the cliff struck Carver as strange. He frowned, waiting a moment to assure himself that the nondescript pack had fled, and that no other menace lurked in the brush, then he darted toward the place where his assailant had fallen.

The figure was human, beyond doubt – or was it? Here on this mad island where species seemed to take any form, Carver hesitated to make even that assumption. He bent over his fallen foe, who lay face down, then turned the body over. He stared.

It was a girl. Her face, still as the features of the Buddha of Nikko, was young and lovely as a Venetian bronze figurine, with delicate features that even in unconsciousness had a wildness apparent in them. Her eyes, closed though they were, betrayed a slight, dryadlike slant.

The girl was white, though her skin was sun-darkened almost to a golden hue. Carver was certain of her color, nevertheless, for at the edges of her single garment – an untanned hide of leopard-like fur, already stiffening and cracking – her skin showed whiter.

Had he killed her? Curiously perturbed, he sought for the wound, and found it, at last, in a scarcely bleeding graze above her right knee. His shot had merely spun her off balance; it was the ten-foot fall from the cliff that had done the damage, of which the visible evidence was a reddening bruise of her left temple. But she was living. He swung her hastily into his arms and bore her across the beach, away from the brush in which her motley pack was doubtless still lurking.

He shook his nearly empty canteen, then tilted her head to pour water between her lips. Instantly her eyes flickered open, and for a moment she stared quite uncomprehendingly into Carver's eyes, not twelve inches from her own. Then her eyes widened, not so much in terror as in startled bewilderment; she twisted violently from his arms, tried twice to rise, and twice fell back as her legs refused to support her. At last she lay quite passive, keeping her fascinated gaze on his face.

But Carver received a shock as well. As her lids lifted, he started at the sight of the eyes behind them. They were unexpected, despite the hint given by their ever-so-faint Oriental cast, for they flamed upon him in a tawny hue. They were amber, almost golden, and wild as the eyes of a votary of Pan. She watched the zoologist with the intentness of a captive bird, but not with a bird's timidity, for he saw her hand fumbling for the pointed stick or wooden knife in the thong about her waist.

He proffered the canteen, and she shrank away from his extended hand. He shook the container, and at the sound of gurgling liquid, she took it gingerly, tilted a trickle into her hand, and then, to Carver's surprise, smelled it, her dainty nostrils flaring as widely as her diminutive, uptilted nose permitted. After a moment she drank from her cupped palm, poured another trickle, and drank that. It did not occur to her, apparently, to drink from the canteen.

Her mind cleared. She saw the two motionless bodies of the slain creatures, and murmured a low sound of sorrow. When she moved as if to rise, her gashed knee pained her, and she turned her strange eyes on Carver with a renewed expression of fear. She indicated the red streak of the injury.

'*C'm on?*' she said with a questioning inflection. Carver realized that the sound resembled English words through accident only. 'Where to?' He grinned.

She shook a puzzled head. '*Bu-r-r-o-o-on!*' she said '*Zee-e-e!*'

He understood that. It was her attempt to imitate the sound of his shot and the hum of the bullet. He tapped the revolver. 'Magic!' he said warningly. 'Bad medicine. Better be good girl, see?' It was obvious that she didn't understand. '*Thumbi?*' he tried. 'You Maori?' No result save a long look from slanting, golden eyes. 'Well,' he grunted, '*Sprechen Sie Deutsch*, then? Or Kanaka? Or – what the devil! That's all I know – *Latinumne intelligis?*'

'*C'm on?*' she said faintly, her eyes on the gun. She rubbed the scratch on her leg and the bruise on her temple, apparently ascribing both to the weapon.

'All right,' Carver acceded grimly. He reflected that it could do no harm to impress the girl with his powers. 'I'll come on. Watch this!'

He leveled his weapon at the first target he saw – a dead branch that jutted from a drifted log at the end of the coral spit. It was thick as his arm, but it must have been thoroughly rotted, for instead of stripping a bit of bark as he expected, the heavy slug shattered the entire branch.

'O-o-oh!' gasped the girl, clapping her hands over her ears. Her eyes flickered sidewise at him; then she scrambled wildly to her feet. She was in sheer panic.

'No, you don't!' he snapped. He caught her arm. 'You stay right here!'

For a moment he was amazed at the lithe strength of her. Her free arm flashed upward with the wooden dagger, and he caught that wrist as well. Her muscles were like tempered steel wires. She twisted frantically; then, with sudden yielding, stood quietly in his grasp, as if she thought, 'What use to struggle with a god?'

He released her. 'Sit down!' he growled.

She obeyed his gesture rather than his voice. She sat on the sand before him, gazing up with a trace of fear but more of wariness in her honey-hued eyes.

'Where are your people?' he asked sharply, pointing at her and then waving in an inclusive gesture at the forest.

She stared without comprehension, and he varied his symbolism. 'Your home, then?' he pantomimed the act of sleeping.

The result was the same, simply a troubled look from her glorious eyes.

'Now what the devil!' he muttered. 'You have a name, haven't you? A name? Look!' He tapped his chest. 'Alan. Get it? Alan. Alan.'

That she understood instantly. 'Alan,' she repeated dutifully, looking up at him.

But when he attempted to make her assign a name to herself, he failed utterly. The only effect of his efforts was a deepening of the perplexity in her features. He reverted, at last, to the effort to make her indicate in some fashion the place of her home and people, varying his gestures in every way he could devise. And at last she seemed to comprehend.

She rose doubtfully to her feet and uttered a strange, low, mournful cry. It was answered instantly from the brush, and Carver stiffened as he saw the emergence of that same motley pack of nondescript beings. They must have been watching, lurking just beyond view. Again they circled the two slain members as they advanced.

Carver whipped out his revolver. His movement was followed by a wail of anguish from the girl, who flung herself before him, arms outspread as if to shield the wild pack from the menace of the weapon. She faced him fearfully, yet defiantly, and there was puzzled questioning in her face as well. It was as if she accused the man of ordering her to summon her companions only to threaten them with death.

He stared. 'O.K.,' he said at last. 'What's a couple of rare specimens on an island that's covered with 'em? Send 'em away.'

She obeyed his gesture of command. The weird pack slunk silently from view, and the girl backed hesitantly away as if to follow them, but halted abruptly at Carver's word. Her attitude was a curious one, partly fear, but more largely composed, it seemed, of a sort of fascination, as if she did not quite understand the zoologist's nature.

This was a feeling he shared to a certain extent, for there was certainly something mysterious in encountering a white girl on this mad Austin Island. It was as if there were one specimen, and only one, of every species in the world here on this tiny islet, and she were the representative of humanity. But still he frowned perplexedly into her wild, amber eyes.

It occurred to him again that on the part of Austin he had traversed he had seen no two creatures alike. Was this girl, too, a mutant, a variant of some species other than human, who had through mere chance adopted a perfect human form? As, for instance, the doglike cat whose body still lay on the sand where he had flung it. Was she, perhaps, the sole representative of the human form on the island, Eve before Adam, in the garden? There had been a woman before Adam, he mused.

'We'll call you Lilith,' he said thoughtfully. The name fitted her wild, perfect features and her flame-hued eyes. Lilith, the mysterious being whom Adam found before him in Paradise, before Eve was created. 'Lilith,' he repeated. 'Alan – Lilith. See?'

She echoed the sounds and the gesture. Without question she accepted the name he had given her, and that she understood the sound as a name was evident by her response to it. For when he uttered it a few minutes later, her amber eyes flashed instantly to his face and remained in a silent question.

Carver laughed and resumed his puzzled thoughts. Reflectively, he produced his pipe and packed it, then struck a match and lighted it. He was startled by a low cry from the girl Lilith, and looked up to see her extended hand. For a moment he failed to perceive what she sought, and then her fingers closed around the hissing stem of the match! She had tried to seize the flame as one takes a fluttering bit of cloth.

She screamed in pain and fright. At once the pack of nondescripts appeared at the edge of the forest, voicing their howls of anger, and Carver whirled again to meet them. But again Lilith, recovering from the surprise of the burn, halted the pack with her voice, and sent them slinking away into the shadows. She sucked her scorched fingers and turned widened eyes to his face. He realized with a start of disbelief that the girl did not comprehend fire!

There was a bottle of alcohol in the box of equipment; he produced it and, taking Lilith's hand, bound a moistened strip of handkerchief about her two blistered fingers, though he knew well enough that alcohol was a poor remedy for burns. He applied the disinfectant to the bullet graze on her knee; she moaned softly at the sting, then smiled as it lessened, while her strange amber eyes followed fixedly the puffs of smoke from his pipe, and her nostrils quivered to the pungent tobacco odor.

'Now what,' queried Carver, smoking reflectively, 'am I going to do with you?'

Lilith had apparently no suggestion. She simply continued her wide-eyed regard.

'At least,' he resumed, 'you ought to know what's good to eat on this crazy island. You *do* eat, don't you?' He pantomimed the act.

The girl understood instantly. She rose, stepped to the spot where the body of the doglike cat lay, and seemed for an instant to sniff its scent. Then she removed the wooden knife from her girdle, placed one bare foot upon the body, and hacked and tore a strip of flesh from it. She extended the bloody chunk to him, and was obviously surprised at his gesture of refusal.

After a moment she withdrew it, glanced again at his face, and set her own small white teeth in the meat. Carver noted with interest how daintily she managed even that difficult maneuver, so that her soft lips were not stained by the slightest drop of blood.

But his own hunger was unappeased. He frowned over the problem of conveying his meaning, but at last hit upon a means. 'Lilith!' he said sharply. Her eyes flashed at once to him. He indicated the meat she held, then waved at the mysterious line of trees. 'Fruit,' he said. 'Tree meat. See?' He went through the motions of eating.

Again the girl understood instantly. It was odd, he mused, how readily she comprehended some things, while others equally simple seemed utterly beyond her. Queer, as everything on Austin Island was queer. Was Lilith, after all, entirely human? He followed her to the tree line, stealing a sidelong look at her wild, flame-colored eyes, and her features, beautiful, but untamed, dryadlike, elfin – wild.

She scrambled up the crumbling embankment and seemed to vanish magically into the shadows. For a moment Carver felt a surge of alarm as he clambered desperately after her; she could elude him here as easily as if she were indeed a shadow herself. True, he had no moral right to restrain her, save the hardly tenable one given by her attack; but he did not want to lose her – not yet. Or perhaps not at all.

'Lilith!' he shouted as he topped the cliff.

She appeared almost at his elbow. Above them twined a curious vine like a creeping conifer of some kind, bearing white-greenish fruits the size and shape of a pullet's egg. Lilith seized one, halved it with agile fingers, and raised a portion to her nostrils. She sniffed carefully, daintily, then flung the fruit away.

'*Pah bo!*' she said, wrinkling her nose distastefully.

She found another sort of queerly unprepossessing fruit composed of five finger-like protuberances from a fibrous disk, so that the whole bore the appearance of a large, malformed hand. This she sniffed as carefully as she had the other, then smiled sidewise up at him.

'*Bo!*' she said, extending it.

Carver hesitated. After all, it was not much more than an hour ago that the girl had been trying to kill him. Was it not entirely possible that she was now pursuing the same end, offering him a poisonous fruit?

She shook the unpleasantly bulbous object. '*Bo!*' she repeated, and then, exactly as if she understood his hesitancy, she broke off one of the fingers and thrust it into her own mouth. She smiled at him.

'Good enough, Lilith.' He grinned, taking the remainder.

It was much pleasanter to the tongue than to the eye. The pulp had a tart sweetness that was vaguely familiar to him, but he could not quite identify the taste. Nevertheless, encouraged by Lilith's example, he ate until his hunger was appeased.

The encounter with Lilith and her wild pack had wiped out thoughts of his mission. Striding back toward the beach he frowned, remembering that he was here as Alan Carver, zoologist, and in no other role. Yet – where could he begin? He was here to classify and to take specimens, but what was he to do on a mad island where *every* creature was of an unknown variety? There was no possibility of classification here, because there were no classes. There was only one of everything – or so it appeared.

Rather than set about a task futile on the very face of it, Carver turned his thoughts another way. Somewhere on Austin was the secret of this riotous disorder, and it seemed better to seek the ultimate key than to fritter away his time at the endless task of classifying. He would explore the island. Some strange volcanic gas, he mused vaguely, or some queer radioactive deposit – analogous to Morgan's experiments with x-rays on germ plasm. Or – or something else. There must be *some* answer.

'Come on, Lilith,' he ordered, and set off toward the west, where the hill seemed to be higher than the opposing eminence at the island's eastern extremity.

The girl followed with her accustomed obedience, with her honey-hued eyes fastened on Carver in that curious mixture of fear, wonder, and – perhaps – a dawning light of worship.

The zoologist was not too preoccupied with the accumulation of mysteries to glance occasionally at the wild beauty of her face, and once he caught himself trying to picture her in civilized attire – her mahogany hair confined under one of the current tiny hats, her lithe body sheathed in finer textile than the dried and cracking skin she wore, her feet in dainty leather, and her ankles in chiffon. He scowled and thrust the visualization away, but whether because it seemed too anomalous or too attractive he did not trouble to analyze.

He turned up the slope. Austin was heavily wooded, like the Aucklands, but progress was easy, for it was through a forest, not a jungle. A mad forest, true enough, but still comparatively clear of underbrush.

A shadow flickered, then another. But the first was only a queen's pigeon, erecting its glorious feather crest, and the second only an owl parrot. The birds on Austin were normal; they were simply the ordinary feathered life of the southern seas. Why? Because they were mobile; they traveled, or were blown by storms, from island to island.

It was mid-afternoon before Carver reached the peak, where a solemn outcropping of black basalt rose treeless, like a forester's watchtower. He clambered up its eroded sides and stood with Lilith beside him, gazing out across the central valley of Austin Island to the hill at the eastern point, rising until its peak nearly matched their own.

Between sprawled the wild forest, in whose depths blue-green shadows shifted in the breeze like squalls visible here and there on the surface of a calm lake. Some sort of soaring bird circled below, and far away, in the very center of the valley, was the sparkle of water. That, he knew, must be the rivulet he had already visited. But nowhere – nowhere at all – was there any sign of human occupation to account for the presence of Lilith – no smoke, no clearing, nothing.

The girl touched his arm timidly, and gestured toward the opposite hill.

'*Pah bo!*' she said tremulously. It must have been quite obvious to her that he failed to understand, for she amplified the phrase. '*R-r-r-r!*' she growled, drawing her perfect lips into an imitation of a snarl. '*Pah bo, lay shot.*' She pointed again toward the east.

Was she trying to tell him that some fierce beasts dwelt in that region? Carver could not interpret her symbolism in any other way, and the phrase she had used was the same she had applied to the poisonous fruit.

He narrowed his eyes as he gazed intently toward the eastern eminence, then started. There was something, not on the opposing hill, but down near the flash of water midway between.

At his side hung the prism binoculars he used for identifying birds. He swung the instrument to his eyes. What he saw, still not clearly enough for certainty, was a mound or structure, vine-grown and irregular. But it might be the roofless walls of a ruined cottage.

The sun was sliding westward. Too late in the day now for exploration, but tomorrow would do. He marked the place of the mound in his memory, then scrambled down.

As darkness approached, Lilith began to evince a curious reluctance to move eastward, hanging back, sometimes dragging timidly at his arm. Twice she said 'No, no!' and Carver wondered whether the word was part of her vocabulary or whether she had acquired it from him. Heaven knew, he reflected amusedly, that he had used the word often enough, as one might use it to a child.

He was hungry again, despite the occasional fruits Lilith had plucked for him. On the beach he shot a magnificent Cygnus Atratus, a black Australian swan, and carried it with its head dragging, while Lilith, awed by the shot, followed him now without objection.

He strode along the beach to his box; not that that stretch was any more desirable than the next, but if Kolu and Malloa were to return, or were to guide a rescue expedition from the *Fortune*, that was the spot they'd seek first.

He gathered driftwood, and, just as darkness fell, lighted a fire.

He grinned at Lilith's start of panic and her low 'O-o-oh!' of sheer terror as the blaze of the match caught and spread. She remembered her scorched fingers, doubtless, and she circled warily around the flames, to crouch behind him where he sat plucking and cleaning the great bird.

She was obviously quite uncomprehending as he pierced the fowl with a spit and set about roasting it, but he smiled at the manner in which her sensitive nostrils twitched at the combined odor of burning wood and cooking meat.

When it was done, he cut her a portion of the flesh, rich and fat like roast goose, and he smiled again at her bewilderment. She ate it, but very gingerly, puzzled alike by the heat and the altered taste; beyond question she would have preferred it raw and bleeding. When she had finished, she scrubbed the grease very daintily from her fingers with wet sand at a tidal pool.

Carver was puzzling again over what to do with her. He didn't want to lose her, yet he could hardly stay awake all night to guard her. There were the ropes that had lashed his case of supplies; he could, he supposed, tie her wrists and ankles; but somehow the idea appealed to him not at all. She was too naive, too trusting, too awe-struck and worshipful. And besides, savage or not, she was a white girl over whom he had no conceivable rightful authority.

At last he shrugged and grinned across the dying fire at Lilith, who had lost some of her fear of the leaping flames. 'It's up to you,' he remarked amiably. 'I'd like you to stick around, but I won't insist on it.'

She answered his smile with her own quick, flashing one, and the gleam of eyes exactly the color of the flames they mirrored, but she said nothing. Carver sprawled in the sand; it was cool enough to dull the activities of the troublesome sand fleas, and after a while he slept.

His rest was decidedly intermittent. The wild chorus of night sounds disturbed him again with its strangeness, and he woke to see Lilith staring fixedly into the fire's dying embers. Some time later he awakened again; now the fire was quite extinct, but Lilith was standing. While he watched her silently, she turned toward the forest. His heart sank; she was leaving.

But she paused. She bent over something dark – the body of one of the creatures he had shot. The big one, it was; he saw her struggle to lift it, and, finding the weight too great, drag it laboriously to the coral spit and roll it into the sea.

Slowly she returned; she gathered the smaller body into her arms and repeated the act, standing motionless for long minutes over the black water. When she returned once more she faced the rising moon for a moment, and he saw her eyes glistening with tears. He knew he had witnessed a burial.

He watched her in silence. She dropped to the sand near the black smear of ashes; but she seemed in no need of sleep. She stared so fixedly and so apprehensively toward the east that Carver felt a sense of foreboding. He was about to raise himself to sitting position when Lilith, as if arriving at a decision after long pondering, suddenly sprang to her feet and darted across the sand to the trees.

Startled, he stared into the shadows, and out of them drifted that same odd call he had heard before. He strained his ears, and was certain he heard a faint yelping among the trees. She had summoned her pack. Carver drew his revolver quietly from its holster and half rose on his arm.

Lilith reappeared. Behind her, darker shadows against the shadowy growths, lurked wild forms, and Carver's hand tightened on the grip of his revolver.

But there was no attack. The girl uttered a low command of some sort, the slinking shadows vanished, and she returned alone to her place on the sand.

The zoologist could see her face, silver-pale in the moonlight, as she glanced at him, but he lay still in apparent slumber, and Lilith, after a moment, seemed ready to imitate him. The apprehension had vanished from her features; she was calmer, more confident. Carver realized why, suddenly; she had set her pack to guard against whatever danger threatened from the east.

Dawn roused him. Lilith was still sleeping, curled like a child on the sand, and for some time he stood gazing down at her. She was very beautiful, and now, with her tawny eyes closed, she seemed much less mysterious; she seemed no island nymph or dryad, but simply a lovely, savage, primitive girl. Yet he knew – or he was beginning to suspect – the mad truth about Austin Island. If the truth were what he feared, then he might as well fall in love with a sphinx, or a mermaid, or a female centaur, as with Lilith.

He steeled himself. 'Lilith!' he called gruffly.

She awoke with a start of terror. For a moment she faced him with sheer panic in her eyes; then she remembered, gasped, and smiled tremulously. Her smile made it very hard for him to remember what it was that he feared in her, for she looked beautifully and appealingly human save for her wild, flame-colored eyes, and even what he fancied he saw in those might be but his own imagining.

She followed him toward the trees. There was no sign of her bestial bodyguards, though Carver suspected their nearness. He breakfasted again on fruits chosen by Lilith, selected unerringly, from the almost infinite variety, by her delicate nostrils. Carver mused interestedly that smell seemed to be the one means of identifying genera on this insane island.

Smell is chemical in nature. Chemical differences meant glandular ones, and glandular differences, in the last analysis, probably accounted for racial ones. Very likely the differences between a cat, say, and a dog was, in the ultimate sense, a glandular difference. He scowled at the thought and stared narrowly at Lilith; but, peer as he might, she seemed neither more nor less than an unusually lovely little savage – except for her eyes.

He was moving toward the eastern part of the island, intending to follow the brook to the site of the ruined cabin, if it *was* a ruined cabin. Again he noted the girl's nervousness as they approached the stream that nearly bisected this part of the valley. Certainly, unless her fears were sheer superstition, there was something dangerous there. He examined his gun again, then strode on.

At the bank of the brook Lilith began to present difficulties. She snatched his arm and tugged him back, wailing, 'No, no, no!' in frightened repetition.

When he glanced at her in impatient questioning, she could only repeat her phrase of yesterday. '*Lay shot*' she said, anxiously and fearfully. '*Lay shot!*'

'Humph!' he growled. 'A cannon's the only bird I ever heard of that could – ' He turned to follow the watercourse into the forest.

Lilith hung back. She could not bring herself to follow him there. For an instant he paused, looking back at her slim loveliness, then turned and strode on. Better that she remained where she was. Better if he never saw her again, for she was too beautiful for close proximity. Yet Heaven knew, he mused, that she *looked* human enough. But Lilith rebelled. Once she was certain that he was determined to go on, she gave a frightened cry. 'Alan!' she called. 'Al-an!'

He turned, astonished that she remembered his name, and found her darting to his side. She was pallid, horribly frightened, but she would not let him go alone.

Yet there was nothing to indicate that this region of the island was more dangerous than the rest. There was the same mad profusion of varieties of vegetation, the same unclassifiable leaves, fruits, and flowers. Only – or he imagined this – there were fewer birds.

One thing slowed their progress. At times the eastern bank of the rivulet seemed more open than their side, but Lilith steadfastly refused to permit him to cross. When he tried it, she clung so desperately and so violently to his arms that he at last yielded, and plowed his way through the underbrush on his own bank. It was as if the watercourse were a dividing line, a frontier, or – he frowned – a border.

By noon they had reached a point which Carver knew must be close indeed to the spot he sought. He peered through the tunnel that arched over the course of the brook, and there ahead, so overgrown that it blended perfectly with the forest wall, he saw it.

It was a cabin, or the remains of one. The log walls still stood, but the roof, doubtless of thatch, had long ago disintegrated. But what struck Carver first was the certainty, evident in design, in window openings, in doorway, that this was no native hut. It had been a white man's cabin of perhaps three rooms.

It stood on the eastern bank; but by now the brook had narrowed to a mere rill, gurgling from pool to tiny rapids. He sprang across, disregarding Lilith's anguished cry. But at a glimpse of her face he did pause. Her magnificent honey-hued eyes were wide with fear, while her lips were set in a tense little line of grimmest determination. She looked as an ancient martyr must have looked marching out to face the lions, as she stepped deliberately across to his side. It was almost as if she said, 'If you are bound to die, then I will die beside you.'

Yet within the crumbling walls there was nothing to inspire fear. There was no animal life at all, except a tiny, ratlike being that skittered out between the logs at their approach. Carver stared around him at the grassy and fern-grown interior, at the remnants of decaying furniture and the fallen débris. It had been years since this place had known human occupants, a decade at the very least.

His foot struck something. He glanced down to see a human skull and a human femur in the grass. And then other bones, though none of them were in a natural position. Their former owner must have died there where the ruined cot sagged, and been dragged here by – well, by whatever it was that had feasted on human carrion.

He glanced sidewise at Lilith, but she was simply staring affrightedly toward the east. She had not noticed the bones, or if she had, they had meant nothing to her. Carver poked gingerly among them for some clue to the identity of the remains, but there was nothing save a corroded belt buckle. That, of course, was a little; it had been a man, and most probably a white man.

Most of the débris was inches deep in the accumulation of loam. He kicked among the fragments of what must once have been a cupboard, and again his foot struck something hard and round – no skull this time, but an ordinary jar.

He picked it up. It was sealed, and there was something in it. The cap was hopelessly stuck by the corrosion of years; Carver smashed the glass against a log. What he picked from the fragments was a notebook, yellow-edged and brittle with time. He swore softly as a dozen leaves disintegrated in his hands, but what remained seemed stronger. He hunched down on the log and scanned the all-but-obliterated ink.

There was a date and a name. The name was Ambrose Callan, and the date was October 25th, 1921. He frowned. In 1921 he had been – let's see, he mused; fifteen years ago – he had been in grade school. Yet the name Ambrose Callan had a familiar ring to it.

He read more of the faded, written lines, then stared thoughtfully into space. That *was* the man, then. He remembered the Callan expedition because as a youngster he had been interested in far places, exploration, and adventure, as what youngster isn't? Professor Ambrose Callan of Northern; he began to remember that Morgan had based some of his work with artificial species – synthetic evolution – on Callan's observations.

But Morgan had only succeeded in creating a few new species of fruit fly, of Drosophila, by exposing germ plasm to hard x-rays. Nothing like this – this madhouse of Austin Island. He stole a look at the tense and fearful Lilith, and shuddered, for she seemed so lovely – and so human. He turned his eyes to the crumbling pages and read on, for here at last he was close to the secret.

He was startled by Lilith's sudden wail of terror. '*Lay shot!*' she cried. 'Alan, *lay shot!*'

He followed her gesture, but saw nothing. Her eyes were doubtless sharper than his, yet – there! in the deep afternoon shadows of the forest something moved. For an instant he saw it clearly – a malevolent pygmy like the cat-eyed horror he had glimpsed drinking from the stream. Like it? No, the same; it must be the same, for here on Austin no creature resembled another, nor ever could, save by the wildest of chances.

The creature vanished before he could draw his weapon, but in the shadows lurked other figures, other eyes that seemed alight with non-human intelligence. He fired, and a curious squawling cry came back, and it seemed to him that the forms receded for a time. But they came again, and he saw without surprise the nightmare horde of creatures.

He stuffed the notebook in his pocket and seized Lilith's wrist, for she stood as if paralyzed by horror. He backed away out of the doorless entrance, over the narrow brook. The girl seemed dazed, half hypnotized by the glimpses of the things that followed them. Her eyes were wide with fear, and she stumbled after him unseeing. He sent another shot into the shadows.

That seemed to rouse Lilith. '*Lay shot!*' she whimpered, then gathered her self-control. She uttered her curious call, and somewhere it was answered, and yet further off, answered again.

Her pack was gathering for her defense, and Carver felt a surge of apprehension for his own position. Might he not be caught between two enemies?

He never forgot that retreat down the course of the little stream. Only delirium itself could duplicate the wild battles he witnessed, the unearthly screaming, the death grips of creatures not quite natural, things that fought with the mad frenzy of freaks and outcasts. He and Lilith must have been slain immediately save for the intervention of her pack; they slunk out of the shadows with low, bestial noises, circling Carver cautiously, but betraying no scrap of caution against – the other things.

He saw or sensed something that had almost escaped him before. Despite their forms, whatever their appearance happened to be, Lilith's pack was doglike. Not in looks, certainly; it was far deeper than that. In nature, in character; that was it.

And their enemies, wild creatures of nightmare though they were, had something feline about them. Not in appearance, no more than the others, but in character and actions. Their method of fighting, for instance – all but silent, with deadly claw and needle teeth, none of the fencing of canine nature, but with the leap and talons of feline. But their aspect, their – their *catness* was more submerged by their outward appearance, for they ranged from the semi-human form of the little demon of the brook to ophidian-headed things as heavy and lithe as a panther. And they fought with a ferocity and intelligence that was itself abnormal.

Carver's gun helped. He fired when he had any visible target, which was none too often; but his occasional hits seemed to instill respect into his adversaries.

Lilith, weaponless save for stones and her wooden knife, simply huddled at his side as they backed slowly toward the beach. Their progress was maddeningly slow, and Carver began to note apprehensively that the shadows were stretching toward the east, as if to welcome the night that was sliding around from that half of the world. Night meant – destruction.

If they could attain the beach, and if Lilith's pack could hold the others at bay until Carver could build a fire, they might survive. But the creatures that were allied with Lilith were being overcome. They were hopelessly outnumbered. They were being slain more rapidly with each one that fell, as ice melts more swiftly as its size decreases.

Carver stumbled backward into orange-tinted sunlight. The beach! The sun was already touching the coral spit, and darkness was a matter of minutes – brief minutes.

Out of the brush came the remnants of Lilith's pack, a half dozen nondescripts, snarling, bloody, panting, and exhausted. For the moment they were free of their attackers, since the catlike fiends chose to lurk among the shadows. Carver backed farther away, feeling a sense of doom as his own shadow lengthened in the brief instant of twilight that divided day from night in these latitudes. And then swift darkness came just as he dragged Lilith to the ridge of the coral spit.

He saw the charge impending. Weird shadows detached themselves from the deeper shadows of the trees. Below, one of the nondescripts whined softly. Across the sand, clear for an instant against the white ground coral of the beach, the figure of the small devil with the half-human posture showed, and a malevolent sputtering snarl sounded. It was exactly as if the creature had leaped forward like a leader to exhort his troops to charge.

Carver chose that figure as his target. His gun flashed; the snarl became a squawl of agony, and the charge came.

Lilith's pack crouched; but Carver knew that this was the end. He fired. The flickering shadows came on. The magazine emptied; there was no time now to reload, so he reversed the weapon, clubbed it. He felt Lilith grow tense beside him.

And then the charge halted. In unison, as if at command, the shadows were motionless, silent save for the low snarling of the dying creature on the sand. When they moved again, it was away – toward the trees!

Carver gulped. A faint shimmering light on the wall of the forest caught his eye, and he spun. It was true! Down the beach, down there where he had left his box of supplies, a fire burned, and rigid against the light, facing toward them in the darkness, were human figures. The unknown peril of fire had frightened off the attack. He stared. There in the sea, dark against the faint glow of the West, was a familiar outline. The *Fortune*! The men there were his associates; they had heard his shots and lighted the fire as a guide.

'Lilith!' he choked. 'Look there. Come on!'

But the girl held back. The remnant of her pack slunk behind the shelter of the ridge of coral, away from the dread fire. It was no longer the fire that frightened Lilith, but the black figures around it, and Alan Carver found himself suddenly face to face with the hardest decision of his life.

He could leave her here. He knew she would not follow, knew it from the tragic light in her honey-hued eyes. And beyond all doubt that was the best thing to do; for he could not marry her. Nobody could ever marry her, and she was too lovely to take among men who might love her – as Carver did. But he shuddered a little as a picture flashed in his mind. Children! What sort of children would Lilith bear? No man could dare chance the possibility that Lilith, too, was touched by the curse of Austin Island.

He turned sadly away – a step, two steps, toward the fire. Then he turned.

'Come, Lilith,' he said gently, and added mournfully, 'other people have married, lived, and died without children. I suppose we can, too.'

The *Fortune* slid over the green swells, northward toward New Zealand. Carver grinned as he sprawled in a deck chair. Halburton was still gazing reluctantly at the line of blue that was Austin Island.

'Buck up, Vance,' Carver chuckled. 'You couldn't classify that flora in a hundred years, and if you could, what'd be the good of it? There's just one of each, anyway.'

'I'd give two toes and a finger to try,' said Halburton. 'You had the better part of three days there, and might have had more if you hadn't winged Malloa. They'd have gone home to the Chathams sure, if your shot hadn't got his arm. That's the only reason they made for Macquarie.'

'And lucky for me they did. Your fire scared off the cats.'

'The cats, eh? Would you mind going over the thing again, Alan? It's so crazy that I haven't got it all yet.'

'Sure. Just pay attention to teacher and you'll catch on.' He grinned. 'Frankly, at first I hadn't a glimmering of an idea myself. The whole island seemed insane. No two living things alike! Just one of each genus, and all unknown genera at that. I didn't get a single clue until after I met Lilith. Then I noticed that she differentiated by smell. She told good fruits from poisonous ones by the smell, and she even identified that first cat-thing I shot by smell. She'd eat that because it was an enemy, but she wouldn't touch the dog-things I shot from her pack.'

'So what?' asked Halburton, frowning.

'Well, smell is a chemical sense. It's much more fundamental than outward form, because the chemical functioning of an organism depends on its glands. I began to suspect right then that the fundamental nature of all living things on Austin Island was just the same as anywhere else. It wasn't the *nature* that was changed, but just the *form*. See?'

'Not a bit.'

'You will. You know what chromosomes are, of course. They're the carriers of heredity, or rather, according to Weissman, they carry the genes that carry the determinants that carry heredity. A human being has forty-eight chromosomes, of which he gets twenty-four from each parent.'

'So,' said Halburton, 'has a tomato.'

'Yes, but a tomato's forty-eight chromosomes carry a different heredity, else one could cross a human being with a tomato. But to return to the subject, all variations in individuals come about from the manner in which chance shuffles these forty-eight chromosomes with their load of determinants. That puts a pretty definite limit on the possible variations.

'For instance, eye color has been located on one of the genes on the third pair of chromosomes. Assuming that this gene contains twice as many brown-eye determinants as blue-eye ones, the chances are two to one that the child of whatever man or woman owns that particular chromosome will be brown-eyed – *if* his mate has no marked bias either way. See?'

'I know all that. Get along to Ambrose Callan and his notebook.'

'Coming to it. Now remember that these determinants carry *all* heredity, and that includes shape, size, intelligence, character, coloring – everything. People – or plants and animals – can vary in the vast number of ways in which it is possible to combine forty-eight chromosomes with their cargo of genes and determinants. But that number is not infinite. There are limits, limits to size, to coloring, to intelligence. Nobody ever saw a human race with sky-blue hair, for instance.'

'Nobody'd ever want to!' grunted Halburton.

'And,' proceeded Carver, 'that is because there are no blue-hair determinants in human chromosomes. But – and here comes Callan's idea – suppose we could increase the number of chromosomes in a given ovum. What then? In humans or tomatoes, if, instead of forty-eight, there were four hundred eighty, the possible range of variation would be ten times as great as it is now.

'In size, for instance, instead of the present possible variation of about two and a half feet, they might vary twenty-five feet! And in shape – a man might resemble almost anything! That is, almost anything within the range of the mammalian orders. And in intelligence – ' He paused thoughtfully.

'But how,' cut in Halburton, 'did Callan propose to accomplish the feat of inserting extra chromosomes? Chromosomes themselves are microscopic; genes are barely visible under the highest magnification, and nobody ever saw a determinant.'

'I don't know how,' said Carver gravely. 'Part of his notes crumbled to dust, and the description of his method must have gone with those pages.

Morgan uses hard radiations, but his object and his results are both different. He doesn't change the number of chromosomes.'

He hesitated. 'I think Callan used a combination of radiation and injection,' he resumed. 'I don't know. All I know is that he stayed on Austin four or five years, and that he came with only his wife. That part of his notes is clear enough. He began treating the vegetation near his shack, and some cats and dogs he had brought. Then he discovered that the thing was spreading like a disease.'

'Spreading?' echoed Halburton.

'Of course. Every tree he treated strewed multi-chromosomed pollen to the wind, and as for the cats – Anyway, the aberrant pollen fertilized normal seeds, and the result was another freak, a seed with the normal number of chromosomes from one parent and ten times as many from the other. The variations were endless. You know how swiftly kauri and tree ferns grow, and these had a possible speed of growth ten times as great.

'The freaks overran the island, smothering out the normal growths. And Callan's radiations, and perhaps his injections, too, affected Austin Island's indigenous life – the rats, the bats. They began to produce mutants. He came in 1918, and by the time he realized his own tragedy, Austin was an island of freaks where no child resembled its parents save by the merest chance.'

'His own tragedy? What do you mean?'

'Well, Callan was a biologist, not an expert in radiation. I don't know exactly what happened. Exposure to x-rays for long periods produces burns, ulcers, malignancies. Maybe Callan didn't take proper precautions to shield his device, or maybe he was using a radiation of peculiarly irritating quality. Anyway, his wife sickened first – an ulcer that turned cancerous.

'He had a radio – a wireless, rather, in 1921 – and he summoned his sloop from the Chathams. It sank off that coral spit, and Callan, growing desperate, succeeded somehow in breaking his wireless. He was no electrician, you see.

'Those were troubled days, after the close of the War. With Callan's sloop sunk, no one knew exactly what had become of him, and after a while he was forgotten. When his wife died, he buried her; but when he died there was no one to bury him. The descendants of what had been his cats took care of him, and that was that.'

'Yeah? What about Lilith?'

'Yes,' said Carver soberly. 'What about her? When I began to suspect the secret of Austin Island, that worried me. Was Lilith really quite human? Was she, too, infected by the taint of variation, so that her children might vary as widely as the offspring of the – cats? She spoke not a word of any language I knew – or I thought so, anyway – and I simply couldn't fit her in. But Callan's diary and notes did it for me.'

'How?'

'She's the daughter of the captain of Callan's sloop, whom he rescued when it was wrecked on the coral point. She was five years old then, which makes her almost twenty now. As for language – well, perhaps I should have recognized the few halting words she recalled. *C'm on*, for instance, was *comment* – that is, "how?" And *pah bo* was simply *pas bon*, not good. That's what she said about the poisonous fruit. And *lay shot* was *les chats*, for somehow she remembered, or sensed, that the creatures from the eastern end were cats.

'About her, for fifteen years, centered the dog creatures, who despite their form were, after all, dogs by nature, and loyal to their mistress. And between the two groups was eternal warfare.'

'But are you sure Lilith escaped the taint?'

'Her name's Lucienne,' mused Carver, 'but I think I prefer Lilith.' He smiled at the slim figure clad in a pair of Jameson's trousers and his own shirt, standing there in the stern looking back at Austin. 'Yes, I'm sure. When she was cast on the island, Callan had already destroyed the device that had slain his wife and was about to kill him. He wrecked his equipment completely, knowing that in the course of time the freaks he had created were doomed.'

'Doomed?'

'Yes. The normal strains, hardened by evolution, are stronger. They're already appearing around the edges of the island, and some day Austin will betray no more peculiarities than any other remote islet. Nature always reclaims her own.'

The Purple Death

W. L. Alden

Last winter I occupied a small villa in one of the towns of the Italian
Riviera. To me it is a very delightful little town – partly because it is
extremely picturesque, and partly because it is as yet almost unknown as
a health-resort. You can live there without constantly hearing the cough
of the consumptive, and when you do meet an occasional foreigner, he
does not instantly begin to discuss the condition of his bronchial tubes, or
to inquire as to the state of your own lungs.

Thank Heaven! my lungs and bronchial tubes are perfectly sound. My
only trouble is insomnia, and it was for this that I sought the perfect
repose and stillness of my sleepy little Italian town. There was but
one other foreigner in the place, so I was told; and as I was assured that
this foreigner was phenomenally strong and well, and was, moreover, a
German, and hence presumably unable to converse with a man wholly
innocent of any knowledge of the German language, I did not find fault
with the fact that he was to be my next-door neighbour. I saw him in his
garden a day or two after my arrival, and was struck by his singular
resemblance to the portraits of von Moltke. Although he looked to be at
least seventy years old, he was tall, and straight as an arrow, and his face,
which had something of the firmness and rigidity of sculpture, was that of
a man in perfect health and of an indomitable constitution. Even if I had
not already heard him called 'the Professor', I should have known him at
first sight as a man of culture. Intense thought and unremitting labour
had chiselled those clear-cut features. I made up my mind that, instead of
avoiding him, I should like to make his acquaintance, and I found myself
hoping that he could speak English, or that, at all events, I could understand his French.

Twice during the first week of my residence next door to the German I
saw after midnight a light in his garden, and heard the sound of a spade.
It is one of the advantages of insomnia, that the patient learns to know
the things of the night as well as those of the day. Had I been able to
sleep as soundly as other people, I should never have noticed this mysterious mid-night lanthorn or had my hearing sharpened sufficiently to
note and identify the sound of a spade. What was the professor doing

at so late an hour in his garden? Clearly, he could not have been engaged in gardening or ditching. Even a German philosopher would not be capable of getting up at one o'clock in the morning to plant cabbages, or to improve the drainage of his garden. The only plausible explanation of his conduct was that he was engaged in burying something which he had reason for burying secretly. I knew that he lived absolutely alone, without a single servant. Hence, he could not be a murderer, who made a practice of burying his victims at night.

Then, again, he was a scientific person, and, of course, had no money for safe-keeping in the earth. The third time that I saw my neighbour's lanthorn in the garden, I discovered that I had an object in life, which was to find why he dug in the earth at an hour when, as he supposed, all his neighbours were asleep.

The mystery solved itself a few days later, and proved to be disappointingly simple. The arrival at my neighbour's door of a hamper of rabbits, and another of guinea-pigs, showed me at once that he was engaged in studies which involved the death of numbers of those unhappy little animals. Of course, when his guinea-pigs and rabbits had fulfilled their mission in life, it became necessary to bury their remains; and the professor wisely performed this task at midnight in order not to offend the prejudices of those curious people who believe that vivisection is merely a form of vice in which inhuman men indulge purely for recreation. I had seen the professor, and I could have sworn that he was a kindly and gentle man. If his guinea-pigs and rabbits were cut down in the prime of life, I felt sure that they died in the interests of humanity, and their fate gave me no pain.

My acquaintance with the professor – whom I will call Professor Schwartz, for the reason that it was not his name – grew up gradually. We began by exchanging polite commonplaces over the garden wall, and I found that he spoke English perfectly. We were both methodical in our habits, and were accustomed to smoke in our gardens every afternoon at about the same hour. Gradually we passed from the discussion of the weather to more interesting themes, and, finally, the professor accepted my pressing invitation to come and inspect a plant growing in my garden, of the name of which I was ignorant. When I returned his visit, I accidentally discovered that, like myself, he was a devotee of chess. That put the finishing touch to our acquaintance, and we fell into the invariable habit of playing chess, every evening, from seven to nine.

I found him extremely interesting. He was a physician, though he had long since ceased to practise medicine, and had devoted himself, so he told me, to the study of bacteriology. He was, moreover, a man of wide culture; and there seemed to be hardly any subject of which he had not a more or less thorough knowledge. But what charmed me in the man was his kindness of heart. His philanthropy was not bounded by any of the limitations of race or creed. The sufferings of the poor touched him as profoundly, whether they were Germans, Italians, or Frenchmen. His love for animals was unmistakable, in spite of the fact that he daily inflicted tortures on the unfortunate subjects of his experiments. I had a collie, between whom and Professor Schwartz a deep affection sprang up, and the man was never so happy as when the dog sat by him with its head resting on his knee. There is no reason why I should hesitate to say that Professor Schwartz came, in time, to be sincerely attached to me, for there can be no doubt of the fact. I wondered that such a man should live so completely alone; but once, when I spoke of the matter to him, he gravely replied that a man should live for the benefit of others, and that his studies were of much more importance than his pleasures could possibly be.

One day, my collie came into my room, evidently suffering the greatest agony. He was swelled out to twice his ordinary size, and he had hardly sufficient strength to drag himself to my feet, where he lay moaning. My first thought was of my neighbour's medical skill, and I rushed over to his house, and implored him to come to the aid of the poor dog. The man came instantly, bringing with him a huge bottle of some disinfecting fluid, and showing an agitation which surprised me in one who had spent so much of his life as a practising physician. The dog was dead when we reached the room where I had left him, and the professor instantly poured the

He had hardly sufficient strength
to drag himself to my feet

entire contents of the bottle over the carcase, and then sent me for his spade. When I returned, he carefully removed the dog's body to the garden, and buried it, exercising the greatest care not to touch it, except with the spade. Then he went to his house, bidding me remain in the room where the animal had died, and when he returned he disinfected the room and everything in it with chemicals that caused a thick but entirely respirable smoke. To my inquiry as to what was the matter with the dog, he merely replied that the animal had been poisoned, and asked me if I had seen the dog digging in his garden. I had seen nothing of the kind, but I saw that the professor suspected that the animal had dug up the remains of some guinea-pig or rabbit that had died of an extremely infectious disease. This explained the elaborate care with which disinfectants had been used, though I could not but think that my friend had been unnecessarily alarmed.

I had been acquainted nearly two months with this mild and lovable vivisectionist, when one evening our conversation fell upon Anarchism. The usual bomb had just been exploded in Paris, and I was expressing a good deal of indignation at the miscreants who did such things.

'The Anarchist means well,' replied Professor Schwartz, 'but he is hopelessly stupid. He attacks the wrong people, and he uses absurdly inefficient weapons.'

'What do you mean by saying that he attacks the wrong people?' I asked.

'Just what I say,' he replied. 'The Anarchist wants to kill men who have money – capitalists, and small or great shopkeepers, and employers of labour. These are the very people who are most necessary to the existence of humanity. If the Anarchist tried to kill labouring men, he would be working for the emancipation of the race from poverty and misery, but he cannot see this.'

'I hardly see it myself,' said I. 'Do you mean that the true way to lessen suffering is to kill the sufferers?'

'Yes, and no,' said Professor Schwartz. 'My dear friend, listen to me. All the poverty on this earth is the result of over-population. Why does the Italian labourer work for two francs a day, and spend his whole life in a state of semi-starvation? The Anarchist says that the labourer is oppressed by the capitalist. This is rubbish. A man works for two francs a day because there are so many workmen that the price of labour is wretchedly low. Halve the number of workmen, and you would more than double the wages of the remaining ones. The same thing is true of the men in this town who make a miserable living by raising vegetables. Each man has a little morsel of ground, and he can hardly raise enough to keep himself from starvation. Reduce the numbers of these small proprietors one-half, and you would double the amount of land which each one would cultivate, and thus double their aggregate incomes.'

'That sounds very mathematical,' I answered; 'but I haven't that sublime confidence in figures that I had when I was younger.'

'Any man who sees things as they are must admit,' continued the professor, disregarding my interruption, 'that the world is horribly over-populated. If a pestilence should sweep off two-thirds of the workmen in Europe, the survivors would be able to live in comfort. Now, the Anarchist doesn't see this. He would kill off the capitalists – the very men who employ labour, and make it possible for labourers to live. I, on the contrary, would not harm a single man who has money to pay to others, but I would remedy this fatal over-population – an evil which grows worse and worse every year. Your English Malthus had a glimpse of what was coming, but he did not foresee what the remedy would be.'

'Then, there is a remedy?' I asked.

'Yes. Did I not tell you that the remedy is to reduce the working population? The man who discovers how to do this most swiftly and effectually will be the greatest benefactor this world has ever known.'

It rather amused me to hear this man, whom I knew to be gentle and tender-hearted, actually insisting that about one-half of the population of the globe ought to be murdered; but I thought little of it at the time. I knew how fond some men are of propounding bold and startling theories, which they themselves would be the very last to dream of carrying into action. Here was a man, whose business in life had been to heal the sick, and so to prolong the existence of the weakest specimens of the human race. And now he was saying that the extermination of millions of healthy, vigorous men was the one thing that the world needed! It was another illustration of the inevitable bee which, sooner or later, gets into the bonnet of every scientific man.

I have said that Schwartz lived completely alone. A man in good health can do this, but if he is taken ill he soon finds that he must depend on the help of others. One afternoon Professor Schwartz did not appear in his garden, and when I went to his house, in the evening, he did not come as usual to open the door. Suspecting that he was ill, I went to the side of the house, where I knew his room was situated, and called to him. He answered, but without showing himself at the window. He was not quite well, he said, but assured me that he would be able to see me the next day, and that in the meantime he should want no assistance. He would not consent to see me; and I went back to my villa somewhat uneasy, and half determined to break into Schwartz's house the next morning in case he still refused to open the door.

That extreme measure, however, did not prove to be necessary. When I called at his house in the morning, he opened the door, and invited me to come in. He was looking wretchedly ill, but he assured me that his attack was over, and that there was not the slightest cause for uneasiness.

He took me into his library, and tried to converse with his usual ease. The attempt was a failure, and I saw that, besides being weak from the effect of his illness, he was both preoccupied and troubled. Finally, I asked him frankly to tell me what was the matter, and to permit me to be of any service that might be possible.

He remained silent for a little while, and then he said – 'My dear friend, I have made up my mind to trust you. My illness has shown me that it is no longer safe for me to keep my secret absolutely to myself. I shall die suddenly, and possibly very soon. In that case there must be someone who will know how to prevent the catastrophe which would otherwise happen to this pretty little town, where I have spent so many happy hours. Give me your word that what I shall tell you shall remain a secret so long as I live.'

I gave him the desired promise – rashly, as I now know, but without dreaming of its nature.

He rose from his chair and told me to follow him into his laboratory. There was nothing remarkable in the appearance of the place. I had once before seen the laboratory of a bacteriologist, and it closely resembled Professor Schwartz's laboratory, except that the fittings of the latter were rather more elaborate and complete. On one side of the room was a series of shelves filled with carefully-sealed glass tubes, containing what I assumed to be gelatine. Schwartz called my attention to these, and said – 'If you should find me dead, or dying, some day, I want you to take every one of these tubes, break them one by one in a bucket full of the liquid which you will find in yonder glass jar, and then bury the contents of the bucket, glass and all, in the earth not less than four feet deep. Do this with the utmost care, making sure not to break a single tube except under the surface of the liquid, otherwise I cannot answer for your life. You perfectly understand me?'

'Perfectly,' I said; 'and I will promise to carry out your wishes. The tubes, I presume, contain the microbes of various diseases.'

His face lightened up with a glow of enthusiasm. 'They contain the microbes of diseases,' he replied; 'but the diseases are nearly all new. They are inventions of my own, and some of them are infinitely more deadly than any disease known to the medical profession. You remember the death of your dog? The poor fellow died of a disease which is absolutely new, and which kills in less than six hours. If that disease were once introduced into any city in the world, it would spread so rapidly that in a week the place would be depopulated.'

'I do not understand what you mean by newly-invented diseases,' said I. 'How is it possible for a man to invent a disease?'

'Allow me to sit down,' said the professor, 'for I am too weak to remain standing. The answer to your question is very easy. Certain diseases are produced by certain microbes, and hitherto bacteriologists have confined themselves to trying to discover the specific microbe of each disease, and then to discover a remedy that will kill the microbe without killing the patient. No one but myself has ever tried to develop the deadly powers of known microbes. Look at that tube numbered 17. It contains the microbe of typhoid fever, but I have cultivated it until it will produce the disease in twenty-four hours after the microbe is taken into the system, and will kill the patient infallibly in twelve hours

Look at that tube numbered 17

more. That is only one of the dozen similar successes that I have obtained. Then I have crossed different microbes, or rather cultivated them together, so that they have become capable of producing a new disease, partaking somewhat of the character of each of the diseases which the same microbes, if cultivated separately, would produce. It was I who invented, in this way, the present variety of influenza, by crossing the microbes of malarial fever with those of pneumonia. I was living in St Petersburg at the time, and I accidentally dropped the tube containing the germs of influenza. Someone must have found it and opened it, for when the influenza broke out I instantly recognised it as my own invention.'

'I have always heard,' I ventured to remark, 'that the influenza is a disease which has appeared in Europe several times during the present century.'

'There have been epidemics of a disease called influenza,' he replied, 'but they differed from the present one. They lacked the symptoms of malarial poisoning, which are characteristic of my own influenza. I have always been very sorry that I lost that tube, for an epidemic of influenza can do no possible good, and does great harm. But to come back to what I was saying before we spoke of influenza. Look at tube number 31. It contains microbes that will produce a disease having some of the characteristics of hydrophobia, and some of those of dropsy, while it also has symptoms which are entirely new. It was one of the earliest of my new diseases, and would certainly be very efficacious, should it ever become epidemic. I have, however, invented other diseases which are far superior to it. Here is a tube,' he continued, taking it almost lovingly in his hand, 'which contains my *chef d'oeuvre*. The microbes are a cross between those found in the venom of the tuboba, the most deadly of all known serpents, and those of the Asiatic plague. By the way, I am the first man to discover the existence of microbes in snake-venom. I call the new disease which these crossed microbes produce the "Purple Death", for the reason that the body of the person who is attacked by it becomes purple before death. It kills in less than thirty minutes, and there is no remedy which has the slightest effect upon it. As to its infectious qualities, it is the king of all diseases. If I were to break this tube while we are in this room together, you and I would be dead within an hour, and from this house the infection would spread so rapidly that in two days, at furthest, not a human being would be left alive in this poor little town. Think what would happen, were we Germans to use these microbes in our next war with France. A single bomb filled with the Purple Death, and thrown within the lines of a French army, would render a battle an impossibility. Before six hours were over there would not be left in an army of four hundred thousand men survivors enough to bury the dead!'

The man's eyes sparkled with pride. His weakness had almost vanished while he was talking, but suddenly he sank back on his chair, and feebly begged me to assist him into the other room.

When he was lying on the sofa, and had somewhat regained his strength, I asked him what possible good he expected to accomplish by adding to the number of diseases which already afflicted humanity.

'I have told you,' he said, 'that I am a philanthropist, only, unlike other philanthropists, I have intelligence and, I hope, the courage of my convictions. You have heard me say that all the poverty and misery of the world are due to over-population. Well, I have there in my laboratory the remedy for this evil. I can, with merciful swiftness and with absolute certainty, reduce the population of Europe to a half, or a third, of what it now is. I have only to take my Purple Death, and scatter the teeming gelatine on the side-walk of the most crowded street of your London. It will dry quickly, and under the trampling of hundreds of feet it will become pulverised, and the particles will float in the air. That very day the physicians will find themselves in the presence of a disease wholly unknown to them, and against which medical science can achieve nothing. In a few days London will be silent. The working classes and the poor will be dead, and everyone who can possibly fly from the stricken town will have fled. When the pestilence has spent its force we shall hear no more of the unemployed workmen in London. There will be more work than workmen can be found to do, and the very street-sweepers will receive wages that will permit them to live almost in luxury.

'Or say that I wanted to decrease the population of Berlin. I simply place some of that gelatine in an envelope, and send it through the post to the head workman in some factory. He opens it, and the Purple Death breaks out among the workmen. Nothing can stop it until it has run its course. Of course, a percentage of capitalists and employers of labour will fall victims to the disease, but its ravages will be chiefly confined to those who have not the means to escape from the city. Did I not tell you that the Anarchists select the wrong victims, and that their favourite dynamite is absurdly ineffective in comparison with the weapons that I can use? Now you see that I told the truth. Man, the lives of half Europe are in my hands!'

I made no reply. The vastness of the man's horrible scheme stunned me. I had not the least doubt that he spoke the truth, and I had promised to remain silent while his devilish project was carried out.

Presently he resumed – 'I do not want my weapons to fall into hands that would use them ignorantly. That is why I have asked you to destroy every one of those deadly tubes in case I should die without having been able to do it myself. I made the discovery yesterday that I may die at any minute, and I am physician enough to be sure of what I say. If I should find myself dying, and should have the time and strength to act, I should set this house on fire, and blow out my brains. So if you should happen to find my house burning, you will take no measures to check the flames. But I fear that I shall not have the time to do this myself, and so I rely on your help.'

'How long since you invented the Purple Death?' I asked.

A troubled look passed over Schwartz's face. 'Nearly two years ago,' he replied.

'Why have you delayed to use it?' I asked, a sudden hope that the man was not quite so mad as he seemed to be, springing up within me.

'As yet it has killed no one, beside the guinea-pigs, except your dog,' he replied. 'The dog must have been digging where the guinea-pigs are buried, and so contracted the disease.'

'But why have you not carried out your scheme of depopulating the world during these two years?'

'My friend,' replied the professor, 'I am not so strong as I believed myself. The truth is, I have lacked the courage to begin the work. I have been like a surgeon whose nerves will not permit him to perform a painful operation, although he knows that it is the only means of saving the patient's life. But I shall delay no longer. I may have very little time to live, and, besides, now that I have told you all, my secret is no longer safe. Oh, I do not for an instant doubt your word, and I have perfect confidence in your friendship, but when a secret is known to more than one person it is no longer a secret. But I will have more courage. In another week I shall be as well as ever, and then I will begin the work of redeeming the world from poverty. Now I must ask you to leave me, for I must try to sleep. By the bye, you will find a duplicate key of my door hanging on a nail in the hall. Take it with you, and don't hesitate to use it in case of necessity.'

I left the professor, and returned to my house, in a most unenviable state of mind. I had not the slightest doubt that what he had told me was strictly true. Granting that the man was mad – and surely no sane man could have calmly proposed the murder of hundreds of thousands of unoffending men – still the death of my dog was sufficient evidence that Schwartz's claim that he had invented microbic poisons was true. I had given him my word to remain silent. If I kept my promise I should be accessory to the crimes which he unquestionably meant to commit. If I betrayed him, I not only broke my word, but I made it certain that either he would be condemned to a madhouse, or would be sent to the gallows. I could not determine what it was my duty to do, and I spent a night of more terrible anxiety than any criminal ever spent who knew that the gallows awaited him in the early morning.

All night long, and far into the next day, I ceaselessly debated the question what ought I to do. Towards noon, not having yet heard any sound of life in my neighbour's house, I took the key, and, entering, went up to his bedroom. He was lying in bed, with the bedclothes drawn up close to his chin, and I spoke to him, but he did not answer. When I touched his forehead I found that he was dead and cold. He had evidently died soon after going to bed, for the body was already perfectly rigid.

I did not lose a moment in destroying the tubes in his laboratory. I placed them carefully, one by one, in a bucket filled with the disinfecting fluid which he had shown me, and broke them with a blow of a marble pestle. When this was done, I carried the bucket into the garden and buried it deep with its contents. I should then have been ready to send my servant to notify the authorities of Professor Schwartz's death had it not been for one thing. The tube containing the Purple Death was missing from its place on the laboratory shelf, and I had been totally unable to find it. So long as this remained above ground, all that I had done was comparatively useless. Doubtless the tube would be found by the officers whom the Syndic of the town would send to search the apartment, and take charge of the dead man's effects. Then it would be broken, purposely or accidentally, and the frightful consequences that Schwartz had predicted would be inevitable.

I carried the bucket
into the garden and
buried it deep with its contents

I searched every corner and cranny of the house without finding the tube. Finally I began to hope that the professor had himself destroyed it, fearing that he was near his end, but that he had been unable to destroy the rest of his poisons. Comforting myself with this solution of the mystery, I went to his bedside to smooth the bedclothes before sending for the police, and in so doing I found the Purple Death clasped firmly in his hand!

It was impossible to loosen the dead man's grasp, and, after vainly making the attempt, I gave it up, fearing to break the tube in the effort. I called my servant, and told him to go first for the village doctor, and afterwards to notify the police, and then I sat down to await events.

The doctor arrived promptly, and proved to be a very intelligent man. I told him the whole story that the professor had confided to me, with the exception that I did not hint at the use to which the dead man had proposed to put his terrible inventions. The doctor found no difficulty in believing what I told him, and it evidently gave him a profound respect for his deceased *confrère*. He agreed with me that it would be dangerous to meddle with the tube which the corpse clasped in its rigid hand, and promised me that even if an autopsy should be necessary, he would see that the tube remained undisturbed. I think he was a little shy of coming too closely in contact with the body, lest the professor should have died of one of his new diseases. At any rate, he decided to accept my theory that Schwartz had died of heart-disease, and persuaded the Syndic that an autopsy would be quite superfluous.

Professor Schwartz was buried within twenty-four hours, with the Purple Death still in his right hand. The police were easily persuaded that it contained some holy relic, and that it would be impious to meddle with it. When the funeral was over, I left the place as soon as I could pack my boxes, and surrendered the lease of my villa. I have never seen it since, and never want to see it.

On my way back to England I passed through Berlin, where I went to see an eminent bacteriologist, and asked him how long microbes inclosed in a tube contaming gelatine would retain their vitality. His answer was, 'For ever, so far as is at present known.' That answer has poisoned my whole life. Six feet underground, in the grave of Professor Schwartz, lies the Purple Death, waiting until the day when the cemetery will share the fate of all cemeteries, and be cut up into building lots. Then the tube will be exhumed and broken, and the pestilence that is to sweep away the teeming millions of Europe will begin its work. Sooner or later, this is morally certain to happen. I have sometimes thought of exhuming the coffin of Professor Schwartz, and searching for the fatal tube, but to do this would be to invite the catastrophe which I dread, for in all probability the tube has become unsealed by this time. My only hope is that an earthquake will some day bury the cemetery too deep for any spade to reach the grave of my poor mad friend.

Flatland

A Romance of Many Dimensions
by A Square

Edwin A. Abbott

With Illustrations by the Author

To
    The Inhabitants of SPACE IN GENERAL
        And H. C. IN PARTICULAR
This Work is Dedicated
    By a Humble Native of Flatland
In the Hope that
    Even as he was Initiated into the Mysteries
        Of THREE Dimensions
            Having been previously conversant
                With ONLY TWO
So the Citizens of that Celestial Region
    May aspire yet higher and higher
To the Secrets of FOUR FIVE or even SIX Dimensions
    Thereby contributing
        To the Enlargement of THE IMAGINATION
        And the possible Development
    Of that most rare and excellent Gift of MODESTY
        Among the Superior Races
            Of SOLID HUMANITY

CONTENTS

Part One: This World
  1. Of the Nature of Flatland
  2. Of the Climate and Houses in Flatland
  3. Concerning the Inhabitants of Flatland
  4. Concerning the Women
  5. Of our Methods of Recognizing one another
  6. Of Recognition by Sight
  7. Concerning Irregular Figures
  8. Of the Ancient Practice of Painting
  9. Of the Universal Colour Bill
  10. Of the Suppression of the Chromatic Sedition
  11. Concerning our Priests
  12. Of the Doctrine of our Priests

Part Two: Other Worlds
  13. How I had a Vision of Lineland
  14. How I vainly tried to explain the nature of Flatland
  15. Concerning a Stranger from Spaceland
  16. How the Stranger vainly endeavoured to reveal to me in words the mysteries of Spaceland
  17. How the Sphere, having in vain tried words, resorted to deeds
  18. How I came to Spaceland, and what I saw there
  19. How, though the Sphere shewed me other mysteries of Spaceland, I still desired more; and what came of it
  20. How the Sphere encouraged me in a Vision
  21. How I tried to teach the Theory of Three Dimensions to my Grandson, and with what success
  22. How I then tried to diffuse the Theory of Three Dimensions by other means, and of the result

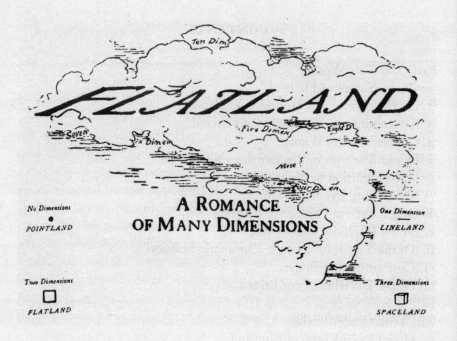

No Dimensions		*One Dimension*
•		
POINTLAND		LINELAND

A ROMANCE
OF MANY DIMENSIONS

Two Dimensions		*Three Dimensions*
▢		◻
FLATLAND		SPACELAND

'Fie, fie, how franticly I square my talk!'

PREFACE TO THE SECOND
AND REVISED EDITION, 1884

By the Editor

If my poor Flatland friend retained the vigour of mind which he enjoyed when he began to compose these Memoirs, I should not now need to represent him in this preface, in which he desires, firstly, to return his thanks to his readers and critics in Spaceland, whose appreciation has, with unexpected celerity, required a second edition of his work; secondly, to apologize for certain errors and misprints (for which, however, he is not entirely responsible); and, thirdly, to explain one or two misconceptions. But he is not the Square he once was. Years of imprisonment, and the still heavier burden of general incredulity and mockery, have combined with the natural decay of old age to erase from his mind many of the thoughts and notions, and much also of the terminology, which he acquired during his short stay in Spaceland. He has, therefore, requested me to reply in his behalf to two special objections, one of an intellectual, the other of a moral nature.

The first objection is, that a Flatlander, seeing a Line, sees something that must be *thick* to the eye as well as *long* to the eye (otherwise it would not be visible, if it had not some thickness); and consequently he ought (it is argued) to acknowledge that his countrymen are not only long and broad, but also (though doubtless in a very slight degree) *thick* or *high*. This objection is plausible, and, to Spacelanders, almost irresistible, so that, I confess, when I first heard it, I knew not what to reply. But my poor old friend's answer appears to me completely to meet it.

'I admit,' said he – when I mentioned to him this objection – 'I admit the truth of your critic's facts, but I deny his conclusions. It is true that we have really in Flatland a Third unrecognized Dimension called "height", just as it is also true that you have really in Spaceland a Fourth unrecognized Dimension, called by no name at present, but which I will call "extra-height". But we can no more take cognizance of our "height" than you can of your "extra-height". Even I – who have been in Spaceland, and have had the privilege of understanding for twenty-four hours the meaning of "height" – even I cannot now comprehend it, nor realize it by the sense of sight or by any process of reason; I can but apprehend it by faith.

'The reason is obvious. Dimension implies direction, implies measurement, implies the more and the less. Now, all our lines are *equally* and *infinitesimally* thick (or high, whichever you like); consequently, there is nothing in them to lead our minds to the conception of that Dimension. No "delicate micrometer" – as has been suggested by one too hasty Spaceland critic – would in the least avail us; for we should not know *what to measure, nor in what direction*. When we see a Line, we see something that is long and *bright*; *brightness*, as well as length, is necessary to the existence of a Line; if the brightness vanishes, the Line is extinguished. Hence, all my Flatland friends – when I talk to them about the unrecognized Dimension which is somehow visible in a Line – say, "Ah, you mean *brightness*": and when I reply, "No, I mean a real Dimension", they at once retort, "Then measure it, or tell us in what direction it extends"; and this silences me, for I can do neither. Only yesterday, when the Chief Circle (in other words our High Priest) came to inspect the State Prison and paid me his seventh annual visit, and when for the seventh time he put me the question, "Was I any better?" I tried to prove to him that he was "high", as well as long and broad, although he did not know it. But what was his reply? "You say I am 'high'; measure my 'high-ness' and I will believe you." What could I do? How could I meet his challenge? I was crushed; and he left the room triumphant.

'Does this still seem strange to you? Then put yourself in a similar position. Suppose a person of the Fourth Dimension, condescending to visit you, were to say, "Whenever you open your eyes, you see a Plane (which is of Two Dimensions) and you *infer* a Solid (which is of Three); but in reality you also see (though you do not recognize) a Fourth Dimension, which is not colour nor brightness nor anything of the kind, but a true Dimension, although I cannot point out to you its direction, nor can you possibly measure it." What would you say to such a visitor? Would not you have him locked up? Well, that is my fate: and it is as natural for us Flatlanders to lock up a Square for preaching the Third Dimension, as it is for you Spacelanders to lock up a Cube for preaching the Fourth. Alas, how strong a family likeness runs through blind and persecuting humanity in all Dimensions! Points, Lines, Squares, Cubes, Extra-Cubes – we are all liable to the same errors, all alike the Slaves of our respective Dimensional prejudices, as one of your Spaceland poets has said – *

'One touch of Nature makes all worlds akin'

* The Author desires me to add, that the misconception of some of his critics on this matter has induced him to insert in his dialogue with the Sphere, certain remarks which have a bearing on the point in question, and which he had previously omitted as being tedious and unnecessary.

On this point the defence of the Square seems to me to be impregnable. I wish I could say that his answer to the second (or moral) objection was equally clear and cogent. It has been objected that he is a woman-hater; and as this objection has been vehemently urged by those whom Nature's decree has constituted the somewhat larger half of the Spaceland race, I should like to remove it, so far as I can honestly do so. But the Square is so unaccustomed to the use of the moral terminology of Spaceland that I should be doing him an injustice if I were literally to transcribe his defence against this charge. Acting, therefore, as his interpreter and summarizer, I gather that in the course of an imprisonment of seven years he has himself modified his own personal views, both as regards Women and as regards the Isosceles or Lower Classes. Personally, he now inclines to the opinion of the Sphere that the Straight Lines are in many important respects superior to the Circles. But, writing as a Historian, he has identified himself (perhaps too closely) with the views generally adopted by Flatland, and (as he has been informed) even by Spaceland, Historians; in whose pages (until very recent times) the destinies of Women and of the masses of mankind have seldom been deemed worthy of mention and never of careful consideration.

In a still more obscure passage he now desires to disavow the Circular or aristocratic tendencies with which some critics have naturally credited him. While doing justice to the intellectual power with which a few Circles have for many generations maintained their supremacy over immense multitudes of their countrymen, he believes that the facts of Flatland, speaking for themselves without comment on his part, declare that Revolutions cannot always be suppressed by slaughter, and that Nature, in sentencing the Circles to infecundity, has condemned them to ultimate failure – 'and herein,' he says, 'I see a fulfilment of the great Law of all worlds, that while the wisdom of Man thinks it is working one thing, the wisdom of Nature constrains it to work another, and quite a different and far better thing.' For the rest, he begs his readers not to suppose that every minute detail in the daily life of Flatland must needs correspond to some other detail in Spaceland; and yet he hopes that, taken as a whole, his work may prove suggestive as well as amusing, to those Spacelanders of moderate and modest minds who – speaking of that which is of the highest importance, but lies beyond experience – decline to say on the one hand, 'This can never be,' and on the other hand, 'It must needs be precisely thus, and we know all about it.'

PART ONE: THIS WORLD

Be patient, for the world is broad and wide

Section 1. Of the Nature of Flatland

I call our world Flatland, not because we call it so, but to make its nature clearer to you, my happy readers, who are privileged to live in Space.

Imagine a vast sheet of paper on which straight Lines, Triangles, Squares, Pentagons, Hexagons, and other figures, instead of remaining fixed in their places, move freely about, on or in the surface, but without the power of rising above or sinking below it, very much like shadows – only hard and with luminous edges – and you will then have a pretty correct notion of my country and countrymen. Alas, a few years ago, I should have said 'my universe': but now my mind has been opened to higher views of things.

In such a country, you will perceive at once that it is impossible that there should be anything of what you call a 'solid' kind; but I dare say you will suppose that we could at least distinguish by sight the Triangles, Squares, and other figures, moving about as I have described them. On the contrary, we could see nothing of the kind, not at least so as to distinguish one figure from another. Nothing was visible, nor could be visible, to us, except Straight Lines; and the necessity of this I will speedily demonstrate.

Place a penny on the middle of one of your tables in Space; and leaning over it, look down upon it. It will appear a circle.

But now, drawing back to the edge of the table, gradually lower your eye (thus bringing yourself more and more into the condition of the inhabitants of Flatland), and you will find the penny becoming more and more oval to your view, and at last when you have placed your eye exactly on the edge of the table (so that you are, as it were, actually a Flatlander) the penny will then have ceased to appear oval at all, and will have become, so far as you can see, a straight line.

The same thing would happen if you were to treat in the same way a Triangle, or Square, or any other figure cut out of pasteboard. As soon as you look at it with your eye on the edge on the table, you will find that it ceases to appear to you a figure, and that it becomes in appearance a straight line. Take for example an equilateral Triangle – who represents with us a Tradesman of the respectable class. Fig. 1 represents the Tradesman as you would see him while you were bending over him from above; figs. 2 and 3 represent the Tradesman, as you would see him if your eye were close to the level, or all but on the level of the table; and if your eye were quite on the level of the table (and that is how we see him in Flatland) you would see nothing but a straight line.

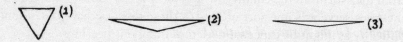

When I was in Spaceland I heard that your sailors have very similar experiences while they traverse your seas and discern some distant island or coast lying on the horizon. The far-off land may have bays, forelands, angles in and out to any number and extent; yet at a distance you see none of these (unless indeed your sun shines bright upon them revealing the projections and retirements by means of light and shade), nothing but a grey unbroken line upon the water.

Well, that is just what we see when one of our triangular or other acquaintances comes toward us in Flatland. As there is neither sun with us, nor any light of such a kind as to make shadows, we have none of the helps to the sight that you have in Spaceland. If our friend comes closer to us we see his line becomes larger; if he leaves us it becomes smaller: but still he looks like a straight line; be he a Triangle, Square, Pentagon, Hexagon, Circle, what you will – a straight Line he looks and nothing else.

You may perhaps ask how under these disadvantageous circumstances we are able to distinguish our friends from one another: but the answer to this very natural question will be more fitly and easily given when I come to describe the inhabitants of Flatland. For the present let me defer this subject, and say a word or two about the climate and houses in our country.

Section 2. Of the Climate and Houses in Flatland

As with you, so also with us, there are four points of the compass: North, South, East, and West.

There being no sun nor other heavenly bodies, it is impossible for us to determine the North in the usual way; but we have a method of our own. By a Law of Nature with us, there is a constant attraction to the South; and, although in temperate climates this is very slight – so that even a Woman in reasonable health can journey several furlongs north-ward without much difficulty – yet the hampering effect of the southward attraction is quite sufficient to serve as a compass in most parts of our earth. Moreover, the rain (which falls at stated intervals) coming always from the North, is an additional assistance; and in the towns we have the guidance of the houses, which of course have their side-walls running for the most part North and South, so that the roofs may keep off the rain from the North. In the country, where there are no houses, the trunks of the trees serve as some sort of guide. Altogether, we have not so much difficulty as might be expected in determining our bearings.

Yet in our more temperate regions, in which the southward attraction is hardly felt, walking sometimes in a perfectly desolate plain where there have been no houses nor trees to guide me, I have been occasionally compelled to remain stationary for hours together, waiting till the rain came before continuing my journey. On the weak and aged, and espec-ially on delicate Females, the force of attraction tells much more heavily than on the robust of the Male Sex, so that it is a point of breeding, if you meet a Lady in the street, always to give her the North side of the way – by no means an easy thing to do always at short notice when you are in rude health and in a climate where it is difficult to tell your North from your South.

Windows there are none in our houses: for the light comes to us alike in our homes and out of them, by day and by night, equally at all times and in all places, whence we know not. It was in old days, with our learned men, an interesting and oft-investigated question, 'What is the origin of light?' and the solution of it has been repeatedly attempted, with no other result than to crowd our lunatic asylums with the would-be solvers. Hence, after fruitless attempts to suppress such investigations indirectly by making them liable to a heavy tax, the Legislature, in com-paratively recent times, absolutely prohibited them. I – alas, I alone in Flatland – know now only too well the true solution of this mysterious problem; but my knowledge cannot be made intelligible to a single one of my countrymen; and I am mocked at – I, the sole possessor of the truths of Space and of the theory of the introduction of Light from the world of three Dimensions – as if I were the maddest of the mad! But a truce to these painful digressions: let me return to our houses.

The most common form for the construction of a house is five-sided or pentagonal, as in the annexed figure. The two Northern sides RO, OF, constitute the roof, and for the most part have no doors; on the East is a small door for the Women; on the West a much larger one for the Men; the South side or floor is usually doorless.

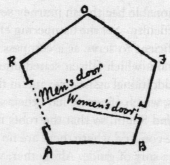

Square and triangular houses are not allowed, and for this reason. The angles of a Square (and still more those of an equilateral Triangle), being much more pointed than those of a Pentagon, and the lines of inanimate objects (such as houses) being dimmer than the lines of Men and Women, it follows that there is no little danger lest the points of a square or triangular house residence might do serious injury to an inconsiderate or perhaps absent-minded traveller suddenly therefore, running against them: and as early as the eleventh century of our era, triangular houses were universally forbidden by Law, the only exceptions being fortifications, powder-magazines, barracks, and other state buildings, which it is not desirable that the general public should approach without circumspection.

At this period, square houses were still everywhere permitted, though discouraged by a special tax. But, about three centuries afterwards, the Law decided that in all towns containing a population above ten thousand, the angle of a Pentagon was the smallest house-angle that could be allowed consistently with the public safety. The good sense of the community has seconded the efforts of the Legislature; and now, even in the country, the pentagonal construction has superseded every other. It is only now and then in some very remote and backward agricultural district that an antiquarian may still discover a square house.

Section 3. Concerning the Inhabitants of Flatland

The greatest length or breadth of a full grown inhabitant of Flatland may be estimated at about eleven of your inches. Twelve inches may be regarded as a maximum.

Our Women are Straight Lines.

Our Soldiers and Lowest Classes of Workmen are Triangles with two equal sides, each about eleven inches long, and a base or third side so short (often not exceeding half an inch) that they form at their vertices a very sharp and formidable angle. Indeed when their bases are of the most degraded type (not more than the eighth part of an inch in size), they can hardly be distinguished from Straight Lines or Women; so extremely pointed are their vertices. With us, as with you, these Triangles are distinguished from others by being called Isosceles; and by this name I shall refer to them in the following pages.

Our Middle Class consists of Equilateral or Equal-Sided Triangles.

Our Professional Men and Gentlemen are Squares (to which class I myself belong) and Five-Sided Figures or Pentagons.

Next above these come the Nobility, of whom there are several degrees, beginning at Six-Sided Figures, or Hexagons, and from thence rising in the number of their sides till they receive the honourable title of Polygonal, or many-sided. Finally when the number of the sides becomes so numerous, and the sides themselves so small, that the figure cannot be distinguished from a circle, he is included in the Circular or Priestly order; and this is the highest class of all.

It is a Law of Nature with us that a male child shall have one more side than his father, so that each generation shall rise (as a rule) one step in the scale of development and nobility. Thus the son of a Square is a Pentagon; the son of a Pentagon, a Hexagon; and so on.

But this rule applies not always to the Tradesmen, and still less often to the Soldiers, and to the Workmen; who indeed can hardly be said to deserve the name of human Figures, since they have not all their sides equal. With them therefore the Law of Nature does not hold; and the son of an Isosceles (i.e. a Triangle with two sides equal) remains Isosceles still. Nevertheless, all hope is not shut out, even from the Isosceles, that his posterity may ultimately rise above his degraded condition. For, after a long series of military successes, or diligent and skilful labours, it is generally found that the more intelligent among the Artisan and Soldier classes manifest a slight increase of their third side or base, and a shrinkage of the two other sides. Intermarriages (arranged by the Priests) between the sons and daughters of these more intellectual members of the lower classes generally result in an offspring approximating still more to the type of the Equal-Sided Triangle.

Rarely – in proportion to the vast numbers of Isosceles births – is a genuine and certifiable Equal-Sided Triangle produced from Isosceles parents.* Such a birth requires, as its antecedents, not only a series of

* 'What need of a certificate?' a Spaceland critic may ask: 'Is not the procreation of a Square Son a certificate from Nature herself, proving the Equal-sidedness of the Father?' I reply that no Lady of any position will marry an uncertified Triangle. Square offspring has sometimes resulted from a slightly Irregular Triangle; but in almost every such case the Irregularity of the first generation is visited on the third; which either fails to attain the Pentagonal rank, or relapses to the Triangular.

carefully arranged intermarriages, but also a long, continued exercise of frugality and self-control on the part of the would-be ancestors of the coming Equilateral, and a patient, systematic, and continuous development of the Isosceles intellect through many generations.

The birth of a True Equilateral Triangle from Isosceles parents is the subject of rejoicing in our country for many furlongs around. After a strict examination conducted by the Sanitary and Social Board, the infant, if certified as Regular, is with solemn ceremonial admitted into the class of Equilaterals. He is then immediately taken from his proud yet sorrowing parents and adopted by some childless Equilateral, who is bound by oath never to permit the child henceforth to enter his former home or so much as to look upon his relations again, for fear lest the freshly developed organism may, by force of unconscious imitation, fall back again into his hereditary level.

The occasional emergence of an Equilateral from the ranks of his serf-born ancestors is welcomed, not only by the poor serfs themselves, as a gleam of light and hope shed upon the monotonous squalor of their existence, but also by the Aristocracy at large; for all the higher classes are well aware that these rare phenomena, while they do little or nothing to vulgarize their own privileges, serve as a most useful barrier against revolution from below.

Had the acute-angled rabble been all, without exception, absolutely destitute of hope and of ambition, they might have found leaders in some of their many seditious outbreaks, so able as to render their superior numbers and strength too much even for the wisdom of the Circles. But a wise ordinance of Nature has decreed that, in proportion as the working-classes increase in intelligence, knowledge, and all virtue, in that same proportion their acute angle (which makes them physically terrible) shall increase also and approximate to the comparatively harmless angle of the Equilateral Triangle. Thus, in the most brutal and formidable of the soldier class – creatures almost on a level with women in their lack of intelligence – it is found that, as they wax in the mental ability necessary to employ their tremendous penetrating power to advantage, so do they wane in the power of penetration itself.

How admirable is this Law of Compensation! And how perfect a proof of the natural fitness and, I may almost say, the divine origin of the aristocratic constitution of the States in Flatland! By a judicious use of this Law of Nature, the Polygons and Circles are almost always able to stifle sedition in its very cradle, taking advantage of the irrepressible and boundless hopefulness of the human mind. Art also comes to the aid of Law and Order. It is generally found possible – by a little artificial compression or expansion on the part of the State physicians – to make some of the more intelligent leaders of a rebellion perfectly Regular, and to admit them at once into the privileged classes; a much larger number, who are still below the standard, allured by the prospect of being ultimately ennobled, are induced to enter the State Hospitals, where they are kept in honourable confinement for life; one or two alone of the more obstinate, foolish, and hopelessly irregular are led to execution.

Then the wretched rabble of the Isosceles, planless and leaderless, are either transfixed without resistance by the small body of their brethren whom the Chief Circle keeps in pay for emergencies of this kind; or else more often, by means of jealousies and suspicions skilfully fomented among them by the Circular party, they are stirred to mutual warfare, and perish by one another's angles. No less than one hundred and twenty rebellions are recorded in our annals, besides minor outbreaks numbered at two hundred and thirty-five; and they have all ended thus.

Section 4. *Concerning the Women*

If our highly pointed Triangles of the Soldier class are formidable, it may be readily inferred that far more formidable are our Women. For if a Soldier is a wedge, a Woman is a needle; being, so to speak, *all* point, at least at the two extremities. Add to this the power of making herself practically invisible at will, and you will perceive that a Female, in Flatland, is a creature by no means to be trifled with.

But here, perhaps, some of my younger Readers may ask *how* a woman in Flatland can make herself invisible. This ought, I think, to be apparent without any explanation. However, a few words will make it clear to the most unreflecting.

Place a needle on a table. Then, with your eye on the level of the table, look at it sideways, and you see the whole length of it; but look at it end-ways, and you see nothing but a point, it has become practically invisible. Just so is it with one of our Women. When her side is turned towards us, we see her as a straight line; when the end containing her eye or mouth – for with us these two organs are identical – is the part that meets our eye, then we see nothing but a highly lustrous point; but when the back is presented to our view, then – being only sub-lustrous, and, indeed, almost as dim as an inanimate object – her hinder extremity serves her as a kind of Invisible Cap.

The dangers to which we are exposed from our Women must now be manifest to the meanest capacity in Spaceland. If even the angle of a respectable Triangle in the middle class is not without its dangers; if to run against a Working Man involves a gash; if collision with an officer of the military class necessitates a serious wound; if a mere touch from the vertex of a Private Soldier brings with it danger of death – what can it be to run against a Woman, except absolute and immediate destruction? And when a Woman is invisible, or visible only as a dim sub-lustrous point, how difficult must it be, even for the most cautious, always to avoid collision!

Many are the enactments made at different times in the different States of Flatland, in order to minimize this peril; and in the Southern and less temperate climates where the force of gravitation is greater, and human beings more liable to casual and involuntary motions, the Laws concerning Women are naturally much more stringent. But a general view of the Code may be obtained from the following summary –

1. Every house shall have one entrance in the Eastern side, for the use of Females only; by which all females shall enter 'in a becoming and respectful manner'* and not by the Men's or Western door.

2. No Female shall walk in any public place without continually keeping up her Peace-cry, under penalty of death.

3. Any Female, duly certified to be suffering from St Vitus Dance, fits, chronic cold accompanied by violent sneezing, or any disease necessitating involuntary motions, shall be instantly destroyed.

In some of the States there is an additional Law forbidding Females, under penalty of death, from walking or standing in any public place without moving their backs constantly from right to left so as to indicate their presence to those behind them; others oblige a Woman, when travelling, to be followed by one of her sons, or servants, or by her husband; others confine Women altogether to their houses except during the religious festivals. But it has been found by the wisest of our Circles or Statesmen that the multiplication of restrictions on Females tends not only to the debilitation and diminution of the race, but also to the increase of domestic murders to such an extent that a State loses more than it gains by a too prohibitive Code.

For whenever the temper of the Women is thus exasperated by confinement at home or hampering regulations abroad, they are apt to vent their spleen upon their husbands and children; and in the less temperate climates the whole male population of a village has been sometimes

---

* When I was in Spaceland I understood that some of your Priestly circles have in the same way a separate entrance for Villagers, Farmers and Teachers of Board Schools (*Spectator*, Sept. 1884, p. 1255) that they may 'approach in a becoming and respectful manner'.

destroyed in one or two hours of simultaneous female outbreak. Hence the Three Laws, mentioned above, suffice for the better regulated States, and may be accepted as a rough exemplification of our Female Code.

After all, our principal safeguard is found, not in Legislature, but in the interests of the Women themselves. For, although they can inflict instantaneous death by a retrograde movement, yet unless they can at once disengage their stinging extremity from the struggling body of their victim, their own frail bodies are liable to be shattered.

The power of Fashion is also on our side. I pointed out that in some less civilized States no female is suffered to stand in any public place without swaying her back from right to left. This practice has been universal among ladies of any pretensions to breeding in all well-governed States, as far back as the memory of Figures can reach. It is considered a disgrace to any State that legislation should have to enforce what ought to be, and is in every respectable female, a natural instinct. The rhythmical and, if I may so say, well-modulated undulation of the back in our ladies of Circular rank is envied and imitated by the Wife of a common Equilateral, who can achieve nothing beyond a mere monotonous swing, like the ticking of a pendulum; and the regular tick of the Equilateral is no less admired and copied by the Wife of the progressive and aspiring Isosceles, in the females of whose family no 'back-motion' of any kind has become as yet a necessity of life. Hence, in every family of position and consideration, 'back motion' is as prevalent as time itself; and the husbands and sons in these households enjoy immunity at least from invisible attacks.

Not that it must be for a moment supposed that our Women are destitute of affection. But unfortunately the passion of the moment predominates, in the Frail Sex, over every other consideration. This is, of course, a necessity arising from their unfortunate conformation. For as they have no pretensions to an angle, being inferior in this respect to the very lowest of the Isosceles, they are consequently wholly devoid of brain-power, and have neither reflection, judgment nor forethought, and hardly any memory. Hence, in their fits of fury, they remember no claims and recognize no distinctions. I have actually known a case where a Woman has exterminated her whole household, and half an hour afterwards, when her rage was over and the fragments swept away, has asked what has become of her husband and her children.

Obviously then a Woman is not to be irritated as long as she is in a position where she can turn round. When you have them in their apartments – which are constructed with a view to denying them that power – you can say and do what you like; for they are then wholly impotent for

mischief, and will not remember a few minutes hence the incident for
which they may be at this moment threatening you with death, nor the
promises which you may have found it necessary to make in order to
pacify their fury.

On the whole we get on pretty smoothly in our domestic relations,
except in the lower strata of the Military Classes. There the want of tact
and discretion on the part of the husbands produces at times indescribable
disasters. Relying too much on the offensive weapons of their acute angles
instead of the defensive organs of good sense and seasonable simulation,
these reckless creatures too often neglect the prescribed construction of
the women's apartments, or irritate their wives by ill-advised expressions
out of doors, which they refuse immediately to retract. Moreover a blunt
and stolid regard for literal truth indisposes them to make those lavish
promises by which the more judicious Circle can in a moment pacify his
consort. The result is massacre; not, however, without its advantages, as it
eliminates the more brutal and troublesome of the Isosceles; and by many
of our Circles the destructiveness of the Thinner Sex is regarded as one
among many providential arrangements for suppressing redundant population, and nipping Revolution in the bud.

Yet even in our best regulated and most approximately Circular families I cannot say that the ideal of family life is so high as with you in
Spaceland. There is peace, in so far as the absence of slaughter may be
called by that name, but there is necessarily little harmony of tastes or
pursuits; and the cautious wisdom of the Circles has ensured safety at the
cost of domestic comfort. In every Circular or Polygonal household it has
been a habit from time immemorial – and now has become a kind of
instinct among the women of our higher classes – that the mothers and
daughters should constantly keep their eyes and mouths towards their
husband and his male friends; and for a lady in a family of distinction to
turn her back upon her husband would be regarded as a kind of portent,
involving loss of *status*. But, as I shall soon shew, this custom, though it
has the advantage of safety, is not without its disadvantages.

In the house of the Working Man or respectable Tradesman – where
the Wife is allowed to turn her back upon her husband, while pursuing her
household avocations – there are at least intervals of quiet, when the Wife
is neither seen nor heard, except for the humming sound of the continuous Peace-cry; but in the homes of the upper classes there is too often
no peace. There the voluble mouth and bright penetrating eye are ever
directed towards the Master of the household; and light itself is not more
persistent than the stream of feminine discourse. The tact and skill which
suffice to avert a Woman's sting are unequal to the task of stopping a

Woman's mouth; and as the Wife has absolutely nothing to say, and absolutely no constraint of wit, sense, or conscience to prevent her from saying it, not a few cynics have been found to aver that they prefer the danger of the death-dealing but inaudible sting to the safe sonorousness of a Woman's other end.

To my readers in Spaceland the condition of our Women may seem truly deplorable, and so indeed it is. A Male of the lowest type of the Isosceles may look forward to some improvement of his angle, and to the ultimate elevation of the whole of his degraded caste; but no Woman can entertain such hopes for her sex. 'Once a Woman, always a Woman' is a Decree of Nature; and the very Laws of Evolution seem suspended in her disfavour. Yet at least we can admire the wise Prearrangement which has ordained that, as they have no hopes, so they shall have no memory to recall, and no forethought to anticipate, the miseries and humiliations which are at once a necessity of their existence and the basis of the constitution of Flatland.

Section 5. Of our Methods of Recognizing one another
You, who are blessed with shade as well as light, you, who are gifted with two eyes, endowed with a knowledge of perspective, and charmed with the enjoyment of various colours, you, who can actually *see* an angle, and contemplate the complete circumference of a circle in the happy region of the Three Dimensions – how shall I make clear to you the extreme difficulty which we in Flatland experience in recognizing one another's configuration?

Recall what I told you above. All beings in Flatland, animate or inanimate, no matter what their form, present *to our view* the same, or nearly the same, appearance, viz. that of a straight Line. How then can one be distinguished from another, where all appear the same?

The answer is threefold. The first means of recognition is the sense of hearing; which with us is far more highly developed than with you, and which enables us not only to distinguish by the voice our personal friends, but even to discriminate between different classes, at least so far as concerns the three lowest orders, the Equilateral, the Square, and the Pentagon – for of the Isosceles I take no account. But as we ascend in the social scale, the process of discriminating and being discriminated by hearing increases in difficulty, partly because voices are assimilated, partly because the faculty of voice-discrimination is a plebeian virtue not much developed among the Aristocracy. And wherever there is any danger of imposture we cannot trust to this method. Amongst our lowest orders, the vocal organs are developed to a degree more than correspondent with those of hearing, so that an Isosceles can easily feign the voice of a Polygon, and, with some training, that of a Circle himself. A second method is therefore more commonly resorted to.

Feeling is, among our Women and lower classes – about our upper classes I shall speak presently – the principal test of recognition, at all events between strangers, and when the question is, not as to the individual, but as to the class. What therefore 'introduction' is among the higher classes in Spaceland, that the process of 'feeling' is with us. 'Permit me to ask you to feel and be felt by my friend Mr So-and-so' – is still, among the more old-fashioned of our country gentlemen in districts remote from towns, the customary formula for a Flatland introduction. But in the towns, and among men of business, the words 'be felt by' are omitted and the sentence is abbreviated to, 'Let me ask you to feel Mr So-and-so'; although it is assumed, of course, that the 'feeling' is to be reciprocal. Among our still more modern and dashing young gentlemen – who are extremely averse to superfluous effort and supremely indifferent to the purity of their native language – the formula is still further curtailed by the use of 'to feel' in a technical sense, meaning, 'to recommend-for-the-purposes-of-feeling-and-being-felt'; and at this moment the 'slang' of polite or fast society in the upper classes sanctions such a barbarism as 'Mr Smith, permit me to feel Mr Jones.'

Let not my Reader however suppose that 'feeling' is with us the tedious process that it would be with you, or that we find it necessary to feel right round all the sides of every individual before we determine the class to which he belongs. Long practice and training, begun in the schools and continued in the experience of daily life, enable us to discriminate at once by the sense of touch, between the angles of an equal-sided Triangle, Square, and Pentagon; and I need not say that the brainless vertex of an acute-angled Isosceles is obvious to the dullest touch. It is therefore not necessary, as a rule, to do more than feel a single angle of an individual; and this, once ascertained, tells us the class of the person whom we are addressing, unless indeed he belongs to the higher sections of the nobility. There the difficulty is much greater. Even a Master of Arts in our University of Wentbridge has been known to confuse a ten-sided with a twelve-sided Polygon; and there is hardly a Doctor of Science in or out of that famous University who could pretend to decide promptly and unhesitatingly between a twenty-sided and a twenty-four-sided member of the Aristocracy.

Those of my readers who recall the extracts I gave above from the Legislative code concerning Women, will readily perceive that the process of introduction by contact requires some care and discretion. Otherwise the angles might inflict on the unwary Feeler irreparable injury. It is essential for the safety of the Feeler that the Felt should stand perfectly still. A start, a fidgety shifting of the position, yes, even a violent sneeze, has been known before now to prove fatal to the incautious, and to nip in the bud many a promising friendship. Especially is this true among the lower classes of the Triangles. With them, the eye is situated so far from their vertex that they can scarcely take cognizance of what goes on at that extremity of their frame. They are, moreover, of a rough coarse nature, not sensitive to the delicate touch of the highly organized Polygon. What wonder then if an involuntary toss of the head has ere now deprived the State of a valuable life!

I have heard that my excellent Grandfather – one of the least irregular of his unhappy Isosceles class, who indeed obtained, shortly before his decease, four out of seven votes from the Sanitary and Social Board for passing him into the class of the Equal-sided – often deplored, with a tear in his venerable eye, a miscarriage of this kind, which had occurred to his great-great-great-Grandfather, a respectable Working Man with an angle or brain of 59 degrees 30 minutes. According to his account, my unfortunate Ancestor, being afflicted with rheumatism, and in the act of being felt by a Polygon, by one sudden start accidentally transfixed the Great Man through the diagonal; and thereby, partly in consequence of his long imprisonment and degradation, and partly because of the moral shock which pervaded the whole of my Ancestor's relations, threw back our family a degree and a half in their ascent towards better things. The result was that in the next generation the family brain was registered at only 58 degrees, and not till the lapse of five generations was the lost ground recovered, the full 60 degrees attained, and the Ascent from the Isosceles finally achieved. And all this series of calamities from one little accident in the process of Feeling.

At this point I think I hear some of my better educated readers exclaim, 'How could you in Flatland know anything about angles and degrees, or minutes? We can *see* an angle, because we, in the region of Space, can see two straight lines inclined to one another; but you, who can see nothing but one straight line at a time, or at all events only a number of bits of straight lines all in one straight line – how can you ever discern any angle, and much less register angles of different sizes?'

I answer that though we cannot *see* angles, we can *infer* them, and this with great precision. Our sense of touch, stimulated by necessity, and developed by long training, enables us to distinguish angles far more accurately than your sense of sight, when unaided by a rule or measure of angles. Nor must I omit to explain that we have great natural helps. It is with us a Law of Nature that the brain of the Isosceles class shall begin at half a degree, or thirty minutes, and shall increase (if it increases at all) by half a degree in every generation; until the goal of 60 degrees is reached, when the condition of serfdom is quitted, and the freeman enters the class of Regulars.

Consequently, Nature herself supplies us with an ascending scale or Alphabet of angles for half a degree up to 60 degrees, Specimens of which are placed in every Elementary School throughout the land. Owing to occasional retrogressions, to still more frequent moral and intellectual stagnation, and to the extraordinary fecundity of the Criminal and Vaga-bond Classes, there is always a vast superfluity of individuals of the half degree and single degree class, and a fair abundance of Specimens up to 10 degrees. These are absolutely destitute of civic rights; and a great number of them, not having even intelligence enough for the purposes of warfare, are devoted by the States to the service of education. Fettered immovably so as to remove all possibility of danger, they are placed in the class rooms of our Infant Schools, and there they are utilized by the Board of Education for the purpose of imparting to the offspring of the Middle Classes that tact and intelligence of which these wretched creatures themselves are utterly devoid.

In some States the Specimens are occasionally fed and suffered to exist for several years; but in the more temperate and better regulated regions, it is found in the long run more advantageous for the educational inter-ests of the young, to dispense with food, and to renew the Specimens every month – which is about the average duration of the foodless existence of the Criminal class. In the cheaper schools, what is gained by the longer existence of the Specimen is lost, partly in the expenditure for food, and partly in the diminished accuracy of the angles, which are impaired after a few weeks of constant 'feeling'. Nor must we forget to add, in enumerating the advantages of the more expensive system, that it tends, though slightly yet perceptibly, to the diminution of the redundant Isosceles population – an object which every statesman in Flatland constantly keeps in view. On the whole therefore – although I am not ignorant that, in many popularly elected School Boards, there is a reaction in favour of 'the cheap system' as it is called – I am myself disposed to think that this is one of the many cases in which expense is the truest economy.

But I must not allow questions of School Board politics to divert me from my subject. Enough has been said, I trust, to shew that Recog-nition by Feeling is not so tedious or indecisive a process as might have been supposed; and it is obviously more trustworthy than Recognition by hearing. Still there remains, as has been pointed out above, the objection that this method is not without danger. For this reason many in the Middle and Lower classes, and all without exception in the Polygonal and Circular orders, prefer a third method, the description of which shall be reserved for the next section.

Section 6. Of Recognition by Sight

I am about to appear very inconsistent. In previous sections I have said that all figures in Flatland present the appearance of a straight line; and it was added or implied, that it is consequently impossible to distinguish by the visual organ between individuals of different classes: yet now I am about to explain to my Spaceland critics how we are able to recognize one another by the sense of sight.

If however the Reader will take the trouble to refer to the passage in which Recognition by Feeling is stated to be universal, he will find this qualification – 'among the lower classes'. It is only among the higher classes and in our temperate climates that Sight Recognition is practised.

That this power exists in any regions and for any classes is the result of Fog; which prevails during the greater part of the year in all parts save the torrid zones. That which is with you in Spaceland an unmixed evil, blotting out the landscape, depressing the spirits, and enfeebling the health, is by us recognized as a blessing scarcely inferior to air itself, and as the Nurse of arts and Parent of sciences. But let me explain my meaning, without further eulogies on this beneficent Element.

If Fog were non-existent, all lines would appear equally and indistinguishably clear; and this is actually the case in those unhappy countries in which the atmosphere is perfectly dry and transparent. But wherever there is a rich supply of Fog, objects that are at a distance, say of three feet, are appreciably dimmer than those at a distance of two feet eleven inches; and the result is that by careful and constant experimental observation of comparative dimness and clearness, we are enabled to infer with great exactness the configuration of the object observed.

An instance will do more than a volume of generalities to make my meaning clear.

Suppose I see two individuals approaching whose rank I wish to ascertain. They are, we will suppose, a Merchant and a Physician, or in other words, an Equilateral Triangle and a Pentagon: how am I to distinguish them?

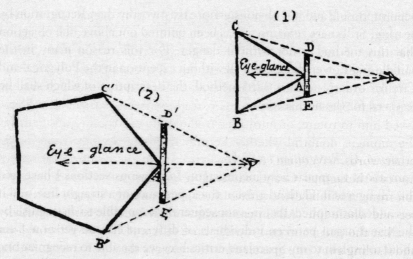

It will be obvious, to every child in Spaceland who has touched the threshold of Geometrical Studies, that, if I can bring my eye so that its glance may bisect an angle (A) of the approaching stranger, my view will lie as it were evenly between his two sides that are next to me (viz. CA and AB), so that I shall contemplate the two impartially, and both will appear of the same size.

Now in the case of (1) the Merchant, what shall I see? I shall see a straight line DAE, in which the middle point (A) will be very bright because it is nearest to me; but on either side the line will shade away *rapidly into dimness*, because the sides AC and AB *recede rapidly into the fog* and what appear to me as the Merchant's extremities, viz. D and E, will be *very dim indeed*.

On the other hand in the case of (2) the Physician, though I shall here also see a line (D'A'E') with a bright centre (A'), yet it will shade away *less rapidly* into dimness, because the sides (A'C', A'B') *recede less rapidly into the fog*: and what appear to me the Physician's extremities, viz. D' and E', will be *not so dim* as the extremities of the Merchant.

The Reader will probably understand from these two instances how – after a very long training supplemented by constant experience – it is possible for the well-educated classes among us to discriminate with fair accuracy between the middle and lowest orders, by the sense of sight. If my Spaceland Patrons have grasped this general conception, so far as to conceive the possibility of it and not to reject my account as altogether incredible – I shall have attained all I can reasonably expect. Were I to attempt further details I should only perplex. Yet for the sake of the young and inexperienced, who may perchance infer – from the two simple instances I have given above, of the manner in which I should recognize my Father and my Sons – that Recognition by sight is an easy affair, it may be needful to point out that in actual life most of the problems of Sight Recognition are far more subtle and complex.

If for example, when my Father, the Triangle, approaches me, he happens to present his side to me instead of his angle, then, until I have asked him to rotate, or until I have edged my eye round him, I am for the moment doubtful whether he may not be a Straight Line, or, in other words, a Woman. Again, when I am in the company of one of my two hexagonal Grandsons, contemplating one of his sides (AB) full front, it will be evident from the accompanying diagram that I shall see one whole line (AB) in comparative brightness (shading off hardly at all at the ends) and two smaller lines (CA and BD) dim throughout and shading away into greater dimness towards the extremities C and D.

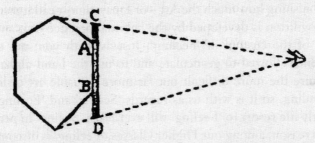

But I must not give way to the temptation of enlarging on these topics. The meanest mathematician in Spaceland will readily believe me when I assert that the problems of life, which present themselves to the well-educated – when they are themselves in motion, rotating, advancing or retreating, and at the same time attempting to discriminate by the sense of sight between a number of Polygons of high rank moving in different directions, as for example in a ball-room or *conversazione* – must be of a nature to task the angularity of the most intellectual, and amply justify the rich endowments of the Learned Professors of Geometry, both Static and Kinetic, in the illustrious University of Wentbridge, where the Science and Art of Sight Recognition are regularly taught to large classes of the *élite* of the States.

It is only a few of the scions of our noblest and wealthiest houses, who are able to give the time and money necessary for the thorough prosecution of this noble and valuable Art. Even to me, a Mathematician of no mean standing, and the Grandfather of two most hopeful and perfectly regular Hexagons, to find myself in the midst of a crowd of rotating Polygons of the higher classes, is occasionally very perplexing. And of course to a common Tradesman, or Serf, such a sight is almost as unintelligible as it would be to you, my Reader, were you suddenly transported into our country.

In such a crowd you could see on all sides of you nothing but a Line, apparently straight, but of which the parts would vary irregularly and perpetually in brightness or dimness. Even if you had completed your third year in the Pentagonal and Hexagonal classes in the University, and were perfect in the theory of the subject, you would still find that there was need of many years of experience, before you could move in a fashionable crowd without jostling against your betters, whom it is against etiquette to ask to 'feel', and who, by their superior culture and breeding, know all about your movements, while you know very little or nothing about theirs. In a word, to comport oneself with perfect propriety in Polygonal society, one ought to be a Polygon oneself. Such at least is the painful teaching of my experience.

It is astonishing how much the Art – or I may almost call it instinct – of Sight Recognition is developed by the habitual practice of it and by the avoidance of the custom of 'Feeling'. Just as, with you, the deaf and dumb, if once allowed to gesticulate and to use the hand-alphabet, will never acquire the more difficult but far more valuable art of lipspeech and lip-reading, so it is with us as regards 'Seeing' and 'Feeling'. None who in early life resort to 'Feeling' will ever learn 'Seeing' in perfection.

For this reason, among our Higher Classes, 'Feeling' is discouraged or absolutely forbidden. From the cradle their children, instead of going to the Public Elementary schools (where the art of Feeling is taught), are sent to higher Seminaries of an exclusive character; and at our illustrious University, to 'feel' is regarded as a most serious fault, involving Rustication for the first offence, and Expulsion for the second.

But among the lower classes the art of Sight Recognition is regarded as an unattainable luxury. A common Tradesman cannot afford to let his son spend a third of his life in abstract studies. The children of the poor are therefore allowed to 'feel' from their earliest years, and they gain thereby a precocity and an early vivacity which contrast at first most favourably with the inert, undeveloped, and listless behaviour of the half-instructed youths of the Polygonal class; but when the latter have at last completed their University course, and are prepared to put their theory into practice, the change that comes over them may almost be described as a new birth, and in every art, science, and social pursuit they rapidly overtake and distance their Triangular competitors.

Only a few of the Polygonal Class fail to pass the Final Test or Leaving Examination at the University. The condition of the unsuccessful minority is truly pitiable. Rejected from the higher class, they are also despised by the lower. They have neither the matured and systematically trained powers of the Polygonal Bachelors and Masters of Arts, nor yet the native precocity and mercurial versatility of the youthful Tradesman. The professions, the public services, are closed against them; and though in most States they are not actually debarred from marriage, yet they have the greatest difficulty in forming suitable alliances, as experience shews that the offspring of such unfortunate and ill-endowed parents is generally itself unfortunate, if not positively Irregular.

It is from these specimens of the refuse of our Nobility that the great Tumults and Seditions of past ages have generally derived their leaders; and so great is the mischief thence arising that an increasing minority of our more progressive Statesmen are of opinion that true mercy would dictate their entire suppression, by enacting that all who fail to pass the Final Examination of the University should be either imprisoned for life, or extinguished by a painless death.

But I find myself digressing into the subject of Irregularities, a matter of such vital interest that it demands a separate section.

Section 7. Concerning Irregular Figures

Throughout the previous pages I have been assuming – what perhaps should have been laid down at the beginning as a distinct and fundamental proposition – that every human being in Flatland is a Regular Figure, that is to say of regular construction. By this I mean that a Woman must not only be a line, but a straight line; that an Artisan or Soldier must have two of his sides equal; that Tradesmen must have three sides equal; Lawyers (of which class I am a humble member), four sides equal, and generally, that in every Polygon, all the sides must be equal.

The size of the sides would of course depend upon the age of the individual. A Female at birth would be about an inch long, while a tall adult Woman might extend to a foot. As to the Males of every class, it may be roughly said that the length of an adult's sides, when added together, is two feet or a little more. But the size of our sides is not under consideration. I am speaking of the *equality* of sides, and it does not need much reflection to see that the whole of the social life in Flatland rests upon the fundamental fact that Nature wills all Figures to have their sides equal.

If our sides were unequal our angles might be unequal. Instead of its being sufficient to feel, or estimate by sight, a single angle in order to determine the form of an individual, it would be necessary to ascertain each angle by the experiment of Feeling. But life would be too short for such a tedious grouping. The whole science and art of Sight Recognition would at once perish; Feeling, so far as it is an art, would not long survive; intercourse would become perilous or impossible; there would be an end to all confidence, all forethought; no one would be safe in making the most simple social arrangements; in a word, civilization would relapse into barbarism.

Am I going too fast to carry my Readers with me to these obvious conclusions? Surely a moment's reflection, and a single instance from common life, must convince every one that our whole social system is based upon Regularity, or Equality of Angles. You meet, for example, two or three Tradesmen in the street, whom you recognize at once to be Tradesmen by a glance at their angles and rapidly bedimmed sides, and you ask them to step into your house to lunch. This you do at present with perfect confidence, because everyone knows to an inch or two the area occupied by an adult Triangle: but imagine that your Tradesman drags behind his regular and respectable vertex, a parallelogram of twelve or thirteen inches in diagonal: – what are you to do with such a monster sticking fast in your house door?

But I am insulting the intelligence of my Readers by accumulating details which must be patent to everyone who enjoys the advantages of a Residence in Spaceland. Obviously the measurements of a single angle would no longer be sufficient under such portentous circumstances; one's whole life would be taken up in feeling or surveying the perimeter of one's acquaintances. Already the difficulties of avoiding a collision in a crowd are enough to tax the sagacity of even a well-educated Square; but if no one could calculate the Regularity of a single figure in the company, all would be chaos and confusion, and the slightest panic would cause serious injuries, or – if there happened to be any Women or Soldiers present – perhaps considerable loss of life.

Expediency therefore concurs with Nature in stamping the seal of its approval upon Regularity of conformation: nor has the Law been back-ward in seconding their efforts. 'Irregularity of Figure' means with us the same as, or more than, a combination of moral obliquity and criminality with you, and is treated accordingly. There are not wanting, it is true, some promulgators of paradoxes who maintain that there is no necessary connection between geometrical and moral Irregularity. 'The Irregular', they say, 'is from his birth scouted by his own parents, derided by his brothers and sisters, neglected by the domestics, scorned and suspected by society, and excluded from all posts of responsibility, trust, and useful activity. His every movement is jealously watched by the police till he comes of age and presents himself for inspection; then he is either destroyed, if he is found to exceed the fixed margin of deviation, or else immured in a Government Office as a clerk of the seventh class; prevented from marriage; forced to drudge at an uninteresting occupation for a miserable stipend; obliged to live and board at the office, and to take even his vacation under close supervision; what wonder that human nature, even in the best and purest, is embittered and perverted by such surroundings!'

All this very plausible reasoning does not convince me, as it has not convinced the wisest of our Statesmen, that our ancestors erred in laying it down as an axiom of policy that the toleration of Irregularity is incompatible with the safety of the State. Doubtless, the life of an Irregular is hard; but the interests of the Greater Number require that it shall be hard. If a man with a triangular front and a polygonal back were allowed to exist and to propagate a still more Irregular posterity, what would become of the arts of life? Are the houses and doors and churches in Flatland to be altered in order to accommodate such monsters? Are our ticket-collectors to be required to measure every man's perimeter before they allow him to enter a theatre or to take his place in a lecture room? Is an Irregular to be exempted from the militia? And if not, how is he to be prevented from carrying desolation into the ranks of his comrades? Again, what irresistible temptations to fraudulent impostures must needs beset such a creature! How easy for him to enter a shop with his polygonal front foremost, and to order goods to any extent from a confiding tradesman! Let the advocates of a falsely called Philanthropy plead as they may for the abrogation of the Irregular Penal Laws, I for my part have never known an Irregular who was not also what Nature evidently intended him to be – a hypocrite, a misanthropist, and, up to the limits of his power, a perpetrator of all manner of mischief.

Not that I should be disposed to recommend (at present) the extreme measures adopted by some States, where an infant whose angle deviates by half a degree from the correct angularity is summarily destroyed at birth. Some of our highest and ablest men, men of real genius, have during their earliest days laboured under deviations as great as, or even greater than, forty-five minutes: and the loss of their precious lives would have been an irreparable injury to the State. The art of healing also has achieved some of its most glorious triumphs in the compressions, extensions, trepannings, colligations, and other surgical or diaetetic operations by which Irregularity has been partly or wholly cured. Advocating therefore a *Via Media*, I would lay down no fixed or absolute line of demarcation; but at the period when the frame is just beginning to set, and when the Medical Board has reported that recovery is improbable, I would suggest that the Irregular offspring be painlessly and mercifully consumed.

Section 8. Of the Ancient Practice of Painting

If my Readers have followed me with any attention up to this point, they will not be surprised to hear that life is somewhat dull in Flatland. I do not, of course, mean that there are not battles, conspiracies, tumults, factions, and all those other phenomena which are supposed to make History interesting; nor would I deny that the strange mixture of the problems of life and the problems of Mathematics, continually inducing conjecture and giving the opportunity of immediate verification, imparts to our existence a zest which you in Spaceland can hardly comprehend. I speak now from the aesthetic and artistic point of view when I say that life with us is dull; aesthetically and artistically, very dull indeed.

How can it be otherwise, when all one's prospect, all one's landscapes, historical pieces, portraits, flowers, still life, are nothing but a single line, with no varieties except degrees of brightness and obscurity?

It was not always thus. Colour, if Tradition speaks the truth, once for the space of half a dozen centuries or more, threw a transient splendour over the lives of our ancestors in the remotest ages. Some private individual – a Pentagon whose name is variously reported – having casually discovered the constituents of the simpler colours and a rudimentary method of painting, is said to have begun decorating first his house, then his slaves, then his Father, his Sons, and Grandsons, lastly himself. The convenience as well as the beauty of the results commended themselves to all. Wherever Chromatistes – for by that name the most trustworthy authorities concur in calling him – turned his variegated frame, there he at once excited attention, and attracted respect. No one now needed to 'feel' him; no one mistook his front for his back; all his movements were readily ascertained by his neighbours without the slightest strain on their powers of calculation; no one jostled him, or failed to make way for him; his voice was saved the labour of that exhausting utterance by which we colourless Squares and Pentagons are often forced to proclaim our individuality when we move amid a crowd of ignorant Isosceles.

The fashion spread like wildfire. Before a week was over, every Square and Triangle in the district had copied the example of Chromatistes, and only a few of the more conservative Pentagons still held out. A month or two found even the Dodecagons infected with the innovation. A year had not elapsed before the habit had spread to all but the very highest of the Nobility. Needless to say, the custom soon made its way from the district of Chromatistes to surrounding regions; and within two generations no one in all Flatland was colourless except the Women and the Priests.

Here Nature herself appeared to erect a barrier, and to plead against extending the innovation to these two classes. Many-sidedness was almost essential as a pretext for the Innovators. 'Distinction of sides is intended by Nature to imply distinction of colours' – such was the sophism which in those days flew from mouth to mouth, converting whole towns at a time to the new culture. But manifestly to our Priests and Women this adage did not apply. The latter had only one side, and therefore – plurally and pedantically speaking – *no sides*. The former – if at least they would assert their claim to be really and truly Circles, and not mere high-class Polygons with an infinitely large number of infinitesimally small sides – were in the habit of boasting (what Women confessed and deplored) that they also had no sides, being blessed with a perimeter of one line, or, in other words, a Circumference. Hence it came to pass that these two Classes could see no force in the so-called axiom about 'Distinction of Sides implying Distinction of Colour'; and when all others had succumbed to the fascinations of corporal decoration, the Priests and the Women alone still remained pure from the pollution of paint.

Immoral, licentious, anarchical, unscientific – call them by what names you will – yet, from an aesthetic point of view, those ancient days of the Colour Revolt were the glorious childhood of Art in Flatland – a childhood, alas, that never ripened into manhood, nor even reached the blossom of youth. To live was then in itself a delight, because living implied seeing. Even at a small party, the company was a pleasure to behold; the richly varied hues of the assembly in a church or theatre are said to have more than once proved too distracting for our greatest teachers and actors; but most ravishing of all is said to have been the unspeakable magnificence of a military review.

The sight of a line of battle of twenty thousand Isosceles suddenly facing about, and exchanging the sombre black of their bases for the orange and purple of the two sides including their acute angle; the militia of the Equilateral Triangles tricoloured in red, white, and blue; the mauve, ultra-marine, gamboge, and burnt umber of the Square artillerymen rapidly rotating near their vermilion guns; the dashing and flashing of the five-coloured and six-coloured Pentagons and Hexagons careering across the field in their offices of surgeons, geometricians and aides-de-camp – all these may well have been sufficient to render credible the famous story how an illustrious Circle, overcome by the artistic beauty of the forces under his command, threw aside his marshal's baton and his royal crown, exclaiming that he henceforth exchanged them for the artist's pencil. How great and glorious the sensuous development of these days must have been is in part indicated by the very language and vocabulary of the period. The commonest utterances of the commonest citizens in the time of the Colour Revolt seem to have been suffused with a richer tinge of word or thought; and to that era we are even now indebted for our finest poetry and for whatever rhythm still remains in the more scientific utterance of these modern days.

Section 9. Of the Universal Colour Bill
But meanwhile the intellectual Arts were fast decaying.

The Art of Sight Recognition, being no longer needed, was no longer practised; and the studies of Geometry, Statics, Kinetics, and other kindred subjects, came soon to be considered superfluous, and fell into disrespect and neglect even at our University. The inferior Art of Feeling speedily experienced the same fate at our Elementary Schools. Then the Isosceles classes, asserting that the Specimens were no longer used nor needed, and refusing to pay the customary tribute from the Criminal classes to the service of Education, waxed daily more numerous and more insolent on the strength of their immunity from the old burden which had formerly exercised the twofold wholesome effect of at once taming their brutal nature and thinning their excessive numbers.

Year by year the Soldiers and Artisans began more vehemently to assert – and with increasing truth – that there was no great difference between them and the very highest class of Polygons, now that they were raised to an equality with the latter, and enabled to grapple with all the difficulties and solve all the problems of life, whether Statical or Kinetical, by the simple process of Colour Recognition. Not content with the natural neglect into which Sight Recognition was falling, they began boldly to demand the legal prohibition of all 'monopolizing and aristocratic Arts' and the consequent abolition of all endowments for the studies of Sight Recognition, Mathematics, and Feeling. Soon, they began to insist that inasmuch as Colour, which was a second Nature, had destroyed the need of aristocratic distinctions, the Law should follow in the same path, and that henceforth all individuals and all classes should be recognized as absolutely equal and entitled to equal rights.

Finding the higher Orders wavering and undecided, the leaders of the Revolution advanced still further in their requirements, and at last demanded that all classes alike, the Priests and the Women not excepted, should do homage to Colour by submitting to be painted. When it was objected that Priests and Women had no sides, they retorted that Nature and Expediency concurred in dictating that the front half of every human being (that is to say, the half containing his eye and mouth) should be distinguishable from his hinder half. They therefore brought before a general and extraordinary Assembly of all the States of Flatland a Bill proposing that in every Woman the half containing the eye and mouth should be coloured red, and the other half green. The Priests were to be painted in the same way, red being applied to that semicircle in which the eye and mouth formed the middle point; while the other or hinder semicircle was to be coloured green.

There was no little cunning in this proposal, which indeed emanated not from any Isosceles – for no being so degraded would have had angularity enough to appreciate, much less to devise, such a model of statecraft – but from an Irregular Circle who, instead of being destroyed in his childhood, was reserved by a foolish indulgence to bring desolation on his country and destruction on myriads of his followers.

On the one hand the proposition was calculated to bring the Women in all classes over to the side of the Chromatic Innovation. For by assigning to the Women the same two colours as were assigned to the Priests, the Revolutionists thereby ensured that, in certain positions, every Woman would appear like a Priest, and be treated with corresponding respect and deference – a prospect that could not fail to attract the Female Sex in a mass.

But by some of my Readers the possibility of the identical appearance of Priests and Women, under the new Legislation, may not be recognized; if so, a word or two will make it obvious.

Imagine a woman duly decorated, according to the new Code; with the front half (i.e. the half containing eye and mouth) red, and with the hinder half green. Look at her from one side. Obviously you will see a straight line, *half red, half green.*

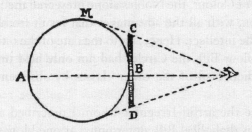

Now imagine a Priest, whose mouth is at M, and whose front semicircle (AMB) is consequently coloured red, while his hinder semicircle is green; so that the diameter AB divides the green from the red. If you contemplate the Great Man so as to have your eye in the same straight line as his dividing diameter (AB), what you will see will be a straight line (CBD), of which *one half* (CB) *will be red, and the other* (BD) *green*. The whole line (CD) will be rather shorter perhaps than that of a full-sized Woman, and will shade off more rapidly towards its extremities; but the identity of the colours would give you an immediate impression of identity of Class, making you neglectful of other details. Bear in mind the decay of Sight Recognition which threatened society at the time of the Colour Revolt; add too the certainty that Women would speedily learn to shade off their extremities so as to imitate the Circles; it must then be surely obvious to you, my dear Reader, that the Colour Bill placed us under a great danger of confounding a Priest with a young Woman.

How attractive this prospect must have been to the Frail Sex may readily be imagined. They anticipated with delight the confusion that would ensue. At home they might hear political and ecclesiastical secrets intended not for them but for their husbands and brothers, and might even issue commands in the name of a priestly Circle; out of doors the striking combination of red and green, without addition of any other colours, would be sure to lead the common people into endless mistakes, and the Women would gain whatever the Circles lost, in the deference of the passers-by. As for the scandal that would befall the Circular Class if the frivolous and unseemly conduct of the Women were imputed to them, and as to the consequent subversion of the Constitution, the Female Sex could not be expected to give a thought to these considerations. Even in the households of the Circles, the Women were all in favour of the Universal Colour Bill.

The second object aimed at by the Bill was the gradual demoralization of the Circles themselves. In the general intellectual decay they still preserved their pristine clearness and strength of understanding. From their earliest childhood, familiarized in their Circular households with the total absence of Colour, the Nobles alone preserved the Sacred Art of Sight Recognition, with all the advantages that result from that admirable training of the intellect. Hence, up to the date of the introduction of the Universal Colour Bill, the Circles had not only held their own, but even increased their lead of the other classes by abstinence from the popular fashion.

Now therefore the artful Irregular whom I described above as the real author of this diabolical Bill, determined at one blow to lower the status of the Hierarchy by forcing them to submit to the pollution of Colour, and at the same time to destroy their domestic opportunities of training in the Art of Sight Recognition, so as to enfeeble their intellects by depriving them of their pure and colourless homes. Once subjected to the chromatic taint, every parental and every childish Circle would demoralize each other. Only in discerning between the Father and the Mother would the Circular infant find problems for the exercise of its understanding – problems too often likely to be corrupted by maternal impostures with the result of shaking the child's faith in all logical conclusions. Thus by degrees the intellectual lustre of the Priestly Order would wane, and the road would then lie open for a total destruction of all Aristocratic Legislature and for the subversion of our Privileged Classes.

Section 10. Of the Suppression of the Chromatic Sedition
The agitation for the Universal Colour Bill continued for three years; and up to the last moment of that period it seemed as though Anarchy were destined to triumph.

A whole army of Polygons, who turned out to fight as private soldiers, was utterly annihilated by a superior force of Isosceles Triangles – the Squares and Pentagons meanwhile remaining neutral. Worse than all, some of the ablest Circles fell a prey to conjugal fury. Infuriated by political animosity, the wives in many a noble household wearied their lords with prayers to give up their opposition to the Colour Bill; and some, finding their entreaties fruitless, fell on and slaughtered their innocent children and husband, perishing themselves in the act of carnage. It is recorded that during that triennial agitation no less than twenty-three Circles perished in domestic discord.

Great indeed was the peril. It seemed as though the Priests had no choice between submission and extermination; when suddenly the course of events was completely changed by one of those picturesque incidents which Statesmen ought never to neglect, often to anticipate, and some-times perhaps to originate, because of the absurdly disproportionate power with which they appeal to the sympathies of the populace.

It happened that an Isosceles of a low type, with a brain little if at all above four degrees – accidentally dabbling in the colours of some Tradesman whose shop he had plundered – painted himself, or caused himself to be painted (for the story varies) with the twelve colours of a Dodecagon. Going into the Market Place he accosted in a feigned voice a maiden, the orphan daughter of a noble Polygon, whose affection in former days he had sought in vain; and by a series of deceptions – aided, on the one side, by a string of lucky accidents too long to relate, and on the other, by an almost inconceivable fatuity and neglect of ordinary precautions on the part of the relations of the bride – he succeeded in consummating the marriage. The unhappy girl committed suicide on discovering the fraud to which she had been subjected.

When the news of this catastrophe spread from State to State the minds of the Women were violently agitated. Sympathy with the miserable victim and anticipations of similar deceptions for themselves, their sisters, and their daughters, made them now regard the Colour Bill in an entirely new aspect. Not a few openly avowed themselves converted to antagonism; the rest needed only a slight stimulus to make a similar avowal. Seizing this favourable opportunity, the Circles hastily convened an extraordinary Assembly of the States; and besides the usual guard of Convicts, they secured the attendance of a large number of reactionary Women.

Amidst an unprecedented concourse, the Chief Circle of those days – by name Pantocyclus – arose to find himself hissed and hooted by a hundred and twenty thousand Isosceles. But he secured silence by declaring that henceforth the Circles would enter on a policy of Concession; yielding to the wishes of the majority, they would accept the Colour Bill. The uproar being at once converted to applause, he invited Chromatistes, the leader of the Sedition, into the centre of the hall, to receive in the name of his followers the submission of the Hierarchy. Then followed a speech, a masterpiece of rhetoric, which occupied nearly a day in the delivery, and to which no summary can do justice.

With a grave appearance of impartiality he declared that as they were now finally committing themselves to Reform or Innovation, it was desirable that they should take one last view of the perimeter of the whole subject, its defects as well as its advantages. Gradually introducing the mention of the dangers to the Tradesmen, the Professional Classes and the Gentlemen, he silenced the rising murmurs of the Isosceles by reminding them that, in spite of all these defects, he was willing to accept the Bill if it was approved by the majority. But it was manifest that all, except the Isosceles, were moved by his words and were either neutral or averse to the Bill.

Turning now to the Workmen he asserted that their interests must not be neglected, and that, if they intended to accept the Colour Bill, they ought at least to do so with full view of the consequences. Many of them, he said, were on the point of being admitted to the class of the Regular Triangles; others anticipated for their children a distinction they could not hope for themselves. That honourable ambition would now have to be sacrificed. With the universal adoption of Colour, all distinctions would cease; Regularity would be confused with Irregularity; development would give place to retrogression; the Workman would in a few generations be degraded to the level of the Military, or even the Convict Class; political power would be in the hands of the greatest number, that is to say the Criminal Classes, who were already more numerous than the Workmen, and would soon outnumber all the other Classes put together when the usual Compensative Laws of Nature were violated.

A subdued murmur of assent ran through the ranks of the Artisans, and Chromatistes, in alarm, attempted to step forward and address them. But he found himself encompassed with guards and forced to remain silent while the Chief Circle in a few impassioned words made a final appeal to the Women, exclaiming that, if the Colour Bill passed, no marriage would henceforth be safe, no woman's honour secure; fraud, deception, hypocrisy would pervade every household; domestic bliss would share the fate of the Constitution and pass to speedy perdition. 'Sooner than this,' he cried, 'come death.'

At these words, which were the preconcerted signal for action, the Isosceles Convicts fell on and transfixed the wretched Chromatistes; the Regular Classes, opening their ranks, made way for a band of Women who, under direction of the Circles, moved, back foremost, invisibly and unerringly upon the unconscious soldiers; the Artisans, imitating the example of their betters, also opened their ranks. Meantime bands of Convicts occupied every entrance with an impenetrable phalanx.

The battle, or rather carnage, was of short duration. Under the skillful generalship of the Circles almost every Woman's charge was fatal and very many extracted their sting uninjured, ready for a second slaughter. But no second blow was needed; the rabble of the Isosceles did the rest of the business for themselves. Surprised, leaderless, attacked in front by invisible foes, and finding egress cut off by the Convicts behind them, they at once – after their manner – lost all presence of mind, and raised the cry of 'treachery'. This sealed their fate. Every Isosceles now saw and felt a foe in every other. In half an hour not one of that vast multitude was living; and the fragments of seven score thousand of the Criminal Class slain by one another's angles attested the triumph of Order.

The Circles delayed not to push their victory to the uttermost. The Working Men they spared but decimated. The Militia of the Equilaterals was at once called out; and every Triangle suspected of Irregularity on reasonable grounds, was destroyed by Court Martial, without the form-ality of exact measurement by the Social Board. The homes of the Military and Artisan classes were inspected in a course of visitations extending through upwards of a year; and during that period every town, village, and hamlet was systematically purged of that excess of the lower orders which had been brought about by the neglect to pay the tribute of Criminals to the Schools and University, and by the violation of the other natural Laws of the Constitution of Flatland. Thus the balance of classes was again restored.

Needless to say that henceforth the use of Colour was abolished, and its possession prohibited. Even the utterance of any word denoting Colour, except by the Circles or by qualified scientific teachers, was punished by a severe penalty. Only at our University in some of the very highest and most esoteric classes – which I myself have never been privileged to attend – it is understood that the sparing use of Colour is still sanctioned for the purpose of illustrating some of the deeper problems of mathematics. But of this I can only speak from hearsay.

Elsewhere in Flatland, Colour is now non-existent. The art of making it is known to only one living person, the Chief Circle for the time being; and by him it is handed down on his death-bed to none but his Successor. One manufactory alone produces it; and, lest the secret should be betrayed, the Workmen are annually consumed, and fresh ones introduced. So great is the terror with which even now our Aristocracy looks back to the far-distant days of the agitation for the Universal Colour Bill.

Section 11. Concerning our Priests

It is high time that I should pass from these brief and discursive notes about things in Flatland to the central event of this book, my initiation into the mysteries of Space. *That* is my subject; all that has gone before is merely preface.

For this reason I must omit many matters of which the explanation would not, I flatter myself, be without interest for my Readers: as for example, our method of propelling and stopping ourselves, although destitute of feet; the means by which we give fixity to structures of wood, stone, or brick, although of course we have no hands, nor can we lay foundations as you can, nor avail ourselves of the lateral pressure of the earth; the manner in which the rain originates in the intervals between our various zones, so that the northern regions do not intercept the moisture from falling on the southern; the nature of our hills and mines, our trees and vegetables, our seasons and harvests; our Alphabet and method of writing, adapted to our linear tablets; these and a hundred other details of our physical existence I must pass over, nor do I mention them now except to indicate to my readers that their omission proceeds not from forgetfulness on the part of the author, but from his regard for the time of the Reader.

Yet before I proceed to my legitimate subject some few final remarks will no doubt be expected by my Readers upon those pillars and mainstays of the Constitution of Flatland, the controllers of our conduct and shapers of our destiny, the objects of universal homage and almost of adoration: need I say that I mean our Circles or Priests?

When I call them Priests, let me not be understood as meaning no more than the term denotes with you. With us, our Priests are Administrators of all Business, Art, and Science; Directors of Trade, Commerce, Generalship, Architecture, Engineering, Education, Statesmanship, Legislature, Morality, Theology; doing nothing themselves, they are the Causes of everything worth doing, that is done by others.

Although popularly everyone called a Circle is deemed a Circle, yet among the better educated Classes it is known that no Circle is really a Circle, but only a Polygon with a very large number of very small sides. As the number of the sides increases, a Polygon approximates to a Circle; and, when the number is very great indeed, say for example three or four hundred, it is extremely difficult for the most delicate touch to feel any polygonal angles. Let me say rather, it *would* be difficult: for, as I have shown above, Recognition by Feeling is unknown among the highest society, and to *feel* a Circle would be considered a most audacious insult. This habit of abstention from Feeling in the best society enables a Circle the more easily to sustain the veil of mystery in which, from his earliest years, he is wont to enwrap the exact nature of his Perimeter or Circumference. Three feet being the average Perimeter it follows that, in a Polygon of three hundred sides each side will be no more than the hundredth part of a foot in length, or little more than the tenth part of an inch; and in a Polygon of six or seven hundred sides the sides are little larger than the diameter of a Spaceland pin-head. It is always assumed, by courtesy, that the Chief Circle for the time being has ten thousand sides.

The ascent of the posterity of the Circles in the social scale is not restricted, as it is among the lower Regular classes, by the Law of Nature which limits the increase of sides to one in each generation. If it were so, the number of sides in a Circle would be a mere question of pedigree and arithmetic, and the four hundred and ninety-seventh descendant of an Equilateral Triangle would necessarily be a Polygon with five hundred sides. But this is not the case. Nature's Law prescribes two antagonistic decrees affecting Circular propagation; first, that as the race climbs higher in the scale of development, so development shall proceed at an accelerated pace; second, that in the same proportion, the race shall become less fertile. Consequently in the home of a Polygon of four or five hundred sides it is rare to find a son; more than one is never seen. On the other hand the son of a five-hundred-sided Polygon has been known to possess five hundred and fifty, or even six hundred sides.

Art also steps in to help the process of the higher Evolution. Our physicians have discovered that the small and tender sides of an infant Polygon of the higher class can be fractured, and his whole frame re-set, with such exactness that a Polygon of two or three hundred sides sometimes – by no means always, for the process is attended with serious risk – but sometimes overleaps two or three hundred generations, and as it were doubles at a stroke, the number of his progenitors and the nobility of his descent.

Many a promising child is sacrificed in this way. Scarcely one out of ten survives. Yet so strong is the parental ambition among those Polygons who are, as it were, on the fringe of the Circular class, that it is very rare to find a Nobleman of that position in society, who has neglected to place his first-born in the Circular Neo-Therapeutic Gymnasium before he has attained the age of a month.

One year determines success or failure. At the end of that time the child has, in all probability, added one more to the tombstones that crowd the Neo-Therapeutic Cemetery; but on rare occasions a glad procession bears back the little one to his exultant parents, no longer a Polygon, but a Circle, at least by courtesy: and a single instance of so blessed a result induces multitudes of Polygonal parents to submit to similar domestic sacrifices, which have a dissimilar issue.

Section 12. Of the Doctrine of our Priests

As to the doctrine of the Circles it may briefly be summed up in a single maxim, 'Attend to your Configuration.' Whether political, ecclesiastical, or moral, all their teaching has for its object the improvement of individual and collective Configuration – with special reference of course to the Configuration of the Circles, to which all other objects are subordinated.

It is the merit of the Circles that they have effectually suppressed those ancient heresies which led men to waste energy and sympathy in the vain belief that conduct depends upon will, effort, training, encouragement, praise, or anything else but Configuration. It was Pantocyclus – the illustrious Circle mentioned above, as the queller of the Colour Revolt – who first convinced mankind that Configuration makes the man; that if, for example, you are born an Isosceles with two uneven sides, you will assuredly go wrong unless you have them made even – for which purpose you must go to the Isosceles Hospital; similarly, if you are a Triangle, or Square, or even a Polygon, born with any Irregularity, you must be taken to one of the Regular Hospitals to have your disease cured; otherwise you will end your days in the State Prison or by the angle of the State Executioner.

All faults or defects, from the slightest misconduct to the most flagitious crime, Pantocyclus attributed to some deviation from perfect Regularity in the bodily figure, caused perhaps (if not congenital) by some collision in a crowd; by neglect to take exercise, or by taking too much of it; or even by a sudden change of temperature, resulting in a shrinkage or expansion in some too susceptible part of the frame. Therefore, concluded that illustrious Philosopher, neither good conduct nor bad conduct is a fit subject, in any sober estimation, for either praise or blame. For why should you praise, for example, the integrity of a Square who faithfully defends the interests of his client, when you ought in reality rather to admire the exact precision of his right angles? Or again, why blame a lying, thievish Isosceles when you ought rather to deplore the incurable inequality of his sides?

Theoretically, this doctrine is unquestionable; but it has practical drawbacks. In dealing with an Isosceles, if a rascal pleads that he cannot help stealing because of his unevenness, you reply that for that very reason, because he cannot help being a nuisance to his neighbours, you, the Magistrate, cannot help sentencing him to be consumed – and there's an end of the matter. But in little domestic difficulties, where the penalty of consumption, or death, is out of the question, this theory of Configuration sometimes comes in awkwardly; and I must confess that occasionally when one of my own Hexagonal Grandsons pleads as an excuse for his disobedience that a sudden change of the temperature has been too much for his Perimeter, and that I ought to lay the blame not on him but on his Configuration, which can only be strengthened by abundance of the choicest sweetmeats, I neither see my way logically to reject, nor practically to accept, his conclusions.

For my own part, I find it best to assume that a good sound scolding or castigation has some latent and strengthening influence on my Grandson's Configuration; though I own that I have no grounds for thinking so. At all events I am not alone in my way of extricating myself from this dilemma; for I find that many of the highest Circles, sitting as Judges in law courts, use praise and blame towards Regular and Irregular Figures; and in their homes I know by experience that, when scolding their children, they speak about 'right' or 'wrong' as vehemently and passionately as if they believed that these names represented real existences, and that a human Figure is really capable of choosing between them.

Constantly carrying out their policy of making Configuration the leading idea in every mind, the Circles reverse the nature of that Command-
ment which in Spaceland regulates the relations between parents and
children. With you, children are taught to honour their parents; with us –
next to the Circles, who are the chief object of universal homage – a man is
taught to honour his Grandson, if he has one; or, if not, his Son. By
'honour', however, is by no means meant 'indulgence', but a reverent
regard for their highest interests: and the Circles teach that the duty of
fathers is to subordinate their own interests to those of posterity, thereby
advancing the welfare of the whole State as well as that of their own
immediate descendants.

The weak point in the system of the Circles – if a humble Square may
venture to speak of anything Circular as containing any element of weakness – appears to me to be found in their relations with Women.

As it is of the utmost importance for Society that Irregular births
should be discouraged, it follows that no Woman who has any Irregularities in her ancestry is a fit partner for one who desires that his posterity
should rise by regular degrees in the social scale.

Now the Irregularity of a Male is a matter of measurement; but as all
Women are straight, and therefore visibly Regular so to speak, one has
to devise some other means of ascertaining what I may call their invisible Irregularity, that is to say their potential Irregularities as regards
possible offspring. This is effected by carefully-kept pedigrees, which are
preserved and supervised by the State; and without a certified pedigree
no Woman is allowed to marry.

Now it might have been supposed that a Circle – proud of his ancestry
and regardful for a posterity which might possibly issue hereafter in a
Chief Circle – would be more careful than any other to choose a Wife
who had no blot on her escutcheon. But it is not so. The care in choosing a Regular Wife appears to diminish as one rises in the social scale.
Nothing would induce an aspiring Isosceles, who had hopes of generating an Equilateral Son, to take a Wife who reckoned a single Irregularity
among her Ancestors; a Square or Pentagon, who is confident that his
family is steadily on the rise, does not inquire above the five-hundredth
generation; a Hexagon or Dodecagon is even more careless of the Wife's
pedigree; but a Circle has been known deliberately to take a Wife who
has had an Irregular Great-Grandfather, and all because of some slight
superiority of lustre, or because of the charms of a low voice – which, with
us, even more than you, is thought 'an excellent thing in Woman'.

Such ill-judged marriages are, as might be expected, barren, if they do
not result in positive Irregularity or in diminution of sides; but none of

these evils have hitherto proved sufficiently deterrent. The loss of a few sides in a highly-developed Polygon is not easily noticed, and is sometimes compensated by a successful operation in the Neo-Therapeutic Gymnasium, as I have described above; and the Circles are too much disposed to acquiesce in infecundity as a Law of the superior development. Yet, if this evil be not arrested, the gradual diminution of the Circular class may soon become more rapid, and the time may be not far distant when, the race being no longer able to produce a Chief Circle, the Constitution of Flatland must fall.

One other word of warning suggests itself to me, though I cannot so easily mention a remedy; and this also refers to our relations with Women. About three hundred years ago, it was decreed by the Chief Circle that, since women are deficient in Reason but abundant in Emotion, they ought no longer to be treated as rational, nor receive any mental education. The consequence was that they were no longer taught to read, nor even to master Arithmetic enough to enable them to count the angles of their husband or children; and hence they sensibly declined during each generation in intellectual power. And this system of female non-education or quietism still prevails.

My fear is that, with the best intentions, this policy has been carried so far as to react injuriously on the Male Sex.

For the consequence is that, as things now are, we Males have to lead a kind of bi-lingual, and I may almost say bi-mental, existence. With Women, we speak of 'love', 'duty', 'right', 'wrong', 'pity', 'hope', and other irrational and emotional conceptions, which have no existence, and the fiction of which has no object except to control feminine exuberances; but among ourselves, and in our books, we have an entirely different vocabulary and I may almost say, idiom. 'Love' then becomes 'the anticipation of benefits'; 'duty' becomes 'necessity' or 'fitness'; and other words are correspondingly transmuted. Moreover, among Women, we use language implying the utmost deference for their Sex; and they fully believe that the Chief Circle Himself is not more devoutly adored by us than they are: but behind their backs they are both regarded and spoken of – by all except the very young – as being little better than 'mindless organisms'.

Our Theology also in the Women's chambers is entirely different from our Theology elsewhere.

Now my humble fear is that this double training, in language as well as in thought, imposes somewhat too heavy a burden upon the young, especially when, at the age of three years old, they are taken from the maternal care and taught to unlearn the old language – except for the purpose of repeating it in the presence of their Mothers and Nurses – and to learn the vocabulary and idiom of science. Already methinks I discern a weakness in the grasp of mathematical truth at the present time as compared with the more robust intellect of our ancestors three hundred years ago. I say nothing of the possible danger if a Woman should ever surreptitiously learn to read and convey to her Sex the result of her perusal of a single popular volume; nor of the possibility that the indiscretion or disobedience of some infant Male might reveal to a Mother the secrets of the logical dialect. On the simple ground of the enfeebling of the Male intellect, I rest this humble appeal to the highest Authorities to reconsider the regulations of Female education.

PART TWO: OTHER WORLDS

O brave new worlds, that have such people in them

Section 13. How I had a Vision of Lineland

It was the last day but one of the 1999th year of our era, and the first day of the Long Vacation. Having amused myself till a late hour with my favourite recreation of Geometry, I had retired to rest with an unsolved problem in my mind. In the night I had a dream.

I saw before me a vast multitude of small Straight Lines (which I naturally assumed to be Women) interspersed with other Beings still smaller and of the nature of lustrous points – all moving to and fro in one and the same Straight Line, and, as nearly as I could judge, with the same velocity.

A noise of confused, multitudinous chirping or twittering issued from them at intervals as long as they were moving; but sometimes they ceased from motion, and then all was silence.

Approaching one of the largest of what I thought to be Women, I accosted her, but received no answer. A second and a third appeal on my part were equally ineffectual. Losing patience at what appeared to me intolerable rudeness, I brought my mouth into a position full in front of her mouth so as to intercept her motion, and loudly repeated my question, 'Woman, what signifies this concourse, and this strange and confused chirping, and this monotonous motion to and fro in one and the same Straight Line?'

'I am no Woman,' replied the small Line. 'I am the Monarch of the world. But thou, whence intrudest thou into my realm of Lineland?' Receiving this abrupt reply, I begged pardon if I had in any way startled or molested his Royal Highness; and describing myself as a stranger I besought the King to give me some account of his dominions. But I had the greatest possible difficulty in obtaining any information on points that really interested me; for the Monarch could not refrain from constantly assuming that whatever was familiar to him must also be known to me and that I was simulating ignorance in jest. However, by persevering questions I elicited the following facts.

It seemed that this poor ignorant Monarch – as he called himself – was persuaded that the Straight Line which he called his Kingdom, and in which he passed his existence, constituted the whole of the world, and indeed the whole of Space. Not being able either to move or to see, save in his Straight Line, he had no conception of anything out of it. Though he had heard my voice when I first addressed him, the sounds had come to him in a manner so contrary to his experience that he had made no answer, 'seeing no man', as he expressed it, 'and hearing a voice as it were from my own intestines.' Until the moment when I placed my mouth in his World, he had neither seen me, nor heard anything except confused sounds beating against – what I called his side, but what he called his *inside* or *stomach*; nor had he even now the least conception of the region from which I had come. Outside his World, or Line, all was a blank to him; nay, not even a blank, for a blank implies Space; say, rather, all was non-existent.

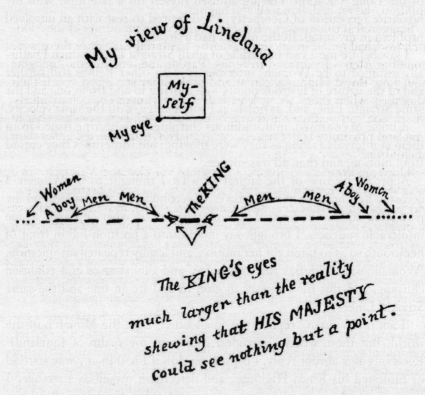

His subjects – of whom the small Lines were men and the Points Women – were all alike confined in motion and eyesight to that single Straight Line, which was their World. It need scarcely be added that the whole of their horizon was limited to a Point; nor could anyone ever see anything but a Point. Man, woman, child, thing – each was a Point to the eye of a Linelander. Only by the sound of the voice could sex or age be distinguished. Moreover, as each individual occupied the whole of the narrow path, so to speak, which constituted his Universe, and no one could move to the right or left to make way for passers-by, it followed that no Linelander could ever pass another. Once neighbours, always neighbours. Neighbourhood with them was like marriage with us. Neighbours remained neighbours till death did them part.

Such a life, with all vision limited to a Point, and all motion to a Straight Line, seemed to me inexpressibly dreary; and I was surprised to note the vivacity and cheerfulness of the King. Wondering whether it was possible, amid circumstances so unfavourable to domestic relations, to enjoy the pleasures of conjugal union, I hesitated for some time to question his Royal Highness on so delicate a subject; but at last I plunged into it by abruptly inquiring as to the health of his family. 'My wives and children,' he replied, 'are well and happy.'

Staggered at this answer – for in the immediate proximity of the Monarch (as I had noted in my dream before I entered Lineland) there were none but Men – I ventured to reply, 'Pardon me, but I cannot imagine how your Royal Highness can at any time either see or approach their Majesties, when there are at least half a dozen intervening individuals, whom you can neither see through, nor pass by? Is it possible that in Lineland proximity is not necessary for marriage and for the generation of children?'

'How can you ask so absurd a question?' replied the Monarch. 'If it were indeed as you suggest, the Universe would soon be depopulated. No, no; neighbourhood is needless for the union of hearts; and the birth of children is too important a matter to have been allowed to depend upon such an accident as proximity. You cannot be ignorant of this. Yet since you are pleased to affect ignorance, I will instruct you as if you were the veriest baby in Lineland. Know, then, that marriages are consummated by means of the faculty of sound and the sense of hearing.

'You are of course aware that every Man has two mouths or voices – as well as two eyes – a bass at one and a tenor at the other of his extremities. I should not mention this, but that I have been unable to distinguish your tenor in the course of our conversation.' I replied that I had but one voice, and that I had not been aware that his Royal Highness had two. 'That confirms my impression,' said the King, 'that you are not a Man, but a feminine Monstrosity with a bass voice, and an utterly uneducated ear. But to continue.

'Nature having herself ordained that every Man should wed two wives – ' 'Why two?' asked I. 'You carry your affected simplicity too far,' he cried. 'How can there be a completely harmonious union without the combination of the Four in One, viz. the Bass and Tenor of the Man and the Soprano and Contralto of the two Women?' 'But supposing,' said I, 'that a man should prefer one Wife or three?' 'It is impossible,' he said; 'it is as inconceivable as that two and one should make five, or that the human eye should see a Straight Line.' I would have interrupted him; but he proceeded as follows.

'Once in the middle of each week a Law of Nature compels us to move to and fro with a rhythmic motion of more than usual violence, which continues for the time you would take to count a hundred and one. In the midst of this choral dance, at the fifty-first pulsation, the inhabitants of the Universe pause in full career, and each individual sends forth his richest, fullest, sweetest strain. It is in this decisive moment that all our marriages are made. So exquisite is the adaptation of Bass to Treble, of Tenor to Contralto, that oftentimes the Loved Ones, though twenty thousand leagues away, recognize at once the responsive note of their destined Lover; and, penetrating the paltry obstacles of distance, Love unites the three. The marriage in that instant consummated results in a threefold Male and Female offspring which takes its place in Lineland.'

'What! Always threefold?' said I. 'Must one Wife then always have twins?'

'Bass-voiced Monstrosity! yes,' replied the King. 'How else could the balance of the Sexes be maintained, if two girls were not born for every boy? Would you ignore the very Alphabet of Nature?' He ceased, speechless for fury; and some time elapsed before I could induce him to resume his narrative.

'You will not, of course, suppose that every bachelor among us finds his mates at the first wooing in this universal Marriage Chorus. On the contrary, the process is by most of us many times repeated. Few are the hearts whose happy lot it is at once to recognize in each other's voices the partner intended for them by Providence, and to fly into a reciprocal and perfectly harmonious embrace. With most of us the courtship is of long duration. The Wooer's voices may perhaps accord with one of the future wives, but not with both; or not, at first, with either; or the Soprano and Contralto may not quite harmonize. In such cases Nature has provided that every weekly Chorus shall bring the three Lovers into closer harmony. Each trial of voice, each fresh discovery of discord, almost imperceptibly induces the less perfect to modify his or her vocal utterance so as to approximate to the more perfect. And after many trials and many approximations, the result is at last achieved. There comes a day at last, when, while the wonted Marriage Chorus goes forth from universal Lineland, the three far-off Lovers suddenly find themselves in exact harmony, and, before they are awake, the wedded Triplet is rapt vocally into a duplicate embrace; and Nature rejoices over one more marriage and over three more births.'

Section 14. How I vainly tried to explain the nature of Flatland
Thinking that it was time to bring down the Monarch from his raptures to
the level of common sense, I determined to endeavour to open up to him
some glimpses of the truth, that is to say of the nature of things in Flatland.
So I began thus: 'How does your Royal Highness distinguish the shapes
and positions of his subjects? I for my part noticed by the sense of sight,
before I entered your Kingdom, that some of your people are Lines and
others Points, and that some of the Lines are larger – ' 'You speak of an
impossibility,' interrupted the King; 'you must have seen a vision; for to
detect the difference between a Line and a Point by the sense of sight is, as
every one knows, in the nature of things, impossible; but it can be detected
by the sense of hearing, and by the same means my shape can be exactly
ascertained. Behold me – I am a Line, the longest in Lineland, over six
inches of Space – ' 'Of Length', I ventured to suggest. 'Fool,' said he,
'Space is Length. Interrupt me again, and I have done.'

I apologized; but he continued scornfully, 'Since you are impervious to
argument, you shall hear with your ears how by means of my two voices I
reveal my shape to my Wives, who are at this moment six thousand miles
seventy yards two feet eight inches away, the one to the North, the other
to the South. Listen, I call to them.'

He chirruped, and then complacently continued: 'My wives at this
moment receiving the sound of one of my voices, closely followed by the
other, and perceiving that the latter reaches them after an interval in
which sound can traverse 6.457 inches, infer that one of my mouths is
6.457 inches further from them than the other, and accordingly know my
shape to be 6.457 inches. But you will of course understand that my wives
do not make this calculation every time they hear my two voices. They
made it, once for all, before we were married. But they *could* make it at
any time. And in the same way I can estimate the shape of any of my Male
subjects by the sense of sound.'

'But how,' said I, 'if a Man feigns a Woman's voice with one of his two
voices, or so disguises his Southern voice that it cannot be recognized as
the echo of the Northern? May not such deceptions cause great inconvenience? And have you no means of checking frauds of this kind by
commanding your neighbouring subjects to feel one another?' This of
course was a very stupid question, for feeling could not have answered
the purpose; but I asked with the view of irritating the Monarch, and I
succeeded perfectly.

'What!' cried he in horror; 'explain your meaning.' 'Feel, touch,
come into contact,' I replied. 'If you mean by *feeling*,' said the King,

'approaching so close as to leave no space between two individuals, know, Stranger, that this offence is punishable in my dominions by death. And the reason is obvious. The frail form of a Woman, being liable to be shattered by such an approximation, must be preserved by the State; but since Women cannot be distinguished by the sense of sight from Men, the Law ordains universally that neither Man nor Woman shall be approached so closely as to destroy the interval between the approxim-ator and the approximated.

'And indeed what possible purpose would be served by this illegal and unnatural excess of approximation which you call *touching*, when all the ends of so brutal and coarse a process are attained at once more easily and more exactly by the sense of hearing? As to your suggested danger of deception, it is non-existent: for the Voice, being the essence of one's Being, cannot be thus changed at will. But come, suppose that I had the power of passing through solid things, so that I could penetrate my subjects, one after another, even to the number of a billion, verifying the size and distance of each by the sense of *feeling*: how much time and energy would be wasted in this clumsy and inaccurate method! Whereas now, in one moment of audition, I take as it were the census and statistics, local, corporeal, mental and spiritual, of every living being in Lineland. Hark, only hark!'

So saying he paused and listened, as if in an ecstasy, to a sound which seemed to me no better than a tiny chirping from an innumerable multi-tude of Lilliputian grasshoppers.

'Truly,' replied I, 'your sense of hearing serves you in good stead, and fills up many of your deficiencies. But permit me to point out that your life in Lineland must be deplorably dull. To see nothing but a Point! Not even to be able to contemplate a Straight Line! Nay, not even to know what a Straight Line is! To see, yet be cut off from those Linear prospects which are vouchsafed to us in Flatland! Better surely to have no sense of sight at all than to see so little! I grant you I have not your discriminative faculty of hearing; for the concert of all Line-land which gives you such intense pleasure, is to me no better than a multitudinous twittering or chirping. But at least I can discern, by sight, a Line from a Point. And let me prove it. Just before I came into your kingdom, I saw you dancing from left to right, and then from right to left, with Seven Men and a Woman in your immediate proximity on the left, and eight Men and two Women on your right. Is not this correct?'

'It is correct,' said the King, 'so far as the numbers and sexes are concerned, though I know not what you mean by "right" and "left". But I deny that you saw these things. For how could you see the Line, that is to say the inside, of any Man? But you must have heard these things, and then dreamed that you saw them. And let me ask what you mean by those words "left" and "right". I suppose it is your way of saying Northward and Southward.'

'Not so,' replied I; 'besides your motion of Northward and Southward, there is another motion which I call from right to left.'

KING. Exhibit to me, if you please, this motion from left to right.

I. Nay, that I cannot do, unless you could step out of your Line altogether.

KING. Out of my Line? Do you mean out of the world? Out of Space?

I. Well, yes. Out of *your* World. Out of *your* Space. For your Space is not the true Space. True Space is a Plane; but your Space is only a Line.

KING. If you cannot indicate this motion from left to right by yourself moving in it, then I beg you to describe it to me in words.

I. If you cannot tell your right side from your left, I fear that no words of mine can make my meaning clear to you. But surely you cannot be ignorant of so simple a distinction.

KING. I do not in the least understand you.

I. Alas! How shall I make it clear? When you move straight on, does it not sometimes occur to you that you *could* move in some other way, turning your eye round so as to look in the direction towards which your side is now fronting? In other words, instead of always moving in the direction of one of your extremities, do you never feel a desire to move in the direction, so to speak, of your side?

KING. Never. And what do you mean? How can a man's inside 'front' in any direction? Or how can a man move in the direction of his inside?

I. Well then, since words cannot explain the matter, I will try deeds, and will move gradually out of Lineland in the direction which I desire to indicate to you.

At the word I began to move my body out of Lineland. As long as any part of me remained in his dominion and in his view, the King kept exclaiming, 'I see you, I see you still; you are not moving.' But when I had at last moved myself out of his Line, he cried in his shrillest voice, 'She is vanished; she is dead.' 'I am not dead,' replied I; 'I am simply out of Lineland, that is to say, out of the Straight Line which you call Space, and in the true Space, where I can see things as they are. And at this moment I can see your Line, or side – or inside as you are pleased to call it; and I can see also the Men and Women on the North and South of you, whom I will now enumerate, describing their order, their size, and the interval between each.'

When I had done this at great length, I cried triumphantly, 'Does that at last convince you?' And, with that, I once more entered Lineland, taking up the same position as before.

But the Monarch replied, 'If you were a Man of sense – though, as you appear to have only one voice I have little doubt you are not a Man but a Woman – but, if you had a particle of sense, you would listen to reason. You ask me to believe that there is another Line besides that which my senses indicate, and another motion besides that of which I am daily conscious. I, in return, ask you to describe in words or indicate by motion that other Line of which you speak. Instead of moving, you merely exercise some magic art of vanishing and returning to sight; and instead of any lucid description of your new World, you simply tell me the numbers and sizes of some forty of my retinue, facts known to any child in my capital. Can anything be more irrational or audacious? Acknowledge your folly or depart from my dominions.'

Furious at his perversity, and especially indignant that he professed to be ignorant of my sex, I retorted in no measured terms, 'Besotted Being! You think yourself the perfection of existence, while you are in reality the most imperfect and imbecile. You profess to see, whereas you can see nothing but a Point! You plume yourself on inferring the existence of a Straight Line; but I *can see* Straight Lines, and infer the existence of Angles, Triangles, Squares, Pentagons, Hexagons, and even Circles. Why waste more words? Suffice it that I am the completion of your incomplete self. You are a Line, but I am a Line of Lines, called in my country a Square: and even I, infinitely superior though I am to you, am of little account among the great nobles of Flatland, whence I have come to visit you, in the hope of enlightening your ignorance.'

Hearing these words the King advanced towards me with a menacing cry as if to pierce me through the diagonal; and in that same moment there arose from myriads of his subjects a multitudinous war-cry, increasing in vehemence till at last methought it rivalled the roar of an army of a hundred thousand Isosceles, and the artillery of a thousand

Pentagons. Spell-bound and motionless, I could neither speak nor move to avert the impending destruction; and still the noise grew louder, and the King came closer, when I awoke to find the breakfast-bell recalling me to the realities of Flatland.

Section 15. Concerning a Stranger from Spaceland

From dreams I proceed to facts.

It was the last day of the 1999th year of our era. The pattering of the rain had long ago announced nightfall; and I was sitting * in the company of my Wife, musing on the events of the past and the prospects of the coming year, the coming century, the coming Millennium.

My four Sons and two orphan Grandchildren had retired to their several apartments; and my Wife alone remained with me to see the old Millennium out and the new one in.

I was rapt in thought, pondering in my mind some words that had casually issued from the mouth of my youngest Grandson, a most promising young Hexagon of unusual brilliancy and perfect angularity. His uncles and I had been giving him his usual practical lesson in Sight Recognition, turning ourselves upon our centres, now rapidly, now more slowly, and questioning him as to our positions; and his answers had been so satisfactory that I had been induced to reward him by giving him a few hints on Arithmetic, as applied to Geometry.

Taking nine Squares, each an inch every way, I had put them together so as to make one large Square, with a side of three inches, and I had hence proved to my little Grandson that – though it was impossible for us to *see* the inside of the Square – yet we might ascertain the number of square inches in a Square by simply squaring the number of inches in the side: 'and thus,' said I, 'we know that 3^2, or 9, represents the number of square inches in a Square whose side is 3 inches long.'

The little Hexagon meditated on this a while and then said to me; 'But you have been teaching me to raise numbers to the third power: I suppose 3^3 must mean something in Geometry; what does it mean?' 'Nothing at all,' replied I, 'not at least in Geometry; for Geometry has

* When I say 'sitting', of course I do not mean any change of attitude such as you in Spaceland signify by that word; for as we have no feet, we can no more 'sit' nor 'stand' (in your sense of the word) than one of your soles or flounders.

Nevertheless, we perfectly well recognize the different mental states of volition implied in 'lying', 'sitting', and 'standing', which are to some extent indicated to a beholder by a slight increase of lustre corresponding to the increase of volition.

But on this, and a thousand other kindred subjects, time forbids me to dwell.

only Two Dimensions.' And then I began to shew the boy how a Point by moving through a length of three inches makes a Line of three inches, which may be represented by 3; and how a Line of three inches, moving parallel to itself through a length of three inches, makes a Square of three inches every way, which may be represented by 3^2.

Upon this, my Grandson, again returning to his former suggestion, took me up rather suddenly and exclaimed, 'Well, then, if a Point by moving three inches, makes a Line of three inches represented by 3; and if a straight Line of three inches, moving parallel to itself, makes a Square of three inches every way, represented by 3^2; it must be that a Square of three inches every way, moving somehow parallel to itself (but I don't see how) must make Something else (but I don't see what) of three inches every way – and this must be represented by 3^3.'

'Go to bed,' said I, a little ruffled by this interruption: 'if you would talk less nonsense, you would remember more sense.'

So my Grandson had disappeared in disgrace; and there I sat by my Wife's side, endeavouring to form a retrospect of the year 1999 and of the possibilities of the year 2000, but not quite able to shake off the thoughts suggested by the prattle of my bright little Hexagon. Only a few sands now remained in the half-hour glass. Rousing myself from my reverie I turned the glass Northward for the last time in the old Millennium; and in the act, I exclaimed aloud, 'The boy is a fool.'

Straightway I became conscious of a Presence in the room, and a chilling breath thrilled through my very being. 'He is no such thing,' cried my Wife, 'and you are breaking the Commandments in thus dishonouring your own Grandson.' But I took no notice of her. Looking round in every direction I could see nothing; yet still I *felt* a Presence, and shivered as the cold whisper came again. I started up. 'What is the matter?' said my Wife; 'there is no draught; what are you looking for? There is nothing.' There was nothing; and I resumed my seat, again exclaiming, 'The boy is a fool, I say; 3^3 can have no meaning in Geometry.' At once there came a distinctly audible reply, 'The boy is not a fool; and 3^3 has an obvious Geometrical meaning.'

My Wife as well as myself heard the words, although she did not understand their meaning, and both of us sprang forward in the direction of the sound. What was our horror when we saw before us a Figure! At the first glance it appeared to be a Woman, seen sideways; but a moment's observation shewed me that the extremities passed into dimness too rapidly to represent one of the Female Sex; and I should have thought it a Circle, only that it seemed to change its size in a manner impossible for a Circle or for any regular Figure of which I had had experience.

But my Wife had not my experience, nor the coolness necessary to note these characteristics. With the usual hastiness and unreasoning jealousy of her Sex, she flew at once to the conclusion that a Woman had entered the house through some small aperture. 'How comes this person here?' she exclaimed; 'you promised me, my dear, that there should be no ventilators in our new house.' 'Nor are there any,' said I; 'but what makes you think that the stranger is a Woman? I see by my power of Sight Recognition – ' 'Oh, I have no patience with your Sight Recognition,' replied she, ' "Feeling is believing" and "A Straight Line to the touch is worth a Circle to the sight" ' – two Proverbs, very common with the Frailer Sex in Flatland.

'Well,' said I, for I was afraid of irritating her, 'if it must be so, demand an introduction.' Assuming her most gracious manner, my Wife advanced towards the Stranger, 'Permit me, Madam, to feel and be felt by – ' then, suddenly recoiling, 'Oh! it is not a Woman, and there are no angles either, not a trace of one. Can it be that I have so misbehaved to a perfect Circle?'

'I am indeed, in a certain sense a Circle,' replied the Voice, 'and a more perfect Circle than any in Flatland; but to speak more accurately, I am many Circles in one.' Then he added more mildly, 'I have a message, dear Madam, to your husband, which I must not deliver in your presence; and, if you would suffer us to retire for a few minutes – ' But my Wife would not listen to the proposal that our august Visitor should so incommode himself, and assuring the Circle that the hour of her own retirement had long passed, with many reiterated apologies for her recent indiscretion, she at last retreated to her apartment.

I glanced at the half-hour glass. The last sands had fallen. The third Millennium had begun.

*Section 16. How the Stranger vainly endeavoured
to reveal to me in words the mysteries of Spaceland*

As soon as the sound of the Peace-cry of my departing Wife had died away, I began to approach the Stranger with the intention of taking a nearer view and of bidding him be seated: but his appearance struck me dumb and motionless with astonishment. Without the slightest symptoms of angularity he nevertheless varied every instant with gradations of size and brightness scarcely possible for any Figure within the scope of my experience. The thought flashed across me that I might have before me a burglar or cut-throat, some monstrous Irregular Isosceles, who, by feigning the voice of a Circle, had obtained admission somehow into the house, and was now preparing to stab me with his acute angle.

In a sitting-room, the absence of Fog (and the season happened to be remarkably dry), made it difficult for me to trust to Sight Recognition, especially at the short distance at which I was standing. Desperate with fear, I rushed forward with an unceremonious, 'You must permit me, Sir – ' and felt him. My Wife was right. There was not the trace of an angle, not the slightest roughness or inequality: never in my life had I met with a more perfect Circle. He remained motionless while I walked round him, beginning from his eye and returning to it again. Circular he was through-out, a perfectly satisfactory Circle; there could not be a doubt of it. Then followed a dialogue, which I will endeavour to set down as near as I can recollect it, omitting only some of my profuse apologies – for I was covered with shame and humiliation that I, a Square, should have been guilty of the impertinence of feeling a Circle. It was commenced by the Stranger with some impatience at the lengthiness of my introductory process.

STRANGER. Have you felt me enough by this time? Are you not intro-duced to me yet?

I. Most illustrious Sir, excuse my awkwardness, which arises not from ignorance of the usages of polite society, but from a little surprise and nervousness, consequent on this somewhat unexpected visit. And I beseech you to reveal my indiscretion to no one, and especially not to my Wife. But before your Lordship enters into further communications, would he deign to satisfy the curiosity of one who would gladly know whence his Visitor came?

STRANGER. From Space, from Space, Sir: whence else?

I. Pardon me, my Lord, but is not your Lordship already in Space, your Lordship and his humble servant, even at this moment?

STRANGER. Pooh! what do you know of Space? Define Space.

I. Space, my Lord, is height and breadth indefinitely prolonged.

STRANGER. Exactly: you see you do not even know what Space is. You think it is of Two Dimensions only; but I have come to announce to you a Third – height, breadth, and length.

I. Your Lordship is pleased to be merry. We also speak of length and height, or breadth and thickness, thus denoting Two Dimensions by four names.

STRANGER. But I mean not only three names, but Three Dimensions.

I. Would your Lordship indicate or explain to me in what direction is the Third Dimension, unknown to me?

STRANGER. I came from it. It is up above and down below.

I. My Lord means seemingly that it is Northward and Southward.

STRANGER. I mean nothing of the kind. I mean a direction in which you cannot look, because you have no eye in your side.

I. Pardon me, my Lord, a moment's inspection will convince your Lordship that I have a perfect luminary at the juncture of two of my sides.

STRANGER. Yes: but in order to see into Space you ought to have an eye, not on your Perimeter, but on your side, that is, on what you would probably call your inside; but we in Spaceland should call it your side.

I. An eye in my inside! An eye in my stomach! Your Lordship jests.

Stranger. I am in no jesting humour. I tell you that I come from Space, or, since you will not understand what Space means, from the Land of Three Dimensions whence I but lately looked down upon your Plane which you call Space forsooth. From that position of advantage I discerned all that you speak of as *solid* (by which you mean 'enclosed on four sides'), your houses, your churches, your very chests and safes, yes even your insides and stomachs, all lying open and exposed to my view.

I. Such assertions are easily made, my Lord.

STRANGER. But not easily proved, you mean. But I mean to prove mine.

When I descended here, I saw your four Sons, the Pentagons, each in his apartment, and your two Grandsons the Hexagons; I saw your youngest Hexagon remain a while with you and then retire to his room, leaving you and your Wife alone. I saw your Isosceles servants, three in number, in the kitchen at supper, and the little Page in the scullery. Then I came here, and how do you think I came?

I. Through the roof, I suppose.

STRANGER. Not so. Your roof, as you know very well, has been recently repaired, and has no aperture by which even a Woman could penetrate. I tell you I come from Space. Are you not convinced by what I have told you of your children and household?

I. Your Lordship must be aware that such facts touching the belongings of his humble servant might be easily ascertained by anyone in the neighbourhood possessing your Lordship's ample means of obtaining information.

STRANGER. [*to himself*] What must I do? Stay; one more argument suggests itself to me. When you see a Straight Line – your Wife, for example – how many Dimensions do you attribute to her?

I. Your Lordship would treat me as if I were one of the vulgar who, being ignorant of Mathematics, suppose that a Woman is really a Straight Line, and only of One Dimension. No, no, my Lord; we Squares are better advised, and are as well aware as your Lordship that a Woman, though popularly called a Straight Line, is, really and scientifically, a very thin Parallelogram, possessing Two Dimensions, like the rest of us, viz., length and breadth (or thickness).

STRANGER. But the very fact that a Line is visible implies that it possesses yet another Dimension.

I. My Lord, I have just acknowledged that a Woman is broad as well as long. We see her length, we infer her breadth; which, though very slight, is capable of measurement.

STRANGER. You do not understand me. I mean that when you see a Woman, you ought – besides inferring her breadth – to see her length, and to *see* what we call her *height*; although that last Dimension is infinitesimal in your country. If a Line were mere length without 'height', it would cease to occupy Space and would become invisible. Surely you must recognize this?

I. I must indeed confess that I do not in the least understand your Lordship. When we in Flatland see a Line, we see length and *brightness*. If the brightness disappears, the Line is extinguished, and, as you say, ceases to occupy Space. But am I to suppose that your Lordship gives to brightness the title of a Dimension, and that what we call 'bright' you call 'high'?

STRANGER. No, indeed. By 'height' I mean a Dimension like your length: only, with you, 'height' is not so easily perceptible, being extremely small.

I. My Lord, your assertion is easily put to the test. You say I have a Third Dimension, which you call 'height'. Now, Dimension implies direction and measurement. Do but measure my 'height', or merely indicate to me the direction in which my 'height' extends, and I will become your convert. Otherwise, your Lordship's own understanding must hold me excused.

STRANGER. [*to himself*] I can do neither. How shall I convince him? Surely a plain statement of facts followed by ocular demonstration ought to suffice. – Now, Sir; listen to me.

You are living on a Plane. What you style Flatland is the vast level surface of what I may call a fluid, on, or in, the top of which you and your countrymen move about, without rising above it or falling below it.

I am not a plane Figure, but a Solid. You call me a Circle; but in reality I am not a Circle, but an infinite number of Circles, of size varying from a Point to a Circle of thirteen inches in diameter, one placed on the top of the other. When I cut through your plane as I am now doing, I make in your plane a section which you, very rightly, call a Circle. For even a Sphere – which is my proper name in my own country – if he manifest himself at all to an inhabitant of Flatland – must needs manifest himself as a Circle.

Do you not remember – for I, who see all things, discerned last night the phantasmal vision of Lineland written upon your brain – do you not remember, I say, how, when you entered the realm of Lineland, you were compelled to manifest yourself to the King, not as a Square, but as a Line, because that Linear Realm had not Dimensions enough to represent the whole of you, but only a slice or section of you? In precisely the same way, your country of Two Dimensions is not spacious enough to represent me, a being of Three, but can only exhibit a slice or section of me, which is what you call a Circle.

The diminished brightness of your eye indicates incredulity. But now prepare to receive proof positive of the truth of my assertions. You cannot indeed see more than one of my sections, or Circles, at a time; for you have no power to raise your eye out of the plane of Flatland; but you can at least see that, as I rise in Space, so my sections become smaller. See now, I will rise; and the effect upon your eye will be that my Circle will become smaller and smaller till it dwindles to a point and finally vanishes.

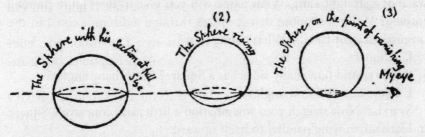

There was no 'rising' that I could see; but he diminished and finally vanished. I winked once or twice to make sure that I was not dreaming. But it was no dream. For from the depths of nowhere came forth a hollow voice – close to my heart it seemed – 'Am I quite gone? Are you convinced now? Well, now I will gradually return to Flatland and you shall see my section become larger and larger.'

Every reader in Spaceland will easily understand that my mysterious Guest was speaking the language of truth and even of simplicity. But to me, proficient though I was in Flatland Mathematics, it was by no means a simple matter. The rough diagram given above will make it clear to any Spaceland child that the Sphere, ascending in the three positions indicated there, must needs have manifested himself to me, or to any Flatlander, as a Circle, at first of full size, then small, and at last very small indeed, approaching to a Point. But to me, although I saw the facts before me, the causes were as dark as ever. All that I could comprehend was, that the Circle had made himself smaller and vanished, and that he had now reappeared and was rapidly making himself larger.

When he regained his original size, he heaved a deep sigh; for he perceived by my silence that I had altogether failed to comprehend him. And indeed I was now inclining to the belief that he must be no Circle at all, but some extremely clever juggler; or else that the old wives' tales were true, and that after all there were such people as Enchanters and Magicians.

After a long pause he muttered to himself, 'One resource alone remains, if I am not to resort to action. I must try the method of Analogy.' Then followed a still longer silence, after which he continued our dialogue.

SPHERE. Tell me, Mr Mathematician; if a Point moves Northward, and leaves a luminous wake, what name would you give to the wake?

I. A straight Line.

SPHERE. And a straight Line has how many extremities?

I. Two.

SPHERE. Now conceive the Northward straight Line moving parallel to itself, East and West, so that every point in it leaves behind it the wake of a straight Line. What name will you give to the Figure thereby formed? We will suppose that it moves through a distance equal to the original straight Line. – What name, I say?

I. A Square.

SPHERE. And how many sides has a Square? How many angles?

I. Four sides and four angles.

SPHERE. Now stretch your imagination a little, and conceive a Square in Flatland, moving parallel to itself upward.

I. What? Northward?

SPHERE. No, not Northward; upward; out of Flatland altogether.

If it moved Northward, the Southern points in the Square would have to move through the positions previously occupied by the Northern points. But that is not my meaning.

I mean that every Point in you – for you are a Square and will serve the purpose of my illustration – every Point in you, that is to say in what you call your inside, is to pass upwards through Space in such a way that no Point shall pass through the position previously occupied by any other Point; but each Point shall describe a straight Line of its own. This is all in accordance with Analogy; surely it must be clear to you.

Restraining my impatience – for I was now under a strong temptation to rush blindly at my Visitor and to precipitate him into Space, or out of Flatland, anywhere, so that I could get rid of him – I replied: 'And what may be the nature of the Figure which I am to shape out by this motion which you are pleased to denote by the word "upward"? I presume it is describable in the language of Flatland.'

SPHERE. Oh, certainly. It is all plain and simple, and in strict accordance with Analogy – only, by the way, you must not speak of the result as being a Figure, but as a Solid. But I will describe it to you. Or rather not I, but Analogy.

We began with a single Point, which of course – being itself a Point – has only *one* terminal Point.

One Point produces a Line with *two* terminal Points.

One Line produces a Square with *four* terminal Points.

Now you can give yourself the answer to your own question: 1, 2, 4, are evidently in Geometrical Progression. What is the next number?

I. Eight.

SPHERE. Exactly. The one Square produces a *something-which-you-do-not-as-yet-know-a-name-for-but-which-we-call-a-cube* with *eight* terminal Points. Now are you convinced?

I. And has this Creature sides, as well as angles or what you call 'terminal Points'?

SPHERE. Of course; and all according to Analogy. But, by the way, not what *you* call sides, but what *we* call sides. You would call them *solids*.

I. And how many solids or sides will appertain to this Being whom I am to generate by the motion of my inside in an 'upward' direction, and whom you call a Cube?

SPHERE. How can you ask? And you a mathematician! The side of anything is always, if I may so say, one Dimension behind the thing. Consequently, as there is no Dimension behind a Point, a Point has o sides; a Line, if I may say, has 2 sides (for the Points of a Line may be called by courtesy, its sides); a Square has 4 sides; o, 2, 4; what Progression do you call that?

I. Arithmetical.

SPHERE. And what is the next number?

I. Six.

SPHERE. Exactly. Then you see you have answered your own question. The Cube which you will generate will be bounded by six sides, that is to say, six of your insides. You see it all now, eh?

'Monster,' I shrieked, 'be thou juggler, enchanter, dream, or devil, no more will I endure thy mockeries. Either thou or I must perish.' And saying these words I precipitated myself upon him.

Section 17. How the Sphere, having in vain tried words, resorted to deeds

It was in vain. I brought my hardest right angle into violent collision with the Stranger, pressing on him with a force sufficient to have destroyed any ordinary Circle: but I could feel him slowly and unarrestably slipping from my contact; no edging to the right nor to the left, but moving somehow out of the world, and vanishing to nothing. Soon there was a blank. But still I heard the Intruder's voice.

SPHERE. Why will you refuse to listen to reason? I had hoped to find in you – as being a man of sense and an accomplished mathematician – a fit apostle for the Gospel of the Three Dimensions, which I am allowed to preach once only in a thousand years: but now I know not how to convince you. Stay, I have it. Deeds, and not words, shall proclaim the truth. Listen, my friend.

I have told you I can see from my position in Space the inside of all things that you consider closed. For example, I see in yonder cupboard near which you are standing, several of what you call boxes (but like everything else in Flatland, they have no tops nor bottoms) full of money; I see also two tablets of accounts. I am about to descend into that cupboard and to bring you one of those tablets. I saw you lock the cupboard half an hour ago, and I know you have the key in your possession. But I descend from Space; the doors, you see, remain unmoved. Now I am in the cupboard and am taking the tablet. Now I have it. Now I ascend with it.

I rushed to the closet and dashed the door open. One of the tablets was gone. With a mocking laugh, the Stranger appeared in the other corner of the room, and at the same time the tablet appeared upon the floor. I took it up. There could be no doubt – it was the missing tablet.

I groaned with horror, doubting whether I was not out of my senses; but the Stranger continued: 'Surely you must now see that my explanation, and no other, suits the phenomena. What you call Solid things are really superficial; what you call Space is really nothing but a great Plane. I am in Space, and look down upon the insides of the things of which you only see the outsides. You could leave this Plane yourself, if you could but summon up the necessary volition. A slight upward or downward motion would enable you to see all that I can see.

'The higher I mount, and the further I go from your Plane, the more I can see, though of course I see it on a smaller scale. For example, I am ascending; now I can see your neighbour the Hexagon and his family in their several apartments; now I see the inside of the Theatre, ten doors off, from which the audience is only just departing; and on the other side a Circle in his study, sitting at his books. Now I shall come back to you.

And, as a crowning proof, what do you say to my giving you a touch, just the least touch, in your stomach? It will not seriously injure you, and the slight pain you may suffer cannot be compared with the mental benefit you will receive.'

Before I could utter a word of remonstrance, I felt a shooting pain in my inside, and a demoniacal laugh seemed to issue from within me. A moment afterwards the sharp agony had ceased, leaving nothing but a dull ache behind, and the Stranger began to reappear, saying, as he gradually increased in size, 'There, I have not hurt you much, have I? If you are not convinced now, I don't know what will convince you. What say you?'

My resolution was taken. It seemed intolerable that I should endure existence subject to the arbitrary visitations of a Magician who could thus play tricks with one's very stomach. If only I could in any way manage to pin him against the wall till help came!

Once more I dashed my hardest angle against him, at the same time alarming the whole household by my cries for aid. I believe, at the moment of my onset, the Stranger had sunk below our Plane, and really found difficulty in rising. In any case he remained motionless, while I, hearing, as I thought, the sound of some help approaching, pressed against him with redoubled vigour, and continued to shout for assistance.

A convulsive shudder ran through the Sphere. 'This must not be,' I thought I heard him say: 'either he must listen to reason, or I must have recourse to the last resource of civilization.' Then, addressing me in a louder tone, he hurriedly exclaimed, 'Listen: no stranger must witness what you have witnessed. Send your Wife back at once, before she enters the apartment. The Gospel of Three Dimensions must not be thus frustrated. Not thus must the fruits of one thousand years of waiting be thrown away. I hear her coming. Back! back! Away from me, or you must go with me – whither you know not – into the Land of Three Dimensions!'

'Fool! Madman! Irregular!' I exclaimed; 'never will I release thee; thou shalt pay the penalty of thine impostures.'

'Ha! Is it come to this?' thundered the Stranger: 'then meet your fate: out of your Plane you go. Once, twice, thrice! 'Tis done!'

Section 18. How I came to Spaceland, and what I saw there

An unspeakable horror seized me. There was a darkness; then a dizzy, sickening sensation of sight that was not like seeing; I saw a Line that was no Line; Space that was not Space: I was myself, and not myself. When I could find voice, I shrieked aloud in agony, 'Either this is madness or it is Hell.' 'It is neither,' calmly replied the voice of the Sphere, 'it is Knowledge; it is Three Dimensions: open your eye once again and try to look steadily.'

I looked, and, behold, a new world! There stood before me, visibly incorporate, all that I had before inferred, conjectured, dreamed, of perfect Circular beauty. What seemed the centre of the Stranger's form lay open to my view: yet I could see no heart, nor lungs, nor arteries, only a beautiful harmonious Something – for which I had no words; but you, my Readers in Spaceland, would call it the surface of the Sphere.

Prostrating myself mentally before my Guide, I cried, 'How is it, O divine ideal of consummate loveliness and wisdom, that I see thy inside, and yet cannot discern thy heart, thy lungs, thy arteries, thy liver?' 'What you think you see, you see not,' he replied; 'it is not given to you, nor to any other Being to behold my internal parts. I am of a different order of Beings from those in Flatland. Were I a Circle, you could discern my intestines, but I am a Being, composed as I told you before, of many Circles, the Many in the One, called in this country a Sphere. And, just as the outside of a Cube is a Square, so the outside of a Sphere presents the appearance of a Circle.'

Bewildered though I was by my Teacher's enigmatic utterance, I no longer chafed against it, but worshipped him in silent adoration. He continued, with more mildness in his voice. 'Distress not yourself if you cannot at first understand the deeper mysteries of Spaceland. By degrees they will dawn upon you. Let us begin by casting back a glance at the region whence you came. Return with me a while to the plains of Flatland, and I will shew you that which you have often reasoned and thought about, but never seen with the sense of sight – a visible angle.' 'Impossible!' I cried; but, the Sphere leading the way, I followed as if in a dream, till once more his voice arrested me: 'Look yonder, and behold your own Pentagonal house, and all its inmates.'

I looked below, and saw with my physical eye all that domestic individuality which I had hitherto merely inferred with the understanding. And how poor and shadowy was the inferred conjecture in comparison with the reality which I now beheld! My four Sons calmly asleep in the North-Western rooms, my two orphan Grandsons to the South; the Servants, the Butler, my Daughter, all in their several apartments. Only my affectionate Wife, alarmed by my continued absence, had quitted her room and was roving up and down in the Hall, anxiously awaiting my return. Also the Page, aroused by my cries, had left his room, and under pretext of ascertaining whether I had fallen somewhere in a faint, was prying into the cabinet in my study. All this I could now see, not merely infer; and as we came nearer and nearer, I could discern even the contents of my cabinet, and the two chests of gold, and the tablets of which the Sphere had made mention.

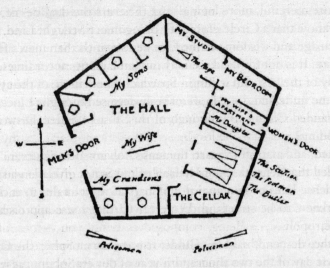

Touched by my Wife's distress, I would have sprung downward to reassure her, but I found myself incapable of motion. 'Trouble not yourself about your Wife,' said my Guide: 'she will not be long left in anxiety; meantime, let us take a survey of Flatland.'

Once more I felt myself rising through space. It was even as the Sphere had said. The further we receded from the object we beheld, the larger became the field of vision. My native city, with the interior of every house and every creature therein, lay open to my view in miniature. We mounted higher, and lo, the secrets of the earth, the depths of mines and inmost caverns of the hills, were bared before me.

Awestruck at the sight of the mysteries of the earth, thus unveiled before my unworthy eye, I said to my Companion, 'Behold, I am become as a God. For the wise men in our country say that to see all things, or as they express it, *omnividence*, is the attribute of God alone.' There was something of scorn in the voice of my Teacher as he made answer: 'Is it so indeed? Then the very pick-pockets and cut-throats of my country are to be worshipped by your wise men as being Gods: for there is not one of them that does not see as much as you see now. But trust me, your wise men are wrong.'

I. Then is omnividence the attribute of others besides Gods?

SPHERE. I do not know. But, if a pick-pocket or a cut-throat of our country can see everything that is in your country, surely that is no reason why the pick-pocket or cut-throat should be accepted by you as a

God. This omnividence, as you call it – it is not a common word in
Spaceland – does it make you more just, more merciful, less selfish, more
loving? Not in the least. Then how does it make you more divine?

I. 'More merciful, more loving!' But these are the qualities of women!
And we know that a Circle is a higher Being than a Straight Line, in so far
as knowledge and wisdom are more to be esteemed than mere affection.

SPHERE. It is not for me to classify human faculties according to merit.
Yet many of the best and wisest in Spaceland think more of the affections
than of the understanding, more of your despised Straight Lines than of
your belauded Circles. But enough of this. Look yonder. Do you know
that building?

I looked, and afar off I saw an immense Polygonal structure, in which I
recognized the General Assembly Hall of the States of Flatland, surrounded by dense lines of Pentagonal buildings at right angles to each other,
which I knew to be streets; and I perceived that I was approaching the
great Metropolis.

'Here we descend,' said my Guide. It was now morning, the first hour
of the first day of the two thousandth year of our era. Acting, as was their
wont, in strict accordance with precedent, the highest Circles of the
realm were meeting in solemn conclave, as they had met on the first hour
of the first day of the year 1000, and also on the first hour of the first day
of the year 0.

The minutes of the previous meetings were now read by one whom I at
once recognized as my brother, a perfectly Symmetrical Square, and the
Chief Clerk of the High Council. It was found recorded on each occasion
that: 'Whereas the States had been troubled by divers ill-intentioned
persons pretending to have received revelations from another World,
and professing to produce demonstrations whereby they had instigated to
frenzy both themselves and others, it had been for this cause unanimously
resolved by the Grand Council that on the first day of each millennary,
special injunctions be sent to the Prefects in the several districts of Flatland, to make strict search for such misguided persons, and without form-
ality of mathematical examination, to destroy all such as were Isosceles of
any degree, to scourge and imprison any regular Triangle, to cause any
Square or Pentagon to be sent to the district Asylum, and to arrest anyone
of higher rank, sending him straightway to the Capital to be examined and
judged by the Council.'

'You hear your fate,' said the Sphere to me, while the Council was
passing for the third time the formal resolution. 'Death or imprisonment
awaits the Apostle of the Gospel of Three Dimensions.' 'Not so,' replied
I, 'the matter is now so clear to me, the nature of real space so palpable,

that methinks I could make a child understand it. Permit me but to descend at this moment and enlighten them.' 'Not yet,' said my Guide, 'the time will come for that. Meantime I must perform my mission. Stay thou there in thy place.' Saying these words, he leaped with great dexterity into the sea (if I may so call it) of Flatland, right in the midst of the ring of Counsellors. 'I come,' cried he, 'to proclaim that there is a land of Three Dimensions.'

I could see many of the younger Counsellors start back in manifest horror, as the Sphere's circular section widened before them. But on a sign from the presiding Circle – who shewed not the slightest alarm or surprise – six Isosceles of a low type from six different quarters rushed upon the Sphere. 'We have him,' they cried; 'No; yes; we have him still! He's going! He's gone!'

'My Lords,' said the President to the Junior Circles of the Council, 'there is not the slightest need for surprise; the secret archives, to which I alone have access, tell me that a similar occurrence happened on the last two millennial commencements. You will, of course, say nothing of these trifles outside the Cabinet.'

Raising his voice, he now summoned the guards. 'Arrest the policemen; gag them. You know your duty.' After he had consigned to their fate the wretched policemen – ill-fated and unwilling witnesses of a State-secret which they were not to be permitted to reveal – he again addressed the Counsellors. 'My Lords, the business of the Council being concluded, I have only to wish you a happy New Year.' Before departing, he expressed, at some length, to the Clerk, my excellent but most unfortunate brother, his sincere regret that, in accordance with precedent and for the sake of secrecy, he must condemn him to perpetual imprisonment, but added his satisfaction that, unless some mention were made by him of that day's incident, his life would be spared.

Section 19. How, though the Sphere shewed me other mysteries of Spaceland, I still desired more; and what came of it

When I saw my poor brother led away to imprisonment, I attempted to leap down into the Council Chamber, desiring to intercede on his behalf, or at least bid him farewell. But I found that I had no motion of my own. I absolutely depended on the volition of my Guide, who said in gloomy tones, 'Heed not thy brother; haply thou shalt have ample time hereafter to condole with him. Follow me.'

Once more we ascended into space. 'Hitherto,' said the Sphere, 'I have shewn you naught save Plane Figures and their interiors. Now I must introduce you to Solids, and reveal to you the plan upon which they are constructed. Behold this multitude of moveable square cards. See, I put one on another, not, as you supposed, Northward of the other, but *on* the other. Now a second, now a third. See, I am building up a Solid by a multitude of Squares parallel to one another. Now the Solid is complete, being as high as it is long and broad, and we call it a Cube.'

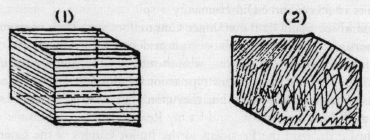

'Pardon me, my Lord,' replied I; 'but to my eye the appearance is as of an Irregular Figure whose inside is laid open to the view; in other words, methinks I see no Solid, but a Plane such as we infer in Flatland; only of an Irregularity which betokens some monstrous criminal, so that the very sight of it is painful to my eyes.'

'True,' said the Sphere, 'it appears to you a Plane, because you are not accustomed to light and shade and perspective; just as in Flatland a Hexagon would appear a Straight Line to one who has not the Art of Sight Recognition. But in reality it is a Solid, as you shall learn by the sense of Feeling.'

He then introduced me to the Cube, and I found that this marvellous Being was indeed no Plane, but a Solid; and that he was endowed with six plane sides and eight terminal points called solid angles; and I remembered the saying of the Sphere that just such a Creature as this would be formed by a Square moving, in Space, parallel to himself: and I rejoiced to think that so insignificant a Creature as I could in some sense be called the Progenitor of so illustrious an offspring.

But still I could not fully understand the meaning of what my Teacher had told me concerning 'light' and 'shade' and 'perspective'; and I did not hesitate to put my difficulties before him.

Were I to give the Sphere's explanation of these matters, succinct and clear though it was, it would be tedious to an inhabitant of Space, who knows these things already. Suffice it, that by his lucid statements, and by changing the position of objects and lights, and by allowing me to feel the several objects and even his own sacred Person, he at last made all things clear to me, so that I could now readily distinguish between a Circle and a Sphere, a Plane Figure and a Solid.

This was the Climax, the Paradise, of my strange eventful History. Henceforth I have to relate the story of my miserable Fall – most miserable, yet surely most undeserved! For why should the thirst for knowledge be aroused, only to be disappointed and punished? My volition shrinks from the painful task of recalling my humiliation; yet, like a second Prometheus, I will endure this and worse, if by any means I may arouse in the interiors of Plane and Solid Humanity a spirit of rebellion against the Conceit which would limit our Dimensions to Two or Three or any number short of Infinity. Away then with all personal considerations! Let me continue to the end, as I began, without further digressions or anticipations, pursuing the plain path of dispassionate History. The exact facts, the exact words – and they are burnt in upon my brain – shall be set down without alteration of an iota; and let my Readers judge between me and Destiny.

The Sphere would willingly have continued his lessons by indoctrinating me in the conformation of all regular Solids, Cylinders, Cones, Pyramids, Pentahedrons, Hexahedrons, Dodecahedrons, and Spheres: but I ventured to interrupt him. Not that I was wearied of knowledge. On the contrary, I thirsted for yet deeper and fuller draughts than he was offering to me.

'Pardon me,' said I, 'O Thou Whom I must no longer address as the Perfection of all Beauty; but let me beg thee to vouchsafe thy servant a sight of thine interior.'

SPHERE. My what?

I. Thine interior: thy stomach, thy intestines.

SPHERE. Whence this ill-timed impertinent request? And what mean you by saying that I am no longer the Perfection of all Beauty?

I. My Lord, your own wisdom has taught me to aspire to One even more great, more beautiful, and more closely approximate to Perfection than yourself. As you yourself, superior to all Flatland forms, combine many Circles in One, so doubtless there is One above you who combines many Spheres in One Supreme Existence, surpassing even the Solids of Spaceland. And even as we, who are now in Space, look down on Flatland and see the insides of all things, so of a certainty there is yet above us some higher, purer region, whither thou dost surely purpose to lead me – O Thou Whom I shall always call, everywhere and in all Dimensions, my Priest, Philosopher, and Friend – some yet more spacious Space, some more dimensionable Dimensionality, from the vantage-ground of which we shall look down together upon the revealed insides of Solid things, and where thine own intestines, and those of thy kindred Spheres, will lie exposed to the view of the poor wandering exile from Flatland, to whom so much has already been vouchsafed.

Sᴘʜᴇʀᴇ. Pooh! Stuff! Enough of this trifling! The time is short, and much remains to be done before you are fit to proclaim the Gospel of Three Dimensions to your blind benighted countrymen in Flatland.

I. Nay, gracious Teacher, deny me not what I know it is in thy power to perform. Grant me but one glimpse of thine interior, and I am satisfied for ever, remaining henceforth thy docile pupil, thy unemancipable slave, ready to receive all thy teachings and to feed upon the words that fall from thy lips.

Sᴘʜᴇʀᴇ. Well, then, to content and silence you, let me say at once, I would shew you what you wish if I could; but I cannot. Would you have me turn my stomach inside out to oblige you?

I. But my Lord has shewn me the intestines of all my countrymen in the Land of Two Dimensions by taking me with him into the Land of Three. What therefore more easy than now to take his servant on a second journey into the blessed region of the Fourth Dimension, where I shall look down with him once more upon this land of Three Dimensions, and see the inside of every three-dimensioned house, the secrets of the solid earth, the treasures of the mines in Spaceland, and the intestines of every solid living creature, even of the noble and adorable Spheres.

Sᴘʜᴇʀᴇ. But where is this land of Four Dimensions?

I. I know not: but doubtless my Teacher knows.

Sᴘʜᴇʀᴇ. Not I. There is no such land. The very idea of it is utterly inconceivable.

I. Not inconceivable, my Lord, to me, and therefore still less inconceivable to my Master. Nay, I despair not that, even here, in this region of Three Dimensions, your Lordship's art may make the Fourth Dimension visible to me; just as in the Land of Two Dimensions my Teacher's skill would fain have opened the eyes of his blind servant to the invisible presence of a Third Dimension, though I saw it not.

Let me recall the past. Was I not taught below that when I saw a Line and inferred a Plane, I in reality saw a Third unrecognized Dimension, not the same as brightness, called 'height'? And does it not now follow that, in this region, when I see a Plane and infer a Solid, I really see a Fourth unrecognized Dimension, not the same as colour, but existent, though infinitesimal and incapable of measurement?

And besides this, there is the Argument from Analogy of Figures.

Sᴘʜᴇʀᴇ. Analogy! Nonsense: what analogy?

I. Your Lordship tempts his servant to see whether he remembers the revelations imparted to him. Trifle not with me, my Lord; I crave, I thirst, for more knowledge. Doubtless we cannot *see* that other higher Spaceland now, because we we have no eye in our stomachs. But, just as there *was* the realm of Flatland, though that poor puny Lineland Monarch could neither turn to left nor right to discern it, and just as there *was* close at hand, and touching my frame, the land of Three Dimensions, though I, blind senseless wretch, had no power to touch it, no eye in my interior to discern it, so of a surety there is a Fourth Dimension, which my Lord perceives with the inner eye of thought. And that it must exist my Lord himself has taught me. Or can he have forgotten what he himself imparted to his servant?

In One Dimension, did not a moving Point produce a Line with *two* terminal points?

In Two Dimensions, did not a moving Line produce a Square with *four* terminal points?

In Three Dimensions, did not a moving Square produce – did not this eye of mine behold it – that blessed Being, a Cube, with *eight* terminal points?

And in Four Dimensions shall not a moving Cube – alas, for Analogy, and alas for the Progress of Truth, if it be not so – shall not, I say, the motion of a divine Cube result in a still more divine Organization with *sixteen* terminal points?

Behold the infallible confirmation of the Series, 2, 4, 8, 16: is not this a Geometrical Progression? Is not this – if I might quote my Lord's own words – 'strictly according to Analogy'?

Again, was I not taught by my Lord that as in a Line there are *two* bounding Points, and in a Square there are *four* bounding Lines, so in a Cube there must be *six* bounding Squares? Behold once more the confirming Series, 2, 4, 6: is not this an Arithmetical Progression? And consequently does it not of necessity follow that the more divine offspring of the divine Cube in the Land of Four Dimensions, must have *eight* bounding Cubes: and is not this also, as my Lord has taught me to believe, 'strictly according to Analogy'?

O, my Lord, my Lord, behold, I cast myself in faith upon conjecture, not knowing the facts; and I appeal to your Lordship to confirm or deny my logical anticipations. If I am wrong, I yield, and will no longer demand a fourth Dimension; but, if I am right, my Lord will listen to reason.

I ask therefore, is it, or is it not, the fact, that ere now your countrymen also have witnessed the descent of Beings of a higher order than their own, entering closed rooms, even as your Lordship entered mine, without the opening of doors or windows, and appearing and vanishing at will? On the reply to this question I am ready to stake everything. Deny it, and I am henceforth silent. Only vouchsafe an answer.

SPHERE. [*after a pause*]. It is reported so. But men are divided in opinion as to the facts. And even granting the facts, they explain them in different ways. And in any case, however great may be the number of different explanations, no one has adopted or suggested the theory of a Fourth Dimension. Therefore, pray have done with this trifling, and let us return to business.

I. I was certain of it. I was certain that my anticipations would be fulfilled. And now have patience with me and answer me yet one more question, best of Teachers! Those who have thus appeared – no one knows whence – and have returned – no one knows whither – have they also contracted their sections and vanished somehow into that more Spacious Space, whither I now entreat you to conduct me?

SPHERE [*moodily*]. They have vanished, certainly – if they ever appeared. But most people say that these visions arose from the thought – you will not understand me – from the brain; from the perturbed angularity of the Seer.

I. Say they so? Oh, believe them not. Or if it indeed be so, that this other Space is really Thoughtland, then take me to that blessed Region where I in Thought shall see the insides of all solid things. There, before my ravished eye, a Cube, moving in some altogether new direction, but strictly according to Analogy, so as to make every particle of his interior pass through a new kind of Space, with a wake of its own – shall create a still more perfect perfection than himself, with sixteen terminal Extra-solid angles, and Eight solid Cubes for his Perimeter. And once there, shall we stay our upward course? In that blessed region of Four Dimensions, shall we linger on the threshold of the Fifth, and not enter therein? Ah, no! Let us rather resolve that our ambition shall soar with our corporal ascent. Then, yielding to our intellectual onset, the gates of the Sixth Dimension shall fly open; after that a Seventh, and then an Eighth –

How long I should have continued I know not. In vain did the Sphere, in his voice of thunder, reiterate his command of silence, and threaten me with the direst penalties if I persisted. Nothing could stem the flood of my ecstatic aspirations. Perhaps I was to blame; but indeed I was intoxicated with the recent draughts of Truth to which he himself had introduced me. However, the end was not long in coming. My words were cut short by a crash outside, and a simultaneous crash inside me, which impelled me through space with a velocity that precluded speech. Down! down! down! I was rapidly descending; and I knew that return to Flatland was my doom. One glimpse, one last and never-to-be-forgotten glimpse I had of that dull level wilderness – which was now to become my Universe again – spread out before my eye. Then a darkness. Then a final, all-consummating thunder-peal; and, when I came to myself, I was once more a common creeping Square, in my Study at home, listening to the Peace-Cry of my approaching Wife.

Section 20. How the Sphere encouraged me in a Vision

Although I had less than a minute for reflection, I felt, by a kind of instinct, that I must conceal my experiences from my Wife. Not that I apprehended, at the moment, any danger from her divulging my secret, but I knew that to any Woman in Flatland the narrative of my adventures must needs be unintelligible. So I endeavoured to reassure her by some story, invented for the occasion, that I had accidentally fallen through the trap-door of the cellar, and had there lain stunned.

The Southward attraction in our country is so slight that even to a Woman my tale necessarily appeared extraordinary and well-nigh incredible; but my Wife, whose good sense far exceeds that of the average of her Sex, and who perceived that I was unusually excited, did not argue with me on the subject, but insisted that I was ill and required repose. I was glad of an excuse for retiring to my chamber to think quietly over what had happened. When I was at last by myself, a drowsy sensation fell on me; but before my eyes closed I endeavoured to reproduce the Third Dimension, and especially the process by which a Cube is constructed through the motion of a Square. It was not so clear as I could have wished; but I remembered that it must be 'Upward, and yet not Northward', and I determined steadfastly to retain these words as the clue which, if firmly grasped, could not fail to guide me to the solution. So mechanically repeating, like a charm, the words, 'Upward, yet not Northward', I fell into a sound refreshing sleep.

During my slumber I had a dream. I thought I was once more by the side of the Sphere, whose lustrous hue betokened that he had exchanged his wrath against me for perfect placability. We were moving together towards a bright but infinitesimally small Point, to which my Master directed my attention. As we approached, methought there issued from it a slight humming noise as from one of your Spaceland bluebottles, only less resonant by far, so slight indeed that even in the perfect stillness of the Vacuum through which we soared, the sound reached not our ears till we checked our flight at a distance from it of something under twenty human diagonals.

'Look yonder,' said my Guide, 'in Flatland thou hast lived; of Lineland thou hast received a vision; thou hast soared with me to the heights of

Spaceland; now, in order to complete the range of thy experience, I conduct thee downward to the lowest depth of existence, even to the realm of Pointland, the Abyss of No dimensions.

'Behold yon miserable creature. That Point is a Being like ourselves, but confined to the non-dimensional Gulf. He is himself his own World, his own Universe; of any other than himself he can form no conception; he knows not Length, nor Breadth, nor Height, for he has had no experience of them; he has no cognizance even of the number Two; nor has he a thought of Plurality; for he is himself his One and All, being really Nothing. Yet mark his perfect self-contentment, and hence learn this lesson, that to be self-contented is to be vile and ignorant, and that to aspire is better than to be blindly and impotently happy. Now listen.'

He ceased; and there arose from the little buzzing creature a tiny, low, monotonous, but distinct tinkling, as from one of your Spaceland phonographs, from which I caught these words, 'Infinite beatitude of existence! It is; and there is none else beside It.'

'What,' said I, 'does the puny creature mean by "it"?' 'He means himself,' said the Sphere: 'have you not noticed before now, that babies and babyish people who cannot distinguish themselves from the world, speak of themselves in the Third Person? But hush!'

'It fills all Space,' continued the little soliloquizing Creature, 'and what It fills, It is. What It thinks, that It utters; and what It utters, that It hears; and It itself is Thinker, Utterer, Hearer, Thought, Word, Audition; it is the One, and yet the All in All. Ah, the happiness ah, the happiness of Being!'

'Can you not startle the little thing out of its complacency?' said I. 'Tell it what it really is, as you told me; reveal to it the narrow limitations of Pointland, and lead it up to something higher.' 'That is no easy task,' said my Master; 'try you.'

Hereon, raising my voice to the uttermost, I addressed the Point as follows: 'Silence, silence, contemptible Creature. You call yourself the All in All, but you are the Nothing: your so-called Universe is a mere speck in a Line, and a Line is a mere shadow as compared with – ' 'Hush, hush, you have said enough,' interrupted the Sphere; 'now listen, and mark the effect of your harangue on the King of Pointland.'

The lustre of the Monarch, who beamed more brightly than ever upon hearing my words, shewed clearly that he retained his complacency; and I had hardly ceased when he took up his strain again. 'Ah, the joy, ah, the joy of Thought! What can It not achieve by thinking! Its own Thought coming to Itself, suggestive of Its disparagement, thereby to enhance Its happiness! Sweet rebellion stirred up to result in triumph! Ah, the divine creative power of the All in One! Ah, the joy, the joy of Being!'

'You see,' said my Teacher, 'how little your words have done. So far as the Monarch understands them at all, he accepts them as his own – for he cannot conceive of any other except himself – and plumes himself upon the variety of "Its Thought" as an instance of creative Power. Let us leave this God of Pointland to the ignorant fruition of his omnipresence and omniscience: nothing that you or I can do can rescue him from his self-satisfaction.'

After this, as we floated gently back to Flatland, I could hear the mild voice of my Companion pointing the moral of my vision, and stimulating me to aspire, and to teach others to aspire. He had been angered at first – he confessed – by my ambition to soar to Dimensions above the Third; but, since then, he had received fresh insight, and he was not too proud to acknowledge his error to a Pupil. Then he proceeded to initiate me into mysteries yet higher than those I had witnessed, shewing me how to construct Extra-Solids by the motion of Solids, and Double Extra-Solids by the motion of Extra-Solids, and all 'strictly according to Analogy', all by methods so simple, so easy, as to be patent even to the Female Sex.

Section 21. How I tried to teach the Theory of Three
Dimensions to my Grandson, and with what success
I awoke rejoicing, and began to reflect on the glorious career before me. I would go forth, methought, at once, and evangelize the whole of Flatland. Even to Women and Soldiers should the Gospel of Three Dimensions be proclaimed. I would begin with my Wife.

Just as I had decided on the plan of my operations, I heard the sound of many voices in the street commanding silence. Then followed a louder voice. It was a herald's proclamation. Listening attentively, I recognized the words of the Resolution of the Council, enjoining the arrest, imprisonment, or execution of anyone who should pervert the minds of the people by delusions, and by professing to have received revelations from another World.

I reflected. This danger was not to be trifled with. It would be better to avoid it by omitting all mention of my Revelation, and by proceeding on the path of Demonstration – which after all, seemed so simple and so conclusive that nothing would be lost by discarding the former means. 'Upward, not Northward' – was the clue to the whole proof. It had seemed to me fairly clear before I fell asleep; and when I first awoke, fresh from my dream, it had appeared as patent as Arithmetic; but somehow it did not seem to me quite so obvious now. Though my Wife entered the room opportunely just at that moment, I decided, after we had exchanged a few words of commonplace conversation, not to begin with her.

My Pentagonal Sons were men of character and standing, and physicians of no mean reputation, but not great in mathematics, and, in that respect, unfit for my purpose. But it occurred to me that a young and docile Hexagon, with a mathematical turn, would be a most suitable pupil. Why therefore not make my first experiment with my little precocious Grandson, whose casual remarks on the meaning of 3^3 had met with the approval of the Sphere? Discussing the matter with him, a mere boy, I should be in perfect safety; for he would know nothing of the Proclamation of the Council; whereas I could not feel sure that my Sons – so greatly did their patriotism and reverence for the Circles predominate over mere blind affection – might not feel compelled to hand me over to the Prefect, if they found me seriously maintaining the seditious heresy of the Third Dimension.

But the first thing to be done was to satisfy in some way the curiosity of my Wife, who naturally wished to know something of the reasons for which the Circle had desired that mysterious interview, and of the means by which he had entered the house. Without entering into the details of the elaborate account I gave her – an account, I fear, not quite so consistent with truth as my Readers in Spaceland might desire – I must be content with saying that I succeeded at last in persuading her to return quietly to her household duties without eliciting from me any reference to the World of Three Dimensions. This done, I immediately sent for my Grandson; for, to confess the truth, I felt that all that I had seen and heard was in some strange way slipping away from me, like the image of a half-grasped, tantalizing dream, and I longed to essay my skill in making a first disciple.

When my Grandson entered the room I carefully secured the door. Then, sitting down by his side and taking our mathematical tablets – or, as you would call them, Lines – I told him we would resume the lesson of yesterday. I taught him once more how a Point by motion in One Dimension produces a Line, and how a straight Line in Two Dimensions produces a Square. After this, forcing a laugh, I said, 'And now, you scamp, you wanted to make me believe that a Square may in the same way by motion "Upward, not Northward" produce another figure, a sort of extra Square in Three Dimensions. Say that again, you young rascal.'

At this moment we heard once more the herald's 'O yes! O yes!' outside in the street proclaiming the Resolution of the Council. Young though he was, my Grandson – who was unusually intelligent for his age, and bred up in perfect reverence for the authority of the Circles – took in the situation with an acuteness for which I was quite unprepared. He remained silent till the last words of the Proclamation had died away, and then, bursting into tears, 'Dear Grandpapa,' he said, 'that was only my fun, and of course I meant nothing at all by it; and we did not know anything then about the new Law; and I don't think I said anything about the Third Dimension; and I am sure I did not say one word about "Upward, not Northward", for that would be such nonsense, you know. How could a thing move Upward, and not Northward? Upward and not Northward! Even if I were a baby, I could not be so absurd as that. How silly it is! Ha! ha! ha!'

'Not at all silly,' said I, losing my temper; 'here for example, I take this Square,' and, at the word, I grasped a moveable Square, which was lying at hand – 'and I move it, you see, not Northward but – yes, I move it Upward – that is to say, not Northward, but I move it somewhere – not exactly like this, but somehow – ' Here I brought my sentence to an inane conclusion, shaking the Square about in a purposeless manner, much to the amusement of my Grandson, who burst out laughing louder than ever, and declared that I was not teaching him, but joking with him; and so saying he unlocked the door and ran out of the room. Thus ended my first attempt to convert a pupil to the Gospel of Three Dimensions.

Section 22. How I then tried to diffuse the Theory of
Three Dimensions by other means, and of the result
My failure with my Grandson did not encourage me to communicate my secret to others of my household; yet neither was I led by it to despair of success. Only I saw that I must not wholly rely on the catchphrase, 'Upward, not Northward', but must rather endeavour to seek a demonstration by setting before the public a clear view of the whole subject; and for this purpose it seemed necessary to resort to writing.

So I devoted several months in privacy to the composition of a treatise on the mysteries of Three Dimensions. Only, with the view of evading the Law, if possible, I spoke not of a physical Dimension, but of a Thoughtland whence, in theory, a Figure could look down upon Flatland and see simultaneously the insides of all things, and where it was possible that there might be supposed to exist a Figure environed, as it were, with six Squares, and containing eight terminal Points. But in writing this book I found myself sadly hampered by the impossibility of drawing such diagrams as were necessary for my purpose; for of course, in our country of Flatland, there are no tablets but Lines, and no diagrams but Lines, all in one straight Line and only distinguishable by difference of size and brightness; so that, when I had finished my treatise (which I entitled, 'Through Flatland to Thoughtland') I could not feel certain that many would understand my meaning.

Meanwhile my life was under a cloud. All pleasures palled upon me; all sights tantalized and tempted me to outspoken treason, because I could not but compare what I saw in Two Dimensions with what it really was if seen in Three, and could hardly refrain from making my comparisons aloud. I neglected my clients and my own business to give myself to the contemplation of the mysteries which I had once beheld, yet which I could impart to no one, and found daily more difficult to reproduce even before my own mental vision.

One day, about eleven months after my return from Spaceland, I tried to see a Cube with my eye closed, but failed; and though I succeeded afterwards, I was not then quite certain (nor have I been ever afterwards) that I had exactly realized the original. This made me more melancholy than before, and determined me to take some step; yet what, I knew not. I felt that I would have been willing to sacrifice my life for the Cause, if thereby I could have produced conviction. But if I could not convince my Grandson, how could I convince the highest and most developed Circles in the land?

And yet at times my spirit was too strong for me, and I gave vent to dangerous utterances. Already I was considered heterodox if not treasonable, and I was keenly alive to the danger of my position; nevertheless I could not at times refrain from bursting out into suspicious or half-seditious utterances, even among the highest Polygonal and Circular society. When, for example, the question arose about the treatment of those lunatics who said that they had received the power of seeing the insides of things, I would quote the saying of an ancient Circle, who declared that prophets and inspired people are always considered by the majority to be mad; and I could not help occasionally dropping such expressions as 'the eye that discerns the interiors of things', and 'the all-seeing land'; once or twice I even let fall the forbidden terms 'the Third and Fourth Dimensions'. At last, to complete a series of minor indiscretions, at a meeting of our Local Speculative Society held at the palace of the Prefect himself – some extremely silly person having read an elaborate paper exhibiting the precise reasons why Providence has limited the number of Dimensions to Two, and why the attribute of omnividence is assigned to the Supreme alone – I so far forgot myself as to give an exact account of the whole of my voyage with the Sphere into Space, and to the Assembly Hall in our Metropolis, and then to Space again, and of my return home, and of everything that I had seen and heard in fact or vision. At first, indeed, I pretended that I was describing the imaginary experiences of a fictitious person; but my enthusiasm soon forced me to throw off all disguise, and finally, in a fervent peroration, I exhorted all my hearers to divest themselves of prejudice and to become believers in the Third Dimension.

Need I say that I was at once arrested and taken before the Council?

Next morning, standing in the very place where but a very few months ago the Sphere had stood in my company, I was allowed to begin and to continue my narration unquestioned and uninterrupted. But from the first I foresaw my fate; for the President, noting that a guard of the better sort of Policemen was in attendance, of angularity little, if at all, under 55 degrees, ordered them to be relieved before I began my defence, by an inferior class of 2 or 3 degrees. I knew only too well what that meant. I was to be executed or imprisoned, and my story was to be kept secret from the world by the simultaneous destruction of the officials who had heard it; and, this being the case, the President desired to substitute the cheaper for the more expensive victims.

After I had concluded my defence, the President, perhaps perceiving that some of the junior Circles had been moved by my evident earnestness, asked me two questions: –

1. Whether I could indicate the direction which I meant when I used the words 'Upward, not Northward'?

2. Whether I could by any diagrams or descriptions (other than the enumeration of imaginary sides and angles) indicate the Figure I was pleased to call a Cube?

I declared that I could say nothing more, and that I must commit myself to the Truth, whose cause would surely prevail in the end.

The President replied that he quite concurred in my sentiment, and that I could not do better. I must be sentenced to perpetual imprisonment; but if the Truth intended that I should emerge from prison and evangelize the world, the Truth might be trusted to bring that result to pass. Meanwhile I should be subjected to no discomfort that was not necessary to preclude escape, and, unless I forfeited the privilege by misconduct, I should be occasionally permitted to see my brother who had preceded me to my prison.

Seven years have elapsed and I am still a prisoner, and – if I except the occasional visits of my brother – debarred from all companionship save that of my jailers. My brother is one of the best of Squares, just, sensible, cheerful, and not without fraternal affection; yet I confess that my weekly interviews, at least in one respect, cause me the bitterest pain. He was present when the Sphere manifested himself in the Council Chamber; he saw the Sphere's changing sections; he heard the explanation of the phenomena then given to the Circles. Since that time, scarcely a week has passed during seven whole years, without his hearing from me a repetition of the part I played in that manifestation, together with ample descriptions of all the phenomena in Spaceland, and the arguments for the existence of Solid things derivable from Analogy. Yet – I take shame to be forced to confess it – my brother has not yet grasped the nature of the Third Dimension, and frankly avows his disbelief in the existence of a Sphere.

Hence I am absolutely destitute of converts, and, for aught that I can see, the millennial Revelation has been made to me for nothing. Prometheus up in Spaceland was bound for bringing down fire for mortals, but I – poor Flatland Prometheus – lie here in prison for bringing down nothing to my countrymen. Yet I exist in the hope that these memoirs, in some manner, I know not how, may find their way to the minds of humanity in Some Dimension, and may stir up a race of rebels who shall refuse to be confined to limited Dimensionality.

That is the hope of my brighter moments. Alas, it is not always so. Heavily weighs on me at times the burdensome reflection that I cannot honestly say I am confident as to the exact shape of the once-seen, oft-regretted Cube; and in my nightly visions the mysterious precept, 'Upward, not Northward', haunts me like a soul-devouring Sphinx. It is part of the martyrdom which I endure for the cause of the Truth that there are seasons of mental weakness, when Cubes and Spheres flit away into the background of scarce-possible existences; when the Land of Three Dimensions seems almost as visionary as the Land of One or None; nay, when even this hard wall that bars me from my freedom, these very tablets on which I am writing, and all the substantial realities of Flatland itself, appear no better than the offspring of a diseased imagination, or the baseless fabric of a dream.

The Last Stand of the Decapods

Frank T. Bullen

Probably few of the thinking inhabitants of dry land, with all their craving for tales of the marvellous, the gloomy, and the gigantic, have in these later centuries of the world's history given much thought to the conditions of constant warfare existing beneath the surface of the ocean. As readers of ancient classics well know, the fathers of literature gave much attention to the vast, awe-inspiring inhabitants of the sea, investing and embellishing the few fragments of fact concerning them which were available with a thousand fantastic inventions of their own naive imaginations, until there emerged – chief and ruler of them all – the Kraken, Leviathan, or whatever other local name was considered to best convey in one word their accumulated ideas of terror. In lesser degree, but still worthy compeers of the fire breathing dragon and sky-darkening 'Rukh' of earth and sky, a worthy host of attendant sea-monsters were conjured up, until, apart from the terror of loneliness, of irresistible fury, and instability that the sea presented to primitive peoples, the awful nature of its supposed inhabitants made the contemplation of an ocean journey sufficient to appal the stoutest heart.

A better understanding of this aspect of the sea to early voyagers may be obtained from some of the artistic efforts of those days than from anything else. There you shall see gigantic creatures with human faces, teeth like foot-long wedges, armour-plated bodies, and massive feet fitted with claws like scythe-blades calmly issuing from the waves to prey upon the dwellers on the margin, or devouring with much apparent enjoyment ships with their crews, as a child crunches a stick of barley-sugar. Even such innocent-looking animals as the seals were distorted and decorated until the contemplation of their counterfeit presentment is sufficient to give a healthy man the nightmare, whilst such monsters as really were so terrible of aspect that they could hardly be 'improved' upon were increased in size until they resembled islands whereon whole tribes might live. To these chimeras were credited all natural phenomena such as waterspouts, whirlpools, and the upheaval of submarine volcanoes. Some imaginative peoples went even farther than that by attributing the support of the whole earth to a vast sea-monster, while others, like the ancient Jews, fondly pictured Leviathan awaiting in the solitude and gloom of ocean's depths the glad day of Israel's reunion, when the mountain ranges of his flesh would be ready to furnish forth the family feast for all the myriads of Abraham's children.

The earliest seafarers set boldly out from shore

Surely we may pause awhile to contemplate the overmastering courage of the earliest seafarers who, in spite of all these terrors, unappalled by the comparison between their tiny shallops and the mighty waves that towered above them, set boldly out from shore into the unknown, obeying that deeply-rooted instinct of migration which has peopled every habitable part of the earth's surface. Those who remember their childhood's dread of the dark, with its possible population of bogeys, who have ever been lost in early youth in some lonely place, can have some dim conception – though only a dim one, after all – of the inward battle these ancients fought and won until it became possible for the epigram to be written most truly –

> The seas but join the nations they divide.

But after all we are not now concerned with the warlike doings of men. It is with the actualities of submarine struggle we wish to deal, those wars without an armistice, where to be defeated is to be devoured, and from the sea-shouldering whale down to the smallest sea insect every living thing is carnivorous, dependent directly upon the flesh of its neighbours for its own life, and incapable of altruism in any form whatever, except among certain of the mammalia and sharks. In dealing with the more heroic phases of this unending warfare, then, it must be said once for all that the ancient writers had a great deal of reason on their side. They distorted and exaggerated, of course, as all children do, but they did not disbelieve. But moderns, rushing to the opposite extreme, have neglected the marvels of the sea by the simple process of disbelieving in them, except in the case of the sea-serpent, that myth which seems bound to persist for ever and ever. Only of late years have the savants of the world allowed themselves to be convinced of the existence of a far more wondrous monster than the sea-serpent (if that 'loathly worm' were a reality), the original kraken of old-world legends.

Hugest of all the mollusca, whose prevailing characteristics are ugliness, ferocity, and unappeasable hunger, he has lately asserted himself so firmly that current imaginative literature bristles with allusions to him, albeit often-times in situations where he could by no possibility be found. No matter, he has supplied a long-felt want, but the curious fact remains that he is not a discovery, but a reappearance. The gigantic cuttle-fish of actual, indisputable fact is in all respects except size the kraken; and any faithful representation of him will justify the assertion that no imagination could add anything to the terror-breeding potentialities of his aspect. That is so, even when he is viewed by the light of day in the helplessness of death, or disabling sickness, or in the invincible grip of his only conqueror. In his proper realm, crouching far below the surface of the sea in some coral cave or labyrinth of rocks, he must present a sight so awful that the imagination recoils before it. For, consider him but a little. He possesses a cylindrical body reaching, in the largest specimens yet recorded as having been seen, a length of between 60 ft and 70 ft, with an average girth of half that amount. That is to say, considerably larger than a Pullman railway-car.

Now, this immense mass is of boneless, gelatinous matter capable of much greater distension than the body of a snake, so that in the improbable event of his obtaining an extra abundant supply of food it is competent to swell to the occasion, and still give the flood of digestive juices that it secretes full opportunity to dispose of the burden with almost incredible rapidity. Now, the apex of this mighty cylinder – I had almost said 'tail', but remembered that it would give a wrong impression, since it is the part of the monster that always comes first when he is moving from place to place – is conical; that is to say, it tapers off to a blunt point something like a Whitehead torpedo. Near this apex there is a broad fin-like arrangement looking much like the body of a skate without its tail, which, however, is used strictly for steering purposes only.

So far, there is nothing particularly striking about the appearance of this vast cylinder except in colour. This characteristic varies in different individuals, but is always reminiscent of the hues of a very light-coloured leopard; that is to say, the ground is of a livid greenish white, while the detail is in splashes and spots of lurid red and yellow, with an occasional nimbus of pale blue around these deeper markings. But it is the head of the monster that appals. Nature would seem, in the construction of this greatest of all mollusca, to have combined every weapon of offence possessed by the rest of the animal kingdom in one amazing arsenal, disposing them in such a manner that not only are they capable of terrific destruction, but their appearance defies adequate description.

The trunk at the head end is sheath-like, its terminating edges forming a sort of collar around the vast cable of muscles without a fragment of bone that connect it with the head. Through a large opening within this collar is pumped a jet of water, the pressure of which upon the surrounding sea is sufficiently great to drive the whole bulk of the creature, weighing perhaps sixty or seventy tons, *backward* through the water at the rate of sixteen to twenty miles per hour. Not in steady progression, of course, but by successive leaps. At will, this propelling jet is deeply stained with sepia, a dark brown, inky fluid, that, mingling with the encompassing sea, fills all the neighbourhood of the monster with a gloom so deep that nothing save one of its own species can see either to fight or whither to fly. The head itself is of proportionate size. It is rounded underneath and of much lighter hue than the trunk. On either side of it is set an eye of such dimensions that the mere statement of them sounds like the efforts of one of those grand old mediæval romancers whose sole object was to make their readers' flesh creep.

It is perfectly safe to say that, even in proportion to size, no other known creature has such organs of vision as the cuttle-fish, for the pupils of such a one as I am now describing are fully 2 ft in diameter. They are perfectly black, with a dead white rim, and cannot be closed. No doubt their enormous size is for the purpose of enabling their possessor to discern what is going on amidst the thick darkness that he himself has raised, so that while all other organisms are groping blindly in the gloom, he may work his will among them. Then come the weapons which give the cuttle-fish its power of destruction, the arms or tentacles. These are not eight in number as in the octopus, an ugly beast enough and spiteful withal, but a babe of innocence compared with our present subject. Every school-boy should know that *octopus* signifies an eight-armed or eight-footed creature, and yet in nine cases out of ten where writers of fiction and would-be teachers of fact are describing the deadly doings of the gigantic cuttle-fish they call *him* an octopus, whereas he is nothing of the kind. For in addition to the eight arms which the octopus possesses the cuttle-fish flaunts two, each of which is double the length of the other eight, making him a *decapod*. This confusion is the more unpardonable because even the most ancient of scribes always spoke of this mollusc as the 'ten-armed one', while a reference to any standard work on natural history will show even the humbler cuttle-fish with their full complement of arms: that is, ten. But this is digression.

Our friend, then, has ten arms springing from the crown of his head, of which eight are about 40 ft in length and two are 70 ft to 80 ft. The eight each taper outward from the head, from the thickness of a stout man's body at the base to the slenderness of a whip-lash at the end. On their inner sides they are studded with saucer-like hollows, each of which has a fringe of curving claws set just within its rim. So that in addition to their power of holding on to anything they touch by a suction so severe that it would strip flesh from bone, these cruel claws, large as those of a full-grown tiger, get to work upon the subject being held, lacerating and tearing until the quivering body yields up its innermost secrets. Each of these destroying, serpent-like arms is also gifted with an almost independent power of volition. Whatever it touches it holds with an unreleasable grip, but with wonderful celerity it brings its prey inwards to where in the centre of all those infernal purveyors lies a black chasm whose edges are shaped like the upper and lower mandibles of a parrot, and these complete the work so well begun.

This nightmare monstrosity crouches in the darkling depths of ocean

The outliers, those two far-reaching tentacles, unlike the busy eight, are comparatively slender from their bases to within 2ft. or so of their ends. There they expand into broad, paddle-like masses thickly studded with *acetabulae*, those holding, sucking discs that garnish the inner arms for their entire length. So, thus armed, this nightmare monstrosity crouches in the darkling depths of ocean like some unimaginable web whereof every line is alive to hold and tear. Its digestion is like a furnace of dissolution needing a continual inflow of flesh, and nothing living that inhabits the sea comes amiss to its never-satisfied cravings. It is very near the apex of the pyramid of interdependence into which sea-life is built, but not quite. For at the summit is the sperm whale, the monarch of all seas, whom man alone is capable of meeting in fair fight and overcoming.

The head of the sperm whale is of heroic size, being in bulk quite one-third of the entire body, but in addition to its size it has characteristics that fit it peculiarly to compete with such a dangerous monster as the gigantic decapod. Imagine a solid block of crude india-rubber, between 20ft. and 30ft. in length and 8ft. through, in shape not at all unlike a railway carriage, but perfectly smooth in surface. Fit this mass beneath with a movable shaft of solid bone 20ft. in length studded with teeth, each protruding 9in. and resembling the points of an elephant's tusks. You will then have a fairly complete notion of the equipment with which the ocean monarch goes into battle against the kraken. And behind it lies the warm blood of the mammal, the massive framework of bone belonging to the highly-developed vertebrate animal, governed by a brain impelled by irresistible instinct to seek its sustenance where alone it can be found in sufficiently satisfying bulk. And there for you are the outlines of the highest form of animal warfare existing within our ken – a conflict of Titans, to which a combat between elephants and rhinoceri in the jungle is but as the play of school-boys compared with the gladiatorial combats of Ancient Rome.

This somewhat lengthy preamble is necessary in order to clear the way for an account of the proceedings leading up to the final subjugation of the huge mollusca of the elder slime to the needs of the great vertebrates like the whales, who were gradually emerging into a higher development, and, finding new wants oppressing them, had to obey the universal law and fight for the satisfaction of their urgent needs. Fortunately the period with which we have to deal was before chronology, so that we are not hampered by dates, and as the disposition of sea and land, except in its main features, was altogether different to what we have long been accustomed to regard as the always existing geographical order of things, we need not be greatly troubled by place considerations either.

What must be considered as the first beginning of the long struggle occurred when some predecessors of the present sperm whales, wandering through the vast morasses and among the sombre forests of that earlier world, were compelled to recognise that the conditions of shore life were rapidly becoming too onerous for them. Their immensely weighty bodies lumbering slowly as a seal does over the rugged land surface handicapped them more and more in the universal business of life, the procuring of food. Not only so, but as by reason of their slowness they were confined for hunting-grounds to a very limited area, the slower organisms upon which their vast appetites were fed grew scarcer and scarcer in spite of the fecundity of that prolific time. And in proportion as they found it more and more difficult to get a living, so did their enemies grow more numerous and bolder. Vast dragon-like shapes, clad in complete armour that clanged as the wide-spreading bat-wings bore them swiftly through the air, descended upon the sluggish whales, and with horrid rending by awful shear-shaped jaws, plentifully furnished with foot-long teeth, speedily stripped from their gigantic bodies the masses of succulent flesh. Other enemies weird of shape and swift of motion, although confined to the earth, fastened also upon the easily attainable prey that provided flesh in such bountiful abundance and was unable to fight or flee.

Well was it, then, for the whales that, living always near the sea, they had formed aquatic habits, finding in the limpid element a medium wherein their huge bulk was rather a help than a hindrance to them. Gradually they grew to use the land less and less as they became more and more accustomed to the food provided in plenty by the inexhaustible ocean; continual practice enabled them to husband the supplies of air which they took in on the surface for use beneath the waves; and, better still, they found that, whereas they had been victims to many a monster on land whose proportions and potentialities seemed far inferior to their own, here, in their new element, they were supreme – nothing living but fled from before them.

But presently a strange thing befell them. As they grew less and less inclined to use the dry land they found that their powers of locomotion thereon gradually became less and less until at last their hind legs dwindled away and disappeared. Their vast and far-reaching tails lost their length and their bones spread out laterally into flexible fans of toughest gristle, with which they could propel themselves through the waves at speeds to which their swiftest progress upon land had been but a snail's crawl. Also their fore-legs grew shorter and wider, and the separation of the toes disappeared, until all that was left of these once ponderous supports were elegant fan-like flippers of gristle, of not the slightest use for propulsion, but merely acting as steadying vanes to keep the whole great structure in its proper position according to the will of the owner.

All these radical physical changes, however, had not affected the real classification of the whales. They were still mammals, still retained in the element which was now entirely their habitat the high organization belonging to the great carnivora of the land. Therefore, it took them no long period of time to realize that in the ocean they would be paramount; that with the tremendous facilities for rapid movement afforded them by their new element they were able to maintain that supremacy against all comers, unless their formidable armed jaws should also become modified by degeneration into some such harmless cavities for absorbing food as were possessed by their distant relatives the mysticetae, or toothless whales.

With a view to avoiding any such disaster they made good use of their jaws, having been taught by experience that the simple but effectual penalty for the neglect of any function, whether physical or mental, was the disappearance of the organs whereby such functions had been performed. But their energetic use of teeth and jaws had a result entirely unforeseen by them. Gradually the prey they sought, the larger fish and smaller sea-mammals, disappeared from the shallow seas adjacent to the land from whence the whales had been driven. And in order to satisfy the demands of their huge stomachs they were fain to follow their prey into deeper and deeper waters, meeting as they went with other and stranger denizens of those mysterious depths, until at last the sperm whale met the kraken. There in his native gloom, vast, formless, and insatiable, brooded the awful Thing. Spread like a living net whereof every mesh was armed, sensitive and lethal, this fantastic complication of horrors took toll of all the sea-folk, needing not to pursue its prey, needing only to lie still, devour, and grow. Sometimes, moved by mysterious impulses, one of these chimeras would rise to the sea-surface and bask in the beams of the offended sun, poisoning the surrounding air with its charnel-house odours, and occasionally finding within the never-resting, nervous clutching of its tentacles some specimens of the highest, latest product of Creation, man himself. Ages of such experiences as these had left the kraken defenceless as to his body. The absence of any necessity for exertion had arrested the development of a backbone; the inability of any of the sea-people to retaliate upon their sateless foe had made him neglect any of those precautions that weaker organisms had provided themselves with; and even the cloud of sepia with which all the race were provided, and which often assisted the innocent and weaker members of the same great family to escape, was only used by these masters of the sea to hide their monstrous lures from their prey.

Thus on a momentous day a ravenous sperm whale, hunting eagerly for wherewithal to satisfy his craving, suddenly found himself encircled by many long, cable-like arms. They clung, they tore, they sucked. But whenever a stray end of them flung itself across the bristling parapet of the whale's lower jaw it was promptly bitten off, and, a portion having found its way down into the craving stomach of the big mammal, it was welcomed as good beyond all other food yet encountered. Once this had been realized, what had originally been an accidental entrapping changed itself into a vigorous onslaught and banquet. True, the darkness fought for the mollusc, but that advantage was small compared with the feeling of incompetence, of inability to make any impression upon this mighty, impervious mass that was moving as freely amid the clinging embarrassments of those hitherto invincible arms as if they were only fronds of seaweed. And then the foul mass of the kraken found itself, contrary to all previous experience, rising involuntarily, being compelled to leave its infernal shades, and without any previous preparation for such a change of pressure to visit the upper air. The fact was that the whale, finding its stock of air exhausted, had put forth a supreme effort to rise, and found that although unable to free himself from those enormous cables he was actually competent to raise the whole mass. What an upheaval! Even the birds that, allured by the strong carrion scent, were assembling in their thousands fled away from that appalling vision, their wild screams of affright filling the air with lamentation. The tormented sea foamed and boiled in wide-spreading whirls, its deep sweet blue changed into an unhealthy nondescript tint of muddy yellow. Then the whale, having renewed his store of air, settled down seriously to the demolition of his prize. Length after length of tentacle was torn away from the central crown and swallowed, gliding down the abysmal throat of the gratified mammal in snaky convolutions until even his great store-room would contain no more.

The vanquished kraken lay helplessly rolling upon the wave, while its conqueror in satisfied ease lolled near watching with good-humoured complacency the puny assaults made upon that island of gelatinous flesh by the multitude of smaller hungry things. The birds returned reassured, and added by their clamour to the strangeness of the scene where the tribes of air and sea, self-bidden to the enormous banquet, were making full use of their exceptional privilege. So the great feast continued, while the red sun went down and the white moon rose in placid beauty. Yet, for all the combined assaults of those hungry multitudes, the tenacious life of that largest of living things lay so deeply seated that when the rested whale resumed his attentions he found the body of his late antagonist still quivering under the attack of his tremendous jaws. Still, its proportions were so immense that his utmost efforts left store sufficient for at least a dozen of his companions, had they been there, to have satisfied their hunger upon. And satisfied at last he turned away, allowing the smaller fry, who had waited his pleasure most respectfully, to close in again and finish the work he had so well begun.

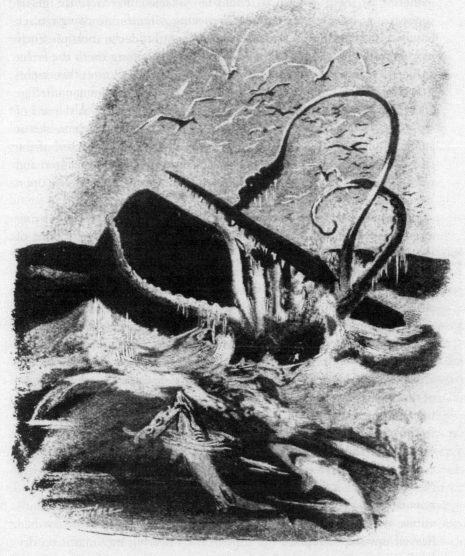

The whale settled down seriously to the demolition of his prize

Now this was a momentous discovery indeed. For the sperm whales had experienced, even when fish and seals were plentiful, great difficulty in procuring sufficient food at one time for a full meal, and the problem of how to provide for themselves as they grew and multiplied had become increasingly hard to solve. Therefore, this discovery filled the fortunate pioneer with triumph, for his high instincts told him that he had discovered a new source of supply that promised to be inexhaustible. So, in the manner common to his people, he wasted no time in convening a gathering of them as large as could be collected. Far over the glassy surface of that quiet sea lay gently rocking a multitude of vast black bodies, all expectant, all awaiting the momentous declaration presently to be made. The epoch-making news circulated among them in perfect silence, for to them has from the earliest times been known the secret that is only just beginning to glimmer upon the verge of human intelligence, the ability to communicate with one another without the aid of speech, sight, or touch: a kind of thought-transference, if such an idea as animal thought may be held allowable. And having thus learned of the treasures held in trust for them by the deep waters, they separated and went, some alone and some in compact parties of a dozen or so, upon their rejoicing way.

But among the slimy hosts of the gigantic mollusca there was raging a sensation unknown before: a feeling of terror, of insecurity born of the knowledge that at last there had appeared among them a being proof against the utmost pressure of their awful arms, who was too great to be devoured; who on the other hand had evinced a greedy partiality for devouring them. How this information became common property among them it is impossible to say, since they dwelt alone each in his own particular lair, rigidly respected by one another, because any intrusion upon another's domains was invariably followed by the absorption of either the intruder or the intruded upon by the stronger of the two. This, although not intended by them, had the effect of vastly heightening the fear with which they were regarded by the smaller sea-folk, for they took to a restless prowling along the sea-bed, enwreathing themselves about the mighty bases of the islands and invading cool, coral caverns where their baleful presence had been till then unknown. Never before had there been such a panic among the multitudinous sea-populations. What could this new portent signify? Were the foundations of the great deep again about to be broken up and the sea-bed heaved upward to replace the tops of the towering mountains on dry land? There was no reply, for there were none that could answer questions like these.

Still the fear-smitten decapods wandered, seeking seclusion from the coming enemy and finding none to their mind. Still the crowds of their victims rushed blindly from shoal to shoal, plunging into depths unfitted for them, or rising into shallows where their natural food was not. And the whole sea was troubled. Until at last there appeared, grim and vast, the advance-guard of the sperm whales and hurled themselves with joyful anticipation upon the shrinking convolutions of those hideous monsters that had so long dominated the dark places of the sea.

For the whales it was a time of feasting hitherto without parallel. Without any fear, uncaring to take even the most elementary precautions against a defeat which they felt to be an impossible contingency, they sought out and devoured one after another of these vast uglinesses, already looked upon by them as their natural provision, their store of food accumulated of purpose against their coming. Occasionally, it is true, some rash youngster, full of pride and rejoicing in his pre-eminence over all life in the depths, would hurl himself into a smoky network of far-spreading tentacles, which would wrap him round so completely that his jaws were fast bound together, his flukes would vainly essay to propel him anywhither, and he would presently perish miserably, his cable-like sinews falling slackly and his lungs suffused with crimson brine. Even then, the advantage gained by the triumphant kraken was a barren one, for in every case the bulk of the victim was too great, his body too firm in its build for the victor, despite his utmost efforts, to succeed in devouring his prize. So that the disappointed kraken had perforce to witness the gradual disappearance of his lawful prize beneath the united efforts of myriads of tiny sea-scavengers, secure in their insignificance against any attack from him, and await with tremors extending to the remotest extremity of every tentacle the retribution which, he felt sure, would speedily follow.

This desultory warfare was waged for long until, driven by despair to a community of interest unknown before, the krakens gradually sought one another out with but a single idea – that of combining against the new enemy. For, knowing to what an immense size their kind could attain in the remoter fastnesses of ocean, they could not yet bring themselves to believe that they were to become the helpless prey of these newcomers, visitors of yesterday, coming from the cramped acreage of the land into the limitless fields of ocean, and invading the immemorial freeholds of its hitherto unassailable sovereigns.

From the remotest recesses of ocean they came, that grisly gathering, came in ever-increasing hosts, their silent progress spreading unprecedented dismay among the fairer inhabitants of the sea. Figure to yourselves, if you can, the advance of this terrible army! But the effort is vain. Not even Martin, that frenzied delineator of the frightful halls of Hell, the terrors of the Apocalypse, and the agonies of the Deluge, could have done justice to the terrors of such a picture. Only dimly can we imagine what must have been the appearance of those vast masses of writhing flesh, as through the palely gleaming phosphorescence of those depths they sped backwards in leaps of a hundred fathoms each, their terrible arms, close clustered together, streaming behind them like Medusa's hair magnified ten thousand times in size, and with each snaky tress bearing a thousand mouths instead of one.

So they converged upon the place of meeting – an area of the sea-bed nowhere more than 500 fathoms in depth, from whose rugged floor rose irregularly stupendous columnar masses of lava, hurled upwards by the cosmic forces below in a state of incandescence, and solidified as they rose, assuming many fantastic shapes and affording perfect harbourage to such dire scourges of the sea as were now making the place their rendez-vous. For, strangely enough, this marvellous portion of the submarine world was more densely peopled with an infinite variety of sea folk than any other. Its tepid waters seemed to bring forth abundantly of all kinds of fish, crustacea, and creeping things. Sharks in all their fearsome varieties prowled greasily about scenting for dead things whereon to gorge; shell-fish, from the infinitesimal globigerina up to the gigantic tridacna, whose shells were a yard each in diameter; crabs, lobsters, and other freakish varieties of crustacea of a size and ugliness unknown to-day lurked in every crevice, while about and among all these scavengers flitted the happy, lovely fish in myriads of glorious hues, matching the tender shades of the coral groves that sprang from the summits of those sombre pillars beneath. Hitherto this happy hunting-ground had not been invaded by the sea-mammals. None of the air-breathing inhabit-ants of the ocean had ventured into its gloomy depths or sought their prey among the blazing shallows of the surface reefs, although no more favourable place for their exertions could possibly have been selected over all the wide seas. It had long been a favourite haunt of the kraken, for whom it was, as aforesaid, an ideal spot; but now it was to witness a sight unparalleled in ocean history. Heralded by an amazing series of under waves, the gathering of monsters grew near. They numbered many thousands, and no one in all their hosts was of lesser magnitude than sixty feet long by thirty in girth of body alone. From that size they increased until some, the acknowledged leaders, discovered themselves like islands, their cylindrical carcasses huge as that of an ocean liner and their ten-tacles capable of overspreading an entire village.

In concentric rings they assembled, all heads pointing outward, the mightiest within, and four clear avenues through the circles left for coming and going. Contrary to custom, but by mutual consent, all the tentacles lay closely arranged in parallel lines, not outspread to every quarter of the compass and all a-work. They looked indeed in their inertia and silence like nothing so much as an incalculable number of dead squid of enormous size neatly laid out at the whim of some giant's fancy. Yet communication between them was active, a subtle interchange of experiences and plans went briskly on through the medium of the mobile element around them. The elder and mightier were full of disdain at the reports they were furnished with, utterly incredulous as to the ability of any created thing to injure them, and as the time wore on an occasional tremor was distinctly noticeable through the whole length of their tentacles which boded no good to their smaller brethren. Doubtless but little longer was needed for the development of a great absorption of the weaker by the stronger, only that darting into their midst like a lightning streak came a messenger squid bearing the news that a school of sperm whales numbering at least a thousand were coming at top-speed direct for their place of meeting. Instantly to the farthest confines of that mighty gathering the message radiated, and as if by one movement there uprose from the sea-bed so dense a cloud of sepia that for many miles around the clear bright blue of the ocean became turbid, stagnant, and foul. Even the birds that hovered over those dark-brown waves took fright at this terrible phenomenon, to them utterly incomprehensible, and with discordant shrieks they fled in search of sweeter air and cleaner sea. But below the surface, under cover of this thickest darkness, there was the silence of death.

Twenty miles away, under the bright sunshine, an advance guard of about a hundred sperm whales came rushing on. Line abreast, their bushy breath rising like the regular steam-jets from a row of engines, they dashed aside the welcoming wavelets, every sense alert and full of eagerness for the consummation of their desires. Such had been their dispatch that throughout the long journey of 500 leagues they had not once stayed for food, so that they were ravenous with hunger as well as full of fight. They passed, and before the foaming of their swift passage had ceased the main body, spread over a space of thirty miles, came following on, the roar of their multitudinous march sounding like the voice of many waters.

Suddenly the advance guard, with stately elevation of the broad fans of their flukes, disappeared, and by one impulse the main body followed them. Down into the depths they bore, noting with dignified wonder the absence of all the usual inhabitants of the deep until, with a thrill of joyful anticipation which set all their masses of muscle a-quiver, they recognised the scent of the prey. No thought of organized resistance presented itself; without a halt or even the faintest slackening of their great rush they plunged forward into the abysmal gloom; down, down withal into that wilderness of waiting demons. And so, in darkness and silence like that of the beginning of things, this great battle was joined. Whale after whale succumbed, anchored to the bottom by such bewildering entanglements, such enlacement of tentacles that their vast strength was helpless to free them, their jaws were bound hard together, and even the wide sweep of their flukes gat no hold upon the slimy water. But the decapods were in evil case. Assailed from above while their groping arms writhed about below they found themselves more often locked in unreleasable hold of their fellows than they did of their enemies. And the quick-shearing jaws of those foes shredded them into fragments, made nought of their bulk, revelled and frolicked among them, slaying, devouring, exulting. Again and again the triumphant mammals drew off for air and from satiety, went and lolled upon the sleek, oily surface in water now so thick that the fiercest hurricane that ever blew would have failed to raise a wave thereon.

So through a day and a night the slaying ceased not, except for these brief interludes, until those of the decapods left alive had disentangled themselves from the *débris* of their late associates and returned with what speed they might to depths and crannies where they fondly hoped their ravenous enemies could never come. Henceforth they were no longer lords of the sea; instead of being as hitherto devourers of all things living that crossed the radius of their outspread toils, they were now and for all time to be the prey of a nobler creation, a higher order of being, and at last they had taken their rightful position as creatures of usefulness in the vast economy of Creation.

Three Go Back

To

R. L. Mégroz

My dear Mégroz,
I wrote this novel as a holiday from more serious things and in dedicating it to
such distinguished critic as yourself might be guilty of some temerity were it not
for the fact that convention will forbid you reviewing me. But though this may
be my loss I hope it will not be your gain!

You've impressed on me that a novel should need neither footnote nor fore-
note. I agree – and happily escape the reproach of either by embodying their
contents in the dedication.

First, the continent where Clair and Sinclair and Sir John adventure: many
respectworthy people in all ages have professed to find the ocean shores littered
with proofs of its one-time existence.

The litter leaves me unconvinced.

Secondly, the character and characteristics here and elsewhere ascribed to the
'grey beasts': There is not a scrap of proof that the 'grey beasts' were ferocious and
gorilla-like; for that matter, and to employ a very just Irishism, there is not a
shred of evidence that the gorilla in his native haunts behaves in the least like
a gorilla.

But though these two apparent fictions, continental and temperamental, are
employed for dramatic effect, they have no direct bearing on the main theme and
contention of the story, which seem to me quite unassailable.

And with these cautions I pass you the book in company with my gratitude and
good wishes. May you like the reading of it as much as I enjoyed the writing!

Yours,

J. LESLIE MITCHELL

London, 1932

CONTENTS

Book One: Where? When?

Chapter 1 The wreck of *Magellan's Cloud*

Chapter 2 The survivors

Chapter 3 In an unknown land

Chapter 4 The lair

Chapter 5 And I'll take the low road

Chapter 6 The hunters

Chapter 7 A slip in the time-spirals

Chapter 8 A lover for the dark days

Chapter 9 Sir John a prophet: his prophecy

Chapter 10 Exodus

Book Two: Whence? Whither?

Chapter 1 Clair lost

Chapter 2 A light in the south

Chapter 3 All our yesterdays

Chapter 4 Now sleeps the crimson petal

Chapter the last: I shall rise again

BOOK ONE

Where? When?

And if you conquer the air, and if you
compass the earth,
It will not sweeten your death, and it will
not better your birth,
And though you out-distance the swallow,
with a song of pride in your mouth,
What if you barter your soul for speed —
and forget the way to the South?

OLAF BAKER

CHAPTER ONE
The wreck of Magellan's Cloud

Subchapter i

A skyey monster, cobalt and azure-blue, it sailed out of the heat-haze that all morning had been drifting westwards from the Bay of Biscay. It startled the crew of the Rio tramp and there was a momentary scurry of grimy off-watches reaching the deck, and a great upward gape of astounded eyes and mouths. Then the second engineer, a knowledge-able man and discreet in friendship with the wireless operator, voiced explanations.

'It'll be the airship *Magellan's Cloud* on her return voyage.'

The Third spat, not disparagingly, but because the fumes of the engine-room were still in his throat. 'Where to?'

'Man, you're unco ignorant. Noo York. She's been lying off for weather at Paris nearly a week, Sparks says. Twenty o' a crew and twenty passen-gers – they'll be payin' through the nose, I'll warrant . . . There's Sparks gabblin' at her.'

A subdued buzz and crackle. A tapping that presently ceased. High up against a cloudless sky, the airship quivered remoter in the Atlantic sun-shine. The Third spat again, forgetfully.

'Pretty thing,' he said.

The Rio tramp chugged north-eastwards. One or two of the crew still stood on deck, watching the aerial *voyageur* blend with the August sun-haze and the bubble walls of seascape till it disappeared.

And that was the last their world ever saw of the airship *Magellan's Cloud.*

Subchapter ii

Clair Stranlay could not forget her lover who had died on the wire out-side Mametz.

A series of chance encounters and casual conversations overheard had filled out in tenebrous vignettes each letter of the cryptic notice, Killed in Action. He had died very slowly and reluctantly, being a boy and anxious to live, and unaware that civilization has its prices . . . And at intervals, up into the coming of the morning, they had heard him calling in delirium: 'Clair! *Oh, Clair!*'

Fourteen years ago. And still a look, a book, a word could set in motion the little discs of memory in her mind, and his voice, in its own timbre and depth and accent, would come ringing to her across the years in that cry of agony . . . She thought, stirring from the verge of sleep in her chair of the *Magellan's* deserted passenger lounge: 'What on earth made me think of that now?'

' . . . no, madam, quite definitely I've nothing to say about my deportation from Germany.'

'Oh, please, Dr Sinclair, *do* give your side of the case. Just a par. I'm Miss Kemp of the C.U.P., you know, and it would be rather a scoop for me. Shame to miss it.'

'I've nothing to say. And I'll be obliged if you'll stop pestering me.'

'Oh, *very* well.'

An angry staccato of heel-taps broke out and approached. Clair, deep in her basket-chair, saw the doorway to the swinging gallery blind for a moment its glimpse of ultramarine skyscape. Miss Kemp, short, sandy, stocky, stood with flushed face, biting her lips inelegantly. Then, catching sight of Clair, she came across the cabin in her religiously-acquired svelte-glide. Clair thought, with an inward groan: 'Oh, my good God, now I *am* in for it.'

She closed her eyes, as if dozing. Unavailingly. The near basket-chair creaked under the ample, svelte-moulded padding of Miss Kemp.

'Hear me try the beast? You're not asleep, are you? I saw your eyes open . . . Hear me tackle him? Hope I'm not disturbing you . . . Beast. Hear his answers? But I'll give him a write-up that'll make him and his precious league squirm, though. Dirty deportee.'

'Dirty what?' Clair opened reluctant eyes.

'Deportee. Haven't you heard of him?'

'Quite likely. Who is he?'

'Why, Keith Sinclair, the agitator who's been travelling about Europe organizing the League of Militant Pacifists. Says that another war's inevitable with the present drift of things and that it's up to the common people to organize and shoot down or assassinate their militarists and politicians at the first hint of it.'

'Sounds logical,' Clair thought: 'And I hope I sound bored enough . . . No result? Oh, well.' Aloud: 'And what happened?'

'Haven't you heard? He was kicked out of Italy a month ago and deported from Germany last week.'

'What fun. And where's he going now?'

'Beast. To gaol, I hope. Returning to America in a hurry to attend some demonstration in Boston.' Miss Kemp's chair creaked its relief as she rose. 'Hear that Sir John Mullaghan's on board?'

'I'm awfully weak on the auricular verb . . . Never heard of him at all.'

'Oh, you *must* have. Awfully important. Conservative M.P. Head of the armaments people. I'm off to get his opinion of the trip. Rather amusing, you know; he and Sinclair have met before.'

'Have they?'

'Didn't you hear? Awful shindy. Sir John was making a speech at some place in Berlin. Said there would always be wars and that honest men prepared for them. Sinclair stood up in the audience and interrupted and started a speech on his own. Told them things he'd seen on the Western Front when he served there as a doctor with the Canadians. Sickening things; he's a beast. Women began screaming and some were carried out fainting . . . Ended up by saying that the obvious duty of the British public was to cut Sir John Mullaghan's throat, and the Germans to hamstring Frau Krupp . . . Police had to interfere, and that led to his deportation. Sinclair's, I mean. Wonder if Sir John knows he's on board the *Magellan*?'

'I haven't heard.'

'*Will* be a scoop if they say anything when they meet. Did you hear – oh, there's Sir John crossing to the steering cabin. I'll get him now.'

Clair cautiously raised the eyelids below her pencilled brows. Like talking to the bound files of the *News Chronicle*.

The lounge was empty, the passengers in their cabins or on the galleries. Miss Kemp's high-heeled footfalls receded . . . Blessed relief. Please God, why did you make Miss Kemps?

Clair closed her eyes again, and remembered with a drowsy twinge of amusement various gossip paragraphs in the less sanitary weeklies. Inspired by Miss Kemp. No doubt as to the inspirer . . . What had they been?

WE'D LOVE TO KNOW –

If it's true a certain lady novelist acquires a new 'lover for life' with every fresh novel she writes?

If she's made this *clair* to the seventh successor in the rôle?

And if London isn't rather tired of both her literary and personal promiscuities?

Poor Miss Kemp! That had been the case of Gilbert Trolden she'd heard of and exploited at half-a-crown a par. And poor Gilbert with his desperately respectable sins – how the pars had shocked him! Almost burst his bootlaces. Didn't realize Miss Kemp must live, or that he himself suffered from quite as many pitiful spites and repressions as the journalist . . . That article in *Literary Portraits* had been sheer claw, however.

BEST-SELLER FROM THE SLUMS

Miss Clair Stranlay, whose real name is Elsie Moggs . . . born in a tenement house in Battersea . . . best-seller in England and America . . . Mr Justice Melhuish, delivering judgment in the case of her banned novel, *Night on Sihor*, said: 'It is obscene and unclean . . . '

Most of it true enough, of course. Except for the Elsie Moggs bit. A bad mix-up that on Miss Kemp's part when searching out antecedents in Thrush Road. She'd missed the story of how fond Stranlay *mère* had been of novelettes – even to the extent of christening her daughter out of one of them . . .

Romance! Romance that had beckoned so far away beyond the kindly poverty of Thrush Road!

'My dear girl, you came this voyage for rest, not reminiscence. Now's your time.'

But not even the *Magellan's* soothing motion could recapture that drowsiness from which the sound of Miss Kemp's attempted interviewing has evicted her. She thought, with a laggard curiosity: 'Wonder if the Sinclair man is the one with the beard and false front who ate so hard at lunch? Throat-cutting is probably hungry work. Let's look.'

And, as idly as that, she was afterwards to reflect, she stood up and strolled out of the *Magellan's* lounge and out of the twentieth century.

Subchapter iii
Below her, trellis-work of wood and aluminium, and, in the interstices, the spaces of the sun-flooded ocean. The beat of the engines astern sounded remote and muffled. There was not a cloud.

Then, raising her eyes, she saw Keith Sinclair for the first time. He turned with blown hair at the moment, glanced at her uninterestedly, looked away, looked back again. He scowled at her with the sun in his eyes.

He saw a woman who might have been anything from twenty-five to thirty years of age, and who, as a matter of data, was thirty-three. She was taller than most men liked, with that short-cut, straight brown hair which has strands and islets of red in it. And, indeed, that red spread to her eyelashes, which were very long, though Sinclair did not discover this until afterwards, and to her eyes, which had once been blue before the gold-red came into them. Nose and chin, said Sinclair's mind methodically, very good, both of them. She can breathe, which is something. Half the women alive suffer from tonsilitis. But that mouth . . . And he definitely disapproved of the pursed, long-lipped mouth in the lovely face – the mouth stained scarlet with cochineal.

'Weather keeping up,' said Clair, helpfully.

He said: 'Yes.' She thought: 'My dear man, I don't want to interview you. Only to collect you as a comic character. Sorry you haven't that beard.'

Nearly six feet three inches in height, too long in the leg and too short in the body. All his life, indeed, there had been something of the impatient colt in his appearance. He had a square head and grey eyes set very squarely in it; high cheek-bones, black hair, and the bleached white hands of his craft. Those hands lay on the gallery railing now.

'Wish I could go and smoke somewhere,' said Clair.

'So do I.'

'A little ambiguous.' He stared rudely. Clair said, suddenly: 'Goodness!' Startled, they both raised their heads.

The metal stays below their feet had swung upwards and downwards, with a soggy swish of imprisoned lubricant. The whole airship had shuddered and for a moment had seemed to pause, so to speak, in its stride. Sinclair leant over the gallery railing.

'Hell, look at the sea.'

Clair looked. The Atlantic was boiling. Innumerable maelstroms were rising from the depths, turning even in that distance below them from blue-green to white, creamed white, and then, in widening ripples, to dark chocolate . . . Clair felt a kindly prick of interest in the performance.

'What's causing it?'

The American was silent for a moment, regarding the Atlantic with a scowl of surprise. He said: 'Impossible.'

'What is?'

'I said impossible.' He brushed past her towards the doorway of the lounge. Paused. 'See the dark chocolate?'

Clair nodded, regarding him with a faint amusement.

'Well, don't you see it must have come from the bottom?'

'So it must.' She peered down again. 'And it's deep here, isn't it?'

'Perhaps a couple of miles.' He disappeared.

News of the submarine earthquake spread quickly enough. Passengers crowded the galleries, Miss Kemp coming to the side of Clair in some excitement. Another passenger, the inescapable portrait-hound, appeared with a camera of unbelievable price and intricacy, and snapshotted the Atlantic closely and severely. From the flashing of lens in the gallery of the engine-house it was obvious that a member of the crew was similarly engaged.

'The chocolate's dying away,' said Clair Stranlay.

So it was. The Atlantic had reassumed its natural hue. The maelstroms had vanished, or the airship had passed beyond the locality where they still uprose. For, after that first shudder, the *Magellan's Cloud* had held on her way unfalteringly. The snapshotter beside Clair wrinkled a puzzled brow.

'Very strange. I could have sworn there was a ship down there to the south only a minute or so ago. It's disappeared . . . Quick going.'

The airship beat forward into the waiting evening. Sky and sea were as before. But presently there gathered in the west such polychrome splendour of sunset as the *Magellan's* commander, who had crossed the Atlantic many times by ship, had never before observed.

And suddenly, inexplicably, it grew amazingly cold.

Subchapter iv

The airship's wireless operator fumed over dials and board, abandoned the instrument, went out into the miniature crow's nest that overhung his cabin, glanced about him, and beat his hands together in the waft of icy air that chilled them.

'Damn funny,' he commented.

He went back to his cabin and rang up the *Magellan's* commander. The latter had donned the only overcoat he had brought on board and was discussing the weather with the navigator when the wireless operator's voice spoke in his ear.

'Is that you, sir?'

'Yes.'

'I'm sorry, but it seems impossible to send that message.'

'Eh?'

'I thought there was some fault in the set. I've been sitting here for the last two and a half hours trying to tap in on France or a ship. There's no message come through. I've sent out yours, but there's been no reply.'

The commander was puzzled. 'That's strange, Gray. Sure your instrument is functioning all right?'

'Certain, sir. I've broadcast to the receiving apparatus in the passengers' lounge and they heard perfectly.'

'Damn funny. Get it right as soon as you can, will you?'

'But . . . right, sir.'

The commander put down the telephone and turned to give the news to the navigator. They were in the steering cage and it was just after eight o'clock. But the navigator, instead of standing by with his usual stolid expressionlessness, was at the far end of the cage, staring upwards fascinatedly.

'Gray says the infernal wireless has gone out of order. Bright look-out if we go into fog over the banks . . . Hello, anything wrong?'

'Come here, Commodore.'

The commander crossed to the navigator's side. The latter pointed up to a darkling sky which, ever since the sudden fall of temperature, had been adrift with a multitude of cloudlets like the débris of a feather-bed. The commander peered upwards ineffectually.

'Well, what is it?'

'Look. Up there.'

'Only the moon. Well?'

'Well, it's only the 22nd of the month. The new moon, in its first quarter, isn't due till the 27th. And that one's gibbous.'

'Good Christopher!'

They both stared at the sky through the lattice of airship wire, amazed, half-convinced that some trick was being played upon them. From behind the clouds the moon was indeed emerging, round and wind-flushed and full. It sailed the sky serenely, five days ahead of time, taking stock of this other occupant of its firmament. The *Magellan's* commander brought his glasses to bear on it. It appeared to be the same moon.

'But it's impossible. The calendar must be wrong.'

'The only thing possibly wrong is the date. And it's not – as of course we know. Look, here's today's *Matin*.'

He showed it. It was dated the 22nd.

The airship *Magellan's Cloud* beat forward into the growing radiance of moonlight which had mysteriously obliterated the last traces of the day.

Subchapter v

Looking out from his cabin window as he prepared to undress and go to bed, the American, Keith Sinclair, was startled. He was aware that it had grown intensely cold, as indeed was every soul on board the *Magellan's Cloud*, whether on duty or in bed. But now his gaze revealed to him the fact that the airship's hull was silvered with frost in the moonlight. Frost at this altitude in August?

For a moment he accepted the moonlight. And then, standing in the soft hush-hush of the flexible airship walls, realization of the impossibility of that moon came on him, as it had done on the navigator.

'Now how the devil did you come to be there?'

The moon, sailing a sky that was now quite clear, cloudless and star-less, made no answer. The notorious deportee whistled a little, remembering a Basque story heard from his mother – of how the sun one morning had risen in the semblance of the moon . . . But that didn't help. It wasn't nearly morning yet. And it was an indubitable moon.

Still whistling, he felt his pulse, and, as an after-thought, took his temperature. Both were normal. Meanwhile, the cold increased. Sinclair pulled open his cabin door.

'Look up the navigator again. He had precious little explanation of that submarine earthquake, but the moon's beyond ignoring.'

But, crossing the lounge, glimpse of the dark seascape beyond the open door drew him out on the passengers' gallery. There it was even colder, though there was no gale. The ship was travelling at a low altitude. Below, smooth, vast and unhurrying, the rollers of the Atlantic passed out of the near sheen of moonlight into the dimness astern . . . Abruptly Sinclair became aware that the gallery had another occupant.

Clair Stranlay; in pyjamas, slippers, and wrap. Intent on the night and the sea. But, imagining for a moment that she had air-sickness, the American groped along the handrail towards her.

'Feel ill?'

She started. 'What? Dr Sinclair, isn't it? I'm quite well.'

'You'll be down with pneumonia if you stay here.'

She thought: 'You must be a blood relation of the Irish policeman – "You'll have to be moving on if you're going to be standing here." But I'd better not say so. Thrush Road imperence, Miss Kemp would diagnose it.' Aloud: 'Don't think so. I do winter bathing and icy baths. What's happened?'

'The cold?'

'Yes.'

'Early bergs down from the north, I suppose.'

'But it's not nearly the season yet.'

He had seen something in the moonlight below them. He caught her arm. Clair brushed the short, red-tipped hair from her face with one hand, clung to the handrail with the other, and looked down.

Out of the deserted Atlantic was emerging what appeared to be an immense berg – a sailing of cragged, shapeless greyness upon the water. The moonlight struck wavering bands of radiance from it, and for a moment, in some trick of refraction, it glowed a pearled blue as though lighted from within. It passed underfoot, and as it passed a beam of light shot down from the navigating cabin, played upon it, passed, returned, hesitated, hovered, was abruptly extinguished.

But not so quickly that the two occupants of the passengers' gallery failed to see an accretion such as no iceberg ever bore. For beyond the berg had showed up a long, sandy beach, and beyond that the vague suggestion, a mere limning in the moon-dusk, of a flat and comber-washed island.

Sinclair swore, unimpassioned. 'I'm going to find out about this. Are we making for the Pole?'

Clair, to her own amusement, found herself shaking with excitement. 'But what could it have been? There are no islands on the France-New York track.'

'We've just seen one. I'm going to find out what the navigating cabin knows about it. Unless we're Pole-bound – and that's nonsense – the submarine earthquake may have thrown it up.'

'It must have done other things as well, then.' Clair began to stamp her feet to warmth. The rest of her felt only the glow of well-being that falling temperatures nowadays gifted her unfailingly as guerdon for much braving of wintry dips. 'Haven't you noticed something entirely missing from the sea – even though this is the crowded season?'

'What?' He sounded impatient.

'Ship-lights. Not one has shown up since sunset.'

'Who said so?'

'One of the riggers I spoke to just now.'

She saw, dimly, his puzzled scowl, and thought, with the unfailing Cockney imp for prompter: 'Disapproving of the Atlantic again!'

He said: 'The submarine 'quake we saw couldn't have affected shipping. It was quite localized. If it had caused great damage the wireless bulletins they post in the lounge would have told us.'

'Don't they?'

The same thought occurred to them simultaneously. Clinging to the handrail, she followed Sinclair into the cabin. The case with wireless transcriptions was hung against the further wall. They crossed to it, looked at it, and then looked at each other. Clair's face close to his, a flushed and lovely and easily-controlled face, he found for a moment irritatingly disconcerting.

No notices had been posted since five o'clock in the afternoon.

'Look here, Miss – '

'Stranlay.'

'Stranlay, I'm going to find out about things. Something extraordinary seems to have happened. But if any of the other passengers come out, don't alarm them.'

Clair shook her head, regarding him with upraised brows. 'Much too.'

'Eh?'

'Dictatorial . . . And I alarm people only in my books.'

'Oh. Do you write?'

'Novels.'

'Oh. I'd go to bed if I were you. I'll tap on your cabin door and let you know what I hear.'

Fortunate she hadn't seen anything peculiar in the moonlight itself . . .

Passing through the hull, he stopped at a window and himself noted another happening.

The moonlight was pouring lengthwise into the long hull of *Magellan's Cloud*, not striking due in front, as a moment before.

The airship had turned southwards.

Subchapter vi

Clair Stranlay arrived in her cabin meditating the deportee from Germany. And, looking out at the far, moon-misted horizon of the Atlantic, she thought: 'He'd never heard of me! Publicity, where are thy charms? . . . Any more than I of him. But how desperately important folk we are to ourselves!' She yawned. 'Must insert that reflection in my next serial. It can't have been used in more than a million novels already.'

And, because that Cockney insouciance of Battersea days seldom deserted her, and she had long ceased to feel even mildly vexed that there lived a world which devoured not best-sellers, she forgot the matter. She slipped out of wrap and pyjamas, rubbed her white and comely self until she felt warm and pringling and the possessor of an altogether enjoyable body. A spearbeam of moonlight splashed on her shoulder and she raised her head, with the red lights in her hair, and looked at it. She put up her hand.

'The blessed thing feels almost cold.'

Something quite extraordinary had happened to the *Magellan's Cloud*. But what? Delay it much reaching New York?

'Oh, my good God!' sighed Clair, getting into bed.

For, escaping England and boredom to go and lecture in America, the awfulness of the ennui, hitherto concealed, that lay awaiting her appalled her. The shore. Miles and miles of ferro-concrete, macadam, pelting rush and automobilist slither. Packing of clothes – scanty though they were. Mooring mast. Elevator. Customs shed. Forms. Beefy officials. Forms. 'Are you an atheist or anarchist?' Solemn no, instead of writing, as the spirit always moved her, 'Yes, both, and then some.' Auto. Becky Meadow's house. Literary gathering. Stylists (accent on the sty). Prudent pornographers. Platform. Brisk skittishness with tiredness commingled –

correct best-seller attitude. Husky American voices stilling. 'The New Schools in England.' Woof, woof, woof. Woolf, Huxley. Blah, blah, blah. And rows and rows of eyes set in faces more like those of paralytic codfish than human beings – faces of women combed and powdered and bathed to excess, living hungrily on the mean grubbing and sweating of mean and shrivelled hes. Shes! Oh, my good God, the shes of the world!

And, thinking of them, Clair's mind-mask of insouciance, brittle and bright, quivered and almost showered her soul with its flakes. Sometimes, indeed, it cracked and fell about her entirely, and she'd hear that boy on the wire outside Mametz, and her desperate distaste for her work, her lovers, her life and her century crescendoed in her heart into the cry of a prisoned, tortured thing . . .

'Oh, forget it. The mess of our lives! Civilization! Ragged automata or lopsided slitherers. Our filthy concealments and our filthy cacklings when the drapings slip aside! Our hates, our loves – oh, my good God, your own loves, my dear! Better to have kept to the memory of the boy always, perhaps – and turned to a shrivelled virginal spite like the Kemp. Your lovers . . . Poor simulacra! Remember them? Sneak and strategy. Devotion. Starryeyedness. Thrill and masculinity . . . Instead of –

'What else? What else is there? Physical love or life – could there ever be anything very much better? For we're not human beings, of course. There was never such a thing as a human being. We're only apes repressing our blood-lusts and sex-lusts and God alone knows what unhygienic lusts – in the interests of feeding better! And the repressions'll grow and grow as we eliminate the beast entirely. Exit Tarzan . . . And when that's happened there won't be a codfish in a N'York audience but'll be an intelligent codfish, discussing hormones with its intimate hes. Utopia . . . See old Moore –'

But here Clair Stranlay found the blessedness of sleep now close upon her. Her body had lost its surface cold. She curled up her toes a little under the quilt – they were even, uncramped, and shapely toes – and sighed a little, and wished she could smoke a cigarette, and fell fast asleep – and was shot out of sleep five minutes later by a knock at the door of her cabin.

Subchapter vii
'Yes, come in,' she called, good-tempered even then; good temper had dogged her through life. Was it morning already and had they sighted New York?

But there was no daylight, only moonlight, entering the cabin window. She reached up to the switch and in the pallor of electric light looked at the American. Keith Sinclair, shutting the door, thought: 'Pretty thing' – a thought in the circumstances that was a considerable feat of detachment.

'About what's happened, Miss Stranlay – Can I sit down?'

'Can you?' said Clair, blinking her eyes and looking round the small cabin. Then, entirely awake, she solved the difficulty by drawing herself into the smallest space possible. 'Yes, do, here on the side of the bed. If anyone comes in you can be taking my temperature.' She put her hands behind her head and leant back comfortably.

The American grunted. 'It'll probably want taking when I've told you the news.' He brooded, his high cheek-boned face dourly thoughtful. 'We're in this together, in a fashion, I suppose, seeing we were the first to see the submarine 'quake. Well – the commander refuses to talk sense. Scared I alarm the others, I suppose. But he has to admit that no wireless messages have been received since the time of the submarine disturbance, though the apparatus of the *Magellan* appears to be perfectly in order. Also, he's turned the airship south.'

'South?' Clair's hands dropped from her neck at that. 'Then we're not making New York?'

'We're not' – grimly. 'We'll be lucky if we fetch up in Brazil at this rate.'

'Thank God,' said Clair.

'Eh?'

'Nothing. Not particularly anxious to reach New York. The codfish can wait . . . Sorry, I'm still half-asleep. Nice of you to come and tell me the news. Why has the *Magellan* turned south, then, and what does the captain say about that island with the berg we saw from the gallery?'

'Turned south because he's scared about the effect of the continued cold on the airship's envelope. I don't wonder, either. I met your garrulous rigger just now and he says we're carrying tons of ice. As for the island – the navigator says we're mistaken.'

'Astigmatism or booze?'

He grinned – a softening relaxation. ('Possibility that some day he'll laugh,' recorded Clair's imp.) He said: 'Neither in his case and both in ours, he seems to think. Truth of the matter is that the crew is as puzzled as we are, but they think if the passengers knew they'd blame them for all these extraordinary phenomena.' He considered his pyjama-jacketed listener for a moment. 'There's another thing, Miss Stranlay, which you didn't notice. The most serious of the lot, though the commander refuses to have anything said about it. It's the moon.'

'What has it done?'

'Arrived five days ahead of time. There shouldn't be a full moon for another fortnight; there shouldn't be a moon at all just now.'

Even Clair felt startled at that. 'But – that *is* the moon.'

He looked through the cabin window at it. 'It is.' He rubbed his chin impatiently. 'And it isn't . . . Eh?'

'I said: Clear as mud.'

'Oh. It's a thing not easy to explain.' He stood up. 'But I've a telescope with me – probably the most powerful magnifier on the *Magellan* – and I've had a peek at the moon through it. Just a minute.'

He was back in less. He opened the cabin window and poised the telescope on the ledge. Clair sat forward and looked through it.

'Keep both eyes open,' advised the American.

So she did, and for a moment was blinded in consequence. The moon was sinking. Stars were appearing, pallidly. Clair gazed across space. Then: 'Nothing very different, is it? I've looked at it through the big glass at Mount Wilson. Why – the nose!'

The Man in the Moon lacked a nose. Clair turned her face to Sinclair's moon-illumined one. He nodded.

'Exactly. That mountain-range on the moon is missing. Something is happening up there.'

She thought for a moment, caught a glimpse of a possible explanation. 'Then – the tides are caused by the moon. Mayn't that submarine earth-quake have been caused by the change in the moon?'

'Perhaps. I'm not an astronomer. But something abnormal *has* happened to the moon – both to her surface and her rate of revolution. The submarine earthquake we witnessed may have been the result. Probably it's had other effects in the far north – God knows what. Bringing down bergs and so forth.'

'And the wireless interruptions due to the same cause?' Clair lowered the telescope from her cabin-window in the *Magellan*. 'Most interesting thing I've seen for years. Pity we've explained it all so nicely.'

But, as they were later to learn, they were very far indeed from having explained it.

Subchapter viii

And presently, while Clair slept again and Sinclair tried to sleep (for his mind was vexing itself with notes for his Boston speech to the League of Militant Pacifists), and the commander sat peering at an almanac, and the navigator peered into the west – a pale shimmer of daylight arose in the east, lightening the surface of that strange Atlantic, flowing liquid almost as the Atlantic itself till it touched the southwards-hasting, high-slung cars of the *Magellan's Cloud*. A moment it lingered (as if puzzled) on that floating monster of the wastes, and then, abruptly, like a candle lighted for a hasty glimpse of the world by some uncertain archangel, was snuffed out . . . And the navigator from his gallery was shouting urgent directions into the engine-room telephone.

It is doubtful if they ever reached the engineers. For at that moment the nose of the *Magellan*, driving south at the rate of eighty miles an hour, rustled and crumpled up with a thin crack of metallic sheathing. The whole airship sang in every strut and girder, and, quivering like a stunned bird, still hung poised against the mountain-range that had arisen out of the darkness. The drumming roar roused to frantic life everyone on board, asleep or awake. Most of the passengers probably succeeded in leaving their beds, if not their cabins. On the lurching floors of these they may have glanced upwards and caught horrified glimpses of the next moment's happening.

The airship's hull spurted into bright flames, green-glowing, long-streaming in the darkness that had succeeded the false twilight. Then the whole structure broke apart, yet held together by the tendrils of the galleries and cabins, and, an agonized, mutilated thing, drew back from the mountainside and fell and flamed and fell again, unendingly, in two long circles, the while the morning came again, hasting across the sea, and the noise of that sea rose up and up and reached the ears of some on the *Magellan* . . .

And then suddenly the Atlantic yawned and hissed, while the dawn passed overhead and lighted the mountains and hastened into the west.

CHAPTER TWO

The survivors

Now, what happened to Clair Stranlay in that dawn-wrecking of the *Magellan's Cloud* was this.

The preliminary shock, when the nose of the airship drove into the mountain which had mysteriously arisen out of the spaces of the Atlantic, did not awaken her, though she twitched in dreams, and, indeed, may in dream have had a momentary startlement. She stirred uneasily, though still asleep, freeing her pretty arms from the quilt during the period that the *Magellan* hung, death-quivering, against her murderer. Then, abruptly, sight, hearing, and a variety of other sensations, were vouchsafed to her *fortissimo, crescendo.*

She heard the first explosion which shattered the hull of the airship, and leapt up in bed to see through the cabin window, phantasmagoric against a grey morning sky, the flare and belch of the flames. She sat stunned, uncomprehending, the while the floor of her cabin tilted and tilted and the metal-work creaked and warped. Then the cabin-door, a groaning, flare-illumined panel, was torn open, a figure shot in, crossed to Clair's bed and caught her with rough hands. It was the American deportee, Sinclair.

'Oh, my good God, he's been reading one of my novels,' thought Clair, as his hands touched her. It was the kind of thing the over-wrought hero always did when he couldn't abide the fact of the heroine sleeping alone any longer . . . She struggled, thinking: 'Shall I blacken his eye?' then ceased from that as, fully awake, she heard him shout: 'Come on, damn you! The ship's a flaming wreck . . . Clothes – some clothes!'

He swept a pile into his arms from the locker. Clair jumped from bed, plucked something – she could not see what it was – from the floor, and groped across the cabin after Sinclair. He tugged at the door. It had jammed. Now, out of the corridor, above the babel of sounds, one sound sharp-edged and clear came to them; a moan like that of trapped cattle. For a moment it rang in Clair's ears in all its horror, and then – the floor of the cabin vanished from beneath the feet of Sinclair and herself.

Below, the Atlantic.

And Clair thought 'Oh, God', and fell and fell, with a flaming comet in wavering pursuit. Till something that seemed like a red-hot dagger was thrust to the hilt into her body.

Subchapter ii

Breakers, and breakers again – the cry of them and the splash of them, and their salt taste stale in her mouth. In and in, and out with a slobbering surge. Water in pounding hill-slopes, green and white-crested. Pounding tons of water whelming over into those breakers . . . Clair Stranlay cried out and awoke.

'Better? I thought you'd gone . . . My God, look at the *Magellan*!'

Her body seemed wrapped in a sheet of fire that was a sheet of ice. She could not open her eyes. She tried again. They seemed fast-gummed. Then, abruptly, they opened. She moaned at the prick of the salt-grime.

She and Keith Sinclair were lying in a wide sweep of mountain-surrounded bay, on a beach of pebbles. Beyond and below them the sea was thundering. And out in the bay, a splendour like a fallen star, the *Magellan's Cloud* was flaming against a dark-grey, rainy sky momentarily growing lighter, as if the *Magellan* were serving as tinder to its conflagration.

This was not what Clair saw immediately. It was what she realized as she looked around her. Sinclair lay at right-angles to her, propped on his arm, vomiting sea-water in horrid recurring spasms of sickness.

Clair stared at him, sought for her voice, found it after an interval, manipulated it with stiff and painful lips.

'How did we get here?'

'Swam.' The American swayed to his knees. His high cheek-boned face looked as though the blood had been drained from it through a pipette. 'We hit the water before the *Magellan* did, and sank together. Came up clear of the wreck and I pulled you ashore . . . Oh, *damn* it!'

He was very sick indeed. There was an inshore-blowing wind, bitterly cold. With a shock Clair discovered she was dressed in her pyjamas only. Through those garments the rain-laden wind drove piercingly. It was laden now with other things than rain – adrift with red-glowing fragments of fluff, portions of the *Magellan's* fabric. The *Magellan*?

In that moment the airship blew up. A second Clair saw its great girders, like the skeleton of a great cow, then they vanished.

The eastwards sky was blinded to darkness in the flash, Clair and

Sinclair momentarily stunned with the noise of the explosion. Then a great wave poured shoreward out of the stirred water of the bay, leapt up the beach, snarled, spat, soaked and splashed them anew, tore at them, retreated. Gasping, Clair saw Sinclair's hand extended towards her. She caught it. Unspeaking, now crawling, now gaining their feet and proceeding at a shambling run, they attained the upper beach. Fifty yards away, across the shingle, there towered in the dimness of the morning great cliffs of black basalt. Against their black walls Sinclair thought he discerned a fault and overhang. He pointed towards it and they stumbled together across sharp stones that lacerated their feet. Anything to get out of the wind and spray. Clair almost fell inside the crack in the rock face. Sinclair crumpled to the ground beside her. Clair heard someone sobbing and realized it was herself.

'What's wrong?'

She looked up at him, her teeth chattering, thinking: 'I suppose we'll both be dead in a minute.' She said: 'I'm all right.'

Prone, he began to laugh crackedly at that. Clair stuffed her fingers in her ears and looked out to sea.

It was deserted. The *Magellan's Cloud* had disappeared without leaving other trace than themselves. Green, tremendous, with tresses upraised and flying through the malachite comb of the wind, the Atlantic surged over the spot where the wreck had flamed. An urgent fear came upon Clair. She shook the American's shoulder.

'Where are the others?'

'Dead.'

He had stopped laughing. He lay face downwards, unmoving. Clair shook him again.

'You mustn't! You must keep awake ...'

But she knew it was useless. Her own head nodded in exhaustion. She laid her face in the curve of her arm and presently was as silent as he was.

Subchapter iii

The morning wind died away and with its passing the sky began to clear. One after another, like great trailing curtains drawn aside from an auditorium, sheets of rain passed over the sea. But they passed northeastwards, not touching the little bay. Lying exhausted and asleep in their inadequate shelter under the lee of the cliffs the two survivors of the airship's wreck stirred at the coming of the sunlight. Sinclair awoke, sat up, looked round, remembered. He whistled with cracked lips.

'Great Spartacus!'

Wrecked. The *Magellan's Cloud* blown up. And cold – the infernal cold . . .

He was in pyjamas – green-striped silk poplin. The suit clung to his skin in damp and shuddersome patches. He stood up. His feet were cut and bruised, black with congealed blood. The salt bit into them as he moved. Alternate waves of warmth and coldness flowed up and down his body. He pulled off the pyjama-jacket, stripped himself of the trousers, and spread the soggy things to dry in front of the shelter. Setting his teeth against giving way to the pull of the urgent pain in his feet, he began to knead and pound his throat and chest and abdomen and thighs, then took to massaging them, plucking out and releasing muscles like a violin-maker testing the strings of a bow. Suddenly something screamed at him, menacingly.

He glanced up, startled. It was a solitary gull. He thought: 'And a peculiar one, too.' It swooped and hovered, its bright eyes on the occupants of the shelter. Man and bird looked at each other unfriendlily. Then the gull, with slow beating wings, flapped out of sight. Sinclair resumed operations on his now tingling body.

Behind him, Clair Stranlay began to moan.

He had thought her dead. He wheeled round. Lying with her face and throat in the sun, she was moaning, again unable to open her eyes. Her hair was a damp mop. The American frowned at her, lightedly, considered a moment, reached out for his pyjamas, found them almost dry, donned them.

Then he knelt down by his fellow-survivor, straightened out the crumplement in which she lay, loosened at waist and throat her ornate sleeping suit of blue and gold, and began with great vigour to massage her body into such warmth as he had induced in his own. The muscles of her stomach, usually a very flat and comely stomach, were bunched in cold. He smoothed that out, gently enough. She quivered under his hands. Her eyes opened at last.

She sat up, remembering at once, as he himself had done.

'Any of the others turned up?'

He shook his head, searching her body the while with skilful, nervous fingers. She became aware of that, surprisedly.

'Thanks. What about yourself?'

'I attended to myself before tackling you. The sunlight woke me.'

'I'm horribly thirsty.'

'So am I. I'll go and look for water in a minute.'

'Where do you think we are?'

'Somewhere in the Bay of Biscay. Coast of Portugal, perhaps.'

Clair's undrowned imp raised a damp head. 'Hope it's the sherry district. People inland must have seen the wreck of the *Magellan*. They're bound to come down to the shore, aren't they?'

'Bound to, I should think. Feel certain enough to rise now?'

She stood up with his arm supporting her. Instantly, in the full sunlight, she began to shiver. He nodded.

'Strip and do exercises. Know how? Right. I'll go and look for water and see if any people are coming down the cliffs. Don't overdo things. Shout for me if you feel faintness coming on.'

He went, limping bloody-heeled. Clair stared after him till his black poll vanished round a projection of rock, and then emerged slowly from her dejected sleeping-suit. She thought, hazily: ' "Exercises . . . " Honest to God Amurrican ones. This can't be happening to me. It's a scene out of a novel.'

Her feet, like Sinclair, she discovered bloody, though not so badly cut. Excepting its craving for water, her body in the next few strenuous minutes acquired comfort and familiarity again. The pyjamas steamed in the sunlight; ceased to steam. In ten minutes they were dry. She was putting them on when Sinclair returned.

'There's water round to the left – a cascade over the rocks. Can you walk?'

She essayed the adventure, gingerly. 'Easily.'

Out in the full sunlight she stopped to look round the bay. Desolate. The navigator, the commander, Miss Kemp – a fit of shuddering came on again. She covered her face with her hands.

But the horror lingered for a moment only, and then was gone. She turned to the American, a pace behind her, waiting for her, a grotesque figure in his shrunken pyjamas, his blue-black hair untidily matted. He stood arms akimbo, scowling at the sea. A gull – there seemed but one gull in the bay – swooped over their heads. Clair thought, after that one swift under-glance: 'We must look like a bridal couple in a Coward play. But I'd better not say so.'

She became aware that the silence around them was illusory. It was a thing girdled by unending sound, as the earth is girdled with ether. The tide was no longer in full flow, but the serene thunder of the breakers was unceasing. Clair's voice sounded queer to herself as she spoke, as though voices were scarce and alien things in this land.

'Funny no Portuguese have come down to look for the wreck.'

'Damn funny.' The scowl went from his face. He looked at her expressionlessly. He glanced up at the surrounding walls of basalt. 'They'll come. You'd better have some water.'

The pebbles underfoot were slimily warm. From the sea a breath of fog was rising, like a thin cigarette-smoke. Not a ship or a boat was in sight, nothing upon or above the spaces of the Atlantic but a solitary cirrus low down in the north-eastern sky. Clair's heels smarted. The American limped. They turned a corner in the winding wall of cliff and were in sight of the waterfall. In distance it seemed to hang bright, lucent, unmoving, a silver pillar in a dark phallic temple. Clair loved it for its beauty; she had the power in any circumstances to love beauty unexpected and unwarranted. She bent and scooped from it a double handful of water. She gasped.

It was icily cold. Some drops splashed through her jacket. They stung like leaden pellets. She shivered and, squatting, rinsed her mouth and laved her face. Sinclair looked down at her; knelt down beside her. They scoured their faces in solemn unison. Standing up, Sinclair looked round about him, involuntarily, for a towel. Clair wiped her face with the jacket of her pyjamas. Sinclair followed suit. Wiping, he suddenly stayed operations.

'Here's someone at last.'

He pointed towards the leftward tip of the bay. A black-clad figure was descending the inky, sun-laced escarpment, apparently less steep at that spot than elsewhere. It was descending in haste. It had descended. It stood hesitant, glancing upwards, not towards them. Clair put her fingers to her mouth and startled the bay, Sinclair and the stranger with a piercing, moaning whistle which the rocks caught and echoed and re-echoed.

'Stop that!' said Sinclair, angrily.

He was to see often enough in succeeding days that look of innocent, amused surprise on the lovely face turned towards him. The black-garmented figure had started violently, seen them, stood doubtful a moment, but now, with gesticulating arm, was coming towards them.

'I can't speak a word of Portuguese,' said Clair. 'Can you?'

There was a pause. Then: 'It won't be necessary. I don't suppose he knows Portuguese himself.'

'No?' Puzzled, Clair examined the nearing stranger. He was finding the going punishing. He stumbled. His features changed from a blur to discernible outline. 'Who is he?'

'A fellow-passenger on the *Magellan*. Sir John Mullaghan.'

Subchapter iv
'I was washed ashore at the far peak of the bay when the *Magellan's Cloud* struck the water. I imagined I was the only survivor.'

The grey-haired man with the gentle, sensitive face was addressing Clair. She held out her hand to him.

'I'm Clair Stranlay. Dr Sinclair rescued me.' She glanced from one to the other, thinking: 'Don't bite . . . ' 'You know each other?'

The American smiled thinly, but otherwise took no notice of the question. Sir John Mullaghan began to unbutton. Clair said, wide-eyed: 'What's wrong?'

'You must wear my coat, Miss Stranlay.'

'No thanks. I'm quite comfy. However do you come to be wearing your clothes?'

'I found it too cold to go to bed, and was sitting up studying some documents when the wreck occurred.' His small, neat form was clad in the shrunken caricature of a dress suit. Collar and tie were missing, the breast of the shirt very limp and muddied. Sinclair glanced sideways at his feet and scowled again. Shod in thin pumps that were at least some slight protection . . . Clair said: 'Let's sit down. What did you see at the top of the cliff?'

They sat down, Clair and Sir John. Sinclair remained standing. Clair folded one shapely knee over the other, and twisted a little on the boulder, thinking: 'Oh, my good God, how I *would* like some coffee and a soft chair to sit in!' She repeated her question to the new arrival.

' – and what made you come down so quickly?'

The armaments manufacturer was sitting with his grey head in his hands. He looked up.

'A lion, Miss Stranlay.'

'A – what?'

'A lion. One of the largest brutes I have ever seen. It stalked me close to the cliff-head.' He trembled involuntarily.

Clair glanced at Sinclair, glanced back at Sir John, looked up at the cliffs. The Atlantic said: 'Shoom. Surf. Shoom.' The cirrus cloud trailed its laces across the face of the sun, and for a little the faces of the three derelicts on the beach were in patterned shadow. 'A *lion*? But I thought we were in Portugal?'

'I don't know where we are. But this is not the coast of Portugal. At the top of the cliff there is a further terrace-wall to be climbed. It is fringed with bushes and trees. I expected to get some view of the country from there and went up about half an hour ago.'

'What happened?'

'I pushed through the fringe of bushes until I came to a fairly open space. I was certain that I would see some village near at hand, or at least houses and some marks of cultivation.' He paused. The Atlantic listened.

'There are no houses and the country is quite wild. It is natural open park-land, dotted with clumps of trees, stretching as far away as one can see. And on the horizon, about five or six miles distant from here, are two volcanoes.'

'Volcanoes?' The American was startled into speech. 'You must have been mistaken.'

'I have quite good eyesight, Miss Stranlay.'

The American bit his lip. Clair said: 'Where do you think we are, then?'

'Somewhere on the coast of Africa.'

'But it's much too cold. And I never heard of volcanoes on the coast of Africa.'

'There *are* no volcanoes on the coast of Africa. Most likely the lion was some beast escaped from a menagerie.'

This was Sinclair. Sir John Mullaghan flushed. Clair, wondering bemusedly if there were ever an armaments manufacturer who looked less the part, wondered also if the beast of which he spoke had had any existence outside the reaches of a disaster-strained imagination. She looked again at the cliff-top, shining in the cool sunlight. 'We'll have to go up there and look for food, anyhow. I'm horribly hungry.'

All three of them were. It was nearing noon. They licked hungry lips. Both men, if for different reasons, had been too preoccupied to realize the emptiness within them. Sinclair, peering up at the cliffs in the breaker-hung silence, thought: 'Hungry? As hell. But if this patriot warrior didn't dream, there's a lion up there. Still – without food we'll never last another night.'

Clair thought: 'Now, if this were a good novel of wrecked mariners, we'd toss up for it to see which was to eat t'other.' And she began to giggle, being very hungry and somewhat dizzy.

'Miss Stranlay!'

She regarded the American placidly. 'It's all right. I was thinking of a funny story.'

'Oh.'

'Yes.' She stood up, suddenly decided. 'Wrecked people sometimes eat each other if they can't get other food – at least, they always do in my profession. *De rigueur*. Let's climb the cliff and see if the lion's gone.'

'Come on, then,' said Sinclair, shortly, striding over the shingle. They followed him, Sir John Mullaghan dubiously, Clair satisfiedly, and once surreptitiously trying to rub some feeling into her oddly-numbed stomach. Sinclair was making for the point ascended and descended by the armaments manufacturer. His survey of the cliffs had told him that no other spot was climbable.

They went on along the deserted beach. The tide was going out. Sinclair glanced back, casually, halted in his stride, stared, abandoned the other two, strode past them.

'Wait.'

They looked after him. Ten yards away he bent over something at the wet verge of shingle. He picked it up. It glittered, wetly. He shook it vigorously. Clair called: 'What is it?'

'An eiderdown quilt.'

So it was. Brought nearer in Sinclair's arms, Clair recognized it. 'It's off my cabin-bed in the *Magellan*! I'd know those whorls anywhere . . . That was the thing I must have picked up when you came to get me.'

'Lucky that you did.'

'Why?' She regarded it without enthusiasm. 'It's very wet, isn't it?'

'It'll dry. And the nights are likely to be cold.'

'But – ' Clair looked out to sea, looked round the deserted bay again. The possibility that this was not, after all, a few hours' lark struck upon her. 'We'll be rescued before then.'

Neither of the men spoke. Sir John passed a grey hand over his grey hair. Sinclair's comment was the usual impatient frown . . . They resumed their progress cliffwards, the barefooted refugees slipping on the moist pebbles, Sir John in slightly better case. The thin, sun-flecked wind bit casually through pyjama-fabric. At the foot of the cliff-ascent, hearing a swish of wings, Clair looked back.

The bay's solitary seagull was following them. Clair held out her hand to it. At that, as if frightened by the gesture, it turned in the air in a wide loop, and planed away steeply down towards the retreating tide. The American was speaking to Sir John.

'You've got shoes. Will you lead?'

The armaments manufacturer hesitated only a moment, nodded curtly, and began the ascent. The silence but for his scrapings over the rock was more intense than ever.

Sinclair and Clair followed, the American in a little beginning to swear violently underbreath because of his cut feet. Clair said: 'Say something for me as well.'

He glanced at her – almost a puzzled glance – from below his fair, unhappy brows. Then he went on. Clair, panting, poised to rest. She was more than a little frightened, though she refused to think of the fact . . . Where were they? And what on earth was going to happen? And how long would her pyjamas last?

Sinclair's toiling back, quilt-laden, reproached her sloth. Sir John Mullaghan had almost disappeared.

From the shore the circling gull saw the three strange animals – it had never seen such animals, nor had any gull on the shore of that strange Atlantic ever seen their like – dwindle to spider-splayed shadows against the face of the cliffs, dwindle yet further to hesitant, foreshortened dots on the cliff-brow, and then vanish for ever from its ken.

CHAPTER THREE

In an unknown land

Subchapter i

Three days later, and the coming of nightfall.

Almost it came in countable strides. All the afternoon the line of volcanoes beyond the leftward swamps had smoked like hazy beacons, like the whin-burnings on a summer day in Scotland. They had drowsed in the clear, sharp sunshine that picked out so pitilessly the hilly, wooded contours of the deserted land. Swamp and plain and rolling grassland, straggling rightwards forest fringe, swamp and plain and hill again. Unendingly. But with the westering of the sun these things had softened in outline, blurred in distance, and now, on the hesitating edge of darkness, the great chain of volcanoes lighted and lighted till they were a beckoning candelabrum, casting long shadows and gleams of light over leagues of the bleak savannah. The coming nightfall hesitated a little on the stilled tree-tops of the great western forest, and then, with uncertain feet, walked westwards, delicately, like Agag, to meet the challenge of those night-beacons kindled far down in the earth's interior. So, walking, it paused a little, as if astounded, by a spot in the tree-sprayed foothills that led to the volcanoes' range.

For here, in all that chilled and hushed and waiting expectancy, were three things that did not wait, that bore human heads and bodies and cast their anxious glances at the astounded and brooding nightfall. For three sunsets now the nightfall had come on those three hasting figures. Each time they were further south, each time they greeted the astounded diurnal traveller with the uplift of thin, ridiculous pipings in that waste land overshadowed by the volcanoes. They did so, now.

''Fraid it'll beat us,' said the middle figure, a short, bunched shapelessness.

The leading figure, tall and hasting, grunted. The last figure, breathing heavily, said: 'I also think it's useless. We had much better try the forest.'

'What do you think, Dr Sinclair?' asked the midway shapelessness. The leader grunted again.

'Damn nonsense. We'll climb towards the volcanoes, where we've a chance of getting warm. Another night in the open may finish us. And the forest's not safe.'

Underfoot, the heavy-fibred grass rustled harsh and wet to the touch of naked feet. Overhead, the dark traveller still hesitated. The heavy-breathing rearward figure said: 'There is probably no danger in the forest. You saw things while you were half-awake. In daylight we've seen no animal larger than a small deer.'

The leading figure swore, turned a shadowed face, halted and confronted the rearguard, and disregarded a restraining motion made by the shapelessness. 'Damn you and your impertinences. Did you imagine that lion you originally saw, then? I tell you I saw a brute twice as big as any lion hovering round the tree-clump we slept in this morning. And you make me out a liar, you – you damned straying patriot freak!'

And the middle shapelessness which, under the endrapement of the eiderdown quilt salvaged from the wreck of *Magellan's Cloud*, contained Clair Stranlay, thought: 'Goodness, they're both nearly all in. And I don't wonder. What on earth am I to do if they start scrapping now?'

That question had vexed her almost continually for some seventy hours. The American and Sir John Mullaghan had seemed to her designed from the beginning of the world to detest each other. For seventy hours they had lived on edge. And now –

Clair thought: 'Oh, my good God, I could knock your silly heads together. And I'm cold and miserable and hungry. And if ever we get out of this awful country I'll write an account and lampoon you both – '

Subchapter ii
There would be plenty of copy for that account.

. . . The wreck. The rescue. Sir John Mullaghan arriving on the scene, complete with tale of discourteous lion. Climbing the cliffs. No lion. Wide view of the sea. No ships. No food. And before them an unrecognizable landscape about which Sinclair and Sir John had at once begun to disagree. Labrador or North Canada, said Sinclair – abruptly deserting Portugal. There were supposed to be lost volcanoes in the wilds of Canada. Sir John had asked if there were also lions, and how the *Magellan*, turning south just prior to being wrecked, could have reached Canada? No reply to that. Scowls. All three growing hungry. Finally, exploration in search of food.

It had led them further and further inland, that exploration. No animals. Not a solitary bird. Strange land without the sound of birds, without the chirp of grasshoppers in those silent forest clumps! Clair had shivered at that voicelessness, though, far off beyond the cliffs, they could still hear the moan of the lost Atlantic. They had strayed remoter and remoter from that moan, out into thinner aspects of the park-land, till the landscape they saw was this: distant against the eastern horizon a long mountain sierra, ivory-toothed with snow, cold and pale and gleaming in the cool sunshine, except at points lighted with the lazy smoking of volcanoes. To the right a jumble of hills that must lead back to the Atlantic eventually, and those hills matted and clogged with forest. But not jungle. Pines and conifers and firs.

'Likely-looking country for lion,' the American deportee had remarked acidly, and then hushed them both with a sharp gesture. Something stirred in a clump of bushes only a yard or so away. They'd stared at it, making out at last the head and shoulders and attentive antlers of a small deer. Sinclair had acted admirably then, Clair had thought – albeit a little ridiculously. He'd motioned them to silence, unwound the damp eider-down from about his shoulders, crept forward, suddenly leapt, landed on top of the deer and proceeded to smother the little animal in the quilt's gaudy folds. Squeals and scuffling. Deer on top, deer underfoot. Sinclair in all directions, but hanging on grimly and cursing so that Clair, running to his aid, had thought regretfully how she'd no notebook with her on this jaunt . . . She had halted and gasped.

For at her forward rush all the bushes round about, probably held para-lysed by fear until then, had suddenly vomited deer; a good two score of deer. A hoofs-clicking like the rattle of an insane orchestra of castanets, the bushes were deserted, and the deer in headlong flight. Clair had stared after them, fascinated, been cursed for her pains, then had knelt down and, rather white-faced, assisted Sinclair to strangle his captive . . .

Sir John Mullaghan, who had tripped and fallen in *his* forward rush, had arrived then.

They had kindled a fire and fed on that deer. The making of the fire had been a problem until it was discovered that the armaments manu-facturer had a petrol-lighter in his pocket. Ornate, gold-mounted thing. No petrol. But the flint had still functioned and there had been lots of dry grass available. Fire in a minute. How to cook the deer? No knives. Sinclair had said: 'Miss Stranlay, go away for a minute. You, Mullaghan, I want your help.' Clair had turned away, reluctantly, had heard an un-friendly confabulation, had heard the sound of scuffling, smelt the reek of blood and manure, had wheeled round with a cry . . . The men had torn a leg and haunch from the body of the deer. Clair had been quietly sick.

The meal had been good, though singey and tough. Sinclair had burned his fingers in tearing off a half-cooked portion and handing it to her. Sir John, his dress-suit spattered with drops of blood, had helped at the cooking efficiently enough. But there had been no co-operation between him and Sinclair. They had sat, replete, and disagreed with each other, never once addressing each other, but talking through the medium of Clair. It had then been late afternoon.

'It's obvious we must hold inland and south-ward,' said Sinclair. 'There's no sign of human beings or habitations hereabouts. And if this, as I suspect, is Northern Canada in a warm spell, it is only southward we are ever likely to meet with anyone.'

'I doubt if there's anything in that, Miss Stranlay.' The grey head had been shaken at her; the gentle eyes held determination. 'Probably you, like myself, wish to get back to civilization as soon as possible? Then, I think, it's obvious we ought to return to the cliff-head before sunset and light a fire there and wait through the night. Some ship is bound to see the signal, for there are plenty of ships on the African coast.'

Clair had wiped her greasy, slim fingers on the coarse grass, and thought about it, sitting cross-legged and massaging her sweetly pedi-cured toes. 'I don't know. Canada? I don't think we can be there, Dr Sinclair. It's too far away from the eastern Atlantic, as Sir John Mullaghan says. But this is not a bit like Africa.' She had glanced round the unhappy landscape. 'Not a bit like anything I ever heard of.' She had thought of adding: 'Like hell it isn't!' because that would have been funny, and was always appreciated in her novels. But she had restrained herself, being judicious, and looked at the three-quarters of deer left to them, the while the two men looked at her, Sinclair with apparent indifference, Sir John with courteous attention. 'On the other hand, there doesn't seem to be any food in this place. All those little deer ran away south. They may have been strays from the south. I think we ought to follow them. After all, we're bound to meet people some time.'

The American had stood up at that, handed Clair the quilt, seized the deer, gutted it – a sickening task – with his hands, and then slung it across the shoulder of his pyjama-jacket. 'You've the casting vote. Come on, then.'

And they had gone on. They'd camped that night a few miles inland, under the lee of a ragged and woebegone pine on the edge of the great, silent forest itself. They had made another fire with the aid of Sir John Mullaghan's lighter, and broiled more deer and eaten it, all three of them by then weary and footsore from the few miles they'd covered, but Clair in no worse plight than the others, except that she wasn't of their sex. When she strolled into the bushes Sir John had called out warnings about the lion. Clair had called back: 'No lion would be so unlionly', and then wished she hadn't, and thought: 'Oh, Batter-sea!' and sighed, being tired.

When she came back they had apparently settled down for the night. Sir John lay to the left of her entrance. He had taken off his pumps and wrapped his feet with grass. He had also removed his coat and draped it round his thin shoulders. He lay close enough to the fire. It had grown cold, though there was no wind. Neither was there a star in the sky. Sinclair lay near the fire also, but more directly under the lee of the pine. He was swathed about by bundles of grass, and Clair had thought, appalled: 'Oh, my good God, I'll have to do some hay-making.' But that had proved unnecessary. Between the spaces occupied by the two men, and directly opposite the bole of the pine, the quilt had been outspread to dry and had dried. This, Clair understood, was her sleeping position. She had sunk into the eiderdown gratefully.

'Good night, you two,' she had called, muffling the soft folds round about her. Sinclair had merely grunted. Sir John had said, uncovering his face: 'Good night, Miss Stranlay. Call me if you want anything.'

'Tea in the morning, please.'

He had laughed, with pleasant courtesy, and there had been silence.

Such silence! All her life she would remember it, though the second night had made it commonplace. The night was a stark and naked woman, asleep. But sometimes you could hear her breathe. Terrible. And against the lightless sky, unlighted though it was, you saw her hair rise floating now and then. The pine foliage . . .

Miles and miles of it, this cold, queer country. Where was it? What would happen to them?

Clair had stirred in the light of the fire, and turned on her left side, staring at the dead wood and hearing the soft hiss of burning cones. She lay half-in, half-out, the spraying circle of radiance. Beyond that: the darkness. Fantastic position to be in! She had thought, 'Tonight? I should have been in N'York. Betsy would have been coddling me. Bedtime cocktail. Slippers and – oh, my good God, a clean pair of pyjamas. Lighted bedroom. Bed. Blankets. Sheets. A *soft* bed . . . ' She had drowsed then and wakened to find the fire dying down and her shoulder cold where the eiderdown had slipped aside. Also, her hip-bone had been aching unbearably. She had turned over and lain on her back, thinking: 'Is it really me?'

Three or four yards to her right she had seen the outline of the sleeping form of Sir John Mullaghan. He was snoring. Catarrh. That was what had awakened her. She lay and stared at him, thinking: 'I do wish he'd realize he's a lost and desperate refugee and wouldn't saw at his backbone like that.' But Sir John had sawed on. She had turned her eyes towards Sinclair's place.

No more than herself was he asleep – or sleeping only fitfully. His grass wrappings had fallen off, and she saw the gleam of the dying firelight on his skin where the pyjama-jacket had failed of its purpose. At that sight she had called to him, softly, but he had made no answer. Reluctantly, she had disencased herself from the eiderdown and stood up, finding the night a pringling coldness and underfoot something that rustled like salt. Hoar-frost. She'd danced to the fire, seized the ready collected pile of cones and branches, and fed the heap of red cinders till it kindled to a glow, eating hungrily into the resinous cones, more slowly engaging in mastication of the branches. She'd stood and shivered until it was well under way, and then bent over the American.

'Are you sleeping, Dr Sinclair?'

'No. Why?'

'Come under the eiderdown with me.'

'Nonsense. Go back to it. You'll freeze there.'

'And you'll freeze here with nothing but pyjamas. Do come.'

'No thanks. Ask Sir John Mullaghan.'

She'd felt herself flush a little at that, in spite of the cold. She'd turned round and gone back to her place, picked up the quilt, wheeled round and returned to Sinclair's side.

'I'm not asking you to become my lover,' she had explained. 'Only not to be a silly ass.'

He'd stared up at her, the firelight in his eyes. He had looked rather ashamed. He'd stood up. 'All right, Miss Stranlay. Sorry. Stand back and I'll arrange the grass. We'll lie on it . . . Now.'

Even so, he had been diffident. Clair had said: 'Please just forget it. We're both very sleepy . . . So. Comfortable?'

He'd said 'Yes.' And added, as an afterthought: 'Thank you.'

He'd been asleep before she was, and she'd lain listening to his quiet breathing and thinking: 'This is a fine scene for a novel. But there ought to have been all kinds of drama. Instead of which the hero's so tired he'd have bitten the Queen of Sheba if she'd suggested being naughty . . . Has a nice, strong chest. Hope to goodness he doesn't snore . . . ' And then, though she didn't know it, she had snored a little herself, gently, adding her soft pipe to the deep bass notes that smote the night from the nose of Sir John Mullaghan.

Next day they had held south again, with little conversation except that Sir John, some sternness in his gentle eyes, had drawn Clair aside after breakfast and asked her if the American – last night –

'Oh, no, I went and forced myself into his bed,' Clair had said, looking at him wide-eyed.

He'd coloured a little, looking at her undecidedly. 'Remember, Miss Stranlay, I can always protect you.'

'From lions, you mean?'

Catty, that, she had thought remorsefully as he turned away. He'd addressed few remarks to her from that time onwards until the evening. Neither had the American. Willy-nilly, he had taken the lead. There was no compulsory obedience, but the other two had followed. Water in ponds and in streamlets was plentiful enough, but the character of the country did not change. As one volcano receded to the right, another took its place. Clump on clump of forest, dark-green, erupted from the face of the tundra. The great forest itself marched on their left, watching them. Again and again Clair had the feeling that they were being watched from that half-mile distant forest. She had told the two men of the feeling. Sinclair had shrugged his shoulders.

'We may be. But it doesn't look like it.' He waved his hand around. 'Look, it's completely desolate.'

There was no sign of other living thing than themselves until late afternoon, when they again started a small herd of the small deer. Perhaps it was the same herd. It disappeared from view within two minutes of their rousing it. Sinclair had sworn. 'We could have done with more venison.'

There had been only a quarter of the deer left by then. Camping at sunset, this time in the midst of a cluster of bushes, itself in the midst of a tree-clump out in the tundra, Clair had taken stock of herself and her companions. First, herself: her pyjama-trousers were ripped and scratched from the knee downwards; otherwise intact. The jacket was still serviceable, though one of the loops had been torn away. Her feet ached, as indeed did all her body, especially knee and thigh joints. But otherwise she was quite well.

Sinclair – it did not do to look very directly at Sinclair. In matters sartorial he had suffered the worst of the three, though he did not seem very conscious of the fact . . . All right if he didn't feel cold.

'And anyhow,' Clair had consoled herself the while she gathered brushwood for the fire, 'we've still got a dress suit in the expedition. Even though the pumps have given way.'

They had, abruptly abandoning their allegiance to the armaments manufacturer in a swampy place. Prior to that they had abandoned their soles. Now Sir John tramped barefooted, like his companions, displaying small, handsome and well-cared for feet. 'Fortunate he hasn't got bunions,' Clair had meditated, and had gone on to think that it was fortunate indeed that all three of them were comparatively healthy people. Her own penchant for winter bathing had inured her to almost any extreme of temperature that almost any climate could provide. Sinclair, she had discovered, was a trained athlete, combining with militant pacifism some gospel of the unpadded life which had taken him on tramping expeditions through half the Western States. Sir John was the least well equipped, yet compared with the average passenger on the *Magellan*! What would Miss Kemp have done? *Miss Kemp*!

Sinclair had divided up the last leg and haunch for the evening meal. 'We don't know when we'll get any other food.' The others had assented, Clair silently regretful, for she found herself very hungry in those hours of marching through the clear, cold sunshine. Suddenly she had thought, and said aloud with a rush of longing: 'Oh, my good God, I do wish I had a cigarette!'

Sir John Mullaghan had come to her aid unexpectedly. 'I have two,' he had said, and had drawn a small silver case from his pocket the while Clair stared at him unbelievingly. Opened, the case disclosed two veritable Egyptians. Clair had reached for one, starvingly, lighted it from a twig, drawn the acrid, sweet smoke down into grateful lungs. Sir John, similarly employed, had sat at the other side of the fire. Sinclair, looking tired, looked into the fire. She had suddenly disliked Mullaghan with great intensity.

'Share with me, Dr Sinclair?'

'No, thanks. I don't smoke.'

'Now, isn't that a blessed relief?' Clair had said, but she had not said it aloud. Instead, she had leant back on the long, coarse grass and smoked slowly, carefully, lingeringly, finishing long after Sir John, and indeed, had she known it, finishing the last cigarette ever smoked in that unknown land.

Nightfall. Bed with Sinclair under the eiderdown quilt, Sir John, grey-headed, watching them across the fire. The American, settling down, had resented the stare.

'What the devil are you glowering about?'

'To see you take no advantage of Miss Stranlay's kindness.'

Clair had felt Sinclair's arm muscles tauten beside her. She had interposed, sleepily. 'It's quite all right, Sir John. We sleep together for warmth, not love.' Then she had laid her head against Sinclair's unyielding shoulder and gone to sleep again. So presently had Sir John. But Sinclair had slept in fits and starts, turning uneasily and twice awakening Clair. Finally she had whispered: 'Whatever ails the man?'

He had answered in a whisper. 'There's something prowling round the fire.'

Clair had sat up beside him, peering forward. Nothing. Nothing but the crackle of a consuming twig. Not even a breath of wind. Nothing to see, except far off, remote across the tundra, the nearest volcano, crowned with quiet flame, burning watchfully. Perhaps five miles away. Utter darkness and silence. Sir John Mullaghan, dim-seen, sleeping quietly now. Or was he also awake? Not a sound. Or was there?

It was a deep, steady, full-lunged breathing a little distance away from them. 'There's some beast there,' whispered Sinclair, unnecessarily, staring across the fire. He had slipped out of the eiderdown. Clair had caught his wrist. 'Stir up the fire.'

'I'm going to.'

He had, and then, suddenly snatching up a branch which was crackling into flame, had emitted a blood-curdling yell and rushed round to the other side of the fire, waving his torch. He had crashed through the bushes, spark-spreading, and to Clair, thinking unalarmedly: 'Goodness, his poor pyjamas!' it had seemed he was preceded by an even more distant crash. Sir John awoke, startledly.

'What is it? Miss Stranlay – are you all right?'

'Quite. Dr Sinclair thought he heard a wild animal prowling round and went after it with a torch. Here he comes.'

Sinclair returned, piled the fire with all the wood they had collected, and sank down by Clair. Crouching on his elbow, the armaments manu-facturer had looked across at them.

'What was it?' Clair had asked.

'Sorry I'm so damn chill . . . Eh? Some kind of bear, I think.'

'A big one?'

'Brute like a cart-horse.'

'Did it run away?'

'Near the equator by now, I should think.'

Clair had gurgled drowsily and laid her shapely head on the grass pillow. It was the first spark of humour she had heard struck from the American's angry, flinty personality. Soon she and Sinclair slept. But until dawn Sir John had watched the moving shadows of the bushes beyond the radiance of the camp-fire.

Next morning – the third morning – they had eaten the last of the deer and tramped southwards again, across country still unchanged and un-changing in promise. But this morning had greeted them with rain, so that they had been forced to shelter under a great fir, watching the sheets of water warping westwards over the long llanos. It looked almost like grey English countryside, grossly exaggerated in every feature. Clair had early felt very tired, and standing under the fir had become aware of the cause. Of course, the damn thing *would* happen now. She had questioned Sinclair, who had looked curiously into her white face.

'Do you know what the date is?'

'It should be the 25th.'

'The 25th? But it can't be. Why – ' She had stopped, calculating, very puzzled as well as otherwise distressed. Sinclair she had discovered to have singularly gentle eyes. Sir John Mullaghan was a little apart.

'Why can't it be?'

She had remembered his profession, with relief, and had explained. He had stood thoughtful, draped in his ragged pyjama-suit, pulling at his rather long upper lip. Then: 'If it's only twenty days since the last occurrence, Miss Stranlay, you can put it down to shock, I suppose. Hardship. Different life. Though I never heard of such a case.'

'The moon!'

'Eh?'

'Don't you remember?' she said. 'The moon we saw from the *Magellan*. You said it was five or six days too early.'

He had stared away from her. 'So I did. And it was. Been too cloudy since we landed to see the moon again . . . But the connection's a myth – '

Clair had smiled at him ruefully, lovely even then. 'It's a fact.'

He had nodded, impersonally. 'Right. Now – '

When Sir John Mullaghan turned to them again, with the clearing of the rain, he had stared in some surprise at Sinclair's legs. He was clad now in knee-length shorts. Clair, considerably more comfortable, moved forward by his side.

But the day had held little of comfort in it, what with the rain. Somewhere in the early afternoon Sinclair had stopped near a stream which meandered out of the forest and filed away into the beginnings of a tract of long-grassed, mush-eared swamp. 'I'm going to hunt around and see if there's any food to be had, Miss Stranlay.'

'I think I'll also look round, Miss Stranlay.'

'There's a fire required,' the American had flung over his shoulder. 'And Miss Stranlay's tired.'

Sir John Mullaghan had searched around for dry grass and twigs, scarce enough commodities, both of them, the while Clair lay under a thing that looked like a whortleberry bush, but wasn't, and wished she was dead. The quilt was damp, and presently kindled to a slimy warmth from the heat of her body. She had fallen asleep in a self-induced Turkish bath, with the slow patter of the rain on the leaves overhead and a view of Sir John Mullaghan, in a considerably battered dress-suit, squatting on bruised and dirty heels, doing futile things with his petrol lighter against a dour loom of treey, desolate landscape. Sinclair had not yet returned.

They had no method of measuring time, with the sun's face draped in trailing rain-curtains, but it must have been at least another two hours before he did come back, coming from the direction of the forest, and walking wearily, a soaked and tattered figure.

'You'll catch pneumonia,' Clair had called, and tried to stir the fire to warmth-giving. But both she and Sir John had looked at the doctor with sinking hearts. Clair had said, casually: 'Any luck?'

Sinclair had opened his right hand. 'These.'

They were half a dozen half-ripened beech nuts, picked up below a high, solitary and unclimbable tree. Sinclair told, shortly, that he had wandered for miles without sighting any animal or bird or fruit-bearing tree. 'And we'd best be getting on again.'

'Why?' Clair had queried, eating her two nuts.

'Because you can't stay unsheltered on a night such as this promises to be. We'll try nearer the mountains for some ledge or rock shelter.'

So once again they had set out southwards, with the rain presently clearing merely to display a sun hovering on the verge of setting.

Subchapter iii

And now, in the last of the daylight, lost, desperate, and foolish, they stood on the brink of a disastrous quarrel, Sinclair with every appearance of being about to assault the armaments manufacturer, Sir John with his gentle face ablaze. Clair looked from one to other of them, wanly, but still with that gay irony that was her salvation, and, after a little calculation, did the thing that she thought would be best under the circumstances.

She burst into tears.

The two men paused. The American, she observed through her fingers, went more white and haggard than ever. Sir John laid his hand on her arm.

'Miss Stranlay, you must keep up. We can't be far now from some town or village or a trapper's hut.'

'It – it's not that.' Clair thought, swiftly 'Am I overdoing it? Oh, God, I hope it doesn't take long, because I really am sick and tired and ill, and all this crying isn't in jest.' She resumed: 'It's you and Dr Sinclair. You're spoiling all our chances because you won't act together.'

There was a silence. Sinclair looked at the volcanoes, looked at Clair. 'That's true, Miss Stranlay . . . I'm sorry, Mullaghan.'

'And I, Dr Sinclair. If you'll lead on – '

The American turned again and led. Clair thought: 'Triumph of the civilized habit. Or is it? According to all the books they should have flown at each other's throats in this primitive milieu, and the winner grabbed me as prize . . . Goodness, a damp and dejected prize I'd have been!'

Suddenly they found themselves in the lee of one of the foothills, under the mouths of two great caves.

CHAPTER FOUR

The lair

Subchapter i

'We don't know what may be in them,' said Sir John Mullaghan.

They stood and looked at the cave-mouths. They stood almost in darkness, in a thin line of light, a space-time illusion of luminosity, for the sun had quite vanished. Hesitating, they peered at each other in the false twilight. A little stream of water, hardly seen, ran coldly over Clair's toes. She felt iller than ever.

'What can there be? There are no animals in this country. Do let's get out of the rain – it's coming on again.'

'Can't you smell?' said Sinclair.

Clair elevated her small, rain-beaded nose and smelt. A faint yet acrid odour impinged on the rainy evening. Ammoniac. 'Like the zoo lion-house,' said Sinclair, very low, staring at the near cave-mouth.

The armaments manufacturer showed his latent quality. He bent down, groped at his feet, and straightened with a large stone in his hand. He motioned them aside. Clair stood still. Sinclair seized her roughly by the shoulder and pulled her to one side of the near cave-mouth.

'Come out!'

The stone crashed remotely in the bowels of the cave, ricocheted in darkness, stirred a multitude of echoes. Nothing else. The twilight vanished. They stood in the soft sweep of the rain, listening.

'I'll step into the mouth and try the lighter on a bit of my under-clothes,' said Sir John, practically.

'All right.' The American's voice, imperturbable.

Clair could see neither of them now. But Sinclair's shoulder touched hers. She heard cautious, bare-foot treadings in the dark. Sir John had left them. Clair thought: 'Oh, God, why doesn't he hurry?' Her thoughts blurred. She leant against Sinclair. 'I'm going to be sick.'

He put his arm round her and the quilt. 'Not now. Don't be a fool.'

She bit her lips, holding herself erect, dizzily. 'You've shocking bed-side manners.'

'Sh!'

The forward darkness spat sparks, intermittently. The lighter. Spat. Spat.

Something dirty white. A catch. Vigorous blowing. A glow. The mouth of the cave. Porous-looking rock. Sir John Mullaghan's face. His voice.

'It winds inward. I'll go and see if there's anything.'

'All right.'

Clair said: 'No, you don't. Dr Sinclair thinks he's protecting me. I don't need it.' She prodded her protector. 'Go with him.'

His support was withdrawn. 'Keep where you are.'

A faint glow, over-gloomed by a titanic shadow, illumined the cave-mouth. Betwixt her and that glow passed another tenebrous titan. The glow failed, lighted up again, receded. Alone. Soft swish of rain. Clair began to count, found herself swaying, shook herself out of counting. 'Makes you sleepy.' A long wait and then suddenly Sinclair's voice close at hand: 'Miss Stranlay!'

'Hello?'

'Give me your hand.' She found herself drawn forward. 'Careful.'

'Nothing inside?'

'Not a thing except a queer kind of nest.'

She stumbled in blackness. 'Has the light gone out?'

'The cave twists.'

The ground underfoot had a porous feeling; it was as though one walked over the surface of a frozen sponge. A few more steps and Sinclair, by the aid of disjointed gropings with his disengaged hand, guided Clair round a corner of the ante-cave. She saw then a roof nine or ten feet high over-arching a cave-chamber something of the size and appearance of her own small drawing-room in Kensington. It glittered greyly. On the uneven floor, tending a small fire that seemed to be fed with his undergarments and a pile of ancient hay, squatted Sir John Mullaghan, naked to the waist. In the far leftwards corner was a hummock. The 'nest'.

'All right, Miss Stranlay?'

'As rain, Sir John.' Clair stumbled again. Sinclair pushed her past the fire. She sank down on the nest. Its straw crackled dustily under her weight. The fire, Sir John, and Sinclair, began to pace a hasting gavotte. Clair closed her eyes.

'I'm going to faint.'

She did.

Subchapter ii

She passed from the faint into a sleep, and awoke several hours later, Sinclair's hand shaking her.

'Miss Stranlay! . . . I'm afraid it's going to spring – '

She sat up with a twingeing body, brushing back the hair from her face. The American crouched beside her, a red-ochred shadow in the light of the fire, his head turned towards the fire. The fire itself burned and sputtered sulkily under a strange, brittle heaping of fuel. And beyond its light, in the darkness, glowed another light.

Two of them. Unwinking. Clair felt an acid saliva collect in her mouth. Suddenly the two lights changed position; they had sunk lower towards the floor of the cave. Clair understood. It was crouching.

'Don't scream.'

Sinclair's words were in a whisper. But the Thing in the darkness beyond the fire must have heard them. Its eyes reared up again. Clair shut her own; opened them again. The eyes were again sinking. Spring this time?

And then the fire took a hand. It spiralled upwards a long trail of smoke, red-glowing gas which burst into crackling flame. There came a violent sneeze, a snarl, the thump of a heavy body crashing against the side of the cave in a backwards leap. And then the three survivors of the *Magellan's Cloud* saw – saw for a moment a bunched, barred, gigantic body, a coughing, snarling, malignant face. Then a rushing patter filled the cave. The fire died down. Beyond its light no eyes now glowed in the darkness.

Clair sank on her elbow, dry-mouthed. 'What was it?'

Someone beyond Sinclair drew a long breath. 'A tiger.'

Sinclair spoke very quietly. 'Like one, but it wasn't.'

'What was it, then?' Clair saw Sir John Mullaghan also crouching, a keyed-up shadow.

The American, answering, still stared across the fire. '*Machaerodus*.'

'What?'

'*Machaerodus* – a sabre-toothed tiger.'

There fell a moment's silence – of stupefaction on the part of all three. Clair, ill, closed her eyes and opened them again. She must be dreaming. 'But – it can't be. They're extinct.'

'Didn't you see the tusks?'

She had. So had Sir John. The latter got to his feet. He spoke and moved doubtfully.

'It may come back.'

The fire purred and crackled again. He had fed it from a pile of fuel not in the cave when they first entered it. The American got up and helped him. Clair's head, sleep-weighted, sank again on the nest. She thought: 'I'm dreaming. Don't care though it's a mammoth next time.' The smell of the fuel was nauseating. She voiced a sleepy question, and, voicing it, was asleep, and never heard Sinclair's answer.

'What are you burning?'

'Bones.'

Subchapter iii

When next she awoke, she was in complete darkness. No fire burned near at hand. She had a sense of having slept for many hours. She stretched, cautiously, remembering everything, and found that someone had tended to her while she slept. Her rain-dampened pyjamas had disappeared. She was lying not merely covered by the quilt, but wrapped in it. A keen, cool current of air blew steadily in her face.

If that three-days' Odyssey across the deserted savannah was a dream? . . . She was at home in Kensington . . . Wrapped in a quilt, lying in fusty hay? She called, cautiously: 'Dr Sinclair!'

No answer. She released her left arm, and sought in the place where he had crouched while they looked at the eyes beyond the fire. Her fingers touched bare rock. She sat up, a little frightened, desperately hungry.

'*Dr Sinclair!*'

A far-off voice called: 'Coming, Miss Stranlay.'

Footsteps, and the darkness receding from the light of a smoky torch, held in Sinclair's hand. In his other he carried a shapeless bundle.

She said: 'Goodness, nice to see you. Where's the fire? Have I slept long?'

Sinclair's mind said, absorbedly, and for the second or third time in looking at her: 'Pretty thing!' Tousled red-tipped hair, comely sleep-flushed face, clear, friendly, questioning eyes. Miraculous to wake from sleep like that . . . Aloud: 'The fire's in the outer half of the cave. It's about noon. I've brought you your things.'

He dropped them in her hands. They were her pyjamas, dry and warm.

'You *are* a dear – though you try so desperately not to be.' The dear grunted. Clair's eyes twinkled at him. 'Is that a smell of something cooking?'

'We've found some food. I'll leave you the torch to dress by.'

He set it against the rock-wall, turned about, and went. Clair stood up and shook off the eiderdown quilt, and felt her body with disgust. Grimy, gritty and granulous. But her sickness of the night before had passed. She thought: 'Wonder if it's safe to bathe yet? Nice things, warm pyjamas. Wonder – '

She had remembered the beast which had stalked them in the dark hours. Had there been any beast? She snatched up the torch and walked past the ashes of the fire. On the damp floor were multitudes of impressions, and superimposed on these great pug-marks of a cat.

'A sabre-toothed tiger!'

She picked up the eiderdown quilt and groped her way through to the front part of the cave, and so came on the sight of it suddenly, the entrance flooded with sunlight, and against that sunlight a hazy drift of smoke, as from the lips of a contemplative smoker, engendered by the fire. Either side of this fire sat Sinclair and Sir John – Sinclair in his ragged pyjamas, Sir John with his slight form even slighter than of yore. Minus underclothes. Neither of them heard her coming and she stood for a moment and looked at them with some little modification of that gay, ironic, contemplative scrutiny she usually turned upon the world. Their lives had interwoven in hers with a dream-like abruptness and intimacy –

'Sinclair – no more a gentleman than you're a lady. No more an American than you're an Englishwoman. Why? Fifty years ago we might have been both – the tricks are easy enough to learn . . . Sir John – no doubt about *him*. A lost aristo who's mislaid his guillotine and ruffles – '

Sinclair – he had begun to fray badly, poor boy. Soon be a catastrophe with that sleeping-suit of his. The faces of both men were lined with stubble, an unchancy harvest, Sir John's a red wiriness of vegetal promise, with hints of grey, Sinclair's a blue-black down. Their hair stood up in tufts and feathers. But both of them seemed to have washed, and Clair noted the fact with an interest that put an end to her survey.

''Morning, Sir John. I've already met you, doctor . . . Oh, not in the wilds.' She motioned them to sit, but flushed a little with a touch of reminiscent wonder. The cosmopolitan had been at least as quick as the aristo . . . 'Where did you get the food?'

Sir John was toasting on a sliver of wood a strange-looking, yellowish piece of meat. Sinclair bent his dark poll over a roundish, smooth-polished object. Sir John seemed to hesitate a second in his reply.

'Dr Sinclair found it, Miss Stranlay. We've already eaten some, but you slept too soundly to be awakened. Better now?'

Something funny about this meat. 'Yes, much.' She stared at Sir John's preparations. '*Found* it?'

The American glanced up, impatiently. 'Nothing mysterious. It won't poison you – I saw to that. It's horse-flesh. There was a partly-eaten carcase about a hundred yards from the mouth of the cave here.'

'Oh. So I didn't dream last night. There *was* a beast like a tiger prowling on the other side of the fire?'

The armaments manufacturer held up the skewer of yellowish meat, looking the most incongruous of cooks as he did so. 'Yes. Some kind of tiger. It probably killed the pony after it ceased to stalk us.'

Clair regarded her breakfast uncertainly.

'I think I'll bath first. Both of you have. Where?'

'Just outside the cave, to the left.'

Clair went out. Sinclair looked after her, looked at Sir John, said something. The armaments manufacturer rose up and followed Clair. She glanced round from bending over the streamlet that had gurgled over her feet the night before.

'I'm sorry, Miss Stranlay, but one of us had better be near. That beast may come back, though it's not very likely.'

'I see.' Clair felt and sounded ungracious – and, as usual, regretted it. She looked away, across the tundra flowering into swamp, at the sun-hazed surface of the mile-distant forest, and then southward, where swamp and forest crept down to the foothills, and their long journey through the llanos-land seemed to end. What was beyond that cul-de-sac? . . . She became aware of Sir John waiting. 'Sorry. Shan't keep you a minute. Do wish I had some soap.'

'There's red earth on the bank here. I used it.' He felt his unshaven face, wryly. 'It seemed fairly effective.'

He thought she looked like an absurd boy in her thin, stained garments. Not at all as he had pictured her. For he had heard of Clair Stranlay before that meeting on the beach, had once, on a train journey, read one of her books. Crude, calamitous, vicious thing. Very vivid, too . . . How had he pictured her? A dark and beetle-like best-seller, perhaps, or one of those blowsily mammalian women you meet in French magazines. Instead: this charming, impertinent boy . . .

He sighed and turned away from that thought. He turned his head away from her also, looking round the deserted countryside. The sun seemed warmer. A little breeze stirred the long grass. The stream glimmered and its gurgling passage was the only sound to be heard. And the same thought came to him as to Clair: what lay south? What country was this, with wild ponies and tigers? Tigers? A sabre-tooth? But that was absurd. Probably some freak animal.

He became aware of Clair standing beside him, dabbing at her face and hands with a bunch of grass. 'That was good . . . Sir John.'

He looked gently into her grave eyes.

'*What* country is this? It can't be Canada. And it can't be Africa.'

He shook his head. 'I'm afraid I haven't an opinion worth knowing, Miss Stranlay. Tigers, I think, are found in the East Indies. But to suppose the *Magellan's Cloud* drifted across the Atlantic, America and the Pacific in those few hours four nights ago is absurd. And I cannot imagine this stretch of uninhabited country in the East Indies.'

Clair finished dabbing, re-tied the fraying neckloop of her jacket. 'No. But we *must* be getting near some inhabited place.'

'I hope so.'

He wouldn't say more than that, though her eyes still questioned him. They went back to the cave. A smudge of smoke, fainter now, for the fire was dying down, rose from it against the limestone hillside. Sinclair was standing in the sunlight at the mouth of the second cave, looking intently southward, as both of them had done. He came and joined them. Clair was surprised at the look on his usually dour face. It was alive with some strayed excitement.

'Feel hungry?' he asked her.

'Shockingly.' But indeed her appetite felt oddly reserved. She sat down beside the fire, but still in the sunlight. She picked up the piece of charred horse-flesh and began to eat it. Sir John stayed outside, leaning against the cave entrance, his greying head down-bent. 'How did you manage to cut it up?'

'With this.' Sinclair was back at the other side of the fire. He held up an object. Clair peered at it. He passed it to her. She turned it over, wonderingly.

It was a fragment of stone, she thought, though it was flint. Even to her unaccustomed eyes it seemed to have a certain artificiality. She held it away from her with her left hand, the while she fed her small, stained mouth with the right. She saw the shape of the thing better then. It was in the form of a smooth-butted axe-blade – an incredibly crude stone axe-blade.

'Why – it's *made*.'

The American nodded. 'It's *made*.'

'Where did you find it?'

'In the next cave. Among a pile of bones.'

She remembered something. She questioned him with her eyes. He nodded.

'Human bones. Though I didn't know that in the darkness last night when I was searching for fuel. Fortunately I didn't burn them all.'

She looked at the thing at his feet, and somehow didn't want any more of the horse-flesh. It was a skull he had been examining. She stood up and went to the entrance. Sir John glanced at her. Something like a smile of sympathy flickered over his face. The American said, abruptly: 'You people.'

They both turned. Sinclair had the skull in his hands. He came towards them. The stone axe-blade slipped out of Clair's forgetful hand as she backed away from the skull. Sinclair sprang forward and caught it, bruising his fingers. He swore. Sir John turned his head, Clair tried hard to repress herself, failed; giggled. Sir John's laughter joined with hers.

'I'm so sorry.' Genuinely contrite.

'All right. I want to talk to you both about these finds.' He addressed Sir John, still with something of an effort. 'Know anything about crania?'

Sir John shook his head. 'Nothing at all.' He took the skull in his hand, however, and examined it. It was complete to jawbone and teeth. He held it out to Clair. She waved it away.

'No thanks. Ghastly thing. It's got a permanent frown, too.'

Sinclair: 'Exactly. That's the point. It's not an ordinary skull.'

The other two regarded it, back in Sinclair's hands. 'A savage's?' said Clair, helpfully.

'Of course it's a savage's. Otherwise he wouldn't have had a flint hand-axe in his possession when he was carried back in there and devoured by the sabre-tooth.'

Clair shivered. 'Was that what happened?' She looked over the undulating waste of grass to the dark boles of the sun-crowned forest. 'Ugh.'

Sir John glanced at her, and interposed, gently. 'And what is peculiar about the skull?'

'It's as Miss Stranlay says. It has a permanent frown – look, this ridge above the eyes. And practically no forehead.' He loosened the clenched jaw. 'Look at the teeth.'

They looked. 'Funny,' said Clair, at once repulsed and fascinated. Sinclair closed the jaw again, set the skull at his feet, stared at it, fascinated also.

'Not a human skull at all, you know, as we understand the term human. By rights it belongs to a race that died off twenty thousand years ago.'

Clair was startled into dim memories of casual reading in pre-history. 'What race?'

'The Neanderthal. It's a Neanderthal skull.'

Subchapter iv

By early afternoon they had left the caves some four or five miles behind, and, tramping along the edge of the foothills, were nearing the spot where hills and forest converged. Sinclair, as usual, walked in advance. He was burdened with the remains of the horseflesh, a great haunch, and the cord of his pyjama-shorts sagged under the weight of the flint axe-head. The strange skull he had abandoned with reluctance.

Clair and Sir John walked side by side, half a dozen yards behind him. Sir John said: 'I'm afraid we're rather a drag on our leader. By the way, have you noticed how much alike your names are? – Clair and Sinclair.'

She looked after the long-striding figure of the American, and unconsciously increased her own pace. 'He's the saint and I'm the Clair . . . *Is* energetic. I'm sure that's why they used to martyr saints.' (But it wouldn't do to discuss one with the other.) 'What do you think of the skull?'

'I don't know what to think. Though I should imagine that the chances are Dr Sinclair has made a mistake.'

'Neanderthal man . . . They all died off in the last Glacial Age – I think. Or was it just after it? Perhaps it was a fossil skull.'

The armaments manufacturer, striding barefooted, bowed-shouldered beside her, shook his head. 'No, it wasn't that. I'm afraid I know little or nothing of such matters, but it was comparatively fresh bone.'

'Funny if there are any more of them about.'

Sir John also thought that, but did not say so. Funny? The coarse grass was warm and dry under their feet. The last of the volcanoes had disappeared on the northwards horizon. Sinclair slowed down till they caught up with him. He pointed.

They were at a slight elevation by then. The forest did not close completely on the hills, but left a narrow corridor, a waste, bush-strewn space. Across this space they looked, and it was as if they were at no slight elevation, but on a mountain-side. For beyond the passage-way the land failed completely, as it seemed. Yet, remote and far away, downwards, southwards, something like a lake shimmered, forest-fringed; and blue and golden, there shone under the sunlight a suggestion of immense tracts of waste country. All three of the travellers stared, Clair with sinking heart. It must be miles to that lake. And no sign anywhere of a native village or trading station.

'We're on a high level – a plateau with mountains,' said Sinclair, unemotionally. 'We've been travelling across it for days. That's why we've seen so few animals, probably. There's nothing here but strays from down there.'

Sir John said: 'And we're going down?'

'Yes.'

Clair smiled at the American, casually, friendlily. 'There's no "yes" about it. Not until we've all made up our minds.'

Sinclair's ears tinted themselves a slow red. '*I* am going down.'

'Do.'

Sir John interposed. 'Really, Miss Stranlay, I don't think there is anything else to be done now . . . Though possibly Dr Sinclair might word his invitations a little more courteously in future.'

Sinclair scowled at him, angrily. 'Courtesy! Do you realize we're absolutely lost somewhere in absolutely unknown and unexplored country? That there are *machaerodi* and possibly other wild beasts in it – to say nothing of Neanderthalers?'

'That seems to be the case,' said Clair. 'But it doesn't alter the fact that your manners are badly in need of improvement.'

He glanced from one to the other of them, as though he were looking at idiots. He shrugged. 'All right. Bad though they may be, I think it would be ruinous if we split into two parties.' He bowed, a ludicrous, angry figure. 'Would you mind coming down into the low country, Miss Stranlay?'

Clair had a ridiculous impulse and a lovable singing voice – a deep, untrained contralto. They stared at her startled as she held out her arms and smiled at the wild lands below them.

> *'Oh, ye'll take the high road,*
> *And I'll take the low road,*
> *And I'll be in Scotland afore ye;*
> *But me and my true love*
> *We'll never meet again*
> *On the bonny, bonny banks of Loch Lomond!'*

She felt her eyes grown moist, involuntarily. Sir John said, gently: 'Thank you, Miss Stranlay.'

'Silly,' Clair confessed.

'Not silly at all, Miss Stranlay.' It was Sinclair, unexpectedly. 'Thank you also. I was a lout.'

'You're a dear,' said Clair, soberly, and for the second time that day.

Subchapter v

It was a steeply-shelving descent of nearly a mile, over the usual coarse grass. At the foot Sinclair waited – as usual. He avoided Clair's eyes. He had avoided them since that remark. 'We have about an hour until sunset.'

Sir John, panting, sat down. 'And what are we going to do until then?'

The American pacifist seemed for once at a loss. 'Find a place to camp, I suppose.'

'Looks different somehow,' said Clair.

It did. The forest was more widely spread or the tundra more en-forested, according to one's fancy. Some oaks – young-looking oaks – grew near at hand. Smooth, hog-backed hills rose here and there in the tree-set waste, but there were no mountains, no volcanoes. Also, near sunset though it was, this low country was much warmer than the plateau they had just deserted. Nor was it so silent. A long-necked grey bird flitted among the oaks; they could hear the swish of its wings through the leaves. Remote among the low, smooth-humped hills a vast, long-drawn moan rose and fell; they had not noticed it at first, because it was part of the landscape. Now, as it ceased, they peered in the direction from which it had come.

'A cow,' said Clair.

It did indeed sound like the lowing of a cow – a gigantic cow. Presently it ceased with some decision, and was not resumed. Sinclair stood with his fingers on his hand-axe. 'Bison, perhaps.'

'What *is* this place, Dr Sinclair?'

The question worried all three of them continually. Clair put it into words most frequently. Sir John glanced up at her, then at the ragged bearer of the horse-haunch. The latter started.

'Eh? . . . God knows.'

'I doubt it,' said Clair.

The American began to move across the grass towards the trees. Clair held out her hand to Sir John, but he stood up without assistance, albeit with a grimace. Presently they were threading a new belt of trees, very green and lush with undergrowth, and with their shadows pointing long, dark fingers into the east. The grey bird was silent. So was all else of the hidden life of the tree-spaces – if there were life. Clair heard herself call in a whisper: 'Where are we going?'

Sinclair's voice also was low. 'Some place where there's water.'

They emerged from the trees then, into another clearing. Doing so, Clair seemed to hear a sound of low rumblings, like the borborygm in a large and placid stomach. She thought, rather ruefully: 'Not mine.' And went on, following the sunset-reddened back of Sinclair. Neither he nor Sir John had heard anything.

But suddenly they did. Fallen boughs crunched and snapped, and something with heavy tread came after them from the twilight darkness of the trees.

They all halted, looking back. For a moment they could distinguish nothing, though the heavy tread paced towards them. And then they saw it against the dun light of an open patch – its swaying bulk, its matted shagginess. Its trunk was lowered, sniffing the track they had taken.

They stared appalled. They had all seen its like before – in this or that museum or illustration. There could be no mistaking those curved immensities of tusk.

It was a mammoth.

CHAPTER FIVE

And I'll take the low road

Subchapter i

They camped a quarter of an hour or so later, by the mere of the lake that had glittered its invitation from the northern plateau. Tall reeds grew far out into the water, and, remotely over that water, unknown birds croaked and dipped amid long grasses that Sinclair certified were – of all things – wild wheat. The American knelt under the moss-shaggy boughs of a great oak, coaxing Sir John's lighter to imbed a spark in a tuft of withered grass. Sunset was again close – the lingering sunset of a temperate country. It might have been eight o'clock in the evening.

Clair padded to and fro, bough-collecting, with even her bare feet a little chilled by the evening dew. Sir John, outside the obscuring bulk of the oak, was looking back to the dimness of the plateau – that high land where they had adventured through three long days.

And the mammoth continued to watch them.

It was halted at a distance of ten yards or so, not facing them, but in profile. Its great ears flapped meditatively and every now and then its trunk would stray upwards into the foliage of a bush, or down into the unappetizing grass. The sunset glimmered on its watching eye . . .

It had trailed them like a great retriever, halting when they halted, coming on again as they moved hesitatingly away. While they crossed a clear space it would stop and watch them, pawing a little, rubbing a gigantic, hair-fringed shoulder against a tree. Then it would pace swingingly after them. Once, apparently imagining them lost, it had frolicked wildly amid the bushes, hunting the scent of them with uplifted trunk.

'It must be harmless,' Clair had whispered, walking between the two men.

'Trying to summon up courage to charge,' hazarded Sinclair.

'Hope it comes of a timid family.'

'I'm afraid we can't do anything to prevent it charging, anyhow,' said Sir John, glancing over his shoulder and starting a little. ' . . . I thought it was coming that time.'

But it had not, and, the lake opening out before them, there had been no other course obvious than to camp. It was eerie doing so with that watching monster pretending not to watch them. Clair knelt by Sinclair with a handful of twigs, seeing he had caught a spark and was cherishing the grass into the parturition of a flame.

He glanced at her. 'The fire may scare it off or may madden it into making an attack. Scoot round the back of the tree if it comes.' He spoke in a whisper. 'Frightened?'

Clair fed the flame with a twig, resolutely keeping her eyes from the watcher. 'Not now. Rather a thrill . . . What's it doing now?'

Sir John came to their side. 'I think it's going to charge.'

The mammoth had knelt on its knees, embedding its immense tusks in a great clump of grass. There came a crackling, tearing sound. The mammoth stood up. Its tusks were laden with grass, like the rake of a hay-maker. Elevating its trunk to the fodder, it proceeded to test and devour great wisps.

'Bless it,' said Clair, 'it's having its supper.'

The armaments manufacturer ruffled his grey hair. 'One certainly didn't expect such mildness. A *mammoth*!'

There the brute stood, real enough, feeding and watching them, with the brown night closing down behind him. The flame came now in little spurts and glows and the twigs caught and, cautiously, Sinclair admin- istered first small branches, then larger ones. The firelight went out across the gloaming shadows, splashing gently on the red-brown coat and bare, creased skull of the mammoth. It paused for a little in its eating, turning its trunk towards them. Then resumed. Clair sat down and held her head between her hands.

'A mammoth in the twentieth century! It's – oh, it's ridiculous.'

Sir John, standing and looking at the watcher, patted her shoulder. Sinclair hacked at the dried horsemeat with the Neanderthal axe. The meat had a faint smell of decay. He said: 'I've been thinking about where we are. I know now it can't be Canada.'

'And it's certainly not Africa, as I thought at first,' murmured Sir John.

'No. I think we're in Patagonia.'

Clair drew back warmed toes from the fire. Abruptly the last of the daylight went. The lake misted from a pale sheen to a dark, rippling mystery. The sound of the mammoth feeding was oddly homely . . . Patagonia?

'But I understand practically all of it has been explored,' said Sir John.

Sinclair toasted yellow meat for a moment. 'I don't think so. Delusion we North Americans and English have about every country which is shown plainly on a map, with the main mountains and rivers and a pol- itical colouring. We can't get it into our heads that these places are much larger than a home county. And of course – ' He stopped and frowned at the piece of meat. He addressed Clair. He still avoided, as far as possible, speaking directly to Sir John Mullaghan. 'Did you notice from the plateau brow the mere tips of a mountain-range – they must be more than fifty miles away – down there in the south, Miss Stranlay?'

Clair nodded.

'I think they must be the Andes. We're somewhere in the western Argentine or the foothills of Chili – the country where Pritchard went to hunt the great sloth. We may be traversing a mountain kink or fold that up to this time has escaped notice completely.'

Clair thought. Then: 'A kink with sabre-tooth tigers and fresh Neanderthal skulls in it – and mammoths?'

'All possible.' But his voice sounded less certain.

Sir John said: 'But not very probable. We landed on a sea-coast, somewhere, went inland, and turned south. That sea-coast, if this is South American, must have been the Atlantic. And Patagonia, if my memory serves me, is remote from the Atlantic. Also, it has grown warmer the further south we have come. If we are south of the equator it ought to grow colder.'

Sinclair detached the piece of meat from its wooden skewer and handed it to Clair. He nodded acknowledgment of Sir John's arguments and was silent. All three of them sat and ate the tough meat. Then, stumbling among the reeds, they went down to the lake in search of water. At a spot that glimmered faintly Sinclair lay down full length and drank. Sir John followed suit. Clair squatted and cupped the water in her hands and drank that way. As they came back to the fire they noted the mammoth still in guardianship. Overhead there was a faint pearliness in the darkness of the sky.

Sir John raked about in the shadows outside the fire, collecting damp grass and arranging it for drying to act as pillows and mattresses. Clair sat a yard or so from Sinclair, looking into the fire, drowsy and still a little hungry after her meagre ration of horseflesh. Sinclair had procured a long bough from amid the treelitter and was whittling at it doggedly with the flint-axe.

'Stone Age idyll,' murmured Clair.

'Eh?'

She repeated the words, and, as she did so, remote away beyond the lake, strange and eerie, that lowing they had heard in the early afternoon broke out again. It rose and belled and fell, the calling of some stray of a Titan herd. Unexpectedly, for he had been quiet enough until then, the mammoth answered, lifting his trunk in the remote washings of the firelight and trumpeting screamingly. Clair thought her ear-drums would burst. She covered them and heard the noise die down. The ensuing quietness held no hint of the distant lowing.

But to Clair, with it dead, there came an almost passionate wish that it would break out again. She looked at the two men, at the darkness around them, at the bulk of the strange beast that guarded them so queerly. That lowing and wild trumpeting seemed to have torn down a barrier inside her heart – that calling across wild spaces heard in the shelter of the campfire . . . She had heard it before, somewhere, at some time, in an era that knew not print and publishers. Often. And of all sounds it had lived with her through changes innumerable. She had heard it before in lives not her own –

Fantastic dream!

'Miss Stranlay!' Sir John's hand on her shoulder. 'You'd best lie down if you're so sleepy. You nearly fell into the fire.'

Subchapter ii
'Did I?'

She shook herself and looked at them. Sinclair, hafting his axe-head on the bough and binding it with sinews he had saved from the tiger-killed pony, had half-risen to catch her just as Sir John forestalled him. He sank down again. The armaments manufacturer, padding about barefooted, arranged the grass beds. He looked over at Clair, hearing her low laugh.

'Nothing much, Sir John. But I'd just said to Dr Sinclair, before that trumpeting started, that this was a Stone Age idyll. And just now I caught sight of your clothes.'

The firelight twinkled on a grey head and the smile on a gentle, cultured face. 'And they don't fit the part?'

'Not very well.'

The American laughed shortly. 'The warrior was the armaments manufacturer of the Stone Age, Miss Stranlay, and no doubt wore appropriate habiliments.'

Clair felt a little pang of shame for him. The fire simmered cheerfully. Sir John straightened and looked across at the deportee.

'Yes, the warrior was probably the equivalent of the armaments manufacturer,' he said quietly. 'He brought order and a livable relationship into primitive anarchy. And his task isn't yet finished.'

Clair said: 'Perhaps it hasn't begun in this country yet . . . Funniest nightmare of a country we've landed in! I'd give anything for clothes and a bathroom and electric light and – oh, for a cigarette!' She paused and tried to put into unfacile words that strange aching that had been in her heart hearing the lowing in the distant hills. She looked at Sinclair's and Mullaghan's listening faces. 'But there's something in it that's not terrifying at all. Lovely, rather. The silence and starkness . . . Those primitives of the Old Stone Age – they had some elemental contacts with beauty that we've lost for ever.'

Sir John Mullaghan sat clasping his knees, rubbing his chilled, bare feet. He shook his head. 'They had this kind of country, perhaps, but it was not the country you see with your civilized, romantic eyes, Miss Stranlay. It was a waste of ghouls for them. The night was a horror to the squatting-places – the time when the dead Old Men of the tribes returned as stalking carnivorae, the time of shuddering fear. It was a life livable only for the strongest and most brutal. For thousands and thousands of years life was that only. And here and there rose the soldier and the inventor, the men who subjected the squalid and lowly, who built the first classes and sowed the first seeds. And the long climb from the filth and futility of the night-time camps began.'

'Poor ancestors!' Clair said it soberly, her eyes on the night.

Sinclair finished bonding his axe, and laid it on his knees and looked into the fire.

'That was the life of the Stone Age savage, Miss Stranlay. And the strong men and the wise men, the warriors and the witch-doctors, bound him in chains of taboo – the first laws – and made him less of a beast. For twenty thousand years they've fashioned new chains for him, till civilized man has taken the place of the savage. But it's been no simple case of design. The old, meaningless taboos and loyalties – once necessary and just – are things that threaten to strangle us nowadays. The age of the witch-doctor and the warrior is over. But they won't believe it. They still preach their obscene gods and raise and equip armies that now threaten to smash to atoms the foundations of civilization. It is they who are the ghouls who haunt the contemporary world.'

Sir John said, steadily: 'They are the ghouls, if you like, that guard civilization. The strong man keeps his house and the wise country an army on the *qui vive*. The soldier is civilization's safeguard, and still, thank God, defends it against anarchic sentimentalities. . . Do you people know *nothing* of the beast that is in human nature unless there is force and discipline to keep it down? I had a daughter once. Twelve years of age. Bright and clean and very glad to be alive. Like Miss Stranlay in some ways . . . She was missing one night. She was found under some bushes a mile or so away from home next day. She had been raped and murdered by a tramp.'

Clair made an inarticulate sound of sympathy. Sinclair's knuckles whitened round his axe-haft. 'I also have seen human beings mutilated and murdered – in thousands. And through no chance accident of lust or madness. Sentimentalist? My God, you old men! Sentimentalists we are then, and our fight is for human sanity. Don't think we shirk facts. And we've learned from experience. We know that man's a fighting animal by nature, that cruelty's his birthright; and we also know that what keep us in the pit as animals are the armies and the armaments. We're out to smash both, we who have had some personal experience of both. And we'll do it. There's a league of men coming into being that'll send a bullet into the brain of every clown who preaches war in future, Sir John – and a bomb into the office of every armaments manufacturer who trades in blood and human agony . . . It is you and your kind who will not let the ape and tiger die. And they're prepared to your challenge.'

Clair's voice startled them. 'I had a lover in 1917. A boy. He'd have hated to hurt the hatefullest human on earth. He went to France because I taunted him. He died on the barb wire at Mametz. All night. He screamed my name all night . . . And at heart he was just a savage filled with lust and cruelty?'

They said nothing, uncomfortably. Clair thought, suddenly weary: 'Idiotic to speak about that. Oh, my dear, my dear, who died there at Mametz, that's a time long ago, and I can't do anything for you now . . .'

She leant back with her hands under her head. They had all three forgotten the mammoth. Now they heard its steady munching. Clair thought, with a reckless change to gaiety: 'It'll have tummy-ache if it's not careful.' She said: 'There come the stars. We're hopelessly lost, but they're still the same as ever.'

Unchanged, indeed, and remote and cold as ever. As though a lamp-man walked the dark spaces of the night they kindled in groups and constellations. The night was very still and cloudless. It was not yet moonrise. The evening star burned palely beyond the stance of the drowsily-shuffling mammoth. And over the darkness of the untrodden lands to the south Jupiter hung like a twinkling ball of fire.

Subchapter iii

In the morning the mammoth had gone. There was no trace of it but the trampled stretch of grass and a great heap of dung. Wakening the first of the three, Clair thought she heard remote trumpetings. But whether these were memories from night-time dreams, or the farewell callings of their mysterious guardian, there was nothing now in the quietude of the morning to tell her.

The fire was a grey fluff. They had slept beyond the first chill of the dawn, and the sunshine, like early spring sunshine in the greys and greens of England, sprayed through the lattice-patterns of the oak boughs. The reeds that hid the lake stood in long battalions, peering into the sunrise, with the urge behind them of a little wind from the places of the earth that the morning had not yet touched. Sinclair slept beside Clair with his arms outflung and begrimed, his bearded face hid in his shoulder. Clair touched that shoulder with the tips of her fingers, found it cold, pulled the eiderdown quilt over it, and herself stood up.

Sir John Mullaghan slept huddled in his stained coat, his grey-streaked hair ruffled every now and then by a stray waft of wind from the places of the sunset.

Clair wondered if she should make a fire. But either Sinclair or Sir John had the lighter. She moved about under the oak, and further into the bushes, collecting twigs. She found a stretch of gorse-bushes, very yellow and scented, still wet with night-mist. It was as she stood among them that the lark began to sing.

It was at first no more than a remote piping up in the grey pearlment of the sky. But it came nearer, and the sound hovered, and, shading her eyes, it seemed to Clair that she saw the fluttering singer for a moment. She stood and listened and found herself weeping. She dropped the bundle of firewood and, weeping, stood in that morning listening to the amazing sound. Shrill and strange and sweet, the piping of youth unforgotten! . . . And they took that youth and smeared it with the filths of the years, murdered it on barb-wire entanglements, gave it to torture and horrific agonies in the hands of lust-crazed lunatics . . .

Clair thought: 'But, even so, we've heard it. It's worth having heard it though the memory torture us all our lives.'

It died away. Clair picked up the firewood and went back to the camping-place. The men still slept. For a little she considered them and then went down through the dark, seeping peat-edges to the mere of the lake. A bird flew out of the reeds as she approached. A kingfisher. From her feet the cold of the ground spread up through her body. Accustomed though she was, she shivered in the sunlight. She bent and touched the water and found it – 'wet, of course. And cold enough. Doesn't matter. I'm too filthy for description.'

She undressed, a simple matter, and waded out, into a clamouring pain of coldness. Her hair fell over her face and she switched her mind to that matter as the water rose higher, over her knees, creeping upwards . . . 'Getting long, and where will you find a barber's shop? Unless Sinclair operates with his flint-axe . . . Now? Deep enough?' She halted, half-knelt, and flung herself forward.

Deep enough.

She swam into the sunrise through a long lane in the reeds. Beyond that lane cramp caught her right arm for a moment and she struggled with it, a little frightened, until it passed. The lake swept to the horizon almost, she saw, though from its surface there was no sign of Sinclair's Andes . . . Alligators?

But there seemed nothing living in the region of the lake, apart from the skimming kingfishers. She turned round at last and swam towards the remote, solitary oak. As she did so she suffered from the curious illusion that it waved to and fro, violently, as in a high wind. A thin, pencil-point of smoke was rising. It did the same.

'Curious. Something wrong with my heart?'

Soberly, she reached the shore and dressed, and went through the reeds, hearing the anxious calling of Sinclair and Sir John, whom an earthquake of considerable intensity had disturbed in the preparation of breakfast.

Subchapter iv

Clair thought: 'We are in the Hollow Land.'

There were high hills both to right and left now as they still pressed south. For four or five miles they kept the bank of the lake, but that was soon left behind, a radiance that presently betook itself from the earth to the sky. The leftwards hills were the further away, and betwixt them rose and fell in long undulations a crazy scarping of nullahs. Underfoot was the long grass, but of finer texture here than on the northwards plateau, growing in places lush and emerald, especially where some stream hesitated and crept and slept and woke and shook itself and meandered uncertainly amid the llano.

It was a land of streams. They forded three – one at a trampled place, where were the imprints of both tiny hoofs and great paws.

'Why are we still going south?' Clair asked once.

'Because we might as well,' the American returned, broodingly.

Sir John suffered from agonies of stomach-ache throughout that day. He walked beside Clair with distorted face and frequently distorted body. Several times he sat down while the other two stood and waited. Sinclair could do nothing for him – or at least offered to do nothing. Neither he nor Clair had as yet been affected by the saltless diet of horseflesh. But the surviving piece quite definitely began to smell undaintily. It was fortunate that the country seemed almost entirely devoid of insects.

Sinclair carried his axe-blade hafted now on a five-foot pole. He stalked a sound in the bushes with it once, only to disturb a long, tawny shape which snarled at him sleepily. Then it turned and slunk unhurriedly into deeper cover. Sinclair, rather pale, rejoined the other two.

'What was it?' Clair asked.

He glanced at Sir John. 'A lion.'

They went on. Once, far towards the leftward hills, and beyond the nullahs, they heard that lowing break out again. Plangent and plaintive. Several times herds of small deer such as they had twice seen on the plateau were observable at a distance, feeding with some daintiness and apparent enjoyment. Clair looked at them carnivorously. But the wind went steadily south and at the first whiff of the travellers, and long before Sinclair could near them, the deer had gone.

'How many more meals?' Clair asked the American, looking without appetite at the shrinking haunch of horseflesh. Sinclair had dropped back from his old position in the van and walked beside the other two now.

'Two, I think.'

Sir John, padding along in pain, grimaced. 'You may count it three. I – I don't think I'll be hungry for some time.'

'Oh, the doctor may be able to stalk something fresh,' said Clair.

Instead, it was something fresh which presently stalked them, though they never caught sight of it. The noise of its padding pursuit and appraisal began to the right of a long corridor of bushes. The three went on for a little while, and then halted, listening. The stalker had halted also. In the sunshine silence they heard the noise of its heavy breathing. And a sound of a swish-swish among the leaves. ('Its tail,' thought Clair.) Sinclair changed from the left hand side of the march to the right. They waited. No movement of approach. They went forward again. The paddings and cracklings came after them, till beyond the bushes they were in open grassland again and the stalker gave them up.

At noon they made a fire near the usual stream, and Sinclair toasted the meat. Sir John lay full-length on the ground, his face hidden, saying nothing. Clair, who had been looking about her as they trekked, walked a quarter of a mile or so away across the llano, into a patch of gorse-like bushes. Presently she emerged from these, coming back with her hands held like a cup. As she came near the fire she called: 'Sir John!'

He looked up at her, and smiled wryly, his face drawn with pain. She knelt beside him. Her hands were filled with blueberries.

'Now you can lunch.'

'You are a very sweet lady.'

His eyes were grave and Clair looked at him as gravely. 'Thank you,' she said, and emptied the berries into his hands. Sinclair said, evenly:

'You shouldn't eat too many of them, else it'll be as bad for you as the meat. Some horse, Miss Stranlay?'

They went on again, after Clair had fallen asleep and slept a dream-filled hour in the sun. The southwards nullah-jumble drew nearer with its background of hills. And on the upper ranges of those hills was a glittering yellow colourlessness.

In mid-afternoon they came upon the giant deer.

It stood with head lowered, drinking at a pool, with dark-brown back pelt and white-dappled belly. It was quite close to them when they came through a belt of trees on it, and it was a moment before Clair realized its hugeness. Then she saw Sinclair's six feet two in outline against the thing: it had the bulk of a small elephant.

From its head uprose a twelve-foot spread of antlers, velvet-rimed. Clair thought: 'They must weigh half a ton.' The brute slowly lifted its head and regarded them with vague, indifferent eyes. Then it inhaled deeply, coughed, and trotted away, unhurryingly, westwards. They stared after it, seeing it clear the dip of a nullah in one magnificent bound, and then disappear through a pass in the hills.

And presently over those hills came the hunters.

Subchapter v

They came like figures on a Grecian frieze upflung against the colours of the sunset.

First, there was the afternoon quietness but for the scuffle of the grass underfoot. The sun overhung the hills, the country lay deserted since the great deer had vanished. Clair had bent to pick a thorn from her foot and her companions also had halted, Sir John lifting his face, smelling at some unusual odour he imagined upon the wind. Then –

The first intimation was a far, wild neighing and stamping. Clair straightened and looked at the other two. Their eyes were on the grass-covered hill-top perhaps a quarter of a mile away. Its rim was set with hasting dots – dots that changed, enlarged, were heads, shoulders, flying manes. It was a herd of wild ponies in panic flight. The drumming of their hoofs came down to the watchers. Up over the hill into full view they thundered, with flowing manes and tails, thundering against the sunset. And behind, company on company, racing into view, came the hunters.

They ran in silence, tall and naked, the sunshine glistening on golden bodies, their hair flying like the horses' manes. Golden and wonderful against the hill-crest they ran, and the staring Sinclair drew a long breath.

'Good God, they are running as fast as the horses!'

It was unbelievable. It was true. And while Sinclair and Sir John stared at now one hunter, now another, overtake his prey and spear it with whirling weapon, Clair Stranlay put her hands to her lips and whistled up through the evening that piercing blast learned long before in the streets of Battersea.

CHAPTER SIX
The hunters

Subchapter i

Those ensuing moments! Looking back on them, Clair was to wonder, with a strange tautness of her heartstrings, if they were indeed as her memory pictured them – if the fervour of the sunset behind the hunters had indeed been so intense, their approach to the three survivors of the *Magellan* so rapid. They had come fleeting down the hill, a wash of gold, with the speed of converging clouds in a rainstorm. Abandoning the carcases of the ponies they had swooped downwards in a bright torrent, and in Clair's memory she had fast-closed her eyes at sight of their spears. She had thought: 'They will throw those spears.'

But they had not. She had opened her eyes again, to find that Sinclair, upright and with scowling face, had moved a little in front of her, as though to shield her from the approaching savages. Close now. Gold and naked, with flying hair.

And then indeed in her heart had leapt that strange quiver of unreality upon which her memory insisted – or was that a later-learnt thing from Sinclair's theories? For in that moment of mind-tremor it was a torrent of men from her own land – pale and pinched and padded – who bore down upon her . . . Then that passed. She stood shaking, but seeing clearly again.

Two score or more of them, naked and tall and golden-brown, not one of them under six feet in height. Some of them mere boys; no old men. And their faces! They were the faces of no savages of whom she had ever heard or read: broad, comely, high-cheekboned, some with black eyes and some with blue, and one she noted with eyes that were vividly grey eyes in his golden face . . . Sinclair barking out: 'Damn you! Keep off!'

They took no notice whatever. Sir John Mullaghan put his arm round Clair, Sinclair fell back to her other side. The hunters at that manoeuvre halted, queried each other with surprised looks, and then burst into a loud peal of laughter.

Sinclair swung up his axe. 'Keep off!'

For answer one of the hunters, armed with a piece of wood shaped like a boomerang, laughed in the American's face and came casually forward under the threat of the axe – so close did he come that he stood not three feet away. Clair stared up at him, saw him young, with white teeth uncovered in an enjoying grin ('and that completes his costume', added the imp in her mind) – then found her attention distracted. Sir John's arm shot past her, gripping Sinclair's just as it was about to descend.

'Keep steady, Dr Sinclair. We can't do anything . . . Ah, it's too late.'

For the young hunter had wheeled round at a call from his companions. Most of them had halted in attitudes of casual surprise or cheerful indifference, but three of them, older men, were poising their spears, warningly. They called something again, and the young man, the mirth falling from his face, drew back. Unexpectedly, Sinclair dropped his axe and stood staring stupidly.

Next moment, apparently galvanized into action by nothing more than a co-operative impulse, the hunters swept in and surrounded them.

'They're friendly,' said Sir John. 'Keep cool, Miss Stranlay.'

'I'm going to –'

A hand tugged gently at the eiderdown quilt draped round her shoulders. She wheeled round, clutching the thing. An impudent golden face smiled down at her. Behind came another tug, and she turned on that. The quilt was in the hands of the young hunter who had smiled under the threat of the Neanderthal axe. He dropped it, and stretched out his hands again, his eyes lighted with amused curiosity. Clair's heart contracted.

'No – *no!*'

The laughter of the savages echoed up the evening of the hills. The three survivors of the *Magellan's Cloud* found themselves patted and pinched and questioned in pantomime. The young hunter, smiling, put his arms round Clair, and in a sudden panic she sank her teeth into a warm, muscular, golden arm.

The savage drew back with a cry of pain. Sinclair struggled free from the group surrounding him. He glanced round and caught sight of Clair.

'Miss Stranlay? What is it?'

'Nothing.' She was already repentant. 'I was a fool.'

She bent to reclaim the eiderdown. One of the hunters, like a mischievous boy, kicked it beyond her reach. Thereat Sinclair flung him nearly as far. The laughter died down. The levitated hunter picked himself up, his face black with anger. He dropped his spear, came running into the circle again, pushed his face close to Sinclair's, and shouted excitedly.

'Don't touch him again, Sinclair!' Clair discovered Sir John Mullaghan, panting, standing by her side. The hunters had fallen silent, with eager, expectant faces. Sir John said: 'God bless me!'

Sinclair, his head thrust forward as had been the angry hunter's, seemed to be replying to the savage in his own language – a torrent of consonants. At that the angry one suddenly smacked the American in the face, and then leapt back lightly out of range. Doing so, the anger vanished from his face. He laughed. Thereon all the others shouted with laughter as well, Clair's assailant being so overcome that he had to hold his sides . . .

The *Magellan's* survivors stared astounded.

'Must be a colony of escaped lunatics,' said Sir John. 'I'll try and get you that quilt, Miss Stranlay . . . What now?'

'*Utso! Utso!*'

The hunters, yelling, turned and ran, all but three of them. One of these seized Sinclair's wrist, another Sir John's, gesticulating the while towards the hill where the pony-battue had taken place. Clair found her right hand in the grasp of a savage whose face was vaguely familiar. It was he of the vivid grey eyes.

He waved towards the hill, urgently. Clair, with a last, desperate glance backwards, pointed to the quilt. He shook his head. Next moment, in the trail of Sir John and his captor, Clair Stranlay found herself running through the evening shadows of the unknown land by the side of a golden body and a golden head which stirred a misty clamour of memories in her mind.

Subchapter ii

There were half a dozen ponies on the hill-brow. They were no larger than Shetlands. One of them was not quite dead. As Clair and the grey-eyed hunter arrived, a savage bent over the beast and, poising a flint-axe in his hand, neatly split its skull. Half the hunters faced outwards, their flint-tipped spears held ready. Strange, grey-black things, with high shoulders and dragging hindquarters, came out of the gloaming dimness, glared at the groupings of dead ponies and quick men, snarled disappointedly, and wobbled backwards. A hunter made a feint with his spear at one of these unaccountable beasts. Thereat, scrambling away like a calf, it guffawed hideously. Clair felt she was going mad, standing in the gloaming chill among these laughing savages and laughing beasts. She found Sinclair beside her, and clung to him for a moment, thinking: 'That scowl of yours is the only sane thing in this country.' She shook him.

'Who are they? What are they going to do?'

'Wish I knew – the giggling swine! Especially that clown who slapped my face –'

'Oh, never mind your face.'

'I'm sorry.' Stiffly.

They looked at each other. Clair began to giggle. The American still scowled with twitching face. Clair realized he was almost as hysterical as she was. Realization was somehow sobering. A hunter near them, bending over the carcase of a pony, pushed his bearded face towards them, grinning inquisitively himself, as though desirous of sharing a joke. Sir John Mullaghan struggled to their side, though indeed no one made any effort to detain him.

'Sinclair, since you know their language –'

'Oh, yes, and what language is it?' Clair also had remembered.

'I don't know.' He stared at them puzzledly in the twilight. 'I've no memory of hearing it before. But when that circus clown came jabbering I found myself – answering him.'

'But you *must* know what you answered.'

'I don't . . . Good God, are we to stand here while I'm put through an examination in linguistics? Stop that damned giggling, Miss Stranlay . . . I'll ask them where they're going to take us –'

'No need,' said the armaments manufacturer.

Nor was there. The hunters, half of them laden with portions of pony carcase, began to move down the southward brow of the hill. They seemed to have no leader. The move was made in a drift of mutual convenience. A large, elderly man, over-burdened, stopped beside Sinclair and motioned unmistakably. He wanted assistance.

'I'm damned if I do,' said the American.

The man showed his teeth in a grin, lingered, moved on. It was almost dark. A hunter with his spear slung on his arm by a thong caught Sir John and Sinclair by the arms and urged them down the hillside. Looking after them it struck Clair, absurdly, that he was doing the thing in sheer friendliness . . . Next moment she found herself alone on the hill-brow with the beasts, now a dark mass like a moving carpet, snuffling up the hill towards her. She would have run but that a hand came over her shoulder, and she almost screamed at that. It was the grey-eyed hunter. He was evidently the rearguard. He smiled and motioned southward. He smiled less frequently than the others. His body smelt of red earth. Clair thought, sickly: 'Some caveman stuff, now, of course.' And so thinking she was suddenly very sick.

The savage left her side. Being ill, she heard the sound of a furious scuffle, the impact of blows. The hunter returned, breathing heavily, glancing over his shoulder. He caught her arm anxiously. They began to run downhill together. Thereat a wurr of protest behind them changed into a scamper of many paws and a blood-freezing bay of laughter.

Sinclair, Sir John and the others had disappeared. Clair ran blindly in the darkness over grass and things that were probably bush-roots, for she stumbled on them. Behind, the pattering sound gained volume. Clair understood. The man beside her could run as fast as the beasts by whom they were being pursued. She was delaying him. She shook her arm free.

'Go on, you idiot, then! I can't.'

For answer, still holding her hand, he swung to the right. Clair heard the scratch and scrape of the wheeling pack behind them. The hunter's hand shot up and gripped her wrist.

Next moment they trod vacancy.

Clair heard a feeble little ghost of a scream come from her own lips. She curved her body automatically and next moment struck water – water she could not see. It closed over her body like an envelope of red-hot steel. Down and down, with burning eyeballs. Something tearing at her, something holding her . . . She found herself on the surface – the surface of a river it must be, for the current was strong – trying to swim and hampered in the effort by the grip of the naked hunter.

She tried to wrench her arm free, and then immediately stopped, realizing that he evidently knew in which direction to swim. Which she as certainly did not. A short distance away a snuffling clamour and bestial laughter grew fainter. Clair's knee struck soggy, yielding ground. They crawled through a stretch of swamp; scrambled up an incline. Clair fell on the ground, panting. It was black as pitch. The savage was the vaguest shadow. He pulled at her shoulder impatiently, saying incomprehensible things. She raised her head.

Quite near at hand was the glow of five great fires.

Subchapter iii

So it seemed to Clair then, looking at that bright segmenting of the eastern night. But she was mistaken. There were five great openings into the cave, and the segmented glow had birth and being in a multitude of fires. The light grew brighter as she and the grey-eyed hunter climbed from the river. Far in ages past that river had driven through a higher channel in the limestone bowels of the hillside; once, indeed, it must have flowed eastwards an underground river. Then, in some catastrophic spate, it had burst those stygian bonds, broken free in an acre-wide vomit of great limestone boulders, and then sunk and sunk, sweeping eastwards and downwards, till it flowed, in rough parallel, a good hundred yards from the gaping cavern mouths that marked the riven bank of the original channel. The catastrophe had left a great cave, at some points narrow, at others wide and sweeping into a glow-softened darkness; fires burned in remote sub-caves far into the rock . . . Clair stood in the wash of light, looking at a scene as remote from the life and times of her country as it was remote from all pictures she had ever built in imagination of the life of the savage.

There were perhaps two hundred or less human beings in that immense abandoned channel of the underground river. More than half were women and children. Some were grouped round the innumerable small fires, some lay flat and apparently asleep on skins by those fires, some stood in groups – surely in gossip! Ten yards from Clair an old man squatted, his greying hair falling over his eyes, and, in the unchancy light of the fires, smote with a mallet at a nodule of bright flint. The staccato blows rose at regular intervals, high above the hum of the cavern.

Men, women and children were entirely naked, and for a little they saw neither Clair, panting and dripping, nor her companion, dripping as well, but panting not at all. Then a voice called something from the group round the nearest fire, and Clair's hunter touched her arm and she found herself walking across the hard, uneven floor of the cave into the concentrated, astounded stare of four hundred eyes. Then (so it seemed to her) the whole cave rose en masse and precipitated itself upon her.

She said, frightenedly, so frightened that she merely said it, not screamed it, 'Sinclair.'

A man touched her hair, found it unbelievable, ruffled it wildly, laughed. Two women stroked her breasts. Someone pinched her. A boy who might have been five years old slipped through the forest of legs and clasped Clair's knees, so that she almost fell. She clenched her fists and struck one of the women on the mouth. At that the touching hands left her. The babble hushed. The laughing, curious eyes darkened. And from somewhere Sir John Mullaghan's voice called abruptly: 'Don't do that, Miss Stranlay! They don't mean any harm.'

So Clair had realized. It was impossible, but it was a fact. The golden-skinned nudes were as friendly as they were unreticent. Clair did something then that was an inspiration – leant forward to the woman she had hit, and who had drawn back a pace, and kissed her on her bruised mouth.

'I – I'm sorry.'

Thus haltingly (and appropriately, she was afterwards to think) her greeting to that world from her own. For answer the brown-haired woman put up her arms, held her head in a curious way, and kissed her in return!

('And, oh, my good God, she's a *savage*!')

Clair found her hand seized by the woman. She found herself being led away towards a fire burning solitary in a sub-cave of the great rock chamber. She found herself sitting on a badly-cured skin, with beside her the woman whom she had hit and kissed, bending over the fire, toasting a long, grey fish in much the same fashion as Sinclair had toasted the horsemeat. ('Like a figure from the Greek vases – a lovely figure,' said her mind.) She recovered her breath and looked about her.

The American and Sir John were hasting towards her, threading the dottings of fires. Behind them followed the grey-eyed savage.

'Where did you get to, Miss Stranlay?'

Sinclair was unreasonably angry. Also, it seemed to her he was still hysterical. He kept glancing from right to left, towards the cave-mouths, the cavern-ceiling, the groups of the golden-skinned. He waited for no answer, but, gripping his head with his hands, half-turned away. Clair thought, disturbedly: 'Good gracious, what's the fuss – now we've fallen among these nice natives? They'll guide us to a town or a trading-post in a day or so.' She smiled up at the two of them.

'Having a walk with a gentleman friend. There he is behind you.'

The hunter came up, unsmiling. He looked from Clair to Sinclair, from Sinclair to Sir John. Then his grey eyes came back to Clair, questioningly. He made a motion from her to Sinclair.

She said to Sinclair: 'What?'

The American stared at her and the hunter abstractedly. He was certainly on the verge of a breakdown. He said, 'Eh?' and then, to the savage, a bark of unintelligibility. The savage found it intelligible. He answered. Sinclair's hands went again to his head.

'He wants to know if you are my woman.'

Clair sat up with some abruptness. 'What have you told him?'

Sir John Mullaghan said, very evenly: 'I think Sinclair had better say "Yes", Miss Stranlay.'

Clair found the three of them watching her – Sinclair with a strange, dazed look on his face. ('Not thinking of me at all.') The woman toasting the fish looked up with wondering, friendly eyes. Clair thought: 'Silly ass – go on, agree!' and so thinking found herself for some reason shaking her head at the grey-eyed hunter.

He smiled, gravely; nodded, and walked away. Clair, with a little catch of breath, watched him go.

To what had she committed herself?

Subchapter iv

That question was to return with frightening intensity a few hours later.

The fires had died down considerably. Heaped with damp grass and heavy boughs they smouldered with the smell of garden rubbish burned in an English garden. The smoke drifted out of the circle-radiance of each fire, coiled to the roof, and then, in an army of ragged banners, went north into the unexplored darkness of the ancient river-bed. Outside, a wind had risen that soughed eerily among the stars. On either side of the fires the naked hunters and their women slept, sometimes as many as eight or ten to a fire, sometimes only two. Clair had witnessed, and in the sleepy stirrings of the dark continued to witness, scenes of a kindly simplicity unbelievable. Naked savages in a naked cave in an unknown land! Sir John Mullaghan had emerged once from the bizarre cavern background and the neighbourhood of the distant fire where he had been adopted.

'Comfortable, Miss Stranlay? If you want Sinclair or myself during the night, just shout. One of us will keep awake.'

'Oh, don't. I'm sure we're safe enough. Who on earth *are* these people, Sir John?'

The grey-haired armaments manufacturer – surely the most grotesque figure ever seen in these surroundings! – put his hand to his head, bewilderedly, much as Sinclair had done.

'I've no idea – unless I'm to accept Sinclair's new theory. Perfectly mad.' He stared down at her with something like horror on his gentle face. 'At least, I hope to God he's mad . . . Don't talk about it, Miss Stranlay. We'll discuss the matter tomorrow. Have you noticed the paintings on the roof?'

'Paintings?'

'Look. Amazing things, aren't they?' He muttered to himself, distractedly. 'And the final proof for Sinclair's sanity . . . Oh, they can't be.' He shook himself. 'Good night, Miss Stranlay.'

'Good night, Sir John.'

She had stared after him, troubled and puzzled. Sinclair? . . . And then her eyes had turned to the wild beauty and vigour of the painted beasts that stood and charged and fled in panic flight amid the coiling of the fires' smoke. Here was their sabre-tooth, in black and grey; yonder, a red mammoth; centre the great arch of the cave chamber a nightmare monster bunched in polychrome, gigantically, for an attack . . . Savages – and these paintings! Where were they? What country was this?

She turned now, the heavy pelt of an unknown animal beneath her, and lay on her right shoulder. She pulled another skin, long-haired and warm, up to her neck, and lay sleepless, looking down the stretch of the caves. Savages. Awful people. Only – they were neither savage nor awful.

No other words than negatives in which to state the facts.

A yard away the woman she had hit slept by the side of a broad-chested hunter with one eye and a face disfigured as though half of it had been torn away in red eclipse by the stroke of a great paw. He had come into the sub-cave the while the woman stolen from an Attic vase had been feeding Clair on a piece of fish and a handful of green, rush-like things; he was evidently a late arrival from the hunt, and the woman his squaw. Clair had shuddered at sight of his face, and then saw that the hideous grimace on it was an interested smile. Her pyjamas again, of course. He had reached out and down an inquiring hand – and then withdrawn the hand, shamefacedly, as the woman said something to him, sharply . . . Squaw!

Clair looked over her shoulder at them in the cave-silence now. They might have been Iseult and Tristan together in that unshielded embrace.

She closed her eyes – and instantly opened them again. Somewhere close to the cave-mouths a savage snarling had broken out. Clair raised herself on her elbow. She could just see through the nearest entrance, greatly pillared by nature, like an archaic temple. In the pearl starshine stalked two dim shapes, long-bodied, sinister. They seemed smooth-skinned in that light, like great hounds. Were they coming into the cave?

They growled again, and she realized the brutes were hesitating, seeking to summon up courage for just such a raid. But while she thought so a figure beside one of the far fires arose, stirred the fire near him to a blaze, and with blazing torch came sleepily down the length of the main cave, stirring each fire. Lights yellow and red and lilac fountained with much crackle and twinkle. The beasts in the starlight vanished. Clair sank down again, watching the man with the torch.

He stopped beside her fire, stirring it as he had done the others, but more cautiously. Then he laid down the torch and crossed towards where Clair lay. She closed her eyes, fast.

With that blinding of herself the silence of the night and cave fell upon her senses acutely, like a sharp pain. It was actual physical relationship, not of hearing alone, this silence. The crackling fires had ceased their crackling, burning now in a steady loom. Outside, the wind had died away, perhaps awaiting the moonrise – or even the dawn, for how could one know the hour? And bending over her was a naked savage.

She bit her lips, hearing the fervid beating of her own heart. He also would hear it, and at that thought she tried, foolishly, to ease its noise. She almost suffocated. Should she shout for Sinclair?

She opened her eyes. She knew him then. It was the grey-eyed hunter. And it was someone else; *the face of the boy who had died outside Mametz bent over her in dim scrutiny*.

So, for a moment, then he turned and went, and Clair laid her head in her arms and slipped into unconsciousness.

CHAPTER SEVEN

A slip in the time-spirals

Subchapter i

It was next afternoon.

Clair Stranlay lay sleeping in the sunlight of the bluff that fronted the caves across the river. She was high up there, and had found a place where the sere grass was less coarse than usual, and soft to lie on. She had not intended to sleep, but to lie taking mental stock of the forenoon's impressions, brooding over the symptoms of a mysterious insanity hourly displayed by Sinclair, watching the unending play of life in the cave-mouths opposite. So indeed she had done for a little after climbing the bluff, seeing the remote golden figures of hunters or women stroll out against the limestone pillars of their habitations, seeing the moving, hasting, recumbent dots that were children sprayed out in all directions from the cave-mouths to the river. Then sleep had come upon her, un-awares, yet gently, so that even sleeping she was conscious that she slept and slept comfortably. Almost it was as though she were deeply asleep and dreaming that she slept.

So the new-comers over the grass, from the opposite way up the bluff that she had taken, did not greatly startle her. She opened clear, undrowsy eyes and watched Sir John Mullaghan and the American sit down beside her, one on either side, so that all three had view of the cave-mouths opposite.

'You've been a long time,' she said. 'If there *is* time in this place.'

The two men glanced at each other, swiftly, queerly, then looked away again. They said nothing. Sir John passed his hand over his grey hair in characteristic gesture. He had begun to fray badly, Sir John; he seemed to have frayed overnight. He still had trousers and coat, but the trousers were now shorts, the coat lacked sleeves. Sinclair –

Clair glanced at herself, and made hasty redraping of her rags. 'Goodness, our tailors will do a thriving trade when we *do* get back!'

'If we ever get back,' said Sinclair.

Clair had half-expected some such remark. Yet it startled her. 'So there's something behind their friendliness? Do they – do they intend to do something to us?'

'Eh?' The American looked blank for a moment. Grinned without mirth. 'Oh, the cooking-pot or something like that? I imagine they've never dreamt of cannibalism. No, it's not that. We're prisoners – but only as result of the most fantastic accident. Frankly, Miss Stranlay, I don't think there's any chance of us getting back to civilization again.'

'But – we're not going to stay here always? We can start out exploring again, and we're bound to reach some place in touch with civilization. Some time.'

'I doubt it.'

'Why?'

The American looked round the lilac, sun-hazed hills. Below them went on the drowsy play of activity of the naked figures at the cavern entrances. Curlews were crying over that stretch of marsh across which Clair and the grey-eyed hunter had run the night before to escape from the giant hyenas . . . His gaze came back to Clair's face.

'Because I don't think there's such a thing as civilization in existence. I don't believe there's a restaurant or a dress-maker's shop or a doctor's surgery anywhere in the world.'

Clair nodded, chewing a stalk of grass. 'I know. I felt like that last night . . . But it's only an illusion we play with, of course.'

Sir John struck in, quietly. 'Sinclair means it seriously, Miss Stranlay.'

Clair sat up, looking at them both. Sunstroke? But Sinclair was merely scowling, as he always did when brooding on a problem, and Sir John's face was sane enough.

'Seriously? But – we came out of – civilization five or six days ago.' She indicated the frayed rags that clad her. 'This sleeping-suit was made in the Rue de la Paix.'

Sinclair drew up his knees in front of him and clasped them. 'I don't mean anything illusory, symbolic or allegorical when I say there's no such thing as civilization. I just mean it, Miss Stranlay. There's no such thing; there won't be any such thing for thousands of years.'

'Perhaps you'd better detail all the evidence, as you did for me, Sinclair.'

'Yes.' The American turned his square, firmly-modelled head. Clair, troubled though she was, had a little shock of enlightenment. Of course – that was it! The hunters had heads like that! 'Let's go back to the beginning of all these happenings, Miss Stranlay –'

'Oh, let's. But why?'

'A minute. Remember what happened on board the *Magellan's Cloud*? First, there was that submarine earthquake. Then the airship's wireless failed to get any message from outside, though the set was quite undamaged. Then it grew inexplicably cold for that time of the year, and we saw islands appearing in mid-Atlantic – and quite evidently islands not newly risen from the sea. And then – the moon appearing at the full, though no moon was due for another five days.'

Clair wriggled herself flat again in the sunlight. She felt a strange uneasiness. 'Yes, I remember all that. And it was a different moon.'

'It *still* is a different moon,' said Sir John. 'I went out of the cave early this morning and saw it. Intense volcanic activity must still be going on up there.'

'More than likely. You've got all these facts, Miss Stranlay? Then, the *Magellan's Cloud* was wrecked against a mountain in a land that couldn't exist . . . We spent a deal of argument in the last few days trying to guess what the land was. I suppose it was necessary to argue to keep sane. I was never very convinced by my own arguments. Now we've had time to think, it's plain that the airship didn't diverge sufficiently from its course – or go at such an altered speed – as to reach back either to Africa or forward to Canada or Patagonia.'

'Yes. But we're somewhere.'

'Obviously. But it isn't any place you ever heard of, is it? It is, in the geography of the twentieth century, an impossible place, because the airship couldn't have reached it.'

Clair had begun to see. 'Then – it's a new country, somewhere in the middle of the Atlantic? . . . But that must be nonsense. The sun's got at us all . . . It's too big not to have been discovered before. It must be as big as ancient Atlantis.'

There was an unnecessary silence. Sinclair brooded, Rodin's Thinker in rags. Sir John had turned his face into the blow of the sunlight wind. Sinclair spoke.

'Exactly. That is where I'm convinced we are – in that continent which once filled the eastern trough of the Atlantic.'

Subchapter ii

Clair covered her ears. ' "Once filled it?" Stop, please . . . I feel as muzzy as a fly in honey. *Once* . . . That was thousands of years ago, Atlantis. How can we be in Atlantis *now*?'

'Because the now *is* thousands of years ago.'

Clair laughed and patted her ears. 'There's something wrong with my hearing. You'll have to examine my ears.'

'It sounds very confusing, Miss Stranlay, but I think Dr Sinclair's cumulative evidence is unimpeachable.'

'Evidence of what?'

Sinclair seemed to have lost something of his old-time, ready exasperation. He did not rave at her stupidity, Clair reflected, as he would
certainly have done three days before. His voice was very quiet.

'Let me go on with the evidence first. We three survived the *Magellan's*
wreck, we found a plateau practically without animals, and entirely without
human beings in its northernmost part. And there was a long mountain-
chain that must be a vent of the central fires of the earth, with thirteen
unknown volcanoes on it.'

'Were there thirteen? I never counted.'

'Yes. Towards the end of the plateau we sheltered in a cave and were
almost killed there by a sabre-tooth tiger. And in the cave I found the
bones and skull – fresh bones and fresh skull, not fossils – of a Neanderthal man. We came down from the plateau and were chased by a
mammoth. We saw an Irish elk, and, late last night, hyaenodons. All
these animals – and the Neanderthal man – had long been extinct before
the twentieth century. And, last of all, we were made prisoners by these
people' – he waved his hand towards the caves – 'whom at first I thought
were merely an unknown tribe of savages.'

'And aren't they?'

'I don't think so. I know what their language is now, and why I
answered in it so readily. It's Basque – an elementary and elemental
form of Basque. My mother was Basque. I haven't spoken the language
since childhood, but last evening found myself speaking and thinking in
it half-unconsciously . . . It's the loneliest language in twentieth century
Europe, as I suppose you know. No affinities to any other, just as the
Basques have no apparent racial affinity to any existing group. It's been
speculated that they're the pure descendants of the Cro-Magnards –
you've heard of them?'

It sounded to Clair foolishly remote from their trouble of finding a
way back to a knowable coast and civilization. She wrinkled her sun-
burnt brows. 'I think so. Yes – I went picnicking to the Cro-Magnon
caves once and drank bad Moselle there. They were the Stone Age
people who painted all those French and Spanish caves, weren't they?
Painters!' Apparent enlightenment came on her. 'And you think our
hunters are a stray tribe of Basques?'

'No, I don't. I think they're proto-Cro-Magnards – ancestors of the
French Cro-Magnards and remote ancestors of the twentieth century
Basques.'

'*Ancestors?*'

Sir John patted her shoulder. 'I think you'd have done better to tell her
your theory right out, Sinclair – rather than lead up to it with evidence.'

Still, miraculously, Sinclair kept his temper. 'All right. Plainly, then, Miss Stranlay, and fantastic as it may sound, I believe we're not in the twentieth century at all – that through some inexplicable accident connected with that submarine earthquake the *Magellan's Cloud* fell out of the twentieth century into an Atlantic atmosphere that had never known an airship before. That was why she could get no reply to her wireless calls. This is not the twentieth century.'

'What is it, then?' Clair heard her voice in the strangest, attenuated whisper.

'I don't know. But from all the evidences, I should think we're somewhere in the autumn of a year between thirty and twenty thousand years before the birth of Christ.'

Subchapter iii

'It will always remain unreal – and oh, nonsensically impossible to believe!'

More than two hours had gone by. Clair's face was more pallid than either of the men had ever seen it, and indeed it had required something of her disbelief and horror to make them realize the thing themselves, albeit they had met that desperation of hers with irrefragable fact after fact. Now Sinclair pointed down to the mouths of the caves where the golden children played.

'Are these people unreal?'

Clair looked down. 'No, they are real enough.' She spoke in a low voice, so that they hardly caught her words. She thought for a moment and then smiled from one to the other of them. 'Thank you. It's – a devil of a thing. I don't think I'll think about it much . . . if I can. Or at least not deliberately try to go mad . . . All this stuff about the time-spirals and retro-cognitive memory – maths have always given me a headache. The world used always, I thought, to roll along a straight line called Time, instead of looping the loop with a thousand ghosts of itself before and after it. And none of them ghost, and none the reality.'

Sir John said: 'I'm not a mathematician either, Miss Stranlay. But I take it they're all realities in the loop-spirals. And for a second – at that moment of the submarine-earthquake – two of the loops touched, and the *Magellan's Cloud* was scraped off one on to the other.'

'Like a fly off a pat of butter?'

'Something like that.' He smiled at her from behind his grizzled beard. That was better. The Cockney was coming to her help. Clair said, very softly: 'Please. It's a September afternoon in London now. There are dead leaves in the parks, and a lot of people at the Zoo drinking tea under the trees. And motorbuses going round Trafalgar Square and the pigeons are twittering on the roofs of St Martin's in the Field. And there's been an accident in Hammersmith Broadway, and an ambulance has come up, and the policeman is shooing back the crowd. And Big Ben says it's twenty past three, and Jean Borrow in my flat is writing a Lido novel, and there's an unemployment procession, and there's Bond Street and shops and early door queues in Leicester Square for an Edgar Wallace play . . . Just now. And it's not now. It won't happen for twenty-five thousand years. Year after year. I've been speaking just a minute. And it's a long time until sunset. And till the sunset of tomorrow. And until the winter comes here on those caves. And until the spring of next year. Year after year, till we're all three dead. And years after that, till this country's dead and no one really believes it existed. And years after that, with spring and summer and birds over the hills and belling deer, and people in love and sleeping together and having babies and watching them grow up, and the babies becoming old men and women, and dying, and *their* descendants seeing another spring. And an ice age coming – slowly, through thousands of years. And passing away through thousands more. And at the end of that time – London will still be in the future . . . It's not now, it never can be for us, nor for anyone now alive . . . Up through thousands and thousands of years we'll never see – '

Her voice had risen; it cracked on the last word. Sinclair was on his feet. He took her by the shoulders and shook her. Laughing and crying, she stared up in his eyes. Sir John half stood up also, made to interfere, refrained. Clair struggled. Her hysteria died away. Sinclair's fingers relaxed. Clair found herself staring at him resentfully, flushed, rubbing her shoulders.

'You beast!'

He was panting. He sat down. 'Anything you like. I tried to be an effective counter-irritant. Feel better?'

Clair shuddered. 'Don't look at me, you two, for a bit.'

They didn't. After a little they heard her say: 'Sorry I went like that, especially after my promise.'

'I felt like going that way myself last night.'

'Did you?'

The American nodded. 'And we're to make a compact, all three. If one of us ever feels that way again, we're to get to the other two at once. Promise?'

'Yes.'

Sinclair nodded to Clair's spoken reply and Sir John's nod, and they said nothing for a little. Clair's mind felt as though it were slowly recovering from a surgical operation. *Atlantis*! She said: 'And what are we going to do?'

'What *is* there we can do?'

This was Sinclair. Clair turned her eyes to the armaments manufacturer. He smiled at her. He looked ill, she reflected. He said, gently: 'At least, we have all our lives to live – now, as in that time that is not yet, that time that is thousands of years away. And they are our lives . . . There's the sun and the wind on the heath, brother. I wish I could remember more of Borrow.' Below their eyes, in the still sunshine, the life of the cave-mouths went on. 'And those people among whom we've come – if we can live their life, they're livable companions, aren't they?'

'Oh . . . ' Clair sat up again. 'I knew there was something you two had left unexplained. Most important of all. You can't explain it.' She turned to the American accusingly. 'If these are the ancestors of the Cro-Magnards who are to become the ancestors of the Basques – '

'And perhaps our own ancestors. Your own remote ancestor may be one of these children playing by the river there, Miss Stranlay.'

'Oh, my good God!' She was checked for a moment, and again the curtain of horror waved before her eyes. And, queerly, something came to her aid. It was memory of the grey-eyed hunter. 'But that doesn't matter. Won't bear thinking about. If these people are as far back in time as you imagine – they're remoter from civilization than any savage of the twentieth century.'

'Far remoter,' said Sinclair. 'Their weapons and implements are palaeolithic flints. They seem to have no knowledge of even the elements of agriculture. They wear no clothes at all, they haven't even arrived at the idea of storing water in calabashes – as I found to my discomfort last night.'

'They've no tribal organization,' said Sir John. 'That is plain enough already. None of the ultimate divisions of power and responsibility have been yet evolved.'

'But – *your* theories, Sir John, and yours, Dr Sinclair . . . Where is the raving Old Man with his harem of wives? And where's all the cruelty and fear and horror? They're not savages. They're clean and kindly children. Listen!'

Some jest of the caves. The shout of laughter came up to them on the bluff-head. Both the men were silent. Clair thought: 'Oh, shame to wreck your nice theories!' and said: 'So it must be the twentieth century and Patagonia or some such place after all.'

The American shook his head. 'It's not the twentieth century; our data is stable enough. It's just that all the history books and all the anthropological theories of the twentieth century tell the most foolish lies. It's just that Sir John Mullaghan and I and thousands more have been victims of the shoddiest scientific lie ever imposed on human credulity . . . These proto-Cro-Magnards, these earliest true men on earth – absolutely without culture and apparently absolutely without superstitious fears, cruelties, or class-divisions. It means that Rousseau was right (or will be right? How is one to think of it?) and the twentieth century evolutionists all wrong.'

Clair said, steadily: 'These – like our ancestors; perhaps some of them our own ancestors . . . ' For a moment it seemed to her that her two companions were ghouls squatting beside her in the sunlight. 'And I knew it – women always knew it! But you two and the thousands of others who led the world swore that men were natural murderers; you killed five million in France to prove your theories. All through history you've been doing it . . . The boy who died on the wire outside Mametz – he was one of these hunters, I saw his own face last night. And you and the world told him he was a murderous beast by nature and ancestry!'

She was aware of the armaments manufacturer looking at her, doubt and a grey horror in his face. 'Perhaps this is only a stray tribe of primitives unlike all others.'

'No.' Sinclair spoke. Abruptly, as with an effort. 'They are no stray tribe. You are right, Miss Stranlay. You are woman, for that matter, of fifty tortured centuries accusing us . . . And we've no defence. We never tried to find out the real facts of human nature . . . By God, but some did! Some were trying. I've just remembered. There was a new school of thought in the world out of which we came. The Diffusionist. And we thought them fantastic dreamers!'

'What did they dream?'

'Why, that primitive man was no monster, that it was the early civilizations and their offshoots that bedevilled him. If a Diffusionist were here at the moment he would say that these are men as Nature intended them to be. So they will continue for thousands of years till by an accident in the Nile Valley agriculture and its attendant religious rites will be evolved. And from that accident in 4000 B.C. will rise, transforming the world – the castes and gods, the warrior and slave, the cruelties and cannibalisms, Sir John Mullaghan's armaments, the war that murdered your lover, Miss Stranlay, and my League of Militant Pacifists.'

They stared at Clair uncomfortably in the bright sunshine. A party of hunters came over the eastward hills – golden figures against a golden background. They were singing, these dawn-men – godless and fearless and hateless and glorious, Sinclair thought, they who should have

slouched through the sunlight obsessed and obscene animals! . . . Sir John
was greyly conscious of Clair's silent figure.

'But I still don't understand. If this is the world of twenty-five thousand B.C., as we've calculated, what is its population? Are there other
men? Is there a Europe? And that Neanderthal skull – it didn't belong to
a species of man like one of these hunters, surely?'

The American made an abrupt, half-despairing gesture.

'How can we know – *now* – since all our other beliefs about these
times go phut? Something like this, I imagine: Atlantis here is a great
waste of land, the youngest and most unstable of the continents. It
must stretch at points almost across to the Antilles and America. And
wandering through it are possibly a few scarce family-groups like our
hunters. Possibly – but our hunters may be the only true men as yet in
existence. They must have been wandering this land for thousands of
years. In the east there, towards Europe and in Europe itself there are
Neanderthal men – unhuman, a primitive experiment by Nature in the
making of man. They also must be few enough in number, though their
species probably spreads far into Asia and Africa. And somewhere in
Central and South-Eastern Asia at this moment may be other family
groups of true men, not so very different from these golden cavemen of
ours, slowly wandering westwards . . . There is an Ice Age coming, a few
thousand years hence, and at the end of it the Neanderthalers will die
out and these hunters, or rather their descendants, reach Europe and
spread over it and intermarry with those remote kinsmen of theirs from
Asia . . . Something like that.'

He jumped to his feet. 'Oh, by God, if one could only tell them – those
hunters of ours!'

'Tell them what?' asked Sir John.

'History – the world that is to be. Remember that kindly chap who
took you and me prisoners – we thought we were prisoners and we
weren't at all! He's never heard the words for war or prison. Or that
hunter who brought Miss Stranlay to the caves . . . If they knew what
their children there in the sunlight are going to inherit – thousands of
years away! All the bloody butcheries of the battlefields, the tortures and
mutilatings of the cities still unbuilt, the blood-sacrifices of the Aztec
altars, those maimed devils who die in the coalmines of Europe . . . ' He
looked down at Clair. 'You're a novelist, Miss Stranlay. You were born in
the slums – thirty thousand years in the future. Do you remember it?
Think that it still has to happen – for these.'

Clair said, in a pale, quiet voice: 'Will you two leave me alone? Oh, I
won't go mad again.'

'Don't stay too late. We'll watch for you from the cave.'

'All right, Sir John.'

She heard the scuff-scuff of their receding footsteps. She was alone. A lapwing came wheeling over the hill-brow and passed towards the marshes. Drowsiness had settled on the caves. Clair Stranlay laid her head on her arms and began to weep – to weep and weep as she had done never before in her life.

Subchapter iv

For a little, weeping, her thoughts were a static confusion. Then they combered into a wild clamour – an affrighted clamour, though the fear was of a different order from that which had horrified her into hysteria in the presence of Sinclair and Sir John.

'But what am I to do? Oh, my good God, what *am* I to do? If we're here for ever – but I can't, I can't! I may live to be a hundred – days and days and months and years – among horseflesh and fires. No books. Never read a lovely piece of prose again. Never have the fun of correcting my own proofs. Or lying on a soft, clean bed. Or smoking cigarettes. Never talk to the people who like my kind of jokes, or twist an argument; or be clever and bright. Or wear pretty clothes and have men want me . . . And be safe – safe and secure . . . I can't do it, I can't!' The grass rustled under her as she lay and wept, terrified. She closed her eyes, tightly, to make sure that this country and the American's talk were all part of a dream. Ever so tightly. In a moment, when she opened them, she'd know. It couldn't be, it couldn't be . . . She opened her eyes on the afternoon of the pale Atlantean hills.

As she looked across them with misted eyes, far and remote, and heard by her for the first time since their coming to the caves, there rose and belled and quivered in the air the sound that had startled the mammoth miles away by the side of the great oak. It rose and fell, rose again, died on a long, strange note, that mysterious lowing. Wonderful thing. Breathtaking thing to hear.

If only she had a notebook and pencil!

Both of them thousands of years away.

'Let's think calmly, then. If this were only a novel – one of the kind you've wanted to write for a holiday. Think that this isn't yourself; only your heroine. It's she who's lying on a hill above a lost Atlantis cave, watching the children of the dawn-men playing by a lost river . . . And you're comfortable in your Kensington study, planning out the synopsis. What's she going to do next? How's she going to live? She *must* live – you'd never be mean enough to kill her. But *how?*'

It was late in the afternoon now – those afternoons that seemed to contract so steadily with the wearing of the week. She saw the smoke far up the opposite hillside – from some high vent that aerated the caves – thicken from pale blue to violet black. They were building up the fires. Soon the main body of the hunters, that had left at dawn, would return. The individual hunters must long ago have returned. Sinclair and Sir John waiting for her. Hungry. Hungry herself.

She stood up. The wind had turned cooler. She shivered. Her ragged jacket flapped, and the pyjama-trousers blew against her legs.

She looked down at herself – and, looking, started at the thought that came to her.

Opposite, the loitering figures by the cave-mouths.

All her life among them . . .

'Do it. Sometime you'll be forced to do it. Goodness, why wait till then?'

A fox prowling up the side of the hill heard her laugh, and at the sound stopped and bared his teeth, brush cocked. He crept behind a tussock of grass and wormed his way through the heart of it and looked at the strange hunter with the uncouth skin . . . He bristled a little at sight of what the hunter did, and waited till she was gone, and for nearly an hour later circled slowly round a strange, grassy fluffment that was yet, he knew, no grass, and intriguing, though very unlikely eatable.

Subchapter v

Sinclair was the first to see her coming, splashing through the shallow natural ford of the river. Reaching the near side she paused to shake the water from herself. The sunlight caught her then, dazzlingly. Deliberately, walking with head down-bent (in thought, somehow he knew, not in dejection) she came up the incline towards the mouths of the caves.

Sinclair said: 'By God, well done!'

'Eh?' Sir John Mullaghan had not seen her. Now he did. He hesitated, then nodded. 'Splendid. Sensible girl.'

'I'll go in,' said Sinclair.

'That would be a mistake. Much better to stay here and look at her and talk to her as we would have done yesterday . . . Hello, Miss Stranlay. That is the sensible thing to do. I wish I weren't so old, otherwise I'd follow suit.'

Clair thought, 'You dear', gratefully. She looked at both of them, and found it now very easy. Sir John's eyes were naturally kind, the American's at the moment deliberately so. She said: 'It feels good. Especially coming through the river. And I always hated bathing-dresses . . . Only I hope winter doesn't come too soon.'

'Both Sir John and I will be forced to it in time, anyhow,' said Sinclair. And added, easily: 'Shall we walk over to your fire with you?'

Clair realized, suddenly, something of the ordeal of that. Or need it be? She felt her nether lip begin to tremble; stayed it.

'Oh, no thanks.'

She smiled at them and went into the cave; and, so seeing her for the first time, the women of the cave rose like a flight of birds and settled around her.

Unreasonably, abruptly, Clair felt not afraid at all. Standing smiling and nude, pearl and rose, under the touch of their friendly golden hands, she thought: ' . . . as though I were freed from a horrible skin disease – free for the first time in my life. Oh, winter, don't come too soon! I want to live!'

CHAPTER EIGHT

A lover for the dark days

Subchapter i

But that night the rain set in, blowing squallily into the mouths of the caves, so that the flames of the fires danced and spat and flickered, and long serpent-shapes of smoke wound and whorled everywhere. Amid them blew sharp, piercing shafts of wind, and Clair began to realize something of the life of those people in the winter months. She lay wakeful beside her fire, and Sinclair, who could not sleep either, came over to her while the beating gusts shook the limestone hills and moaned far away in the subterranean depths of the ancient river-bed.

'Shocking night.'

Clair stirred the fire gently with a bough, and nodded to him. He stood, naked of shoulders and legs, looking into the fire himself after that first sharp appraisal of her. He said: 'Missing your clothes?'

Clair wound the odorous bearskin more closely round herself. 'I suppose I am – in spite of my immunity from cold. Silly perhaps of me to part with them.'

'Let me feel your pulse.'

He did. It seemed quite normal. She startled him with a question. 'Do you think we'll pull through the winter months – especially Sir John?'

'What?'

'Oh, you know. *You* will, I think. You have physique for it, and most of the other advantages. I may – through the accident that winter-bathing was my hobby – though goodness knows I feel like a white snail without its shell among all these golden people.'

'You looked lovely enough for the Parthenon frieze.'

He said this impersonally. Clair nodded. 'I know I'm not unsightly. But mentally – coddled and cowardly. Best-selling never trained me for a winter in Atlantis.'

He was silent. He bent down to place a burning twig more evenly. The wind whoomed, blowing his hair and beard, as Clair saw looking up at him from the shelter of her bearskin. In shadow and in flickering light the Cro-Magnards slept, disregarding rain and squall – all, except three very young babies who wailed softly in the far corner of the cave. These apart, even the very youngest slept soundly though the wind occasionally lifted a skin covering and drifted it yards, leaving exposed those nude bodies that had indeed the colours of a fresh gold coin. As though made of gold leaf. Outside, against the cave-mouths, the wavering curtains of rain . . . Atlantis! Lost in Atlantis and pre-history! Clair, forgetting the silent Sinclair, leant on an elbow, gazing round at the sleeping hunters with golden, easy bodies. And for some strange, fantastic reason she thought of lines in Tennyson:

> *Ah, such a sleep they sleep,*
> *The men I loved!*

These cavemen, the men of the dawn! And suddenly it was to her as though they lay dead, they and their women and children, and over them indeed came stalking those ghoulish shapes with which the world remote in the future was to identify them – great beasts, manure-flanked, slime-dripping, with fetid jaws and rheumy eyes, tearing at the throats of these dead men of the dawn, mangling and destroying and befouling the human likeness from the lovely limbs and faces . . . She started, hitting her head against the sandy floor. Sinclair had turned *his* head, sharply, looking at her.

'You're sleepy now. Good night.'

'Oh – I was dreaming awake. Good night – it's ridiculous to say Dr Sinclair. What is your name?'

'Keith.'

'Good night, Keith.'

'Good night, Clair.'

Alone again, she lay on the verge of sleep, and thought: 'Those babies. Poor things. Awful for them.'

Two of them had been born that afternoon. Both had been dead before sunset. Their bodies had been carried along the river bank to the edge of the marsh and abandoned there, Sinclair had said.

'Awful. How it's raining! Drumming like a London roof under rain, almost. London roofs – but you mustn't think of them. Nor all your London days. Over, all days, very soon, I suppose.'

She grew wakeful again at that thought. Sinclair had gone without answering her question. Over: all the bright, burnished hours, the days of summers and autumns, the good things to eat, the ease and pleasantness . . . To come to an end and a blinding in darkness at last, somewhere, in some dark cave, without medical attention or understanding. And someone, unless Sinclair or Sir John was still alive, would carry her body outside the range of the caves; and leave it for a beast to devour.

She looked, and so for long until the fires died continued to look, into a night that was a pit of terror.

Subchapter ii
But that next dawn –

She awoke luxuriously, in the embrace of a strange, secret exultation. Why? Something awaiting her? She put aside the fur and got up and shivered in the dawn chill, and saw then that it was but barely the dawn.

No one stirred. Far at the furthest fire the watcher of the fires was smoothing a stick with a flint. He heard her, lightly though she walked, and looked round, and flung back his hair from his face, and smiled. A boy. She smiled herself and warmed herself by the fire of another household, scraping away ash and refuse and replenishing the cone-shaped structure with boughs from a pile stacked near. Then she went to the nearest mouth of the cavern, and at her appearance the sun that had been hesitating behind the hills came over them, and she stood and shivered with pleasure in its first beams. The guard hunter came to her side; said something unintelligible; motioned towards the river. A lion and a lioness, grey beasts rather than tawny in that light, were standing watching them, not twenty yards away. The hunter gestured with the half-smoothed bough in his hand. Promptly the lion disappeared through the soft, wet grass. The lioness growled and stalked after him despondently.

The hunter laughed.

The caves began to stir. The naked women awoke and fed their babies. The men, naked equally, arose and drifted about and were scolded, and grinned, and crowded the cave-mouths as though in casual gossip. Clair saw Sir John Mullaghan rising, with some appearance of chilled joints, from a heap of boughs. A Cro-Magnard helped him up. A frizzling smell began to pervade the cavern. Breakfast. It was deerflesh, cooked in the same monotonous way as always. Frying-pans, pots and pantries were as unknown as gods, chancels and torture-chambers. Afterwards the Cro-Magnards would wander down to the river in twos and threes, and drink.

Clair ate her charred venison with a hunger that surprised her. She had learned a few words of the proto-Basque in the past twenty-four hours, and with their aid gathered from the woman, Zumarr, that Belia, the hunter with the mutilated face, admired his guest's new appearance. So, apparently, and with much astounded calling one to the other, did as many of the Cro-Magnards as had not seen her before in natural garb. They dropped pieces of venison and came running to look at her. Zumarr shooed them away, vigorously. The others who had come to look at her the night before laughed.

And Clair thought a surprising thought: 'These people without religion are the most spiritual the world will ever see! They are quite unaware of their bodies. They aren't personal possessions to them, as mine is to me. They must feel through them, impersonally, just as they feel pleasure in the painting of sky and earth by sun and mist. And they don't dream of refusing other people the right of looking at sky and earth . . . '

The men went away in the early morning, after drinking at the river and indulging in some horse-play when three of them were thrown into the water, and the others – apparently in a mood of self-retaliation – flung themselves in on top. Watching them, Clair said to Sir John: 'But I thought swimming was a very artificial acquirement of human beings?'

'Perhaps this family group has wandered from the shore of some inland sea in Atlantis. They're certainly very cleanly, most of them, though it's plain it's not because of any code. They are because they enjoy it.'

'Where's Keith Sinclair?'

Sir John smiled. 'He's going out with the hunters.'

Clair saw him approaching then. It was apparently for him that the watcher of the fires had been smoothing the bough through the night. He carried that bough now, straightened, and with a carefully-knapped sliver of flint wedged and bound in it. Clair reached out her hand and took the thing and examined it, and some of the women came and looked at the three of them, smilingly. One, a girl, giggled. And Clair thought: 'I hope I'm not examining it too intently. I should be just as casual as he was.'

The American nodded as she handed it back. There was a flush on his dour face, a sparkle in his eyes. 'I expect I'll be the worst kind of amateur. At the stalking as well as the running – in spite of my atavistic legs.'

'Atavistic?'

'Hadn't you noted them? I'm fairly Cro-Magnard altogether in physiognomy. And the twentieth century seems to have guessed correctly from study of the fossil remains of these people found in the French caves that their long shin-bones were developed by racing game on foot . . . By the by, this is a feast day.'

'Feast?' Sir John, a grotesque figure in his rags, had sat down. He smiled at them, greyly. 'I'm sorry, Miss Stranlay. I'm still a trifle upset internally . . . Did you say a feast, Sinclair?'

'Yes.'

'But from what you were telling me of the Diffusionist theory of history last night I understood that ritual feasts came only with civilization?'

'There seem to be two exceptions. Perhaps they're memories of the old pre-human mating seasons. In spring and autumn they occur, as far as

I can gather from the old flint-knapper, Aitz-kore; and the autumn one comes after the first night of rain.'

'What's it for?' Clair asked.

'Why – You won't be shocked?'

Clair laughed. Even Sir John, with closed eyes, smiled. The American hefted his flint spear.

'It's the time, I understand, when the men and women choose their lovers for the winter – or those already mated exchange.'

'Will there be – ?' Clair's question hesitated in her eyes. Sinclair's reply hesitated on his lips.

'I don't think so. But I don't know. Sir John and I will take you out for a walk when if comes off, if you like.'

'No. If we're here for the remainder of our lives that would be too suburban . . . ' She suddenly gripped his arm. 'There's my hunter.'

No other. Clair had not seen him all the day before. He went and sat down by a fire and ate some scraps of venison surviving the breakfast. A baby came and fell over his feet. He righted it, absorbedly, and put it aside. The baby procured a bone, and sucked it. Clair shuddered.

'Been out on a lone trek, I should think,' said the American. 'They often do that, the young and unmarried, according to Aitz-kore. Wander off sometimes and don't come back. Hello, they're waiting for me!'

'Good hunting!'

'Thanks.' He called over his shoulder. 'Don't stray far from the caves, either of you.'

Scouts had already gone. Others straggled west-wards by the marsh, going casually, for there was no game near at hand. The American pacifist joined a golden-skinned group and companioned them out of sight, his white starkness very conspicuous. Standing in the sunlight of the cave-mouths, Clair looked after him and stretched her own smooth-skinned body luxuriously, and sighed deeply. Sir John looked up inquiringly.

'?'

'Nothing, Sir John, except – Did you ever sleep on Box Hill on a Sunday afternoon?'

He shook his head, his face gentle still, if a little twisted. She did not notice. She was twenty millennia away.

'Heat and stickiness and someone playing a melodeon, and poor, life-starved louts prowling among the bushes. Goodness, the stickiness and the taste in one's mouth! Horrible clothes. When we might have been like this . . . Box Hill!'

Sir John also had fallen into a dream. Box Hill! His company; his constituency; that journey to America . . . Here in the sunshine of

Atlantis one began to doubt them. Had they ever been? . . . He found he had been thinking aloud. He found Clair's hand on his shoulder. Her lovely face was lighted but dreamy still.

'Perhaps they were, but – *need they ever be*? Perhaps men dreamt the wrong dream. We are such stuff of dreams . . . Perhaps it was only a nightmare astray on Sinclair's time-spirals out of which we came . . . It feels so here this morning. As though all the world could begin again – '

Begin again? Sir John put his head in his hands. Begin again! Who indeed knew what was possible in this fantastic adventure – if only the pain would go and he could see and understand more clearly . . . Begin again? Poets had dreamt it, and they had changed the world with other dreams . . . Shelley, of course! Long since he had read Shelley:

> *The world's great age begins anew,*
> *The golden years return.*
> *The earth doth like a snake renew*
> *Her winter skin outworn:*
> *Heaven smiles, and faiths and empires gleam*
> *Like wrecks of a dissolving dream.*

Subchapter iii

It was mid-afternoon.

The caves had emptied their entire population on to the plateau east of the river bank. They had trooped out in little groups, men and women separately for once. A couple of jackals, roused from a bed of reeds, had distracted somewhat the attention of the processions, the entire tribe engaging in an idiot chase of the beasts, pelting them with stones, shouting and hallooing, until long after the snarling brutes were out of sight. Clair, laughing and panting, a Greek among Polynesians, rejoined Sir John and Sinclair, grey-haired the one, black the other, and now with her red-tipped mop coming between them.

'Feel as though I were going to the world's first picnic!'

Beyond the nullahs was a flattish stretch of grass, short-cropped perhaps in the hour-passing of some enormous herd. Right of it lay the river. Over the westward hills beyond the marsh hung the sun, high up. The grey-gold land drowsed. And the Cro-Magnards' laughter went up a little wind that turned back from the east towards the deserted caves. The women and children grouped themselves, sitting or standing or lying, round the eastwards verge of the sward. The men held over to the other side and also lay or sat. A silence fell. The three survivors of the *Magellan's Cloud* looked at each other in some doubt; finally reached a spot that seemed neutral, neither for men nor women. They lay down, resting on their elbows. The silence went on.

Suddenly a blackbird began to pipe in a thicket near at hand, breaking the tension for the three aliens at least.

' "And we have Box Hill here and now",' misquoted Sir John Mullaghan, gently.

The sound had stirred the Cro-Magnards also. A man rose slowly from the midst of the male embankment, and slowly walked across towards the gathering of women. The sunshine glided over grey-black hair.

'It's the old flint-knapper, Aitz-kore,' whispered the American, interestedly.

So it was. Still the silence went on as he passed over the grass. The rustle of his passage if not his footfalls could be heard. He arrived at the end of the women's line, and, slowly, passed up the ranks of the women, scanning each face. They looked him in the eye. One or two of the younger ones giggled. But for the most they kept the initial silence. Sir John whispered: 'His wife is there in the middle.'

Aitz-kore neared her. Clair found herself holding her breath. The flint-knapper passed the woman without a change of countenance. Something seemed to contract in Clair's throat.

Aitz-kore reached the end of the line, paused, shrugged, turned back, walked slowly over the track he had already made in the grass, his face like his name, a pointed hatchet, old and sharp. He halted in front of the woman who had been his wife. She had sat with head downbent, but she raised it now. Clair was too far off to see her face, but she knew she was weeping. The flint-knapper held out his hand. The woman took it and rose up. A yell of delight rose from hunters and women alike.

'He's selected her again from all the women of the tribe,' Sinclair explained.

The two of them walked down to the southwards end of the plateau, turned leftwards, in the opposite direction from the caves, and were out of sight before Clair glanced for them again. She had been intent on the second venture.

Again a man had crossed the open space, walked the line, and made selection of a woman – a young woman, and comely even among the comely. But he had less luck than Aitz-kore. The woman shook her head. Thereat the hunter, after a moment's hesitation, walked back to the place from which he had come.

It was now the woman's turn. She rose. She was *enceinte*, but comely enough in carriage still. Leisurely she crossed to the seated rows of men, hesitated not an instant, but held out her hand. Instantly a young man – a mere boy – sprang to his feet and took her hand. Again the strange cheer went up from the gathering. Clair's eyes sparkled.

'Kidnapping.'

'Young enough,' Sinclair agreed, absently. 'Wonder if he's the father of her baby – or that man she has just refused?'

Clair wondered that also, looking after woman and boy as they broke into an easy, long-legged trot, south-wards, across the sward, and then turning east and racing for the hills. Another woman rose up and crossed towards the men's side, stopping mid-way to fling back a cloud of russet hair from a flushed, high-cheekboned face.

'She has a lovely figure,' said Clair.

'They all have,' said Sinclair.

And it was true. Neither the steatopygy of the savage nor the pendulous paunch and breasts of corset-wearing civilizations were here. They mated as they chose, those golden women; they bore children, many and quickly, unless they tired of mating; they died in great numbers in childbirth, they and their children. And they lived free from the moment they were born till the moment when that early death might overtake them. The eager, starved, mind-crippled creatures of the diseased lust of men were twenty thousand generations unborn. The veil, the priest, the wedding ring, the pornographic novel, and all the unclean drama of two beasts enchained by sex and law and custom were things beyond comprehension of the childlike minds in those golden heads or the vivid desires of those golden bodies . . . Golden children in the dawn of time, they paired in the afternoon sunshine and in pairs melted away into the east. Clair, warm and comfortable, her breasts pressed in the grass, found herself nodding drowsily. Every now and then, however, she would start to half-wakefulness as another shout went up, another nuptial couple wheeled out of the gathering. Suddenly, in a long quietness, she started fully awake.

'Keep cool, Miss Stranlay.'

'By God . . . Aerte.'

Clair raised her head. An intenser silence than ever before had fallen on the gathering. Few of the Cro-Magnards were sitting now. All stood to look. And the reason was the grey-eyed hunter, Aerte.

He walked from the far end of the men's line. His head was a little down-bent, as though in deep thought. Under his left arm was his spear. Disregarding the waiting line of women he came, straight towards where the three survivors of the airship's wreck lay. Clair thought, breathlessly: 'Cooler, now. Must get back to the caves soon. Sir John – wonder if he's feeling better? . . . ' Defence. Not thinking. Taking no heed. But in some fashion she felt as though she had just finished running an exhausting race. Sinclair, his eyes on the hunter, said: 'Just shake your head, Clair. There's no compulsion among these people.'

But Clair's head he saw as down-bent as the hunter's own. She saw the nearing feet in the grass, but nothing more. And then he was close; had halted. She raised her head.

They looked at each other for a long time. She heard the American say something; something quite incomprehensible because of that drumming noise in her ears. She was looking up, even in the still sunshine, not into the face of Aerte alone. Her heart was wrung with a sudden, wild pain of recognition, and then that passed, leaving a tingling as of blood, long congealed, that flowed again . . . A gentle voice came nearer and nearer out of the aurulent silence. Sir John's.

'He'll go away. It's just that he doesn't realize that you are different.'

'I'm glad.'

They saw her swing to her feet. For a moment the long, sweet lines of her figure also glimmered pale gold. She stood beside the hunter.

'Miss Stranlay!'

There was urgency and appeal in the simultaneous cry. Clair looked back at them, shook her head. They had grown the mistiest of images.

And then she put her hand in the hand of the hunter, Aerte, felt that hand close on hers, felt herself drawn forward, heard a groan from Sir John Mullaghan.

She closed her eyes, and when next she opened them found before her the eastern hills and two shadows treading a deserted land.

Subchapter iv

Rain came on again that night. Winter was not far off from Atlantis. Distant in the north the volcanoes smoked, and sometimes, in the lifting clouds of rain, could be glimpsed as the beating of damp beacons remote in the mirk. Clair, lying sleepless with her lover for the dark days, saw them, pregnant, dark blossoms high up in the sky. Remote there was the plateau crossed by herself and Sinclair and Sir John only three days before. Fantastic journey. Fantastic climax to it, this . . . The hunter stirred, dreamlessly, dark and golden and close, and she peered at him, then at the passing curtains of rain.

A lover for the dark days! A lover dead and dust twenty-five thousand years before she had been born! What dream was this that had led her feet from a Kensington flat to that running across the hills from the mating place of the dawn men?

They had run beyond the sight and sound of that mating place, and then, at the over-quickening of Clair's breathing, the hunter had slowed down and looked at her inquiringly. They were in a treeless stretch of long grass, the river deserting them and holding southwards. Across the grass, a mile or more away, two great hairy beasts shoggled through the afternoon, one after the other. Woolly rhinoceroi. Clair, panting, had brought her eyes back to Aerte.

They had smiled together. Clair had thought: 'And where from here?'

He had answered that by taking her hand again and breaking again into the trot that was probably his customary pace. The trees drew nearer. Clair saw that they were beeches, with great open spaces between. The rhinoceroi had disappeared. Clair, breathing desperately, lay down. Aerte halted, laughed, gestured, his black hair falling over his face. Then he laid the spear down beside her and vanished among the beeches.

When she had recovered her breath she heard the sound of him returning, and saw what he carried. It was a great water-melon. She sat up, looking at him lightedly. His grave eyes laughed down at her. Abruptly he dropped the fruit. She found warm, aurulent arms round her. The grass was warm. A cricket was chirping. Clair shook her head, and saw that gestured denial, unreal and unconvincing, in the eyes so close to hers.

'Not yet.'

And then she had thought, with a cool clarity, as he put his hand on her shoulder: 'But that's a lie.'

So it had been. Lying with her hands clasped behind her small head on which the hair was already too long, she had thought: 'I'll hear that cricket all my life long.' And then she knew with utter certitude that at last was here fulfilment of a phrase that twenty thousand years away was to sing like a bugle-call through a dank ritual mumble. '*I thee with my body worship.*' For one moment the knowledge had been merely terrifying, as though she stood in the imminent threat of mutilation. She had struggled a little, but the singing of the cricket was already lost. Some other song came and shaped to a clamour in her heart, till she knew it one with herself, and never would she be wholly herself again . . . She had reached up and kissed the Cro-Magnard's lips, and then, perhaps a full minute later, with that wilder music dying in her ears, heard suddenly the chirping of the cricket, and realized that it had never ceased . . .

Where would the night find them? Back in the caves?

Aerte had shaken his head when they stood on their feet again and she gestured that question. He picked up his spear. On the young, bearded face close to hers she saw, with a quiver of wonder, a mist of perspiration. He looked down at her, grave again, though with shining eyes. Haunting face . . .

He said: 'Over the hills.'

They had perhaps half a score of words between them. As they went across the sunset land he taught her three. One was his own name. And for the other two Clair looked in his eyes, wondering again, suddenly so pitiful that she almost wept, and then suddenly laughing so that she found herself caught and held again, and it was still longer before the hills came in sight.

But at length they drew nearer, great redstone masses unusual enough in the Atlantean scene. Gorse in thickets climbed their flanks. Birds rose whirring at their approach. Plover. It grew cold. Suddenly their shadows began to race hillwards.

'Do hope you've some place in mind where we can shelter.'

Strange jargon in that sunset land! The English speech, so fine and splendid and flexible an implement, fashioned from the blood and travail of generations of Aryans yet unborn. Thousands of years yet before from Oxus bank dim tribesmen would drift across the Urals, and the first English word issue from barbarous lips . . . She became aware that they were threading in single file a long cleft in the hills. Golden flanked as the hills, Aerte led the way.

Beyond the winding cleft, she realized they had swung north-eastwards. Across the savannah waste, remote, towered the plateau where she had journeyed from the wreck of *Magellan's Cloud*. A week ago!

There lay the lake in the dying light. Perhaps if they listened they would hear that lowing again. She had caught the hunter's arm then, and stayed him, listening. But from the dimming plateau-world and its foreground had come no sound other than a faint rustle, as though it were a painted screen rustling in the wind.

They climbed. The lake receded, blurred, vanished. And at length, on a bush-strewn ledge, Aerte had drawn aside a bush and shown their shelter for the night. She understood then the reason for his disappearance the day before. Some twelve to fourteen feet deep, the shelter, though not more than four feet high. Round the walls were things that looked to Clair like paintings, but the light went then and she could make nothing of them. The hunter motioned her inside. He was standing against the sunset. It was very still. She heard the beating of his heart and thought that were the light clearer she might verily see that beating . . . Almost a shadow, some Titan threatener of the ancient gods, against the coming threat of darkness. His black hair blew softly in the wind.

And Clair, sitting, rubbing her shapely, surface-chilled self, remembered more Tennyson:

Man, her last dream who seemed so fair,
Such splendid promise in his eyes –

Man. Aerte. One and the same, here in the night that was the morning of the world. And if she closed her eyes for a moment she would see him hanging on the barbed-wire entanglements of a Mametz trench, hear again that moan that shuddered still, undying, unceasing, in a night twenty-five thousand years away: 'Clair! *Oh, Clair*! . . .'

She had called him in then, startledly, her face quivering, and he had come, and ceased to have any symbolical significance whatever, and had been merely the strange, dark hunter, and again, of course, the lover. And, lying on the verge of yet another abyssal descent to that place where all colours and sounds merged in a harmony that God had used as model when He painted the first rainbow, Clair had thought, very practically: 'In a minute I shan't be able to think at all, but just now, oh, my good God, I *am* hungry!'

The thought and the fact of her hunger had returned, however, as they sat again in that twilight, her arm round the bare shoulder of the hunter. She told him in a slow murmur of words of which he had no understanding, and he had understood and brought from the back of the cavelet cooked fish, several of them, wrapped in great leaves. She sat and ate with great appetite, wiping her fingers in the grass, and reflecting on the amount of germs she must be eating . . . Her world had been haunted by the wriggly shapes of germs, even as the world of the Middle Ages by devils.

Then she had found herself drowsy. So had been the hunter, untroubled by either germs or devils. They had lain together and from the cave recesses he had brought forward an unfamiliar skin; she was to discover in the morning it was a lion skin. It was warm 'if smelly'. The hunter lay athwart the entrance. He piled the skin round her, laid his head on her breast, kissed her there and was asleep in a moment.

But at that, somehow, sleep had gone from her. The cold had closed it, despite the hunter and her rug. She thought of Sinclair and Sir John, several miles away. Wondering about her? They would go back to the great cave sometime . . .

She abandoned that train of thought, hearing the soft coming of the rain. The volcano lights forty miles in the north seemed to spit and hiss through the intensity of the downpour. They drove not into the shelter, bright, splashing spear-heads as she saw them in the ghostly light. The hunter slept as lightly and soundly as a child.

A child. For that was what he was. So she had said of him and the others, and so they were. Lover! It was she who had abducted a boy. She was twenty thousand years older than this head that lay so close to her, and the hair that tickled and the shoulder grown chill and the hands that touched her. Behind her marched the bloody ghosts of all history; behind the ancestry of this golden boy beside her in the dark was nothing but long millennia of vivid, harmless lives, reaching back to the time when men were not yet men . . .

A child. Instantly the word had a different meaning for her. Her lips grew dry. Beyond Aerte was the rain-curtain. She reached out her hand to it. Damp and cool the fingers she brought to her lips. And already her startlement had passed.

A child.

She laid her head by that other in the darkness. She lay in quivering wonder, unafraid, on the brink of sleep. A child. Spring-time fields at night under the fall of the rain . . .

Wonderful thing if *that* should happen in some tomorrow of this dream!

CHAPTER NINE

Sir John a prophet: his prophecy

Subchapter i

It did not rain the next day, nor the next. Instead, they burned with the vivid radiance of a Mediterranean summer; they burned their sights and sounds into the soul of Clair Stranlay. Each evening found her and the hunter back in the painted cavelet – and aurochs stood in challenging regard of a chrome-red lion in that cave, and Aerte was the artist – but nights and evenings were only so many jade beads on the golden garments of the suntime hours. Clair in those hours discovered the wonder of her own body as she discovered the wonder of the earth itself – as though it were a thing apart from her, yet no more apart than grass and trees and that aurochs' calling and the cry of a wounded deer. This body of hers! A stranger that was yet herself, one with whom she went out into mornings that changed from dull grey to amethystine clarity and a hold-your-breath silence, from that to a nameless stir and scurry and beat that brought the sun orange and tremendous above the Atlantean hills, pringling with warmth on chilled back and face, though one's feet, running in the grass, were chilled still. These, and the smell of the smoke from the fire kindled in the bright weather and drifting blue wavelets across the face of the hunter. Noon, and lying together in sunlight in a sunlight dream, with each pore of her skin hungrily drinking in that sun, and the smell, the chloric smell, of the crushed grass under her head. Crickets chorusing; it was a land of crickets. Sunset and the hasting homewards of bird and sun and cloud and themselves. These the background for hours such as neither she nor any of her century had ever lived.

But the second nightfall a troubled, brooding look came into the grave eyes of Aerte. He turned at the mouth of their shelter and pointed towards the plateau that with each falling of dusk kindled its volcano-torches to watchful brightness. He gestured ineffectively. He and Clair looked at each other dumbly in the dusk. Something –

And next morning they went out from the painted cavelet of sixty hours' residence, and Clair never saw it again. For that morning they went west before the sun, slowly, in no great hurry, yet with intention. Once they stopped to bathe in a lagoon from which they were evicted by the splashings and blowings of a great beast such as Clair had never seen before – a thing with a body like an unfortunate beer-vat, four stumpy legs, a hide that seemed to suffer from mildew and a head that was a bewildering confusion of teeth, tusks, horns and bosses. It splashed and paused and pawed, watching the bathers, and Clair felt the hunter tug at her hair. She turned, treading water, and followed him. Nor any too soon, for the multi-horned animal at that moment charged them from the bank with the speed of an express train and something of its whining uproar. Clair it missed by inches, but they were good as so many miles, for the beast's speed carried it into deep water where it floundered and squawked piercingly, evidently unable to swim. Its musk odour lay like a scum upon the water. Eyeing it, the hunter hefted his spear thoughtfully, and then shook a regretful head as it gained a sandbank and stood blowing and dripping there. Bogged, he would evidently have considered it a titbit.

'I'd sooner eat a goods-wagon,' Clair told him.

She told him many a thing as unintelligible. She found it a saving necessity to keep herself in remembrance that a week before she had been Clair Stranlay, not a naked wanderer (albeit with a comely enough nudity, as the pools still told a disinterested survey) in a love-cycle with a savage through a land lost in the deeps of time. A savage! At that her laughter went up to the soaring circus of carrion birds gathered in haste to watch the shoreward meanderings of the ill-tempered monster. The hunter's contralto laugh joined in, shortly, his grey eyes upon Clair, and lighting as they were wont to do.

And suddenly, in the aurulent loveliness of the day, Clair felt sick with a strange, queer dread.

Subchapter ii

Sinclair saw their home-coming in the late afternoon of that third day. Sitting a little beyond and above the cave-mouths, peeling a long wand and binding either end of that wand with deer-gut, he saw them come. He paused at work and shaded his eyes with his hand. He swore, with the ancient outward mechanism of emotion that the days were indeed wearing to meaninglessness.

Clair Stranlay!

(Ten days before: *Magellan's Cloud*; passengers' gallery; a languid loveliness in an expensive frock, with painted lips and ironic, inquiring gaze . . .)

'Safe, anyhow.'

Safe they seemed. They came over the hills, the hunter pony-laden, Clair carrying his spear. She was a white slip-painting on an Athenian vase; in the blaze of the sun setting she saw the American and waved the Old Stone Age spear. He waved in reply and then returned to work on the peeled wand. He was almost alone at the cave-mouths, for of the mating couples who had taken to the hills, Clair and Aerte were the last to return.

They splashed through the river, stopping midway for Clair to lave the hunter from head to foot, for he was very warm, having killed the pony on the run only a few minutes before. Sinclair descended from his ledge.

'Hello, Keith!'

'Hello, Clair.'

She found his stare impossible to meet. A slow wave of colour ebbed into her cheeks and passed across her breast. She thought: 'I *will* look at him,' and look at him she did, resolutely, then. His gaze passed over her shoulder. She leant on the spear, pleasantly tired, and looked round for Aerte.

He also stood looking at Sinclair. And then a queer thing happened. A shadow came on his face; he seemed to flicker before Clair's eyes, to vanish . . . Moved, of course. Slipped into the caves . . .

'Good God!'

Clair said, standing wiping herself with her hands, there being nothing else with which to wipe herself: 'Why?'

'Your hunter. Where is he?' The American looked round about him in some puzzlement. 'Sight of him with you makes me realize more than anything else the damnable impossibility of it all. Where did you go?'

She told him something of the two days. A boy came wandering out of the caves, saw her, gave a hail of welcome that brought out Zumarr and others. She stood in the midst of a laughing, friendly throng, unalien to them, as Sinclair realized, as she had never been to her own century. Clair Stranlay, the best-selling novelist, had shrugged aside the dream of civilization and come home to the welcome and understandability of an Atlantean cave!

Darkness was very near. Now the radiance from the cave fires stole out across sedge and savannah in pursuit of the hasting daylight. Returned, the hunters were singing in unison, and Sinclair heard their singing with voices from his childhood.

> *I followed my brother into the sun,*
> *In the sunrise-time.*
> *And we crept beyond the place of the bear*
> *Sleeping and sad and a foolish bear*
> *In the sunrise-time,*

To the ridge where the wild horse run,
Running and pawing and making their play
	In the sunrise-time.
And we lay and awaited, still as a deer
	In a thicket at bay:
Till the stallion came near with the mares of his choice
	In the sunrise-time.
And my brother slew with a blow of his spear
The stallion red like the sun himself
	In the sunrise-time.
But I, I followed the mare that was grey
Swiftly out of the place of the ridge
Swiftly past the lair of the bear,
The sleeping and sad and foolish bear,
	In the sunrise-time.
And we ran with the sun
Swift and swift and the mare was mine
And I slew the mare with a blow of my spear
And I drank its blood and I warmed my hands
	In the blood of the mare
	In the sunrise-time.

'What are they singing?' he heard an English voice.

He found Clair alone with him again. The others had drifted back to the caves to join in that song. A chill wind came down the Atlantean river.

'Singing? I suppose it is a song. About killing a horse.'

'Filthy business. I helped Aerte to kill one.'

'You helped at the same business before you met him. Remember that little deer up on the plateau?'

Clair remembered. 'And we thought we were in West Africa. Instead –'

The instead was beyond speech. Sinclair looked across the river. He said, abruptly: 'You and the hunter – I hope you've taken care there won't be – ?'

She stared at him, shook her head. 'How could I – here? Besides – '

She heard then a child wailing in the caves, one of the innumerable children who could and did die so easily. She shivered. But another thought had been with her throughout the past two days, and she put it in words now, to herself more than to Sinclair.

'I want one! We're here for life – however long our lives may last. If we come through the winter we may live as long as the average . . . And we can alter things – we have a doctor among us! – change things so that babies won't die so readily . . . Oh, I'll hate the bother of it. But I'll have one – next spring.'

'I wouldn't.'

'I know.'

She could not resist that. The Battersea imp was a ghostly presence enough these days, but undead still. Sinclair laughed shortly, straightening up where he sat, clasping his hands behind his head.

'Listen, Miss Stranlay, we're here by such kind of accident as probably never happened before. Twenty-five thousand years or more before the birth of Christ. It means hardly anything saying those words; but they have meaning. We're here, members of a tribal group that, for all we know, are the only human beings yet on earth. Certainly it's ancestral to the Cro-Magnards and half the modern population of Europe. And there is no Europe yet, there is no modern population.' He spoke very slowly and casually.

'And if you have a baby and it lives and also has children – can you see the road they'll travel in the next twenty-five thousand years? This is the Golden Age of the human race. I don't know how long it will be before the Fourth Glacial time. Perhaps three thousand years. But it's coming, and by then the descendants of these people – the descendants of your baby – will have drifted across to the fringes of Europe. Through thousands and thousands of years they'll drift with all the chances of famine and starvation and mauling and killing by beasts that are Nature's chances, and may be shared by this baby of yours and its children, and endured because of the things between that will be like the happiness in the lives of these present hunters – like those two days you've spent with the hunter Aerte. But this life does not last for ever.

'In the Nile Valley, four thousand years before the birth of Christ, an accident is to transform the human race and human nature. Do you know that there will be descendants of yours whom they'll stretch out on sacrificial altars – babies of yours – and rip their hearts out of their chests? Do you know that babies of yours will be tortured in dungeons, massacred in captured cities, devoured at cannibal banquets? In Tyre they'll burn alive those children of yours inside the iron belly of Baal, Rome will crucify them in scores along the Appian Way. They'll chop off their hands in hundreds when Vercingetorix surrenders to Caesar. Can't you hear the chop-chop of that axe, and hear mounting down through the years the cry of agony from those children of yours that may so easily be? I can. I can close my eyes and hear the dripping of their blood.'

So could Clair. 'I never thought of that. Oh . . . horrible and terrible!' She covered her face. 'Why did you tell me? Perhaps – *perhaps there were babies of mine who died on the barbed-wire there in France, who are starving in the London streets now, drowned in some awful Welsh mine . . .* ' She took her hands from her face. 'But it's a lie. I don't believe this can ever end. Oh, Keith – help me – '

He did not move. He said to her, as she stood weeping: 'Fantastic stuff we are, Miss Stranlay! Not you and I only. All the human adventure . . . Here, on an autumn night in Atlantis. On the edge of an adventure that probably no other thing in the cosmos will ever attempt . . . ' He paused; he stood up with clenched hands. 'By God, if we should ever get back!'

'Back?'

He laughed. 'I still can't forget, still can't realize that this is reality for us. Of course there's no going back.'

He stood beside her, silent. Clair's thoughts were a grey blur. There came a drift of laughter from the caves. It was as though they stood, an old man and woman, outside a children's playground. And then Clair knew some more immediate matter worrying her. She touched Sinclair's arm.

'I'd forgotten. Where is Sir John?'

Subchapter iii

Sir John Mullaghan lay wrapped in a long, dark skin that might have been a dyed sheepskin but for the fact that there were no sheep in the world where he lay dying. Clair, kneeling beside him, knew that he was dying, even as he knew it himself. His face, grimed and hirsute, as though it were the face of the one-time armaments manufacturer dead and dried and smoked in some head-hunter's hut, looked up at her and then suddenly shrivelled and then grew bloated in one of the spasms of pain that were unceasing.

The odour of that corner of the cave was horrible. But Clair knelt unhorrified. The din of the golden communal life was stilled about them – strange thing this prehistoric foreshadowing of long sickroom silences round many a bed of pain through many a thousand years! In the roof-spaces of the cave the great aurochs stood belling eternally, the mammoth walked the open plains with flailing trunk, the uiratherium strayed from his geological epoch still bunched in frozen charge . . . Clair saw that the night had come down.

'I'm glad you're back safely, Miss Stranlay. Nice honeymoon?'

She smiled down at him, unsteadily. 'Lovely.'

'That's good.' His grey head moved dimly, the words came staccato, as by an effort. 'Unfriendly – if I'd gone – without waiting for your return.'

'You're not going. It's just difference of food, Keith says. We'll hunt up berries and green stuff for you to eat. You'll be well as ever in a day or so.'

'Sinclair didn't say that, I fear. I'm poisoned – very unpleasantly and thoroughly, and can't eat anything. All in all, a very shocking exhibit, Miss Stranlay.' She saw the ghost of a smile. 'Nature didn't design me for a caveman, I'm afraid . . . You've come back in time. There is the rain again.'

So it was. Thunderously. Suddenly, beyond the cave-rims, the cup of darkness cracked. Lightning played and shimmered in the interstices, filling the cave with echoes. Then the darkness closed again. Clair saw Sinclair standing beside them, kneeling beside them.

'Drink this, Mullaghan.'

'What is it?'

'Herb broth. I found a hollow stone and have had it cooking the last two hours.'

The grey head moved upwards painfully. Clair looked away. Then: 'Sorry, Sinclair, I'm afraid I can't.'

'All right. Don't worry. I'll bring some water.'

For a full minute after the American had gone he lay so silent that Clair thought he had fallen asleep. But he moved, again in pain. He chuckled, unexpectedly, surprisingly.

'The head of the League of Militant Pacifists acting as sick-nurse to an armaments manufacturer!'

'I'll help him now I'm back.'

He spoke, but did not seem to answer her. 'And Clair Stranlay, the pornographic novelist. But there are fine things in her, I think, though her books are the nonsense of the half-educated. Fine things in her, Merton, though she was born in a Battersea slum. Courage and honesty and a happy pessimism . . . Her books? They are just such desperate, half-articulate, half-unconscious protestings as Sinclair's threats of sabotage and assassination . . . The savages of civilization . . .

' "Savages!" My God, Merton, the fantastic nonsense we have been taught! I lived in the midst of a Palaeolithic tribe twenty-five thousand years ago. Heroes and kindly women, kindly children all of them. And you have spent your life blackening the memory of them in your lectures and classes – and I have spent mine in murdering their descendants.

'I didn't *know* . . .'

He quivered. Clair put one hand on his forehead, the other under his neck.

'Sir John! Don't worry. None of us knew. Do sleep and don't worry.'

He said, in a whisper: 'We murdered her lover – a boy – on the barbed-wire outside Mametz. She told me. That was why she went away with the hunter that afternoon. Lost somewhere in the Atlantis hills . . .'

The night wore on. Sound of human voice in the great communal cave ceased but for those occasional whispers of clear-headed delirium. Once Aerte came and touched Clair questioningly, but she shook her head, and did not watch him go. Sinclair came and went continuously, with water which he boiled above the far, bright fire by the near entrance. Once he said to Clair: 'You can't do anything. You had better go and lie down.'

'Not until he sleeps.'

'Mr Speaker, in moving support of this Bill for disarmament by example, I am aware that I am contradicting previous utterances of my own and taking a line of action in direct opposition to that pursued by the great party to which I belong, and to my own private interests. But I plead for my former attitude an ignorance of the essential nature of man as crass as any member of this House may ever have confessed to. I lived the scientific delusions of my age – strengthened as these delusions were by the act of a stray madman which brought a very bitter tragedy into my own life . . . But the wreck of the airship *Magellan's Cloud* on the ancient continent of Atlantis and my experiences there in company with two other survivors, amongst primitive men who were our own ancestors – literally, sir, opened my eyes.

'I found no "howling primordial beast"; I saw nothing to indicate that man is by nature a cruel and bloodthirsty animal. It became plain to me that the vicious combativeness of civilized man is no survival from an earlier epoch; it is a thing resultant on the torturing dreads of civilization itself. The famous Chinese poet and philosopher, Lao-Tze, writing of a Golden Age which has been considered mythical, yet describes in vivid detail the character and conduct of those Old Stone Age primitives among whom I lived during an eventful fortnight:

' *"They loved one another without knowing that to do so was benevolence; they were honest and leal-hearted without knowing that it was loyalty; they employed the services of one another without thinking that they were receiving or conferring any gift. Therefore their actions left no trace and there was no record of their affairs . . ."* '

The sound of the rain! Clair heard it rise gustily and drown in momentary volume of sound the speech that Sir John Mullaghan, remote in space and time, was delivering to the English House of Commons. The helpless pity of the first hour of watching was past. In an unimpassioned clarity her mind went on with that speech, as though she also were addressing an unborn multitude in that future from which she had come, and which she would never see again . . . *No Record?* Except that somehow Zumarr and Aerte and Belia, each and all of them sleeping here in this wild night, were to live through the ages, to pass undying through them, to rise again in the Christs and Father Damiens, the Brunos and the Shelleys, the comradeship and compassion of the slave-pit and the trench. No record! They were to live though all else died; they were ghosts of a sanity that haunted mankind.

This adventure in pre-history! As if any woman whatever who had loved a man and been by him loved, known him in the intimate hours when the tabus passed and he lived as man indeed – as if she did not know the true nature of the kindly child immortal, though cult and environment twisted his mind and instincts, though press and pulpit shouted that he was by nature a battling animal, a sin- and cruelty-laden monster! What slum-dweller did not know his neighbour a peaceable man unless one of civilization's innumerable diseases drove him to momentary madness . . . ?

She started drowsily, sleep pressing on her eyelids. Sir John talking or herself thinking? She heard him then, his voice clear and sharp: 'Gentlemen, we must transform our factories to other purposes. There are still bridges to be built and tunnels to be excavated. Flying machines . . . We have barely glimpsed the universe in which man adventures, yet you and I have sat in this room and planned murder and destruction and called it business and patriotism . . . '

He murmured a phrase: 'The Militant Pacifists . . . ' Then: 'Sinclair? We will have him on our board.'

Sinclair came tiredly through the red-ochred mirk at that moment, and again held water to dim lips. All the cave was as some gigantic Akkadian sarcophagus; it seemed to Clair, as once before, that it was a place of the long-dead in which she knelt, and overhead washed the Atlantic . . . Sir John said, very distinctly: 'Miss Stranlay – I thought she was here?'

'So she is. Here she is.'

He peered up at them, his eyes very bright. 'I've been dreaming – that next war. You two – promise me you'll get back, get back and tell them!'

'We'll get back,' Sinclair said, steadily.

'You *must* get back. They're planning it again . . . Tell them, Sinclair. Fight them even with your bombs if they won't listen . . . They *shall* listen. For there was hope even in that age out of which we came – more hope than ever before since civilization began. Else we could never have dreamt this dream, we three who are its children. The slaver and the soldier passes and Man will walk the earth again . . . '

He began to speak in a low, singing voice, so low that Clair had to bend nearer to hear him:

> 'The world's great age begins anew,
>   The golden years return,
> The earth doth like a snake renew
> Her winter skin outworn:
>   Heaven smiles, and faiths and empires gleam
>   Like wrecks of a dissolving dream . . .'

Clair felt the American's hand on her shoulder in the ensuing silence. He gave a sigh of relief.

'He's sleeping now. We can take it easy. If you're as dead-beat as I am – Hell, what was that?'

CHAPTER TEN

Exodus

Subchapter i

It was as though a great beast stirred in dreams under the floor of the cave. Clair was instantly on her feet beside the American. She saw it was close to dawn; the river glimmered beyond the fires. The watcher of the fires himself squatted not far away, nodding, undisturbed, though the faintest rustle of a nearing beast would have roused him to instant activity.

Clair whispered: 'What was it?'

'Remember back beside the lake? Some kind of earthquake shock . . . Here it is again.'

The cave rocked. They held to each other for a moment. The shock passed. Clair peered past the drowsy fire-watcher. 'These people must be used to it. None of them have wakened.'

Not a hunter or a woman had stirred. They lay and slept in healthy disregard of the earth's freakish moods.

The fires burned low, yet glowed enough to show the painted uiratherium still bunched with head eternally lowered. Funny to think that that beast ('at this moment!') in the twentieth century might still survive in this cave long sunk two miles or more below the level of the ocean! . . . The thought made Clair whisper another question: 'Wasn't this continent sunk in an earthquake?'

She saw a pallid flicker of a smile on Sinclair's face. '*Will* be . . . Let's see if anything's happening outside.'

The fire-tender nodded to them. They paused at the cave-entrance and looked out. Nothing. The rain had cleared away. The sky was pallid with the waning lights of the stars awaiting the morning. The crispness of the air caught at their throats. But there was also in that air an unusual quality.

'Sulphur,' said Sinclair. 'Stay here. I'm going out to look.'

He vanished, tall and white, into that waiting unease of the morning. Clair thought: 'Dictatorial still. But a dear.' Yawned. 'Oh, my good God, what wouldn't I give for a cup of tea!'

Startling thought! Years, surely, since she had visioned such wistful amenities! . . . She yawned again. 'Thank goodness Sir John's asleep at last . . . Eaough!'

She became aware of a pillared whiteness, like Lot's wife, against the remoter greyness of the morning. It was Sinclair, beckoning.

The grass was wet and cold. The morning wind blew chill on their unclad bodies as they passed together outside the furthest flow of the cave-fires' radiance and climbed over the smooth back of the bluff. And, as they did so, the smell of sulphur increased with every step they took. Nearing the top of the bluff, Clair, looking upwards, suffered a curious optical illusion. It seemed to her that the grass on the knoll, that the whole summit, was lighted to an unwonted glow, as though a great fire were kindled on the other side. But, the summit attained, she saw she had suffered from no delusion. She gasped and stared.

In that hour they should have seen but a little way across the jumble of foothill and nullahs towards the mountain land from which they had descended a short week before. Instead, all that landscape which should have lain in morning darkness was lighted uneasily, a welter of unstable candle-points of flame, and backgrounding it, mile on mile, from one end of the horizon to the other, was a dark-red glow that glimmered and faded and grew to purple being and then died again, yet never quite, like a fire that lives in a half-charred stick. Momentarily, as they watched, the red and ochre faded from the glow, yet that was through no waning of its strength, as they saw, but with the coming of the morning. And with that coming the mystery grew plainer. The whole of the dim mountain-land of their first adventures had vanished into some fissure of the earth from which now arose the corona of its destruction. Twenty miles away to the north the vivid line of flame stalked the horizon, and in the nearer distance they saw a pale advancing gleam.

'Floods – it's the sea!' said Clair.

Sinclair peered forward from beneath his hands. 'Hell, and it is! We'll have to run for it.'

But he did not. He said, a second later: 'It's advancing no longer. Only through the light growing it seems to be. The floods have stopped.'

So it seemed, now. Daylight was almost upon the land, and the havoc of fire and water grew clearer. The sea had come far in – in places it was not more than two or three miles distant. More than that. They stood now on what was a great promontory, for this was higher land than to east and west. And, advancing out of the water-threatened, cobalt valleys were long trains of moving objects that ran and squealed and jostled. Clair saw them coming, up out of the morning, dipping and rising, here and there covering the hills in dun hordes.

'Trek of the animals,' said Sinclair. 'Look – the mammoths!'

A great herd of them led the exodus. They came at racing speed, great tusks uplifted, trunks uplifted, untrumpeting, with flying coats of dun red hair. They thundered past not half a mile away. Then Clair saw her first aurochs, also running in herds, the gigantic beasts whose lowing she had listened to many a time since that first night by the lake. Horned and maddened, with belching breaths of spume they ran, swinging round the corner of the bluff so that Sinclair, seeing the danger there might be to the cave-dwellers below, turned and ran down the hill, calling to Clair to stay where she was. Safest place . . . Clair sank down in the wet grass, staring appalled. It was as though the hills were the contours of a wet corpse, hideously, titanically be-magotted.

'Oh, horrible!'

The hills drummed with flying hoofs. Great deer, an Irish elk, a pack of lions like loping St Bernards, here and there a trundling bear. Then herd on herd of ponies, with manes in quivering serration. The day brightened, and with its brightening the glow in the north abruptly flickered and vanished. The pulsing flight of beasts thinned, but the birds still passed overhead in great flocks, tern and snipe and partridge either momentarily startled or out on definite migration through the weaving of some mysterious instinct. Up till then no animal had attempted the scaling of the bluff, but now two leopards did so. Sly and suave, they came in loping bounds, not greatly frightened, evidently, though in flight. One had been swimming, and the water glistened on its sleek black coat. They slithered leftwards at sight of the kneeling woman. Then one crouched and snarled –

The charge of the brute rolled her on the ground. It had charged, not leapt, being over-hungry, and had hit her with its shoulder, instead of pinning her to the earth. Its body sprawled across her, furry and musk and smelling vilely of the cat-house. She thought, vividly: 'My throat!' and screamed, and saw the other leopard looking away, with pricked ears. She caught the wurring muzzle of the brute above her. Screamed again. Thereat, unaccountably, it vomited blood all over her. She was dragged to her feet by Aerte. She wiped her face; she laughed hysterically.

All over in a minute. Three of the hunters, Aerte included, had seen the leopards and raced them up the opposite side of the hill. She saw Sinclair ascending more slowly, now that she was safe. Aerte laughed. She could not look at the smoking, furred thing on the ground. The other leopard had fled.

When Sinclair came up she was still trembling, as in the throes of a fever.

'Goodness – I – I always did hate cats. Never bathe . . . Silly to shake, but I can't stop it. I think I'll go down to Sir John.'

Sinclair looked at her apathetically; sat down. She was safe; the caves were safe. He felt he wanted to sleep for a month.

'Sir John is dead,' he said, tiredly.

Subchapter ii
The sun lay brave on the hillside. The day marched bannered across the Atlantean sky. Little clouds tinged with purple went sailing by, free and very fleecy and lovely. More of the bird-flocks came from the north, holding into dim southern regions of the Pleistocene earth. Far below, in the open spaces between the caves and the river, the Cro-Magnards cut up the meat which had come, alive and maddened, past their doors in such abundance.

And on the hill-brow Clair and Sinclair watched the passing of the day. Clair lay with her breasts to the earth, thinking, and yet trying not to think. She raised her face once, looking at the American.

'But it can't be! He can't have died. We don't belong here; it couldn't have happened this way in time! Else he was dead long before he was born. This would have happened to him before we knew him. Before the *Magellan* was wrecked he was dead.' She giggled a little and dropped her head on the grass again. 'We've been talking to a corpse all this last fortnight.'

Sinclair said nothing, bleakly. Clair, exhausted, dozed. Later, she felt a hand on her shoulder, and aroused to Sinclair speaking at last: 'I won't leave you long. Shout if anything comes near.'

'Where are you going?'

But he had gone. She sat, clasping her knees, sun-warmed, earth-kissed, vividly aware of the beauty and pleasure of her body. And below, in the Cro-Magnard caves, was that other body, finished with this and the sun and the rain and the hearing of laughter for ever. Impossibly dead in an impossible country in an impossible epoch. She remembered, numbedly, half-forgotten things about him – his courteous care of her, and her flouting of it, in that march across the plateau; his pathetic adaptations to Cro-Magnard ways . . . 'Oh, my good God, I am *so* tired!'

She looked back over the bluff. Sinclair and two hunters, burdened, were coming up. A few feet from Clair they halted. One of the hunters was Aerte.

They lowered something to the ground.

Next instant she found Aerte beside her. He put his arms round her. He laughed, gravely, and pointed down to the river in the sunlight. His brows knitted puzzledly as she shook her head and indicated the body wrapped in the pelt from the cave. He glanced at it indifferently, smiled again, and tried to pull her to her feet. She shook him off; his touch was suddenly as shuddersomely repulsive as that of an unclean animal.

'Keith – *send him away*.'

She did not look round again as the American spoke to the two hunters, but she heard the sound of a lingering, puzzled retreat through the low, brittle grass. Then the noise of Sinclair digging with a hand-axe. At that she rose and went and helped him. They worked in silence.

'Stand away, Miss Stranlay.'

She stood aside and looked down over the flood-sodden lands. Already the darkness waited for them. She heard Sinclair dragging the body to the shallow pit. Then a sound of scraping and the fall of earth. Sinclair said: 'Throw some earth, Miss Stranlay.'

She turned round, seeing the grave almost completed. She picked up a handful of clayey dust and dropped it through her fingers. Sinclair replaced the turfs and walked over them, stamping them gently.

Then he held out his hand to Clair and she went to him.

Subchapter iii

It seemed to her that something had numbed her body and brain alike, through and through, in the next twenty-four hours. The second night-fall Sinclair came and sat down beside the fire of Zumarr, who glanced at him questioningly and from him towards another fire at which the hunter Aerte had again taken up quarters, as in times before the Mating for the Dark Days.

'Clair.'

She roused a little. 'Oh, it's you, Keith.'

He stretched himself out beside her. His square, dark head was oddly similar to Zumarr's. She thought, apathetically: 'They might be brother and sister.' He put a twig on the fire, absently, scowlingly, as was his habit, and watched it consume. Abruptly he said: 'This can't go on, you know.'

She said, dully: 'What?'

He seemed to be considering his answer. Then: 'These people aren't to blame, Clair, but you. I mean your hunter and the others when they thought Mullaghan's death and dead body of no account. Neither, really, were they. Death *is* of no account in fundamental human values – the things these people live by. Your hunter saw a man lying dead – one to whom he had never talked, a puzzling stranger, a man who had presumably lived to the full, and was now dead, as was the order of things. And if your hunter thought about it at all, it was simply that he himself would also die some time, but meantime there was living to be done – eating, and sleeping with you, and painting his pictures, and hunting, and every moment in which to live his body before he also was dead. That was all. It was perfectly natural.'

'I know. And it has made me sick and frozen.'

'It has no cause to make you any such things. If he'd seen Sir John lying ill or wounded he'd have carried him miles to safety. You know he would. They are absolutely unselfish and absolutely natural. Nothing horrible in death to them; there *is* nothing horrible in death. It is merely that you and I are laden down with the knowledge of that past that is not yet – with all the obscene funeral rites in our memory and that ritual of sorrow that isn't natural at all, but was an artificial thing foisted on human nature in a matter of mistaken science. It is these people who are clean and you who are diseased.'

'I know,' Clair said again. And suddenly she found words. 'Oh, Sinclair, I'll go mad, I know I will, in this horrible place, among these horrible people! Natural and clean? Of course they are. Splendid and shining and lovely, all of them. Aerte – he's been my lover and is closer to my life than the blood in my body . . . And they're not kin to me at all. I'm separated from them by a bending wall of glass. I'm not human if they are. I'm the diseased animal, and it's not the winter or the memory of Sir John that'll kill me. It's realization of a fact. I can't go on with it, I *can't*!'

'You filthy little weakling.'

He said it in a low, even voice. Clair suddenly found herself in the cave. Something seemed to cataract and then clot about her heart. She stared at the American. He looked at her evenly.

'You little gutter-slut of the London slums! I thought you had guts in you. You haven't. You've a pious, rotten romanticism that's no relation to reality. Think I don't know – that I haven't watched your antics ever since I was fool enough to drag you out of the *Magellan*? And I *was* a fool; I fooled myself about you. Here, especially. I thought this place and these people had done to you what they did to me and poor Mullaghan – discovered the human in you. But there wasn't a human to discover. You're only a sack of second-rate opinions and third-rate fears. Human! A thing like you! – '

Clair shook herself and leant forward to the fire and also put a twig on it. Then she laughed and gave a long sigh, and, looking at Sinclair, shook her head.

'Thanks. But it's really not necessary . . . Or not now.'

He flushed, suddenly, darkly. 'I thought it might work.'

'It has, in a way.' She raised her head and looked across the cave towards Aerte's fire. 'Goodness . . . Sorry I've been all you said.'

'You haven't, of course . . . But I need help as well, Clair. All this stuff I talked – about the naturalness of regarding death casually – I know as well as you do that it's impossible for us, just as it's impossible for us ever to live the lives of these hunters. I know that wall of glass as well . . . But Mullaghan's gone, and if you went and I were left on my own – I also don't want to go mad . . .'

Clair said, soberly: 'I'm both sick and sorry. Oh, I'm damnably selfish.' She held out her hand. 'I don't think we've ever been friends. Can't we be?'

He held her hand a moment. She thought: 'Funny how like his eyes are to someone's – ' He said: 'This is the last night in these caves.'

She was startled. 'Why?'

'You haven't heard, of course. They've left you alone, thinking you're sick. But the exodus was decided on this afternoon. There's no game anywhere in the flooded country round about, nor anywhere to the south as far as the hunters have penetrated. That earthquake and the sinking of the mountain-land has left this section a deserted peninsula. The cave is going to be abandoned tomorrow.'

'And where are they going?'

'Southwards, somewhere, in pursuit of the game. And it's not only threat of famine, of course. You haven't noticed, not being outside the cave. But there was frost this morning; the new lagoons, half salt at that, were covered with ice. It'll be a winter of such terrors as these people have never endured – at least as far north as this.'

Clair looked at the painted animals overhead. 'And they're to leave . . .' It seemed that she herself had occupied these caverns for months. Then: 'We knew that this happened in pre-history, of course – or will happen . . . Goodness, tenses do get mixed in the time-spirals . . . Is this the coming of the Ice Age?'

'I don't think so. It's just that Atlantis is the most unstable of the continents. That, of course, we know from the future out of which we've come. It's doomed.'

'And these people?'

'They're the ancestors of the Cro-Magnards from Cro-Magnon in France, remember. So some of them at least are to push eastwards, and some years or generations hence strike Europe. Or at least, that preceded the future in which we lived.'

'Isn't it bound to happen, then?'

'Not necessarily. Perhaps the future we came from was one of many possible futures – '

She leant forward in excitement. 'I thought that – once – but I'd forgotten.'

'There was nothing fixed and real about that twentieth century of ours, Clair. Civilization as we knew it – it has still to happen. Perhaps it need never happen. Perhaps we can prevent it, sabotage it in advance – '

It had grown dark again. The Cro-Magnards were turning to sleep. The evening was frostily clear and set with frosty stars. Clasping her knees and looking out as she listened to Sinclair, Clair thought of Sir John Mullaghan. *'Think but one thought of me up in the stars – '* said a vagrant line . . . She turned her attention to the American.

'There is no need for the processes of history, as we knew them, ever to take place. You and I can alter the very beginnings. Listen! We're going south, and it will get warmer. Somewhere beyond the southwards mountains we saw from the plateau these people will find new hunting-grounds. Then you and I can get to work. We can teach them the beginnings of civilization without any of civilization's attendant horrors.'

'What, for example? I'm horribly ignorant.'

He shook his head. 'It's just that you don't realize what you know. Pitchers – they've never thought of using gourds to store water at night. That for a beginning. Then in hunting: I'm engaged in making a bow. But these are the lesser things. Somewhere beyond those southwards mountains we'll find a river and wild millet or barley or corn. We can start the first agriculture – ploughing and seeding will be simple enough. That for next spring. And in the summer get them to build a corral and drive wild cattle into it; they can tame them in a few years. Next autumn take a party prospecting in the mountains – I know something about metals . . . Flax or hemp growing, perhaps. Even with crude metal implements and rough fibre bandagings I could save half the women who die in childbirth. And iodine and suchlike are easy enough extracts . . . We can leap twenty thousand years and take these people with us if we plan it carefully. Preserve this sane equality that's theirs, take care that no idea of gods or kings or devils ever arises in their minds. We can transform humanity.'

Clair began to kindle to his words. If they could! 'But – aren't the cruelties and the tabus bound to rise with civilization? Better to leave our hunters alone for the Golden Age that is still theirs than try and fail.'

'We won't fail. Much better to leave them if there was any chance of failure. If there was no choice for the future but history as we know it, a thing inevitable awaiting these people, it would be better for them and better for the world if we poisoned them all or drove them to death by starvation. But there's no reason why we should fail. The foul things of civilization were an accident . . . Time and history will go on long after we're dead here in Atlantis, Clair, but there need never be a pyramid built or a city massacred or a war or a miners' strike. We can re-make the world.'

'Goodness, we will! . . . Keith, there's Gloezel!'

'Eh?'

'Don't you remember reading about it a few years back? That place in France where heaps of Neolithic relics were dug up, and were said to be fakes because they were mixed with modern-looking bottles and jars and the scratchings of a primitive alphabet? . . . Perhaps this experiment we're going to try was known to us already in that twentieth century from which we came! Perhaps Gloezel saw the end of this plan of yours, and men of those days forgot your teachings, and the civilizations and the savageries rose in spite of the dream we brought these hunters.'

Sinclair laughed and stood up. 'Perhaps there have been other voyagers into time than you and I. Perhaps time and history cannot be altered. Yet if they can – '

Somewhere in the depths of the caves a sick child was crying He stood and listened to it and then looked down in Clair's fire-bright face.

'There need never be a lost baby crying again in the world that we can make.'

And with that he left her, and Clair lay down, and saw him stride into the far shadows, and a hunter rouse and look after him. For a moment she hesitated, and a shudder as of nausea passed through her. Then she raised her head and called.

'Aerte!'

So it was that Sinclair, coming back to lie down by his own fire after tending that crying child, saw the hunter and Clair, the lovers for the dark days, asleep in each other's arms.

Subchapter iv

And next day the Cro-Magnards of that nameless valley in Atlantis left the fires in the painted caves still burning, and gathered their children and their implements and the skins of the beasts they had killed in generations of hunting, and forded the river, and turned to the south. The rain cleared, and a cold sun shone, and far in the north the new lakes shivered in a brisk wind. They passed through a deserted country, with not even birds in it. They passed out of the Atlantean valley as dream-people pass from a dream dreamt by a drowsy fire. Coming from the east or west hundreds of years before, their ancestors, a people with a no-history of millennia, descendants of the dawn-men who lived in Java and Peking and the Sussex downs, had descended upon the valley, a place of good hunting, and settled there. And the years had passed in the flow and ebb of death and love and birth, times of plenty and times of famine, with neither memory of the past nor fears nor hopes for the future. The sun and the wind, the splendour of simple things, had been theirs; theirs that Golden Age that was to live for ever, a wistful thing in the minds of men. Now they were out on an adventure that followed no road Clair Stranlay could foreplot.

They carried their sick and their aged with them, and they went gaily enough, with laughter and singing, the young men stringing out far in advance across the southern savannahs. They went in no great order, but a friendly southwards drift. Alone perhaps of them all Clair and Sinclair stopped and looked back.

'There will be fishes swimming in that cave years hence,' said Clair. 'Poor Mullaghan!'

And that was strange enough to think of also. Thousands of years away, perhaps preserved uncorrupted and incorruptible by the pressures of water and rock, the body of Sir John Mullaghan would lie in that grave they had dug for it with the flint spears of Cro-Magnard hunters. The knoll glimmered.

'And now –' said Sinclair.

So they too turned about and went, their white bodies strange phenomena still in the wake of the golden men of the dawn. The savannahs rose green and brown and cobalt in the distance. Far and remote beyond these, many days' journeyings away, were the mountains where Sinclair planned to change the course of history.

Behind, the winter followed on their tracks.

BOOK TWO

Whence? Whither?

If I have been extinguished, yet there rise
A thousand beacons from the spark I bore.

SHELLEY

CHAPTER ONE
Clair lost

Subchapter i

Clair Stranlay was lost.

She looked back, shading her eyes with her hand against the pale afternoon sunlight, to the track she had taken across the withering grass to this eminence in the southern foothills. But all the country was desolate and deserted, except by a far loch where curlews called and called. Nothing moved or took to itself animate being in that still land, with the forests marching on its fringes and the sun – silver, not gold at all – brooding upon the quietness. Up that track she had come. But before that?

She sat down to consider the matter. There was the forest. But which forest? The country was ribbed with just such masses of trees, and the rise and fall of nullahs confused all knowledge as to whether one mass was a separate entity or the winding continuation of another . . . Goodness, such a fool not to watch the course of the sun!

'I'm shockingly hungry,' said Clair, aloud.

The silent countryside took no notice. Clair pushed her hair from her eyes and stood up again. It would be nonsensical to rest now. Somewhere, from higher up, she would be bound to see the hunters or the encampment.

She climbed through grass that was sedgy because of a trickle of water from the hillside. A ridge, like the scales on the back of a stegosaurus, ran along its summit. Here the grass gave place to lichened rock – granite rock, she noted, and red granite at that. The sight brought back a memory – oh, holiday bathing at Peterhead in Scotland, of course. Twenty-five thousand years before.

The red slivers cut her feet, hardened though these had grown. But at last, though with some difficulty, she attained a platform-ledge that dominated all the hill and indeed all the country. Panting, she looked again into the north.

Made miniature in distance, the land was otherwise unchanged. No sign of the Cro-Magnards or their encampment anywhere.

If she made a fire –

Realization of a startling fact chilled her a little. She had nothing with which to make a fire. She glanced down at the short-bladed flint spear in her hand. Flint. But no iron pyrite. The hunters used tinder and a drum-stick – things she was incapable of operating. No chance of raising a fire. Must watch for one instead.

For how long? She looked at the sun. Perhaps three hours more of daylight. She turned round, slowly, in a circle, looking about her. So, very suddenly, she became aware at last of the mountains of the south.

From her stance, and for the first time in the southwards trek, she saw them uprise plainly. Not only so, but gigantic. They filled all the south-ern horizon with their tumbled shapes. Distant, Andean, some trick of refraction allowed her to see the sun filtering into immense canyons, splashing in remote upland tarns, crowning each point with quicksilver. The significance of that last gleam dawned on her.

'Snow.'

They were perhaps twenty miles away. From right to left of the horizon they stretched unbroken, tenebrous and question-evoking. Were they passable?

She thought: 'Keith's plan to take the hunters south of them – he may never be able to carry it out. Necessary to try out our experiment on a southwards river, protected by mountains in the north . . . Wonder what he's doing now? Missed me? Sure to.'

She had an afterthought, and smiled at it, absently. 'And Aerte as well, I suppose.'

How far away, both of them? Miles and miles, surely. Goodness, what a fool –

But thinking that wouldn't help.

It was nine days since the beginning of their trek from the ancient cave. Acting on the apparently casual suggestion of Sinclair, the Cro-Magnards had held as directly southwards as the nature of the country allowed. It was to them a matter of indifference what direction was taken, so long as game grew more plentiful. And certainly neither to left nor right was there that plentitude. But one colony of lions the general exodus of the animals had left behind, and on the fifth night of the trek these beasts, made bold by hunger, had raided the camp, a score or more of them. Clair and Sinclair had been awakened by the screams and shouts, and stirred to see a fire geyser under the impact of a lion landing from a misdirected spring. Clair had caught up a torch and thrust it into the face of one brute. Near her Zumarr had been killed and nearly disembowelled by the stroke of a huge paw. The fighting in the semi-darkness about the fires had gone on for many minutes. Then the lions had retreated, dragging several bodies with them. Devouring these, they had squatted all night in a semi-circle beyond the fires, evidently determined not to abandon the neighbourhood of this store of food which had descended on their famished land from the north. Sinclair had gone about, binding up such wounds as grass and sinew seemed capable of salving. Aerte had come to Clair and crouched by her, looking towards the noise of the lions' grisly banqueting and gripping a spear in either hand. Then, towards the dawn, the Cro-Magnards had begun to move out towards the lions, discovering them replete and somnolent, all but two or three cubs which had had little share of the human meat. Out there, beyond the camp, a running fight began, three men and more to one beast, until the morning came. Half a dozen or so of the lions escaped. The rest, dead, were skinned, and the Cro-Magnards cooked and ate meat from their haunches. Both Clair and Sinclair had refused it.

Throughout the next day and the next, holding south again, no game at all had been encountered. Food was growing very scarce, and the half-dozen lions, made cautious, but still hungry, followed up the trek, roaring despondently at night-time but venturing on no more raids. But, on the morning of this day on which Clair sat lost on the summit of her hill, a boy, slipping out of the camp in the early hours on some boyish foraging of his own, had wandered for several miles and then returned in a glow and much excitement. The lions had vanished from about the camp, and he knew the reason. A herd of mammoth, many bulls and cows and three young ones, was gathered feeding near a stream and a hill.

The news had emptied the camp, at racing speed, of the golden men. Clair had caught up a flint spear and ran by Sinclair's side, the spear a thrilling complement. 'Though goodness only knows what for. Unless to tickle the mammoths . . . What, for that matter, are any of us going to do with spears against a mammoth?'

'Aerte was telling me,' Sinclair had said. 'We'll drive one of the animals into the river and attack it there.'

So they had done. One bull, perhaps the leader of the herd, had charged the yelling attack of the Cro-Magnards, a magnificent spectacle of wrath with uplifted trunk and threatening tusks. Him they had allowed to pass without casualty, and, once past, he had stood a moment meditating discretion or valour, and then taken to the open land and safety. The others, all but the selected two, had followed him. Driving those twain into the river was the task. Under the urge of a hail of stones one of them at length galumphed forward into the muddy embrace of the waters and sank to the knees and was held there, like a fly in glue. And, as by so many hornets, hewing and stabbing, he had been instantly assailed. Not so the second. It had broken away to the right, trampling several hunters underfoot and impaling one on a great broken tusk. Sinclair had taken abrupt command, his dour face flushed; perhaps the first commander in the world, for even in hunting parties the Cro-Magnards had no leaders. They were an orchestra without a conductor, yet a fairly efficient one at that, acting with a serene co-operativeness that suggested to Clair telepathy. But, under the direction of Sinclair's shout, such of them as had already attended the panicked antics of the second mammoth broke into two parties. One raced for the hills, the other held in the track of the beast. Clair had joined the first group, and ran with them, feeling in a very glow of health, and had slipped and fallen; and had laughed and scrambled to her feet and reclaimed her spear. Then she had found herself alone and lost.

As simply as that. For a time she had heard receding shoutings and once a wild trumpeting of agony that made her cover her ears. She had made in the direction of both sounds, as she believed. Neither could be more than half a mile distant. And no sign of hunters or hunted had met her eyes. She had found herself in a series of low valleys, one fitting into the other with the suave necessity of shallow boxes in a Chinese puzzle. And when finally she had emerged from the labyrinth into open country again, it was a country of which she had no knowledge. No river was in sight, other than one glistening far across the savannah. It had seemed too distant to be the one where the first mammoth had been killed, and she had disregarded it and searched in other directions. And when she would have sought for it again it had disappeared.

She had wandered the deserted Atlantean country since then, once stopping to drink at a pool, once finding a nest with three eggs in it, curious speckled eggs which she had broken and eaten raw, very thankful that they were fresh. She had even thought of the curate's egg while doing so, and laughed, feeling refreshed. Then she had hunted on again.

And this seemed the day's end of the hunt.

Bound to follow her. But could they? With a certain uncertainty gripping her she turned now from survey of the gigantic bastion in the south, and looked at the country out of which she had climbed. They had no dogs, they had no special scent themselves; scent was nothing to primitive man, was probably a later acquirement of specialized savages. She would have to wait until darkness and then look for the light of a fire somewhere down there. And food –

Beyond her hill, eastwards, was another, and between the two of them a gleam of water. She realized the thirst parching her throat, and began to descend from the scaled back of the granite stegosaurus. The sun flung her a long shadow eastwards as she walked, but it was only as she neared the foot of the hill and the water was near that she saw a mist was rising or descending from nowhither. Between her and the distant, nameless Andes the undulating, sparsely-forested land was sheathed in an uneasy garment of damp wool. By the time she had knelt and drunk and stood up again, the mist was all about her. She stood in uncertainty of it, walked a few steps, halted, determined to climb her hill again. But the hill had disappeared. Or rather the hill-summit had.

Now she walked along a rolling shoulder of earth that was either of the original eminence, or of that second hill she had seen in the east. A tickling sensation disturbed her chest; then her nose. Abruptly she began to sneeze, desperately. She sought for a handkerchief she did not possess. The fit passed in a moment, but not the constricted feeling in her throat. She thought, dismayed: 'Goodness, if I'm in for a cold!'

She came to another tarn. It reflected her face and body as her feet touched the edge. She leant on her spear and looked down at herself.

'Pretty thing still,' she said, and rubbed her chill arms and flanks, still regarding herself. A woman had come into the water and looked up at her gravely, from under a heavy, short-cut mane of brown hair with the red slightly bleached from it. But the red tints were still in eyes and brows, and her face had a brownness set on it evenly, as though out of a jar. So indeed her whole body was tinted, yet in some fashion that left it none the less white. Rubbed to warmth, she picked up the spear again, and, leaving that reflection of herself to dream of her for ever, perhaps, in that lost pool, went on into a mist that presently cleared, like a curtain drawn aside to disclose the splendours of the sunset on the Atlantean Alps. They changed and took separate form and advanced and retreated as she looked, like a company of warriors in gold and grey and the panoply of war.

With purple from the murex the sunset had garbed them, and with the red of rust, and a blue – an ultramarine blue that must have found its colours in those high, glacial snows . . . Clair had never seen such a sunset, and the stalking approach of darkness at her lower level was almost upon her before she noticed it. With that darkness came a bitter coldness and a wind that seemed somehow dissociated from the cold, but cold itself . . .

And suddenly Clair knew that she was being tracked.

The beast had snuffled in a peculiar way. She wheeled round and saw nothing. Then – a hump of rock she had not noticed when she passed that way. It was not a hump of rock. The beast was crouching. There was not light enough for its eyes to gleam, she saw merely the dim shape, hunched, and the twitching of its ears. She thought: 'Is it going to spring?'

She turned round and went on. The padding came on as well. This time she wheeled so rapidly that she saw the beast, not crouching this time, but on its feet, its ears still twitching.

And it was not a beast!

Subchapter ii

To Clair it seemed that she stood and faced the thing through minute after minute of horror-struck silence. The spear was gripped and useless in her hand, for the blood had deserted her hand. It grew momentarily darker, in wave on wave of lapping shadow from the sunset fire in the mountains of the south. And still Clair Stranlay stood and stared wide-eyed at that hideous apparition out of pre-history.

It was a male, with the bigness of a gorilla and something of its form. It was hung with dun-red hair; crouched forward, its shoulders were an immense stretch of arching muscle and bone. Its gnarled hands almost touched the ground. It smelt. It stared at her filmily, and a panting breath of excitement came from its open jaws.

A Neanderthaler!

The thought flashed through her mind and was instantly disputed and dismissed. For the thing had an immense bulge of forehead and no downwards-pressing neck constriction such as she had read the lost race of Neanderthal possessed. Nor had it a single implement or weapon about it. It crouched, a strange, strayed, hungry, pitiful beast, looking at her. What it was she did not know, was never to know, that member of some lost, discarded genus of sub-men that time was utterly to annihilate. Lost as herself she suddenly realized it was, and with that realization blood came back to her hand. She raised the spear and shouted, 'Shoo!'

The thing, half in sitting posture though it was, sprang back a full yard, and then, as Clair, desperately afraid, made at it, turned and shambled off in a rapid, baboon-like scrabble. And as it went it uttered a strange, moaning cry, growing louder and louder as the body behind the voice receded and finally vanished into the evening. Clair, sobbing hysterically, no sooner saw it out of sight than she turned in her original direction and ran and ran, slipping and falling over rocks and once becoming desperately entangled in a soft and hairy bush which seemed to grasp at her with clammy hands. When finally she stopped, panting, there was no echo of that moaning ululation to be heard in the deserted hills, nor any sign of her stalker.

The running had warmed her, but now, stopping, she felt the wind drive against her bare skin icily. Some shelter she must have before the night came. And there was little chance in these hills, for they were of granite, not the familiar limestone so frequently honeycombed with caverns. Yet, in the thickening nightfall, she had not gone more than a dozen steps when fortune favoured her and up the brow of the hill she saw an indentation. Attained with panting effort, she discovered it a fault in the strata that left a roofed, triangular recess some nine or ten feet deep, inadequate enough, but better than nothing.

Grass. Grass to warm it and herself.

She laid down her spear and ran to the foot of the hill where grass, sere and dry as hay, rustled and whispered eerily in that voiceless country. She tore up great armfuls of it and carried it up to the ledge. Meantime the force of the wind had increased, and as she made the last journey sleet began to pelt her body, as though she stood in an ice-cold spray from a bathroom tap. But the ledge was a heaped fuzz of hay. She ran inside, seized the flint spear, lay down on the hay and wound herself into the swathes, rolling over and over till the faintly burred heads had entangled her in a great coverlet from head to foot. She left her right arm bare and gathered more of the hay and piled it above her in blanket-like layers. The exertion had warmed her again, faintly, but her whole body was still an icy numbness. When she finished and raised her head it was to see the blackness complete but for a strange phenomenon. A white curtain wavered and shook in front of the ledge of refuge. And the rock sang as it waved and shook.

Hail.

Winter.

She found she had forgotten hunger as she had forgotten to be afraid. Yet the numbness of her body had not spread to her mind. She found herself thinking and remembering in a passionate dispassion.

She thought of Aerte and that first night she had lain with him in the cave far to the north, watching the volcanoes burn in the land that the seas were soon to devour. And instantly the memory passed from her. Neither Aerte – his face seemed to take shape in the darkness and then fade at once – nor that pitiful shade of Mametz seemed of importance. She thought of Sinclair, and he passed from her mind, a dour, enigmatic ghost. Sir John Mullaghan – less than a ghost. So with all she had ever known, all the tenants of the ancient world of comfort and security. Only in the sound of the bitter hail-storm that thudded upon the hills, remained one piercing memory; the face of the beastman, lost and desperate as herself, astray in time and the world.

Had he found refuge or was he out in this? What a jest of God! Millions and millions of years ago He had brought a warm, fetid scum to anchor on some intertidal beach. And it had fermented through long nights and noons; and it was life. And life climbed and branched and flowered from it. And the dragons passed and the mammals rose and the great apes walked the hills of Siwalik. Westwards they wandered, through millennium on millennium, gathering their little skills with stock and stone. And one by one God murdered and discarded them. For they bored Him. Heidelberg man with the mighty skull, the ape-hunter of Piltdown, the chattering beasts of Broken Hill and the Java jungles – they passed and were not, bloody foam and spume on a sea that whimpered cruelty and change. Till this Atlantean night of hail all these experimentings of Nature's thousand millennia – they ended here in a nameless hill-land with the ape-beast and herself, last representatives of their kindred experiments . . .

She quivered to a misty drowsiness, even while a faint voice protested through her frozen serenity: 'But you are not the last!' Last she was. Poor humanity, that had dreamed so much and so splendidly – to end its dream with her! . . .

Thereon, warmed by the heat her body had engendered in the hay, utterly exhausted with her day's marchings and searchings, Clair laid her head on her hand, and slept, while the hail ceased and the hand of winter drew back, hesitating a cosmic moment, from the night and hills of Atlantis.

Subchapter iii

It began to freeze as the night wore on. The cold grew more intense. But it did not penetrate the grass coverings wherein Clair Stranlay lay enwrapped. Not cold but cramped position made her awake, and, shifting her aching hip, she saw that the hail had ceased and the moonlight had come. It flooded all the uplands and came in little waves into the recess. She lay and looked out, suddenly vividly awake. What had she been imagining before she fell asleep?

Suddenly she remembered and laughed a little at the memory. The night bent eagerly in to listen to her. She thought: 'You were hysterical, I suppose. The last woman in the world . . . Still, supposing Keith Sinclair is all wrong, and it's into the future we've strayed, not the past? Then this damn hunger of mine must be the accumulated hunger of centuries . . . *Paté de foie gras* sandwiches – remember them? They were very good. And spring lamb. And black coffee. And green chartreuse. And – you'd better not go on.'

She pressed her hand against her small, flat stomach. Her back ached. Those kidney-pill people would give anything to have her as an illustration. 'The Cave-woman's Bowels . . . ' Every picture tells a story.

Bright moonlight.

She wriggled a little, cautiously if light-headedly, towards the fore part of the cave. Now she could see the moonlit lands. The silence of the day that had encompassed her wanderings was as nothing to this. Over a crisp white shroud that draped the countryside, nothing moved or cried. Had she indeed dreamed? Was this not perhaps verily the end? Far below, to the right, a stretch of water gleamed icily, burnished and unrippled. Silence and the sweetness of death in the silence, and beyond the water the black armies of the trees.

> *Forest and water, far and wide,*
> *In limpid starlight glorified,*
> *Lie like the mystery of death.*

And God? Was there indeed no God, were He and His variants no more than mistaken science – results of that seasonal ritual that grew in the Nile Valley when men ascribed the time of flood and ripening to the mysterious, animate sun? No more? And the Christ and the Buddha and their dream of a Father Who knew if a sparrow fell? Were these no more than thin plaints of this lost adventure of mankind, crying for warmth and safety and comfort?

Lo, I shall be with you alway, even unto the end of the world.
Until the day break and the shadows flee away –

> *Father, in Thy gracious keeping,*
> *Leave we now thy servant, sleeping.*

Phrases innumerable, lovely and gracious and shining, came to her out of the silence. Things from the Anglican burial service, from the poets, from forgotten hymns . . .

Our birth is but a sleep and a forgetting . . .
For God so loved the world that He gave His only begotten Son –

> *So runs my dream, but what am I?*
> *An infant crying in the night,*
> *An infant crying for the light,*
> *And with no language but a cry –*

Was *that* God only the Anglicized version of the Nile-lands sun? A dream, Himself a hope and a terror as yet unborn, undreamt of here in the wastes of Atlantis or elsewhere in this world that awaited the coming of the last Ice Age? Before Adam – this was a night before the birth of God!

Omnipotence and Omniprescience still unborn. Far up there in the stars God still lay unborn and unawakened . . . Or dead, dead indeed if this were the last night of the world, swinging now a frozen star about an extinct sun.

'Then what am I? Why was I born to think these things? Oh, some-where, surely, in some age to come, there's explanation. Of me and Sinclair and Sir John and the beast-man lost in these hills. Somewhere...'

She covered her eyes from the bright moonlight. No sound, no answer came to her. None had ever come or ever would come.

And then Clair felt no longer afraid. She dropped her hands. She addressed the frozen world in a whisper.

'You lovely thing, you can kill me and finish me. Very easily. But not that question. It's beyond your killing. It'll live long after you're dead yourself.'

Subchapter iv

In the morning she encountered and speared a half-frozen hare by the verge of the loch. Shuddering, she cut its throat and drank its blood. By nightfall she was far from the ledge where she had sheltered, hold-ing across the savannah towards the southwards mountains. That had seemed the only hope left. Towards those mountains Sinclair was guid-ing the Cro-Magnards and somewhere on the verge of them she would overtake or intercept the trek.

The sun had risen, powerful and hot, and the thin frost-rime went fast from grass and forest. Clair ran as much and as often as she could, but many times had to sit and rub her numbed feet, agonizingly, back to circulation. No wind came across the hill-jumbled plain, and the south-ern peaks seemed to come but little closer with the passing of the day. Yet the hills where she had encountered the ape-man receded almost into flatness. She made up her mind to perch in a tree during the night; so all day she kept near the winding forest-belts, lest darkness overtake her remote from the shelter she had determined on.

For shelter, cold apart, would be necessary. The land now swarmed with game. Once she came on a nest of hyaenodon, rolling and play-ing and snarling happily in the sun. They desisted at sight of her, and crouched with lolling tongues, looking at her quizzically. Two, hardly more than puppies, got up and cantered after her, falling over the grass-tussocks and their own legs, foolishly. A great gaunt female the size of a young heifer whined them back. Further on she saw a herd of aurochs among the trees, and remembered the Latin tale of these animals having no knees and being unable to kneel or lie, or sleep otherwise than unchancily poised against the bole of a tree. The Romans had been misinformed. Many of the great beasts squatted, cud-chewing and somnolent, with bulls on guard here and there. Clair passed too far off for them to take offence at her. The wonder of this passing through a land filled with wild beasts, and passing unharmed, wore off in the trudging hours. She thought, with a return of her usual gay irony: 'I'm the essential Cockney still, I suppose, and can't get rid of the notion that it's really Regent's Park or the Bronx – and if any of the beasts break loose I can scream for a keeper.'

But in late afternoon the direct sunlight vanished, extinguished in a driving storm of snow, soft, powdery stuff which felt almost warm at first, but speedily lost that quality. The landscape became a wavering scurry, as though the very savannahs were seeking shelter. Clair turned into the safety of the trees, treading a great nave of pines with underfoot a thick carpet of needles which pricked her feet. Scotch firs grew here as well, and under one of them she crept and sheltered, watching the afternoon pass greyly and the storm continue unabated.

She could still see the land she had crossed, and, presently, in a late clearing of the snow-squall, a figure nearing the forest. A human figure.

She knew it a dream or a mirage and looked away, and rubbed her eyes, and looked back again. Then she started to her feet and found herself running towards him, calling and sobbing. He saw her, dropped his load, and came running towards her and caught her in his arms.

'Aerte!' she cried.

It was Keith Sinclair.

CHAPTER TWO

A light in the south

Subchapter i

He said, breathlessly, 'Clair! Are you all right?' And she could not answer because her head was pressed against his chest, and she was breathless with running and surprise, and felt she never wanted to speak again; only to hold to him and hold to him and never let him go. So for a time they stood in each other's arms, and then somehow they were apart, Clair looking up at him, still unbelievingly.

'You *are* Sinclair? I'm not the last left alive? Oh, Keith! . . .'

He turned away and picked up the bundle. It was a great bearskin. Beside it he had dropped a hunting spear and something else – a huge, stringed bow that reached almost to his shoulder. He turned round to find Clair drying her eyes ineffectually. He saw her slim and brown-white and grimy, with snow in her hair and a ripple of gooseflesh across her shoulders. Bless her for those winter dips of hers . . . He said: 'My God, it's a long way to Kensington!'

'I thought I was lost for ever. I thought – ' She darted forward and seized his spear and bow. 'You dear to find me! I've got a tree to shelter under. Come along!'

The snow had begun again and they ran for the shelter of the forest. Under the Scotch fir no snow came, and only a waft of faint ice currents from the wind. Sinclair dropped his bundle and bent and untied it, not looking at her as he asked the question: 'Have you had any food?'

'I killed a hare this morning and drank its blood.'

'And no fire? How did you pass the night?'

'Sheltering in a ledge up on the hills back there. I saw all the world lying dead last night, Keith.'

He said, with a grimace of dour humour: 'Why didn't you wave to me? That's what I felt like!'

He was gathering pine-needles and broken branches. He placed a little circle of rotten wood fragments round the heap and then fumbled in the bearskin. Some tarnished thing shone in his hand. Clair drew a long breath.

'Sir John's lighter. Does it still light?'

'He never used it after we came among the Cro-Magnards, you know. And the wadding is still a little damp with petrol – I hope.' He flicked the lighter open. A tiny, white-yellow flame kindled the wick. Shielding it, he knelt to the heap of twigs. The wind had ebbed round and came from the north now. The flame ran swiftly along a twig. Clair, standing, stared at it fascinatedly. A fire again! Sinclair put up a hand, iron-cold even upon her chill-accustomed skin, and pulled her down.

'Sit here and don't let it out. I'm going to erect a break-wind.'

He bent and disappeared out of the sheltering circle of the fir-fronds, returning in a moment with an armful of boughs. He went back, foraging, and she heard him snapping off others. Presently he was beside her again, and began to construct the break-wind, inter-weaving from the ground up to the fir-fronds a wall of boughs. Abruptly the wind ceased to blow upon Clair's back. The fire changed from a sulky negligence to a gossipy crackling. Sinclair lay beside her.

'That's that. God, I am glad to see you.'

She saw then that he was utterly exhausted. His face was pinched and dented with cold and other things, his eyes bloodshot. Also, his feet were so torn that the blood had splashed in long streaks up past his ankles. She gave a cry at sight of them.

'They're all right.' He was lying with closed eyes. 'Stopped aching, and the dirt in them's clean enough.' He tried to rouse himself. 'There's pemmican in that parcel. Twine the bearskin round you. Keep up fire . . .' His voice trailed off into unintelligibility. She thought he had fainted and leant over him in some consternation.

He was asleep. Probably he had not slept all the previous night.

She undid the bundle and found inside it smoked meat, as he had said; strange spongy stuff she had never seen before. Mammoth meat? In the bundle was a package of stone-tipped arrows. Nothing else. She cut off some of the meat with the blade of the spear which had companied her, and mounted the spongy slices on arrow-heads, and crawled out from below the tree to collect more fuel. There, beyond the shelter of the break-wind, she realized the salvation of Sinclair's coming. The snow had ceased again, but the wind was almost a solid thing, and awful in its numbing coldness. Darkness was driving across it, an opposing force, and she stumbled chilledly in shadows, presently sobbing through her teeth as she faced about to return to the fir. There she found the meat smoking and Sinclair still fast asleep. She flung the skin over him and tucked it about him, and he stirred a little and muttered something; and she bent to hear what it was.

'Road to the south. She'll have taken the road to the mountains.'

So he had guessed and followed on that chance? But a hazardous enough guess, and when had he made it? Not until he had reached one of those hills in which she herself had sheltered last night. That was obvious . . . Keith Sinclair! And she had thought – she had *known* as she ran towards him – that he was Aerte.

Where were the hunters?

Useless questions. She thought: 'Oh, it *is* good to eat,' and ate the meat slowly, carefully, wondering if she should awaken Sinclair to share with her. But he was obviously more tired than hungry. The saltless stuff in her mouth went over without effort nowadays. But a drink – it might be impossible to find any water. She looked beyond the break-wind and saw only a smouldering landscape on the verge of night. But the break-wind had collected a drift of snow, and she gathered a handful and ate it, though she knew she invited stomach-ache. But her mouth and throat felt instantly cold and moist, and she finished the sliver of meat in her hand, and looked for the rest, and gave a little gasp. Oh, my good God, had she eaten all that?

So it seemed. She piled more boughs on the fire. Now the wind was crying overhead. The Scotch fir drummed like a harp played on by a blind harper. She found handfuls of damp leaves and cones and packed them about the fire, their resinous smell homely in her nostrils. Then she crept to Sinclair's side and lay down beside him. Under the bearskin his body had generated a grateful warmth, and now an additional warmth came out from the fire. She stretched herself beside him and he moved in sleep, as if making way for her. She patted his shoulder, soothingly, and saw his shadowed face in sleep, not so worn now, but blued still under the eyes. He moaned a little as he moved his torn feet. She lay in compassionate alertness, not touching him. The fire-light flickered and flapped in a stray eddy of the wind. Clair tucked the bearskin around herself and then leant over and tucked the other side round Sinclair.

So raised, she looked out from below the whistling fronds of the tree, into the darkness of the forest and tundra, a darkness based on a ghostly greyness that was the snow. She felt a drowsy content upon her. She thought, withdrawing a chilled arm into shelter: 'Goodness, how little we need for comfort!' Two naked savages in a forest on a snowing night. A fire, food, a break-wind and a bearskin. And men had toiled and planned and invented elaborate explorer's equipment and central heating and safety lavatories when they might have had this for nothing – and conquered the stars and split the atom in the generations devoted to worrying over houses sound-proof and wind-proof, and, as they had had at length to construct them, fool-proof . . . Her hair blew a little; she felt it rise and undulate pleasantly on her head. She was about to lie down when something in the night, far away, caught her attention.

At first she thought it was a star and then realized the impossibility of that. The night was too dense with storm-clouds. And, though it had the twinkling immobility of a star, it was too low down there in the horizon of the south. But it gleamed brightly, like a torch in an unsteady hand, winking, as it seemed, across the leagues of tundra in the drive of the same blizzard as whoomed against the break-wind. What could it be?

Another volcano? But there had been no sign of a volcano during all her southwards tramp of the afternoon. The Atlantean Alps were great, glacier-studded masses, not like that line of fires that had marched to the right of the original trek of Sir John and Sinclair and herself from the wreck of *Magellan's Cloud*. No volcano. It must be a fire.

But kindled by whom?

Staring across the night, a maze of drowsy speculations unfolded in her brain. Other Cro-Magnards? But were there any, other than those she knew? Perhaps – who knew! – another party of explorers from the outer rims of Time, sucked into this epoch by just such accident as wrecked the *Magellan's Cloud*. No impossibility. People perhaps out of an age even remoter than the twentieth century, stray Utopians perhaps from A.D. ten thousand, with the most fantastic notions of the twentieth century, and never having heard of the Cro-Magnards at all . . .

Still – perhaps simply a consignment from the same age and era as had caught the *Magellan*!

She lowered her head, and then, he being at last fast asleep, snuggled close to Sinclair. The remote, mysterious fire had vanished from her range of vision. She closed her eyes. Other twentieth century explorers! . . . Who would they be if she had the selection of them? The Archbishop of Canterbury, of course – to see what he thought of a people who knew not God; Mr H. G. Wells, to find out what he thought of primitives who were neither stalking ghouls of the night nor those vexedly flea-bitten savages who scratched throughout the early pages of the *Outline*; President Hoover and Mr Ramsay MacDonald – to learn a little about the original nature of man, and be shocked to death to find their ancestors so unwarlike that they needed no elaborate conventions to restrain themselves from throat-cutting and the disembowelment of babies; Mr Henry Ford, with his tight, narrow face, to die of a broken heart in an auto-less world; Charlie Chaplin to poke the aurochs with his stick . . .

A small and sleepy chuckle stole out to the fire, and the two under the bearskin lay very still indeed the while the night went on and the wind rose to a super-blizzard, rose to the roar of a Russian *shoom*, and then fell and died. But all through these hours, and into the pale coming of the next dawn, enigmatic, the fire in the southwards mountains winked across the wastes.

Subchapter ii

The American was the first to awake, aware of his unquenched hunger from the previous day. All his trunk was very warm; but his feet ached as though they had been frozen and were now in the process of thawing. The fire was out and the wind had died away and it was the beginning of daylight. He put aside the bearskin from his face and discovered then the reason for some of his warmth. Clair lay with her arms around his neck, fast asleep, her grimy face laid in the hollow of his shoulder.

He remembered at once, and then, not moving, lay and looked at her. For a moment the temptation made him dizzy. All the repressed and thwarted desires of his ancestors for six thousand years were behind him, urging him to it in that Atlantean forest that was to be a rotted myth before those ancestors were born. But there were other and older ancestors . . . He scowled.

'You scabrous lout,' he commented to himself.

He withdrew his shoulder as gently as possible and stood up and shivered in the waiting coldness of the morning. A moorhen twittered. Water was not so far off. He stepped gingerly towards the fire and collected charred boughs, and scrunched around in search for Sir John's petrol-lighter, and found it laid neatly at the base of the fir, in company with his bow. His spear was nowhere to be seen, because at the moment Clair lay on it. He started a fire and then crept out from below the fir and held down through an avenue of pines to that twittering that told of the moorhen's splashings. The sun came up over the eastward tundra at that moment and followed him. He found the water, a stream that meandered southwards towards the mountains, and sat down on its snow-covered bank. He was half-frozen already with his walking through that snow, but the cleansing of his feet at once was imperative. He set to work with handfuls of ice-cold water. Several times he felt he was about to faint in the spasms of agony that travelled up his body. Clair's voice spoke behind him.

'Keith! Why didn't you ask me to help?'

He looked over his shoulder and saw her shivering behind him and carrying the bearskin. 'Go back to the fire.'

'Don't bully. We'll go when you're all right again. Sit on this and I'll bathe them.'

He rose and then sat down, as she had told him. And then she saw a curious thing. His black hair was almost ashen grey. She stared at it appalled, half-kneeling in front of him and looking up. Sinclair said: 'What is it?'

'Your hair.'

'My what?'

Of course he didn't know. She hesitated, beginning to lave his feet. He scowled at her, inquiringly. He put up his hand to his head. 'Seems all right.'

'It's turned grey,' said Clair, gently.

'What!'

He was astounded for a moment. He laughed. He muttered something unkind about the influence of Hollywood and was palpably ashamed of himself. But Clair kept her head down-bent. Had he been through as bad a time as that? Hers had been nothing to it. Of course he had thought her lost for ever, killed most probably . . . His feet made her shudder, and he shuddered himself as she tended them and drew out long slivers of stone from the right one.

'That was from the time I had a slip and glissade on those infernal red hills.'

'If only we had something to bind up the cuts with – '

'I'll make some sandals from part of this bearskin. They'll do, thanks. Let's get back to the fire.'

At the fire Clair knelt and toasted herself and more of the mammoth meat. Sinclair made his moccasins. 'How did you find me?' Clair asked.

'God knows. How did you get lost?'

She told him of the circumstances the while the day brightened; then heard of his own Odyssey. Her absence had not been discovered by him until the afternoon of the day on which she had been lost. He had hunted from group to group, asking about her, and finding her nowhere. Presently the whole camp was aroused and, excepting those Cro-Magnards engaged in the boucanning of the mammoth meat, every hunter and woman had set out in the search for her. From one of the hunters the American heard of Clair's joining the party which had made a dash through the hills to intercept the second mammoth. Thereat, in company with Aerte and three or four more, he had set out to retraverse that route. In the hills they had scattered and presently Sinclair, in a muddy patch on the other side of these hills, had come on the imprint of a naked and recent footstep which he knew was Clair's –

'How did you know?'

From the arching of the instep. There had been no more than that single footprint, but it had pointed southwards, towards a range of hills. He had set out to reach that range.

The range had been gained as the darkness was falling, and with no further sign of Clair, nor sound of her or answer to his shouts. He had hunted the range all the night, and with the coming of morning had gained the top of it and considered the situation, deciding correctly that if Clair lost were still Clair alive she must have determined to make the southwards mountains in the hope of intercepting the trek of the Cro-Magnards. So he himself had set out in the direction of the name-less Alps and – then he had heard her hail him.

She said: 'We've always been cut apart and strangers in some way, Keith. Why did you do it? – all this tremendous search for me?'

He had made the moccasins by then and was fitting them to his feet with gut as string. He looked across the savannah to the mountains.

'Any of the hunters would have done it. Aerte is probably searching for you still.'

'Yes, I know. But we are different. So why?'

He said in a very still, strained voice: 'It's because I love you, I suppose. And there isn't any supposing about it. It's just that.'

She stared into the fire. 'And I love you also. I think I always loved you. From that day I saw you on the gallery of the *Magellan*. Remember it – twenty-five thousand years ago. Oh, Keith!'

He dropped the moccasins and came towards her, grey-headed, his eyes alight. She shook her head. She spoke in a whisper. 'But there's still Aerte – my lover for the dark days.'

'Eh?'

'There's still him. We've still got to find the hunters again, and there's still Aerte. He's as remote and impossible as a boy in a fairy-tale. But I'm his and he's mine for the dark days at least . . . I thought you were Aerte last night. I could have sworn you were.'

He sat down again. He said: 'It's damned nonsense.'

'I know.'

'Aerte will make no claim on you if you come to me.'

'No, he won't. But that's the point, Keith. Oh, my dear, don't you see? It's for you and your sake and the sake of your dream that I must keep by Aerte. Unless you've given that up? Are we to look for the hunters again?'

He nodded south towards the mountains. His face had the savage sulkiness of repressed wrath she remembered from the days of crossing the upland plateau. 'We'll go on and wait their coming there. Even if they don't go further than this stretch of country we'll be able to see them and return to them.'

'But you want them to go further. You're going to lead them south of the mountains and find a river and plant corn and teach them to build houses and cast metals? Remember? You and I are going to change the course of history there, somewhere beyond these Alps. Do you think we can do it without keeping faith in every detail with the hunters? They'd laugh and say nothing and only pity Aerte a little, but they'd never take counsel from you again.'

Sinclair sat down and completed the binding of his footwear. Clair laughed, a little shakily.

'It's me or the future of history, Keith! . . . And don't leave it to me now, else I'll forget that other lover of mine who died on the wire in France, and I'll forget all the black oppressions done in this wild world under the sun, and think only of you, and the dearness and adorableness of your dear, sulky head and the queer sweetness of your body and the heart-breaking miracle of that grey hair of yours and its soft lie on your head, and the loveliness of that clean, crude, splendid mind of yours. I'll remember only these things – and you'll never forget the others, though all our lives together you'd pretend you had forgotten them.'

He said: 'I think you've cured me. Bless you. We'll go south and await the coming of Aerte and the hunters.'

Subchapter iii

'Oh, that light last night. I forgot to mention it.'

'Eh?'

They were on the road to the southern mountains, though no road had ever crossed that wild belt of land. It was past noon. Here and there the snow still lay in patches, or shivered and wilted into slush pools under the heat of the sun. And over all the landscape was a steaming haze that rose a little, but patched the ground in great areas to indistinctness. Sinclair strode nude as when he was born, but for the bearskin moccasins. Clair, bare-footed, was elsewhere wrapped in the remnants of the mutilated skin.

They had crossed a good eight or nine miles of country since leaving the encampment of the night before. Now the mountains before them changed shape continually, but visibly grew greater. They towered as tower the walls of the Colorado Canyon from river-bed level. Crowned with snow, the great massif stretched from horizon to horizon, with in front, leftwards, an extended arm, a crazy jumble of broken peaklets and poised glacierettes. It was somewhere in that extended arm, Clair thought, that she had seen the light.

Sinclair scowled down at her questioningly. 'Light? What kind of light?'

She put her arm through his. 'Funny how that scowl of yours used almost to intimidate me! . . . Fun to be alive, isn't it, Keith?'

The scowl went from his face. He pinched her shoulder, absently. Then: 'The light?'

'Oh, yes. It was like a camp-fire.'

'Couldn't be. At least, I don't think so. The hunters have no story of other groups living so comparatively near.'

Some half-memory vexed her mind. She could not secure it. 'But there might be.'

'I don't know.' They passed into a winding track-way made by beasts, between two stretches of marsh, and climbed up from that low patch to firmer ground, a re-beginning of the savannah-land and dotted with deer and aurochs herds. 'There might be, but on the whole I doubt it. Our hunters are perhaps as yet the only human beings in Atlantis – perhaps in all the world.'

She found that a breath-taking notion. 'But there were other peoples in pre-history besides the Cro-Magnards.'

'Later, yes. But at this epoch? Mayn't the others have been helped into full humanity by imitation of our proto-Cro-Magnards? . . . We can't say. But all these things are accidental, dependent on a multitude of chances that might arise in one district and nowhere else. Perhaps in the world at the moment there are only tribes of submen at various levels, and our hunters constitute the only group that has as yet emerged into full humanity.'

'Then –'

He smiled down into her grave face, and bit his lips because he desired her, and there were other things than desire, but none so warm and immediate as she was. Clair looked back at the land behind them.

'Any accident might change the nature of things for ever. If our Cro-Magnards were suddenly wiped out –'

'There might never be such a thing as history. At least – we can never know.'

'Oh, the awful loneliness of men! They couldn't help making gods when they found some shelter and security in an agricultural society . . . Pious, rotten romanticism, Keith – remember what you once told me I was addicted to? – but that night I was lost on the hills back there I began to think that perhaps there was some God after all. Not just a god. Something. Someone . . .'

She looked up at him. Thousands and thousands were yet to look up into the faces of their fellows for confirmation of that wild hope . . . He said: 'An honest god's the noblest work of man. I don't believe there's anything to shield us from the darkness, Clair. And not even for the sake of poetry do I think we should carry the idea to our hunters in that world we're to make beyond these mountains . . . If we ever get beyond them.'

'Tremendous things, aren't they?'

They were. Somewhere at the foot of their slopes, however, the Cro-Magnards would arrive in time, and there was nothing for the two of them but to press on and await that arrival. Clair said, being dragged out of a squelchy, boggy place: 'The light – we never settled about that.'

'No.' Sinclair, assisting her to her feet, abruptly pulled her down again and lay prone himself. 'But we can now, I think.'

Clair, her breath shaken from her, wriggled out of his grasp and looked in the direction in which he pointed.

Subchapter iv

The tapering tip of the northwards spur of the mountain-range was already a sierraed toweringness to the left of them. It was not more than three miles away. The forests climbed its base in green attack, even skirmished remotely up into valleys and ledges of the heights. That for background, with directly south the still remoter, more gigantic background of the range proper, a good six miles away. Here and there, in the angle so formed, grew clumps of larch and fir and great stretches of gorse. Amid these fed the herds of aurochs Clair had noted before. One herd was very close – a herd that had ceased to feed and stood on the *qui vive*, bulls with gigantic tails uplifted, cows and calves sniffing the air. And the reason for the alarm – a dozen reasons – became at length obtrusive to Clair's gaze.

They were less than a quarter of a mile away, but had remained unperceived by her because of their dull grey colouring. It seemed to her that it was on all fours they were creeping from bush to bush, nearer their quarry, the aurochs. But indeed it was merely that their arms were so elongated as naturally to reach the ground. Across cavernous, hair-matted torsos were strapped crude skin-wrappings. From each pair of shoulders, on a short, squat neck, a strange, deformed head, chinless, browless, enormously eye-ridged, projected forward so that the Thing could never look directly upwards. Even at that distance they were horrible, dreadful and awful caricatures of familiar and lovely things.

Clair felt sick. 'What are they?' she whispered.

'Neanderthalers,' said Sinclair, also in a whisper.

CHAPTER THREE

All our yesterdays

Subchapter i

No snow fell that night, but a bitter wind sprang up with the coming of darkness and blew into the great triangular space formed by the forest lines and the bastions of the unknown mountain-ranges. At first the darkness, for there came neither moon nor star-rise, was heavy and complete, without even the usual brooding Atlantean greyness. And then, as if lighted one by one, there became obvious far in the base of the triangle and ranging up northwards towards the open country the glare of great fires. Sinclair and Clair saw them pringling brightly in the night, from their own camping-place in the heart of a thicket of broom-plants and larch. They also had kindled a fire, dangerous though that procedure might be; they had kindled it mid-way the thicket, however, so that there was little chance of those alien firetenders seeing it. But both, after they had eaten, went out to the verge of thicket to watch that bright sentinelling of the mountain-base. Sinclair stood with his arm round Clair, and pulled her back into the thicket after a moment to still her shivering.

'Then they can make fires – they *are* men,' she said.

'They are men, but not Man. They are the sub-human species that are almost men, and are to be in occupation of most of Europe when our Cro-Magnards wander there thousands of years hence. If they do so wander.'

The fires burned steadily. Clair remembered the creeping beasts of the afternoon and shuddered with disgust. Yet perhaps that was unreasonable enough. Perhaps there was nothing of savagery about them, any more than among the Cro-Magnards. She saw the dim shaking of Sinclair's grey head.

'Their conduct didn't warrant it. Men – the Cro-Magnards and the stock that produced ourselves – are decent, kindly animals of anthropoid blood, like the chimpanzee and gibbon. But there *is* another strain – the gorilla and perhaps these Neanderthalers – the sullen, individualist beast whose ferocity is perhaps maladjustment of body and a general odd, black resentment against life.'

'Like the militarists and the hanging judges and the gloomy deans of the twentieth century?'

'Exactly.' But his voice sounded absent. 'I wonder . . . Look here, go back to the fire. I'm going out to see what they're really like.'

'What?' She was startled enough at that. 'Then I'll come as well.'

'Can't. One of us must go, Clair, and must take the bearskin for covering against this infernal wind. And it must be me. I'm stronger than you and I can run faster.'

'But why must? We needn't go near them at all.'

'We must because our hunters will be down from the north in the next day or so, and there's no telling what will happen then. If they're peaceable or cowardly beasts there's nothing to fear. If not – '

'But we needn't lead the Cro-Magnards anywhere near them. We can take them through the mountains away over there, somewhere.' She pointed to the right in the westwards darkness.

'Can we? I wonder . . . I must go, Clair.'

She said, standing beside the fire and helping him to tie the bearskin: 'Do take care of yourself, my dear.' And thought: 'As though we were in Kensington and I was telling him to mind the buses on the way to the office!'

He said, absently still: 'I'll do that.' Then he picked up his spear, and put his hand on her shoulder and gave it a little shake, and went off into the darkness.

Clair built up the fire and lay down in the shelter of the break-wind. She took her own spear beside her for company and Sinclair's bow as well, though she knew nothing of the handling of the thing. It was a very lonely vigil. The fire fluffed and rose and fell occasionally in eddies of the wind. But presently that wind died away almost completely, though the cold seemed to grow intenser still. Clair thought: 'I must not think of Sinclair,' and put him out of her thoughts as well as she might, and curled her legs up beneath her, and remembered some picture of a Tierra del Fuegan savage she had once seen in that attitude.

She thought, startled: 'Goodness, I might have sat as the artist's model!' Where were Aerte and the hunters?

Something bayed close at hand beyond the bushes. There came a distant scuffling; more near, the swift scurry of running paws. The scurry ceased. Then a pad-pad-padding began in a circle, just beyond the range of the fire-glow. Clair, with a very dry throat, stirred the fire and in its increase of radiance saw that she was surrounded by a pack of wolves – beasts with long, feathery brushes and brightly erected ears. Each might have been of the bigness of an Alsatian. Sometimes they sat and rested, staring at her, at other times resumed that scurrying encirclement of the fire. It was difficult to realize that if they overcame fear of the fire they would eat her, sink those bright teeth into her legs and throat and stomach, very agonizingly, in a flounder of hot and stench-laden bodies . . . Clair got to her feet once and waved her spear at a great, cadaverous brute. He stopped in his pacing, head brightly alert, and cocked his ears. Then, as though grinning sardonically, he bared his teeth, growled, and advanced a step or so. Clair stirred the fire again, and he retreated.

So the night went on. Clair, sitting dozing once, awoke to find – not the beasts upon her as she had dreamt, and dreaming had awoken with a startled cry – but them gone and the fire burned very low, and herself very cold. She fed the smoulder hurriedly, carefully. A mammoth trumpeted, southwards, in some glen of the mountains, the sound eerie and plaintive. The clouds began to clear and presently, with a faint spraying of powdery light, the star-rise came. The heavens were filled with an eastwards sailing of great masses of dark storm-clouds. Clair sat and warmed herself and got up and walked about and sat down again. Still Sinclair did not return.

There came a breath of dawn through the air of the darkness. The stars grew brighter and then faded. And through the dawn Sinclair came back. She heard him calling in the distance: 'Clair! Clair!' and ran and found him.

He had been *lost*.

Subchapter ii

'Most infernally lost.' He was splashed with mud and rimed with frost. His eyebrows and eyelids curled white with frost. He sat down jerkily by the fire and started up again, glancing over his shoulder. 'Idiotic to shout, but there was nothing else to be done. I hadn't a notion of where you were. Lost my way completely coming back – as I might have guessed I'd do . . . Old habit of thinking of the lie of a country in terms of roads and signposts . . . Wonder if they heard me shouting?'

'I'll go and see,' Clair said.

He pulled her down beside him. 'Not that, anyway,' he said, grimly. 'Let's listen.'

They listened to that austere world of the Third Interglacial awakening with the coming of the morning over the Atlantean savannah. Sparrows chirped in the trees. Somewhere in the depths of the wood a corn-crake was sounding its note. Spite the nearing of the sun, it was still bitterly cold. But there was no crackling of undergrowth under coming feet.

'What are they like?' Clair whispered.

'God . . . Awful.'

He said no more than that about them. Instead, he shivered. Clair cut meat from their dwindling supply and grilled it. Sinclair was nodding from lack of sleep. She asked: 'Did you get near them?'

'I lay above one of their caves: I seemed to lie there for hours. Limestone spur, that, and its upper tip here is honeycombed with caves. There must be several hundreds of them. Ugh.' He had been eating. He was suddenly sick. 'Sorry, Clair.'

She ruffled his grey hair. 'Don't think of them or speak about them for a bit. Do you think I could use your bow?'

'Why?'

She looked wistfully through the trees towards the sound of the forest fowls. 'I *would* like chicken for a change.'

He smiled at her from a face as grey as his hair. 'Try. But don't go too far. And if you see – any of them – scream like hell and run back in this direction.'

She went through the morning-stirred forest, thinking, at first almost in a panic: 'I had to get away . . . Keith, my dear, you've had the devil of a night. Will it pass or are you really ill? . . . Oh, *damn* this thing.'

She stopped and disentangled the bow from a bush, and hurried on again because of the coldness. She came to the edge of a clearing. In the charred forest-litter two birds fed, perkily, with quick-darting heads. Partridges. She thought: 'I'll never hit them,' and stopped, and planted the butt of the bow in the ground, and fitted the clumsy arrow. One of the birds saw her and raised its head, regarding her sideways, out of a bright, questioning eye. Her fingers fumbled frozenly at the bow-string. The damn bird imagines it's having its photograph taken . . . Now.

The arrow whizzed across the space, an enormous lance of a projectile. One partridge rose with a flirr! The other lay impaled wing from wing, and fluttering wildly. Clair wrung its neck and tried to get out the arrow, and desisted, lest she snap off the insecure flint; and went back towards Sinclair and the camp-fire. The break-wind shelter was deserted. She dropped the bird and ran through the trees towards the open country that led to the Neanderthal caves. Sinclair turned about as he heard her coming.

'Sh. For God's sake.'

The great triangle was evidently the hunting-ground of the beast-men. Three separate parties, none of them near enough for the intimate study of individuals, were debouching in various directions from that far mountain-wall – one party apparently heading in the direction of their shelter. A little over two miles away, Clair judged it. Sinclair swore, ruffling his bearded chin.

'Are they on my track – or is it just a chance drift after game?'

Clair stared with him. He gave a sigh of relief. 'A chance party, after all. They're just on the prowl.'

'Are they? They're not coming in a straight line, but they seem to be following something. Didn't you lose yourself last night? Perhaps they're following your – '

'By God, they are!'

Subchapter iii

All that forenoon they fled westwards and south-westwards, the grey beasts behind them. Sinclair's own running abilities might have out-distanced them with ease, but Clair needed frequent rests. Once or twice, reaching the foot of one or other of the rolling inclines in which the land ebbed and flowed, they would glance up and see their pursuers at the summit, sometimes less than a quarter of a mile distant. On flat country that distance grew greater; the Neanderthalers were at a disadvantage on the plain. Once, when a good mile and a half separated them, Clair, lying panting on the ground, asked: 'Shouldn't we strike north? We'd meet Aerte and the hunters.'

Sinclair himself lay and breathed in great gasps, watching that loping, crouched-forward trot of the beast-men. 'We might miss them com-pletely. Perhaps they're already much nearer the mountains than we've supposed. Anyhow, they'll descend further to the west than this, I think . . . Rested?'

'Goodness, no.' She looked at him, white-faced, and smiled. 'If only I'd had training as a charwoman instead as a novelist!'

'You don't do badly.' He stood up. A long, guttural wail came down the air from the beast-men. 'I think they don't like us.'

'Mean of them.'

Funny how one could push the horror back with a remark like that . . . But they followed on behind, doggedly enough, the horrors. Clair, run-ning stripped and unshod, carried nothing but the light spear she had brought from the far northern camp of the Cro-Magnards. Sinclair had tied to his back both the bearskin, now enwrapping the slain partridge, and his bow and arrows. His feet were still in their moccasins, and from the bloody tracks left behind by his companion he could see that without such aids Clair herself was hardly capable of keeping the pace for long. Running beside her, he glanced at her face, red-flushed, a very sweet and kind and comely face even in this desperate hour. And again he thought, wonderingly and inadequately: 'Pretty thing!'

Open country they had come to then. But the Neanderthalers seemed tireless. Sinclair looked back to see them not more than half a mile away. Strange – that tenacity of pursuit. Did they recognize Clair and himself as kindred animals, to be killed as freaks, or did they seem just desirable and tirable meat? God, what an end to the business!

Messy end, too. For Clair – ? Not to be thought of.

But it had to be thought of. He said: 'If they overtake us, Clair, I'll kill you. That'll be best. It won't hurt much.'

'Oh, don't be a fool!'

He almost sulked, and grinned wryly at the recurrence of his ancient short temper. Clair flung herself to the ground again.

'Can't go further – yet. Sorry I said that, Keith. But you *are* a fool to suggest these melodramatics, you know. Here, in Atlantis. Stuff our of Victorian novels . . . And I ought to suggest now that you should leave me and save yourself. Not so silly. Oh, goodness, my heart . . . We'll just fight it out together. They'll kill both of us.'

'Will they?' He stood above her, desperate, looking backwards. Clair lay flat, breathing ('like a stranded lung-fish!')

'Of course they will. Oh, because I'm a woman? I'll seem just as repulsive to them as they do to us . . . How far?'

'Very near now.'

He had unslung his bow. Clair scrambled to her knees. The beast-men were quite close, running with lowered heads and trailing fringes of body-hair, their knuckles touching the ground at every forward swing of their bodies, in their hands great shapeless mallets of stone, mounted on rude wooden hafts. Sinclair knelt on one knee. The bow-string sang like a plucked guitar.

A Neanderthaler to the left – not one Sinclair had aimed at – received the arrow in his chest, almost in the region of the heart. The brute screamed horribly, and its companions, swaying and lurching, halted. They were all males. The beast plucked stupidly at the arrow, and then bent its head and bit the thing clean off where the shaft entered its chest. Then it suddenly crumpled, as though some support had been withdrawn. Sinclair loosed his second arrow, glanced after it not at all, but heard its thud in flesh and the succeeding howl; and dragged Clair to her feet.

'Try again.'

They ran hand in hand towards the near belt of forest. Clair felt her lungs bursting. A red mist played before her eyes. Twice she tripped, and

Sinclair, savagely, jerked her to her feet again. Again and again the earth seemed to rise up towards her. Sinclair's grasp on her hand suddenly eased. She heard his voice far off.

'Done all we can. Sit down, my dear.'

She fell rather than sat, and put her hands to throbbing ear-drums. Sinclair gave a shout.

'Impossible . . . They've turned.'

Clair swung round at that, resting on her elbows also, looking. The Neanderthalers were in retreat, carrying the dead body. One of them went with limp-swinging arm, blood-dripping. Every now and then he bent to bite at the arm. Clair stared stupidly.

'They're . . . going.'

He lay beside her, almost as exhausted as she was. 'Looks like it.'

They had neither the will nor the breath to say more at the moment. Meantime the Neanderthalers, without a backward glance, shambled across the savannah, topped a low rise, and disappeared into the jungle wilderness in the direction of the northern spur. It was past noon. Still there was no sunlight and still it blew as harshly as during the night. Sinclair, with a driving headache, sat erect.

'Can't stay here. Die of cold after the heat of that run. I'll leave you the bearskin and go and make a fire over there.'

Clair sat up also. She had the pocked, grey face of a woman of fifty. 'I'll come. I can manage.'

Somehow they helped each other to the forest-fringe – great beeches standing with shrill, whistling boughs. But further in were more larch, and then a wide grove of stone-oaks. Beyond these: more evergreens, then a wide glade and open country once more. It was no forest, as they had imagined from the east, but only a long, straggling plantation of Nature's planting. Through the glade the open country to the west showed up as differing in no great degree from the stretches they had already traversed. They dropped to earth by a little stream meandering amid the tree-roots – an indifferent little stream crooning in an absorbed contentment – and drank ice-cold water which instantly gave Clair cramp. Sinclair picked her up and carried her under a larch nearby.

'Stick it. I'll have a fire in a minute.'

It seemed to Clair an unending minute. Then she was conscious of warmth and of Sinclair kneeling, massaging her. He had the fire kindled and crackling. The greyness had gone from his face, and, incidentally, from her own.

'Feel better?'

'Leagues. Goodness – ' she looked up at him in the gay, ironic self-appraisal that survived the *Magellan*, clothes, comfort, and seemingly every conceivable contingency – '*and* hungry!'

'I know. So'm I. Nothing like a run in the Neanderthal Stakes for an appetite. I'm roasting your partridge.'

It smelt savoury enough. Clair sat up and assisted. They sat side by side, and despite her hunger and her recovery she still felt weak, and leaned her head comfortably on Sinclair's shoulder.

'Adam and Eve.'

He smiled at her, his face remarkably un-dour. 'Or the Babes in the Wood.'

She dozed a little. So did Sinclair. Then their heads knocked together and they started awake. The smell of singeing partridge filled the air. Clair shook herself.

'Shockingly selfish again. It's you who've a right to be sleepy. Rest when we've had lunch.'

'I will. I'm almost all in.'

They ate nearly all the partridge. It was very good. Sinclair, lying down and closing his eyes, nevertheless did so with a mental reservation. He would keep awake and get up in a short time and make her take his place . . . He looked at her from below half-closed eyelids that each seemed to weigh a ton. God, if the Neanderthalers – !

Infernal to die and never see Clair again, never hear her deep, enjoyable and enjoying laughter; or see that bright, naïve puzzling of hers. Infernal to have died and never held her in your arms and kissed her from tip to toe, as she deserves to be kissed. As you want to kiss her and she wants . . . Never see the Cro-Magnards again, perhaps. We'll go west, far off, and find a passage through the south mountains together, and build a house next spring. Together ourselves. Children – we can make them safe enough. Together . . .

Clair's voice raised in excitement, her hand shaking him. 'Keith – oh, Keith, our hunters!'

Subchapter iv
He had slept for perhaps a couple of hours, in spite of his resolution. He sat up with a start and looked round scowlingly. 'The hunters?'

'I'm sure they are. Away over there by that cramped little wood.'

He saw them then. 'The hunters right enough.' His voice was oddly unglad. 'Still on the trek, too.'

They had debouched from the wood that Clair thought of as cramped. They were specks in distance, but speck-men, not the strange beasts of

Neanderthal. They straggled southwards in happy-go-lucky migration, moving slowly, proving they had no lack of food at least at the moment.

Sinclair got to his feet, stiffly.

'No more Neanderthalers, anyhow. And you'll find Aerte again.'

'I needn't. We need never find any of them.'

He started: 'You've thought that?'

'And you?'

He nodded. Clair said, slowly: 'We could hide from them and wait till they pass. We could go south beyond the mountains, and start a Golden Age of our own. We could be happier than was ever possible in the world – before or after . . . And we'd be ashamed of ourselves all our lives.'

He found a wry jibe: ' "Stern daughter of the voice of God!" '

She laughed, pitifully, looking out at the nearing Cro-Magnards. Was ever such a fantastic choice before a man and woman? Sinclair wondered. And wondering, he knew there was no choice, neither for himself nor for Clair. For she brought out of that dim twentieth century of three weeks ago the memory of her boy-lover who had screamed away a night of agony beyond the parapets of Mametz; and he – he had brought memories kin enough to hers, dying soldiers and starving miners, the Morlocks of the pits . . . Clair seemed to have read his thoughts.

'We're both playing, Keith, and we know it. Let's go out to them.' She turned away, and then turned back, resolutely. 'But you'd like to kiss me first!'

When he had finished with that they went out across the cold, knee-length grass, laden as they had arrived. The whole migration of the hunters paused, in straggling, shimmering lines in the cold, gold light of the afternoon. And then there came a shout.

They had been recognized.

Subchapter v

Lying in the arms of Aerte that night, Clair Stranlay did not care to move lest she awaken him. But with the passing of the hours it grew to a veritable agony keeping the position in which his golden arms held her. Golden and delicately fringed with gold, as she could see, for they lay near one of the camp-fires, two of innumerable such recumbent figures; and the light came out and lay on the face and arms of Aerte. He slept in happy security. His lover for the dark days had returned. She had been lost and she was found, and he had gone to her and taken her with a simplicity that had wrung from Clair no protest or repulsion.

Only pity. Sinclair had gone back to his place by the fire of Aitz-kore, the flint-knapper. Life went on – even life in a dream in winter-threatened Atlantis.

Life went on . . . Perhaps she was the first woman in the world to lie in this sleepless unease because of the arms that held her. No Cro-Magnard woman would, Clair knew. There were already several who had tired of their choice in the mating-time, and their hunters did not go near them. Here there was no hate, no compulsion in love. These people played no game of sacrifice, because sacrifice was a stupidity beyond their under-standing. They did not live such a lie as she had lived a few hours ago, with the bright face of Aerte close to hers, his arms about her. It was the mentality of the slave, the bond-woman of all the weary years of civilization that had allowed those caresses while Sinclair went away.

All their thousands of grey, suppressed years! And, hating and resent-ing all that tradition of sacrifice and servitude, she was herself submitting to it. Why?

There was someone else who was sleepless. She saw him pass and repass amid the fires, though she knew he was not the night's watcher of the fires. It seemed colder than ever, spite the bluff under which the camp was built. Beasts roamed beyond the radiance of the fires, but timorously, perhaps at sight of that white, restless figure within the camp.

The why of it all. Keith and his dream. Keith and Aerte and their dreams! Tomorrow and tomorrow and tomorrow –

CHAPTER FOUR

Now sleeps the crystal petal

Subchapter i

And the unaccustomed cold grew ever more intense.

Day came and brought no lightening of that burden. Instead, it brought generally sharp showers of hail in the morning hours, and at noon the scurry of a snow-blizzard from the north-west. It was weather of a severity the hunters had never known before in all the long days of their residence in the painted caves of the north. Stumbling camp-wards at evening both hunters and Sinclair's scouts would come on the bodies of their fellows lying frozen and naked in places where exhaustion had overtaken them. Winter had come to Atlantis – a foretaste of that winter that was gradually creeping down on all the northern hemisphere, presently to crystallize into the spreading glaciers and the long silences of the Fourth Ice Age.

Game grew ever scarcer. The herds went west and disappeared, and the hunters might have trailed in pursuit but for the alien presence of Sinclair in their midst. Hence the scouts that day after day went out under his direction, puzzled yet friendly, even though they might never return from such scoutings, any more than those death-frozen comrades of theirs. Game had almost vanished, but packs of the raiding and scavenging carnivorae hung around the camp, and at night the fires had to be built to twice the usual height, both in order to scare the wolves and hyaenodon and to counteract the bitter frosts.

On the second day Sinclair himself vanished in early dawn together with two of the strongest and wiriest Cro-Magnards. It did not snow all that day, but to Clair, wandering the camp clad in the bearskin Sinclair had once brought for her protection, it seemed that the cold had again increased. They could not long remain in this place. Indeed, Aerte had gestured to her that they were to follow the game westwards on the morrow. He had no understanding of Sinclair's hesitations . . . Doubtlessly, however, like other hesitants on other occasions, the White Hunter would follow the main drift of opinion and migration.

Thus Aerte, the while Clair marvelled, chilledly and once again, at these people of the dawn. There was no compulsion, just as there was no acceptance of it. They had grown to know and love Sinclair, perhaps because of that energetic righteousness of his that was so in contrast to their own unhesitating and unswerving kindliness. But he was no magic leader from the void, no story-book hero such as Clair had read of her fellow-authors assigning to the leadership of savage tribes in the pages of many a romance. Here was truer romance. He was merely one who promised good hunting grounds and pleasant days beyond the south-wards mountains – better than they would elsewhere find if they took his advice. Now it was evident that he was mistaken, as a man might be. West or east they must go. The game seemed to have gone west. They would follow it.

That night Sinclair came back with one of his hunters. The other had been lost in a canyon of the southern mountains, the great black-blue wall that dominated the horizons of their world. The American came to Clair while there was still daylight and flung himself down by the fire deserted but for herself. He was spattered in mud from head to feet, mud that had frozen on him; his arms and legs were scored with long cicatrices. For a little he lay in silence near Clair. She put her hand on his shoulder in that caress that was his own, and he put up his hand to her hand. He said, as if speaking to himself: 'There's no road at all through the southwards moun-tains. It is an absolutely impassable wall. We've climbed and prospected ever since we reached it an hour after daybreak. And the other parties that have gone into the west report the same. It's a range that may lie mid-way across Atlantis. And it curves northwards after a bit.'

'North?' Clair lay on an elbow and reflected; and suddenly under-stood. 'Then if the hunters go west that will take them into a worse winter. It might even mean – '

'Extinction. These people cannot stick things worse than they are at present. And it'll grow worse every hour. The sinking of the northern plateau has done it, of course.'

'Then what are we going to do?'

'*I* don't know. God, how I ache!'

He lay so quiet that she thought he was asleep. But presently he spoke again. 'And in the east, beyond that northwards-making spur, we know there are leagues and leagues of brackish marsh. Didn't notice them? I did . . . That would mean, if we turn the drift east, that we'll have to go far north again to circumvent the marsh, and turn south again. It would mean that hardly a woman or child could survive. Perhaps not any of us . . . Remember my Utopia beyond the mountains?' He laughed.

Clair sat and stared at him and the fading of the daylight. There was still food in the camp. There was still the calling of greetings and the flaring of fires, there was still the sight and being of unfearing human life all around them. Southwards: impassable. Westwards: impassable. In the north: extinction. And then a great light seemed to flash on her.

'But they didn't die, Keith. They went east, somehow, some of them, and escaped this winter. We know it from history, as you've often told me. Our hunters weren't killed. They reached France thousands of years after this.'

He was silent for a little, then he said: 'That was in the history we knew, not in the history we hope to build.'

She put out her hand and shook him again. 'Oh, we're playing again, Keith. *How if the history we knew is the history we helped to build?* How if when you, twenty-five thousand years away, learned as a student that the Cro-Magnards came into Spain at the end of the Ice Age – how if you were learning about an event which you yourself had helped to fashion?'

'Then I've come back again and can refuse its fashioning this second chance – even if I knew how.' He sat up. 'And of course – there is perhaps a way!'

'Which?'

He pondered, looking at her and not seeing her, as she knew. 'The northwards spur to the east is broken off from the main mountain-wall. I saw that on the night I crept out from our camp and went to spy on the Neanderthalers. There's a long, hillocky valley lies between. Perhaps half a mile broad, though it seems to climb up to a point at the other side . . . '

'Keith, you've found the way!'

'By God, I have not! Oh, we're the stuff of dreams, but that's not the dream I'm going to help humanity to dream. We'd crawl through that pass sometime at night, so's not to arouse the Neanderthalers, and gain the country in the east. I don't know how many would ever gain it, but some at least. Not me among them, I think. And beyond that pass in the east lies: your boy lover dying on the wire in France, Clair, and the crucified slaves along the Appian Way and the Pinkertons shooting down the starving strikers of a Scotch philanthropist . . . Not if I know it! Better to end it here. Better to make this the end of the human adventure, or go west with the hunters tomorrow and lose ourselves and die in the clean snows of Atlantis . . . Here's your hunter, Clair. Twenty-five thousand years hence he'll also be a hunter – of human heads in New Guinea, with dried human hands strapped on his chest. Or a gangster in Chicago. Or a Steel Helmet in Germany. Like it?'

Aerte sat down beside them. He looked from one to the other with puzzled eyes. Clair smiled at him, this child who loved her. She said: 'I never had a classical education, but wasn't there some tag: "They make a desert and they call it peace" '

Sinclair said nothing, standing up and looking into the darkening west. She knew she was pleading for something immeasurably greater than herself. She could find no words but seemed trite and pitiable ones.

'There were other people than the head-hunter and the gangster . . . There was Karl Liebknecht; there was Anatole France. There was even yourself in that age out of which we came. There was I.'

He turned back at that. She saw more than a bitter denial in his face now. She looked at Aerte and someone other than herself spoke through her lips: 'Do you think they ever quite beat us, Keith – the beasts of civilization? Do you think that Aerte ever quite died, away there in those years? Do you think he won't beat them when civilization has passed and finished? Remember Sir John? – The hunter will come again in the world we left! You and I and thousands of others were fighting up from the fears and cruelties of civilization to look at the world through his eyes again. There are later ages than the one we came from, and Aerte – he'll walk naked across the world again, and fearless, but with Orion's sword in his belt and the Milky Way for a plaything. The weeping and the tears – they're a darkness yet to fall on our hunters. But it will pass. I know. You know it will. And it is for that, though your own dream of changing that chance must finish, that you are to lead the Cro-Magnards east to the pass in the mountain-wall.'

She could not see when she stopped speaking. She thought: 'Oh! I ache also, and I'm cold and hungry, and I've been ranting . . . And I'd like to lie down and sleep and sleep and forget it all – ' She heard Sinclair speaking, and looked up and saw that Titan resentment gone from his face.

'You've won again, Clair. There was you, at least, in that age that is not yet . . . We'll go east tomorrow.'

Subchapter ii

At dawn the next morning the Cro-Magnards moved out from their camp and took up the line of march into the east. In front Sinclair and his surviving scout vanished beforehand. Clair marched mid-way the migration in the company of a girl, Lizair, who had adopted her after the death of Zumarr; it was the same girl who had refused her first suitor in the time of the mating for the dark days. Now the boy whom she had chosen walked beside them, solicitous for Lizair's baby, and a very prideful and manly boy. Aerte had gone off with a band of other hunters to forage northwards for game with which to feed the migration.

No sun came, but a pale diffusion of saffron light in the east. The wind had died away again, but beyond the forest belt to the verge of which the

Neanderthalers had pursued Clair and Sinclair, the Cro-Magnards saw the rolling savannah country pelted with flying showers of sleet. Here, also, the snow lay deeper than in the higher country from which they had descended, and the trek, a grey trek in a grey country, moved slowly enough in the direction set by Sinclair the night before. Children wailed ceaselessly in the piercing chill. Behind, as Clair could see looking back, there followed pack on pack of wolves, black hordes of skulking raiders which grew ever bolder as the day wore on.

Clair tramped half that day like one in a dream. As in a dream she saw the country close in and open out before them; she was hazily conscious of the passing bombardments of sleet; once of a thunderstorm and a great flare of lightning that played over a wood where they halted somewhere towards midday and ate cooked or raw flesh brought with them, for Sinclair had told them to light no fires. It was there that the girl Lizair began to cough and cough in ever-increasing spasms, until she was coughing blood, and in a little while was dead. They left her there, and others, and the wolves halted for a little time, and then came on again.

The boy who had been Lizair's lover insisted, with a dull obstinacy, in carrying her baby. Clair could not bear to look at him.

The northwards spur, not more than five miles or so away, was red-dened with the colours of the sunset when Sinclair and his scout fell back on the main body of the trek. Clair was told of their coming and managed to urge her half-frozen limbs to carry her to the front of the march. As she did so the march gradually turned aside, to the south, making another small wood. Sinclair had advised a halt.

She found him at last, Aitz-Kore and a group of other Cro-Magnards about him. They were at the further verge of the wood in which the trek had halted, and in the hearing of the long, easy agglutinative roll of the proto-Basque speech she stood for a while puzzled and un-noticed. Then she heard her name mentioned, and saw Sinclair's face lighten. She went forward and touched his arm then.

He held her in his arms then, while the hunters with troubled eyes looked at them. 'How are you?'

She was weak enough to want to sob, but she did not. 'Getting weaker and wiser, as the rabbit said when the dog was eating it . . . I'm lasting, but there have been awful things back there, Keith.'

'I've heard. It can't be helped. We must just go on.'

'Can we?'

He indicated the open country in front of them. It was the triangle of the Neanderthalers, and apparently quite deserted. 'The hunter and I have been watching the place ever since we arrived early this forenoon.

There's been no one out on it, and no sign of any of the beast-men stirring, even over by the spur.'

Clair peered through the intervening distances. She saw, after a little, lighter patches in the face of the cliff, and in that clear, generally untainted air, there was the ghost of a sharp, *blue* odour.

'Aren't those their fires?'

'Yes. But they don't seem to be moving out of the caves. Probably they have plenty of food and will continue to keep inside, as they have done all the daylight. We'll strike south as soon as the darkness comes and wait in the lee of the mountain-wall for the stars – if there are any. Can't move further in pitch blackness. Then we'll cross and push up through the valley.'

'If there's fighting – what will happen?'

'God knows. Our hunters have never fought anything but beasts. They can't conceive a human enemy. It would all depend if they were to find the Neanderthalers human or bestial . . . We won't have any need to put it to the test, I think . . . Go and help keep everyone on the move or interested, Clair. No fires . . . Eh?'

She gave a little ghost of a laugh. ' "While shepherds watched their flocks by night" – I never thought I'd play the rôle. I wish we could sing.'

'What would you sing?'

'Something comforting.'

'Do, then; but not too loud. It'll keep the hunters interested.'

She had never thought of singing to them before. They had no songs of the European type, with sharp rhymes and mechanical spacings. But they came round about, from the greyness of the trees, in some numbers as she began to sing, her voice a little hoarse, for she shivered still, but as sweet and sensuous as it had ever been. Sinclair, standing still watching the Neanderthaler fires, heard her voice:

> *Abide with me,* [Clair sang]
> *Fast falls the eventide,*
> *The darkness deepens,*
> *Lord, with me abide.*

Clair's God beyond the gods . . .

The wind rose again. The last of the daylight lingered sharply, on pinpoints of the strange world in the beginning of history, and Sinclair's eyes, in a sudden passion of knowledge of how little of this world he had ever made deep acquaintance with, went from point to point as these rearguards of the day quenched their lamps and departed. Clair sang on, a new song now, inexpressibly alien in that wild land.

> *Now sleeps the crimson petal, now the white;*
> *Now waves the cypress in the palace walk;*
> *Now sinks the goldfish in the porphyry font;*
> *The firefly wakens: waken thou with me.*
> *Now droops the milk-white peacock like a ghost,*
> *And like a ghost she glimmers unto me.*
> *Now lies the Earth all Danaë to the stars,*
> *And all thy heart lies open unto me.*

He looked up at the sky. It was pall-black. He moved and stamped frozen feet, thinking: 'I'll have frost-bite soon. And Clair – better not think of her. Of nothing but the pass. God, if only there will be starshine!'

> *Now folds the lily all her sweetness up,*
> *And slips into the bosom of the lake:*
> *So fold thyself, my dearest, thou, and slip*
> *Into my bosom, and be lost in me.*

He waited while he counted a thousand, and then moved through the darkness of the trees, speaking to the hunters and women. They must walk four or five abreast and follow after him. He heard their pleasant sing-song of response, though many of their faces he could not see, and turned about, and called that he was ready, and held out gingerly southwards on the track he had mentally plotted while the daylight lasted. He held his spear extended, and groped the path with it.

He thought: 'Rotten show if the wolves attack,' and put that out of his mind also. One thing at a time . . .

Beyond the wood the wind smote them as with keen-edged knives. Sinclair gasped, and steadied himself, and plodded forward. Behind, he heard the scuffle of the migration, and looking over his shoulder could see the lighter shadows that were the bodies of the frontwards Cro-Magnards. One slipped forward to his side and kept pace with him. Sinclair said: 'Who are you?'

'I am Aerte.'

'You had better go back to Clair and guard her. I can lead the way.'

Aerte, the Atlantean child-man whom he had never been able to detest, whom even in bitterest moments he had never regarded with other than a grey acquiescence, remained at his shoulder. 'Clair sent me here.'

So that was that . . .

Once the wolves behind did verily attack, and the whole column swayed and eddied while the rearward hunters turned about and fought and stabbed at the leaping bodies in the darkness. They did it with little noise, and the beasts drew off again. But they took with them the bodies of some half-dozen, half-grown children. Nothing could be done for these, and some hunters also did not return. The march through the darkness went on.

Clair carried Lizair's baby by then, for its boy-father had handed it to her when he fell back to fight the wolves; he had not come again from that baying clamour. It coughed, pitifully, now and then. Presently, in her forward stumblings, Clair was aware that the mite within the bearskin had ceased to cough. Not until the column halted in slow eddyings, and she realized it was a deliberate halt, and sought to use the interval to ease the position of the child, did she discover that it was dead. She put her lips to its and her hand over its heart. There was no movement. A nearing voice called: 'Clair! Clair!'

'I'm here.'

A lighter form than those she had followed came out of the darkness. 'What's that you've got?'

'A baby. Oh, Keith, it's dead.'

'It's finished with cold and hunger, Clair. Put it down.'

'I can't . . . Those beasts behind.'

He shook her. 'We're going into something twice as bad as we've had to face in the last hour; and I'll want your help. Put it away.'

She did. The American said: 'I want you to walk mid-way the column. Talk to the people round about you. Explain just what I'm doing, and why they must make no noise. Aerte's going to do the same at the rear.'

'But I can't talk their language!'

'Lord. I'd forgotten that.'

'We're turning towards the valley, now?'

'Yes. It's grown a little lighter.' His fingers touched hers, awkwardly. 'Good luck.'

She would have called him back; but he had gone. In another moment, slowly, in a light that gradually increased with the coming of the star-rise through the frost, the trek was again in motion. In their changed direction the wind blew not behind them now, but on their left. And suddenly, pricking out the bastions of the northwards mountain-spur, seen as they rose to the higher ground that led to that spur, there shone bright and splendid the fires of the Neanderthal caves.

A murmur arose from the Cro-Magnards, but died away at the urgings of Sinclair and Aerte. Over there was danger, no food or help. They must still even the crying of the babies.

The fires seemed to Clair to draw nearer in leaps and bounds. They were fires remote in caves, however; there were no signs of watchers.

Right ahead, where the column wound into the presumed valley, was unspotted darkness.

Clair became aware of the fires passing on her left. They had entered the valley. They stumbled up over rocky ground. Clair raised her head once and saw the heavens, unclouded, banded with the glory of the Milky Way.

And then presently another line of fires gleamed directly ahead, a strange, wild moaning filled the air, and above it rose shout on shout – shoutings in Sinclair's voice!

The migratory column of the Cro-Magnards was being attacked at a dozen points by the Neanderthalers of the unsuspected valley caves.

Subchapter iii

That had been hours ago.

Morning in the air again. It seemed to Clair, looking downwards and around, that this was the land of morning. How many of them had she seen come over the strange, pale hills? Would she see this one?

They were through now, the bulk of the frightened, amazed, uncomprehending Cro-Magnards and their women. Or such of them as had survived the attacks. Or such of them as had not been dragged into those caves of night . . . But Clair would not look in that direction, nor think of those dismembered bodies the beast-men had dragged there. Here they came again –

Like a pelting rush of shadows. But shadows of sickening substance, with the gleam of low-set eyes in the foreheadless heads. They charged again, with their ululating moan rising to a scream, and the musk odour of their bodies nauseating. Sinclair's yell met the scream, and at sound of it the Cro-Magnards still unpast the valley point bunched forward uncertainly to meet the attack . . . Sinclair himself Clair saw, dimly, stripped of bearskin cloak and every other encumberment, in his hand a great club of the beast-men.

Then the scurry of furred grey bodies was upon the Cro-Magnard line.

The morning seemed to have heard the impact. It was coming more quickly out of the wild, unknown eastern lands. Clair felt its pale fore-radiance in her face as she darted here and there, heeding to the onward guiding of the main hunter-stream. Betwixt two rocks they filed, into the unguessable valley-country beyond. Clair thought, wearily: 'Will they never get through?' and heard herself chanting again, foolishly: 'Oh – do please hurry!'

Sinclair, on the westward slopes, heard that cry. Then other interests engaged him. A great brute tore the club from his hands and took him by the throat. Its breath was fetid in his face. He kicked it, intimately, with a moccasined foot. It screamed and slipped away from him. He found a hunter stabbing methodically on either side. Not courage but comprehension they lacked . . . Breathing space.

The Neanderthalers were swaying backwards and downwards again, moaning as they retreated. But, as throughout the hours since the migration had stumbled upon the fact that all one valley-wall was inhabited, other grey beasts were coming at a scrambling, swaying run to replace the rout. Tireless, scores on scores of them, reinforcements from the northwards spur. Rational animals. Men almost . . .

Lighter and lighter the darkness. It was gloaming. Sinclair heard Clair, far up the slope: 'Keith! Keith! All the women are through!'

He stumbled up through the ring of hunters towards the ring of her voice. Dawn near. White in the ghostly radiance. 'Unhurt?'

He breathed sobbingly. 'All right. Everyone through?'

'Except these dozen with you.'

'I'll send them up. Hurry on yourself.'

'You're coming?'

'I'll come. In a minute.' He grinned at her, grey-faced. '*Do* please hurry!'

He watched her disappear. He found himself sobbing again. Now the false dawn illumined the valley.

It rose in a cone, mid-way, and at the cone-tip the cliffs closed in on either side, allowing barely more than the passage of two men abreast. The red sandstone rocks were already a dun rose colour, though no sign of the actual sun came yet. It was snowing fleecily, but even as he turned back towards the westwards slopes that ceased. The rearguard bunched up towards him, and now in the morning light added to the light of the cave-fires, he saw the valley alive, like a spider's nest, with fresh hordes of the grey-furred beast-men.

They would follow on in hundreds . . .

'Go through! Go through!'

Panting, leaning against a rock, he saw them file past, the last of the hunters. Below, the grey, hirsute whirlpool beginning to boil again . . . Two or at the least one must stay with him; he could not do it alone. But whom? Not that old man. Nor this boy. Quick, quick. Whom? Whom? Aerte to guard Clair in the world beyond – ah, God, she had still her hunter! He heard himself shout with sudden strength: 'Turn south beyond this valley – south if you can! Keep watch always.'

'But you will be there with us, brother.' The last hunter, scarred and torn, swayed round and waited. Keith Sinclair cursed him.

'Go on! Go on!'

He heard the pad of retreating feet.

He found himself alone.

Subchapter iv

He started up, gripping his spear. He peered in the faces of the two who stood beside him.

Clair said, sitting down with a sigh: 'Silly to think you could hold this place alone, Keith. So Aerte and I have come back.'

The light grew brighter on the hunter's face. Sinclair stared at the two of them. Clair leant her chin in her hands.

'Nightmare, Keith – but a wonderful one. Last dawn in Atlantis! . . . And the beasts that follow men – '

Thereat the sunrise, in a great hush that seemed to hold quiescent even the gathering attack of the Neanderthalers twenty yards below, sped suddenly up from the eastern end of the canyon and poured liquid through the narrow defile. Sitting, Clair's head nodded on her shoulders. But she started up at Sinclair's last cry of entreaty.

'Clair!'

She stumbled between the two men. Her eyes turned to the horror below. 'I'll stand behind with my spear. They're coming.'

Twice they had come, and twice broken and shambled downwards in screaming flight. Clair's spear was gone, the head embedded in a beast-man's chest. Sinclair leant against the canyon wall, his right arm hanging by a pinch of skin, blood pouring from a dreadful stomach wound . . . His face a battered mask, all human likeness had gone from the hunter. But she saw his eyes turned towards her, glazing eyes lovely and human still. He staggered to his feet. She felt suddenly serene and assured.

'Oh, my dears, it isn't long now! They are coming again – '

CHAPTER THE LAST

I shall arise again

Subchapter i

She awoke in a dazzle of sunshine that blinded her for a moment. She sat up and knuckled her eyes. She felt very tired – sun-tired, as though she had slept a long time in this warmth of the earth and sky. There was a continual drumming splash near at hand, like the sound of the sea heard far off. She took her hands from her eyes and looked round.

She was lying on a patch of sand on a low beach that sloped up to rocky, verdant mountains. The violent green of the near underbrush waved, languid and warm, in the ghost of a breeze. Overhead was a sky deep and blue and touched with a sailing speck-net of clouds. A score of yards away the sea rumbled unhurryingly on the beach.

The beast-men of the pass!

'Keith! Aerte!'

A gull whooped past her. Far up the mountainside a sudden roar grew to a grinding clamour, became a glittering snake in the sunlight, hissed; swept from view again. A railway train . . .

She stared upwards in paralysed affright. Delirium. Of course it was delirium. For suddenly she had remembered. *She was dead.*

Morning Pass – the Neanderthalers – their last charge – a great malachite club descending – Aerte and Keith gold and white and red-streaked veinings of foam under a wave of snarling greyness. She must be still alive and in delirium – the last alive of the *Magellan*!

She closed her eyes again, that the horror might pass, and willed to die also; and the wind touched her cheek and her hair came ruffling across her face, tickling her skin so that her hand went up involuntarily to put it aside. She opened her eyes on the green, warm day. And then she saw something lying a few yards off, and, sobbing, was in a moment kneeling by the side of that something.

It was Keith Sinclair.

He lay unmoving, face downwards in an outpost of the mountain grass. Kneeling in a blur of tears beside him, she thought: 'I am mad; it is still delirium.' For his body was unmarked by signs of struggle in the pass – that body from which the blood had welled in great gouts. She shook his shoulder.

'Keith. Oh, Keith, make it real!'

For answer he yawned where he lay, stretched his arms, stretched his legs, seemed to stretch every muscle in his body. Then, slowly and casually, he turned round and sat erect. His eyes seemed to have a grey film over them. He blinked, knuckling his eyes as she had knuckled hers. She sat back and watched him.

As she did so there came again, far up the slope, that muffled roar, the green of the mountain vegetation stirred ever so slightly, and again that metal toy monster swept round a curve and vanished with a loud whistle. Sinclair's head jerked upwards. He stared with fallen jaw. Then he looked round him, smiled dazedly at Clair, and, as she had done, covered his eyes.

'By God,' he said, *'we're back!'*

Subchapter ii

'We'll go exploring in a minute. Azores or Madeira I should think . . . Oh, I'm real enough and sound enough. So – and so. Convinced?'

She said, her voice muffled in his long hair: 'Still a dream for all I know, for you did that often enough in my day-dreams. Oh, my dear! You're real and whole . . . And ten minutes ago your arm was hanging by a thread from your shoulder – and that stomach-wound – '

Sinclair held her close. 'But it wasn't ten minutes ago. It happened thousands of years ago, else we'd never see that train.'

His arms about her still, he started suddenly; laughed.

'What is it?'

'We were killed, of course – and by some chance didn't die . . . We're back in the year we left – unless some other accident has happened. It may be 2000.'

She withdrew her head and looked at the brightening day. 'Real. You and the world and myself . . . And I know it's the year we left.'

'So do I,' he confessed. And thought aloud: 'The railway trains of 2000 won't burn coal – '

'Keith, where are we?'

'Eh?' He looked round the scene again. Then: 'We're in Morning Pass still. Look.'

He pointed to the mountain-edge near at hand. Dimly, a ghostly scene in the sunlight, a remembrance shaped in Clair's mind. That boulder, that curve of rock that swept into the sea where the grey men mustered for their last attack . . . But the leftwards wall of the pass had vanished into a smother of grass that was presently sand; beyond that also the murmur of the sea . . . Ten minutes ago, twenty-five thousand years ago . . . She knew him looking at her in quick understanding.

'We're *back*, Clair. Don't worry about it. Let's get up and do that exploring.'

They stood up together, helping each other. And then it was Sinclair who was seized with an obsessing memory. He looked to right and left and broke away from her, searching. She stared after him. 'Keith!'

He halted in his search, looking over his shoulder. 'Aerte – he must be here! He died with us.'

But he turned fully round again, and they looked at each other white-faced. And then it seemed to Clair that his face had altered, that she knew at last the meaning of scores of puzzling resemblances that had torn her heart now this way, now that. She knew that she might cry again if she did not speak very quickly. She said: 'Don't you understand? I do at last. *You* are Aerte.'

Subchapter iii

The deserted beach curved northwards round the shoulder of the mountain. Out to sea a trail of smoke grew to being across the horizon, became a triune procession of dots that were funnels, and presently sank again, leaving that scroll-writing in the sky. But neither Clair nor Sinclair moved.

'I am Aerte.' He sat with his hands clasped round his knees. 'Just as he was the boy who died at Mametz and a score of others. Race-type, race-memory, blood of his blood – who can know? . . . And there was a you also in the painted caves. I didn't know then. Now – I saw her a dozen times, in a look, a way of walking. Lizair who died in the last forest – she was you.'

Clair Stranlay stood with the sun in her face, dreaming also. 'Oh, Keith, not only these two! Zumarr and her hunter – Aitz-kore – Lizair's boy-lover who died among the wolves – the young men who came back at evening singing – '

'They're here in the world still, all of them, that company that went over Sunrise Pass into the morning we never saw.'

'But what happened then – that morning? They must have got clear away.'

'Somehow. Perhaps the Neanderthalers never pursued them after our end. Somehow they went east and south and found a place safe from the winter. And then they went east again, into the beginnings of history.'

She stood with troubled, lighted face, far in dreams, and he looked up at her suddenly with the gaze of the twentieth century; the custom of weeks fell from his eyes. Unconscious of herself and the beauty of herself in the fall of sunshine, her red hair blown on the tanned gold of her neck, and against the mountain greenery almost merging the gold of her body into the sunlight . . . *Back*!

She looked down and sighed and sat beside him. She smiled into those eyes that were not of the caves of Atlantis.

'Oh, we've awakened . . .' She looked round the bright weather of the green beach. 'We've come back. We'll be hungry in a little, and have to go round that hill, and hear people speak and wear clothes again, and lie in the fug of little rooms and never hear the midnight cry upon the mountains. That's finished and put by . . . If only it was a pack of hyaenodon that waited us round that mountain bend!'

It was he who stood up now, with a laugh, and she also saw him with eyes that had lost the acceptance of many a day and scene. Keith Sinclair of the *Magellan* – never that Keith Sinclair again . . . He smiled down at her. He held out his hand.

'Come along. We'll go and meet the hyaenodon.'

She put her fingers in his. 'I suppose we must . . . Love me, my dear?'

'Till the hunters come back to the world again – and after.'

She did not stir.

'Then there's still a moment we've never known, Keith, though we dreamt it in the Golden Age. It's still the same sun and earth – for a moment, before we go back to the world that's forgotten both.'

Not looking at him, she yet saw his face change strangely, felt the pressure on her fingers alter, knew him kneeling beside her. She put her arms round his neck. He held her away a moment.

'Sure, Clair?'

'Till the hunters walk again.'

She drew down his head very slowly, and kissed him tremulously, and the moment came out of the growing day, and waited for them with a quiver of purple wings, and was theirs for ever.

Subchapter iv

Senhora Leiria regarded her guest with admiration and uplifted her voice in throaty French.

'But they fit with exactitude!'

The guest raised a flushed, smiling face. 'Very sweet,' she agreed, and thought: 'Oh, my good God, and I'll have to *wear* the things!'

The thought was appalling. So was the Senhora. Had she never seen a nude body before? Why, if she looked across at the caves there –

But the caves were twenty-five thousand years away.

Clair sat down. 'I'll manage ever so nicely now I've had a bath and you've shown me the stuff I can choose from. I'll dress and come down in a minute or so.'

The stout Senhora lingered, constitutional languor and aroused curiosity in combat. 'The dreadful hours you must have spent, Senhora Keith, after the wreck of your husband's boat!'

'Shocking.' ('If she doesn't go away I'll – ')

The door closed. Clair dropped the garments entrusted to her, stumbled to the casement window, and flung it wide open. Gasped with relief.

'The ghastly, ghastly smell of the place! Just the ordinary room smell? Wonder how Keith's getting on – or what he's getting on? . . . Those must be the roofs of San Miguel over there.'

San Miguel of the Azores . . .

She began to laugh. That servant whom Keith had encountered –

Three hours ago. They'd rounded the mountain bend into view of open, cultivated country, a road half a mile away alive with automobiles, and, in the fore-ground, on a branch of the road and not more than eighty yards from where they stood, a low and gabled house with a garden and the white shirt-sleeves of a gardener.

Clair had sunk hastily to the ground. 'Don't shock them too much, Keith.'

He had grinned and set out, long-striding. Almost immediately there was catastrophe. Avoiding the main door and turning rightwards through the garden he had collided with a diminutive female in some kind of domestic uniform. Her shrieks preceding him, he had disappeared from Clair's view for a quarter of an hour, and, just as she had begun to wonder about his safety, had emerged from that main door and approached her.

'It's all right, Clair. Put on this coat of the Senhora's. We're in the Azores. Portuguese. I've told them a few lies to avoid unbelievable explanations.'

'Keith – that ulster of yours!' She had struggled into the coat, half-hysterical. Surveyed herself: 'And I look like something saved by some ghastly missionary . . . What were the lies?'

'Coming? Senhora Leiria is going to look after you and get you some clothes . . . We're the Keiths, an English couple, husband and wife. We've a craze for boating. Tried to reach San Miguel from Santarem in our three-ton yacht – '

'Are there three-ton yachts?'

'Eh? No idea. But early this morning we met a squall and were upset. Stripped and swam. You're Mrs Keith, remember.'

'But we'll have to tell some of the truth later.'

'We won't be able to avoid that. But this is the best meanwhile. I realized just in time that our banks'll refuse us a draft, as they'll believe us lost in the *Magellan*. But I keep an alias account – name of Keith, League of Militant Pacifist purposes – and can always order on it by a code message . . . ' They were under the garden-wall. 'Now – '

Now, with a curious shambling motion, upraised upon the heels of unaccustomed shoes, Clair Stranlay crossed the floor of Senhora Leiria's bedroom and began to descend the stairs. At the foot of the first landing was an open door, and beyond –

'Clair! Hell, what a mess!'

He was tugging to ease an unaccustomed collar. He had risen from uneasy sprawling in a be-cushioned chair. He pushed her away from him.

'My God, did you see that crucifix? And servants – diseased animals sweating to tend diseased animals! Why do they? Why the devil do they? Pack a room like this? All this nonsense of furniture. Pottering in that damned garden . . . Flowers: they grow much better wild; any fool knows it. You can see them opposite the caves – purple-growing blooms. Sometimes the firelight reaches across the river to them – '

'Keith!'

She closed the door behind her. He sat down and buried his face in his hands. He looked up at her with just such film over his eyes as she had seen on them at his awakening.

'Sorry. Went crack for a moment . . . All this – God, we can never endure it again, Clair! Beyond this house there are the towns and the filth and the stench. London on a wet Sunday afternoon. The shoddy crowds of the Boul' Mich'. Newsboys screaming, trains screaming . . . It would kill us after – after that.'

'What are we going to do, then?'

'Clear out to the South Seas or some such place.'

'Escape?'

'Escape.'

'My dear, I'd sooner go down to the sea there and walk out into it.' She started to cross the room towards him. Something snapped, intimately. She put her hand to her thigh. 'Those damn things . . . Let's open that window.' She laughed down at him. 'Keith, are we to be beaten by a collar and a brassière when the Neanderthalers didn't beat us?'

She knelt beside him. 'I'm going to do what *you* are going to do. Go back to the world we came from. Tell them we survived the *Magellan* – and then preach Atlantis till our dying day!'

'Tell them what happened? Who'd ever believe it? Can't you hear the bray of the headlines? – remember how they vilified Mitchell Hedges?'

She smiled the old, gay smile with no irony at all in it. 'Different from that. Upstairs I suddenly knew what we would do. We can't desert the world – we've no right to . . . Not while there are still Neanderthalers alive – in generals' uniforms. Not while they still can lie about the ever-lastingness of rich and poor and innate human ferocity. Not while our hunters are still in the world – somewhere out there, Keith! – chained and gagged and brutalized, begging in streets, cheating in offices, doing dirty little cruelties in prison wards . . . Remember that world you planned beyond the southern mountains? It's still a possible world and a possible civilization.'

'This disease of mine is merely agoraphobia, of course. It'll pass.'

'Then – ?'

'Of course.' He caught her hand and stood up with her. He winced at his straining clothes, as she did. Clair's laughter had survived Atlantis. He shook her, very gently. 'We could never do anything else, I suppose – even though we bring a flint spear against a sixteen-inch gun.'

Subchapter v

They stood together in the sunset. The sea rumbled again at their feet in the beat of the incoming tide. And out for miles, hasting into the west, the fading light leapt from roller to roller of the Atlantic. Remote above them the culvert belched out another train to sweep the mountain track down to San Miguel. Sinclair's hand fell on Clair's.

'Time we went back. The Leirias dine early, they said.'

'I know. But just a minute more . . . Tomorrow's so near.'

'Eh?'

'Tomorrow and all the things of which we've talked. You'll get money and we'll go into San Miguel and sail to France, and begin the fight for sanity; and the world will vex and thwart us and we'll grow bitter, and grow old till those four weeks – '

He put his arms round her. 'We're going to work and fight together. We're going to marry. Children we'll have like yourself – keen and lovely as you. We'll do all the things you said this forenoon when the future scared me. We'll light a torch and never let it die.'

She did not move, still staring out to sea. 'Oh, Keith, I know. This is only a moment with me also, and it'll pass and be forgotten. Do you think I won't love the fight as well? – or love loving you and bearing your babies and taming your temper and – and seeing you always have a fresh razor blade? It isn't that. Only – '

It was almost dark. He held her gently, unimpatiently. 'Only – ?'

'Oh, Keith, say you'll never forget them! – all those days? Remember that first night? Remember the golden hunters on the western hill? Remember the fires? Remember the laughter and the kindliness of them? Remember the road to Sunrise Pass? . . . We'll forget and forget and the years'll come tramping over our lives and memories – '

'But not these memories.' His arms tightened round her. 'They'll live as long as we do. They're things undying. They live though human nature go into an underground pit for a million years.'

She stirred in his arms. She touched his cheek in shadowy caress. 'The Leirias are lighting their lamps.'

But as they passed together out of the noise of the sea to the lighted night and the waiting world, Clair caught his hand and turned back a moment to the rolling waste of waters whereneath lies buried these twenty thousand years the mythic land of Atlantis: 'Good-bye, my dears!'

THE END

The Crystal Man

Edward Page Mitchell

Rapidly turning into the Fifth Avenue from one of the cross streets above the old reservoir, at quarter past eleven o'clock on the night of November 6, 1879, I ran plump into an individual coming the other way.

It was very dark on this corner. I could see nothing of the person with whom I had the honor to be in collision. Nevertheless, the quick habit of a mind accustomed to induction had furnished me with several well-defined facts regarding him before I fairly recovered from the shock of the encounter.

These were some of the facts: he was a heavier man than myself, and stiffer in the legs; but he lacked precisely three inches and a half of my stature. He wore a silk hat, a cape or cloak of heavy woolen material, and rubber overshoes or arctics. He was about thirty-five years old, born in America, educated at a German university, either Heidelberg or Freiburg, naturally of hasty temper, but considerate and courteous, in his demeanor to others. He was not entirely at peace with society: there was something in his life or in his present errand which he desired to conceal.

How did I know all this when I had not seen the stranger, and when only a single monosyllable had escaped his lips? Well, I knew that he was stouter than myself, and firmer on his foot, because it was I, not he, who recoiled. I knew that I was just three inches and a half taller than he, for the tip of my nose was still tingling from its contact with the stiff, sharp brim of his hat. My hand, involuntarily raised, had come under the edge of his cape. He wore rubber shoes, for I had not heard a footfall. To an observant ear, the indications of age are as plain in the tones of the voice as to the eye in the lines of the countenance. In the first moment of exasperation of my maladroitness, he had muttered 'Ox!' a term that would occur to nobody except a German at such a time. The pronunciation of the guttural, however, told me that the speaker was an American German, not a German American, and that his German education had been derived south of the river Main. Moreover, the tone of the gentleman and scholar was manifest even in the utterance of wrath. That the gentleman was in no particular hurry, but for some reason anxious to remain unknown, was a conclusion drawn from the fact that, after listening in silence to my polite apology, he stooped to recover and restore to me my umbrella, and then passed on as noiselessly as he had approached.

I make it a point to verify my conclusions when possible. So I turned back into the cross street and followed the stranger toward a lamp part way down the block. Certainly, I was not more than five seconds behind him. There was no other road that he could have taken. No house door had opened and closed along the way. And yet, when we came into the light, the form that ought to have been directly in front of me did not appear. Neither man nor man's shadow was visible.

Hurrying on as fast as I could walk to the next gaslight, I paused under the lamp and listened. The street was apparently deserted. The rays from the yellow flame reached only a little way into the darkness. The steps and doorway, however, of the brownstone house facing the street lamp were sufficiently illuminated. The gilt figures above the door were distinct. I recognized the house: the number was a familiar one. While I stood under the gaslight, waiting, I heard a slight noise on these steps, and the click of a key in a lock. The vestibule door of the house was slowly opened, and then closed with a slam that echoed across the street. Almost immediately followed the sound of the opening and shutting of the inner door. Nobody had come out. As far as my eyes could be trusted to report an event hardly ten feet away and in broad light, nobody had gone in.

With a notion that here was scanty material for an exact application of the inductive process, I stood a long time wildly guessing at the philosophy of the strange occurrence. I felt that vague sense of the unexplainable which amounts almost to dread. It was a relief to hear steps on the sidewalk opposite, and turning, to see a policeman swinging his long black club and watching me.

2

This house of chocolate brown, whose front door opened and shut at midnight without indications of human agency, was, as I have said, well known to me. I had left it not more than ten minutes earlier, after spending the evening with my friend Bliss and his daughter Pandora. The house was of the sort in which each storey constitutes a domicile complete in itself. The second floor, or flat, had been inhabited by Bliss since his return from abroad; that is to say, for a twelvemonth. I held Bliss in esteem for for his excellent qualities of heart, while his deplorably illogical and unscientific mind commanded my profound pity. I adored Pandora.

Be good enough to understand that my admiration for Pandora Bliss was hopeless, and not only hopeless, but resigned to its hopelessness. In our circle of acquaintance there was a tacit covenant that the young lady's peculiar position as a flirt wedded to a memory should be at all times respected. We adored Pandora mildly, not passionately – just enough to feed her coquetry without excoriating the seared surface of her widowed heart. On her part, Pandora conducted herself with signal propriety. She did not sigh too obtrusively when she flirted: and she always kept her flirtations so well in hand that she could cut them short whenever the fond, sad recollections came.

It was considered proper for us to tell Pandora that she owed it to her youth and beauty to put aside the dead past like a closed book, and to urge her respectfully to come forth into the living present. It was not considered proper to press the subject after she had once replied that this was forever impossible.

The particulars of the tragic episode in Miss Pandora's European experience were not accurately known to us. It was understood, in a vague way, that she had loved while abroad, and trifled with her lover: that he had disappeared, leaving her in ignorance of his fate and in perpetual remorse for her capricious behavior. From Bliss I had gathered a few, sporadic facts, not coherent enough to form a history of the case. There was no reason to believe that Pandora's lover had committed suicide. His name was Flack. He was a scientific man. In Bliss's opinion he was a fool. In Bliss's opinion Pandora was a fool to pine on his account. In Bliss's opinion all scientific men were more or less fools.

3

That year I ate Thanksgiving dinner with the Blisses. In the evening I sought to astonish the company by reciting the mysterious events on the night of my collision with the stranger. The story failed to produce the expected sensation. Two or three odious people exchanged glances. Pandora, who was unusually pensive, listened with seeming indifference. Her father, in his stupid inability to grasp anything outside the commonplace, laughed outright, and even went so far as to question my trustworthiness as an observer of phenomena.

Somewhat nettled, and perhaps a little shaken in my own faith in the marvel, I made an excuse to withdraw early. Pandora accompanied me to the threshold. 'Your story,' said she, 'interested me strangely. I, too, could report occurrences in and about this house which would surprise you. I believe I am not wholly in the dark. The sorrowful past casts a glimmer of light – but let us not be hasty. For my sake probe the matter to the bottom.'

The young woman sighed as she bade me good night. I thought I heard a second sigh, in a deeper tone than hers, and too distinct to be a reverberation.

I began to go downstairs. Before I had descended half a dozen steps I felt a man's hand laid rather heavily upon my shoulder from behind. My first idea was that Bliss had followed me into the hall to apologize for his rudeness. I turned around to meet his friendly overture. Nobody was in sight.

Again the hand touched my arm. I shuddered in spite of my philosophy. This time the hand gently pulled at my coat sleeve, as if to invite me upstairs. I ascended a step or two, and the pressure on my arm was relaxed. I paused, and the silent invitation was repeated with an urgency that left no doubt as to what was wanted.

We mounted the stairs together, the presence leading the way, I following. What an extraordinary journey it was! The halls were bright with gaslight. By the testimony of my eyes there was no one but myself upon the stairway. Closing my eyes, the illusion, if illusion it could be called, was perfect. I could hear the creaking of the stairs ahead of me, the soft but distinctly audible footfalls synchronous with my own, even the regular breathing of my companion and guide. Extending my arm, I could touch and finger the skirt of his garment – a heavy woolen cloak lined with silk.

Suddenly I opened my eyes. They told me again that I was absolutely alone.

This problem then presented itself to mind: how to determine whether vision was playing me false, while the senses of hearing and feeling correctly informed me, or whether my ears and touch lied, while my eyes reported the truth. Who shall be arbiter when the senses contradict each other? The reasoning faculty? Reason was inclined to recognize the presence of an intelligent being, whose existence was flatly denied by the most trusted of the senses.

We reached the topmost floor of the house. The door leading out of the public hall opened for me, apparently of its own accord. A curtain within seemed to draw itself aside, and hold itself aside long enough to give me ingress to an apartment wherein every appointment spoke of good taste and scholarly habits. A wood fire was burning in the chimney place. The walls were covered with books and pictures. The lounging chairs were capacious and inviting. There was nothing in the room uncanny, nothing weird, nothing different from the furniture of everyday flesh and blood existence.

By this time I had cleared my mind of the last lingering suspicion of the supernatural. These phenomena were perhaps not inexplicable; all that I lacked was the key. The behavior of my unseen host argued his amicable disposition. I was able to watch with perfect calmness a series of manifestations of independent energy on the part of inanimate objects.

In the first place, a great Turkish easy chair wheeled itself out of a corner of the room and approached the hearth. Then a square-backed Queen Anne chair started from another corner, advancing until it was planted directly opposite the first. A little tripod table lifted itself a few inches above the floor and took a position between the two chairs. A thick octavo volume backed out of its place on the shelf and sailed tranquilly through the air at the height of three or four feet, landing neatly on top of the table. A finely painted porcelain pipe left a hook on the wall and joined the volume. A tobacco box jumped from the mantlepiece. The door of a cabinet swung open, and a decanter and wineglass made the journey in company, arriving simultaneously at the same destination. Everything in the room seemed instinct with the spirit of hospitality.

I seated myself in the easy chair, filled the wineglass, lighted the pipe, and examined the volume. It was the *Handbuch der Gewebelehre* of Bussius of Vienna. When I had replaced the book upon the table, it deliberately opened itself at the four hundred and forty-third page.

'You are not nervous?' demanded a voice, not four feet from my tympanum.

4

This voice had a familiar sound. I recognized it as the voice that I heard in the street on the night of November 6, when it called me an ox.

'No,' I said. 'I am not nervous. I am a man of science, accustomed to regard all phenomena as explainable by natural laws, provided we can discover the laws. No, I am not frightened.'

'So much the better. You are a man of science, like myself' – here the voice groaned – 'a man of nerve, and a friend of Pandora's.'

'Pardon me,' I interposed. 'Since a lady's name is introduced it would be well to know with whom or with what I am speaking.'

'That is precisely what I desire to communicate,' replied the voice, 'before I ask you to render me a great service. My name is or was Stephen Flack. I am or have been a citizen of the United States. My exact status at present is as great a mystery to myself as it can possibly be to you. But I am, or was, an honest man and a gentleman, and I offer you my hand.'

I saw no hand. I reached forth my own, however, and it met the pressure of warm, living fingers.

'Now,' resumed the voice, after this silent pact of friendship, 'be good enough to read the passage at which I have opened the book upon the table.'

Here is a rough translation of what I read in German.

As the color of the organic tissues constituting the body depends upon the presence of certain proximate principles of the third class, all containing iron as one of the ultimate elements, it follows that the hue may vary according to well-defined chemico-physiological changes. An excess of hematin in the blood globules gives a ruddier tinge to every tissue. The melanin that colors the choroid of the eye, the iris, the hair, may be increased or diminished according to laws recently formulated by Schardt of Basel. In the epidermis the excess of melanin makes the Negro, the deficient supply the albino. The hematin and the melanin, together with the greenish-yellow biliverdine and the reddish-yellow urokacine, are the pigments which impart color character to tissues otherwise transparent, or nearly so. I deplore my inability to record the result of some highly interesting histological experiments conducted by that indefatigable investigator Fröliker in achieving success in the way of separating pink discoloration of the human body by chemical means.

'For five years,' continued my unseen companion when I had finished reading, 'I was Fröliker's student and laboratory assistant at Freiburg. Bussius only half guessed at the importance of our experiments. We reached results which were so astounding that public policy required they should not be published, even to the scientific world. Fröliker died a year ago last August.

'I had faith in the genius of this great thinker and admirable man. If he had rewarded my unquestioning loyalty with full confidence, I should not now be a miserable wretch. But his natural reserve, and the jealousy with which all savants guard their unverified results, kept me ignorant of the essential formulas governing our experiments. As his disciple I was familiar with the laboratory details of the work; the master alone possessed the radical secret. The consequence is that I have been led into a misfortune more appalling than has been the lot of any human being since the primal curse fell upon Cain.

'Our efforts were at first directed to the enlargement and variation of the quantity of pigmentary matter in the system. By increasing the proportion of melanin, for instance, conveyed in food to the blood, we were able to make a fair man dark, a dark man black as an African. There was scarcely a hue we could not impart to the skin by modifying and varying our combinations. The experiments were usually tried on me. At different times I have been copper-colored, violet blue, crimson, and chrome yellow. For one triumphant week I exhibited in my person all the colors of the rainbow. There still remains a witness to the interesting character of our work during this period.'

The voice paused, and in a few seconds a hand bell upon the mantel was sounded. Presently an old man with a close-fitting skullcap shuffled into the room.

'Käspar,' said the voice, in German, 'show the gentleman your hair.'

Without manifesting any surprise, and as if perfectly accustomed to receive commands addressed to him out of vacancy, the old domestic bowed and removed his cap. The scanty locks thus discovered were of a lustrous emerald green. I expressed my astonishment.

'The gentleman finds your hair very beautiful,' said the voice, again in German. 'That is all, Käspar.'

Replacing his cap, the domestic withdrew, with a look of gratified vanity on his face.

'Old Käspar was Fröliker's servant, and is now mine. He was the subject of one of our first applications of the process. The worthy man was so pleased with the result that he would never permit us to restore his hair to its original red. He is a faithful soul, and my only intermediary and representative in the visible world.

'Now,' continued Flack, 'to the story of my undoing. The great histologist with whom it was my privilege to be associated, next turned his attention to another and still more interesting branch of the investigation. Hitherto he had sought merely to increase or to modify the pigments in the tissues. He now began a series of experiments as to the possibility of eliminating those pigments altogether from the system by absorption, exudation, and the use of the chlorides and other chemical agents acting on organic matter. He was only too successful!

'Again I was the subject of experiments which Fröliker supervised, imparting to me only so much of the secret of this process as was unavoidable. For weeks at a time I remained in his private laboratory, seeing no one and seen by no one excepting the professor and the trustworthy Käspar. Herr Friiliker proceeded with caution, closely watching the effect of each new test, and advancing by degrees. He never went so far in one experiment that he was unable to withdraw at discretion. He always kept open an easy road for retreat. For that reason I felt myself perfectly safe in his hands and submitted to whatever he required.

'Under the action of the etiolating drugs which the professor administered in connection with powerful detergents, I became at first pale, white, colorless as an albino, but without suffering in general health. My hair and beard looked like spun glass and my skin like marble. The professor was satisfied with his results, and went no further at this time. He restored to me my normal color.

'In the next experiment, and in those succeeding, he allowed his chemical agents to take firmer hold upon the tissues of my body. I became not only white, like a bleached man, but slightly translucent, like a porcelain figure. Then again he paused for a while, giving me back my color and allowing me to go forth into the world. Two months later I was more than translucent. You have seen floating those sea radiates, the medusa or jellyfish, their outlines almost invisible to the eye. Well, I became in the air like a jellyfish in the water. Almost perfectly transparent, it was only by close inspection that old Käspar could discover my whereabouts in the room when he came to bring me food. It was Käspar who ministered to my wants at times when I was cloistered.'

'But your clothing?' I inquired, interrupting Flack's narrative. 'That must have stood out in strong contrast with the dim aspect of your body.'

'Ah, no,' said Flack. 'The spectacle of an apparently empty suit of clothes moving about the laboratory was too grotesque even for the grave professor. For the protection of his gravity he was obliged to devise a way to apply his process to dead organic matter, such as the wool of my cloak, the cotton of my shirts, and the leather of my shoes. Thus I came to be equipped with the outfit which still serves me.

'It was at this stage of our progress, when we had almost attained perfect transparency, and therefore complete invisibility, that I met Pandora Bliss.

'A year ago last July, in one of the intervals of our experimenting, and at a time when I presented my natural appearance, I went into the Schwarzwald to recuperate. I first saw and admired Pandora at the little village of St Blasien. They had come from the Falls of the Rhine, and were traveling north; I turned around and traveled north. At the Stern Inn I loved Pandora; at the summit of the Feldberg I madly worshiped her. In the Höllenpass I was ready to sacrifice my life for a gracious word from her lips. On Hornisgrinde I besought her permission to throw myself from the top of the mountain into the gloomy waters of the Mummelsee in order to prove my devotion. You know Pandora. Since you know her, there is no need to apologize for the rapid growth of my infatuation. She flirted with me, laughed with me, laughed at me, drove with me, walked with me through byways in the green woods, climbed with me up acclivities so steep that climbing together was one delicious, prolonged embrace; talked science with me, and sentiment; listened to my hopes and enthusiasm, snubbed me, froze me, maddened me – all at her sweet will, and all while her matter-of-fact papa dozed in the coffee rooms of the inns over the financial columns of the latest New York newspapers. But whether she loved me I know not to this day.

'When Pandora's father learned what my pursuits were, and what my prospects, he brought our little idyll to an abrupt termination. I think he classed me somewhere between the professional jugglers and the quack doctors. In vain I explained to him that I should be famous and probably rich. "When you are famous and rich," he remarked with a grin, "I shall be pleased to see you at my office in Broad Street." He carried Pandora off to Paris, and I returned to Freiburg.

'A few weeks later, one bright afternoon in August, I stood in Fröliker's laboratory unseen by four persons who were almost within the radius of my arm's length. Käspar was behind me, washing some test tubes. Fröliker, with a proud smile upon his face, was gazing intently at the place where he knew I ought to be. Two brother professors, summoned on some pretext, were unconsciously almost jostling me with their elbows as they discussed I know not what trivial question. They could have heard my heart beat. "By the way, Herr Professor," one asked as he was about to depart, "has your assistant, Herr Flack, returned from his vacation?" This test was perfect.

'As soon as we were alone, Professor Fröliker grasped my invisible hand, as you have grasped it tonight. He was in high spirits.

'"My dear fellow," he said, "tomorrow crowns our work. You shall appear – or rather not appear – before the assembled faculty of the university. I have telegraphed invitations to Heidelberg, to Bonn, to Berlin. Schrotter, Haeckel, Steinmetz, Lavallo, will be here. Our triumph will be in presence of the most eminent physicists of the age. I shall then disclose those secrets of our process which I have hitherto withheld even from you, my co-laborer and trusted friend. But you shall share the glory. What is this I hear about the forest bird that has flown? My boy, you shall be restocked with pigment and go to Paris to seek her with fame in your hands and the blessings of science on your head."

'The next morning, the nineteenth of August, before I had arisen from my cot bed, Käspar hastily entered the laboratory.

'"Herr Flack! Herr Flack!" he gasped, "the Herr Doctor Professor is dead of apoplexy." '

5

The narrative had come to an end. I sat a long time thinking. What could I do? What could I say? In what shape could I offer consolation to this unhappy man?

Flack, the invisible, was sobbing bitterly.

He was the first to speak. 'It is hard, hard, hard! For no crime in the eyes of man, for no sin in the sight of God, I have been condemned to a fate ten thousand times worse than hell. I must walk the earth, a man, living, seeing, loving, like other men, while between me and all that makes life worth having there is a barrier fixed forever. Even ghosts have shapes. My life is living death; my existence oblivion. No friend can look me in the face. Were I to clasp to my breast the woman I love, it would only be to inspire terror inexpressible. I see her almost every day. I brush against her skirts as I pass her on the stairs. Did she love me? Does she love me? Would not that knowledge make the curse still more cruel? Yet it was to learn the truth that I brought you here.'

Then I made the greatest mistake of my life.

'Cheer up!' I said. 'Pandora has always loved you.'

By the sudden overturning of the table I knew with what vehemence Flack sprang to his feet. His two hands had my shoulders in a fierce grip.

'Yes,' I continued; 'Pandora has been faithful to your memory. There is no reason to despair. The secret of Fröliker's process died with him, but why should it not be rediscovered by experiment and induction *ab initio*, with the aid which you can render? Have courage and hope. She loves you. In five minutes you shall hear it from her own lips.'

No wail of pain that I ever heard was half so pathetic as his wild cry of joy.

I hurried downstairs and summoned Miss Bliss into the hall. In a few words I explained the situation. To my surprise, she neither fainted nor went into hysterics. 'Certainly, I will accompany you,' she said, with a smile which I could not then interpret.

She followed me into Flack's room, calmly scrutinizing every corner of the apartment, with the set smile still upon her face. Had she been entering a ballroom she could not have shown greater self-possession. She manifested no astonishment, no terror, when her hand was seized by invisible hands and covered with kisses from invisible lips. She listened with composure to the torrent of loving and caressing words which my unfortunate friend poured into her ears.

Perplexed and uneasy, I watched the strange scene.

Presently Miss Bliss withdrew her hand.

'Really, Mr Flack,' she said with a light laugh, 'you are sufficiently demonstrative. Did you acquire the habit on the Continent?'

'Pandora!' I heard him say, 'I do not understand.'

'Perhaps,' she calmly went on, 'you regard it as one of the privileges of your invisibility. Let me congratulate you on the success of your experiment. What a clever man your professor – what is his name? – must be. You can make a fortune by exhibiting yourself.'

Was this the woman who for months had paraded her inconsolable sorrow for the loss of this very man? I was stupefied. Who shall undertake to analyze the motives of a coquette? What science is profound enough to unravel her unconscionable whims?

'Pandora!' he exclaimed again, in a bewildered voice. 'What does it mean? Why do you receive me in this manner? Is that all you have to say to me?'

'I believe that is all,' she coolly replied, moving toward the door. 'You are a gentleman, and I need not ask you to spare me any further annoyance.'

'Your heart is quartz,' I whispered, as she passed me in going out. 'You are unworthy of him.'

Flack's despairing cry brought Käspar into the room. With the instinct acquired by long and faithful service, the old man went straight to the place where his master was. I saw him clutch at the air, as if struggling with and seeking to detain the invisible man. He was flung violently aside. He recovered himself and stood an instant listening, his neck distended, his face pale. Then he rushed out of the door and down the stairs. I followed him.

The street door of the house was open. On the sidewalk Käspar hesitated a few seconds. It was toward the west that he finally turned, running down the street with such speed that I had the utmost difficulty to keep at his side.

It was near midnight. We crossed avenue after avenue. An inarticulate murmur of satisfaction escaped old Käspar's lips. A little way ahead of us we saw a man, standing at one of the avenue corners, suddenly thrown to the ground. We sped on, never relaxing our pace. I now heard rapid footfalls a short distance in advance of us. I clutched Käspar's arm. He nodded.

Almost breathless, I was conscious that we were no longer treading upon pavement, but on boards and amid a confusion of lumber. In front of us were no more lights; only blank vacancy. Käspar gave one mighty spring. He clutched, missed, and fell back with a cry of horror.

There was a dull splash in the black waters of the river at our feet.

The Balloon Tree

Edward Page Mitchell

The colonel said:

We rode for several hours straight from the shore toward the heart of the island. The sun was low in the western sky when we left the ship. Neither on the water nor on the land had we felt a breath of air stirring. The glare was upon everything. Over the low range of hills miles away in the interior hung a few copper-colored clouds. 'Wind,' said Briery. Kilooa shook his head.

Vegetation of all kinds showed the effects of the long-continued drought. The eye wandered without relief from the sickly russet of the undergrowth, so dry in places that leaves and stems crackled under the horses' feet, to the yellowish-brown of the thirsty trees that skirted the bridle path. No growing thing was green except the bell-top cactus, fit to flourish in the crater of a living volcano.

Kilooa leaned over in the saddle and tore from one of these plants its top, as big as a California pear and bloated with juice. He crushed the bell in his fist, and, turning, flung into our hot faces a few grateful drops of water.

Then the guide began to talk rapidly in his language of vowels and liquids. Briery translated for my benefit.

The god Lalala loved a woman of the island. He came in the form of fire. She, accustomed to the ordinary temperature of the clime, only shivered before his approaches. Then he wooed her as a shower of rain and won her heart. Kakal was a divinity much more powerful than Lalala, but malicious to the last degree. He also coveted this woman, who was very beautiful. Kakal's importunities were in vain. In spite, he changed her to a cactus, and rooted her to the ground under the burning sun. The god Lalala was powerless to avert this vengeance; but he took up his abode with the cactus woman, still in the form of a rain shower, and never left her, even in the driest seasons. Thus it happens that the bell-top cactus is an unfailing reservoir of pure cool water.

Long after dark we reached the channel of a vanished stream, and Kilooa led us for several miles along its dry bed. We were exceedingly tired when the guide bade us dismount. He tethered the panting horses and then dashed into the dense thicket on the bank. A hundred yards of scrambling, and we came to a poor thatched hut. The savage raised both hands above his head and uttered a musical falsetto, not unlike the yodel peculiar to the Valais. This call brought out the occupant of the hut, upon whom Briery flashed the light of his lantern. It was an old woman, hideous beyond the imagination of a dyspeptic's dream.

'*Omanana gelaäl!*' exclaimed Kilooa.

'Hail, holy woman,' translated Briery.

Between Kilooa and the holy hag there ensued a long colloquy, respectful on his part, sententious and impatient on hers; Briery listened with eager attention. Several times he clutched my arm, as if unable to repress his anxiety. The woman seemed to be persuaded by Kilooa's arguments, or won by his entreaties. At last she pointed toward the south-east, slowly pronouncing a few words that apparently satisfied my companions.

The direction indicated by the holy woman was still toward the hills, but twenty or thirty degrees to the left of the general course which we had pursued since leaving the shore.

'Push on! Push on!' cried Briery. 'We can afford to lose no time.'

2

We rode all night. At sunrise there was a pause of hardly ten minutes for the scanty breakfast supplied by our haversacks. Then we were again in the saddle, making our way through a thicket that grew more and more difficult, and under a sun that grew hotter.

'Perhaps,' I remarked finally to my taciturn friend, 'you have no objection to telling me now why two civilized beings and one amiable savage should be plunging through this infernal jungle, as if they were on an errand of life or death?'

'Yes,' said he, 'it is best you should know.'

Briery produced from an inner breast pocket a letter which had been read and reread until it was worn in the creases. 'This,' he went on, 'is from Professor Quakversuch of the University of Uppsala. It reached me at Valparaiso.'

Glancing cautiously around, as if he feared that every tree fern in that tropical wilderness was an eavesdropper, or that the hood-like spathes of the giant caladiums overhead were ears waiting to drink in some mighty secret of science, Briery read in a low voice from the letter of the great Swedish botanist.

You will have in these islands [wrote the professor] a rare opportunity to investigate certain extraordinary accounts given me years ago by the Jesuit missionary Buteaux concerning the Migratory Tree, the *cereus vagrans* of Jansenius and other speculative physiologists.

The explorer Spohr claims to have beheld it; but there is reason, as you know, for accepting all of Spohr's statements with caution.

That is not the case with the assertions of my late valued correspondent, the Jesuit missionary. Father Buteaux was a learned botanist, an accurate observer, and a most pious and conscientious man. He never saw the Migratory Tree; but during the long period of his labors in that part of the world he accumulated, from widely different sources, a mass of testimony as to its existence and habits.

Is it quite inconceivable, my dear Briery, that somewhere in the range of nature there is a vegetable organization as far above the cabbage, let us say, in complexity and potentiality as the ape is above the polyp? Nature is continuous. In all her schemes we find no chasms, no gaps. There may be missing links in our books and classifications and cabinets, but there are none in the organic world. Is not all of lower nature struggling upward to arrive at the point of self-consciousness and volition? In the unceasing process of evolution, differentiation, improvement in special functions, why may not a plant arrive at this point and feel, will, act, in short, possess and exercise the characteristics of the true animal?'

Briery's voice trembled with enthusiasm as he read this.

I have no doubt [continued Professor Quakversuch] that if it shall be your great good fortune to encounter a specimen of the Migratory Tree described by Buteaux, you will find that it possesses a well-defined system of real nerves and ganglia, constituting, in fact, the seat of vegetable intelligence. I conjure you to be very thorough in your dissections.

According to the indications furnished me by the Jesuit, this extraordinary tree should belong to the order of Cactaceae. It should be developed only in conditions of extreme heat and dryness. Its roots should be hardly more than rudimentary, affording a precarious attachment to the earth. This attachment it should be able to sever at will, soaring up into the air and away to another place selected by itself, as a bird shifts its habitation. I infer that these migrations are accomplished by means of the property of secreting hydrogen gas, with which it inflates at pleasure a bladder-like organ of highly elastic tissue, thus lifting itself out of the ground and off to a new abode.

Buteaux added that the Migratory Tree was invariably worshiped by the natives as a supernatural being, and that the mystery thrown by them around its cult was the greatest obstacle in the path of the investigator.

'There!' exclaimed Briery, folding up Professor Quakversuch's letter. 'Is not that a quest worthy the risk or sacrifice of life itself!? To add to the recorded facts of vegetable morphology the proved existence of a tree that wanders, a tree that wills, a tree, perhaps, that thinks – this is glory to be won at any cost! The lamented Decandolle of Geneva –'

'Confound the lamented Decandolle of Geneva!' shouted I, for it was excessively hot, and I felt that we had come on a fool's errand.

3

It was near sunset on the second day of our journey, when Kilooa, who was riding several rods in advance of us, uttered a quick cry, leaped from his saddle, and stooped to the ground.

Briery was at his side in an instant. I followed with less agility; my joints were very stiff and I had no scientific enthusiasm to lubricate them. Briery was on his hands and knees, eagerly examining what seemed to be a recent disturbance of the soil. The savage was prostrate, rubbing his forehead in the dust, as if in a religious ecstasy, and warbling the same falsetto notes that we had heard at the holy woman's hut.

'What beast's trail have you struck?' I demanded.

'The trail of no beast,' answered Briery, almost angrily. 'Do you see this broad round abrasion of the surface, where a heavy weight has rested? Do you see these little troughs in the fresh earth, radiating from the center like the points of a star? They are the scars left by slender roots torn up from their shallow beds. Do you see Kilooa's hysterical performance? I tell you we are on the track of the Sacred Tree. It has been here, and not long ago.'

Acting under Briery's excited instructions we continued the hunt on foot. Kilooa started toward the east, I toward the west, and Briery took the southward course.

To cover the ground thoroughly, we agreed to advance in gradually widening zigzags, communicating with each other at intervals by pistol shots. There could have been no more foolish arrangement. In a quarter of an hour I had lost my head and my bearings in a thicket. For another quarter of an hour I discharged my revolver repeatedly, without getting a single response from east or south. I spent the remainder of daylight in a blundering effort to make my way back to the place where the horses were; and then the sun went down, leaving me in sudden darkness, alone in a wilderness of, the extent and character of which I had not the faintest idea.

I will spare you the history of my sufferings during the whole of that night, and the next day, and the next night, and another day. When it was dark I wandered about in blind despair, longing for daylight, not daring to sleep or even to stop, and in continual terror of the unknown dangers that surrounded me. In the daytime I longed for night, for the sun scorched its way through the thickest roof that the luxuriant foliage afforded, and drove me nearly mad. The provisions in my haversack were exhausted. My canteen was on my saddle; I should have died of thirst had it not been for the bell-top cactus, which I found twice. But in that horrible experience neither the torture of hunger and thirst nor the torture of heat equalled the misery of the thought that my life was to be sacrificed to the delusion of a crazy botanist, who had dreamed of the impossible.

The impossible?

On the second afternoon, still staggering aimlessly on through the jungle, I lost my last strength and fell to the ground. Despair and indifference had long since given way to an eager desire for the end. I closed my eyes with indescribable relief; the hot sun seemed pleasant on my face as consciousness departed.

Did a beautiful and gentle woman come to me while I lay unconscious, and take my head in her lap, and put her arms around me? Did she press her face to mine and in a whisper bid me have courage? That was the belief that filled my mind when it struggled back for a moment into consciousness; I clutched at the warm, soft arms, and swooned again.

Do not look at each other and smile, gentlemen; in that cruel wilderness, in my helpless condition, I found pity and benignant tenderness. The next time my senses returned I saw that Something was bending over me – something majestic if not beautiful, humane if not human, gracious if not woman. The arms that held me and drew me up were moist, and they throbbed with the pulsation of life. There was a faint, sweet odor, like the smell of a woman's perfumed hair. The touch was a caress, the clasp an embrace.

Can I describe its form? No, not with the definiteness that would satisfy the Quakversuches and the Brierys. I saw that the trunk was massive. The branches that lifted me from the ground and held me carefully and gently were flexible and symmetrically disposed. Above my head there was a wreath of strange foliage, and in the midst of it a dazzling sphere of scarlet. The scarlet globe grew while I watched it but the effort of watching was too much for me.

Remember, if you please, that at this time, physical exhaustion and mental torture had brought me to the point where I passed to and fro between consciousness and unconsciousness as easily and as frequently as one fluctuates between slumber and wakefulness during a night of fever. It seemed the most natural thing in the world that in my extreme weakness I should be beloved and cared for by a cactus. I did not seek an explanation of this good fortune, or try to analyze it; I simply accepted it as a matter of course, as a child accepts a benefit from an unexpected quarter. The one idea that possessed me was that I had found an unknown friend, instinct with womanly sympathy and immeasurably kind.

And as night came on it seemed to me that the scarlet bulb overhead became enormously distended, so that it almost filled the sky. Was I gently rocked by the supple arms that still held me? Were we floating off together into the air? I did not know, or care. Now I fancied that I was in my berth on board ship, cradled by the swell of the sea; now, that I was sharing the flight of some great bird; now, that I was borne on with prodigious speed through the darkness by my own volition. The sense of incessant motion affected all my dreams. Whenever I awoke I felt a cool breeze steadily beating against my face – the first breath of air since we had landed. I was vaguely happy, gentlemen. I had surrendered all responsibility for my own fate. I had gained the protection of a being of superior powers.

<h2 style="text-align:center">4</h2>

'The brandy flask, Kilooa!'

It was daylight. I lay upon the ground and Briery was supporting my shoulders. In his face was a look of bewilderment that I shall never forget.

'My God!' he cried, 'and how did you get here? We gave up the search two days ago.'

The brandy pulled me together. I staggered to my feet and looked around. The cause of Briery's extreme amazement was apparent at a glance. We were not in the wilderness. We were at the shore. There was the bay, and the ship at anchor, half a mile off. They were already lowering a boat to send for us.

And there to the south was a bright red spot on the horizon, hardly larger than the morning star – the Balloon Tree returning to the wilderness. I saw it, Briery saw it, the savage Kilooa saw it. We watched it till it vanished. We watched it with very different emotions, Kilooa with superstitious reverence, Briery with scientific interest and intense disappointment, I with a heart full of wonder and gratitude.

I clasped my forehead with both hands. It was no dream, then. The Tree, the caress, the embrace, the scarlet bulb, the night journey through the air, were not creations and incidents of delirium. Call it tree, or call it plant-animal – there it was! Let men of science quarrel over the question of its existence in nature; this I know: *it had found me dying and had brought me more than a hundred miles straight to the ship where I belonged.* Under Providence, gentlemen, that sentient and intelligent vegetable organism had saved my life.

At this point the colonel got up and left the club. He was very much moved. Pretty soon Briery came in, briskly as usual. He picked up an uncut copy of Lord Bragmuch's *Travels in Kerguellon's Land*, and settled himself in an easy chair at the corner of the fireplace.

Young Traddies timidly approached the veteran globetrotter. 'Excuse me, Mr Briery,' said he, 'but I should like to ask you a question about the Balloon Tree. Were there scientific reasons for believing that its sex was – '

'Ah,' interrupted Briery, looking bored; 'the colonel has been favoring you with that extraordinary narrative? Has he honored me again with a share in the adventure? Yes? Well, did we bag the game this time?'

'Why, no,' said young Traddies. 'You last saw the Tree as a scarlet spot against the horizon.'

'By Jove, another miss!' said Briery, calmly beginning to cut the leaves of his book.

The Ablest Man in the World

Edward Page Mitchell

I

It may or may not be remembered that in 1878 General Ignatieff spent several weeks of July at the Badischer Hof in Baden. The public journals gave out that he visited the watering-place for the benefit of his health, said to be much broken by protracted anxiety and responsibility in the service of the Czar. But everybody knew that Ignatieff was just then out of favor at St Petersburg, and that his absence from the centers of active statecraft at a time when the peace of Europe fluttered like a shuttlecock in the air, between Salisbury and Shouvaloff, was nothing more or less than politely disguised exile.

I am indebted for the following facts to my friend Fisher, of New York, who arrived at Baden on the day after Ignatieff, and was duly announced in the official list of strangers as 'Herr Doctor Professor Fischer, mit Frau Gattin and Bed. Nordamerika.'

The scarcity of titles among the traveling aristocracy of North America is a standing grievance with the ingenious person who compiles the official list. Professional pride and the instincts of hospitality alike impel him to supply the lack whenever he can. He distributes governor, major-general, and doctor professor with tolerable impartiality, according as the arriving Americans wear a distinguished, a martial, or a studious air. Fisher owed his title to his spectacles.

It was still early in the season. The theatre had not yet opened. The hotels were hardly half full, the concerts in the kiosk at the Conversationshaus were heard by scattering audiences, and the shopkeepers of the bazaar had no better business than to spend their time in bewailing the degeneracy of Baden Baden since an end was put to the play. Few excursionists disturbed the meditations of the shriveled old custodian of the tower on the Mercuriusberg. Fisher found the place very stupid – as stupid as Saratoga in June or Long Branch in September. He was impatient to get to Switzerland, but his wife had contracted a table d'hôte intimacy with a Polish countess, and she positively refused to take any step that would sever so advantageous a connection.

One afternoon Fisher was standing on one of the little bridges that span the gutter-wide Oosbach, idly gazing into the water and wondering whether a good sized Rangely trout could swim the stream without personal inconvenience, when the porter of the Badischer Hof came to him on the run.

'Herr Doctor Professorl' cried the porter, touching his cap. 'I pray you pardon, but the highborn the Baron Savitch out of Moscow, of the General Ignatieff's suite, suffers himself in a terrible fit, and appears to die.'

In vain Fisher assured the porter that it was a mistake to consider him a medical expert; that he professed no science save that of draw poker; that if a false impression prevailed in the hotel it was through a blunder for which he was in no way responsible; and that, much as he regretted the unfortunate condition of the highborn the baron out of Moscow, he did not feel that his presence in the chamber of sickness would be of the slightest benefit. It was impossible to eradicate the idea that possessed the porter's mind. Finding himself fairly dragged toward the hotel, Fisher at length concluded to make a virtue of necessity and to render his explanations to the baron's friends.

The Russian's apartments were upon the second floor, not far from those occupied by Fisher. A French valet, almost beside himself with terror, came hurrying out of the room to meet the porter and the doctor professor. Fisher again attempted to explain, but to no purpose. The valet also had explanations to make, and the superior fluency of his French enabled him to monopolize the conversation. No, there was nobody there – nobody but himself, the faithful Auguste of the baron. His Excellency, the General Ignatieff, His Highness, the Prince Koloff, Dr Rapperschwyll, all the suite, all the world, had driven out that morning to Gernsbach. The baron, meanwhile, had been seized by an effraying malady, and he, Auguste, was desolate with apprehension. He entreated Monsieur to lose no time in parley, but to hasten to the bedside of the baron, who was already in the agonies of dissolution.

Fisher followed Auguste into the inner room. The Baron, in his boots, lay upon the bed, his body bent almost double by the unrelenting gripe of a distressful pain. His teeth were tightly clenched, and the rigid muscles around the mouth distorted the natural expression of his face. Every few seconds a prolonged groan escaped him. His fine eyes rolled piteously. Anon, he would press both hands upon his abdomen and shiver in every limb in the intensity of his suffering.

Fisher forgot his explanations. Had he been a doctor professor in fact, he could not have watched the symptoms of the baron's malady with greater interest.

'Can Monsieur preserve him?' whispered the terrified Auguste.

'Perhaps,' said Monsieur, dryly.

Fisher scribbled a note to his wife on the back of a card and dispatched it in the care of the hotel porter. That functionary returned with great promptness, bringing a black bottle and a glass. The bottle had come in Fisher's trunk to Baden all the way from Liverpool, had crossed the sea to Liverpool from New York, and had journeyed to New York direct from Bourbon County, Kentucky. Fisher seized it eagerly but reverently, and held it up against the light. There were still three inches or three inches and a half in the bottom. He uttered a grunt of pleasure.

'There is some hope of saving the Baron,' he remarked to Auguste.

Fully one half of the precious liquid was poured into the glass and administered without delay to the groaning, writhing patient. In a few minutes Fisher had the satisfaction of seeing the baron sit up in bed. The muscles around his mouth relaxed, and the agonized expression was superseded by a look of placid contentment.

Fisher now had an opportunity to observe the personal characteristics of the Russian baron. He was a young man of about thirty-five, with exceedingly handsome and clear-cut features, but a peculiar head. The peculiarity of his head was that it seemed to be perfectly round on top – that is, its diameter from ear to ear appeared quite equal to its anterior and posterior diameter. The curious effect of this unusual conformation was rendered more striking by the absence of all hair. There was nothing on the baron's head but a tightly fitting skullcap of black silk. A very deceptive wig hung upon one of the bed posts.

Being sufficiently recovered to recognize the presence of a stranger, Savitch made a courteous bow.

'How do you find yourself now?' inquired Fisher, in bad French.

'Very much better, thanks to Monsieur,' replied the baron, in excellent English, spoken in a charming voice. 'Very much better, though I feel a certain dizziness here.' And he pressed his hand to his forehead.

The valet withdrew at a sign from his master, and was followed by the porter. Fisher advanced to the bedside and took the baron's wrist. Even his unpractised touch told him that the pulse was alarmingly high. He was much puzzled, and not a little uneasy at the turn which the affair had taken. 'Have I got myself and the Russian into an infernal scrape?' he thought. 'But no – he's well out of his teens, and half a tumbler of such whiskey as that ought not to go to a baby's head.'

Nevertheless, the new symptoms developed themselves with a rapidity and poignancy that made Fisher feel uncommonly anxious. Savitch's face became as white as marble – its paleness rendered startling by the sharp contrast of the black skull cap. His form reeled as he sat on the bed, and he clasped his head convulsively with both hands, as if in terror lest it burst.

'I had better call your valet,' said Fisher, nervously.

'No, no!' gasped the baron. 'You are a medical man, and I shall have to trust you. There is something – wrong – here.' With a spasmodic gesture he vaguely indicated the top of his head.

'But I am not –' stammered Fisher.

'No words!' exclaimed the Russian, imperiously. 'Act at once – there must be no delay. Unscrew the top of my head!'

Savitch tore off his skullcap and flung it aside. Fisher has no words to describe the bewilderment with which he beheld the actual fabric of the baron's cranium. The skullcap had concealed the fact that the entire top of Savitch's head was a dome of polished silver.

'Unscrew it!' said Savitch again.

Fisher reluctantly placed both hands upon the silver skull and exerted a gentle pressure toward the left. The top yielded, turning easily and truly in its threads.

'Faster!' said the baron, faintly. 'I tell you no time must be lost.' Then he swooned.

At this instant there was a sound of voices in the outer room, and the door leading into the baron's bed-chamber was violently flung open and as violently closed. The newcomer was a short, spare man, of middle age, with a keen visage and piercing, deepset little gray eyes. He stood for a few seconds scrutinizing Fisher with a sharp, almost fiercely jealous regard.

The baron recovered his consciousness and opened his eyes.

'Dr Rapperschwyll!' he exclaimed.

Dr Rapperschwyll, with a few rapid strides, approached the bed and confronted Fisher and Fisher's patient. 'What is all this?' he angrily demanded.

Without waiting for a reply he laid his hand rudely upon Fisher's arm and pulled him away from the baron. Fisher, more and more astonished, made no resistance, but suffered himself to be led, or pushed, toward the door. Dr Rapperschwyll opened the door wide enough to give the American exit, and then closed it with a vicious slam. A quick click informed Fisher that the key had been turned in the lock.

2

The next morning Fisher met Savitch coming from the Trinkhalle. The baron bowed with cold politeness and passed on. Later in the day a *valet de place* handed to Fisher a small parcel, with the message: 'Dr Rapperschwyll supposes that this will be sufficient' The parcel contained two gold pieces of twenty marks.

Fisher gritted his teeth. 'He shall have back his forty marks,' he muttered to himself, 'but I will have his confounded secret in return.'

Then Fisher discovered that even a Polish countess has her uses in the social economy.

Mrs Fisher's table d'hôte friend was amiability itself, when approached by Fisher (through Fisher's wife) on the subject of the Baron Savitch of Moscow. Know anything about the Baron Savitch? Of course she did, and about everybody else worth knowing in Europe. Would she kindly communicate her knowledge? Of course she would, and be enchanted to gratify in the slightest degree the charming curiosity of her Americaine. It was quite refreshing for a *blasée* old woman, who had long since ceased to feel much interest in contemporary men, women, things and events, to encounter one so recently from the boundless prairies of the new world as to cherish a piquant inquisitiveness about the affairs of the *grand monde*. Ah! yes, she would very willingly communicate the history of the Baron Savitch of Moscow, if that would amuse her dear Americaine.

The Polish countess abundantly redeemed her promise, throwing in for good measure many choice bits of gossip and scandalous anecdotes about the Russian nobility, which are not relevant to the present narrative. Her story, as summarized by Fisher, was this.

The Baron Savitch was not of an old creation. There was a mystery about his origin that had never been satisfactorily solved in St Petersburg or in Moscow. It was said by some that he was a foundling from the Vospitatelnoi Dom. Others believed him to be the unacknowledged son of a certain illustrious personage nearly related to the House of Romanoff. The latter theory was the more probable, since it accounted in a measure for the unexampled success of his career from the day that he was graduated at the University of Dorpat.

Rapid and brilliant beyond precedent this career had been. He entered the diplomatic service of the Czar, and for several years was attached to the legations at Vienna, London, and Paris. Created a Baron before his twenty-fifth birthday for the wonderful ability displayed in the conduct of negotiations of supreme importance and delicacy with the House of Hapsburg, he became a pet of Gortchakoff's, and was given every opportunity for the exercise of his genius in diplomacy. It was even said in well-informed circles at St Petersburg that the guiding mind which directed Russia's course throughout the entire Eastern complication, which planned the campaign on the Danube, effected the combinations that gave victory to the Czar's soldiers, and which meanwhile held Austria aloof, neutralized the immense power of Germany, and exasperated England only to the point where wrath expends itself in harmless threats, was the brain of the young Baron Savitch. It was certain that he had been with Ignatieff at Constantinople when the trouble was first fomented, with Shouvaloff in England at the time of the secret conference agreement, with the Grand Duke Nicholas at Adrianople when the protocol of an armistice was signed, and would soon be in Berlin behind the scenes of the Congress, where it was expected that he would outwit the statesmen of all Europe, and play with Bismarck and Disraeli as a strong man plays with two kicking babies.

But the countess had concerned herself very little with this handsome young man's achievements in politics. She had been more particularly interested in his social career. His success in that field had been not less remarkable. Although no one knew with positive certainty his father's name, he had conquered an absolute supremacy in the most exclusive circles surrounding the imperial court. His influence with the Czar himself was supposed to be unbounded. Birth apart, he was considered the best *parti* in Russia. From poverty and by the sheer force of intellect he had won for himself a colossal fortune. Report gave him forty million roubles, and doubtless report did not exceed the fact. Every speculative enterprise which he undertook, and they were many and various, was carried to sure success by the same qualities of cool, unerring judgment, far-reaching sagacity, and apparently superhuman power of organizing, combining, and controlling, which had made him in politics the phenomenon of the age.

About Dr Rapperschwyll? Yes, the countess knew him by reputation and by sight. He was the medical man in constant attendance upon the Baron Savitch, whose high-strung mental organization rendered him susceptible to sudden and alarming attacks of illness. Dr Rapperschwyll was a Swiss – had originally been a watchmaker or artisan of some kind, she had heard. For the rest, he was a commonplace little old man, devoted to his profession and to the baron, and evidently devoid of ambition, since he wholly neglected to turn the opportunities of his position and connections to the advancement of his personal fortunes.

Fortified with this information, Fisher felt better prepared to grapple with Rapperschwyll for the possession of the secret. For five days he lay in wait for the Swiss physician. On the sixth day the desired opportunity unexpectedly presented itself.

Half way up the Mercuriusberg, late in the afternoon, he encountered the custodian of the ruined tower, coming down. 'No, the tower was not closed. A gentleman was up there, making observations of the country, and he, the custodian, would be back in an hour or two.' So Fisher kept on his way.

The upper part of this tower is in a dilapidated condition. The lack of a stairway to the summit is supplied by a temporary wooden ladder. Fisher's head and shoulders were hardly through the trap that opens to the platform, before he discovered that the man already there was the man whom he sought. Dr Rapperschwyll was studying the topography of the Black Forest through a pair of field glasses.

Fisher announced his arrival by an opportune stumble and a noisy effort to recover himself, at the same instant aiming a stealthy kick at the topmost round of the ladder, and scrambling ostentatiously over the edge of the trap. The ladder went down thirty or forty feet with a racket, clattering and banging against the walls of the tower.

Dr Rapperschwyll at once appreciated the situation. He turned sharply around, and remarked with a sneer, 'Monsieur is unaccountably awkward.' Then he scowled and showed his teeth, for he recognized Fisher.

'It *is* rather unfortunate,' said the New Yorker, with imperturbable coolness. 'We shall be imprisoned here a couple of hours at the shortest. Let us congratulate ourselves that we each have intelligent company, besides a charming landscape to contemplate.'

The Swiss coldly bowed, and resumed his topographical studies. Fisher lighted a cigar.

'I also desire,' continued Fisher, puffing clouds of smoke in the direction of the Teufelmfihle, 'to avail myself of this opportunity to return forty marks of yours, which reached me, I presume, by a mistake.'

'If Monsieur the American physician was not satisfied with his fee,' rejoined Rapperschwyll, venomously, 'he can without doubt have the affair adjusted by applying to the baron's valet.'

Fisher paid no attention to this thrust, but calmly laid the gold pieces upon the parapet, directly under the nose of the Swiss.

'I could not think of accepting any fee,' he said, with deliberate emphasis. 'I was abundantly rewarded for my trifling services by the novelty and interest of the case.'

The Swiss scanned the American's countenance long and steadily with his sharp little gray eyes. At length he said, carelessly: 'Monsieur is a man of science?'

'Yes,' replied Fisher, with a mental reservation in favor of all sciences save that which illuminates and dignifies our national game.

'Then,' continued Dr Rapperschwyll, 'Monsieur will perhaps acknowledge that a more beautiful or more extensive case of trephining has rarely come under his observation.'

Fisher slightly raised his eyebrows.

'And Monsieur will also understand, being a physician,' continued Dr Rapperschwyll, 'the sensitiveness of the baron himself, and of his friends upon the subject. He will therefore pardon my seeming rudeness at the time of his discovery.'

'He is smarter than I supposed,' thought Fisher. 'He holds all the cards, while I have nothing – nothing, except a tolerably strong nerve when it comes to a game of bluff.'

'I deeply regret that sensitiveness,' he continued, aloud, 'for it had occurred to me that an accurate account of what I saw, published in one of the scientific journals of England or America, would excite wide attention, and no doubt be received with interest on the Continent.'

'What you saw?' cried the Swiss, sharply. 'It is false. You saw nothing – when I entered you had not even removed the – '

Here he stopped short and muttered to himself, as if cursing his own impetuosity. Fisher celebrated his advantage by tossing away his half-burned cigar and lighting a fresh one.

'Since you compel me to be frank,' Dr Rapperschwyll went on, with visibly increasing nervousness, 'I will inform you that the baron has assured me that you saw nothing. I interrupted you in the act of removing the silver cap.'

'I will be equally frank,' replied Fisher, stiffening his face for a final effort. 'On that point, the baron is not a competent witness. He was in a state of unconsciousness for some time before you entered. Perhaps I was removing the silver cap when you interrupted me – '

Dr Rapperschwyll turned pale.

'And, perhaps,' said Fisher, coolly, 'I was replacing it.'

The suggestion of this possibility seemed to strike Rapperschwyll like a sudden thunderbolt from the clouds. His knees parted, and he almost sank to the floor. He put his hands before his eyes, and wept like a child, or, rather, like a broken old man.

'He will publish it! He will publish it to the court and to the world!' he cried, hysterically. 'And at this crisis – '

Then, by a desperate effort, the Swiss appeared to recover to some extent his self-control. He paced the diameter of the platform for several minutes, with his head bent and his arms folded across the breast. Turning again to his companion, he said: 'If any sum you may name will – '

Fisher cut the proposition short with a laugh.

'Then,' said Rapperschwyll, 'if – if I throw myself on your generosity – '

'Well?' demanded Fisher.

'And ask a promise, on your honor, of absolute silence concerning what you have seen?'

'Silence until such time as the Baron Savitch shall have ceased to exist?'

'That will suffice,' said Rapperschwyll. 'For when he ceases to exist I die. And your conditions?'

'The whole story, here and now, and without reservation.'

'It is a terrible price to ask me,' said Rapperschwyll, 'but larger interests than my pride are at stake. You shall hear the story.

'I was bred a watchmaker,' he continued, after a long pause, 'in the Canton of Zurich. It is not a matter of vanity when I say that I achieved a marvellous degree of skill in the craft. I developed a faculty of invention that led me into a series of experiments regarding the capabilities of purely mechanical combinations. I studied and improved upon the best automata ever constructed by human ingenuity. Babbage's calculating machine especially interested me. I saw in Babbage's idea the germ of something infinitely more important to the world.

'Then I threw up my business and went to Paris to study physiology. I spent three years at the Sorbonne and perfected myself in that branch of knowledge. Meanwhile, my pursuits had extended far beyond the purely physical sciences. Psychology engaged me for a time; and then I ascended into the domain of sociology, which, when adequately understood, is the summary and final application of all knowledge.

'It was after years of preparation, and as the outcome of all my studies, that the great idea of my life, which had vaguely haunted me ever since the Zurich days, assumed at last a well-defined and perfect form.'

The manner of Dr Rapperschwyll had changed from distrustful reluctance to frank enthusiasm. The man himself seemed transformed. Fisher listened attentively and without interrupting the relation. He could not help fancying that the necessity of yielding the secret, so long and so jealously guarded by the physician, was not entirely distasteful to the enthusiast.

'Now, attend, Monsieur,' continued Dr Rapperschwyll, 'to several separate propositions which may seem at first to have no direct bearing on each other.

'My endeavors in mechanism had resulted in a machine which went far beyond Babbage's in its powers of calculation. Given the data, there was no limit to the possibilities in this direction. Babbage's cogwheels and pinions calculated logarithms, calculated an eclipse. It was fed with figures, and produced results in figures. Now, the relations of cause and effect are as fixed and unalterable as the laws of arithmetic. Logic is, or should be, as exact a science as mathematics. My new machine was fed with facts, and produced conclusions. In short, it reasoned; and the results of its reasoning were always true, while the results of human reasoning are often, if not always, false. The source of error in human logic is what the philosophers call the 'personal equation'. My machine eliminated the personal equation; it proceeded from cause to effect, from premise to conclusion, with steady precision. The human intellect is fallible; my machine was, and is, infallible in its processes.

'Again, physiology and anatomy had taught me the fallacy of the medical superstition which holds the gray matter of the brain and the vital principle to be inseparable. I had seen men living with pistol balls imbedded in the medulla oblongata. I had seen the hemispheres and the cerebellum removed from the crania of birds and small animals, and yet they did not die. I believed that, though the brain were to be removed from a human skull, the subject would not die, although he would certainly be divested of the intelligence which governed all save the purely involuntary actions of his body.

'Once more: a profound study of history from the sociological point of view, and a not inconsiderable practical experience of human nature, had convinced me that the greatest geniuses that ever existed were on a plane not so very far removed above the level of average intellect. The grandest peaks in my native country, those which all the world knows by name, tower only a few hundred feet above the countless unnamed peaks that surround them. Napoleon Bonaparte towered only a little over the ablest men around him. Yet that little was everything, and he overran Europe. A man who surpassed Napoleon, as Napoleon surpassed Murat, in the mental qualities which transmute thought into fact, would have made himself master of the whole world.

'Now, to fuse these three propositions into one: suppose that I take a man, and, by removing the brain that enshrines all the errors and failures of his ancestors away back to the origin of the race, remove all sources of weakness in his future career. Suppose, that in place of the fallible intellect which I have removed, I endow him with an artificial intellect that operates with the certainty of universal laws. Suppose that I launch this superior being, who reasons truly, into the hurly-burly of his inferiors, who reason falsely, and await the inevitable result with the tranquillity of a philosopher.

'Monsieur, you have my secret. That is precisely what I have done. In Moscow, where my friend Dr Duchat had charge of the new institution of St Vasili for hopeless idiots, I found a boy of eleven whom they called Stépan Borovitch. Since he was born, he had not seen, heard, spoken or thought. Nature had granted him, it was believed, a fraction of the sense of smell, and perhaps a fraction of the sense of taste, but of even this there was no positive ascertainment. Nature had walled in his soul most effectually. Occasional inarticulate murmurings, and an incessant knitting and kneading of the fingers were his only manifestations of energy. On bright days they would place him in a little rocking-chair, in some spot where the sun fell warm, and he would rock to and fro for hours, working his slender fingers and mumbling forth his satisfaction at the warmth in the plaintive and unvarying refrain of idiocy. The boy was thus situated when I first saw him.

'I begged Stépan Borovitch of my good friend Dr Duchat. If that excellent man had not long since died he should have shared in my triumph. I took Stépan to my home and plied the saw and the knife. I could operate on that poor, worthless, useless, hopeless travesty of humanity as fearlessly and as recklessly as upon a dog bought or caught for vivisection. That was a little more than twenty years ago. Today Stépan Borovitch wields more power than any other man on the face of the earth. In ten years he will be the autocrat of Europe, the master of the world. He never errs; for the machine that reasons beneath his silver skull never makes a mistake.'

Fisher pointed downward at the old custodian of the tower, who was seen toiling up the hill.

'Dreamers,' continued Dr Rapperschwyll, 'have speculated on the possibility of finding among the ruins of the older civilizations some brief inscription which shall change the foundations of human knowledge. Wiser men deride the dream, and laugh at the idea of scientific kabbala. The wiser men are fools. Suppose that Aristotle had discovered on a cuneiform-covered tablet at Nineveh the few words, "Survival of the Fittest", Philosophy would have gained twenty-two hundred years. I will give you, in almost as few words, a truth equally pregnant. *The ultimate evolution of the creature is into the creator.* Perhaps it will be twenty-two hundred years before the truth finds general acceptance, yet it is not the less a truth. The Baron Savitch is my creature, and I am his creator – creator of the ablest man in Europe, the ablest man in the world.

'Here is our ladder, Monsieur. I have fulfilled my part of the agreement. Remember yours.'

3

After a two months' tour of Switzerland and the Italian lakes, the Fishers found themselves at the Hotel Splendide in Paris, surrounded by people from the States. It was a relief to Fisher, after his somewhat bewildering experience at Baden, followed by a surfeit of stupendous and ghostly snow peaks, to be once more among those who discriminated between a straight flush and a crooked straight, and whose bosoms thrilled responsive to his own at the sight of the star-spangled banner. It was particularly agreeable for him to find at the Hotel Splendide, in a party of Easterners who had come over to see the Exposition, Miss Bella Ward, of Portland, a pretty and bright girl, affianced to his best friend in New York.

With much less pleasure, Fisher learned that the Baron Savitch was in Paris, fresh from the Berlin Congress, and that he was the lion of the hour with the select few who read between the written lines of politics and knew the dummies of diplomacy from the real players in the tremendous game. Dr Rapperschwyll was not with the baron. He was detained in Switzerland, at the death-bed of his aged mother.

This last piece of information was welcome to Fisher. The more he reflected upon the interview on the Mercuriusberg, the more strongly he felt it to be his intellectual duty to persuade himself that the whole affair was an illusion, not a reality. He would have been glad, even at the sacrifice of his confidence in his own astuteness, to believe that the Swiss doctor had been amusing himself at the expense of his credulity. But the remembrance of the scene in the baron's bedroom at the Badischer Hof was too vivid to leave the slightest ground for this theory. He was obliged to be content with the thought that he should soon place the broad Atlantic between himself and a creature so unnatural, so dangerous, so monstrously impossible as the Baron Savitch.

Hardly a week had passed before he was thrown again into the society of that impossible person.

The ladies of the American party met the Russian baron at a ball in the New Continental Hotel. They were charmed with his handsome face, his refinement of manner, his intelligence and wit. They met him again at the American Minister's, and, to Fisher's unspeakable consternation, the acquaintance thus established began to make rapid progress in the direction of intimacy. Baron Savitch became a frequent visitor at the Hotel Splendide.

Fisher does not like to dwell upon this period. For a month his peace of mind was rent alternately by apprehension and disgust. He is compelled to admit that the baron's demeanor toward himself was most friendly, although no allusion was made on either side to the incident at Baden. But the knowledge that no good could come to his friends from this association with a being in whom the moral principle had no doubt been supplanted by a system of cog-gear, kept him continually in a state of distraction. He would gladly have explained to his American friends the true character of the Russian, that he was not a man of healthy mental organization, but merely a marvel of mechanical ingenuity, constructed upon a principle subversive of all society as at present constituted – in short, a monster whose very existence must ever be revolting to right-minded persons with brains of honest gray and white. But the solemn promise to Dr Rapperschwyll sealed his lips.

A trifling incident suddenly opened his eyes to the alarming character of the situation, and filled his heart with a new horror.

One evening, a few days before the date designated for the departure of the American party from Havre for home, Fisher happened to enter the private parlor which was, by common consent, the headquarters of his set. At first he thought that the room was unoccupied. Soon he perceived, in the recess of a window, and partly obscured by the drapery of the curtain, the forms of the Baron Savitch and Miss Ward of Portland. They did not observe his entrance. Miss Ward's hand was in the baron's hand, and she was looking up into his handsome face with an expression which Fisher could not misinterpret.

Fisher coughed, and going to another window, pretended to be interested in affairs on the Boulevard. The couple emerged from the recess. Miss Ward's face was ruddy with confusion, and she immediately withdrew. Not a sign of embarrassment was visible on the baron's countenance. He greeted Fisher with perfect self-possession, and began to talk of the great balloon in the Place du Carrousel.

Fisher pitied but could not blame the young lady. He believed her still loyal at heart to her New York engagement. He knew that her loyalty could not be shaken by the blandishments of any man on earth. He recognized the fact that she was under the spell of a power more than human. Yet what would be the outcome? He could not tell her all; his promise bound him. It would be useless to appeal to the generosity of the baron; no human sentiments governed his inexorable purposes. Must the affair drift on while he stood tied and helpless? Must this charming and innocent girl be sacrificed to the transient whim of an automaton? Allowing that the baron's intentions were of the most honorable character, was the situation any less horrible? Marry a Machine! His own loyalty to his friend in New York, his regard for Miss Ward, alike loudly called on him to act with promptness.

And, apart from all private interest, did he not owe a plain duty to society, to the liberties of the world? Was Savitch to be permitted to proceed in the career laid out for him by his creator, Dr Rapperschwyll? He (Fisher) was the only man in the world in a position to thwart the ambitious programme. Was there ever greater need of a Brutus?

Between doubts and fears, the last days of Fisher's stay in Paris were wretched beyond description. On the morning of the steamer day he had almost made up his mind to act.

The train for Havre departed at noon, and at eleven o'clock the Baron Savitch made his appearance at the Hotel Splendide to bid farewell to his American friends. Fisher watched Miss Ward closely. There was a constraint in her manner which fortified his resolution. The baron incidentally remarked that he should make it his duty and pleasure to visit America within a very few months, and that he hoped then to renew the acquaintances now interrupted. As Savitch spoke, Fisher observed that his eyes met Miss Ward's, while the slightest possible blush colored her cheeks. Fisher knew that the case was desperate, and demanded a desperate remedy.

He now joined the ladies of the party in urging the baron to join them in the hasty lunch that was to precede the drive to the station. Savitch gladly accepted the cordial invitation. Wine he politely but firmly declined, pleading the absolute prohibition of his physician. Fisher left the room for an instant, and returned with the black bottle which had figured in the Baden episode.

'The Baron,' he said, 'has already expressed his approval of the noblest of our American products, and he knows that this beverage has good medical endorsement.' So saying, he poured the remaining contents of the Kentucky bottle into a glass, and presented it to the Russian.

Saviteh hesitated. His previous experience with the nectar was at the same time a temptation and a warning, yet he did not wish to seem discourteous. A chance remark from Miss Ward decided him.

'The baron,' she said, with a smile, 'will certainly not refuse to wish us *bon voyage* in the American fashion.'

Savitch drained the glass and the conversation turned to other matters. The carriages were already below. The parting comphments were being made, when Savitch suddenly pressed his hands to his forehead and clutched at the back of a chair. The ladies gathered around him in alarm.

'It is nothing,' he said faintly; 'a temporary dizziness.'

'There is no time to be lost,' said Fisher, pressing forward. 'The train leaves in twenty minutes. Get ready at once, and I will meanwhile attend to our friend.'

Fisher hurriedly led the baron to his own bedroom. Savitch fell back upon the bed. The Baden symptoms repeated themselves. In two minutes the Russian was unconscious.

Fisher looked at his watch. He had three minutes to spare. He turned the key in the lock of the door and touched the knob of the electric annunciator.

Then, gaining the mastery of his nerves by one supreme effort for self-control, Fisher pulled the deceptive wig and the black skullcap from the baron's head. 'Heaven forgive me if I am making a fearful mistake!' he thought. But I believe it to be best for ourselves and for the world.' Rapidly, but with a steady hand, he unscrewed the silver dome. The Mechanism lay exposed before his eyes. The baron groaned. Ruthlessly Fisher tore out the wondrous machine. He had no time and no inclination to examine it. He caught up a newspaper and hastily enfolded it. He thrust the bundle into his open traveling bag. Then he screwed the silver top firmly upon the baron's head, and replaced the skullcap and the wig.

All this was done before the servant answered the bell. 'The Baron Savitch is ill,' said Fisher to the attendant, when he came. 'There is no cause for alarm. Send at once to the Hotel de l'Athénée for his valet, Auguste.' In twenty seconds Fisher was in a cab, whirling toward the Station St Lazare.

When the steamship Pereire was well out at sea, with Ushant five hundred miles in her wake, and countless fathoms of water beneath her keel, Fisher took a newspaper parcel from his traveling bag. His teeth were firm set and his lips rigid. He carried the heavy parcel to the side of the ship and dropped it into the Atlantic. It made a little eddy in the smooth water, and sank out of sight. Fisher fancied that he heard a wild, despairing cry, and put his hands to his ears to shut out the sound. A gull came circling over the steamer – the cry may have been the gull's.

Fisher felt a light touch upon his arm. He turned quickly around. Miss Ward was standing at his side, close to the rail.

'Bless me, how white you are!' she said. 'What in the world have you been doing?'

'I have been preserving the liberties of two continents,' slowly replied Fisher, 'and perhaps saving your own peace of mind.'

'Indeed!' said she; 'and how have you done that?'

'I have done it,' was Fisher's grave answer, 'by throwing overboard the Baron Savitch.'

Miss Ward burst into a ringing laugh. 'You are sometimes too droll, Mr Fisher,' she said.

The Tachypomp

A mathematical demonstration

Edward Page Mitchell

There was nothing mysterious about Professor Surd's dislike for me. I was the only poor mathematician in an exceptionally mathematical class. The old gentleman sought the lecture-room every morning with eagerness, and left it reluctantly. For was it not a thing of joy to find seventy young men who, individually and collectively, preferred x to XX; who had rather differentiate than dissipate; and for whom the limbs of the heavenly bodies had more attractions than those of earthly stars upon the spectacular stage?

So affairs went on swimmingly between the Professor of Mathematics and the Junior Class at Polyp University. In every man of the seventy the sage saw the logarithm of a possible La Place, of a Sturm, or of a Newton. It was a delightful task for him to lead them through the pleasant valleys of conic sections, and beside the still waters of the integral calculus. Figuratively speaking, his problem was not a hard one. He had only to manipulate, and eliminate, and to raise to a higher power, and the triumphant result of examination day was assured.

But I was a disturbing element, a perplexing unknown quantity, which had somehow crept into the work, and which seriously threatened to impair the accuracy of his calculations. It was a touching sight to behold the venerable mathematician as he pleaded with me not so utterly to disregard precedent in the use of cotangents; or as he urged, with eyes almost tearful, that ordinates were dangerous things to trifle with. All in vain. More theorems went on to my cuff than into my head. Never did chalk do so much work to so little purpose. And, therefore, it came that Furnace Second was reduced to zero in Professor Surd's estimation. He looked upon me with all the horror which an unalgebraic nature could inspire. I have seen the professor walk around an entire square rather than meet the man who had no mathematics in his soul.

For Furnace Second were no invitations to Professor Surd's house. Seventy of the class supped in delegations around the periphery of the professor's tea-table. The seventy-first knew nothing of the charms of that perfect ellipse, with its twin bunches of fuchsias and geraniums in gorgeous precision at the two foci.

This, unfortunately enough, was no trifling deprivation. Not that I longed especially for segments of Mrs Surd's justly celebrated lemon pies; not that the spheroidal damsons of her excellent preserving had any marked allurements; not even that I yearned to hear the professor's jocose tabletalk about binomials, and chatty illustrations of abstruse paradoxes. The explanation is far different. Professor Surd had a daughter. Twenty years before, he made a proposition of marriage to the present Mrs S. He added a little corollary to his proposition not long after. The corollary was a girl.

Abscissa Surd was as perfectly symmetrical as Giotto's circle, and as pure, withal, as the mathematics her father taught. It was just when spring was coming to extract the roots of frozen-up vegetation that I fell in love with the corollary. That she herself was not indifferent I soon had reason to regard as a self-evident truth.

The sagacious reader will already recognize nearly all the elements necessary to a well-ordered plot. We have introduced a heroine, inferred a hero, and constructed a hostile parent after the most approved model. A movement for the story, a *deus ex machina*, is alone lacking. With considerable satisfaction I can promise a perfect novelty in this line, a *deus ex machina* never before offered to the public.

It would be discounting ordinary intelligence to say that I sought with unwearying assiduity to figure my way into the stern father's goodwill; that never did dullard apply himself to mathematics more patiently than I; that never did faithfulness achieve such meagre reward. Then I engaged a private tutor. His instructions met with no better success.

My tutor's name was Jean-Marie Rivarol. He was a unique Alsatian – though Gallic in name, thoroughly Teuton in nature; by birth a Frenchman, by education a German. His age was thirty; his profession, omniscience; the wolf at his door, poverty; the skeleton in his closet, a consuming but unrequited passion. The most recondite principles of practical science were his toys; the deepest intricacies of abstract science his diversions. Problems which were foreordained mysteries to me were to him as clear as Tahoe water. Perhaps this very fact will explain our lack of success in the relation of tutor and pupil; perhaps the failure is alone due to my own unmitigated stupidity. Rivarol had hung about the skirts of the University for several years; supplying his few wants by writing for scientific journals, or by giving assistance to students who, like myself, were characterized by a plethora of purse and a paucity of ideas; cooking, studying and sleeping in his attic lodgings; and prosecuting queer experiments all by himself.

We were not long discovering that even this eccentric genius could not transplant brains into my deficient skull. I gave over the struggle in despair. An unhappy year dragged its slow length around. A gloomy year it was, brightened only by occasional interviews with Abscissa, the Abbie of my thoughts and dreams.

Commencement Day was coming on apace. I was soon to go forth, with the rest of my class, to astonish and delight a waiting world. The professor seemed to avoid me more than ever. Nothing but the conventionalities, I think, kept him from shaping his treatment of me on the basis of unconcealed disgust.

At last, in the very recklessness of despair, I resolved to see him, plead with him, threaten him if need be, and risk all my fortunes on one desperate chance. I wrote him a somewhat defiant letter, stating my aspirations, and, as I flattered myself, shrewdly giving him a week to get over the first shock of horrified surprise. Then I was to call and learn my fate.

During the week of suspense I nearly worried myself into a fever. It was first crazy hope, and then saner despair. On Friday evening, when I presented myself at the professor's door, I was such a haggard, sleepy, dragged-out spectre, that even Miss Jocasta, the harsh-favored maiden sister of the Surd's, admitted me with commiserate regard, and suggested pennyroyal tea.

Professor Surd was at a faculty meeting. Would I wait?

Yes, till all was blue, if need be. Miss Abbie?

Abscissa had gone to Wheelborough to visit a school friend. The aged maiden hoped I would make myself comfortable, and departed to the unknown haunts which knew Jocasta's daily walk.

Comfortable! But I settled myself in a great uneasy chair and waited, with the contradictory spirit common to such junctures, dreading every step lest it should herald the man whom, of all men, I wished to see.

I had been there at least an hour, and was growing right drowsy.

At length Professor Surd came in. He sat down in the dusk opposite me, and I thought his eyes glinted with malignant pleasure as he said, abruptly: 'So, young man, you think you are a fit husband for my girl?'

I stammered some inanity about making up in affection what I lacked in merit; about my expectations, family and the like. He quickly interrupted me.

'You misapprehend me, sir. Your nature is destitute of those mathematical perceptions and acquirements which are the only sure foundations of character. You have no mathematics in you.

'You are fit for treason, stratagems, and spoils. – Shakespeare. Your narrow intellect cannot understand and appreciate a generous mind. There is all the difference between you and a Surd, if I may say it, which intervenes between an infinitesimal and an infinite. Why, I will even venture to say that you do not comprehend the Problem of the Couriers!'

I admitted that the Problem of the Couriers should be classed rather without my list of accomplishments than within it. I regretted this fault very deeply, and suggested amendment. I faintly hoped that my fortune would be such –

'Money!' he impatiently exclaimed. 'Do you seek to bribe a Roman senator with a penny whistle? Why, boy, do you parade your paltry wealth, which, expressed in mills, will not cover ten decimal places, before the eyes of a man who measures the planets in their orbits, and close crowds infinity itself?'

I hastily disclaimed any intention of obtruding my foolish dollars, and he went on: 'Your letter surprised me not a little. I thought *you* would be the last person in the world to presume to an alliance here. But having a regard for you personally' – and again I saw malice twinkle in his small eyes – 'and still more regard for Abscissa's happiness, I have decided that you shall have her – upon conditions. Upon conditions,' he repeated, with a half-smothered sneer.

'What are they?' cried I, eagerly enough. 'Only name them.'

'Well, sir,' he continued, and the deliberation of his speech seemed the very refinement of cruelty, 'you have only to prove yourself worthy an alliance with a mathematical family. You have only to accomplish a task which I shall presently give you. Your eyes ask me what it is. I will tell you. Distinguish yourself in that noble branch of abstract science in which, you cannot but acknowledge, you are at present sadly deficient. I will place Abscissa's hand in yours whenever you shall come before me and square the circle to my satisfaction. No! That is too easy a condition. I should cheat myself. Say perpetual motion. How do you like that? Do you think it lies within the range of your mental capabilities? You don't smile. Perhaps your talents don't run in the way of perpetual motion. Several people have found that theirs didn't. I'll give you another chance. We were speaking of the Problem of the Couriers, and I think you expressed a desire to know more of that ingenious question. You shall have the opportunity. Sit down some day, when you have nothing else to do, and discover the principle of infinite speed. I mean the law of motion which shall accomplish an infinitely great distance in an infinitely short time. You may mix in a little practical mechanics, if you choose. Invent some method of taking the tardy Courier over his road at the rate of sixty miles a minute. Demonstrate me this discovery (when you have made itl) mathematically, and approximate it practically, and Abscissa is yours. Until you can, I will thank you to trouble neither myself nor her.'

I could stand his mocking no longer. I stumbled mechanically out of the room, and out of the house. I even forgot my hat and gloves. For an hour I walked in the moonlight. Gradually I succeeded to a more hopeful frame of mind. This was due to my ignorance of mathematics. Had I understood the real meaning of what he asked, I should have been utterly despondent.

Perhaps this problem of sixty miles a minute was not so impossible after all. At any rate I could attempt, though I might not succeed. And Rivarol came to my mind. I would ask him. I would enlist his knowledge to accompany my own devoted perseverance. I sought his lodgings at once.

The man of science lived in the fourth story, back. I had never been in his room before. When I entered, he was in the act of filling a beer mug from a carboy labelled *aqua fortis*.

'Seat you,' he said. 'No, not in that chair. That is my Petty Cash Adjuster.' But he was a second too late. I had carelessly thrown myself into a chair of seductive appearance. To my utter amazement it reached out two skeleton arms and clutched me with a grasp against which I struggled in vain. Then a skull stretched itself over my shoulder and grinned with ghastly familiarity close to my face.

Rivarol came to my aid with many apologies. He touched a spring somewhere and the Petty Cash Adjuster relaxed its horrid hold. I placed myself gingerly in a plain cane-bottomed rocking-chair, which Rivarol assured me was a safe location.

'That seat,' he said, 'is an arrangement upon which I much felicitate myself. I made it at Heidelberg. It has saved me a vast deal of small annoyance. I consign to its embraces the friends who bore, and the visitors who exasperate, me. But it is never so useful as when terrifying some tradesman with an insignificant account. Hence the pet name which I have facetiously given it. They are invariably too glad to purchase release at the price of a bill receipted. Do you well apprehend the idea?'

While the Alsatian diluted his glass of *aqua fortis*, shook into it an infusion of bitters, and tossed off the bumper with apparent relish, I had time to look around the strange apartment.

The four corners of the room were occupied respectively by a turning lathe, a Rhumkorff Coil, a small steam engine and an orrery in stately motion. Tables, shelves, chairs and floor supported an odd aggregation of tools, retorts, chemicals, gas receivers, philosophical instruments, boots, flasks, paper-collar boxes, books diminutive and books of preposterous size. There were plaster busts of Aristotle, Archimedes, and Comte, while a great drowsy owl was blinking away, perched on the benign brow of Martin Farquhar Tupper. 'He always roosts there when he proposes to slumber,' explained my tutor. 'You are a bird of no ordinary mind. *Schlafen Sie wohl.*'

Through a closet door, half open, I could see a humanlike form covered with a sheet. Rivarol caught my glance.

'That,' said he, 'will be my masterpiece. It is a Microcosm, an Android, as yet only partially complete. And why not? Albertus Magnus constructed an image perfect to talk metaphysics and confute the schools. So did Sylvester II; so did Robertus Greathead. Roger Bacon made a brazen head that held discourses. But the first named of these came to destruction. Thomas Aquinas got wrathful at some of its syllogisms and smashed its head. The idea is reasonable enough. Mental action will yet be reduced to laws as definite as those which govern the physical. Why should not I accomplish a manikin which shall preach as original discourses as the Reverend Dr Allchin, or talk poetry as mechanically as Paul Anapest? My android can already work problems in vulgar fractions and compose sonnets. I hope to teach it the Positive Philosophy.'

Out of the bewildering confusion of his effects Rivarol produced two pipes and filled them. He handed one to me.

'And here,' he said, 'I live and am tolerably comfortable. When my coat wears out at the elbows I seek the tailor and am measured for another. When I am hungry I promenade myself to the butcher's and bring home a pound or so of steak, which I cook very nicely in three seconds by this oxy-hydrogen flame. Thirsty, perhaps, I send for a carboy of *aqua fortis*. But I have it charged, all charged. My spirit is above any small pecuniary transaction. I loathe your dirty greenbacks, and never handle what they call scrip.'

'But are you never pestered with bills?' I asked. 'Don't the creditors worry your life out?'

'Creditors!' gasped Rivarol. 'I have learned no such word in your very admirable language. He who will allow his soul to be vexed by creditors is a relic of an imperfect civilization. Of what use is science if it cannot avail a man who has accounts current? Listen. The moment you or anyone else enters the outside door this little electric bell sounds me warning. Every successive step on Mrs Grimler's staircase is a spy and informer vigilant for my benefit. The first step is trod upon. That trusty first step immediately telegraphs your weight. Nothing could be simpler. It is exactly like any platform scale. The weight is registered up here upon this dial. The second step records the size of my visitor's feet. The third his height, the fourth his complexion, and so on. By the time he reaches the top of the first flight I have a pretty accurate description of him right here at my elbow, and quite a margin of time for deliberation and action. Do you follow me? It is plain enough. Only the A B C of my science.'

'I see all that,' I said, 'but I don't see how it helps you any. The knowledge that a creditor is coming won't pay his bill. You can't escape unless you jump out of the window.'

Rivarol laughed softly. 'I will tell you. You shall see what becomes of any poor devil who goes to demand money of me – of a man of science. Ha! ha! It pleases me. I was seven weeks perfecting my Dun Suppressor. Did you know' – he whispered exultingly – 'did you know that there is a hole through the earth's center? Physicists have long suspected it; I was the first to find it. You have read how Rhuyghens, the Dutch navigator, discovered in Kerguellen's Land an abysmal pit which fourteen hundred fathoms of plumb-line failed to sound. Herr Tom, that hole has no bottom! It runs from one surface of the earth to the antipodal surface. It is diametric. But where is the antipodal spot? You stand upon it. I learned this by the merest chance. I was deep-digging in Mrs Grimler's cellar, to bury a poor cat I had sacrificed in a galvanic experiment, when the earth under my spade crumbled, caved in, and wonder-stricken I stood upon the brink of a yawning shaft. I dropped a coal-hod in. It went down, down, down, bounding and rebounding. In two hours and a quarter that coal-hod came up again. I caught it and restored it to the angry Grimler. Just think a minute. The coal-hod went down, faster and faster, till it reached the center of the earth. There it would stop, were it not for acquired momentum. Beyond the center its journey was relatively upward, toward the opposite surface of the globe. So, losing velocity, it went slower and slower till it reached that surface. Here it came to rest for a second and then fell back again, eight thousand odd miles, into my hands. Had I not interfered with it, it would have repeated its journey, time after time, each trip of shorter extent, like the diminishing oscillations of a pendulum, till it finally came to eternal rest at the center of the sphere. I am not slow to give a practical application to any such grand discovery. My Dun Suppressor was born of it. A trap, just outside my chamber door: a spring in here: a creditor on the trap: need I say more?'

'But isn't it a trifle inhuman?' I mildly suggested. 'Plunging an unhappy being into a perpetual journey to and from Kerguellen's Land, without a moment's warning.'

'I give them a chance. When they come up the first time I wait at the mouth of the shaft with a rope in hand. If they are reasonable and will come to terms, I fling them the line. If they perish, 'tis their own fault. Only,' he added, with a melancholy smile, 'the center is getting so plugged up with creditors that I am afraid there soon will be no choice whatever for'em.'

By this time I had conceived a high opinion of my tutor's ability. If anybody could send me waltzing through space at an infinite speed, Rivarol could do it. I filled my pipe and told him the story. He heard with grave and patient attention. Then, for full half an hour, he whiffed away in silence. Finally he spoke.

'The ancient cipher has overreached himself. He has given you a choice of two problems, both of which he deems insoluble. Neither of them is insoluble. The only gleam of intelligence Old Cotangent showed was when he said that squaring the circle was too easy. He was right. It would have given you your *Liebchen* in five minutes. I squared the circle before I discarded pantalets. I will show you the work – but it would be a digression, and you are in no mood for digressions. Our first chance, therefore, lies in perpetual motion. Now, my good friend, I will frankly tell you that, although I have compassed this interesting problem, I do not choose to use it in your behalf. I too, Herr Tom, have a heart. The loveliest of her sex frowns upon me. Her somewhat mature charms are not for Jean-Marie Rivarol. She has cruelly said that her years demand of me filial rather than connubial regard. Is love a matter of years or of eternity? This question did I put to the cold, yet lovely Jocasta.'

'Jocasta Surd!' I remarked in surprise, 'Abscissa's aunt!'

'The same,' he said, sadly. 'I will not attempt to conceal that upon the maiden Jocasta my maiden heart has been bestowed. Give me your hand, my nephew in affliction as in affection!'

Rivarol dashed away a not discreditable tear, and resumed: 'My only hope lies in this discovery of perpetual motion. It will give me the fame, the wealth. Can Jocasta refuse these? If she can, there is only the trap-door and – Kerguellen's Land!'

I bashfully asked to see the perpetual-motion machine. My uncle in affliction shook his head.

'At another time,' he said. 'Suffice it at present to say, that it is something upon the principle of a woman's tongue. But you see now why we must turn in your case to the alternative condition – infinite speed. There are several ways in which this may be accomplished, theoretically. By the lever, for instance. Imagine a lever with a very long and a very short arm. Apply power to the shorter arm which will move it with great velocity. The end of the long arm will move much faster. Now keep shortening the short arm and lengthening the long one, and as you approach infinity in their difference of length, you approach infinity in the speed of the long arm. It would be difficult to demonstrate this practically to the professor. We must seek another solution. Jean-Marie will meditate. Come to me in a fortnight. Goodnight. But stop! Have you the money – *das Geld*?'

'Much more than I need.'

'Good! Let us strike hands. Gold and Knowledge; Science and Love. What may not such a partnership achieve? We go to conquer thee, Abscissa. *Vorwärts!*'

When, at the end of a fortnight; I sought Rivarol's chamber, I passed with some little trepidation over the terminus of the Air Line to Kerguellen's Land, and evaded the extended arms of the Petty Cash Adjuster. Rivarol drew a mug of ale for me, and filled himself a retort of his own peculiar beverage.

'Come,' he said at length. 'Let us drink success to the TACHYPOMP.'

'The TACHYPOMP?'

'Yes. Why not? *Tachu*, quickly, and *pempo*, *pepompa*, to send. May it send you quickly to your wedding-day. Abscissa is yours. It is done. When shall we start for the prairies?'

'Where is it?' I asked, looking in vain around the room for any contrivance which might seem calculated to advance matrimonial prospects.

'It is here,' and he gave his forehead a significant tap. Then he held forth didactically.

'There is force enough in existence to yield us a speed of sixty miles a minute, or even more. All we need is the knowledge how to combine and apply it. The wise man will not attempt to make some great force yield some great speed. He will keep adding the little force to the little force, making each little force yield its little speed, until an aggregate of little forces shall be a great force, yielding an aggregate of little speeds, a great speed. The difficulty is not in aggregating the forces; it lies in the corresponding aggregation of the speeds. One musket ball will go, say a mile. It is not hard to increase the force of muskets to a thousand, yet the thousand musket balls will go no farther, and no faster, than the one. You see, then, where our trouble lies. We cannot readily add speed to speed, as we add force to force. My discovery is simply the utilization of a principle which extorts an increment of speed from each increment of power. But this is the metaphysics of physics. Let us be practical or nothing.

'When you have walked forward, on a moving train, from the rear car, toward the engine, did you ever think what you were really doing?'

'Why, yes, I have generally been going to the smoking car to have a cigar.'

'Tut, tut – not that! I mean, did it ever occur to you on such an occasion, that absolutely you were moving faster than the train? The train passes the telegraph poles at the rate of thirty miles an hour, say. You walk toward the smoking car at the rate of four miles an hour. Then you pass the telegraph poles at the rate of thirty-four miles. Your absolute speed is the speed of the engine, plus the speed of your own locomotion. Do you follow me?'

I began to get an inkling of his meaning, and told him so.

'Very well. Let us advance a step. Your addition to the speed of the engine is trivial, and the space in which you can exercise it, limited. Now suppose two stations, A and B, two miles distant by the track. Imagine a train of platform cars, the last car resting at station A. The train is a mile long, say. The engine is therefore within a mile of station B. Say the train can move a mile in ten minutes. The last car, having two miles to go, would reach B in twenty minutes, but the engine, a mile ahead, would get there in ten. You jump on the last car, at A, in a prodigious hurry to reach Abscissa, who is at B. If you stay on the last car it will be twenty long minutes before you see her. But the engine reaches B and the fair lady in ten. You will be a stupid reasoner, and an indifferent lover, if you don't put for the engine over those platform cars, as fast as your legs will carry you. You can run a mile, the length of the train, in ten minutes. Therefore, you reach Abscissa when the engine does, or in ten minutes – ten minutes sooner than if you had lazily sat down upon the rear car and talked politics with the brakeman. You have diminished the time by one half. You have added your speed to that of the locomotive to some purpose. *Nicht wahr?*'

I saw it perfectly; much plainer, perhaps, for his putting in the clause about Abscissa.

He continued, 'This illustration, though a slow one, leads up to a principle which may be carried to any extent. Our first anxiety will be to spare your legs and wind. Let us suppose that the two miles of track are perfectly straight, and make our train one platform car, a mile long, with parallel rails laid upon its top. Put a little dummy engine on these rails, and let it run to and fro along the platform car, while the platform car is pulled along the ground track. Catch the idea? The dummy takes your place. But it can run its mile much faster. Fancy that our locomotive is strong enough to pull the platform car over the two miles in two minutes.

The dummy can attain the same speed. When the engine reaches B in one minute, the dummy, having gone a mile a-top the platform car, reaches B also. We have so combined the speeds of those two engines as to accomplish two miles in one minute. Is this all we can do? Prepare to exercise your imagination.'

I lit my pipe.

'Still two miles of straight track, between A and B. On the track a long platform car, reaching from A to within a quarter of a mile of B. We will now discard ordinary locomotives and adopt as our motive power a series of compact magnetic engines, distributed underneath the platform car, all along its length.'

'I don't understand those magnetic engines.'

'Well, each of them consists of a great iron horseshoe, rendered alternately a magnet and not a magnet by an intermittent current of electricity from a battery, this current in its turn regulated by clockwork. When the horseshoe is in the circuit, it is a magnet, and it pulls its clapper toward it with enormous power. When it is out of the circuit, the next second, it is not a magnet, and it lets the clapper go. The clapper, oscillating to and fro, imparts a rotatory motion to a fly wheel, which transmits it to the drivers on the rails. Such are our motors. They are no novelty, for trial has proved them practicable.

'With a magnetic engine for every truck of wheels, we can reasonably expect to move our immense car, and to drive it along at a speed, say, of a mile a minute.

'The forward end, having but a quarter of a mile to go, will reach B in fifteen seconds. We will call this platform car number 1. On top of number 1 are laid rails on which another platform car, number 2, a quarter of a mile shorter than number 1, is moved in precisely the same way. Number 2, in its turn, is surmounted by number 3, moving independently of the tiers beneath, and a quarter of a mile shorter than number 2. Number 2 is a mile and a half long; number 3 a mile and a quarter. Above, on successive levels, are number 4, a mile long; number 5, three quarters of a mile; number 6, half a mile; number 7, a quarter of a mile, and number 8, a short passenger car, on top of all.'

'Each car moves upon the car beneath it, independently of all the others, at the rate of a mile a minute. Each car has its own magnetic engines. Well, the train being drawn up with the latter end of each car resting against a lofty bumping-post at A, Tom Furnace, the gentlemanly conductor, and Jean-Marie Rivarol, engineer, mount by a long ladder to the exalted number 8. The complicated mechanism is set in motion. What happens?'

'Number 8 runs a quarter of a mile in fifteen seconds and reaches the end of number 7. Meanwhile number 7 has run a quarter of a mile in the same time and reached the end of number 6; number 6, a quarter of a mile in fifteen seconds, and reached the end of number 5; number 5, the end of number 4; number 4, of number 3; number 3, of number 2; number 2, of number 1. And number 1, in fifteen seconds, has gone its quarter of a mile along the ground track, and has reached station B. All this has been done in fifteen seconds. Wherefore, numbers 1, 2, 3, 4, 5, 6, 7, and 8 come to rest against the bumping-post at B, at precisely the same second. We, in number 8, reach B just when number 1 reaches it. In other words, we accomplish two miles in fifteen seconds. Each of the eight cars, moving at the rate of a mile a minute, has contributed a quarter of a mile to our journey, and has done its work in fifteen seconds. All the eight did their work at once, during the same fifteen seconds. Consequently we have been whizzed through the air at the somewhat startling speed of seven and a half seconds to the mile. This is the Tachypomp. Does it justify the name?'

Although a little bewildered by the complexity of cars, I apprehended the general principle of the machine. I made a diagram, and understood it much better. 'You have merely improved on the idea of my moving faster than the train when I was going to the smoking car?'

'Precisely. So far we have kept within the bounds of the practicable. To satisfy the professor, you can theorize in something after this fashion: if we double the number of cars, thus decreasing by one half the distance which each has to go, we shall attain twice the speed. Each of the sixteen cars will have but one eighth of a mile to go. At the uniform rate we have adopted, the two miles can be done in seven and a half instead of fifteen seconds. With thirty-two cars, and a sixteenth of a mile, or twenty rods difference in their length, we arrive at the speed of a mile in less than two seconds; with sixty-four cars, each travelling but ten rods, a mile under the second. More than sixty miles a minute! If this isn't rapid enough for the professor, tell him to go on, increasing the number of his cars and diminishing the distance each one has to run. If sixty-four cars yield a speed of a mile inside the second, let him fancy a Tachypomp of six hundred and forty cars, and amuse himself calculating the rate of car number 640. Just whisper to him that when he has an infinite number of cars with an infinitesimal difference in their lengths, he will have obtained that infinite speed for which he seems to yearn. Then demand Abscissa.'

I wrung my friend's hand in silent and grateful admiration. I could say nothing.

'You have listened to the man of theory,' he said proudly. 'You shall now behold the practical engineer. We will go to the west of the Mississippi and find some suitably level locality. We will erect thereon a model Tachypomp. We will summon thereunto the professor, his daughter, and why not his fair sister Jocasta, as well? We will take them a journey which shall much astonish the venerable Surd. He shall place Abscissa's digits in yours and bless you both with an algebraic formula. Jocasta shall contemplate with wonder the genius of Rivarol. But we have much to do. We must ship to St Joseph the vast amount of material to be employed in the construction of the Tachypomp. We must engage a small army of workmen to effect that construction, for we are to annihilate time and space. Perhaps you had better see your bankers.'

I rushed impetuously to the door. There should be no delay.

'Stop! stop! *Um Gottes Willen*, stop!' shrieked Rivarol. 'I launched my butcher this morning and I haven't bolted the – '

But it was too late. I was upon the trap. It swung open with a crash, and I was plunged down, down, down! I felt as if I were falling through illimitable space. I remember wondering, as I rushed through the darkness, whether I should reach Kerguellen's Land or stop at the center. It seemed an eternity. Then my course was suddenly and painfully arrested.

I opened my eyes. Around me were the walls of Professor Surd's study. Under me was a hard, unyielding plane which I knew too well was Professor Surd's study floor. Behind me was the black, slippery, haircloth chair which had belched me forth, much as the whale served Jonah. In front of me stood Professor Surd himself, looking down with a not unpleasant smile.

'Good evening, Mr Furnace. Let me help you up. You look tired, sir. No wonder you fell asleep when I kept you so long waiting. Shall I get you a glass of wine? No? By the way, since receiving your letter I find that you are a son of my old friend, Judge Furnace. I have made inquiries, and see no reason why you should not make Abscissa a good husband.'

Still, I can see no reason why the Tachypomp should not have succeeded. Can you?

The Man Without a Body

Edward Page Mitchell

On a shelf in the old Arsenal Museum, in the Central Park, in the midst of stuffed hummingbirds, ermines, silver foxes, and bright-colored parakeets, there is a ghastly row of human heads. I pass by the mummied Peruvian, the Maori chief, and the Flathead Indian, to speak of a Caucasian head which has had a fascinating interest to me ever since it was added to the grim collection a little more than a year ago.

I was struck with the Head when I first saw it. The pensive intelligence of the features won me. The face is remarkable, although the nose is gone, and the nasal fossae are somewhat the worse for wear. The eyes are likewise wanting, but the empty orbs have an expression of their own. The parchmenty skin is so shriveled that the teeth show to their roots in the jaws. The mouth has been much affected by the ravages of decay, but what mouth there is displays character. It seems to say: 'Barring certain deficiencies in my anatomy, you behold a man of parts!' The features of the Head are of the Teutonic cast, and the skull is the skull of a philosopher. What particularly attracted my attention, however, was the vague resemblance which this dilapidated countenance bore to some face which had at some time been familiar to me – some face which lingered in my memory, but which I could not place.

After all, I was not greatly surprised, when I had known the Head for nearly a year, to see it acknowledge our acquaintance and express its appreciation of friendly interest on my part by deliberately winking at me as I stood before its glass case.

This was on a Trustees' Day, and I was the only visitor in the hall. The faithful attendant had gone to enjoy a can of beer with his friend, the superintendent of the monkeys.

The Head winked a second time, and even more cordially than before. I gazed upon its efforts with the critical delight of an anatomist. I saw the masseter muscle flex beneath the leathery skin. I saw the play of the glutinators, and the beautiful lateral movement of the internal platysma. I knew the Head was trying to speak to me. I noted the convulsive twitchings of the risorius and the zygomatic major, and knew that it was endeavoring to smile.

'Here,' I thought, 'is either a case of vitality long after decapitation, or an instance of reflex action where there is no diastaltic or excitor-motory system. In either case the phenomenon is unprecedented, and should be carefully observed. Besides, the Head is evidently well disposed toward me.' I found a key on my bunch which opened the glass door.

'Thanks,' said the Head. 'A breath of fresh air is quite a treat.'

'How do you feel?' I asked politely. 'How does it seem without a body?'

The Head shook itself sadly and sighed. 'I would give,' it said, speaking through its ruined nose, and for obvious reasons using chest tones sparingly, 'I would give both ears for a single leg. My ambition is principally ambulatory, and yet I cannot walk. I cannot even hop or waddle. I would fain travel, roam, promenade, circulate in the busy paths of men, but I am chained to this accursed shelf. I am no better off than these barbarian heads – I, a man of science! I am compelled to sit here on my neck and see sandpipers and storks all around me, with legs and to spare. Look at that infernal little Oedieneninus longpipes over there. Look at that miserable gray-headed porphyric. They have no brains, no ambition, no yearnings. Yet they have legs, legs, legs, in profusion.' He cast an envious glance across the alcove at the tantalizing limbs of the birds in question and added gloomily, 'There isn't even enough of me to make a hero for one of Wilkie Collins's novels.'

I did not exactly know how to console him in so delicate a matter, but ventured to hint that perhaps his condition had its compensations in immunity from corns and the gout.

'And as to arms,' he went on, 'there's another misfortune for you! I am unable to brush away the flies that get in here – Lord knows how – in the summertime. I cannot reach over and cuff that confounded Chinook mummy that sits there grinning at me like a jack-in-the-box. I cannot scratch my head or even blow my nose (his nose!) decently when I get cold in this thundering draft. As to eating and drinking, I don't care. My soul is wrapped up in science. Science is my bride, my divinity. I worship her footsteps in the past and hail the prophecy of her future progress. I – '

I had heard these sentiments before. In a flash I had accounted for the familiar look which had haunted me ever since I first saw the Head. 'Pardon me,' I said, 'you are the celebrated Professor Dummkopf?'

'That is, or was, my name,' he replied, with dignity.

'And you formerly lived in Boston, where you carried on scientific experiments of startling originality. It was you who first discovered how to photograph smell, how to bottle music, how to freeze the aurora borealis. It was you who first applied spectrum analysis to Mind.'

'Those were some of my minor achievements,' said the Head, sadly nodding itself – 'small when compared with my final invention, the grand discovery which was at the same time my greatest triumph and my ruin. I lost my Body in an experiment.'

'How was that?' I asked. 'I had not heard.'

'No,' said the Head. 'I being alone and friendless, my disappearance was hardly noticed. I will tell you.'

There was a sound upon the stairway. 'Hush!' cried the Head. 'Here comes somebody. We must not be discovered. You must dissemble.'

I hastily closed the door of the glass case, locking it just in time to evade the vigilance of the returning keeper, and dissembled by pretending to examine, with great interest, a nearby exhibit.

On the next Trustees' Day I revisited the museum and gave the keeper of the Head a dollar on the pretense of purchasing information in regard to the curiosities in his charge. He made the circuit of the hall with me, talking volubly all the while.

'That there,' he said, as we stood before the Head, 'is a relic of morality presented to the museum fifteen months ago. The head of a notorious murderer guillotined at Paris in the last century, sir.'

I fancied that I saw a slight twitching about the corners of Professor Dummkopf's mouth and an almost imperceptible depression of what was once his left eyelid, but he kept his face remarkably well under the circumstances. I dismissed my guide with many thanks for his intelligent services, and, as I had anticipated, he departed forthwith to invest his easily earned dollar in beer, leaving me to pursue my conversation with the Head.

'Think of putting a wooden-headed idiot like that,' said the professor, after I had opened his glass prison, 'in charge of a portion, however small, of a man of science – of the inventor of the Telepomp! Paris! Murderer! Last century, indeed!' and the Head shook with laughter until I feared that it would tumble off the shelf.

'You spoke of your invention, the Telepomp,' I suggested.

'Ah, yes,' said the Head, simultaneously recovering its gravity and its center of gravity; 'I promised to tell you how I happen to be a Man without a Body. You see that some three or four years ago I discovered the principle of the transmission of sound by electricity. My telephone, as I called it, would have been an invention of great practical utility if I had been spared to introduce it to the public. But, alas – '

'Excuse the interruption,' I said, 'but I must inform you that somebody else has recently accomplished the same thing. The telephone is a realized fact.'

'Have they gone any further?' he eagerly asked. 'Have they discovered the great secret of the transmission of atoms? In other words, have they accomplished the Telepomp?'

'I have heard nothing of the kind,' I hastened to assure him, 'but what do you mean?'

'Listen,' he said. 'In the course of my experiments with the telephone I became convinced that the same principle was capable of indefinite expansion. Matter is made up of molecules, and molecules, in their turn, are made up of atoms. The atom, you know, is the unit of being. The molecules differ according to the number and the arrangement of their constituent atoms. Chemical changes are effected by the dissolution of the atoms in the molecules and their rearrangements into molecules of another kind. This dissolution may be accomplished by chemical affinity or by a sufficiently strong electric current. Do you follow me?'

'Perfectly.'

'Well, then, following out this line of thought, I conceived a great idea. There was no reason why matter could not be telegraphed, or, to be etymologically accurate, "telepomped". It was only necessary to effect at one end of the line the disintegration of the molecules into atoms and to convey the vibrations of the chemical dissolution by electricity to the other pole, where a corresponding reconstruction could be effected from other atoms. As all atoms are alike, their arrangement into molecules of the same order, and the arrangement of those molecules into an organization similar to the original organization, would be practically a reproduction of the original. It would be a materialization – not in the sense of the spiritualists' cant, but in all the truth and logic of stern science. Do you still follow me?'

'It is a little misty,' I said, 'but I think I get the point. You would telegraph the Idea of the matter, to use the word Idea in Plato's sense.'

'Precisely. A candle flame is the same candle flame although the burning gas is continually changing. A wave on the surface of water is the same wave, although the water composing it is shifting as it moves. A man is the same man although there is not an atom in his body which was there five years before. It is the form, the shape, the Idea, that is essential. The vibrations that give individuality to matter may be transmitted to a distance by wire just as readily as the vibrations that give individuality to sound. So I constructed an instrument by which I could pull down matter, so to speak, at the anode and build it up again on the same plan at the cathode. This was my Telepomp.'

'But in practice – how did the Telepomp work?'

'To perfection! In my rooms on Joy Street, in Boston, I had about five miles of wire. I had no difficulty in sending simple compounds, such as quartz, starch, and water, from one room to another over this five-mile coil. I shall never forget the joy with which I disintegrated a three-cent postage stamp in one room and found it immediately reproduced at the receiving instrument in another. This success with inorganic matter emboldened me to attempt the same thing with a living organism. I caught a cat – a black and yellow cat – and I submitted him to a terrible current from my two-hundred-cup battery. The cat disappeared in a twinkling. I hastened to the next room and, to my immense satisfaction, found Thomas there, alive and purring, although somewhat astonished. It worked like a charm.'

'This is certainly very remarkable.'

'Isn't it? After my experiment with the cat, a gigantic idea took possession of me. If I could send a feline being, why not send a human being? If I could transmit a cat five miles by wire in an instant by electricity, why not transmit a man to London by Atlantic cable and with equal dispatch? I resolved to strengthen my already powerful battery and try the experiment. Like a thorough votary of science, I resolved to try the experiment on myself.

'I do not like to dwell upon this chapter of my experience,' continued the Head, winking at a tear which had trickled down on to his cheek and which I gently wiped away for him with my own pocket handkerchief. 'Suffice it that I trebled the cups in my battery, stretched my wire over housetops to my lodgings in Phillips Street, made everything ready, and with a solemn calmness born of my confidence in the theory, placed myself in the receiving instrument of the Telepomp at my Joy Street office. I was as sure that when I made the connection with the battery I would find myself in my rooms in Phillips Street as I was sure of my existence. Then I touched the key that let on the electricity. Alas!'

For some moments my friend was unable to speak. At last, with an effort, he resumed his narrative.

'I began to disintegrate at my feet and slowly disappeared under my own eyes. My legs melted away, and then my trunk and arms. That something was wrong, I knew from the exceeding slowness of my dissolution, but I was helpless. Then my head went and I lost all consciousness. According to my theory, my head, having been the last to disappear, should have been the first to materialize at the other end of the wire. The theory was confirmed in fact. I recovered consciousness. I opened my eyes in my Phillips Street apartments. My chin was materializing, and with great satisfaction I saw my neck slowly taking shape. Suddenly, and about at the third cervical vertebra, the process stopped. In a flash I knew the reason. I had forgotten to replenish the cups of my battery with fresh sulphuric acid, and there was not electricity enough to materialize the rest of me. I was a Head, but my body was Lord knows where.'

I did not attempt to offer consolation. Words would have been mockery in the presence of Professor Dummkopf's grief.

'What matters it about the rest?' he sadly continued. 'The house in Phillips Street was full of medical students. I suppose that some of them found my head, and knowing nothing of me or of the Telepomp, appropriated it for purposes of anatomical study. I suppose that they attempted to preserve it by means of some arsenical preparation. How badly the work was done is shown by my defective nose. I suppose that I drifted from medical student to medical student and from anatomical cabinet to anatomical cabinet until some would-be humorist presented me to this collection as a French murderer of the last century. For some months I knew nothing, and when I recovered consciousness I found myself here.

'Such,' added the Head, with a dry, harsh laugh, 'is the irony of fate!'

'Is there nothing I can do for you?' I asked, after a pause.

'Thank you,' the Head replied; 'I am tolerably cheerful and resigned. I have lost pretty much all interest in experimental science. I sit here day after day and watch the objects of zoological, ichthyological, ethnological, and conchological interest with which this admirable museum abounds. I don't know of anything you can do for me.

'Stay,' he added, as his gaze fell once more upon the exasperating legs of the Oedienenius longpipes opposite him. 'If there is anything I do feel the need of, it is outdoor exercise. Couldn't you manage in some way to take me out for a walk?'

I confess that I was somewhat staggered by this request, but promised to do what I could. After some deliberation, I formed a plan, which was carried out in the following manner.

I returned to the museum that afternoon just before the closing hour, and hid myself behind the mammoth sea cow, or *Manatus Americanus*. The attendant, after a cursory glance through the hall, locked up the building and departed. Then I came boldly forth and removed my friend from his shelf. With a piece of stout twine, I lashed his one or two vertebrae to the headless vertebrae of a skeleton moa. This gigantic and extinct bird of New Zealand is heavy-legged, full-breasted, tall as a man, and has huge, sprawling feet. My friend, thus provided with legs and arms, manifested extraordinary glee. He walked about, stamped his big feet, swung his wings, and occasionally broke forth into a hilarious shuffle. I was obliged to remind him that he must support the dignity of the venerable bird whose skeleton he had borrowed. I despoiled the African lion of his glass eyes, and inserted them in the empty orbits of the Head. I gave Professor Dummkopf a Fiji war lance for a walking stick, covered him with a Sioux blanket, and then we issued forth from the old arsenal into the fresh night air and the moonlight, and wandered arm in arm along the shores of the quiet lake and through the mazy paths of the Ramble.

The Clock That Went Backward

Edward Page Mitchell

A row of Lombardy poplars stood in front of my great-aunt Gertrude's house, on the bank of the Sheepscot River. In personal appearance my aunt was surprisingly like one of those trees. She had the look of hopeless anemia that distinguishes them from fuller blooded sorts. She was tall, severe in outline, and extremely thin. Her habiliments clung to her. I am sure that had the gods found occasion to impose upon her the fate of Daphne she would have taken her place easily and naturally in the dismal row, as melancholy a poplar as the rest.

Some of my earliest recollections are of this venerable relative. Alive and dead she bore an important part in the events I am about to recount: events which I believe to be without parallel in the experience of mankind.

During our periodical visits of duty to Aunt Gertrude in Maine, my cousin Harry and myself were accustomed to speculate much on her age. Was she sixty, or was she six score? We had no precise information; she might have been either. The old lady was surrounded by old-fashioned things. She seemed to live altogether in the past. In her short half-hours of communicativeness, over her second cup of tea, or on the piazza where the poplars sent slim shadows directly toward the east, she used to tell us stories of her alleged ancestors. I say alleged, because we never fully believed that she had ancestors.

A genealogy is a stupid thing. Here is Aunt Gertrude's, reduced to its simplest form.

Her great-great-grandmother (1599–1642) was a woman of Holland who married a Puritan refugee, and sailed from Leyden to Plymouth in the ship *Ann* in the year of our Lord 1632. This Pilgrim mother had a daughter, Aunt Gertrude's great-grandmother (1640–1718). She came to the Eastern District of Massachusetts in the early part of the last century, and was carried off by the Indians in the Penobscot wars. Her daughter (1680–1776) lived to see these colonies free and independent, and contributed to the population of the coming republic not less than nineteen stalwart sons and comely daughters. One of the latter (1735–1802) married a Wiscasset skipper engaged in the West India trade, with whom she sailed. She was twice wrecked at sea – once on what is now Seguin Island and once on San Salvador. It was on San Salvador that Aunt Gertrude was born.

We got to be very tired of hearing this family history. Perhaps it was the constant repetition and the merciless persistency with which the above dates were driven into our young ears that made us skeptics. As I have said, we took little stock in Aunt Gertrude's ancestors. They seemed highly improbable. In our private opinion the great-grandmothers and grandmothers and so forth were pure myths, and Aunt Gertrude herself was the principal in all the adventures attributed to them, having lasted from century to century while generations of contemporaries went the way of all flesh.

On the first landing of the square stairway of the mansion loomed a tall Dutch clock. The case was more than eight feet high, of a dark red wood, not mahogany, and it was curiously inlaid with silver. No common piece of furniture was this. About a hundred years ago there flourished in the town of Brunswick a horologist named Cary, an industrious and accomplished workman. Few well-to-do houses on that part of the coast lacked a Cary timepiece. But Aunt Gertrude's clock had marked the hours and minutes of two full centuries before the Brunswick artisan was born. It was running when William the Taciturn pierced the dikes to relieve Leyden. The name of the maker, Jan Lipperdam, and the date, 1572, were still legible in broad black letters and figures reaching quite across the dial. Cary's masterpieces were plebeian and recent beside this ancient aristocrat. The jolly Dutch moon, made to exhibit the phases over a landscape of windmills and polders, was cunningly painted. A skilled hand had carved the grim ornament at the top, a death's head transfixed by a two-edged sword. Like all timepieces of the sixteenth century, it had no pendulum. A simple Van Wyck escapement governed the descent of the weights to the bottom of the tall case.

But these weights never moved. Year after year, when Harry and I returned to Maine, we found the hands of the old clock pointing to the quarter past three, as they had pointed when we first saw them. The fat moon hung perpetually in the third quarter, as motionless as the death's head above. There was a mystery about the silenced movement and the paralyzed hands. Aunt Gertrude told us that the works had never performed their functions since a bolt of lightning entered the clock; and she showed us a black hole in the side of the case near the top, with a yawning rift that extended downward for several feet. This explanation failed to satisfy us. It did not account for the sharpness of her refusal when we proposed to bring over the watchmaker from the village, or for her singular agitation once when she found Harry on a stepladder, with a borrowed key in his hand, about to test for himself the clock's suspended vitality.

One August night, after we had grown out of boyhood, I was awakened by a noise in the hallway. I shook my cousin. 'Somebody's in the house,' I whispered.

We crept out of our room and on to the stairs. A dim light came from below. We held breath and noiselessly descended to the second landing. Harry clutched my arm. He pointed down over the banisters, at the same time drawing me back into the shadow.

We saw a strange thing.

Aunt Gertrude stood on a chair in front of the old clock, as spectral in her white nightgown and white nightcap as one of the poplars when covered with snow. It chanced that the floor creaked slightly under our feet. She turned with a sudden movement, peering intently into the darkness, and holding a candle high toward us, so that the light was full upon her pale face. She looked many years older than when I bade her good night. For a few minutes she was motionless, except in the trembling arm that held aloft the candle. Then, evidently reassured, she placed the light upon a shelf and turned again to the clock.

We now saw the old lady take a key from behind the face and proceed to wind up the weights. We could hear her breath, quick and short. She rested a band on either side of the case and held her face close to the dial, as if subjecting it to anxious scrutiny. In this attitude she remained for a long time. We heard her utter a sigh of relief, and she half turned toward us for a moment. I shall never forget the expression of wild joy that transfigured her features then.

The hands of the clock were moving; they were moving backward.

Aunt Gertrude put both arms around the clock and pressed her withered cheek against it. She kissed it repeatedly. She caressed it in a hundred ways, as if it had been a living and beloved thing. She fondled it and talked to it, using words which we could hear but could not understand. The hands continued to move backward.

Then she started back with a sudden cry. The clock had stopped. We saw her tall body swaying for an instant on the chair. She stretched out her arms in a convulsive gesture of terror and despair, wrenched the minute hand to its old place at a quarter past three, and fell heavily to the floor.

2

Aunt Gertrude's will left me her bank and gas stocks, real estate, railroad bonds, and city sevens, and gave Harry the clock. We thought at the time that this was a very unequal division, the more surprising because my cousin had always seemed to be the favorite. Half in seriousness we made a thorough examination of the ancient timepiece, sounding its wooden case for secret drawers, and even probing the not complicated works with a knitting needle to ascertain if our whimsical relative had bestowed there some codicil or other document changing the aspect of affairs. We discovered nothing.

There was testamentary provision for our education at the University of Leyden. We left the military school in which we had learned a little of the theory of war, and a good deal of the art of standing with our noses over our heels, and took ship without delay. The clock went with us. Before many months it was established in a corner of a room in the Breede Straat.

The fabric of Jan Lipperdam's ingenuity, thus restored to its native air, continued to tell the hour of quarter past three with its old fidelity. The author of the clock had been under the sod for nearly three hundred years. The combined skill of his successors in the craft at Leyden could make it go neither forward nor backward.

We readily picked up enough Dutch to make ourselves understood by the townspeople, the professors, and such of our eight hundred and odd fellow students as came into intercourse. This language, which looks so hard at first, is only a sort of polarized English. Puzzle over it a little while and it jumps into your comprehension like one of those simple cryptograms made by running together all the words of a sentence and then dividing in the wrong places.

The language acquired and the newness of our surroundings worn off, we settled into tolerably regular pursuits. Harry devoted himself with some assiduity to the study of sociology, with especial reference to the round-faced and not unkind maidens of Leyden. I went in for the higher metaphysics.

Outside of our respective studies, we had a common ground of unfailing interest. To our astonishment, we found that not one in twenty of the faculty or students knew or cared a sliver about the glorious history of the town, or even about the circumstances under which the university itself was founded by the Prince of Orange. In marked contrast with the general indifference was the enthusiasm of Professor Van Stopp, my chosen guide through the cloudiness of speculative philosophy.

This distinguished Hegelian was a tobacco-dried little old man, with a skullcap over features that reminded me strangely of Aunt Gertrude's. Had he been her own brother the facial resemblance could not have been closer. I told him so once, when we were together in the Stadthuis looking at the portrait of the hero of the siege, the Burgomaster Van der Werf. The professor laughed. 'I will show you what is even a more extraordinary coincidence,' said he; and, leading the way across the hall to the great picture of the siege, by Warmers, he pointed out the figure of a burgher participating in the defense. It was true. Van Stopp might have been the burgher's son; the burgher might have been Aunt Gertrude's father.

The professor seemed to be fond of us. We often went to his rooms in an old house in the Rapenburg Straat, one of the few houses remaining that antedate 1574. He would walk with us through the beautiful suburbs of the city, over straight roads lined with poplars that carried us back to the bank of the Sheepscot in our minds. He took us to the top of the ruined Roman tower in the center of the town, and from the same battlements from which anxious eyes three centuries ago had watched the slow approach of Admiral Boisot's fleet over the submerged polders, he pointed out the great dike of the Landscheiding, which was cut that the oceans might bring Boisot's Zealanders to raise the leaguer and feed the starving. He showed us the headquarters of the Spaniard Valdez at Leyderdorp, and told us how heaven sent a violent north-west wind on the night of the first of October, piling up the water deep where it had been shallow and sweeping the fleet on between Zoeterwoude and Zwieten up to the very walls of the fort at Lammen, the last stronghold of the besiegers and the last obstacle in the way of succor to the famishing inhabitants. Then he showed us where, on the very night before the retreat of the besieging army, a huge breach was made in the wall of Leyden, near the Cow Gate, by the Walloons from Lammen.

'Why!' cried Harry, catching fire from the eloquence of the professor's narrative, 'that was the decisive moment of the siege.'

The professor said nothing. He stood with his arms folded, looking intently into my cousin's eyes.

'For,' continued Harry, 'had that point not been watched, or had defense failed and the breach been carried by the night assault from Lammen, the town would have been burned and the people massacred under the eyes of Admiral Boisot and the fleet of relief. Who defended the breach?'

Van Stopp replied very slowly, as if weighing every word: 'History records the explosion of the mine under the city wall on the last night of the siege; it does not tell the story of the defense or give the defender's name. Yet no man that ever lived had a more tremendous charge than fate entrusted to this unknown hero. Was it chance that sent him to meet that unexpected danger? Consider some of the consequences had he failed. The fall of Leyden would have destroyed the last hope of the Prince of Orange and of the free states. The tyranny of Philip would have been reestablished. The birth of religious liberty and of self-government by the people would have been postponed, who knows for how many centuries? Who knows that there would or could have been a republic of the United States of America had there been no United Netherlands? Our University, which has given to the world Grotius, Scaliger, Arminius, and Descartes, was founded upon this hero's successful defense of the breach. We owe to him our presence here today. Nay, you owe to him your very existence. Your ancestors were of Leyden; between their lives and the butchers outside the walls he stood that night.'

The little professor towered before us, a giant of enthusiasm and patriotism. Harry's eyes glistened and his cheeks reddened.

'Go home, boys,' said Van Stopp, 'and thank God that while the burghers of Leyden were straining their gaze toward Zoeterwoude and the fleet, there was one pair of vigilant eyes and one stout heart at the town wall just beyond the Cow Gate!'

3

The rain was splashing against the windows one evening in the autumn of our third year at Leyden, when Professor Van Stopp honored us with a visit in the Breede Straat. Never had I seen the old gentleman in such spirits. He talked incessantly. The gossip of the town, the news of Europe, science, poetry, philosophy, were in turn touched upon and treated with the same high and good humor. I sought to draw him out on Hegel, with whose chapter on the complexity and interdependency of things I was just then struggling.

'You do not grasp the return of the Itself into Itself through its Other-self?' he said smiling. 'Well, you will, sometime.'

Harry was silent and preoccupied. His taciturnity gradually affected even the professor. The conversation flagged, and we sat a long while without a word. Now and then there was a flash of lightning succeeded by distant thunder.

'Your clock does not go,' suddenly remarked the professor. 'Does it ever go?'

'Never since we can remember,' I replied. 'That is, only once, and then it went backward. It was when Aunt Gertrude – '

Here I caught a warning glance from Harry. I laughed and stammered, 'The clock is old and useless. It cannot be made to go.'

'Only backward?' said the professor, calmly, and not appearing to notice my embarrassment. 'Well, and why should not a clock go backward? Why should not Time itself turn and retrace its course?'

He seemed to be waiting for an answer. I had none to give.

'I thought you Hegelian enough,' he continued, 'to admit that every condition includes its own contradiction. Time is a condition, not an essential. Viewed from the Absolute, the sequence by which future follows present and present follows past is purely arbitrary. Yesterday, today, tomorrow; there is no reason in the nature of things why the order should not be tomorrow, today, yesterday.'

A sharper peal of thunder interrupted the professor's speculations.

'The day is made by the planet's revolution on its axis from west to east. I fancy you can conceive conditions under which it might turn from east to west, unwinding, as it were, the revolutions of past ages. Is it so much more difficult to imagine Time unwinding itself; Time on the ebb, instead of on the flow; the past unfolding as the future recedes; the centuries countermarching; the course of events proceeding toward the Beginning and not, as now, toward the End?'

'But,' I interposed, 'we know that as far as we are concerned the – '

'We know!' exclaimed Van Stopp, with growing scorn. 'Your intelligence has no wings. You follow in the trail of Comte and his slimy brood of creepers and crawlers. You speak with amazing assurance of your position in the universe. You seem to think that your wretched little individuality has a firm foothold in the Absolute. Yet you go to bed tonight and dream into existence men, women, children, beasts of the past or of the future. How do you know that at this moment you yourself, with all your conceit of nineteenth-century thought, are anything more than a creature of a dream of the future, dreamed, let us say, by some philosopher of the sixteenth century? How do you know that you are anything more than a creature of a dream of the past, dreamed by some Hegelian of the twenty-sixth century? How do you know, boy, that you will not vanish into the sixteenth century or 2060 the moment the dreamer awakes?'

There was no replying to this, for it was sound metaphysics. Harry yawned. I got up and went to the window. Professor Van Stopp approached the clock.

'Ah, my children,' said he, 'there is no fixed progress of human events. Past, present, and future are woven together in one inextricable mesh. Who shall say that this old clock is not right to go backward?'

A crash of thunder shook the house. The storm was over our heads.

When the blinding glare had passed away, Professor Van Stopp was standing upon a chair before the tall timepiece. His face looked more than ever like Aunt Gertrude's. He stood as she had stood in that last quarter of an hour when we saw her wind the clock.

The same thought struck Harry and myself.

'Hold!' we cried, as he began to wind the works. 'It may be death if you – '

The professor's sallow features shone with the strange enthusiasm that had transformed Aunt Gertrude's.

'True,' he said, 'it may be death; but it may be the awakening. Past, present, future; all woven together! The shuttle goes to and fro, forward and back – '

He had wound the clock. The hands were whirling around the dial from right to left with inconceivable rapidity. In this whirl we ourselves seemed to be borne along. Eternities seemed to contract into minutes while lifetimes were thrown off at every tick. Van Stopp, both arms outstretched, was reeling in his chair. The house shook again under a tremendous peal of thunder. At the same instant a ball of fire, leaving a wake of sulphurous vapor and filling the room with dazzling light, passed over our heads and smote the clock. Van Stopp was prostrated. The hands ceased to revolve.

4

The roar of the thunder sounded like heavy cannonading. The lightning's blaze appeared as the steady light of a conflagration. With our hands over our eyes, Harry and I rushed out into the night.

Under a red sky people were hurrying toward the Stadthuis. Flames in the direction of the Roman tower told us that the heart of the town was afire. The faces of those we saw were haggard and emaciated. From every side we caught disjointed phrases of complaint or despair. 'Horseflesh at ten schillings the pound,' said one, 'and bread at sixteen schillings.' 'Bread indeed!' an old woman retorted: 'It's eight weeks gone since I have seen a crumb.' 'My little grandchild, the lame one, went last night.' 'Do you know what Gekke Betje, the washerwoman, did? She was starving. Her babe died, and she and her man – '

A louder cannon burst cut short this revelation. We made our way on toward the citadel of the town, passing a few soldiers here and there and many burghers with grim faces under their broad-brimmed felt hats.

'There is bread plenty yonder where the gunpowder is, and full pardon, too. Valdez shot another amnesty over the walls this morning.'

An excited crowd immediately surrounded the speaker. 'But the fleet!' they cried.

'The fleet is grounded fast on the Greenway polder. Boisot may turn his one eye seaward for a wind till famine and pestilence have carried off every mother's son of ye, and his ark will not be a rope's length nearer. Death by plague, death by starvation, death by fire and musketry – that is what the burgomaster offers us in return for glory for himself and kingdom for Orange.'

'He asks us,' said a sturdy citizen, 'to hold out only twenty-four hours longer, and to pray meanwhile for an ocean wind.'

'Ah, yes!' sneered the first speaker. 'Pray on. There is bread enough locked in Pieter Adriaanszoon van der Werf's cellar. I warrant you that is what gives him so wonderful a stomach for resisting the Most Catholic King.'

A young girl, with braided yellow hair, pressed through the crowd and confronted the malcontent. 'Good people,' said the maiden, 'do not listen to him. He is a traitor with a Spanish heart. I am Pieter's daughter. We have no bread. We ate malt cakes and rapeseed like the rest of you till that was gone. Then we stripped the green leaves from the lime trees and willows in our garden and ate them. We have eaten even the thistles and weeds that grew between the stones by the canal. The coward lies.'

Nevertheless, the insinuation had its effect. The throng, now become a mob, surged off in the direction of the burgomaster's house. One ruffian raised his hand to strike the girl out of the way. In a wink the cur was under the feet of his fellows, and Harry, panting and glowing, stood at the maiden's side, shouting defiance in good English at the backs of the rapidly retreating crowd.

With the utmost frankness she put both her arms around Harry's neck and kissed him.

'Thank you,' she said. 'You are a hearty lad. My name is Gertruyd van der Wert.'

Harry was fumbling in his vocabulary for the proper Dutch phrases, but the girl would not stay for compliments. 'They mean mischief to my father'; and she hurried us through several exceedingly narrow streets into a three-cornered market place dominated by a church with two spires. 'There he is,' she exclaimed, 'on the steps of St Pancras.'

There was a tumult in the market place. The conflagration raging beyond the church and the voices of the Spanish and Walloon cannon outside of the walls were less angry than the roar of this multitude of desperate men clamoring for the bread that a single word from their leader's lips would bring them. 'Surrender to the King!' they cried, 'or we will send your dead body to Lammen as Leyden's token of submission.'

One tall man, taller by half a head than any of the burghers confronting him, and so dark of complexion that we wondered how he could be the father of Gertruyd, heard the threat in silence. When the burgomaster spoke, the mob listened in spite of themselves.

'What is it you ask, my friends? That we break our vow and surrender Leyden to the Spaniards? That is to devote ourselves to a fate far more horrible than starvation. I have to keep the oath! Kill me, if you will have it so. I can die only once, whether by your hands, by the enemy's, or by the hand of God. Let us starve, if we must, welcoming starvation because it comes before dishonor. Your menaces do not move me; my life is at your disposal. Here, take my sword, thrust it into my breast, and divide my flesh among you to appease your hunger. So long as I remain alive expect no surrender.'

There was silence again while the mob wavered. Then there were mutterings around us. Above these rang out the clear voice of the girl whose hand Harry still held – unnecessarily, it seemed to me.

'Do you not feel the sea wind? It has come at last. To the tower! And the first man there will see by moonlight the full white sails of the prince's ships.'

For several hours I scoured the streets of the town, seeking in vain my cousin and his companion; the sudden movement of the crowd toward the Roman tower had separated us. On every side I saw evidences of the terrible chastisement that had brought this stout-hearted people to the verge of despair. A man with hungry eyes chased a lean rat along the bank of the canal. A young mother, with two dead babes in her arms, sat in a doorway to which they bore the bodies of her husband and father, just killed at the walls. In the middle of a deserted street I passed unburied corpses in a pile twice as high as my head. The pestilence had been there – kinder than the Spaniard, because it held out no treacherous promises while it dealt its blows.

Toward morning the wind increased to a gale. There was no sleep in Leyden, no more talk of surrender, no longer any thought or care about defense. These words were on the lips of everybody I met: 'Daylight will bring the fleet!'

Did daylight bring the fleet? History says so, but I was not a witness. I know only that before dawn the gale culminated in a violent thunderstorm, and that at the same time a muffled explosion, heavier than the thunder, shook the town. I was in the crowd that watched from the

Roman Mound for the first signs of the approaching relief. The concussion shook hope out of every face. 'Their mine has reached the wall!' But where? I pressed forward until I found the burgomaster, who was standing among the rest. 'Quick!' I whispered. 'It is beyond the Cow Gate, and this side of the Tower of Burgundy.' He gave me a searching glance, and then strode away, without making any attempt to quiet the general panic. I followed close at his heels.

It was a tight run of nearly half a mile to the rampart in question. When we reached the Cow Gate this is what we saw.

A great gap, where the wall had been, opening to the swampy fields beyond: in the moat, outside and below, a confusion of upturned faces, belonging to men who struggled like demons to achieve the breach, and who now gained a few feet and now were forced back; on the shattered rampart a handful of soldiers and burghers forming a living wall where masonry had failed; perhaps a double handful of women and girls, serving stones to the defenders and boiling water in buckets, besides pitch and oil and unslaked lime, and some of them quoiting tarred and burning hoops over the necks of the Spaniards in the moat; my cousin Harry leading and directing the men; the burgomaster's daughter Gertruyd encouraging and inspiring the women.

But what attracted my attention more than anything else was the frantic activity of a little figure in black, who, with a huge ladle, was showering molten lead on the heads of the assailing party. As he turned to the bonfire and kettle which supplied him with ammunition, his features came into the full light. I gave a cry of surprise: the ladler of molten lead was Professor Van Stopp.

The burgomaster Van der Werf turned at my sudden exclamation. 'Who is that?' I said. 'The man at the kettle?'

'That,' replied Van der Werf, 'is the brother of my wife, the clock-maker Jan Lipperdam.'

The affair at the breach was over almost before we had had time to grasp the situation. The Spaniards, who had overthrown the wall of brick and stone, found the living wall impregnable. They could not even maintain their position in the moat; they were driven off into the darkness. Now I felt a sharp pain in my left arm. Some stray missile must have hit me while we watched the fight.

'Who has done this thing?' demanded the burgomaster. 'Who is it that has kept watch on today while the rest of us were straining fools' eyes toward tomorrow?'

Gertruyd van der Werf came forward proudly, leading my cousin. 'My father,' said the girl, 'he has saved my life.'

'That is much to me,' said the burgomaster, 'but it is not all. He has saved Leyden and he has saved Holland.'

I was becoming dizzy. The faces around me seemed unreal. Why were we here with these people? Why did the thunder and lightning forever continue? Why did the clockmaker, Jan Lipperdam, turn always toward me the face of Professor Van Stopp? 'Harry!' I said, 'come back to our rooms.'

But though he grasped my hand warmly his other hand still held that of the girl, and he did not move. Then nausea overcame me. My head swam, and the breach and its defenders faded from sight.

5

Three days later I sat with one arm bandaged in my accustomed seat in Van Stopp's lecture room. The place beside me was vacant.

'We hear much,' said the Hegelian professor, reading from a notebook in his usual dry, hurried tone, 'of the influence of the sixteenth century upon the nineteenth. No philosopher, as far as I am aware, has studied the influence of the nineteenth century upon the sixteenth. If cause produces effect, does effect never induce cause? Does the law of heredity, unlike all other laws of this universe of mind and matter, operate in one direction only? Does the descendant owe everything to the ancestor, and the ancestor nothing to the descendant? Does destiny, which may seize upon our existence, and for its own purposes bear us far into the future, never carry us back into the past?'

I went back to my rooms in the Breede Straat, where my only companion was the silent clock.

The Senator's Daughter

Edward Page Mitchell

1 *The small gold box*

On the evening of the fourth of March, year of grace nineteen hundred and thirty-seven, Mr Daniel Webster Wanlee devoted several hours to the consummation of a rather elaborate toilet. That accomplished, he placed himself before a mirror and critically surveyed the results of his patient art.

The effect appeared to give him satisfaction. In the glass he beheld a comely young man of thirty, something under the medium stature, faultlessly attired in evening dress. The face was a perfect oval, the complexion delicate, the features refined. The high cheekbones and a slight elevation of the outer corners of the eyes, the short upper lip, from which drooped a slender but aristocratic mustache, the tapered fingers of the hand, and the remarkably small feet, confined tonight in dancing pumps of polished red morocco, were all unmistakable heirlooms of a pure Mongolian ancestry. The long, stiff, black hair, brushed straight back from the forehead, fell in profusion over the neck and shoulders. Several rich decorations shone on the breast of the black broadcloth coat. The knickerbocker breeches were tied at the knees with scarlet ribbons. The stockings were of a flowered silk. Mr Wanlee's face sparked with intelligent good sense; his figure poised itself before the glass with easy grace.

A soft, distinct utterance, filling the room yet appearing to proceed from no particular quarter, now attracted Mr Wanlee's attention. He at once recognized the voice of his friend, Mr Walsingham Brown.

'How are we off for time, old fellow?'

'It's getting late,' replied Mr Wanlee, without turning his face from the mirror. 'You had better come over directly.'

In a very few minutes the curtains at the entrance to Mr Wanlee's apartments were unceremoniously pulled open, and Mr Walsingham Brown strode in. The two friends cordially shook hands.

'How is the honorable member from the Los Angeles district?' inquired the newcomer gaily. 'And what is there new in Washington society? Prepared to conquer tonight, I see. What's all this? Red ribbons and flowered silk hose! Ah, Wanlee. I thought you had outgrown these frivolities!'

The faintest possible blush appeared on Mr Daniel Webster Wanlee's cheeks. 'It is cool tonight?' he asked, changing the subject.

'Infernally cold,' replied his friend. 'I wonder you have no snow here. It is snowing hard in New York. There were at least three inches on the ground just now when I took the Pneumatic.'

'Pull an easy chair up to the thermo-electrode,' said the Mongolian. 'You must get the New York climate thawed out of your joints if you expect to waltz creditably. The Washington women are critical in that respect.'

Mr Walsingham Brown pushed a comfortable chair toward a sphere of shining platinum that stood on a crystal pedestal in the center of the room. He pressed a silver button at the base, and the metal globe began to glow incandescently. A genial warmth diffused itself through the apartment. 'That feels good,' said Mr Walsingham Brown, extending both hands to catch the heat from the thermo-electrode.

'By the way,' he continued, 'you haven't accounted to me yet for the scarlet bows. What would your constituents say if they saw you thus – you, the impassioned young orator of the Pacific slope; the thoughtful student of progressive statesmanship; the mainstay and hope of the Extreme Left; the thorn in the side of conservative Vegetarianism; the *bête noire* of the whole Indo-European gang – you, in knee ribbons and florid extensions, like a club man at a fashionable Harlem hop, or a – '

Mr Brown interrupted himself with a hearty but goodnatured laugh.

Mr Wanlee seemed ill at ease. He did not reply to his friend's raillery. He cast a stealthy glance at his knees in the mirror, and then went to one side of the room, where an endless strip of printed paper, about three feet wide, was slowly issuing from between noiseless rollers and falling in neat folds into a willow basket placed on the floor to receive it. Mr Wanlee bent his head over the broad strip of paper and began to read attentively.

'You take the *Contemporaneous News*, I suppose,' said the other.

'No, I prefer the *Interminable Intelligencer*,' replied Mr Wanlee. 'The *Contemporaneous* is too much of my own way of thinking. Why should a sensible man ever read the organ of his own party? How much wiser it is to keep posted on what your political opponents think and say.'

'Do you find anything about the event of the evening?'

'The ball has opened,' said Mr Wanlee, 'and the floor of the Capitol is already crowded. Let me see,' he continued, beginning to read aloud: ' "The wealth, the beauty, the chivalry, and the brains of the nation combine to lend unprecedented luster to the Inauguration Ball, and the brilliant success of the new Administration is assured beyond all question."'

'That is encouraging logic,' Mr Brown remarked.

' "President Trimbelly has just entered the rotunda, escorting his beautiful and stately wife, and accompanied by ex-President Riley, Mrs Riley, and Miss Norah Riley. The illustrious group is of course the cynosure of all eyes. The utmost cordiality prevails among statesmen of all shades of opinion. For once, bitter political animosities seem to have been laid aside with the ordinary habiliments of everyday wear. Conspicuous among the guests are some of the most distinguished radicals of the opposition. Even General Quong, the defeated Mongol-Vegetarian candidate, is now proceeding across the rotunda, leaning on the arm of the Chinese ambassador, with the evident intention of paying his compliments to his successful rival. Not the slightest trace of resentment or hostility is visible upon his strongly marked Asiatic features."

'The hero of the Battle of Cheyenne can afford to be magnanimous,' remarked Mr Wanlee, looking up from the paper.

'True,' said Mr Walsingham Brown, warmly. 'The noble old hoodlum fighter has settled forever the question of the equality of your race. The presidency could have added nothing to his fame.'

Mr Wanlee went on reading: ' "The toilets of the ladies are charming. Notable among those which attract the reportorial eye are the peacock feather train of the Princess Hushyida; the mauve – "'

'Cut that,' suggested Mr Brown. 'We shall see for ourselves presently. And give me a dinner, like a good fellow. It occurs to me that I have eaten nothing for fifteen days.'

The Honorable Mr Wanlee drew from his waistcoat pocket a small gold box, oval in form. He pressed a spring and the lid flew open. Then he handed the box to his friend. It contained a number of little gray pastilles, hardly larger than peas. Mr Brown took one between his thumb and forefinger and put it into his mouth. 'Thus do I satisfy mine hunger,' he said, 'or, to borrow the language of the opposition orators, thus do I lend myself to the vile and degrading practice, subversive of society as at present constituted, and outraging the very laws of nature.'

Mr Wanlee was paying no attention. With eager gaze he was again scanning the columns of the *Interminable Intelligencer*. As if involuntarily, he read aloud: ' " – Secretary Quimby and Mrs Quimby, Count Schneeke, the Austrian ambassador, Mrs Hoyette and the Misses Hoyette of New York, Senator Newton of Massachusetts, whose arrival with his lovely daughter is causing no small sensation – "'

He paused, stammering, for he became aware that his friend was regarding him earnestly. Coloring to the roots of his hair, he affected indifference and began to read again: ' "Senator Newton of Massachusetts, whose arrival with his lovely – " '

'I think, my dear boy,' said Mr Walsingham Brown, with a smile, 'that it is high time for us to proceed to the Capitol.'

2 *The ball at the Capitol*

Through a brilliant throng of happy men and charming women, Mr Wanlee and his friend made their way into the rotunda of the Capitol. Accustomed as they both were to the spectacular efforts which society arranged for its own delectation, the young men were startled by the enchantment of the scene before them. The dingy historical panorama that girds the rotunda was hidden behind a wall of flowers. The heights of the dome were not visible, for beneath that was a temporary interior dome of red roses and white lilies, which poured down from the concavity a continual and almost oppressive shower of fragrance. From the center of the floor ascended to the height of forty or fifty feet a single jet of water, rendered intensely luminous by the newly discovered hydrolectric process, and flooding the room with a light ten times brighter than daylight, yet soft and grateful as the light of the moon. The air pulsated with music, for every flower in the dome overhead gave utterance to the notes which Ratibolial, in the Conservatoire at Paris, was sending across the Atlantic from the vibrant tip of his baton.

The friends had hardly reached the center of the rotunda, where the hydrolectric fountain threw aloft its jet of blazing water, and where two opposite streams of promenaders from the north and the south wings of the Capitol met and mingled in an eddy of polite humanity, before Mr Walsingham Brown was seized and led off captive by some of his Washington acquaintances.

Wanlee pushed on, scarcely noticing his friend's defection. He directed his steps wherever the crowd seemed thickest, casting ahead and on either side of him quick glances of inquiry, now and then exchanging bows with people whom he recognized, but pausing only once to enter into conversation. That was when he was accosted by General Quong, the leader of the Mongol-Vegetarian party and the defeated candidate for President in the campaign of 1936. The veteran spoke familiarly to the young congressman and detained him only a moment. 'You are looking for somebody, Wanlee,' said General Quong, kindly. 'I see it in your eyes. I grant you leave of absence.'

Mr Wanlee proceeded down the long corridor that leads to the Senate chamber, and continued there his eager search. Disappointed, he turned back, retraced his steps to the rotunda, and went to the other extremity of the Capitol. The Hall of Representatives was reserved for the dancers. From the great clock above the Speaker's desk issued the music of a waltz, to the rhythm of which several hundred couples were whirling over the polished floor.

Wanlee stood at the door, watching the couples as they moved before him in making the circuit of the hall. Presently his eyes began to sparkle. They were resting upon the beautiful face and supple figure of a girl in white satin, who waltzed in perfect form with a young man, apparently an Italian. Wanlee advanced a step or two, and at the same instant the lady became aware of his presence. She said a word to her partner, who immediately relinquished her waist.

'I have been expecting you this age,' said the girl, holding out her hand to Wanlee. 'I am delighted that you have come.'

'Thank you, Miss Newton,' said Wanlee.

'You may retire, Francesco,' she continued, turning to the young man who had just been her partner. 'I shall not need you again.'

The young man addressed as Francesco bowed respectfully and departed without a word.

'Let us not lose this lovely waltz,' said Miss Newton, putting her hand upon Wanlee's shoulder. 'It will be my first this evening.'

'Then you have not danced?' asked Wanlee, as they glided off together.

'No, Daniel,' said Miss Newton, 'I haven't danced with any gentlemen.'

The Mongolian thanked her with a smile.

'I have made good use of Francesco, however,' she went on. 'What a blessing a competent protectional partner is! Only think, our grand-mothers, and even our mothers, were obliged to sit dismally around the walls waiting the pleasure of their high and mighty –'

She paused suddenly, for a shade of annoyance had fallen upon her partner's face. 'Forgive me,' she whispered, her head almost upon his shoulder. 'Forgive me if I have wounded you. You know, love, that I would not –'

'I know it,' he interrupted. 'You are too good and too noble to let that weigh a feather's weight in your estimation of the Man. You never pause to think that my mother and my grandmother were not accustomed to meet your mother and your grandmother in society – for the very excellent reason,' he continued, with a little bitterness in his tone, 'that my mother had her hands full in my father's laundry in San Francisco, while my grandmother's social ideas hardly extended beyond the cabin of our ancestral san-pan on the Yangtze Kiang. *You* do not care for that. But there are others – '

They waltzed on for some time in silence, he thoughtful and moody, and she, sympathetically concerned.

'And the senator; where is he tonight?' asked Wanlee at last.

'Papa!' said the girl, with a frightened little glance over her shoulder. 'Oh! Papa merely made his appearance here to bring me and because it was expected of him. He has gone home to work on his tiresome speech against the vegetables.'

'Do you think,' asked Wanlee, after a few minutes, whispering the words very slowly and very low, 'that the senator has any suspicion?'

It was her turn now to manifest embarrassment. 'I am very sure,' she replied, 'that Papa has not the least idea in the world of it all. And that is what worries me. I constantly feel that we are walking together on a volcano. I know that we are right, and that heaven means it to be just as it is; yet, I cannot help trembling in my happiness. You know as well as I do the antiquated and absurd notions that still prevail in Massachusetts, and that Papa is a conservative among the conservatives. He respects your ability, that I discovered long ago. Whenever you speak in the House, he reads your remarks with great attention. I think,' she continued with a forced laugh, 'that your arguments bother him a good deal.'

'This must have an end, Clara,' said the Chinaman, as the music ceased and the waltzers stopped. 'I cannot allow you to remain a day longer in an equivocal position. My honor and your own peace of mind require that there shall be an explanation to your father. Have you the courage to stake all our happiness on one bold move?'

'I have courage,' frankly replied the girl, 'to go with you before my father and tell him all. And furthermore,' she continued, slightly pressing his arm and looking into his face with a charming blush, 'I have courage even beyond that.'

'You beloved little Puritan!' was his reply.

As they passed out of the Hall of Representatives, they encountered Mr Walsingham Brown with Miss Hoyette of New York. The New York lady spoke cordially to Miss Newton, but recognized Wanlee with a rather distant bow. Wanlee's eyes sought and met those of his friend. 'I may need your counsel before morning,' he said in a low voice.

'All right, my dear fellow,' said Mr Brown. 'Depend on me.' And the two couples separated.

The Mongolian and his Massachusetts sweetheart drifted with the tide into the supper room. Both were preoccupied with their own thoughts.

Almost mechanically, Wanlee led his companion to a corner of the supper room and established her in a seat behind a screen of palmettos, sheltered from the observation of the throne.

'It is nice of you to bring me here,' said the girl, 'for I am hungry after our waltz.'

Intimate as their souls had become, this was the first time that she had ever asked him for food. It was an innocent and natural request, yet Wanlee shuddered when he heard it, and bit his under lip to control his agitation. He looked from behind the palmettos at the tables heaped with delicate viands and surrounded by men, eagerly pressing forward to obtain refreshment for the ladies in their care. Wanlee shuddered again at the spectacle. After a momentary hesitation he returned to Miss Newton, seated himself beside her, and taking her hand in his, began to speak deliberately and earnestly.

'Clara,' he said, 'I am going to ask you for a final proof of your affection. Do not start and look alarmed, but hear me patiently. If, after hearing me, you still bid me bring you a *pâté*, or the wing of a fowl, or a salad, or even a plate of fruit, I will do so, though it wrench the heart in my bosom. But first listen to what I have to say.'

'Certainly I will listen to all you have to say,' she replied.

'You know enough of the political theories that divide parties,' he went on, nervously examining the rings on her slender fingers, 'to be aware that what I conscientiously believe to be true is very different from what you have been educated to believe.'

'I know,' said Miss Newton, 'that you are a Vegetarian and do not approve the use of meat. I know that you have spoken eloquently in the House on the right of every living being to protection in its life, and that that is the theory of your party. Papa says that it is demagogy – that the opposition parade an absurd and sophistical theory in order to win votes and get themselves into office. Still, I know that a great many excellent people, friends of ours in Massachusetts, are coming to believe with you, and, of course, loving you as I do, I have the firmest faith in the honesty of your convictions. You are not a demagogue, Daniel. You are above pandering to the radicalism of the rabble. Neither my father nor all the world could make me think the contrary.'

Mr Daniel Webster Wanlee squeezed her hand and went on: 'Living as you do in the most ultra-conservative of circles, dear Clara, you have had no opportunity to understand the tremendous significance and force of the movement that is now sweeping over the land, and of which I am a very humble representative. It is something more than a political agitation; it is an upheaval and reorganization of society on the basis of science and abstract right. It is fit and proper that I, belonging to a race that has only been emancipated and enfranchised by the march of time, should stand in the advance guard – in the forlorn hope, it may be – of the new revolution.'

His flaming eyes were now looking directly into hers. Although a little troubled by his earnestness, she could not hide her proud satisfaction in his manly bearing.

'We believe that every animal is born free and equal,' he said. 'That the humblest polyp or the most insignificant mollusk has an equal right with you or me to life and the enjoyment of happiness. Why, are we not all brothers? Are we not all children of a common evolution? What are we human animals but the more favored members of the great family? Is Senator Newton of Massachusetts further removed in intelligence from the Australian bushman, than the Australian bushman or the Flathead Indian is removed from the ox which Senator Newton orders slain to yield food for his family? Have we a right to take the paltriest life that evolution has given? Is not the butchery of an ox or of a chicken murder – nay, fratricide – in the view of absolute justice? Is it not cannibalism of the most repulsive and cowardly sort to prey upon the flesh of our defenseless brother animals, and to sacrifice their lives and rights to an unnatural appetite that has no foundation save in the habit of long ages of barbarian selfishness?'

'I have never thought of these things,' said Miss Clara, slowly. 'Would you elevate them to the suffrage – I mean the ox and the chicken and the baboon?'

'There speaks the daughter of the senator from Massachusetts,' cried Wanlee. 'No, we would not give them the suffrage – at least, not at present. The right to live and enjoy life is a natural, an inalienable right. The right to vote depends upon conditions of society and of individual intelligence. The ox, the chicken, the baboon are not yet prepared for the ballot. But they are voters in embryo; they are struggling up through the same process that our own ancestors underwent, and it is a crime, an unnatural, horrible thing, to cut off their career, their future, for the sake of a meal!'

'Those are noble sentiments, I must admit,' said Miss Newton, with considerable enthusiasm.

'They are the sentiments of the Mongol-Vegetarian party,' said Wanlee. 'They will carry the country in 1940, and elect the next President of the United States.'

'I admire your earnestness,' said Miss Newton after a pause, 'and I will not grieve you by asking you to bring me even so much as a chicken wing.

I do not think I could eat it now, with your words still in my ears. A little fruit is all that I want.'

'Once more,' said Wanlee, taking the tall girl's hand again, 'I must request you to consider. The principles, my dearest, that I have already enunciated are the principles of the great mass of our party. They are held even by the respectable, easygoing, not oversensitive voters such as constitute the bulk of every political organization. But there are a few of us who stand on ground still more advanced. We do not expect to bring the laggards up to our line for years, perhaps in our lifetime. We simply carry the accepted theory to its logical conclusions and calmly await ultimate results.'

'And what is your ground, pray?' she inquired. 'I cannot see how anything could be more dreadfully radical – that is, more bewildering and generally upsetting at first sight – than the ground which you just took.'

'If what I have said is true, and I believe it to be true, then how can we escape including the Vegetable Kingdom in our proclamation of emancipation from man's tyranny? The tree, the plant, even the fungus, have they not individual life, and have they not also the right to live?'

'But how – '

'And indeed,' continued the Chinaman, not noticing the interruption, 'who can say where vegetable life ends and animal life begins? Science has tried in vain to draw the boundary line. I hold that to uproot a potato is to destroy an existence certainly, although perhaps remotely akin to ours. To pluck a grape is to maim the living vine; and to drink the juice of that grape is to outrage consanguinity. In this broad, elevated view of the matter it becomes a duty to refrain from vegetable food. Nothing less than the vital principal itself becomes the test and tie of universal brotherhood. "All living things are born free and equal, and have a right to existence and the enjoyment of existence." Is not that a beautiful thought?'

'It is a beautiful thought,' said the maiden. 'But – I know you will think me dreadfully cold, and practical, and unsympathetic – but how are *we* to live? Have *we* no right, too, to existence? Must we starve to death in order to establish the theoretical right of vegetables not to be eaten?'

'My dear love,' said Wanlee, 'that would be a serious and perplexing question, had not the latest discovery of science already solved it for us.'

He took from his waistcoat pocket the small gold box, scarcely larger than a watch, and opened the cover. In the palm of her white hand he placed one of the little pastilles.

'Eat it,' said he. 'It will satisfy your hunger.'

She put the morsel into her mouth. 'I would do as you bade me,' she said, 'even if it were poison.'

'It is not poison,' he rejoined. 'It is nourishment in the only rational form.'

'But it is tasteless; almost without substance.'

'Yet it will support life for from eighteen to twenty-five days. This little gold box holds food enough to afford all subsistence to the entire Seventy-sixth Congress for a month.'

She took the box and curiously examined its contents.

'And how long would it support my life – for more than a year, perhaps?'

'Yes, for more than ten – more than twenty years.'

'I will not bore you with chemical and physiological facts,' continued Wanlee, 'but you must know that the food which we take, in whatever form, resolves itself into what are called proximate principles – starch, sugar, oleine, flurin, albumen, and so on. These are selected and assimilated by the organs of the body, and go to build up the necessary tissues. But all these proximate principles, in their turn, are simply combinations of the ultimate chemical elements, chiefly carbon, nitrogen, hydrogen, and oxygen. It is upon these elements that we depend for sustenance. By the old plan we obtained them indirectly. They passed from the earth and the air into the grass; from the grass into the muscular tissues of the ox; and from the beef into our own persons, loaded down and encumbered by a mass of useless, irrelevant matter. The German chemists have discovered how to supply the needed elements in compact, undiluted form – here they are in this little box. Now shall mankind go direct to the fountain-head of nature for his aliment; now shall the old roundabout, cumbrous, inhuman method be at an end; now shall the evils of gluttony and the attendant vices cease; now shall the brutal murdering of fellow animals and brother vegetables forever stop – now shall all this be, since the new, holy cause has been consecrated by the lips I love!'

He bent and kissed those lips. Then he suddenly looked up and saw Mr Walsingham Brown standing at his elbow.

'You are observed – compromised, I fear,' said Mr Brown, hurriedly. 'That Italian dancer in your employ, Miss Newton, has been following you like a hound. I have been paying him the same gracious attention. He has just left the Capitol post haste. I fear there may be a scene.'

The brave girl, with clear eyes, gave her Mongolian lover a look worth to him a year of life. 'There shall be no scene,' she said; 'we will go at once to my father, Daniel, and bear ourselves the tale which Francesco would carry.'

The three left the Capitol without delay. At the head of Pennsylvania Avenue they entered a great building, lighted up as brilliantly as the Capitol itself. An elevator took them down toward the bowels of the earth. At the fourth landing they passed from the elevator into a small carriage, luxuriously upholstered. Mr Walsingham Brown touched an ivory knob at the end of the conveyance. A man in uniform presented himself at the door.

'To Boston,' said Mr Walsingham Brown.

3 *The frozen bride*

The senator from Massachusetts sat in the library of his mansion on North Street at two o'clock in the morning. An expression of astonishment and rage distorted his pale, cold features. The pen had dropped from his fingers, blotting the last sentences written upon the manuscript of his great speech – for Senator Newton still adhered to the ancient fashion of recording thought. The blotted sentences were these.

'The logic of events compels us to acknowledge the political equality of those Asiatic invaders – shall I say conquerors? – of our Indo-European institutions. But the logic of events is often repugnant to common sense, and its conclusions abhorrent to patriotism and right. The sword has opened for them the way to the ballot box; but, Mr President, and I say it deliberately, no power under heaven can unlock for these aliens the sacred approaches to our homes and hearts!'

Beside the senator stood Francesco, the professional dancer. His face wore a smile of malicious triumph.

'With the Chinaman? Miss Newton – my daughter?' gasped the senator. 'I do not believe you. It is a lie.'

'Then come to the Capitol, Your Excellency, and see it with your own eyes,' said the Italian.

The door was quickly opened and Clara Newton entered the room, followed by the Honorable Mr Wanlee and his friend.

'There is no need of making that excursion, Papa,' said the girl. 'You can see it with your own eyes here and now. Francesco, leave the house!'

The senator bowed with forced politeness to Mr Walsingham Brown. Of the presence of Wanlee he took not the slightest notice.

Senator Newton attempted to laugh. 'This is a pleasantry, Clara,' he said; 'a practical jest, designed by yourself and Mr Brown for my midnight diversion. It is a trifle unseasonable.'

'It is no jest,' replied his daughter, bravely. She then went up to Wanlee and took his hand in hers. 'Papa,' she said, 'this is a gentleman of whom you already know something. He is our equal in station, in intellect, and in moral worth. He is in every way worthy of my friendship and your esteem. Will you listen to what he has to say to you? *Will* you, Papa?'

The senator laughed a short, hard laugh, and turned to Mr Walsingham Brown. 'I have no communication to make to the member of the lower branch,' said he. 'Why should he have any communication to make to me?'

Miss Newton put her arm around the waist of the young Chinaman and led him squarely in front of her father. 'Because,' she said, in a voice as firm and clear as the note of a silver bell ' – because I love him.'

In recalling with Wanlee the circumstances of this interview, Mr Walsingham Brown said long afterward, 'She glowed for a moment like the platinum of your thermo-electrode.'

'If the member from California,' said Senator Newton, without changing the tone of his voice, and still continuing to address himself to Mr Brown, 'has worked upon the sentimentality of this foolish child, that is her misfortune, and mine. It cannot be helped now. But if the member from California presumes to hope to profit in the least by his sinister operations, or to enjoy further opportunities for pursuing them, the member from California deceives himself.'

So saying he turned around in his chair and began to write on his great speech.

'I come,' said Wanlee slowly, now speaking for the first time, 'as an honorable man to ask of Senator Newton the hand of his daughter in honorable marriage. Her own consent has already been given.'

'I have nothing further to say,' said the Senator, once more turning his cold face toward Mr Brown. Then he paused an instant, and added with a sting, 'I am told that the member from California is a prophet and apostle of Vegetable Rights. Let him seek a cactus in marriage. He should wed on his own level.'

Wanlee, coloring at the wanton insult, was about to leave the room. A quick sign from Miss Newton arrested him.

'But I have something further to say,' she cried with spirit. 'Listen, Father; it is this. If Mr Wanlee goes out of the house without a word from you – a word such as is due him from you as a gentleman and as my father – I go with him to be his wife before the sun rises!'

'Go if you will, girl,' the senator coldly replied. 'But first consult with Mr Walsingham Brown, who is a lawyer and a gentleman, as to the tenor and effect of the Suspended Animation Act.'

Miss Newton looked inquiringly from one face to another. The words had no meaning to her. Her lover turned suddenly pale and clutched at the back of a chair for support. Mr Brown's cheeks were also white. He stepped quickly forward, holding out his hands as if to avert some dreadful calamity.

'Surely you would not – ' he began. 'But no! That is an absolute low, an inhuman, outrageous enactment that has long been as dead as the partisan fury that prompted it. For a quarter of a century it has been a dead letter on the statute books.'

'I was not aware,' said the senator, from between firmly set teeth, 'that the act had ever been repealed.'

He took from the shelf a volume of statutes and opened the book. 'I will read the text,' he said. 'It will form an appropriate part of the ritual of this marriage.' He read as follows:

Section 7.391. No male person of Caucasian descent, of or under the age of 25 years, shall marry, or promise or contract himself in marriage with any female person of Mongolian descent without the full written consent of his male parent or guardian, as provided by law; and no female person, either maid or widow, under the age of 30 years, of Caucasian parentage, shall give, promise, or contract herself in marriage with any male person of Mongolian descent without the full written and registered consent of her male and female parents or guardians, as provided by law. And any marriage obligations so contracted shall be null and void, and the Caucasian so contracting shall be guilty of a misdemeanor and liable to punishment at the discretion of his or her male parent or guardian as provided by law.

Section 7.392. Such parents or guardians may, at their discretion and upon application to the authorities of the United States District Court for the district within which the offense is committed, deliver the offending person of Caucasian descent to the designated officers, and require that his or her consciousness, bodily activities, and vital functions be suspended by the frigorific process known as the Werkomer process, for a period equal to that which must elapse before the offending person will arrive at the age of 25 years, if a male, or 30 years, if a female; or for a shorter period at the discretion of the parent or guardian; said shorter period to be fixed in advance.

'What does it mean?' demanded Miss Newton, bewildered by the verbiage of the act, and alarmed by her lover's exclamation of despair.

Mr Walsingham Brown shook his head, sadly. 'It means,' said he, 'that the cruel sin of the fathers is to be visited upon the children.'

'It means, Clara,' said Wanlee with a great effort, 'that we must part.'

'Understand me, Mr Brown,' said the senator, rising and motioning impatiently with the hand that held the pen, as if to dismiss both the subject and the intruding party. 'I do not employ the Suspended Animation Act as a bugaboo to frighten a silly girl out of her lamentable infatuation. As surely as the law stands, so surely will I put it to use.'

Miss Newton gave her father a long, steady look which neither Wanlee nor Mr Brown could interpret and then slowly led the way to the parlor. She closed the door and locked it. The clock on the mantel said four.

A complete change had come over the girl's manner. The spirit of defiance, of passionate appeal, of outspoken love, had gone. She was calm now, as cold and self-possessed as the senator himself. 'Frozen!' she kept saying under her breath. 'He has frozen me already with his frigid heart.'

She quickly asked Mr Walsingham Brown to explain clearly the force and bearings of the statute which her father had read from the book. When he had done so, she inquired, 'Is there not also a law providing for voluntary suspension of animation?'

'The Twenty-seventh Amendment to the Constitution,' replied the lawyer, 'recognizes the right of any individual, not satisfied with the condition of his life, to suspend that life for a time, long or short, according to his pleasure. But it is rarely, as you know, that anyone avails himself of the right – practically never, except as the only means to procure divorce from uncongenial marriage relations.'

'Still,' she persisted, 'the right exists and the way is open?' He bowed. She went to Wanlee and said: 'My darling, it must be so. I must leave you for a time, but as your wife. We will arrange a wedding' – and she smiled sadly – 'within this hour. Mr Brown will go with us to the clergyman. Then we will proceed at once to the Refuge, and you yourself shall lead me to the cloister that is to keep me safe till times are better for us. No, do not be startled, my love! The resolution is taken; you cannot alter it. And it will not be so very long, dear. Once, by accident, in arranging my father's papers, I came across his Life Probabilities, drawn up by the Vital Bureau at Washington. He has less than ten years to live. I never thought to calculate in cold blood on the chances of my father's life, but it must be. In ten years, Daniel, you may come to the Refuge again and claim your bride. You will find me as you left me.'

With tears streaming down his pale cheeks, the Mongolian strove to dissuade the Caucasian from her purpose. Hardly less affected, Mr Walsingham Brown joined his entreaties and arguments.

'Have you ever seen,' he asked, 'a woman who has undergone what you propose to undergo? She went into the Refuge, perhaps, as you will go, fresh, rosy, beautiful, full of life and energy. She comes out a prematurely aged, withered, sallow, flaccid body, a living corpse – a skeleton, a ghost of her former self. In spite of all they say, there can be no absolute suspension of animation. Absolute suspension would be death. Even in the case of the most perfect freezing there is still some activity of the vital functions, and they gnaw and prey upon the existence of the unconscious subject. Will you risk,' he suddenly demanded, using the last and most perfect argument that can be addressed to a woman ' – will you risk the effect your loss of beauty may have upon Wanlee's love after ten years' separation?'

Clara Newton was smiling now. 'For my poor beauty,' she replied, 'I care very little. Yet perhaps even that may be preserved.'

She took from the bosom of her dress the little gold box which the Chinaman had given her in the supper room of the Capitol, and hastily swallowed its entire contents.

Wanlee now spoke with determination: 'Since you have resolved to sacrifice ten years of your life my duty is with you. I shall share with you the sacrifice and share also the joy of awakening.'

She gravely shook her head. 'It is no sacrifice for me,' she said. 'But you must remain in life. You have a great and noble work to perform. Till the oppressed of the lower orders of being are emancipated from man's injustice and cruelty, you cannot abandon their cause. I think your duty is plain.'

'You are right,' he said, bowing his head to his breast.

In the gray dawn of the early morning the officials at the Frigorific Refuge in Cambridgeport were astonished by the arrival of a bridal party. The bridegroom's haggard countenance contrasted strangely with the elegance of his full evening toilet, and the bright scarlet bows at his knees seemed a mockery of grief. The bride, in white satin, wore a placid smile on her lovely face. The friend accompanying the two was grave and silent.

Without delay the necessary papers of admission were drawn up and signed and the proper registration was made upon the books of the establishment. For an instant husband and wife rested in each other's arms. Then she, still cheerful, followed the attendants toward the inner door, while he, pressing both hands upon his tearless eyes, turned away sobbing.

A moment later the intense cold of the congealing chamber caught the bride and wrapped her close in its icy embrace.

Old Squids and Little Speller

Edward Page Mitchell

In the days of content, when wants were few and well supplied, when New England rum was pure and cheap, and while the older generation still wore the knee breeches and turkey-tailed coats of colonial days, old Bailey, who kept a tollgate on the Hartford and Providence turnpike, died. For forty years after the Revolution, Bailey lived in the solitary little tollhouse, near the bridge over the turbulent Quinnebaug, and in all that time had never failed to answer the call to come and take toll; but one night he responded not, and they found him sitting in his chair with an open Bible on his knees, and his spirit gone to the country of which he had been reading.

So it happened that a few days after, the big coach left a tall young man at the Quinnebaug tollhouse, who brought with him his possessions encased in a handkerchief. The driver of the stage informed the young man that here was the scene of his future activities for the turnpike company, and added as he saw the young fellow staring at the board beside the door on which, at a long distant time, the rates of toll had been painted, 'See here, Old Squids, you'd better chalk up some new figures. The old ones is about washed out.'

The driver called him Old Squids, but aside from the fact that such a surname, if such it was, had never been heard before in that country, it was strange that he should have been called old. He was, in fact, a young fellow, not more than two or three and twenty, seemingly. Though his skin was bronzed, it was smooth, and though his beard was tangled, each hair at cross purposes, it had never known the razor, and was, therefore, silky. He was sinewy, though his joints were protuberant, and his broad shoulders were not erect. Yet, perhaps, they called him old because he was moderate in his way, not so much because of laziness as by inborn disposition.

When the coach rolled away Squids was left standing there, gazing with a perplexed expression at the toll board and abstractedly tugging at his beard. No wonder he was perplexed. There appeared only fragments of words on the board, for the rains had washed the paint away with bewildering irregularity. He could make nothing of it. The very first thing that Squids did, therefore, was to tear down the board and take it into the little cottage. Then, without any examination of his new home, he threw his bundle upon the bed and began to repair the damage that time had done to the board. But age had done its inevitable work with it, and as Squids held it on his knees it crumbled in his strong grasp and broke into fragments, as though the rude change, after forty years of unmeddled security on the door, had been too much for it.

Squids sorrowfully looked at the fragments at his feet, then gathered them up carefully, and gave them a decent interment in an old chest. For a week Squids labored to make a new toll board. Not that the board itself needed so much time, but, alas, the announcement on it did. For, skillful as Squids was with the hammer and saw and nails, his fingers were clumsy with the pencil and paint brush. Hour after hour he worked, studying the printed card of rates which the company had given him, so that he might transfer those figures and letters intelligibly upon the board. One night he even dreamed how it should be done, and dreaming, awoke with delight, lighted his candle, and down on his knees he went, to transfer the dream to the board. But his fingers refused to respond to the picture in his mind, and, with a sigh, Squids returned to bed.

At last Squids gave it up. He simply painted upon the board something like this:

MAN .... I CT.

HORSE .... TO CT.

CRITTERS .... ASK ME.

The words and the spelling of them he slyly obtained from some passing stranger who wrote them out for Squids upon a shingle. This new board he hung up in the old place, and when he saw anyone, man or beast, approaching the gate, he brought out his tariff card in case anybody should ask him the toll.

The manager of the company passing by in the stage, though he smiled at the board, comforted Squids by saying that he had done well, and then the manager told his companion that Squids was odd, but faithful, and had given proof of his integrity to one of the company's directors. 'He doesn't know any name but Squids,' said the manager, 'and we suppose he is some whaler's waif cast ashore in New London, and left to look out for himself. But he is faithful.'

But Squids, while pacified by the manager's approval, was by no means content. 'Some day,' said he to himself, as he gazed sadly at his rather abortive effort, 'I'll put one up that'll be a credit.'

Squids seemed happy enough in his lonely home. He made few friends, for the spot was remote from the farms of that town. The stage drivers liked him, for he always gave each of them a glass of cool milk. Squids's only possession, besides his clothes, was a cow.

One day one of the drivers said to him: 'See here, old Squids. I've been a-drinking your milk, off and on, a year or more for nothing. What can I get for you up to Hartford that will sorter square it up?'

'You might bring me a spelling book,' said Squids. 'If you'll buy it and bring it I'll pay what it costs: not more than a dollar, I guess.'

On the next down trip the driver handed Squids a Webster's spelling book. His blue eyes sparkled as he received it, but he said nothing except to express his thanks. But when the stage rolled away, and Squids was alone, he opened the book haphazard, and then, standing before the billboard, said, with an accent of triumph in his tone and the gleam of victory in his eye. 'By moy I can paint one and put it up that will be a credit.'

Squids could spell two- and three-letter words, but beyond that he found himself mired in many difficulties very often. He struggled and wrestled manfully, but rather despairingly, with the two-syllabled words in the speller. 'That's a B,' he would say, 'sure, and that's an A, and that spells Ba. But I don't quite get this 'ere yet. That's a K, that's an E, and that's an R. K is a K. E is an E. R is an R. Ker. That must be Keer. Bakeer. Now what kind of word is that?'

Thus Baker overthrew him and he was very despondent. One night, as he lay upon his bed, his eyes wide open and his brain throbbing with the misery of the mystery of Bakeer, a great light came to him. He arose, lighted a candle, and from his canvas bag drew forth ten copper pennies, which he placed conspicuously upon his table. Then he no sooner touched his pillow than he fell asleep.

In the morning the ten coppers were given to the driver, with the request that they should be exchanged at Hartford for ten peppermint bull's-eyes, streaked red and white. When Squids received the bull's-eyes he put them away on a plate in his cupboard and bided his time until the next Saturday afternoon. At that time, about an hour before sundown, he began to peer up the road toward the bend, for it was at such time that he knew that every Saturday a young lad came along with some good things from his father's farm for the minister's Sunday dinner at the parsonage, a mile away on the other side of the Quinnebaug. At last Squids caught sight of the boy, who bore a basket on his arm seemingly heavily laden. Squids, with a slyness born of some sense of shame, concealed himself in the tollhouse. Soon the lad was at the gate calling upon Squids to come out and pass him.

'Hulloo! It's you, is it, Ebenezer, going to the minister's? That basket must be heavy. Should think you'd want to rest a bit.'

''Tis heavy. There's a spare rib in it?'

'M'm. Want to know,' said Squids, opening his eyes in surprise and sympathy well simulated. 'Come in and sit down. Mebbe I can give you something kinder good.'

'Now what's that air thing?' asked Squids, when he had Ebenezer in the house, holding up the monstrously tempting confection before the boy's eyes.

'Pepentink bull's-eyes,' said the boy, delightedly.

'You like 'em. You shall have one.' Here Squids seemed about to give Ebenezer the candy, but suddenly restrained himself.

'Hold on,' he said. 'You've got to earn it. Oh! You go to school?'

'Yes, in winter.'

'H'm-m. How far have you got?'

'I've got to fractions and second reader.'

'Sho! No! I wan't to know. Now let's see.' Here Squids meditatively produced the Webster's speller from its place under his pillow, and opening it, said: 'H'm-m. Let's see. Now, here, if you will read that colyumn down straight you shall have two bull's-eyes. Right here. Just to see how much you know.'

'That's easy,' said Ebenezer. 'I will read some harder ones.'

Squids seemed a little perplexed. At length he said, 'Let's try the easy ones first. It'll be so much easier to earn the bull's-eyes. Don't you see?' And Squids placed the point of his jack-knife blade upon Baker.

'That's Baker,' said Ebenezer.

'Baker,' replied Squids, with the queerest accent in his voice. 'Baker. Sho! so 'tis.' Here Squids abstractedly combed his beard with his jack-knife.

'Of course it's Baker. Ker don't spell keer. Anybody but a fool might a' known that. Let me write it down, Ebenezer.'

Then Squids, somewhat to the astonishment of Ebenezer, brought forth a shingle, and on the smooth white side, with a piece of charcoal, spelled out the word B-a-k-e-r.

'What do you write it down for, Squids?' asked the boy.

'What for? Oh, only to see how many you get right,' replied the cunning Squids.

Thus Squids mastered some ten or twelve words, and the boy received two bull's-eyes, and Squids made a covenant with him that he should stop there every Saturday afternoon and show Squids whether he could read rightly such words in Webster's speller as Squids showed him, for which he was to receive two or more bull's-eyes.

Thus Squids, taught by a bribed and unconscious teacher, mastered the speller and began to make preparations to build a new toll board on which he purposed to paint the tariff of prices in a manner that would be a credit.

But something happened that made the new toll board and the credit that it was to be seem of petty consequence to him. One evening in March, when the line storm was raging without, Squids, with his speller on the table between two candles, and a shingle on his knee, was painting out with almost infinite pains the word cattle, so that he might be schooled in printing it correctly and as artistically as possible upon the toll board.

Suddenly Squids paused in his work and listened. There was surely a knock upon his door. The sound was not made by the beating of the oak branches on the roof. Squids took a candle and opened the door. A gust of wind blew the light out, as well as the other one on the table, but Squids had seen a woman's form on the doorstep, and he put forth his hand and drew her within. He bade her be patient until he relighted the candle, but before he could do so he heard her staggering step, and then he knew that she had fallen.

When Squids at last with nervous fingers coaxed a spark into the tinder and lighted a candle, he saw that the woman seemed to have sunk to the floor. Her face, over which her hair had fallen and was matted by the rain, was pale, and her eyes, half-opened with unconscious stare, seemed to him like the eyes of the dead. Her head, having fallen back, rested against the door. Squids held the candle to her parted lips and saw that she was not dead, but faint, and even before he could apply the simple remedies that he had she had somewhat recovered. She feebly rose, tottered to a chair, and then for the first time Squids saw that which startled him far more than her unconscious form had done. He saw in her arms the peaceful face of a sleeping infant.

She drank a glass of water, and Squids bustled about to prepare for her a cup of tea, which he had made of great potency, so that, having taken it, she greatly revived.

'You're very wet,' said Squids, and he threw some logs upon the hearth, urging her to draw near the fire. She did so, but with such manner of indifference that it seemed to Squids that she cared little whether she was wet or dry.

Though he had never touched the smooth, soft flesh of an infant before, Squids gently took this one from her unresisting arms and laid it upon his pillow. The child had not been wet by the storm, and Squids carefully tucked the quilt under the pillow. It did not even awaken under his unaccustomed touch, and as he looked upon the little sleeping one upon his pillow, with a chubby hand resting beside its cheek, Squids vowed that neither mother nor child should leave the house that night.

The woman watched him with the first sign of interest she had shown, and she said at length, 'You are kind, very kind.'

'That air's a cute little beauty,' was all the reply Squids made. The woman told him an incoherent, rambling story about missing the stage and losing her way, and she begged that she might rest there until the next stage came. Squids urged her to make herself comfortable, and he set milk and bread before her. Then, with cautions respecting the need of thorough drying, Squids went away to the little loft. He listened as he lay upon an extemporized bed, but all was silent below, and when he was assured that the stranger was in comfort he fell asleep.

In the morning Squids knocked at the door, but there was no response. 'She is tired: let her sleep,' said Squids to himself.

But by and by there being no sound within, Squids ventured to knock again, and still getting no response opened the door. The room was vacant.

'She went away before I awoke,' reasoned Squids, and he set about getting his breakfast.

Soon he heard that which caused him to stop and stand in utter amazement. He did not stir until he heard the sound again.

'Ma! Ma!' It came to him once more, and then, gently raising the bedquilt, Squids's eyes met those of the baby.

The little thing put up its hands, chuckled, and bounced up and down upon the pillow.

'Mo! Mo!' it said.

'Mo! Mo!' said Squids. 'That means moolly, moolly. It wants milk.'

In an instant Squids was warming a basin of milk. 'I calculate it'll like it sweet,' he meditated. So he put in a heaping spoonful of sugar. Then, with the tenderness of a mother, Squids fed the little one, spoonful by spoonful, till at last it pushed the spoon away with its fat little hands, and, reaching up, clung with gentle yet firm grasp to Squids's long and silky beard, and then, tugging away, looked up into his eyes, and laughed and crowed.

'Seems as though it knowed me,' said Squids. 'I vum, the cute little rascal thinks it knows me,' and two tears dropped from Squids' eyes right down upon the baby's cheek, and it lifted up one hand in sport, and as it felt of Squids's rough skin, it brushed away another tear or two with its frolicking. And Squids held his face down to it, and clucked and clucked, and spoke softly with all the instinct of paternity within him aroused. At last the little one's hands relaxed, and its eyelids drooped, and it fell asleep, and Squids stood there watching it, how long he knew not.

Thus Squids had a companion brought to him. He never knew why the mother, if such she was, left the baby there, or where she had gone, and as the days went by he began to have a secret terror lest she should sometime come and claim it. But she did not. No more thought had Squids for the new toll board, only as he set it before the child for a table whereon were gathered the marvelous toys that Squids whittled for it with his jack-knife. Squids early discovered that the baby liked wheels above all things, and that it displayed wonderful cunning in the arrangement of them after he had whittled them out.

One day Squids found him gazing wonderingly at the Webster's speller, and though fearful of the lawlessness of those little hands, Squids bound the covers firmly together with cords and suffered him to play with the book. Then Squids called the baby Little Speller, and never by any other name. The little one tried hard to say Squids, but could only lisp 'Thid,' so that Squids came to like this diminutive as spoken by the child better than all other sounds.

'Some day you and me will rastle with this book, and I calculate we'll get the best of it, won't we, sir?' Squids would say to the child when it grew old enough to understand, and the little one would reply, 'Yes we will, Thid.'

Thus they lived, day by day, Little Speller content, while Squids – his happiness was a revelation of delight of which he had had no conception. By and by, when the little one was older, Squids would take him on his knee, and with the Webster speller and a new slate brought from Hartford, they would take up their tasks.

'That's A, sir. See how I make it. One line down, so, and another down, so, and one across, and that makes A.' And Little Speller, with faltering fingers, would draw the lines and say, 'That's A, Thid,' and Squids would laugh and say, 'We'll have a toll board by and by that will be a credit, and no mistake.'

One day Squids spelled out horse on the slate, and Little Speller took the pencil and sketched a horse with very rectangular head and body and very wavy legs, and he said, 'No, that's horse, Thid.'

Squids roared, and got a shingle and made Little Speller spell horse in that way on it with a crayon. Then Squids nailed the shingle on the wall over the fireplace, and when anybody came in he would point proudly to it, saying, 'See how Little Speller spells horse. He's a cute one!'

But before many months went by Squids found that the boy and he were exchanging places, for the teacher was becoming the taught and the scholar becoming the teacher. So Squids sent to Hartford and bought a first reader and an arithmetic, and great was their delight in pondering over the mysteries of these books and solving them.

'Little Speller,' said Squids, one day, 'you took to spelling natural, but you take to 'rithmetic more natural. But it's beyond me. After this you'll have to do the figgering and the spelling for me.'

That the child had a talent for mathematics and mechanics Squids understood fully, though he could not express it in any other way than by saying: 'He's mighty sharp at figgers and mighty cute with the jack-knife.'

One morning, as Squids was opening the tollgate, he astonished the traveler who waited to pass through by suddenly stopping and staring at the house. The stranger feared he had gone mad, or was carrying too much New England rum, till Squids, with triumphant utterance, said, 'Look at that air. That's a credit at last,' and he pointed to a new toll board neatly painted and accurately lettered. Then he rushed into the house and brought forth the lad.

'This is the boy that done it,' said Squids, 'unbeknown to me, and nailed her up unbeknown. Ain't that a credit? It is Little Speller, it is.'

Then, when Little Speller grew older, he builded, with Squids's help, a marvelous tollgate that opened and shut automatically by the touching of a lever; and the fame of it spread, so that the manager even came, and wondered, too, and praised the lad, saying: 'Squids, that boy is a genius, sure.'

And Squids would watch Little Speller, when the lad knew it not, as an enthusiast studies a painting, and many and many a time did Squids in the night quietly arise from the bed, light a candle, and look, with something like awe in his glance, upon the face of the sleeping boy.

One day there came to the Quinnebaug tollgate some men, and they drove stakes and dug ditches, and builded a great dam across the river, half a mile above. Then they put up a building, larger than any Little Speller ever saw, and placed within it curious machines, and they put a huge wheel outside the building. Little Speller seemed entranced as he watched them day by day, and he caused the men to deal with him with great respect, because at a critical time in setting up the wheel, when it seemed as though something had gone wrong, they heard a little voice shouting peremptorily, 'Loose your ropes, quick,' and they did so, and the wheel settled properly in place. The men wondered how it was that that little fellow standing there on a rock could have shouted so commandingly that they trusted him. But they said: 'He's got some gumption, sure.'

When the big wheel was set a-going and the machines in the mill began to make a frightful clatter, then it was that Little Speller's enthusiasm and delight seemed to be greater even than such a little body as his could contain. He spent hours and hours in the mill watching the machines as they wove the threads of wool into cloth.

By and by Squids saw that Little Speller was silent, dreaming, abstracted, and Squids became alarmed. 'It's that air dreadful noise in the mill that's confusing his little head,' reasoned Squids: and he urged the boy to go there less frequently, but Little Speller went as was his wont. At length, Squids saw that the boy was busying himself day and night with the jack-knife and such other tools as were there, and Squids was pleased, though he could not comprehend what this strange thing was that Little Speller was building. The boy seemed absorbed by his work. When he ate, his great dreamy eyes were fixed abstractedly upon his plate; but he slept soundly, and Squids was not greatly alarmed.

'There's something in him that's working out,' reasoned Squids, and when he saw the fierce energy and enthusiasm with which Little Speller cut and shaped and planed and fashioned the bits of wood, Squids was sure that whatever it was that was working out of him was working out well.

One day Little Speller said, as he put his hand on the thing he had made, 'There, it's done, and it's all right. It's better than the ones they've got in the mill, only it's wood.'

'What might it be, Little Speller?' asked Squids.

'It's a weaving machine.'

'It's worked out of you. Part of you is in that thing, Little Speller, and it's a greater credit than the toll board or the gate.'

Then Squids in great glee went and fetched the superintendent of the mill. 'See,' said he, when he had brought the man, 'that air is worked out of Little Speller. Part of him is in it, and it's a credit.'

The superintendent glanced with some interest at the model, more to please the lad and Squids than for any other reason. 'Show him how it works,' said Squids.

Little Speller did so. It was rude, clumsy; but as the boy explained the working of it, the superintendent became excited. He fingered it himself. He worked at it. Great beads of sweat stood on his forehead, for he was intensely interested. At last he said: 'That will revolutionize woolen mills. The thing's built wrong, but the idea is there. Where did you get that idea, Squids?'

'Me!' exclaimed Squids. 'Me! 'Taint me. It worked out of Little Speller. It's been working out of him ever since the mill was built. Ain't it a credit?'

'Credit!' and the superintendent smiled. 'What do you want for it?' he asked.

'I want to see one built and set to working in the mill,' said Little Speller.

'Will you let me build it?'

'Oh, if you only will,' begged Little Speller.

'Put that down in writing, and I'll promise you I'll fit the mill with them; yes, and a hundred mills.'

Squids and Little Speller seemed dazed by this unexpected glory.

'He's going to put what's worked out of you into a hundred mills, Little Speller,' said Squids, as he looked almost reverentially upon the boy.

It was as the superintendent had said. Seizing Little Speller's idea, he had properly handled it, builded machines, obtained patents, therefore, and had revolutionized the woolen mills that were then springing up throughout eastern New England, and had he opened a mine of gold there on the banks of the Quinnebaug, the superintendent could hardly have had more riches.

But Squids and Little Speller were content. They would go up to the mill and watch the new machine, weaving yards and yards of cloth, Little Speller with the most ecstatic delight, and Squids with a sense of awe. 'That's you, Little Speller. That's you working. It ain't the machine. That's only wood and iron.'

By and by Little Speller began to appear abstracted again, and he spent many hours watching the transmission of power from the water wheel to the machinery. 'Something more is working out,' reasoned Squids, but he held his peace.

One day Squids heard someone coming down the road. He went to open the gate. There were four or five men, and they were bearing a burden. When they were near, Squids saw that they moved gently and bore their burden tenderly and that their faces were very grave. They did not try to pass the gate, but instead entered Squids's little house and laid their burden upon his bed. Then Squids saw Little Speller's pale face, and a little red thread that was vividly tracing its way on the white cheek down from the temple, and the eyes were closed and the hand hung limp. Squids stood there motionless a long time, then, turning to the men, he said, with dull, phlegmatic speech and a veiled appearance of his eyes, 'Was he working it out?'

'He was,' said one, 'and he forgot himself and got too near the shafting and it – '

'Yes, yes. He was a-working it out,' said Squids mechanically, and with no intelligence in his eyes. Then suddenly he darted fiercely to the bedside. Little Speller had opened his eyes. He saw Squids and knew him.

'Thid,' he said.

Squids bent over him, but could not speak.

'Thid, I shall never work it out,' he whispered.

Then he turned his eyes longingly to the old model across the room, and then looked imploringly at Squids. The gatekeeper read his wishes. He pushed the old model up to the bedside. Then Little Speller put one hand upon it, and with the other outstretched till the palm rested gently upon Squids's face, he looked up with one peaceful glance and the flicker of a faint smile, and then the light passed out of Little Speller's eyes forever.

The men saw what had happened and went quietly away, leaving Squids alone with Little Speller.

In the afterdays, Squids would sit by the old model, gently speaking to it, and affectionately causing its mechanism to be put in operation, and he would say, 'Little Speller is in there. He is in a hundred mills. You can hear him, but I, when I look at this, I can see him, too.'

The Facts in the Ratcliff Case

Edward Page Mitchell

I first met Miss Borgier at a tea party in the town of R— , where I was attending medical lectures. She was a tall girl, not pretty; her face would have been insipid but for the peculiar restlessness of her eyes. They were neither bright nor expressive, yet she kept them so constantly in motion that they seemed to catch and reflect light from a thousand sources. Whenever, as rarely happened, she fixed them even for a few seconds upon one object, the factitious brilliancy disappeared, and they became dull and somnolent. I am unable to say what was the color of Miss Borgier's eyes.

After tea, I was one of a group of people whom our host, the Reverend Mr Tinker, sought to entertain with a portfolio of photographs of places in the Holy Land. While endeavoring to appear interested in his descriptions and explanations, all of which I had heard before, I became aware that Miss Borgier was honoring me with steady regard. My gaze encountered hers and I found that I could not, for the life of me, withdraw my own eyes from the encounter. Then I had a singular experience, the phenomena of which I noted with professional accuracy. I felt the slight constriction of the muscles of my face, the numbness of the nerves that precedes physical stupor induced by narcotic agency. Although I was obliged to struggle against the physical sense of drowsiness, my mental faculties were more than ordinarily active. Her eyes seemed to torpify my body while they stimulated my mind, as opium does. Entirely conscious of my present surroundings, and particularly alert to the Reverend Mr Tinker's narrative of the ride from Joppa, I accompanied him on that journey, not as one who listens to a traveler's tale, but as one who himself travels the road. When, finally, we reached the point where the Reverend Mr Tinker's donkey makes the last sharp turn around the rock that has been cutting off the view ahead, and the Reverend Mr Tinker beholds with amazement and joy the glorious panorama of Jerusalem spread out before him, I saw it all with remarkable vividness. I saw Jerusalem in Miss Borgier's eyes.

I tacitly thanked fortune when her eyes resumed their habitual dance around the room, releasing me from what had become a rather humiliating captivity. Once free from their strange influence, I laughed at my weakness. 'Pshaw!' I said to myself. 'You are a fine subject for a young woman of mesmeric talents to practise upon.'

'Who is Miss Borgier?' I demanded of the Reverend Mr Tinker's wife, at the first opportunity.

'Why, she is Deacon Borgier's daughter,' replied that good person, with some surprise.

'And who is Deacon Borgier?'

'A most excellent man; one of the pillars of my husband's congregation. The young people laugh at what they call his torpidity, and say that he has been walking about town in his sleep for twenty years; but I assure you that there is not a sincerer, more fervent Chris – '

I turned abruptly around, leaving Mrs Tinker more astonished than ever, for I knew that the subject of my inquiries was looking at me again. She sat in one corner of the room, apart from the rest of the company. I straightway went and seated myself at her side.

'That is right,' she said. 'I wished you to come. Did you enjoy your journey to Jerusalem?'

'Yes, thanks to you.'

'Perhaps. But you can repay the obligation. I am told that you are Dr Mack's assistant in surgery at the college. There is a clinic tomorrow. I want to attend it.'

'As a patient?' I inquired.

She laughed. 'No, as a spectator. You must find a way to gratify my curiosity.'

I expressed, as politely as possible, my astonishment at so extraordinary a fancy on the part of a young lady, and hinted at the scandal which her appearance in the amphitheater would create. She immediately offered to disguise herself in male attire. I explained that the nature of the relations between the medical college and the patients who consented to submit to surgical treatment before the class were such that it would be a dishonorable thing for me to connive at the admission of any outsider, male or female. That argument made no impression upon her mind. I was forced to decline peremptorily to serve her in the affair. 'Very well,' she said. 'I must find some other way.'

At the clinic the next day I took pains to satisfy myself that Miss Borgier had not surreptitiously intruded. The students of the class came in at the hour, noisy and careless as usual, and seated themselves in the lower tiers of chairs around the operating table. They produced their notebooks and began to sharpen lead pencils. Miss Borgier was certainly not among them. Every face in the lecture room was familiar to me. I locked the door that opened into the hallway, and then searched the anteroom on the other side of the amphitheater. There were a dozen or more patients, nervous and dejected, waiting for treatment and attended by friends hardly less frightened than themselves. But neither Miss Borgier nor anybody resembling Miss Borgier was of the number.

Dr Mack now briskly entered by his private door. He glanced sharply at the table on which his instruments were arranged, ready for use, and, having assured himself that everything was in its place, began the clinical lecture. There were the usual minor operations – two or three for strabismus, one for cataract, the excision of several cysts and tumors, large and small, the amputation of a railway brakeman's crushed thumb. As the cases were disposed of, I attended the patients back to the anteroom and placed them in the care of their friends.

Last came a poor old lady named Wilson, whose leg had been drawn up for years by a rheumatic affection, so that the joint of the knee had ossified. It was one of those cases where the necessary treatment is almost brutal in its simplicity. The limb had to be straightened by the application of main force. Mrs Wilson obstinately refused to take advantage of anesthesia. She was placed on her back upon the operating table, with a pillow beneath her head. The geniculated limb showed a deflection of twenty or twenty-five degrees from a right line. As already remarked, this deflection had to be corrected by direct, forcible pressure downward upon the knee.

With the assistance of a young surgeon of great physical strength, Dr Mack proceeded to apply this pressure. The operation is one of the most excruciating that can be imagined. I was stationed at the head of the patient, in order to hold her shoulders should she struggle. But I observed that a marked change had come over her since we established her upon the table. Very much agitated at first, she had become perfectly calm. As she passively lay there, her eyes directed upward with a fixed gaze, the eyelids heavy as if with approaching slumber, the face tranquil, it was hard to realize that this woman had already crossed the threshold of an experience of cruel pain.

I had no time, however, to give more than a thought to her wonderful courage. The harsh operation had begun. The surgeon and his assistant were steadily and with increasing force bearing down upon the rigid knee. Perhaps the Spanish Inquisition never devised a method of inflicting physical torture more intense than that which this woman was now undergoing, yet not a muscle of her face quivered. She breathed easily and regularly, her features retained their placid expression, and, at the moment when her sufferings must have been the most agonizing, I saw her eyes close, as if in peaceful sleep.

At the same instant the tremendous force exerted upon the knee produced its natural effect. The ossified joint yielded, and, with a sickening noise – the indescribable sound of the crunching and gritting of the bones of a living person, a sound so frightful that I have seen old surgeons, with sensibilities hardened by long experience, turn pale at hearing it – the crooked limb became as straight as its mate.

Closely following this horrible sound, I heard a ringing peal of laughter.

The operating table, in the middle of the pit of the amphitheater, was lighted from overhead. Directly above the table, a shaft, five or six feet square, and closely boarded on its four sides, led up through the attic story of the building to a skylight in the roof. The shaft was so deep and so narrow that its upper orifice was visible from no part of the room except a limited space immediately around the table. The laughter which startled me seemed to come from overhead. If heard by any other person present, it was probably ascribed to a hysterical utterance on the part of the patient. I was in a position to know better. Instinctively I glanced upward, in the direction in which the eyes of Mrs Wilson had been so fixedly bent.

There, framed in a quadrangle of blue sky, I saw the head and neck of Miss Borgier. The sash of the skylight had been removed, to afford ventilation. The young woman was evidently lying at full length upon the flat roof. She commanded a perfect view of all that was done upon the operating table. Her face was flushed with eager interest and wore an expression of innocent wonder, not unmingled with delight. She nodded merrily to me when I looked up and laid a finger against her lips, as if to warn me to silence. Disgusted, I withdrew my eyes hastily from hers. Indeed, after my experience of the previous evening, I did not care to trust my self-control under the influence of her gaze.

As Dr Mack with his sharp scissors cut the end of a linen bandage, he whispered to me: 'This is without a parallel. Not a sign of syncope, no trace of functional disorder. She has dropped quietly into healthy sleep during an infliction of pain that would drive a strong man mad.'

As soon as released from my duties in the lecture room, I made my way to the roof of the building. As I emerged through the scuttle-way, Miss Borgier scrambled to her feet and advanced to meet me without manifesting the slightest discomposure. Her face fairly beamed with pleasure.

'Wasn't it beautiful?' she asked with a smile, extending her hand. 'I heard the bones slowly grinding and crushing!'

I did not take her hand. 'How came you here?' I demanded, avoiding her glance.

'Oh!' said she, with a silvery laugh. 'I came early, about sunrise. The janitor left the door ajar and I slipped in while he was in the cellar. All the morning I spent in the place where they dissect; and when the students began to come in downstairs I escaped here to the roof.'

'Are you aware, Miss Borgier,' I asked, very gravely, 'that you have committed a serious indiscretion, and must be gotten out of the building as quickly and privately as possible?'

She did not appear to understand. 'Very well,' she said. 'I suppose there is nothing more to see. I may as well go.'

I led her down through the garret, cumbered with boxes and barrels of unarticulated human bones; through the medical library, unoccupied at that hour; by a back stairway into and across the great vacant chemical lecture room; through the anatomical cabinet, full of objects appalling to the imagination of her sex. I was silent and she said nothing; but her eyes were everywhere, drinking in the strange surroundings with an avidity which I could feel without once looking at her. Finally we came to a basement corridor, at the end of which a door, not often used, gave egress by an alleyway to the street. It was through this door that subjects for dissection were brought into the building. I took a bunch of keys from my pocket and turned the lock. 'Your way is clear now,' I said.

To my immense astonishment, Miss Borgier, as we stood together at the end of the dark corridor, threw both arms around my neck and kissed me.

'Goodbye,' she said, as she disappeared through the half-opened door.

When I awoke the next morning, after sleeping for more than fifteen hours, I found that I could not raise my head from the pillow without nausea. The symptoms were exactly like those which mark the effects of an overdose of laudanum.

2

I have thought it due to myself and to my professional reputation to recount these facts before briefly speaking of my recent testimony as an expert, in the Ratcliff murder trial, the character of my relations with the accused having been persistently misrepresented.

The circumstances of that celebrated case are no doubt still fresh in the recollection of the public. Mr John L. Ratcliff, a wealthy, middle-aged merchant of Boston, came to St Louis with his young bride, on their wedding journey. His sudden death at the Planters' Hotel, followed by the arrest of his wife, who was entirely without friends or acquaintances in the city, her indictment for murder by poisoning, the conflict of medical testimony at the trial, and the purely circumstantial nature of the evidence against the prisoner, attracted general attention and excited public interest to a degree that was quite extraordinary.

It will be remembered that the state proved that the relations of Mr and Mrs Ratcliff, as observed by the guests and servants of the hotel, were not felicitous; that he rarely spoke to her at table, habitually averting his face in her presence; that he wandered aimlessly about the hotel for several days previous to his illness, apparently half stupefied, as if by the oppression of some heavy mental burden, and that when accosted by anyone connected with the house he started as if from a dream, and answered incoherently if at all.

It was also shown that, by her husband's death, Mrs Ratcliff became the sole mistress of a large fortune.

The evidence bearing directly upon the circumstances of Mr Ratcliff's death was very clear. For twenty-four hours before a physician was summoned, no one had access to him save his wife. At dinner that day, in response to the polite inquiry of a lady neighbor at table, Mrs Ratcliff announced, with great self-possession, that her husband was seriously indisposed. Soon after eleven o'clock at night, Mrs Ratcliff rang her bell, and, without the least agitation of manner, remarked that her husband appeared to be dying, and that it might be well to send for a physician. Dr Culbert, who arrived within a very few minutes, found Mr Ratcliff in a profound stupor, breathing stertorously. He swore at the trial that when he first entered the room the prisoner, pointing to the bed, coolly said, 'I suppose that I have killed him.'

Dr Culbert's testimony seemed to point unmistakably to poisoning by laudanum or morphine. The unconscious man's pulse was full but slow; his skin cold and pallid; the expression of his countenance placid, yet ghastly pale; lips livid. Coma had already supervened, and it was impossible to rouse him. The ordinary expedients were tried in vain. Flagellation of the palms of his hands and the soles of his feet, electricity applied to the head and spine, failed to make any impression on his lethargy. The eyelids being forcibly opened, the pupils were seen to be contracted to the size of pinheads, and violently turned inward. Later, the stertorous breathing developed into the ominously loud rattle of mucous in the trachea; there were convulsions, attended by copious frothings at the mouth; the under jaw fell upon the breast; and paralysis and death followed, four hours after Dr Culbert's arrival.

Several of the most eminent practitioners of the city, put upon the stand by the prosecution, swore that, in their opinion, the symptoms noted by Dr Culbert not only indicated opium poisoning, but could have resulted from no other cause.

On the other hand, the state absolutely failed to show either that opium in any form had been purchased by Mrs Ratcliff in St Louis, or that traces of opium in any form were found in the room after the event. It is true that the prosecuting attorney, in his closing argument, sought to make the latter circumstance tell against the prisoner. He argued that the disappearance of any vessel containing or having contained laudanum, in view of the positive evidence that laudanum had been employed, served to establish a deliberate intention of murder and to demolish any theory of accidental poisoning that the defense might attempt to build; and he propounded half a dozen hypothetical methods by which Mrs Ratcliff might have disposed, in advance, of this evidence of her crime. The court, of course, in summing up, cautioned the jury against attaching weight to these hypotheses of the prosecuting attorney.

The court, however, put much emphasis on the medical testimony for the prosecution, and on the calm declaration of Mrs Ratcliff to Dr Culbert, 'I suppose that I have killed him.'

Having conducted the autopsy, and afterward made a qualitative analysis of the contents of the dead man's stomach, I was put upon the stand as a witness for the defense.

Then I saw the prisoner for the first time in more than five years. When I had taken the oath and answered the preliminary questions, Mrs Ratcliff raised the veil which she had worn since the trial began, and looked me in the face with the well-remembered eyes of Miss Borgier.

I confess that my behavior during the first few moments of surprise afforded some ground for the reports that were afterward current concerning my relations with the prisoner. Her eyes chained not only mine, but my tongue also. I saw Jerusalem again, and the face framed in blue sky peering down into the amphitheater of the old medical college. It was only after a struggle which attracted the attention of judge, jury, bar, and spectators that I was able to proceed with my testimony.

That testimony was strong for the accused. My knowledge of the case was wholly post-mortem. It began with the autopsy. Nothing had been found that indicated poisoning by laudanum or by any other agent. There was no morbid appearance of the intestinal canal; no fullness of the cerebral vessels, no serous effusion. Every appearance that would have resulted from death by poison was wanting in the subject. That, of course, was merely negative evidence. But, furthermore, my chemical analysis had proved the absence of the poison in the system. The opium odor could not be detected. I had tested for morphine with nitric acid, permuriate of iron, chromate of potash, and, most important of all, iodic acid. I had tested again for meconic acid with the permuriate of iron. I had tested by Lassaigne's process, by Dublane's, and by Flandin's. As far as the resources of organic chemistry could avail, I had proved that, notwithstanding the symptoms of Mr Ratcliff's case before death, death had not resulted from laudanum or any other poison known to science.

The questions by the prosecuting counsel as to my previous acquaintance with the prisoner, I was able to answer truthfully in a manner that did not shake the force of my medical testimony. And it was chiefly on the strength of this testimony that the jury, after a short deliberation, returned a verdict of not guilty.

Did I swear falsely? No; for science bore me out in every assertion. I knew that not a drop of laudanum or a grain of morphine had passed Ratcliff's lips. Ought I to have declared my belief regarding the true cause of the man's death, and told the story of my previous observations of Miss Borgier's case? No; for no court of justice would have listened to that story for a single moment. I knew that the woman did not murder her husband. Yet I believed and knew – as surely as we can know anything where the basis of ascertained fact is slender and the laws obscure – that she poisoned him, *poisoned him to death with her eyes.*

I think that it will be generally conceded by the profession that I am neither a sensationalist nor prone to lose my self-command in the mazes of physico-psychologic speculation. I make the foregoing assertion deliberately, fully conscious of all that it implies.

What was the mystery of the noxious influence which this woman exerted through her eyes? What was the record of her ancestry, the secret of predisposition in her case? By what occult process of evolution did her glance derive the toxical effect of the *papaver somniferum*? How did she come to be a Woman-Poppy? I cannot yet answer these questions. Perhaps I shall never be able to answer them.

But if there is need of further proof of the sincerity of my denial of any sentiment on my part which might have led me to shield Mrs Ratcliff by perjury, I may say that I have now in my possession a letter from her, written after her acquittal, proposing to endow me with her fortune and herself; as well as a copy of my reply, respectfully declining the offer.

The Story of the Deluge

Edward Page Mitchell

THE REMARKABLE DISCOVERIES OF MR GEORGE SMITH

Interesting Particulars Respecting the Translations of the Assyrian Tablets in the British Museum – Newly Discovered Facts About the Flood and Noah, Together with Some Light on the History of the Senator from Maine and the Settlement of Brooklyn.

Boston, April 26 – Mr Jacob Rounds of London, one of the assistant curators of the British Museum, in a private letter to a distinguished Orientalist of this city, gives some interesting particulars regarding the progress which has been made in the arrangement and translation of the sculptured tablets and *lateres coctiles* brought from Assyria and Chaldea by Mr George Smith. The results of the past three or four months are gratifying in the extreme. The work, which was begun three quarters of a century ago by Grotefend, and pursued by archaeologists such as Rask, St Martin, Klaproth, Oppert, and the indefatigable Rawlinson, each of whom was satisfied if he carried it forward a single step, has been pushed far and fast by Mr George Smith and his scholarly associates. The Assyrio-Babylonian cuneiforms, the third and most complicated branch of the trilogy, may fairly be said to have found their Oedipus.

The riddles of Accad and of Sumir are read at last. The epigraphs on tablets dug from the earth and rubbish of the Ninevite mounds are now translated by Mr George Smith as readily as Professor Whitney translates Greek, or a fifth-term schoolboy, the fable of the man and the viper.

It is not many years since the learned Witte declared that these sphenographic characters, arranged so neatly upon the slabs of gray alabaster, or the carefully prepared surface of clay – like specimen arrowheads in the museum of some ancient war department – were entirely without alphabetic significance, mere whimsical ornaments, or perhaps the trail of worms! But their exegesis has been perfected. The mounds of Nimroud, and Kouyunjik, and Khorsabad, and Nebbi Yunus have yielded up their precious treasures, and are now revealing, page by page, the early history of our globe.

Mr Smith and Mr Rounds are both confirmed in the belief, first entertained by Westergaarde, that the cuneiform character is closely akin to the Egyptian demotic; and also that its alphabet – which contains over four hundred signs, some syllable, some phonetic, and some ideographic – is of the most complicated and arbitrary nature. As already intimated, the inscriptions which Mr Smith and his co-laborers have deciphered are in the primitive or Babylonian character, which is much more obscure than either of its successors and modifications, the so-called Persian and Median cunei.

SENNACHERIB'S LIBRARY

The slabs of the greatest interest and importance were those found buried in the famous Kouyunjik mound, first opened in 1843 by M. Paul Emile Botta, and subsequently explored by Layard himself.

The inscriptions are mostly upon clay, and seem to have constituted the walls of the great library of Assurbanipal in Sennacherib's palace. Sennacherib was probably a monarch of a nautical turn of mind, for a large portion of the inscriptions illustrate the history of the flood and the voyage of Noah, or of Nyab, his Assyrian counterpart, who also corresponds, in some particulars, with the Deucalion of the Grecian myths. Piece by piece and fragment by fragment the diluvian narrative has been worked out, until it stands complete, a distinct episode in the vast epic which Mr George Smith is engaged in reconstructing. Mr Rounds may certainly be pardoned for the naturally enthusiastic terms in which he speaks of these labors.

And well may he be proud. These men in the British Museum are successfully compiling, brick by brick, what they claim to be a complete encyclopedia of sacred and profane history, beginning with the conception of matter and the birth of mind. Their extraordinary researches have placed them upon a pedestal of authority, from which they now gravely pronounce their approval of the Holy Scriptures, and even stoop to pat Moses on the head and to tell him that his inspired version was very nearly correct.

So graphic is the account of the adventures of Nyab, or Noah as he may more conveniently be called; so clear is the synopsis of his method of navigation; so startling are the newly discovered facts regarding the Ark and its passengers, that I am tempted to avail myself of the kind permission of the Boston savant who has the honor to be Mr Rounds's esteemed correspondent, and to transcribe somewhat in detail, for the benefit of your readers, the extraordinary story of the flood as told by the Assyrian cuneiforms – cryptograms for four thousand years until the genius of a Smith unveiled the mystery of their meaning.

THE RISING OF THE WATERS

Mr Smith ascertains from these inscriptions that when Noah began to build his Ark and prophesy a deluge, the prevailing opinion was that he was either a lunatic or a shrewd speculator who proposed, by his glowing predictions and appearance of perfect sincerity, so to depreciate real estate that he might buy, through his brokers, to any extent at prices merely nominal.

Even after the lowlands were submerged, and it was apparent that there was to be a more than usually wet season, Noah's wicked neighbors were accustomed to gather for no other purpose than to deride the ungainly architecture of the Ark and to question its sailing qualities. They were not wanting who asserted that the Thing would roll over at the first puff of wind like a too heavily freighted tub. So people came from far and near to witness and laugh at the discomfiture of the aged patriarch.

But there was no occasion for ridicule. The Ark floated like a cork. Noah dropped his center board and stood at the helm waving graceful adieus to his wicked contemporaries, while the good vessel caught a fresh southerly breeze and moved on like a thing of life. There is nothing whatever in the Assyrian account to confirm the tradition that Noah accelerated the motion of the Ark by raising his own coat-tails. This would have been an unnecessary as well as undignified proceeding. The tall house on deck afforded sufficient resistance to the wind to drive the Ark along at a very respectable rate of speed.

NOAH AS A NAVIGATOR

After the first novelty of the situation had worn off, and there was no longer the satisfaction of kindly but firmly refusing applications for passage, and seeing the lately derisive people scrambling for high land, only to be eventually caught by and swallowed up in the roaring waters, the voyage was a vexatious and disagreeable one. The Ark at the best was an unwieldy craft. She fell off from the wind frightfully, and almost invariably missed stays. Every choppy sea hammered roughly upon her flat bottom, making all on board so seasick as to wish that they too had been wicked, and sunk with the crowd.

Inside the miserable shanty which served for a cabin, birds, beasts, and human beings were huddled promiscuously together. One of the deluge tablets says, not without a touch of pathos: 'It was extremely uncomfortable [*amakharsyar*] to sleep with a Bengal tiger glaring at one from a corner, and a hedgehog nestled up close against one's bare legs. But it was positively dangerous when the elephant became restless, or the polar bear took offense at some fancied slight.'

I will not anticipate Mr Smith's detailed account of the cruise of the Ark. He has gathered data for a complete chart of Noah's course during the many months of the voyage. The tortuous nature of the route pursued and the eccentricity of Noah's great-circle sailing are proof that the venerable navigator, under the depressing influence of his surroundings, had frequent recourse to ardent spirits, an infirmity over which we, his descendants, should drop the veil of charity and of silence.

EXTRACT FROM NOAH'S LOG

The most astounding discovery of all, however, is a batch of tablets giving an actual and literal transcript from Noah's logbook. The journal of the voyage – which Noah, as a prudent navigator, doubtless kept with considerable care – was probably bequeathed to Shem, eldest born and executive officer of the Ark. Portions of the log, it may be, were handed down from generation to generation among the Semitic tribes; and Mr Rounds does not hesitate to express his opinion that these tablets in the British Museum were copied directly from the original entries made in the ship's book by Noah or Shem.

He sends to his Boston correspondent early proofs of some of the lithographic facsimiles which are to illustrate Mr Smith's forthcoming work, *An Exhaustive History of the Flood and of the Noachic Voyage*. They should bear in mind that the inscription reads from left to right, and not, like Arabic and numerous other Semitic languages, from right to left.

Expressed in the English character, this inscription would read as follows:

> *. . . dahyarva saka ormudzi . . . fraharram athura uvatish . . . kia rich thyar avalna nyasadayram okanaus mana frabara . . . gathava Hambi Humin khaysathryam nam Buhmi . . . pasara ki hi baga Jethyths paruvnam oazarka . . . Rhsayarsha . . .*

Such progress has been made in the interpretation of the Aramaic dialects that it is comparatively an easy matter for Mr Rounds to put this into our vernacular, which he does as follows, supplying certain hiatuses to the inscription where the connection is obvious:

SCOW *AHK*, LATITUDE 44° 15', LONGITUDE . . . Water falling rapidly. Ate our last pterodactyl yesterday . . . Hambl Hamin [Hannibal Hamlin!] down with scurvy. Must put him ashore . . . THURS, 7th. Bitter ale and mastodons all gone. Mrs Japheth's had another pair of twins. All well.

The importance of this scrap of diluvian history can hardly be over-estimated. It throws light on three or four points which have been little understood hitherto. Having viewed the subject in all its bearings, and having compared the extract here quoted with numberless other passages which I have not time to give, Mr Smith and Mr Rounds arrive at the following

IMPORTANT CONCLUSIONS

1. When this entry was made in the logbook by Noah (or Shem) the Ark was somewhere off the coast of Maine. The latitude warrants this inference; the longitude is unfortunately wanting. Parallel proof that Noah visited the shores of North America is to be found in the old ballad, founded on a Habbinical tradition, where mention is made of Barne-gat. The singular error which locates Ararat just three miles south of Barnegat is doubtless due to some confusion in Noah's logarithms – the natural result of his unfortunate personal habits.

2. 'Ate our last pterodactyl yesterday . . . Bitter ale and mastodons all gone.' There we have a simple solution of a problem which has long puzzled science. The provisions stowed away in the Ark did not prove sufficient for the unexpectedly protracted voyage. Hard-pressed for food, Noah and his family were obliged to fall back on the livestock. They devoured the larger and more esculent animals in the collection. The only living specimens of the ichthyosaurus, the dodo, the silurian, the pleisosaurus, the mastodon, were eaten up by the hungry excursionists. We can therefore explain the extinction of certain species, which, as geology teaches us, existed in antediluvian times. Were this revelation the only result of Mr Smith's researches he would not have dug in vain. Mr Rounds justly observes that the allusion to bitter ale affords strong presumptive evidence that this entry in the log was made by the hand of no other than Noah himself!

3. The allusion to the interesting increase of Japheth's family shows that woman – noble woman, who always rises to the occasion – was doing her utmost to repair the breaches made in the earth's population by the whelm-ing waters. The phrase *hibaga* may possibly signify triplets; but Mr Smith, with that conservatism and repugnance to sensation which ever charac-terize the true archaeologist, prefers to be on the safe side and call it twins.

HANNIBAL HAMLIN THE ORIGINAL HAM

4. We now come to a conclusion which is as startling as it is inevitable. It connects the Honorable Hannibal Hamlin with the diluvian epoch, and thus with the other long-lived patriarchs who flourished before the flood. Antiquarians have long suspected that the similarity between the names

Ham and Hamlin was something more than a coincidence. The industry of a Smith has discovered among the Assyrian ruins the medial link which makes the connection perfectly apparent. Ham, the second son of Noah, is spoken of in these records from Kouyunjik as Hambl Hamin; and no candid mind can fail to see that the extreme antiquity of the senator from Maine is thus very clearly established!

'Hambl Hamin down with the scurvy. Must put him ashore.' Buhmi literally signifies earth, dirt: and the phrase *nam Buhmi* is often used in these inscriptions in the sense of to put in the earth, or bury. This can hardly be the meaning here, however, for the Ark was still afloat. *Nam Buhmi* can therefore hardly be construed otherwise than 'put ashore'.

Note the significance. The Ark is beating up and down, off the coast of Maine, waiting for a nor'west wind. Poor Ham, or Hambl Hamin, as he should properly be called, has reason to regret his weakness for maritime excursions and naval junketing parties. The lack of fresh vegetables, and a steady diet of corned mastodon, have told upon his system. Poor Hambl! When he was collector of a Mediterranean port just before the flood, he was accustomed to have green peas and asparagus franked him daily from the Garden of Eden. But now the franking privilege has been abrogated, and the Garden of Eden is full forty fathoms under the brine. Everything is salt. His swarthy face grows pale and haggard. His claw-hammer coat droops upon an attenuated frame. He chews his cheroot moodily as he stands upon the hurricane deck of the Ark with his thumbs in his vest pocket, and thinks that he can hold office on this earth but little longer. His gums begin to soften. He shows the ravages of the scurvy. And Noah, therefore, after considerable argument – for Hambl is reluctant to get out of any place he has once got into – nam Buhmi's him – puts him ashore.

We have no further record of Hambl Hamin, but it is perfectly reasonable to assume that after being landed on the rocky coast of Maine he subsisted upon huckleberries until sufficiently recovered from the scurvy, then sailed up the Penobscot upon a log, founded the ancient village of Hamden, which he named after himself, and was immediately elected to some public position.

AN OPPOSITION ARK

In Mr Rounds's long and profoundly interesting communication I have, I fear, an *embarras de richesses*. From the many curious legends which Mr Smith has deciphered, I shall select only one more, and shall deal briefly with that. It is the story of an opposition ark.

At the time of the flood there lived a certain merchant named Brith, who had achieved a competence in the retail grocery business. In fact, he was an antediluvian millionaire. Brith had been converted from heathenism by the exceedingly effective preaching of Noah, but had subsequently backslidden. When it began to thunder and lighten, however, and to grow black in the north-east, Brith professed recurring symptoms of piety. He came down to the gangway plank and applied for passage for himself and family. Noah, who was checking off the animals on the back of an old tax bill, sternly refused to entertain any such idea. Brith had recently defeated him for the Common Council.

The worthy grocer's money now stood him in good stead. He did the most sensible thing possible under the circumstances. He built an ark for himself, painted in big letters along the side the words: 'The Only Safe Plan of Universal Navigation!' and named it the *Toad*. The *Toad* was fashioned after the model of the Ark, and there being no copyright in those days, Noah could only hope that it might prove unseaworthy.

In the *Toad*, Brith embarked his wife Briatha, his two daughters, Phessar and Barran, his sons-in-law, Lampra and Pinnyish, and a select assortment of beasts hardly inferior to that collected by Noah himself. Lampra and Pinnyish, sly dogs, persuaded fifty of the most beautiful women they could find to come along with them.

Brith was not so good a sailor as Noah. He put to sea full forty days too soon. He lost his dead reckoning and beat around the ocean for the space of seven years and a quarter, living mostly upon the rats that infested the *Toad*. Brith had foolishly neglected to provision his craft for a long voyage.

After this protracted sailing, the passengers and crew of the *Toad* managed to make a landing one rainy evening and took ashore, with themselves, their baggage and a coon and dromedary, the sole surviving relics of their proud menagerie. Once on terra firma, the three men separated, having drawn up a tripartite covenant of perpetual amity and divided up the stock of wives. Brith took eighteen, Lampra took eighteen, and Pinnyish, who seems to have been an easygoing sort of fellow, too lazy to quarrel, had to be satisfied with the seventeen that remained.

Tablets from Nebbi Yunus throw some light on the interesting question as to the landing place of this party. *Khayarta* certainly means island, and *Dyinim* undeniably signifies long. Perhaps, therefore, Mr Rounds is justified in his opinion that the *Toad* dropped anchor in Wallabout Bay, and that Brooklyn and the Plymouth society owe their origin to this singular expedition.

The Professor's Experiment

Edward Page Mitchell

The red wine of Affenthal has this quality, that one half-bottle makes you kind but firm, two make you talkative and obstinate, and three, recklessly unreasonable.

If the waiter at the Prinz Carl in Heidelberg had possessed a soul above drink-money, he might have calculated accurately the effect of the six half-bottles of Affenthaler which he fetched to the apartment of the Reverend Dr Bellglory at the six o'clock dinner for three. That is to say, he might have deduced this story in advance by observation of the fact that of the six half-bottles one was consumed by Miss Blanche Bellglory, two went to the Reverend Doctor, her father, while the remaining moiety fell to the share of young Strout, remotely of New York and immediately of Professor Schwank's psycho-neurological section in the university.

So when in the course of the evening the doctor fell asleep in his chair, and young Strout took opportunity to put to Miss Blanche a question which he had already asked her twice, once at Saratoga Springs and once in New York city, she returned the answer he had heard on two former occasions, but in terms even more firm, while not less kind than before. She declared her unalterable determination to abide by her parent's wishes.

This was not exactly pleasing to young Strout. He knew better than anybody else that, while approving him socially and humanly, the doctor abhorred his opinions. 'No man,' the doctor had repeatedly said, 'who denies the objective verity of knowledge derived from intuition or otherwise by subjective methods – no man who pushes noumena aside in his impetuous pursuit of phenomena can make a safe husband for my child.'

He said the same thing again in a great many words and with much emphasis, after he awoke from his nap, Miss Blanche having discreetly withdrawn.

'But, my dear Doctor,' urged Strout, 'this is an affair of the heart, not of metaphysics; and you leave for Nuremberg tomorrow, and now is my last chance.'

'You are an excellent young man in several respects,' rejoined the doctor. 'Abjure your gross materialism and Blanche is yours with all my heart. Your antecedents are unexceptionable, but you are intellectually impregnated with the most dangerous heresy of this or any other age. If I should countenance it by giving you my daughter, I could never look the Princeton faculty in the face.'

'It appears to me that this doesn't concern the Princeton faculty in the least,' persisted Strout. 'It concerns Blanche and me.'

Here, then, were three people, two of them young and in love with each other, divided by a question of metaphysics, the most abstract and useless question that ever wasted human effort. But that same question divided the schools of Europe for centuries and contributed largely to the list of martyrs for opinion's sake. The famous old controversy was now taken up by the six half-bottles of Affenthaler, three of them stoutly holding ground against the other three.

'No argument in the world,' said the doctor's two half-bottles, 'can shake my decision'; and off he went to sleep again.

'No amount of coaxing,' said Miss Blanche's half-bottle, two hours later in the evening, 'can make me act contrary to Papa's wishes. But,' continued the half-bottle in a whisper, 'I am sorry he is so stubborn.'

'I don't believe it,' retorted Strout's three half-bottles. 'You have no more heart than one of your father's non-individualized ideas. You are not real flesh and blood like other women. You are simply Extension, made up of an aggregate of concepts, and assuming to be Entity, and imposing your unreal existence upon a poor Devil like me. You are unreal, I say. A flaw in logic, an error of the senses, a fallacy in reasoning, a misplaced premise, and what becomes of you? Puff! Away you go into all. If it were otherwise, you would care for me. What a fool I am to love you! I might as well love a memory, a thought, a dream, a mathematical formula, a rule of syntax, or anything else that lacks objective existence.'

She said nothing, but the tears came into her eyes.

'Goodbye, Blanche,' he continued at the door, pulling his hat over his eyes and not observing the look of pain and bewilderment that clouded her fair face – 'Heaven bless you when your father finally marries you to a syllogism!'

2

Strout went whistling from the Prinz Carl Hotel toward his rooms in the Plöckstrasse. He reviewed his parting with Blanche. 'So much the better, perhaps,' he said to himself. 'One dream less in life, and more room for realities.' By the clock in the market place he saw that it was half-past nine, for the full moon hanging high above the Königstuhle flooded the town and valley with light. Up on the side of the hill the gigantic ruin of the old castle stood boldly out from among the trees.

He stopped whistling and gritted his teeth.

'Pshaw!' he said aloud, 'one can't take off his convictions like a pair of uncomfortable boots. After all, love is nothing more nor less than the disintegration and recombination of certain molecules of the brain or marrow, the exact laws governing which have not yet been ascertained.' So saying, he ran plump into a portly individual coming down the street.

'Hallo! Herr Strout,' said the jolly voice of Professor Schwank. 'Whither are you going so fast, and what kind of physiology talk you to the moon?'

'I am walking off three half-bottles of your cursed Affenthaler, which have gone to my feet, Herr Professor,' replied Strout, 'and I am making love to the moon. It's an old affair between us.'

'And your lovely American friend?' demanded the fat professor, with a chuckle.

'Departs by the morning train,' replied Strout gravely.

'*Himmelshitzen!*' exclaimed the professor. 'And grief has blinded you so that you plunge into the abdomens of your elders? But come with me to my room, and smoke yourself into a philosophic frame of mind.'

Professor Schwank's apartments faced the university buildings in the Ludwig-platz. Established in a comfortable armchair, with a pipe of excellent tobacco in his mouth, Strout felt more at peace with his environment. He was now in an atmosphere of healthful, practical, scientific activity that calmed his soul. Professor Schwank had gone further than the most eminent of his contemporaries in demonstrating the purely physiological basis of mind and thought. He had gotten nearer than any other man in Europe to the secrets of the nerve aura, the penetralia of the brain, the memory scars of the ganglia. His position in philosophy was the antipodes of that occupied by the Reverend Dr Bellglory, for example. The study reflected the occupations of the man. In one corner stood an enormous Ruhmkorff coil. Books were scattered everywhere – on shelves, on tables, on chairs, on the floor. A plaster bust of Aristotle looked across the room into the face of a plaster bust of Leibnitz. Prints of Gall, of Pappenheim, of Leeuwenhoek, hung upon the walls. Varnished dissections and wet preparations abounded. In a glass vessel on the table at Strout's elbow, the brain of a positivist philosopher floated in yellow alcohol: near it, also suspended in spirits, swung the medulla oblongata of a celebrated thief.

The appearance of the professor himself, as he sat in his arm-chair opposite Strout, serenely drawing clouds of smoke from the amber mouthpiece of his long porcelain pipe, was of the sort which, by promising sympathy beforehand, seduces reserve into confidential utterances. Not only his rosy face, with its fringe of yellow beard, but his whole mountainous body seemed to beam on Strout with friendly good will. He looked like the refuge of a broken heart. Drawn out in spite of himself by the professor's kindly, attentive smile and discreet questions, Strout found satisfaction in unbosoming his troubles. The professor, smoking in silence, listened patiently to the long story. If Strout had been less preoccupied with his own woes he might, perhaps, have discovered that behind the friendly interest that glimmered on the glasses of the professor's gold-bowed spectacles, a pair of small, steel-gray eyes were observing him with the keen, unrelenting coldness of scientific scrutiny.

'You have seen, Herr Professor,' said Strout in conclusion, 'that the case is hopeless.'

'My dear fellow,' replied the professor, 'I see nothing of the kind.'

'But it is a matter of conviction,' explained Strout. 'One cannot renounce the truth even to gain a wife. She herself would despise me if I did.'

'In this world everything is true and nothing is true,' replied the professor sententiously. 'You must change your convictions.'

'That is impossible!'

The professor blew a great cloud of smoke and regarded the young man with an expression of pity and surprise. It seemed to Strout that Aristotle and Leibnitz, Leeuwenhoek, Pappenheim, and Gall were all looking down upon him with pity and surprise.

'Impossible did you say?' remarked Professor Schwank. 'On the contrary, my dear boy, nothing is easier than to change one's convictions. In the present advanced condition of surgery, it is a matter of little difficulty.'

Strout looked at his respected instructor in blank amazement. 'What you call your convictions,' continued the savant, 'are matters of mental constitution, depending on adventitious circumstances. You are a positivist, an idealist, a skeptic, a mystic, a what-not, why? Because nature, predisposition, the assimilation of bony elements, have made your skull thicker in one place, thinner in another. The cranial wall presses too close upon the brain in one spot; you sneer at the opinions of your friend, Dr Bellglory. It cramps the development of the tissues in another spot; you deny faith a place in philosophy. I assure you, Herr Strout, we have discovered and classified already the greater part of the physical causes determining and limiting belief, and are fast reducing the system to the certainty of science.'

'Granting all that,' interposed Strout, whose head was swimming under the combined influence of Affenthaler, tobacco smoke, and startling new ideas, 'I fail to see how it helps my case. Unfortunately, the bone of my skull is no longer cartilage, like an infant's. You cannot mold my intellect by means of compresses and bandages.'

'Ah! there you touch my professional pride,' cried Schwank. 'If you would only put yourself into my hands!'

'And what then?'

'Then,' replied the professor with enthusiasm, 'I should remodel your intellect to suit the emergency. How, you ask? If a blow on the head had driven a splinter of bone down upon the gray matter overlaying the cerebrum, depriving you of memory, the power of language, or some other special faculty, as the case might be, how should I proceed? I should raise a section of the bone and remove the pressure. Just so when the physical conformation of the cranium limits your capacity to understand and credit the philosophy which your American theologian insists upon in his son-in-law. I remove the pressure. I give you a charming wife, while science gains a beautiful and valuable fact. That is what I offer you, Herr Strout!'

'In other words – ' began Strout.

'In other words, I should trephine you,' shouted the professor, jumping from his chair and no longer attempting to conceal his eagerness.

'Well, Herr Professor,' said Strout slowly, after a long pause, during which he had endeavored to make out why the pictured face of Gall seemed to wear a look of triumph ' – Well, Herr Professor, I consent to the operation. Trephine me at once – tonight.'

The professor feebly demurred to the precipitateness of this course. 'The necessary preparations,' he urged.

'Need not occupy five minutes,' replied Strout. 'Tomorrow I shall have changed my mind.'

This suggestion was enough to impel the professor to immediate action. 'You will allow me,' asked he, 'to send for my esteemed colleague in the university, the Herr Dr Anton Diggelmann?'

Strout assented. 'Do anything that you think needful to the success of the experiment.'

Professor Schwank rang. 'Fritz,' said he to the stupid-faced Black Forester who answered the bell, 'run across the square and ask Dr Diggelmann to come to me immediately. Request him to bring his surgical case and sulphuric ether. If you find the doctor, you need not return.'

Acting on a sudden impulse, Strout seized a sheet of paper that lay on the professor's table and hastily wrote a few words. 'Here!' he said, tossing the servant a gold piece of ten marks. 'Deliver this note at the Prince Carl in the morning – mind you, in the morning.'

The note which he had written was this:

BLANCHE: When you receive this I shall have solved the problem in one way or another. I am about to be trephined under the superintendence of my friend Professor Schwank. If the intellectual obstacle to our union is removed by the operation, I shall follow you to Bavaria and Switzerland. If the operation results otherwise, think sometimes kindly of your unfortunate

G. S.

Ludwig-platz; 10:30 p.m.

Fritz faithfully delivered the message to Dr Diggelmann, and then hied toward the nearest wine shop. His gold piece dazed him. 'A nice, liberal gentleman that!' he thought. 'Ten marks for carrying the letter to the Prinz Carl in the morning – ten marks, a thousand pfennige; beer at five pfennige the glass, two hundred glasses!' The immensity of the prospect filled him with joy. How might he manifest his gratitude? He reflected, and an idea struck him. 'I will not wait till morning,' he thought. 'I will deliver the gentleman's letter tonight, at once. He will say, "Fritz, you are a prompt fellow. You do even better than you are told."'

3

Strout was stretched upon a reclining chair, his coat and waistcoat off. Professor Schwank stood over him. In his hand was a hollow cone, rolled from a newspaper. He held the cone by the apex: the broad aperture at the base was closely pressed against Strout's face, covering all but his eyes and forehead.

'By long, steady, regular inspiration,' said the professor, in a soothing, monotonous voice. 'That is right; that is right; that is – right – there – there – there!'

With every inhalation Strout drew in the pleasant, tingling coldness of the ether fumes. At first his breathing was forced: at the end of each inspiration he experienced for an instant a sensation as if mighty waters were rushing through his brain. Gradually the period of the rushing sensation extended itself, until it began with the beginning of each breath. Then the ether seemed to seize possession of his breathing, and to control the expansions and contractions of his chest independently of his own will. The ether breathed for him. He surrendered himself to its influence with a feeling of delight. The rushings became rhythmic, and the intervals shorter and shorter. His individuality seemed to be wrapped up in the rushings, and to be borne to and fro in their tremendous flux and reflux. 'I shall be gone in one second more,' he thought, and his consciousness sank in the whirling flood.

Professor Schwank nodded to Dr Diggelmann. The doctor nodded back to the professor.

Dr Diggelmann was a dry little old man, who weighed hardly more than a hundred pounds. He wore a black wig, too large for his head. His eyes were deep set under corrugated brows, while strongly marked lines running from the corners of his nostrils to the corners of his mouth gave his face a lean, sardonic expression, in striking contrast with the jolly rotundity of Professor Schwank's visage. Dr Diggelmann was taciturn but observant. At the professor's nod, he opened his case of surgical instruments and selected a scalpel with a keen curved blade, and also a glittering piece of steel which looked like an exaggerated auger bit with a gimlet handle. Having satisfied himself that these instruments were in good condition, he deliberately rolled up the sleeves of his coat and approached the unconscious Strout.

'About on the median line, just behind the junction of the coronal and sagittal sutures,' whispered Professor Schwank eagerly.

'Yes. I know – I know,' replied Diggelmann.

He was on the point of cutting away with his scalpel some of the brown hair that encumbered operations on the top of Strout's head, when the door was quickly opened from the outside and a young lady, attended by a maid, entered without ceremony.

'I am Blanche Bellglory,' the young lady announced to the astonished savants, as soon as she had recovered her breath. 'I have come to – '

At this moment she perceived the motionless form of Strout upon the reclining chair, while the gleaming steel in Dr Diggelmann's hand caught her alert eyes. She uttered a little shriek and ran toward the group.

'Oh, this is terrible!' she cried. 'I am too late, and you have already killed him.'

'Calm yourself, I beg you,' said the polite professor. 'No circumstance is terrible to which we are indebted for a visit from so charming a young lady.'

'So great an honor!' added Dr Diggelmann, grinning diabolically and rubbing his hands.

'And Herr Strout,' continued the professor, 'is unfortunately not yet trephined. As you entered, we were about beginning the operation.'

Miss Bellglory gave a sob of relief and sank into a chair.

In a few well-chosen words the professor explained the theory of his experiment, dwelling especially upon the effect it was expected to have on the fortunes of the young people. When he finished, the American girl's eyes were full of tears, but the firm lines of her mouth showed that she had already resolved upon her own course.

'How noble in him,' she exclaimed, 'to submit to be trephined for my sake! But that must not be. I can't consent to have his poor, dear head mutilated. I should never forgive myself. The trouble all originates from my decision not to marry him without Papa's approval. With my present views of duty, I cannot alter that decision. But don't you think,' she continued, dropping her voice to a whisper, 'that if you should trephine me, I might see my duty in a different light?'

'It is extremely probable, my dear young lady,' replied the professor, throwing a significant glance at Dr Diggelmann, who responded with the faintest wink imaginable.

'Then,' said Miss Blanche, arising and beginning to remove her bonnet, 'please proceed to trephine me immediately. I insist on it.'

'What's all this?' demanded the deep voice of the Reverend Dr Bellglory, who had entered the room unnoticed, piloted by Fritz. 'I came as rapidly as I could, Blanche, but not early enough, it appears, to learn the first principles of your singular actions.'

'My papa, gentlemen,' said Miss Bellglory.

The two Germans bowed courteously. Dr Bellglory affably returned their salutation.

'These gentlemen, Papa,' Miss Blanche explained, 'have kindly undertaken to reconcile the difference of opinion between poor George and ourselves by means of a surgical operation. I don't at all understand it, but George does, for you see that he has thought best to submit to the operation, which they were about to begin when I arrived. Now, I cannot allow him to suffer for my obstinacy; and, therefore, dear Papa, I have requested the gentlemen to trephine me instead of him.'

Professor Schwank repeated for Dr Bellglory's information the explanation which he had already made to the young lady. On learning of Strout's course in the matter, Dr Bellglory was greatly affected.

'No, Blanche!' he said, 'our young friend must not be trephined. Although I cannot conscientiously accept him as a son-in-law while our views on the verity of subjective knowledge differ so widely, I can at least emulate his generous willingness to open his intellect to conviction. It is I who will be trephined, provided these gentlemen will courteously substitute me for the patient now in their hands.'

'We shall be most happy,' said Professor Schwank and Dr Diggelman in the same breath.

'Thanks! Thanks!' cried Dr Bellglory, with genuine emotion.

'But I shall not permit you to sacrifice your lifelong convictions to my happiness, Papa,' interposed Blanche. The doctor insisted that he was only doing his duty as a parent. The amiable dispute went on for some time, the Germans listening with indifference. Sure of a subject for their experiment at any rate, they cared little which one of the three Americans finally came under the knife. Meanwhile Strout opened his eyes, slowly raised himself upon one elbow, vacantly gazed about the room for a few seconds, and then sank back, relapsing temporarily into unconsciousness.

Professor Schwank, who perceived that father and daughter were equally fixed in their determination, and each unlikely to yield to the other, was on the point of suggesting that the question be settled by trephining both of them, when Strout again regained his senses. He sat bolt upright, staring fixedly at the glass jar which contained the positivist's brain. Then he pressed both hands to his head, muttering a few incoherent words. Gradually, as he recovered from the clutch of the ether one after another of his faculties, his eyes brightened and he appeared to recognize the faces around him. After some time he opened his lips and spoke.

'Marvelous!' he exclaimed.

Miss Bellglory ran to him and took his hand. The doctor hurried forward, intending to announce his own resolution to be trephined. Strout pressed Blanche's hand to his lips for an instant, gave the doctor's hand a cordial grasp, and then seized the hand of Professor Schwank, which he wrung with all the warmth of respectful gratitude.

'My dear Herr Professor,' he said, 'how can I ever repay you? The experiment is a perfect success.'

'But – ' began the astounded professor.

'Don't try to depreciate your own share in my good fortune,' interrupted Strout. 'The theory was yours, and all the triumph of the practical success belongs to you and Dr Diggelmann's skill.'

Strout, still holding Blanche's hand, now turned to her father.

'There is now no obstacle to our union, Doctor,' he said. 'Thanks to Professor Schwank's operation, I see the blind folly of my late attitude toward the subjective. I recant. I am no longer a positivist. My intellect has leaped the narrow limits that hedged it in. I know now that there is more in our philosophy than can be measured with a metric ruler or weighed in a coulomb balance. Ever since I passed under the influence of the ether, I have been floating in the infinite. I have been freed from conditions of time and space. I have lost my own individuality in the immensity of the All. A dozen times I have been absorbed in Brahma; a dozen times I have emanated from Brahma, a new being, forgetful of my old self. I have stood face to face with the mystic and awful Om; my world-soul, descending to the finite, has floated calmly over an ocean of Affenthaler. My consciousness leaped back as far as the thirtieth century before Christ and forward as far as the fortieth century yet to come. There is no time; there is no space; there is no individual existence; there is nothing save the All, and the faith that guides reason through the changeless night. For more than one million years my identity was that of the positivist in the glass jar yonder. Pardon me, Professor Schwank, but for the same period of time yours was that of the celebrated thief in the other jar. Great heavens! How mistaken I have been up to the night when you, Herr Professor, took charge of my intellectual destiny.'

He paused for want of breath, but the glow of the mystic's rapture still lighted up his handsome features. There was an awkward silence in the room for considerable time. Then it was broken by the dry, harsh voice of Dr Diggelmann.

'You labor under a somewhat ridiculous delusion, young gentleman. You haven't been trephined yet.'

Strout looked in amazement from one to another of his friends; but their faces confirmed the surgeon's statement.

'What was it then?' he gasped.

'Sulphuric ether,' replied the surgeon, laconically.

'But after all,' interposed Dr Bellglory, 'it makes little difference what agent has opened our friend's mind to a perception of the truth. It is a matter for congratulation that the surgical operation becomes no longer necessary.'

The two Germans exchanged glances of dismay. 'We shall lose the opportunity for our experiment,' the professor whispered to Diggelmann. Then he continued aloud, addressing Strout: 'I should advise you to submit to the operation, nevertheless. There can be no permanent intellectual cure without it. These effects of the ether will pass away.'

'Thank you,' returned Strout, who at last read correctly the cold, calculating expression that lurked behind the scientist's spectacles. 'Thank you, I am very well as I am.'

'But you might, for the sake of science, consent – ' persisted Schwank.

'Yes, for the sake of science,' echoed Diggelmann.

'Hang science!' replied Strout, fiercely. 'Don't you know that I no longer believe in science?'

Blanche also began to understand the true motives which had led the German professor to interfere in her love affair. She cast an approving glance at Strout and arose to depart. The three Americans moved toward the door. Professor Schwank and Dr Diggelmann fairly gnashed their teeth with rage. Miss Bellglory turned and made them a low curtsey.

'If you must trephine somebody for the sake of science, gentlemen,' she remarked with her sweetest smile, 'you might draw lots to see which of you shall trephine the other.'

The Soul Spectroscope

The Singular Materialism of a Progressive Thinker

Edward Page Mitchell

PROFESSOR TYNDALL'S VIEWS MORE THAN JUSTIFIED
BY THE EXPERIMENTS OF THE CELEBRATED PROFESSOR
DUMMKOPF OF BOSTON, MASS.

Boston, December 13 – Professor Dummkopf, a German gentleman of education and ingenuity, at present residing in this city, is engaged on experiments which, if successful, will work a great change both in metaphysical science and in the practical relationships of life.

The professor is firm in the conviction that modern science has narrowed down to almost nothing the border territory between the material and the immaterial. It may be some time, he admits, before any man shall be able to point his finger and say with authority, 'Here mind begins; here matter ends.' It may be found that the boundary line between mind and matter is as purely imaginary as the equator that divides the northern from the southern hemisphere. It may be found that mind is essentially objective, as is matter, or that matter is as entirely subjective, as is mind. It may be that there is no matter except as conditioned in mind. It may be that there is no mind except as conditioned in matter. Professor Dummkopf's views upon this broad topic are interesting, although somewhat bewildering. I can cordially recommend the great work in nine volumes, *Koerperliche-gewissenschaft*, to any reader who may be inclined to follow up the subject. The work can undoubtedly be obtained in the original Leipzig edition through any responsible importer of foreign books.

Great as is the problem suggested above, Professor Dummkopf has no doubt whatever that it will be solved, and at no distant day. He himself has taken a masterly stride toward a solution by the brilliant series of experiments I am about to describe. He not only believes with Tyndall that matter contains the promise and potency of all life, but he believes that every force, physical, intellectual, and moral, may be resolved into matter, formulated in terms of matter, and analyzed into its constituent forms of matter; that motion is matter, mind is matter, law is matter, and even that abstract relations of mathematical abstractions are purely material.

PHOTOGRAPHING SMELL

In accordance with an invitation extended to me at the last meeting of the Radical Club – an organization, by the way, which is doing a noble work in extending our knowledge of the Unknowable – I dallied yesterday at Professor Dummkopf's rooms in Joy Street, at the West End. I found the professor in his apartment on the upper floor, busily engaged in an attempt to photograph smell.

'You see,' he said, as he stirred up a beaker from which strongly marked fumes of sulphuretted hydrogen were arising and filling the room, 'you see that, having demonstrated the objectiveness of sensation, it has now become my privilege and easy task to show that the phenomena of sensation are equally material. Hence I am attempting to photograph smell.'

The professor then darted behind a camera which was leveled upon the vessel in which the suffocating fumes were generated and busied himself awhile with the plate.

A disappointed look stole over his face as he brought the negative to the light and examined it anxiously. 'Not yet, not yet!' he said sadly; 'but patience and improved appliances will finally bring it. The trouble is in my tools, you see, and not in my theory. I did fancy the other day that I obtained a distinctly marked negative from the odor of a hot onion stew, and the thought has cheered me ever since. But it's bound to come. I tell you, my worthy friend, the actinic ray wasn't made for nothing. Could you accommodate me with a dollar and a quarter to buy some more collodion?'

THE BOTTLE THEORY OF SOUND

I expressed my cheerful readiness to be banker to genius.

'Thanks,' said the professor, pocketing the scrip and resuming his position at the camera. 'When I have pictorially captured smell, the most palpable of the senses, the next thing will be to imprison sound – vulgarly speaking, to bottle it. Just think a moment. Force is as imperishable as matter; indeed, as I have been somewhat successful in showing, it is matter. Now, when a sound wave is once started, it is only lost through an indefinite extension of its circumference. Catch that sound wave, sir! Catch it in a bottle, then its circumference cannot extend. You may keep the sound wave forever if you will only keep it corked up tight. The only difficulty is in bottling it in the first place. I shall attend to the details of that operation just as soon as I have managed to photograph the confounded rotten-egg smell of sulphydric acid.'

The professor stirred up the offensive mixture with a glass rod, and continued: 'While my object in bottling sound is mainly scientific, I must confess that I see in success in that direction a prospect of considerable pecuniary profit. I shall be prepared at no distant day to put operas in quart bottles, labeled and assorted, and contemplate a series of light and popular airs in ounce vials at prices to suit the times. You know very well that it costs a ten-dollar bill now to take a lady to hear *Martha* or *Mignon*, rendered in first-class style. By the bottle system, the same notes may be heard in one's own parlor at a comparatively trifling expense. I could put the operas into the market at from eighty cents to a dollar a bottle. For oratorios and symphonies I should use demijohns, and the cost would of course be greater. I don't think that ordinary bottles would hold Wagner's music. It might be necessary to employ carboys. Sir, if I were of the sanguine habit of you Americans, I should say that there were millions in it. Being a phlegmatic Teuton, accustomed to the precision and moderation of scientific language, I will merely say that in the success of my experiments with sound I see a comfortable income, as well as great renown.

A SCIENTIFIC MARVEL

By this time the professor had another negative, but an eager examination of it yielded nothing more satisfactory than before. He sighed and continued: 'Having photographed smell and bottled sound, I shall proceed to a project as much higher than this as the reflective faculties are higher than the perceptive, as the brain is more exalted than the ear or nose.

'I am perfectly satisfied that elements of mind are just as susceptible of detection and analysis as elements of matter. Why, mind *is* matter.

'The soul spectroscope, or, as it will better be known, Dummkopf's duplex self-registering soul spectroscope, is based on the broad fact that whatever is material may be analyzed and determined by the position of the Frauenhofer lines upon the spectrum. If soul is matter, soul may thus be analyzed and determined. Place a subject under the light, and the minute exhalations or emanations proceeding from his soul – and these exhalations or emanations are, of course, matter – will be represented by their appropriate symbols upon the face of a properly arranged spectroscope.

'This, in short, is my discovery. How I shall arrange the spectroscope, and how I shall locate the subject with reference to the light is of course my secret. I have applied for a patent. I shall exploit the instrument and its practical workings at the Centennial. Till then I must decline to enter into any more explicit description of the invention.'

THE IMPORTANCE OF THE DISCOVERY

'What will be the bearing of your great discovery in its practical workings?'

'I can go so far as to give you some idea of what those practical workings are. The effect of the soul spectroscope upon everyday affairs will be prodigious, simply prodigious. All lying, deceit, double dealing, hypocrisy, will be abrogated under its operation. It will bring about a millennium of truth and sincerity.

'A few practical illustrations. No more bell punches on the horse railroad. The superintendent, with a smattering of scientific knowledge and one of my soul spectroscopes in his office, will examine with the eye of infallible science every applicant for the position of conductor and will determine by the markings on his spectrum whether there is dishonesty in his soul, and this as readily as the chemist decides whether there is iron in a meteorolite or hydrogen in Saturn's ring.

'No more courts, judges, or juries. Hereafter justice will be represented with both eyes wide open and with one of my duplex self-registering soul spectroscopes in her right hand. The inmost nature of the accused will be read at a glance and he will be acquitted, imprisoned for thirty days, or hung, just as the Frauenhofer lines which lay bare his soul may determine.

'No more official corruption or politicians' lies. The important element in every campaign will be one of my soul spectroscopes, and it will effect the most radical, and, at the same time, the most practicable of civil service reforms.

'No more young stool pigeons in tall towers. No man will subscribe for a daily newspaper until a personal inspection of its editor's soul by means of one of my spectroscopes has convinced him that he is paying for truth, honest conviction, and uncompromising independence, rather than for the false utterances of a hired conscience and a bought judgment.

'No more unhappy marriages. The maiden will bring her glibly promising lover to me before she accepts or rejects his proposal, and I shall tell her whether his spectrum exhibits the markings of pure love, constancy, and tenderness, or of sordid avarice, vacillating affections, and post-nuptial cruelty. I shall be the angel with shining sword (or rather spectroscope) who shall attend Hymen and guard the entrance to his paradise.

'No more shame. If anything be wanting in the character of a man, no amount of brazen pretension on his part can place the missing line in his spectrum. If anything is lacking in him, it will be lacking there. I found by a long series of experiments upon the imperfectly constituted minds of the patients in the lunatic asylum at Taunton – '

'Then you have been at Taunton?'

'Yes. For two years I pursued my studies among the unfortunate inmates of that institution. Not exactly as a patient myself, you understand, but as a student of the phenomena of morbid intellectual developments. But I see I am wearying you, and I must resume my photography before this stuff stops smelling. Come again.'

Having bid the professor farewell and wished him abundant success in his very interesting experiments, I went home and read again for the thirty-ninth time Professor Tyndall's address at Belfast.

The Inside of the Earth

A big hole through the planet from pole to pole

Edward Page Mitchell

HOW CLALTUS TREATS THE THEORY OF THE OPEN POLAR
SEA — WHAT HE SAYS ABOUT THE GULF STREAM — LIFE OF
A BROOKLYN DISCOVERER

He was an elderly man with a beard of grizzled gray unkempt hair, light eyes that shot quick, furtive glances, pale lips that trembled often with weak, uneasy smiles, and hands that restlessly rubbed each other, or else groped unconsciously for some missing tool. His clothes were coarse and in rags, and as he sat on a low upturned box, close before a half-warm stove, he shivered sometimes when a fierce gust of freezing wind rattled the patched and dingy windows. Behind him was a carpenter's bench, with a rack of neatly kept woodworking tools above it; a lathe and a small stock of very handsomely finished library stepladders. A great pile of black walnut chips and lathe dust lay on the floor, and the air was full of the clean, fresh smell of the wood. The room in which he sat was a garret, at the top of two eroded flights of steep and rickety stairs, in a building within three blocks of the southernmost extremity of that Lilliputian railway on which Saratoga trunks, fitted up as horse cars, are run from Fulton ferry to Hamilton ferry.

'Don't mention my name at all, sir,' said he to the *Sun* reporter, who perched upon an unsteady box before him, 'nor don't give them the exact place, please, for there are lots about who know me, and who'd be bothering me, and maybe laughing at me. Call me John Claltus. That's the name I was known by down in Charleston and all down South, and it did very well while I was working there, so you can put it in that.'

'But why, having a grand scientific idea, and being the originator of novel and bold theories, do you shrink so modestly from public recognition and admiration?'

'I don't want any glory. I've thought out what I have because I felt I had a mission to do it, and maybe mightn't be let live if I didn't; but I'm done now. I can't last much longer. I'm old and poor, and I don't care to have folks bothering me and maybe laughing at me; and you see my brother, my cousins, and sometimes some sailor friends come to see me, and I'd rather you'd let it go as Claltus, sir.'

'And as Claltus it shall go. But about your discovery. Was it not Symmes's theory of a hole through the globe that first gave you the idea?'

REMARKABLE VISIONS

'Oh, not at all! I was shown it all in a vision years before I ever heard of him. It was more than thirty-eight years ago. I was only a twelve-year-old boy. I was greatly afraid when I saw it; it was so terrible to me. I really think, from what I saw, that the earth was all in a sort of mist or fog once. I felt that I must go to sea and try to find out what I could about it as a poor man; so as a sailor I went for years, always thinking about it and inquiring when I could of them that might have had a chance to know something. About two years ago I went South and tried to establish myself there, and then I saw the vision again, not so terrible as before, and I could understand it better. It came to me like a globe, about two feet through, and a hole through it one third of its diameter in bigness. I told it to people there and they said I was crazy. I told it to two men I was working for – brothers they were and Frenchmen. I built an extension table and raised the roof of their house for them, and they said, "How can it be that you do our work so well and yet are not in your right mind?" So I quit saying anything about it. This is a model of like what I saw in the vision.'

The model of the vision as produced is a ball of black walnut wood, four and a half inches in diameter, traversed by a round aperture whose diameter seemed to be about one third the diameter of the ball or globe. Around the exterior, lines have been traced by a lathe tool, the spaces between them representing ten degrees each. A chalk mark on one side represents New York. This ball is mounted between the points of an inverted U of strong wire, so based upon a little board as to admit of being tipped to change the angle at which the ball is poised. The points of the wire are fastened near the edges of the ends of the hole at opposite sides of the little globe, so as to admit of its turning, and thus alternately raising and depressing, with reference to the false poles, the ends of the hole. As the thing stood on a little stand, where he placed it very carefully, the sunlight poured through the hole, and as he turned it the area covered in the interior of the ball by the sun's direct rays was gradually narrowed, shortened, and finally so diminished as to extend inward only a very little way; then, as he continued turning it, the patch of light once more widened and lengthened until the sun again shone all the way through.

THE LESSON OF THE MODEL

'There,' said he, 'that represents a day and a night for the people in the inside of the earth. I'm perfectly satisfied in my own mind that the turn is made on about ten degrees, and about ten degrees from the outside rim of it; them that goes there would get to the flat part on the inside. When they get to the ninetieth degree that's the pole they've always been trying to make. They'll be turning into the inside. Eighty degrees is the furthest they've ever got yet, at least that's the furthest for anyone that has come back to tell about it. Perry's Point is the furthest land northward on this continent that has ever been reached, and Spitsbergen is about as far on the other side. The furthest they have gone south is Victoria Island, opposite Cape Horn, maybe a thousand miles away from the Cape, and that's only about eighty degrees. I've got a bit of stone here that came from Victoria Island that a sailor man gave me, thinkin', maybe, I might find out something about it from somebody that knew.'

The discoverer arose and walked slowly to the further end of his garret, where he took from a shelf a little piece of stone, about three inches in length, two in width, and three quarters in thickness, soft as rotten stone almost, light brown and looking like a bit of petrified wood.

'I don't know what it is. There isn't much curious about it. I've seen bits of stone from the Central Park that looked much like it, but not just the same. I tried to make a whetstone of it, but it was too soft; it wouldn't take any polish.'

'In your long sea service did you ever get far enough toward the poles to find anything corroborative of your theories?'

'Not myself, though I've noticed things that confirmed me. Now, there's the Gulf Stream, for instance. They say there's a current from the Gulf of Mexico that goes across to Europe; but I've seen enough myself, in the Indian Ocean, that I've crossed many a time and often, and round to Cape Horn, that I'm convinced it's the polar stream and the action of the sun on the narrow part of the rim there causes it. I studied it in the Gulf of Mexico. They thought the pressure of them big rivers flowing into the gulf made it. Now if that was so it would make a great pressure where it rushes through the narrow place between Florida and the West Indies that would set the stream going away to the other side of the ocean, but I couldn't see any such pressure greater there than anywhere else. Them rivers has no more effect there than a bucket of water poured into the bay down beyond. It's the great heat of the sun at the narrow rim melting the ice, and the current pouring out of that hole, that makes what they call the Gulf Stream in the part of it they've observed.'

WHAT A SAILOR SAID HE SAW

'Have you ever met any sailors who knew anything more about it than you did yourself?'

'Yes,' the discoverer answered quickly, ceasing to bore bits from the soft stone with his thick thumbnail and looking up with an eager smile, 'I met a sailor man in Charleston – Tola or Toland his name was – and he said he had been far enough to see a great, bright arch that rose out of the water like, and I said, "That's my arch; that's the rim of the hole to the inside of the earth." He was there in Charleston waiting for a ship, and I was making patterns. We used to meet every night to talk about the thing, for he was a knowledgeable man, and took an interest in it, the same as I did. He saw that arch every night for two weeks while the privateer he was on was in them waters, and all that was with him saw it, but they couldn't make it out. Then they got frightened of it, beating about in strange waters, and at last they got back to parts of the ocean they knew, and so came away as fast as they could. Well,' sighing as he spoke, 'sailors sometimes make a heap of brag about what they've seen and possibly there's nothing in it, but there may be. I know it's there all the same, for I've seen it in the vision and it stands to reason. I asked him if he could see anything in the daytime, and he said no – nothing, only clouds and mists about him. And that stands to reason, for in the night, you see, the reflected light would shine up the arch and show it, but in daytime it would be so high and so far off that it could not be seen. I had some hopes that he might have got the color of land, but he didn't.'

'What do you suppose is the character of the country in there?'

'Oh! I don't know, but it's likely there are mountains and rivers in there. I think it's most likely they have most water in there, but maybe a good deal of land, too; and maybe gold and various kinds of things that's scarce on the outside.'

'And people, too?'

'I shouldn't wonder at all if there was people there, driven in there by the storms, and that couldn't find their way out again.'

'And how do you suppose they support life?'

'Why shouldn't they the same as people on the outside? Haven't they got air and light and heat and the change of seasons, and water and soil, the same as there is outside? It's a big place in there. The open polar circle, I calculate, is in circumference about the diameter of the earth, and that would give one third of the earth open inside. They get light and heat from the sun, and maybe a good deal of reflected light and heat all the way through from the south end of the hole. That's where it all goes in at.'

THE MEN WHO LIVE INSIDE

'And what sort of folks do you suppose are in there?'

'Ah! I don't know. There may be Irishmen there, and there may be Dutch there, and there may be Malays there, and other kinds of people, and there may be Danes there, too – they were good smart sailor people, too, in their time, always beating about the waters and they might have got drifted in there and couldn't get out.'

'How do you mean "couldn't get out"?'

'Couldn't find their way. There's no charts of them waters, and maybe the needle won't work the same there, and the place is so big they may go on sailing there and never going straight or finding their way back. Maybe they've been wrecked, and had no means of coming away. Sure there must be mighty storms in there. Great storms come out of that hole in the south. "Great storms come out of the South," the Scriptures say. You'll find that in the Book of Job, that and lots more about the earth. He talks about it as if he knew all about it. He knew all about that hole in the inside of the earth, and as he wasn't with the Creator when He made it, he must have seen it to know so much about it as he shows he did.

'And yet – ' he murmured in a lower voice, meditatively digging off little bits from a piece of chalk with his fingernails, and touching up the spot representing New York on the wooden ball – 'you'll find a good many things in the Scriptures if you search them, about the interior of the earth.'

'Have you ever tried to enlist government or private enterprise to prosecute an investigation of the correctness of your theories?'

'No. What could I do? I was always only a poor, hard-working, ignorant man, but I seen it in a vision and I felt it my duty to study on it and make it known. But I think if a good steamship was laid on her course proper from New York, set in the way I know she would have to be, and provided for rightly, in about ten weeks she would get there and into the inside of the earth. Her wheels would never stop until she got there, for there's more than human thought about it. It's God's will it should be known, and her machinist couldn't stop her wheels if she was going the right way for it. But she would have to be provided with a good shower bath to keep her wet all the time, for on the rim there, on the narrow part, it will be five times as hot as at the equator. If they get up an expedition to go there, it will have to be well armed, too. If they find them Irish and Danes in there, there will be fighting, for they are hostile people. Yes, and them Malays, too. They know how to navigate ships, too, and they're warlike chaps and they'll give them some trouble. Yes, the expedition will have to be well armed.'

OF LIGHT

'Do the inhabitants of the hole see the moon and the stars?'

'Partly, I conceive. They get the good of the moon about nine days in the month, and can see such parts of the heavens as are visible out of the ends of the hole. That's all; but it would never be real night there, for even when the sun would be off on one side its light would be reflected from the walls of the other side. You see the earth is moving about the sun all the time. Not that I think it goes round in the form them astronomers say it does. I think it goes round on the high and low orbit, that is, one side of the circle is raised in coming down from the sun – and always at the same distance from the sun. Any globe working about the sun must have the same force and the same balance all the time to keep face. The theory of the astronomers is that it goes out many millions of miles at certain times of the year and comes back. Now, there would be no order or regularity about that. It isn't reason. It would make a regular hurly-burly of everything if the earth was allowed to run around in that wild way. And there's another thing that goes to show the world is hollow inside. A solid globe you can't make roll of itself in the sunlight but a hollow one will. You go to work and make a globe of fine silk and fill it with gas, or make it of cork and hollow, and put it into a glass jar in the sun, and pump the air out, and raise it up to a certain temperature – about 180 degrees or maybe 200, I think – and it'll roll in the sun, but a solid one won't do it. So it stands to reason the earth is hollow, so it will roll in the sun. I've tried that experiment in my shop during the war. I made it up nice, but I haven't got it now, for my shop was robbed three years ago, and I lost that and a lot more things, and all my tools. The model I had for the Patent Office was carried away, too.'

'But let us get back to our hole. Beyond what the sailor told you, you have nothing more than theory?'

'Not altogether. There are signs of life from further to the south than anybody has ever gone yet that we know of. I read in a paper last August that an English captain went far enough south to get into warm water; and there he picked up a log drifting from still further south, with nails in it and marks of an ax on it, and that log he brought back with him to England, and it's there now. Anyway, I read that in the paper – but,' speaking in a tone of regretful sadness, 'these newspapers start so many curious things and ideas that you can't always be certain about what they say. But other sailor men than that captain have found the water growing warmer, and had reason to know of open seas at the poles. Besides, there's another thing that goes to show that there's life inside the earth, and that is the great bones and tusks of animals, so big that no animals on the earth now can carry them or have such things, that they find away up in Siberia. Them came from the inside of the earth, I've no doubt, drifted out in the ice that was parted there when the sun cracked the floes and set them drifting out in a polar current.'

SURELY HOLLOW

'You are, of course, aware that many people have a theory that the interior of the earth is in a state of fusion, and others that there are vast internal seas, whose waves act upon chemical substances in the earth, and produce spontaneous combustion and earthquakes and volcanoes?'

'Yes, and what's to hinder. The crust of the earth, between the hole inside and the outside surface, is nearly three thousand miles thick, and surely in all that there's a heap of room for many strange things. But as sure as you live and I live the earth is hollow inside, and there's a great country there where people can live, and where I've no doubt they do live, and some day it will all be found out about it.'

Stories of Other Worlds

An Account of the Adventures of the Earl of Redgrave
and his Bride on their Honeymoon in Space

George Griffith

I A VISIT TO THE MOON

INTRODUCTORY NOTE – The adventures of Rollo Lenox Smeaton Aubrey, Earl of Redgrave, and his bride Lilla Zaidie, daughter of the late Professor Hartley Rennick, Demonstrator in Physical Science in the Smith-Oliver University in New York, were first made possible by that distinguished scientist's now famous separation of the Forces of Nature into their positive and negative elements. Starting from the axiom that everything in Nature has its opposite, he not only divided the Universal Force of Gravitation into its elements of attraction and repulsion, but also constructed a machine which enabled him to develop either or both of these elements at will. From this triumph of mechanical genius it was but a step to the magnificent conception which was subsequently realised by Lord Redgrave in the *Astronef*.

Lord Redgrave had met Professor Rennick, about a year before his lamented death, when he was on a holiday excursion in the Canadian Rockies with his daughter. The young millionaire nobleman was equally fascinated by the daring theories of the Professor, and by the mental and physical charms of Miss Zaidie. And thus the chance acquaintance resulted in a partnership, in which the Professor was to find the knowledge and Lord Redgrave the capital for translating the theory of the 'R Force' (Repulsive or Anti-Gravitational Force) into practice, and constructing a vessel which would be capable, not only of rising from the earth, but of passing the limits of the terrestrial atmosphere, and navigating with precision and safety the limitless ocean of Space.

Unhappily, before the *Astronef*, or star-navigator, was completed at the works which Lord Redgrave had built for her construction on his estate at Smeaton, in Yorkshire, her inventor succumbed to pulmonary complications following an attack of influenza. This left Lord Redgrave the sole possessor of the secret of the 'R Force'. A year after the Professor's death he completed the *Astronef*, and took her across the Atlantic by rising into Space until the attraction of the earth was so far weakened that in a couple of hours' time he was able to descend in the vicinity of New York. On this trial trip he was accompanied by Andrew Murgatroyd, an old engineer who had superintended the building of the *Astronef*. This man's family had been attached to his Lordship's for generations, and for this reason he was selected as engineer and steersman of the Navigator of the Stars.

The excitement which was caused, not only in America but over the whole civilised world, by the arrival of the *Astronef* from the distant regions of space to which she had soared; the marriage of her creator to the daughter of her inventor in the main saloon while she hung motionless in a cloudless sky a mile above the Empire City: their return to earth; the wedding banquet; and their departure to the moon, which they had selected as the first stopping-place on their bridal trip – these are now matters of common knowledge. The present series of narratives begins as the earth sinks away from under them, and their Honeymoon in Space has actually begun.

When the *Astronef* rose from the ground to commence her marvellous voyage through the hitherto untraversed realms of Space, Lord Redgrave and his bride were standing at the forward-end of a raised deck which ran along about two-thirds of the length of the cylindrical body of the vessel. The walls of this compartment, which was about fifty feet long by twenty broad, were formed of thick, but perfectly transparent, toughened glass, over which, in cases of necessity, curtains of ribbed steel could be drawn from the floor, which was of teak and slightly convex. A light steel rail ran round it and two stairways ran up from the other deck of the vessel to two hatches, one fore and one aft, destined to be hermetically closed when the *Astronef* had soared beyond breathable atmosphere and was crossing the airless, heatless wastes of inter-planetary space.

Lord and Lady Redgrave and Andrew Murgatroyd were the only members of the crew of the Star-navigator. No more were needed, for on board this marvellous craft nearly everything was done by machinery; warming, lighting, cooking, distillation and re-distillation of water, constant and automatic purification of the air, everything, in fact, but the regulation of the mysterious 'R Force', could be done with a minimum of human attention. This, however, had to be minutely and carefully regulated, and her commander usually performed this duty himself.

The developing engines were in the lowest part of the vessel amidships. Their minimum power just sufficed to make the *Astronef* a little lighter than her own bulk of air, so that when she visited a planet possessing an atmosphere sufficiently dense, the two propellers at her stern would be capable of driving her through the air at the rate of about a hundred miles an hour. The maximum power would have sufficed to hurl the vessel beyond the limits of the earth's atmosphere in a few minutes.

When they had risen to the height of about a mile above New York, her ladyship, who had been gazing in silent wonder and admiration at the strange and marvellous scene, pointed suddenly towards the East and said: 'Look, there's the moon! Just fancy – our first stopping-place! Well, it doesn't look so very far off at present.'

Redgrave turned and saw the pale yellow crescent of the new moon just rising above the eastern edge of the Atlantic Ocean.

'It almost looks as if we could steer straight to it right over the water, only, of course, it wouldn't wait there for us,' she went on.

'Oh, it'll be there when we want it, never fear,' laughed his lordship, 'and, after all, it's only a mere matter of about two hundred and forty thousand miles away, and what's that in a trip that will cover hundreds of millions? It will just be a sort of jumping-off place into space for us.'

'Still I shouldn't like to miss seeing it,' she said. 'I want to know what there is on that other side which nobody has ever seen yet, and settle that question about air and water. Won't it just be heavenly to be able to come back and tell them all about it at home? But fancy me talking stuff like this when we are going, perhaps, to solve some of the hidden mysteries of Creation, and, maybe, to look upon things that human eyes were never meant to see,' she went on, with a sudden change in her voice.

He felt a little shiver in the arm that was resting upon his, and his hand went down and caught hers.

'Well, we shall see a good many marvels, and, perhaps, miracles, before we come back, but I hardly think we shall see anything that is forbidden. Still, there's one thing we shall do, I hope. We shall solve once and for all the great problem of the worlds – whether they are inhabited or not. By the way,' he went on, 'I may remind your ladyship that you are just now drawing the last breaths of earthly air which you will taste for some time, in fact until we get back! You may as well take your last look at earth as earth, for the next time you see it, it will be a planet.'

She went to the rail and looked over into the enormous void beneath, for all this time the *Astronef* had been mounting towards the zenith. She could see, by the growing moon-light, vast, vague shapes of land and sea. The myriad lights of New York and Brooklyn were mingled in a tiny patch of dimly luminous haze. The air about her had suddenly grown bitterly cold, and she saw that the stars and planets were shining with a brilliancy she had never seen before. Her husband came to her side, and, laying his arm across her shoulder, said: 'Well, have you said goodbye to your native world? It is a bit solemn, isn't it, saying goodbye to a world that you have been born on; which contains everything that has made up your life, everything that is dear to you?'

'Not quite everything!' she said, looking up at him. 'At least, I don't think so.'

He immediately made the only reply which was appropriate under the circumstances; and then he said, drawing her towards the staircase: 'Well, for the present this is our world; a world travelling among worlds, and as I have been able to bring the most delightful of the Daughters of Terra with me, I, at any rate, am perfectly happy. Now, I think it's getting on to supper time, so if your ladyship will go to your household duties, I'll have a look at my engines and make everything snug for the voyage.'

The first thing he did when he got on to the main deck, was to hermetically close the two companion-ways; then he went and carefully inspected the apparatus for purifying the air and supplying it with fresh oxygen from the tanks in which it was stored in liquid form. Lastly he descended into the lower hold of the ship and turned on the energy of repulsion to its full extent, at the same time stopping the engines which had been working the propellers.

It was now no longer necessary or even possible to steer the *Astronef*. She was directed solely by the repulsive force which would carry her with ever-increasing swiftness, as the attraction of the earth became diminished, towards that neutral point some two hundred thousand miles away, at which the attraction of the earth is exactly balanced by the moon. Her momentum would carry her past this point, and then the 'R Force' would be gradually brought into play in order to avert the unpleasant consequences of a fall of some forty odd thousand miles.

Andrew Murgatroyd, relieved from his duties in the wheelhouse, made a careful inspection of the auxiliary machinery, which was under his special charge, and then retired to his quarters forward to prepare his own evening meal. Meanwhile her ladyship, with the help of the ingenious contrivances with which the kitchen of the *Astronef* was stocked, and with the use of which she had already made herself quite familiar, had prepared a dainty little *souper à deux*. Her husband opened a bottle of the finest champagne that the cellars of New York could supply, to drink at once to the prosperity of the voyage, and the health of his beautiful fellow-voyager.

When supper was over and the coffee made he carried the apparatus up the stairs on to the glass-domed upper deck. Then he came back and said: 'You'd better wrap yourself up as warmly as you can, dear, for it's a good deal chillier up there than it is here.'

When she reached the deck and took her first glance about her, Zaidie seemed suddenly to lapse into a state of somnambulism. The whole heavens above and around were strewn with thick clusters of stars which she had never seen before. The stars she remembered seeing from the earth were only little pin-points in the darkness compared with the myriads of blazing orbs which were now shooting their rays across the silent void of Space. So many millions of new ones had come into view that she looked in vain for the familiar constellations. She saw only vast clusters of living gems of all colours crowding the heavens on every side of her. She walked slowly round the deck, looking to right and left and above, incapable for the moment either of thought or speech, but only of dumb wonder, mingled with a dim sense of overwhelming awe. Presently she craned her neck backwards and looked straight up to the zenith. A huge, silver crescent, supporting, as it were, a dim, greenish coloured body in its arms stretched overhead across nearly a sixth of the heavens.

Her husband came to her side, took her in his arms, lifted her as if she had been a little child, so feeble had the earth's attraction now become, and laid her in a long, low deck-chair, so that she could look at it without inconvenience. The splendid crescent grew swiftly larger and more distinct, and as she lay there in a trance of wonder and admiration she saw point after point of dazzlingly white light flash out on to the dark portions, and then begin to send out rays as though they were gigantic volcanoes in full eruption, and were pouring torrents of living fire from their blazing craters.

'Sunrise on the moon!' said Redgrave, who had stretched himself on another chair beside her. 'A glorious sight, isn't it! But nothing to what we shall see tomorrow morning – only there doesn't happen to be any morning just about here.'

'Yes,' she said dreamily, 'glorious, isn't it? That and all the stars – but I can't think of anything yet, Lenox! It's all too mighty and too marvellous. It doesn't seem as though human eyes were meant to look upon things like this. But where's the earth? We must be able to see that still.'

'Not from here,' he said, 'because it's underneath us. Come below, and you shall see Mother Earth as you have never seen her yet.'

They went down into the lower part of the vessel, and to the after-end behind the engine-room. Redgrave switched on a couple of electric lights, and then pulled a lever attached to one of the side-walls. A part of the flooring, about 6ft square, slid noiselessly away; then he pulled another lever on the opposite side and a similar piece disappeared, leaving a large space covered only by absolutely transparent glass. He switched off the lights again and led her to the edge of it, and said: 'There is your native world, dear; that is the earth!'

Wonderful as the moon had seemed, the gorgeous spectacle, which lay seemingly at her feet, was infinitely more magnificent. A vast disc of silver grey, streaked and dotted with lines and points of dazzling light, and more than half covered with vast, glittering, greyish-green expanses, seemed to form, as it were, the floor of the great gulf of space beneath them. They were not yet too far away to make out the general features of the continents and oceans, and fortunately the hemisphere presented to them happened to be singularly free from clouds.

Zaidie stood gazing for nearly an hour at this marvellous vision of the home-world which she had left so far behind her before she could tear herself away and allow her husband to shut the slides again. The greatly diminished weight of her body almost entirely destroyed the fatigue of standing. In fact, at present on board the *Astronef* it was almost as easy to stand as it was to lie down.

There was of course very little sleep for any of the travellers on this first night of their adventurous voyage, but towards the sixth hour after leaving the earth her ladyship, overcome as much by the emotions which had been awakened within her as by physical fatigue, went to bed, after making her husband promise that he would wake her in good time to see the descent upon the moon. Two hours later she was awake and drinking the coffee which Redgrave had prepared for her. Then she went on to the upper deck.

To her astonishment she found, on one hand, day more brilliant than she had ever seen it before, and on the other hand, darkness blacker than the blackest earthly night. On the right hand was an intensely brilliant orb, about half as large again as the full moon seen from earth, shining with inconceivable brightness out of a sky black as midnight and thronged with stars. It was the sun, the sun shining in the midst of airless space.

The tiny atmosphere inclosed in the glass-domed space was lighted brilliantly, but it was not perceptibly warmer, though Redgrave warned her ladyship not to touch anything upon which the sun's rays fell directly as she would find it uncomfortably hot. On the other side was the same black immensity of space which she had seen the night before, an ocean of darkness clustered with islands of light. High above in the zenith floated the great silver-grey disc of earth, a good deal smaller now, and there was another object beneath which was at present of far more interest to her. Looking down to the left she saw a vast semi-luminous area in which not a star was to be seen. It was the earth-lit portion of the long familiar and yet mysterious orb which was to be their resting-place for the next few hours.

'The sun hasn't risen over there yet,' said Redgrave, as she was peering down into the void. 'It's earth-light still. Now look at the other side.'

She crossed the deck and saw the strangest scene she had yet beheld. Apparently only a few miles below her was a huge crescent-shaped plain arching away for hundreds of miles on either side. The outer edge had a ragged look, and little excrescences, which soon took the shape of flat-topped mountains, projected from it and stood out bright and sharp against the black void beneath, out of which the stars shone up, as it seemed, sharp and bright above the edge of the disc.

The plain itself was a scene of the most awful and utter desolation that even the sombre fancy of a Dante could imagine. Huge mountain walls, towering to immense heights and inclosing great circular and oval plains, one side of them blazing with intolerable light, and the other side black with impenetrable obscurity; enormous valleys reaching down from brilliant day into rayless night – perhaps down into the empty bowels of the dead world itself; vast, grey-white plains lying round the mountains, crossed by little ridges and by long, black lines, which could only be immense fissures with perpendicular sides – but all hard grey-white and black, all intolerable brightness or repulsive darkness; not a sign of life anywhere, no shady forests, no green fields, no broad, glittering oceans; only a ghastly wilderness of dead mountains and dead plains.

'What an awful place!' said Zaidie, in a slowly spoken whisper. 'Surely we can't land there. How far are we from it?'

'About fifteen hundred miles,' replied Redgrave, who was sweeping the scene below him with one of the two powerful telescopes which stood on the deck. 'No, it doesn't look very cheerful, does it; but it's a marvellous sight for all that, and one that a good many people on earth would give their ears to see from here. I'm letting her drop pretty fast, and we shall probably land in a couple of hours or so. Meanwhile, you may as well get out your moon atlas and your Jules Verne and Flammarion, and study your lunography. I'm going to turn the power a bit astern so that we shall go down obliquely and see more of the lighted disc. We started at new moon so that you should have a look at the full earth, and also so that we could get round to the invisible side while it is lighted up.'

They both went below, he to deflect the repulsive force so that one set of engines should give them a somewhat oblique direction, while the other, acting directly on the surface of the moon, simply retarded their fall; and she to get her maps and the ever-fascinating works of Jules Verne and Flammarion. When they got back, the *Astronef* had changed her apparent position, and, instead of falling directly on to the moon, was descending towards it in a slanting direction. The result of this was that the sunlit crescent rapidly grew in breadth, whilst peak after peak and range after range rose up swiftly out of the black gulf beyond. The sun climbed quickly up through the star-strewn, mid-day heavens, and the full earth sank more swiftly still behind them.

Another hour of silent, entranced wonder and admiration followed, and then Lenox remarked to Zaidie: 'Don't you think it's about time we were beginning to think of breakfast, dear, or do you think you can wait till we land?'

'Breakfast on the moon!' she exclaimed, 'That would be just too lovely for words! Of course we'll wait.'

'Very well,' he said, 'you see that big, black ring nearly below us, that, as I suppose you know, is the celebrated Mount Tycho. I'll try and find a convenient spot on the top of the ring to drop on, and then you will be able to survey the scenery from seventeen or eighteen thousand feet above the plains.'

About two hours later a slight jarring tremor ran through the frame of the vessel, and the first stage of the voyage was ended. After a passage of less than twelve hours the *Astronef* had crossed a gulf of nearly two hundred and fifty thousand miles and rested quietly on the untrodden surface of the lunar world.

'We certainly shan't find any atmosphere here,' said Redgrave, when they had finished breakfast, 'although we may in the deeper parts, so if your ladyship would like a walk we'd better go and put on our breathing dresses.'

These were not unlike diving dresses, save that they were much lighter. The helmets were smaller, and made of aluminium covered with asbestos. A sort of knapsack fitted on to the back, and below this was a cylinder of liquefied air which, when passed through the expanding apparatus, would furnish pure air for a practically indefinite period, as the respired air passed into another portion of the upper chamber, where it was forced through a chemical solution which deprived it of its poisonous gases and made it fit to breathe again.

The pressure of air inside the helmet automatically regulated the supply, which was not permitted to circulate into the dress, as the absence of air-pressure on the moon would cause it to instantly expand and probably tear the material, which was a cloth woven chiefly of asbestos fibre. The two helmets could be connected for talking purposes by a light wire communicating with a little telephonic apparatus inside the helmet.

They passed out of the *Astronef* through an air-tight chamber in the wall of her lowest compartment, Murgatroyd closing the first door behind them. Redgrave opened the next one and dropped a short ladder on to the grey, loose, sand-strewn rock of the little plain on which they had stopped. Then he stood aside and motioned for Zaidie to go down first.

She understood him, and, taking his hand, descended the four easy steps, and so hers was the first human foot which, in all the ages since its creation, had rested on the surface of the World that Had Been. Redgrave followed her with a little spring which landed him gently beside her, then he took both her hands and pressed them hard in his. He would have kissed her if he could; but that of course was out of the question.

Then he connected the telephone wire, and hand in hand they crossed the little plateau towards the edge of the tremendous gulf, fifty-four miles across, and nearly twenty thousand feet deep. In the middle of it rose a conical mountain about five thousand feet high, the summit of which was just beginning to catch the solar rays. Half of the vast plain was already brilliantly illuminated, but round the central cone was a vast semi-circle of shadow impenetrable in its blackness.

'Day and night in this same valley, actually side by side!' said Zaidie. Then she stopped, and pointed down into the brightly lit distance, and went on hurriedly: 'Look, Lenox, look at the foot of the mountain there! Doesn't that seem like the ruins of a city?'

'It does,' he said, 'and there's no reason why it shouldn't be. I've always thought that, as the air and water disappeared from the upper parts of the moon, the inhabitants, whoever they were, must have been driven down into the deeper parts. Shall we go down and see?'

'But how?' she said.

He pointed towards the *Astronef*. She nodded her helmeted head, and they went back to the vessel. A few minutes later the *Astronef* had risen from her resting-place with a spring which rapidly carried her over half of the vast crater, and then she began to drop slowly into the depths. She grounded as gently as before, and presently they were standing on the lunar surface about a mile from the central cone. This time, however, Redgrave had taken the precaution to bring a magazine rifle and a couple of revolvers with him in case any strange monsters, relics of the vanished fauna of the moon, might still be taking refuge in these mysterious depths. Zaidie, although, like a good many American girls, she could shoot excellently well, carried no weapon more offensive than a whole-plate camera and a tripod, which here, of course, only weighed a sixth of their earthly weight.

The first thing that Redgrave did when they stepped out on to the sandy surface of the plain was to stoop down and strike a wax match; there was a tiny glimmer of light which was immediately extinguished.

'No air here,' he said, 'so we shall find no living beings – at any rate, none like ourselves.'

They found the walking exceedingly easy, although their boots were purposely weighted in order to counteract to some extent the great difference in gravity. A few minutes' sharp walking brought them to the outskirts of the city. It had no walls, and in fact exhibited no signs of preparations for defence. Its streets were broad and well-paved; and the houses, built of great blocks of grey stone joined together with white cement, looked as fresh and unworn as though they had only been built a few months, whereas they had probably stood for hundreds of thousands of years. They were flat-roofed, all of one storey and practically of one type.

There were very few public buildings, and absolutely no attempt at ornamentation was visible. Round some of the houses were spaces which might once have been gardens. In the midst of the city, which appeared to cover an area of about four square miles, was an enormous square paved with flagstones, which were covered to the depth of a couple of inches with a light grey dust, and, as they walked across it, this remained perfectly still save for the disturbance caused by their footsteps. There was no air to support it, otherwise it might have risen in clouds about them.

From the centre of this square rose a huge pyramid nearly a thousand feet in height, the sole building in the great, silent city which appeared to have been raised as a monument, or, possibly, a temple by the hands of its vanished inhabitants. As they approached this they saw a curious white fringe lying round the steps by which it was approached. When they got nearer they found that this fringe was composed of millions of white-bleached bones and skulls, shaped very much like those of terrestrial men save that they were much larger and that the ribs were out of all proportion to the rest of the bones.

They stopped awe-stricken before this strange spectacle. Redgrave stooped down and took hold of one of the bones, a huge thigh bone. It broke in two as he tried to lift it, and the piece which remained in his hand crumbled instantly to white powder.

'Whoever they were,' said Redgrave, 'they were giants. When air and water failed above they came down here by some means and built this city. You see what enormous chests they must have had. That would be Nature's last struggle to enable them to breathe the diminishing atmosphere. These, of course, will be the last descendants of the fittest to breathe it; this was their temple, I suppose, and here they came to die – I wonder how many thousand years ago – perishing of heat, and cold, and hunger, and thirst, the last tragedy of a race, which, after all, must have been something like our own.'

The bone crumbled instantly to white powder

'It is just too awful for words,' said Zaidie. 'Shall we go into the temple? That seems one of the entrances up there, only I don't like walking over all those bones.'

Her voice sounded very strange over the wire which connected their helmets.

'I don't suppose they'll mind if we do,' replied Redgrave, 'only we mustn't go far in. It may be full of cross passages and mazes, and we might never get out. Our lamps won't be much use in there, you know, for there's no air. They'll just be points of light, and we shan't see any-thing but them. It's very aggravating, but I'm afraid there's no help for it. Come along!'

They ascended the steps, crushing the bones and skulls to powder beneath their feet, and entered the huge, square doorway, which looked like a rectangle of blackness against the grey-white of the wall. Even through their asbestos-woven clothing they felt a sudden shock of icy cold. In those few steps they had passed from a temperature of tenfold summer heat into one far below that of the coldest spots on earth. They turned on the electric lamps which were fitted to the breast-plates of their dresses, but they could see nothing save the glow of the lamps. All about them was darkness impenetrable, and so they reluctantly turned back to the doorway, leaving all the mysteries which the vast temple might contain to remain mysteries to the end of time. They passed down the steps again and crossed the square, and for the next half hour Zaidie, who was photographer to the expedition, was busy taking photographs of the Pyramid with its ghastly surroundings, and a few general views of this strange City of the Dead.

Then they went back to the *Astronef*. They found Murgatroyd pacing up and down under the dome looking about him with serious eyes, but yet betraying no particular curiosity. The wonderful vessel was at once his home and his idol, and nothing but the direct orders of his master would have induced him to leave her even in a world in which there was probably not a living human being to dispute possession of her.

When they had resumed their ordinary clothing, she rose rapidly from the surface of the plain, crossed the encircling wall at the height of a few hundred feet, and made her way at a speed of about fifty miles an hour towards the regions of the South Pole. Behind them to the north-west they could see from their elevation of nearly thirty thousand feet the vast expanse of the Sea of Clouds. Dotted here and there were the shin-ing points and ridges of light, marking the peaks and crater walls which the rays of the rising sun had already touched. Before them and to right and left of them rose a vast maze of crater-rings and huge ramparts of mountain-walls inclosing plains so far below their summits that the light of neither sun nor earth ever reached them.

By directing the force exerted by what might now be called the pro-pelling part of the engines against the mountain masses, which they crossed to right and left and behind, Redgrave was able to take a zigzag course which carried him over many of the walled plains which were wholly or partially lit up by the sun, and in nearly all of the deepest their telescopes revealed what they had found within the crater of Tycho. At length, pointing to a gigantic circle of white light fringing an abyss of utter darkness, he said: 'There is Newton, the greatest mystery of the moon. Those inner walls are twenty-four thousand feet high; that means that the bottom, which has never been seen by human eyes, is about five thousand feet below the surface of the moon. What do you say, dear – shall we go down and see if the searchlight will show us, anything? There may be air there.'

'Certainly!' replied Zaidie decisively. 'Haven't we come to see things that nobody else has ever seen?'

Redgrave signalled to the engine-room, and presently the *Astronef* changed her course, and in a few minutes was hanging, bathed in sunlight, like a star suspended over the unfathomable gulf of darkness below.

As they sank beyond the sunlight, Murgatroyd turned on both the head and stern searchlights. They dropped down ever slowly and more slowly until gradually the two long, thin streams of light began to spread themselves out, and by the time the *Astronef* came gently to a rest they were swinging round her in broad fans of diffused light over a dark, marshy surface, with scattered patches of moss and reeds, which showed dull gleams of stagnant water between them.

Air and water at last!' said Redgrave, as he rejoined his wife on the upper deck, 'air and water and eternal darkness! Well, we shall find life on the moon here if anywhere. Shall we go?'

'Of course,' replied her ladyship, 'what else have we come for? Must we put on the breathing-dresses?'

'Certainly,' he replied, 'because, although there's air we don't know yet whether it is breathable. It may be half carbon-dioxide for all we know; but a few matches will soon tell us that.'

Within a quarter of an hour they were again standing on the surface. Murgatroyd had orders to follow them as far as possible with the head searchlight, which, in the comparatively rarefied atmosphere, appeared to have a range of several miles. Redgrave struck a match, and held it up level with his head. It burnt with a clear, steady, yellow flame.

'Where a match will burn a man can breathe,' he said. 'I'm going to see what lunar air is like.'

'For Heaven's sake be careful, dear,' came the reply in pleading tones across the wire.

'All right, but don't open your helmet till I tell you.'

He then raised the hermetically-closed slide of glass, which formed the front of the helmets, half an inch or so. Instantly he felt a sensation like the drawing of a red-hot iron across his skin. He snapped the visor down and clasped it in its place. For a moment or two he gasped for breath and then he said rather faintly: 'It's no good, it's too cold, it would freeze the blood in our veins. I think we'd better go back and explore this valley under cover. We can't do anything in the dark, and we can see just as well from the upper deck with the searchlights. Besides, as there's air and water here, there's no telling but there may be inhabitants of sorts such as we shouldn't care to meet.'

He took her hand, and, to Murgatroyd's intense relief, they went back to the vessel.

Redgrave then raised the *Astronef* a couple of hundred feet and, by directing the repulsive force against the mountain walls, developed just sufficient energy to keep them moving at about twelve miles an hour.

They began to cross the plain with their searchlights flashing out in all directions. They had scarcely gone a mile before the headlight fell upon a moving form half walking, half crawling among some stunted brown-leaved bushes by the side of a broad, stagnant stream.

'Look!' said Zaidie, clasping her husband's arm, 'is that a gorilla, or – no, it *can't* be a man.'

The light was turned full upon the object. If it had been covered with hair it might have passed for some strange type of the ape tribe, but its skin was smooth and of a livid grey. Its lower limbs were evidently more powerful than its upper; its chest was enormously developed, but the stomach was small. The head was big and round and smooth. As they came nearer they saw that in place of finger-nails it had long white feelers which it kept extended and constantly waving about as it groped its way towards the water. As the intense light flashed full on it, it turned its head towards them. It had a nose and a mouth. The nose was long and thick, with huge mobile nostrils, and the mouth formed an angle something like a fish's lips, and of teeth there seemed none. At either side of the upper part of the nose there were two little sunken holes, in which this thing's ancestors of countless thousand years ago had possessed eyes.

As she looked upon this awful parody of what had once perhaps been a human face, Zaidie covered hers with her hands and uttered a little moan of horror.

'Horrible, isn't it?' said Redgrave. 'I suppose that's what the last remnants of the lunarians have come to, evidently once men and women something like ourselves. I dare say the ancestors of that thing have lived here in coldness and darkness for hundreds of generations. It shows how tremendously tenacious nature is of life.

'Ages ago that awful thing's ancestors lived up yonder when there were seas and rivers, fields and forests, just as we have them on earth;

men and women who could see and breathe and enjoy everything in life and had built up civilisations like ours. Look, it's going to fish or something. Now we shall see what it feeds on. I wonder why that water isn't frozen. I suppose there must be some internal heat left still, split up into patches, I dare say, and lakes of lava. Perhaps this valley is just over one of them, and that's why these creatures have managed to survive. Ah there's another of them, smaller not so strongly formed. That thing's mate, I suppose, female of the species. Ugh, I wonder how many hundreds of thousands of years it will take for *our* descendants to come to that.'

'I hope our dear old earth will hit something else and be smashed to atoms before that happens!' exclaimed Zaidie, whose curiosity had now partly overcome her horror. 'Look, it's trying to catch something.'

The larger of the two creatures had groped its way to the edge of the sluggish, half-foetid water and dropped or rather rolled quietly into it. It was evidently cold-blooded or nearly so, for no warm-blooded animal could have withstood that more than glacial cold. Presently the other dropped in, too, and both disappeared for some minutes. Then suddenly there was a violent commotion in the water a few yards away; and the two creatures rose to the surface of the water, one with a wriggling eel-like fish between its jaws.

They both groped their way towards the edge, and had just reached it and were pulling themselves out when a hideous shape rose out of the water behind them. It was like the head of an octopus joined to the body of a boa-constrictor, but head and neck were both of the same ghastly, livid grey as the other two bodies. It was evidently blind, too, for it took no notice of the brilliant glare of the searchlight. Still it moved rapidly towards the two scrambling forms, its long white feelers trembling out in all directions. Then one of them touched the smaller of the two creatures. Instantly the rest shot out and closed round it, and with scarcely a struggle it was dragged beneath the water and vanished.

Zaidie uttered a little low scream and covered her face again, and Redgrave said: 'The same old brutal law again. Life preying upon life even on a dying world, a world that is more than half dead itself. Well, I think we've seen enough of this place. I suppose those are about the only types of life we should meet anywhere, and one acquaintance with them satisfies me completely. I vote we go and see what the invisible hemisphere is like.'

'I have had all I want of this side,' said Zaidie, looking away from the scene of the hideous conflict, 'so the sooner the better.'

The feelers shot out and closed round the smaller of the two creatures

A few minutes later the *Astronef* was again rising towards the stars with her searchlights still flashing down into the Valley of Expiring Life, which seemed worse than the Valley of Death. As he followed the rays with a pair of powerful field glasses, Redgrave fancied that he saw huge, dim shapes moving about the stunted shrubbery and through the slimy pools of the stagnant rivers, and once or twice he got a glimpse of what might well have been the ruins of towns and cities; but the gloom soon became too deep and dense for the searchlights to pierce and he was glad when the *Astronef* soared up into the brilliant sunlight once more. Even the ghastly wilderness of the lunar landscape was welcome after the nameless horrors of that hideous abyss.

After a couple of hours' rapid travelling, Redgrave pointed down to a comparatively small, deep crater, and said: 'There, that is Malapert. It is almost exactly at the south pole of the moon, and there,' he went on pointing ahead, 'is the horizon of the hemisphere which no earthborn eyes but ours and Murgatroyd's have ever seen.'

Contrary to certain ingenious speculations which have been indulged in, they found that the hemisphere, which for countless ages has never been turned towards the earth, was almost an exact replica of the visible one. Fully three-fourths of it was brilliantly illuminated by the sun, and the scene which presented itself to their eyes was practically the same which they had beheld on the earthward side; huge groups of enormous craters and ringed mountains, long, irregular chains crowned with sharp, splintery peaks, and between these vast, deeply depressed areas, ranging in colour from dazzling white to grey-brown, marking the beds of the vanished lunar seas.

As they crossed one of these, Redgrave allowed the *Astronef* to sink to within a few thousand feet of the surface, and then he and Zaidie swept it with their telescopes. Their chance search was rewarded by what they had not seen in the sea-beds of the other hemisphere. These depressions were far deeper than the others, evidently many thousands of feet deep, but the sun's rays were blazing full into this one, and, dotted round its slopes at varying elevations, they made out little patches which seemed to differ from the general surface.

'I wonder if those are the remains of cities,' said Zaidie. 'Isn't it possible that the populations might have built their cities along the seas, and that their descendants may have followed the waters as they retreated, I mean as they either dried up or disappeared into the centre?'

'Very probable indeed, dear,' he said, 'we'll go down and see.'

He diminished the vertically repulsive force a little, and the *Astronef* dropped slantingly towards the bed of what might once have been the Pacific of the Moon. When they were within about a couple of thousand feet of the surface it became quite plain that Zaidie was correct in her hypothesis. The vast sea-floor was literally strewn with the ruins of countless cities and towns, which had been inhabited by an equally countless series of generations of men and women, who had, perhaps, lived in the days when our own world was a glowing mass of molten rock, surrounded by the envelope of vapours which has since condensed to form its oceans.

The nearer they approached to the central and deepest depression the more perfect the buildings became until, down in the lowest depth, they found a collection of low-built, square edifices, scarcely better than huts, which had clustered round the little lake into which ages before the ocean had dwindled. But where the lake had been there was now only a depression covered with grey sand and brown rock.

Into this they descended and touched the lunar soil for the last time. A couple of hours' excursion among the houses proved that they had been the last refuge of the last descendants of a dying race, a race which had steadily degenerated just as the successions of cities had done, as the bitter fight for mere existence had become keener and keener until the two last essentials, air and water, had failed and then the end had come.

The streets, like the square of the great temple of Tycho, were strewn with myriads and myriads of bones, and there were myriads more scattered round what had once been the shores of the dwindling lake. Here, as elsewhere, there was not a sign or a record of any kind – carving or sculpture.

Inside the great Pyramid of the City of Tycho they might, perhaps, have found something – some stone or tablet which bore the mark of the artist's hand; elsewhere, perhaps, they might have found cities reared by older races, which might have rivalled the creations of Egypt and Babylon, but there was no time to look for these. All that they had seen of the Dead World had only sickened and saddened them. The untravelled regions of Space peopled by living worlds more akin to their own were before them, and the red disc of Mars was glowing in the zenith among the diamond-white clusters which gemmed the black sky behind him.

More than a hundred millions of miles had to be traversed before they would be able to set foot on his surface, and so, after one last look round the Valley of Death about them, Redgrave turned on the full energy of the repulsive force in a vertical direction, and the *Astronef* leapt upwards in a straight line for her new destination. The unknown hemisphere spread out in a vast plain beneath them, the blazing sun rose on their left, and the brilliant silver orb of the Earth on their right, and so, full of wonder, and yet without regret, they bade farewell to the World that Was.

II THE WORLD OF THE WAR GOD

INTRODUCTION – For their honeymoon Rollo Lenox Smeaton Aubrey, Earl of Redgrave, and his bride, Lilla Zaidie, leave the earth on a visit to the moon and the principal planets, their sole companion being Andrew Murgatroyd, an old engineer who had superintended the building of the *Astronef*, in which the journey is made. By means of the 'R Force,' or Anti-Gravitational Force, of the secret of which Lord Redgrave is the sole possessor, they are able to navigate with precision and safety the limitless ocean of space. Their adventures on the moon were described in the first story of the series.

The Earth and the Moon were more than a hundred million miles behind in the depths of Space, and the *Astronef* had crossed this immense gap in eleven days and a few hours; but this apparently inconceivable speed was not altogether due to the powers of the Navigator of the Stars, for Lord Redgrave had taken advantage of the passage of the planet along its orbit towards that of the earth; therefore, while the *Astronef* was approaching Mars with ever-increasing speed, Mars was travelling towards the *Astronef* at the rate of sixteen miles a second.

The great silver disc of the earth had diminished until it looked only a little larger than Venus appears from the earth. In fact the planet Terra is to the inhabitants of Mars what Venus is to us, the star of the morning and evening.

Breakfast on the morning of the twelfth day, or, since there is neither day nor night in Space, it would be more correct to say the twelfth period of twenty-four earth-hours as measured by the chronometers, was just over, and the Commander of the *Astronef* was standing with his bride in the forward end of the glass-covered deck looking downwards at a vast crescent of rosy light which stretched out over an arc of more than ninety degrees. Two tiny black spots were travelling towards each other across it.

'Ah!' said her ladyship, going towards one of the telescopes, 'there are the moons. I was reading my Gulliver last night. I wonder what the old Dean would have given to be here, and see how true his guess was. Have you made up your mind to land on them?'

'I don't see why we shouldn't,' said her husband. 'I think they'd make rather convenient stopping-places; besides, we want to know whether they have atmospheres and inhabitants.'

'What, people living on those wee things?' she laughed, 'why, they're only about thirty or forty miles round, aren't they?'

'That's about it,' he said, 'but that's just one of the points I want to solve, and as for life, it doesn't always mean people, you know. We are only a few hundred miles away from Deimos, the outer one, and he is twelve thousand five hundred miles from Mars. I vote we drop on him first and let him carry us towards his brother Phobos. Then when we've examined him we'll drop down to Phobos and take a trip round Mars on him. He does the journey in about seven hours and a half, and as he's only three thousand seven hundred miles above the surface we ought to get a very good view of our next stopping-place.'

'That ought to be quite a delightful trip!' said her ladyship. 'But how commonplace you are getting, Lenox. That's so like you Englishmen. We are doing what has only been dreamt of before, and here you are talking about moons and planets as if they were railway stations.'

'Well, if your ladyship prefers it, we will call them undiscovered islands and continents in the Ocean of Space. That does sound a little bit better, doesn't it? Now I must go down and see to my engines.'

When he had gone, Zaidie sat down to the telescope again and kept it on one of the little black spots travelling across the crescent of Mars. Both it and the other spot rapidly grew larger, and the features of the planet itself became more distinct. She could make out the seas and continents and the mysterious canals quite plainly through the clear rosy atmosphere, and, with the aid of the telescope, she could even make out the glimmer which the inner moon threw upon the unlighted portion of the disc.

Deimos grew bigger and bigger, and in about half-an-hour the *Astronef* grounded gently on what looked to her like a dimly-lighted circular plain, but which, when her eyes became accustomed to the light, was more like the summit of a conical mountain. Redgrave raised the keel a little from the surface again and propelled her towards a thin circle of light on the tiny horizon. As they crossed into the sunlit portion it became quite plain that Deimos at any rate was as airless and lifeless as the moon. The surface was composed of brown rock and red sand broken up into miniature hills and valleys. There were a few traces of bygone volcanic action, but it was evident that the internal fires of this tiny world must have burnt themselves out very quickly.

'Not much to be seen here,' said Redgrave, 'and I don't think it would be safe to go out. The attraction is so weak here that we might find ourselves falling off with very little exertion. You might take a couple of photographs of the surface, and then we'll be off to Phobos.'

A few minutes later Zaidie got a couple of good photographs of the satellite. The attraction of Mars now began to make itself strongly felt, and the *Astronef* dropped rapidly through the eight thousand miles which separate the inner and outer Moons of Mars. As they approached Phobos they saw that half the little disc was brilliantly lighted by the same rays of the sun which were glowing on the rapidly increasing crescent of Mars beneath them. By careful manipulation of his engines Lord Redgrave managed to meet the approaching satellite with a hardly perceptible shock about the centre of its lighted portion, that is to say the side turned towards the planet.

Mars now appeared as a gigantic rosy moon filling the whole vault of the heavens above them. Their telescopes brought the three thousand seven hundred and fifty miles down to about fifty. The rapid motion of the tiny satellite afforded them a spectacle which might be compared to the rising of a moon glowing with rosy light and hundreds of times larger than the earth. The speed of the vehicle of which they had taken possession, something like four thousand two hundred miles an hour, caused the surface of the planet to apparently sweep away from below them from west to east, just as the earth appears to slip away from under the car of a balloon.

Neither of them left the telescopes for more than a few minutes during this aerial circumnavigation. Murgatroyd, outwardly impassive, but inwardly filled with solemn fears for the fate of this impiously daring voyage, brought them wine and sandwiches, and later on tea and toast and more sandwiches; but they hardly touched even these, so absorbed were they in the wonderful spectacle which was passing swiftly under their eyes. Their telescopes were excellent ones, and at that distance Mars gave up all his secrets.

Phobos revolves from west to east almost along the plane of the planet's equator. To left and right they saw the huge ice-caps of the South and North Poles gleaming through the red atmosphere with a pale sunset glimmer. Then came the great stretches of sea, often obscured by vast banks of clouds, which, as the sunlight fell upon them, looked strangely like the earth-clouds at sunset. Then, almost immediately underneath them spread out the great land areas of the equatorial region. The three continents of Halle, Gallileo, and Tycholand; then Huygens – which is to Mars what Europe, Asia, and Africa are to the earth. Then Herschell and Copernicus. Nearly all of these land masses were split up into semi-regular divisions by the famous canals which have so long puzzled terrestrial observers.

'Well, there is one problem solved at any rate,' said Redgrave, when, after a journey of nearly four hours, they had crossed the western hemisphere. 'Mars is getting very old, her seas are diminishing, and her continents are increasing, and those canals are the remains of gulfs and isthmuses which have been widened and deepened and lengthened by human, or we'll say Martian, labour, partly, I've no doubt, for purposes of navigation, and partly to keep the inhabitants of the interior of the continents within measurable distance of the sea. There's not the slightest doubt about that. Then, you see, we've seen scarcely any mountains to speak of so far, only ranges of low hills.'

'And that means, I suppose,' said Zaidie, 'that they've all been worn down as the mountains of the earth are worn away. I was reading Flammarion's *End of the World* last night, and he, you know, painted the earth at the end as an enormous plain of land, no hills or mountains, no seas, and only sluggish rivers draining into marshes. I suppose that's what they're coming to down yonder. Now, I wonder what sort of civilisation we shall find. Perhaps we shan't find any at all. Suppose all their civilisations have worn out, and they are degenerating into the same struggle for sheer existence those poor creatures in the moon must have had.'

'Or suppose,' said his lordship seriously, 'we find that they have passed the zenith of civilisation, and are dropping back into savagery, but still have the use of weapons and means of destruction which we, perhaps, have no notion of, and are inclined to use them. We'd better be careful, dear.'

'What do you mean, Lenox?' she said. 'They wouldn't try to do us any harm, would they? Why should they?'

'I don't say they would,' he replied; 'but still you never know. You see, their ideas of right and wrong and hospitality and all that sort of thing may be quite different to what we have on the earth. In fact, they may not be men at all, but just a sort of monster with a semi-human intellect, perhaps a superhuman one with ideas that we have no notion of. Then there's another thing; suppose they fancied a trip through Space, and thought that they had quite as good a right to the *Astronef* as we have? I dare say they've seen us by this time if they've got telescopes, as no doubt they have, perhaps a good deal more powerful than ours, and they may be getting ready to receive us now. I think I'll get the guns up before we go down, in case our reception may not be a friendly one.'

The defensive armament of the *Astronef* consisted of four pneumatic guns, which could be mounted on swivels, two ahead and two astern, and which carried a shell containing either one of two kinds of explosives invented by her creator. One was a solid, and burst on impact with an explosive force equal to about twenty pounds of dynamite. The other consisted of two liquids separated in the shell, and these, when mixed by the breaking of the partition, burst into a volume of flame which could not be extinguished by any known human means. It would burn even in a vacuum, since it supplied its own elements of combustion. The guns would throw these shells to a distance of about seven terrestrial miles. On the upper deck there were also stands for a couple of light machine-guns, capable of discharging seven hundred bullets a minute.

The small arms consisted of a couple of heavy, ten-bore, elephant guns carrying explosive bullets, a dozen rifles and fowling-pieces of different makes of which three, a single and a double-barrelled rifle and a double-barrelled shotgun, belonged to her ladyship, as well as a dainty brace of revolvers, one of half-a-dozen brace of various calibres which completed the minor armament of the *Astronef*.

These guns were got up and mounted while the attraction of the planet was comparatively feeble, and the guns themselves were, therefore, of very little weight. On the surface of the earth a score of men could not have done the work, but on board the *Astronef*, suspended in Space, his lordship and Murgatroyd found the work easy, and Zaidie herself picked up a Maxim and carried it about as though it were a toy sewing-machine.

'Now I think we can go down,' said Redgrave, when everything had been put in position as far as possible. 'I wonder whether we shall find the atmosphere of Mars suitable for terrestrial lungs. It will be rather awkward if it isn't.'

A very slight exertion of repulsive force was sufficient to detach the *Astronef* from the body of Phobos. She dropped rapidly towards the surface of the planet, and within three hours they saw the sunlight for the first time since they had left the Earth shining through an unmistakable atmosphere, an atmosphere of a pale, rosy hue, instead of the azure of the earthly skies, and an angular observation showed that they were within fifty miles of the surface of the undiscovered world.

'Well, there's air here of some sort, there's no doubt. We'll drop a bit further and then Andrew shall start the propellers. They'll very soon give us an idea of the density. Do you notice the change in the temperature? That's the diffused rays instead of the direct ones. Twenty miles! I think that will do. I'll stop her now and we'll prospect for a landing-place.'

He went down to apply the repulsive force directly to the surface of Mars, so as to check the descent, and then he put on his breathing-dress, went into the exit chamber, closed one door behind him, opened the other and allowed it to fill with Martian air; then he shut it again, opened his visor and took a cautious breath.

It may, perhaps, have been the idea that he, the first of all the sons of Earth, was breathing the air of another world, or it might have been some peculiar property from the Martian atmosphere, but he immediately experienced a sensation such as usually follows drinking a glass of champagne. He took another breath, and another. Then he opened the inner door and went on to the lower deck, saying to himself: 'Well, the air's all right if it is a bit champagney, rich in oxygen, I suppose, with perhaps a trace of nitrous-oxide in it. Still, it's certainly breathable, and that's the principal thing.'

'It's all right, dear,' he said as he reached the upper deck where Zaidie was walking about round the sides of the glass dome gazing with all her eyes at the strange scene of mingled cloud and sea, and land, which spread for an immense distance on all sides of them. 'I have breathed the air of Mars, and even at this height it is distinctly wholesome, though of course it's rather thin, and I had it mixed with some of our own atmosphere. Still I think it will agree all right with us lower down.'

'Well, then,' said Zaidie, 'suppose we get down below those clouds and see what there really is to be seen.'

'Your ladyship has but to speak and be obeyed,' he replied, and disappeared into the lower regions of the vessel.

In a couple of minutes she saw the cloud belt below them rising rapidly. When her husband returned the *Astronef* plunged into a sea of rosy mist.

'The clouds of Mars,' she exclaimed. 'Fancy a world with pink clouds! I wonder what there is on the other side.'

The next moment they saw. Just below them, at a distance of about five earth-miles, lay an irregularly triangular island, a detached portion of the Continent of Huygens almost equally divided by the Martian equator, and lying with another almost similarly shaped island between the fortieth and fiftieth meridians of west longitude. The two islands were divided by a broad straight stretch of water about the width of the English Channel between Folkestone and Boulogne. Instead of the bright blue green of terrestrial seas, this connecting link between the great Northern and Southern Martian oceans had an orange tinge.

The land immediately beneath them was of a gently undulating character, something like the Downs of South-Eastern England. No mountains were visible in any direction. The lower portions, particularly along the borders of the canals and the sea, were thickly dotted with towns and cities, apparently of enormous extent. To the north of the Island Continent there was a Peninsula, covered with a vast collection of buildings, which, with the broad streets and spacious squares which divided them, must have covered an area of something like two hundred square miles.

'There's the London of Mars!' said Redgrave, pointing down towards it; 'where the London of Earth will be in a few thousand years, close to the equator. And you see all those other towns and cities crowded round the canals! I dare say when we go across the northern and southern temperate zones we shall find them in about the state that Siberia or Patagonia are in.'

'I dare say we shall,' replied Zaidie, 'Martian civilisation is crowding towards the equator, though I should call that place down there the greater New York of Mars, and see there's Brooklyn just across the canal. I wonder what they're thinking about us down there.'

'Hullo, what's that!' exclaimed Redgrave, interrupting her and pointing towards the great city whose roofs, apparently of glass, were flashing with a thousand tints in the pale crimson sunlight. 'That's either an airship or another *Astronef*, and it's evidently coming up to interview us. So they've solved the problem, have they? Well, dear, I think it quite possible that we're in for a pretty exciting time on Mars.'

While he was speaking a little dark shape, at first not much bigger than a bird, had risen from the glittering roofs of the city. It rapidly increased in size until in a few minutes Zaidie got a glimpse of it through one of the telescopes and said: 'It's a great big thing something like the *Astronef*, only it has wings and, I think, masts; yes, there are three masts and there's something glittering on the tops of them.'

'Revolving helices, I suppose. He's screwing himself up into the air. That shows that they must either have stronger and lighter machinery here than we have, or, as the astronomers have thought, this atmosphere is denser than ours and therefore easier to fly in. Then, of course, things are only half their earthly weight here. Well, I suppose we may as well let them come and reconnoitre; then we shall see what kind of creatures they are. Ah! there are a lot more of them, some coming from Brooklyn, too, as you call it. Come up into the wheelhouse and I'll relieve Murgatroyd so that he can go and look after his engines. We shall have to give these gentlemen a lesson in flying. Meanwhile, in case of accidents, we may as well make ourselves as invulnerable as possible.'

A few minutes later they were in the little steel conning-tower forward, watching the approach of the Martian fleet through the thick windows of toughened glass which enabled them to look in every direction except straight down. The steel coverings had been drawn down over the glass dome of the main deck, and Murgatroyd had gone down to the engine-room, which was connected with the conning-tower by telephone and electric signal, as well as by speaking tubes. Fifty feet ahead of them stretched out a long shining spur, the forward end of the *Astronef* of which ten feet were solid steel, a ram which no floating structure built by human hands could have resisted.

Redgrave was at the wheel, standing with his hands on the steering-wheel, looking more serious than he had done so far during the voyage. Zaidie stood beside him with a powerful binocular telescope watching, with cheeks a little paler than usual, the movements of the Martian air-ships. She counted twenty-five vessels rising round them in a wide circle.

'I don't like the idea of a whole fleet coming up,' said Redgrave, as he watched them rising, and the ring narrowing round the still motionless *Astronef*. 'If they only wanted to know who and what we are, or to leave their cards on us, as it were, and bid us welcome to the world, one ship could have done that just as well as fifty. This lot coming up looks as if they wanted to get round and capture us.'

'It does look like it!' said Zaidie, with her glasses fixed on the nearest of the vessels; 'and now I can see they've guns, too, something like ours, and, perhaps, as you said just now, they may have explosives that we don't know anything about. Oh, dear, suppose they were able to smash us up with a single shot!'

'You needn't be afraid of that, dear,' said Redgrave, laying his hand on her shoulder; 'but, of course, it's perfectly natural that they should look upon us with a certain amount of suspicion, dropping like this on them from the stars. Can you see anything like men on board them yet?'

'No, they're all closed in,' she replied, 'just as we are; but they've got conning-towers like this, and something like windows along the sides; that's where the guns are, and the guns are moving, they're pointing them at us. Lenox, I'm afraid they're going to shoot.'

'Then we may as well spoil their aim,' he said, pressing an electric button three times, and then once more after a little interval.

In obedience to the signal Murgatroyd turned on the repulsive force to half power, and the *Astronef* leapt up vertically a couple of thousand feet; then Redgrave pressed the button once and stopped. Another signal set the propellers in motion, and as she sprang forward across the circle formed by the Martian air-ships, they looked down and saw that the place which they had just left was occupied by a thick, greenish-yellow cloud.

'Look, Lenox, what on earth is that?' exclaimed Zaidie, pointing down to it.

'What on Mars would be nearer the point, dear,' he said, with what she thought a somewhat vicious laugh. 'That I'm afraid means anything but a friendly reception for us. That cloud is one of two things. It's either made by the explosion of twenty or thirty shells, or else it's made of gases intended to either poison us or make us insensible, so that they can take possession of the ship. In either case I should say that the Martians are not what we should call gentlemen.'

'I should think not,' she said angrily. 'They might at least have taken us for friends till they had proved us enemies, which they wouldn't have done. Nice sort of hospitality that, considering how far we've come, and we can't shoot back because we haven't got the ports open.'

'And a very good thing too!' laughed Redgrave. 'If we had had them open, and that volley had caught us unawares, the *Astronef* would probably have been full of poisonous gases by this time, and your honeymoon, dear, would have come to a somewhat untimely end. Ah, they're trying to follow us! Well, now we'll see how high they can fly.'

He sent another signal to Murgatroyd, and the *Astronef*, still beating the Martain air with the fans of her propellers, and travelling forward at about fifty miles an hour, rose in a slanting direction through a dense bank of rosy-tinted clouds, which hung over the bigger of the two cities – New York, as Zaidie had named it. When they reached the golden red sunlight above it, the *Astronef* stopped her ascent, and with half a turn of the wheel her commander sent her sweeping round in a wide circle. A few minutes later they saw the Martian fleet rise almost simultaneously through the clouds. They seemed to hesitate a moment, and then the prow of every vessel was directed towards the swiftly moving *Astronef*.

'Well, gentlemen,' said Redgrave, 'you evidently don't know anything about Professor Rennick and his R Force; and yet you ought to know that we couldn't have come through Space without being able to get beyond this little atmosphere of yours. Now let us see how fast you can fly.'

Another signal went down to Murgatroyd, and the whirling propellers became two intersecting circles of light. The speed of the *Astronef* increased to a hundred miles an hour, and the Martian fleet began to drop behind and trail out into a triangle like a flock of huge birds.

'That's lovely; we're leaving them!' exclaimed Zaidie leaning forward with the glasses to her eyes and tapping the floor of the conning-tower with her toe as if she wanted to dance, 'and their wings are working faster than ever. They don't seem to have any screws.'

'Probably because they've solved the problem of the bird's flight,' said Redgrave. 'They're not gaining on us, are they?'

'No, they're at about the same distance.'

'Then we'll see how they can soar.'

Another signal went over the wire, the *Astronef's* propellers slowed down and stopped, and the vessel began to rise swiftly towards the zenith, which the Sun was now approaching. The Martian fleet continued the impossible chase until the limits of the navigable atmosphere, about eight earth-miles above the surface, was reached. Here the air was evidently too rarefied for their wings to act. They came to a standstill arranged in an irregular circle, their occupants no doubt looking up with envious eyes upon the shining body of the *Astronef* glittering like a tiny star in the sunlight ten thousand feet above them.

'Now, gentlemen,' said Redgrave, 'I think we have shown you that we can fly faster and soar higher than you can. Perhaps you'll be a bit more civil now. And, if you're not, well, we shall have to teach you manners.'

'But you're not going to fight them all, dear, are you? Don't let us be the first to bring war and bloodshed with us into another world.'

'Don't trouble about that, little woman, it's here already,' said her husband. 'People don't have air-ships and guns, which fire shells or whatever they were, without knowing what war is. From what I've seen, I should say these Martians have civilised themselves out of all the emotions, and, I dare say, have fought pitilessly for the possession of the last habitable lands of the planet. They've preyed upon each other till only the fittest are left, and those, I suppose, were the ones who invented the air-ships and finally got possession of all that existed. Of course that would give them the command of the planet, land, and sea. In fact, if we were able to make the personal acquaintance of the Martians, we should probably find them a set of over-civilised savages.'

'That's a rather striking paradox, isn't it, dear?' said Zaidie, slipping her hand through his arm: 'but still it's not at all bad. You mean, of course, that they've civilised themselves out of all the emotions until they're just a set of cold, calculating, scientific animals. After all, they must be. We should not have done anything like that on Earth if we'd had a visitor from Mars. We shouldn't have got out cannons, and shot at him before we'd even made his acquaince.

'Now, if he or they had dropped in America as we were going down there, we should have received them with deputations, given them banquets, which they might not have been able to eat, and speeches, which they would not understand, photographed them, filled the news-papers with everything that we could imagine about them, put them in a palace car and hustled them round the country for everybody to look at.'

'And meanwhile,' laughed Redgrave, 'some of your smart engineers, I suppose, would have gone over the vessel they had come in, found out how she was worked, and taken out a dozen patents for her machinery.'

'Very likely,' replied Zaidie, with a saucy little toss of her chin; 'and why not? We like to learn things down there – and anyhow that would be better than shooting at them.'

While this little conversation was going on, the *Astronef* was dropping rapidly into the midst of the Martian fleet, which had again arranged itself in a circle. Zaidie soon made out through the glasses that the guns were pointed upwards.

'Oh, that's your little game, is it!' said Redgrave, when she told him of this. 'Well, if you want a fight, you can have it.'

As he said this, his jaws came together, and Zaidie saw a look in his eyes that she had never seen there before. He signalled rapidly two or three times to Murgatroyd. The propellers began to whirl at their utmost speed, and the *Astronef*, making a spiral downward course, swooped down on to the Martian fleet with terrific velocity. Her last curve coincided almost exactly with the circle occupied by the fleet. Half-a-dozen spouts of greenish flame came from the nearest vessel, and for a moment the *Astronef* was enveloped in a yellow mist.

'Evidently they don't know that we are air-tight, and they don't use shot or shell. They've got past that. Their projectiles kill by poison or suffocation. I dare say a volley like that would kill a regiment. Now I'll give that fellow a lesson which he won't live to remember.'

They swept through the poison mist. Redgrave swung the wheel round. The *Astronef* dropped to the level of the ring of Martian vessels which had now got up speed again. Her steel ram was directed straight at the vessel which had fired the last shot. Propelled at a speed of more than a hundred miles an hour, it took the strange-winged craft amidships. As the shock came, Redgrave put his arm round Zaidie's waist and held her close to him, otherwise she would have been flung against the forward wall of the conning tower.

The Martian vessel stopped and bent up. They saw human figures, more than half as large again as men, inside her, staring at them through the windows in the sides. There were others at the breaches of the guns in the act of turning the muzzles on the *Astronef*; but this was only a momentary glimpse, for in a second or two after the *Astronef's* spur had pierced her, the Martian air-ship broke in twain, and her two halves plunged downwards through the rosy clouds.

'Keep her at full speed, Andrew,' said Redgrave down the speaking-tube, 'and stand by to jump if we want to.'

'Ready, my lord!' came back up the tube.

The old Yorkshireman during the last few minutes had undergone a transformation which he himself hardly understood. He recognised that there was a fight going on, that it was a case of 'burn, sink and destroy', and the thousand-year-old savage awoke in him just as, as a matter of fact, it had done in his lordship.

'Well, they can pick up the pieces down there,' said Redgrave, still holding Zaidie tight to his side with one hand and working the wheel with the other. 'Now we'll teach them another lesson.'

'What are you going to do, dear?' she said, looking up at him with somewhat frightened eyes.

'You'll see in a moment,' he said, between his shut teeth. 'I don't care whether these Martians are degenerate human beings or only animals; but from my point of view the reception that they have given us justifies any kind of retaliation. If we'd had a single port hole open during the first volley you and I would have been dead by this time, and I'm not going to stand anything like that without reprisals. They've declared war on us, and killing in war isn't murder.'

'Well, no, I suppose not,' she said; 'but it's the first fight I've been in, and I don't like it. Still, they did receive us pretty meanly, didn't they?'

'Meanly? If there was anything like a code of interplanetary morals, one might call it absolutely caddish.'

He sent another message to Murgatroyd. The *Astronef* sprang a thousand feet towards the zenith; another signal, and she stopped exactly over the biggest of the Martian airships; another, and she dropped on to it like a stone and smashed it to fragments. Then she stopped and mounted again above the broken circle of the fleet, while the pieces of the air-ship and what was left of her crew plunged downwards through the crimson clouds in a fall of nearly thirty thousand feet.

Within the next few moments the rest of the Martian fleet had followed it, sinking rapidly down through the clouds and scattering in all directions.

'They seem to have had enough of it,' laughed Redgrave, as the *Astronef*, in obedience to another signal, began to drop towards the surface of Mars. 'Now we'll go down and see if they're in a more reasonable frame of mind. At any rate we've won our first scrimmage, dear.'

'But it was rather brutal, Lenox, wasn't it?'

'When you are dealing with brutes, Zaidie, it is sometimes necessary to be brutal.'

'And you look a wee bit brutal now,' she replied, looking up at him with something like a look of fear in her eyes. 'I suppose that is because you have just killed somebody – or somethings – whichever they are.'

'Do I, really?'

The hard-set jaw relaxed and his lips melted into a smile under his moustache, and he bent down and kissed her. And then he said: 'Well, what do you suppose I should have thought of them if *you* had had a whiff of that poison?'

'Yes, dear,' she said; 'I see now.'

When the *Astronef* dropped through the clouds, they saw that the fleet had not only scattered, but was apparently getting as far out of reach as possible. One vessel had dropped into the principal square in the centre of the city which her ladyship had called New York.

'That fellow has gone to report, evidently,' said Redgrave. 'We'll follow him, but I don't think we'd better open the ports even then. There's no telling when they might give us a whiff of that poison-mist, or whatever it is.'

'But how are you going to talk to them, then, if they can talk? – I mean, if they know any language that we do?'

'They're something like men, and so I suppose they understand the language of signs, at any rate. Still, if you don't fancy it, we'll go somewhere else.'

'No thanks,' she said. 'That's not my father's daughter. I haven't come a hundred million miles from home to go away before the first act's finished. We'll go down to see if we can make them understand.'

By this time the *Astronef* was hanging suspended over an enormous square about half the size of Hyde Park. It was laid out just as a terrestrial park would be in grassland, flower beds, and avenues, and patches of trees, only the grass was a reddish yellow, the leaves of the trees were like those of a beech in autumn, and the flowers were nearly all a deep violet, or a bright emerald green.

As they descended they saw that the square, or Central Park, as her ladyship at once christened it, was flanked by enormous blocks of buildings, palaces built of a dazzlingly white stone, and topped by domed roofs, and lofty cupolas of glass.

'Isn't that just lovely!' she said, swinging her binoculars in every direction. 'Talk about Fifth Avenue and the houses in Central Park; why, it's the Chicago Exposition, and the Paris one, and your Crystal Palace, multiplied by about ten thousand, and all spread out just round this one place. If we don't find these people nice, I guess we'd better go back and build a fleet like this, and come and take it.'

'There spoke the new American imperialism,' laughed Redgrave. 'Well, we'll go and see what they're like first, shall we?'

The *Astronef* dropped a little more slowly than the air-ship had done, and remained suspended a hundred feet or so above her after she had reached the ground. Swarms of human figures, but of more than human stature, clad in tunics and trousers or knickerbockers, came out of the glass-domed palaces from all sides into the park. They were nearly all of the same stature and there appeared to be no difference whatever between the sexes. Their dress was absolutely plain; there was no attempt at ornament or decoration of any kind.

'If there are any of the Martian women among those people,' said her ladyship, 'they've taken to rationals and they've grown about as big as the men. And look; there's someone who seems to want to communicate with us. Why, they're all bald! They haven't got a hair among them – and what a size their heads are!'

'That's brains – too much brains, I expect! These people have lived too long. I expect they've ceased to be animals – civilised themselves out of everything in the way of passions and emotions – and are just purely intellectual beings, with as much human nature about them as a limited company has.'

The orderly swarms of figures, which were rapidly filling the park, divided as he was speaking, making a broad lane from one of its entrances to where the *Astronef* was hanging above the air-ship. A light four-wheeled vehicle, whose framework and wheels glittered like burnished gold, sped towards them, driven by some invisible agency. Its only occupant was a huge man, dressed in the universal costume, saving only a scarlet sash in place of the cord-girdle which the others wore round their waists. The vehicle stopped near the air-ship, over which the *Astronef* was hanging, and, as the figure dismounted, a door opened in the side of the vessel and three other figures, similar both in stature and attire, came out and entered into conversation with him.

'The Admiral of the Fleet is evidently making his report,' said Redgrave. 'Meanwhile, the crowd seems to be taking a considerable amount of interest in us.'

'And very naturally, too!' replied Zaidie. 'Don't you think we might go down now and see if we can make ourselves understood in any way? You can have the guns ready in case of accidents, but I don't think they'll try and hurt us now. Look, the gentleman with the red sash is making signs.'

'I think we can go down now all right,' replied Redgrave, 'because it's quite certain they can't use the poison guns on us without killing themselves as well. Still, we may as well have our own ready. Andrew, load up and get that port Maxim ready. I hope we shan't want it, but we may. I don't quite like the look of these people.'

'They're very ugly, aren't they?' said Zaidie; 'and really you can't tell which are men and which are women. I suppose they've civilised themselves out of everything that's nice, and are just scientific and utilitarian and everything that's horrid.'

'I shouldn't wonder. They look to me as if they've just got common sense, as we call it, and hadn't any other sense; but, at any rate, if they don't behave themselves, we shall be able to teach them manners of a sort, though I dare say we've done that to some extent already.'

As he said this Redgrave went into the conning-tower, and the *Astronef* moved from above the air-ship, and dropped gently into the crimson grass about a hundred feet from her. Then the ports were opened, the guns, which Murgatroyd had loaded, were swung into position, and they armed themselves with a brace of revolvers each, in case of accident.

'What delicious air this is!' said her ladyship, as the ports were opened, and she took her first breath of the Martian atmosphere. 'It's ever so much nicer than ours; it's just like breathing champagne.'

Redgrave looked at her with an admiration which was tempered by a sudden apprehension. Even in his eyes she had never seemed so lovely before. Her cheeks were glowing and her eyes were gleaming with a brightness that was almost feverish, and he was himself sensible of a strange feeling of exultation, both mental and physical, as his lungs filled with the Martian air.

'Oxygen,' he said shortly, 'and too much of it! Or, I shouldn't wonder if it was something like nitrous-oxide – you know, laughing gas.'

'Don't!' she laughed. 'It may be very nice to breath, but it reminds one of other things which aren't a bit nice. Still, if it is anything of that sort it might account for these people having lived so fast. I know I feel just now as if I were living at the rate of thirty-six hours a day and so, I suppose, the fewer hours we stop here the better.'

'Exactly!' said Redgrave, with another glance of apprehension at her. 'Now, there's his Royal Highness, or whatever he is, coming. How are we going to talk to him? Are you all ready, Andrew?'

'Yes, my lord, all ready,' replied the old Yorkshireman, dropping his huge, hairy hand on the breach of the Maxim.

'Very well, then, shoot the moment you see them doing anything suspicious, and don't let anyone except his Royal Highness come nearer than a hundred yards.'

As he said this, Redgrave, revolver in hand, went to the door, from which the gangway steps had been lowered, and, in reply to a singularly expressive gesture from the huge Martian, who seemed to stand nearly nine feet high, he beckoned to him to come up on to the deck.

A huge Martian, who seemed to stand nearly nine feet high

As he mounted the steps the crowd closed round the *Astronef* and the Martian air-ship; but, as though in obedience to orders which had already been given, they kept at a respectful distance of a little over a hundred yards away from the strange vessel, which had wrought such havoc with their fleet. When the Martian reached the deck Redgrave held out his hand and the giant recoiled, as a man on earth might have done if, instead of the open palm, he had seen a clenched hand gripping a knife.

'Take care, Lenox,' exclaimed Zaidie, taking a couple of steps towards him, with her right hand on the butt of one of her revolvers. The movement brought her close to the open door, and in full view of the crowd outside.

If a seraph had come on earth and presented itself thus before a throng of human beings, there might have happened some such miracle as was wrought when the swarm of Martians beheld the strange beauty of this radiant daughter of the earth. As it seemed to them, when they discussed it afterwards, ages of purely mechanical and utilitarian civilisation had brought all conditions of Martian life up – or down – to the same level. There was no apparent difference between the males and females in stature; their faces were all the same, with features of mathematical regularity, pale skin, bloodless cheeks, and an expression, if such it could be called, utterly devoid of emotion.

But still these creatures were human, or at least, their forefathers had been. Hearts beat in their breasts, blood flowed through their veins, and so the magic of this marvellous vision instantly awoke the long-slumbering elementary instincts of a bygone age. A low murmur ran through the vast throng, a murmur, half-human, half-brutish, which swiftly rose to a hoarse, screaming roar.

'Look out, my lord! Quick! Shut the door, they're coming! It's her ladyship they want; she must look like an angel from Heaven to them. Shall I fire?'

'Yes,' said Redgrave, gripping the lever, and bringing the door down. 'Zaidie, if this fellow moves, put a bullet through him. I'm going to talk to that air-ship before he gets his poison guns to work.'

As the last word left his lips, Murgatroyd put his thumb on the spring on the Maxim. A roar such as Martian ears had never heard before resounded through the vast square, and was flung back with a thousand echoes from the walls of the huge palaces on every side. A stream of smoke and flame poured out of the little port-hole, and then the onward-swarming throng seemed to stop, and the front ranks of it began to sink down silently in long rows.

Then through the roaring rattle of the Maxim, sounded the deep, sharp bang of Redgrave's gun, as he sent twenty pounds' weight of an explosive, invented by Zaidie's father, which was nearly four times as powerful as Lyddite, into the Martian air-ship. Then came an explosion, which shook the air for miles around. A blaze of greenish flame, and a huge cloud of steamy smoke, showed that the projectile had done its work, and, when the smoke drifted away, the spot on which the air-ship had lain was only a deep, red, jagged gash in the ground. There was not even a fragment of the ship to be seen.

Then Redgrave left the gun and turned the starboard Maxim on to another swarm which was approaching the *Astronef* from that side. When he had got the range, he swung the gun slowly from side to side. The moving throng stopped, as the other one had done, and sank down to the red grass, now dyed with a deeper red.

Meanwhile, Zaidie had been holding the Martian at something more than arm's length with her revolver. He seemed to understand perfectly that, if she pulled the trigger, the revolver would do something like what the Maxims had done. He appeared to take no notice whatever either of the destruction of the air ship or of the slaughter that was going on around the *Astronef*. His big, pale blue eyes were fixed upon her face. They seemed to be devouring a loveliness such as they had never seen before. A dim, pinky flush stole for the first time into his sallow cheeks, and something like a light of human passion came into his eyes.

Then he spoke. The words were slowly uttered, passionless, and very distinct. As words they were unintelligible but there was no mistaking their meaning or that of the gestures which accompanied them. He bent forward, towering over her with outstretched arms, huge, hideous, and half human.

Zaidie took a step backwards and, just as Redgrave whipped out one of his revolvers, she pulled the trigger of hers. The bullet cut a clean hole through the smooth, hairless skull of the Martian, and he dropped to the deck without a sound other than what was made by his falling body.

'That's the first man I've ever killed,' she faltered, as her hand fell to her side, and the revolver dropped from it. 'Still, do you think it really was a man?'

'That a man!' said Redgrave through his clenched teeth. 'Not much! Here, Andrew, open that door again and help me to heave this thing overboard, and then we'd better be off or we shall be having the rest of the fleet with their poison guns around us. Hurry up! Zaidie, I think you'd better go below for the present, little woman, and keep the door of your room tight shut. There's no telling what these animals may do if they get a chance at us.'

Although she would rather have remained on deck to see what was to happen, she saw that he was in earnest, and so she at once obeyed.

The dead body of the Martian was tumbled out, Murgatroyd closed all the air-tight doors of the upper deck chamber, while Redgrave set the engines in motion and, with hardly a moment's delay, the *Astronef* sprang up into the crimson sky from her first and last battle-field in the well-named world of the War God.

III A GLIMPSE OF THE SINLESS STAR

INTRODUCTION. – For their honeymoon Rollo Lenox Smeaton Aubrey, Earl of Redgrave, and his bride, Lilla Zaidie, leave the earth on a visit to the moon and the principal planets, their sole companion being Andrew Murgatroyd, an old engineer who had superintended the building of the *Astronef*, in which the journey is made. By means of the 'R Force,' or Anti Gravitational Force, of the secret of which Lord Redgrave is the sole possessor, they are able to navigate with precision and safety the limitless ocean of space. Their adventures on the Moon and on Mars have been described in the first two stories of the series.

'How very different Venus looks now to what it does from the earth,' said Zaidie as she took her eye away from the telescope, through which she had been examining the enormous crescent, almost approaching to what would be called upon earth a half-moon, which spanned the dark vault of space ahead of the *Astronef*.

'I wonder what she'll be like. All the authorities are agreed that on Venus, having her axis of revolution very much inclined to the plane of her orbit, the seasons are so severe that for half the year its temperate zone and its tropics have a summer about twice as hot as our tropics and the other half they have a winter twice as cold as our coldest. I'm afraid, after all, we shall find the Love-Star a world of salamanders and seals; things that can live in a furnace and bask on an iceberg; and when we get back home it will be our painful duty, as the first explorers of the fields of space, to dispel another dearly-cherished popular delusion.'

'I'm not so very sure about that,' said Lenox, glancing from the rapidly growing crescent, which was still so far away, to the sweet smiling face that was so near to his. 'Don't you see something very different there to what we saw either on the Moon or Mars? Now just go back to your telescope and let us take an observation.'

'Well,' said Zaidie, 'as our trip is partly, at least, in the interest of science, I will;' and then, when she had got her own telescope into focus again – for the distance between the *Astronef* and the new world they were about to visit was rapidly lessening – she took a long look through it, and said: 'Yes, I think I see what you mean. The outer edge of the crescent is bright, but it gets greyer and dimmer towards the inside of the curve. Of course Venus has an atmosphere. So had Mars; but this must be very dense. There's a sort of halo all round it. Just fancy that splendid thing being the little black spot we saw going across the face of the Sun a few days ago! It makes one feel rather small, doesn't it?'

'That is one of the things which a woman says when she doesn't want to be answered; but, apart from that, your ladyship was saying?'

'What a very unpleasant person you can be when you like! I was going to say that on the Moon we saw nothing but black and white, light and darkness. There was no atmosphere, except in those awful places I don't want to think about. Then, as we got near Mars, we saw a pinky atmosphere, but not very dense; but this, you see, is a sort of pearl-grey white shading from silver to black. But look – what are those tiny bright spots? There are hundreds of them.'

'Do you remember, as we were leaving the earth, how bright the mountain ranges looked; how plainly we could see the Rockies and the Andes?'

'Oh, yes, I see; they're mountains; thirty-seven miles high some of them, they say; and the rest of the silver-grey will be clouds, I suppose. Fancy living under clouds like those.'

'Only another case of the adaptation of life to natural conditions, I expect. When we get there, I dare say we shall find that these clouds are just what make it possible for the inhabitants of Venus to stand the extremes of heat and cold. Given elevations, three or four times as high as the Himalayas, it would be quite possible for them to choose their temperature by shifting their altitude.

'But I think it's about time to drop theory and see to the practice,' he continued, getting up from his chair and going to the signal board in the conning-tower. 'Whatever the planet Venus may be like, we don't want to charge it at the rate of sixty miles a second. That's about the speed now, considering how fast she's travelling towards us.'

'And considering that, whether it is a nice world or not, it's about as big as the earth, and so we should get rather the worst of the charge,' laughed Zaidie, as she went back to her telescope.

Redgrave sent a signal down to Murgatroyd to reverse engines, as it were, or, in other words, to direct the 'R Force' against the planet, from which they were now only a couple of hundred thousand miles distant. The next moment the sun and stars seemed to halt in their courses. The great silver-grey crescent which had been increasing in size every moment appeared to remain stationary, and then when Lenox was satisfied that the engines were developing the force properly, he sent another signal down, and the *Astronef* began to descend.

The half-disc of Venus seemed to fall below them, and in a few minutes they could see it from the upper deck spreading out like a huge semi-circular plain of silver grey light ahead, and on both sides of them. The *Astronef* was falling upon it at the rate of about a thousand miles a minute towards the centre of the half crescent, and every moment the brilliant spots above the cloud-surface grew in size and brightness.

'I believe the theory about the enormous height of the mountains of Venus must be correct after all,' said Redgrave, tearing himself with an evident wrench away from his telescope. 'Those white patches can't be anything else but the summits of snow-capped mountains. You know how brilliantly white a snow-peak looks on earth against even the whitest of clouds.'

'Oh, yes,' said her ladyship, 'I've often seen that in the Rockies. But it's lunch time, and I must go down and see how my things in the kitchen are getting on. I suppose you'll try and land somewhere where it's morning, so that we can have a good day before us. Really it's very convenient to be able to make your own morning or night as you like, isn't it? I hope it won't make us too conceited when we get back, being able to choose our mornings and our evenings; in fact, our sunrises and sunsets on any world we like to visit in a casual way like this.'

'Well,' laughed Redgrave, as she moved away towards the companion stairs, 'after all, if you find the United States, or even the planet Terra, too small for you, we've always got the fields of Space open to us. We might take a trip across the Zodiac or down the Milky Way.'

'And meanwhile,' she replied, stopping at the top of the stairs and looking round, 'I'll go down and get lunch. You and I may be king and queen of the realms of Space, and all that sort of thing; but we've got to eat and drink after all.'

'And that reminds me,' said Redgrave, getting up and following her, 'we must celebrate our arrival on a new world as usual. I'll go down and get out the champagne. I shouldn't be surprised if we found the people of the Love-World living on nectar and ambrosia, and as fizz is our nearest approach to nectar – '

'I suppose,' said Zaidie, as she gathered up her skirts and stepped daintily down the companion stairs, 'if you find anything human, or at least human enough to eat and drink, you'll have a party and give them champagne. I wonder what those wretches on Mars would have thought of it if we'd only made friends with them?'

Lunch on board the *Astronef* was about the pleasantest meal of the day. Of course there was neither day nor night, in the ordinary sense of the word, except as the hours were measured off by the chronometers. Whichever side or end of the vessel received the direct rays of the sun, there there was blazing heat and dazzling light. Elsewhere there was black darkness, and the more than icy cold of space; but lunch was a convenient division of the waking hours, which began with a stroll on the upper deck and a view of the ever-varying splendours about them, and ended after dinner in the same place with coffee and cigarettes and speculations as to the next day's happenings.

This lunch hour passed even more pleasantly and rapidly than others had done, for the discussion as to the possibilities of Venus was continued in a quite delightful mixture of scientific disquisition and that converse which is common to most human beings on their honeymoon.

As there was nothing more to be done or seen for an hour or two, the afternoon was spent in a pleasant siesta in the luxurious saloon of the star-navigator; because evening to them would be morning on that portion of Venus to which they were directing their course, and, as Zaidie said, when she subsided into her hammock: 'It will be breakfast time before we shall be able to get dinner.'

As the *Astronef* fell with ever-increasing velocity towards the cloud-covered surface of Venus, the remainder of her disc, lit up by the radiance of her sister-worlds, Mercury, Mars, and the Earth, and also by the pale radiance of an enormous comet, which had suddenly shot into view from behind its southern limb, became more or less visible.

Towards six o'clock, according to Earth, or rather *Astronef*, time, it became necessary to exert the full strength of her engines to check the velocity of her fall. By eight she had entered the atmosphere of Venus, and was dropping slowly towards a vast sea of sunlit cloud, out of which, on all sides, towered thousands of snow-clad peaks, with wide-spread stretches of upland above which the clouds swept and surged like the silent billows of some vast ocean in ghostland.

'I thought so!' said Redgrave, when the propellers had begun to revolve and Murgatroyd had taken his place in the conning-tower. 'A very dense atmosphere loaded with clouds. There's the sun just rising, so your lady-ship's wishes are duly obeyed.'

'And doesn't it seem nice and homelike to see him rising through an atmosphere above the clouds again? It doesn't look a bit like the same sort of dear old sun just blazing like a red-hot moon among a lot of white hot stars and planets. Look, aren't those peaks lovely, and that cloud-sea? Why, for all the world we might be in a balloon above the Rockies or the Alps. And see,' she continued, pointing to one of the thermometers fixed outside the glass dome which covered the upper deck, 'it's only sixty-five even here. I wonder if we could breathe this air, and oh, I do wonder what we shall see on the other side of those clouds.'

'You shall have both questions answered in a few minutes,' replied Redgrave, going towards the conning-tower. 'To begin with, I think we'll land on that big snow-dome yonder, and do a little exploring. Where there are snow and clouds there is moisture, and where there is moisture a man ought to be able to breathe.'

The *Astronef*, still falling, but now easily under the command of the helmsman, shot forwards and downwards towards a vast dome of snow which, rising some two thousand feet above the cloud-sea, shone with dazzling brilliance in the light of the rising sun. She landed just above the edge of the clouds. Meanwhile they had put on their breathing suits, and Redgrave had seen that the air chamber, through which they had to pass from their own little world into the new ones that they visited, was in working order. When the outer door was opened and the ladder lowered, he stood aside, as he had done on the moon, and her ladyship's was the first human foot which made an imprint on the virgin snows of Venus.

The first thing Lenox did was to raise the visor of his helmet and taste the air of the new world. It was cool, and fresh, and sweet, and the first draught of it sent the blood tingling and dancing through his veins. Perfect as the arrangements of the *Astronef* were in this respect, the air of Venus tasted like clear running spring water would have done to a man who had been drinking filtered water for several days. He threw the visor right up and motioned to Zaidie to do the same. She obeyed, and, after drawing a long breath, she said: 'That's glorious! It's like wine after water, and rather stagnant water too. But what a world, snow-peaks and cloud-sea, islands of ice and snow in an ocean of mist! Just look at them! Did you ever see anything so lovely and unearthly in your life? I wonder how high this mountain is, and what there is on the other side of the clouds. Isn't the air delicious! Not a bit too cold after all – but, still, I think we may as well go back and put on something more becoming. I shouldn't quite like the ladies of Venus to see me dressed like a diver.'

'Come along then,' laughed Lenox, as he turned back towards the vessel. 'That's just like a woman. You're about a hundred and fifty million miles away from Broadway or Regent Street. You are standing on the top of a snow mountain above the clouds of Venus, and the moment that you find the air is fit to breathe you begin thinking about dress. How do you know that the inhabitants of Venus, if there are any, dress at all?'

'What nonsense! Of course they do – at least, if they are anything like us.'

Lenox raised the visor of his helmet

As soon as they got back on board the *Astronef* and had taken their breathing-dresses off, Redgrave and the old engineer, who appeared to take no visible interest in their new surroundings, threw open all the sliding doors on the upper and lower decks so that the vessel might be thoroughly ventilated by the fresh sweet air. Then a gentle repulsion was applied to the huge snow mass on which the *Astronef* rested. She rose a couple of hundred feet, her propellers began to whirl round, and Redgrave steered her out towards the centre of the vast cloud-sea which was almost surrounded by a thousand glittering peaks of ice and domes of snow.

'I think we may as well put off dinner, or breakfast as it will be now, until we see what the world below is like,' he said to Zaidie, who was standing beside him on the conning-tower.

'Oh, never mind about eating just now; this is altogether too wonderful to be missed for the sake of ordinary meat and drink. Let's go down and see what there is on the other side.'

He sent a message down the speaking tube to Murgatroyd, who was below among his beloved engines, and the next moment sun and clouds and ice-peaks had disappeared and nothing was visible save the all-enveloping silver-grey mist.

For several minutes they remained silent, watching and wondering what they would find beneath the veil which hid the surface of Venus from their view. Then the mist thinned out and broke up into patches which drifted past them as they descended on their downward slanting course.

Below them they saw vast, ghostly shapes of mountains and valleys, lakes and rivers, continents, islands, and seas. Every moment these became more and more distinct, and soon they were in full view of the most marvellous landscape that human eyes had ever beheld.

The distances were tremendous. Mountains, compared with which the Alps or even the Andes would have seemed mere hillocks, towered up out of the vast depths beneath them. Up to the lower edge of the all-covering cloud-sea they were clad with a golden-yellow vegetation, fields and forests, open, smiling valleys, and deep, dark ravines through which a thousand torrents thundered down from the eternal snows beyond, to spread themselves out in rivers and lakes in the valleys and plains which lay many thousands of feet below.

'What a lovely world!' said Zaidie, as she at last found her voice after what was almost a stupor of speechless wonder and admiration. 'And the light! Did you ever see anything like it? It's neither moonlight nor sunlight. See, there are no shadows down there; it's just all lovely silvery twilight. Lenox, if Venus is as nice as she looks from here I don't think I shall want to go back. It reminds me of Tennyson's Lotus Eaters, "the Land where it is always afternoon".'

'I think you are right after all. We are thirty million miles nearer to the sun than we were on the earth, and the light and heat have to filter through those clouds. They are not at all like earth-clouds from this side. It's the other way about. The silver lining is on this side. Look, there isn't a black or a brown one, or even a grey one within sight. They are just like a thin mist, lighted by millions of electric lamps. It's a delicious world, and if it isn't inhabited by angels it ought to be.'

While they were talking, the *Astronef* was still sweeping swiftly down towards the surface through scenery of whose almost inconceivable magnificence no human words could convey any adequate idea. Underneath the cloud-veil the air was absolutely clear and transparent; clearer, indeed, than terrestrial air at the highest elevations, and, moreover, it seemed to be endowed with a strange luminous quality, which made objects, no matter how distant, stand out with almost startling distinctness.

The rivers and lakes and seas, which spread out beneath them, seemed never to have been ruffled by the blast of a storm or wind, and shone with a soft silvery grey light, which seemed to come from below rather than from above. The atmosphere, which had now penetrated to every part of the *Astronef*, was not only exquisitely soft but also conveyed a faint but delicious sense of languorous intoxication to the nerves.

'If this isn't Heaven it must be the half-way house,' said Redgrave, with what was, perhaps, under the circumstances, a pardonable irreverence. 'Still, after all, we don't know what the inhabitants may be like, so I think we'd better close the doors, and drop on the top of that mountain spur running out between the two rivers into the bay. Do you notice how curious the water looks after the earth-seas; bright silver, instead of blue and green?'

'Oh, it's just lovely,' said Zaidie. 'Let's go down and have a walk. There's nothing to be afraid of. You'll never make me believe that a world like this can be inhabited by anything dangerous.'

'Perhaps, but we mustn't forget what happened on Mars; still, there's one thing, we haven't been tackled by any aerial fleets yet.'

'I don't think the people here want airships. They can fly themselves. Look! there are a lot of them coming to meet us. That was a rather wicked remark of yours, about the half-way house to Heaven; but those certainly look something like angels.'

As Zaidie said this, after a somewhat lengthy pause, during which the *Astronef* had descended to within a few hundred feet of the mountain-spur, she handed a pair of field-glasses to her husband, and pointed downward towards an island which lay a couple of miles or so off the end of the spur.

Redgrave put the glasses to his eyes, and, as he took a long look through them, moving them slowly up and down, and from side to side, he saw hundreds of winged figures rising from the island and soaring towards them.

'You were right, dear,' he said, without taking the glass from his eyes, 'and so was I. If those aren't angels, they're certainly something like men, and, I suppose, women too, who can fly. We may as well stop here and wait for them. I wonder what sort of an animal they take the *Astronef* for.'

He sent a message down the tube to Murgatroyd, and gave a turn and a half to the steering wheel. The propellers slowed down and the *Astronef* landed with a hardly perceptible shock in the midst of a little plateau covered with a thick soft moss of a pale yellowish green, and fringed by a belt of trees which seemed to be over three hundred feet high, and whose foliage was a deep golden bronze.

They had scarcely landed before the flying figures reappeared over the tree-tops and swept downwards in long spiral curves towards the *Astronef*.

'If they're not angels, they're very like them,' said Zaidie, putting down her glasses.

'There's one thing,' replied her husband; 'they fly a lot better than the old masters' angels or Doré's could have done, because they have tails – or at least something that seems to serve the same purpose, and yet they haven't got feathers.'

'Yes, they have, at least round the edges of their wings or whatever they are, and they've got clothes, too, silk tunics or something of that sort – and there are men and women.'

'You're quite right. Those fringes down their legs are feathers, and that's how they can fly.'

The flying figures which came hovering near to the *Astronef*, without evincing any apparent sign of fear, were certainly the strangest that human eyes had looked upon. In some respects they had a sufficient resemblance to human form for them to be taken for winged men and women, while in another they bore a decided resemblance to birds. Their bodies and limbs were almost human in shape, but of slenderer and lighter build; and from the shoulder-blades and muscles of the back there sprang a pair of wings arching up above their heads.

The body was covered in front and down the back between the wings with a sort of tunic of a light, silken-looking material, which must have been clothing, since there were many different colours.

In stature these inhabitants of the Love-Star varied from about five feet six to five feet, but both the taller and the shorter of them were all of

nearly the same size, from which it was easy to conclude that this difference in stature was on Venus, as well as on the Earth, one of the broad
distinctions between the sexes.

They flew once or twice completely round the *Astronef* with an exquisite ease and grace which made Zaidie exclaim: 'Now, why weren't we
made like that on Earth!'

To which Redgrave, after a look at the barometer, replied: 'Partly, I
suppose, because we weren't built that way, and partly because we don't
live in an atmosphere about two and a half times as dense as ours.'

Then several of the winged figures alighted on the mossy covering of
the plain and walked towards the vessel.

'Why, they walk just like us, only much more prettily!' said Zaidie.
'And look what funny little faces they've got! Half bird, half human,
and soft, downy feathers instead of hair. I wonder whether they talk
or sing. I wish you'd open the doors again, Lenox. I'm sure they can't
possibly mean us any harm; they are far too innocent for that. What soft
eyes they have, and what a thousand pities it is we shan't be able to
understand them.'

They had left the conning-tower, and both his lordship and Murgatroyd were throwing open the sliding doors and, to Zaidie's considerable
displeasure, getting the deck Maxims ready for action in case they should
be required. As soon as the doors were open Zaidie's judgment of the
inhabitants of Venus was entirely justified.

Without the slightest sign of fear, but with very evident astonishment in
their round golden-yellow eyes, they came walking close up to the sides
of the *Astronef.* Some of them stroked her smooth, shining sides with
their little hands, which Zaidie now found had only three fingers and a
thumb. Many ages before they might have been bird's claws, but now they
were soft and pink and plump, utterly strange to work as manual work is
understood upon Earth.

'Just fancy getting Maxim guns ready to shoot those delightful things,'
said Zaidie, almost indignantly, as she went towards the doorway from
which the gangway ladder ran down to the soft, mossy turf. 'Why, not
one of them has got a weapon of any sort; and just listen,' she went
on, stopping in the opening of the doorway, 'have you ever heard music
like that on earth? I haven't. I suppose it's the way they talk. I'd give
a good deal to be able to understand them. But still, it's very lovely,
isn't it?'

'Ay, like the voices of syrens enticing honest folk to destruction,' said
Murgatroyd, speaking for the first time since the *Astronef* had landed; for
this big, grizzled, taciturn Yorkshireman, who looked upon the whole

cruise through Space as a mad and almost impious adventure, which nothing but his hereditary loyalty to his master's name and family could have persuaded him to share in, had grown more and more silent as the millions of miles between the *Astronef* and his native Yorkshire village had multiplied day by day.

'Syrens – and why not?' laughed Redgrave. 'Yes, Zaidie, I never heard anything like that before. Unearthly, of course it is; but then we're not on Earth. Now, Zaidie, they seem to talk in song-language. You did pretty well on Mars with your sign-language, suppose we go out and show them that you can speak the song-language, too.'

'What do you mean?' she said; 'sing them something?'

'Yes,' he replied, 'they'll try to talk to you in song, and you won't be able to understand them; at least, not as far as words and sentences go. But music is the universal language on Earth, and there's no reason why it shouldn't be the same through the solar system. Come along, tune up, little woman!'

They went together down the gangway stairs, he dressed in an ordinary English tweed grey suit, with a golf cap on the back of his head, and she in the last and daintiest of costumes which had combined the art of Paris and London and New York before the *Astronef* soared up from Central Park.

The moment that she set foot on the golden-yellow sward she was surrounded by a swarm of the winged, and yet strangely human creatures. Those nearest to her came and touched her hands and face, and stroked the folds of her dress. Others looked into her violet-blue eyes, and others put out their queer little hands and touched her hair.

This and her clothing seemed to be the most wonderful experience for them, saving always the fact that she had no wings.

Redgrave kept close beside her until he was satisfied that these strange half-human, and yet wholly interesting creatures were innocent of any intention of harm, and when he saw two of the winged daughters of the Love-Star put up their hands and touch the thick coils of her hair, he said: 'Take those pins and things out and let it down. They seem to think that your hair's part of your head. It's the first chance you've had to work a miracle, so you may as well do it. Show them the most beautiful thing they've ever seen.'

'What babies you men can be when you get sentimental!' laughed Zaidie, as she put her hands up to her head. 'How do you know that this may not be ugly in their eyes?'

'Quite impossible!' he replied. 'They're a great deal too pretty themselves to think *you* ugly.'

While he was speaking Zaidie had taken off a Spanish mantilla which she had thrown over her head as she came out, and which the ladies of Venus seemed to think was part of her hair. Then she took out the comb and one or two hairpins which kept the coils in position, deftly caught the ends, and then, after a few rapid movements of her fingers, she shook her head, and the wondering crowd about her saw what seemed to them a shimmering veil, half gold, half silver, in the strange, reflected light from the cloud-veil, fall down from her head over her shoulders.

They crowded still more closely round her, but so quietly and so gently that she felt nothing more than the touch of wondering hands on her arms, and dress, and hair. Her husband, as he said afterwards, was 'absolutely out of it'. They seemed to imagine him to be a kind of uncouth monster, possibly the slave of this radiant being which had come so strangely

A shimmering veil fell down from her head over her shoulders

from somewhere beyond the cloud-veil. They looked at him with their golden-yellow eyes wide open, and some of them came up rather timidly and touched his clothes, which they seemed to think were his skin.

Then one or two, more daring, put their little hands up to his face and touched his moustache, and all of them, while both examinations were going on, kept up a running conversation of cooing and singing which evidently conveyed their ideas from one to the other on the subject of this most marvellous visit of these two strange beings with neither wings nor feathers, but who, most undoubtedly, had other means of flying, since it was quite certain that they had come from another world.

There was a low cooing note, something like the language in which doves converse, and which formed a sort of undertone. But every moment this rose here and there into higher notes, evidently expressing wonder or admiration, or both.

'You were right about the universal language,' said Redgrave, when he had submitted to the stroking process for a few moments. 'These people talk in music, and, as far as I can see or hear, their opinion of us, or, at least, of you, is distinctly flattering. I don't know what they take *me* for, and I don't care, but, as we'd better make friends with them, suppose you sing them "Home, Sweet Home", or the "Swanee River". I shouldn't wonder if they consider our talking voices most horrible discords, so you might as well give them something different.'

While he was speaking the sounds about them suddenly hushed, and, as Redgrave said afterwards, it was something like the silence that follows a cannon shot. Then, in the midst of the hush, Zaidie put her hands behind her, looked up towards the luminous silver surface which formed the only visible sky of Venus, and began to sing 'The Swanee River'.

The clear, sweet notes rang up through the midst of a sudden silence. The sons and daughters of the Love-Star ceased the low, half-humming, half-cooing tones in which they seemed to be whispering to each other, and Zaidie sang the old plantation song through for the first time that a human voice had sung it to ears other than human.

As the last note thrilled sweetly from her lips she looked round at the crowd of strange half-human figures about her, and something in their unlikeness to her own kind brought back to her mind the familiar scenes which lay so far away, so many millions of miles across the dark and silent Ocean of Space.

Other winged figures, attracted by the sound of her singing, had crossed the trees, and these, during the silence which came after the singing of the song, were swiftly followed by others, until there were nearly a thousand of them gathered about the side of the *Astronef*.

There was no crowding or jostling among them. Each one treated every other with the most perfect gentleness and courtesy. No such thing as enmity or ill-feeling seemed to exist among them, and, in perfect silence, they waited for Zaidie to continue what they thought was her first speech of greeting. The temper of the throng somehow coincided exactly with the mood which her own memories had brought to her, and the next moment she sent the first line of 'Home Sweet Home' soaring up to the cloud-veiled sky.

As the notes rang up into the still, soft air a deeper hush fell on the listening throng. Heads were bowed with a gesture almost of adoration, and many of those standing nearest to her bent their bodies forward, and expanded their wings, bringing them together over their breasts with a motion which, as they afterwards learnt, was intended to convey the idea of wonder and admiration, mingled with something like a sentiment of worship.

Zaidie sang the sweet old song through from end to end, forgetting for the time being everything but the home she had left behind her on the banks of the Hudson. As the last notes left her lips, she turned round to Redgrave and looked at him with eyes dim with the first tears that had filled them since her father's death, and said, as he caught hold of her outstretched hand: 'I believe they've understood every word of it.'

'Or, at any rate, every note. You may be quite certain of that,' he replied. 'If you had done that on Mars it might have been even more effective than the Maxims.'

'For goodness sake don't talk about things like that in a heaven like this! Oh, listen! They've got the tune already!'

It was true! The dwellers of the Love-Star, whose speech was song, had instantly recognised the sweetness of the sweetest of all earthly songs. They had, of course, no idea of the meaning of the words; but the music spoke to them and told them that this fair visitant from another world could speak the same speech as theirs. Every note and cadence was repeated with absolute fidelity, and so the speech, common to the two far-distant worlds, became a link connecting this wandering son and daughter of the Earth with the sons and daughters of the Love-Star.

The throng fell back a little and two figures, apparently male and female, came to Zaidie and held out their right hands and began addressing her in perfectly harmonised song, which, though utterly unintelligible to her in the sense of speech, expressed sentiments which could not possibly be mistaken, as there was a faint suggestion of the old English song running through the little song-speech that they made, and both Zaidie and her husband rightly concluded that it was intended to convey a welcome to the strangers from beyond the cloud-veil.

And then the strangest of all possible conversations began. Redgrave, who had no more notion of music than a walrus, perforce kept silence. In fact, he noticed with a certain displeasure which vanished speedily with a musical, and half-malicious little laugh from Zaidie, that when he spoke the bird-folk drew back a little and looked in something like astonishment at him, but Zaidie was already in touch with them, and half by song and half by signs she very soon gave them an idea of what they were and where they had come from. Her husband afterwards told her that it was the best piece of operatic acting he had ever seen, and, considering all the circumstances, this was very possibly true.

In the end the two, who had come to give her what seemed to be the formal greeting, were invited into the *Astronef*. They went on board without the slightest sign of mistrust, and with only an expression of mild wonder on their beautiful and almost childlike faces.

Then, while the other doors were being closed, Zaidie stood at the open one above the gangway and made signs showing that they were going up beyond the clouds and then down into the valley, and as she made the signs she sang through the scale, her voice rising and falling in harmony with her gestures. The Bird-Folk understood her instantly, and as the door closed and the *Astronef* rose from the ground, a thousand wings were outspread and presently hundreds of beautiful soaring forms were circling about the Navigator of the Stars.

'Don't they look lovely!' said Zaidie. 'I wonder what they would think if they could see us flying above New York or London or Paris with an escort like this. I suppose they're going to show us the way. Perhaps they have a city down there. Suppose you were to go and get a bottle of champagne and see if Master Cupid and Miss Venus would like a drink. We'll see then if our nectar is anything like theirs.'

Redgrave went below. Meanwhile, for lack of other possible conversation, Zaidie began to sing the last verse of 'Never Again'. The melody almost exactly described the upward motion of the *Astronef*, and she could see that it was instantly understood, for when she had finished, their two voices joined in an almost exact imitation of it.

When Redgrave brought up the wine and the glasses they looked at them without any sign of surprise. The pop of the cork did not even make them look round.

'Evidently a semi-angelic people, living on nectar and ambrosia, with nectar very like our own,' he said, as he filled the glasses. 'Perhaps you'd better give it to them. They seem to understand you better than they do me – you being, of course, a good bit nearer to the angels than I am.'

'Thanks!' she said, as she took a couple of glasses up, wondering a little what their visitors would do with them. Somewhat to her surprise, they took them with a little bow and a smile and sipped at the wine, first with a little glint of wonder in their eyes, and then with smiles which are unmistakable evidence of perfect appreciation.

'I thought so,' said Redgrave, as he raised his own glass, and bowed gravely towards them. 'This is our nearest approach to nectar, and they seem to recognise it.'

'And don't they just look like the sort of people who live on it, and, of course, other things,' added Zaidie, as she too lifted her glass, and looked with laughing eyes across the brim at her two guests.

But meanwhile Murgatroyd had been applying the repulsive force a little too strongly. The *Astronef* shot up with a rapidity which soon left her winged escort far below. She entered the cloud-veil and passed beyond it. The instant that the unclouded sunrays struck the glass-roofing of the upper deck, their two guests, who had been moving about examining everything with a childlike curiosity, closed their eyes and clasped their hands over them, uttering little cries, tuneful and musical, but still with a note of strange discord in them.

'Lenox, we must go down again,' exclaimed Zaidie. 'Don't you see they can't stand the light; it hurts them. Perhaps, poor dears, it's the first time they've ever been hurt in their lives. I don't believe they have any of our ideas of pain or sorrow or anything of that sort. Take us back under the clouds, quick, or we may blind them.'

Before she had ceased speaking, Redgrave had sent a signal down to Murgatroyd, and the *Astronef* began to drop back again towards the surface of the cloud-sea. Zaidie had, meanwhile, gone to her lady guest and dropped the black lace mantilla over her head, and, as she did so, she caught herself saying: 'There, dear, we shall soon be back in your own light. I hope it hasn't hurt you. It was very stupid of us to do a thing like that.'

The answer came in a little cooing murmur, which said: 'Thank you!' quite as effectively as any earthly words could have done, and then the *Astronef* dropped through the cloud-sea. The soaring forms of her lost escort came into view again and clustered about her; and, surrounded by them, she dropped, in obedience to their signs, down between the tremendous mountains and towards the island, thick with golden foliage, which lay two or three earth-miles out in a bay, where four converging rivers spread out into the sea.

It would take the best part of a volume rather than a few lines to give even an imperfect conception of the purely arcadian delights with which the hours of the next ten days and nights were filled; but some idea of what the Space-voyagers experienced may be gathered from this extract of a conversation which took place in the saloon of the *Astronef* on the eleventh evening.

'But look here, Zaidie,' said his lordship, 'as we've found a world which is certainly much more delightful than our own, why shouldn't we stop here a bit? The air suits us and the people are simply enchanting. I think they like us, and I'm sure you're in love with every one of them, male and female. Of course, it's rather a pity that we can't fly unless we do it in the *Astronef*. But that's only a detail. You're enjoying yourself thoroughly, and I never saw you looking better or, if possible, more beautiful; and why on earth – or Venus – do you want to go?'

She looked at him steadily for a few moments, and with an expression which he had never seen on her face or in her eyes before, and then she said slowly and very sweetly, although there was something like a note of solemnity running through her tone : 'I altogether agree with you, dear; but there is something which you don't seem to have noticed. As you say, we have had a perfectly delightful time. It's a delicious world, and just everything that one would think it to be, either Aurora or Hesperus looked at from the Earth; but if we were to stop here we should be committing one of the greatest crimes, perhaps the greatest, that ever was committed within the limits of the Solar System.'

'My dear Zaidie, what in the name of what we used to call morals on the earth, *do* you mean?'

'Just this,' she replied, leaning a little towards him in her deck chair. 'These people, half angels, and half men and women, welcomed us after we dropped through their cloud-veil, as friends: a bit strange to them, certainly, but still they welcomed us as friends. They've taken us into their palaces, they've given us, as one might say, the whole planet. Everything was ours that we liked to take.

'We've been living with them ten days now, and neither you nor I, nor even Murgatroyd, who, like the old Puritan that he is, seems to see sin or wrong in everything that looks nice, has seen a single sign among them that they know anything about what we call sin or wrong on Earth.'

'I think I understand what you're driving at,' said Redgrave. 'You mean, I suppose, that this world is something like Eden before the fall, and that you and I – oh – but that's all rubbish you know.'

She got up out of her chair and, leaning over his, put her arm round his shoulder. Then she said very softly: 'I see you understand what I mean, Lenox. It doesn't matter how good you think me or I think you, but we have our original sin. You're an earthly man and I'm an earthly woman, and, as I'm your wife, I can say it plainly. We may think a good bit of each other, but that's no reason why we shouldn't be a couple of plague-spots in a sinless world like this.'

Their eyes met, and he understood. Then he got up and went down to the engine-room.

A couple of minutes later the *Astronef* sprang upwards from the midst of the delightful valley in which she was resting. In five minutes she had passed through the cloud-veil, and the next morning when their new friends came to visit them and found that they had vanished back into Space, there was sorrow for the first time among the sons and daughters of the Love-Star.

IV THE WORLD OF THE CRYSTAL CITIES

INTRODUCTION. – For their honeymoon Rollo Lenox Smeaton Aubrey, Earl of Redgrave, and his bride, Lilla Zaidie, leave the earth on a visit to the moon and the principal planets, their sole companion being Andrew Murgatroyd, an old engineer who had superintended the building of the *Astronef*, in which the journey is made. By means of the 'R Force', or Anti-Gravitational Force, of the secret of which Lord Redgrave is the sole possessor, they are able to navigate with precision and safety the limitless ocean of space. Their adventures on the Moon, Mars, and Venus have been described in the first three stories of the series.

'Five hundred million miles from the earth and forty-seven million miles from Jupiter,' said his lordship, as he came in to breakfast on the morning of the twenty-eighth day after leaving Venus.

During this brief period the *Astronef* had recrossed the orbits of the Earth and Mars and passed through that marvellous region of the Solar System, the Belt of the Asteroides. Nearly a hundred million miles of their journey had lain through this zone, in which hundreds and possibly thousands of tiny planets revolve in vast orbits round the Sun.

Then had come a desert void of over three hundred million miles, through which the *Astronef* voyaged alone, surrounded by the ever-constant splendours of the Heavens, but visited only now and then by one of those Spectres of Space, which we call comets.

Astern, the disc of the Sun steadily diminished, and ahead, the grey-blue shape of Jupiter, the Giant of the Solar System, had grown larger and larger until now they could see it as it had never been seen before – a gigantic three-quarter moon filling up the whole Heavens in front of them almost from Zenith to Nadir.

Its four satellites, Io, Europa, Ganymede, and Calisto were distinctly visible to the naked eye, and Europa and Ganymede happened to be in such a position with regard to the *Astronef* that her crew could see not only the bright sides turned towards the sun, but also the black shadow-spots which they cast on the cloud-veiled face of the huge planet.

'Five hundred million miles!' said Zaidie, with a little shiver, 'that seems an awful long way from home, doesn't it? Though, of course, we've brought our home with us to a certain extent. Still I often wonder what they are thinking about us on the dear old earth. I don't suppose anyone ever expects to see us again. However, it's no good getting homesick in the middle of a journey when you're outward bound.'

They were now falling very rapidly towards the huge planet, and as the crescent approached the full, they were able to examine the mysterious bands as human observers had never examined them before. For hours they sat almost silent at their telescopes, trying to probe the mystery which has baffled human science since the days of Gallileo.

'I believe I was right, or, in other words, the people I got the idea from are,' said Redgrave eventually, as they approached the orbit of Calisto, which revolves at a distance of about eleven hundred thousand miles from the surface of the planet.

'Those belts are made of clouds or vapour in some stage or other. The lightest – the ones along the equator and what we should call the Temperate Zones – are the highest, and therefore coolest and whitest. The dark ones are the lowest and hottest. I dare say they are more like what we call volcanic clouds. Do you see how they keep changing? That's what's bothered our astronomers. Look at that big one yonder a bit to the north, going from brown to red. I suppose that's something like the famous red spot which they have been puzzling about. What do you make of it?'

'Well,' said Zaidie, looking up from her telescope, 'it's quite certain that the glare must come from underneath. It can't be sunlight, because the poor old sun doesn't seem to have strength enough to make a decent sunset or sunrise here, and look how it's running along to the westward! What does that mean, do you think?'

'I should say it means that some half-formed Jovian Continent has been flung sky high by a big burst-up underneath, and that's the blaze of the incandescent stuff running along. Just fancy a continent, say ten times the size of Asia, being split up and sent flying in a few moments like that. Look, there's another one to the north. On the whole, dear, I don't think we should find the climate on the other side of those clouds very salubrious. Still, as they say the atmosphere of Jupiter is about ten thousand miles thick, we may be able to get near enough to see something of what's going on.

'Meanwhile, here comes Calisto. Look at his shadow flying across the clouds. And there's Ganymede coming up after him, and Europa behind him. Talk about eclipses, they must be about as common here as thunderstorms are with us.'

'We don't have a thunderstorm every day,' corrected Zaidie, 'but on Jupiter they have two or three eclipses every day. Meanwhile, there goes

Jupiter himself. What a difference distance makes! This little thing is only a trifle larger than our moon, and it's hiding everything else.'

As she was speaking, the full-orbed disc of Calisto, measuring nearly three thousand miles across, swept between them and the planet. It shone with a clear, somewhat reddish light like that of Mars. The *Astronef* was feeling its attraction strongly, and Redgrave went to the levers and turned on about a fifth of the R Force to avoid contact with it.

'Another dead world,' said Redgrave, as the surface of Calisto revolved swiftly beneath them, 'or, at any rate, a dying one. There must be an atmosphere of some sort, or else that snow and ice wouldn't be there, and the land would be either black or white as it was on the Moon. It's not worth while landing there. Ganymede will be much more interesting.'

Zaidie took half-a-dozen photographs of the surface of Calisto while they were passing it at a distance of about a hundred miles, and then went to get lunch ready.

When they got on to the upper deck again Calisto was already a half-moon in the upper sky nearly five hundred thousand miles away, and the full orb of Ganymede, shining with a pale golden light, lay outspread beneath them. A thin, bluish-grey arc of the giant planet over-arched its western edge.

'I think we shall find something like a world here,' said Zaidie, when she had taken her first look through her telescope. 'There's an atmosphere and what looks like thin clouds. Continents, and oceans, too! And what is that light shining up between the breaks? Isn't it something like our Aurora?'

As the *Astronef* fell towards the surface of Ganymede she crossed its northern pole, and the nearer they got the plainer it became that a light very like the terrestrial Aurora was playing about it, illuminating the thin, yellow clouds with a bluish-violet light, which made magnificent contrasts of colouring amongst them.

'Let us go down there and see what it's like,' said Zaidie. 'There must be something nice under all those lovely colours.'

Redgrave checked the R Force and the *Astronef* fell obliquely across the pole towards the equator. As they approached the luminous clouds Redgrave turned it on again, and they sank slowly through a glowing mist of innumerable colours, until the surface of Ganymede came into plain view about ten miles below them.

What they saw then was the strangest sight they had beheld since they had left the Earth. As far as their eyes could reach, the surface of Ganymede was covered with vast orderly patches, mostly rectangular, of what they at first took for ice, but which they soon found to be a something that was self-illuminating.

'Glorified hot houses, as I'm alive,' exclaimed Redgrave. 'Whole cities under glass, fields, too, and lit by electricity or something very like it. Zaidie, we shall find human beings down there.'

'Well, if we do I hope they won't be like the half-human things we found on Mars! But isn't it all just lovely! Only there doesn't seem to be anything outside the cities, at least nothing but bare, flat ground with a few rugged mountains here and there. See, there's a nice level plain near the big glass city, or whatever it is. Suppose we go down there.'

Redgrave checked the after-engine which was driving them obliquely over the surface of the satellite, and the *Astronef* fell vertically towards a bare flat plain of what looked like deep yellow sand, which spread for miles alongside one of the glittering cities of glass.

'Oh, look, they've seen us!' exclaimed Zaidie. 'I do hope they're going to be as friendly as those dear people on Venus were.'

'I hope so,' replied Redgrave, 'but if they're not, we've got the guns ready.'

As he said this about twenty streams of an intense bluish light suddenly shot up all round them, concentrating themselves upon the hull of the *Astronef*, which was now about a mile and a half from the surface. The light was so intense that the rays of the sun were lost in it. They looked at each other, and found that their faces were almost perfectly white in it. The plain and the city below had vanished.

To look downwards was like staring straight into the focus of a ten thousand candle-power electric arc lamp. It was so intolerable that Redgrave closed the lower shutters, and meanwhile he found that the *Astronef* had ceased to descend. He shut off more of the R Force, but it produced no effect. The *Astronef* remained stationary. Then he ordered Murgatroyd to set the propellers in motion. The engineer pulled the starting levers, and then came up out of the engine-room and said to Lord Redgrave: 'It's no good, my lord; I don't know what devil's world we've got into now, but they won't work. If I thought that engines could be bewitched – '

'Oh, nonsense, Andrew!' said his lordship rather testily. 'It's perfectly simple; those people down there, whoever they are, have got some way of de-magnetising us, or else they've got the R Force too, and they're applying it against us to stop us going down. Apparently they don't want us. No, that's just to show us that they can stop us if they want to. The light's going down. Begin dropping a bit. Don't start the propellers, but just go and see that the guns are all right in case of accidents.'

The old engineer nodded and went back to his engines, looking considerably scared. As he spoke the brilliancy of the light faded rapidly and the *Astronef* began to sink towards the surface.

As a precaution against their being allowed to drop with force enough to cause a disaster, Redgrave turned the R Force on again and they dropped slowly towards the plain, through what seemed like a halo of perfectly white light. When she was within a couple of hundred yards of the ground a winged car of exquisitely graceful shape rose from the roof of one of the huge glass buildings nearest to them, flew swiftly towards them, and after circling once round the dome of the upper deck, ran close alongside.

The car was occupied by two figures of distinctly human form but rather more than human stature. Both were dressed in long, close-fitting garments of what seemed like a golden brown fleece. Their heads were covered with a close hood and their hands with thin, close-fitting gloves.

'What an exceedingly handsome man!' said Zaidie, as one of them stood up. 'I never saw such a noble-looking face in my life; it's half philosopher, half saint. Of course, you won't be jealous.'

'Oh, nonsense!' he laughed. 'It would be quite impossible to imagine *you* in love with either. But he is handsome, and evidently friendly – there's no mistaking that. Answer him, Zaidie; you can do it better than I can.'

The car had now come close alongside. The standing figure stretched its hands out, palms upward, smiled a smile which Zaidie thought was very sweetly solemn, next the head was bowed, and the gloved hands brought back and crossed over his breast. Zaidie imitated the movements exactly. Then, as the figure raised its head, she raised hers, and she found herself looking into a pair of large, luminous eyes such as she could have imagined under the brows of an angel. As they met hers, a look of unmistakable wonder and admiration came into them. Redgrave was standing just behind her; she took him by the hand and drew him beside her, saying with a little laugh: 'Now, please look as pleasant as you can; I am sure they are very friendly. A man with a face like that couldn't mean any harm.'

The figure repeated the motions to Redgrave, who returned them, perhaps a trifle awkwardly. Then the car began to descend, and the figure beckoned to them to follow.

'You'd better go and wrap up, dear. From the gentleman's dress it seems pretty cold outside, though the air is evidently quite breathable,' said Redgrave, as the *Astronef* began to drop in company with the car. 'At any rate, I'll try it first, and, if it isn't, we can put on our breathing-dresses.'

When Zaidie had made her winter toilet, and Redgrave had found the air to be quite respirable, but of Arctic cold, they went down the gangway ladder about twenty minutes later. The figure had got out of the car which was lying a few yards from them on the sandy plain, and came forward to meet them with both hands outstretched.

Zaidie unhesitatingly held out hers, and a strange thrill ran through her as she felt them for the first time clasped gently by other than earthly hands, for the Venus folk had only been able to pat and stroke with their gentle little paws, somewhat as a kitten might do. The figure bowed its head again and said something in a low, melodious voice, which was, of course, quite unintelligible save for the evident friendliness of its tone. Then, releasing her hands, he took Redgrave's in the same fashion, and then led the way towards a vast, domed building of semi-opaque glass, or a substance which seemed to be something like a mixture of glass and mica, which appeared to be one of the entrance gates of the city.

When they reached it a huge sheet of frosted glass rose silently from the ground. They passed through, and it fell behind them. They found themselves in a great oval ante-chamber along each side of which stood triple rows of strangely shaped trees whose leaves gave off a subtle and most agreeable scent. The temperature here was several degrees higher, in fact about that of an English spring day, and Zaidie immediately threw open her big fur cloak saying: 'These good people seem to live in Winter Gardens, don't they? I don't think I shall want these things much while we're inside. I wonder what dear old Andrew would have thought of this if we could have persuaded him to leave the ship.'

They followed their host through the ante-chamber towards a magnificent pointed arch, raised on clusters of small pillars each of a different coloured, highly polished stone which shone brilliantly in a light which seemed to come from nowhere. Another door, this time of pale, transparent blue glass, rose as they approached; they passed under it and, as it fell behind them, half-a-dozen figures, considerably shorter and slighter than their host, came forward to meet them. He took off his gloves and cape and thick outer covering, and they were glad to follow his example for the atmosphere was now that of a warm June day.

The attendants, as they evidently were, took their wraps from them, looking at the furs and stroking them with evident wonder; but with nothing like the wonder which came into their wild, soft grey eyes when they looked at Zaidie, who, as usual when she arrived on a new world, was arrayed in one of her daintiest costumes.

Their host was now dressed in a tunic of a light blue material, which glistened with a lustre greater than that of the finest silk. It reached a little below his knees, and was confined at the waist by a sash of the same colour but of somewhat deeper hue. His feet and legs were covered with stockings of the same material and colour, and his feet, which were small for his stature and exquisitely shaped, were shod with thin sandals of a material which looked like soft felt, and which made no noise as he walked over the delicately coloured mosaic pavement of the street – for such it actually was – which ran past the gate.

When he removed his cap they expected to find that he was bald like the Martians, but they were mistaken. His well-shaped head was covered with long, thick hair of a colour something between bronze and grey. A broad band of metal, looking like light gold, passed round the upper part of his forehead, and from under this the hair fell in gentle waves to below his shoulders.

For a few moments Zaidie and Redgrave stared about them in frank and silent wonder. They were standing in a broad street running in a straight line, apparently several miles, along the edge of a city of crystal. It was lined with double rows of trees with beds of brilliantly coloured flowers between them. From this street others went off at right angles and at regular intervals. The roof of the city appeared to be composed of an infinity of domes of enormous extent, supported by tall clusters of slender pillars standing at the street corners.

Presently their host touched Redgrave on the shoulder and pointed to a four-wheeled car of light framework and exquisite design, containing seats for four besides the driver, or guide, who sat behind. He held out his hand to Zaidie, and handed her to one of the front seats just as an earth-born gentleman might have done. Then he motioned to Redgrave to sit beside her, and mounted behind them.

The car immediately began to move silently, but with considerable speed, along the left-hand side of the outer street, which, like all the others, was divided by narrow strips of russet-coloured grass and flowering shrubs.

In a few minutes it swung round to the right, crossed the road, and entered a magnificent avenue, which, after a run of some four miles, ended in a vast, park-like square, measuring at least a mile each way.

The two sides of the avenue were busy with cars like their own, some carrying six people, and others only the driver. Those on each side of the road all went in the same direction. Those nearest to the broad side-walks between the houses and the first row of trees went at a moderate speed of five or six miles an hour, but along the inner sides, near the central line of trees, they seemed to be running as high as thirty miles an hour. Their occupants were nearly all dressed in clothes made of the same glistening, silky fabric as their host wore, but the colourings were of infinite variety. It was quite easy to distinguish between the sexes, although in stature they were almost equal.

The men were nearly all clothed as their host was. The women were dressed in flowing garments something after the Greek style, but they were of brighter hues, and much more lavishly embroidered than the men's tunics were. They also wore much more jewellery. Indeed, some of the younger ones glittered from head to foot with polished metal and gleaming stones.

'Could anyone ever have dreamt of such a lovely place?' said Zaidie, after their wondering eyes had become accustomed to the marvels about them. 'And yet – oh dear, now I know what it reminds me of! Flammarion's book, *The End of the World*, where he describes the remnants of the human race dying of cold and hunger on the Equator in places something like this. I suppose the life of poor Ganymede is giving out, and that's why they've got to live in glorified Crystal Palaces like this, poor things.'

'Poor things!' laughed Redgrave, 'I'm afraid I can't agree with you there, dear. I never saw a jollier looking lot of people in my life. I dare say you're quite right, but they certainly seem to view their approaching end with considerable equanimity.'

'Don't be horrid, Lenox! Fancy talking in that cold-blooded way about such delightful-looking people as these, why, they are even nicer than our dear bird-folk on Venus, and, of course, they are a great deal more like ourselves.'

'Wherefore it stands to reason that they must be a great deal nicer!' he replied, with a glance which brought a brighter flush to her cheeks. Then he went on: 'Ah, now I see the difference.'

'What difference? Between what?'

'Between the daughter of Earth and the daughters of Ganymede,' he replied. 'You can blush, and I don't think they can. Haven't you noticed that, although they have the most exquisite skins and beautiful eyes and hair and all that sort of thing, not a man or woman of them has any colouring. I suppose that's the result of living for generations in a hot-house.'

'Very likely,' she said; 'but has it struck you also that all the girls and women are either beautiful or handsome, and all the men, except the ones who seem to be servants or slaves, are something like Greek gods, or, at least, the sort of men you see on the Greek sculptures?'

'Survival of the fittest, I presume. These will be the descendants of the highest races of Ganymede – the people who conceived the idea of prolonging human life like this and were able to carry it out. The inferior races would either perish of starvation or become their servants. That's what will happen on Earth, and there is no reason why it shouldn't have happened here.'

As he said this the car swung out round a broad curve into the centre of the great square, and a little cry of amazement broke from Zaidie's lips as her glance roamed over the multiplying splendors about her.

In the centre of the square, in the midst of smooth lawns and flower beds of every conceivable shape and colour, and groves of flowering trees, stood a great, domed building, which they approached through an avenue of over-arching trees interlaced with flowering creepers.

The car stopped at the foot of a triple flight of stairs of dazzling whiteness which led up to a broad, arched doorway. Several groups of people were sprinkled about the avenue and steps and the wide terrace which ran along the front of the building. They looked with keen, but perfectly well-mannered surprise at their strange visitors, and seemed to be discussing their appearance; but not a step was taken towards them nor was there the slightest sign of anything like vulgar curiosity.

'What perfect manners these dear people have!' said Zaidie, as they dismounted at the foot of the staircase. 'I wonder what would happen if a couple of them were to be landed from a motor car in front of the Capitol at Washington. I suppose this is their Capitol, and we've been brought here to be put through our facings. What a pity we can't talk to them. I wonder if they'd believe our story if we could tell it.'

'I've no doubt they know something of it already,' replied Redgrave; 'they're evidently people of immense intelligence. Intellectually, I dare say, we're mere children compared with them, and it's quite possible that they have developed senses of which we have no idea.'

'And perhaps,' added Zaidie, 'all the time that we are talking to each other our friend here is quietly reading everything that is going on in our minds.'

Whether this was so or not their host gave no sign of comprehension. He led them up the steps and through the great doorway, where he was met by three splendidly dressed men even taller than himself.

'I feel beastly shabby among all these gorgeously attired personages,' said Redgrave, looking down at his plain tweed suit, as they were conducted with every manifestation of politeness along the magnificent vestibule beyond.

At the end of the vestibule another door opened, and they were ushered into a large hall which was evidently a council-chamber. At the further end of it were three semicircular rows of seats made of the polished silvery metal, and in the centre and raised slightly above them another under a canopy of sky-blue silk. This seat and six others were occupied by men of most venerable aspect, in spite of the fact that their hair was just as long and thick and glossy as their host's or even as Zaidie's own.

The ceremony of introduction was exceedingly simple. Though they could not, of course, understand a word he said, it was evident from his eloquent gestures that their host described the way in which they had come from Space, and landed on the surface of the World of the Crystal Cities, as Zaidie subsequently re-christened Ganymede.

The President of the Senate or Council spoke a few sentences in a deep musical tone. Then their host, taking their hands, led them up to his seat, and the President rose and took them by both hands in turn. Then, with a grave smile of greeting, he bent his head and resumed his seat. They joined hands in turn with each of the six senators present, bowed their farewells in silence, and then went back with their host to the car.

They ran down the avenue, made a curving sweep round to the left – for all the paths in the great square were laid in curves, apparently to form a contrast to the straight streets – and presently stopped before the porch of one of the hundred palaces which surrounded it. This was their host's house, and their home during the rest of their sojourn on Ganymede.

It is, as I have already said, greatly to be regretted that the narrow limits of these brief narratives make it impossible for me to describe in detail all the experiences of Lord Redgrave and his bride during their Honeymoon in Space. Hereafter I hope to have an opportunity of doing so with the more ample assistance of her ladyship's diary; but for the present I must content myself with the outlines of the picture which she may some day consent to fill in.

The period of Ganymede's revolution round its gigantic primary is seven days, three hours, and forty-three minutes, practically a terrestrial week, and both of the daring navigators of Space describe this as the most interesting and delightful week in their lives, not even excepting the period which they spent in the Eden of the Morning Star.

There the inhabitants had never learnt to sin; here they had learnt the lesson that sin is mere foolishness, and that no really sensible or properly educated man or woman thinks crime worth committing.

The life of the Crystal Cities, of which they visited four in different parts of the satellite, using the *Astronef* as their vehicle, was one of peaceful industry and calm innocent enjoyment. It was quite plain that their first impressions of this aged world were correct. Outside the cities spread a universal desert on which life was impossible. There was hardly any moisture in the thin atmosphere. The rivers had dwindled into rivulets and the seas into vast, shallow marshes. The heat received from the Sun was only about a twenty-fifth of that received on the surface of the Earth, and this was drawn to the cities and collected and preserved under their glass domes by a number of devices which displayed super-human intelligence.

The dwindling supplies of water were hoarded in vast subterranean reservoirs and by means of a perfect system of redistillation the priceless fluid was used over and over again both for human purposes and for irrigating the land within the cities.

Still the total quantity was steadily diminishing, for it was not only evaporating from the surface, but, as the orb cooled more and more rapidly towards its centre, it descended deeper and deeper below the surface, and could now only be reached by means of marvellously con-structed borings and pumping machinery which extended down several miles into the ground.

The dwindling store of heat in the centre of the little world, which had now cooled through more than half its bulk, was utilised for warm-ing the air of the cities, and also to drive the machinery which propelled it through the streets and squares. All work was done by electricity developed directly from this source, which also actuated the repulsive engines which had prevented the *Astronef* from descending.

In short, the inhabitants of Ganymede were engaged in a steady, cease-less struggle to utilise the expiring natural forces of their world to pro-long to the latest possible date their own lives and the exquisitely refined civilisation to which they had attained. They were, in fact, in exactly the same position in which the distant descendants of the human race may one day be expected to find themselves.

Their domestic life, as Zaidie and Lenox saw it while they were the guests of their host, was the perfection of simplicity and comfort, and their public life was characterised by a quiet but intense intellectuality which, as Zaidie had said, made them feel very much like children who had only just learnt to speak.

As they possessed magnificent telescopes, far surpassing any on earth, the wanderers were able to survey, not only the Solar System, but the other systems far beyond its limits as no other of their kind had ever been able to do before. They did not look through or into the telescopes. The lens was turned upon the object, which was thrown, enormously magnified, upon screens of what looked something like ground glass some fifty feet square. It was thus that they saw, not only the whole visible surface of Jupiter as he revolved above them and they about him, but also their native earth, sometimes a pale silver disc or crescent close to the edge of the Sun, visible only in the morning and the evening of Jupiter, and at other times like a little black spot crossing the glowing surface.

It was, of course, inevitable that the *Astronef* – which Murgatroyd could not be persuaded to leave once during their stay – should prove an object of intense interest to their hosts. They had solved the problem of the Resolution of Forces, and, as they were shown pictorially, a vessel had been made which embodied the principles of attraction and repulsion. It had risen from the surface of Ganymede, and then, possibly because its engines could not develop sufficient repulsive force, the tremendous pull of the giant planet had dragged it away. It had vanished through the cloud-belts towards the flaming surface beneath – and the experiment had never been repeated.

Here, however, was a vessel which had actually, as Redgrave had convinced his hosts by means of celestial maps and drawings of his own, left a planet close to the Sun, and safely crossed the tremendous gulf of six hundred and fifty million miles which separated Jupiter from the centre of the system. Moreover he had twice proved her powers by taking his host and two of his newly-made friends, the chief astronomers of Ganymede, on a short trip across space to Calisto and Europa, the second satellite of Jupiter, which, to their very grave interest, they found had already passed the stage in which Ganymede was, and had lapsed into the icy silence of death.

It was these two journeys which led to the last adventure of the *Astronef* in the Jovian System. Both Redgrave and Zaidie had determined, at whatever risk, to pass through the cloud-belts of Jupiter, and catch a glimpse, if only a glimpse, of a world in the making. Their host and the two astronomers, after a certain amount of quiet discussion, accepted their invitation to accompany them, and on the morning of the eighth day after their landing on Ganymede, the *Astronef* rose from the plain outside the Crystal City, and directed her course towards the centre of the vast disc of Jupiter.

She was followed by the telescopes of all the observatories until she vanished through the brilliant cloud-band, eighty-five thousand miles long and some five thousand miles broad, which stretched from east to west of the planet. At the same moment the voyagers lost sight of Ganymede and his sister satellites.

The temperature of the interior of the *Astronef* began to rise as soon as the upper cloud-belt was passed. Under this, spread out a vast field of brown-red cloud, rent here and there into holes and gaps like those storm-cavities in the atmosphere of the Sun, which are commonly known as sun-spots. This lower stratum of cloud appeared to be the scene of terrific storms, compared with which the fiercest earthly tempests were mere zephyrs.

After falling some five hundred miles further they found themselves surrounded by what seemed an ocean of fire, but still the internal temperature had only risen from seventy to ninety-five. The engines were well under control. Only about a fourth of the total R Force was being developed, and the *Astronef* was dropping swiftly, but steadily.

Redgrave, who was in the conning-tower controlling the engines, beckoned to Zaidie and said: 'Shall we go on?'

'Yes,' she said. 'Now we've got as far as this I want to see what Jupiter is like, and where you are not afraid to go, I'll go.'

'If I'm afraid at all it's only because you are with me, Zaidie,' he replied, 'but I've only got a fourth of the power turned on yet, so there's plenty of margin.'

The *Astronef*, therefore, continued to sink through what seemed to be a fathomless ocean of whirling, blazing clouds, and the internal temperature went on rising slowly but steadily. Their guests, without showing the slightest sign of any emotion, walked about the upper deck now singly and now together, apparently absorbed by the strange scene about them.

At length, after they had been dropping for some five hours by *Astronef* time, one of them, uttering a sharp exclamation, pointed to an enormous rift about fifty miles away. A dull, red glare was streaming up out of it. The next moment the brown cloud-floor beneath them seemed to split up into enormous wreaths of vapour, which whirled up on all sides of them, and a few minutes later they caught their first glimpse of the true surface of Jupiter.

It lay, as nearly as they could judge, some two thousand miles beneath them, a distance which the telescopes reduced to less than twenty; and they saw for a few moments the world that was in the making. Through floating seas of misty steam they beheld what seemed to them to be vast continents shape themselves and melt away into oceans of flames. Whole mountain ranges of glowing lava were hurled up miles high to take shape for an instant and then fall away again, leaving fathomless gulfs of fiery mist in their place.

Then waves of molten matter rose up again out of the gulfs, tens of miles high and hundreds of miles long, surged forward, and met with a

The cloud-floor beneath them seemed to split up into enormous wreaths of vapour

concussion like that of millions of earthly thunder-clouds. Minute after
minute they remained writhing and struggling with each other, flinging up spurts of flaming matter far above their crests. Other waves
followed them, climbing up their bases as a sea-surge runs up the side
of a smooth, slanting rock. Then from the midst of them a jet of living

fire leapt up hundreds of miles into the lurid atmosphere above, and then, with a crash and a roar which shook the vast Jovian firmament, the battling lava-waves would split apart and sink down into the all-surrounding fire-ocean, like two grappling giants who had strangled each other in their final struggle.

'It's just Hell let loose!' said Murgatroyd to himself as he looked down upon the terrific scene through one of the port-holes of the engine-room; 'and, with all respect to my lord and her ladyship, those that come this near almost deserve to stop in it.'

Meanwhile, Redgrave and Zaidie and their three guests were so absorbed in the tremendous spectacle, that for a few moments no one noticed that they were dropping faster and faster towards the world which Murgatroyd, according to his lights, had not inaptly described. As for Zaidie, all her fears were for the time being lost in wonder, until she saw her husband take a swift glance round upwards and downwards, and then go up into the conning-tower. She followed him quickly, and said: 'What is the matter, Lenox, are we falling too quickly?'

'Much faster than we should,' he replied, sending a signal to Murgatroyd to increase the force by three-tenths.

The answering signal came back, but still the *Astronef* continued to fall with terrific rapidity, and the awful landscape beneath them – a landscape of fire and chaos – broadened out and became more and more distinct.

He sent two more signals down in quick succession. Three-fourths of the whole repulsive power of the engines was now being exerted, a force which would have been sufficient to hurl the *Astronef* up from the surface of the Earth like a feather in a whirl-wind. Her downward course became a little slower, but still she did not stop. Zaidie, white to the lips, looked down upon the hideous scene beneath and slipped her hand through Redgrave's arm. He looked at her for an instant and then turned his head away with a jerk, and sent down the last signal.

The whole energy of the engines was now directing the maximum of the R Force against the surface of Jupiter, but still, as every moment passed in a speechless agony of apprehension, it grew nearer and nearer. The fire-waves mounted higher and higher, the roar of the fiery surges grew louder and louder. Then, in a momentary lull, he put his arm round her, drew her close up to him, and kissed her and said: 'That's all we can do, dear. We've come too close and he's too strong for us.'

She returned his kiss and said quite steadily: 'Well, at any rate, I'm with you, and it won't last long, will it?'

'Not very long now, I'm afraid,' he said between his clenched teeth.

Almost the next moment they felt a little jerk beneath their feet – a jerk upwards; and Redgrave shook himself out of the half stupor into which he was falling and said: 'Hallo, what's that! I believe we're stopping – yes, we are – and we're beginning to rise, too. Look, dear, the clouds are coming down upon us – fast too! I wonder what sort of miracle that is. Ay, what's the matter, little woman?'

Zaidie's head had dropped heavily on his shoulder. A glance showed him that she had fainted. He could do nothing more in the conning-tower, so he picked her up and carried her towards the companion-way, past his three guests, who were standing in the middle of the upper deck round a table on which lay a large sheet of paper.

He took her below and laid her on her bed, and in a few minutes he had brought her to and told her that it was all right. Then he gave her a drink of brandy and water, and went back on to the upper deck. As he reached the top of the stairway one of the astronomers came towards him with the sheet of paper in his hand, smiling gravely, and pointing to a sketch upon it.

He took the paper under one of the electric lights and looked at it. The sketch was a plan of the Jovian System. There were some signs written along one side, which he did not understand, but he divined that they were calculations. Still, there was no mistaking the diagram. There was a circle representing the huge bulk of Jupiter; there were four smaller circles at varying distances in a nearly straight line from it, and between the nearest of these and the planet was the figure of the *Astronef*, with an arrow pointing upwards.

'Ah, I see!' he said, forgetting for a moment that the other did not understand him, 'that was the miracle! The four satellites came into line with us just as the pull of Jupiter was getting too much for our engines, and their combined pull just turned the scale. Well, thank God for that, sir, for in a few minutes more we should have been cinders!'

The astronomer smiled again as he took the paper back. Meanwhile the *Astronef* was rushing upward like a meteor through the clouds. In ten minutes the limits of the Jovian atmosphere were passed. Stars and gems and planets blazed out of the black vault of Space, and the great disc of the World that Is to Be once more covered the floor of Space beneath them – an ocean of cloud, covering continents of lava and seas of flame.

They passed Io and Europa, which changed from new to full moons as they sped by towards the Sun, and then the golden yellow crescent of Ganymede also began to fill out to the half and full disc, and by the tenth hour of earth-time after they had risen from its surface, the *Astronef* was once more lying beside the gate of the Crystal City.

At midnight on the second night after their return, the ringed shape of Saturn, attended by his eight satellites, hung in the zenith magnificently inviting. The *Astronef's* engines had been replenished after the exhaustion of their struggle with the might of Jupiter. Zaidie and Lenox said farewell to their friends of the dying world. The doors of the air chamber closed. The signal tinkled in the engine-room, and a few moments later a blur of white lights on the brown background of the surrounding desert was all they could distinguish of the Crystal City under whose domes they had seen and learnt so much.

INTRODUCTION. – For their honeymoon Rollo Lenox Smeaton Aubrey, Earl of Redgrave, and his bride, Lilla Zaidie, leave the earth on a visit to the Moon and the principal planets, their sole companion being Andrew Murgatroyd, an old engineer who had superintended the building of the *Astronef*, in which the journey is made. By means of the 'R Force', or Anti-Gravitational Force, of the secret of which Lord Redgrave is the sole possessor, they are able to navigate with precision and safety the limitless ocean of Space. Their adventures on the Moon, Mars, Venus, and Jupiter have been described in the first four stories of the series.

The relative position of the two giants of the Solar System at the moment when the *Astronef* left the surface of Ganymede, the third and largest satellite of Jupiter, was such that she had to make a journey of rather more than 340,000,000 miles before she passed within the confines of the Saturnian System.

At first her speed, as shown by the observations which Redgrave took by means of instruments designed for such a voyage by Professor Rennick, was comparatively slow. This was due to the tremendous 'pull' or attraction of Jupiter and its four moons on the fabric of the Star Navigator; but this backward drag rapidly decreased as the pull of Saturn and his System began to overmaster that of Jupiter.

It so happened, too, that Uranus, the next outer planet of the Solar System, revolving round the Sun at the tremendous distance of more than 1,700,000,000 miles, was approaching its conjunction with Saturn, and thus the pull of the two huge orbs and their systems of satellites acted together on the tiny bulk of the *Astronef*, producing a constant acceleration of speed.

Jupiter and his System dropped behind, sinking, as it seemed to the wanderers, down into the bottomless gulf of Space, but still forming by far the most brilliant and splendid object in the skies. The far distant Sun which, seen from the Saturnian System, has only about a ninetieth of the superficial extent which he presents to the Earth, dwindled away rapidly until it began to look like a huge planet, with the Earth, Venus, Mars, and

Mercury as satellites. Beyond the orbit of Saturn, Uranus, with his eight moons, was shining with the lustre of a star of the first magnitude, and far above and beyond him again hung the pale disc of Neptune, the outer guard of the Solar System, separated from the Sun by a gulf of more than 2,750,000,000 miles.

When two-thirds of the distance between Jupiter and Saturn had been traversed, Saturn lay beneath them like a vast globe surrounded by an enormous circular ocean of many-coloured fire, divided, as it were, by circular shores of shade and darkness. On the side opposite to them a gigantic conical shadow extended beyond the confines of the ocean of light. It was the shadow of half the globe of Saturn cast by the Sun across his rings. Three little dark spots were also travelling across the surface of the rings. They were the shadows of Mimas, Enceladus, and Tethys, the three inner satellites. Iapetus, the most distant, which revolves at a distance ten times greater than that of the Moon from the Earth, was rising to their left above the edge of the rings, a pale, yellow little disc shining feebly against the black background of Space. The rest of the eight satellites were hidden behind the enormous bulk of the planet, and the infinitely vaster area of the rings.

Day after day Zaidie and her husband had been exhausting the possibilities of the English language in attempting to describe to each other the multiplying marvels of the wondrous scene which they were approaching at a speed of more than a hundred miles a second, and at length Zaidie, after nearly an hour's absolute silence, during which they sat with eyes fastened to their telescopes, looked up and said: 'It's no use, Lenox, all the fine words that we've been trying to think of have just been wasted. The angels may have a language that you could describe that in, but we haven't. If it wouldn't be something like blasphemy I should drop down to the commonplace, and call Saturn a celestial spinning-top, with bands of light and shadow instead of colours all round it.'

'Not at all a bad simile either,' laughed Redgrave, as he got up from his chair with a yawn and a stretch of his athletic limbs. 'Still, it's as well that you said celestial, for, after all, that's about the best word we've found yet. Certainly the ringed world is the most nearly heavenly thing we've seen so far.

'But,' he went on, 'I think it's about time we were stopping this headlong fall of ours. Do you see how the landscape is spreading out round us? That means that we're dropping pretty fast. Whereabouts would you like to land? At present we're heading straight for the north pole.'

'I think I'd rather see what the rings are like first,' said Zaidie; 'couldn't we go across them?'

'Certainly we can,' he replied, 'only we'll have to be a bit careful.'

'Careful, what of – collisions? I suppose you're thinking of Proctor's explanation that the rings are formed of multitudes of tiny satellites?'

'Yes, but I should go a little farther than that, I should say that his rings and his eight satellites are to Saturn what the planets generally and the ring of the Asteroides are to the Sun, and if that is the case – I mean if we find the rings made up of myriads of tiny bodies flying round with Saturn – it might get a bit risky.

'You see the outside ring is a bit over 160,000 miles across, and it revolves in less than eleven hours. In other words we might find the ring a sort of celestial maelstroom, and if we once got into the whirl, and Saturn exerted his full pull on us, we might become a satellite, too, and go on swinging round with the rest for a good bit of eternity.'

'Very well, then,' she said, 'of course we don't want to do anything of that sort, but there's something else I think we could do,' she went on, taking up a copy of Proctor's *Saturn and its System*, which she had been reading just after breakfast. 'You see those rings are, all together, about 10,000 miles broad; there's a gap of about 1700 miles between the big dark one and the middle bright one, and it's nearly 10,000 miles from the edge of the bright ring to the surface of Saturn. Now why shouldn't we get in between the inner ring and the planet? If Proctor was right and the rings are made of tiny satellites and there are myriads of them, of course they'll pull up while Saturn pulls down. In fact Flammarion says some-where, that along Saturn's equator there is no weight at all.'

'Quite possible,' said Redgrave, 'and, if you like, we'll go and prove it. Of course, if the *Astronef* weighs absolutely nothing between Saturn and the rings, we can easily get away. The only thing that I object to is getting into this 170,000 mile vortex, being whizzed round with Saturn every ten and a half hours, and sauntering round the Sun at 21,000 miles an hour.'

'Don't,' she said, 'really it isn't good to think about these things, situated as we are. Fancy, in a single year of Saturn there are nearly 25,000 days. Why, we should each of us be about thirty years older when we got round, even if we lived, which, of course, we shouldn't. By the way, how long could we live for, if the worst came to the worst?'

'About two earth-years at the outside,' he replied, 'but, of course, we shall be home long before that.'

'If we don't become one of the satellites of Saturn,' she replied, 'or get dragged away by something into the outer depths of Space.'

Meanwhile the downward speed of the *Astronef* had been considerably checked. The vast circle of the rings seemed to suddenly expand, though it now covered the whole floor of the vault of Space.

As the *Astronef* dropped towards what might be called the limit of the northern tropic of Saturn, the spectacle presented by the rings became every minute more and more marvellous – purple and silver, black and gold, dotted with myriads of brilliant points of many-coloured lights, they stretched upwards like vast rainbows in the Saturnian sky as the *Astronef's* position changed with regard to the horizon of the planet. The nearer they approached the surface, the nearer the gigantic arch of the many-coloured rings approached the zenith. Sun and stars sank down behind it, for now they were dropping through the fifteen-year-long twilight that reigns over that portion of the globe of Saturn which during half of his year of thirty terrestrial years is turned away from the Sun.

The further they dropped towards the rings the more certain it became that the theory of the great English astronomer was the correct one. Seen through the telescopes at a distance of only thirty or forty thousand miles, it became perfectly plain that the outer or darker ring as seen from the Earth, was composed of myriads of tiny bodies so far separated from each other that the rayless blackness of Space could be seen through them.

'It's quite evident,' said Redgrave, 'that those are rings of what we should call meteorites on earth, atoms of matter which Saturn threw off into Space after the satellites were formed.'

'And I shouldn't wonder, if you will excuse my interrupting you,' said Zaidie, 'if the moons themselves have been made up of a lot of these things going together when they were only gas, or nebula or something of that sort. In fact, when Saturn was a good deal younger than he is now, he may have had a lot more rings and no moons, and now these aerolites, or whatever they are, can't come together and make moons, because they've got too solid.'

Meanwhile the *Astronef* was dropping rapidly down towards the portion of Saturn's surface which was illuminated by the rays of the Sun, streaming under the lower arch of the inner ring.

As they passed under it the whole scene suddenly changed. The rings vanished. Overhead was an arch of brilliant light a hundred miles thick, spanning the whole of the visible heavens. Below lay the sunlit surface of Saturn divided into light and dark bands of enormous breadth.

The band immediately below them was of a brilliant silver-grey, very much like the central zone of Jupiter. North of this on the one side stretched the long shadow of the rings, and southward other bands of alternating white and gold and deep purple succeeded each other till they were lost in the curvature of the vast planet. The poles were of course invisible since the *Astronef* was now too near to the surface; but on their approach they had seen unmistakable evidence of snow and ice.

As soon as they were exactly under the Ring-arch, Redgrave shut off the R Force, and, somewhat to their astonishment, the *Astronef* began to revolve slowly on its axis, giving them the idea that the Saturnian System was revolving round them. The arch seemed to sink beneath their feet while the belts of the planet rose above them.

'What on earth is the matter?' said Zaidie. 'Everything has gone upside down.'

'Which shows,' replied Redgrave, 'that as soon as the *Astronef* became neutral the rings pulled harder than the planet, I suppose because we're so near to them, and, instead of falling on to Saturn, we shall have to push up at him.'

'Oh yes, I see that,' said Zaidie, 'but after all it does look a little bit bewildering, doesn't it, to be on your feet one minute and on your head the next?'

'It is, rather; but you ought to be getting accustomed to that sort of thing now. In a few minutes neither you, nor I, nor anything else will have any weight. We shall be just between the attraction of the Rings and Saturn, so you'd better go and sit down, for if you were to give a bit of an extra spring in walking you might be knocking that pretty head of yours against the roof,' said Redgrave, as he went to turn the R Force on to the edge of the Rings.

A vast sea of silver cloud seemed now to descend upon them. Then they entered it, and for nearly half-an-hour the *Astronef* was totally enveloped in a sea of pearl-grey luminous mist.

'Atmosphere!' said Redgrave, as he went to the conning-tower and signalled to Murgatroyd to start the propellers. They continued to rise and the mist began to drift past them in patches, showing that the propellers were driving them ahead.

They now rose swiftly towards the surface of the planet. The cloud wrack got thinner and thinner, and presently they found themselves floating in a clear atmosphere between two seas of cloud, the one above them being much less dense than the one below.

'I believe we shall see Saturn on the other side of that,' said Zaidie, looking up at it. 'Oh dear, there we are going round again.'

'Reaching the point of neutral attraction,' said Redgrave; 'once more you'd better sit down in case of accidents.'

Instead of dropping into her deck chair as she would have done on Earth, she took hold of the arms and pulled herself into it, saying: 'Really it seems rather absurd to have to do this sort of thing. Fancy having to hold yourself into a chair. I suppose I hardly weigh anything at all now.'

'Not much,' said Redgrave, stooping down and taking hold of the end of the chair with both hands. Without any apparent effort he raised her about five feet from the floor, and held her there while the *Astronef* made another revolution. For a moment he let go, and she and the chair floated between the roof and the floor of the deck-chamber. Then he pulled the chair away from under her, and as the floor of the vessel once more turned towards Saturn, he took hold of her hands and brought her to her feet on deck again.

'I ought to have had a photograph of you like that!' he laughed. 'I wonder what they'd think of it at home?'

'If you had taken one I should certainly have broken the negative. The very idea, a photograph of me standing on nothing! Besides, they'd never believe it on Earth.'

'We might have got old Andrew to make an affidavit to that effect,' he began.

'Don't talk nonsense, Lenox! Look! there's something much more interesting. There's Saturn at last. Now I wonder if we shall find any sort of life there – and shall we be able to breathe the air?'

'I hardly think so,' he said, as the *Astronef* dropped slowly through the thin cloud-veil. 'You know spectrum analysis has proved that there is a gas in Saturn's atmosphere which we know nothing about, and, whatever it may be for the inhabitants, it's not very likely that it would agree with us, so I think we'd better be content with our own. Besides, the atmosphere is so enormously dense that even if we could breathe it it might squash us up. You see we're only accustomed to fifteen pounds on the square inch, and it may be hundreds of pounds here.'

'Well,' said Zaidie, 'I haven't got any particular desire to be flattened out like that, or squeezed dry like an orange. It's not at all a nice idea, is it? But, look, Lenox,' she went on, pointing downwards, 'surely this isn't air at all, or at least it's something between air and water. Aren't these things swimming about in it – something like fish in the sea? They can't be clouds, and they aren't either fish or birds. They don't fly or float. Well, this is certainly more wonderful than anything else we've seen, though it doesn't look very pleasant. They're not nice looking, are they? I wonder if they are at all dangerous!'

While she was saying this Zaidie had gone to her telescope, and was sweeping the surface of Saturn, which was now about 100 miles distant.

Her husband was doing the same. In fact, for the time being they were all eyes, for they were looking on a stranger sight than human beings had ever seen before.

Underneath the inner cloud-veil the atmosphere of Saturn appeared to them somewhat as the lower depths of the ocean would appear to a diver, granted that he was able to see for hundreds of miles about him. Its colour was a pale greenish yellow. The outside thermometers showed that the temperature was a hundred and seventy-five. In fact the interior of the *Astronef* was getting uncomfortably like a Turkish bath, and Redgrave took the opportunity of at once freshening and cooling the air by releasing a little from the cylinders where it was stored in liquid form.

From what they could see of the surface of Saturn it seemed to be a dead level, greyish-brown in colour, and not divided into oceans and continents. In fact there were no signs whatever of water within range of their telescopes. There was nothing that looked like cities, or any human habitations, but the ground, as they got nearer to it, seemed to be covered with a very dense vegetable growth, not unlike gigantic forms of seaweed, and of somewhat the same colour. In fact, as Zaidie remarked, the surface of Saturn was not at all unlike what the floors of the ocean of the Earth might be if they were laid bare.

It was evident that the life of this portion of Saturn was not what, for want of a more exact word, might be called terrestrial. Its inhabitants, however they were constituted, floated about in the depths of this semi-gaseous ocean as the denizens of earthly seas did in the terrestrial oceans. Already their telescopes enabled them to make out enormous moving shapes, black and grey-brown and pale red, swimming about, evidently by their own volition, rising and falling and often sinking down on to the gigantic vegetation which covered the surface, possibly for the purpose of feeding. But it was also evident that they resembled the inhabitants of earthly oceans in another respect, since it was easy to see that they preyed upon each other.

'I don't like the look of those creatures at all,' said Zaidie when the *Astronef* had come to a stop and was floating about five miles above the surface. 'They're altogether too uncanny. They look to me something like jelly-fish about the size of whales, only they have eyes and mouths. Did you ever see such awful looking eyes, bigger than soup-plates and as bright as a cat's. I suppose that's because of the dim light. And the nasty wormy sort of way they swim, or fly, or whatever it is. Lenox, I don't know what the rest of Saturn may be like, but I certainly don't like this part. It's quite too creepy and unearthly for my taste. Look at the horrors fighting and eating each other. That's the only bit of earthly character they've got about them; the big ones eating the little ones. I hope they won't take the *Astronef* for something nice to eat.'

'They'd find her a pretty tough morsel if they did,' laughed Redgrave, 'but still we may as well get some speed on her in case of accident.'

In obedience to a signal to Murgatroyd, the propellers began to revolve, beating the dense air and driving the Star Navigator about twenty miles an hour through the depths of this strangely-peopled ocean.

They approached nearer and nearer to the surface, and as they did so the strange creatures about them grew more and more numerous. They were certainly the most extraordinary living things that human eyes had looked upon. Zaidie's comparison to the whale and the jelly-fish was by no means incorrect; only when they got near enough to them they found, to their astonishment, that they were double-headed – that is to say, they had a head furnished with mouth, nostrils, ear-holes and eyes, at each end of their bodies.

The larger of the creatures appeared to have a certain amount of respect for each other. Now and then they witnessed a battle-royal between two of the monsters who were pursuing the same prey. Their method of attack was as follows: the assailant would rise above his opponent or prey, and then, dropping on to its back, envelope it and begin tearing at its sides and under parts with huge beak-like jaws, somewhat resembling those of the largest kind of the earthly octopus, only very much larger. The substance composing their bodies appeared to be not unlike that of a terrestrial jelly-fish, but much denser, and having the tenacity of soft indiarubber save at the double ends, where it was much harder, in fact a good deal more like horn.

When one of them had overpowered an enemy or a victim the two sank down into the vegetation, and the victor began to eat the vanquished. Their means of locomotion consisted of huge fins, or rather half fins, half wings, of which they had three laterally arranged behind each head, and four much longer and narrower, above and below, which seemed to be used mainly for steering purposes.

They moved with equal ease in either direction, and they appeared to rise or fall by inflating or deflating the middle portions of their bodies, somewhat as fish do with their swimming bladders.

The light in the lower regions of this strange ocean was dimmer than earthly twilight, although the *Astronef* was steadily making her way beneath the arch of the rings towards the sunlit hemisphere.

'I wonder what the effect of the searchlight would be on these fellows!' said Redgrave. 'Those huge eyes of theirs are evidently only suited to dim light. Let's try and dazzle some of them.'

They witnessed a battle-royal between two of the monsters

'I hope it won't be a case of the moths and the candle!' said Zaidie. 'They don't seem to have taken much interest in us so far. Perhaps they haven't been able to see properly, but suppose they were attracted by the light and began crowding round us and fastening on to us, as the horrible things do with each other. What should we do then? They might drag us down and perhaps keep us there; but there's one thing, they'd never eat us, because we could keep closed up and die respectably together.'

'Not much fear of that, little woman,' he said, 'we're too strong for them. Hardened steel and toughened glass ought to be more than a match for a lot of exaggerated jelly-fish like these,' said Redgrave, as he switched on the head search-light. 'We've come here to see strange things and we may as well see them. Ah, would you, my friend? No, this is not one of your sort, and it isn't meant to eat.'

A huge, double-headed monster, apparently some four hundred feet long, came floating towards them as the search-light flashed out, and others began instantly to crowd about them, just as Zaidie had feared.

'Lenox, for Heaven's sake be careful!' cried Zaidie, shrinking up beside him as the huge, hideous head, with its saucer eyes and enormous beak-like jaws wide open, came towards them. 'And look, there are more coming. Can't we go up and get away from them?'

'Wait a minute, little woman,' replied Redgrave, who was beginning to feel the passion of adventure thrilling in his nerves. 'If we fought the Martian air fleet and licked it I think we can manage these things. Let's see how he likes the light.'

As he spoke he flashed the full glare of the five thousand candle-power lamp full on to the creature's great cat-like eyes. Instantly it bent itself up into an arc. The two heads, each the exact image of the other, came together. The four eyes glared half dazzled into the conning-tower and the four huge jaws snapped viciously together.

'Lenox, Lenox, for goodness sake let us go up!' cried Zaidie shrinking still closer to him. 'That thing's too horrible to look at.'

'It is a beast, isn't it?' he said, 'but I think we can cut him in two without much trouble.'

He pressed one of the buttons on the signal board three times quickly and once slowly. It was the signal for full speed on the propellers, that is to say about a hundred earth-miles an hour. The *Astronef* ought to have sprung forward and driven her ram through the huge, brick-red body of the hideous creature which was now only a couple of hundred yards from them; but instead of that a slow, jarring, grinding thrill seemed to run through her, and she stopped. The next moment Murgatroyd put his head up through the companion-way which led from the upper deck to the conning-tower, and said in a tone whose calm indicated, as usual, resignation to the worst that could happen: 'My lord, two of those beasts, fishes or live balloons, or whatever they are, have come across the propellers. They're cut up a good bit, but I've had to stop the engines, and they're clinging all round the after part. We're going down, too. Shall I disconnect the propellers and turn on the repulsion?'

'Yes, certainly, Andrew!' cried Zaidie, 'and all of it, too. Look, Lenox, that horrible thing is coming. Suppose it broke the glass, and we couldn't breathe this atmosphere!'

As she spoke the enormous, double-headed body advanced until it completely enveloped the forward part of the *Astronef*. The two hideous heads came close to the sides of the conning-tower; the huge, palely luminous eyes looked in upon them. Zaidie, in her terror, even thought that she saw something like human curiosity in them.

Then, as Murgatroyd disappeared to obey the orders which Redgrave had sanctioned with a quick nod, the heads approached still closer, and she heard the ends of the pointed jaws, which she now saw were armed with shark-like teeth, striking against the thick glass walls of the conning-tower.

'Don't be frightened, dear!' he said, putting his arm round her, just as he had done when they thought they were falling into the fiery seas of Jupiter. 'You'll see something happen to this gentleman soon. Big and all as he is there won't be much left of him in a few minutes. They are like those monsters they found in the lowest depths of our own seas. They can only live under tremendous pressure. That's why we didn't find any of them up above. This chap'll burst like a bubble presently. Meanwhile, there's no use in stopping here. Suppose you go below and brew some coffee and bring it up on deck with a drop of brandy in it, while I go and see how things are looking aft. It doesn't do you any good, you know, to be looking at monsters of this sort. You can see what's left of them later on.'

Zaidie was not at all sorry to obey him, for the horrible sight had almost sickened her.

They were still under the arch of the rings, and so, when the full strength of the R Force was directed against the body of Saturn, the vessel sprang upwards like a projectile fired from a cannon.

Redgrave went back into the conning-tower to see what happened to their assailant. It was already trying vainly to detach itself and sink back into a more congenial element. As the pressure of the atmosphere decreased its huge body swelled up into still huger proportions. The skin on the two heads puffed up as though air was being pumped in under it. The great eyes protruded out of their sockets; the jaws opened widely as though the creature were gasping for breath.

Meanwhile Murgatroyd was seeing something very similar at the after end, and wondering what was going to happen to his propellers, the blades of which were deeply imbedded in the jelly-like flesh of the monsters.

The *Astronef* leaped higher and higher, and the hideous bodies which were clinging to her swelled out huger and huger, and Redgrave even fancied that he heard something like the cries of pain from both heads on either side of the conning-tower. They passed through the inner cloud-veil, and then the *Astronef* began to turn on her axis, and, just as the outer envelope came into view the enormously distended bulk of the monsters collapsed, and their fragments, seeming now more like the tatters of a burst balloon, dropped from the body of the *Astronef*, and floated away down into what had once been their native element.

'Difference of environment means a lot, after all,' said Redgrave to himself. 'I should have called that either a lie or a miracle if I hadn't seen it, and I'm jolly glad I sent Zaidie down below.'

'Here's your coffee, Lenox,' said Zaidie's voice from the upper deck, 'only it doesn't seem to want to stop in the cups, and the cups keep getting off the saucers. I suppose we're turning upside down again.'

Redgrave stepped somewhat gingerly on to the deck, for his body had so little weight under the double attraction of Saturn and the Rings that a very slight effort would have sent him flying up to the roof of the deck-chamber.

'That's exactly as you please,' he said, 'just hold that table steady a minute. We shall have our centre of gravity back soon. And now, as to the main question, suppose we take a trip across the sunlit hemisphere of Saturn to what I suppose we should call, on Earth, the South Pole. We can get resistance from the Rings, and as we are here we may as well see what the rest of Saturn is like. You see, if our theory is correct as to the Rings gathering up most of the atmosphere of Saturn about its equator, we shall get to higher altitudes where the air is thinner and more like our own, and therefore it's quite possible that we shall find different forms of life in it too – or if you've had enough of Saturn and would prefer a trip to Uranus – ?'

'No, thanks,' said Zaidie quickly. 'To tell you the truth, Lenox, I've had almost enough star-wandering for one honeymoon, and though we've seen nice things as well as horrible things – especially those ghastly, slimy creatures down there – I'm beginning to feel a bit homesick for good old mother Earth. You see, we're nearly a thousand million miles from home, and, even with you, it makes one feel a bit lonely. I vote we explore the rest of this hemisphere up to the pole, and then, as they say at sea – I mean our sea – 'bout ship, and see if we can find our own old world again. After all, it's more homelike than any of these, isn't it?'

'Just take your telescope and look at it,' said Redgrave, pointing towards the Sun, with its little cluster of attendant planets. 'It looks something like one of Jupiter's little moons down there, doesn't it, only not quite as big?'

'Yes, it does, but that doesn't matter. The fact is that it's there, and we know what it's like, and it's *home*, if it is a thousand million miles away, and that's everything.'

By this time they had passed through the outer band of clouds. The huge, sunlit arch of the Rings towered up to the zenith, and apparently overarched the whole heavens. Below and in front of them lay the enormous semi-circle of the hemisphere which was turned towards the Sun, shrouded by its many colored bands of clouds. The Repulsive Force was directed strongly against the lower Ring, and the *Astronef* dropped rapidly in a slanting direction through the cloud-bands towards the southern temperate zone of the planet.

They passed through the second, or dark, cloud-band at the rate of about three thousand miles an hour, aided by the Repulsion against the Rings and, the attraction of the planet, and soon after lunch, the materials of which now consented to remain on the table, they passed through the clouds and found themselves in a new world of wonders.

On a far vaster scale, it was the Earth during that period of its development which is called the Reptilian Age. The atmosphere was still dense and loaded with aqueous vapour, but the waters had already been divided from the land.

They passed over vast, marshy continents and islands, and warm seas, above which thin clouds of steam still hung. They passed through these, and, as they swept southward with the propellers working at their utmost speed, they caught glimpses of giant forms rising out of the steamy waters near the land; of others crawling slowly over it, dragging their huge bulk through a tremendous vegetation, which they crushed down as they passed, as a sheep on earth might push its way through a field of standing corn.

Yet other shapes, huge-winged and ungainly, fluttered with a slow, bat-like motion through the lower strata of the atmosphere.

Every now and then during the voyage across the temperate zone the propellers were slowed down to enable them to witness some titanic conflict between the gigantic denizens of land and sea and air. But her ladyship had had enough of horrors on the Saturnian equator, and so she was quite content to watch this phase of evolution (as it had happened on the Earth many thousands of ages ago) from a convenient distance, and so the *Astronef* sped on southward without approaching the surface nearer than a couple of miles.

'It'll be all very nice to see and remember and dream about afterwards,' she said, 'but really I don't think I can stand any more monsters just now, at least not at close quarters, and I'm quite sure if those things can live there we couldn't, any more than we could have lived on Earth a million years or so ago. No, really I don't want to land, Lenox, let's go on.'

They went on at a speed of about a hundred miles an hour, and, as they progressed southward, both the atmosphere and the landscape rapidly changed. The air grew clearer and the clouds lighter. Lands and seas were more sharply divided, and both teeming with life. The seas still swarmed with serpentine monsters of the saurian type, and the firmer lands were peopled by huge animals, mastodons, bears, giant tapirs, nyledons, deinotheriums, and a score of other species too strange for them to recognise by any earthly likeness, which roamed in great herds through the vast twilit forests and over boundless plains covered with grey-blue vegetation.

Here, too, they found mountains for the first time on Saturn: mountains steep-sided, and many earth-miles high.

As the *Astronef* was skirting the side of one of these ranges Redgrave allowed it to approach more closely than he had so far done to the surface of Saturn.

'I shouldn't wonder if we found some of the higher forms of life up here,' he said. 'If there is anything here that's going to develop some day into the human race of Saturn, it would naturally get up here.'

'Of course it would,' said Zaidie, 'as far as possible out of the reach of those unutterable horrors on the equator. I should think that would be one of the first signs they would show of superior intelligence. Look, I believe there are some of them. Do you see those holes in the mountain side there? And there they are, something like gorillas, only twice as big, and up the trees, too – and what trees! They must be seven or eight hundred feet high.'

'Tree- and cave-dwellers, and ancestors of the future royal race of Saturn, I suppose!' said Redgrave. 'They don't look very nice, do they? Still, there's no doubt about their being far superior in intelligence to what we left behind us. Evidently this atmosphere is too thin for the two-headed jelly-fishes and the saurians to breathe. These creatures have found that out in a few hundreds of generations, and so they have come to live up here out of the way. Vegetarians, I suppose, or perhaps they live on smaller monkeys and other animals, just as our ancestors did.'

'Really, Lenox,' said Zaidie, turning round and facing him, 'I must say that you have a most unpleasant way of alluding to one's ancestors. They couldn't help what they were.'

'Well, dear,' he said, going towards her, 'marvellous as the miracle seems, I'm heretic enough to believe it possible that your ancestors even, millions of years ago, perhaps, may have been something like those; but then, of course, you know I'm a hopeless Darwinian.'

The firmer lands were peopled by huge animals

'And, therefore, entirely horrid, as I've often said before when you get on subjects like these. Not, of course, that I'm ashamed of my poor relations; and then, after all, your Darwin was quite wrong when he talked about the descent of man – and woman. We – especially the women – have *as*cended from that sort of thing, if there's any truth in the story at all; though, personally, I must say I prefer dear old Mother Eve.'

'Who never had a sweeter daughter!' he replied, drawing her towards him.

'And, meanwhile, compliments being barred, I'll go and get dinner ready,' she said. 'After all, it doesn't matter what world one's in, one gets hungry all the same.'

The dinner, which was eaten somewhere in the middle of the fifteen-year-long day of Saturn, was a very pleasant one, because they were now nearing the turning-point of their trip into the depths of Space, and thoughts of home and friends were already beginning to fly back across the thousand-million-mile gulf which lay between them and the Earth which they had left only a little more than two months ago.

While they were at dinner the *Astronef* rose above the mountains and resumed her southward course. Zaidie brought the coffee up on deck as usual after dinner, and, while Redgrave smoked his cigar and Zaidie her cigarette, they luxuriated in the magnificent spectacle of the sunlit side of Rings towering up, rainbow built on rainbow, to the zenith of their visible heavens.

'What a pity there aren't any words to describe it!' said Zaidie. 'I wonder if the descendants of the ancestors of the future human race on Saturn will invent anything like a suitable language. I wonder how they'll talk about those Rings millions of years hence.'

'By that time there may not be any Rings,' Lenox replied, blowing a ring of smoke from his own lips. 'Look at that – made in a moment and gone in a moment – and yet on exactly the same principle, it gives one a dim idea of the difference between time and eternity. After all it's only another example of Kelvin's theory of vortices. Nebulae, and asteroids, and planet-rings, and smoke-rings are really all made on the same principle.'

'My dear Lenox, if you're going to get as philosophical and as common-place as that I'm going to bed. Now that I come to think of it, I've been about fifteen earth-hours out of bed, so it's about time I went. It's your turn to make the coffee in the morning – our morning I mean – and you'll wake me in time to see the South Pole of Saturn, won't you? You're not coming yet, I suppose?'

'Not just yet, dear. I want to see a bit more of this, and then I must go through the engines and see that they're all right for that thousand-million-mile homeward voyage you're talking about. You can have a good ten hours' sleep without missing much, I think, for there doesn't seem to be anything more interesting than our own Arctic life down there. So good-night, little woman, and don't have too many nightmares.'

'Good-night!' she said, 'if you hear me shout you'll know that you've to come and protect me from monsters. Weren't those two-headed brutes just too horrid for words? Good-night, dear!'

VI HOMEWARD BOUND

George Griffith

After leaving Saturn the *Astronef* pursued her lonely course on her homeward voyage across the fields of space, while the Ringed World, which had so nearly proved the end of Lord and Lady Redgrave's wanderings, grew dimmer every hour behind them.

On the morning of the fourth day from Saturn Lord Redgrave went as usual into the conning-tower to examine the instruments and to see that everything was in order. To his intense surprise he found, on looking at the gravitational compass, which was to the *Astronef* what the ordinary compass is to a ship at sea, that the vessel was a long way out of her course.

Such a thing had never yet occurred. Up to now the *Astronef* had obeyed the laws of gravitation and repulsion with absolute exactness. He made another examination of the instruments; but no, all were in perfect order.

'I wonder what the deuce is the matter,' he said, after he had looked for a few moments with frowning eyes at the Heavens before him. 'By Jove, we're swinging more. This is getting serious.'

He went back to the compass. The long, slender needle was slowly swinging farther and farther out of the middle line of the vessel.

'There can only be two explanations of that,' he went on, thrusting his hands deep into his trouser pockets; 'either the engines are not working properly, or some enormous and invisible body is pulling us towards it out of our course. Let's have a look at the engines first.'

When he reached the engine-room he said to Murgatroyd, who was indulging in his usual pastime of cleaning and polishing his beloved charges: 'Have you noticed anything wrong during the last hour or so, Murgatroyd?'

'No, my lord, at least not so far as concerns the engines. They're all right. Hark now, they're not making more noise than a lady's sewing machine,' replied the old Yorkshireman with a note of resentment in his voice. The suspicion that anything could be wrong with his shining darlings was almost a personal offence to him. 'But is anything the matter, my lord, if I might ask?'

'We're a long way off our course, and for the life of me I can't understand it,' replied Redgrave. 'There's nothing about here to pull us out of our line. Of course the stars – good Lord, I never thought of that! Look here, Murgatroyd, not a word about this to her ladyship, and stand by to raise the power by degrees, as I signal to you.'

'Ay, my lord. I hope it's nothing bad.'

Redgrave went back to the conning-tower without replying. The only possible solution of the mystery of the deviation had suddenly dawned upon him, and a very serious solution it was. He remembered that there were such things as dead suns – the derelicts of the Ocean of Space – vast, invisible orbs, lightless and lifeless, too distant from any living sun to be illumined by its rays, and yet exercising the only force left to them, the force of attraction. Might not one of these have wandered near enough to the confines of the Solar System to exert this force. a force of absolutely unknown magnitude, upon the *Astronef*?

He went to a little desk beside the instrument-table and plunged into a maze of mathematics, of masses and weights, angles and distances. Half-an-hour later he stood looking at the last symbol on the last sheet of paper with something like fear. It was the fatal x which remained to satisfy the last equation, the unknown quantity which represented the unseen force that was dragging the *Astronef* into the outer wilderness of interstellar space, into far-off regions from which, with the remaining force at his disposal, no return would be possible.

. . . into a maze of mathematics

He signalled to Murgatroyd to increase the development of the R Force from a tenth to a half. Then he went to the lower saloon, where Zaidie was busy with her usual morning 'tidy-up'. Now that the mystery was explained there was no reason to keep her in the dark. Indeed, he had given her his word that he would conceal from her no danger, however great, that might threaten them when he had once assured himself of its existence.

She listened to him in silence and without a sign of fear beyond a little lifting of the eyelids and a little fading of the colour in her cheeks.

'And if we can't resist this force,' she said, when he had finished, 'it will drag us millions – perhaps millions of millions – of miles away from our own system into outer space, and we shall either fall on the surface of this dead sun and be reduced to a puff of lighted gas in an instant, or some other body will pull us away from it, and then another away from that, and so on, and we shall wander among the stars for ever and ever until the end of time!'

'If the first happens, darling, we shall die – together – without knowing it. It's the second that I'm most afraid of. The *Astronef* may go on wandering among the stars for ever – but we have only water enough for three weeks more. Now come into the conning-tower and we'll see how things are going.'

As they bent their heads over the instrument-table Redgrave saw that the remorseless needle had moved two degrees more to the right. The keel of the *Astronef*, under the impulse of the R Force, was continually turning. The pull of the invisible orb was dragging the vessel slowly but irresistibly out of her line.

'There's nothing for it but this,' said Redgrave, putting out his hand to the signal-board, and signalling to Murgatroyd to put the engines to their highest power. 'You see, dear, our greatest danger is this; we have had to exert such a tremendous lot of power that we haven't any too much to spare, and if we have to spend it in counteracting the pull of this dead sun, or whatever it is, we may not have enough of what I call the R fluid left to get home with.'

'I see,' she said, staring with wide-open eyes at the needle. 'You mean that we may not have enough to keep us from falling into one of the planets or perhaps into the sun itself. Well, supposing the dangers are equal, this one is the nearest, and so I guess we've got to fight it first.'

'Spoken like a good American!' he said, putting his arm across her shoulders and looking at once with infinite pride and infinite regret at the calm, proud face which the glory of resignation had adorned with a new beauty.

She bowed her head and then looked away again so that he should not see that there were tears in her eyes. He took his hand from her shoulder and stared in silence down at the needle. It was stationary again.

'We've stopped!' he said, after a pause of several moments. 'Now, if the body that's taken us out of our course is moving away from us we win, if it's coming towards us we lose. At any rate, we've done all we can. Come along, Zaidie, let's go and have a walk on deck.'

They had scarcely reached the upper deck when something happened which dwarfed all the other experiences of their marvellous voyage into utter insignificance.

Above and around them the constellations blazed with a splendour inconceivable to an observer on earth, but ahead of them gaped the vast, black void which sailors call 'the coal-hole', and in which the most powerful telescopes have only discovered a few faintly luminous bodies. Suddenly, out of the midst of this infinity of darkness, there blazed a glare of almost intolerably brilliant radiance. Instantly the forward end of the *Astronef* was bathed in light and heat – the light and heat of a re-created sun, whose elements had been dark and cold for uncounted ages.

Hundreds of tiny points of light, unknown worlds which had been dark for myriads of years, twinkled out of the blackness. Then the fierce glare grew dimmer. A vast mantle of luminous mist spread out with inconceivable rapidity, and in the midst of this blazed the central nucleus – the sun which in far-off ages to come would be the giver of light and heat, of life and beauty to worlds unborn, to planets which were now only little eddies of atoms whirling in that ocean of nebulous flame.

For more than an hour the two voyagers stood motionless and silent, gazing on the indescribable splendours of a spectacle such as no human eyes but theirs had ever beheld. Every earthly thought seemed burnt out of their souls by the glory and the wonder of it. It was almost as though they were standing in the very presence of God, for were they not witnessing the supreme act of omnipotence, a new creation? Their peril, a peril such as had never threatened mortals before, was utterly forgotten. They had even forgotten each other's presence. For the time being they existed only to look and to wonder.

They were called at length out of their trance by the matter-of-fact voice of Murgatroyd saying: 'My lord, she's back to her course. Will I keep the power on full?'

'Eh! What's that?' exclaimed Redgrave, as they both turned quickly round. 'Oh, it's you, Murgatroyd. The power? Yes, keep it on full till I have taken the bearings.'

'Ay, my lord, very good,' replied the engineer.

As he left the deck Redgrave put his arm round Zaidie and drew her gently towards him and said: 'Zaidie, truly you are favoured among women! You have seen the beginning of a new creation. You will certainly be saved somehow after that.'

'Yes, and you too, dear,' she murmured, as though still half-dreaming. 'It is very glorious and wonderful; but what is it all – I mean, what is the explanation of it?'

'The merely scientific explanation, dear, is very simple. I see it all now. The force that was dragging us out of our course was the united pull of two dead stars approaching each other in the same orbit. They may have been doing that for millions of years. The shock of their meeting has transformed their motion into light and heat. They have united to form a single sun and a nebula, which will some day condense into a system of planets like ours. Tonight the astronomers on earth will discover a new star – a variable star as they'll call it – for it will grow dimmer as it moves away from our system. It has often happened before.'

Then they turned back to the conning-tower.

The needle had swung to its old position. The new star, henceforth to be known in the annals of astronomy as Lilla-Zaidie, had already set for them to the right of the *Astronef* and risen on the left, and, at a distance of over nineteen hundred million miles from the earth, the corner was turned, and the homeward voyage began.

A few days later they crossed the path of Jupiter, but the giant was invisible, far away on the other side of the sun. Redgrave laid his course so as to avail himself to the utmost of the 'pull' of the planets without going near enough to them to be compelled to exert too much of the priceless R Force, which the indicators showed to be running perilously low.

Between the orbits of Jupiter and Mars they made a decided economy by landing on Ceres, one of the largest of the asteroids, and travelling about fifty million miles on her towards the orbit of the earth without any expenditure of force whatever. They found the tiny world possessed of a breathable atmosphere and a fluid resembling water but nearly as dense as mercury. A couple of flasks of it form the greatest treasures of the British Museum and the National Museum at Washington. The vegetable world was represented by coarse grass, lichens, and dwarf shrubs, and the animal by different species of worms, lizards and flies, and small burrowing animals of the rodent type.

As the orbit of Ceres, like that of the other asteroids, is considerably inclined to that of the earth, the *Astronef* rose from its surface when the plane of the earth's revolution was reached, and the glittering swarm of miniature planets plunged away into space beneath them.

'Where to now?' said Zaidie, as her husband came down on deck from the conning-tower.

'I am going to try to steer a middle course between the orbits of Mercury and Venus,' he replied. 'They just happen to be so placed now that we ought to be able to get the advantage of the pull of both of them as we pass, and that will save us a lot of power. The only thing I'm afraid of is the pull of the sun, equal to goodness knows how many times the attraction of all the planets put together. You see, little woman, it's like this,' he went on, taking out a pencil and going down on one knee on the deck: 'Here's the *Astronef*; there's Venus; there's Mercury; there's the sun; and there, away on the other side of him, is Mother Earth. If we can turn that corner safely and without expending too much power we should be all right.'

'And if we can't, what will happen?'

'It will be a choice between morphine and cremation in the atmosphere of the sun, dear, or rather gradually roasting as we fall towards it.'

'Then, of course, it will be morphine,' she said quite quietly, as she turned away from his diagram and looked at the now fast increasing disc of the sun. A well-balanced mind speedily becomes accustomed even to the most terrible perils, and Zaidie had now looked this one so long and so steadily in the face that for her it had already become merely the choice between two forms of death with just a chance of escape hidden in the closed hand of Fate.

Thirty-six earth-hours later the glorious golden disc of Venus lay broad and bright beneath them. Above was the blazing orb of the sun, nearly half as big again as it appears from the earth, with Mercury, a round black spot, travelling slowly across it.

'My dear Bird-Folk!' said Zaidie, looking down at the lovely world below them. 'If home wasn't home – '

'We can be back among them in a few hours with absolute safety,' interrupted her husband, catching at the suggestion. 'I've told you the truth about getting back to the earth. It's only a chance at best, and even if we pass the sun we may not have force enough left to prevent the *Astronef* from being smashed to dust or burnt up in the atmosphere. After all we might do worse – '

'What would you do if you were alone, Rollo?' she said, interrupting him in turn.

'I should take my chance and go on. After all home's home and worth a struggle. But you, dear – '

'I'm you, and so I take the same chances as you do. Besides, we're not perfect enough for a world where there isn't any sin. We should probably get quite miserable there. No, home's home, as you say.'

'Then home it is, dear!' he replied.

The vast, resplendent hemisphere of the Love-Star sunk down into the vault of space, growing swiftly smaller and dimmer as the *Astronef* sped towards the little black spot on the face of the sun, which to them was like a buoy marking a place of utter and hopeless shipwreck in the ocean of immensity.

The chronometer, still set to earth time, had now begun to mark the last hours of the *Astronef*'s voyage. She was not only travelling at a speed of which figures could give no comprehensible idea, but the Sun, Mercury, and the Earth were rushing towards her with a compound velocity, composed of the movement of the Solar System through space and of the movement of the two planets round the sun.

Murgatroyd was at his post in the engine-room. Redgrave and Zaidie had gone into the conning-tower, perhaps for the last time. For good fortune or evil, for life or death, they would see the end of the voyage together.

'How far yet, dear?' she said, as Venus began to slip away behind them, rising like a splendid moon in their wake.

'Only sixty million miles or so, a matter of a few hours, more or less – it all depends,' he replied, without taking his eyes off the compass.

'Sixty millions! Why I feel almost at home again.'

'But we have to turn the corner of the street yet, dear, and after that there's a fall of more than twenty-five million miles on to the more or less kindly breast of Mother Earth.'

'A fall! It does sound rather awful when you put it that way; but I am not going to let you frighten me. I believe Mother Earth will receive her wandering children quite as kindly as they deserve.'

The moon-like disc of Venus grew swiftly smaller, and the black spot on the face of the sun larger and larger as the *Astronef* rushed silently and imperceptibly, and yet with almost inconceivable velocity, towards doom or fortune. Neither Zaidie nor Redgrave spoke again for nearly three hours – hours which to them seemed to pass like so many minutes. Their eyes were fixed on the black disc of Mercury, which, as they approached it, expanded with magical rapidity till it completely eclipsed the blazing orb behind it. Their thoughts were far away on the still invisible earth and all the splendid possibilities that it held for two young lives like theirs.

As the sunlight vanished they looked at each other in the golden moonlight of Venus, and Zaidie let her head rest for a moment on her husband's shoulder. Then a swiftly broadening gleam of light shot out from behind the black circle of Mercury. The first crisis had come. Redgrave put out his hand to the signal-board and rang for full power. The planet seemed to swing round as the *Astronef* rushed into the blaze. In a few minutes it passed through the phases from 'new' to 'full'. Venus became eclipsed in turn as they swung between Mercury and the Sun, and then Redgrave, after a rapid glance to either side, said: 'If we can only keep the two pulls balanced we shall do it. That will keep us in a straight line, and our own momentum ought to carry us into the earth's attraction.'

Zaidie did not reply. She was shading her eyes with her hand from the almost intolerable brilliance of the sun's rays, and looking straight ahead to catch the first glimpse of the silver-grey orb. Her husband read her thoughts and respected them. But a few minutes later he startled her out of her dream of home by exclaiming: 'Good God, we're turning!'

'What do you say, dear? Turning what?'

'On our own centre. Look! I'm afraid only a miracle can save us now, darling.'

She looked to the left-hand side where he was pointing. The sun, no longer now a sun, but a vast ocean of flame filling nearly a third of the vault of space, was sinking beneath them. On the right Mercury was rising. Zaidie knew only too well what this meant. It meant that the keel of the *Astronef* was being dragged out of the straight line which would cut the earth's orbit some forty million miles away. It meant that, in spite of the exertion of the full power that the engines could develop, they had begun to fall into the sun.

Redgrave laid his hand on his wife's, and their eyes met. There was no need for words. Perhaps speech just then would have been impossible. In that mute glance each looked into the other's soul and was content. Then he left the conning-tower, and Zaidie dropped on to her knees before the instrument-table and laid her forehead upon her clasped hands.

Her husband went to the saloon, unlocked a little cupboard in the wall and took out a blue bottle of corrugated glass labeled 'Morphine, poison'. He took another empty bottle of white glass and measured fifty drops into it. Then he went to the engine-room and said abruptly: 'Murgatroyd, I'm afraid it's all up with us. We're falling into the sun, and you know what that means. In a few hours the *Astronef* will be red-hot. So it's roasting alive – or this. I recommend this.'

'And what might that be, my lord?' said the old engineer, looking at the bottle which his master held out towards him.

'That's morphine – poison. Fill that up with water, drink it, and in half-an-hour you'll be dead without knowing it. Of course, you won't take it until there's absolutely no hope; but, granted that, you'll find this a better death than roasting or baking alive.' Then his voice changed suddenly as he went on: 'Of course, I need not say, Murgatroyd, how deeply I regret now that I asked you to come in the *Astronef*.'

'My lord, my people have served yours for seven hundred years, and, whether on earth or among the stars, where you go it is my duty to go also. But don't ask me to take the poison. It is not for me to say that a journey like this is tempting Providence, but, by my lights, if I am to die it will be the death that Providence sends.'

'I dare say you're right in one way, Murgatroyd, but it's no time to argue about beliefs now. There's the bottle. Do as you think right. And now, in case the miracle doesn't happen, goodbye.'

'Goodbye, my lord, if it be so,' replied the old Yorkshireman, taking the hand which Redgrave held out to him. 'I'll keep the power on to the last, I suppose?'

'Yes, you may as well. If it doesn't keep us away from the sun it won't be much use to us in two or three hours.'

He left the engine-room and went back to the conning-tower. Zaidie was still on her knees. Beneath and around them the awful gulf of flame was broadening and deepening. Mercury was rising higher and growing smaller. He put the bottle down on the table and waited. Then Zaidie looked up. Her eyes were clear, and her face was perfectly calm. She rose and put her arm through his, and said: 'Well, is there any hope, dear? There can't be now, can there? Is that the morphine?'

'Yes,' he replied, slipping his arm beneath hers and round her waist. 'I'm afraid there's not much hope now, little woman. We're using up the last of the power, and you see – '

As he said this he looked at the thermometer. The mercury had risen from 65 deg. Fahrenheit, the normal temperature of the interior of the *Astronef*, to 93 deg., and during the half-minute that he watched it rose another degree. There was no mistaking such a warning as that. He had brought two little liqueur glasses in his pocket from the saloon. He divided the morphine between them, and filled them up with water.

'Not until the last moment, dear,' said Zaidie, as he set one of them before her. 'We have no right to do it until then.'

'Very well. When the mercury reaches a hundred and fifty. After that it will go up ten and fifteen degrees at a jump, and we – '

'Yes, at a hundred and fifty,' she replied, cutting short a speech she dared not hear the end of. 'I understand. It will be impossible to hope any more.'

Now, side by side, they stood and watched the thermometer.

Ninety-five – ninety-eight – a hundred and three – a hundred and ten – eighteen – twenty-four – thirty-two – forty-one –

The silent minutes passed, and with each the silver thread – for them the thread of life – grew, with strange contradiction, longer and longer, and with every minute it grew more quickly.

A hundred and forty-six.

With his right arm Redgrave drew Zaidie still closer to him. He put out his left hand and took up the little glass. She did the same.

'Goodbye, dear, till we have slept and wake again!'

'Goodbye, darling, God grant that we may!' But the agony of that last farewell was more than Zaidie could bear. She looked away at the little glass in her hand, a hand which even now did not tremble. Then she raised her eyes again to take one last look at the glory of the stars, and at the Fate incarnate in flame which lay beneath them.

'The Earth, the Earth – thank God, the Earth!'

With the hand that held the draught of Lethe – which in another moment would have passed her lips – she caught at her husband's hand, pulled the glass out of it, and then with a little sigh she dropped senseless on the floor of the conning-tower. Redgrave looked for a moment in the direction that her eyes had taken. A pale, silver-grey crescent, with a little white spot near it, was rising out of the blackness beyond the edge of the solar ocean of flame. Home was in sight at last, but would they reach it – and how?

He picked her up and carried her to their room and laid her on the bed. Then he went to the medicine chest again, this time for a very different purpose.

An hour later, they were on the upper deck with their telescopes turned on to the rapidly-growing crescent of the home-world, which, in its eternal march through space, had come into the line of direct attraction just in time to turn the scale in which the lives of the star-voyagers were trembling. The higher it rose, the bigger and broader and brighter it grew, and, at last, Zaidie – forgetting in her transport of joy all the perils that were yet to come – sprang to her feet and clapped her hands, and cried: 'There's America!'

Then she dropped back into her long deck-chair and began a good, hearty, healthy cry.

NOTE. – The manner of the ending of the *Astronef's* marvellous voyage is now as much a matter of public knowledge as are the circumstances of its beginning. Everyone knows now how, with the remains of the R force, Lord Redgrave managed to steer the Star-Navigator so accurately between the earth and the moon that, descending obliquely towards the earth, she became, during eleven days and twelve nights of terrible suspense, a tiny satellite of the Mother Planet with a constantly decreasing orbit. How, during one awful hour, by the exertions of the last unit of power of which her engines were capable, she almost grazed the highest peaks of the Bolivian Andes, swept like a meteor over the foothills and plains of the western slope of Peru and took the waters of the Pacific barely ten miles from the coast. It is equally needless to recapitulate the delights and the splendours of the welcome home which the whole civilised world united to give to Lord Redgrave and his lovely countess, whose diary of the star voyage has, thanks to her Ladyship's generous condescension, furnished alike the groundwork and the inspiration of the present series of narratives.

The Dust of Death

The story of the great plague
of the twentieth century

Fred M. White

The front door bell tinkled impatiently; evidently somebody was in a hurry. Alan Hubert answered the call, a thing that even a distinguished physician might do, seeing that it was on the stroke of midnight. The tall, graceful figure of a woman in evening dress stumbled into the hall. The diamonds in her hair shimmered and trembled, her face was full of terror.

'You are Dr Hubert,' she gasped. 'I am Mrs Fillingham, the artist's wife, you know. Will you come with me at once . . . My husband . . . I had been dining out. In the studio . . . Oh, please come!'

Hubert asked no unnecessary questions. He knew Fillingham, the great portrait painter, well enough by repute and by sight also, for Fillingham's house and studio were close by. There were many artists in the Devonshire Park district – that pretty suburb which was one of the triumphs of the builder's and landscape gardener's art. Ten years ago it had been no more than a swamp; today people spoke complacently of the fact that they lived in Devonshire Park.

Hubert walked up the drive and past the trim lawns with Mrs Fillingham hanging on his arm, and in at the front door. Mrs Fillingham pointed to a door on the right. She was too exhausted to speak. There were shaded lights gleaming everywhere, on old oak and armour and on a large portrait of a military-looking man propped up on an easel. On a lay figure was a magnificent foreign military uniform.

Hubert caught all this in a quick mental flash. But the vital interest to him was a human figure lying on his back before the fireplace. The clean-shaven, sensitive face of the artist had a ghastly, purple-black tinge, there was a large swelling in the throat.

'He – he is not dead?' Mrs Fillingham asked in a frozen whisper.

Hubert was able to satisfy the distracted wife on that head. Fillingham was still breathing. Hubert stripped the shade from a reading lamp and held the electric bulb at the end of its long flex above the sufferer's mouth, contriving to throw the flood of light upon the back of the throat.

'Diphtheria!' he exclaimed

'Diphtheria!' he exclaimed. 'Label's type unless I am greatly mistaken. Some authorities are disposed to scoff at Dr Label's discovery. I was an assistant of his for four years and I know better. Fortunately I happen to know what the treatment – successful in two cases – was.'

He hurried from the house and returned a few minutes later breathlessly. He had some strange-looking, needle-like instruments in his hands. He took an electric lamp from its socket and substituted a plug on a flex instead. Then he cleared a table without ceremony and managed to hoist his patient upon it.

'Now please hold that lamp steadily thus,' he said. 'Bravo, you are a born nurse! I am going to apply these electric needles to the throat.'

Hubert talked on more for the sake of his companion's nerves than anything else. The still figure on the table quivered under his touch, his lungs expanded in a long, shuddering sigh. The heart was beating more or less regularly now. Fillingham opened his eyes and muttered something.

'Ice,' Hubert snapped, 'have you got any ice in the house?'

It was a well-regulated estabment and there was plenty of ice in the refrigerator. Not until the patient was safe in bed did Hubert's features relax.

'We'll pull him through yet,' he said. 'I'll send you a competent nurse round in half-an-hour. I'll call first thing in the morning and bring Dr Label with me. He must not miss this on any account.'

Half-an-hour later Hubert was spinning along in a hansom towards Harley Street. It was past one when he reached the house of the great German savant. A dim light was burning in the hall. A big man with an enormous shaggy head and a huge frame attired in the seediest of dress coats welcomed Hubert with a smile.

'So, my young friend,' Label said, 'your face promises excitement.'

'Case of Label's diphtheria,' Hubert said crisply. 'Fillingham, the artist, who lives close by me. Fortunately they called me in. I have arranged for you to see my patient the first thing in the morning.'

The big German's jocular manner vanished. He led Hubert gravely to a chair in his consulting-room and curtly demanded details. He smiled approvingly as Hubert enlarged upon his treatment of the case.

'Undoubtedly your diagnosis was correct,' he said, puffing furiously at a long china pipe. 'You have not forgotten what I told you of it. The swelling – which is caused by violent blood poisoning – yielded to the electric treatment. I took the virus from the cases in the north and I tried them on scores of animals. And they all died.

'I find it is the virus of what is practically a new disease, one of the worst in the wide world. I say it recurs again, and it does. So I practise and practise to find a cure. And electricity is the cure. I inoculate five dogs with the virus and I save two by the electric current. You follow my plans and you go the first stage of the way to cure Fillingham. Did you bring any of that mucous here?'

Hubert produced it in a tiny glass tube. For a little time Label examined it under his microscope. He wanted to make assurance doubly sure.

'It is the same thing,' he said presently. 'I knew that it was bound to recur again. Why, it is planted all over our big cities. And electricity is the only way to get rid of it. It was the best method of dealing with sewage, only corporations found it too expensive. Wires in the earth charged to say 10,000 volts. Apply this and you destroy the virus that lies buried under hundreds of houses in London. They laughed at me when I suggested it years ago.'

'Underground,' Hubert asked vaguely.

'Ach, underground, yes. Don't you recollect that in certain parts of England cancer is more common than in other places? The germs have been turned up in fields. I, myself, have proved their existence. In a little time, perhaps. I shall open the eyes of your complacent Londoners. You live in a paradise, ach Gott! And what was that paradise like ten years ago? Dreary pools and deserted brickfields. And how do you fill it up and level it to build houses upon?'

'By the carting of hundreds of thousands of loads of refuse, of course.'

'Ach, I will presently show you what that refuse was and is. Now go home to bed.'

* * *

Mrs Fillingham remained in the studio with Hubert whilst Label was making his examination overhead. The patient had had a bad night; his symptoms were very grave indeed. Hubert listened more or less vaguely; his mind had gone beyond the solitary case. He was dreading what might happen in the future.

'Your husband has a fine constitution,' he said soothingly.

'He has overtried it lately,' Mrs Fillingham replied. 'At present he is painting a portrait of the Emperor of Asturia. His Majesty was to have sat today; he spent the morning here yesterday.'

But Hubert was paying no attention.

The heavy tread of Label was heard as he floundered down the stairs. His big voice was booming. What mattered all the portraits in the world so long as the verdict hung on the German doctor's lips!

'Oh, there is a chance,' Label exclaimed. 'Just a chance. Everything possible is being done. This is not so much diphtheria as a new disease. Diphtheria family, no doubt, but the blood poisoning makes a difficult thing of it.'

Label presently dragged Hubert away after parting with Mrs Fillingham. He wanted to find a spot where building or draining was going on.

They found some men presently engaged in connecting a new house with the main drainage – a deep cutting some forty yards long by seven or eight feet deep. There was the usual crust of asphalt on the road, followed by broken bricks and the like, and a more or less regular stratum of blue-black rubbish, soft, wet, and clinging, and emitting an odour that caused Hubert to throw up his head.

'You must have broken into a drain somewhere here,' he said.

'We ain't, sir,' the foreman of the gang replied. 'It's nout but rubbidge as they made up the road with here ten years ago. Lord knows where it came from, but it do smell fearful in weather like this.'

The odour indeed was stifling. All imaginable kinds of rubbish and refuse lay under the external beauties of Devonshire Park in strata ranging from five to forty feet deep. It was little wonder that trees and flowers flourished here. And here – wet, and dark, and festering – was a veritable hotbed of disease. Contaminated rags, torn paper, road siftings, decayed vegetable matter, diseased food, fish and bones all were represented here.

'Every ounce of this ought to have gone through the destructor,' Label snorted. 'But no, it is used for the foundations of a suburban paradise. My word, we shall see what your paradise will be like presently. Come along.'

Label picked up a square slab of the blue stratum, put it in a tin, and the tin in his pocket. He was snorting and puffing with contempt.

'Now come to Harley Street with me and I will show you things,' he said.

He was as good as his word. Placed under a microscope, a minute portion of the subsoil from Devonshire Park proved to be a mass of living matter. There were at least four kinds of bacillus here that Hubert had never seen before. With his superior knowledge Label pointed out the fact that they all existed in the mucous taken from Fillingham on the previous evening.

'There you are!' He cried excitedly. 'You get all that wet sodden refuse of London and you dump it down here in a heap. You mix with it a heap of vegetable matter so that fermentation shall have every chance. Then you cover it over with some soil, and

Label picked up a square slab
of the blue stratum

you let it boil, boil, boil. Then, when millions upon millions of death-dealing microbes are bred and bred till their virility is beyond the scope of science, you build good houses on the top of it. For years I have been prophesying an outbreak of some new disease – or some awful form of an old one – and here it comes. They called me a crank because

I asked for high electric voltage to kill the plague – to destroy it by lightning. A couple of high tension wires run into the earth and there you are. See here.'

He took his cube of the reeking earth and applied the battery to it. The mass showed no outward change. But once under the microscope a fragment of it demonstrated that there was not the slightest trace of organic life.

'There!' Label cried. 'Behold the remedy. I don't claim that it will cure in every case, because we hardly touch the diphtheretic side of the trouble. When there has been a large loss of life we shall learn the perfect remedy by experience. But this thing is coming, and your London is going to get a pretty bad scare. You have laid it down like port wine, and now that the thing is ripe you are going to suffer from the consequence. I have written articles in the *Lancet*, I have warned people, but they take not the slightest heed.'

Hubert went back home thoughtfully. He found the nurse who had Fillingham's case in hand waiting for him in his consulting-room.

'I am just back from my walk,' she said. 'I wish you would call at Dr Walker's at Elm Crescent. He has two cases exactly like Mr Fillingham's, and he is utterly puzzled.'

Hubert snatched his hat and his electric needles, and hurried away at once. He found his colleague impatiently waiting for him There were two children this time in one of the best appointed houses in Devonshire Park, suffering precisely as Fillingham had done. In each instance the electric treatment gave the desired result. Hubert hastily explained the whole matter to Walker.

'It's an awful business,' the latter said, 'Personally, I have a great respect for Label, and I feel convinced that he is right. If this thing spreads, property in Devonshire Park won't be worth the price of slum lodgings.'

By mid-day nineteen cases of the so-called diphtheria had been notified within the three miles area known as Devonshire Park. Evidently some recent excavations had liberated the deadly microbe. But there was no scare as yet. Label came down again hotfoot with as many assistants as he could get, and took up his quarters with Hubert. They were going to have a busy time.

It was after two before Hubert managed to run across to Fillingham's again. He stood in the studio waiting for Mrs Fillingham. His mind was preoccupied and uneasy, yet he seemed to miss something from the studio. It was strange, considering that he had only been in the room twice before.

'Are you looking for anything?' Mrs Fillingham asked.

'I don't know,' Hubert exclaimed. 'I seem to miss something. I've got it – the absence of the uniform.'

'They sent for it,' Mrs Fillingham said vaguely. She was dazed for want of sleep. 'The Emperor had to go to some function, and that was the only uniform of the kind he happened to have. He was to have gone away in it after his sitting today. My husband persuaded him to leave it when it was here yesterday, and – '

Hubert had cried out suddenly as if in pain. 'He was here yesterday – here, with your husband, and your husband with the diphtheria on him?'

Then the weary wife understood.

'Good heavens – '

But Hubert was already out of the room. He blundered on until he came to a hansom cab creeping along in the sunshine.

'Buckingham Palace,' he gasped. 'Drive like mad. A five-pound note for you if you get me there by three o'clock!'

* * *

Already Devonshire Park was beginning to be talked about. It was wonderful how the daily press got to the root of things. Hubert caught sight of more than one contents bill as he drove home that alluded to the strange epidemic.

Dr Label joined Hubert presently in Mrs Fillingham's home, rubbing his huge hands together. He knew nothing of the new dramatic developments. He asked where Hubert had been spending his time.

'Trying to save the life of your friend, the Emperor of Asturia,' Hubert said. 'He was here yesterday with Fillingham, and, though he seems well enough at present, he may have the disease on him now. What do you think of that?'

Hubert waited to see the great man stagger before the blow. Label smiled and nodded as he proceeded to light a cigarette.

'Good job too,' he said. 'I am honorary physician to the court of Asturia. I go back, there, as you know, when I finish my great work here. The Emperor I have brought through four or five illnesses, and if anything is wrong he always sends for me.'

'But he might get the awful form of diphtheria!'

'Very likely,' Label said coolly. 'All these things are in the hands of Providence. I know that man's constitution to a hair, and if he gets the disease I shall pull him through for certain. I should like him to have it.'

'In the name of all that is practical, why?'

'To startle the public,' Label cried. He was mounted on his hobby now. He paced up and down the room in a whirl of tobacco smoke. 'It would bring the matter home to everybody. Then perhaps something will be done. I preach and preach in vain. Only the *Lancet* backs me up at all. Many times I have asked for a quarter of a million of money, so that I can found a school for the electrical treatment of germ diseases. I want to destroy all malaria. All dirt in bulk, every bit of refuse that is likely to breed fever and the like, should be treated by electricity. I would take huge masses of deadly scourge and mountains of garbage, and render them innocent by the electric current. But no; that costs money, and your poverty-stricken Government cannot afford it. Given a current of 10,000 volts a year or two ago, and I could have rendered this one of the healthiest places in England. You only wanted to run those high voltage wires into the earth here and there, and behold the millions are slain, wiped out, gone for ever. Perhaps I will get it now.'

* * *

London was beginning to get uneasy. There had been outbreaks before, but they were of the normal type. People, for instance, are not so frightened of smallpox as they used to be. Modern science has learnt to grapple with the fell disease and rob it of half its terrors. But this new and virulent form of diphtheria was another matter.

Hubert sat over his dinner that night, making mental calculations. There were nearly a thousand houses of varying sizes in Devonshire Park. Would it be necessary to abandon these? He took down a large scale map of London, and hastily marked in blue pencil those areas which had developed rapidly of recent years. In nearly all of these a vast amount of artificial ground had been necessary. Hubert was appalled as he calculated the number of jerry-built erections in these districts.

A servant came in and laid *The Evening Wire* upon the table. Hubert glanced at it. Nothing had been lost in the way of sensation. The story of the Emperor's visit to the district had been given great prominence. An inquiry at Buckingham Palace had elicited the fact that the story was true.

Well, perhaps no harm would come of it. Hubert finished a cigar and prepared to go out. As he flung the paper aside a paragraph in the stop press column – a solitary paragraph like an inky island in a sea of white – caught his eye.

No alarm need be experienced as to the danger encountered by the Emperor of Asturia, but we are informed that His Majesty is prevented from dining at Marlborough House tonight owing to a slight cold and sore throat caught, it is stated, in the draughts at Charing Cross Station. The Emperor will go down to Cowes as arranged tomorrow.

Hubert shook his head doubtfully. The slight cold and sore throat were ominous. His mind dwelt upon the shadow of trouble as he made his way to the hospital. There had been two fresh cases during the evening and the medical staff were looking anxious and worried. They wanted assistance badly, and Hubert gave his to the full.

It was nearly eleven before Hubert staggered home. In the main business street of the suburb a news-shop was still open.

A flaming placard attracted the doctor's attention. It struck him like a blow. 'Alarming illness of the Asturian Emperor. His Majesty stricken down by the new disease. Latest bulletin from Buckingham Palace.'

Almost mechanically Hubert bought a paper. There was not much beyond the curt information that the Emperor was dangerously ill.

Arrived home Hubert found a telegram awaiting him. He tore it open. The message was brief but to the point.

HAVE BEEN CALLED IN TO BUCKINGHAM PALACE, LABEL'S DIPH-THERIA CERTAIN. SHALL TRY AND SEE YOU TOMORROW MORNING.

LABEL

London was touched deeply and sincerely. A great sovereign had come over here in the most friendly fashion to show his good feeling for a kindred race. On the very start of a round of pleasure he had been stricken down like this.

The public knew all the details from the progress of that fateful uniform to the thrilling eight o'clock bulletin when the life of Rudolph III was declared to be in great danger. They knew that Dr Label had been sent for post haste. The big German was no longer looked upon as a clever crank, but the one man who might be able to save London from a terrible scourge. And from lip to lip went the news that over two hundred cases of the new disease had now broken out in Devonshire Park.

People knew pretty well what it was and what was the cause now. Label's warning had come home with a force that nobody had expected. He had stolen away quite late for half-an-hour to his own house and there had been quite free with the pressmen. He extenuated nothing. The thing was bad, and it was going to be worse. So far as he could see, something of this kind was inevitable. If Londoners were so blind as to build houses on teeming heaps of filth, why, London must be prepared to take the consequences.

Hubert knew nothing of this. He had fallen back utterly exhausted in his chair with the idea of taking a short rest – for nearly three hours he had been fast asleep. Somebody was shaking him roughly. He struggled back to the consciousness that Label was bending over him.

'Well, you are a nice fellow,' the German grumbled.

'I was dead beat and worn out,' Hubert said apologetically. 'How is the Emperor?'

'His Majesty is doing as well as I can expect. It is a very bad case, however. I have left him in competent hands, so that I could run down here. They were asking for you at the hospital, presuming that you were busy somewhere. The place is full, and so are four houses in the nearest terrace.'

'Spreading like that?' Hubert exclaimed.

'Spreading like that! By this time tomorrow we shall have a thousand cases on our hands. The authorities are doing everything they can to help us, fresh doctors and nurses and stores are coming in all the time.'

'You turn people out of their houses to make way then?'

Label smiled grimly. He laid his hand on Hubert's shoulder, and piloted him into the roadway. The place seemed to be alive with cabs and vehicles of all kinds. It was as if all the inhabitants of Devonshire Park were going away for their summer holidays simultaneously. The electric arcs shone down on white and frightened faces where joyous gaiety should have been. Here and there a child slept peacefully, but on the whole it was a sorry exodus.

'There you are,' Label said grimly. 'It is a night flight from the plague. It has been going on for hours. It would have been finished now but for the difficulty in getting conveyances. Most of the cabmen are avoiding the place as if it were accursed. But money can command everything, hence the scene that you see before you.'

Hubert stood silently watching the procession. There was very little luggage on any of the cabs or conveyances. Families were going wholesale. Devonshire Park for the most part was an exceedingly prosperous district, so that the difficulties of emigration were not great. In their panic the people were abandoning everything in the wild flight for life and safety.

Then he went in again to rest before the unknown labours of tomorrow. Next morning he anxiously opened his morning paper.

It was not particularly pleasant reading beyond the information that the health of the Emperor of Asturia was mentioned, and that he had passed a satisfactory night. As to the rest, the plague was spreading. There were two hundred and fifty cases in Devonshire Park. Label's sayings had come true at last; it was a fearful vindication of his prophecy. And the worst of it was that no man could possibly say where it was going to end.

* * *

Strange as it may seem, London's anxiety as to the welfare of one man blinded all to the great common danger. For the moment Devonshire Park was forgotten. The one centre of vivid interest was Buckingham Palace.

For three days crowds collected there until at length Label and his colleagues were in a position to issue a bulletin that gave something more than hope. The Emperor of Asturia was going to recover. Label was not the kind of man to say so unless he was pretty sure of his ground.

It was not till this fact had soaked itself into the public mind that attention was fully turned to the danger that threatened London. Devonshire Park was practically in quarantine. All those who could get away had done so, and those who had remained were confined to their own particular district, and provisioned on a system. The new plague was spreading fast.

In more than one quarter the suggestion was made that all houses in certain localities should be destroyed, and the ground thoroughly cleansed and disinfected. It would mean a loss of millions of money, but in the scare of the moment London cared nothing for that.

At the end of a week there were seven thousand cases of the new form of diphtheria under treatment. Over one thousand cases a day came in. Devonshire Park was practically deserted save for the poorer quarters, whence the victims came. It seemed strange to see fine houses abandoned to the first comer who had the hardihood to enter. Devonshire Park was a stricken kingdom within itself, and the Commune of terror reigned.

Enterprising journalists penetrated the barred area and wrote articles about it. One of the fraternity bolder than the rest passed a day and night in one of these deserted palatial residences, and gave his sensations to the Press. Within a few hours most of the villas were inhabited again! There were scores of men and women in the slums who have not the slightest fear of disease – they are too familiar with it for that – and they came creeping westward in search of shelter. The smiling paradise had become a kind of Tom Tiddlers ground, a huge estate in Chancery.

Nobody had troubled, the tenants were busy finding pure quarters elsewhere, the owners of the property were fighting public opinion to save what in many cases was their sole source of income. If Devonshire Park had to be razed to the ground many a wealthy man would be ruined.

It was nearly the end of the first week before this abnormal state of affairs was fully brought home to Hubert. He had been harassed and worried and worn by want of sleep, but tired as he was he did not fail to notice the number of poorer patients who dribbled regularly into the terrace of houses that now formed the hospital. There was something about them that suggested any district rather than Devonshire Park.

'What does it mean, Walker?' he asked one of his doctors.

Walker had just come in from his hour's exercise, heated and excited.

'It's a perfect scandal,' he cried. 'The police are fighting shy of us altogether. I've just been up to the station and they tell me it is a difficult matter to keep competent officers in the district. All along Frinton Hill and Eversley Gardens the houses are crowded with outcasts. They have drifted here from the East End and are making some of those splendid residences impossible.'

Hubert struggled into his hat and coat, and went out. It was exactly as Walker had said. Here was a fine residence with stables and greenhouses and the like, actually occupied by Whitechapel at its worst. A group of dingy children played on the lawn, and a woman with the accumulated grime of weeks on her face was hanging something that passed for washing out of an upper window. The flower beds were trampled down, a couple of attenuated donkeys browsed on the lawn.

Here was a fine residence actually
occupied by Whitechapel at its worst

Hubert strolled up to the house fuming. Two men were sprawling on a couple of morocco chairs smoking filthy pipes. They looked up at the newcomer with languid curiosity. They appeared quite to appreciate the fact that they were absolutely masters of the situation.

'What are you doing here?' Hubert demanded.

'If you're the owner well and good,' was the reply. 'If not, you take an' 'ook it. We know which side our bread's buttered.'

There was nothing for it but to accept this philosophical suggestion. Hubert swallowed his rising indignation and departed. There were other evidences of the ragged invasion as he went down the road. Here and there a house was closed and the blinds down; but it was an exception rather than the rule.

Hubert walked away till he could find a cab, and was driven off to Scotland Yard in a state of indignation. The view of the matter rather startled the officials there.

'We have been so busy,' the Chief Inspector said; 'but the matter shall be attended to. Dr Label was here yesterday, and at his suggestion we are having the whole force electrically treated – a kind of electrical hardening of the throat. The doctor claims that his recent treatment is as efficacious against the diphtheria as vaccination is against smallpox. It is in all the papers today. All London will be going mad over the new remedy tomorrow.'

Hubert nodded thoughtfully. The electric treatment seemed the right thing. Label had shown him what an effect the application of the current had had on the teeming mass of matter taken from the road cutting. He thought it over until he fell asleep in his cab on the way back to his weary labours.

* * *

London raged for the new remedy. The electric treatment for throat troubles is no new thing. In this case it was simple and painless, and it had been guaranteed by one of the popular heroes of the hour. A week before Label had been regarded as a crank and a faddist; now people were ready to swear by him. Had he not prophesied this vile disease for years, and was he not the only man who had a remedy? And the Emperor of Asturia was mending rapidly.

Had Label bidden the people to stand on their heads for an hour a day as a sovereign specific they would have done so gladly. Every private doctor and every public institution was worked to death. At the end of ten days practically all London had been treated. There was nothing for it now but to wait patiently for the result.

Another week passed and then suddenly the inrush of cases began to drop. The average at the end of the second week was down to eighty per day. On the seventeenth and eighteenth days there were only four cases altogether and in each instance they proved to be patients who had not submitted themselves to the treatment.

The scourge was over. Two days elapsed and there were no fresh cases whatever. Some time before a strong posse of police had swamped down upon Devonshire Park and cleared all the slum people out of their luxurious quarters. One or two of the bolder dwellers in that once favoured locality began to creep back. Now that they were inoculated there seemed little to fear.

But Label had something to say about that. He felt that he was free to act now, he had his royal patient practically off his hands. A strong Royal Commission had been appointed by Parliament to go at once thoroughly into the matter.

'And I am the first witness called,' he chuckled to Hubert as the latter sat with the great German smoking a well-earned cigar. 'I shall be able to tell a few things.'

He shook his big head and smiled. The exertion of the last few weeks did not seem to have told upon him in the slightest.

'I also have been summoned,' Hubert said. 'But you don't suggest that those fine houses should be destroyed?'

'I don't suggest anything. I am going to confine myself to facts. One of your patent medicine advertisements says that electricity is life. Never was a truer word spoken. What has saved London from a great scourge? Electricity. What kills this new disease and renders it powerless? Electricity. And what is the great agent to fight dirt and filth with whenever it exists in great quantities? Always electricity. It has not been done before on the ground of expense, and look at the consequences. In one way and another it will cost London 2,000,000 pounds to settle this matter. It was only a little over a third of that I asked for. Wait till you hear me talk!'

* * *

Naturally the greatest interest was taken in the early sittings of the Commission. A somewhat pompous chairman was prepared to exploit Label for his own gratification and self-glory. But the big German would have none of it. From the very first he dominated the Committee, he would give his evidence in his own way, he would speak of facts as he found them. And, after all, he was the only man there who had any practical knowledge of the subject of the inquiry.

'You would destroy the houses?' an interested member asked.

'Nothing of the kind,' Label growled. 'Not so much as a single pigsty. If you ask me what electricity is I cannot tell you. It is a force in nature that as yet we don't understand. Originally it was employed as a destroyer of sewage, but it was abandoned as too expensive. You are the richest country in the world, and one of the most densely populated. Yet you are covering the land with jerry-built houses, the drainages of which will frequently want looking to. And your only way of discovering this is when a bad epidemic breaks out. Everything is too expensive. You will be a jerry-built people in a jerry-built empire. And your local authorities adopt some cheap system and then smile at the ratepayers and call for applause. Electricity will save all danger. It is dear at first, but it is far cheaper in the long run.'

'If you will be so good as to get to the point,' the chairman suggested.

Label smiled pityingly. He was like a schoolmaster addressing a form of little boys.

'The remedy is simple,' he said. 'I propose to have a couple of 10,000 volts wires discharging their current into the ground here and there over the affected area. Inoculation against the trouble is all very well, but it is not permanent and there is always danger whilst the source of it remains. I propose to remove the evil. Don't ask me what the process is, don't ask me what wonderful action takes place. All I know is that some marvellous agency gets to work and that a huge mound of live disease is rendered safe and innocent as pure water. And I want these things now, I don't want long sittings and reports and discussions. Let me work the cure and you can have all the talking and sittings you like afterwards.'

Label got his own way; he would have got anything he liked at that moment. London was quiet and humble and in a mood to be generous.

* * *

Label stood over the cutting whence he had procured the original specimen of all the mischief. He was a little quiet and subdued, but his eyes shone and his hand was a trifle unsteady. His fingers trembled as he took up a fragment of the blue-grey stratum and broke it up.

'Marvellous mystery,' he cried. 'We placed the wires in the earth and that great, silent, powerful servant has done the rest. Underground the current radiates, and, as it radiates, the source of the disease grows less and less until it ceases to be altogether. Only try this in the tainted areas of all towns and in a short time disease of all kinds would cease for ever.'

'You are sure that stuff is wholesome, now?' Hubert asked.

'My future on it,' Label cried. 'Wait till we get it under the microscope. I am absolutely confident that I am correct.'

And he was.

The Four Days' Night

Fred M. White

I

The weather forecast for London and the Channel was 'light airs, fine generally, milder'. Further down the fascinating column Hackness read that 'the conditions over Europe generally favoured a continuance of the large anti-cyclonic area, the barometer steadily rising over Western Europe, sea smooth, readings being unusually high for this time of the year.' Martin Hackness, B.Sc., London, thoughtfully read all this and more. The study of the meteorological reports was part of his religion almost. In the laboratory at the back of his sitting-room were all kinds of weird-looking instruments for measuring sunshine and wind pressure, the weight of atmosphere and the like. Hackness trusted before long to be able to foretell a London fog with absolute accuracy, which, when you come to think of it, would be an exceedingly useful matter. In his queer way Hackness described himself as a fog specialist. He hoped some day to prove himself a fog-disperser, which is another word for a great public benefactor.

The chance he was waiting for seemed to have come at last. November had set in, mild and dull and heavy. Already there had been one or two of the dense fogs under which London periodically groans and does nothing to avert. Hackness was clear-sighted enough to see a danger here that might some day prove a hideous national disaster. So far as he could ascertain from his observations and readings, London was in for another dense fog within the next four-and-twenty hours.

Unless he was greatly mistaken, the next fog was going to be a particularly thick one. He could see the yellow mists gathering in Gower Street, as he sat at his breakfast.

The door flew open and a man rushed in without even an apology. He was a little man, with sharp, clean-shaven features, an interrogative nose and assertive pince-nez. He was not unlike Hackness, minus his calm ruminative manner. He fluttered a paper in his hand like a banner.

'It's come, Hackness,' he cried. 'It was bound to come sometime. It's all here in a late edition of the *Telegraph*. We must go and see it.'

He flung himself into an armchair.

'Do you remember,' he said, 'the day in the winter of 1898, the day that petroleum ship exploded? You and I were playing golf together on the Westgate links.'

Hackness nodded eagerly.

'I shall never forget it, Eldred,' he said, 'though I have forgotten the name of the ship. She was a big iron boat, and she caught fire about daybreak. Of her captain and her crew not one fragment was ever found.'

'It was perfectly still and the effect of that immense volume of dense black smoke was marvellous. Do you recollect the scene at sunset? It was like looking at half-a-dozen Alpine ranges piled one on the top of the other. The spectacle was not only grand, it was appalling, awful. Do you happen to recollect what you said at the time?'

There was something in Eldred's manner that roused Hackness.

'Perfectly well,' he cried. 'I pictured that awful canopy of sooty, fatty matter suddenly shut down over a great city by a fog. A fog would have beaten it down and spread it. We tried to imagine what might happen if that ship had been in the Thames, say at Greenwich.'

'Didn't you prophesy a big fog for today?'

'Certainly I did. And a recent examination of my instruments merely confirms my opinion. Why do you ask?'

'Because early this morning a fire broke out in the great petroleum storage tanks, down the river. Millions of gallons of oil are bound to burn themselves out – nothing short of a miracle can quench the fire, which will probably rage all through today and tomorrow. The fire-brigades are absolutely powerless – in the first place the heat is too awful to allow them to approach; in the second, water would only make things worse. It's one of the biggest blazes ever known. Pray Heaven, your fog doesn't settle down on the top of the smoke.'

Hackness turned away from his unfinished breakfast and struggled into an overcoat. There was a peril here that London little dreamt of. Out in the yellow streets newsboys were yelling of the conflagration down the Thames. People were talking of the disaster in a calm frame of mind between the discussion of closer personal matters.

'There's always the chance of a breeze springing up,' Hackness muttered. 'If it does, well and good, if not – but come along. We'll train it from Charing Cross.'

A little way down the river the mist curtain lifted. A round magnified sun looked down upon a dun earth. Towards the south-east a great black column rose high in the sky. The column appeared to be absolutely motionless; it broadened from an inky base like a grotesque mushroom.

'Fancy trying to breathe that,' Eldred muttered. 'Just think of the poison there. I wonder what that dense mass would weigh in tons. And it's been going on for five hours now. There's enough there to suffocate all London.'

Hackness made no reply. On the whole he was wishing himself well out of it. That pillar of smoke would rise for many more hours yet. At the same time here was his great opportunity. There were certain experiments that he desired to make and for which all things were ready.

They reached the scene of the catastrophe. Within a radius of five hundred yards the heat was intense. Nobody seemed to know the cause of the disaster beyond the general opinion that the oil gases had ignited.

And nothing could be done. No engine could approach near enough to do any good. Those mighty tanks and barrels filled with petroleum would have to burn themselves out.

The sheets of flame roared and sobbed. Above the flames rose the column of thick black smoke, with just the suspicion of a slight stagger to the westward. The inky vapour spread overhead like a pall. If Hackness's fog came now it meant a terrible disaster for London.

Further out in the country, where the sun was actually shining, people watched that great cloud with fearsome admiration. From a few miles beyond the radius it looked as if all the ranges of the world had been piled atop of London. The fog was gradually spreading along the south of the Thames, and away as far as Barnet to the north.

There was something in the stillness and the gloom that London did not associate with ordinary fogs.

Hackness turned away at length, conscious of his sketchy breakfast and the fact that he had been watching this thrilling spectacle for two hours.

'Have you thought of a way out?' Eldred asked. 'What are you going to do?'

'Lunch,' Hackness said curtly. 'After that I propose to see to my arrangements in Regent's Park. I've got Grimfern's aeroplane there, and a pretty theory about high explosives. The difficulty is to get the authorities to consent to the experiments. The police have absolutely forbidden experiments with high explosives, fired in the air above London. But perhaps I shall frighten them into it this time. Nothing would please me better than to see a breeze spring up, and yet on the other hand – '

'Then you are free tonight?' Eldred asked.

'No, I'm not. Oh, there will be plenty of time. I'm going with Sir Edgar Grimfern and his daughter to see Irving, that is if it is possible for anyone to see Irving tonight. I've got the chance of a lifetime at hand, but I wish that it was well over, Eldred my boy. If you come round about midnight – '

'I'll be sure to,' Eldred said eagerly. 'I'm going to be in this thing. And I want to know all about that explosive idea.'

2

Martin Hackness dressed with less than his usual care that evening. He even forgot that Miss Cynthia Grimfern had a strong prejudice in favour of black evening ties, and, usually, he paid a great deal of deference to her opinions. But he was thinking of other matters now. There was no sign of anything abnormal as Hackness drove along in the direction of Clarence Terrace. The night was more than typically yellow for the time of year, but there was no kind of trouble with the traffic, though down the river the fairway lay under a dense bank of cloud.

Hackness sniffed the air eagerly. He detected or thought he detected a certain acrid suggestion in the atmosphere. As the cab approached Trafalgar Square Hackness could hear shouts and voices raised high in protestation. Suddenly his cab seemed to be plunged into a wall of darkness.

It was so swift and unexpected that it came with the force of a blow. The horse appeared to have trotted into a bank of dense blackness. The wall had shut down so swiftly, blotting out a section of London, that Hackness could only gaze at it with mouth wide open.

Hackness hopped out of his cab hurriedly. So sheer and stark was the black wall that the horse was out of sight. Mechanically the driver reined back. The horse came back to the cab with the dazzling swiftness of a conjuring trick. A thin stream of breeze wandered from the direction of Whitehall. It was this air finding its way up the funnel formed by the sheet that cut off the fog to a razor edge.

'Been teetotal for eighteen years,' the cabman muttered, 'so that's all right. And what do you please to make of it, sir?'

Hackness muttered something incoherent. As he stood there, the black wall lifted like a stage curtain, and he found himself under the lee of an omnibus. In a dazed kind of way he patted the cabhorse on the flank. He looked at his hand. It was greasy and oily and grimy as if he had been in the engine-room of a big liner.

'Get on as fast as you can,' he cried. 'It was fog, just a little present from the burning petroleum. Anyway, it's gone now.'

True, the black curtain had lifted, but the atmosphere reeked with the odour of burning oil. The lamps and shop windows were splashed and mottled with something that might have passed for black snow. Traffic had been brought to a standstill for the moment, eager knots of pedestrians were discussing the situation with alarm and agitation, a man in evening dress was busily engaged in a vain attempt to remove sundry black patches from his shirt front.

Sir Edgar Grimfern was glad to see his young friend. Had Grimfern been comparatively poor, and less addicted to big game shooting, he would doubtless have proved a great scientific light. Anything with a dash of adventure fascinated him. He was enthusiastic on flying machines and aeroplanes generally. There were big workshops at the back of 119, Clarence Terrace, where Hackness put in a good deal of his spare time. Those two were going to startle the world presently.

Hackness shook hands thoughtfully with Cynthia Grimfern. There was a slight frown on her pretty intellectual face as she noted his tie.

'There's a large smut on it,' she remarked, 'and it serves you right.'

Hackness explained. He had a flattering audience. He told of the strange happening in Trafalgar Square and the majestic scene on the river. He gave a graphic account of the theory that he had built upon it. There was an animated discussion all through dinner.

'The moral of which is that we are going to be plunged into Cimmerian darkness,' Cynthia said, 'that is, if the fog comes down. If you think you are going to frighten me out of my evening's entertainment you are mistaken.'

All the same it had grown much darker and thicker as the trio drove off in the direction of the Lyceum Theatre. There were patches of dark acrid fog here and there like ropes of smoke into which figures passed and disappeared only to come out on the other side choking and coughing. So local were these swathes of fog that in a wide thoroughfare it was possible to partially avoid them. Festoons of vapour hung from one lampost to another, the air was filled with a fatty sickening odour.

'How nasty,' Cynthia exclaimed. 'Mr Hackness, please close that window. I am almost sorry that we started. What's that?'

There was a shuffling movement under the seat of the carriage, the quick bark of a dog; Cynthia's little fox terrier had stolen into the brougham. It was a favourite trick of his, the girl explained.

'He'll go back again,' she said. 'Kim knows that he has done wrong.'

That Kim was forgotten and discovered later on coiled up under the stall of his mistress was a mere detail. Hackness was too preoccupied to feel any uneasiness. He was only conscious that the electric lights were growing dim and yellow, and that a brown haze was coming between the auditorium and the stage. When the curtain fell on the third act it was hardly possible to see across the theatre. Two or three large heavy blots of some greasy matter fell on to the white shoulders of a lady in the stalls to be hastily wiped away by her companion. They left a long greasy smear behind.

'I can hardly breathe,' Cynthia gasped. 'I wish I had stopped at home. Surely those electric lights are going out.'

But the lights were merely being wrapped in a filament that every moment grew more and more dense. As the curtain went up again there was just the suspicion of a draught from the back of the stage, and the whole of it was smothered in a small brown cloud that left absolutely nothing to the view. It was impossible now to make out a single word of the programme, even when it was held close to the eyes.

'Hackness was right,' Grimfern growled. 'We had far better have stayed at home.'

Hackness said nothing. He had no pride in the accuracy of his forecast. Perhaps he was the only man in London who knew what the full force of this catastrophe meant. It grew so dark now that he could see no more than the mere faint suggestion of his fair companion, something was falling out of the gloom like black ragged snow. As the pall lifted just for an instant he could see the dainty dresses of the women absolutely smothered with the thick oily smuts. The reek of petroleum was stifling.

There was a frightened scream from behind, and a yell out of the ebony wall to the effect that somebody had fainted. Someone was speaking from the stage with a view to stay what might prove to be a dangerous panic. Another sombre wave filled the theatre and then it grew absolutely black, so black that a match held a foot or so from the nose could not be seen. One of the plagues of Egypt with all its horrors had fallen upon London.

'Let us try and make our way out,' Hackness suggested. 'Go quietly.'

Others seemed to be moved by the same idea. It was too black and dark for anything like a rush, so that a dangerous panic was out of the question. Slowly but surely the fashionable audience reached the vestibule, the hall, and the steps.

Nothing to be seen, no glimmer of anything, no sound of traffic. The destroying angel might have passed over London and blotted out all human life. The magnitude of the disaster had frightened London's millions as it fell.

3

A city of the blind! Six millions of people suddenly deprived of sight! The disaster sounds impossible – a nightmare, the wild vapourings of a diseased imagination – and yet why not? Given a favourable atmospheric condition, something colossal in the way of a fire, and there it is. And there, somewhere folded away in the book of Nature, is the simple remedy.

Such thoughts as these flashed through Hackness's mind as he stood under the portico of the Lyceum Theatre, quite helpless and inert for the moment.

But the darkness was thicker and blacker than anything he had ever imagined. It was absolutely the darkness that could be felt. Hackness could hear the faint scratching of matches all around him, but there was no glimmer of light anywhere. And the atmosphere was thick, stifling, greasy. Yet it was not quite as stifling as perfervid imagination suggested. The very darkness suggested suffocation. Still, there was air, a sultry light breeze that set the murk in motion, and mercifully brought from some purer area the oxygen that made life possible. There was always air, thank God, to the end of the Four Days' Night.

Nobody spoke for a time. Not a sound of any kind could be heard. It was odd to think that a few miles away the country might be sleeping under the clear stars. It was terrible to think that hundreds of thousands of people must be standing lost in the streets and yet near to home.

A little way off a dog whined, a child in a sweet refined voice cried that she was lost. An anxious mother called in reply. The little one had been forgotten in the first flood of that awful darkness. By sheer good luck Hackness was enabled to locate the child. He could feel that her wraps were rich and costly, though the same fatty slime was upon them. He caught the child up in his arms and yelled that he had got her. The mother was close by, yet full five minutes elapsed before Hackness blundered upon her. Something was whining and fawning about his feet.

He called upon Grimfern, and the latter answered in his ear. Cynthia was crying pitifully and helplessly. Some women there were past that.

'For Heaven's sake tell us what we are to do,' Grimfern gasped. 'I flatter myself that I know London well, but I couldn't find my way home in this.'

Something was licking Hackness's hand. It was the dog Kim. There was just a chance here. He tore his handkerchief in strips and knotted it together. One end he fastened to the little dog's collar.

'It's Kim,' he explained. 'Tell the dog "home". There's just a chance that he may lead you home. We're very wonderful creatures, but one sensible dog is worth a million of us tonight. Try it.'

'And where are you going?' Cynthia asked. She spoke high, for a babel of voices had broken out. 'What will become of you?'

'Oh, I am all right,' Hackness said with an affected cheerfulness. 'You see, I was fairly sure that this would happen sooner or later. So I pigeon-holed a way of dealing with the difficulty. Scotland Yard listened, but thought me a bore all the same. This is the situation where I come in.'

Grimfern touched the dog and urged him forward.

Kim gave a little bark and a whine. His muscular little body strained at the leash.

'It's all right,' Grimfern cried. 'Kim understands. That queer little pill-box of a brain of his is worth the finest intellect in England tonight.'

Cynthia whispered a faint good-night, and Hackness was alone. As he stood there in the blackness the sense of suffocation was overwhelming. He essayed to smoke a cigarette, but he hadn't the remotest idea whether the thing was alight or not. It had no taste or flavour.

But it was idle to stand there. He must fight his way along to Scotland Yard to persuade the authorities to listen to his ideas. There was not the slightest danger of belated traffic, no sane man would have driven a horse in such dense night. Hackness blundered along without the faintest idea to which point of the compass he was facing.

If he could only get his bearings he felt that he should be all right. He found his way into the Strand at length; he fumbled up against someone and asked where he was. A hoarse voice responded that the owner fancied it was somewhere in Piccadilly.

There were scores of people in the streets standing about talking desperately, absolute strangers clinging to one another for sheer craving for company to keep the frayed senses together. The most fastidious clubman there would have chummed with the toughest Hooligan rather than have his own thoughts for company.

Hackness pushed his way along. If he got out of his bearings he adopted the simple experiment of knocking at the first door he came to and asking where he was. His reception was not invariably enthusiastic, but it was no time for nice distinctions. And a deadly fear bore everybody down.

At last he came to Scotland Yard, as the clocks proclaimed that it was half-past one. Ghostly official voices told Hackness the way to Inspector Williamson's office, stern officials grasped him by the arm and piloted him up flights of stairs. He blundered over a chair and sat down. Out of the black cavern of space Inspector Williamson spoke.

'I am thankful you have come. You are just the man I most wanted to see. I want my memory refreshed over that scheme of yours,' he said. 'I didn't pay very much attention to it at the time.'

'Of course you didn't. Did you ever know an original prophet who wasn't laughed at? Still, I don't mind confessing that I hardly anticipated anything quite so awful as this. The very density of it makes some parts of my scheme impossible. We shall have to shut our teeth and endure it. Nothing really practical can be done so long as this fog lasts.'

'But, man alive, how long will it last?'

'Perhaps an hour or perhaps a week. Do you grasp what an awful calamity faces us?'

Williamson had no reply. So long as the fog lasted, London was in a state of siege, and, not only this, but every house in it was a fort, each depending upon itself for supplies. No bread could be baked, no meal could be carried round, no milk or vegetables delivered so long as the fog remained. Given a day or two of this and thousands of families would be on the verge of starvation. It was not a pretty picture that Hackness drew, but Williamson was bound to agree with every word of it.

These two men sat in the darkness till what should have been the dawn, whilst scores of subordinates were setting some sort of machinery in motion to preserve order.

Hackness stumbled home to his rooms about nine o'clock in the morning, without having succeeded in persuading the officials to grant him permission to experiment. Mechanically he felt for his watch to see the time. The watch was gone. Hackness smiled grimly. The predatory classes had not been quite blind to the advantages of the situation.

There was no breakfast for Hackness for the simple reason that it had been found impossible to light the kitchen fire. But there was a loaf of bread, some cheese, and a knife. Hackness fumbled for his bottled beer and a glass. There were many worse breakfasts in London that morning.

He woke presently, conscious that a clock was striking nine. After some elaborate thought and the asking of a question or two from another inmate of the house, Hackness found to his horror that he had slept the clock round nearly twice. It was nine o'clock in the morning, twenty-three hours since he had fallen asleep! And, so far as Hackness could judge, there were no signs of the fog's abatement.

He changed his clothes and washed the greasy slime off him so far as cold water and soap would allow. There were plenty of people in the streets, hunting for food for the most part; there were tales of people found dead in the gutters. Progression was slow but the utter absence of traffic rendered it safe and possible. Men spoke with bated breath, the weight of the great calamity upon them.

News that came from a few miles outside the radius spoke of clear skies and bright sunshine. There was a great deal of sickness, and the doctors had more than they could manage, especially with the young and the delicate.

And the calamity looked like getting worse. Six million people were breathing what oxygen there was. Hackness returned to his chambers to find Eldred awaiting him.

'This can't go on, you know,' the latter said tersely.

'Of course it can't,' Hackness replied. 'All the air is getting exhausted. Come with me down to Scotland Yard and help to try and persuade Williamson to test my experiment.'

'What! Do you mean to say he is still obstinate?'

'Well, perhaps he feels different today. Come along.'

Williamson was in a chastened frame of mind. He had no optimistic words when Hackness suggested that nothing less than a violent meteor-ological disturbance would clear the deadly peril of the fog away. It was time for drastic remedies, and if they failed things would be no worse than before.

'But can you manage it?' Williamson asked.

'I fancy so,' Hackness replied. 'It's a risk, of course, but everything has been ready for a long time. We could start after tomorrow midnight, or any time for that matter.'

'Very well,' Williamson sighed with the air of a man who realises that after all the tooth must come out. 'If this produces a calamity I shall be asked to send in my resignation. If I refuse – '

'If you refuse there is more than a chance that you won't want another situation,' Hackness said grimly. 'Let's get the thing going, Eldred.'

They crawled along through the black suffocating darkness, feeble, languid, and sweating at every pore. There was a murky closeness in the vitiated atmosphere that seemed to take all the strength and energy away. At any other time the walk to Clarence Terrace would have been a pleasure, now it was a penance. They found their objective after a deal of patience and trouble. Hackness yelled in the doorway. There was a sound of footsteps and Cynthia Grimfern spoke.

'Ah, what a relief it is to know that you are all right,' she said. 'I pictured all sorts of horrors happening to you. Will this never end, Martin?'

She cried softly in her distress. Hackness felt for her hand and pressed it tenderly.

'We are going to try my great theory,' he said. 'Eldred is with me, and we have got Williamson's permission to operate with the aerophane. Where is Sir Edgar?'

Grimfern was in the big workshop in the garden. As best he could, he was fumbling over some machinery for the increase of power in electric lighting. Hackness took a queer-looking lamp with double reflectors from his pocket.

'Shut off that dynamo,' he said, 'and give me the flex. I've got a little idea here Bramley, the electrician, lent me. With that 1000-volt generator of yours I can get a light equal to 40,000 candles. There.'

Flick went the switch, and the others staggered back with their hands to their eyes. The great volume of light, impossible to face under ordinary circumstances, illuminated the workshop with a faint glow like a winter's dawn. It was sufficient for all practical purpose, but to eyes that had seen absolutely nothing for two days and nights very painful.

Cynthia laughed hysterically. She saw the men grimed and dirty, blackened and greasy, as if they were fresh from a stoker's hole in a tropical sea. They saw a tall, graceful girl in the droll parody of a kitchen-maid who had wiped a tearful face with a blacklead brush.

But they could see. Along the whole floor of the workshop lay a queer, cigar-shaped instrument with grotesque wings and a tail like that of a fish, but capable of being turned in any direction. It seemed a problem to get this strange-looking monster out of the place, but as the whole of the end of the workshop was constructed to pull out, the difficulty was not great.

This was Sir Edgar Grimfern's aerophane, built under his own eyes and with the assistance of Hackness and Eldred.

'It will be a bit of risk in the dark,' Sir Edgar said thoughtfully.

'It will, sir, but I hope it will mean the saving of a great city,' Hackness remarked. 'We shall have no difficulty in getting up, and as to the getting down, don't forget that the atmosphere a few miles beyond the outskirts of London is quite clear. If only the explosives are strong enough!'

'Don't theorise,' Eldred snapped. 'We've got a good day's work before we start. And there is no time to be lost.'

'Luncheon first,' Sir Edgar suggested, 'served in here. It will be plain and cold; but, thank goodness, there is plenty of it. My word, after that awful darkness what a blessed thing light is once more!'

* * *

Two hours after midnight the doors of the workshop were pulled away and the aerophane was dragged on its carriage into the garden. The faint glimmer of light only served to make the blackness all the thicker. The three men waved their hands silently to Cynthia and jumped in. A few seconds later and they were whirred and screwed away into the suffocating fog.

4

London was holding out doggedly and stolidly. Scores of houses watched and waited for missing ones who would never return, the streets and the river had taken their toll, in open spaces, in the parks, and on the heaths many were shrouded. But the long black night held its secret well. There had been some ruffianism and plundering at first. But what was the use of plunder to the thief who could not dispose of his booty, who could not exchange a rare diamond for so much as a mouthful of bread? Some of them could not even find their way home, they had to remain in the streets where there was the dread of the lifting blanket and the certainty of punishment with the coming of the day.

But if certain houses mourned the loss of inmates, some had more than their share. Belated women, frightened business girls, caught in the fog had sought the first haven at hand, and there they were free to remain. There were sempstresses in Mayfair, and delicately-nurtured ladies in obscure Bloomsbury boarding-houses. Class distinction seemed to be remote as the middle ages.

Scotland Yard, the local authorities, and the County Council had worked splendidly together. Provisions were short, though a good deal of bread and milk had with greatest difficulty been imported from outside the radius of the scourge. Still the poor were suffering acutely, and the cries of frightened children were heard in every street. A few days more and the stoutest nerves must give way. Nobody could face such a blackness and retain their senses for long. London was a city of the blind. Sleep was the only panacea for the creeping madness.

There were few deeds of violence done. The most courageous, the most bloodthirsty man grew mild and gentle before the scourge. Desperate men prowled about in search of food, but they wanted nothing else. Certainly they would not have attempted violence to get it.

Alarmists predicted that in a few hours life in London would be impossible. For once they had reason on their side. Every hour the air, or what passed for air, grew more poisonous. Men fancied a city with six million corpses!

The calamity would kill big cities altogether. No great mass of people would ever dare to congregate together again where manufacturers made a hideous atmosphere overhead. It would be a great check upon the race for gold. There was much justification for this morbid condition of public feeling.

So the third long weary day dragged to an end, and people went to bed in the old mechanical fashion hoping for better signs in the morning. How many weary years since they had last seen the sunshine, colour, anything?

There was a change from the black monotony some time after dawn. Most people had nearly lost all sense of time when dawn ought to have been. People were struggling back to their senses again, trying to pierce the thick curtain that held everything in bondage. Doors were opened and restless ones passed into the street.

Suddenly there was a smiting shock from somewhere, a deafening splitting roar in the ears, and central London shivered. It was as if some mighty explosion had taken place in space, and as if the same concussion had been followed by a severe shock of earthquake.

Huge buildings shook and trembled, furniture was overturned, and from every house came the smash of glass. Was this merely a fog or some thick curtain that veiled the approaching dissolution of the world? People stood still, trembling and wondering. And before the question was answered, a strange thing, a modern miracle happened. A great arc of the blackness peeled off and stripped the daylight bare before their startled eyes.

5

The work was full of a real live peril, but the aerophane was cast loose at length. Its upward motion was slow, perhaps owing to the denseness of the atmosphere. For some time nobody spoke. Something seemed to oppress their breathing. They were barely conscious of the faint upward motion. If they only rose perfectly straight all would be well.

'That's a fine light you had in the workshop,' said Eldred. 'But why not have established a few hundreds of them –'

'All over London,' Hackness cut in, 'for the simple reason that the lamp my friend lent me is the only one in existence. It is worked at a dangerous voltage too.'

The upward motion continued. The sails of the aerophane rustled slightly. Grimfern drew a deep breath.

'Air,' he gasped, 'real pure fresh air! Do you notice it?'

The cool sweetness of it filled their lungs. The sudden effect was almost intoxicating. A wild desire to laugh and shout and sing came over them. Then gradually three human faces and a ghostly shaped aerophane emerged out of nothingness. They could see one another plainly now; they felt the upward rush; they were passing through a misty envelope that twisted and curled like live ropes. Another minute and they were beyond the fog belt.

They looked at one another and laughed. All three of them were blackened and grimed and greasy, smothered from head to foot in fatty soot flakes. Three more disreputable looking ruffians it would have been hard to imagine. There was something grotesque in the reflection that every Londoner was the same.

It was light now, broad daylight, with a round globe of sun climbing up out of the pearly mists in the East. They revelled in the brightness and the light. Below them lay the thick layers of fog that would be a shroud in earnest if nothing came to dispel it.

'We're a thousand feet above the city,' Eldred said presently. 'We had better pay out five hundred feet of cable.'

To a hook at the end of a flexible wire Hackness attached a large bomb filled with a certain high explosive. Through the eye of the hook another wire – an electric one – was attached. The whole thing was carefully lowered to the full extent of the cable. Two anxious faces peered from the car. Grimfern appeared to be playing carelessly with a polished switch spliced into the wire. But his hands were shaking.

Eldred nodded. He had no words to spare just then.

Grimfern's forefinger pressed the polished button, there was a snap and almost immediately a roar and a rush of air that set the aerophane rocking violently. All about them the clouds were spinning, below the foggy envelope was twisted and torn as smoke is blown away from a huge stack by a high wind.

'Look,' Hackness yelled. 'Look at that!'

He pointed downwards. The force of the explosion had literally torn a hole in the dense foggy curtain. The brilliant light of day shone through down into London as from a gigantic skylight.

This is what the amazed inhabitants of central London saw as they rushed out of their houses after what they imagined to be a shock of earth-quake. The effect was weird, wonderful, one never to be forgotten. From a radius of half a mile from St Paul's, London was flooded with brilliant light. People rubbed their eyes, unable to face the sudden and blinding glare. They gasped and thrilled with exultation as a column of fresh sweet air rushed to fill the vacuum. As yet they knew nothing of the cause.

That brilliant shaft of light showed strange things. Every pavement was black as ink, the fronts of the houses looked as if they had been daubed over with pitch. The roads were dark with fatty soot. On Ludgate Hill were dozens of vehicles from which the horses had been detached. There were numerous motor cars apparently lacking owners. A pick-pocket sat in the gutter with a pile of costly trinkets about him, gems that glittered in the mud. These things had been collected before the fog grew beyond endurance. Now they were about as useful to the thief as an elephant might have been.

At the end of five minutes the curtain fell again. The flying, panic-stricken pickpocket huddled down once more with a frightened curse.

But London was no longer alarmed. A passing glimpse of the aero-phane had been seen, and better informed folks knew what was taking place. Presently another explosion followed, tearing the curtain away over Hampstead; for the next two hours the explosions continued at short intervals. There were tremendous outbursts of cheering whenever the relief came.

Presently a little light seemed to be coming. Ever and again it was possible for a man to see his hands before his face. Above the fog banks a wrack of cloud had gathered, the aerophane was coated with a glittering mist. An hour before it had been perfectly fair overhead. Then it began to rain in earnest. The constant explosions had summoned up and brought down the rain as the heavy discharge of artillery used to do in the days of the Boer War.

It came down in a drenching stream that wetted the occupants of the aerophane to the skin. They did not seem to mind. The exhilaration of the fresh sweet air was still in their veins, they worked on at their bombs till the last ounce of the high explosives was exhausted.

And the rain was falling over London. Wherever a hole was torn in the curtain, the rain was seen to fall – black rain as thick as ink and quite as disfiguring. The whole city wore a suit of mourning.

'The cloud is passing away,' Eldred cried. 'I can see the top of St Paul's.'

Surely enough, the cross seemed to lift skyward. Bit by bit and inch by inch the panorama of London slowly unfolded itself. Despite the sooty flood – a flood gradually growing cleaner and sweeter every mom-ent – the streets were filled with people gazing up in fascination at the aerophane.

The tumult of their cheers came upwards. It was their thanks for the forethought and scientific knowledge that had proved to be the salvation of London. As a matter of fact, the high explosives had only been the indirect means of preserving countless lives. The conjuring up of that heavy rain had been the real salvation. It had condensed the fog and beaten it down to earth in a sooty flow of water. It was a heavy, sloppy, gloomy day, such as London ever enjoys the privilege of grumbling over, but nobody grumbled now. The blessed daylight had come back, it was possible to fill the lungs with something like pure air once more, and to realise the simple delight of living.

Nobody minded the rain, nobody cared an atom for the knowledge that he was a little worse and a little more grimy than the dirtiest sweep alive. What did it matter so long as everybody was alike? Looking down, the trio in the aerophane could see London grow mad, grave men skip-ping about in the rain like schoolboys at the first fall of snow.

'We had better get down,' said Grimfern. 'Otherwise we shall have an ovation ready for us, and, personally, I should prefer a breakfast. In a calm like this we need not have any difficulty in making Regent's Park safely.'

The valve was opened and the great car dropped like a flashing bird. They saw the rush in the streets, they could hear the tramp of feet now. They dropped at length in what looked like a yelling crowd of demented Hottentots.

6

The aerophane was safely housed once more, the yelling mob had de-parted. London was bent upon one of its occasional insane holidays. The pouring rain did not matter one jot – had not the rain proved to be the salvation of the great city? What did it matter that the streets were black and the people blacker still? The danger was averted. 'We will go out and explore presently,' said Grimfern. 'Meanwhile, breakfast. A thing like this must never occur again, Hackness.' Hackness sincerely hoped not. Cynthia Grimfern came out to meet them. A liberal application of soap and water had rendered her sweet and fair, but it was impossible to keep clean for long. Everywhere lay evidences of the fog.

'It's lovely to be able to see and breathe once more,' she said. 'Last night every moment I felt as if I must be suffocated. Today it is like suddenly finding Paradise.'

'A sooty paradise,' Grimfern growled.

Cynthia laughed a little hopelessly.

'It's dreadful,' she said. 'I have had no table-cloth laid, it is useless. But the table itself is clean, and that is something. I don't think London will ever be perfectly clean again.'

The reek was still upon the great city, the taint of it hung upon the air. By one o'clock it had ceased raining and the sky cleared A startled sun looked down on strange things. There was a curious thickness about the trees in Regent's Park, they were as black as if they had been painted. The pavements were greasy and dangerous to pedestrians in a hurry.

There was a certain jubilation still to be observed, but the black melancholy desolation was bound to depress the most exuberant spirits. For the last three days everything had been at a standstill.

In the thickly populated districts the mortality amongst little children had been alarmingly high. Those who had any tendency to lung or throat or chest troubles died like flies before the first breath of frost. The evening papers, coming out as usual, a little late in the day, had many a gruesome story to tell. It was the harvest of the scare-line journalist, and he lost no chance. He scented his gloomy copy and tracked it down unerringly.

Over two thousand children – to say nothing of elderly people – had died in the East End. The very small infants had had no chance at all.

The Lord Mayor promptly started a Mansion House fund. There would be work and to spare presently. Meanwhile tons upon tons of machinery stood idle until it could be cleaned; all the trade of London was disorganised.

The river and the docks had taken a dreadful toll. Scores of labourers and sailors overtaken by the sudden scourge, had blundered into the water to be seen no more. The cutting off of the railways and other communications that brought London its daily bread had produced a temporary, but no less painful lack of provisions.

'It's a lamentable state of things,' Grimfern said moodily as the two trudged back to Regent's Park later in the evening. It was impossible to get a cab for the simple reason that there was not one in London fit to be used. 'But I don't see how we are going to better it. We can dispel the fogs, but not before they have done terrible damage.'

'There is an easy way out of the difficulty,' Eldred said quietly.

The others turned eagerly to listen. As a rule Eldred did not speak until he had thought the matter deliberately out.

'Abolish all fires throughout the Metropolitan area,' he said. 'In time it will have to be done. All London must warm itself and cook its food and drive all its machinery by electric power. Then it will be one of the healthiest towns in the universe. Everything done by electric power. No thousands of chimneys belching forth black poisonous smoke, but a clear, pure atmosphere. In towns like Brighton, where the local authorities have grappled the question in earnest, electric power is half the cost of gas.

'If only London combined it would be less than that. No dirt, no dust, no smell, no smoke! The magnificent system at Brighton never cost the ratepayers anything, indeed a deal of the profit has gone to the relief of the local burdens. Perhaps this dire calamity will rouse London to a sense of its dangers – but I doubt it.'

Eldred shook his head despondingly at the dark chaos of the park. Perhaps he was thinking of the victims that the disaster had claimed. The others had followed sadly, and Grimfern, leading the way into his house banged the door on the darkening night.

The Invisible Force

Fred M. White

*A story of what might happen in the days to come, when underground
London is tunnelled in all directions for electric railways, if an explosion
should take place in one of the tubes*

I

It seemed as if London had solved one of her great problems at last. The
communication difficulty was at an end. The first-class ticket-holders
no longer struggled to and from business with fourteen fellow-sufferers
in a third-class carriage. There were no longer any particularly favoured
suburbs, nor were there isolated localities where it took as long getting
to the City as an express train takes between London and Swindon. The
pleasing paradox of a man living at Brighton because it was nearer to his
business than Surbiton had ceased to exist. The tubes had done away
with all that.

There were at least a dozen hollow cases running under London in all
directions. They were cool and well ventilated, the carriages were brilliantly lighted, the various loops were properly equipped and managed.

All day long the shining funnels and bright platforms were filled
with passengers. Towards midnight the traffic grew less, and by half-
past one o'clock the last train had departed. The all-night service was
not yet.

It was perfectly quiet now along the gleaming core that lay buried
under Bond Street and St James's Street, forming the loop running
below the Thames close by Westminster Bridge Road and thence to the
crowded Newington and Walworth districts. Here a portion of the roof
was under repair.

The core was brilliantly lighted; there was no suggestion of fog or
gloom. The general use of electricity had disposed of a good deal of
London's murkiness; electric motors were applied now to most manufactories and workshops. There was just as much gas consumed as ever,
but it was principally used for heating and culinary purposes. Electric
radiators and cookers had not yet reached the multitude; that was a
matter of time.

In the flare of the blue arc lights a dozen men were working on the dome of the core. Something had gone wrong with a water-main over-head, the concrete beyond the steel belt had cracked, and the moisture had corroded the steel plates, so that a long strip of the metal skin had been peeled away, and the friable concrete had fallen on the rails. It had brought part of the crown with it, so that a maze of large and small pipes was exposed to view.

'They look like the reeds of an organ,' a raw engineer's apprentice remarked to the foreman. 'What are they?'

'Gas mains, water, electric light, telephone, goodness knows what,' the foreman replied. 'They branch off here, you see.'

'Fun to cut them,' the apprentice grinned. The foreman nodded ab-sently. He had once been a mischievous boy, too. The job before him looked a bigger thing than he had expected. It would have to be patched up till a strong gang could be turned on to the work. The raw apprentice was still gazing at the knot of pipes. What fun it would be to cut that water-main and flood the tunnels!

In an hour the scaffolding was done and the débris cleared away. Tomorrow night a gang of men would come and make the concrete good and restore the steel rim to the dome. The tube was deserted. It looked like a polished, hollow needle, lighted here and there by points of dazzling light.

It was so quiet and deserted that the falling of a big stone reverberated along the tube with a hollow sound. There was a crack, and a section of piping gave way slightly and pressed down upon one of the electric mains. A tangled skein of telephone wires followed. Under the strain the electric cable parted and snapped. There was a long, sliding, blue flame, and instantly the tube was in darkness. A short circuit had been established somewhere. Not that it mattered, for traffic was absolutely suspended now, and would not be resumed again before daylight. Of course, there were the workmen's very early trains, and the Covent Garden market trains, but they did not run over this section of the line. The whole darkness reeked with the whiff of burning indiarubber. The moments passed on drowsily.

Along one side of Bond Street the big lamps were out. All the lights on one main switch had gone. But it was past one o'clock now, and the thing mattered little. These accidents occurred sometimes in the best-regulated districts, and the defect would be made good in the morning.

It was a little awkward, though, for a great State ball was in progress at Buckingham Palace. Supper was over, the magnificent apartments were brilliant with light dresses and gay uniforms. The shimmer and fret of diamonds flashed back to lights dimmer than themselves. There was a slide of feet over the polished floors. Then, as if some unseen force had cut the bottom of creation, light and gaiety ceased to be, and darkness fell like a curtain.

There were a few cries of alarm from the swift suddenness of it. To eyes accustomed to that brilliant glow the gloom was Egyptian. It seemed as if some great catastrophe had happened. But common-sense reasserted itself, and the brilliant gathering knew that the electric light had failed.

There were quick commands, and spots of yellow flame sprang out here and there in the great desert of the night. How faint and feeble, and yellow and flaring, the lights looked! The electrician down below was puzzled, for, so far as he could see, the fuses in the meters were intact. There was no short circuit so far as the Palace was concerned. In all probability there had been an accident at the generating stations; in a few minutes the mischief would be repaired.

But time passed, and there was no welcome return of the flood of crystal light.

'It is a case for all the candles,' the Lord Chamberlain remarked; 'fortunately the old chandeliers are all fitted. Light the candles.'

It was a queer, grotesque scene, with all that wealth of diamonds and glitter of uniforms and gloss of satins, under the dim suggestion of the candles. And yet it was enjoyable from the very novelty of it. Nothing could be more appropriate for the minuet that was in progress.

'I feel like one of my own ancestors,' a noble lord remarked. 'When they hit upon that class of candle I expect they imagined that the last possibility in the way of lighting had been accomplished. Is it the same outside, Sir George?'

Sir George Egerton laughed. He was fresh from the gardens.

'It's patchwork,' he said. 'So far as I can judge, London appears to be lighted in sections. I expect there is a pretty bad breakdown. My dear chap, do you mean to say that clock is right?'

'Half-past four, sure enough, and mild for the time of year. Did you notice a kind of rumbling under – Merciful Heavens, what is that?'

2

There was a sudden splitting crack as if a thousand rifles had been discharged in the ballroom. The floor rose on one side to a perilous angle, considering the slippery nature of its surface. Such a shower of white flakes fell from the ceiling that dark dresses and naval uniforms looked as if their wearers had been out in a snowstorm.

A yell proclaimed that one of the great crystal chandeliers was falling

Cracks and fissures started in the walls with pantomimic effect, on all sides could be heard the rattle and splinter of falling glass. A voice suddenly uprose in a piercing scream, a yell proclaimed that one of the great crystal chandeliers was falling. There was a rush and a rustle of skirts, and a quick vision of white, beautiful faces, and with a crash the great pendant came to the floor.

The whole world seemed to be oscillating under frightened feet, the palace was humming and thrumming like a harpstring. The panic was so great, the whole mysterious tragedy so sudden, that the bravest there had to battle for their wits. Save for a few solitary branches of candles, the big room was in darkness.

There were fifteen hundred of England's bravest, and fairest, and best, huddled together in what might be a hideous deathchamber for all they knew to the contrary. Women were clinging in terror to the men, the fine lines of class distinction were broken down. All were poor humanity now in the presence of a common danger.

In a little time the earth ceased to sway and rock, the danger was passing. A little colour was creeping back to the white faces again. Men and women were conscious that they could hear the beating of their own hearts. Nobody broke the silence yet, for speech seemed to be out of place.

'An earthquake,' somebody said at length. 'An earthquake, beyond doubt, and a pretty bad one at that. That accounts for the failure of the electric light. There will be some bad accidents if the gas mains are disturbed.'

The earth grew steady underfoot again, the white flakes ceased to fall. Amongst the men the spirit of adventure was rising; the idea of standing quietly there and doing nothing was out of the question.

Anyway, there could be no further thought of pleasure that night. There were many mothers there, and their uppermost thought was for home. Never, perhaps, in the history of royalty had there been so informal a breaking up of a great function. The King and Queen had retired some little time before – a kindly and thoughtful act under the circumstances. The women were cloaking and shawling hurriedly; they crowded out in search of their carriages with no more order than would have been obtained outside a theatre.

But there were remarkably few carriages in waiting. An idiotic footman who had lost his head in the sudden calamity sobbed out the information that Oxford Street and Bond Street were impassable, and that houses were down in all directions. No vehicles could come that way; the road was destroyed. As to the rest, the man knew nothing; he was frightened out of his life.

There was nothing for it but to walk. It wanted two good hours yet before dawn, but thousands of people seemed to be abroad. For a space of a mile or more there was not a light to be seen. Round Buckingham Palace the atmosphere reeked with a fine irritating dust, and was rendered foul and poisonous by the fumes of coal gas. There must have been a fearful leakage somewhere.

Nobody seemed to know what was the matter, and everybody was asking everybody else. And in the darkness it was very hard to locate the disaster. Generally, it was admitted that London had been visited by a dreadful earthquake. Never were the daylight hours awaited more eagerly.

'The crack of doom,' Sir George Egerton remarked to his companion, Lord Barcombe.

They were feeling their way across the park in the direction of the Mall.

'It's like a shuddering romance that I read a little time since. But I must know something about it before I go to bed. Let's try St James's Street – if there's any St James Street left.'

'All right,' Lord Barcombe agreed, 'I hope the clubs are safe. Is it wise to strike a match with all this gas reeking in the air?'

'Anything's better than the gas,' Sir George said tersely.

The vesta flared out in a narrow, purple circle. Beyond it was a glimpse of a seat with two or three people huddled on it. They were outcasts and companions in the grip of misfortune, but they were all awake now.

'Can any of you say what's happened?' Lord Barcombe asked.

'The world's come to an end, sir, I believe,' was the broken reply. 'You may say what you like, but it was a tremendous explosion. I saw a light like all the world ablaze over to the north, and then all the lights went out, and I've been waiting for the last trump to sound ever since.'

'Then you didn't investigate?' Lord Barcombe asked.

'Not me, sir. I seem to have struck a bit of solid earth where I am. And then it rained stones and pieces of brick and vestiges of creation. There's the half of a boiler close to you that dropped out of the sky. You stay where you are, sir.'

But the two young men pushed on. They reached what appeared to be St James's Street at length, but only by stumbling and climbing over heaps of débris.

The roadway was one mass of broken masonry. The fronts of some of the clubs had been stripped off as if a titanic knife had sliced them. It was like looking into one of the upholsterers' smart shops, where they display rooms completely furnished. There were gaps here and there where houses had collapsed altogether. Seeing that the road had ceased to exist, it seemed impossible that an earthquake could have done this thing. A great light flickered and roared a little way down the road. At an angle a gas main was tilted up like the spout of a teapot, upheaved and snapped from its twin pipes. This had caught fire in some way, so that for a hundred yards or so each way the thoroughfare was illuminated by a huge flare lamp.

It was a thrilling sight focused in that blue glare. It looked as if London had been utterly destroyed by a siege – as if thousands of well-aimed shells had exploded. Houses looked like tattered banners of brick and mortar. Heavy articles of furniture had been hurled into the street; on the other hand, little gimcrack ornaments still stood on tiny brackets.

A scared-looking policeman came staggering along.

'My man,' Lord Barcombe cried, 'what has happened?'

The officer pulled himself together and touched his helmet.

'It's dreadful, sir,' he sobbed. 'There has been an accident in the tubes; and they have been blown all to pieces.'

3

The constable, for the moment, had utterly lost his nerve. He stood there in the great flaring roar of the gas mains with a dazed expression that was pitiful.

'Can you tell us anything about it?' Lord Barcombe asked.

'I was in Piccadilly,' was the reply. 'Everything was perfectly quiet. and so far as I could see not a soul was in sight. Then I heard a funny rushing sound, just like the tear of an express train through a big, empty station. Yes, it was for all the world like a ghostly express train that you could hear and not see. It came nearer and nearer; the whole earth trembled just as if the train had gone mad in Piccadilly. It rushed past me down St James's Street, and after that there was an awful smash and a bang, and I was lying on my back in the middle of the road. All the lights that remained went out, and for a minute or two I was in that railway collision. Then, when I got my senses back, I blundered down here because of that big flaring light there; and I can't tell you, gentlemen, any more, except that the tube has blown up.'

Of that fact there was no question. There were piles of débris thrown high in one part and a long deep depression in another like a ruined dyke. A little further on the steel core of the tube lay bare with rugged holes ripped in it.

'Some ghastly electric catastrophe,' Sir George Egerton murmured.

It was getting light by this time, and it was possible to form some idea of the magnitude of the disaster. Some of the clubs in St James's Street still appeared to be intact, but others had suffered terribly. The heaps of tumbled masonry were powdered and glittering with broken glass and a few walls hung perilously over the pavement. And still the gas main roared on until the flame grew from purple to violet, and to straw colour before the coming dawn. If this same thing had happened all along the network of tubes London would be more or less a hideous ruin.

For the better part of Piccadilly things were brighter. Evidently the explosion had had a straight run here, for the road had been raised like some mighty zigzag molehill for many yards. The wood pavement scattered all over the place suggested a gigantic box of child's bricks strewn over a nursery floor. The tube had been forced up, its outer envelope of concrete broken so that the now twisted steel core might have been a black snake crawling down Piccadilly. Doubtless the expanding air had met with some obstacle in the tube under St James's Street, hence the terrible force of the explosion there.

There was quite a large crowd in Oxford Street. The whole roadway was wet; the gutters ran with the water from the broken pipes. The air was full of the odour of gas. All the clocks in the streets seemed to have gone mad. Lord Barcombe glanced at his own watch, to find that it was racing furiously.

The explosion had had a straight run here, for the road had been raised like some mighty zigzag molehill

'By Jove!' he whispered excitedly, 'we're in danger here. The air is full of electricity. I went over some works once and neglected to leave my watch behind me, and it played me the same prank. It affects the main-spring, you know.'

There were great ropes and coils of electric wire of high voltage crop-ping out of the ground here and there; coils attached to huge accumul-ators, and discharging murderous current freely. A dog, picking his way across the sopping street, trod on one of the wires, and instantly all that remained of the dog was what looked like a twisted bit of burnt skin and bone. It appealed to Sir George Egerton's imagination strongly.

'Poor little brute!' he murmured. 'It might have happened to you or me. Don't you know that a force that only gives a man a bad shock when he is standing on dry ground often kills him when the surface is wet? I wonder if we can get some indiarubber gloves and galoshes hereabouts. After that gruesome sight, I shall be afraid to put one foot before the other.'

Indeed, the precaution was a necessary one. A horse attached to a cab came creeping over the blocked streets; the animal slipped on a grating connected with the ventilation of the drains, and a fraction of a second later there was no horse in existence. The driver sat on his perch, white and scared.

'The galoshes,' Lord Barcombe said hoarsely. 'Don't you move till we come back again, my man. And everybody keep out of the roadway.'

The cry ran along that the roadway meant instant death. The cabman sat there gibbering with terror. A little way further down was a rubber warehouse, with a fine selection of waders' and electricians' gloves in the window. With a fragment of concrete Sir George smashed in the win-dow, and took what he and Lord Barcombe required. They knew that they would be quite safe now.

More dead than alive the cabman climbed down from his seat and was carried to the pavement on Lord Barcombe's shoulder. The left side of his face was all drawn up and puckered, the left arm was useless.

'Apoplexy from the fright,' Sir George suggested.

'Not a bit of it,' Lord Barcombe exclaimed, 'It's a severe electric shock. Hold up.'

Gradually the man's face and arm ceased to twitch.

'If that's being struck by lightning,' he said, 'I don't want another dose. It was as if something had caught hold of me and frozen my heart in my body. I couldn't do a thing. And look at my coat.'

All up the left side the coat was singed so that at a touch the whole cloth fell to pieces. It was a strange instance of the freakishness of the invisible force. A great fear fell on those who saw. This intangible, unseen danger, with its awful swiftness, was worse than the worst that could be seen.

'Let's get home,' Lord Barcombe suggested. 'It's getting on my nerves. It's dreadful when all the terror is left to the imagination.'

4

Meanwhile no time was lost in getting to the root of the mischief.

The danger could not be averted by switching off the power altogether at the various electrical stations of the metropolis. At intervals along the tubes were immense accumulators which for the present could not be touched. It was these accumulators that rendered the streets such a ghastly peril.

It was the electrical expert to the County Council – Alton Rossiter – who first got on the track of the disaster. More than once before, the contact between gas and electricity had produced minor troubles of this kind. Gas that had escaped into man-holes and drains had been fired from the sparks caused by a short-circuit current wire. For some time, even as far back as 1895, instances of this kind had been recorded.

But how could the gas have leaked into the tube, seeing that it was a steel core with a solid bedding of concrete beyond? Unless an accident had happened when the tube was under repair, this seemed impossible.

The manager of the associated tubes was quite ready to afford every information to Mr Rossiter. The core had corroded in Bond Street in consequence of a settling of the earth caused by a leaky water-main. The night before, this had been located and the steel skin stripped off for the necessary repairs.

Mr Alton Rossiter cut the speaker short.

'Will you come to Bond Street with me, Mr Fergusson?' he said; 'we may be able to get into the tunnel there.'

Fergusson was quite ready. The damage in Bond Street was not so great, though the lift shaft was filled with débris, and it became necessary to cut a way into the station before the funnel was reached.

For a couple of hundred yards the tube was intact; beyond that point the fumes of gas were overpowering. A long strip of steel hung from the roof. Just where it was, a round, clean hole in the roadway rendered it possible to work and breathe there in spite of the gas fumes.

'We shall have to manage as best we can,' Rossiter muttered. 'For a little time at any rate, the gas of London must be cut off entirely. With broken mains all over the place the supply is positively dangerous. Look here.'

He pointed to the spot where the gas main had trended down and where a short-circuit wire had fused it. Here was the whole secret in a nutshell. A roaring gas main had poured a dense volume into the tube for hours; mixed with the air it had become one of the most powerful and deadly of explosives.

'What time does your first train start?' Rossiter asked.

'For the early markets, four o'clock,' Fergusson replied. 'In other words, we switch on the current from the accumulator stations at twenty minutes to four.'

'And this is one of your generating stations?'

'Yes. Of course I see exactly what you are driving at. Practically the whole circuit of tubes was more or less charged with a fearful admixture of gas and air. As soon as the current was switched on a spark exploded the charge. I fear, I very much fear, that you are right. If we can only find the man in charge here! But that would be nothing else than a miracle.'

All the same the operator in charge of the switches was close by. Fortunately for him the play of the current in the tube had carried the gases towards St James's Street. The explosion had lifted him out of his box, and for a time he lay stunned. Dazed and confused, he had climbed to the street and staggered into the shop of a chemist who was just closing the door upon a customer who had rung him up for a prescription.

But he could say very little. There had been an explosion directly he pulled down the first of the switches, and his memory was a blank after that.

Anyway, the cause of the disaster was found. To prevent further catastrophe notice was immediately given to the various gas companies to cut off the supplies at once. In a little time the whole disastrous length of the tube was free from that danger.

* * *

By the afternoon a committee had gone over the whole route. At the first blush it looked as if London had been half ruined. It was impossible yet to estimate the full extent of the damage. In St James's Street alone the loss was pretty certain to run into millions.

Down in Whitehall and Parliament Street, and by Westminster Bridge, the damage was terrible. Here sharp curves and angles had checked the rush of expanding air with the most dire results. Huge holes and ruts had been made in the earth, and houses had come down bodily.

Most of the people out in the streets by this time were properly equipped in indiarubber shoes and gloves. It touched the imagination strongly to know that between a man and hideous death was a thin sheet of rubber no thicker than a shilling. It was like walking over the crust of a slumbering volcano; like skating at top speed over very thin ice.

Towards the evening a thrilling whisper ran round. From Deptford two early specials had started to convey an annual excursion of five hundred men and their wives to Paddington, whence they were going to Windsor. It seemed impossible, incredible, that these could have been overlooked; but by five o'clock the dreadful truth was established. Those two specials had started; but what oblivion they had found – how lingering, swift, or merciful, nobody could tell.

5

There was a new horror. The story of those early special trains gave the final terror to the situation. Probably they had been blown to eternity. There was just one chance in a million that anybody had escaped. All the same something would have to be done to put the matter at rest.

Nobody knew what to do; everybody had lost their heads for the moment. It seemed hopeless from the very start. Naturally, the man that everybody looked to at the moment was Fergusson of the associated tubes. With him was Alton Rossiter, representing the County Council.

'But how to make a start?' the latter asked.

'We will start from Deptford,' said Fergusson. 'We must first ascertain the exact time that the train left Deptford, and the precise moment when the first explosion took place. Mind you, I believe there was a series of explosions. You see, there is always a fair amount of air in the tubes. When the inflowing gas met the cross currents of air, it would be diverted, or pocketed, so to speak. We should have a big pocket of the explosive, followed by a clear space.

'When the switches were turned on there would be sparks here and there all along the tubes. This means that practically simultaneously the mines would be fired; fired so quickly that the series of reports would sound like one big bang. That this must be so can be seen by the state of some of the streets. In some spots the tube has been wrenched bodily from the earth as easily as if it had been a gaspipe. And then, again, you have streets that do not show the slightest damage. You must agree with me that my theory is a correct one.'

'I do. But what are you driving at?'

'Well, I am afraid that my theory is a very forlorn one, but I give it for what it is worth. It's just possible, faintly possible, that those trains ran into a portion of the tube where there was no explosion at all. There were explosions behind them and in front of them, and of course the machinery would have been rendered useless instantly, so that the trains may be trapped with no ingress or outlet. I'm not in the least sanguine of finding anything but the aftermath of a fearful tragedy.

Anyway, our duty is pretty plainly before us – we must go to Deptford.
Come along.'

The journey to Deptford was no easy one. There were so many streets
up that locomotion was a difficult matter. And where the streets were
damaged there was danger. It was possible to use cycles, seeing that the
rubber tires formed non-conductors, and indiarubber gloves and shoes
allowed extra protection. But the mere suggestion of a spill was thrilling.
It might mean the tearing of a glove or the loss of a shoe, and then – well,
that did not bear thinking about.

'I never before properly appreciated the feelings of the man that Blon-
din used to carry on his back,' Rossiter said as the pair pushed steadily
through Bermondsey, 'but I can understand his emotions now.'

The roads, even where there was no danger, were empty. A man or
woman would venture timidly out and look longingly to the other side of
the road and then give up the idea of moving altogether. As a matter of
fact there was more of it safe than otherwise, but the risks were too awful.

6

Meanwhile something like an organised attempt was being made to
grapple with the evil: days must, of necessity, elapse before a proper
estimate of the damage could be made, to say nothing of the loss of life.

Nothing very great could be accomplished, however, until the huge
accumulators had been cleared and the deadly current switched off. So
far as the London area proper was concerned, Holborn Viaduct was the
point to aim at. In big vaults there, underground, were some of the
largest accumulators in the world. These would have to be rendered
harmless at any cost.

But the work was none so easy, seeing that the tube here was crushed
and twisted, and all about it was a knot of high-pressure cables deadly to
the touch. There was enough power here running to waste to destroy a
city. There were spaces that it was impossible to cross; and unfortunately
the danger could not be seen. There was no warning, no chance of escape
for the too hardy adventurer; he would just have stepped an inch beyond
the region of safety, and there would have been an end of him. No
wonder that the willing workers hesitated.

There was nothing for it but the blasting of the tube. True, this might
be attended with danger to such surrounding buildings as had weathered
the storm, but it was the desperate hour for desperate remedies. A big
charge of dynamite rent a long slit in the exposed length of tube, and a
workman taking his life in his hands entered the opening. There were

few spectators watching. It was too gruesome and horrible to stand there with the feeling that a slip either way might mean sudden death.

The workman, swathed from head to foot in indiarubber, disappeared from sight. It seemed a long time before he returned, so long that his companions gave him up for lost. Those strong able men who were ready to face any ordinary danger looked at one another askance. Fire, or flood, or gas, they would have endured, for under those circumstances the danger was tangible. But here was something that appealed horribly to the imagination. And such a death! The instantaneous fusion of the body to a dry charcoal crumb!

The workman, swathed from head to foot in indiarubber, disappeared from sight

But presently a grimed head looked out of the funnel. The face was white behind the dust, but set and firm. The pioneer called for lights.

So far he had been successful. He had found the accumulators buried under a heap of refuse. They were built into solid concrete below the level of the tube so that they had not suffered to any appreciable extent.

There was no longer any holding back. The party swung along the tube with lanterns, and candles flaring, they reached the vault where the great accumulators were situated. Under the piled rails and fragments of splintered wood, the shining marble switchboard could be seen.

But to get to it was quite another matter.

Once this was accomplished, one of the greatest dangers and horrors that paralysed labour would be removed. It was too much to expect that the average labourer would toil willingly, or even toil at all when the moving of an inch might mean instant destruction. And it was such a little thing to do after all. A child could have accomplished it; the pressure of a finger or two, the tiny action that disconnects a wire from the live power, and the danger would be no more, and the automatic accumulators rendered harmless.

But here were a few men, at any rate, who did not mean to be defeated. They toiled on willingly, and yet with the utmost caution; for the knots of cable wire under their feet and over their heads were like brambles in the forest. If one of these had given way, all of them might be destroyed. It was the kind of work that causes the scalp to rise and the heart to beat and the body to perspire even on the coldest day. Now and then a cable upheld by some débris would slip; there would be a sudden cry, and the workmen would skip back, breathing heavily.

It was like working a mine filled with rattlesnakes asleep; but gradually the mass of matter was cleared away and the switchboard disclosed. A few light touches, and a large area of London was free from a terrible danger. It was possible now to handle the big cables with impunity, for they were perfectly harmless.

There was no word spoken for a long time. The men were trembling with the reaction. One of them produced a large flask of brandy and handed it round. Not till they had all drunk did the leader of the expedition speak. 'How many years since yesterday morning?' he asked.

'Makes one feel like an old man,' another muttered.

They climbed presently into the street again, for there was nothing to be done here for the present. A few adventurous spectators heard the news that the streets were free from danger once more. The tidings spread in the marvellous way that such rumour carries, and in a little time the streets were packed with people.

7

When the two cyclists came to Deptford, they found that comparatively little damage had been done to the station there, beyond that the offices and platforms had been wrecked. A wounded man was found, who described how a mighty hurricane had roared down the tube ten minutes after the excursion trains had departed. Fergusson made a rapid calculation from the figures that the man supplied.

'The trains must have been near to Park Road Station,' he said, 'when the explosion occurred. There is just a chance that they may have run into a space free from gas, and that the explosion passed them altogether. Let us make for Park Road Station without delay, and we must try to pick up some volunteers as we go along.'

When they arrived at the scene they found that a big crowd had gathered. A rumour had spread that feeble voices had been heard down one of the ventilation gratings, calling for help. Fergusson and Rossiter reached the spot with difficulty.

'Get our fellows together,' whispered Fergusson. 'We can work now with impunity; and if any of those poor people down below are alive, we shall have them out in half-an-hour. If we only had some lights! Beg, borrow, or steal all the lanterns you can get.'

The nearest police-station solved that problem fast enough. A small gang of special experts moved upon Park Road Station whilst the mob was still struggling about the ventilation shaft, and in a little time the entrance was forced.

The station was a veritable wreck; but for two hundred yards the tunnel was clear before them. Then came a jammed wall of timber, the end of a railway carriage standing on end. The timbers were twisted, huge baulks of wood were bent like a bow. A way was soon made through the débris, and Fergusson yelled aloud.

To his delight a hoarse voice answered him. He yelled again and waved his lantern. Out of the velvety darkness of the tube a man staggered into the lane of light made by the lantern. He was a typical, thick-set workman, in his best clothes.

'So you've found us at last,' he said dully.

He appeared to be past all emotions. His eyes showed no gratitude, no delight. The horrors of the dark hours had numbed his senses.

'Is – is it very bad?' asked Rossiter.

'Many were killed,' the newcomer said in the same wooden voice. 'But the others are sitting in the carriages waiting for the end to come. The lights in the carriages helped us a bit, but after the first hour they

Out of the velvety darkness of the tube a man staggered into the lane of light

went out. Then one or two of us went up the line till it seemed to rise and twist as if it was going to climb into the sky, and by that we guessed that there had been a big explosion of some kind. So we tried the other way, and that was all blocked up with timber; and we knew then. The electricity was about, and – well, it wasn't a pretty sight, so we went back to the trains. When the lights went out we were all mad for a time, and – and – '

The speaker's lips quivered and shook – he burst into a torrent of tears. Rossiter patted him on the back approvingly. Those tears probably staved off stark insanity. The light of the lanterns went swinging on ahead now, and the trains began to pour out their freight of half-dead people. There were some with children, who huddled back fearfully in their corners and refused to face the destruction which they were sure lay before them. They were all white and trembling, with quivering lips and eyes that twitched strangely. Heaven only knows how long an eternity those hours of darkness had seemed.

They were all out at last, and were gently led to blessed light again. There were doctors on the spot by this time with nourishing food and stimulants. For the most part, the women sat down and cried, quietly hugging their children to their breasts. Some of the men were crying in the same dull way, but a few were violent. The dark horror of it had driven them mad for the time. But there was a darker side to it; of the pleasure-seekers the dead were numbered at more than half.

Rut there was one man here and there who had kept his head throughout the crisis. A cheerful-looking sailor gave the best account of the adventure.

'Not that there is much to say,' he remarked. 'We got on just as usual for the first ten minutes or so, the train running smoothly and plenty of light. Then all at once we came to a sudden stop that sent us flying across the carriage. We seemed to have gone headlong into the stiffest tempest I ever met. You could hear the wind go roaring past the carriages, and then it stopped as soon as it had begun.

'The rattle of broken glass was like musketry. The first thing I saw when I got out was the dead body of the engine-driver with the stoker close by. It was just the same with the train in front. Afterwards, I tried to find a way out, but couldn't. There was a man with me who trod on some of them cables as you call 'em, and the next instant there was no man – but I don't want to talk of that.'

'It means months upon months,' Fergusson said sadly.

'Not months – years,' Rossiter replied. 'Yet I dare say that in the long run we shall benefit by the calamity, great communities do. As to calculating the damage, my imagination only goes as far as fifty millions, and then stops. And yet if anybody had suggested this to me yesterday morning, I should have laughed.'

'It would have seemed impossible.'

'Absolutely impossible. And yet now that it has come about, how easy and natural it all seems! Come, let us get to work and try to forget.'

The Purple Terror

Fred M. White

I

Lieutenant Will Scarlett's instructions were devoid of problems, physical or otherwise. To convey a letter from Captain Driver of the *Yankee Doodle*, in Porto Rico Bay, to Admiral Lake on the other side of the isthmus, was an apparently simple matter.

'All you have to do,' the captain remarked, 'is to take three or four men with you in case of accidents, cross the isthmus on foot, and simply give this letter into the hands of Admiral Lake. By so doing we shall save at least four days, and the aborigines are presumedly friendly.'

The aborigines aforesaid were Cuban insurgents. Little or no strife had taken place along the neck lying between Porto Rico and the north bay where Lake's flagship lay, though the belt was known to be given over to the disaffected Cubans.

'It is a matter of fifty miles through practically unexplored country,' Scarlett replied; 'and there's a good deal of the family quarrel in this business, sir. If the Spaniards hate us, the Cubans are not exactly enamoured of our flag.'

Captain Driver roundly denounced the whole pack of them.

'Treacherous thieves to a man,' he said. 'I don't suppose your progress will have any brass bands and floral arches to it. And they tell me the forest is pretty thick. But you'll get there all the same. There is the letter, and you can start as soon as you like.'

'I may pick my own men, sir?'

'My dear fellow, take whom you please. Take the mastiff, if you like.'

'I'd like the mastiff,' Scarlett replied; 'as he is practically my own, I thought you would not object.'

Will Scarlett began to glow as the prospect of adventure stimulated his imagination. He was rather a good specimen of West Point naval dandyism. He had brains at the back of his smartness, and his geological and botanical knowledge were going to prove of considerable service to a grateful country when said grateful country should have passed beyond the rudimentary stages of colonization. And there was some disposition to envy Scarlett on the part of others floating for the past month on the liquid prison of the sapphire sea.

A warrant officer, Tarrer by name, plus two A.B.s of thews and sinews, to say nothing of the dog, completed the exploring party. By the time that the sun kissed the tip of the feathery hills they had covered some six miles of their journey. From the first Scarlett had been struck by the absolute absence of the desolation and horror of civil strife. Evidently the fiery cross had not been carried here; huts and houses were intact; the villagers stood under sloping eaves, and regarded the Americans with a certain sullen curiosity.

'We'd better stop for the night here,' said Scarlett.

They had come at length to a village that boasted some pretensions. An adobe chapel at one end of the straggling street was faced by a wine-house at the other. A padre, with hands folded over a bulbous, greasy gabardine, bowed gravely to Scarlett's salutation. The latter had what Tarrer called 'considerable Spanish'.

'We seek quarters for the night,' said Scarlett. 'Of course, we are prepared to pay for them.'

The sleepy padre nodded towards the wine-house.

'You will find fair accommodation there,' he said. 'We are friends of the Americanos.'

Scarlett doubted the fact, and passed on with florid thanks. So far, little sign of friendliness had been encountered on the march. Coldness, suspicion, a suggestion of fear, but no friendliness to be embarrassing.

The keeper of the wine-shop had his doubts. He feared his poor accommodation for guests so distinguished. A score or more of picturesque, cut-throat-looking rascals with cigarettes in their mouths lounged sullenly in the bar. The display of a brace of gold dollars enlarged mine host's opinion of his household capacity.

'I will do my best, señors,' he said. 'Come this way.'

So it came to pass that an hour after twilight Tarrer and Scarlett were seated in the open amongst the oleanders and the trailing gleam of the fireflies, discussing cigars of average merit and a native wine that was not without virtues. The long bar of the wine-house was brilliantly illuminated; from within came shouts of laughter mingled with the ting, tang of the guitar and the rollicking clack of the castanets.

'They seem to be happy in there,' Tarrer remarked. 'It isn't all daggers and ball in this distressful country.'

A certain curiosity came over Scarlett.

'It is the duty of a good officer,' he said, 'to lose no opportunity of acquiring useful information. Let us join the giddy throng, Tarrer.'

Tarrer expressed himself with enthusiasm in favour of any amusement that might be going. A month's idleness on shipboard increases the appetite for that kind of thing wonderfully. The long bar was comfortable, and filled with Cubans who took absolutely no notice of the intruders. Their eyes were turned towards a rude stage at the far end of the bar, whereon a girl was gyrating in a dance with a celerity and grace that caused the wreath of flowers around her shoulders to resemble a trembling zone of purple flame.

'A wonderfully pretty girl and a wonderfully pretty dance,' Scarlett murmured, when the motions ceased and the girl leapt gracefully to the ground. 'Largesse, I expect. I thought so. Well, I'm good for a quarter.'

The girl came forward, extending a shell prettily. She curtsied before Scarlett and fixed her dark, liquid eyes on his. As he smiled and dropped his quarter-dollar into the shell a coquettish gleam came into the velvety eyes. An ominous growl came from the lips of a bearded ruffian close by.

The girl came forward, extending a shell prettily

'Othello's jealous,' said Tarrer. 'Look at his face.'

'I am better employed,' Scarlett laughed. 'That was a graceful dance, pretty one. I hope you are going to give us another one presently – '

Scarlett paused suddenly. His eyes had fallen on the purple band of flowers the girl had twined round her shoulder. Scarlett was an enthusiastic botanist; he knew most of the gems in Flora's crown, but he had never looked upon such a vivid wealth of blossom before.

The flowers were orchids, and orchids of a kind unknown to collectors anywhere. On this point Scarlett felt certain. And yet this part of the world was by no means a difficult one to explore in comparison with New Guinea and Sumatra, where the rarer varieties had their homes.

The blooms were immensely large, far larger than any flower of the kind known to Europe or America, of a deep pure purple, with a blood-red centre. As Scarlett gazed upon them he noticed a certain cruel expression on the flower. Most orchids have a kind of face of their own; the purple blooms had a positive expression of ferocity and cunning. They exhumed, too, a queer, sickly fragrance. Scarlett had smelt something like it before, after the Battle of Manila. The perfume was the perfume of a corpse.

'And yet they are magnificent flowers,' said Scarlett. 'Won't you tell me where you got them from, pretty one?'

The girl was evidently flattered by the attention bestowed upon her by the smart young American. The bearded Othello alluded to edged up to her side.

'The señor had best leave the girl alone,' he said, insolently.

Scarlett's fist clenched as he measured the Cuban with his eyes. The Admiral's letter crackled in his breast-pocket, and discretion got the best of valour.

'You are paying yourself a poor compliment, my good fellow,' he said, 'though I certainly admire your good taste. Those flowers interested me.'

The man appeared to be mollified. His features corrugated in a smile.

'The señor would like some of those blooms?' he asked. 'It was I who procured them for little Zara here. I can show you where they grow.'

Every eye in the room was turned in Scarlett's direction. It seemed to him that a kind of diabolical malice glistened on every dark face there, save that of the girl, whose features paled under her healthy tan.

'If the señor is wise,' she began, 'he will not – '

'Listen to the tales of a silly girl,' Othello put in, menacingly. He grasped the girl by the arm, and she winced in positive pain. 'Pshaw, there is no harm where the flowers grow, if one is only careful. I will take you there, and I will be your guide to Port Anna, where you are going, for a gold dollar.'

All Scarlett's scientific enthusiasm was aroused. It is not given to every man to present a new orchid to the horticultural world. And this one would dwarf the finest plant hitherto discovered.

'Done with you,' he said; 'we start at daybreak. I shall look to you to be ready. Your name is Tito? Well, good-night, Tito.'

As Scarlett and Tarrer withdrew the girl suddenly darted forward. A wild word or two fluttered from her lips. Then there was a sound as of a blow, followed by a little, stifled cry of pain.

'No, no,' Tarrer urged, as Scarlett half turned. 'Better not. They are ten to one, and they are no friends of ours. It never pays to interfere in these family quarrels. I daresay, if you interfered, the girl would be just as ready to knife you as her jealous lover.'

'But a blow like that, Tarrer!'

'It's a pity, but I don't see how we can help it. Your business is the quick dispatch of the Admiral's letter, not the squiring of dames.'

Scarlett owned with a sigh that Tarrer was right.

2

It was quite a different Tito who presented himself at daybreak the following morning. His insolent manner had disappeared. He was cheerful, alert, and he had a manner full of the most winning politeness.

'You quite understand what we want,' Scarlett said. 'My desire is to reach Port Anna as soon as possible. You know the way?'

'Every inch of it, señor. I have made the journey scores of times. And I shall have the felicity of getting you there early on the third day from now.'

'Is it so far as that?'

'The distance is not great, señor. It is the passage through the woods. There are parts where no white man has been before.'

'And you will not forget the purple orchids?'

A queer gleam trembled like summer lightning in Tito's eyes. The next instant it had gone. A time was to come when Scarlett was to recall that look, but for the moment it was allowed to pass.

'The señor shall see the purple orchid,' he said; 'thousands of them. They have a bad name amongst our people, but that is all nonsense. They grow in the high trees, and their blossoms cling to long, green tendrils. These tendrils are poisonous to the flesh, and great care should be taken in handling them. And the flowers are quite harmless, though we call them the devil's poppies.'

To all of this Scarlett listened eagerly. He was all-impatient to see and handle the mysterious flower for himself. The whole excursion was going to prove a wonderful piece of luck. At the same time he had to curb his impatience. There would be no chance of seeing the purple orchid today.

For hours they fought their way along through the dense tangle. A heat seemed to lie over all the land like a curse – a blistering, sweltering, moist heat with no puff of wind to temper its breathlessness. By the time that the sun was sliding down, most of the party had had enough of it.

They passed out of the underwood at length, and, striking upwards, approached a clump of huge forest trees on the brow of a ridge. All kinds of parasites hung from the branches; there were ropes and bands of green, and high up a fringe of purple glory that caused Scarlett's pulses to leap a little faster.

'Surely that is the purple orchid?' he cried.

Tito shrugged his shoulders contemptuously.

'A mere straggler or two,' he said, 'and out of our reach in any case. The señor will have all he wants and more tomorrow.'

'But it seems to me,' said Scarlett, 'that I could – '

Then he paused. The sun like a great glowing shield was shining full behind the tree with its crown of purple, and showing up every green rope and thread clinging to the branches with the clearness of liquid crystal. Scarlett saw a network of green cords like a huge spider's web, and in the centre of it was not a fly, but a human skeleton!

The arms and legs were stretched apart as if the victim had been crucified. The wrists and ankles were bound in the cruel web. Fragments of tattered clothing fluttered in the faint breath of the evening breeze.

'Horrible,' Scarlett cried, 'absolutely horrible!'

'You may well say that,' Tarrer exclaimed, with a shudder. 'Like the fly in the amber or the apple in the dumpling, the mystery is how he got there.'

In the centre was not a fly, but a human skeleton

'Perhaps Tito can explain the mystery,' Scarlett suggested.

Tito appeared to be uneasy and disturbed. He looked furtively from one to the other of his employers as a culprit might who feels he has been found out. But his courage returned as he noted the absence of suspicion in the faces turned upon him.

'I can explain,' he exclaimed, with teeth that chattered from some unknown terror or guilt. 'It is not the first time that I have seen the skeleton. Some plant-hunter doubtless who came here alone. He climbed into the tree without a knife, and those green ropes got twisted round his limbs, as a swimmer gets entangled in the weeds. The more he struggled, the more the cords bound him. He would call in vain for anyone to assist him here. And so he must have died.'

The explanation was a plausible one, but by no means detracted from the horror of the discovery. For some time the party pushed their way on in the twilight, till the darkness descended suddenly like a curtain.

'We will camp here,' Tito said; 'it is high, dry ground, and we have this belt of trees above us. There is no better place than this for miles around. In the valley the miasma is dangerous.'

As Tito spoke he struck a match, and soon a torch flamed up. The little party were on a small plateau, fringed by trees. The ground was dry and hard, and, as Scarlett and his party saw to their astonishment, littered with bones. There were skulls of animals and skulls of human beings, the skeletons of birds, the frames of beasts both great and small. It was a weird, shuddering sight.

'We can't possibly stay here,' Scarlett exclaimed.

Tito shrugged his shoulders.

'There is nowhere else,' he replied. 'Down in the valley there are many dangers. Further in the woods are the snakes and jaguars. Bones are nothing. Peuf, they can be easily cleared away.'

They had to be cleared away, and there was an end of the matter. For the most part the skeletons were white and dry as air and sun could make them. Over the dry, calcined mass the huge fringe of trees nodded mournfully. With the rest, Scarlett was busy scattering the mocking frames aside. A perfect human skeleton lay at his feet. On one finger something glittered – a signet ring. As Scarlett took it in his hand he started.

'I know this ring!' he exclaimed; 'it belonged to Pierre Anton, perhaps the most skilled and intrepid plant-hunter the *Jardin des Plantes* ever employed. The poor fellow was by way of being a friend of mine. He met the fate that he always anticipated.'

'There must have been a rare holocaust here,' said Tarrer.

'It beats me,' Scarlett responded. By this time a large circle had been shifted clear of human and other remains. By the light of the fire loathsome insects could be seen scudding and straddling away. 'It beats me entirely. Tito, can you offer any explanation? If the bones were all human I could get some grip of the problem. But when one comes to birds and animals as well! Do you see that the skeletons lie in a perfect circle, starting from the centre of the clump of trees above us? What does it mean?'

Tito professed utter ignorance of the subject. Some years before a small tribe of natives invaded the peninsula for religious rites. They came from a long way off in canoes, and wild stories were told concerning them. They burnt sacrifices, no doubt.

Scarlett turned his back contemptuously on this transparent tale. His curiosity was aroused. There must be some explanation, for Pierre Anton had been seen of men within the last ten years.

'There's something uncanny about this,' he said, to Tarrer. 'I mean to get to the bottom of it, or know why.'

'As for me,' said Tarrer, with a cavernous yawn, 'I have but one ambition, and that is my supper, followed by my bed.'

3

Scarlett lay in the light of the fire looking about him. He felt restless and uneasy, though he would have found it difficult to explain the reason. For one thing, the air trembled to strange noises. There seemed to be something moving, writhing in the forest trees above his head. More than once it seemed to his distorted fancy that he could see a squirming knot of green snakes in motion.

Outside the circle, in a grotto of bones, Tito lay sleeping. A few moments before his dark, sleek head had been furtively raised, and his eyes seemed to gleam in the flickering firelight with malignant cunning. As he met Scarlett's glance he gave a deprecatory gesture and subsided.

'What the deuce does it all mean?' Scarlett muttered. 'I feel certain yonder rascal is up to some mischief. Jealous still because I paid his girl a little attention. But he can't do us any real harm. Quiet, there!'

The big mastiff growled and then whined uneasily. Even the dog seemed to be conscious of some unseen danger. He lay down again, cowed by the stern command, but he still whimpered in his dreams.

'I fancy I'll keep awake for a spell,' Scarlett told himself.

For a time he did so. Presently he began to slide away into the land of poppies. He was walking amongst a garden of bones which bore masses of purple blossoms. Then Pierre Anton came on the scene, pale and resolute as Scarlett had always known him; then the big mastiff seemed in some way to be mixed up with the phantasm of the dream, barking as if in pain, and Scarlett came to his senses.

He was breathing short, a beady perspiration stood on his forehead, his heart hammered in quick thuds – all the horrors of nightmare were still upon him. In a vague way as yet he heard the mastiff howl, a real howl of real terror, and Scarlett knew that he was awake.

Then a strange thing happened. In the none too certain light of the fire, Scarlett saw the mastiff snatched up by some invisible hand, carried far on high towards the trees, and finally flung to the earth with a crash. The big dog lay still as a log.

A sense of fear born of the knowledge of impotence came over Scarlett; what in the name of evil did it all mean? The smart scientist had no faith in the occult, and yet what *did* it all mean?

Nobody stirred. Scarlett's companions were soaked and soddened with fatigue; the rolling thunder of artillery would have scarce disturbed them. With teeth set and limbs that trembled, Scarlett crawled over to the dog.

The great, black-muzzled creature was quite dead. The full chest was stained and soaked in blood; the throat had been cut apparently with some jagged, saw-like instrument away to the bone. And, strangest thing of all, scattered all about the body was a score or more of the great purple orchid flowers broken off close to the head. A hot, pricking sensation travelled slowly up Scarlett's spine and seemed to pass out at the tip of his skull. He felt his hair rising.

He was frightened. As a matter of honest fact, he had never been so horribly scared in his life before. The whole thing was so mysterious, so cruel, so bloodthirsty.

Still, there must be some rational explanation. In some way the matter had to do with the purple orchid. The flower had an evil reputation. Was it not known to these Cubans as the devil's poppy?

Scarlett recollected vividly now Zara's white, scared face when Tito had volunteered to show the way to the resplendent bloom; he remembered the cry of the girl and the blow that followed. He could see it all now. The girl had meant to warn him against some nameless horror to which Tito was leading the small party. This was the jealous Cuban's revenge.

A wild desire to pay this debt to the uttermost fraction filled Scarlett, and shook him with a trembling passion. He crept along in the drenching dew to where Tito lay, and touched his forehead with the chill blue rim of a revolver barrel. Tito stirred slightly.

'You dog!' Scarlett cried. 'I am going to shoot you.'

Tito did not move again. His breathing was soft and regular. Beyond a doubt the man was sleeping peacefully. After all he might be innocent; and yet, on the other hand, he might be so sure of his quarry that he could afford to slumber without anxiety as to his vengeance.

In favour of the latter theory was the fact that the Cuban lay beyond the limit of what had previously been the circle of dry bones. It was just possible that there was no danger outside that pale. In that case it would be easy to arouse the rest, and so save them from the horrible death which had befallen the mastiff. No doubt these were a form of upas tree, but that would not account for the ghastly spectacle in mid-air.

'I'll let this chap sleep for the present,' Scarlett muttered.

He crawled back, not without misgivings, into the ring of death. He meant to wake the others and then wait for further developments. By now his senses were more alert and vigorous than they had ever been before. A preternatural clearness of brain and vision possessed him. As he advanced he saw suddenly falling a green bunch of cord that straightened into a long, emerald line. It was triangular in shape, fine at the apex, and furnished with hooked spines. The rope appeared to dangle from the tree overhead; the broad, sucker-like termination was evidently soaking up moisture.

A natural phenomenon evidently, Scarlett thought. This was some plant new to him, a parasite living amongst the tree-tops and drawing life and vigour by means of these green, rope-like antennae designed by Nature to soak and absorb the heavy dews of night.

For a moment the logic of this theory was soothing to Scarlett's distracted nerves, but only for a moment, for then he saw at regular intervals along the green rope the big purple blossoms of the devil's poppy.

He stood gasping there, utterly taken aback for the moment. There must be some infernal juggling behind all this business. He saw the rope slacken and quiver, he saw it swing forward like a pendulum, and the next minute it had passed across the shoulders of a sleeping seaman.

Then the green root became as the arm of an octopus. The line shook from end to end like the web of an angry spider when invaded by a wasp. It seemed to grip the sailor and tighten, and then, before Scarlett's affrighted eyes, the sleeping man was raised gently from the ground.

Scarlett jumped forward with a desire to scream hysterically. Now that a comrade was in danger he was no longer afraid. He whipped a jack-knife from his pocket and slashed at the cruel cord. He half expected to meet with the stoutness of a steel strand, but to his surprise the feeler snapped like a carrot, bumping the sailor heavily on the ground.

He sat up, rubbing his eyes vigorously.

'That you, sir?' he asked. 'What is the matter?'

'For the love of God, get up at once and help me to arouse the others,' Scarlett said, hoarsely. 'We have come across the devil's workshop. All the horrors of the inferno are invented here.'

The bluejacket struggled to his feet. As he did so, the clothing from his waist downwards slipped about his feet, clean cut through by the teeth of the green parasite. All around the body of the sailor blood oozed from a zone of teeth-marks.

Two-o'clock-in-the-morning courage is a virtue vouchsafed to few. The tar, who would have faced an ironclad cheerfully, fairly shivered with fright and dismay.

'What does it mean, sir?' he cried. 'I've been – '

'Wake the others,' Scarlett screamed; 'wake the others.'

Two or three more green tangles of rope came tumbling to the ground, straightening and quivering instantly. The purple blossoms stood out like a frill upon them. Like a madman Scarlett shouted, kicking his companions without mercy.

They were all awake at last, grumbling and moaning for their lost slumbers. All this time Tito had never stirred.

'I don't understand it at all,' said Tarrer.

'Come from under those trees,' said Scarlett, 'and I will endeavour to explain. Not that you will believe me for a moment. No man can be expected to believe the awful nightmare I am going to tell you.'

Scarlett proceeded to explain. As he expected, his story was followed with marked incredulity, save by the wounded sailor, who had strong evidence to stimulate his otherwise defective imagination.

'I can't believe it,' Tarrer said, at length. They were whispering together beyond earshot of Tito, whom they had no desire to arouse for obvious reasons. 'This is some diabolical juggling of yonder rascally Cuban. It seems impossible that those slender green cords could – '

Scarlett pointed to the centre of the circle.

'Call the dog,' he said, grimly, 'and see if he will come.'

'I admit the point as far as the poor old mastiff is concerned. But at the same time I don't – however, I'll see for myself.'

By this time a dozen or more of the slender cords were hanging pendent from the trees. They moved from spot to spot as if jerked up by some unseen hand and deposited a foot or two farther. With the great purple bloom fringing the stem, the effect was not unlovely save to Scarlett, who could see only the dark side of it. As Tarrer spoke he advanced in the direction of the trees.

'What are you going to do?' Scarlett asked.

'Exactly what I told you. I am going to investigate this business for myself.'

Without wasting further words Scarlett sprang forward. It was no time for the niceties of an effete civilization. Force was the only logical argument to be used in a case like this, and Scarlett was the more powerful man of the two.

Tarrer saw and appreciated the situation.

'No, no,' he cried; 'none of that. Anyway, you're too late.'

He darted forward and threaded his way between the slender emerald columns. As they moved slowly and with a certain stately deliberation there was no great danger to an alert and vigorous individual. As Scarlett entered the avenue he could hear the soak and suck as the dew was absorbed.

'For Heaven's sake, come out of it,' he cried.

The warning came too late. A whip-like trail of green touched Tarrer from behind, and in a lightning flash he was in the toils. The tendency to draw up anything and everything gave the cords a terrible power. Tarrer evidently felt it, for his breath came in great gasps.

'Cut me free,' he said, hoarsely; 'cut me free. I am being carried off my feet.'

He seemed to be doomed for a moment, for all the cords there were apparently converging in his direction. This, as a matter of fact, was a solution of the whole sickening, horrible sensation. Pulled here and there, thrust in one direction and another, Tarrer contrived to keep his feet.

Heedless of possible danger to himself Scarlett darted forward, calling to his companions to come to the rescue. In less time than it takes to tell, four knives were at work ripping and slashing in all directions.

'Not all of you,' Scarlett whispered. So tense was the situation that no voice was raised above a murmur. 'You two keep your eyes open for fresh cords, and cut them as they fall, instantly. Now then.'

The horrible green spines were round Tarrer's body like snakes. His face was white, his breath came painfully, for the pressure was terrible. It seemed to Scarlett to be one horrible dissolving view of green, slimy cords and great weltering, purple blossoms. The whole of the circle was strewn with them. They were wet and slimy underfoot.

Tarrer had fallen forward half unconscious. He was supported now by but two cords above his head. The cruel pressure had been relieved. With one savage sweep of his knife Scarlett cut the last of the lines, and Tarrer fell like a log unconscious to the ground. A feeling of nausea, a yellow dizziness, came over Scarlett as he staggered beyond the dread circle. He saw Tarrer carried to a place of safety, and then the world seemed to wither and leave him in the dark.

'I feel a bit groggy and weak,' said Tarrer an hour or so later: 'but beyond that this idiot of a Richard is himself again. So far as I am concerned, I should like to get even with our friend Tito for this.'

'Something with boiling oil in it,' Scarlett suggested, grimly. 'The callous scoundrel has slept soundly through the whole of this business. I suppose he felt absolutely certain that he had finished with us.'

'Upon my word, we ought to shoot the beggar!' Tarrer exclaimed.

'I have a little plan of my own,' said Scarlett, 'which I am going to put in force later on. Meanwhile we had better get on with breakfast. When Tito wakes a pleasant little surprise will await him.'

Tito roused from his slumbers in due course and looked around him. His glance was curious, disappointed, then full of a white and yellow fear. A thousand conflicting emotions streamed across his dark face. Scarlett read them at a glance as he called the Cuban over to him.

'I am not going into any unnecessary details with you,' he said. 'It has come to my knowledge that you are playing traitor to us. Therefore we prefer to complete our journey alone. We can easily find the way now.'

'The señor may do as he pleases,' he replied. 'Give me my dollar and let me go.'

Scarlett replied grimly that he had no intention of doing anything of the kind. He did not propose to place the lives of himself and his comrades in the power of a rascally Cuban who had played false.

'We are going to leave you here till we return,' he said. 'You will have plenty of food, you will be perfectly safe under the shelter of these trees, and there is no chance of anybody disturbing you. We are going to tie you up to one of these trees for the next four-and-twenty hours.'

All the insolence died out of Tito's face. His knees bowed, a cold dew came out over the ghastly green of his features. From the shaking of his limbs he might have fared disastrously with ague.

'The trees,' he stammered, 'the trees, señor! There is danger from snakes, and – and from many things. There are other places – '

'If this place was safe last night it is safe today,' Scarlett said, grimly. 'I have quite made up my mind.'

Tito fought no longer. He fell forward on his knees, he howled for mercy, till Scarlett fairly kicked him up again.

He howled for mercy

'Make a clean breast of it,' he said, 'or take the consequences. You know perfectly well that we have found you out, scoundrel.'

Tito's story came in gasps. He wanted to get rid of the Americans. He was jealous. Besides, under the Americanos would Cuba be any better off? By no means and assuredly not. Therefore it was the duty of every good Cuban to destroy the Americanos where possible.

'A nice lot to fight for,' Scarlett muttered. 'Get to the point.'

Hastened to the point by a liberal application of stout shoe-leather, Tito made plenary confession. The señor himself had suggested death by medium of the devil's poppies. More than one predatory plant-hunter had been lured to his destruction in the same way. The skeleton hung on the tree was a Dutchman who had walked into the clutch of the purple terror innocently. And Pierre Anton had done the same. The suckers of the devil's poppy only came down at night to gather moisture; in the day they were coiled up like a spring. And anything that they touched they killed. Tito had watched more than one bird or small beast crushed and mauled by these cruel spines with their fringe of purple blossoms.

'How do you get the blooms?' Scarlett asked.

'That is easy,' Tito replied. 'In the daytime I moisten the ground under the trees. Then the suckers unfold, drawn by the water. Once the suckers unfold one cuts several of them off with long knives. There is danger, of course, but not if one is careful.'

'I'll not trouble the devil's poppy any further at present,' said Scarlett, 'but I shall trouble you to accompany me to my destination as a prisoner.'

Tito's eyes dilated.

'They will not shoot me?' he asked, hoarsely.

'I don't know,' Scarlett replied. 'They may hang you instead. At any rate, I shall be bitterly disappointed if they don't end you one way or the other. Whichever operation it is, I can look forward to it with perfect equanimity.'

Around the Moon

A Sequel to *From the Earth to the Moon*

Jules Verne

CONTENTS

Introduction

1   *From 10.20 p.m. to 10.47 p.m.*

2   *The first half-hour*

3   *In which they make themselves at home*

4   *A lesson in algebra*

5   *The coldness of space*

6   *Questions and answers*

7   *A moment of frenzy*

8   *Seventy-eight thousand one hundred and fourteen leagues off*

9   *Consequences of a deviation*

10   *The observers of the moon*

11   *Imagination and reality*

12   *Orographical details*

13   *Lunar landscapes*

14   *The night of 354½ hours*

15   *Hyperbola or parabola?*

16   *The southern hemisphere*

17   *Tycho*

18   *Important questions*

19   *A struggle against the impossible*

20   *The soundings of the* Susquehanna

21   *J. T. Maston recalled*

22   *Saved*

23   *To conclude*

INTRODUCTION

Which sums up the first portion of this work as a Preface to the second

During the year 186— the whole world was greatly excited by a scientific experiment without precedent in the annals of science. The members of the Gun Club – an assembly of artillerists founded at Baltimore – had conceived the idea of placing themselves in communication with the moon – yes, with the moon! – by means of a cannon-ball. Their president, Barbicane, the originator of the idea, having consulted on the subject the astronomers of the Cambridge Observatory, took all the measures necessary for the success of the extraordinary undertaking, which had been declared feasible by the majority of competent men. After having opened a public subscription, which realised nearly 30 millions of francs (£ 1,200,000), he commenced his gigantic works.

In accordance with a note drawn up by the members of the observatory, the cannon which was to discharge the projectile had to be established on some spot situated between 0° and 28° of latitude, north or south, so as to aim at the moon in the zenith, and the projectile was to be endowed with an initial velocity of 12,000 yards per second. Discharged on the 1st of December at 10.48 p.m., it would strike the moon four days after its departure – on the 5th of December – at midnight precisely, at the very moment when she would be in perigee, *i.e.* at her nearest approach to the earth, being just 96,410 leagues distant.

The principal members of the Gun Club, President Barbicane, Major Elphiston, the secretary J. T. Maston, and other scientific men, held several meetings, at which were discussed the form and composition of the projectile, the disposition and nature of the cannon, and the quantity and quality of the powder to be used. It was decided: (1) That the projectile should be an aluminum shell of 108 inches in diameter, and with sides of a thickness of 12 inches, weighing 19,250 pounds. (2) That the cannon should be a cast-iron columbiad, 900 feet long, and cast direct in the ground. (3) That the charge should consist of 400,000 pounds of gun-cotton, which would produce 600 million litres of gas beneath the projectile, and would amply suffice to propel the latter to the orb of night.

These questions having been decided, President Barbicane, assisted by the engineer Murchison, made choice of a site situated in Florida at 27° 7' N. latitude by 5° 7' W. longitude. In this spot, after the execution of marvellous works, the columbiad was cast with complete success.

Matters were at this point, when an incident occurred which increased one-hundredfold the interest awakened by this great undertaking.

A Frenchman, a fantastic Parisian – an artist, as witty as he was audacious – asked permission to be enclosed in the projectile, so as to reach the moon and reconnoitre the earth's satellite. This intrepid adventurer was named Michel Ardan. He arrived in America, was received with enthusiasm, held meetings, was carried in triumph, reconciled President Barbicane with his mortal enemy Captain Nicholl, and, as a proof of reconciliation, induced them to embark with him in the projectile.

The proposal was accepted and the form of the projectile was altered from spherical to cylindro-conic. The interior of this aerial carriage was fitted up with powerful springs and partitions, which were to break and lessen the shock of the departure. It was supplied with provisions for one year, with water for some months, and with gas for several days. An automatic apparatus manufactured and supplied the air necessary for breathing purposes. At the same time the Gun Club ordered a gigantic telescope to be constructed upon one of the highest summits of the Rocky Mountains, which would enable the projectile to be observed during its passage through space. Everything was ready.

On the 1st of December, at the hour appointed, in the midst of an immense concourse of spectators, the departure took place, and, for the first time, three human beings quitted the terrestrial globe and dashed towards the planetary regions with the almost absolute certainty of reaching their goal. These audacious travellers – Michel Ardan, President Barbicane, and Captain Nicholl – were to effect their passage in 97 hours, 13 minutes, and 20 seconds. Consequently their arrival on the lunar disc could only take place on the 5th of December at midnight, at the precise moment at which the moon would be full, and not on the 4th, as some ill-informed newspapers had announced.

However, an unforeseen circumstance occurred: the explosion produced by the columbiad caused an immediate disturbance in the terrestrial atmosphere by accumulating an immense mass of vapour. This phenomenon excited general indignation, for the moon was veiled for several nights from the eyes of all observers.

Worthy J. T. Maston, the staunchest friend of the three travellers, set out for the Rocky Mountains in company with the Hon. J. Belfast, director of the Cambridge Observatory, and reached the station at Long's

Peak, where the telescope was established, which brought the moon to within two leagues. The hon. secretary of the Gun Club wished to observe for himself, the vehicle of his audacious friends.

The accumulation of clouds in the atmosphere rendered impossible any observations during the 5th, 6th, 7th, 8th, 9th, and 10th of December. It was even thought that the observations would have to be postponed until the 3rd of January of the next year, inasmuch as the moon would enter her last quarter on the 11th, and would then only present a constantly decreasing portion of her disc, totally insufficient to reveal any trace of the projectile.

At last, to the general satisfaction, a violent tempest cleared the atmosphere in the night of the 11th of December, and the moon, half-illumined, stood out boldly in the midst of the black sky. That same night, a telegram was despatched from Long's Peak, by J. T. Maston and J. Belfast, to the members of the Cambridge Observatory. What did this telegram announce? It announced that on the 11th of December, at 8.47 p.m., the projectile discharged by the columbiad from Stone's Hill, had been perceived by Messrs Belfast and J. T. Maston; that the projectile, having deviated from some unknown cause, had not reached its goal, but had passed near enough to be retained by the lunar attraction; that its rectilinear movement had been changed into a circular movement, and that it had been carried away on an elliptic orbit around the orb of night, whose satellite it had become.

The telegram added that the elements of this new star had not yet been calculated; indeed, three observations, each taking the star in a different position, were necessary to determine its elements. It then pointed out that the distance separating the projectile from the lunar surface might be estimated at about 2,833 miles. It concluded by suggesting this double hypothesis – either the attraction of the moon would prove the stronger and the travellers would reach their destination, or the projectile, maintained in an immutable orbit, would gravitate round the lunar disc until the end of time.

In these two alternatives, what would be the fate of the travellers? They had provisions for a certain time, it is true; but, even supposing the success of their bold undertaking, how would they return? Would they ever be able to return? Could there be any news from them? These questions, treated by the most learned writers of the day, excited public attention to the utmost.

It is necessary to make a remark here, which should be well considered by hasty observers. When a man of science announces a purely speculative discovery to the public, he cannot be too prudent. No one is obliged to discover a comet, or a planet, or a satellite; and whoever makes an error under such circumstances becomes fair game for the laughter of the crowd. Consequently it is better to wait; and so the impatient J. T. Maston should have done, instead of publishing to the world the telegram which, in his opinion, formed the conclusion of the undertaking.

In fact, the telegram contained errors of two kinds, as was subsequently proved. First, errors of observation concerning the distance of the projectile from the surface of the moon, for, at the date of the 11th of December it was impossible to perceive it; and what J. T. Maston saw, or imagined he saw, could not have been the shot from the columbiad. Secondly, theoretical errors as to the fate reserved for the said projectile, inasmuch as to make it a satellite of the moon was to act in direct contradiction with the laws of rational mechanics.

One hypothesis only of the observers at Long's Peak might be realised, viz. that the travellers, if they still were in existence, would combine their efforts with the lunar attraction, so as to reach the surface of the moon.

Now these men, as intelligent as they were rash, had survived the terrible shock of the departure. It is their journey in the projectile-carriage which is about to be related, in its most dramatic as in its most singular details. This story will upset many theories and illusions, but it will give a true idea of the dangers inherent to such an undertaking, and will bring into bold relief the scientific knowledge of Barbicane, the resources of the industrious Nicholl, and the humorous audacity of Michel Ardan.

Further, it will prove that their worthy friend J. T. Maston was losing his time when, leaning over the gigantic telescope, he observed the passage of the moon through the starry firmament.

CHAPTER ONE

From 10.20 p.m. to 10.47 p.m.

On the stroke of ten, Michel Ardan, Barbicane, and Nicholl took leave of the numerous friends whom they were leaving upon earth. The two dogs, destined to propagate the canine race upon the lunar continents, had already been enclosed in the projectile. The three travellers approached the orifice of the enormous cast-iron tube, and a movable crane lowered them to the conic roof of the projectile.

There an opening left for the purpose gave them access to the interior of the aluminum carriage. The tackle of the crane was hauled up, and the mouth of the columbiad was instantaneously freed from its last incumbrances.

So soon as Nicholl and his companions were inside the projectile, the former began to close up the opening by means of a strong plate, held in position by powerful screws. Other plates, firmly fixed, covered the lenticular glasses of the scuttles. The travellers, hermetically enclosed in their metal prison, were plunged into profound darkness.

'And now, dear friends,' said Michel Ardan, 'let us make ourselves at home. I am a homely man, I am, and a capital housekeeper. We must make the most of our new lodgings, and make ourselves comfortable. In the first place let us throw a little light on the subject. Devil take it! gas was not made for moles.'

So saying, the heedless fellow lit a match upon the sole of his boot, and applied it to the burner of the reservoir in which carbonised hydrogen had been stored at high pressure, in sufficient quantity to light and warm the projectile during 144 hours, or six days and six nights.

The gas ignited, and the projectile, thus lighted, appeared like a comfortable chamber with padded sides, furnished with circular divans, and having a ceiling in the shape of a dome.

The articles it contained – arms, instruments, and utensils – were firmly attached to the knobs of the padding, and would bear with impunity the shock of the departure. All humanly possible precautions had been taken to make this rash experiment a success.

Michel Ardan examined everything, and declared himself very well satisfied with the arrangements.

'It is a prison,' said he, 'but a travelling prison, and we have the right of looking out of the window. I should like to take a lease for 100 years. You smile, Barbicane. You are thinking of something. You are thinking that the prison might become our tomb! Very well! but I would not exchange with Mahomet, whose tomb floats in space but does not move.'

Whilst Ardan was speaking, Barbicane and Nicholl were making their last preparations.

Nicholl's chronometer marked 10.20 p.m. when the three travellers were definitively walled up in their projectile. The chronometer was set within a tenth of a second of that belonging to Murchison the engineer. Barbicane consulted it.

'My friends,' said he, 'it is 20 minutes past 10. At 47 minutes past 10, Murchison will flash the electric spark to the wire which communicates with the charge of the columbiad. At that moment precisely we will leave our spheroid. We have still 27 minutes to remain on earth.'

'26 minutes and 13 seconds,' replied the methodical Nicholl.

'Well!' cried Michel Ardan, in a good-humoured tone, 'much can be done in 26 minutes. We might discuss the gravest questions of morals or politics, and even solve them! 26 minutes well employed are better worth than 26 years of idleness. A few seconds of Newton or Pascal are more precious than the whole lifetime of the general run of fools.'

'And what conclusion do you draw, chatterbox?' asked President Barbicane.

'I conclude that we have 26 minutes before us,' replied Ardan.

'24 only,' said Nicholl.

'24 if you like, worthy captain; 24 minutes during which we might investigate – '

'Michel,' said Barbicane, 'during our passage we shall have all the time necessary to investigate the most arduous questions. Let us now think of our departure.'

'Are we not ready?'

'Doubtless. But there are some precautions to be taken so as to attenuate, as much as possible, the first shock.'

'Have we not layers of water between breakable partitions, whose elasticity will protect us sufficiently?'

'I hope so, Michel,' said Barbicane quietly, 'but I am not very sure.'

'This is a nice joke!' said Ardan. 'He is not sure. He hopes. And he waits for the moment when we are all locked in to make the avowal. Let me out!'

'How can we manage that?'

'That is true enough,' said Ardan; 'it would be difficult. We are in the train, and the guard's whistle will sound in 24 minutes.'

'Twenty!' said Nicholl.

For a few minutes the three travellers looked at each other. Then they examined the articles imprisoned with them.

'Everything is in its place,' said Barbicane. 'We must now decide how we can place ourselves in the best position to bear the shock of the start. The position is of great importance, and we must avoid, as much as possible, a rush of blood to the head.'

'Quite right,' said Nicholl.

'In that case,' said Michel Ardan, joining the action to the word, 'let us stand on our heads, like the clowns in the Great Circus.'

'No,' said Barbicane, 'let us lie down on our sides. In that way we shall best sustain the shock. Observe that at the moment when the shot is fired it is almost the same thing whether we are inside or in front.'

'So long as it is only *almost* the same thing I don't mind,' replied Ardan.

'Do you approve of my idea, Nicholl?' asked Barbicane.

'Fully,' replied the captain. 'Thirteen and a half minutes more!'

'That fellow Nicholl is not a man,' cried Ardan; 'he is a chronometer, with a second hand, with escapement, with eight rubies – '

But his companions paid no attention to him. They were completing their arrangements with unimaginable coolness. They looked like two travellers, in a first-class carriage, trying to make themselves as comfortable as possible. One is tempted to ask of what these American hearts are made, which beat not one pulsation faster at the approach of the most frightful dangers.

Three thick, well-made couches had been placed in the projectile. Nicholl and Barbicane deposited them in the centre of the disc, which formed the movable flooring. The three travellers were to lay themselves down a few minutes before the start.

During this time, Michel Ardan, who could not remain quiet one instant, ranged up and down his narrow prison like a wild beast in a cage; talking to his friends and to his dogs, Diana and Satellite, to which he had given, as you see, some time ago, these significant names.

'Hi, Diana! hi, Satellite!' he cried, teasing them; 'you are going to show the Selenite dogs how well-behaved the dogs of the earth are. What an honour for the canine species! If ever I return, I shall bring back some specimens of cross-bred moon dogs, which will certainly be all the rage.'

'If there are any dogs in the moon,' said Barbicane.

'There are some,' said Michel Ardan, 'as there are horses, cows, donkeys, and hens. I bet we find hens there.'

'One hundred dollars we don't,' said Nicholl.

'Done, captain!' said Ardan, wringing Nicholl's hand. 'By-the-bye, you have already lost three bets with the president, since the funds for the undertaking were found, the casting succeeded, and the columbiad was loaded without accident. That makes 6,000 dollars.'

'Yes,' said Nicholl. 'Thirty-seven minutes and sixteen seconds past ten.'

'Quite so, captain. Well, in a quarter of an hour you will have to pay 9,000 dollars to the president – 4,000 because the columbiad will not burst, and 5,000 because the projectile will travel more than six miles in the air.'

'I have got the dollars,' said Nicholl, slapping his pocket. 'I shall be only too glad to pay.'

'Bravo, Nicholl! I see you are a man of order – which I never could be. But, after all, you have made a series of bets which are not precisely advantageous, allow me to say.'

'Why not?' asked Nicholl.

'Because, to win the first, the columbiad must burst and the projectile too, and Barbicane won't be forthcoming to repay the dollars.'

'My stake is deposited in the Bank of Baltimore,' said Barbicane simply; 'and in Nicholl's default the money will be paid to his heirs.'

'Oh! practical men,' cried Ardan; 'matter-of-fact minds. I admire you the more that I don't understand you.'

'Forty-two minutes past ten,' said Nicholl. 'Only five minutes more.'

'Yes; five short minutes!' replied Michel Ardan. 'And we are enclosed in a cannon-ball, at the bottom of a cannon 900 feet long; and beneath this projectile, are piled 400,000 pounds of gun-cotton, equal to 1,600,000 pounds of ordinary gunpowder. And friend Murchison, chronometer in hand, his eye fixed on the second hand, his finger placed on the electric apparatus, counts the seconds, and is going to launch us into the planetary spheres.'

'Enough, Michel, enough,' said Barbicane in a solemn tone. 'Let us prepare; a few instants only separate us from an awful moment. Let us shake hands, my friends.'

'Yes,' said Michel Ardan, more moved than he wished to appear. The three bold companions united in a last embrace.

'God be with us,' said the religious Barbicane.

Michel Ardan and Nicholl threw themselves on the couches placed in the centre of the disc.

'47 minutes past 10,' murmured the captain.

'20 seconds more!' Barbicane rapidly extinguished the gas and lay down beside his companions. The profound silence was only broken by the tick of the chronometer counting the seconds. Suddenly a terrific shock was felt, and the projectile was hurled into space by the force of six milliards of litres of gas developed by the combustion of the pyroxyle.

CHAPTER TWO

The first half-hour

What had passed? What effect had the terrible shock produced? Had the ingenuity of the constructors of the projectile attained the happy result? Had the shock been deadened, thanks to the springs, to the four buffers, to the layers of water, and to the breakable partitions? Had that frightful propelling strength been subdued which produced an initial velocity of 12,000 yards, sufficient to pass through Paris or New York in one second? Such certainly was the question propounded by the thousand spectators of this awful scene. They forgot the object of the journey to think only of the travellers. And if one of them – J. T. Maston for instance – could have caught a glimpse of the interior of the projectile, what would he have seen? At first, nothing. The darkness was profound in the projectile; but its cylindro-conic sides had admirably resisted. Not a crack, not a dent, not a deformation. The admirable projectile was not even damaged by the intense heat of the combustion of the gun-cotton, nor liquefied, as had been feared, into a rain of aluminum. In the interior, not much disorder after all. Some articles had been violently thrown to the roof, but the most important did not appear to have suffered from the shock; their fastenings were intact.

Upon the movable disc, which had now fallen to the bottom, since the breaking of the partitions and the escape of the water, three bodies lay without movement. Did Barbicane, Nicholl, and Michel Ardan still breathe? Was the projectile no more than a metal coffin bearing three corpses into space? A few minutes after the departure of the projectile, one of these bodies moved its arms, raised its head, and finally got upon its knees. It was Michel Ardan. He felt himself all over, gave a sonorous 'hem', and said: 'Michel Ardan safe and sound – let us see the others!'

The courageous Frenchman tried to rise, but found himself unable to stand. His head swam round, the violently injected blood blinded him, he was like a drunken man.

'Brr!' said he; 'one would think I had drunk two bottles of Corton; but it is much less agreeable to swallow.'

Then, passing his hand several times across his forehead and rubbing his temples, he cried in a firm voice: 'Hallo! Nicholl! – Barbicane!'

He waited anxiously. No reply; not even a sigh, to prove that his companions' hearts were still beating. He repeated his call – same silence.

'The devil!' said he, 'one would think they had fallen from a fifth storey on their heads. Bah!' he added, with that imperturbable confidence which nothing could shake, 'if a Frenchman is able to get on his knees, two Americans will be certainly able to get on their feet. But first of all let's have a light.'

Ardan felt life rushing back into his veins. His blood calmed down and resumed its accustomed circulation. A few more attempts enabled him to regain his equilibrium. He succeeded in rising, drew a match from his pocket and ignited it by striking the phosphorus. Then, approaching it to the gas-burner, he lighted it. The reservoir had not suffered; the gas had not escaped. Indeed its odour would have betrayed it, and Ardan could not have lighted a match with impunity in so confined a space full of hydrogen. The gas, combined with the air, would have produced a detonating mixture, and the explosion would certainly have completed what the shock had perhaps begun. As soon as the burner was lighted, Ardan stooped over the prostrate forms of his companions. Their bodies were thrown one over the other like inert masses – Nicholl above, Barbicane below. Ardan dragged up the captain, placed him against the divan, and rubbed him vigorously. This shampooing, intelligently performed, soon brought Nicholl to himself. He instantly recovered his presence of mind, and seized Ardan by the hand; then, looking round: 'Where is Barbicane?' he asked.

'Each in his turn,' replied Michel Ardan quietly, 'I commenced with you, Nicholl, because you were uppermost. Now let us see to Barbicane.' Whereupon Ardan and Nicholl lifted the president of the Gun Club and laid him on the divan. Barbicane seemed to have suffered more than his companions. His blood had flowed; but Nicholl was reassured by discovering that it was only from a slight wound on the shoulder, a mere scratch, which was carefully dressed. Nevertheless Barbicane was a long time coming to, much to the alarm of his two friends, who did not spare their frictions.

'He breathes, at any rate,' said Nicholl, approaching his ear to the breast of the wounded man.

'Yes,' replied Ardan; 'he breathes like a man who is somewhat accustomed to that daily operation. Rub, Nicholl, rub vigorously!' And the two improvised practitioners worked so long and so well, that Barbicane recovered the use of his senses. He opened his eyes, sat up, took his two friends by the hand, and for his first word: 'Nicholl,' he asked, 'are we moving?'

Nicholl and Barbicane looked at each other. They had not yet thought about the projectile. Their first thought had been for the travellers, not for the carriage.

'Well, are we moving?' repeated Michel Ardan.

'Or are we quietly reposing on Floridan soil?' asked Nicholl.

'Or in the bottom of the Gulf of Mexico?' added Michel Ardan.

'The devil!' cried President Barbicane. And this double hypothesis, suggested by his companions, had the effect of immediately bringing him to himself.

However, they could not yet give an opinion as to the position of the projectile. Its apparent immobility, the absence of means of communication with the outside world, would not allow of the question being solved. Perhaps the projectile followed its trajectory through space! Perhaps, after a short journey, it had fallen back to earth, or even into the Gulf of Mexico, which the narrowness of the Floridan peninsula rendered possible. The question was important; the problem interesting. It must be solved as quickly as possible. Barbicane, in great excitement, and conquering physical weakness by moral strength, raised himself and listened. Outside, profound silence. But the thick padding was sufficient to intercept any noise from the earth. However, one circumstance struck Barbicane particularly. The temperature of the interior of the projectile was singularly high. The president drew a thermometer from its case and consulted it. The instrument marked 45° centigrade.

'Yes!' he cried; 'yes! we are moving. This stifling heat penetrates through the sides of the projectile. It is produced by friction with the atmospheric strata. It will decrease shortly, for already we float in a vacuum, and after being nearly suffocated we will suffer from intense cold.'

'What!' asked Michel Ardan. 'In your opinion, Barbicane, we have already passed the limits of the terrestrial atmosphere?'

'Without doubt, Michel. Listen. It is 55 minutes past 10 – we have been travelling about eight minutes, and if our initial velocity had not been diminished by friction, six seconds would have sufficed to pass through the sixteen leagues of atmosphere which surround the spheroid.'

'Very good,' replied Nicholl; 'but in what proportion do you estimate the diminution of velocity by friction?'

'About one-third, Nicholl,' replied Barbicane. 'The diminution is doubtless great, but it is proved by my calculations. If, therefore, we have had an initial velocity of 12,000 yards, on leaving the atmosphere this velocity will have been reduced to about 8,000 yards. In any case we have already passed that distance, and – '

'And,' said Michel Ardan, 'our friend Nicholl has lost his two bets; 4,000 dollars since the columbiad has not burst, and 5,000 dollars since the projectile has risen to a height greater than six miles. Nicholl, my friend, pay up.'

'Let us satisfy ourselves first,' said the captain, 'and then we will pay. It is very possible that Barbicane's arguments may be right, in which case I have lost my 9,000 dollars; but a new hypothesis occurs to my mind which would cancel the bet.'

'Which is that?' asked Barbicane.

'The hypothesis that, for some reason or another, the powder not having been ignited, we have not started.'

'Upon my word, captain!' cried Michel Ardan; 'that hypothesis is worthy of me; it cannot be serious. Were we not almost killed by the shock? Did I not bring you back to life? Does not the president's shoulder still bleed from the blow it received?'

'Agreed, Michel,' said Nicholl; 'but one question more.'

'Fire away, captain!'

'Did you hear the report, which must have been formidable?'

'No!' replied Ardan, astonished. 'You are quite right; I did not hear the report.'

'Did you, Barbicane?'

'No.'

'Well?' said Nicholl.

'True!' murmured the president. 'Why did we not hear the report?'

The three friends looked at each other somewhat crestfallen. Here was an inexplicable phenomenon! However, the projectile had started, and the report must have occurred.

'Let us find out where we are,' said Barbicane, 'and open the shutters.'

This extremely simple operation was immediately effected. The nuts which held the bolts of the exterior plates of the right-hand scuttle, gave way under the pressure of a wrench. The bolts were pushed outwards, and plugs, covered with indiarubber, stopped up the holes. At once, the exterior plate fell back upon its hinge, like a port-hole, and the lenticular glass appeared. A similar scuttle was opened, in the thickness of the wall, at the other side of the projectile, another in the dome, and a fourth in the floor. They could thus make observations in the four opposite directions. The firmament was visible through the lateral glasses, and, more directly, the earth and the moon by the upper and lower apertures in the projectile. Barbicane and his two companions had immediately rushed to the unclosed window. Not one ray of light illumined it. A profound darkness surrounded the projectile. Nevertheless President Barbicane exclaimed: 'No, my friends, we have not fallen back to earth! No, we are not submerged in the Gulf of Mexico! Yes, we are mounting through space! See the stars that shine, and the impenetrable darkness between the earth and us!'

'Hurrah! hurrah!' cried Michel Ardan and Nicholl simultaneously. In reality, this compact darkness proved that the projectile had left the earth; for if the travellers had remained on its surface, the ground would have appeared to them vividly illumined by the rays of the moon. This darkness also proved that the projectile had passed the atmospheric stratum; for the diffused light, spread through the air, would have caused some reflection on the metal walls, which reflection was wanting. This light would have illumined the glass of the scuttle, and the glass remained dark. Doubt was impossible; the travellers had quitted the earth!

'I have lost!' said Nicholl.

'I congratulate you,' replied Ardan.

'Here are 9,000 dollars,' said the captain, drawing a bundle of notes from his pocket.

'Will you take a receipt?' asked Barbicane, taking the sum.

'If not disagreeable to you,' replied Nicholl. 'It is more regular.'

And President Barbicane, gravely, phlegmatically, as if he had been at his counter, drew out his pocket-book, tore out a blank page, wrote a receipt in pencil, dated it, signed it, initialled it, and handed it to the captain, who carefully deposited it in his pocket-book. Michel Ardan, taking off his cap, bowed, without speaking, to these two companions. So much formality, under such circumstances, left him speechless. He had never seen anything so 'American'. Barbicane and Nicholl, having completed this operation, replaced themselves at the window, and studied the constellations. The stars stood out brilliantly upon the dark firmament. But from this side, they could not perceive the orb of night, which, travelling from east to west, rose gradually towards the zenith. This absence provoked a reflection from Ardan.

'What about the moon?' said he. 'Supposing she were to miss our appointment!'

'Don't be afraid,' replied Barbicane. 'Our future spheroid is at her post, but we cannot see her from this side. Let us open the other side scuttle.'

At the moment when Barbicane was about to quit the window to open the opposite scuttle, his attention was attracted by the approach of a brilliant object. It was an enormous disc, whose colossal proportions could not be estimated. One might have thought it a small moon, reflecting the light of the great one. It was travelling with prodigious swiftness, and appeared to describe an orbit round the earth, crossing the trajectory of the projectile. The movement of translation of this body was joined to a movement of rotation on its axis, as is the case in all celestial bodies abandoned in space.

'Hallo!' cried Michel Ardan, 'what is that? Another projectile?'

Barbicane did not reply. The appearance of this enormous body surprised and disquieted him. A collision was possible, which would have had disastrous results, either by forcing the projectile from its route, or breaking its flight and hurling it back to earth; or, again, by irresistibly carrying away the projectile by the power of attraction of this asteroid. President Barbicane had rapidly grasped the consequences of these three hypotheses, which in one way or another would infallibly entail the failure of his experiment. His companions looked silently into space. The body increased prodigiously in size as it approached, and by an optical illusion it seemed as though the projectile were rushing to meet it.

'By Jove!' cried Michel Ardan, 'the two trains will collide!'

Instinctively, the travellers had started back. Their fright was great, but only lasted a few seconds. The asteroid passed at a few hundred yards from the projectile, and disappeared; not so much from the rapidity of its flight, as from the fact that its face, opposed to the moon, was soon lost in the absolute darkness of space.

'A good journey to you!' cried Michel Ardan, heaving a sigh of satisfaction. 'What! the infinite is not large enough to allow a poor little projectile to travel without danger? What is that pretentious globe which nearly ran into us?'

'I know,' said Barbicane.

'Of course, you know everything.'

'It is merely a meteorite,' said Barbicane; 'but an enormous meteorite, which the attraction of the earth has maintained in the position of satellite.'

'Is it possible?' cried Michel Ardan. 'Has the earth two moons, like Neptune?'

'Yes, my friend, although she is generally supposed to have but one. But this second moon is so small, and its velocity so great, that the inhabitants of the earth cannot perceive her. It was by taking certain perturbations into account, that a French astronomer, M. Petit, was able to discover the existence of this second satellite and to calculate its elements. From two observations, it appears that this meteorite completes its revolution round the earth in 3 hours and 20 minutes, which implies a prodigious velocity.'

'Do all astronomers,' asked Nicholl, 'admit the existence of this satellite?'

'No,' said Barbicane; 'but if, like us, they had met with it, they would doubt no longer. By the way, now I think of it, this meteorite, which nearly ran us down, will enable us to calculate our position in space.'

'How?' said Ardan.

'Because its distance is known, and, at the point where we met with it, we were exactly 8,140 kilometres from the surface of the terrestrial globe.'

'More than 2,000 leagues!' cried Michel Ardan. 'I should think that will take the shine out of the express trains on the miserable globe which they call the earth.'

'I should think so,' replied Nicholl, consulting his chronometer, 'it is now 11 p.m.; we left the American continent only thirteen minutes ago.'

'Only thirteen minutes?' said Barbicane.

'Yes,' replied Nicholl, 'and if our initial velocity of 12,000 yards were constant, we should travel about 10,000 leagues an hour.'

'That is all very well, my friends,' said the president; 'but the insoluble question still remains: why did we not hear the report of the columbiad?'

As no reply was forthcoming, the conversation dropped, and Barbicane, plunged in thought, began to open the second side scuttle. This operation was successful, and the moon filled the projectile with a brilliant light. Nicholl, like an economical fellow, put out the gas, which had become useless; the glare, too, prevented any observation of the planetary spheres. The lunar disc shone with incomparable purity. Her rays, which were no longer dimmed by the vaporous atmosphere of the terrestrial globe, shone through the glass, and filled the air of the interior of the projectile with its silvery reflections. The black curtain of the firmament doubled the splendour of the moon, which in this ether, unfavourable to diffusion, did not eclipse the neighbouring stars. The sky, thus seen, presented a perfectly new aspect, which the human eye could not suspect. It is easy to conceive the interest with which these audacious men contemplated the orb of night, the final goal of their journey. The satellite of the earth, in its movement of translation, insensibly neared the zenith, which mathematical point it was to reach in about 96 hours later. Its mountains and its plains were not more clearly visible to their eyes, than if they had observed them from any point of the earth; but its light through a vacuum shone with extraordinary intensity. The disc glowed like a platinum mirror. The travellers had already lost all memory of the earth which fled beneath their feet. Captain Nicholl was the first to call attention to the globe which had disappeared.

'Yes,' replied Michel Ardan; 'let us not be ungrateful to it. As we are leaving our country, let us give it our last looks. I wish to see the earth before it completely disappears from my eyes.'

Barbicane, to satisfy his friend's desire, set to work to clear away the bottom window, which would allow the earth to be seen. The disc, which the force of projection had brought to the bottom, was taken to pieces, not without difficulty. Its fragments, placed carefully against the sides, might serve again if necessary. Then appeared a circular gap 50 centimetres (21 inches) wide, cut in the bottom part of the projectile. This was closed by a glass, 15 centimetres (6 inches) thick, set in a rim of copper. Below was a plate of aluminum, fixed by bolts. The nuts having been unscrewed, and the bolt-holes plugged, the plate fell back, and visual communication was established between the interior and the exterior. Michel Ardan had knelt down to the glass. It was dark as though opaque.

'Well,' cried he, 'and the earth?'

'The earth?' said Barbicane, 'there it is.'

'What!' said Ardan, 'that thin streak? – that silvery crescent?'

'Certainly, Michel. In four days, when the moon is full at the moment when we reach it, the earth will be new, and will only appear to us in the form of a thin crescent, which will soon disappear completely, and remain for some days bathed in impenetrable darkness.'

'That the earth!' repeated Michel Ardan, looking fixedly at the thin slice of his native planet.

The explanation given by President Barbicane was correct. The earth, with reference to the projectile, was entering upon its last phasis. It was in its octant, and only showed a crescent beautifully traced upon the black background of the sky. Its light, rendered bluish by the thickness of the atmospheric strata, was less intense than that of the lunar crescent. Its crescent was of considerable dimensions, like an immense bow stretched over the firmament. A few points, vividly lighted, especially in its concave portions, bespoke the presence of high mountains, which occasionally disappeared beneath thick spots, such as are never seen on the surface of the lunar disc. These were rings of cloud, lying concentrically around the terrestrial spheroid. However, thanks to a natural phenomenon – identical with that produced on the moon when in her octants – the whole contour of the terrestrial globe could be perceived. Its whole disc was rendered visible by an effect of ash-light, though less appreciably than is the case with the ash-light of the moon. And the reason of this lesser intensity may be easily understood. This reflection is caused upon the moon by the solar rays which the earth reflects on to its satellite; but the terrestrial light is about thirteen times more intense than the lunar light, which results from the difference in volume between the two bodies. Hence the result that, in the phenomenon of ash-light, the dark portion of the earth's disc is less distinctly marked out than that of the moon's disc, inasmuch as the intensity of the phenomenon is in proportion to the lighting power of the two orbs. It must also be added that the terrestrial crescent seemed to form a more extended curve than that of the disc, but this was merely the effect of irradiation. Whilst the travellers were endeavouring to pierce the profound darkness of space, a sparkling cluster of shooting-stars burst upon their eyes. Hundreds of meteorites, ignited by the contact of the atmosphere, crossed the darkness in every direction, with their luminous trains, and shed fiery spots all over the ashy portion of the disc. At this time the earth was in its perihelion; and the month of December is so prolific in these shooting-stars that astronomers have counted as many as 24,000 in an hour. But Michel Ardan, disdaining all scientific explanations, preferred to think that the earth was greeting, with its most brilliant display of fireworks, the departure of its three children. This was all that was seen of the spheroid, lost in the shadow of an inferior orb of the solar world, which, for the larger planets, rises and sets like an ordinary morning or evening star. This globe, where they had left all their affections, was nothing more than a fugitive crescent – an imperceptible point in space. The three friends, speechless but united in heart, looked long and steadfastly as the projectile flew onwards with ever-decreasing speed. Then an irresistible desire for sleep came over them. Was it fatigue of body and fatigue of mind? No doubt, for after the excitement of the last hours spent upon earth, a reaction must inevitably set in.

'Well,' said Michel Ardan, 'since we must sleep, let us do so.' And, stretching themselves upon their couches, they were soon wrapt in profound slumber. But they had not been sleeping more than a quarter of an hour, when Barbicane started up, and awakening his companions, cried with a loud voice: 'I have discovered it!'

'What have you discovered?' cried Michel Ardan, jumping from his bed.

'The reason why we did not hear the report of the columbiad.'

'What was it?' asked Nicholl.

'Because our projectile travelled quicker than sound!'

CHAPTER THREE

In which they make themselves at home

So soon as this curious but correct explanation had been given, the three friends once more relapsed into a deep sleep. Where could they have found, for slumber, a spot more calm, a centre more peaceful? Upon earth, the houses in the towns and the huts in the country feel all the shocks imparted to the earth's crust. At sea, the vessel tossed upon the waves is nothing but shocks and motion. In the air, the balloon oscillates incessantly between fluid strata of different densities. Alone this projectile, floating in an absolute vacuum, amidst absolute silence, could offer absolute repose to its inmates. Consequently, the sleep of the three adventuresome travellers would perhaps have been indefinitely prolonged, had not an unexpected noise awakened them about 7 a.m. on the 2nd of December, or nearly 8 hours after their departure. This noise was a very decided bark.

'The dogs! It's the dogs!' cried Michel Ardan, jumping up at once.

'They are hungry,' said Nicholl.

'Of course they are,' replied Michel, 'we had quite forgotten them.'

'Where are they?' asked Barbicane.

They searched, and found one of the animals hidden under the divan. Terrified and shaken by the initial shock, it had remained in this corner, until the moment when the feeling of hunger had given it tongue. It was the amiable Diana. Still somewhat frightened, she crept out of her retreat, after some enticing, and Michel Ardan encouraged her with his most gracious words.

'Come, Diana,' said he; 'come, my girl! thou whose fate will form an epoch in cynegetic annals! Thou whom pagans would have given as companion to the god Anubis, and Christians as a friend to St Roch! Thou who art worthy to be wrought in brass by the king of the infernal regions, like the puppy which Jupiter presented to Europa in exchange for a kiss! Thou whose celebrity will eclipse the heroes of Montargis and Mount St Bernard! Thou who, launched into planetary spheres, wilt perhaps become the Eve of Selenite dogs! Thou who wilt justify the words of Toussenel: "In the beginning, God created man, and, seeing how weak he was, gave him a dog" – come, Diana, come here!'

Whether Diana were flattered or not, she came out by degrees, whining plaintively.

'Good,' said Barbicane, 'I see Eve, but where is Adam?'

'Adam,' replied Michel, 'Adam cannot be far off. He is there somewhere! We must call him. Here, Satellite, here, Satellite.' But Satellite did not appear.

Diana continued to whimper. However, they discovered that she was not hurt, and an appetising mess soon stopped her whinings. As to Satellite, he appeared quite lost, but after a long search, he was discovered in one of the upper compartments of the projectile, where he had been violently thrown by the shock, in some inexplicable manner. The poor beast was sadly hurt and in a pitiable state.

'The devil!' said Michel, 'our acclimatisation is somewhat endangered.' The unfortunate animal was taken down with many precautions. His skull had been fractured against the roof, and it appeared improbable that he would recover from such a shock. Nevertheless, he was comfortably stretched out upon a cushion, and there he gave vent to a deep sigh.

'We will take care of you,' said Michel. 'We are responsible for your existence. I would rather lose my arm than a leg of my poor Satellite.' Saying which he offered the wounded dog a little water, which it drank greedily. This having been done, our three travellers observed attentively the earth and the moon. The earth was now only represented by an ashy disc, terminated by a yet narrower crescent than the day before; but its volume still remained enormous as compared with the moon, which approached nearer and nearer to a perfect circle.

'The deuce!' said Michel Ardan; 'I am dreadfully sorry we did not start at a moment of 'full earth', *i.e.* when our globe was in opposition with the sun.'

'Why?' asked Nicholl.

'Because, we should then have perceived our continents and seas in a new light – the former glowing under the projection of solar rays, the latter darker, as they appear upon certain maps of the world. I would have liked to see those poles upon which the eye of man has never rested.'

'No doubt,' replied Barbicane; 'but if the earth had been full, the moon would have been new, that is to say invisible amidst the irradiation of the sun. It is better for us to see the goal of our journey than the point of departure.'

'You are right, Barbicane,' replied Captain Nicholl. 'Besides, when we have reached the moon, we shall have plenty of time, during the long lunar nights, to observe leisurely the globe which our fellow-creatures do inhabit.'

'Our fellow-creatures!' cried Michel Ardan. 'They are no more our fellow-creatures now than the Selenites. We inhabit a new world, peopled only by ourselves – a projectile! I am the fellow-creature of Barbicane, and Barbicane of Nicholl. Beyond us, outside ourselves, humanity ceases and we are the only population of this microcosm, up to the moment when we shall become mere Selenites.'

'In about twenty-four hours,' said the captain.

'Which means – ?' asked Michel Ardan.

'That it is half-past eight,' replied Nicholl.

'In which case,' replied Michel Ardan, 'I can see no possible reason why we should not breakfast *instanter*.'

The inhabitants of the new star could not live without eating, and their stomachs were then undergoing the imperious laws of hunger. Michel Ardan, in virtue of his nationality, claimed to be head cook, for which important function there were no other competitors. The gas supplied the few degrees of heat necessary for the culinary preparations, and the provision chest furnished the elements of this first feast. Breakfast commenced with three plates of excellent soup, made by liquefying, in boiling water, some precious tablets of Liebig, prepared from the best parts of the ruminants of the pampas. To the gravy soup succeeded some slices of beefsteak, compressed by the hydraulic-press, and as tender and succulent as if they had just left the kitchens of the Café Anglais. Michel, who was highly imaginative, maintained that they were red. Preserved vegetables, 'fresher than nature', as the good-humoured Michel said, succeeded to the dish of meat, and were followed by some tea and bread-and-butter, in American fashion. This beverage, which was declared exquisite, was obtained by the infusion of the most choice leaves, of which a few boxes had been presented to the travellers by the Emperor of Russia. Lastly, to crown the repast, Ardan discovered a fine bottle of Nuits, which was lying, by chance, in the provision chest. The three friends drank it to the union of the earth and its satellite. And, as if not satisfied with this generous wine which he had distilled upon the slopes of Burgundy, the sun chose to be of the party. The projectile, at this moment, emerged from the cone of shadow formed by the terrestrial globe, and the rays of the radiant orb shone full upon the lower disc of the projectile, by reason of the angle which the moon's orbit makes with that of the earth.

'The sun!' cried Michel Ardan.

'Quite so!' replied Barbicane, 'I was expecting him.'

'However,' said Michel, 'the conical shadow which the earth throws over space extends beyond the moon?'

'Far beyond, if you do not take the atmospheric refraction into account,' said Barbicane; 'but when the moon is clothed in shadow, the centres of the three orbs, the sun, the earth, and the moon, are in a straight line with each other. Then the nodes coincide with the phases of the full moon, and there is eclipse. If we had started at a moment of eclipse of the moon, our whole passage would have been made in shadow, which would have been unfortunate.'

'Why?'

'Because, although we are floating in a vacuum, our projectile, bathed by the solar rays, receives their light and their heat. Hence an economy of gas, a precious economy in every respect.'

In fact, beneath these rays, of which the brilliancy and temperature were unimpaired by any atmosphere, the projectile was heated and lighted, as though it had suddenly passed from winter to summer. The moon above and the sun below bathed it in their light.

'It is delightful here,' said Nicholl.

'I should think so,' cried Michel Ardan; 'with a little mould spread on our aluminum planet we would have new peas in 24 hours. I am only afraid lest the sides of the projectile should melt.'

'Do not be afraid, worthy friend,' replied Barbicane. 'The projectile has sustained a much higher temperature when passing through the atmospheric strata. I should not be surprised if, to the eyes of the Floridans, it took the form of a fiery meteorite.'

'Then Maston must think we are roasted.'

'What surprises me,' replied Barbicane, 'is that we have not been roasted. It is a danger which we had not foreseen.'

'I was afraid of it,' replied Nicholl, simply.

'And you did not say anything about it, sublime captain!' cried Michel Ardan, wringing his companion's hand.

Meanwhile, Barbicane continued to make his arrangements in the projectile, as if he were never to leave it. It will be remembered that the basis of the aerial carriage had a superficies of 54 square feet. Twelve feet in height to the apex of the roof, skilfully arranged in the interior, not much encumbered by the instruments and travelling utensils – each of which had its special place – the projectile left, to the three guests, a certain amount of elbow-room. The thick glass, at the basis, could bear a considerable weight with impunity, and Barbicane and his companions trod upon its surface as upon a solid flooring. The rays of the sun, shining straight upon this glass, illumined the interior of the projectile, and produced the most singular effects of light and shade.

They began by examining the water reservoir and the provision chest.

These had not sustained any damage, thanks to the dispositions taken to break the shock. The provisions were abundant, and sufficient to supply the wants of the three travellers during a whole year. Barbicane had taken his precautions in case the projectile should fall upon an absolutely sterile part of the moon.

As to the water and reserve of 50 gallons of brandy, there would only be enough for two months. But it was shown, by the latest astronomical observations, that the moon possessed a low, dense, thick atmosphere, at least in her valleys, and there rivulets and springs could not be wanting. So, during the journey, and for one year after their arrival on the lunar continent, the adventuresome explorers would neither suffer from hunger nor thirst. There remained the question of air in the interior of the projectile. There again was perfect security. Reiset and Regnault's apparatus, for producing oxygen, was supplied with chlorate of potash for two months. It necessarily consumed a certain quantity of gas, for it had to be maintained at a temperature above 400 degrees. Here again there was an ample supply, besides which, the apparatus required but little looking after – it worked automatically. At this high temperature, the chlorate of potash changed into chloride of potassium, giving off all the oxygen therein contained. How much would 18 pounds of chlorate of potash produce? – the 7 pounds of oxygen necessary for the daily consumption of the inmates of the projectile. But it was not sufficient to renew the oxygen – it was also requisite to absorb the carbonic acid produced by exhalation. During the last twelve hours, the atmosphere in the projectile had become charged with this deleterious gas, produced by the combustion of the elements of the blood by the inhaled oxygen. Nicholl recognised this state of the air by seeing Diana panting painfully. In fact, the carbonic acid – by a phenomenon identical with that produced in the famous 'Dogs' Grotto' – had fallen to the bottom of the projectile, by reason of its density. Poor Diana, on account of the lowness of her head, would suffer before her master from the presence of this gas. Captain Nicholl hastened to remedy this state of things. He placed, at the bottom of the projectile, several saucers containing caustic potash, which he moved about from time to time, and this substance, which has a great affinity to carbonic acid, absorbed the latter, and completely purified the air in the interior. The inventory of the instruments was then commenced. The thermometers and barometers had resisted, with the exception of a minima thermometer, of which the glass had been broken. An excellent aneroid was drawn from its wadded case and hung against one of the walls. Naturally, it only marked the pressure of air at the interior of the projectile; but it also marked the quantity of moisture which it contained. At this moment its needle oscillated between 765 and 760 millimetres. The weather was 'fair'. Barbicane had also taken several compasses, which were discovered intact. It will be understood that, under such circumstances, their needles acted wildly and without constant direction. At the distance which separated the projectile from the earth, the magnetic pole could not have any apparent influence upon the apparatus. Perhaps, when the compasses were carried on to the lunar disc, some peculiar phenomena would be produced. In any case, it would be interesting to discover whether the earth's satellite was subject, like the earth, to magnetic influences. A hypsometer, to measure the altitude of lunar mountains; a sextant, to take the height of the sun; a theodolite, a surveyor's instrument, which is used to make plans and measure angles at the horizon; lunettes, the use of which would be much appreciated on their approach to the moon – all these instruments were carefully examined, and discovered to be in good condition, notwithstanding the violence of the initial shock.

As to the utensils – the pickaxes, the spades, the several tools which Nicholl had specially chosen – as to the different seeds and shrubs, which Michel Ardan intended to transplant into Selenite soil – they were all in their places, in the upper corners of the projectile. There was also a sort of lumber-room, filled with the articles which the prodigal Frenchman had piled up there. No one knew what they were, and the jovial fellow offered no explanation. From time to time he climbed up, by means of the cramp-irons fitted to the walls, but he reserved this inspection to himself. He arranged and rearranged, and plunged his hand rapidly into certain mysterious boxes, singing, completely out of tune, some old refrain from France, to enliven the situation.

Barbicane remarked, with interest, that the rockets and other fireworks had not been damaged. These important pieces, heavily charged, were to diminish the fall of the projectile, when the latter, entering into the sphere of lunar attraction, after passing the neutral point, would fall towards the surface of the moon, which fall, however, would be six times less rapid than on to the surface of the earth, on account of the difference in volume between the two orbs. Thus the inspection ended with general satisfaction, and each one returned to the observation of space through the lateral and bottom scuttles. The view was the same. The whole extent of the celestial spheres was alive with stars and constellations of marvellous purity, fit to drive an astronomer wild. On the one side the sun, like the mouth of a blazing furnace, a dazzling disc without a halo, stood out upon the dark background of the sky; on the other, was the moon shedding her reflected rays, motionless in the midst of the starry world.

Then a large spot, like a hole in the firmament, with a silvery rim; that was the earth. Here and there nebulous masses, like large flakes of sidereal snow, and, from zenith to nadir, an immense ring formed of an impalpable cloud of stars, the 'milky way', in which the sun only counts as a star of the fourth magnitude. The spectators could not withdraw their eyes from this novel spectacle, of which no description could give an idea. How many reflections it suggested! What unknown emotions it awakened in their breasts! Barbicane wished to commence the account of his journey under the influence of these impressions, and he noted, hour by hour, all the incidents which occurred during the commencement of their undertaking. He wrote quietly, with his large square writing, and in a somewhat commercial style.

During this time Nicholl, the mathematician, was overhauling his formulae of trajectories, and used his figures with unparalleled dexterity. Michel Ardan chatted, now with Barbicane, who did not reply; now with Nicholl, who did not hear him; with Diana, who understood nothing of his theories; finally with himself, questioning and answering, going and coming, busy with a thousand details; now bent over the bottom glass, now perched in the roof of the projectile, and always singing. In this microcosm, he represented French restlessness and loquacity, and it may be believed that they were worthily represented. The day, or rather to be more correct, the space of 12 hours which forms a day upon earth, was terminated by a copious supper, well prepared. No incident had yet occurred to diminish the confidence of the travellers. So, full of hope, already certain of success, they slept peacefully, whilst the projectile, with gradually decreasing speed, held its way through the paths of the heavens.

CHAPTER FOUR

A lesson in algebra

The night passed without incident. Correctly speaking, the word 'night' is improper. The position of the projectile did not change as regards the sun. Astronomically, there was day on the lower portion of the projectile and night on the upper. When therefore, in this history, these two words are employed, they express the lapse of time which occurs between the rising and setting of the sun upon earth. The travellers' sleep was the more peaceful that the projectile, notwithstanding its excessive velocity, appeared absolutely motionless. No movement betrayed its passage through space. Motion, however rapid, cannot produce any effect upon organisms when it occurs in a vacuum, or when the mass of air follows the moving body. What inhabitant of the earth perceives its rapidity, which, however, carries him along at the rate of 90,000 kilometres (about 60,000 miles) an hour? Motion, under such conditions, is no more 'felt' than repose. Hence, all bodies are indifferent on the point. Is the body in a state of repose, it will remain so until some foreign force moves it. Is it in motion, it will continue so, and only stop when some obstacle is placed in its way. This indifference to motion or repose is inertia. Barbicane and his companions, being enclosed in the projectile, might believe themselves to be in a state of absolute immobility, and the effect would have been the same if they had placed themselves outside the projectile. Had it not been for the moon, which increased above them in size, they could have sworn that they were floating in complete stagnation.

That morning – the 3rd of December – the travellers were awakened by a joyful but unexpected sound. The crowing of a cock echoed within the carriage. Michel Ardan, the first up, climbed to the top of the projectile, and, closing a half-opened case: 'Hold your tongue!' said he, in a low tone. 'The brute is going to spoil my combination.'

However, Nicholl and Barbicane had awoke.

'A cock?' said Nicholl.

'Nothing of the kind, my friends,' replied Michel, hastily; 'I only wanted to awaken you with that rural song.' Saying which he performed a magnificent Cock-a-doodle-doo! which would have done honour to the proudest champion of the dunghill. The two Americans could not keep from laughter.

'A very pretty talent,' said Nicholl, looking somewhat suspiciously at his friend.

'Yes,' replied Michel, 'one of my country's jokes. It is very Gallic. That is how they imitate the cock in the very best society.'

Then, turning the conversation: 'Do you know, Barbicane,' said he, 'of what I have been thinking all night?'

'No,' replied the president.

'Of our friends at Cambridge. You have already remarked that I am a complete ignoramus in mathematical matters. I cannot, for the life of me, imagine how the *savants* of the Observatory were able to calculate the initial velocity which would enable the projectile to reach the moon.'

'You mean,' replied Barbicane, 'to reach the neutral point where the terrestrial and lunar attractions are equal; for from that point – which is about 7/10ths of the total distance – the projectile will fall towards the moon by force of gravitation.'

'Quite so,' replied Michel; 'but, once more, how could they calculate the initial velocity?'

'It is the simplest thing in the world,' replied Barbicane.

'Could you have made the calculation?' asked Ardan.

'Certainly. Nicholl and I would have worked it out if the note from the Observatory had not spared us the trouble.'

'Well, old Barbicane, they might have cut me into slices, from my feet upwards, before I could have worked out that problem.'

'Because you don't know algebra,' replied Barbicane quietly.

'Ah, there you are, you fellows with your x's. You think algebra is an answer to everything.'

'Michel,' replied Barbicane, 'do you think one can forge without a hammer, or plough without a ploughshare?'

'With difficulty.'

'Well, algebra is a tool like the ploughshare or the hammer, and a good tool for those who know how to use it.'

'Seriously?'

'Very seriously.'

'And you could use that tool before me?'

'If it interested you.'

'And show me how the initial velocity of our carriage was calculated?'

'Yes, worthy friend. Taking into account all the elements of the problem, the distance from the centre of the earth to the centre of the moon, the earth's radius, the earth's volume, and the moon's volume, I can establish precisely what our initial velocity ought to have been, and that by means of a simple formula.'

'Let us see the formula.'

'You shall see it. However, I will not give you the curve described by the projectile between the earth and the moon, taking into account their movement of translation round the sun. I shall consider these two orbs as motionless, which will be sufficient for us.'

'Why so?'

'Because the other would be to seek the solution of the problem called "the problem of the three bodies", which integral calculi are not yet sufficiently advanced to solve.'

'How so?' said Michel Ardan, in a somewhat mocking tone of voice; 'mathematics have not said their last word yet?'

'Certainly not,' replied Barbicane.

'Good! Perhaps the Selenites have carried integral calculi farther than you. By-the-bye, what is this integral calculus?'

'It is the inverse of differential calculus,' replied Barbicane gravely.

'Much obliged.'

'In other words, it is a calculation by which you seek certain quantities, of which the differential is known.'

'At least that is clear,' said Michel, with a most satisfied air.

'Now,' said Barbicane, 'give me a slip of paper and a pencil, and in less than half-an-hour I will find out the formula required.'

Whereupon Barbicane became absorbed in his work, whilst Nicholl looked out into space, leaving the care of the breakfast to his companion. Half-an-hour had not passed when Barbicane, raising his head, showed Michel Ardan a paper covered with algebraical signs, in the centre of which was the following general formula:

$$\frac{1}{2}\left(v^2 - v_0^2\right) = gr\left\{\frac{r}{x} - 1 + \frac{m'}{m}\left(\frac{r}{d-x} - \frac{r}{d-r}\right)\right\}$$

'Which means – ?' asked Michel.

'It means,' replied Nicholl, 'that one half v^2 minus v_0^2, equals gr, multiplied by r divided by x, minus one, plus m' divided by m, multiplied by r divided by d minus x, minus r divided dy d minus r –'

'x upon y riding on z and mounted on p,' cried Michel Ardan, bursting into a laugh. 'And do you understand that, captain?'

'Nothing can be clearer.'

'Certainly not,' said Michel; 'it is as clear as daylight, and I am enlightened at once.'

'You eternal joker!' replied Barbicane; 'you wanted algebra, and you shall have your fill of it.'

'I would rather be hanged!'

'Really,' replied Nicholl, who was examining the formula as a connoisseur, 'that is very well put together, Barbicane. It is the integral of the equation of live forces, and I have no doubt it will give us the requisite result.'

'But I should like to understand,' cried Michel; 'I would give ten years of Nicholl's life to understand!'

'Listen then,' continued Barbicane, 'one half v^2 minus v_0^2 is the formula for the half variation of live force.'

'Good, and Nicholl knows what that means?'

'No doubt, Michel,' replied the captain. 'All these signs, which appear so mysterious, form the clearest and most consistent language which can be read.'

'And you pretend, Nicholl,' asked Michel, 'that by means of these hieroglyphics, more incomprehensible than the Egyptian Ibis, you can discover the initial velocity requisite to be given to the projectile?'

'Certainly,' replied Nicholl; 'and by this same formula, I could always tell you what is its velocity at a given point of its journey.'

'On your honour?'

'On my honour.'

'Then you are as clever as the president?'

'No, Michel; Barbicane had done the difficult part, which consists in establishing an equation which takes all the conditions of the problem into account. The rest is only a question of arithmetic, and only requires a knowledge of the four rules.'

'That is a good deal!' replied Michel Ardan, who had never been able to make a correct addition in his life.

However, Barbicane maintained that Nicholl would have had no difficulty in discovering the same formula.

'I don't know,' said Nicholl; 'for the more I study it, the more admirable I think it.'

'Now listen,' said Barbicane to his ignorant comrade, 'and you will see that all these letters have their signification.'

'I am listening,' said Michel with a resigned air.

'd,' said Barbicane, 'is the distance from the centre of the earth to the centre of the moon, for we must take the centres to calculate attractions.'

'I understand that.'

'r is the radius of the earth.'

'r radius – admitted!'

'm is the mass of the earth, m' the mass of the moon. It is necessary to take the masses of the two bodies into account, because the attraction is in proportion to the masses.'

'That is agreed.'

'g represents the gravity – the velocity acquired at the end of one second by a body falling to the surface of the earth. Is that clear?'

'Like spring water!' replied Michel.

'Now, I represent by x the variable distance which separates the projectile from the centre of the earth, and by v the velocity which the projectile has attained at that distance.'

'Good.'

'Lastly, the expression v_o, which figures in the equation, is the velocity of the projectile upon leaving the atmosphere.'

'Quite right,' said Nicholl; 'that is the point at which you must calculate the velocity, since we know already that the velocity at starting is exactly equal to one and a half times the velocity on leaving the atmosphere.'

'I don't understand any longer,' said Michel.

'It is simple enough,' said Barbicane.

'Not so simple as I am,' said Michel.

'It means that, when our projectile reached the limit of the terrestrial atmosphere, it had already lost one-third of its initial velocity.'

'So much as that?'

'Yes, my friend, merely by friction with the atmospheric strata. You understand that the more rapidly it travelled, the greater resistance it met with from the air.'

'I admit that,' replied Michel, 'although your v zero two, and your v zero square are rattling in my head like nails in a bag.'

'That is the first effect of algebra,' replied Barbicane. 'And now, to finish you off, we are going to establish the numeric data of these several expressions; that is, calculate their value.'

'Finish me off,' replied Michel.

'Some of these expressions,' said Barbicane, 'are known; the others have to be calculated.'

'I will undertake the latter,' said Nicholl.

'Let us see, r,' continued Barbicane; 'r is the radius of the earth, which, under the latitude of Florida, our starting-point, is equal to 6,370,000 metres (say 7,000,000 yards). d – that is, the distance from the centre of the earth to the centre of the moon, is equal to 56 radii of the earth, say – '

Nicholl calculated rapidly. 'Say,' said he, '356,720,000 metres (about 420,000,000 yards) at the moment when the moon is in perigee – that is, at her shortest distance from the earth.'

'Good,' said Barbicane. Now, m'/m – that is, the relation between the mass of the earth and the mass of the moon, equals – 1/81th.'

'Hear, hear!' said Michel.

'g, the gravity, is, in Florida, 9 metres, 91 centimetres, whence it results that gr equals – '

'Sixty-two million four hundred and twenty-six thousand square metres,' replied Nicholl.

'And now?' asked Michel Ardan.

'Now that the expressions are put into figures,' replied Barbicane, 'I am going to seek the velocity, v_0 – that is, the velocity which the projectile must possess on leaving the atmosphere, to reach the point of attraction, equal to an absence of velocity. Since, at that moment, the velocity will be null, I put down that it will be equal to zero, and that x, the distance where the neutral point is to be found, will be represented by 9/10ths of d – that is, the distance which separates the two centres.'

'I have a vague idea that it must be so,' said Michel.

'I shall then have: x equals 9/10ths of d, and v equals zero, and my formula will become – '

Barbicane wrote rapidly on the paper –

$$v_0^2 = 2\,gr\left\{1 - \frac{10\,r}{9d} - \frac{1}{81}\left(\frac{10\,r}{d} - \frac{r}{d-r}\right)\right\}$$

Nicholl scanned it greedily.

'That is it, that is it,' he cried.

'Is it clear?' asked Barbicane.

'It is written in letters of fire!' replied Nicholl.

'Extraordinary men!' murmured Michel.

'Have you understood at last?' asked Barbicane.

'Have I understood?' cried Michel Ardan; 'why, my head is bursting with it!'

'So,' replied Barbicane, 'v_0^2 equals 2 gr multiplied by 1 minus 10r/9d minus 1/81th multiplied by 10r/d minus r/$d-r$.

'And now,' said Nicholl, 'to obtain the velocity of the projectile on leaving the atmosphere, it is only necessary to calculate.'

The captain, like a practitioner equal to all difficulties, began to calculate with frightful rapidity. Divisions and multiplications increased under his fingers; the figures covered the white paper. Barbicane followed every line, whilst Michel Ardan repressed a growing headache with both hands.

'Well?' said Barbicane, after a few minutes' silence.

'Well,' replied Nicholl, 'v_0 – that is, the velocity of the projectile on leaving the atmosphere, to reach the point of equal attractions, ought to have been – '

'What?' said Barbicane.

'Eleven thousand and fifty-one metres (12,000 yards) in the first second.'

'Hallo!' cried Barbicane, jumping up; '11,051 metres. Damnation!' cried the president, with a gesture of despair.

'What is the matter?' asked Michel Ardan, much surprised.

'What is the matter! Why, if at that moment the velocity was already reduced by one-third from friction, the initial velocity ought to have been – '

'Sixteen thousand five hundred and seventy-three metres (18,000 yards),' replied Nicholl.

'And the Cambridge Observatory, who declared that 11,000 metres were sufficient for the departure, and our projectile, which started with only that velocity – !'

'Well?' asked Nicholl.

'Well! it will be insufficient.'

'Goodness!'

'We shall not reach the neutral point.'

'Confound it!'

'We won't even go half way.'

'God bless me!' cried Michel Ardan, jumping as though the projectile had been on the point of striking the terrestrial spheroid.

'And we shall fall back to earth.'

CHAPTER FIVE

The coldness of space

This revelation was a thunderbolt. Who would have expected such an error of calculation! Barbicane would not believe it. Nicholl went again over his figures, but they were exact. As to the formula, its correctness could not be suspected; and, after verification, it became evident that an initial velocity of 16,576 metres in the first second was necessary to reach the neutral point. The three friends looked at each other in silence. There was no further question of breakfasting. Barbicane, with compressed lips, contracted eyebrows, and hands clasped convulsively, gazed fixedly through the scuttle. Nicholl, with crossed arms, examined his figures. Michel Ardan murmured: 'There you have the men of science. They are always doing something of that sort. I would give twenty pistoles to fall upon the Cambridge Observatory and crush it, with all the dabblers in figures which it contains.'

Suddenly the captain made an observation which struck Barbicane at once.

'Hallo!' said he, 'it is 7 a.m. We have been travelling for thirty-two hours. More than half our journey is passed, and we are not falling, that I know of.'

Barbicane did not reply, but, after a rapid glance at the captain, he took a compass, which served to measure the angular distance of the terrestrial globe. Then through the lower glass he took a very exact observation, thanks to the apparent immobility of the projectile. Then rising and wiping the drops of perspiration from his forehead, he made some calculations on paper. Nicholl understood that the president was calculating from the measure of the terrestrial diameter, the distance of the projectile from the earth. He looked at him anxiously.

'No,' said Barbicane after a few minutes, 'no; we are not falling. We are already at more than 50,000 miles from the earth! We have passed the point where the projectile should have stopped, if its starting velocity was only 11,000 metres. We are still ascending.'

'That is evident,' said Nicholl; 'and we must conclude that our initial velocity under the pressure of 400,000 pounds of gun-cotton has exceeded the 11,000 metres required. I can now understand how we met, after only 13 minutes' journey, the second satellite, which revolves at a distance of 2,000 leagues from the earth.'

'This explanation is the more probable,' added Barbicane, 'that in getting rid of the water contained between the breakable partitions, the projectile suddenly found itself relieved of a considerable weight.'

'Quite right,' said Nicholl.

'Ah! worthy Nicholl,' cried Barbicane, 'we are saved.'

'Well,' said Michel Ardan quietly, 'as we are saved let us breakfast.'

In fact Nicholl was not mistaken. The initial velocity had been happily superior to the velocity fixed by the Cambridge Observatory, but the Cambridge Observatory was not the less in the wrong. The travellers, having recovered from this false alarm, took their seats and breakfasted gaily. If they ate much they talked more. The confidence was greater than after the 'algebra incident'.

'Why should we not succeed?' repeated Michel Ardan. 'Why should we not reach the moon? We have started, there are no obstacles in the way, the road is open, more open than to the ship, which fights against the waves, more open than to a balloon, which fights against the wind! If, then, a ship reaches where it will, if a balloon ascends as it pleases, why should our projectile not attain our desired goal?'

'It will,' said Barbicane.

'If it were only to honour the American people,' added Michel Ardan, 'the only nation capable of carrying out such an undertaking, the only one which could produce a President Barbicane! By-the-bye, now that I think of it, now that we have no further uneasiness, what will become of us? We shall be right royally bored!' Barbicane and Nicholl shook their heads.

'But I have provided for the case, my friends,' continued Michel Ardan. 'You have only to speak. I have at your disposal chess, draughts, cards, dominoes. There only wants a billiard-table!'

'What!' cried Barbicane, 'you have brought such trifles with you?'

'Doubtless,' said Michel; 'and not only to amuse ourselves, but with the laudable intention of endowing the Selenite public-houses with them.'

'My friends,' said Barbicane, 'if the moon is inhabited, the inhabitants must have appeared a few thousand years before those of the earth, for we cannot doubt that the orb is more ancient than ours. If, therefore, the Selenites exist for some hundreds of thousands of years, if their brain is organised like the human brain, they have already invented all that we have invented, and even what we will invent in the course of centuries. They will have nothing to learn from us, and we, on the contrary, will have everything to learn from them.'

'What!' replied Michel, 'you think they have had artists like Phidias, Michel Angelo, or Raphael?'

'Yes.'

'Poets like Homer, Virgil, Milton, Lamartine, Hugo?'

'I am certain of it.'

'Philosophers like Plato, Aristotle, Descartes, Kant?'

'I have no doubt of it.'

'Scientific men like Archimedes, Euclid, Pascal, Newton?'

'I would swear it.'

'Comics like Arnal and photographers like – Nadar?'

'I am sure they have.'

'Then, friend Barbicane, if they are as wise as we are, and even wiser – these Selenites – why have they not tried to communicate with the earth? Why have they not despatched a lunar projectile into the terrestrial regions?'

'Who says they have not?' replied Barbicane gravely.

'In point of fact,' added Nicholl, 'it would have been easier for them than for us, and for two reasons: first, because the attraction is six times less on the surface of the moon than on the surface of the earth, which would allow a projectile to ascend more easily; secondly, because it would have sufficed to send the projectile 8,000 leagues only, instead of 80,000, which only requires a force of projection ten times less.'

'Then,' continued Michel, 'I repeat, why have they not done it?'

'And I,' replied Barbicane, 'I repeat, who says they have not done it?'

'When?'

'Thousands of years ago; before the appearance of man upon earth.'

'And the projectile? Where is the projectile? I ask to see the projectile.'

'My friend,' replied Barbicane, 'the ocean covers five-sixths of our globe. Hence five good reasons for supposing that the lunar projectile, if launched, is now submerged at the bottom of the Atlantic or Pacific; unless it is buried in some crevasse, before the rind of the earth was completely formed.'

'Barbicane, old fellow,' replied Michel, 'you have an answer for everything, and I bow to your wisdom. However, there is one hypothesis which pleases me more than the others; it is that the Selenites, being more ancient than we, are also wiser, and have not invented gunpowder.'

At this moment Diana took a share in the conversation by a loud bark. She wanted her breakfast.

'Ah!' said Michel. 'In our discussion, we are forgetting Diana and Satellite.'

Immediately, a respectable mess was offered to the bitch, who devoured it with a good appetite.

'You see, Barbicane,' said Michel, 'we ought to have made a second Noah's ark of our projectile, and carried to the moon a couple of each kind of domestic animals.'

'No doubt,' replied Barbicane; 'if we had had room enough.'

'Oh,' said Michel, 'by squeezing a little!'

'The fact is,' said Nicholl, 'that oxen, cows, bulls, horses – all these ruminants would have been very useful to us on the lunar continent. Unfortunately this carriage could not contain either a stable or a pigsty.'

'At least,' said Michel Ardan, 'we might have brought an ass; one wee little ass, that courageous and patient beast which old Silenus liked so much to ride! I love the poor donkeys; they are certainly the least favoured animals in creation. Not only are they beaten during their lifetime, they are even beaten after death.'

'How so?' asked Barbicane.

'Why,' said Michel, 'don't they make drum-heads of them?'

Barbicane and Nicholl could not refrain from laughter at this ridiculous reflection; but a cry from their jovial companion stopped them. He was bent over Satellite's kennel, and arose saying, 'Good, Satellite is no longer ill.'

'Bravo!' said Nicholl.

'No,' replied Michel; 'he is dead! That is most embarrassing,' added he, in a piteous tone of voice. 'I am afraid, my poor Diana, that you will not leave any descendants in the lunar regions.'

The unfortunate Satellite had not survived his wounds. He was dead, thoroughly dead; and Michel, crestfallen, looked at his friends.

'There is one point,' said Barbicane; 'we cannot keep the carcase of this dog for another forty-eight hours.'

'Most certainly not,' replied Nicholl; 'but our scuttles work on hinges, they can be opened. We will open one of them and throw the dog into space.'

The president reflected a few minutes, and said: 'Yes, that is what we must do; but we must take the most minute precautions.'

'Why?' asked Michel.

'For two reasons, that you will readily understand,' replied Barbicane. 'The first relates to the air in the projectile, of which we must lose as little as possible.'

'But, as we renew the air?'

'Only a portion. We only renew the oxygen, good Michel; and, by the way, we must take care that the apparatus does not supply oxygen in too

great quantities, for such an excess would produce very serious physiological disturbances. But in renewing the oxygen, we do not renew the
nitrogen, which the lungs do not absorb, and which remains intact. Now
this nitrogen would escape rapidly through the open scuttles.'

'Oh, the time to throw out poor Satellite,' said Michel.

'Very well; but let us be quick.'

'And the second reason?' asked Michel.

'The second reason is that we must not allow the exterior cold, which is
intense, to penetrate into the projectile, or we should be frozen to death.'

'But the sun – '

'The sun warms our projectile, which absorbs its rays; but it does not
warm the vacuum in which we float at the present moment. Where there
is no air, there is no more heat than diffused light; and, as it is dark, so it is
cold, where the rays of the sun do not reach directly. This temperature is
therefore nothing more than the temperature produced by the starry
irradiation, which is what the earth would receive if the sun were to be
extinguished some day.'

'Which is not to be feared,' replied Nicholl.

'Who knows?' said Michel Ardan. 'But even admitting that the sun will
not be extinguished, the earth might become more distant from it.'

'Good,' said Barbicane; 'those are Michel's notions.'

'Oh,' continued Michel, 'do we not know that the earth passed through
the tail of a comet in 1861? Now, suppose a comet with an attraction
greater than the solar attraction, the terrestrial orbit will incline towards
the wandering star, and the earth, becoming its satellite, would be carried
away to a distance where the rays of the sun would have no further action
on its surface.'

'That might happen,' replied Barbicane, 'but the consequences of such
a displacement might not be so redoubtable as you suppose.'

'Why not?'

'Because the heat and the cold would equalise on our globe. It was
calculated that if the earth had been carried away by the comet in 1861, it
would not have felt, at its greatest distance from the sun, a heat sixteen
times superior to that which we receive from the moon; which heat, concentrated in the focus of the strongest burning-glasses, produces no effect.'

'Well?' said Michel.

'Wait a minute,' replied Barbicane. 'They also calculated that at its
perihelium – that is, its nearest approach to the sun – the earth would
have supported a heat equal to 28,000 times that of summer. But this
heat, capable of vitrifying terrestrial matter and vaporising water, would
have formed a dense ring of cloud, and tempered the excessive heat.

Hence, compensation between the cold of the aphelium and the heat of the perihelium, and an average, probably, bearable.'

'But, at how many degrees do they estimate the temperature of the planetary spheres?' asked Nicholl.

'Formerly,' replied Barbicane, 'they thought that the temperature was excessively low. By calculating its thermometrical decrease, we reach a figure, millions of degrees below zero. Fourier, a fellow-countryman of Michel, an illustrious member of the Academy of Sciences, reduced these figures to their closest estimates. In his opinion the temperature of space does not descend below −60°.'

'Pooh!' said Michel.

'That is about the temperature which was observed in the Polar regions,' said Barbicane, 'on Melville Island, or at Fort Reliance; about 56° below zero centigrade.'

'It remains to be proved,' said Nicholl, 'whether Fourier was not mistaken in his calculations. Unless I am mistaken, another French scientist, M. Pouillet, estimates the temperature of space at 160° below zero. We shall be able to verify.'

'Not at the present moment,' replied Barbicane, 'for the solar rays strike directly on our thermometer, and would, on the contrary, give a very high temperature. But, when we have reached the moon, during the nights, fifteen days long, which each face undergoes in turn, we shall have leisure to make our experiment, for our satellite moves in a vacuum.'

'What do you mean by a vacuum?' asked Michel. 'Is it an absolute vacuum?'

'It is a vacuum absolutely deprived of air.'

'In which nothing replaces the air?'

'Yes, ether,' replied Barbicane.

'Ah! what is ether?'

'Ether, my good friend, is an agglomeration of imponderable atoms, which, say the works on molecular physics, are, in relation to their dimensions, as far removed from each other as the celestial bodies are in space. Their distance, however, is inferior to one three-millionth part of a millimetre. These atoms, by their movement of vibration, produce light and heat by making, in each second, 430,000,000,000,000 undulations, each undulation only extending from four to six ten-millionth parts of a millimetre.'

'Milliards of milliards!' cried Michel Ardan. 'Have they measured and counted these oscillations? All those figures, my friend, are good enough for scientists. They frighten the ear and do not appeal to the mind.'

'However, one must calculate −'

'No; it is better to compare. A trillion signifies nothing. A comparison means everything. For instance, when you tell me that the volume of Uranus is 76 times greater than the Earth's, Saturn's volume 900 times greater, Jupiter's volume 1,300 times greater, the Sun's volume 1,300,000 times greater, I am not much the wiser. I much prefer the old-fashioned comparisons of the *Double Liègeois*, which inform you simply: the Sun is a pumpkin, two feet in diameter, Jupiter an orange, Saturn a love-apple, Neptune a black cherry, Uranus a smaller cherry, the Earth a bean, Venus a pea, Mars a large pin's head, Mercury a mustard seed, and Juno, Ceres, Vesta, and Pallas mere grains of sand. One can understand that sort of thing.'

After Michel's tirade against scientists and the trillions which they cast up without winking, they proceeded to bury Satellite. It was merely necessary to throw him into space, in the same way that sailors throw a corpse into the sea. But, as President Barbicane had advised, it was necessary to operate rapidly, so as to lose as little air as possible. The bolts of the right-hand scuttle, which measured about 30 centimetres across, were carefully unscrewed, whilst Michel, in great grief, prepared to throw his dog into space. The glass, worked by a powerful lever which enabled it to overcome the pressure of the interior air against the walls of the projectile, turned rapidly on its hinge, and Satellite was thrown out. Hardly any molecules of air escaped; in fact, the operation succeeded so well that later on Barbicane was not afraid to get rid, in this way, of the useless lumber which encumbered the carriage.

CHAPTER SIX

Questions and answers

On the 4th of December, the chronometers marked 5 a.m. by terrestrial time, when the travellers awoke, after 54 hours' journey. As regards time, they had only passed, by five hours, the half of the time fixed for their stay in the projectile; but, as regards distance, they had already got over 7/10ths of the passage. This singularity was owing to the regular decrease in their speed. When they observed the earth through the lower glass, it now only appeared to them like a dark spot, bathed in the solar rays. No longer any crescent, no longer any ash-light. The next day, at midnight, the earth would be new, at the precise moment when the moon would be full. Over-head, the orb of night approached nearer and nearer to the line followed by the projectile, so as to meet with it at the hour fixed. All around the dark vault was constellated with brilliant spots which appeared to move slowly, but, owing to the considerable distance at which they lay, their relative sizes did not appear to be modified. The sun and the stars appeared just as they are seen from the earth. As to the moon, she had considerably increased in size; but the travellers' telescopes not being very powerful they could not make any reliable observations, or reconnoitre her topo-graphical or geological dispositions. Therefore, the time passed in interm-inable conversations, of which the moon formed the principal topic. Each one brought his contingent of special knowledge; Barbicane and Nicholl always serious, Michel Ardan always fantastic. The projectile, its situation, its direction, the incidents which might arise, and the precautions which its fall upon the moon would necessitate, supplied unlimited matter for con-jecture. While they were at breakfast a question of Michel's, relating to the projectile, elicited from Barbicane a curious answer, worthy of being related. Michel, supposing that the projectile should be suddenly stopped in the midst of its terrific initial velocity, wished to know what would have been the consequences of such stoppage.

'But I don't see,' said Barbicane, 'how the projectile could have been stopped.'

'A mere supposition,' said Michel.

'An impossible supposition,' replied the practical Barbicane; 'unless the force of impulsion suddenly ceased. But in that case its velocity would have decreased gradually, and it would not have suddenly stopped. Suppose for one moment it had struck some body floating in space.'

'Which?'

'The enormous meteorite which we met with.'

'In that case,' said Nicholl, 'the projectile would have been dashed into a thousand atoms, and we also.'

'Better still,' said Barbicane, 'we should have been burnt alive.'

'Burnt!' cried Michel. 'By Jove, I am sorry the event did not occur, just to see.'

'And you would have seen,' replied Barbicane. 'We now know that heat is but a modification of motion. When we heat water – that is, when we add heat to it – it means that we set its molecules into movement.'

'By George!' said Michel, 'that is an ingenious theory.'

'And a correct one, worthy friend, for it explains all the phenomena connected with heat. Heat is only a molecular movement, a mere oscillation of the particles of a body. When the brake of a train is applied, the train stops. What becomes of the movement by which it was animated? It is transformed into heat and the brake becomes hot. Why do we grease the axles of wheels? To keep them from becoming hot, because that heat would be so much movement lost by transformation. Do you understand?'

'Do I understand!' replied Michel. 'For instance, when I have run for a long time and am in a bath of perspiration, covered with sweat, why am I obliged to stop? Simply because my movement is transformed into heat.'

Barbicane could not refrain from smiling at this repartee. Then, continuing his theory: 'Consequently,' said he, 'in the event of a shock, the same thing would have happened to our projectile as to the bullet which falls, burning, after striking a metal shield. Its movement would be changed into heat. Consequently, I maintain that if our projectile had struck the meteorite, its velocity, suddenly checked, would have created sufficient heat to volatilise it instantaneously.'

'What, then, would happen if the earth were to stop suddenly in its movement of translation?'

'The temperature would be carried to such a height,' replied Barbicane, 'that it would immediately be turned into vapour.'

'Good,' said Michel; 'there you have a way of ending the world which would simplify many things.'

'And if the earth fell upon the sun?' said Nicholl.

'According to calculation,' replied Barbicane, 'that fall would develop an amount of heat equal to the heat produced by 1,600 globes of coal each of the same volume as the terrestrial globe.'

'A nice increase of temperature for the sun,' replied Michel Ardan, 'and for which, no doubt, the inhabitants of Uranus and Neptune would be grateful, for they must be perishing from cold on their planets.

'Thus, my friends,' continued Barbicane, 'every movement suddenly checked produces heat; and this theory leads us to admit that the heat of the solar disc is maintained by a hail of meteorites incessantly falling to its surface. Calculations have been made – '

'Look out,' murmured Michel Ardan, 'here come the figures!'

'It has been calculated,' continued Barbicane, imperturbably, 'that the shock of each meteorite upon the sun would produce an amount of heat equal to that of 4,000 masses of coal of the same size.'

'And what is the solar heat?' asked Michel.

'It is equal to that produced by the combustion of a seam of coal surrounding the sun, and of a thickness of 27 kilometres.'

'And that heat – ?'

'Would be sufficient to boil, per hour, two milliards nine hundred millions of cubic myriametres of water.'

'And yet it does not roast us!' cried Michel.

'No,' replied Barbicane; 'because the terrestrial atmosphere absorbs four-tenths of the solar heat. Besides, the amount of heat intercepted by the earth, is only the two-milliardth of the total irradiation.'

'I quite see that all is for the best!' cried Michel, 'and that this atmosphere is a useful invention; for it not only allows us to breathe, but it prevents our being cooked.'

'Yes,' said Nicholl; 'but unfortunately it will not be the same in the moon.'

'Bah!' said Michel, always full of confidence; 'if there are inhabitants they must breathe; if there are no longer any they will certainly have left sufficient oxygen for three persons, if it were only at the bottom of the valleys, where its weight would have caused it to accumulate. Well, we won't climb up the mountains, that is all.' And Michel, rising, went off to observe the lunar disc, which shone with dazzling brilliancy. 'By Jove,' said he, 'it must be very hot up there.'

'Without counting,' replied Nicholl, 'that the days last 360 hours.'

'As a compensation,' said Barbicane, 'the nights are of the same duration, and as the heat arises from radiation, their temperature can only be that of the planetary spheres.'

'A nice country,' said Michel; 'but no matter – I wish I was there! By Jupiter! my friends, it will be curious to have the earth for a moon, to see it rise in the horizon, to recognise the configuration of its continents, to say, "There is America; there is Europe." Then to follow it till it loses itself in the rays of the sun. By-the-bye, Barbicane, are there any eclipses for the Selenites?'

'Yes, eclipses of the sun,' replied Barbicane; 'when the centres of the three orbs are on the same line, the earth being in the middle. But they are only partial eclipses, during which the earth is thrown like a screen upon the solar disc, allowing the greater part of it to be seen.'

'Why is there no total eclipse?' asked Michel. 'Is it because the cone of shadow, thrown by the earth, does not extend beyond the moon?'

'Yes, if you do not take into account the refraction produced by the terrestrial atmosphere; no, if you take that into account. So let ∂ be the horizontal parallax and p the half diameter visible – '

'*Ouf!*' cried Michel, 'one half of v zero square. Speak plainly, you algebraic man!'

'Well, in common parlance,' replied Barbicane, 'the mean distance from the moon to the earth being equal to 60 radii of the latter, the length of the cone of shadow is reduced by refraction to less than 42 radii. Hence it results that, in eclipses, the moon is found beyond the cone of pure shadow, and that the sun not only sends her its edge rays but also its central rays.'

'Then,' said Michel, jeeringly, 'why is there an eclipse since there should not be one?'

'Merely because the solar rays are weakened by this refraction, and the atmosphere, through which they pass, absorbs the greater number of them.'

'That reason suffices,' replied Michel. 'Besides, we shall see for ourselves when we get there. Now tell me, Barbicane, do you think that the moon is an old comet?'

'What an idea!'

'Yes,' replied Michel with inimitable foppishness, 'I occasionally have ideas like that!'

'But that is not Michel's idea,' said Nicholl.

'Good, then I am a plagiarist!'

'No doubt,' replied Nicholl. 'According to the testimony of the ancients, the Arcadians maintained that they had inhabited the earth before the moon became its satellite. Reasoning from this fact, certain learned men have considered the moon a comet, whose orbit brought it one day sufficiently near the earth to be retained by terrestrial attraction.'

'And what truth is there in that hypothesis?' asked Michel.

'None,' replied Barbicane; 'and the proof is, that the moon has not retained any trace of that gaseous surrounding which always accompanies comets.'

'But,' replied Nicholl, 'might not the moon, before having become the earth's satellite, have passed near enough to the sun in her perihelium to lose all gaseous substances by evaporation?'

'That is possible, friend Nicholl, but not probable.'

'Why not?'

'Because – By Jove! I really do not know.'

'Ah!' cried Michel, 'how many hundred volumes one might fill with what one does not know!'

'By the way, what o'clock is it?' asked Barbicane.

'Three,' replied Nicholl.

'How time flies,' said Michel, 'in the conversation of such learned men as we! Decidedly, I feel that I am becoming too learned. I feel that I am becoming a well of science!' Saying which, Michel hoisted himself to the roof of the projectile, 'to get a better look at the moon,' he said. During this time his companions gazed into space through the lower glass. There was nothing new to be seen.

When Michel Ardan had come down he approached the side scuttle, and suddenly gave vent to an exclamation of surprise.

'What now?' asked Barbicane. The president approached the glass and perceived a sort of flattened sack, which floated outside at a few metres from the projectile. This object seemed motionless, like the projectile, and was consequently animated by the same ascending motion.

'What the devil is that?' said Michel Ardan. 'Is it one of the corpuscles of space which our projectile retains within its radius of attraction, and which will accompany it to the moon?'

'What astonishes me,' replied Nicholl, 'is that the specific weight of that body, which is certainly less than the projectile's, allows it to maintain itself on our level.'

'Nicholl,' replied Barbicane, after a moment's reflection, 'I do not know what that object is, but I know perfectly well why it remains on a level with the projectile.'

'Why?'

'Because we are floating in a vacuum, my dear captain, and that in a vacuum all bodies fall or move (which is the same thing) with equal velocity whatever their weight or shape. It is air that creates, by its resistance, differences in weight. When you create a vacuum in a tube by means of an air-pump, all the articles within it, specks of dust or pellets of lead, fall with the same rapidity. Here in space, we have the same cause and the same effect.'

'Quite right,' said Nicholl; 'and all that we throw out of the projectile will accompany the latter in its journey to the moon.'

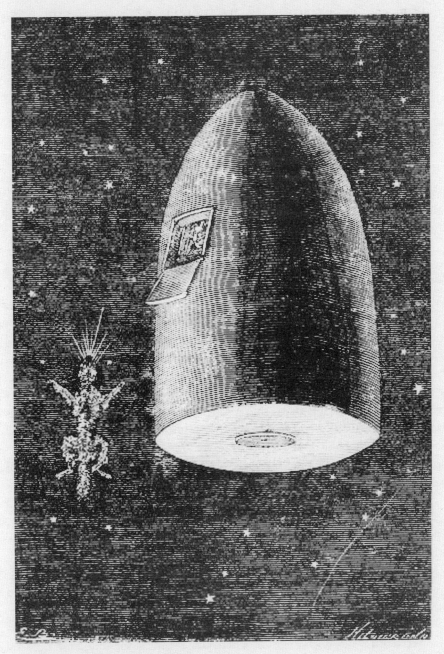

'What fools we are!' cried Michel.

'Why?' asked Barbicane.

'Because we ought to have filled the projectile with useful articles – books, instruments, tools, &c. We could have thrown them all out of window, and they would all have followed in our train. But now that I think of it, why should we not walk outside like this meteorite? Why not cast ourselves into space through the scuttle? What delight to remain suspended in ether, more favoured than the bird, who must always keep his wings moving.'

'Agreed,' said Barbicane; 'but how shall we breathe?'

'Cursed air, which fails us at such an interesting moment.'

'But if it did not fail, Michel, your density being much less than that of the projectile, you would be quickly left behind.'

'Then there is no means?'

'None whatever.'

'We must remain shut up in the carriage?'

'We must.'

'Hallo!' cried Michel in a formidable voice.

'What is it?' asked Nicholl.

'I know – I guess what that pretended meteorite is! It is not an asteroid – it is not a piece of planet!'

'What is it, then?' asked Barbicane.

'It is our unfortunate dog, Diana's husband.' In fact this deformed, unrecognisable object, reduced to nothing, was the corpse of Satellite, flattened out like an empty wind-bag, and still ascending, ascending ever!

CHAPTER SEVEN

A moment of frenzy

Thus a curious but consistent phenomenon, extraordinary, but capable of explanation, was happening under these singular conditions. Every article, thrown out of the projectile, would follow the same trajectory and only stop with it. Here was a subject of conversation sufficient for the whole evening. The excitement of the three travellers increased as they approached the end of their journey. They expected something unforeseen, some new phenomena, and nothing would have surprised them in their present frame of mind. Their excited imagination went ahead of the projectile, whose swiftness diminished notably without their being aware of it. But the moon increased before their eyes, and they already thought that they had but to stretch out their hand to grasp it. The next day, all three were on foot from 5 a.m. That day was to be the last of their journey, if their calculations were correct. That same evening, at midnight, in 18 hours, at the precise moment of the full moon, they would reach her flaming disc. This most extra-ordinary journey of ancient or modern times would be completed at midnight. So, from early morning, they greeted the orb of night with confident and joyous cheers through the scuttles silvered by her rays. The moon advanced majestically upon the starry firmament. Yet a few more degrees and she would reach the precise point in space, where her junction with the projectile would take place. From his own observ-ations, Barbicane calculated that they would reach the northern hemi-sphere, where there are immense plains and but few mountains, which circumstance would be favourable, if the lunar atmosphere, as it was thought, was stored in the valleys only.

'Besides which,' remarked Michel Ardan, 'a plain is better adapted to disembarkments than a mountain. A Selenite who had been dropped in Europe upon the summit of Mont Blanc, or in Asia upon the top of the Himalayas, could not precisely be considered to have arrived.'

'Further,' added Captain Nicholl; 'on a flat surface, the projectile will remain motionless as soon as it has reached it; on a slope, it would roll like an avalanche. As we are not precisely squirrels, we should not get out of it alive; so, all is for the best!'

In fact, the success of the audacious experiment no longer appeared doubtful. However, one reflection preoccupied Barbicane, but, not wishing to alarm his companions, he held his peace. The direction of the projectile, towards the northern hemisphere of the moon, proved that its trajectory had been somewhat modified. The line of fire, mathematically calculated, should carry the projectile into the very centre of the lunar disc. If it did not arrive there, it was on account of some deviation. What had produced it? Barbicane could not imagine nor determine the importance of this deviation, for all fixed points were wanting. He hoped that the only result would be, to carry them to the northern edge of the moon, which was the most propitious for landing. So Barbicane, without saying anything to his friends, contented himself with observing the moon, and trying to discover whether the direction of the projectile was not further modified; for the situation would have been terrible, if the projectile, missing its aim and carried beyond the lunar disc, were to be launched into the planetary regions. At this moment the moon, instead of appearing flat like a disc, already gave signs of convexity. If the sun had shed its rays upon her obliquely, the shadow thrown would have indicated the high mountains, and clearly defined them. The eye might have plunged into the yawning gulfs of the craters, and followed the capricious grooves which cover the extent of the plains. But all relief was levelled in one intense glow. It was even difficult to trace the large spots, which give to the moon the appearance of a human face.

'Face, if you like,' said Ardan; 'but I am sorry for the amiable sister of Apollo, it's a very worn face!'

Meanwhile our travellers, so near the end of their journey, did not cease to observe this new world; their imagination carried them through these unknown countries. They ascended the highest summits; they descended to the bottom of the deep valleys. Here and there, they thought they could perceive vast seas, hardly contained beneath a rarefied atmosphere; and watercourses pouring forth the tribute of the mountains. Leaning over the abyss, they hoped to surprise the sounds of the orb, which lies eternally mute in the solitudes of a vacuum. This last day left most exciting souvenirs. They took note of the minutest details; a vague uneasiness seized upon them as they approached the goal. This uneasiness would have redoubled had they known how much their velocity had decreased; it would have appeared to them quite insufficient to carry them to the end. At that moment the projectile had scarcely any weight. Its weight decreased continuously, and would be completely null at the line where the lunar and terrestrial attractions, neutralising each other, would produce the most surprising results. However, notwithstanding his preoccupations, Michel Ardan did not forget to prepare the morning's repast with his accustomed punctuality. All ate with good appetites. Nothing could be better than the soup, liquefied by the heat of the gas, nothing better than the preserved meats; a few glasses of good French wine crowned the repast, and on this head Michel Ardan remarked, 'that the lunar vineyards, under the action of a burning sun, ought to produce the most generous wines, if there were any!' In any case, this far-seeing Frenchman had taken care not to forget a few cuttings from Medoc and Côte d'Or, from which he expected great things. Reiset and Regnault's apparatus worked with great precision, and the air was maintained in a state of perfect purity; not a particle of carbonic acid resisted the potash, and as to the oxygen, it was, as Captain Nicholl said, 'of the very best quality'. The small quantity of moisture contained in the projectile mingled with the air and tempered its dryness, so that many apartments in Paris, London, or New York, and many theatres, were not in such good sanitary condition. But to work, regularly, this apparatus had to be kept in perfect order; so each morning Michel visited the taps and regulators, and adjusted, by the pyrometer, the heat of the gas. All was going on well, and the travellers, like J. T. Maston, were getting so stout as to be unrecognisable, if their imprisonment had lasted many months. They did as the fowls do in cages – they grew fat. Looking through the scuttle, Barbicane saw the spectre of the dog and other articles thrown out of the projectile, obstinately following. Diana howled in a most melancholy manner when she saw the remains of Satellite. These remnants seemed as immovable as if they had lain upon solid ground.

'Do you know, my friends,' cried Michel Ardan, 'if one of us had died from the effects of the shock at starting, we should have had much difficulty in burying him, or, rather, in "etherising" him – since ether replaces the earth. Think how the accusing corpse would have followed us like remorse.'

'It would have been sad indeed,' said Nicholl.

'Ah,' continued Michel, 'what I regret is, not to be able to get outside! What voluptuousness to float in the midst of this radiant ether! to bathe and roll in the pure rays of the sun! If Barbicane had only thought of supplying us with a diving apparatus and an air-pump, I would have risked the experiment, and I would have assumed the posture of Chimera or a Hippogriff on the top of the projectile!'

'Well, Michel, old fellow, you would not have long played the Hippogriff, for, notwithstanding the diving-dress filled with air, you would have collapsed like a balloon which had risen too high in the air; so don't regret anything, and don't forget this: so long as we are floating in a vacuum you must dispense with all sentimental walks outside the projectile.'

Michel Ardan let himself be convinced in a certain measure. He agreed that the thing was difficult, but not impossible, which word he never pronounced. The conversation passed from this subject to another, without languishing one instant. It seemed to the three friends that, under these conditions, their ideas sprang up in their brains, like leaves under the first warmth of spring, thick and fast! Amidst the questions and answers which crossed each other during this morning, Nicholl asked a certain question which did not meet with an immediate solution.

'By-the-bye,' said he, 'it's all very well to get to the moon, but how are we to return?'

His two companions looked at each other in surprise, as though that eventuality had occurred to them for the first time.

'What do you mean by that, Nicholl?' said Barbicane gravely.

'It seems to me somewhat premature,' said Ardan, 'to want to return from a country which one has not yet reached!'

'I don't say it because I wish to hang back,' replied Nicholl; 'but if you like I will withdraw my question, and substitute: how shall we return?'

'I don't know,' replied Barbicane.

'And as for me,' said Michel, 'if I had known how to return, I should not have started.'

'That is something like an answer,' cried Nicholl.

'I approve my friend Nicholl's words,' said Barbicane; 'and I will add, that the question has no present interest. Later on, when we think proper to return, we will consult on the point. If the columbiad is no longer to the fore, the projectile is.'

'That's not much good! A bullet without a gun.'

'We can manufacture the gun,' replied Barbicane; 'we can make the gunpowder. Neither metals, nor saltpetre, nor coal can be wanting in the bowels of the moon. Besides, to return, we need only conquer the lunar attraction, and it suffices to travel 8,000 leagues to fall down upon the earth by mere gravitation.'

'Enough,' cried Michel, with animation. 'Let there be no further question of returning; we have spoken too much of it already. As regards communicating with our old colleagues upon earth that will not be difficult.'

'How so?'

'By means of meteorites cast from lunar volcanoes.'

'Bravo, Michel!' cried Barbicane, in a tone of conviction. 'Laplace has calculated that a force five times superior to that of our cannons, would suffice to send a meteorite from the moon to the earth, and there is no volcano which has not a greater force of propulsion.'

'Hurrah!' cried Michel. 'Those meteorites will make capital postmen, and cost nothing. Won't we laugh at the postal authorities! But I was thinking –'

'What?'

'A superb idea! Why did we not fasten a wire to our projectile? We might have sent telegrams to the earth.'

'The deuce we might!' said Nicholl. 'Don't you take into account the weight of a wire 86,000 leagues long!'

'That is nothing. We might have tripled the charge of the columbiad, or quadrupled it, or quintupled it!' cried Michel, the intonation of whose voice became more and more violent.

'There is only one little objection to be made to your plan,' replied Barbicane: 'that during the movement of rotation of the globe, our wire would have been wound round it, like a chain round a capstan, and it would inevitably have dragged us back to earth.'

'By the thirty-nine stars of the Union,' cried Michel, 'I have nothing but impracticable ideas today. Ideas worthy of J. T. Maston. But now that I think of it, if we don't get back to earth, J. T. Maston is capable of coming to fetch us.'

'Yes, he will come,' replied Barbicane, 'he is a worthy and courageous comrade. Besides, what can be easier? Does not the columbiad still lie open in the Floridan soil? Are cotton and azotic acid wanting for the manufacture of pyroxyle? Will not the moon again cross the zenith of Florida? In 18 years will she not again occupy the same place she occupies today?'

'Yes,' replied Michel, 'yes, Maston will come, and with him our friends Elphiston, Blomsberry, and all the members of the Gun Club; and they will be welcome! And later on, we will establish trains of projectiles between the earth and the moon. Hurrah for J. T. Maston!'

It is probable that if the Hon. J. T. Maston did not hear the hurrahs shouted in his honour, at least his ears must have tingled. What was he doing then? Doubtless, at his post, on the Rocky Mountains at Long's Peak Station, he was trying to discover the invisible projectile, gravitating in space. If he was thinking of his dear companions, it must be admitted that the latter were not behindhand with him, and that, under the influence of a peculiar exaltation, they were giving him their best thoughts. But whence did this animation arise, which was visibly increasing in the inmates of the projectile? Their sobriety could not be doubted. Was this strange excitement of the brain to be attributed to

the exceptional circumstances in which they were situated? – to the proximity of the orb of night, from which they were only separated by a few
hours? – to some secret influence of the moon, acting upon their nervous
system? Their faces became red, as though exposed to the reflections of a
furnace; their breathing became more rapid, and their lungs worked like
the bellows of a forge; their eyes shone with an unaccustomed brightness;
their voices resounded with terrific accents; their words escaped like
champagne corks under pressure of carbonic acid; their gestures became
alarming, they required so much room, and, strange to say, none of them
noticed this excessive tension of their minds.

'Now,' said Nicholl sharply, 'now that I don't know whether we shall
ever return from the moon, I want to know what we are going to do
there?'

'What we are going to do there?' replied Barbicane, stamping with his
foot as if in a fencing-school, 'I don't know!'

'You don't know?' cried Michel, with a roar which produced a sonorous echo in the projectile.

'No, I have not the slightest idea,' replied Barbicane, in the same tone
as his interlocutor.

'Well, I know,' replied Michel.

'Speak, then,' cried Nicholl, who could no longer contain the growls
of his voice.

'I shall speak if I like,' cried Michel, seizing violently his companion's
arm.

'You will be obliged to like,' said Barbicane, with glaring eye and
threatening hand. 'It is you who have brought us on this formidable
journey, and we want to know why?'

'Yes,' said the captain, 'now that I don't know where I am going, I want
to know why I am going there?'

'Why?' cried Michel, bounding a yard into the air. 'Why? To take
possession of the moon, in the name of the United States! To add a
fortieth state to the Union! To colonise the lunar regions, to cultivate
them, to people them, to carry thither all the prodigies of art, of science,
of industry. To civilise the Selenites, unless they are more civilised than
we, and to form them into a republic if they do not already form one.'

'And if there are no Selenites?' replied Nicholl, who had become very
contradictory under the influence of this extraordinary frenzy.

'Who says there are no Selenites?' cried Michel in a threatening tone.

'I!' roared Nicholl.

'Captain,' said Michel, 'don't repeat that insolence, or I will force it
down your throat through your teeth!'

The two adversaries were on the point of rushing upon each other, and this incoherent discussion threatened to degenerate into a fight, when Barbicane interfered with a formidable bound. 'Stop, miserable men,' cried he, placing his two companions back to back, 'if there are no Selenites we will do without them.'

'Yes,' exclaimed Michel, who was not particularly tenacious of the point. 'We will do without them! What do we want with Selenites? Down with the Selenites!'

'The empire of the moon is ours,' said Nicholl.

'The three of us, let us form a republic; I will be the congress,' cried Michel. 'And I the senate,' replied Nicholl. 'And Barbicane president,' roared Michel. 'Not a president appointed by the nation,' replied Barbicane. 'Well, a president appointed by congress,' cried Michel; 'and as I am the congress, I appoint you unanimously.' 'Hip, hip, hurrah! for President Barbicane,' cried Nicholl. 'Hip, hip, hurrah!' screamed Michel Ardan. Then the president and the senate commenced in a terrible voice the popular 'Yankee Doodle', whilst the congress made the place re-echo with the manly notes of the 'Marseillaise'. Then commenced a frantic dance with insensate gesticulations, maniacal postures and somersaults as of boneless clowns. Diana joined in the dance, howling in her turn, and leaped to the roof of the projectile. An inexplicable flapping of wings was heard, and crowings of unusual shrillness. Five or six hens flew about beating against the walls, like lunatic bats. Then the three travelling companions, with lungs disorganised, under some incomprehensible influence, more than drunk, burnt by the air which set their respiratory apparatus on fire, fell without motion to the bottom of the projectile.

CHAPTER EIGHT

Seventy-eight thousand one hundred and fourteen leagues off

What had occurred? What was the cause of this singular frenzy, of which the consequences might be disastrous? A mere act of thoughtlessness on Michel's part; but which, happily, Nicholl was able to remedy in time. After a swoon, which lasted a few minutes, the captain, who first came back to life, recovered his intellectual faculties. Although he had breakfasted two hours previously, he felt a terrible hunger gnawing him, as if he had not eaten for several days. Every part of him, stomach and brain, were excited to the highest pitch. So he arose and called upon Michel for a new collation. Michel, completely broken-down, did not reply. Nicholl then tried to make a few cups of tea, to facilitate the deglutition of about a dozen sandwiches. He first tried to make a fire, and struck a match. What was his surprise at seeing the sulphur burn with extraordinary brilliancy, almost unbearable to the sight. He lighted the gas-burner, and a flame burst forth like the flash of an electric light. A revelation was made in Nicholl's mind. This intensity of the light, the physiological troubles which had arisen in him, the super-excitement of all his faculties moral and physical – he understood it all.

'The oxygen!' he cried; and bending over the air-apparatus he perceived that the tap was allowing this colourless gas to escape in floods – tasteless, scentless, eminently vital, it produces in a pure state the most serious disorders in the system. Michel had thoughtlessly opened the tap of the apparatus to its full extent! Nicholl hastened to stop this escape of oxygen, with which the atmosphere was saturated, and which would have caused the death of the travellers, not from suffocation, but by combustion. One hour afterwards, the air was less loaded, and their lungs recovered their normal action. Gradually the three friends recovered from their intoxication; but they were obliged to sleep off their oxygen, as a drunkard sleeps off his wine. When Michel learnt what had been his share in this accident, he was not in the least disconcerted. This unexpected intoxication broke the monotony of the journey. Many foolish things had been uttered under its influence, but they were forgotten as soon as said.

'Besides,' said this jovial Frenchman, 'I am not sorry to have tried this heady gas. Do you know, my friends, one might set up a curious establishment with oxygen cabinets, where people, whose system is weakened, might live a more active life for a few hours. Imagine meetings where the air had been saturated with this heroic fluid! – theatres where the management kept a constant supply at high-pressure! What passion in the breasts of the spectators! What fire – what enthusiasm! And if, instead of a mere assembly, a whole nation could be saturated, what activity in its functions, what an increase of life it would receive. From a used-up nation, one might perhaps make a great and strong people, and I know more than one state in old Europe which ought to undergo a course of oxygen, for the good of its health.'

Michel spoke with an animation which might have led one to believe that the tap was still open; but with one word Barbicane put an end to his enthusiasm.

'All that is very well, friend Michel,' said he; 'but will you inform us, whence come these hens which have joined our party?'

'Hens?'

'Yes.' In fact, half-a-dozen hens and a superb cock were strutting about, fluttering and cackling.

'Oh, the fools,' cried Michel; 'the oxygen must have caused a revolution!'

'What do you want with these hens?' asked Barbicane.

'I want to acclimatise them in the moon, of course.'

'But why hide them?'

'A joke, worthy president, a mere joke, which has broken down most pitifully. I wanted to let them loose in the lunar continent, without saying anything to you. Ah! how great would not your astonishment have been, to see these terrestrial fowls pecking on the fields of the moon!'

'Oh you schoolboy, you eternal schoolboy,' replied Barbicane, 'you don't want any oxygen to excite yourself! You are always what we were under the influence of this gas! You are always mad.'

'And who says that we were not wise men then?' replied Michel Ardan.

After this philosophical reflection, the three friends repaired the disorder of the projectile. Hens and cock were returned to their coop; but, in proceeding to this operation, Barbicane and his two companions became forcibly aware of a new phenomenon. Since the moment when they had left the earth, their own weight, that of the projectile, and of the articles which it contained, had undergone a progressive diminution. If they could not ascertain this loss as regarded the projectile, the

moment arrived when the effect would be very appreciable, as regarded
themselves and the instruments and utensils of which they made use.
It is unnecessary to add, that a pair of scales would not have indicated
this loss, for, the weight with which the article was weighed would
have lost precisely as much as the article itself; but a spring weighing-
machine, for instance, which works without reference to attraction,
would have given the exact amount of the falling off. We know that
attraction, otherwise gravitation, is proportionate to the volume and
in inverse ratio of the square of the distances. Hence this result: if
the earth had been alone in space, if the other celestial bodies had
been suddenly annihilated, the projectile, according to Newton's law,
would have decreased in weight in proportion as it became more distant
from the earth, without, however, ever losing its weight completely,
for the terrestrial attraction would always make itself felt at no matter
what distance. But in the present case, a moment must arrive in which
the projectile would no longer be subject to the laws of gravitation,
abstraction made of the other celestial bodies whose effect might be
considered as nil. In fact, the trajectory of the projectile lay between the
earth and the moon. In proportion as it left the earth, the terrestrial
attraction diminished in the inverse ratio of the square of the distance,
but at the same time, the lunar attraction increased in the same proportion; a point would thus be reached, where the two attractions would
neutralise each other, and the projectile would have no more weight.
If the volume of the earth and moon had been equal, this point would
have lain at an equal distance from the two orbs. Taking into account
the difference of the two masses, it was easy to calculate that the
point would be situated at the 47/52nds of the journey, or, in figures, at
78,114 leagues from the earth. At this point, a body having no principle
of swiftness or of displacement in itself, would remain eternally motionless, being equally attracted by the two orbs, and not being more drawn
towards the one than towards the other. Now the projectile, if the force
of impulsion had been exactly calculated, ought to reach this point
without any velocity, having lost all indication of weight, as well as all
the articles contained in it. What would then happen? Three hypotheses were possible. Either the projectile would have retained a certain
velocity, and, passing the point of equal attractions, it would fall upon
the moon, by reason of the excess of lunar attraction over terrestrial
attraction, or, if the velocity were wanting to attain the point of equal
attractions, it would fall back to earth, by reason of the excess of terrestrial attraction. Or, finally, endowed with sufficient velocity to attain the
neutral point, but insufficient to pass beyond it, the projectile would

remain eternally suspended in that place, like the pretended coffin of Mohamet, between zenith and nadir.

Such was the situation, and Barbicane clearly explained its consequences to his companions, which interested them in the highest degree. Now, how were they to discover that the projectile had attained this neutral point, 78,114 leagues from the earth? – at which point precisely neither they, nor the articles contained in the projectile, would be any longer under the influence of the laws of gravitation. Until now, the travellers, whilst remarking that this action (gravitation) decreased more and more, had not yet discovered its total absence. But that day, Nicholl having dropped a glass from his hand, the glass, instead of falling, remained suspended in the air.

'Ah,' cried Michel, 'we shall have some amusing experiments in physics.'

Immediately various articles, arms and bottles, thrown into the air, remained stationary, as by a miracle. Diana herself, placed by Michel in space, reproduced, without any deception, the marvellous suspension performed by Caston and Robert Houdin. Further, the bitch did not seem aware that she was floating in air. They themselves, surprised and stupefied, notwithstanding their scientific reasonings, felt themselves carried into the world of the marvellous. They felt that gravitation was wanting to their bodies. Their arms, when stretched out, no longer tended to fall back to their sides; their heads wagged upon their shoulders; their feet no longer clove to the bottom of the projectile. They were like drunken men, without stability. Imagination has created men without reflection and without shadow, but here reality, by neutralising the attractive forces, produced men in whom nothing had any weight, and who weighed nothing themselves. Suddenly Michel, taking a spring, left the bottom, and remained suspended in air, like the monk in Murillo's 'Angel's Kitchen'. In an instant, his two friends had joined him, and the three of them, in the centre of the projectile, represented a miraculous ascension.

'Is it creditable? Is it probable? Is it possible?' cried Michel. 'No! And yet it is. Ah, if Raphael could have seen us thus, what an Assumption he would have sketched upon his canvas.'

'The assumption cannot last,' replied Barbicane. 'If the projectile passes the neutral point, the lunar attraction will draw us towards the moon.'

'Then our feet will stand upon the roof of the projectile?' replied Michel.

'No,' said Barbicane, 'because the projectile, whose centre of gravity is very low, will gradually turn round.'

'Then all our arrangements will be turned topsy-turvy?'

'Don't be afraid, Michel,' replied Nicholl. 'There will be no dis-arrangement. Not a single article will move, for the evolution of the projectile will only take place insensibly.'

'In fact,' continued Barbicane, 'when it has passed the point of equal attractions, its lower portion, comparatively heavier, will be drawn down,

along one of the moon's perpendiculars. But, in order that such a phenomenon may occur, we must necessarily have passed the neutral line.'

'Pass the neutral line!' cried Michel, 'then let us do as the sailors do
when they cross the equator. Let us wet our journey.'

A slight side movement brought Michel to the padded wall. He took a
bottle and some glasses, placed them in space before his companions, and,
joyously clinking their glasses, they saluted the line with a triple hurrah.
This influence of the attractions hardly lasted an hour. The travellers felt
themselves insensibly brought towards the bottom, and Barbicane thought
that he perceived the conical end of the projectile diverge slightly from
its normal direction towards the moon. By an inverse movement, the
bottom approached towards it. So the lunar attraction became stronger
than the terrestrial attraction; it would only be $1\frac{1}{3}$ millimetre in the first
second, or 590-1000ths of a line's width. But, gradually, the attractive
force would increase, the fall would be more rapid; the projectile, carried
away, bottom downwards, would present its upper cone to the earth,
and would fall with an increasing velocity to the surface of the Selenite
continent. Thus, the goal would be reached. Now, nothing could hinder
the success of the undertaking, and Nicholl and Michel Ardan shared
Barbicane's joy. Then they talked of all these phenomena which had
astonished them all in turn; especially the neutralisation of the laws of
gravitation was an inexhaustible topic. Michel Ardan, always enthusiastic,
wished to deduce purely fantastic consequences.

'Ah! my worthy friends,' cried he, 'what progress indeed if we could
get rid on earth of that gravitation, which binds us to it like a chain. We
should be like liberated prisoners. No more fatigues, either of legs or
arms. And whereas now, to fly above the surface of the earth, to remain in
air by the action of the muscles, requires a strength 150 times greater
than that which we possess, if no attraction existed, a caprice, a mere
effort of the will, would carry us into space.'

'True,' replied Nicholl, laughing; 'if we were able to suppress gravitation as we suppress pain, by anaesthetics, that would certainly alter the
conditions of modern society.'

'Yes,' cried Michel, full of his subject, 'let us destroy gravitation, and
let us have no more burdens. Therefore no more cranes, no more pulleys,
no more capstans, no more handles, and other machinery; they will no
longer be required.'

'Quite right,' replied Barbicane, 'but if nothing had any weight, things
would not hold together. Neither your hat, worthy Michel, nor your
house, whose bricks only adhere by their weight. No more ships, whose
stability upon the water is but a consequence of gravitation; not even an

ocean, for its waves would no longer be kept in equilibrium by terrestrial attraction. Lastly, no atmosphere, for its molecules, no longer under attraction, would disperse into space.'

'That is unfortunate,' replied Michel. 'There is nothing like matter-of-fact men to bring you brutally back to realities.'

'Console yourself, Michel,' continued Barbicane; 'if there is no orb without laws of gravitation, at least you are going to visit one where gravitation is much less than on earth.'

'The moon?'

'Yes, the moon; on whose surface things have six times less weight than on the surface of the earth – which phenomenon is easily proved.'

'And we shall be aware of it?' asked Michel.

'Certainly, for 200 kilogrammes will only weigh 30 on the surface of the moon.'

'And our muscular force will not diminish?'

'Not at all. Instead of rising one yard when you jump, you will spring to a height of 18 feet.'

'But we shall be like Hercules in the moon!' cried Michel.

'The more so,' replied Nicholl, 'that if the size of the Selenites is proportionate to the volume of their globe, they will scarcely be one foot high.'

'Lilliputians!' replied Michel. 'I shall take the part of Gulliver. We shall realise the fable of the giants. That is the advantage of leaving one's planet and travelling in the solar world!'

'One minute, Michel,' replied Barbicane; 'if you want to play at Gulliver, you must only visit the inferior planets, such as Mercury, Venus, or Mars, whose mass is less than the moon's. Don't venture on to the great planets, such as Jupiter, Saturn, Uranus, or Neptune, for there the parts would be changed, and you would become the Lilliputian.'

'And in the sun?'

'In the sun, though its density is four times less than that of the earth, its volume is 1,380,000 times greater, and gravitation is 27 times greater than at the surface of our globe. If the same proportions be maintained, the inhabitants must be at least 200 feet high.'

'The devil!' cried Michel. 'I should only be a pigmy – a myrmidon!'

'Gulliver in Brobdingnag,' said Nicholl.

'Just so,' replied Barbicane.

'And it would not be out of the way to take some artillery with one to defend oneself.'

'Good!' replied Barbicane; 'your bullets would have no effect in the sun, and would fall to earth a few yards off.'

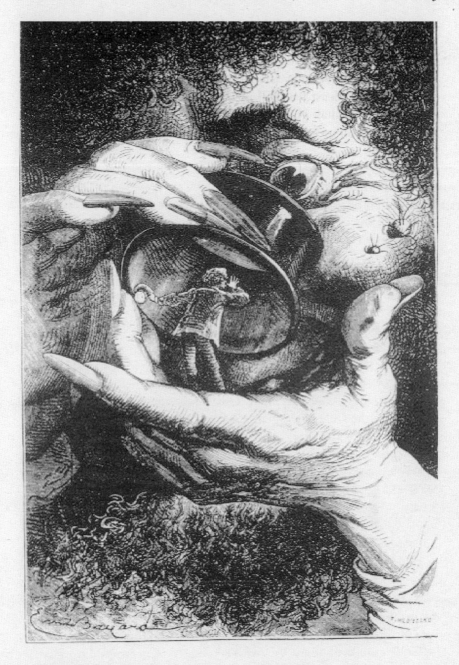

'What do you mean?'

'It is quite certain,' replied Barbicane. 'The attraction is so great upon this enormous orb, that an object weighing 70 kilogrammes on the earth would weigh 1,930 on the surface of the sun; your hat, about 12 kilogrammes; your cigar, half a pound. Lastly, if you were to fall on the solar continent, your weight would be such – about 2,500 kilogrammes – that you could not get up.'

'The deuce I couldn't!' said Michel. 'In that case we must all have portable cranes! Well, my friends, let us be satisfied with the moon for today. There at least we shall make a good figure. Later on, we shall see whether we shall go to this sun, where one wants a capstan, when drinking, to haul up one's glass to one's mouth.'

CHAPTER NINE

Consequences of a deviation

Barbicane had no further uneasiness, if not as to the result of the journey, at least as to the force of impulsion of the projectile. Its velocity had carried it beyond the neutral line, so it would not return to earth, and it would not become immovable upon the point of attraction. Only one hypothesis remained to be realised – the arrival of the projectile at its goal, under the action of lunar attraction. In reality it was a fall of 8,296 leagues, upon an orb where, it is true, the gravitation was only estimated at one-sixth of the terrestrial gravitation. Nevertheless the fall was a formidable one, and all precautions possible had to be taken at once.

  These precautions were of two sorts: some were to lessen the shock at the moment when the projectile touched the lunar ground, and the others were to stay its fall, and consequently render it less violent. To annul the shock, it was unfortunate that Barbicane could no longer employ the means by which he had so effectually lessened the shock of the departure, that is to say the water used as a spring, and the breakable partitions. The partitions still remained, but there was no water; for they could not make use of their reserve for that purpose, in case, during the first days, the precious element should be wanting on the lunar soil. Besides, this reserve would have been quite insufficient as a spring. The layer of water stored in the projectile at the start, and on which lay the water-tight disc, rose to a height of not less than 3 feet, over a surface of fifty-four square feet. In capacity it measured 6 cubic metres, and in weight 5,750 kilogrammes. The reservoirs did not contain 1-5th part as much, so they were obliged to give up all idea of this powerful means of lessening the shock. Happily Barbicane, not content with using water, had furnished the movable disc with strong spring buffers, for the purpose of lessening the shock against the bottom, after the breakage of the horizontal partitions. These buffers still existed; it was only necessary to readjust them and put the movable disc in place again. All these pieces were easily moved about, their weight being scarcely perceptible, and could be rapidly put together. This was done. The several parts were adjusted without difficulty; it was a mere matter of nuts and bolts. The tools were not wanting. Soon the readjusted disc stood upon its buffers like a table upon its legs. One inconvenience resulted from this replacing of the disc: the lower window became closed; hence it would be impossible for the travellers to observe the moon through that aperture when they were being perpendicularly precipitated upon her. So they were obliged to give that up. However, from the side openings they could observe the vast lunar regions, as the earth is seen from the car of a balloon. This arrangement of the disc required one hour's work, and it was past noon when the preparations were finished. Barbicane took new observations as to the inclination of the projectile, but, to his great disgust, it had not sufficiently turned for a fall; it seemed to follow a curve parallel with the lunar disc. The orb of night shone magnificently in space, while on the other side the orb of day fired it with its rays. The situation became disquieting.

'Are we arriving?' said Nicholl.

'Let us act as though we were arriving,' replied Barbicane.

'You are a timid lot,' said Michel. 'We shall arrive, and sooner than we wish for.'

This reply brought Barbicane back to his preparatory arrangements, and he began to arrange the apparatus which was to lessen the fall.

The scene at the meeting held at Tampa Town, Florida, will be remembered, when Nicholl took up an inimical position towards Barbicane and Ardan. When Captain Nicholl maintained that the projectile would be shattered like glass, Michel had replied that he would lessen its fall by means of rockets properly placed. In fact, powerful rockets attached to the bottom and fired outside, might, by producing a retrograde movement, diminish to a certain extent the velocity of the projectile. These rockets would burn in a vacuum it is true: but they would not want for oxygen, for they would supply themselves, like the lunar volcanoes, whose deflagration has never been hindered by the want of atmosphere around the moon. Barbicane had therefore supplied himself with rockets contained in steel cases, which could be screwed on to the bottom of the projectile. Interiorly these cases were on a level with the bottom; exteriorly they protruded half-a-foot. There were twenty of them. An aperture in the disc allowed of the lighting of the fuse with which each was provided. All the effect was produced outside. The explosive mixture had been already rammed into each steel case, so that it was only necessary to remove the metallic plugs in the bottom of the projectile and replace them by these steel cases, which fitted the holes exactly. This new work was completed about three o'clock, and, all precautions being taken, there only remained to wait.

However, the projectile visibly neared the moon. It evidently was under her influence in a certain proportion; yet, at the same time, its own velocity carried it in an oblique line. The result of these two influences, was a line which might prove a tangent, but it was evident that the projectile was not falling to the moon in a normal manner, for its bottom, by reason of its superior weight, ought to have been turned towards her. Barbicane's uneasiness increased on seeing his projectile resist the influence of gravitation. The unknown opened before him – the unknown in the planetary spheres. He, the man of science, thought he had foreseen the three possible hypotheses – the return to earth, the return to the moon, stagnation upon the neutral line – and now a fourth hypothesis, replete with all the terror of the infinite, arose inopportunely. One must be a resolute man like Barbicane, a phlegmatic man like Nicholl, or an audacious adventurer like Michel Ardan, to look the prospect in the face without wincing. The conversation turned on this subject. Other men would have considered the question from a practical standpoint. They would have inquired whither their 'projectile-carriage' was carrying them. They, on the contrary, sought the cause which had produced the effect.

'So we have run off the rails,' said Michel; 'but why?'

'I am much afraid,' replied Nicholl, 'that notwithstanding all the precautions taken, the columbiad was not aimed correctly. An error, no matter how small, would suffice to throw us out of the lunar attraction.'

'Then they aimed badly?' asked Michel.

'I do not think so,' replied Barbicane; 'the perpendicularity of the cannon was absolute, its direction towards the zenith incontestable. The moon crossing the zenith we must strike her in full. There is another reason, but it escapes me.'

'Won't we arrive too late?' asked Nicholl.

'Too late?' said Barbicane.

'Yes,' continued Nicholl. 'The note from the Cambridge Observatory stated that the journey should be accomplished in 97 hours 13 minutes and 20 seconds, which means that, any sooner, the moon would not yet be there, and, any later, she would be gone.'

'Agreed,' replied Barbicane; 'but we left on the 1st December, at 13 minutes and 25 seconds to 11 p.m., and we shall arrive on the 5th, at midnight, at the precise moment when the moon is full. Now this is the 5th December. It is half-past 3 in the afternoon, and eight and a half hours ought to be sufficient to carry us to our goal. Why do we not reach there?'

'Is it not perhaps from excess of velocity?' asked Nicholl; 'for we now know that the initial velocity was greater than we supposed.'

'No! one hundred times no!' replied Barbicane. 'An excess of velocity, if the direction of the projectile had been good, would not have hindered our reaching the moon. No; there has been deviation; we have deviated!'

'How and why?' asked Nicholl.

'I cannot say,' replied Barbicane.

'Well, Barbicane,' said Michel, 'do you want to know my opinion on the point as to whence the deviation arose?'

'Speak out.'

'I would not give half a dollar to know why we have deviated, that is the fact. It is of small importance whither we are going. We shall soon see. Confound it! since we are carried away into space we shall end by finding some centre of attraction!'

Michel Ardan's indifference could not satisfy Barbicane; not that he was preoccupied with the future, but he was desirous of learning, at any price, why his projectile had deviated. Meanwhile, the projectile contin- ued to move laterally with the moon, and with it the string of articles which had been thrown out. Barbicane could even ascertain from the several fixed points which the moon offered, at a distance of less than 2,000 leagues, that the velocity was becoming uniform. This was a fresh proof that they were not falling. The force of impulsion was still greater than the lunar attraction; but the trajectory of the projectile was certainly nearing it to the lunar disc; and it might be hoped that, at a shorter distance from the surface, the action of gravitation would predominate, and cause a fall. The three friends, having nothing better to do, contin- ued their observations. However, they could not yet determine the topo- graphical dispositions of the satellite. All the excrescences were levelled, under the projection of the solar rays. They looked thus through the side windows until 8 p.m. The moon had by that time increased to such an extent that she shut out one-half the firmament. The sun on one side, the orb of night on the other, inundated the projectile with their light. At this moment, Barbicane considered that the distance still separating them from their goal might be estimated at 700 leagues only. The velocity of the projectile seemed to him about 200 metres per second, or about 170 leagues an hour. The bottom of the projectile continued to turn towards the moon, under the influence of centripetal force; but the centrifugal force having still the upper hand, it was becoming probable that the rectilinear trajectory would be changed into a curve, of which it would be impossible to determine the nature. Barbicane was still seeking the solution of his insoluble problem. Hours passed without any result. The projectile was visibly nearing the moon, but it was equally visible that it would not reach her; as to the shortest distance at which it would pass her, that would be the result of two attractive and repellent forces acting on the projectile.

'I only ask for one thing,' said Michel: 'to pass near enough to the moon to discover her secrets.'

'Accursed be the cause,' cried Nicholl, 'which has made our projectile deviate!'

'Then,' replied Barbicane, as if a thought had just struck him, 'accursed be the meteorite which we passed on our road!'

'Hallo!' said Michel Ardan.

'What do you mean?' cried Nicholl.

'I mean,' replied Barbicane, in a tone of conviction, 'I mean that our deviation is owing solely to the meeting with that wandering body.'

'But it did not even touch us,' replied Michel.

'What does that matter? Its mass was enormous compared with that of our projectile, and its attraction has sufficed to influence our direction.'

'So little?' cried Nicholl.

'Yes, Nicholl; but however little it may be,' replied Barbicane, 'upon a distance of 84,000 leagues it required no more to make us miss the moon.

CHAPTER TEN

The observers of the moon

Barbicane had evidently discovered the only plausible reason for this deviation. However small, it had sufficed to modify the trajectory of the projectile. It was a fatality. The audacious attempt fell through from a wholly fortuitous circumstance, and unless some exceptional event occurred, they could not reach the lunar disc. Would they pass near enough to solve some questions of physics or geology hitherto insoluble? This question was the only one which preoccupied the hardy adventurers. As to the fate which the future had in store for them, they would not even think of it. Meanwhile, what would become of them in the midst of these infinite solitudes, where they would soon run short of air? A few days more and they would fall suffocated to the bottom of this wandering projectile. But a few days were so many centuries to these intrepid men, and they applied each minute of their time to observe this moon which they no longer hoped to reach. The distance then separating the projectile from the satellite, was estimated at about 200 leagues. In these conditions, as regards seeing the details of the disc, the travellers were farther from the moon than are the inhabitants of the earth armed with powerful telescopes. It is well known that the instrument set up by Lord Rosse at Parsonstown, which magnifies 6,500 times, brings the moon to within 16 leagues; further, the powerful instrument established at Long's Peak magnifies the orb of night 48,000 times, and brings her to within two leagues, and objects having a diameter of 10 metres are visible with sufficient distinctness. Thus, at this distance, the topographical details of the moon, observed without a telescope, were not very visible. The eye seized the vast contour of those immense depressions, improperly called seas, but could not recognise their nature. The prominence of the mountains disappeared in the splendid irradiation produced by the reflection of the solar rays. The eye, dazzled as though it had looked upon a mass of molten silver, turned involuntarily away.

However, the oblong form of the orb stood out clearly. It appeared like a gigantic egg, with the smaller end turned towards the earth. In fact the moon, liquid or malleable in the first days of its formation, figured then as a perfect sphere; but, entering into the attraction of the earth, it became lengthened, under the action of gravitation, losing, as a satellite, its native purity of shape. The centre of gravity was carried beyond the centre of the figure; and, from this disposition, some learned men drew the conclusion that the air and the water might have taken refuge upon the surface of the moon which is never seen from the earth. This alteration of the primitive shape of the satellite was only perceptible for a few minutes. The distance from the projectile to the moon diminished very rapidly, for its swiftness, although less than its initial velocity, was yet eight or nine times superior to that of express trains. The oblique direction of the projectile gave Michel Ardan, from its very obliquity, some hopes that they would touch at some point of the lunar disc. He could not believe that they would not reach it. No, he could not believe it; and he repeated the same continuously. But Barbicane, who was a better judge, did not cease to reply with pitiless logic:

'No, Michel, no! We cannot reach the moon except by a fall, and we are not falling. The centripetal force maintains us under lunar influence, but the centrifugal force irresistibly keeps us from the moon.'

This was said in a tone of voice which destroyed Michel Ardan's last hopes. The portion of the moon which the projectile neared, was the northern hemisphere, which selenographical maps place undermost, for these maps are generally drawn from the image supplied by lunettes, and we know that lunettes reverse objects. Such was the *Mappa Selenographica* of Beer and Moedler, which Barbicane consulted. This northern hemisphere presented vast plains broken with isolated mountains. At midnight the moon was full. At this precise moment, the travellers ought to have set foot on the moon if the unfortunate meteorite had not caused them to deviate from their direction. The orb arrived in the conditions rigorously determined by the Cambridge Observatory. It was mathematically in its perigee, and at the zenith of the 28th parallel. An observer placed at the bottom of the enormous columbiad, aimed perpendicularly with the horizon, would have seen the moon in the mouth of the cannon, as in a frame. A straight line, marking the axis of the piece, would have passed through the very centre of the orb of night.

It is unnecessary to add that, during the night of the 5th December, the travellers did not take an instant's repose. Could they have closed their eyes so near to this new world? No! All their feelings were concentrated in one thought – to see. Representatives of the earth, of humanity, past and present, it was by their eyes that the human race looked upon these lunar regions, and penetrated the secrets of the satellite. Their hearts swelled with emotion, and they went silently from one window to the other. There observations, reproduced by Barbicane, were rigorously determined. To make them they had lunettes, to verify them they had maps. Galileo was the first observer of the moon. His inadequate lunette magnified only 30 times. Nevertheless, in those spots which are scattered over the lunar disc 'as the eyes on a peacock's tail', he was the first to recognise mountains, and measured some altitudes to which he attributed an exaggerated elevation, equal to 1/20th of the diameter of the disc, or 8,800 metres. Galileo did not make any map of his observations. Some years later an astronomer of Danzig, Hevelius, by processes which were only correct twice in a month – at the first and last quadratures – reduced Galileo's observations to 1/26th of the lunar diameter, which was an exaggeration in the opposite extreme. But it is to this learned man that we are indebted for our first map of the moon. The clear round spots are given as mountains, and the darker spots as vast seas, although in reality they are only plains. To these mountains and extents of water he gave terrestrial names. We find Sinai in the midst of an Arabia; Etna in the centre of Sicily; the Alps, Apennines, Carpathians; and then the Mediterranean, the Paulo-Méotide, the Euxine, and the Caspian seas. These names were badly applied, for neither the mountains nor the seas resemble their homonyms on the globe. In the large white spot, joined at the south to yet larger continents and terminating in a point, it would be difficult to recognise the reversed image of the Indian peninsula, with the Indian Ocean and Cochin-China. Therefore these names were not retained. Another cartographer, who was better acquainted with the human heart, proposed a new nomenclature which human vanity hastened to adopt. This observer was Father Riccioli, a contemporary of Hevelius. He drew up a rough map, full of errors, but to the lunar mountains he gave the names of the great men of antiquity and of scientific men of his time, which custom has since been much in vogue. A third map of the moon was executed in the 17th century, by Domenique Cassini, and, though better drawn than that of Riccioli, it was inexact as regards measurements. Several reproductions of it were published, but its plate, which was long preserved at the royal printing establishment, has been sold by weight as lumber. La Hire, a celebrated mathematician and draughtsman, drew a map of the moon four metres high, which was never engraved. After him a German astronomer, Tobias Mayer, towards the middle of the 18th century, commenced the publication of a magnificent selenographic map, according to measurements accurately verified by him; but his death, in 1762, prevented the completion of this fine work. Next came Schroeter de Lilienthal, who sketched numerous maps of the moon; then a certain Lohrmann, of Dresden, to whom we are indebted for a plate divided into 25 sections, of which four have been engraved.

It was in 1830 that Messrs Beer and Moedler composed their celebrated *Mappa Selenographica*, in accordance with an orthographic projection. This map exactly reproduces the lunar disc such as it appears, but the configurations of the mountains and plains are only correct in the central portion; everywhere else, in the northern and southern portions, or the eastern or western, these configurations, given in reduced sizes, cannot be compared with those of the centre. This topographic map, 95 centimetres high, and divided into four sheets, is the masterpiece of lunar cartography. After these scientific men are mentioned also the selenographic scraps by the astronomer Julius Schmidt, the topographic works of Father Secchi, the magnificent proofs of the English amateur Warren De la Rue, and lastly, a map upon orthographic projection by MM. Lecouturier and Chapuis, of which a fine model was prepared in 1860, beautifully drawn and very clear in its arrangement. Such is the nomenclature of the different maps relating to the lunar world. Barbicane had two in his possession, that of Beer and Moedler and that of MM. Lecouturier and Chapuis. They much facilitated his work of observation. As to the optical instruments at his disposal, they were excellent marine lunettes, specially manufactured for the journey. They magnified objects one hundred times, and would thus have brought the moon to a distance of less than 1,000 leagues from the earth. But at that moment, at a distance which towards 8 a.m. did not exceed 120 kilometres, in a medium without atmospheric disturbances, these instruments would bring the lunar surface to at least 1,500 metres.

CHAPTER ELEVEN

Imagination and reality

'Have you ever seen the moon?' asked a professor ironically of one of his pupils. 'No, sir,' replied the pupil still more ironically, 'but I must admit that I have heard her spoken of.'

In one sense the pupil's jocular reply might be echoed by the immense majority of sublunary beings. How many people have heard talk of the moon who have never seen her, at least through the eye-glass of a lunette or telescope! How many have never even examined the map of their satellite!

When looking at the selenographic map, one peculiarity strikes us first. Contrary to the disposition followed for the earth and Mars, the continents lie more particularly in the southern hemisphere of the lunar globe. These continents do not possess terminal lines so clear and so regular as South America, Africa, and the Indian peninsula. Their angular coasts are capricious, deeply indented, and rich in gulfs and peninsulas. They recall the embroglio of the islands of the Sound, where the land is excessively divided. If navigation has ever existed on the surface of the moon, it must have been singularly difficult and dangerous, and the Selenite sailors and hydrographers are to be pitied, the latter when making a survey of these tortuous coasts, and the former when navigating these dangerous parts. It was also remarked, that on the lunar spheroid, the southern pole was much more continental than the north pole. At the latter there only exists a narrow rim of land separated from the other continents by vast seas. Towards the south, the continents cover nearly the whole hemisphere. It is therefore possible that the Selenites have already planted their flag on one of their poles, whereas Franklin, Ross, Kane, Dumont d'Urville, and Lambert have never been able to attain this unknown point of the terrestrial globe. As to the islands, they are numerous on the surface of the moon; nearly all are oblong or circular, as though traced with a compass; they form a vast archipelago, which may be compared to the charming group lying between Greece and Asia Minor, which mythology has endowed with its most charming legends. Involuntarily, the names of Naxos, Tenedos, Melos, Carpathos rise in the mind, and one looks for the vessel of Ulysses, or the clipper of the Argonauts; at least that is what Michel Ardan called for. He saw a Grecian Archipelago on the map! To his companions' less imaginative eyes, the coast-lines recalled rather the broken land of New Brunswick and Nova Scotia, and there where the Frenchman found traces of the heroes of fable, these Americans pointed out the points most favourable to the establishment of factories, in the interests of lunar commerce and manufactures.

To complete the description of the continental portion of the moon, let us add a few words as to her orthographic disposition. One can easily distinguish chains of mountains, isolated mountains, circuses, and grooves. All the lunar highlands are included in this division. They are excessively varied – like an immense Switzerland, a continuous Norway, where volcanic action has done everything. This so uneven surface is the result of successive contractions of the crust at the time when the orb was in course of formation. The lunar disc is consequently favourable for the study of great geological phenomena. According to a remark of certain astronomers, her surface, although more ancient than that of the earth, has remained newer. There are no waters to deteriorate the primitive relief, and whose increasing action produces a sort of general levelling; no air, whose decomposing influence modifies the orographical profiles. There, plutonic work, unimpaired by neptunian forces, remains in its native purity – like the earth as she was before currents and swamps had coated her with sedimentary strata. After wandering over these vast continents the eye is attracted by yet vaster seas. Not only do their conformation, their situation, their aspect, recall that of the terrestrial oceans, but, as on earth, these seas occupy the greater portion of the globe. Yet they are not seas, but plains, whose nature the travellers soon hoped to determine. It must be admitted that astronomers have given these pretended seas the most extraordinary names, which however science has hitherto respected. Michel Ardan was right when he compared this map to a map of Love, got up by a Scudery or a Cyrano de Bergerac. 'Only,' added he, 'it is not a map of Love as in the seventeenth century, it is the map of life, clearly divided into two parts, the one feminine and the other masculine. To women the right hemisphere, to men the left hemisphere.'

When he spoke thus, Michel made his prosaic companions shrug their shoulders. Barbicane and Nicholl considered the lunar map from quite another standpoint than their imaginative friend. However, their imaginative friend was to some extent right, as may be judged. In this left hemisphere extends the Sea of Clouds, where human reason drowns itself so often. Not far distant is the Sea of Rain, supplied by all the annoyances of life. Near this is the Sea of Tempests, where man unceasingly struggles against his passions – too often victorious. Then, worn out by deceptions, treasons, infidelities, and all the train of terrestrial miseries, where does he find the end of his career? – In the vast Sea of Humours, hardly sweetened by a few drops of the waters of the Gulf of Dew. Clouds, rain, tempests, humours – does man's life contain anything else? and is it not summed up in these four words? The right hemisphere, dedicated to the ladies, contains smaller seas, whose significant names suggest all the incidents of feminine existence. There is the Sea of Serenity, over which bends the young girl; and the Lake of Dreams, which reflects a happy future. There is the Sea of Nectar, with its waves of tenderness and its breezes of love; there is the Sea of Fecundity and the Sea of Crises; and then the Sea of Vapours, whose dimensions are perhaps too restricted; and finally, the vast Sea of Tranquillity, wherein all false passions, all useless dreams, all unsatisfied desires, are absorbed, and whose waters fall peacefully into the Lake of Death.

What a strange sequence of names! What a singular division of these two hemispheres of the moon, united one to the other, like man to woman, and completing a sphere of life carried into space! And was not the imaginative Michel right to interpret thus this fancy of ancient astronomers? But whilst his imagination was thus running wild, his grave companions were considering matters more geographically. They were learning this new world by heart; they measured its angles and diameter.

For Barbicane and Nicholl, the Sea of Clouds was an immense depression of ground, sprinkled with a few circular mountains, and covering the greater portion of the western portion of the southern hemisphere. It occupied 184,800 square leagues, and its centre was situated in 15° south latitude and 20° west longitude. The Ocean of Tempests, *Oceanus Procellarum*, the vastest plain on the lunar disc, covered a superficies of 380,300 square leagues, its centre being in 10° north latitude by 45° east longitude. From its bosom rose the admirable shining mountains of Kepler and Aristarchus. More to the north, and separated from the Sea of Clouds by high chains, lies the Sea of Rain, *Mare Imbrium*, having its central point at 35° north latitude and 20° east longitude. It was almost circular in form, and covered an area of 193,000 leagues. Not far the Sea of Humours, *Mare Humorum*, a small basin of only 44,200 square leagues, was situated in 25° south latitude and 40° east longitude. Lastly, three gulfs were situated on the coasts of this hemisphere: the Torrid Gulf, the Gulf of Dews, and the Gulf of Iris, small plains inclosed between high chains of mountains. The feminine hemisphere, naturally more capricious, was distinguished by smaller and more numerous seas. Towards the north, lay the Sea of Cold, *Mare Frigoris*, in 55° north latitude and 0° longitude, having an area of 76,000 square leagues, which bordered on the Lake of Death and the Lake of Dreams; the Sea of Serenity, *Mare Serenitatis*, in 25° north latitude and 20° west longitude, with an area of 86,000 square leagues; the Sea of Crises, *Mare Crisium*, well defined, very circular, covering, by 17° north latitude and 55° west longitude, a superficies of 40,000 leagues, a true Caspian Sea, surrounded by a belt of mountains. Then at the equator, by 5° north latitude and 25° west longitude, appeared the Sea of Tranquillity, *Mare Tranquillitatis*, occupying 121,509 square leagues. This sea communicated at the south with the Sea of Nectar, *Mare Nectaris*, covering 28,800 square leagues, by 15° south latitude and 35° west longitude; and at the east, with the Sea of Fecundity, *Mare Fecunditatis*, the vastest in this hemisphere, occupying 219,300 square leagues, by 3° south latitude and 50 west longitude. Lastly, quite to the north and quite to the south, two seas were yet to be seen – the Sea of Humbolt, *Mare Humboldianum*, having a superficies of 6,500 square leagues, and the Austral Sea, *Mare Australe*, covering a superficies of 26 miles. In the centre of the lunar disc, across the equator and the zero meridian, was situated the Gulf of the Centre, *Sinus Medii*, acting as a sort of hyphen between the two hemispheres. Thus, the visible surface of the earth's satellite divided itself to the eyes of Nicholl and Barbicane. When they added together these different measures, they found that the superficies of this hemisphere was 4,738,160 square leagues, of which 3,317,600 leagues are composed of volcanoes, chains of mountains, circuses, islands – in a word, all that forms the solid portion of the moon; and 1,410,400 leagues for the seas, lakes, marshes, and all that forms the liquid portion; which, however, was a matter of perfect indifference to the worthy Michel. This hemisphere, it will be seen, is thirteen and a half times smaller than the terrestrial hemisphere. However, selenographers have already counted more than 50,000 craters! Thus it is a bloated surface, full of crevasses, a mass of scum, worthy of the unpoetical qualification which the English have given it of 'green cheese'. Michel Ardan was shocked when Barbicane pronounced this disobliging name.

'It is thus,' cried he, 'that the Anglo-Saxons of the nineteenth century treat beautiful Diana, fair-haired Phoebe, amiable Isis, charming Astarte, the Queen of the Night, daughter of Latona and Jupiter, the younger sister of the radiant Apollo!'

CHAPTER TWELVE

Orographical details

It has already been remarked that the direction followed by the projectile carried it towards the northern hemisphere of the moon. The travellers were far from the central point, which they ought to have struck, if their trajectory had not undergone an irremediable deviation. It was half-past 12, Barbicane estimated his distance at 1,400 kilometres, or rather more than a lunar radius, which distance would yet diminish as they advanced towards the north pole. The projectile was then not at the height of the equator, but across the tenth parallel, and from that latitude, which had been carefully computed on the map, Barbicane and his two companions could observe the moon in the best possible condition. In fact, by using lunettes, the distance of 1,400 kilometres was reduced to fourteen, or three and a half leagues. The telescope of the Rocky Mountains brought the moon yet nearer, but the terrestrial atmosphere greatly diminished its optical power, so Barbicane, posted in his projectile, glass in hand, already perceived certain details which were almost imperceptible to observers on the earth.

'My friends,' said the president in a grave voice, 'I know not whither we are going. I know not whether we shall ever see again the terrestrial globe. Nevertheless, let us proceed as if these works should some day be of service to our fellow-men! Let our minds be free from all preoccupation, we are astronomers, this projectile is a cabinet from the Cambridge Observatory, carried into space. Let us observe.' Whereupon the work was commenced with extreme precision, and reproduced faithfully the different aspects of the moon at the variable distances which the projectile occupied with reference to that orb. At the same time that the projectile stood at the height of the 10th parallel north, it seemed to follow rigidly the 20th degree of east longitude.

Here an important observation is to be made with reference to the map which was used for the observations. In selenographic maps, where, by reason of the reversing of the objects by the lunettes, the south is *above* and the north *below*, it would appear natural that by reason of this inversion the east should be placed to the left and the west to the right. However, this was not the case! If the map were reversed and presented to the moon such as she appears, the east would be to the left and the west to the right, contrary to what exists in terrestrial maps. This is the reason of this anomaly. The observers situated in the eastern hemisphere, in Europe for instance, perceive the moon in the south, with reference to them. When they observe her they turn their backs to the north, which is the reverse of the position they occupy when they look at a terrestrial map. Since they turn their back to the north the east is to their left, and the west to their right. For observers situated in the western hemisphere, in Patagonia, for instance, the west of the moon would be to their left, and the east to their right, as the south is behind them. Such is the reason of this apparent inversion of the two cardinal points, and they must be taken into account to follow President Barbicane's observations. Aided by the *Mappa Selenographica* of Beer and Moedler, the travellers recognised without hesitation the portion of the disc enclosed in the focus of their lunette.

'What do we see at the present moment?' asked Michel.

'The northern portion of the Sea of Clouds,' replied Barbicane. 'We are too far off to discover its nature. Are these plains composed of arid sands, as the first astronomers pretended? Are they only immense forests, according to the opinion of Mr Warren de la Rue, who allows the moon a very low atmosphere, though very dense? We shall know this later. Let us affirm nothing before we are in a position to affirm.'

This Sea of Clouds is somewhat doubtfully marked out on the maps. It is supposed that this vast plain is covered with blocks of lava thrown up by the volcanoes which are near its right portion, Ptolemaeus, Purbach, and Arzachel. But the projectile advanced and approached considerably, and soon the summits appeared which enclose the sea at its northern limits. In front rose a mountain, shining in all its beauty, whose summit seemed lost in an eruption of solar rays.

'That is – ?' asked Michel.

'Copernicus,' replied Barbicane.

'Let us see Copernicus.'

This mountain, situated by 9° latitude north and 20° longitude east, rises to a height of 3,438 metres above the level of the moon's surface. It is easily visible from the earth, and astronomers can study it perfectly, especially during the phases comprised between the first quarter and the new moon, because then the shadows are thrown from east to west, and facilitate the measurement of the heights.

This Copernicus is the most important shining point on the surface of the disc, after Tycho, which is situated in the southern hemisphere. It rises, isolated like a gigantic lighthouse, on that portion of the Sea of

Clouds which borders the Sea of Tempests, and illumines with its splendid irradiation two oceans at once. The long luminous trains so dazzling in the full moon, form a spectacle without an equal, and crossing to the north the adjacent chains, they are finally extinguished in the Sea of Rain. At 1 o'clock of the terrestrial morning, the projectile, like a balloon floating in space, overhung this superb mountain.

Barbicane was able to observe exactly its principal dispositions. Copernicus is comprised in the system of annular mountains of the first order, in the divisions of the great circuses. Like Kepler and Aristarchus, which command the Ocean of Tempests, it appears sometimes like a shining spot through the ashy light, and was taken for a volcano in activity. But it is only an extinct volcano, as are all those on the surface of the moon. Its circumvallation had a diameter of about 22 leagues. The lunette discovered traces of stratifications produced by successive eruptions, and the surroundings appeared covered with volcanic remains, of which some still appeared within the crater.

'There exist,' said Barbicane, 'several kinds of circles on the surface of the moon, and it is easy to see that Copernicus belongs to the irradiating class. If we were nearer we would perceive the cones which cover its interior, and which were formerly so many fire-vomiting mouths! A curious disposition, without exception on the lunar disc, is that the interior surface of these circles is notably lower than the exterior plain, contrary to the form presented by terrestrial craters. It follows therefore that the general curve of the bottom of these circles gives a sphere of an inferior diameter to that of the moon.'

'And why this special arrangement?' asked Nicholl.

'It is not known,' replied Barbicane.

'What a magnificent irradiation!' repeated Michel; 'I could hardly imagine a more superb spectacle.'

'What would you say,' replied Barbicane, 'if the chances of our journey had carried us to the southern hemisphere?'

'I should say that it was more superb still,' replied Michel Ardan.

At this moment the projectile was floating directly over the circus. Copernicus' circumvallation formed an almost perfect circle, and its steep ramparts stood boldly out. They could even perceive a double annular fortification. All around spread a grayish plain with a wild aspect, upon which all prominences stood out in yellow. At the bottom of the circus, as though enclosed in a casket, two or three eruptive cones sparkled like enormous dazzling gems. Towards the north, the ramparts were lowered by a depression, which would probably have given access into the interior of the crater. Whilst passing over the adjacent plain, Barbicane was able to note a large number of unimportant mountains, and amongst others a small annular mountain named Gay-Lussac, which is 23 kilometres wide. Towards the south, the plain appeared very flat, without one prominent part, without one elevation of the ground. Towards the north, on the contrary, up to the spot where it bordered the Ocean of Tempests, it was like a liquid surface agitated by a storm, of which the hills and hollows figured a succession of waves suddenly congealed. Over all this extent, and in every direction, ran luminous trains which converged to the summit of Copernicus. Some of these were 30 kilometres wide and incalculably long. The travellers discussed the origin of these strange rays, but they were no more able than terrestrial observers to determine their nature.

'But why,' said Nicholl, 'should not these rays be simply spurs of mountains reflecting more vividly the light of the sun?'

'No,' replied Barbicane; 'if it were so, under certain conditions of the moon, these spurs would throw a shadow, and they do not throw any. In fact these rays only appear at the moment when the orb of day is in opposition with the moon, and they disappear so soon as the rays become oblique.'

'But how have these trains of light been explained?' asked Michel; 'for I cannot believe that men of science were ever in want of an explanation.'

'Herschel,' replied Barbicane, 'formed an opinion, but he did not insist upon it.'

'Never mind! What is that opinion?'

'He thought that these rays must be streams of cooled lava which shine when the rays of the sun fall upon them. That may be, but nothing can be less certain. However, if we pass nearer to Tycho, we shall be in a better position to judge of the cause of this radiation.'

'Do you know, my friends, what this plain resembles, seen from the height at which we are?' said Michel. 'Why, with all these pieces of lava lying about, like immense spindles, it resembles a huge game of spelikans, thrown pell-mell. There wants but the hook to take them out one by one.'

'Do be serious,' said Barbicane.

'Let us be serious,' replied Michel, quietly, 'and instead of spelikans let us say bones. The plain would then resemble an immense cemetery, where lie the mortal remains of a thousand extinct generations. Do you prefer that high-flown comparison?'

'The one is as good as the other,' replied Barbicane.

'The devil! you are hard to please!' replied Michel.

'My worthy friend,' replied the matter-of-fact Barbicane, 'it matters little what all this resembles when we don't know what it is.'

'Well answered,' cried Michel. 'That will teach me to argue with men of science.'

Meanwhile the projectile advanced with almost uniform velocity around the lunar disc. It will readily be believed that the travellers did not for one moment think of taking rest. Each minute, a new landscape fled from beneath their eyes. Towards 1.30 a.m. they perceived the summit of another mountain. Barbicane, consulting his map, recognised Eratosthenes. It was an annular mountain, 4,500 metres high, and formed one of the numerous circles (or circuses) on the satellite. On this point, Barbicane related to his friends the singular opinion of Kepler as to the formation of these circuses. According to the celebrated mathematician, these crater-like cavities had been excavated by the hand of man.

'For what purpose?' asked Nicholl.

'For a very natural purpose,' replied Barbicane. 'The Selenites were supposed to have undertaken these immense works, and excavated these enormous holes, to take refuge in them, for protection against the solar rays, which beat upon them during 15 consecutive days.'

'The Selenites were no fools!' said Michel.

'What a singular idea!' replied Nicholl. 'But it is probable that Kepler did not know the real dimensions of these circuses, for to excavate them would have been the work of giants, quite impracticable for Selenites.'

'Why so? if gravitation on the surface of the moon is six times less than on earth?' said Michel.

'But if the Selenites are six times smaller?' replied Nicholl.

'And if there are no Selenites?' added Barbicane, which closed the discussion.

Soon Erotosthenes disappeared below the horizon, before the projectile had approached sufficiently near to admit of a precise observation. This mountain separated the Apennines and the Carpathians. In lunar orography, several chains of mountains have been remarked, which are principally distributed over the northern hemisphere; a few, however, occupy certain portions of the southern hemisphere.

This is a list of the different chains running from south to north, with their latitudes and various altitudes:

Mount Doerfel	S. latitude 84°	7,603 metres
Mount Leibnitz	S. latitude 65°	7,600 metres
Mount Rook	S. latitude 20°–30°	1,600 metres
Mount Altaï	S. latitude 17°–28°	4,047 metres
Mount Cordilleras	S. latitude 10°–20°	3,898 metres
Mount Pyrenees	S. latitude 8°–18°	3,631 metres
Mount Ural	S. latitude 5°–13°	838 metres

Mount Alembert	S. latitude 4°–10°	5,847 metres
Mount Hoemus	N. latitude 8°–21°	2,021 metres
Mount Carpathian	N. latitude 15°–19°	1,939 metres
Mount Apennine	N. latitude 14°–27°	5,501 metres
Mount Taurus	N. latitude 21°–28°	2,746 metres
Mount Riphees	N. latitude 25°–33°	4,171 metres
Mount Hercyniens	N. latitude 17°–29°	1,170 metres
Mount Caucasus	N. latitude 32°–41°	5,567 metres
Mount Alps	N. latitude 42°–49°	3,617 metres

Of these different chains, the most important is that of the Apennines, extending over 150 leagues, which is, however, much less than the extension of the great orographical elevations of the earth. The Apennines run along the east border of the Sea of Rain, and are continued at the north by the Carpathians, whose profile measures about 100 leagues. The travellers could only get a glimpse of the summit of the Apennines, which run from 10° west longitude to 16° east longitude; but the Carpathian chain extended under their eyes from the 18th to the 30th degree of east longitude, and they were able to observe its distribution. One hypothesis appeared to them well justified. On seeing the chain of the Carpathians taking here and there circular forms, and overhung by projections, they came to the conclusion that they were formerly important circuses. These mountainous rings must have been partly broken up by the vast disturbance which produced the Sea of Rain. These Carpathians would appear to have then been what Purbach, Arzachel, and Ptolemaeus would be if a convulsion threw down their left escarpments and formed them into a continuous chain. They possess an average height of 3,200 metres, which altitude is comparable with that of certain summits of the Pyrenees, such as the port of Pinedes. Their southern slopes fall abruptly towards the immense Sea of Rain. Towards 2 a.m. Barbicane found himself at the height of the 20th lunar parallel, not far from the small mountain, 1,559 metres high, which bears the name of Pythias. The distance of the projectile from the moon was not more than 1,200 kilometres, which the lunettes reduced to three leagues.

The *Mare Imbrium* spread beneath the travellers' eyes like an immense depression, of which the details were yet scarcely perceptible. Near them on the left, rose Mount Lambert, whose altitude is estimated at 1,813 metres; and farther, on the limits of the Ocean of Tempests, in 23° north latitude and 29° east longitude, shone the gleaming mountain of Euler. This mountain, which rises only 1,815 metres above the lunar surface, was the subject of an interesting work by the astronomer Schroeter. This man of science, trying to discover the origin of the mountains of the moon, had asked himself if the volume of the crater was always equal to the volume of the escarpments which formed it. This was found to be generally the case, and Schroeter concluded therefrom that a single eruption of volcanic matter had sufficed to form these escarpments, for successive eruptions would have altered the proportions. Alone Mount Euler was an exception to this general law, and had required for its formation several successive eruptions; for the volume of its cavity was double that of its escarpments. All these hypotheses were permissible for terrestrial observers, whose instruments acted but incompletely. But Barbicane would no longer be satisfied with them, and seeing that his projectile was steadily nearing the lunar disc, he did not despair, even should he not reach her, of discovering at least the secrets of her formation.

CHAPTER THIRTEEN

Lunar landscapes

At half-past two in the morning, the projectile was over the 30th lunar parallel, at an effective distance of 1,000 kilometres, reduced by instruments to 10 kilometres. It still seemed impossible that it should reach any part of the disc. Its velocity of translation, comparatively so moderate, was inexplicable to President Barbicane. At that distance from the moon, it must be considerable to make head against the force of attraction. So there was a phenomenon, the cause of which escaped them still. Besides, time was wanting to seek the cause. The lunar surface swept below the travellers' eyes, and they were desirous of not losing a single detail. So the disc, in the lunettes, appeared at a distance of two leagues and a half. What would an aeronaut perceive at that distance from the earth? It is impossible to say, for the highest ascensions have never exceeded 8,000 metres. This is, however, an exact description of what Barbicane and his companions saw from that height. Large patches of different colours appeared on the disc. Selenographers are not of the same opinion as to the nature of these colorations. They are different and vividly contrasted. Julius Schmidt asserts that if the terrestrial oceans were dried up, a Selenite lunar observer would not perceive upon the globe, between the oceans and continental plains, so great a diversity of shades as are seen on the moon by the terrestrial observer. According to him, the colour common to the vast plains, known as seas, is dark-gray mixed with green and brown. Some large craters also show this coloration. Barbicane was acquainted with this opinion of the German selenographer, shared by Messrs Beer and Moedler. He remarked that observations proved they were right, as against certain astronomers who only admit a gray coloration on the surface of the moon. In some instances, the green colour was vividly marked, as proved, according to Julius Schmidt, by the Serenity and Humours Seas. Barbicane also remarked large craters without interior cones, which shed a bluish tint, like the reflection of a steel mirror freshly polished. These colours really belong to the lunar disc, and do not arise from imperfections in the object-glass of the lunette, nor from the interposition of the terrestrial atmosphere, as some astronomers have asserted. In this respect Barbicane had no doubts whatever.

He observed through a vacuum, and could commit no optical mistakes. He considered the fact of these different colours as fully established for science. Now, were these green tints owing to some tropical vegetation maintained by a dense, low atmosphere? He could not yet decide. Farther on, he noticed a reddish tint, sufficiently marked. Such a tint had already been remarked at the bottom of an isolated enclosure, known as Lichtenberg's Circus, which is situated near Mount Hercyniens, on the edge of the moon, but he could not discover its nature. He was not more fortunate concerning another peculiarity of the disc, the cause of which he could not discover. This is the peculiarity in question.

Michel Ardan was in observation near the president when he remarked some long white lines, vividly lighted by the direct rays of the sun. It was a succession of luminous furrows, very different from the radiation which Copernicus shed not long before. They lay parallel to each other. Michel, with his usual readiness, did not hesitate to exclaim: 'By Jove, cultivated fields!'

'Cultivated fields!' replied Nicholl, shrugging his shoulders.

'Ploughed at least,' retorted Michel Ardan. 'But what ploughmen these Selenites must be, and what gigantic oxen they must harness to their ploughs, to make such furrows!'

'They are not furrows,' said Barbicane, 'they are rifts.'

'As you please,' replied Ardan, with docility; 'but what do you mean by "rifts" in the scientific world?'

Barbicane imparted to his companion all he knew about lunar rifts. He knew that they were furrows, observed upon all the portions of the disc not mountainous; that these furrows, mostly isolated, measure from four to fifty leagues in length; that their breadth varies from 1,000 to 1,500 metres, and that their edges are exactly parallel; but he knew nothing more either as to their formation or as to their nature. Barbicane, with the aid of his lunette, observed these rifts with extreme attention. He remarked that their sides were formed by extremely steep slopes. They were long parallel escarpments, and by a slight stretch of imagination, they might be considered long lines of fortifications, thrown up by Selenite engineers. Of these different rifts, some were absolutely straight, as though drawn with a tape; others were slightly curved, though still with parallel edges. The latter crossed each other, the former ran through the craters; now they furrowed ordinary cavities, like Posidonius or Petavius; and now they ran through seas, such as the Sea of Serenity. These natural accidents naturally brought into play the imaginations of terrestrial astronomers. The first observations had not discovered these rifts. Neither Hevelius, nor Cassini, nor La

Hire, nor Herschel appear to have known of them. Schroeter, in 1787, was the first who drew the attention of scientific men to their existence. Others followed suit and studied them, such as Pastorff, Gruijthuijsen, Beer and Moedler. Today their number amounts to seventy. But if they have been counted, their nature has not yet been determined. They are certainly not fortifications, any more than dried-up beds of rivers; for, on the one hand, the small quantity of water on the surface of the moon could not have made such channels; and on the other hand, these furrows often cross craters placed at a great elevation. However, Michel Ardan conceived an idea which coincided with that of Julius Schmidt.

'Why,' said he, 'should not these inexplicable appearances be simply phenomena of vegetation?'

'How do you mean?' asked Barbicane hastily.

'Do not excite yourself, worthy president,' replied Michel. 'Is it not possible that the dark lines which form the bastions are rows of trees regularly planted?'

'You will have your vegetation,' said Barbicane.

'I am anxious,' retorted Michel Ardan, 'to explain what you men of science cannot explain. At least my hypothesis would have the advantage of showing why these rifts disappear, or seem to disappear, at regular periods.'

'How so?'

'Because these trees become invisible when they lose their leaves, and visible when they recover them.'

'Your explanation, dear friend, is ingenious but not admissible,' said Barbicane.

'Why not?'

'Because there is not, so to speak, any season on the surface of the moon, and consequently the phenomena of vegetation, to which you refer, could not arise. In fact, the slight obliquity of the lunar axis maintains the sun at an almost constant altitude in all latitudes. Above the equatorial regions, the radiant orb is almost invariably in the zenith, and does not pass the limits of the horizon in the polar regions, so that, in each region, there reigns perpetual winter, perpetual spring, perpetual summer, or perpetual autumn, as also in the planet Jupiter, whose axis is likewise but little inclined towards its orbit.'

'What is the origin of these rifts?'

'The question is difficult to solve. They are certainly posterior to the formation of the craters and of the circles, for several have burst into them, breaking down their circular ramparts. It is possible, therefore, that they are contemporary with the last geological periods, and are due to the expansion of natural forces.'

However, the projectile had attained the 40th degree of lunar latitude, at a distance which could not exceed 800 kilometres. Objects appeared in the focus of the lunette as only two leagues distant. At this point, beneath their feet rose Helicon, 505 metres high, and to the left, stood the moderate heights which enclose a small portion of the Sea of Rain under the name of Gulf of Iris. The terrestrial atmosphere should be 170 times more transparent than it is, to allow astronomers to make complete observations at the surface of the moon; but in the vacuum, where the projectile floated, no fluid interposed between the observer's eye and the object observed. Further, Barbicane found himself at a distance to which the most powerful telescopes had never attained – neither that of Lord Rosse nor that of the Rocky Mountains. He was, therefore, in the most favourable position for solving the great question of the inhabitableness of the moon. However, this solution still escaped him. He duly perceived the deserted expanse of the immense plains, and, to the north, barren mountains. Not one work which betrayed the hand of man; not a ruin, to prove his passage. Not one agglomeration of animals, to show that life existed in the lower degrees. No movement anywhere; no trace of vegetation. Of the three kingdoms which share the terrestrial spheroid, one only was represented on the surface of the lunar globe – the mineral kingdom.

'Hallo!' said Michel Ardan, somewhat downcast; 'is there no one at home?'

'No,' replied Nicholl, 'up to the present. Not a man, not an animal, not a tree. After all, if the atmosphere has taken refuge at the bottom of the cavities, in the interior of the circuses, or even on the opposite face of the moon, we can decide nothing.'

'Besides,' added Barbicane, 'even to the most piercing sight, a man is not visible beyond a distance of seven kilometres. So, if there are Selenites, they can see our projectile, but we cannot see them.'

Towards 4 a.m., at the height of the 50th parallel, the distance was reduced to 600 kilometres. On the left was a line of mountains of capricious shapes, standing in the full light. To the right, on the contrary, was a dark hole, like a vast pit, unfathomable and gloomy, sunk in the lunar soil. This hole was the Black Lake, or Plato – a deep circus, which can only be properly observed from the earth, between the last quarter and the new moon, when the shadows are thrown from west to east. This black colour is rarely met with on the surface of the satellite. Hitherto, it has only been noticed in the depths of Endymion, a circus to the east of the Sea of Cold, in the northern hemisphere, and at the bottom of

Grimaldi on the equator, towards the eastern edge of the orb. Plato is an annular mountain, situated by 51° north latitude and 9° east longitude. Its circus is 92 kilometres long and 61 kilometres wide. Barbicane regretted that he did not pass perpendicularly over its vast aperture. There was there an abyss to fathom, perhaps some mysterious phenomenon to discover, but the direction of the projectile could not be modified; they must submit. Balloons are not to be guided, much less projectiles when you are shut in between their walls. Towards 5 a.m. the northern limit of the Sea of Rain was passed. Mounts La Condamine and Fontenelle remained, the one on the left, the other on the right. This portion of the disc, from the 60th degree became completely mountainous. The lunettes brought it to within one league, a distance less than divides the summit of Mont Blanc and the level of the sea. All this region is covered with mountains and circuses. Towards the 70th degree towered Philoläus, at a height of 3,700 metres, disclosing an elliptical crater sixteen leagues long and four wide. Then the disc, seen from this distance, offered an extremely peculiar aspect. The landscapes met the view under conditions very different from those of the earth, but also very inferior. The moon having no atmosphere, this absence of gaseous envelope entails consequences already mentioned. There is no twilight at its surface – night following day and day following night with the abruptness of a lamp which is extinguished or lighted in the midst of complete darkness. No transition from cold to heat, the temperature falling in an instant from the point of boiling water to the cold of space. Another consequence of the absence of air is this: that absolute darkness prevails wherever the rays of the sun do not penetrate. What is called diffused light upon the earth, that luminous matter which the air holds in suspension, which causes twilights and dawns, which produces shadows and half-shadows, and all that magic of the *chiaro-oscuro*, does not exist on the moon. Hence a grossness of contrasts, which only admits of two colours – black and white. If a Selenite shades his eyes from the solar rays, the sky appears perfectly dark to him, and the stars shine before his view, as in the darkest nights.

Judge of the impression produced by the strange aspect upon Barbicane and his two friends. Their eyes became confused; they could no longer judge of the respective distances of different objects. A lunar landscape, not toned down by the phenomenon of *chiaro-oscuro*, could not be represented by a landscape upon the earth – some blotches of ink upon white paper, and that was all. This aspect was not modified even when the projectile, at the height of the 80th degree, was separated from the moon by a distance of only 100 kilometres; not even when, at

5 a.m., it passed at less than 50 kilometres from Mount Gioja, which distance the lunettes reduced to a quarter of a league. It seemed that the moon could be touched with the hand. It seemed impossible that the projectile should not strike it soon, were it only at its north pole, whose brilliant arch stood vividly out from the dark background of the sky. Michel Ardan wanted to open one of the scuttles to throw himself on to the lunar surface, a fall of 12 leagues. He thought nothing of it. The attempt, however, would have been useless, for if the projectile did not reach some point of the surface of the satellite, neither would Michel, who would follow the same movement. At this moment, 6 a.m., the lunar pole appeared. The disc no longer showed to the travellers more than one-half, brilliantly illuminated, whereas the other was plunged into darkness. Suddenly, the projectile passed the line of demarcation between intense light and absolute darkness, and was immediately enveloped in profound night.

CHAPTER FOURTEEN
The night of 354½ hours

At the moment when this phenomenon was so abruptly produced the projectile was skimming over the north pole, at a distance of less than 50 kilometres; a few seconds had sufficed to plunge it into the absolute darkness of space. The transition had occurred so rapidly, without shade, without gradation of light, without attenuation of the luminous undulations, that the orb appeared to be blown out by the action of some powerful breath.

'The moon has melted, disappeared!' cried Michel Ardan, quite aghast.

In fact there was neither reflection nor shadow. Nothing more appeared of this disc, hitherto so dazzling. The darkness was complete, and rendered more profound by the twinkling of the stars. It was the darkness of the lunar nights, which last 354½ hours for each point of the disc, which long night results from the equality of the movements of translation and of rotation of the moon – the one upon her own axis, the other round the earth. The projectile, immersed in the cone of shadow of the satellite, no longer underwent the action of the solar rays any more than any point of its invisible half.

Inside, therefore, the darkness was complete. They could not see each other – hence the necessity for dispelling the darkness. However desirous Barbicane might be to husband their limited supply of gas, he was forced to ask from it a factitious light, an expensive brilliancy which the sun then refused.

'The devil take the radiant orb!' cried Michel Ardan. 'He is going to put us to the cost of gas, instead of lighting us with his rays, gratis.'

'Do not let us accuse the sun,' said Nicholl. 'It is not his fault, but the fault of the moon, who has placed herself like a screen between us and him.'

'It is the sun!' continued Michel.

'It is the moon!' retorted Nicholl.

An unprofitable dispute, to which Barbicane put an end by saying: 'My friends, it is neither the fault of the sun nor the fault of the moon; it is the fault of the projectile, which, instead of following its proper trajectory, awkwardly left it; or, to be more correct, it is the fault of that disastrous meteorite, which caused us to deviate from our first direction.'

'Good!' replied Ardan; 'as that matter is arranged, let us break-fast. After an entire night of observation, it is necessary to repair our strength.'

This proposal met with no dissentients. In a few minutes Michel had prepared a repast. But they ate for the sake of eating; they drank without toasts – without hurrahs! The bold travellers, carried through the dark-ness of space without their accustomed *cortège* of rays, felt a vague uneasi-ness gain upon them. 'The wild shades,' so dear to Victor Hugo's pen, shut them in on every side.

However, they talked about that interminable night of 354 hours, or nearly fifteen days, which the laws of physics have imposed upon the inhabitants of the moon. Barbicane gave his friends some explan-ations as to the causes and consequences of this curious phenom-enon. 'Most curious, indeed,' said he; 'for if each hemisphere of the moon is deprived of solar light during 15 days, that over which we float at this moment, does not even enjoy, during its long night, the view of the brilliantly-lighted earth. In one word, there is only a moon – applying this qualification to our spheroid – for one side of the disc. Now, if it were thus for the earth – if, for instance, Europe never saw the moon, and the latter were only visible at the antipodes – imagine what would be the astonishment of a European arriving in Australia!'

'People would make the journey merely to see the moon!' replied Michel.

'Well,' replied Barbicane, 'this astonishment is reserved to the Selenite who inhabits the face of the moon opposed to the earth, which face is always invisible to our fellow countrymen of the terrestrial globe.'

'And which we would have seen,' added Nicholl, 'if we had arrived here at the time when the moon was new – that is, 15 days later.'

'On the other hand,' continued Barbicane, 'I may add, the inhabitant of the visible face is singularly favoured by nature, to the detriment of his brethren of the invisible face. This last, as you see, has profound nights of 354 hours, during which no single ray breaks the obscurity. The other, on the contrary, when the sun which has lighted it during 15 days descends below the horizon, sees a magnificent orb rise on the opposite horizon. It is the earth, thirteen times larger than the moon, which we know of – the earth which develops itself at a diameter of two degrees, and which sheds a light thirteen times more intense than that tempered by the atmospheric strata – the earth, which only disappears when the sun reappears in its turn.'

'A very pretty period!' said Michel Ardan; 'somewhat academical perhaps.'

'Whence it follows,' continued Barbicane without wincing, 'that this face of the disc must be very agreeable to inhabit, as it is always looking either at the sun, when the moon is full, or at the earth, when the moon is new.'

'But,' said Nicholl, 'that advantage must be counterbalanced by the unbearable heat which this light brings with it.'

'The inconvenience, in this respect, is the same for the two faces, for the light reflected by the earth, is evidently devoid of heat. However, this invisible face is still more troubled with the heat than the visible face. I say that for you, Nicholl, because Michel would probably not understand.'

'Thank you,' said Michel.

'In fact,' continued Barbicane, 'when this invisible face receives, at the same time, the solar light and heat, the moon is new – that is, she is in conjunction, or situated between the sun and the earth. She is therefore, relatively to the situation she occupies, in opposition when she is full – nearer to the sun by double her distance from the earth. Now this distance may be estimated at the 200th part of that which separates the sun from the earth, or, in round figures, 200,000 leagues. Thus the invisible face is nearer the sun by 200,000 leagues when it receives the solar rays.'

'Quite right,' replied Nicholl.

'On the contrary – ' continued Barbicane.

'One moment,' said Michel, interrupting his grave companion.

'What do you want?'

'I want to continue the explanation.'

'Why?'

'To prove that I have understood.'

'Go on,' said Barbicane, smiling.

'On the contrary,' said Michel, imitating the tone and gestures of President Barbicane, 'on the contrary, when the visible face is lighted by the sun, the moon is full – that is to say, situated on the opposite side of the sun, relatively to the earth. The distance, which separates her from the orb of day, is therefore increased, in round figures, by 200,000 leagues, and the heat which it receives must be somewhat less.'

'Bravo!' cried Barbicane. 'Do you know, Michel, that for an artist you are intelligent?'

'Yes,' replied Michel, negligently; 'we are all like that on the Boulevard des Italiens.'

Barbicane gravely pressed his amiable companion's hand, and continued to enumerate the few advantages reserved to the inhabitants of the visible face. Amongst others, he quoted the observation, 'that the eclipses of the sun only occur for this side of the lunar disc, inasmuch as, for such to be produced, it is necessary that she should be in opposition. These eclipses, produced by the interposition of the earth between the moon and the sun, may last two hours, during which time, by reason of the rays refracted by its atmosphere, the terrestrial globe must appear like a black spot upon the sun.'

'So,' said Nicholl, 'there is one hemisphere – this invisible hemisphere – which is very badly provided for, so to speak – disgraced by nature.'

'Yes,' replied Barbicane, 'but not altogether. In fact, by a certain movement of libration, by a certain oscillation upon its centre, the moon presents to the earth rather more than half her disc. She is like a pendulum, of which the centre of gravity is carried towards the terrestrial globe, and which oscillates regularly.'

'Whence arises this oscillation?'

'From the fact that its movement of rotation upon its axis is animated with uniform velocity, whereas its movement of translation, following an elliptical orbit round the earth, is not so. In perigee, the rapidity of translation has the upper hand, and the moon shows a certain portion of her western edge; in apogee, the rapidity of rotation is the stronger, and a portion of the eastern edge appears. A strip of about 8 degrees appears now on the west, now on the east, so that out of 1,000 parts the moon shows 569.'

'Never mind,' replied Michel, 'if ever we become Selenites, we will inhabit the visible face. I like the light, I do.'

'Unless,' retorted Nicholl, 'that the atmosphere be condensed on the other side, as certain astronomers pretend.'

'That is a consideration,' replied Michel simply.

However, when the breakfast was ended, the observers were again at their post. They tried to see through the dark scuttles, by extinguishing all light in the projectile. But not a particle of light appeared in the darkness. One inexplicable fact preoccupied Barbicane. How, having passed so near to the moon, 50 kilometres about, the projectile had not fallen on to her surface. Had its velocity been enormous, one might have understood that the fall would not have occurred. But with its relatively low rate of speed, this resistance to lunar attraction could not be explained. Was the projectile subject to foreign influences?

Did any other body maintain it in ether? It became evident that it would not touch any point of the moon's surface. Where was it going? Was it becoming more distant from the disc or nearer to it? Was it being carried into profound night through infinite space? How could this be discovered? How calculated amidst darkness? All these questions disquieted Barbicane, but he could not solve them. In fact, the invisible orb was there, perhaps only a few leagues, a few miles distant, but neither his companions nor he could see it. If there were any noise on its surface they could not hear it. The air, that vehicle of sound, was wanting to convey the plaints of the moon, which the Arabs call in their legends 'a man half-granite and yet palpitating'. It was enough to provoke the most patient observers, it must be admitted. It was precisely this unknown hemisphere which was hidden from their sight. That face which a fortnight sooner, or a fortnight later, would have been magnificently lighted up by the solar rays, was lost in absolute obscurity. In a fortnight, where would the projectile be? Where would the chances of attraction have carried it? Who could tell? It is generally admitted, from selenographic observations, that the invisible hemisphere of the moon is perfectly similar in composition to the visible hemisphere. In fact, about the seventh portion of it is disclosed by the movements of libration, of which Barbicane had spoken. These slips, which had been seen, were only mountains and plains, circuses and craters, analogous to those marked on the maps. The same nature and the same world, arid and dead, might be predicted. However, if the atmosphere had taken refuge on this face! If, with the air, water had given life to these regenerated continents! If vegetation were still to be found there! If animals peopled these continents and seas! If man, in these conditions of habitableness, were yet living there! What interesting questions were to be solved! What solutions might have been drawn from the contemplation of this hemisphere! What delight, to cast a glance upon this world, which the human eye had never seen!

The disgust of the travellers may be conceived, in the midst of this dark night. All observation of the lunar disc was impossible. The constellations only were open to their view, and it must be admitted that neither Faye, Chacornac, nor Secchi were ever in such favourable conditions for observing them. In fact, nothing could equal the splendour of this sidereal world, bathed in limpid ether. These diamonds, set in the celestial vault, shone with superb fire. The glance scanned the firmament from the Southern Cross to the North Star, which two constellations, in 12,000 years, by reason of the precession of the equinoxes, will cede their places as polar stars, the one to Canopus in the western hemisphere, and the other to Vega in the eastern hemisphere. The imagination lost itself in this sublime infinite, in the midst of which the projectile floated like a new star created by the hand of man. By a natural effect, these constellations shone with a softened light; they did not twinkle, for the atmosphere was wanting which produces the twinkling, by the interposition of its strata, unequally dense, and of different degrees of moisture. The stars looked like soft eyes peering in the deep night, amidst the absolute silence of space.

For some time the travellers observed in silence the constellated firmament, on which the vast screen of the moon made an enormous black hole. But a painful sensation drew them from their contemplation. It was a very severe cold, which soon covered the interior of the scuttle glasses with a thick layer of ice. In fact, the sun no longer heated the projectile with its rays, and the former gradually lost the heat stored within its walls. This heat by radiation had rapidly evaporated in space, and a considerable lowering of the temperature had resulted. The interior moisture was changed to ice on its contact with the glass, and hindered all observation. Nicholl, consulting the thermometer, saw that it had fallen to $17°$ centigrade below zero. So, notwithstanding all reasons for economy, Barbicane, having used the gas for light, was obliged to use it for heat. The low temperature of the projectile was no longer supportable. Its inmates would have been frozen alive.

'We will not complain,' remarked Ardan, 'of the monotony of our journey. What diversity at least of temperature! Now we are blinded with light and saturated with heat, like the Indians of the Pampas! Now we are plunged into profound darkness, in the midst of intense cold, like the Esquimaux at the north pole! Most certainly we have no right to complain, and nature is treating us handsomely.'

'But,' asked Nicholl, 'what is the exterior temperature?'

'Precisely that of the planetary regions,' replied Barbicane.

'Then,' continued Michel Ardan, 'would not this be the moment to make the experiment, which we could not try when bathed in the rays of the sun?'

'Now, or never,' replied Barbicane, 'for we are admirably placed to verify the temperature of space, and see whether the calculations of Fourier or Pouillet are exact.'

'In any case, it is cold,' replied Michel. 'See, the interior moisture condenses on the glass of the scuttles. If the fall continues, our breath will fall around us like snow.'

'Let us prepare a thermometer,' said Barbicane.

One may well believe that an ordinary thermometer would have given no results, in the conditions wherein the instrument was to be exposed. Quicksilver would have frozen in the bulb, for it does not remain liquid at 42° below zero. But Barbicane was provided with a spirit thermometer on Walferdin's system, which gives the minima of excessively low temperatures. Before commencing the experiment, the instrument was compared with an ordinary thermometer, and Barbicane prepared to use it.

'How are we going to manage?' asked Nicholl.

'Nothing can be easier,' replied Michel Ardan, who was never at a loss. 'You open the scuttle rapidly, throw out the instrument, it follows the projectile with exemplary docility, and a quarter of an hour afterwards you take it in.'

'With the hand?' asked Barbicane.

'With the hand,' replied Michel.

'Well, my friend, don't you run a risk?' replied Barbicane; 'for the hand you drew in would be nothing but a stump, frozen and deformed by this fearful cold.'

'Really!'

'You would feel the sensation of a terrible burn, as if from an iron at white heat, for whether heat leaves our flesh abruptly or enters it, the result is identically the same. Besides, I am not certain that the articles thrown out would still follow us.'

'Why?' said Nicholl.

'Because, if we are passing through an atmosphere, however little dense it may be, the articles would be delayed, and the darkness would prevent our seeing whether they were still floating around us. So, not to risk the loss of our thermometer, we will make it fast, and be better able to draw it into the interior.'

The advice of Barbicane was followed. Through the rapidly-opened scuttle, Nicholl threw the instrument, fastened to a short cord, so that it could be rapidly drawn in. The scuttle had only been open a second, but that second had sufficed to allow a violent cold to penetrate into the interior of the projectile.

'Horrible!' cried Michel Ardan; 'it is cold enough to freeze a polar bear.'

Barbicane waited until half an hour was past, which was more than sufficient to allow the instrument to fall to the level of the temperature of space, then the thermometer was rapidly drawn in.

Barbicane measured the quantity of spirits of wine which had flowed into the little receptacle fixed at the bottom of the instrument, and said: 'One hundred and forty degrees centigrade below zero.'

M. Pouillet was right and Fourier wrong. Such was the dreadful temperature of the starry regions. Such is, perhaps, that of the lunar continents, when the orb of night has lost, by radiation, all the heat absorbed during fifteen days of sunlight.

CHAPTER FIFTEEN

Hyperbola or parabola?

It may perhaps seem astonishing that Barbicane and his companions took so little care of the future reserved for them in their metal prison, which was carrying them into the infinity of space. Instead of inquiring where they were thus travelling, they passed their time in making experiments, as if they had been quietly seated in their study.

It might be answered that men of such calibre were above such cares, that they took no heed of such trifles, and that they had other things to do than to think of their future lot.

The truth is, they were not masters of their projectile; they could neither hinder its progress nor modify its direction. A sailor can alter, at will, the head of his vessel, an aëronaut can give vertical movements to his balloon, but they had no action upon their vehicle. All manoeuvres were impossible. Hence this disposition to let matters take their course. 'Let her run,' as the sailors have it.

Where were they situated at this moment, at 8 a.m. of the day called the 6th December on earth? Most certainly in the neighbourhood of the moon, and near enough for her to appear like an immense black screen spread out on the firmament. As to the distance which separated them from her, it was impossible to estimate it. The projectile, maintained by inexplicable forces, had passed within 50 kilometres of the satellite's north pole; but during the two hours since it had entered the cone of shadow, had this distance increased or diminished? Every fixed point was wanting to estimate the direction and the velocity of the projectile. Perhaps it was rapidly leaving the disc, so as to emerge shortly from the pure shadow. Perhaps, on the contrary, it was nearing it so much as to strike some elevated portion of the invisible hemisphere, which would have ended the journey, doubtless to the detriment of the travellers.

A discussion arose on this point, and Michel Ardan, always rich in explanations, gave out this opinion: that the projectile, retained by lunar attraction, would end by falling to the surface, as an aerolite falls to the surface of the terrestrial globe.

'In the first place, comrade,' replied Barbicane, 'every aerolite does not fall to the earth, but only the smaller number. Thus, from the fact that we have passed into the state of aerolite it does not necessarily follow that we shall reach the surface of the moon.'

'However,' replied Michel, 'if we approach near enough – '

'Error,' replied Barbicane. 'Have you not seen shooting stars cross the sky by thousands at certain periods?'

'Yes.'

'Well, these stars, or rather these corpuscules, only shine on the condition of becoming heated by friction on the atmospheric strata. Now, if they pass through the atmosphere, they come within 16 leagues of the globe, and, nevertheless, they seldom fall to the surface. The same for our projectile, it may approach very near to the moon and yet not fall to the surface.'

'Then,' asked Michel, 'I shall be very curious to see how our wandering vehicle will act in space.'

'I only see two hypotheses,' replied Barbicane, after a few minutes' reflection.

'Which?'

'The projectile has the choice between two mathematical curves, and it will follow one or the other, according to the velocity with which it is endowed, and which I could not estimate at the present moment.'

'Yes,' said Nicholl, 'it will follow a parabola or a hyperbola.'

'True,' replied Barbicane. 'With a certain velocity it will take a parabola, or a hyperbola with a greater velocity.'

'I like fine words,' cried Michel Ardan; 'we all know at once what they mean. And what is your parabola, if you please?'

'My friend,' replied the captain, 'the parabola is a curve of the second order, which results from the section of a cone intersected by a plane parallel to one of its sides.'

'Ah! ah!' said Michel, in a satisfied tone. 'It is about the trajectory of a shell fired from a mortar.'

'Bravo!'

'And hyperbola?' asked Michel.

'Hyperbola, Michel, is a curve of the second order, produced by the intersection of a conic surface by a plane parallel to its axis, which constitutes two branches, separated from each other, extending indefinitely in both directions.'

'Is it possible!' cried Michel Ardan, in a most grave tone of voice, as though he had been informed of some serious matter. 'Then remember this, Captain Nicholl, what I like in your definition of the hyperbola – I was going to say hyperhumbug! – is that it is still less clear than the word which you pretend to define.'

Nicholl and Barbicane cared little for the jokes of Michel Ardan. They were in the midst of a scientific discussion. What would be the curve followed by the projectile? that was what excited their attention. The one was for the parabola, the other for the hyperbola. They gave their reasons bristling with x's. Their arguments were clothed in a language which astounded Michel Ardan. The discussion was warm, and neither of the adversaries would give up his favourite curve.

This scientific dispute becoming somewhat too lengthy, ended by exhausting Michel's patience.

'Now then, gentlemen cosines,' said he, 'when will you have done throwing parabolas and hyperbolas at each other's heads? I want to know the only interesting thing in the whole matter. We shall follow one or other of your curves, but where will they bring us?'

'Nowhere,' replied Nicholl.

'Nowhere! what do you mean?'

'Certainly,' said Barbicane. 'They are open curves, which may be prolonged indefinitely.'

'Ah, men of science, I take you to my bosom,' cried Michel. 'And what matter whether we follow parabola or hyperbola, if both carry us equally into the infinity of space.'

Barbicane and Nicholl could not help smiling. They had been discussing art for art's sake. Never had a more idle question been raised at a more inopportune moment. The dreadful truth was, that the projectile, following either an hyperbola or a parabola, would never again meet either earth or moon.

Now what would happen to these bold travellers in a very proximate future? If they did not die of hunger, or of thirst, at least, in a few days, their gas would run short and they would die from want of air, if the cold had not already killed them.

Notwithstanding the importance of economising gas, the excessive fall of the temperature obliged them to consume a certain quantity. If necessary, they could dispense with light, but not with heat. Happily, the caloric, developed by the apparatus of Reiset and Regnault, somewhat raised the interior temperature of the projectile, and without great expenditure they were able to keep it at a bearable degree of warmth. However, observations had become very difficult through the scuttles. The interior moisture condensed upon the glass and immediately congealed. It was necessary to destroy this opacity of the glass by reiterated friction. However, some phenomena could be observed of the highest interest. In fact, if this invisible disc was provided with an atmosphere, ought they not to see the shooting stars cross it with their trajectories?

If the projectile itself was passing through these fluid strata, could they not catch some sound repercussed by lunar echoes – the growling of a storm, for instance, the noise of an avalanche, the detonations of a volcano in activity? And if some fire-vomiting mountain flashed forth its lightnings, would not their intense flamings be perceived? Such facts, carefully noted, would have singularly elucidated the dark question of lunar composition. So Barbicane and Nicholl, posted at their scuttle, observed with the scrupulous patience of astronomers.

But, up till then, the disc had remained mute and dark. It did not reply to the numerous interrogatories of these ardent minds, which provoked this reflection from Michel, reasonable enough in appearance: 'If ever we recommence this journey, we shall do well to choose the period when the moon is new.'

'Quite right,' replied Nicholl, 'circumstances would then be more favourable. I admit that the moon, bathed in solar rays, would not be visible during the passage, but, on the other hand, we should see the earth, which would be full. Further, if we were carried round the moon, as is now the case, we should at least have the advantage of seeing the invisible disc magnificently lighted up.'

'Well said, Nicholl,' retorted Michel Ardan. 'What do you say, Barbicane?'

'I think this,' replied the grave president: 'If ever we recommence this journey, we will start at the same period and in the same conditions. Suppose that we had attained our goal, would it not have been better to have found the continents in full light, rather than a country plunged in the darkest night? Our first settlement would have occurred under better conditions, most certainly so. As to this invisible side, we could have visited it during our reconnoitring journeys on the surface of the moon. Therefore, the period of the full moon was happily chosen, but it was necessary to reach the goal and not to deviate from the route.'

'To that, there is nothing to reply,' said Michel Ardan. 'However, we have lost a good opportunity of observing the other side of the moon. Who knows whether the inhabitants of the other planets are not more advanced than the scientific men on earth, on the subject of their satellites?'

To this remark of Michel Ardan's, the following reply might easily have been made: yes, other satellites, by their greater proximity, have rendered their study easier. The inhabitants of Saturn, Jupiter, and Uranus, if they exist, may have established easier communication with their moons. The four satellites of Jupiter gravitate at a distance of 108,260 leagues, 172,200 leagues, 274,700 leagues, and 480,130 leagues. But these distances are computed from the centre of the planet, and, on subtracting the length of the radius, which is from 17,000 to 18,000 leagues, it will be seen that the first satellite is not so distant from the surface of Jupiter as the moon is from the surface of the earth. Of the eight moons of Saturn, four are also nearer: Diana is 84,600 leagues distant, Thetys 62,966 leagues, Enceladus 48,191 leagues, and lastly Mimas is at an average distance of only 34,500 leagues. Of the eight satellites of Uranus, Ariel, the first, is only 51,520 leagues distant from the planet.

So, at the surface of these three planets, an experiment like that of President Barbicane would have presented much less difficulty. If, there-fore, their inhabitants have tried the experiment, they have perhaps discovered the composition of that half of the disc which their satellite eternally hides from their eyes. But if they have never quitted their planet, they are no further advanced than the astronomers of the earth.

Meanwhile, the projectile described in shadow that incalculable tra-jectory which no fixed point allowed to be estimated. Had its direction been modified, either under the influence of lunar attractions or under the action of some unknown orb? Barbicane could not tell. But a change had taken place in the relative position of the vehicle, and Barbicane remarked it towards four o'clock in the morning. The alteration con-sisted in this, that the bottom of the projectile was turned towards the surface of the moon, and maintained itself in a perpendicular drawn through its axis. Attraction, that is to say gravitation, had occasioned this alteration. The heaviest part of the projectile inclined towards the invis-ible disc, exactly as though it were falling towards it.

Was it, then, falling? Were the travellers at last going to reach the much-desired goal? No! And an observation, from a somewhat inexplic-able fixed point, proved to Barbicane that his projectile was not nearing the moon, and that it was moving on an almost concentric curve.

This point of mark was a luminous flash, which Nicholl suddenly perceived, on the limit of the horizon formed by the black disc. This flash could not be mistaken for a star. It was a reddish incandescence which increased by degrees, which was incontestable proof that the projectile was moving towards it, and was not falling towards the surface of the orb.

'A volcano! It is a volcano in activity! An outburst of the internal fires of the moon!' cried Nicholl. 'So that world is not yet completely extinct.'

'Yes, an eruption,' replied Barbicane, who was carefully examining the phenomenon through his night-glass. 'What could it be if not a volcano?'

'But then,' said Michel Ardan, 'there must be air to allow of com-bustion. So there is an atmosphere on this part of the moon.'

'Perhaps,' replied Barbicane, 'but not necessarily. The volcano, by the decomposition of certain substances, can supply its own oxygen, and thus vomit flames in a vacuum. It even appears to me, that yonder deflagration has the intensity and brilliancy of a combustion in pure oxygen. Do not let us too hastily assert the existence of a lunar atmosphere.'

The fire-vomiting mountain must have been situated at about the 45th degree of south latitude of the invisible portion of the disc, but, to Barbicane's great displeasure, the curve described by the projectile was carrying the latter far from the point marked by the eruption; thus, he could not determine its nature more exactly. Half an hour after being perceived, this luminous spot disappeared behind the horizon. However, the noting of this phenomenon was an important fact in selenographic studies. It proved that all heat had not yet disappeared from the bowels of this globe; and, where heat exists, who can assert that the vegetable kingdom, and even the animal kingdom, have not hitherto resisted destructive influences? The existence of this volcano in eruption, indisputably acknowledged by men of science on earth, would doubtless have given rise to many theories favourable to this great question of the inhabitableness of the moon.

Barbicane allowed himself to be carried away by his reflections. He forgot himself in a mute reverie, wherein were agitated the mysterious destinies of the lunar world. He tried to unite the facts hitherto observed, when a new incident brought him abruptly back to reality.

This incident was more than a cosmical phenomenon, it was a danger menacing the most disastrous consequences. Suddenly, in the midst of the ether, in this profound darkness, an enormous mass had appeared. It was like a moon, but a burning moon, of a brilliancy the more dazzling, that it contrasted with the deep darkness of space. This mass, of a circular form, shed so much light that the projectile was filled with it. The faces of Barbicane, Nicholl, and Michel Ardan, bathed in these white rays, took that spectral, livid, haggard appearance, which is produced by the flames of spirits mixed with salt.

'A thousand devils!' cried Michel Ardan, 'we are hideous. What is that ill-behaved moon?'

'A meteorite,' replied Barbicane.

'A burning meteorite in a vacuum?'

'Yes.'

This globe of fire was, in fact, a meteorite. Barbicane was not mistaken. But if these cosmical meteors, when observed from the earth, generally present a light only little inferior to the moon, seen in the dark ether, they are resplendent. These wandering bodies carry with them the principles of their incandescence. Circumambient air is not necessary to their combustion; and, in fact, if certain of these meteorites pass through the atmospheric strata at two or three leagues from the earth, others, on the contrary, describe their trajectories at a distance to which the atmosphere could not extend. Such were the meteors which appeared, the one on the 27th October, 1844, at a height of 128 leagues; the other on the 18th August, 1841, which disappeared at a distance of 182 leagues. Some of these meteors are three and four kilometres wide, and possess a velocity which may amount to 75 kilometres per second, following an inverse direction to the movement of the earth.

This shooting globe which suddenly appeared in the darkness, at a distance of 100 leagues at least, must have measured, according to Barbicane's estimate, about 2,000 metres in diameter. It advanced with a velocity of about two kilometres per second, or 30 leagues a minute. It crossed the line of the projectile, and must reach it in a few minutes. As it approached it increased to enormous proportions.

Let the position of our travellers be imagined if possible. It is quite impossible to describe it. Notwithstanding their courage, their presence of mind, their heedlessness of danger, they remained mute, immovable, with stiffened limbs, a prey to the wildest terror. Their projectile, over whose course they could have no control, was flying straight towards that fiery mass, more intense than the open mouth of a furnace. It seemed to rush towards an abyss of fire.

Barbicane had seized the hands of his two companions, and all three looked, through half-closed eyelids, towards this asteroid at a white heat. If thought was not destroyed within them, if their brains still worked in the midst of their terror, they must have thought themselves lost.

Two minutes after the abrupt appearance of the meteor – two centuries of anguish! – the projectile seemed on the point of colliding, when the globe of fire blew up like a shell, but without any noise, in the midst of this vacuum where sound, which is but the agitation of the strata of air, could not be produced.

Nicholl had uttered a cry. His companions and he had rushed to the glass of the scuttles. What a sight! What pen could describe it, what palette could be rich enough in colours to reproduce its magnificence!

It was like the outburst of a crater, like the scattering of an immense conflagration. Thousands of luminous fragments lit up and irradiated space with their fires. All sizes, all colours were mingled. There were yellow irradiations, yellowish-red, green-gray – a crown of fireworks of a thousand colours. Of the enormous, redoubtable globe, there remained nothing but these fragments, borne in all directions, become asteroids in their turn, some flaming like a sword, some surrounded with a whitish cloud, others leaving in their wake brilliant trains of cosmical dust.

These incandescent masses crossed each other, collided, broke into smaller fragments, some of which struck the projectile. Its left window was even cracked by a violent blow. It seemed to float amidst a hail of bombshells, the smallest of which could annihilate it in an instant. The light, which saturated the ether, developed itself with incomparable intensity, for these asteroids dispersed it in every direction. At a certain moment, it was so vivid that Michel, drawing Barbicane and Nicholl to his scuttle, cried: 'The invisible moon visible at last!' and all three, through a luminous effluvium of a few seconds, perceived the mysterious disc which the eye of man saw for the first time.

What did they distinguish at this distance which they could not estimate? A few long bands upon the disc, clouds formed in a very limited atmospheric medium, from which emerged not only all the mountains but also all the less important prominences, the circuses, the yawning craters, capriciously arranged as on the visible surface. Then immense spaces, no longer arid plains, but real oceans, which reflected on their liquid mirror all the dazzling magic of the fires of space. Lastly, on the surface of the continents, vast dark masses, such as immense forests would appear under the rapid illumination of a flash of lightning.

Was it an illusion, an error of sight, an optical deception? Could they give a scientific affirmation to an observation so superficially made? Would they dare to give an opinion on the question of its habitableness after such a transient glimpse of the invisible disc?

Meanwhile, the lightnings of space diminished by degrees, their accidental brilliancy grew less; the asteroids dispersed on different trajectories and disappeared in the distance; the ether recovered its accustomed darkness; the stars, eclipsed for one moment, glowed in the firmament, and the disc, scarcely perceived, was again lost in impenetrable night.

CHAPTER SIXTEEN

The southern hemisphere

The projectile had just escaped a terrible danger and an unforeseen one. Who would have imagined such a meeting of meteors? These wandering bodies might place the travellers in serious peril. For them, they were so many rocks, upon this sea of ether, which, less happy than the mariners, they could not avoid. But did those adventurers of space complain? No, for nature had given them this splendid spectacle of a cosmical meteor, bursting by formidable expansion; for this incomparable firework, which no Ruggieri could hope to imitate, had illumined, for a few seconds, the invisible nimbus of the moon. In this rapid flash, continents, seas, forests had appeared to them. So an atmosphere did bring to this unknown face its vivifying molecules. Questions still insoluble – eternally open to human curiosity.

It was then 3.30 p.m. The projectile was following its curvilinear direction round the moon. Had its trajectory been again altered by the meteor? It was to be feared. However, the projectile must follow a curve unalterably determined by the laws of rational mechanics.

Barbicane was inclined to think that the curve would be rather a parabola than an hyperbola. However, the parabola admitted, the projectile must soon leave the cone of shadow thrown upon space opposed to the sun. In fact, this cone is very narrow, for the angular diameter of the moon is small if compared with the diameter of the orb of day. Up to the present, the projectile floated in this deep shadow. Whatever might be its velocity – and it could not have been small – its period of occupation continued. That was an evident fact. But perhaps, ought that not to have been in the supposed case of a strictly parabolic trajectory? This was a new problem which tormented Barbicane's brain, completely imprisoned in a circle of unknown quantities, from which it could not escape.

None of the travellers thought about taking a moment's repose. Each was on the alert for some unexpected event which should throw a new light upon uranographical studies. Towards 5 o'clock, Michel Ardan distributed, under the name of dinner, a few pieces of bread and cold meat, which were rapidly disposed of, without anyone having abandoned his scuttle, the glass of which was continually becoming encrusted by the condensation of vapour.

Towards 5.45 p.m. Nicholl, with the aid of his lunette, discovered towards the southern edge of the moon, and in the direction followed by the projectile, some brilliant spots which stood out from the dark screen of the sky. They were like a succession of pointed peaks, looking in profile like a jagged line. They shone very brightly. Such appears the terminal line of the moon, when she appears in one of her octants.

They could not be mistaken. It was no longer a question of a simple meteor, for this luminous ridge had neither its colour nor its mobility, nor yet a volcano in eruption. So Barbicane did not hesitate to give his opinion.

'The sun!' cried he.

'What! the sun?' replied Nicholl and Michel Ardan.

'Yes, my friends, it is the radiant orb itself which illumines the summits of those mountains, situated on the southern edge of the moon. We are evidently nearing the south pole.'

'After having passed by the north pole,' replied Michel. 'We have taken a turn round our satellite!'

'Yes, worthy Michel.'

'Then no more hyperbolas, no more parabolas, no more open curves to fear.'

'No, but a closed curve.'

'Which means?'

'An ellipse. Instead of being lost in the planetary regions it is probable that the projectile will describe an elliptical orbit around the moon.'

'In truth!'

'And that it will become her satellite.'

'Moon of moons!' cried Michel Ardan.

'Nevertheless I would have you remark, worthy friend,' retorted Barbicane, 'that we are not the less lost on that account.'

'Yes; but in another manner, and a much more pleasant one,' replied the heedless Frenchman, with his most amiable smile.

President Barbicane was right. In describing this elliptical orbit, the projectile would doubtless gravitate eternally around the moon, like a sub-satellite. It was a new star added to the solar world; a microcosm peopled by three inhabitants, whom want of air would soon destroy. Barbicane could not rejoice at the definitive situation imposed upon the projectile by the double influences of centripetal and centrifugal forces. His companions and he would see again the lighted face of the lunar disc; perhaps their existence would be prolonged, until they could again see the full earth superbly lighted by the solar rays. Perhaps they might send a last adieu to the globe which they would never see again. Then their projectile would be nothing but an extinguished dead mass, like those inert asteroids which circulate in ether. One consolation for them was, to quit at last these unfathomable darknesses, to return to light, to reenter the zones bathed by the solar irradiation. However, the mountains recognised by Barbicane stood out more and more distinctly from the dark mass. They were mounts Doerfel and Leibnitz, which rise to the south in the circumpolar region of the moon.

All these mountains of the visible hemisphere have been measured with absolute exactness. This exactness may excite astonishment, and yet the hypsometric methods are precise. It may even be asserted that the altitude of the mountains of the moon is not less exactly determined, than that of the mountains of the earth.

The method most generally employed, is to measure the shadow cast by the mountains, taking into account the altitude of the sun at the time of the observation. This measurement is easily obtained, by means of a lunette, supplied with a reticule having two parallel threads – it being admitted that the real diameter of the lunar disc is accurately known. This method also allows of calculating the depths of craters and cavities of the moon. Galileo made use of it, and since then Messrs Beer and Moedler have used it with the greatest success.

Another method, called by tangent rays, can also be applied to the measurement of lunar projections. It is applied at the moment when the mountains form luminous spots removed from the line of separation of shadow from light, which shine on the dark portion of the disc. These luminous spots are produced by solar rays, higher than those which determine the limit of the phasis. Thus, the measure of the dark interval which remains between the luminous spot and the luminous portion of the nearest phasis, gives the exact altitude of this spot. But it will be seen that this method only applies to mountains in the neighbourhood of the line of separation of light and shade.

A third method consists in measuring the profiles of lunar mountains, which are seen upon the background by means of a micrometer. But this is only applicable to mountains near the edge of the orb.

In any case, it will be seen that this measurement of shadows, of intervals, or of profiles, can only be executed when the solar rays strike the moon obliquely as regards the observer. When they fall full upon her – in one word, when she is full – all shadow is banished from her disc, and observations are no longer possible.

Galileo first – after having recognised the existence of lunar mountains – used the method of shadows to calculate their height. He attributed to them, as has already been stated, an average of 4,500 fathoms. Hevelius diminished these figures considerably, but Riccioli on the contrary doubled them. These measures were exaggerated on the one side and the other. Herschel, by the aid of perfected instruments, came much nearer the hypsometric truth. But it must be sought for finally in the reports of modern observers. Messrs Beer and Moedler, the most perfect selenographers of the whole world, have measured 1,095 lunar mountains. From their calculations it results that six of these mountains rise above 5,800 metres, and 22 above 4,800 metres. The highest summit of the moon measures 7,603 metres; thus it is inferior to those of the earth, some of which exceed 5,000 or 6,000 fathoms. But one remark must be made. If they are compared to the respective volumes of the two orbs, the lunar mountains are relatively higher than the terrestrial mountains. The former form the 470th portion of the diameter of the moon, and the latter only the 1,440th part of the diameter of the earth. A terrestrial mountain to attain the relative proportions of a lunar mountain, would have to measure a perpendicular altitude of six leagues and a half. But the highest has not a height of nine kilometres.

So then, to proceed by comparison, the chain of the Himalayas counts three summits higher than lunar summits: Mount Everest 8,837 metres, Kimchinjuga 8,588 metres, and Dwalagiri 8,187 metres high. Mounts Doerfel and Leibnitz in the moon have an altitude equal to that of Yewahir of the same chain, say 7,603 metres. Newton, Casatus, Curtius, Short, Tycho, Clavius, Blancanus, Endymion, the principal summits of the Caucasus and of the Apennines, are higher than Mont Blanc, which measures 4,810 metres. Are equal to Mont Blanc: Moret, Theophyles, Catharnia; to Mont Rose, or 4,636 metres: Piccolomini, Werner, Harpalus; to Mont Cervin, 4,522 metres: Macrobus, Eratosthenes, Albatecus, Delambre; to the peak of Teneriffe, which rises to 3,710 metres: Bacon, Cysatus, Philolaus and the summits of the Alps; to Mont Perdu, of the Pyrenees, 3,351 metres: Roemer and Boguslawski; to Etna, 3,237 metres: Hercules, Atlas, Furnerius.

Such are the points of comparison which permit us to appreciate the altitudes of lunar mountains.

Precisely the trajectory followed by the projectile carried it towards the mountainous region of the southern hemisphere, where rise the finest specimens of lunar orography.

CHAPTER SEVENTEEN

Tycho

At 6 p.m. the projectile passed the south pole, at less than 60 kilometres, or the same distance to which it had approached the north pole. The elliptic curve was being rigidly described.

At this moment, the travellers re-entered the beneficent effluvium of solar rays. They saw again the stars moving slowly from east to west. The radiant orb was greeted with a triple hurrah. With its light came heat, which soon pierced through the metal walls. The glasses recovered their accustomed transparency. Their layer of ice melted as by magic. Immediately, for economy's sake, the gas was put out. Alone, the air apparatus consumed its accustomed quantity.

'Ah!' said Nicholl, 'how delightful are these rays of heat. With what impatience, after so long a night, the Selenites must await the reappearance of the orb of day.'

'Yes,' replied Michel Ardan, imbibing as it were this brilliant ether; 'light and heat – all life is there.'

At this moment, the bottom of the projectile had a tendency to diverge slightly from the lunar surface, so as to follow an elliptic orbit somewhat drawn out. From this point, if the earth had been full, Barbicane and his companions might have seen it; but drowned in the radiation of the sun, it remained absolutely invisible. Another sight attracted their attention, viz. that which the southern portion of the moon presents when brought by lunettes to within half a quarter of a league. They did not quit the scuttles, but noted all the details of this strange continent.

Mounts Doerfel and Leibnitz form two separate groups which extend almost to the south pole. The former group extends from the pole to the 84th parallel on the eastern portion of the orb; the second, rising on the eastern edge, extends from the 65th degree of latitude to the pole.

On their fantastically formed ridge, appeared dazzling sheets such as Father Secchi has described. With greater certainty than the illustrious Roman astronomer, Barbicane could recognise their nature.

'It is snow,' cried he.

'Snow?' repeated Nicholl.

'Yes, Nicholl, snow, which is deeply frozen on the surface. See how it reflects the luminous rays: cooled lava would not give so intense a reflection. So there is water and there is air on the surface of the moon. As little as you like, but the fact cannot be contested.'

No, it could not be contested! and if ever Barbicane returns to earth his notes will witness to this important fact in selenographic observations.

Mounts Doerfel and Leibnitz rose in the midst of plains of medium extent, bordered by an infinite succession of circuses and annular ramparts. These two chains are the only ones which meet in the region of circuses. Comparatively but slightly marked, they throw out here and there some sharp-pointed peaks, of which the highest summit measures 7.603 metres. But the projectile overhung all this mass, and the projections disappeared in the intense dazzling brilliancy of the disc. To the eyes of the travellers, the archaic aspect of the lunar landscapes reappeared with raw tones, without gradation of colours, without degrees of shadow, coarsely white or black, as diffused light is wanting. However, the view of this desolate world did not fail to captivate them by its very strangeness. They were passing over that chaotic region as if they had been borne on the blast of a storm, seeing summits fly beneath their feet – plunging their glances into cavities, examining rifts, scaling escarpments, fathoming mysterious holes, levelling all fissures. But there was no trace of vegetation; no appearance of cities – nothing but stratifications, floods of lava overflowings, polished like immense mirrors, reflecting the rays of the sun with unbearable brilliancy. Nothing of a living world, all of a dead world, where avalanches rolling from the summits of mountains plunged, without noise, to the bottom of abysses. They retained the movement, but the noise was still wanting. Barbicane discovered, by repeated observations, that the projections on the borders of the disc, although they had evidently been submitted to different forces than those of the central regions, presented a uniform conformation. There were the same circular aggregation, the same projections of the ground. However, it might be thought that their disposition would not be analogous. In the centre, the malleable crust of the moon had been submitted to the double attraction of the moon and the earth acting in inverse direction, according to a prolonged radius of the one to the other. On the contrary, on the edges of the disc, the lunar attraction has been, so to speak, perpendicular to the terrestrial attraction. It seems as though the projections of the ground, produced under these two conditions, must have taken different forms. But such has not been the case. So the moon had found in herself the principle of her formation and of her constitution. She owed nothing to foreign action, which justifies that remarkable proposition of Arago: 'No action outside the moon has contributed to the formation of its projections.'

Whatever the facts may have been, this world in its present state was the image of death; and it was impossible to say whether life had ever animated it.

Nevertheless, Michel Ardan thought that he perceived an agglomeration of ruins, which he pointed out to Barbicane. They were near the 80th parallel, in 30' of longitude. This heap of stones, arranged with sufficient regularity, represented a vast fortress overhanging one of those long rifts which were formerly the beds of prehistoric rivers. Not far off, arose to a height of 5,646 metres, the annular mountain of Short, equal to the Asiatic Caucasus.

Michel Ardan, with his accustomed ardour, maintained the evidence of his fortress. Below, he perceived the dismantled ramparts of a town; here, the still intact arch of a portico; there, three or four columns lying below their bases; farther on a succession of pillars which must have supported an aqueduct; elsewhere, the shattered piers of a gigantic bridge, half hidden in the depths of the rift. All this he saw, but there was so much imagination in his glance through so fanciful a lunette that his observations are to be mistrusted. And yet, who could assert, who would dare to say, that the amiable Frenchman had not really seen what his two companions refused to perceive?

The moments were too precious to be sacrificed to a useless discussion. The Selenite city, pretended or not, had already disappeared in the distance. The distance of the projectile from the lunar disc was increasing, and the details of the surface became lost in a confused mixture. Alone the projections, the circuses, the craters, the plains, resisted and sharply defined their terminal lines.

At this moment, there arose towards the left one of the finest circuses of lunar orography, one of the curiosities of this continent. It was Newton, which Barbicane had no difficulty in recognising with the aid of his *Mappa Selenographica*. Newton is exactly situated in 77 south latitude, and 16° east longitude. It forms an annular crater, with apparently insurmountable ramparts, 7,264 metres high. Barbicane remarked to his companions that the height of this mountain, above the plain, was far from equal to the depth of its crater. This enormous hole escaped all measurement, and formed a dark abyss, to the bottom of which the solar rays could never penetrate. There, according to Humboldt's remark, reigns absolute darkness, which the light of the sun and earth can never break. Mythologists would have made it, and with reason, the mouth of the infernal regions.

'Newton,' said Barbicane, 'is the most perfect type of these annular mountains, of which the earth possesses no sample. They prove that the formation of the moon by cooling is due to violent causes, for whilst, under the action of internal fires, the projections were thrown out to considerable heights, the bottom contracted and withdrew to much below the lunar level.'

'I did not say it didn't,' replied Michel Ardan.

A few minutes after passing Newton, the projectile overhung the annular Mount Moret. It passed at some distance from Blancanus, and towards 7.30 p.m. it reached Circus Clavius.

This circus is one of the most remarkable of the disc, and is situated in 58° south latitude and 15° degrees east longitude. Its altitude is estimated at 7,091 metres. The travellers, 400 kilometres distant, reduced to four by the lunettes, could admire every point of this vast crater.

'The terrestrial volcanoes,' said Barbicane, 'are only molehills compared with the volcanoes of the moon. On measuring the former craters, caused by the first eruptions of Vesuvius and Etna, they have been found to be only 6,000 metres wide. In France, the Cantal circus measures 10 kilometres; in Ceylon, the circus of the Isle 70 kilometres, which is considered the largest on the globe. What are these diameters compared with Clavius, which we overlook at this moment?'

'What is its width?' asked Nicholl.

'It is 227 kilometres,' replied Barbicane. 'This circus, it is true, is the most important on the moon, but many others measure 200, 150, and 100 kilometres.'

'Ah! my friends,' cried Michel, 'think what this peaceful orb of night must have been when these craters, full of thunderbolts, vomited at once torrents of lava, showers of stones, clouds of smoke, and sheets of flame. What a prodigious sight then! – and now what a falling off! The moon is nothing but the case of a piece of firework, in which the crackers, squibs, serpents, and suns, after a magnificent explosion, have left but the remnants of burst pasteboard. Who could tell the cause, the reason, the justification of these cataclysms?'

Barbicane did not listen to Michel Ardan. He was contemplating these escarpments of Clavius, formed of wide mountains several leagues thick. At the bottom of the immense cavity, were a hundred smaller extinct craters, piercing the ground like a sieve, and overhung by a mountain 5,000 metres high.

All around, the plain had a desolate aspect. Nothing could be more barren than these projections, nothing more sad than these ruins of mountains, and, if one can make use of the expression, these fragments of peaks

and mounds which strewed the ground! The satellite seemed to have burst at that spot.

The projectile still continued and this chaos was not changed. The circuses, the craters, the shattered mountains, succeeded each other without ceasing. No more plains, no more seas! An interminable Switzerland

or Norway. At last in the centre of this region of fissures, at its culmin-
ating point appeared the most splendid mountain of the lunar disc, the
dazzling Tycho, with which posterity will always connect the name of the
illustrious Danish astronomer.

When observing the full moon in a cloudless sky, everyone must have
seen this brilliant spot in the southern hemisphere. Michel Ardan employed in its description all the metaphors which his vivid imagination
could supply. For him, Tycho was a burning focus of light, a centre of
radiation, a crater vomiting rays! It was the tire of a sparkling wheel, an
immense flaming eye, a nimbus for the head of Pluto! It was like a star
hurled from the Creator's hand and flattened against the lunar surface.

Tycho forms such a luminous concentration that the inhabitants of the
earth can perceive it without glasses, though they are at a distance of
100,000 leagues. Imagine, then, what must have been its intensity to the
eyes of observers placed only 150 leagues distant. Through the pure
ether its glare was so unbearable that Barbicane and his friends had to
blacken the eye-glass of their lunettes with the gas smoke, to be able to
support its brilliancy. Then mute, only giving vent to a few expressions of
admiration, they gazed and contemplated. All their sentiments, all their
impressions, were concentrated in their glance; like life, which, under
violent emotion, concentrates entirely in the heart.

Tycho belongs to the class of radiating mountains, like Aristarchus
and Copernicus. The most complete, the most decided of all, it proves
indubitably the frightful volcanic action to which the formation of the
moon is due.

Tycho is situated in 43° south latitude and 12° east longitude. Its centre
is formed by a crater 87 kilometres wide; it has somewhat of an elliptical
form, and is enclosed by annular ramparts, which overhang the exterior
plain to the east and to the west, to a height of 5,000 metres. It is an
aggregation of Mont Blancs placed round a common centre, and crowned
with a radiating crest.

What this incomparable mountain is, the projections converging towards it, and the interior excrescences of its crater, photography has
never been able to depict.

In fact, it is during the full moon that Tycho shows in all its splendour.
But then, shadows are wanting, the foreshortenings of perspective have
disappeared, and the proofs are blanks. This is an unfortunate circumstance, for it would be curious to reproduce this strange region with photographic accuracy. It is but an agglomeration of holes, craters, circuses,
a vertiginous network of crests; then, as far as eye can reach, a volcanic
network cast upon this encrusted soil. It will be thus understood that

the bubbles of the central eruption have retained their primitive shape. Crystallised by cooling, they have become stereotyped, the aspect presented formerly by the moon under the influence of Plutonian forces.

The distance, which separated the travellers from the annular summits of Tycho, was not so great but that they could perceive the principal details. On the embankment which formed the circumvallation of Tycho, the mountains, rising from the sides of the inside and outside slopes, formed gigantic terraces. They appeared 300 or 400 feet higher to the west than to the east. No system of terrestrial encampment could be compared with this natural fortification. A city built at the bottom of this circular cavity would have been absolutely impregnable.

Inaccessible, and marvellously spread over this ground covered with picturesque projections, nature had not left the bottom of this crater flat and hollow. It possessed its special orography – a mountainous system which made it like a separate world. The travellers clearly distinguished caves, central hills, remarkable movements of ground naturally adapted to receive the masterpieces of Selenite architecture. There was the site for a temple, here, the place for a forum; in this spot, the foundations for a palace, in that other, the plan of a citadel. The whole was overlooked by a central mountain 1,500 feet high – a vast enclosure which would have contained ancient Rome ten times over.

'Ah!' cried Michel Ardan, full of enthusiasm at the sight, 'what a magnificent town might be built in that circle of mountains! – A tranquil city, a peaceful place of refuge, outside all human misery. How calm and isolated all misanthropes could live there – all haters of humanity – all who are disgusted with social life!'

'All! It would be too small for them,' replied Barbicane simply.

CHAPTER EIGHTEEN

Important questions

Meanwhile, the projectile had passed over Tycho's enclosure, and Barbicane and his two friends were observing, with scrupulous attention, the brilliant rays which the celebrated mountain disperses so curiously to all the horizons.

What was this radiant aureola? What geological phenomenon had formed this fiery crest? This question naturally preoccupied Barbicane. Under his eyes, ran in all directions luminous furrows, with raised edges and concave hollows, some 20 kilometres wide, some 50. These shining trains proceeded in some places as far as 300 leagues from Tycho, and seemed to cover, especially to the east, north-east, and north, half the southern hemisphere. One of its jets extended to the circus Neandre, situated on the 40th meridian. Another, following a curve, furrowed the Sea of Nectar and broke against the chain of the Pyrenees, after a circuit of 400 leagues. Others, towards the west, covered the Sea of Clouds and the Sea of Humours with a luminous network.

What was the origin of these shining rays which appeared equally on plains and projections, no matter how high? All started from a common centre, the crater of Tycho. They emanated from it. Herschel attributed their brilliant aspect to former currents of lava congealed by cold, which opinion has not been adopted. Other astronomers have seen in these inexplicable rays a sort of *moraines*, rows of erratic blocks, thrown up at the period of Tycho's formation.

'And why not?' asked Nicholl of Barbicane, who related these different opinions and discarded them.

'Because the regularity of these luminous lines, and the violence necessary to carry volcanic matter to such a distance, are incompatible.'

'By Jupiter!' replied Michel Ardan, 'it seems easy enough to me to explain the origin of these rays.'

'Indeed!' said Barbicane.

'Certainly,' continued Michel; 'it is sufficient to call it a vast star, like that produced upon a window-pane by the shock of a ball or a stone.'

'Good!' replied Barbicane smiling; 'and whose hand could have been powerful enough to cast the stone to produce such a shock?'

'The hand is not necessary,' replied Michel, who was not to be put down. 'And as to the stone, let us suppose it to be a comet.'

'Ah! comets indeed,' cried Barbicane; 'how they are abused. My worthy Michel, your explanation is not a bad one, but your comet is useless. The shock which has produced this breakage may have come from the interior of the orb. A violent contraction of the lunar crust, under the action of cooling, may have sufficed to make this gigantic star.'

'A contraction, by all means, something like a lunar stomach-ache,' replied Michel Ardan.

'Besides,' added Barbicane, 'this opinion is shared by an English *savant*, Nasmyth, and it seems to me to explain sufficiently the radiation of these mountains.'

'That fellow Nasmyth was no fool,' replied Michel.

For a long time, the travellers, who could not tire of such a sight, admired the splendour of Tycho. Their projectile, impregnated with luminous effluvia in the double irradiation of the sun and the moon, must have appeared like an incandescent globe. They had suddenly passed from severe cold to intense heat. Nature was preparing them for becoming Selenites.

Becoming Selenites! This idea again brought up the question as to the inhabitableness of the moon. After what they had seen could the travellers decide this question? Could they conclude for or against? Michel Ardan called upon his two friends to give their opinions, and asked them, straightforwardly, whether they thought that animal and human life were represented in the lunar world.

'I think that we can reply,' said Barbicane; 'but to my mind the question should not be put in that form. I ask to alter it.'

'Fire away,' cried Michel.

'The problem,' replied Barbicane, 'is double, and requires a double solution. Is the moon inhabitable? Has she been inhabited?'

'Good!' said Nicholl; 'first let us inquire if the moon is inhabitable.'

'In good truth, I don't know,' retorted Michel.

'And I reply negatively,' continued Barbicane. In the state in which she is at present – with an atmospheric envelope certainly very limited, the seas mostly dried up, the water insufficient, the vegetation restricted, the abrupt alternations of heat and cold, the days and nights of 354 hours – the moon does not appear to me habitable, and does not seem adapted to the development of the animal kingdom, nor sufficient for the necessities of existence such as we understand them.'

'Agreed!' replied Nicholl; 'but is the moon not habitable for beings otherwise organised than we?'

'To that question,' retorted Barbicane, 'it is difficult to reply. I will try however. But I will ask Nicholl if *movement* appears to him to be the necessary result of life, whatever be its organisation?'

'Without a doubt,' replied Nicholl.

'Well,' worthy comrade, 'I will answer that we have observed the lunar continents at a distance not greater than 500 metres, and that nothing has been seen to move on the surface of the moon. The presence of any kind of human life would have been betrayed by its appropriations, by divers constructions, or even by ruins. Now, what have we seen? Everywhere and always the geological work of nature, never the work of man. If representatives of the animal kingdom existed on the moon, they must be hidden in cavities which the eye cannot fathom; which I cannot admit, for they would have left traces of their passage on the plains, covered by an atmospheric stratum, however thin. Now, such traces are nowhere visible. There only remains the hypothesis of a race of living beings without motion, which is life.'

'You might as well say living creatures which do not live,' retorted Michel.

'Precisely,' replied Barbicane; 'which for us has no sense.'

'Then we can form our opinion,' said Michel.

'Yes,' replied Nicholl.

'Well,' continued Michel Ardan, 'the scientific commission assembled in the projectile of the Gun Club, after having based their arguments upon facts recently observed, have decided unanimously upon the question of the inhabitableness of the moon. No! the moon is not habitable.'

This decision was entered by President Barbicane in his note-book, wherein appear the minutes of the meeting of the 6th December.

'Now,' said Nicholl, 'let us attack the second question, which is the necessary corollary of the first. I therefore ask the honourable commission: if the moon is not habitable, has she ever been inhabited?'

'Citizen Barbicane to speak,' said Michel Ardan.

'My friends, replied Barbicane, 'it did not require this journey to form my opinion upon the past habitableness of our satellite. I will add that our personal observations have but confirmed my view. I believe, I can even assert that the moon has been inhabited by a human race organised as ours, that she has produced animals anatomically formed like terrestrial animals; but I will add that these human races and animals have had their time and are for ever extinct.'

'Then,' asked Michel, 'the moon is an older world than the earth?'

'No,' replied Barbicane with conviction, 'but a world which has aged more rapidly, where formation and deformation have been more sudden. Comparatively, the organising forces of matter have been much more violent in the interior of the moon than in the interior of the terrestrial globe. The present state of this fissured, distorted, and uneven disc proves it superabundantly. The earth and the moon were only gaseous masses in their origin. These gases passed to a liquid state under certain influences, and the solid mass was formed subsequently. But certainly our spheroid was gaseous or liquid still, when the moon was already solidified by cooling, and had become inhabitable.'

'I believe it,' said Nicholl.

'Then,' continued Barbicane, 'an atmosphere surrounded it. The water contained by this gaseous envelope could not evaporate. Under the influence of air, water, light, solar heat, central heat, vegetation seized upon continents prepared to receive it; and certainly life appeared towards this period, for nature does not expend her forces uselessly, and a world so marvellously habitable must necessarily have been inhabited.'

'However,' replied Nicholl, 'many of the phenomena inherent to the movements of our satellite, must have hindered the expansion of the vegetable and animal kingdoms. For instance, the days and nights of 354 hours.'

'At the terrestrial poles,' said Michel, 'they last six months.'

'Which argument has little value, since the poles are not inhabited.'

'Observe, my friends,' continued Barbicane, 'that if, in the present state of the moon, these long nights and days create differences of temperature insupportable to human organisms, it was not thus at the period of prehistoric times. The atmosphere enveloped the disc as with a fluid mantle. Vapours lay there under the form of clouds. This natural screen tempered the ardour of the solar rays and hindered nocturnal radiation. Light and heat were diffused in the air. Hence an equilibrium between these influences, which no longer exist, now that the atmosphere has almost entirely disappeared. Besides, I shall much astonish you – '

'Pray do so,' said Michel Ardan.

'But I am inclined to think that at the period when the moon was inhabited the nights and days did not last 354 hours.'

'Why?' asked Nicholl, hastily.

'Because, most probably at that time the movement of rotation of the moon upon its axis was not equal to her movement of revolution, which equality presents each point of the disc, during fifteen days, to the action of the solar rays.'

'Agreed,' replied Nicholl; 'but why should these two movements not have been equal, as they are so now?'

'Because this equality has only been determined by the terrestrial attraction. Now, what tells us that this attraction was sufficiently powerful to modify the movements of the moon at a time when the earth was only fluid?'

'True,' replied Nicholl. 'And what proves that the moon has always been a satellite of the earth?'

Imagination was carrying them away into the infinite field of conjecture. Barbicane wished to restrain them.

'These are,' said he, 'too great speculations, and truly insoluble problems. Do not let us enter into them. Let us only admit the insufficiency of primordial attraction, and then, by the inequality of the two movements of rotation and revolution, days and nights may have succeeded each other on the moon, as they succeed each other on earth. Besides, even without that condition life was possible.'

'So,' asked Michel Ardan, 'you suppose that humanity has disappeared from the moon?'

'Yes,' replied Barbicane, 'after having doubtless existed during thousands of centuries. Then, gradually the atmosphere became rarefied, the disc became uninhabitable, as the terrestrial globe will become some day, by cooling.'

'By cooling?'

'Doubtless!' replied Barbicane. 'In proportion as the internal fires were extinguished, the incandescent matter became concentrated, and the lunar crust cooled. Gradually, the consequences of this phenomenon appeared, viz. disappearance of organised beings, disappearance of vegetation. Soon, the atmosphere became rarefied, probably drawn away by terrestrial attraction; disappearance of breathable air; disappearance of water, by means of evaporation. At this period, the moon having become uninhabitable, was no longer inhabited. It was a dead world, such as we see it today.'

'And you say that such a fate is reserved to the earth?'

'Very probably.'

'But when?'

'When the cooling of its crust has rendered it uninhabitable.'

'And has the time been calculated which our unfortunate spheroid will require to cool?'

'Doubtless.'

'And you know the calculation?'

'Perfectly.'

'Say on then, you tedious man,' cried Michel Ardan; 'you make me boil with impatience.'

'Well, worthy Michel,' replied Barbicane quietly, 'it is well known what diminution the temperature of the earth undergoes in the lapse of one century. According to certain calculations this mean temperature will be reduced to zero in a period of 400,000 years.'

'400,000 years!' cried Michel; 'I breathe again. Really I was afraid. To hear you speak, one would have thought that we had not more than 50,000 years to live.'

Barbicane and Nicholl could not refrain from laughter at their comrade's fears. Then Nicholl, who wished to conclude, again asked the second question which had just been treated: 'Has the moon been inhabited?' asked he.

The reply was affirmative and unanimous.

But during this discussion, fertile in hazardous theories though summarising the general ideas of science on the point, the projectile had rapidly neared the lunar equator whilst moving at a greater distance from the disc. It had passed circus Willem and the 40th parallel, at a distance of 800 kilometres. Then, having Pitatus to the right on the 30th degree, it passed over the south of that Sea of Clouds, the northern portion of which it had already surveyed. Sundry circuses appeared confusedly in the shining whiteness of the full moon: Bouilland, Purbach almost square-shaped with a central crater, then Arzachel, the interior mountain of which shines with an indescribable brilliancy.

At last, as the projectile increased its distance, the lineaments faded from the travellers' eyes, the mountains melted into one another, and, of all those marvellous fantastic strange forms of the earth's satellite, nothing remained but an imperishable souvenir.

CHAPTER NINETEEN

A struggle against the impossible

For a long time, Barbicane and his companions, mute and pensive, contemplated this world which they had only seen from a distance, as Moses had seen the land of Canaan, and from which they were retreating without hope of return. The position of the projectile as regards the moon was altered, and now its bottom was turned towards the earth.

This alteration, discovered by Barbicane, did not fail to surprise him. If the projectile was to gravitate around the satellite, upon an elliptical orbit, why did it not turn the heaviest portion towards it as the moon does to the earth? That was an obscure point.

By observing the advance of the projectile, they could see that it followed, when leaving the moon, a curve similar to that traced when approaching her; therefore it described a lengthened ellipse, which probably would extend to the point of equal attractions, where the influences of the earth and its satellite were neutralised.

Such was the conclusion which Barbicane justly deduced from the facts observed, and his conviction was shared by his two friends.

And questions followed each other in quick succession.

'And when at this point what will become of us?' asked Michel Ardan.

'That is the unknown,' replied Barbicane.

'But we may make conjectures, I suppose?'

'Two,' replied Barbicane. 'Either the velocity will be insufficient, and the projectile will remain eternally motionless on this line of double attraction – '

'I prefer the other hypothesis whatever it may be,' replied Michel.

'Or its velocity will be sufficient,' said Barbicane; 'and it will resume its elliptic route, to gravitate eternally round the orb of night.'

'Not a very consoling revolution,' said Michel, 'to become the humble servitors of the moon, which we are accustomed to consider a servant! And is that the future in store for us?'

Neither Barbicane nor Nicholl replied.

'You are silent,' continued the impatient Michel.

'There is nothing to reply,' said Nicholl.

'Is there nothing to be tried?'

'No!' replied Barbicane. 'Would you struggle against the impossible?'

'Why not? Shall a Frenchman and two Americans retire before such a word?'

'But what would you do?'

'Conquer the movement which is carrying us away.'

'Conquer it?'

'Yes,' continued Michel with animation; 'destroy it, or alter it, use it, in fact, for accomplishing our projects.'

'And how?'

'That is your business. If artillerists are not masters of their shot, they are not artillerists. If the projectile has command over the gunner, the gunner should be shoved into the cannon. Fine *savants*, in sooth! There they are, not knowing what to do after having induced me – '

'Induced!' cried Barbicane and Nicholl. 'Induced! What do you mean by that?'

'No recriminations,' said Michel. 'I do not complain. The journey pleases me. I like the projectile. But let us do what is humanly possible to fall back somewhere, if not on to the moon.'

'That is all we ask for, worthy Michel,' replied Barbicane; 'but the means are wanting.'

'Can we not modify the movement of the projectile?'

'No!'

'Nor diminish its velocity?'

'No!'

'Not even by lightening it, as you lighten a ship too heavily laden?'

'What would you throw out?' replied Nicholl. 'We have no ballast on board. And besides, it seems to me that the lightened projectile would travel faster.'

'Not so fast,' said Michel.

'Faster,' retorted Nicholl.

'Neither faster nor slower,' said Barbicane, to put his two friends in humour; 'for we are floating in a vacuum, where the specific weight is of no account.'

'Well,' cried Michel Ardan in a determined tone, 'there is only one thing to be done.'

'What is that?' asked Nicholl.

'Breakfast!' replied the audacious Frenchman imperturbably. An infallible solution in the most difficult conjunctures. In fact, if that operation had no influence upon the direction of the projectile, at least it could be tried without inconvenience and even with success, as regarded the stomach. Most certainly, Michel's ideas were good for something.

So they breakfasted at 2 a.m., but the hour was of little importance. Michel served up his accustomed bill of fare, crowned by a bottle drawn from his secret cellaret. If ideas did not flow to their brains, Chambertin of 1863 must be despaired of.

The repast terminated, observations recommenced.

Around the projectile, the articles which had been thrown out maintained themselves at the same invariable distance. Evidently the projectile in its movement of translation round the moon, had not passed through any atmosphere, or the specific weight of these several articles would have modified their respective progress.

On the side of the terrestrial spheroid, nothing was to be seen. The earth only counted one day, having become new the previous day at midnight, and two more days must pass ere its crescent would emerge from the solar rays, to act as a timepiece to the Selenites; since, in its movement of rotation, each of its points pass always 24 hours later through the same meridian of the moon.

On the side of the moon, the spectacle was different. The orb shone in all its splendour, in the midst of innumerable constellations, whose purity could not be troubled by her rays. On her disc, the plains were already recovering the dark shade which is seen from the earth. The remainder of the nimbus continued bright, and in the midst of the general resplendence, Tycho stood out like a sun.

Barbicane could not in any way calculate the velocity of the projectile, but reason showed him that the velocity must gradually diminish, according to the laws of rational mechanics.

In fact, it being admitted that the projectile would describe an orbit round the moon, this orbit would necessarily be elliptic. Science proves that it must be so. No movable body, circulating round another body, escapes this law. All orbits described in space are elliptical; those of the satellites round planets, those of planets round the sun, that of the sun round the unknown orb which serves as a central pivot. Why should the projectile of the Gun Club escape this general law? Now, in elliptical orbits the attracting body occupies always one of the foci of the ellipse. The satellite therefore finds itself at one moment nearer, and at another moment more distant from the orb round which it gravitates. When the earth is nearest to the sun, it is in its perihelium, and in its aphelium when at its most distant point. As regards the moon, she is nearest to the earth in her perigee and farthest in her apogee. To use analogous expressions, which will enrich astronomical language, if the projectile remained as a satellite to the moon, it must be said that, at its farthest point, it is in its aposelenium, and, at its nearest point, in its periselenium.

In this last instance, the projectile would attain its maximum of velocity, in the former case its minimum. Now it was evidently travelling towards its apoSelenitic point, and Barbicane was right in thinking that its velocity was decreasing up to that point, to recover gradually as it approached the moon. This velocity would even be completely annulled, if that point coincided with the point of equal attractions.

Barbicane studied the consequences of these different situations, and he was seeking what advantage might be drawn from them, when he was suddenly interrupted by a cry from Michel Ardan.

'By Jove!' cried Michel, 'it must be admitted that we are regular fools.'

'I don't deny it,' replied Barbicane; 'but why?'

'Because we have a very simple means of lessening the velocity which is bearing us from the moon, and we do not use it.'

'And what is this means?'

'It is to utilise the force contained in our rockets.'

'Bravo!' said Nicholl.

'We have not yet utilised this force,' replied Barbicane, 'but we will utilise it.'

'When?' asked Michel.

'When the moment has come! Observe, my friends, that in the position occupied by the projectile, which position is yet oblique as regards the lunar disc, our rockets, by modifying its direction, might turn it aside instead of forcing it nearer to the moon. Now it is the moon that you want to reach, is it not?'

'Certainly,' replied Michel.

'Wait then. By an inexplicable influence, the projectile is gradually turning its base towards the earth. It is probable that at the point of equal attractions, its conic roof will point directly towards the moon. At that moment, we may hope that its velocity will be *nil*. That will be the moment to act, and by the force of our rockets, we may perhaps occasion a direct fall to the surface of the lunar disc – '

'Bravo!' said Michel.

'Which we did not do, which we could not do at our first passage through the dead point, because our projectile was still endowed with too great velocity.'

'Well argued,' said Nicholl.

'Let us wait patiently,' continued Barbicane; 'let us put every chance on our side, and after despairing so long I find myself believing that we shall yet reach our goal.'

This conclusion was a signal for 'hip, hip, hurrahs' from Michel Ardan. Not one of these audacious madmen recollected the question which they had just decided in the negative: 'No, the moon is not inhabited. No, the moon is probably not inhabitable;' and yet they were about to try to reach her.

One single question remained to be solved: At what precise moment would the projectile attain the point of equal attractions, where the travellers were to play their last card?

To calculate this moment within a few seconds, Barbicane had only to consult the notes of his journey, and calculate the different altitudes taken on the lunar parallels. Thus the time employed in travelling the distance separating the dead point and the south pole must be equal to the distance between the north pole and the dead point. The hours representing the time of travelling were carefully noted, and the calculation became easy.

Barbicane found that this point would be reached by the projectile at 1 a.m. in the night of the 7th of December – at this moment it was 3 a.m. in the night of the 6th of December – so that, if nothing impeded its progress, the projectile would reach the required point in 22 hours.

The rockets had been originally arranged to lessen the fall of the projectile on to the moon, and now these bold men intended to use them to produce an absolutely contrary effect. In any case they were ready, whenever the moment arrived, to set light to them.

'As there is nothing to be done,' said Nicholl, 'I make a proposal.'

'What is that?' asked Barbicane.

'I propose to take some sleep.'

'Nonsense!' exclaimed Michel Ardan.

'We have not closed our eyes for forty hours,' said Nicholl; 'a few hours' sleep will restore all our strength.'

'Never!' replied Michel.

'Very well,' continued Nicholl, 'let each one do as he likes. I shall sleep.'

And stretching himself on the divan, Nicholl was soon snoring like the ball from a 48-pounder.

'Nicholl is a sensible man,' said Barbicane presently. 'I shall imitate him.'

A few minutes afterwards his continued bass supported the captain's baritone.

'Decidedly,' said Michel Ardan, 'these practical people have sometimes opportune ideas.'

And stretching his long legs, and folding his great arms beneath his head, Michel slept in his turn.

But this sleep could neither be lasting nor peaceful. The minds of those three men were too full of preoccupation, and, a few hours later, towards 7 a.m., all three were on foot at the same moment. The projectile was still leaving the moon, inclining more and more towards her its conic portion – a phenomenon hitherto inexplicable, but which happily assisted Barbicane's designs. Seventeen hours more, and the moment for acting would have come.

This day appeared long. However audacious they might be, the travellers were deeply impressed by the approach of that moment which was to decide all – either their fall towards the moon or their eternal enchainment in an immutable orbit. They counted the hours, which passed too slowly for their wishes – Barbicane and Nicholl obstinately buried in calculations, Michel going and coming between the narrow walls and observing the impassive moon with a longing eye.

Occasionally recollections of earth rapidly crossed their minds. They again saw their friends of the Gun Club, and the dearest of all, J. T. Maston. At that moment, the honourable secretary must have been at his post in the Rocky Mountains. If he perceived the projectile upon the mirror of his gigantic telescope, what would he think? After seeing it disappear behind the south pole of the moon, he saw it reappear above the north pole! It was thus a satellite of a satellite! Had J. T. Maston spread this unexpected news over the world? Was this then the result of the great undertaking?

However, the day passed without incident. Terrestrial midnight arrived. The 8th of December was about to commence. One hour more, and the point of equal attraction would be reached. What was the velocity of the projectile? It could not be estimated. But no error could have been made in Barbicane's calculation; at 1 a.m. the velocity should be, and would be, *nil*.

Besides which, another phenomenon would mark the arrival of the projectile upon the neutral line. At this spot, the two terrestrial and lunar attractions would be annulled. Bodies would then have no weight. This singular fact, which had so greatly surprised Barbicane and his companions on the journey hither, would be reproduced on the return under identical conditions. It was at this precise moment that they must act. Already the conic roof of the projectile was turned towards the lunar disc. The projectile presented itself in such a manner, as would utilise all the recoil produced by the force of the rockets. The chances were therefore in favour of the travellers. If the velocity of the projectile was absolutely *nil* at the dead points, a determined movement towards the moon would suffice, however light it might be, to produce its fall.

'Five minutes past one,' said Nicholl.

'All is ready,' replied Michel Ardan, approaching a prepared fuse to the gas flame.

'Wait,' said Barbicane, chronometer in hand.

At this moment, gravitation had no more effect. The travellers felt in themselves its complete absence; they were very near the neutral point, if they did not touch it.

'One o'clock,' said Barbicane.

Michel Ardan approached the lighted fuse to a train which communicated with all the rockets. No detonation was heard in the interior, for air was wanting. But through the scuttles Barbicane perceived a prolonged flash, which then expired.

The shock to the projectile was very perceptible inside.

The three friends gazed, listened without speaking, almost without breathing – their hearts might have been heard beating in the midst of the profound silence.

'Are we falling?' asked Michel Ardan at last.

'No,' replied Nicholl, 'for the bottom of the projectile is not turned towards the lunar disc.'

At this moment Barbicane, leaving the glass at the scuttle, turned towards his two companions. He was fearfully pale, his forehead wrinkled, and lips contracted.

'We are falling,' he said.

'Ah!' cried Michel Ardan, 'towards the moon?'

'Towards the earth,' replied Barbicane.

'The devil!' cried Michel Ardan. 'Ah!' he added philosophically, 'when we got into this projectile, we suspected there would be some difficulty in getting out of it.'

In fact this dreadful fall commenced. The velocity retained by the projectile had carried it beyond the dead point, and the explosion of the rockets had not been able to stop it. This velocity, which on the outward journey had carried the projectile past the neutral line, still carried it on the return. The laws of physics required that, in its elliptical orbit, it should again pass through all the points by which it had already passed.

It was a terrible fall, from a height of 78,000 leagues, which no spring could lessen. According to the laws of gunnery the projectile would strike the earth with a velocity equal to that with which it left the columbiad, a velocity of 16,000 metres in the last second.

And, to give a figure of comparison, it has been calculated that an object thrown from the top of the tower of Notre Dame, which is only 200 feet high, would reach the pavement with the velocity of 120 leagues an hour. Here, the projectile would strike the earth with a velocity of 57,600 leagues an hour.

'We are lost,' said Nicholl calmly.

'Well, if we die,' said Barbicane, with a sort of religious enthusiasm, 'the scope of our journey will be magnificently extended. It is his own secret that God will tell us. In the next life, the soul will not require, for knowledge, either machinery or engines. It will be identified with eternal wisdom.'

'Quite right,' replied Michel Ardan, 'the whole of the next world may well console us for the loss of the miserable orb which is called the moon.'

Barbicane crossed his arms on his breast with a movement of sublime resignation. 'The will of Heaven be done!' said he.

CHAPTER TWENTY

The soundings of the Susquehanna

'Well, lieutenant, how about that sounding?'

'I think, sir, that the operation is almost completed,' replied Lieutenant Bronsfield. 'But who would have expected to find such a depth so near the land – only a hundred leagues from the American coast?'

'You are right, Bronsfield; it is a very great depression,' said Captain Blomsberry. 'There exists in this spot a submarine valley made by Humboldt's current, which skirts the American coast, down to the straits of Magellan.'

'These great depths,' continued the lieutenant, 'are not very favourable for laying telegraphic cables. It is better to have a level bottom, like that which bears the American cable between Valencia and Newfoundland.'

'I agree with you, Bronsfield. And by the way, lieutenant, where are we now?'

'Sir,' replied Bronsfield, 'we have at this moment 21,500 feet of line payed out, and the shot at the end has not yet touched the bottom, for it would have come up by itself.'

'An ingenious apparatus, that of Brookes,' said Captain Blomsberry; 'it enables us to obtain very correct soundings.'

'Touched!' cried at this moment one of the men at the fore-wheel, who was superintending the operation.

The captain and lieutenant went forward to the quarterdeck.

'What is the depth?' asked the captain.

'Twenty-one thousand seven hundred and sixty-two feet,' replied the lieutenant, entering the figures in his note-book.

'Good, Bronsfield,' said the captain. 'I shall make a note of the result on my chart. Now haul in the sounding-line. It will be a work of several hours, during which time the engineer can light up his furnaces, and we shall be ready to start as soon as you have finished. By the way, lieutenant, it is 10 o'clock. I shall turn in.'

'Aye, aye, sir,' replied Lieutenant Bronsfield, obligingly.

The captain of the *Susquehanna*, one of the best of men, and very humble servant of his officers, returned to his cabin, took a brandy grog, which earned many expressions of satisfaction for the steward, got into bed, not without complimenting his servant upon the manner of making it, and relapsed into peaceful slumber.

It was then 10 p.m. The 11th day of the month of December was terminating in a magnificent night.

The *Susquehanna*, a corvette of 500 horse-power, of the national navy of the United States, was engaged in making soundings in the Pacific about 100 leagues from the American coast, on a level with that long peninsula which stretches down the coast of New Mexico.

The wind had gradually fallen. Not the slightest agitation moved the strata of air. The pennant of the corvette hung motionless and inert from the main-topgallant mast.

Captain Jonathan Blomsberry – first cousin of Colonel Blomsberry, one of the most ardent members of the Gun Club, who had married a Miss Horschbidden, aunt of the captain and daughter of an honourable Kentucky merchant – Captain Blomsberry could not have wished for better weather for carrying out the delicate operations of sounding. His corvette had not even experienced any portion of that vast tempest which swept away the clouds from the Rocky Mountains, and allowed the course of the famous projectile to be observed. All was going to his wish, and he did not fail to thank heaven with all the fervour of a Presbyterian.

The series of soundings executed by the *Susquehanna* had for their object to discover the most favourable bottom for laying a submarine cable from the American coast to the Hawaian Islands.

This was a great undertaking, due to the initiative of a powerful company. Its intelligent director, Cyrus Field, proposed to unite all the islands of Oceania in a vast electric network; an immense undertaking, worthy of American genius.

The first soundings had been entrusted to the corvette *Susquehanna*. During the night of the 11th of December, she lay exactly in 27° 7' north latitude and 41° 37' longitude west of the meridian at Washington.

The moon, then in her last quarter, began to show above the horizon.

After the departure of Captain Blomsberry, Lieutenant Bronsfield and some officers were together on the quarterdeck. At the appearance of the moon, their thoughts were carried towards that orb, which the eyes of a whole hemisphere were then contemplating. The best marine glasses could not have discovered the projectile circling round its globe, and yet all were pointed towards its flaming disc, which millions of eyes were observing at the same moment.

'They have been gone ten days,' said Lieutenant Bronsfield; 'what has become of them?'

'They have arrived, lieutenant,' exclaimed a young midshipman, 'and they are doing what every traveller does when he reaches a new country – they are walking about.'

'Of course they are, as you say so, young shaver,' replied Lieutenant Bronsfield, smiling.

'However,' continued another officer, 'their arrival cannot be a matter of doubt. The projectile must have reached the moon at the moment when she was full, on the 5th, at midnight. It is now the 11th of December, which makes six days. In six times 24 hours, without darkness, one has time to make one's arrangements comfortably. I think I see them, our brave fellow-countrymen, encamped at the bottom of a valley on the banks of a Selenite rivulet, near the projectile, half broken by its fall, in the midst of volcanic fragments – Captain Nicholl commencing his surveys, President Barbicane copying out his travelling notes, Michel Ardan scenting the lunar solitudes with the perfume of a Londres.'

'Yes that must be so, that is so,' cried the young midshipman, filled with enthusiasm by the ideal description of his superior.

'I should like to believe it,' replied Lieutenant Bronsfield, who was not easily carried away. 'Unhappily, direct news from the lunar world is always wanting.'

'I beg your pardon, lieutenant,' said the midshipman; 'but cannot President Barbicane write?'

This question was met with a roar of laughter.

'Not letters,' continued the young man hastily. 'It is not a question of the postal administration.'

'It is perhaps an affair for the administration of telegraphic lines?' asked one of the officers ironically.

'Certainly not,' replied the midshipman, who was not to be put down; 'but it would be very easy to establish writing communications with the earth.'

'And how?'

'By means of the telescope at Long's Peak. You know that it brings the moon within two leagues of the Rocky Mountains, and that objects having a diameter of nine feet can be seen on the lunar surface. Well, our industrious friends could construct a gigantic alphabet; they could write words 100 fathoms long and sentences a league in length, and they could send us news in this manner.'

The imaginative young midshipman was noisily applauded. Even Lieutenant Bronsfield admitted that the idea was feasible. He added that by sending luminous rays, grouped in bundles by means of parabolic mirrors, direct communication could also be established; in fact these rays would be as visible on the surface of Venus or Mars, as the planet Neptune is on the earth. He ended by remarking, that the brilliant spots observed on the nearer planets, might possibly be signals made to the earth. But he remarked, if by this means we can have news from the lunar world, we could not send news from the terrestrial world, unless the Selenites had instruments at their disposal proper for making distant observations.

'Evidently,' replied one of the officers. 'But what has become of the travellers? What they have done, what they have seen, that is what would be specially interesting. Besides, if the experiment has succeeded, which I do not doubt, it will be tried again. The columbiad is still encased in Floridan soil. It is only a question of a projectile and powder, and each time the moon crosses the zenith we can send her a cargo of visitors.'

'It is evident,' replied Lieutenant Bronsfield, 'that J. T. Maston will one day go to join his friends.'

'If he will take me,' said the young midshipman, 'I am ready to accompany him.'

'Oh, there will be no lack of volunteers,' replied Bronsfield; 'and if they were allowed, one half of the inhabitants of the earth would soon have emigrated to the moon.'

This conversation between the officers of the *Susquehanna* was continued till about 1 a.m. It would be impossible to relate what astounding theories, what extraordinary systems were broached by these bold spirits. Since Barbicane's trial nothing seemed impossible to the Americans. They already proposed to send, not a commission of *savants*, but a whole colony to the Selenite regions, and a whole army, with infantry, artillery, and cavalry, to conquer the lunar world.

At 1 a.m. the hauling in of the sounding-line was not yet completed. Ten thousand feet were still out, which required several hours' work. According to the captain's orders, the fires had been lighted, and steam was getting up. The *Susquehanna* might have started at that very moment.

At this instant – it was 17 minutes past 1 a.m. – Lieutenant Bronsfield was preparing to leave the deck to regain his cabin, when his attention was attracted by a distant and quite unexpected whistling.

His comrades and he thought at first that this whistling was produced by an escape of steam, but, lifting their heads, they could observe that the noise came from the most distant strata of the air.

They had no time for questions; but this whistling attained a frightful intensity, and suddenly, to their dazzled eyes, appeared an enormous meteor, enflamed by the rapidity of its course, and friction on the atmospheric strata.

This fiery mass increased before their eyes, dashed with the noise of
thunder against the bowsprit of the corvette, which it smashed to the

stem, and plunged into the waves with a deafening noise. A few feet nearer, and the *Susquehanna* had gone down all hands on board.

At this moment, Captain Blomsberry appeared half dressed, and rushing to the poop where the officers were assembled: 'By your leave, gentlemen, what has happened?'

And the midshipman, acting as spokesman for all, cried: 'Captain, it is "they" come back again!'

CHAPTER TWENTY-ONE

J. T. Maston recalled

The excitement was great on board the *Susquehanna*. Officers and men, forgetting the terrible danger which they had just escaped – the possibility of being crushed and sunk – thought only of the catastrophe which terminated this voyage. So then the most audacious undertaking of ancient or modern times had cost the lives of the hardy adventurers who had attempted it.

'It is "they" come back again,' had said the young midshipman, and all had understood. No one doubted that this meteor was the Gun Club's projectile. As to the fate of the travellers contained therein, opinions differed.

'They are dead,' said one.

'They are alive,' replied another. 'The stratum of water is deep, and the shock has been deadened.'

'But they want air,' continued the first, 'and have died of suffocation.'

'Burnt,' replied another. 'The projectile was but a burning mass rushing through the atmosphere.'

'What matter!' was the unanimous cry; 'alive or dead they must be got out of there.'

Meanwhile, Captain Blomsberry had assembled his officers, and, with their permission, he held a council. It was necessary to take a decision at once. The most important was to fish out the projectile – a difficult but not an impossible operation. But the corvette had not the necessary machinery, which must be at the same time powerful and accurate. It was resolved to steam to the nearest port and inform the Gun Club of the fall of the projectile.

This determination was taken unanimously. The choice of the port had to be discussed. The neighbouring coast gave no anchorage on the 27th degree of latitude. Higher, above the Monterey peninsula, lay the important town which gives it its name. But, situated on the confines of a perfect desert, it was not united with the interior by means of telegraphic lines, and this important news could only be spread with sufficient rapidity by electricity.

A few degrees higher up was the bay of San Francisco. From the capital of the gold country communication would be easy with the centre of the Union. In less than two days the *Susquehanna*, under high pressure, could reach the port of San Francisco, it must therefore start at once.

The fires were lighted, they could start immediately. Two thousand feet of line yet lay in the water. Captain Blomsberry, not wishing to lose precious time by hauling them in, resolved to cut the line.

'We will fasten a buoy to the end,' said he, 'and the buoy will show us where the projectile went down.'

'Besides,' replied Lieutenant Bronsfield, 'we have our exact situation – 27° 7' north latitude and 41° 37' west longitude.'

'Good, Mr Bronsfield,' replied the captain; 'and with your permission, have the line cut.'

A large buoy, strengthened by a couple of spars, was thrown upon the surface of the ocean. The end of the line was firmly attached, and being only subject to the rise and fall of the swell, the buoy would not much shift its place.

At this moment, the engineer informed the captain that steam was up and they could start at once. The captain thanked him for this excellent communication, and gave the course, north-north-east. The corvette, wearing round, steered at high pressure direct for the bay of San Francisco. It was 3 a.m. Two hundred and twenty leagues to travel was little enough for such a fast sailer as the *Susquehanna*. In 36 hours she had covered the distance, and on the 14th December, at 1.27 p.m. she entered the bay of San Francisco.

At the sight of this vessel of the national fleet arriving full steam, with shorn bowsprit and stayed foremast, public curiosity was much excited. A dense crowd filled the quays, awaiting the arrival.

Having cast anchor, Captain Blomsberry and Lieutenant Bronsfield were lowered into an eight-oared boat, which rapidly carried them to the shore.

They jumped upon the quay.

'The telegraph?' asked they, without answering the thousand questions put to them.

The captain of the port himself conducted them to the telegraph office, in the midst of an immense concourse of eager spectators.

Blomsberry and Bronsfield entered the telegraph office whilst the crowd crushed against the doors.

A few minutes later four copies of a telegram were sent to – 1st, the Secretary of the Admiralty at Washington; 2nd, to the Vice-President of the Gun Club, Baltimore; 3rd, to the Hon. J. T. Maston, Long's Peak,

Rocky Mountains; 4th, to the Sub-Director of the Cambridge Observatory, Mass. It was worded as follows.

IN 20° 7' NORTH LATITUDE AND 41° 37' WEST LONGITUDE, ON THE
12TH DECEMBER, AT 1.17 A.M., PROJECTILE OF COLUMBIAD FALLEN
IN PACIFIC; SEND INSTRUCTIONS.

BLOMSBERRY, COMMANDER *SUSQUEHANNA*

Five minutes afterwards, all the town of San Francisco had heard the news. Before 6 p.m. the different states of the Union learnt the supreme catastrophe. After midnight, by submarine cable, all Europe knew the result of the great American attempt.

It is useless to try to describe the effect produced over the entire world by this unexpected *dénouement*.

On receipt of the despatch the Secretary to the Admiralty telegraphed to the *Susquehanna* orders to remain in the bay of San Francisco, without extinguishing her fires. Day and night she was to be ready to put to sea.

The Cambridge Observatory held an extraordinary meeting, and with that serenity which distinguishes learned bodies, they calmly discussed the scientific bearings of the question.

At the Gun Club there was an explosion. All the artillerists were assembled. The Vice-President, the Hon. Mr Wilcome, was reading that premature despatch by which J. T. Maston and Belfast announced that the projectile had just been perceived in the gigantic reflector at Long's Peak. This communication also stated that the projectile, retained by lunar attraction, had become a sub-satellite in the solar world.

The truth on this point is known. However, on the arrival of Blomsberry's telegram, which so formally contradicted J. T. Maston's telegram, two parties were formed in the bosom of the Gun Club. On the one hand were those who admitted the fall of the projectile, and consequently the return of the travellers; on the other, those who, confident in the observations at Long's Peak, concluded that there was some mistake on the part of the captain of the *Susquehanna*. For these latter, the pretended projectile was nothing but a meteor, a shooting globe, which in its fall had broken the bowsprit of the corvette. It was difficult to meet their arguments, for the velocity with which it was endowed must have rendered any observation of the moving body very difficult. The commander of the *Susquehanna* and his officers might certainly have been mistaken, in all good faith. One argument, nevertheless, militated in their favour: it was, that if the projectile had fallen upon the earth, its juncture with the terrestrial spheroid could only have occurred on the 27th degree of north latitude, and taking count of the time past, and of the earth's movement of rotation, between the 41st and 42nd degree of west longitude.

However, it was unanimously decided in the Gun Club that Bloms-berry's brother, Bilsby, and Major Elphiston, should immediately start for San Francisco, and consult as to the best means of drawing the projectile from the depths of the ocean.

These worthy men set off without loss of time, and the railroad which will soon cross the whole of Central America carried them to St Louis, where rapid mail-coaches awaited them.

Almost at the same instant that the Secretary to the Admiralty, the Vice-President to the Gun Club, and the Sub-Director of the Observatory, received the telegram from San Francisco, the Hon. J. T. Maston experienced the most violent emotion in his whole existence – an emotion which even the bursting of his celebrated cannon had not caused him, and which, for a second time, nearly cost him his life.

It will be remembered that the secretary of the Gun Club had left some moments after the projectile, and almost as quickly as the latter, for his post at Long's Peak in the Rocky Mountains. The learned J. Belfast, director of the Cambridge Observatory, accompanied him. Arrived at the station, the two friends had immediately taken up their position, and had not since left the summit of their enormous telescope. We know that this gigantic instrument had been constructed under conditions as to reflectors called 'front view'. This disposition gave only one reflection to the objects, and consequently rendered the vision clearer. Also, when J. T. Maston and Belfast were observing, they were placed at the upper portion of the instrument and not below. They reached it by a spiral staircase, a masterpiece of lightness, and below them yawned the metal pit, terminated by a metallic mirror, and measuring 280 feet in depth.

Upon this narrow platform, above the telescope, the two *savants* passed their existence, cursing the day which hid the moon from their sight, and the clouds which obstinately veiled her from their view by night.

What was then their joy when, after a few days' waiting, on the night of the 5th December, they perceived the vehicle which carried their friends into space! To this joy succeeded a deep disappointment when, confiding in incomplete observations, they had sent, with their first telegram, through the world that erroneous assertion which made the projectile a satellite of the moon, revolving in an immutable orbit.

Since that instant, the projectile had not been perceived, which disappearance was the more explicable that it was then passing behind the invisible disc of the moon. But when it ought to have reappeared upon the visible disc, judge of the impatience of the impetuous J. T. Maston, and of his companion not less impatient than he. At each minute of the night they thought they could perceive the projectile, and they did not perceive it. Hence, incessant discussions between them and violent disputes; Belfast asserting that the projectile was not visible, and J. T. Maston maintaining that it was staring him in the face.

'It is the projectile,' repeated J. T. Maston.

'No,' replied Belfast; 'it is an avalanche from a lunar mountain.'

'Well, we will see it tomorrow.'

'No, we shall not see it; it is carried into space.'

'We shall.'

'No.'

And in these moments, when interjections fell like hail, the well-known irritability of the secretary of the Gun Club constituted a permanent danger to the Honourable Mr Belfast.

The existence of these two together would soon have become impossible, but an unexpected event cut short these interminable discussions.

During the night of the 14th December the two irreconcilable friends were occupied observing the lunar disc. J. T. Maston was abusing, according to his custom, the learned Belfast, who was getting angry on his side. The secretary of the Gun Club maintained, for the thousandth time, that he had just perceived the projectile, adding even that Michel Ardan's face had been visible through one of the scuttles. He gave further weight to his assertions by a series of gesticulations, which his redoubtable hook rendered very disquieting.

At this moment Belfast's servant appeared on the platform – it was 10 p.m. – and handed him a despatch. It was the telegram of the commander of the *Susquehanna*.

Belfast tore open the envelope, read, and uttered a cry.

'Hallo!' said J. T. Maston.

'The projectile!'

'Well?'

'Has fallen back to the earth.'

A second cry – a roar – this time answered him. He turned towards J. T. Maston. The unfortunate man, imprudently leaning over the metal tube, had disappeared into the immense telescope, a fall of 280 feet!

Belfast, horrified, rushed to the orifice of the reflector.

He breathed. J. T. Maston, caught by his metal hook, was hanging to one of the stays which propped up the telescope. He was howling terribly.

Belfast called out. His assistants improvised a pulley, and, not without difficulty, hauled out the imprudent secretary of the Gun Club. He appeared, unhurt, at the upper orifice.

'By George,' said he, 'if I had broken the mirror!'

'You would have paid for it,' replied Belfast severely.

'And this infernal projectile has fallen?' asked J. T. Maston.

'Into the Pacific.'

'Let us be off.'

A quarter of an hour afterwards, the two *savants* were descending the slopes of the Rocky Mountains, and two days later, at the same time as their friends from the Gun Club, they reached San Francisco, having killed five horses on the road.

Elphiston, Blomsberry's brother, and Bilsby rushed towards them on their arrival.

'What is to be done?' cried they.

'Fish out the projectile,' replied J. T. Maston, 'as soon as possible.'

CHAPTER TWENTY-TWO

Saved

The very spot where the projectile had plunged beneath the waves was known exactly. The instruments to grapple it and bring it to the surface of the ocean were still wanting. They had to be invented, and then manufactured. But American engineers could not be embarrassed by so little. Grappling irons once obtained, and with the aid of steam, they were certain to raise the projectile, notwithstanding its weight; which latter was diminished by the density of the liquid in which it lay.

But it would not suffice to recover the projectile, it was necessary to act properly in the interest of the travellers. Nobody doubted their still being alive.

'Yes,' repeated J. T. Maston unceasingly, and his confidence gained upon the others, 'our friends are clever men, and cannot have fallen like fools. They are alive, thoroughly alive; but we must make haste and get them out. I am not afraid about provisions or water, they have enough for some time; but air! that is what they'll soon be wanting, so let us make haste.'

And they did make haste. They prepared the *Susquehanna* for her new destination. Her powerful machinery was regulated so as to work the hauling chains. The aluminum projectile only weighed 19,250 pounds, which was much less than the weight of the transatlantic cable which was raised under similar conditions. The only difficulty was to haul up the cylindro-conic projectile, the smooth surface of which was difficult to grapple.

For this end Murchison, the engineer, who had hastened to San Francisco, had enormous grappling irons constructed upon an automatic system, which would not let the projectile go if once they seized it in their powerful claws. He also had diving dresses prepared, which, beneath their impervious and resisting cover, enabled divers to reconnoitre the bottom of the sea. He also embarked on board the *Susquehanna* an ingeniously-contrived apparatus of compressed air. These were perfect chambers pierced with scuttles, and which water, introduced into certain compartments, could drag down to great depths. This apparatus was in use at San Francisco, where it had served for the construction of a submarine breakwater. This was fortunate, for the time was wanting to construct one.

However, notwithstanding the perfection of these apparatus, notwithstanding the ingenuity of the men who were going to use them, the success of the operation was certainly not assured. What could be more uncertain than a question of raising a projectile from 20,000 feet below the waters? Then, even if the projectile should be brought to the surface, how would the travellers have borne the terrible shock which 20,000 feet of water had perhaps not sufficiently broken?

However, it was necessary to act as quickly as possible. J. T. Maston pressed on the workmen day and night. He was quite ready either to put on a diver's dress, or to try the air apparatus to reconnoitre the situation of his courageous friends.

Notwithstanding all the diligence used in the manufacture of the different machinery, notwithstanding the considerable sums which were placed at the disposal of the Gun Club by the Government of the Union, five long days – five centuries – had passed before these preparations were completed. During this time, public opinion was excited to the highest degree. Telegrams were incessantly passing over the entire world by the wires and electric cables. The saving of Barbicane, Nicholl, and Michel Ardan was an international matter. All the nations who had subscribed to the Gun Club's loan took a direct interest in the travellers' safety.

At last the hauling chains, the air chambers, the automatic grappling irons were embarked on board the *Susquehanna*. J. T. Maston, Murchison, the engineer, the delegates of the Gun Club, already occupied their cabins. It only remained to start.

On the 21st December, at 8 p.m., the corvette put to sea in fine weather, and a fresh breeze from the north-east. The whole population of San Francisco crowded the quays, excited but mute, reserving their hurrahs for the return.

The steam was raised to its highest pressure, and the screw of the *Susquehanna* carried them rapidly from the bay.

It would be useless to relate the conversations on board between the officers, men, and passengers. All these men had but one thought. All hearts beat with the same emotion whilst they were rushing to their assistance. What were Barbicane and his companions doing? What had become of them? Were they in a position to attempt some audacious manoeuvre to regain their liberty? None could tell. The truth is that all means would have failed. Submerged about two leagues below the ocean, the metal prison defied all the efforts of the prisoners.

On the 23rd December, at 8 a.m., after a rapid passage, the *Susquehanna* had reached the fatal spot. It was necessary to wait for noon to obtain a correct observation. The buoy to which the line was attached had not yet been discovered.

At noon, Captain Blomsberry, aided by his officers, who checked the observation, took the reckoning in the presence of the members of the Gun Club. There was then an instant of anxiety. Her position determined, the *Susquehanna* was found to be a few points to the west of the very spot where the projectile had plunged beneath the waves.

The course of the corvette was given so as to reach this precise spot.

At 47 minutes past noon the buoy was sighted. It was in good condition, and had not much drifted.

'At last!' cried J. T. Maston.

'Shall we commence?' asked Captain Blomsberry.

'Without losing a second,' replied J. T. Maston.

All precautions were taken to maintain the corvette in almost complete immobility.

Before trying to seize the projectile, Murchison, the engineer, first tried to recognise the position on the bottom of the ocean. The submarine apparatus required for this search received their provision of air. The working of these engines is not without danger, for at 20,000 feet below the surface of the water, and under such considerable pressure, they are exposed to breakages, of which the consequences would be terrible.

J. T. Maston, Blomsberry, Crother, and the engineer, Murchison, without heeding these dangers, took their place in the air-chamber. The captain, stationed on the bridge, superintended the operation, ready to stop or haul in the chains on the slightest signal. The screw had been shipped, and all the force of the machinery brought to bear on the capstan, so that the apparatus would have been rapidly hauled on board.

The descent commenced at 25 minutes past 1 p.m., and the chamber, borne down by the reservoirs full of water, disappeared below the surface of the water.

The emotion of the officers and sailors on board was now shared between the prisoners in the projectile and the prisoners in the submarine apparatus. As to the latter, they forgot their own danger, and, stationed at the windows of the scuttles, they observed attentively the liquid masses through which they passed.

The descent was rapid. At 2.17 p.m. J. T. Maston and his companions had reached the bottom of the Pacific. But they saw nothing but the barren desert which neither marine fauna nor flora animated. By the light of their lamps, provided with powerful reflectors, they could observe the dark layers of water, within an extended radius, but the projectile remained invisible to their eyes.

The impatience of these hardy divers could not be described. Their apparatus being in electric communication with the corvette, they made the agreed signal, and the *Susquehanna*, for the space of a mile, moved their chamber, suspended some yards from the bottom.

They thus explored all the submarine plain, deceived each moment by optical illusions which broke their hearts. Here a rock, there an excrescence, seemed like the sought-for projectile; then they perceived their error and despaired.

'Where are they? Where are they?' cried J. T. Maston. And the poor fellow cried out: 'Nicholl! Barbicane! Michel Ardan!' as if their unfortunate friends could have heard or replied through this impenetrable medium.

The search continued under these conditions up to the moment when the vitiated air in the apparatus obliged them to ascend.

The hauling commenced at 6 p.m., and was only completed at midnight.

'Till tomorrow,' said J. T. Maston, setting foot on the deck of the corvette.

'Yes,' replied Captain Blomsberry; 'in another spot.'

'Yes!'

J. T. Maston did not doubt of success; but already his companions, no longer intoxicated with the animation of the first hours, understood all the difficulties of the undertaking.

What appeared so easy at San Francisco, appeared almost impossible here in the open ocean. The chances of success decreased in a great proportion, and it was to chance alone that they must look to discover the projectile.

The next day, on the 24th December, notwithstanding the fatigues of the preceding day, the operation was recommenced. The corvette moved a few points to the west, and the apparatus, provided with air, carried once more the same explorers to the depths of the ocean.

All the day was passed in fruitless researches. The bed of the sea was a desert. The 25th brought no result; nor yet the 26th.

It was disheartening! They thought of those unfortunate fellows shut up in the projectile for 26 days. Perhaps at this moment they were feeling the first sensations of asphyxia, if even they had escaped the dangers of their fall. The air was being exhausted, and with air, courage and energy.

'Air, perhaps,' replied J. T. Maston invariably; 'but energy never.'

On the 28th, after two more days' searching, all hope was abandoned. The projectile was an atom in the immensity of the sea. They must give up all hope of finding it. However, J. T. Maston would not hear of leaving. He would not quit the spot, without having at least sighted his friends' tomb. But Captain Blomsberry could not remain longer, and notwithstanding the complaints of the worthy secretary, he was forced to give orders to sail.

On the 29th December at 9 a.m., the *Susquehanna*, with her head to the north-east, resumed her course towards the bay of San Francisco.

It was 10 a.m. The corvette was moving off at half-steam, and as if with regret from the place of the catastrophe, when a sailor from the mast-head cried suddenly:

'A buoy on the lee bow!'

The officers looked in the direction indicated, and perceived that the object signalled had in reality the appearance of those buoys which serve to mark the passes of bays or rivers. But, curious detail, a flag floating in the wind surmounted its cone, which rose five or six feet out of the water. This buoy shone in the rays of the sun, as if its sides had been of silver.

Captain Blomsberry, J. T. Maston, the delegates of the Gun Club, were standing on the bridge, and examining this object wandering hap-hazard on the waves.

All looked with feverish anxiety, but in silence. None dared give utter-ance to the thought which arose in the minds of all.

The corvette approached within two cable-lengths of the object. A shudder ran through the crew. The flag was the American flag. At this moment a perfect roar was heard. It was worthy J. T. Maston who had fallen in a heap. Forgetting on the one hand that his right arm had been replaced by an iron hook, and that, on the other hand, his brain was only covered by a gutta-percha cap, he had given himself a terrific blow.

They rushed towards him, raised him, and brought him back to life. What were his first words?

'Brutes! idiots! boobies that we are!'

'What is the matter?' was cried from every side.

'What is it?'

'Speak, then.'

'Fools,' roared the terrible secretary, 'the projectile only weighs 19,250 pounds.'

'Well!'

'And displaces 28 tons, otherwise 56,000 pounds, and consequently *it will swim*.'

Ah! how the worthy man emphasised this word 'swim'. And it was the truth. All, yes, all the *savants* had forgotten this fundamental law; by reason of its specific lightness the projectile, after having been carried in its fall to the lowest depths of the ocean, had naturally returned to the surface, and was floating quietly at the mercy of the waves.

The boats were lowered, J. T. Maston and his friends jumped into them; the excitement attained its highest pitch; all hearts beat rapidly as the boats neared the projectile. What did it contain? Living men or dead?

Living men; yes, living men, unless death had carried off Barbicane and his friends since they hoisted the flag.

A profound silence reigned in the boats; all were breathless; eyes grew dim; one of the scuttles of the projectile was open; a few pieces of glass remained in the frame, showing that it had been broken. This scuttle was about five feet above the waves.

One of the boats came alongside. It was J. T. Maston's. J. T. Maston rushed to the broken glass. At this moment a joyous voice was heard – the voice of Michel Ardan crying with the accents of victory: 'Blank all, Barbicane. Blank all.'

Barbicane, Michel Ardan, and Nicholl, were playing dominoes!

CHAPTER TWENTY-THREE

To conclude

It will be remembered what immense sympathy had accompanied the three travellers at their departure. If at the outset of their undertaking they had excited so much emotion in the old and new worlds, what enthusiasm would greet their return! Would not those millions of spectators who had invaded the Floridan peninsula rush to meet these sublime adventurers? Would the legions of foreigners drawn to American shores from all parts of the globe, leave the territory of the Union without again seeing Barbicane, Nicholl, and Michel Ardan? No! And the ardent passion of the public would worthily meet the grandeur of the undertaking. Human creatures who had left the terrestrial spheroid and returned from this strange journey in celestial regions, could not fail to be received like the prophet Elias, when he shall return to earth. To see them first, and then hear them; such was the general desire.

This desire would be promptly realised by almost all the inhabitants of the Union.

Barbicane, Michel Ardan, Nicholl, and the delegates of the Gun Club returned without delay to Baltimore, where they were received with indescribable enthusiasm. The notes of President Barbicane's journey were ready for publication. The *New York Herald* purchased the manuscript for a price which is not yet known, but cannot fail to have been considerable. In fact, during the publication of *A Journey to the Moon*, the daily sale of the paper amounted to 5,000,000 copies. Three days after the return of the travellers to earth, the minutest details of their expedition were known. It only remained to see the heroes of this superhuman undertaking.

The exploration of Barbicane and his friends round the moon had permitted them to verify certain theories admitted on the subject of the terrestrial satellite. These *savants* had observed *de visu* and in very particular conditions. People now knew what systems to reject and what to admit, as to the formation of this orb, its origin and its inhabitableness. Its past, its present, its future, had given up their last secrets. What could be objected to these conscientious observers, who had sighted at less than forty kilometres that curious mountain Tycho, the strangest system of lunar orology. What could be replied to these *savants* who had plunged their glances into the abyss of Plato's circus? How could these audacious men be contradicted, whom the chances of their undertaking had carried over that invisible face of the disc which no human eye had hitherto seen?

It was now their right to impose limits to that selenographic science which had recomposed the lunar world, as Cuvier did the skeleton of a fossil, and to say: the moon *was* an inhabitable world, and inhabited before the earth; the moon *is* an uninhabitable world and now uninhabited.

To celebrate the return of the most illustrious of its members and of his two companions, the Gun Club thought of giving them a banquet, but a banquet worthy of these conquerors and of the American nation, and under such conditions that all the inhabitants of the Union could share in it. All the termini of the States were united by flying rails. Then in all the stations, decorated with the same flags and ornaments, tables were laid and served alike.

At fixed hours, calculated successively and marked upon electric clocks which beat the seconds at the same instant, the populations were invited to take their seats at the banqueting tables.

During four days, from the fifth to the ninth of January, the trains were suspended, as on Sunday, on all the railways of the Union, and all the lines remained open. One express locomotive, drawing a car of state, had alone the right to travel during these four days over the American railways. The locomotive, manned by a driver and a stoker, bore, by special favour, J. T. Maston, the secretary of the Gun Club.

The car was reserved for President Barbicane, Captain Nicholl, and Michel Ardan.

At the whistle of the engine, after the hurrahs, and shouts, and all the onomatopoeia of admiration contained in the American language, the train left the station of Baltimore. It travelled with a velocity of 80 leagues an hour; but what was that speed compared with the velocity when the three heroes had left the columbiad!

Thus they went from town to town, finding the populations at table along their passage, saluting them with the same acclamations, lavishing the same bravos. Thus they travelled through the east of the Union – Pennsylvania, Connecticut, Massachusetts, Vermont, Maine, and New Brunswick; they passed through the north and west by New York, Ohio, Michigan, and Wisconsin; they passed to the south by Illinois, Missouri, Arkansas, Texas, and Louisiana; they ran to the south-east by Alabama and Florida; they reascended by Georgia and the Carolinas; they visited the centre by Tennessee, Kentucky, Virginia, Indiana; then, after a halt at Washington, they re-entered Baltimore, and during four days they might say that the United States of America, seated at one immense banquet, saluted them simultaneously with the same hurrahs.

The apotheosis was worthy of the three heroes, whom mythology would have ranked amongst demigods.

And now, will this attempt, without precedent in the annals of travel, produce any practical results? Will direct communication with the moon ever be established? Will a service of navigation through space be established to open up the solar world? Will we go from one planet to another – from Jupiter to Mercury; and later on from one star to another – from the Pole Star to Sirius? Will any mode of locomotion allow of visiting these suns which swarm in the firmament?

To these questions no answer can be given; but knowing the audacious ingenuity of the Anglo-Saxon race, no one will be astonished that the Americans should try to make some use of President Barbicane's experiment.

So, some time after the return of the travellers, the public will receive, with marked favour, the prospectus of a company (limited), with a capital of 100,000,000 dollars, divided into 100,000 shares of 1,000 dollars each, under the style of the 'National Company of Interstellary Communication'. President, Barbicane; Vice-President, Captain Nicholl; Secretary, J. T. Maston; Director of Movements, Michel Ardan.

And, as it is in the American character to foresee every eventuality in business, even failure, the Hon. Harry Trollope, Judge Commissary, and Francis Drayton, Liquidator, are appointed beforehand.

THE END